❖WRAETHTHU❖

The Enchantments of Flesh and Spirit
✦
The Bewitchments of Love and Hate
✦
The Fulfilments of Fate and Desire

STORM CONSTANTINE

ORB

A TOM DOHERTY ASSOCIATES BOOK

NEW YORK

WRAETHTHU

This book is an omnibus edition, consisting of the novels: *The Enchantments of Flesh and Spirit,* copyright © 1987 by Storm Constantine, first Tor edition January 1990; *The Bewitchments of Love and Hate,* copyright © 1988 by Storm Constantine, first Tor edition August 1990; and *The Fulfilments of Fate and Desire,* copyright © 1988 by Storm Constantinc, first Tor edition March 1991.

Reprinted by arrangement with Macdonald & Co. (Publishers) Ltd.

This book is printed on acid-free paper.

Cover art by Sam Rakeland
Map by Ellisa Mitchell
Design by Junie Lee

An Orb Edition
Published by Tom Doherty Associates, Inc.
175 Fifth Avenue
New York, NY 10010

ISBN: 0-312-89000-1

First Orb edition: November 1993

Printed in the United States of America

0 9 8 7 6 5 4 3

❦WRAETHTHU❦

Camphac

HADASSAJ
• Caraway
• Jasminia

ELHMEN

(SAHALE)
• Kar Tatang
• Shappa

THAINE

Lemarath

WRAKE
TAMYD

GIMRAH
Strabaloth •

SYKES

Ardith •
Kapre

• Clereness
• Jael

Sea
g

FERIKE

• Saphrax

FLORINADA

1993
Ellisa Mitchell

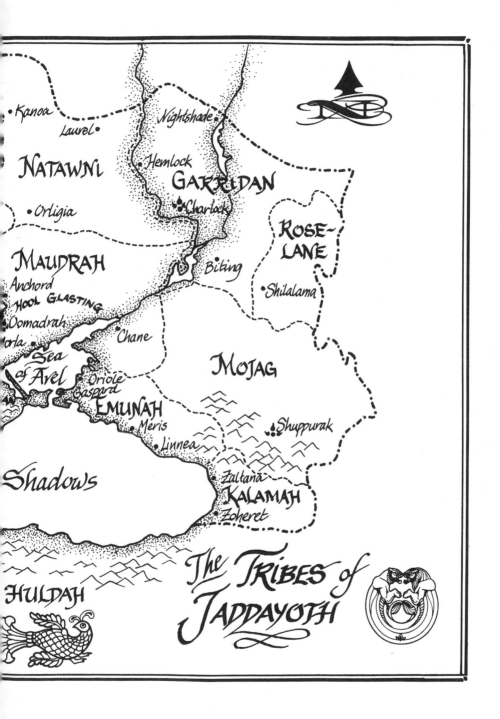

Kanoa

Laurel

NATAWNI

Nightshade

Hemlock GARRIDAN

Orligia

Charlock

ROSE-
LANE

MAUDRAH
Anchord
HOOL GLASTING
Oomadrah
orla
Sea
of Avel

Biting

Shilalama

Chane

MOJAG

Oriole
Gaspard
EMUNAH
Meris

Linnea

Shuppurak

Shadows

Zaltana

KALAMAH
Zoheret

The Tribes of
Jaddayoth

HULDAH

THE ENCHANTMENTS OF
FLESH AND SPIRIT

The First Book of Wraeththu

This book is dedicated to the almond eyes . . .

With thanks to Dave Weight for liaising,
Heidi for her incisive vision,
The Closets of Emily Child for music to write by,
Gillan Paris for the loan of a "Forever" surrogate to photograph
and Jag for the sake of his art and being harshly beautiful.

Our next meeting will be in the lodge, where,
beneath the soft radiance of the everburning flame above you,
and with the light upon the altar casting
its wavering radiance upon the symbols thereon, you will take the
Oath of the Mysteries, and I, ruling in the East,
will accept that oath, and, by virtue of my office, bring you
into our brotherhood.

The gates stand open; enter into light.

W. E. Butler
(Apprenticed to magic)

BOOK ONE

INTRODUCTION

Today: a perfect day for thinking back. It must all be said, now, before time takes an axe to my memory. Outside, on the balcony the air begins to chill. The season changes. Curled leaves, brazen with death, scratch along the marble terrace and the clear, golden sunlight is rustling with ghosts. Remember: laughter; fear; delight; courage. I walked out to the balcony to write. It was difficult to begin. For some minutes I sat gazing at the distant mountains, smudged in a lilac haze. Someone has turned all the fountains off. Below me, the gardens are mostly silent.

They say to me: "What tales you could tell," and if I tell them; "again, more. There must be more." This may become a history book, but remember, it is only my history.

CHAPTER ONE

>━┥◀❭╼❍╾❬▶┝━◄

He faces northwest,
the direction of the unknown

My name is Pellaz. I have no age. I have died and lived again. This is my testament.

At the age of fifteen, I lived in a dusty, scorched town at the edge of a desert. I was the son of a peasant, whose family for centuries had worked the cable crop for the Richards family. Our town was really just a farm, and to call it that lends it an undeserved glamor. Huts upon red dirt; there is little else to imagine. The cable crop, a hardy, stringy, tasteless vegetable, used for everything from bulk food to bed springs, straggled meanly over the parched ground. It did not grow high and its unattractive, pitted fruits burst with a sound like gunfire to release pale seeds in yellow jelly and fill the air with the odor of putrescence. The grand house of Sefton Richards, a stern, northern man, whose reclusiveness was supposed to shelter insanity, squatted against the horizon, far from our own humble dwellings. Every year, ten of us were summoned to the Great House and ordered to whitewash it. Through the windows, we could see that it had very little furniture inside.

We lived in a cruel, bitter, petty country and it was inevitable that we shared many of these characteristics. Only when I escaped did I learn to dislike it. Then, I existed in a mindless, innocent way, ignorant of the world outside our narrow territories and content to stretch and pound the cable fiber with the rest of my kind. I don't suppose I ever did really think about things. The closest I came to this was a dim appreciation of the setting sun dyeing all the world purple and rose, lending the land an ephemeral beauty. Even the eye of a true artist would have had difficulty in finding beauty in that place, but the sunsets were pleasantly deceptive.

We first heard of what were timidly termed "the upsets" by travelers passing hurriedly through our lands. Nobody liked to stay long in this part of the country, but my family were an affable, hospitable crowd; and their hospitality was difficult to evade. They loved visitors and entertained them lavishly, and it would have taken a hard brute indeed to resist their advances. The trouble had started in the north, some years ago. Nobody was exactly sure when it had begun. Different travelers opined different reasons for its cause. Some favored the specter of unemployment and its attendant poverty; others waved the flag of continuing moral decline; others claimed power plants were responsible by insinuating noxious fumes into the air that warped the mind. "The world we know is disappearing," they ranted. "Not the final, sudden death we all envisaged, but a slow sinking to nothing." Squatting in the dirt, I felt none of this would ever touch me. I listened to their tales with the same ghoulish pleasure as I listened to my grandmother's tales of werewolves in the desert.

It was said it had started as small groups of youths. *Something* had happened to them. Perhaps it was just one group. Perhaps, once, on a street corner of a damp, dimly-lit city suburb, an essence strange and huge had reached out from somewhere and touched them, that first group. A catalyst to touch their boredom and their bitterness transforming it to a breathing, half-visible sentience. Oh yes, they changed. They became something like the werewolves my grandmother remembered tales of. Spurning the society that had bred them, rebelling totally, haunting the towns with their gaunt and drug-poisoned bodies; all night-time streets became places of fear. They dressed in strange uniforms to signify their groups, spitting obscenities upon the sacred cows of men, living rough in all the shunned places. The final act of outrage became their fornication amongst themselves amid the debris they had created. The name that they took for themselves was Wraeththu. To distraught mothers and splintered communities, this spelt three things: death, rape and darkness. The Wraeththu hated mankind. They were different; on the inside and on the outside. Hungry, baleful fire smouldered in their skins, you could see it looking out at you. They drank blood and burned the sanctity, the security of society, infecting others like a plague. Some even died, it is said, at their touch. But those who survived and joined them were strong and proud. Werewolves really would walk the desert again.

Listening to all this no invisible wind prickled my skin. I never shivered and looked nervously out at the vast stillness of the desert, wondering. One man who came to us warned my father he should chain his sons to the hut at night. We all just laughed. Nettled, the man pointed out that others, families in villages farther north, did just that. No, no-one had actually been taken, but it was only a matter of time. I looked at my brother, Terez, and we rolled our eyes and giggled. The man turned on us swiftly. Death looked Mankind in the face, he cried, and we were too stupid to save ourselves. Would I laugh as the Wraeththu corrupted my body and destroyed my mind? Would I laugh as I watched my mother and sisters slaughtered? I turned away from him, stung by humiliation for a moment. No, not even then did I stop and feel Fate's breath on our necks. I took out my sharp knife, a cruel little thorn, and declared this was what any of these weird types would get from me, if by some mischance they should wander so far south, and I stabbed the air explicitly. My father smiled. He patted my arm but his eyes were troubled.

After our visitor had gone, my sister Mima asked our father what he thought of these tales. He told her he believed them to be wildly exaggerated. Rumors such as these have been circulating for many years: "Wraeththu they say! If the world sinks, it is not because of them!" Mima and I must have looked unconvinced, so my father smiled. "We are far from the northern cities here," he said, his voice gentle with logic. "A gang of unruly, discontented boys has grown into a pack of demons somewhere between the minds and tongues of travelers. They think us fools, easily fooled. No, the Wraeththu are the payment we receive for food and lodging. People on the road have little money, but they have plenty of imagination, that is all. We have nothing to fear. It is all too far from us."

Mima and I walked in the cable fields that evening. Everything was beautifully red and purple, Mima a stunning ravenhaired wraith in the half-light. We talked again of the Wraeththu.

"What would you do, Pell, if they did come here, if just one of them came here . . .?"

"And I fell under their terrible spell?" I butted in with a laugh.

Mima did not laugh. "You are not quite a man, Pell. You act so young sometimes. I know you would be vulnerable."

I felt I ought to be annoyed with her. "Mima! I am nearly sixteen years old. I'm really not such a baby. Anyway, they will never come here."

"How do you know? You can't be sure." She squatted down among the cable stalks, her beautiful dark eyes almost wet with tears. Sometimes, she made me ache to look at her, yet I never really noticed girls. I was very backward in that respect.

"Mima, you're over-imaginative," I told her.

"I wish you'd believe me," she said, under her breath. But that was an end to the subject for quite a while.

The season had changed, and it was a gloomy day when Cal first came to our home. I was sitting in the doorway, sharpening my mother's knives. The silvery, grating noise I made suited well the warm, clammy air. Nothing could take the metallic taste from my mouth. The skies were overcast, the ground damp and steaming, insects sheltered miserably under the eaves of the hut. He rode in alone on a fine-looking pony. Later I learned it was stolen. I watched him come slowly down the muddy road toward me; past the other huts where other families looked out, past the lithe figure of Mima who was hurrying home through the stream. She stopped and looked at him, inquiry written all over her, but he never looked, just came straight on down to me. He wore a rust-colored poncho, that covered his knees and most of the pony's back. Suddenly a knife-like depression entered me. The world seemed to change before my eyes. All the huts looked empty and sad, the dampness stung like acid. I think I knew then, in that brief instant, that my destiny had been set. Already the land around me had acknowledged my farewell. Then it had gone, that lightening realization, and I looked up at the rider who had halted in front of me. As he leaned down from the saddle, I noticed he was deeply tanned, with wild, yellow hair flattened by

the humid air, and blue, almost purple, eyes. He leaned down and held out
his hand to me. I took it.

"I am Cal," he said and then I knew what he was. I could not hide my
fear, my eyes were as wide as a kitten's.

"I'm Pellaz," I told him and added rather fatuously, "Are you a traveler?" His mirthless smile told me I did not fool him.

"Of sorts. I've been traveling across country for about a week, I think.
Time's gone crazy. I have no money . . ."

This was familiar ground. At once I offered him the hospitality of our
home.

While we ate that evening, the rest of my family treated Cal with wary
respect. They felt he was different from the usual wanderers we encountered. For one thing, his manner seemed quite cultured and he treated my
mother and sisters with flattering courtesy. My father, being overseer of the
farm, owned a hut more splendid than the rest. Separate bedrooms and a
water tap in the wash-room. Because of the weather, my mother had laid
out the meal indoors. We sat around a large and worn wooden table, our
faces softened by the flickering lamplight, flasks of wine stood empty round
our plates. Cal hypnotized us with his voice. I watched him very carefully
as he talked. His face was lean and very mobile, emotions flowing across
his features like the movement of moths. He told stories exceptionally well
and spoke of things he had seen in the north. Everyone wanted to know
more lurid tales about the Wraeththu. Only I knew he was one of them: his
hands were never still, and I could tell half the things he said were lies. But
that was what they wanted to hear, of course. He never told us why he was
traveling or where to. He told us nothing about himself. My sisters were
especially enchanted by him. He was typical of the strange, fey, yet masculine beauty I learned to recognize as Wraeththu. (That look, so disquieting;
it made me uncomfortable to glance at him.) They were very selective in
their choice of converts, I presumed. My father asked him about his family.
He was silent for a moment, troubled, and then the warmth of his smile
moved the silence.

"You are very lucky, sir," he said smoothly. "Your family are all with
you and in good health, and," (his eyes flicked for the slightest instant at
me), "they are all very fine to look upon."

We all laughed then, and respected his reticence.

Mima and I carried the dishes out to the wash-place after the meal.
From the main room came the faint sounds of people bidding each other
goodnight. The washroom was dark and we did not light the lamp. Only
the special light of the sky spun whitely, palely into the little room as we
washed out the pots. We habitually washed up in the dark when it was our
turn. It was easy to confide in each other then.

"I have heard folk call you beautiful," she told me in a vaguely troubled
voice and reached with damp fingers for my hair, tracing its length over my
shoulder. "Hardly even human, are you . . . a changeling child."

I smiled at her, which she did not return.

"There's something strange about that boy," she remarked to me, rolling up her sleeves with wet hands and gazing at the dishes.

"Who? Cal?" I answered her without looking up.

"You know very well!" she said sharply and I glanced up at her. In the half-light her eyes were knowing and showed traces of contempt. She looked much older than her seventeen years. I shrugged and attempted to change the atmosphere with a smile.

"Don't!" she snapped and then, "Oh, Pell, I'm afraid for you. I don't know why. God, what is happening? Something is happening, isn't it?" Suddenly, she was young again and I put my arms around her.

"I'm afraid too," I whispered, "And I don't know why either . . . but in a way it feels nice." We looked hard at each other.

"No-one else knows," she murmured in a small, husky voice. How lost she looked. She always hated not being able to understand things. Our mother just called her nosy.

"Knows what?" I wanted her to say something definite. I wanted to hear something terrible.

"That boy . . . Cal. I don't know. It's the way he looked at you. He's barely human; so strange. It's almost as if he's finished his journey coming here. Pell, I'm sure of it. It's you. It has to be you. The stories are true in a way. They do steal people. But not in the way we thought. They're very clever . . . I'm not prepared. I have no defense for you . . . Pell, is it just me? Am I imagining things?"

I turned away from her and pressed my forehead against the window. Was it just Mima's imagination? I felt numb. My fate was no longer in my own hands, I thought, and I did not really care. I strained to be truly frightened but I could not. For a while the only sound was the clink and scrape of Mima cleaning the pots by herself, until I said; "We have to go back in there." My voice sounded like someone else.

"You do," she answered. "But I'm not going to!" Wiping her hands, she started to leave the room in the direction of the small bedchamber she shared with two of our sisters. At the doorway she paused. It was so dark I could not see her properly. Her voice came to me out of the shadows. "I love you, Pell." Husky and forlorn.

I waited a while before going to my room. Cal had been offered a place on the floor there and when I went in, he was lying under a blanket with one arm thrown over his face. Terez and I slept on an ancient wooden bed that groaned as if in pain whenever one of us moved. Terez had waited for me to come in before he put out the light. We did not speak afterwards, because of Cal being there. Lying there in the muted owl-light I dared not look at him. I knew I would see his eyes glittering in the darkness and if he saw I was awake he might say something. I had to prepare myself. I was feeling scared now. Presently, Terez's gentle snores came from the other side of the bed. I lay and waited, knowing that if nothing happened now, tomorrow Cal would be gone, no matter what Mima thought. It had to come from me. He would say nothing otherwise.

My right arm lay outside the coverlet. It felt cold and sensitive and cumbersome. For a moment or two I clenched my fingers with reluctance before letting it move slowly by itself toward the edge of the bed. I must have been bewitched. I was normally such a coward. We had laughed at the tales we had heard. Now I wanted to be part of them. I was excited and curious. In my head I had already left the farm and carved a highway of adventures into the wilderness. My hand hit the wooden floor without a sound. What could I do now? Prod him? Wake him somehow? What could I say? I want to go with you. What if he did not want anyone with him? What if he laughed at me? My toes curled at the thought of it.

I lay, tense and still, my mind racing, and, as I struggled with a hundred impressive words of persuasion in my head, he curled his fingers around my own and gently pressed.

I did not dare look down at him and stayed like that for what seemed hours until my arm screamed for release. Until Cal pulled my hand toward him and I slipped weightlessly to the floor. He wrapped his blanket around us and told me where we would go tomorrow.

"At the moment, I belong to no particular tribe," he told me. "Most of my people were murdered by soldiers in the north. Few of us escaped. I'm making for Immanion. That's where the Gelaming, a Wraeththu tribe, are building their city. The Gelaming are powerful and can work strong magic. I will take you there. What have you heard about us?"

I could not stop trembling, so he put his arms round me as Mima had done earlier. "Come on, speak, speak. Tell me, what do you know?"

"Only what travelers tell us," I replied through teeth clattering like stones on a tin roof. I am half dead, I thought. Shriveled by the touch of his almost alien flesh: a wolf in man's clothing, something beneath the skin. His smell, pungent, alien, stifling the breath out of me, like a cat over the face of a child.

"And what do the travelers tell you?" Wicked amusement. (Here I have a child to pollute, torment, seduce.)

"They said it was a youth cult, and then more than that. Like a mutation. They said Wraeththu can have strange powers, but we didn't really believe that. . . . They say you want to kill all mankind. . . . They say you are fearless warriors . . . that you murder all women. Many things like that. Not all of it is true . . . is it?"

"How do you feel about women?" he asked abruptly.

"I know what it means to be Wraeththu," I murmured, hoping that would suffice.

"Answer!" he demanded and I was afraid Terez would wake.

"I've never known them," I spluttered quickly. "I never think about things like that. Never. It doesn't matter. Inside. Nothing. It doesn't matter." I struggled in his hold.

"It will," he said quietly, relaxing his grip on me. "But not yet, and certainly not here. You will be Wraeththu. Perhaps you always have been, waiting here at the end of the world. You've just been asleep, that's all. But you will wake, one day."

We lay in silence for a while, listening to Terez rattling away on the bed. For the first time I opened my eyes and looked at Cal. He noticed and smiled at me. I did not feel strange lying there with him. He was like an old friend.

"For now, I shall give you something very special. It is a rare thing among us and not given lightly. You will learn its significance as time goes on. I'm doing it because you fascinate me. Because there's something important inside you. I don't know what it is yet. But I know it was no accident I found you." He leant on his elbow, over me. "This is called the Sharing of Breath. It is sacred and powerful."

I was nearly sick with fright as his face loomed above me, satanic with shadows. I closed my eyes and felt his breath upon me. I expected a vast vampiric drain on my lungs, pain of some kind. I felt his lips, dry and firm, touch my own. His tongue like a thread of fire touched my teeth. He called it a sharing of breath. My arms curled around his back, which was hardened with stress and muscle. He called it a sharing of breath. Where I came from, we called it a kiss.

Before dawn, before anyone would notice our leaving, Cal and I went away from the farm. Cal was riding the pony and I walked beside. I have never been far into the desert before and the vast stony wilderness spread out in front of us appalled me. We had filled every available and portable container we could find with fresh water and I had plundered my mother's larder mercilessly. I asked Cal why we had to branch out into the desert, why we could not follow the road. I did not think anyone from home would come after me. I felt sure Mima would stop them, somehow. Cal only replied that there was only one way to go and we were on it. He seemed to be in a bad mood, his voice was terse, so I did not press him further.

After maybe half an hour of walking, I stopped and looked back for the first time. On the horizon, the Richards' house bulked huge and desolate against the faintest flush of dawn. I could not see my old home, but I knew that presently Mima would be stirring. Would she know immediately what I had done? That I had realized her fears. I felt a needling pang of remorse. Maybe I should have left her a farewell note, some kind of explanation. Only we two had ever been taught to write; our father had known us to be the brightest of his children. Whatever I could have written for her would have been understood by her alone; a last shared secret between us. But it was too late now. Cal called me sharply. "Regrets already?" he asked cruelly, but his eyes were amused. I shook my head.

"This is probably the last time I'll see this place. I've never lived anywhere else . . ." I finished lamely and began walking again.

The desert had a peculiar barbaric beauty. Gray rocks rose like frozen dragons from the reddish, stony ground, and sometimes, strange warped plants sprouted rampantly like unkempt heads of hair or discarded rags. Lizards with flashing scales skidded away from us and wide-winged carrion-birds rode the hot air high above. By noon, it was too hot to travel and Cal unpacked a blanket to make a canopy. I was drenched with sweat because I was wearing all the clothes I owned. It was easier to wear them than carry them. The only shoes I possessed were canvas plimsolls, which I envisaged dropping apart after about three days. Luckily, the feet inside them were quite hardwearing. We stretched out under the shade of the makeshift canopy and ate sparingly of the food we had brought; cheese, fruit and bread. All our water tasted tepid and sour. Hungry insects gorged themselves dizzy on our blood.

I was still very wary of Cal. He appeared cheerful and easy going most of the time, but other times he drifted off into tense, quiet moods, when he stared fixedly at the sky. I could only guess at what he might have suffered in the north. Perhaps he had witnessed things I could not even imagine. Northern society had been disintegrating for years. Even we knew that, safe in our far-away farms. The people now had Wraeththu for a scapegoat. I could almost visualize the brutality that must go on in those gray, mad cities. The people must see Wraeththu as perverted wretches sinking further into decay. Perhaps I too had thought that for a time. Panic and fear blinded them to the cleansing fire that Wraeththu could be. From the ashes new things would grow; not quite the same as they had been before the fire. It annoyed me though, when Cal ignored me and angered me when he would not discuss his life with me. He thought I was naive and sheltered, I supposed, and had no experience to console him. At first, I also dreaded any physical contact with him. In the dark, in the middle of the night, his unexpected kiss had seemed a fitting start to my grand adventure. Here, in daylight, things were different. Most of my reticence, I admit, was due to a fear of making a fool of myself. I was not sufficiently bothered by sex to find him either attractive or repellent. I would accept Wraeththu proclivities because it was necessary if I wanted to be with them; it really did not arouse my interest. Perhaps Cal knew this. On that first day, it was as if what had happened in the night had never been. In my innocence I thought I understood the context of Wraeththu sexuality. It was this way or that way; nothing abstract. "Cal is strange, being around him feels strange, because he craves the bodies of his own kind," I thought cleverly. "That's all it is."

Once the sun had begun its way back to the horizon, we packed up our things and headed out farther into the desert. Far away, bony mountains rose like black spines into the lavender haze. Beneath our feet the ground had become more uneven and sharp stones plunged into my feet through my thin shoes. Cal rode ahead of me, staring into the distance. Annoyance and finally anger gradually unfurled within me. I was carrying a heavy bag of food; my back ached furiously, my ankles were grazed and bleeding and my skin was rubbed raw by sweat and sweaty clothes. There was no way I had begun this journey just to be Cal's unpaid servant. Caught up in a storm of selfishness, that was how I felt. Foaming with wrath, I threw down my baggage, which clattered onto the rocks. Surprisingly, Cal reined the pony in immediately and looked at me. I ranted for a while about my discomfort, feeling both hopeless and abandoned. Sheer willpower kept the tears inside me. "Pellaz, I'm sorry," Cal interrupted me. "Sometimes I don't think. We will take turns upon the pony. Come on." Stunned into silence, I sheepishly hoisted myself onto the animal's back, who immediately sensed an incompetent rider and began tensing its haunches. Cal swung the heavy bag of food over his shoulder and, holding the pony's bridle, walked beside me.

"You must forgive me for being insensitive," he told me. "I've been alone for months now. It's easy to forget how to share things."

I was going through a phase of being uneasy with him, which came about every two hours, and struggled for something to say. Eventually, "Where have you come from?" burbled out. He ran his hand down the pony's sleek orange neck, his face troubled.

"About ten miles north of your place, I came to another farm. It was huge, expensive. You know—palm trees, verandas, drinks on the terrace, that sort of thing. They were into horses in a big way: and I was in a bad way. God knows what they thought when I lurched into their polite little tea-party! My arm was cut to the bone and stank like a carcase. I was sweating, swearing, hallucinating!" He laughed and so did I, but I did not think it was funny. "God, I was nearly dead," he continued. "Two days before that I had been traveling on the road with a friend. We stopped while I went into the bushes. We had a car, you know, and a whole tank of petrol. Anyway, I was only gone for a minute or two, but when I went back, the car was on fire and my friend was lying beside it—what was left of him. Raw meat! God! Two men, a woman and a child were watching. They didn't smile, not anything. But their hands were red with his blood . . ."

I did not like him talking like this. My heart was beating fast and I wanted him to stop. I did not want to hear any more. It made me nervous and sick. He spoke of the life I had now chosen. I was so fickle; one moment I begrudged his silence, the next I loathed his confiding in me. He did not see me though, did not see my discomfort, just kept stroking and stroking the pony's neck and carried on exorcising his bitter ghosts.

"I ran and I ran and I ran," he said, his voice getting fainter, "and I fell, got up, ran and fell again. That's how I hurt my arm. I can't remember doing it . . ." He straightened up and smiled. "Anyway, I was lucky, the fine people at that very white, clean, prosperous farm weren't prejudiced. They knew I was Wraeththu, but they were only curious. Wonderful liberals. Fools. They cleaned me, fed me, healed me and then, can you believe it, even offered me a job! Decorative as the palm trees, that's me. It would have been easy to stay, forget who and what I was for a time, but I had to keep going. I couldn't stay. So I repaid their hospitality and kindness by stealing this very expensive pony—and money. Look." He burrowed in his shirt and held out a crumpled bundle of paper. Silver stripes in it caught the sun.

"You said you had no money!" I gasped in one of my common moments of pathetic innocence.

"I know," he said wryly, smiling, and put it away again. "We'll need money later, really need it. I wasn't going to waste it."

After that, the atmosphere between us improved greatly. He had not crossed the gulf, but at least he had thrown me a rope.

For many days we traveled towards the mountains, conserving our supplies as best we could and resting only when absolutely necessary. We were lucky to find water on several occasions and the pony was content to pick at the sparse vegetation along the way. On the evening of the seventh day, we clambered through the foothills of the crags. Plants were becoming fewer, so we gathered as much as we could carry to feed the pony later on. Cliffs reared black and gaunt in impressive silence toward the darkening sky. Splintered rocks littered the ground, and strangely, brackish, milky pools of water lay in the hollows of them. Cal warned me not to touch it. As there was neither brush nor wood to gather, we could not light a fire when we camped for the night. We huddled uncomfortably under a blanket, too tired to keep going, too discomforted to sleep. For the first time since that first night, Cal deigned to touch me. We sat with our backs pressed into an overhanging rock with the blankets swathed around us. Awkwardly, Cal had put his arm around me, more because he was feeling miserable than because he wanted to hold me, I think. I realized that now I was absurdly disappointed that he had initiated nothing physical between us. It is difficult to work out why I had changed my mind about that. I thought that Wraeththu were on the way to not being exactly human, and it was part of their glamor, I suppose, that forbidden and secret sensuality they shrouded in ritual and reverence. Cal had spoken only briefly of such things and then only dropping meager hints; to test my reaction, I think. He once said, as we lay in a sandy hollow at night, that I possessed a rare and stunning beauty. His words had come to me out of the darkness, I could barely see him, and I had laughed, too loud, immediately, in sheer embarassment.

"Don't be ridiculous!" I had cried, more aggressively than I had intended, because I felt nervous, and just a little scared. He had smiled in a horrible, sneery way.

"Pell, that's one thing about you that is unattractive," he said. "You must know you are beautiful. It is more conceited to deny it. If you think that kind of modesty is becoming, you're wrong. It's just pathetically human. When someone tells you you're beautiful, you don't have to say anything at all."

I squirmed in humiliation for hours afterwards, and would not speak to him, but I knew he was right. Mima and I had always thought ourselves superior to all our peers, and not just in looks. But I had always thought it ill-mannered to let people know that. Cal was of a different world. His kind are proud of themselves and because none of them are truly ugly, Wraeththu are never ashamed to admit they are beautiful. Only in a world where ugliness prevails is it a shame to be vain, a cruelty to appreciate loveliness in oneself. Just being around Cal kindled my sexuality. I must admit this worried me. Had I possessed, unknown within myself, the inclination to desire another male? Perhaps I was being subtly brainwashed, and yet . . . sometimes, when I looked at Cal, out of the corner of my eye, in the evening, in the red light, it seemed a woman stood there; a woman who might have green hair or wings; something strange, unearthly. Sometimes I was frightened, sometimes just confused. Was my mind losing its grip on reality? The heat of the desert. . . ? I was in awe of Cal's magic; that which I could sense beneath the surface and his precise yet languid movements; his cat-like pride in himself, called to me, softly but insistent, like an enchantment. His eyes mirrored an intimacy long-gone, but it was caught within him for ever. That night, crouched under the gaunt, black cliffs, I longed to touch his face, to make him look at me, instead of the middle distance where old memories replayed themselves on the night, but I could not bring myself to move. My previous life had been cut off and had floated away from me, Mima's face was fading and her hands were mere wisps that reached for me, but I was still young, inexperienced and frightened. The beast slept within me but I was not ready to wake it.

The next day, we made our way up into the mountains. Starting at dawn, we followed a winding, stony path between the rocks, always traveling upwards. Cal told me he thought that once water had flowed down the mountains and had cut this convenient little road for us. In that time, the desert would have been lush and fertile. People would have lived there. I wondered how long it had been since others had climbed this path. It might have been centuries. The mountains had been attacked by huge pressures. We passed through a canyon, so deep it seemed we walked underwater and, looking up, we could see stars. The sides of it looked as if they had been hacked by a giant axe. Huge, scrawny birds, wheeled high above us in the light, their ragged voices reaching us as mournful cries.

"They are lost souls who cannot give up this world," said Cal. "They will not pass to the other side."

I shivered, even though I felt he was joking. "Will we have to leave Red behind?" I asked. By this time, our pony had a name.

"Oh no, it's not very far now," Cal replied vaguely. "Look at this." He had found a fossil in the canyon wall.

A thought struck me. "Have you been this way before?"

"Yes. Once."

My theory of us venturing into territory untouched by man for centuries abruptly evaporated. "Are we near Immanion, then?"

"Oh no, nowhere near." He was now sorting through some interesting stones that glittered pink and blue along the path. "Look at this. It could be anything." He held a rough crystal up to me. I was riding the pony more expertly now and it stopped when I wanted it to.

"Cal!" I said with a slight whine in my voice. "Where are we going?" My trousers had ripped at the knees because I had fallen over earlier in the day. While I waited for an answer he thoughtfully licked his forefinger and rubbed the graze on my knee.

"Hopefully, by tonight, we will reach the end of this pass. We will come to what looks like a vast moon crater mostly filled with a rather unpleasant soda lake. On the shores of that lake is a rough little Wraeththu town called Saltrock. It's been there about eighteen months, and yes, I have been there before. I have friends there. Good friends who have pioneered their way to this hellish spot to build a safe haven. At the moment it's not much, but it will be . . ." He was annoyed with me. I can see why now, but at the time I went sulky. "Is that all you want to know?"

I shrugged in the most irritating way I could. Was that all I wanted to know? I wanted to know everything and he told me as little as he had to. I was a willing convert to the way of Wraeththu, yet I knew so little about them. Cal's alien strangeness had become familiar because I was used to him, not because I understood him.

By twilight, the cliffs suddenly fell away beneath us and we stood at the lip of what once must have been a waterfall. Two figures, almost completely covered in sand-colored cloth, appeared in our path. They were armed with long knives. I felt as if my heart had leapt into my throat and I jerked Red's head savagely. But Cal spoke softly to them and they melted away again. For once I held my tongue. A path had been hewn out of the rock to the valley floor. It was narrow and difficult to follow. A strange, acrid stench reached my nostrils as we descended. Only when we reached the bottom did I dare look up. Ahead of us a vast sheet of what looked like molten gold reflected the sinking sun. Steams and vapours coiled and leapt off the surface. Everywhere, grotesque mineral deposits stood like sculptures, the models for which I would not care to meet. The lake was ringed by mountains and not too far away I could see fresh water cascading down the black rock. Saltrock town, a ragged silhouette in the twilight, was lit by flickering yellow and orange fingers of flame.

Someone came to meet us. A thin, rangy horse galloped toward us along the lake's stony shore. Cal stopped dead. He was smiling.

"Behold exotica, Pell!" he exclaimed, with a grin from ear to ear. He who rode the thin horse skidded it to a halt in front of us. Pebbles flew everywhere. When he leapt from the animal's back, it was in a wild tangle of flying rags, tassels and flying red, yellow and black hair. (Another reality shift shocked me cold as the sexes mingled. Was this creature male or female, or could it be both. . .?!)

"Cal! They signaled it was you!" he cried and, with restrained enthusiasm, they embraced.

In the twilight I could just see his amazing, purposefully tattered clothing and incredible hair. If Cal had ever seemed alien to me, there are no words to describe my first impressions of the second Wraeththu I had ever met. A twinge of despair wriggled through me as I waited, small and silent, while they greeted each other. Fumes rose off the lake like ghosts and the smell was making me feel sick. Cal suddenly remembered me. Partly disentangling himself, he said, with a wave of his arm, "Seel, this is Pell. I abducted him from a peasant farm." (Laughter). Nettled, and feeling this was wildly exaggerated, I moved my head in acknowledgment. Seel assessed me in an instant, fixing a huge, disarming grin across his face. "Welcome to Saltrock," he said in a way that let me know I was irrelevant. We strolled toward the town. Seel linked his arm through Cal's and chattered continuously about things and people I did not know. The horses plodded behind. Seel overwhelmed me. He burned with an undeniable dynamism, eclipsing even Cal's charisma, although he was not as tall. When he noticed I was trailing behind, he decided to make a good impression on Cal. I was swooped upon and wrapped in leather-strapped, metal-studded arms. "You look so tired. It's not far. Lean on me."

It pains me to remember what a bad-tempered wretch I was then. The only thing that kept me from shrugging Seel off with a curse, was that I lacked the guts.

Saltrock was my first true encounter with the Wraeththu way of life. I cannot deny it astounded me. I cannot remember what I was expecting, but Saltrock was a real town, or the beginnings of one. Admittedly the buildings were constructed of a mad variety of materials, with seemingly little organization. Some were quite large and made of solid wood, others little more than thrown-together metal sheeting or mere tents of animal hides. Light was provided by flaming torches that gave off an oily reek, hurricane lamps and thick candles. The inhabitants, creatures as startling as Seel, exuded spirit and energy. Many recognized Cal as we passed among them. Everywhere the drabness and disarray was disguised by gaudy decoration. Wraeththu boys of bizarre appearance with painted faces strutted through the crazy streets; some were still working into the night. There was a sound of hammering. All carried guns or knives. I once caught a glimpse of a rusting, flashy car sagging in a sheltered corner and a corral with a high fence teeming with restless horses. Nobody looked at me and the atmosphere, though strange, did not feel hostile.

Seel's house was a little way out of the center of Saltrock, set apart from the other buildings. It was an incredible sight; a large wooden, gothic anachronism. Only skilled carpenters could have produced such a thing. The doors were not locked. Seel said to me, as yet unaware of the simplicity of my origins, "Sorry, we have no electricity here yet." Someone, with a crazy, spiked mop of black hair, had taken our horses from us. I had seen the whites of his eyes, like a mad beast, gleaming and the grin he had fleered at me was nothing other than feral.

We went into the house. "Eventually, we'll get some kind of generator,"

Seel continued conversationally, "but it takes time. We have to steal things bit by bit. We don't have much to barter with as yet."

The entrance hall was fairly bare, but smelled of clean wood. Stairs led to an upper gallery with doors leading off. Three more doors led off the hall. A boy, who looked a little younger than myself, sauntered out from the back of the house, wiping his hands on a cloth. He was very pale, almost white, with an exquisite pixie face. His head was shaved, except for a long black ponytail growing from the top which fell over his shoulder.

"Flick, where's the food? Cal's starving. Get back in the kitchen," Seel ordered with a dismissive wave of his hand. The boy retreated with a shrug.

"Equality, equality," Cal said, rolling his eyes.

"Oh, I know, I know. I'm an ill-humoured bastard who should make a living out of slavery," Seel replied with humor. "If he wants to live here, he works. He's lazy as fuck half the time." He ushered us into one of the rooms. "My nest," he said. We dumped what luggage we were carrying in the hall and followed him in.

"Seel, you Sybarite!" Cal exclaimed with a laugh. Silks and tassels hung everwhere. Lights, suspended from the ceiling in bowls of intricately worked oriental metal, threw out a dim, cozy glow. Perfumes smouldered in corners, exuding a silvery smoke.

"Sit down, sit down," Seel urged impatiently. He tried to hide from us that he was proud of his home and pleased that Cal had admired it. Cautiously, I lowered myself into a heap of black and gold cushions. Protesting, a Siamese cat wriggled from underneath me and shot out through the door. Incense burned behind me with a perfume so strong it made my head ache, although the soda-stink still burned my throat.

"I'll get you some refreshment," Seel told us. Moments later, we could hear him arguing with Flick in the kitchen.

Left alone with Cal, I did not know what to say to him. The last half-hour had passed like a dream. I was dazed. Cal looked awkward.

"Well!" he began, with a pitiful attempt at forced heartiness. "Seel has improved this place since I was last here. He was living in a tent then! What do you think of him?"

He did not look at me when he said it and did not see me shrug helplessly. I was thinking, "Oh God, he's wishing he hadn't brought me here," and decided I knew now why he had never touched me. He had been waiting for Seel. I had a lot to learn.

"Seel's the top dog around here," he said. "This place wouldn't exist if it wasn't for him." He stood up and walked around the room, examining things. "God, it's good to be back!"

Seel came back in clutching a bottle in one hand and three long-stemmed glasses in the other. "Champagne, gentlemen?" he queried.

"Seel, how do you get this stuff?" Cal asked him, impressed.

Seel winked at him. "Treachery, corruption and thievery of course, how else?"

He offered me a glass. I had never even heard of champagne and did not like the taste much. It was very difficult not to keep staring at Seel, but he did not seem to mind. He was dressed mostly in thin, torn leather and had the same build as Cal, sleek and fit, and that same shifting male/female ambience. His olive-skinned face was almost inhumanly symmetrical and the almond-shaped eyes were lined with kohl. Inadequacy swamped me. It was inconceivable I could ever feel equal to Wraeththu strangeness, and, as fear prodded me sharply, I wondered: "How did they become so alien?" Presumably, most, if not all, had come from humble origins like mine once. Something other than human blood coursed through their veins now, I concluded. A thought that proved uncannily perceptive.

"Colt and Stringer might call in later," Seel told Cal. "But if you want to crash out somewhere, that's OK."

Cal rubbed his face. "No. I'd like to see them again. Just kick me if I drop off." The wine had got to him. His eyes were half closed.

Seel looked puzzled about something, as if he had only just thought of it. "Cal?" A careful question.

"What?" Cal suddenly looked defensive.

Seel's eyes flickered over me. "I've a feeling you're going to hate this, but what happened to Zack?" It would have taken more than a knife to cut the atmosphere. I cringed in discomfort.

Cal made a strange, hissing noise through his teeth. "Not now, Seel. Not now," he replied, his voice strained and tired. Never had I felt so out of place. I should not be there. Another's place, not mine.

"Hell, I knew I was going to regret that," Seel sighed, smiling ruefully at Cal. He deftly changed the subject, talking with wit and vigor. Saltrock gossip. I did not really hear him and neither, I think, did Cal. Zack. I had a feeling he was the one who ended up as raw meat.

Flick brought us food. I was hungry but still shy and only nibbled at what was offered; chunks of meat cooked in herbs, and baked potatoes. Hot, melted butter spiced with garlic dripped over them. I regretted my throat was closed. Seel kept glancing at me. "Flick, go talk with Pell," he said, after a while, and turned back to Cal. Flick threw himself into the cushions beside me. He was dressed in ripped jeans and a tattered T-shirt and looked absurdly graceful. He regarded first my mussed plate and then my flushed face.

"Finish your wine. Come with me," he whispered. "You need some air."

The wine hit my stomach like hot ashes. The room lurched as I stood up and I bumped into things as I followed him across the room. I was grateful to get out although I was convinced Cal would start talking about me as soon as I was gone. Half-drunk, I could not be sure if I was really there. Maybe it was a dream and we were still in the desert. Soon I would wake and Cal would be staring at the stars, dead people in his eyes.

Flick steadied me and led me out into the open air. We were in a kind of courtyard. Low buildings shambled around its edge and the air stung my tongue anew with the faint acridity of soda. Above us the sky was rich, dark blue, vividly studded with stars. The eyes of the dead. Raw meat. Dreams.

To my left the roofs of the buildings were touched with a weak luminescence that rose from the lake. An underground, sulphurous light. My chest was tight with painful, intoxicated misery. Flick hovered like a phantom, watching. I sat down heavily on the sandy ground. I could not contain it. Like a burst abscess my fear and discomfort spurted out of me. I wept and wept, hearing my sobs echo like the cries of a child waking from nightmare. I hated this place. The strangeness, the stench, the outlandishness of the people. They are not people. Something else. I was alone. Cal was a stranger, remote and calculating. I had been a fool to go with him. Why had I not thought of what I was getting into? I could never be one of them, never. I did not trust Cal and was terrified of what might happen to me. Raw meat. Into the soda, into the limepits. Curling up as tight as I could, trembling animal howls shuddered out of me. And then, there were arms around me. Then the warmth of another body, a living thing, dream whispers in my hair. No language I had ever heard. Flick, an unlikely comforter, crooning reassurance.

"Come on, come on, get it all out," he urged, as if I was being sick.

Through my tears, I managed a bleak laugh. It was the first time in my life, however, that I had wept and not felt ashamed. Flick asked me what the matter was.

"Scared," I bleated, and all my fears tumbled out, mostly incomprehensible, even to myself. Flick listened patiently, saying nothing, until I had finished.

"Many feel like this at first," he told me. A wistful smile quivered across his face. "You have given up everything you had, everything you knew. It's bound to feel strange. Look at it like this: you come to the world of Wraeththu as naked and helpless as a human baby. You will learn, gradually, just as babies do. Don't expect everything to happen at once. It takes time and there are reasons for that. The Wraeththu are mostly good people. Here at Saltrock they are; you are safe. They will not harm you, especially as you're with Cal."

I thumped the ground angrily with my hand. "Cal!" I spat bitterly. "Safe? With him? He doesn't even live in this world. I hardly know him. My welfare is nothing to him!"

Flick's face was perplexed. He could not think of anything to say. I thought it was because he presumed Cal and I to be closer than we actually were. "He and Seel are laughing at me!" I announced, hating the petty whine in my voice, but powerless to control it.

"No, they're not!" Flick answered sharply. His eyes looked hurt. "Why should they?" He thought I was an idiot.

"Because . . . because I'm nothing, a peasant. I know nothing, and because I was fool enough to let Cal take me away from home . . . and for what?!" I was so angry I could not keep still. I stood up, unsteadily, to continue my ravings. "Why did he do this? Why did he entice me away with him? I don't understand. I'm no use to him or to anyone here. I have no skill to offer you. Cal won't even listen to my questions half the time, let alone answer them. I want answers! What happens next? Where do I go and how do I live?"

Flick would not shout back at me. "You must trust Cal a little more," he said quietly. "He won't abandon you, if that's what you're frightened of. There's so much you don't know. Ignore the fear, it's nothing. I know Cal better than you. He's sick. He's not himself. Give him time." I shrugged and glowered at the floor. "Look, I can't tell you the things you want to know, Pell. It's not my place to. All I can say is that Cal wouldn't have brought you here unless he was sure you were the right person. You must learn to be patient." Looking at his face the anger went out of me. I knew I had made a fool of myself, and was thankful only Flick had witnessed it. "You OK now?"

"Yes." My voice was a sulky mumble. "I'm sorry."

"Forget it. You're tired. You're wrecked. Moan again tomorrow and I'll break your head." His smile, so genuine, I felt like crying again.

Wraeththu; growing. Something great stirring. My perspective was all wrong. Self-centered. I had to learn, or unlearn, my own importance. Only then, could I begin to see. Only then could Wraeththu touch me.

CHAPTER TWO

The light beneath the door

Self-discipline must be the hardest principle to master. Second is tolerance and then acceptance. That first night at Saltrock, I began my education. Something that Flick had said to me made me face myself; a facet of maturing I might never have encountered at home on the cable farm. Wrapped up in the small bit of the world that our ego experiences, it is easy to lose track of absolute reality, to warp actual events to suit ourselves. Wraeththu have an almost clinically straight view of things; from the very beginning they strive to rid themselves of self-delusion. Once this has been accomplished one's instincts are infallible, the mind is finely honed for survival. The first law of Wraeththu is selflessness. It is true that not many can perfect this in themselves, (as became all too clear later on in my life), but as a personal goal it is very important. When faced with the hostility of enemies however, there is no more ferocious killer than the Wraeththu warrior. Therefore, I think the second law of Wraeththu must be physical perfection. The body must run like a well-tended machine; be as trust-worthy as a blade or a bullet.

Colt and Stringer, those people that Seel had mentioned, were as close to these ideals as it is possible to get. At that time I was under the happy delusion that all Wraeththu must be like them. When Flick and I went back into the house, they had already arrived and were speaking in low voices to Cal. I realized something that had gone over my head in the desert. Cal was weary and shaken to the core of his being. Only now, as he relaxed, was it truly apparent. His friends could sense it at once; their whole manner toward him was one of calm and healing. How my sniping temperament must have chafed at his nerves during our journey I could only guess. How lucky I was he had not throttled me! Me: so used to being the center of attention. The beautiful, cherished brother of Mima, the adored, bright son of my doting parents. Now I had to learn that respect had to be earned.

Flick and I sat apart from the others. They barely acknowledged my presence. Flick told me it was because I was Unhar and of no caste.

"What is Unhar?" I asked him.

"You will learn that later," he replied. "I really can't tell you. But I am Har, and my caste is Kaimana. My level is Neoma. Cal and Seel and the others are Ulani; that is a higher caste. I'm not sure, but I think Cal's level is Pyralis, that's second level Ulani. He would be known as Pyralisit. Do you understand?"

"No," I said, "but I'm tired and the wine was strong. Tell me again tomorrow."

Flick laughed in a strange, shy way. "Perhaps," he said. Some moments later, he offered to show me to my room. As we left, no-one bid us good-night. Cal did not even look up. It annoyed me but I tried to ignore it.

"I expect you'd like to take a bath first," Flick remarked casually, as he led me upstairs. "Some things we have to do without, but we do have hot, running water here." I was obviously meant to be impressed by this.

My room was palatial compared to what I was used to. Goatskins covered the floor, opalescent lamps glimmered in corners and the bed was enormous. Thick, striped blankets drooped to the floor on either side and swathes of netting formed a nebulous curtain to keep insects away. Luxury indeed!

"The bathroom's over here," Flick instructed, indicating a door on the far side of the room. "There should be towels in there. I'll give you half an hour or so, then I'll bring you some coffee up, OK?" Once he had gone, I just stood in the middle of the room, marvelling.

Later, Flick not only brought me coffee, dark as sump oil but with a surprisingly mild flavor, but cigarettes as well. I rarely smoked at home, but this was a luxury not to be foregone. Feeling clean and relaxed I sat on the bed while Flick brushed out my wet and tangled hair. I began to tell him about the cable farm (how fascinating) and afterwards he told me he had come from a city farther north. His family had been quite rich and he had brought a lot of money to Saltrock with him. Seel had put it to good use, he said. (Yes, I thought, looking again around the room.) I wanted to know what had induced Flick to run away from a home that had obviously been so comfortable, to join the Wraeththu and live rough by comparison. His mouth twisted with thought. "It just seemed . . . I don't know . . . right. As if I had no choice. I had to do it. Surely you know what I mean." I did. The Wraeththu of Saltrock seemed remarkably adept at procuring luxuries. Flick implied to me that a lot of what they had was stolen, groups of Saltrock inhabitants going out into the world beyond the desert on looting forays, or else commodities were brought into the community by newcomers. I also felt impelled to explain, with much stammering, just what the extent of my relationship with Cal was. Contrary to what I expected, Flick was not at all surprised. "Of course, you are Unhar," was all he said. Some demon made me ask; "Flick. Cal . . . Seel . . . you know . . . Are they . . .?"

Flick gave me a guarded look that melted to a smile. "Now why should you want to know that, Pellaz?" I shrugged helplessly, wishing to God that I had not opened my mouth. Flick patted my face. "Classified information at the moment," he said with a grin.

Once Flick had gone, and I had settled, almost purring, into the canopied bed, I thought about Cal. I was wracked with guilt. I had not noticed his exhaustion, his torment. Perhaps Seel was soothing him now. I could not bear to think about it. Seel and Cal. But it was not my place to wonder. I was Unhar. I was nothing. I awoke from habit just after dawn. Outside, Saltrock was stirring. I suppose I must have thought, "What am I doing here?" Thoughts like that did cross my mind a lot at that time, but I became adept at ejecting them. Pale, lemon light filtered in through the gauzy curtains. I lay there, revelling in the comfort and warmth. Only when something moved and touched me did I turn over. Cal was asleep beside me, two cats slumbering contentedly on his chest. It made me jump. I am not a heavy sleeper, yet I had not heard him come to bed. He was frowning, arms thrown up over his head. He always slept like that. I could see the long, white scar on his arm. It was the first time I had looked at him for so long. Usually, he caught me doing it and I turned away. I desperately wanted to talk to him and spoke his name. Wrinkling his nose, he only mumbled and twitched. Never had he looked so perfect.

"Cal," I said again. He groaned, half-conscious. "I was talking to Flick last night. Listen!"

He sighed. "I am."

"I've been a brat. I'm sorry. Flick told me what I am: Unhar, uncaste. I've been so selfish . . . oh hell!" I could not find the words for what I wanted to say. It all sounded so trite.

Cal was looking at me now, thoughtfully, "Pellaz, shut up. Come here." I put my head upon his chest and clung to him. The cats half rose, looking at me with disgust. "Look, I don't keep you in the dark about things out of spite. In two days time, you will take the Harhune. Then you will be Har. Then you can begin to learn, but not till then." His arm tightened around me, the muscles trembling.

"You're sick," I looked up at him but he would not meet my eyes.

"Like hell. I'm tired, that's all. Don't start, Pell, I can't stand it. And lie still, or you'll be out of that window in a moment. Just go back to sleep, OK?"

We slept till noon.

We breakfasted, or more truthfully, lunched with Seel and Flick in the kitchen. It was a low-ceilinged, dark room dominated by a huge, black cooking-range. We ate fried chicken and salad. I was curious as to how Saltrock obtained vegetables and Seel explained they had one or two acres of irrigated land behind the town where it was possible to grow things. Flick said it was more like a jungle of exotic flowers; they thrived horribly on the mineral cocktail in the soil. It was true that the food did have a faint acrid tang to it. Flick asked me if I would like to ride out along the shores of the soda lake with him and I accepted with enthusiasm. I had decided to goad him for information.

Saltrock, by day, was revealed to be a lot shabbier than I had first imagined. However, everyone I saw seemed to be engaged in some kind of purposeful activity; there were few loiterers. Flick took me on a tour of the town, before we headed out along the shores of the lake. There were no proper shops to be seen, but some of the wooden and corrugated iron dwellings had items for sale spread out beside their doors; mainly mis-matched clothing, rather tired-looking canned food with faded labels or crude utensils for the home. I was curious about what was used as currency and Flick explained that nearly all trade was conducted on a barter system, for the simple reason that the majority of Saltrock's inhabitants rarely ventured out into the world to places where money was still used. I realized, with a pang, how isolated my family had been (and still was, no doubt), living obliviously at the edge of the desert, happily unaware of the huge changes stirring across the face of the world. Sefton Richards, of course, must have felt it; locked away in his great, white house; he must have had accurate news of what was going on. Eventually, the crops we'd grown must become unsaleable. What would happen then? I thought briefly, painfully, of Mima and the others and pushed it out of my mind. I was now in Saltrock, a different reality, my life had changed or begun to; the past was gone forever. Flick called out to people that he knew who would raise their heads from whatever work they were engrossed in and wave. Very few of the buildings were anywhere near as grand as Seel's residence, most being sprawling, single-storied and obviously occupied by large groups of Wraeththu. We passed one large, church-like construction in the middle of the town, but Flick seemed reluctant to discuss its function. It was surpris-ing how many people appeared to be hurrying around, laden with building materials or driving animals here and there. What drew them to this place? I wasn't yet sure whether I liked Saltrock or not.

It was very hot outside and the fumes stung my eyes. Red made an-guished noises through his nose. How exhilarating, though, to gallop through the brittle sands. Strange, lumbering lizards heaved themselves from our path and honking flocks of wading birds lifted from the surface of the lake in alarm. Everything sparkled and crystals of salt formed in my hair. Flick told me I had better make the most of it.

"Of what?" I enquired, shaking the salty locks off my shoulders, making the air glitter.

"Your hair, you peacock! You won't have all that for much longer!"

I yanked Red to a reluctant halt, fighting with his head. "What?" My hand fluttered up automatically to touch it, my crowning glory. "Why not?"

Flick looked furious with himself. "Oh, don't worry, I spoke out of turn." I must have looked demented; I dreaded being disfigured in even the slightest way. "Oh well, I don't suppose it will do any harm; what I meant was, they'll cut your hair. It's part of the ritual, the Harhune. Like mine, not all of it."

"Why?" I squeaked, aghast.

"As I said, it's just part of the ritual, that's all. You can grow it back afterwards."

"Oh. I see." My hair . . . I could remember in the evening, back home, my sister Mima brushing it out for me. "A hundred strokes to make it shine," she had said. Once she had caught me looking in her mirror, admiring and swishing the tumbling blackness, and I can still recall her laughter. "God, you should have been born a girl, Pell." There was a bleak echo to those words now.

I pressed Red with my heels. He put his ears back as he skipped sideways into a trot. There was a strained air around us now. I was so prickly, and unconsciously, so vain.

Finally, I relented and spoke. "How long have you been . . . har, Flick?" My voice sounded imperious and prim even to me.

Flick suppressed a mocking smile. "About a year, I think. I progressed from Ara to Neoma pretty quickly. I had a good teacher." I did not ask him who that was as I was obviously supposed to.

"What is Harhune?" I said instead, to be awkward. I guessed he was forbidden to answer.

He pulled a face. "Pellaz, I wish you wouldn't ask me things. It's so horrible when I can't tell you. Seel would have my skin if I did."

Rage ignited in my throat. "Oh, for God's sake!" I cried. "Why is everything so damn secret. Don't tell Pell this, don't tell him that! He mustn't *know* anything. It's pathetic!" I was sick of the constant air of mystery; I thought it such a pose.

"Look," Flick strained to be patient, "tomorrow you will begin Forale. It's a day of fasting before the Harhune. Seel or someone will instruct you then."

"Why didn't anyone tell me?!" I raged. "If you hadn't, would I have woken up tomorrow and stuffed myself rigid before anyone mentioned I was supposed to be fasting? Hell, hell, bloody hell!!"

"No, no, tonight—they'll tell you tonight!" Flick was unsure of how to handle me, my tempers could be very colorful. I was pleased inside though.

The end of my frustrating, innocent unHarness was in sight. I had an idea what the Harhune actually was and I told Flick about it. He denied it vehemently.

"Oh, come on," I goaded mercilessly, "it's sex, isn't it. That's what it is."

"God, Pell, what cloud are you on?! Sex is important, yes, but it certainly isn't the be-all and end-all of our existence and it definitely isn't what the Harhune is all about. Stop provoking me; I'm not going to tell you."

He kicked his pony into a scrabbling canter and darted away from me. Red bucked as I made him catch up. Flick's pony was no match for him. Ahead of us the black cliffs reared to the sky and water thundered down their glistening flanks. Steam roiled about us like smoke.

"Flick! I want to ask you another question!" I shouted.

Flick screwed up his face again. "Oh no!"

"It's not a forbidden one." I sidled Red up against Flick's pony so I would not have to scream at him. "Did you ever meet Zack?"

Flick gave me another of his strange, guarded looks. "Yes. Why?"

"I'm just curious, that's all. What was he like?" I tried to keep an insouciant note in my voice.

"What was he like? Wild . . . wild and reckless. Witty, courageous, fierce, gorgeous . . . do you want me to go on?"

"Yes. What did he look like?" My heart was thudding; I felt breathless. Flick had warmed to the subject.

"He looked like . . . like, I don't know. He was a bit like Cal, only as dark as Cal is fair. High cheekbones, sulky eyes. In a way you remind me of him; the same temperament I think. That's probably why Cal is kelos over you. He and Zack were chesna."

"Flick," I said, shaking my head at him. "What the hell are you talking about. You must know I don't understand half of it."

He grinned. "Yes, I know. Kelos is crazy, chesna is . . . well, more than friends." A fatuous smile spread across my face. I could not get rid of it.

"Cal is not . . . not kelos, crazy about me, Flick. Surely I'd know if he was."

"Sure. Like you know everything else about Wraeththu."

I could say nothing more. With an ear-splitting screech, I panicked Red into a mad gallop; the stinging, flying air lathering my exhilaration. Tomorrow, tomorrow it would begin. My un-harness would soon be nothing but a frustrating memory. The consequences? Oh, I banished them, what I knew, banished them from my mind. It was too much of an exquisite torment to think of them.

Supper was a subdued affair. I avoided looking at Cal, and Flick avidly watched what I was doing. Seel smoked cigarette after cigarette, I had never met such an addict, and Cal looked so glum he did not even notice I was avoiding him. Not exactly a party atmosphere. Surely, we should have been celebrating my approaching Harhune. When we had finished eating, Cal and Flick discreetly left the room. We were in Seel's exotic little salon.

"Pellaz, we have to talk," he said gravely.

I was feeling edgy and hysterical and wished he would smile. I half knew what he wanted to say, but I still felt stricken, petrified inside. He took my hand. His was cool, long-fingered and dry; mine was shaky and sweaty. He turned it over and half-heartedly examined the palm as he spoke.

"You want to be Wraeththu, don't you?" It was not a question and I said nothing, but swallowed noisily. "Tomorrow you can begin your initiation into our way of life. I have to warn you, it will not be easy, and for that reason, you must be absolutely sure you want to go through with it." His dark eyes seemed enormous; I was hypnotized. They stared right into me, peeling away the constructions of ego. I nodded.

"I'm sure. I've come this far . . ."

"That was nothing!" Seel snorted and let go of my hand, which hit the table like a dead fish. He leaned back into the cushions. I felt foolish. It was all so unreal. I longed to laugh whilst still stretched transparent by nerves. "You know very little and, frankly, that is the best way to be. I expect you find it very irritating."

"Yes. A bit," I confessed in a quiet voice.

"Hmmm. Well, at midnight, tonight, I will take you to the Forale-house. The Forale is what we call the day before Harhune. You will be cleansed and given instructions. You must eat nothing. Do you understand?"

"Yes." He was so cold, so unlike the Seel I had come to expect over the last day.

"Now, all you need to know is that the Harhune itself is painless. You don't have to be afraid." That was one thing I had not anticipated: pain. It unnerved me that Seel should mention it. "Just think of it like this. In a few days' time it will all be over and you'll know everything you want to. Now, you have an hour or so yet. Do you want to see Cal before I take you away?" His voice was less harsh.

I glanced up at him; a face inscrutable with restrained amusement. "Yes . . . please."

He laughed then and patted my shoulder, reaching for another cigarette. "Treat him gently, he's as nervous as you are."

Yes, I thought, probably because he knows what is going to happen to me.

Cal slunk in like a guilty dog and Seel left us alone. When our eyes met it was like being scalded and we both looked away quickly.

"I brought you into this," Cal said with a grimace and a weak attempt at humor.

As usual, all the wrong things started pouring from my mouth. "I don't know what's happening, but the way everyone's carrying on, it must be worse than I think. Unhealthy for me, anyway!"

Cal sat down beside me. "Oh, fuck! Fuck! Fuck!" he profaned. I had never heard him swear before; he was so fastidious. "Oh, God, I don't care what the law says. I'm not supposed to tell you anything but, yes, in a way, it is unhealthy. You must have heard the stories; some of them even died. . . . It's not all exaggeration, you know."

"Oh Cal!" I gasped. "Thanks! Thanks!" I put my head in my hands, arrowed by shock. Possible death was a consequence of becoming Wraeththu I had not considered.

"You had to know. There is a risk, but I think knowing that will make you stronger. You are strong, Pell." I looked at him through my fingers. He was sallow with worry. "It's necessary," he said. "We cannot afford to carry dead wood."

"I know." I straightened my back and closed my eyes. I could feel my hair, soon to be gone, heavy on my shoulders; the first time I had even noticed its weight. "I want to be Wraeththu," I murmured.

"I want you to be as well," said Cal and inevitably we fumbled toward each other. Nearly every time we had touched, I had clung to him like a mewling brat. Tonight was no exception. He wound his fingers in my hair and stroked my neck. I could feel him sighing. His smell was clean and musky, like new-mown hay.

"You've only known me a week, or so," I said.

"A week, a lifetime; what difference?" He held me so tightly, I nearly choked.

Seel walked in and found us like that, just holding onto each other as if for the last time. He passed no comment, but he obviously did not trust Cal not to blab everything to me. We had been alone for about ten minutes.

Just before midnight, Seel stood up and signaled to me. "Now, Pell," he said.

"Just bring him back in one piece," Cal told him, not smiling.

"Oh come on, Calanthe, my dear, you'll be there, watching, I know you will." Seel started herding me toward the door. As we left, he called back over his shoulder. "Just start thinking about aruna, Cal!" And he laughed.

"What's that?" I asked him, not really expecting an answer.

"The finest time of your life, little Pellaz. If only I could be you."

A sentiment I was not averse to sharing, adding drily, "If I get through the Harhune, of course."

Seel made a small noise of annoyance. "You're not safe for a minute, are you. I might have known he'd tell you something. Cal's so emotional, I sometimes think he's still half human."

There is a point when facing the unknown stops being a longed-for adventure and becomes a terrifying reality. When you are young, it is so easy to blunder into situations when misplaced heroism is no substitute for good sense. As I followed Seel to the Forale-house, I started doubting. I had no idea what they would do to me. I had given myself into the hands of strangers with no assurance that they were concerned about my well-being. Cal had glamorized me. His wistful and haunting beauty, his mysterious and perhaps violent past, appealed to me, an inexperienced and immature boy, as make-believe superheroes had appealed to young boys throughout the ages. As much as I realized my impulsive folly, I also knew that it was too late to back out. I would never have been able to find my way home, even if the Wraeththu had allowed it. Perhaps, too, I now knew too much, little as it was, for them to let me go. As Seel opened the door to my fate, the brief intimacy with Cal and the way I had felt about him, had faded. All I knew was that stultifying, indescribable sensation that is the one true fear.

The light inside was dim, but I could make out a bare room, furnished with as little as was practical. A narrow bed stuck out from the far wall. There was a strong smell of creosote. All I wanted to do was curl up on the floor and shut my eyes tight until everything went away.

"Pellaz." Seel's touch on my shoulder brought me around a little. His eyes told me all I needed to know. Once, he had been in my place. Once even Seel had stood at the threshhold of acceptance, doubting. For the first time, I noticed the faint lines around his eyes and the shadow within them that told of the fighting, the struggle. What were Wraeththu?

"Pell, this is Mur and Garis. They are here to help you through the next few days. They will attend to you."

Two figures were standing in the doorway to another room. Neither looked at me with sympathy, only a kind of resigned boredom. They moved, with slouching ennui, to either side of Seel, sharp and angular strangers, dressed in dull gray. Seel lifted his head, his face shadowed yet luminous in the yellow light.

"Pellaz Unhar, now is the time of your Inception. It is decreed that you shall be prepared in your physical, mental and spiritual states for your approaching Harhune. Do you deliver yourself into our hands for this time, your Forale?"

"Yes." My voice was faint, but what else could I have said.

"Then we may commence." He relaxed and rubbed his face, casting off the incongruous image of high priest. Normally, I would have laughed at it all; arcane words and special effects. At the time, it was deadly serious.

"Garis and Mur will bathe you now," he said. "I can promise you, by the end of all this you will hate the sight of a bath. See you tomorrow."

Without a further glance at me he went out, letting the door swing shut with a horrible finality behind him.

"This way," the one called Garis drawled at me. Gray shirt, gray trousers, iron-gray hair, like the color of a horse, half plaited and held up on his head with loose combs. His feet were bare, the toe-nails more like claws. Mur was similarly attired, only his hair was dyed black, mostly cut short and spiked everywhere except at the nape of his neck, where it was braided to below his shoulder-blades. I followed them into the other room which was lit more brilliantly. Two lamps. It was a bathroom that looked more like a dissecting chamber. Two scrubbed tables, a deep, narrow bath and a sink that looked like steel. All that was missing were the knives and the rubber gloves. Chatting to each other, not even looking at me, Mur and

Garis pulled off my clothes. I stood there, shivering and naked, while they busied themselves about the room. Even if they had actually shouted, "Pellaz, you are absolutely worthless!," it would not have been more clear. Thoughts of my old home echoed through my mind. Mima's smile, a dim colorless replay; squeaky sounds I could not understand. Somewhere nearby, Cal was sitting or standing, talking, drinking. Laughing? Did he think of me? Tears of a child dewed my lashes but did not fall. I let the strangers put me into the bath. Salt water licked at all my old cuts and scratches. Garis wrenched my arms as he scrubbed at me. It felt like they were rubbing slivers of glass into my skin.

At the end of it, I was lifted out, impersonally, and dried off with a coarse towel, red and smarting from head to toe.

"Here, put that on!" Garis threw me a bundle of cloth. As I struggled wretchedly to dress myself, the other two laughed together. I dared say nothing, but I hated them. The kind of hate you can nearly see, it is so strong.

"You can go to bed now," Mur mentioned, throwing a cold glance over his shoulder as he folded the towels. Garis leaned against the sink, preening his fingernails, looking at me through slitted eyes. He held me in utter contempt. I burned at the humiliation, the unfairness. They had several days during which to torment me. Hitching up the unflattering robe I was wearing, I shuffled back through the door. They started talking as soon as I had gone.

"Human bodies are so disgusting, like animals," Mur said.

"How lucky for you you never had one!" I heard Garis remind him sarcastically. Disgusting? Animal? To me I looked no different from them. They extinguished the lamps before they left. Not a word of farewell. I huddled on the hard bed trying to warm myself with the thin blanket that covered it. Rough material chafed my skin and scratching myself only made it worse. A window, high up, showed me a perfect sky sequinned with lustrous stars. Moonlight fell across my face. I wanted to weep, but I was numb. Why were they so cruel? I could not understand, innocent as I was. Nobody had ever been actively hostile to me in my life before. Too beaten to be angry anymore, I sank into a restless sleep and the dreams, when they came, were ranting horrors, perverse possibilities.

I had been awake for what seemed hours when Seel sauntered in. He gave me a flask of water, and did not ask how I was feeling. Already my stomach was protesting furiously at not being fed. I had eaten poorly the day before and regretted it deeply now. Sitting dejectedly on the bed, still scratching, I sipped the water.

"Pellaz thinks he's in hell." Seel regarded me inscrutably. I said nothing. "I can remember," he continued. "One day, perhaps, you will be in my position. Soon, you will see . . ."

"It is necessary," I said dully.

Seel chewed his cheek thoughtfully. "You must be purified. To do that you must suffer humiliation. Only from trial may the spirit flower," he quoted, from something.

"Is this a lesson?" My spirit was far from flowering.

Seel raised an eyebrow. "As a matter of fact, yes. Someone else is coming to instruct you fully, though. He's a high ranking Ulani, called Orien. Don't antagonize him, Pell. He may turn you into a frog."

I could see he was struggling to be patient with me. I was supposed to be the abject supplicant awaiting enlightenment, but at the moment, I was slipping the other way.

Orien, however, did much to dispel my petulance. He was blessed with the kind of manner that instantly lightens the atmosphere. His clothes were threadbare and his hair, half tied back with a black ribbon, was escaping confinement over his shoulders. He rarely stopped smiling. Before beginning my lessons, he told me we would meditate together. "Try to empty your mind," he said, as we sat cross-legged on the floor. For me, that was an impossibility. I did not really know what meditation was and my mind was buzzing like a nest of wasps. I could not keep still. After a while, Orien sighed and rummaged in the bag he had brought with him. "Put out your tongue, Pell." He touched me with a bitter paste from a tiny glass pot. I grimaced and he smile at me. "Come on, swallow." My throat burned, but in a short time a pleasant coolness seeped through my limbs and crawled toward my mind. "Now, we shall try again."

This time it was easy. Gradually, I was eased into a white and soothing blankness and I began to drift, high above my troubles. Intelligence welled within me, as my situation hardened into sharp focus in my brain. I was so earthbound, so wrapped up in myself, I was blind to essential truths. Emotion filled me. It was there; the truth was within my grasp. The door was opening to me . . .

Orien's hands snapped together sharply. The wrench of coming back took my breath away. "You are privileged, Pellaz," he said, nodding. (What did he mean?) "But you have a lot to learn. It is all strange to you and you have so much to overcome. Human prejudices, human bonds, human greed . . ."

"Human frailty," I could not help adding. I remembered it from church.

Orien reached out to ruffle my hair. "Pretty child, yes, that too," he laughed. "Now. Tell me what you think Wraeththu is."

I was totally unprepared.

"Well?"

"I . . . I don't know." It was feeble.

Orien was exhibiting that unfailing Wraeththu patience. "Oh, come on. I can't believe you haven't thought about it. Tell me what you think."

Next to him, Seel shifted his position on the floor and cleared his throat. He was either bored or embarassed.

"Well," I began, leaning forward to clasp my toes. "I suppose I think it started like a gang of boys . . . I don't know . . . something like that, and then it just grew. You don't think of yourselves as human though, do you,

but I'm not sure what the difference is. . . . You all seem so . . . so . . . *old.*
It sounds stupid . . . you look young, but you're not . . ." My mind was full
of ideas but I did not have the words to voice them. I shook my head. Orien
did not press me further. "Old? I'm twenty-one, Seel's nineteen, aren't
you?"

Seel did not look amused. "No, twenty now, if it really is that important."

"How old were you . . ." I began, but Orien waved his hand to
silence me.

"Questions later," he said. "Now, I am going to tell you exactly what
you are getting into."

Some years ago, in the north, a child was born. A mutant. Its body was
strangely malformed in some respects. As it grew, this child exhibited many
unusual traits that foxed both its parents and the doctors they consulted in
their concern. Their son conversed earnestly with people they could not see;
some of their neighbors' dogs feared him; other children shrank from him
in horror. His mother complained she simply did not like the child; he was
unlovable, withdrawn. Even as a baby he had snarled at her, refusing the
breast. Once, some years later, as she had prepared his dinner, all the
saucepans had risen off the stove and flown at her. Turning round, a silent
scream frozen on her face, she had seen him standing in the doorway,
watching.

On reaching puberty, the boy disappeared from home, and despite
massive police investigation (accompanied by an insidious sense of relief
experienced by the grieving parents), no clue to his fate was ever
found . . . for some time.

Months later, officials were baffled by a bizarre murder case in Carmine
City. A young man, apparently having been sexually assaulted, had been
found dead in a disused building. But it was far from the simple case it
appeared; such killings commonplace in the city. The young man's insides
had been eroded away as if by a powerful and caustic substance. Post
mortem investigation revealed the presence of an unknown material in the
body tissues, something that kept on burning even as it dried on the
dissecting table. Under the microscope, it teemed with life like sperm, but
unlike the sperm of any creature the scientists had seen before.

A mutant runaway had come alive in the city; alone, frightened and
dangerous in his fear. He had learned just how different he was. His touch
could mean death to those that offered him shelter, the sub-society of the
city. He kept away from them, hiding in the terrible gaunt carcases of
forgotten tenements; on the run, shivering in the dark.

Freaks roamed the steaming tips, the rubble. One came across him as he
slept; lifted aside the foul sacks that covered him; gazed at his translucent
glowing beauty. The veins on his neck showed blue through pearl, pumping
with life. Some people are so far gone they would do anything to eat. One
more day on the planet, one more day for the fleas, the rats, the sores.

Freak lips on a mutant throat, broken teeth to tear. The mutant opened his eyes, relaxed beneath the lapping suction. He did not want to die. He knew he could not die.

For three days the freak writhed, gibbered and screamed on the soiled floor. Passively the mutant watched him, faint interest painted across his bland face. On the third day, the filth peeled away and the mutant was given an angel. An angel like himself, brimming with mysteries that alone he had had no inclination to explore.

The rest of it is now the legends of Wraeththu. Wraeththu, born in hate and bitterness, flexing their young, animal-strong muscles in the cities of the north. Always learning, always increasing their craft and cunning. Increasing. It was inevitable that eventually it touched someone who had the curiosity, the intelligence to probe within the mystery. Wraeththu lost its ungoverned, adolescent wildness; it became an occult society, hungry for knowledge. But what they found within the Temple appalled them; its vastness scared them. Some broke away from the search for truth and fell back into the old ways of fighting and living for the day. Those that remained faced the unavoidable truth: Mankind was on the wane, Wraeth-thu waxed to replace it. The first mutant faded into anonymity. Nobody was quite sure what had happened to him, but he had left strong leaders behind him. Now he had become a creature of legend, revered and feared as a god. Wraeththu did not believe he was dead, but that he'd elevated to a superior form of existence, monitoring or manipulating the development of his race. The Wraeththu grouped into tribes, each ascribing to varying beliefs, but all united in the Wraeththu spirit. They had the power to change the sons of men to be like themselves. As with the first, within three days of being infected with Wraeththu blood, the convert's body has completed the necessary changes. Many of them develop extra-sensory faculties. All are a supreme manifestation of the combined feminine and masculine spiritual constituents present in Mankind. Humanity has abused and abandoned its natural strengths: in Wraeththu it begins to bloom. Wraeththu are also known as hara, as Mankind are called men. Hara are ageless. Their allotted lifespan has not yet been assessed, but their bodies are immune to cellular destruction through time. As they are physically perfect, so must they strive toward spiritual perfection. If power is riches, then the treasure-chests of Wraeththu are depthless. Purity of spirit is the key; few ever attain it. But one day, when the ravages of man is just a memory, then the Few that have succeeded shall be the kings of the Earth.

I learned later on that all of this was Wraeththu perfection as Orien saw it. At the time, I believed all that he told me of Wraeththu's potential greatness because he seemed infinitely wiser than me. Only bitter experience taught me that he was misled, if not misleading himself. Nothing can be perfect in this world. I was curious about the different Wraeththu tribes, although Orien's knowledge on this subject was far from comprehensive. Owing to varying degrees of civil strife across the country, it had been possible for determined groups of Wraeththu to seize towns from humans or else take over towns that had been deserted. Some had maintained a serious belief in occultism and were interested in furthering their powers, whilst others (and these Orien mentioned only briefly) were not so concerned about this aspect of themselves. What they *were* interested in, he neglected to mention.

The sun had traveled to its zenith; I was approaching mine. When Orien ceased speaking the hush still throbbed with his words. What I have told you is only the essence of it; there was much, much more. There was no question of my disbelieving him. To be there was to believe. My doubts were quenched.

"Tomorrow, Pellaz, a Wraeththu of Nahir-Nuri caste, the highest caste, shall come to Saltrock. He is known as the Hienama and it is his task to initiate new converts. A Hienama comes to Saltrock about twice a year. This time there will only be one conversion: yours. At the Harhune, he shall infect you with his blood. That is all. Admittedly, the whole thing will be dressed up in a lot of ritual, which gives everyone a good spectacle." His voice was dry and I smiled at his irony. "Now, do you have any questions?"

"Which hundred do you want first?" I replied. We all laughed, me louder than the others.

"Just start at the beginning," Seel advised.

"Right. Why must I fast today?" This was punctuated by a timely growl from my stomach.

"So that your body will find it easier to cope with the Harhune. For medical reasons."

"And how will I change?" I could tell this was the question Orien liked least of all. He twisted his mouth and looked at the ceiling.

"I must admit, I prefer this question to be answered by experience. I don't want to alarm you.

I looked at him steadily. "Please. I would prefer to know."

He sighed. "Yes. Very well. Most of the changes are internal. You must have realized that Wraeththu can reproduce amongst themselves (I hadn't), but not in the same way as humankind do. It involves the physical union of two hara, yes, but to to conceive life takes more than mere copulation. Essentially, our young are not formed within ourselves in the accepted sense. Only those of high caste may procreate. Sex is also important for reasons other than reproduction. We do not even call it that. When hara have a high regard for each other they can take aruna: that is pleasure, the exchange of essences. Grissecon is a communion of bodies for occult purposes, but I doubt whether that will concern you for quite some time. Inside you, new parts will begin to grow and externally, your organs of generation shall be improved, refined."

I felt faint. Images of castration brought a taste of blood to my mouth. Orien smiled grimly at my pallor. "Now you may wish you had not asked. But there is nothing to fear; it is not as bad as you imagine. Nothing will be taken away; nothing. One thing you must realize, Pellaz; what you will become is not Man, it is something different. Male, female as separate entities must lose its meaning for you. You must stop thinking of yourself as human."

I barely heard him. I was still listening to what had been said before, wanting to shout, "Show me! Show me!", but lacking the nerve. What was hidden from my view? Repulsion filled my throat, but I swallowed and closed my mind: from this point there was no returning.

A knock on the door signaled Mur's arrival bearing a flask of saffron-water for me to drink. I was shaking so much I could hardly manage it. There were no more questions inside me. Nothing seemed important now; my elation had dissipated. I needed to think. Sensing my inner turmoil, Orien and Seel exchanged a glance and stood up. Seel yawned, stretched and turned away from me, no doubt already thinking of his lunch. At that point I realized how much I envied him, simultaneously remembering his words: "You may be in my position one day." I could not imagine it.

"We shall leave you now," Orien announced. "Think about what you have learned." It seemed they could not wait to get away. Left alone, I gave myself up to grief. Harhune. Wraeththu. Much more than I had imagined, so much more. It was impossible my sobs could not be heard outside. I was held fast in the jaws of the trap, awaiting only the heavy, inevitable tread of the hunter. What was beyond the darkness? I fantasized Cal bursting in. He would tell me we were leaving, now, and our flight would be speed-trails of dust to the south. But Cal was one of them. A freak. One of them. Human once. Was he? Was he? I had touched him. Arms around each other like creatures that are the same. (Male, female; which one? Both?) Bile scalded the back of my tongue. Cal. A monster who had brought me to this. At Seel's house, he had known. He had known and he had not told me. It was a wicked, evil trick. I would avenge myself, avenge the humanity within me so soon to die. Death. I even contemplated it, looking wildly round the room for some tool of self-destruction. But they had foreseen that, hadn't they? Did they trust me not to destroy myself? I curled tight on the floor. Tight. Into the darkness. Whimpering.

That was how they found me at night-fall. Mur and Garis. They lifted me up without warmth. "Drink this." I swallowed and tore myself away, wretching and coughing. Steel-strong hands clamped the back of my neck. "Drink it all, damn you." My throat worked. Liquid spilled over my chin. Almost immediately, the drug began to work. I was calm. Light-headed, but lucid. Scrambling, I made my way to the bed and sat there.

Garis, hands on hips, shook his head as he looked at me. "You can hate us all you want, little animal," he said.

"Shut up!" Mur snapped at him. "Get him in the other room."

I would not wait for them to force me. I stood up and stalked through by myself, submitted myself to their attentions without a sound. As they would not look at me, so I did not look at them. They did not mock me again.

Seel came in to see me later on. I had been half-dozing on the bed, lulled by the philter I had been given. There was no grief left inside me, only resignation. All I retained of myself was dignity. Whatever they took from me they could not destroy that. Pride that was the essence of me. "We will come for you mid-morning," Seel said, pacing the room. He smelled of nicotine, wine and, faintly, of cooking.

"I wanted to kill myself this afternoon," I remarked in a flat voice.

Seel stopped pacing and looked at me. "You didn't though."

Angrily, I turned over so I could not see him.

"Pell, I know all this. Every little goddamn bit of it. It may only be a small comfort, but once I felt just as bad as you do now."

"Small comfort," I agreed.

"I was fourteen," he said. "Incepted in a filthy cellar, my arms cut with glass. You don't know how lucky you are!"

I said nothing. I did not care.

Seel decided to continue with his instructions. "The Harhune will take place in the Nayati. That's a kind of hall . . ."

"Yes. Yes. Thanks for the vocabulary," I butted in coldly. What did I care what the damn place was called. Abattoir was enough.

"Look, you wanted this!" Seel erupted. I turned back to look at him. His face said: spoilt brat. He was tired of me.

"Did I?" We stared at each other and it was me that relented. "Yes. Yes I did."

Seel's shoulders slumped and he sighed through his nose. "Don't be bitter, Pell. You will regret nothing, I promise you."

I could not tell whether he wanted to console me or justify himself. But, of course, one kind word and my control began to slip. I began to shake uncontrollably. Seel was beside me in an instant. I could imagine him wondering how he had come to be shouting at me. It was not part of the ritual.

"Seel," I said, "if you mean that . . . about no regrets . . . you must tell me again and again and again. Make me believe it. But it has to be the truth."

He held me in his arms and told me and told me and told me. I had led a sheltered, barricaded life, and was young for my years in so many ways. I cannot stress enough how ignorant and confused I was. One minute the Wraeththu seemed to me like sassy street kids, just dressed up and then the next minute they were creatures I was afraid of, inhuman monsters, speaking words that sounded old. The truth was they were actually both of these things. They did not know themselves exactly what they were or would become. All I needed at the time, though, was what Seel gave me. Comforting arms and proof that Wraeththu were warm with real flesh and real blood. He must have stayed with me until I fell asleep. I did not wake till morning, and when I did I was alone.

CHAPTER THREE

>━!━◆>━•Ⓞ━•◆>━!━◀

The gates stand open, enter into light

The greatest virtue in Man is his undying sense of hope. A hidden reserve of optimism woke with me that day. I would not dishonor myself. My life was caught upon the Wheel of Fate, but I would face my future with dignity and strength. I was apprehensive, yes, but still almost light-hearted by the time Mur and Garis came to bathe me for the last time. Gone was the corroding salt, the rough towels. I was sluiced with hot, smoky perfume and patted dry with purified linen. Aromatic oils were kneaded into my skin, gold powder shaken onto my shoulders and my hair brushed and brushed until even the split ends shone like dull silk. A new robe, of somber black, was wrapped around me; eyes were dabbed with balm to take away the swelling my tears had left behind. Mur and Garis, almost pleasant with the sense of achievement, stood back to inspect their work. I was ready.

When Seel and Orien arrived they were dressed splendidly for the occasion. They seemed taller than I remembered, proud and graceful, and treated me like a bride, which I supposed, in a sense, I was. Seel put white lilies in my hair, avoiding my eyes, and offered me a goblet of blue glass. The liquid inside it looked murky and tasted foul. I downed it as quickly as I could. They would take no chances with me; I would be drugged almost senseless.

The white light outside stung my eyes and I winced, although the taint of soda no longer bothered me. I barely noticed it. Before I could take a single step forward, I wobbled. Seel and Orien swiftly took hold of my arms. They had brought me a chariot, strewn with flowers and ribbons; pale horses fidgeted, festooned with color, plaited with silk and tassels. Wraeththu had already gathered to line the streets we would take to the Nayati. An air of festival vibrated up the sky; they all shone, these supernatural, hypernatural folk, and strange, ululating cries fluted round our heads. Otherworld melodies, and the horses pranced forward, sand skirling in our wake. The hot breezes were intoxicating with the fresh, green smell of cut garlands, petals crushed beneath the capering hooves. I was wedged upright, but nobody could see that. My hair streamed back like a black flag, dappled with fragments of crushed blossoms, palest pink, white and lemon-colored. Exultation fountained through me. I felt like a king.

Shallow white steps led to the main doors of the Nayati. Petals still danced in the hot air like confetti. The moment my feet hit the ground I felt like I was walking upsidedown. Only willpower kept nausea where it belonged, in my imagination. I had never been really drunk, but thought it must have been like that. Nothing mattered and responsibility had been taken from me. We walked into the solemn and sacred gloom of the Nayati. It took some moments for my eyes to adjust to the poor light, but soon the high, narrow hall materialized before me out of the gloom. Tiers of seats reared into the shadows on both sides; from flank entrances the hara of Saltrock filed into their places. All voices were muted, but the whispering quiet could not hide the mounting fever, the heights of expectation implied by half-seen movements above me. I stood between Seel and Orien at the threshold. Light streamed in behind us, dust-moted bars. Gilden metal flashed in the dimness beyond. Seel lifted a long, carven staff from a bracket by the door. He struck the ground three times and the congregation rose, rumbling, to its feet. "Harhune! Harhune!" It began as a soft crooning, and we advanced among them. And then it was a mighty clamor, my skin prickled, voices ringing like clarions as they bayed me forward. I? I was not there really. I was someone else's dream carried forward on the strength of their tuneless cry.

We came to a place where patterns had been chalked onto the floor, and they pushed me to my knees. White dust sprayed my robe, and Seel spoke; softly, it seemed, but his voice filled the hall.

"Today we witness the inception of Pellaz Unhar. He is deemed fit by myself, Seel Griselming and my colleague Orien Farnell."

He raised his arms above his head and the soft white cloth of his sleeves slipped back. Henna patterns were painted on his skin; designs similar to those beneath my knees. "Does the Harhune take place?!" he demanded and a mighty, "Aye!" shook the walls. They blessed me with fire, with water, earth and air, ripped my robe to below my shoulders and wrote on my skin. Henna again, aromatic and gritty. Seel's voice was gutteral; I could not understand what he said, but the crowd were mouthing silently along with him, howling the responses, half-rising from their seats in excitement. I hated to think of Cal being one of them, but he kept creeping into my mind. I kept thinking, "They want my blood, they want my blood," but, of course, the opposite was true. They wanted me to have theirs. This was their ceremony. Mine was yet to come.

Hours later, moments later, two young hara, sparkling in white and gold, came out of the smoky dark at the back of the hall. Soft cloth falling to their feet made them glide like ghosts. One carried a shallow metal dish, his companion holding out the instruments of my hair's death. Seel was before me. He raised my head with a firm hand. "The Shicawm, Pellaz. Be still." I could not shudder but my teeth ached, I had clenched them so. Cold metal touched my brow and I shut my eyes. The sound was terrible, sickening. I could feel it all falling away and hear the silvery swish as it landed on the shallow dish. So quick. It was gone. "Open your eyes," Seel told me, barely audible. It was like looking at an execution. Under my nose, long black locks spilled over the plate, still adorned with waxen, wilted lilies. I half expected to see blood and a thread of hysteria cracked the numbness. It was an effort not to reach up and touch my head. I started to shiver then.

Hands were upon my shoulders and I shook beneath their warmth. Light flared up ahead of me and the dark rafters of the Nayati loomed above, suddenly visible, encrusted with gargoyles who laughed and screamed forever in silence. Tall metal stands made an avenue, topped by filigreed bowls of incense; smoke so heavy it drifted downwards in matted shrouds. At the end a white table gleamed like marble; and beyond that?

A slim reed of light opening out like a flower. Tall. A halo of fiery red-gold hair. An angel. A demon. The hienama. (I heard Seel gasp: "Him? Him?!," urgent with surprise, and Orien's sober answer: "I know.") The congregation crooned once more, upon their knees, and the hienama moved; arms peeling out from his sides, one stretched straight, the other slightly curved, his body half turned toward me. I should have known then who he was. But it took years and years, and even then somebody had to tell me. He never tried to deceive anyone, they were just blind, I think. Looking back, it was obvious. He was more than all of them, and he knew about me. He put his mark on me that day, made me his pawn, but, like I said, it took years for him to put me into play.

I was lifted to my feet. Led forward. No, carried. My legs would not work and my feet dragged as if my ankles were broken. As we went toward him, he grew. Not in actual height, but in magnificence. Slanting, gold-flecked violet eyes lasered straight to my soul. Fire seemed to burn in his hair and flicker over his skin. Nahir-nuri. He had the compassion of a vivisectionist.

They lifted me onto the stone table and all I could do was look at him. (Cold bit into me; the caress of a sepulcher.) His voice is almost impossible to describe. It was full of music but with darker tones, like the sound of gunfire or shatterable things that were breaking. "Welcome, Pellaz. I am Thiede." Like night falling, black draperies softly descended. There was a sound like falling snow, hardly a sound at all, more a feeling, and the crowd could no longer see us. Only Orien and Seel remained. He signaled to them, tying his own arm above the elbow with a knotted cord, always looking at me, inspecting me carefully. I had seen that expression before, a life-time before, on my father's face as he chose a mule for himself. The dealer had been untrustworthy and he had not been sure if the mule was sound. I doubted that Thiede often made mistakes, though. His assessment of me was realized in one short glance.

"Don't be afraid," he said indifferently. "Seel, prepare him. Hurry up."

The veins on my arms stood out like cords. They took away my robe and Thiede looked me up and down with the same indifference, and then he smiled at Seel.

"Yes. Very good."

Seel moved half of his mouth in response. He did not look comfortable.

Thiede's glance whipped back to my face, the movement of a snake. "You know what we're going to do?"

I blinked in reply.

"Are you here of your own free will?"

I think an insignificant "yes" escaped the constriction of my throat.

Thiede nodded, stroking his arm. "Give him the dope," he said, which I found incongruous. He turned away.

Something sharp slid into my arm, an unexpected medical shard in this arcane setting, and the cold poured into me. I had not expected that and was grateful. I thought the last thing I heard was "Open his veins and drink from his heart," but common-sense tells me it was something else. There was no pain.

By late afternoon of the third day, my fever had abated. I was still weak, my eyes hurt most at first, but I was alive. Mur and Garis, in attendance once again, sat me in a chair by the window while they stripped and changed my bedding. I mulled over what I could remember of the last three days.

It had been early evening of my Harhune day when I regained consciousness, not knowing who, where or what I was. I had stared at the ceiling, breathing carefully, aware of pinpricks of pain, like flashes of light, darting round inside me. Red light streamed into the room and a dark shadow hovered at my side.

"Pell, can you hear me?" Flick's voice.

It was all over. I was back at Seel's house in my own room.

"Pell?"

I could not move, my throat felt sewn up and I could not rip the threads. Flick pressed a beaker against my lips. It tasted like sugared water, warm, and my shriveled mouth turned to slime.

"How long?" I croaked.

Flick dabbed at my face with a wet cloth smelling of lemons. "About six hours or so. Do you feel any pain?"

"I don't know." My body was still numbed by drugs. I might have imagined the pricklings. "I can't feel anything."

Flick sat down on the bed and examined my face carefully, pulling down my eyelids. I did not like the expression on his face. It was worse than I felt.

"I've seen quite a few through althaia," he told me. "Don't worry."

I had not, till then. "Althaia . . .?"

Flick sponged my face again. "The changing. It will take about three days. The thing is, Pell, when the drugs wear off, you're going to feel quite ill."

"And I may die."

Flick started to clean between my fingers, concentrating hard and not looking at me. "A small risk, but you're a fighter. I told you, don't worry."

My eyes felt hot. I closed them and tried to swallow. Flick offered me a drink. "Where's Cal?" A sudden, irrational terror shot through me that he had left Saltrock without me. I tried to sit up and my limbs shrieked with pain and displeasure.

Flick pressed me back into the pillows. "Stop it! Don't move!"

I struggled, oblivious of the discomfort. "He's gone!" I half moaned, half screamed, threshing against Flick's restraining arms.

"No! No. It's alright. He's here. In the house. Downstairs. He's here. But you can't see him yet."

Still fringed by hysteria I stopped moving, slumped beneath Flick's hands, which were hot and trembling. It was almost as painful to be still, but the struggle had tired me out. I had to close my eyes, and when I did, the darkness was shot with vague, pulsing colors.

"There, that's better. Lie still, Pell and rest. I'll be back later."

I heard Flick leave the room, slowly. I heard him close the door, oh, so quietly. He would have run down the stairs.

Inside me, irreversible processes had begun to work, yet I could not feel it. No churnings, no bubblings, no strange movements. A sigh escaped me, high and lisping, and childhood tunes scampered from my memory. Now I skipped naked in the red dirt of the cable fields, Mima at my side, both of us laughing. Now the pink sky arced over us, a symbol of innocence; the dark was beneath the horizon.

The first assault, when it came, hurtled rudely through my half-sleep. It felt like a knife turning in my stomach, wrenching, pulling, tearing. My entrails were being torn from me. I shot upright in the bed, the room filled with a high, unearthly sound. My own scream. Half-blind with pain, I squinted at my stomach, terrified of what I might see. Nothing. No blood, no spilling, shining ropes. With sobbing breath I lowered myself back under the blankets. Tears ran down my face. The room was so quiet, not even an echo of my cry. Only quick, shallow breaths hissing in my head. As soon as I shut my eyes the invisible weapon plunged into me again. My body threw itself to the ground, arching in agony. Lights zig-zagged across my vision. I clawed the floor, the edge of the bed, myself, anything. (Stop this. Stop this!) A hard surface, cool and smooth, slapped against the back of my hand. I heaved myself forward and rested my cheek against it. (Somebody come. Somebody please come!) Eyes open, movement on the edge of my vision. I turned my head quickly, and looked. Looked into the hideous face of. . . . Something. Oh, that something! A fiend. A creature; ghastly. Screeching, I backed away, flailing my arms, falling, helpless. Oh God! The gray-faced demon did the same. Mimicking, mocking. And then I realized. No demon, no creature. Hallucination? No. Just this: a mirror. That is all. As the pain ebbed from me once more, sick fascination made me look again. This . . .? This! Whimpering, I crawled closer to the glass my half-naked scalp gleamed damp and white, a long matted plume of hair fell over my face. My face! Bloated, gray, the eyes rimmed with red, the mouth wet, purpled and slack. My body was bruised and discolored, the left arm nearly twice its normal size. I could look no more. Crumpling onto the floor as a new spasm of incisive pain ripped through me, upwards, from my vitals to my throat. Mucus and blood and frenzied sound sprayed from me. My eyes were blinded by black, marching shapes and ziggurats of light.

Suddenly, activity, voices. "Get him back on the bed!" Strident, unrecognizable. A softer tone: "It's started."

Hands lifted me and where they touched, raw skin seemed to be peeling away like charred paper. Distorted faces peered down at me, eyes like saucers. And then a thin trickle of bitter juice was forced between my swollen lips. My jaws were clenched so tightly, someone had to hit me hard to force them apart. The agony was indescribable. Death would have been preferable, and fight to the death it was. Thiede's blood and mine, and if mine won I knew there would be no me left. As suddenly as it came, the pain shot back to a hidden place to brood. The room flickered, lurched and then settled, perspective see-sawing back to reality. I was gulping breath, swallowing foulness.

"A short respite, Pell." Seel's face hovered over me, disembodied, pale. "This is just the beginning, but we are with you."

Smells of fading years, years of innocence, came back to tease me. An untimely stillness of Autumn changed the room. Mellow light. The changing; it had begun. My changing. Within myself, within myself.

That was the last thing I could remember clearly. Afterwards, it was horror, pain, fever, filth and sickness. Occasionally, I would feel lucid enough to understand what was happening around me, usually in the afternoon or dead of night. Then the stillness would make me weep as they changed my bedding yet again with weary, fraying patience. Faces haunted my delirium: faces of the future and the past. Sometimes they fought beside me, hands on the same torn banner, but sometimes they only chittered on the edge of my awareness, mere observers.

Mur rubbed my flaking skin with balm. Weeping sores and blisters burst beneath his fingers. He never spoke, only pushing his braided hair back over his shoulder when it fell forward, a frown between his eyes. Once, I remember, vomit flew from my mouth in a great arc and my body constricted like a bow. I was shrieking, "I'm full of insects!" or some such nonsense. Another time, I was convinced the room was alive with squeaking bats, or something like bats, and I was afraid they would settle on my face to block my nose and mouth. Every time I awoke the room was completely different. When the bats were there, it looked just like a cave. Often I hit out at those who tried to help me. Garis lost his temper when I blacked his eye and smacked me across the face. When he did that, the room exploded with stars and I spiralled, laughing hysterically, like a helix-shaped atom on the air. Sometimes, if they left me alone for even a second, I would get out of bed and crawl, gibbering round the room. I kept wanting to get in corners because I felt more comfortable with walls on two sides of me. They would find me, crouched and demented, blood and bile running out of me across the floor. That was some of it. There was more, perhaps worse; thankfully, most of it now forgotten. But I lived to tell the tale, coming out of it; exhausted, wasted, yet alive.

Mur and Garis whispered about me across the bed. I felt they no longer despised me but their presence was still no comfort. A cat jumped in through the window with a musical greeting and leapt into my lap. I tensed, but there was no pain. The animal crawled up my chest and butted my chin with his head, purring rapturously. I hugged him fiercely and he did not struggle. Then I dared to think it: why had Cal not been to see me? A thought I had been rejecting for some time. Was the althaia so repulsive to him? On reflection, it was probably better that he had kept away. Sleek Pellaz of the desert journey was no longer in residence. I had zealously avoided glancing into mirrors because I was sure my appearance still bordered on horrific. I had still not examined my body for outward changes. When Mur, or one of the others attended to me, I kept my eyes shut. I really did not feel any different, apart from ill. I knew I would have to face Cal again soon and it filled me with different tremors. Fear, anger, pleasure and, something else. Something I examined least of all.

The chair was uncomfortable. I squirmed. Mur was beside me. He was kinder toward me than Garis, less harsh, although just as quick with sarcasm. Because of my condition any riposte I attempted was usually embarrassingly feeble. Though I now knew that their cruel treatment of me had been for a purpose, that of bringing me down to a level from which I could rise afresh, they never completely warmed to me. Could beings as perfect as Wraeththu were supposed to be behave in such a way? Part of my ignorance was that I never questioned this.

"Pellaz, try to stand," he told me. I just looked up at him stupidly. "Come on!" He stood in front of me, offering his hands. Stand? My legs felt as supportive as thin gristle, but I clasped the arms of the chair. It wobbled beneath me as I struggled to rise. The room swerved around me and nausea punched my ribs.

"I can't!" Sweat bubbled from my pores.

"Yes you can. Come on, you have to walk to the bathroom with me."

No mercy, as usual. He held my elbow. "Lean on me." I did not feel pain exactly, but the sensation was sickening. All my guts seemed loose and my loins tingled. Mur half dragged me across the room, accompanied by Garis's spiteful amusement.

I was bathed again. Mur laughed without cruelty and told me to open my eyes, but I would not.

"You should wash yourself now," he said. "Stop trying to be ill." He left me sitting there in the cooling water. "When you've finished, call me," he remarked over his shoulder. "Don't be scared, it's perfect."

Blood scorched my face, but he did not see. He was already complaining to Garis in the other room. "Help me, will you!" The rustle of my sheets being bundled into the linen basket.

I sat there for about five minutes before I dared to open my eyes. Even then I stared at the wall for a while. It was getting dark. Goose pimples invaded my skin. "Hurry up!" Garis called. I could smell food cooking somewhere below. Horses neighed outside, in the distance. All the light was dim and the air was fragrant with herbs. I looked, and looked, and looked again. There was no damage, no scars. Just this exquisite instrument of magic and pleasure. Not changed too much, just redesigned. An orchid on a feathered, velvet shaft. It is something like that. When I touched it, it opened up like a flower, something moved in the heart of it, but I had seen enough for now. I knelt up in the bath, shivering and called, "Mur!" When he stood in the doorway, our eyes met and a great sense of recognition went through me. That which marked us more indelibly than anything else as Men, a crudity, was transformed in Wraeththu to something alien and beautiful. If it is hidden, it is not from modesty or the fear of giving offense, but because the revealing of it is that much more delightful for its secrecy. Men did not know about this, but we knew. Mur smiled. Relief melted something hard and cold inside me.

Back in the bedroom, Mur and Garis set about pampering me. They massaged my skin with oil, fluffed my hair, scented me with pungent essences and disguised my eyes with kohl.

I was a little suspicious. "What is all this for? More rituals?" I think Garis would have liked to have given me the back of his hand, hard, across the mouth, but he contented himself with ignoring my questions and curtly silencing Mur if he opened his mouth to answer me.

Tidying away their things, Mur said, "You must rest now, Pellaz. Go back to bed. Don't overdo it yet."

I felt he was trying to communicate something to me without Garis knowing, but I could not fathom it out. Mur was beginning to like me, or feel sorry for me. He arranged the pillows behind my shoulders before he left.

Once alone, I struggled out of the blankets and weaved over to the mirror. Spots of light speckled my vision, but when the dizziness cleared, I could see myself. Once I would have been ashamed at the rush of pleasure my own reflection gave me, but Cal had done something toward dispelling that attitude. Now, I instinctively drew myself up taller, throwing back my head, gazing haughtily back at myself. I liked the shape of my head, and the sides of it shaved, and the shape of my jaw. I looked leaner and somehow older. Ironically, I remembered my sixteenth birthday had past forgotten two days before. Was I now a woman, a woman who needed no breasts to nurse her young, no swelling hips to carry them? And was I not also a man, a man that needed no woman? They had told me there was nothing to fear; nothing.

A knock on the door made me jump. I did not want to be caught posing, and scrabbled, panicking back to the bed. I was beneath the blankets by the time it opened. Then fear and awe and shyness converged within me; it was Thiede. He was standing there in the doorway, so blatantly, unashamedly inhuman, a towering monolith of potency and power. He flicked his fingers and Mur hurried past him into the room, carrying a tray of food. He virtually threw it on the bed and rushed out again without speaking. Thiede closed the door behind him. I cringed beneath his stare, unable to look away. He was, and always is, marvelous to look at. He prolonged the silence, maybe unintentionally, just gazing at me implacably. When he spoke, his voice made me jump again. "Well. How are you Pellaz?" "Oh, fine." I could not clear my throat properly and my voice sounded squeaky. He nodded disinterestedly, turning away, examining the room. How could he be curious about it? "Eat, eat!" he said, waving his hand. I looked at the tray of food with aversion. Thiede's presence did nothing to stimulate the appetite, but I obediently picked up a hunk of bread. It turned to glue in my mouth, and I struggled to swallow.

"Pellaz, now that you are har, there is one final ceremony to be undergone. A ceremony that will make you truly har, and one, I might add, that will make permanent those transformations that have taken place within you." Where was this leading? "They will have told you what aruna is," he stated flatly. A dreadful suspicion flashed through me. Not him! He knew what I was thinking, of course, and fixed me with an indignant scowl.

"No," he said, drily, and then with humor, "not that I wouldn't like to, but in your present state, well, I do not want to be responsible for your death . . ."

He came to sit on the bed and I hated him being so close. It was like a fear of being scorched.

"You're so quiet, Pellaz, and so scared. Terror of the unknown, I suppose, and so attractive in the newly har."

He settled himself more comfortably.

"My task as hienama is to prepare you for what comes next. We shall have an intimate little talk, Pellaz."

I still could not speak. Surely he could hear my heart.

"Aruna: the exchange of essences. First you shall be soume, shall I say the least demanding role? Accept the essence as an elixir; you need it . . . I am pleased with you Pellaz, very pleased."

He stretched out a hand to touch my face. I could understand nothing of what he was saying.

"Now listen to me carefully," he continued. "Aruna can be a powerful thing. It is not merely the basic thing it appears, but a coming together of two dynamic beings, a mingling of their inner forces. A drawing together. Hear this, Pellaz. One day a stranger will recognize you and you shall recognize him. You will both *know*. Inexorably you will gravitate toward each other and only in aruna express your innate need. Not only the exchange of essences, achieved through that elevating state aruna is, but something more. One day, your seed will become a pearl in the nurturing organs of another. Then you will sire your first son . . . then. But for now . . ." He stood up again, smoothed the soft material of his trousers, shook out his hair and turned to look at me again. "Do not confuse what may happen to you with the self-destructive emotions of Mankind. They once called it love, didn't they? So true, so special, so rotten. Hara may come together for aruna; their friendships may be loyal, but there is never the greed of possession to blacken the heart. Never. Does it frighten you to hear me say we can never fall in love?" I shook my head, wishing he would leave. "I'm glad you understand me. They have chosen for you, Pellaz. You are in good hands, or so Seel tells me." He was no longer looking at me, walking to the middle of the room. "Surpass yourself, Pellaz. Take hold of the life I have given you."

I had not spoken once. Perhaps drowsiness overtook me, perhaps the door opened, perhaps the air fractured around me. . . . The next time I looked at that place in the room where Thiede had stood, he had gone. I tried hard to think about what he had said but could not understand most of it. I shivered. Aruna. The word that sounded whispering, blue-green, shadowed. I put the tray of food down on the floor and lay back on the bed. Outside, the sun sank lower and lower until the light in the room had nearly faded away. No-one came to light my lamp or to take my tray away. The house felt empty. Not even a cat to keep me company. I kept thinking of Thiede and suddenly the gloom frightened me. I jumped off the bed too quickly and reeled over to the table. Dizzy and shaking, I fumbled with the matches, heart pounding. As a welcome petal of light bloomed in the glass the door opened behind me.

I felt it rather than heard it, expecting "What are you doing? Get back on the bed!" or some such outburst, but it did not come. Before I turned, I knew it would be Cal. His face was a mirror: me in the caressing lamp-light.

"Oh, it's you." My voice barely shook. I could not bear to look at him and went back to sit on the bed where the light was dimmer. Actors on a stage, playing out this premeditated performance. He knew his part well. I did not even know my lines. Anger made me itch. I wanted to look up at him with welcome in my eyes, but shyness and embarrassment had frozen all sensation. Encased in ice it glowed there inside me.

"Hello, Pell," he said, in a voice which told me he knew I was going to be difficult.

Fists clenched in my lap, I launched into the attack. "Well, as you see, I am alive. Had they told you? I thought, perhaps, you'd left Saltrock." I had my back to him, but could vividly imagine his eyes rolling upward in exasperation. No reaction. I brought out the big guns. "Why are you here?"

"It's my room. While you were ill, I was sleeping elsewhere. I'm moving back in now, if you don't mind."

Well countered, I thought. His voice gave nothing away. I wondered how long he would wait. Was he ordered to produce results? He sauntered over to my window chair and flamboyantly threw himself down in it, steepling his hands, tapping his lips with his fingers, staring passively out at the yard below. I would have given anything for Thiede's talent of perception. Cal's thoughts were barred by stronger locks than I could break through. Huge, white moths batted moistly against the window, trying to reach the halo of my lamp, or the halo of Cal's bright hair. I wanted him to beat down my defenses, but guessed instinctively he never would. Cal was a great believer in letting other people take the initiative. He made them work for him, just conceited enough to know that they always would. (How could I have known that Cal's darker side went a lot deeper than mere conceit?) Sitting there, sparring and sniping and circling each other, we both knew what the score was. It was just a question of who would back down first. It might easily have gone on for days. I wanted to say, "Cal, look at me. I am har. I am one of you. We are equal, you cannot treat me as less." My mind was racing in the awkward silence. He would say nothing. I would have to provoke him again. "Cal," I began, and his eyes lashed up and caught me, calculating, without warmth, challenging. The merest implication of a smile hovered over his face. "Go on," he was thinking, "go on."

"I . . ." (Oh God, what?), "I still get tired easily. Thiede was here . . . I'm . . . well, goodnight." I could feel him studying me as I burrowed into the blankets, lying there, heart pounding, reciting childhood prayers; I think those few moments are among the worst I have ever lived through. Something hit my pillow, softly. Through slitted eyes I saw a single perfect crocus inches from my nose. Deep purple fading to lilac at the petals' tip, an aching yellow flame within its heart.

"Where did you get it?" I asked. No answer. Seel's flower garden, I thought. His ritual flowers. I felt Cal sit down heavily on the other side of the bed, humming quietly to himself; thuds as his boots hit the floor. I could not resist looking at him. He was lifting his loose white shirt over his head, brown skin and white linen, standing up to finish undressing. He had his back to me, stretching like a cat. All the Wraeththu things inside me that needed aruna were going berserk. He looked over his shoulder at me and I shut my eyes. I heard him laugh, quietly. My body felt uncomfortable. I wanted to run away. I wanted Cal. I could not cope. He could so easily have put me out of my misery with a single word of reassurance. When I could bear it no longer and looked at him again, he was lying beside me, some distance away, arms behind his head, just gazing at the ceiling.

"We were friends once," he said, conversationally.

"You didn't come . . ."

"I couldn't. You should know that."

"Why?"

I heard him sigh.

"Because . . . I had my own rituals to go through."

"Cal."

He looked at me and laughed. "Oh, I know, I know. I'm sorry. Why do you make me so angry? I know. You make me feel inadequate, can you believe that?" I shook my head, confused. "Oh, God, you're incredible. I can't get used to having found you. Come here." He pulled my nightshirt over my head. "There, that's better. Skin to skin." His hands stroked my back, while I clung to him as usual, scared to move. "It is an enormous privilege to share breath, Pell," he told me. "You can even get power over someone that way."

"How?" I could only say the right things. He made it happen that way.

"Oh, like this." Now I was no longer Unhar, it was different. I could taste his soul. I knew then that we had not shared breath before, no matter what he had told me that first night back on the cable farm. It had been nothing in comparison. Would it have poisoned me then if we had?

"Even aruna is not quite like that," he said, "What do you think?"

"What do *you* think!?" We laughed, hugging like children, sharing our breath again, getting mixed up in each other, like overlapping colors, tasting each other; his a taste of ripening corn and sunlight on fur. He pulled away to look at me.

"In the desert, I nearly killed you. I nearly jumped on you," he said. "You're exquisite. The crocus. Let me look at you; all of you." He tossed back the bedclothes and cool air hit my skin with his eyes. "Thiede is interested in you," he remarked. "He knows something about you. Too perfect. What are you?"

"Yours," I told him, making him laugh.

"Oh, I don't think so. But just for now I'll happily believe that."

I asked him, "Cal, why have I done this? What made me do this? Was it Fate that I've become Wraeththu? Did I have a choice? Will I . . .?"

"Hush," he answered. "If there are a thousand reasons or only one, the outcome is the same."

"Is that an answer?!"

"Not really," he said, smiling. "Believe the answer is merely that I wanted you, that I bewitched you into coming with me. Perhaps you didn't have a choice . . ."

"Are you telling me the truth?"

"Perhaps." He laughed and folded his arms around me like wings.

I never asked those questions again.

There is no coupling in eternity that can rival aruna. After a while we did not talk again; there was no need. Thoughts transferred between us like kisses. It was like dreaming and being in someone else's dream all at the same time. A star of pain inside me shot out light like a comet. It was a signal. His face was serious, but he did not speak, just culminated our foreplay by laying me back gently on the pillows. I was in agony, but for a while he did nothing, almost afraid. Feverishly, I reached for him, calling his name. End this torment. Dark flower. Touch. The star of pain fizzed wildly and went out. Tides of another ocean washed me delirious. Inside me, deep inside me, a nerve, a second heart, throbbed, itched, desperate to be stilled. Something snaked out from the heart of the flower and licked it like a bee's tongue. The heat of liquid fire engulfed us, sizzling our sweat and I cried out. Aruna. Ecstasy that can kill. The poison fire that is narcotic. I could never have imagined so much. The finest time of my life? There was something in what Seel had said. Later, others would bring sparks to my eyes, but that time, that first time . . . I could speak of it forever and never fully convey the magic, the power, the union that makes us strong. Nothing like the affairs of men: it is quite different.

We recovered and Cal said, "Be ouana for me, Pell," shining, lazy, passive. We blazed again, and I bloomed within him. When the dawn came, we slept, but even in my dreams, it was the fires of aruna flaring and flickering, a dense inferno, the heart of the volcano, flowers and ashes.

CHAPTER FOUR

>─┤◆>─○─<◆┤─<

On the learning of craft, and beyond sanctuary

My caste was Kaimana, my level Ara. The beginning. Kaimana progresses through three levels; Ara, Neoma and Brynie. Ara means altar and signifies a time of learning and preparation. I had many things to learn; basic occultism as I found out later. Its strange and lavish ritual intrigued me and I took the Oath that bound me to secrecy. There have been books based upon the codes of our religion. This is not one of them. As I speak to you directly through these pages, so I take heed of my vows. To those who already know the truth, there is no need for me to enlighten them. At that time, I had also to come to terms with the biology of my body, to understand its limitations and abilities. I learned to flex the muscles of my mind, so long unused.

Cal and I lived in Saltrock for about eighteen months and during that time I progressed from Ara to Neoma. Everything I learned came mainly from Orien, a patient and wise teacher. Seel taught me the mysteries and uses of plants (that knowledge was invaluable), whilst Cal, never less than that first time, explored with me the horizons of my sexuality. I suppose I was living in a kind of comfortable vacuum. Saltrock is cut off from the real world in a sense, if only by its location. Often, Wraeththu from other places would make their way there, some hideously scarred in mind and body by the wars and skirmishes beyond the mountains. One thing was clear: Wraeththu was becoming more powerful and Mankind responded valiantly to its threat, but the old world was disappearing fast.

We sometimes heard tales of the Gelaming; they that fought hardest of all and were rumored to have the most sophisticated technology known on Earth.

"At the beginning," Cal told me, "Gelaming were the finest, the brightest; in secret, so long ago. Men did not know about us then; that came later, with the killing. They may never know our true nature. (It was incredible to you too once, wasn't it?) They that joined us, the lucky ones, will be the only survivors."

Immanion reared, splendid and shining, somewhere faraway. One day, Cal vowed, we would find it. Saltrock, meantime, grew more solid, more stable with every day that passed. As Seel predicted, a generator was somehow procured and flickering electricity soon lit the lengthening streets and sturdier houses of the town. Saltrock would never be a proud and haughty temple city like Immanion, but it became a place, where even to this day, I could go to find peace and good company.

During that time I heard no more from Thiede. Sometimes, if I stopped to think about it, a threatening prickle of apprehension would scare me. Thiede had made no secret of his interest in me and he was stronger and more dangerous than we all knew. Several weeks after my Harhune, I was talking to Flick about Thiede's visit to my bedroom and how it had disturbed me. For a moment or two Flick looked at me as if I was mad.

"You must have been hallucinating still," he said. I laughed, although a little annoyed that he did not believe me.

"It's true," I insisted. "Thiede did come to see me and he said strange things. I wasn't hallucinating. Mur was there as well."

"But, Pell," Flick replied, his voice beginning to falter with bewilderment. "We all saw it. The day after your Harhune. Thiede left Saltrock. Everyone turned out to see him go; he rode away on a great, white horse . . ."

"Then . . ." My skin freckled with goose-bumps and Flick rubbed his bare arms as if he were cold.

"Then . . . well, he is Nahir-Nuri. That's all there is to say."

But it was more than that. Thiede is a law unto himself. It is possible, though difficult, to handle him, but not an exercise I would recommend. At that time I looked on him as a kind of god, now I know better. He has his limitations; they are just farther than everybody else's.

One day, a young emaciated Har stumbled, half-dead, into Saltrock. His body was in an appalling state and those proficient in medicine were perplexed by its cause. Orien read the crystals to find the answer. Oh, the ways of Men. How they revel in destruction. Now they had discovered a virus lethal to Wraeththu-kind and had lost no time in exploiting it. I was terrified. I thought it would be the end of everything.

Cal laughed at my fears. "It is a mere tick on the skin of Wraeththu," he professed.

I was amazed at his optimism. "How can we combat such a thing?" I argued.

"Simple," he told me. "Our strength can eradicate it easily."

We had to wait for the next full moon. A week and a half. During that time, three hara of Saltrock fell sick with the killer virus. The carrier could not be saved; he was dead two days after his arrival, already two-thirds decomposed.

One day Cal said to me, "Tonight, Grissecon shall be performed. Then you shall see. There is nothing men can throw at us we cannot handle effectively."

He had taken me to the shores of the soda lake to tell me. Instinctively I knew there was something more.

"Why bring me here to tell me this?" I asked. He put his hands upon my shoulders.

"I'm not sure how you'll feel about this. It will be Seel and myself who will perform the Grissecon." For a moment I did not realize what he meant and stared blankly at him. "Pell, you would have to face this sooner or later. We cannot be selfish with each other. Here, in Saltrock, it is easy. Many hara are paired off . . . but this, this is different. Orien has told me it will have to be Seel's essences and mine. We are the only combination here that will work."

He did not know that I had been anticipating something like this happening for some time. Cal often expected me to react in a humanly jealous way to a lot of things. Probably because my temperament had made such an impact on him before my Harhune, in the desert, when he was still raw from what had happened in the North. I was different now; almost detached from emotional matters. I felt a lot for Cal and always will, but I was not possessive about him. Outside, a lot of Wraeththu have degenerated from the True Spirit, and are once again the prey of their own emotions. Thiede's blood ran in my veins, his words stamped indelibly in my head. Unbeknown to anyone, I was more Wraeththu than most, and my emotions were slave to me rather than the other way around. I put my arms round Cal's neck and kissed his cheek.

"Your essence is healing," I told him. "I know you will destroy this curse." I could feel his relief like a golden rain in my eyes. I would watch him work magic with Seel and be proud. Grissecon, simply, is sex magic. Power is a natural result of aruna, which is normally wasted, dissipating into the air. Now I would have the opportunity of seeing this power harnessed, the potent essence of Seel and Cal combined, taken as a living force and directed back against those that cursed us. Somewhere, a resistant pocket of humankind had combined their own efforts in an attempt to destroy us, ignorant (as indeed I was at first) of Wraeththu's ability to fight back.

Saltrock has a sandy central square. It is often used for various meetings or ceremonies, and also for social gatherings. Everyone clustered there that night. I went with Flick. Seel and Cal had been absent from the house for two days to undergo purification. We all sat in a wide circle around a central fire. Orien, as shaman, conducted the preliminaries and we all chanted along with him. He threw grains into the fire and it flared up blue. When Seel and Cal were brought out to us, magnificent and clothed in gossamer, everyone cried out. We were drunk on excitement and pride. Seel's hair had been unbound from its usual rags and ribbons confinement and it seemed to me as if it had a life of its own; all those different colors catching the light of the fire. Cal was simply the primeval embodiment of Wraeththu, his violet eyes shining like midnight from the first days of Eden. By the light of the sapphire flames and the starcrusted, indigo sky above, Cal and Seel sank down together in the dust. They spoke the language of angels and their draperies blew away, into the fire, crackling up into the air like will-o-the-wisps. The throbbing of drums, hand-beaten, rose up behind the crowd; a deep, passionate growling like thunder. We, the gathered, thumped the ground with our fists, our bodies aroused in tune with the workers of magic. When the moment came for the flower to strike, Seel uttered a cry, strange and echoing and I seemed to see it drift from his mouth like an azure smoke, glowing as if a strong light shone through it. Did I see that? I saw Orien hold aloft a glass ball and the blue vapour seemed to coil into it. Cal stood up. In the flickering shadows, Seel still writhed on the sand, half replete, his hair lashing like angry snakes in the dirt. Orien's acolytes rushed forward to milk his essence into a curling glass tube. Cal and Seel mixed. When they held the tube out for us to inspect, I could see it glowing gold and red and purple. Then Orien took it away. He would use this elixir to work on the bodies of the sick and send the soul of the sacred seed speeding out on the ether to do battle. Everything has a life-force; even evil sickness conceived beneath the long eye of the microscope. Back in the square, we thought no more about it for a time. Seel had clawed Cal back to his arms and around us everyone fell to the same activity. I looked at Flick, his little anxious face looking up at me. Only a short time ago, I had felt inadequate beside him. I cupped my hand behind his neck and he closed his eyes.

By morning, it was as if the sickness had never been. I had been shown a little of what we were capable of. In a way, it was hard for me to grasp what I had witnessed, hard to believe that it was real. Did I possess this power too? Was it waiting within me? The sickness had gone. One death to remind us; that was all.

As I had pointed out before, I had no particular skills to offer the hara of Saltrock, yet I could not expect to live there without making some contribution toward the town. I turned my hand to many things: working in the strange, lush gardens under the black cliffs, where vegetables and flowering plants grew with grisly splendor and hugeness; assisting in the construction of new buildings (gradually the tents and makeshift cabins were disappearing); grasping the rudiments of vehicle technology (we had several ailing cars to work with, but lacked many of the tools needed to make them run, and what fuel we had was precious). Sometimes, I would climb alone to the lip of the glossy, dark cliffs, the staunch wall of Saltrock, and gaze out over the landscape. In the distance, rough abandoned farmland wrinkled the surface of the Earth; a pale road cut through it. Beyond that I would often see lights winking in the haze or vague movements. One day I would pass that way, and when I thought that, a deep and thrilling wave would shiver me.

In the mornings I worked, but most afternoons were set aside for study. Orien's house was made of stone, small inside and dark. He lived alone. It was rumored that when the first Wraeththu had come to the soda lake, this little stone building had already been there. Lost, abandoned; who had lived there? No bones had been found, but several fine cats were existing comfortably in what was left of the sparse furnishings. Orien said it was improbable that they had built the place. When I laughed at this, I had the uncanny suspicion that he had not been making a joke. Orien often came out with outlandish suggestions that I later regretted having been amused at. Anyway, since the beginnings of Saltrock, the cats had mysteriously multiplied in numbers. By mysteriously I mean that it happened too quickly to have been by natural means. They are now the familiar spirits of Saltrock. When other Hara came bringing with them other types of animal, the cats showed no hostility to the invaders of their territory. How they had lived untended in that cruel, barren countryside, with so little to hunt and eat, is an enigma, as is their philosophical tolerance of other animals. That was the first thing that Orien and I talked about.

He would give me books to read and then ask me later for my opinions of them. Often I had had difficulty with the language; some of the books were so old. He studied me very carefully as I talked, watching my face more intently than listening to my voice, I thought. Something puzzled him and he told me about it.

"I get a feeling about you, Pell. What is it? What's so different about you? I've instructed dozens of newly-incepted hara, but you. . . . Your beauty is uncanny. It's more inside you than on the surface."

I still could not accept such talk without embarrassment. "No, no, not more than many others," I pointed out quickly. "There is nothing different about me. I was born a peasant . . ."

"You do not talk like a peasant," Orien suggested, awaiting my response.

Something made me say, "It is Thiede," and Orien raised an immaculate eyebrow.

"Perhaps?"

"What is he?" I asked, somehow frightened, like looking into a huge space, dark and cold; somehow sure Orien would know the answer.

"No-one knows for sure," he said, guardedly. "Thiede is certainly *different* to any other Nahir-Nuri I've met. Sometimes he seems barely even Wraeththu. But then, we are a new race. Those of Nahir-Nuri caste are relatively few at present. One day I shall understand perhaps. However, Thiede has only been here twice before and then never as Hienama."

I was shocked. "You mean I am the first. . . ?" (A memory: Seel surprised. "Him?!")

"Yes," Orien confirmed. "He has never performed a Harhune here before. Yet here he was, as if by magic, when you were ready for yours. Pell, I feel I should warn you, but I don't know what against."

As if by common consent, Orien and I never mentioned Thiede again to each other. By now, I realized it was important to progress, for my own protection perhaps. Aspects of my training would often leave me unnerved, like waking from a bad dream. The first time, for example, that my own unsuspecting mind made contact with another's, filled me with disquieting anxiety. Orien spoke to me without words. He touched my brow lightly and I heard him say, "Rise, Pell, rise . . ." His lips never moved. I tried to communicate back and he laughed and stepped away, telling me that my thoughts were as confusing as a whirlwind. It took time for me to relax enough to touch his mind with calm and confidence. I learned also how to manipulate matter to my will, the concentration for which is exhausting. Many times, I was at the point of giving up, only Orien's soothing encouragement keeping me going. The first time I managed to shift a small cup along a tabletop by sheer willpower alone, I nearly wept with relief. I was learning to flex my muscles, the muscles of my own power. Lack of confidence was the worst handicap, and the first that Orien was anxious to help me overcome. To his credit, through patience and understanding, he succeeded. I studied hard and within six months passed to Neoma. Then Orien told me that I would have to continue my studies elsewhere to ascend to Brynie. Saltrock did not have enough hara of third-level Ulani to conduct the ceremony. I did not want to leave. My life at Saltrock had been nothing other than blissful. I had learned many things and made many friends. When we worked together, I revelled in the shared sense of achievement. I did not want to lose that. Yet I also knew that I must go on. Neoma was not enough. It was obvious to myself and to everybody, that I had great reserves of ability. I had no intention of letting it atrophy from disuse before I even discovered it fully.

Cal was still obsessed with finding Immanion. Often, when we lay in the afterglow of aruna, curled around each other like sleepy snakes, he would relate at great length all he believed Immanion to be. A place of great beauty, calm and symmetry; certainly a place where Wraeththu had disassociated themselves from the violence and chaos of the world and had built up a superior society, tranquil and affluent. It would be a place of soaring crystal towers, glistening in the brilliance of perpetual sunlight. Cal thought it was somewhere all hara should naturally head for. I was shrewd enough to realize that the Gelaming hid its location because they preferred to seek out themselves the people they wanted within its walls; nobody would ever find it by chance. However, I humored him. It would have been presumptuous of me to contradict him. He would say, "Don't get uppity, Pell, you've seen nothing yet. Saltrock's a haven," if ever I did pass an opinion he considered was founded on imagination. I knew I had acquired knowledge Cal could never learn, and I also knew where it sprang from. Something made me hide it; respect for Cal was not the least of the reasons.

One day Seel had to go to another town for supplies. It was decided Cal and I would go with him. The time had come for us to go on. We would not return to Saltrock with Seel. On the last night, we had a farewell party in the square. I was nearly heartbroken. It was possible we would never see our friends again; anything could happen Outside. Everyone was there. Mur and Garis, lean, gothic and sharp as needles to the end. Mur shared breath with me and I could taste ice and metal. Flick, I could only hug to me, genuinely sorry to leave him. His was a taste of welcoming fire in a cosy room and soft animal fur. He was a true friend, and when the time came, I turned the world upsidedown to find him again.

The fire had sunk low and nearly everyone had drifted back to their homes when Orien bid me farewell. He gave me a talisman, which I still have, of a sacred eye.

"Be strong, Pell," he said, and I could feel tears behind my eyes. It was difficult to speak.

"Only you know . . ." My voice quavered; I could not help it. Orien nodded, firelight shining through his hair, his face in darkness.

"Be wise as well," he said. "The time will come . . ." I threw myself against him, my chest tight with grief.

"I know, I know!"

Orien knew more of my fate than he cared to tell me, but he could not see all of it. Somewhere, out there, my future hovered like a poison insect. Orien let me weep out my fear.

"After this time, Pell, never show your tears. Never! You are a child no longer."

It was advice I took to heart. In the cold light of pre-dawn, I saddled up Red outside Seel's house. All the windows were dark with farewell, as if we had already gone. Cal had used a little of our money to buy another horse off Seel, bigger and showier than Red, but not as hardy and, surprisingly, not as fast. Seel had been going to use a pickup truck for the journey, but because we were going as well, and on horseback, he settled for a covered cart drawn by two heavy horses. Because it was a slower and more vulnerable method of transport, he took three armed hara with him as protection. All our good-byes had been concluded the night before, and no-one came out to see us off. When I had come to Saltrock my clothes had been barely more than rags covering the gangling awkwardness of youth. Now, when I caught a glimpse of myself in Seel's windows, I realized I had changed beyond all recognition. Gone was the tatty-haired, grubby child with the luminous eyes, bony knees and bony shoulders. I was a year and a half older and a year and a half taller. My hair was still cropped close at the sides of my head, but long down my back and combed high over the crown and wisping into my eyes. Clad in leather and black linen, silver hoops hung through my hair, three in each ear. I spared a thought for Mima and the rest of my family. Would they have recognized me? No. For the essence of the Pellaz they had nurtured had gone. All I retained of my former self was the memory of it.

I had had to leave most of the belongings I had collected behind. Cal refused to waste money on a pack horse. Also, it would have slowed us down. I had not got much, but I was sad to leave it at Saltrock and reluctantly gave it all to Flick. We set off at a brisk trot, down to the farthest shore of the lake where a guarded pass led to the outside world. The rising sun gilded the sulphurous surfaces of the lake; drowsy birds clustered on crystal spars, gaunt, black shadows. Behind us, a dog barked to greet the morning. I did not look back; never again did I look back.

Greenling was not strictly a Wraeththu town. Men existed in surly, wary alliance with hara. We arrived there, mid-afternoon, three days after leaving Saltrock. The land around it was dry, with desert encroaching from the south, but grudgingly fertile and the Wraeththu folk much more urbane. Two women were walking down the road toward us and one of them recognized Seel. She waved and ran over to us. Seel, being the charmer that he is, has an easy, friendly manner with humankind. The woman jumped up on the cart beside him. I realized with some amazement, even disgust, that they were flirting with each other. The men of Greenling, whether by accident or by commonsense, were clever in their acceptance of Wraeththu. Although their kind were dwindling, they would carry on unmolested and in peace until the end. Needless to say, this was not a common circumstance. In other areas humankind would not give up the idea that they were meant to rule the world. In those places, men and hara fought each other like dogs for territory, for commodities, for fuel. Not many places had the calm air of Greenling, where the two races existed alongside each other, somewhat reluctantly sharing resources.

Seel called me forward. "Pell, this is Kate. I usually stay with her family when I come here."

She began to smile, then looked alarmed. "We haven't got room for all of you!"

"I know, I know," Seel teased her. "We'll put up at Feeny's place. Anyway, your father would see us off with a shotgun. He can only handle Wraeththu when they're in a minority."

Kate's smile came back again then and she relaxed against the seat, proud to be seen with us.

Feeny's was a small hostel-come-bar and seedy in the extreme. The proprietor, a large, oily man and an apparent stranger to the concept of hygiene, grumbled at having to find room for six. While Cal organized our rooms, Kate grabbed my arm and flounced me off to buy a drink. She bought me a beer (uncannily enough one of the first things she did next time we met). Boyish in her manner, barely older then myself, she sprawled on a stool like an ungainly colt, appraising me with green eyes. "I curse the day I was born a woman," she told me.

"I can see that," I muttered drily. She unnerved me because she reminded me of Mima, although in appearance they were entirely dissimilar. Kate had blond hair, the kind that is almost green, and not such a bony face as my sister.

"It's so unfair," she continued, wiping her mouth with the back of her hand (a hardened beer drinker!), "I know I would make a brilliant har."

What could I say to that? I could not tease her like Seel. She could sense my discomfort and hated it. She asked me my name, how old I was, where I was born, even how I did my hair!

"Why me?" I asked her, attempting to stem the flow of her questions. "Have you pestered all the others like this?"

"Oh no!" she exclaimed with an endearing innocence, and shaking her head vigorously. "You were the most beautiful."

"I shall have to wear a mask then," I laughed, "Otherwise I might be hounded by inquisitive girls to the ends of the earth."

"Wear a mask?" she grimaced with a careless wave of her hand and taking another gulp of her drink. "What makes you think that will hide it?"

There was some truth in what she said. It wasn't beauty that marked me though, but something else. Something that would draw trouble toward me like a magnet when the time came.

As the sun sank, Greenling hara came to drink at the bar. Sultry and rather unsociable creatures, festooned with decoration; heavy earrings, thick bangles laced with spikes and chains. Seel and Cal and I sat apart in a corner. Tomorrow we would part and there was little conversation between us. Cal reached out and curled his fingers round Seel's arm where it lay on the wet tabletop. "Stay with us tonight," he said. He kicked me on the ankle, sharply, pressing me to silence. Seel said nothing to Cal but turned to look at me. I briefly touched their hands where they lay.

"We both want you to," I said, not really sure if that was true. I still had fears of showing myself up. Cal and Flick were the only ones I had taken aruna with. But I need not have worried. Seel wanted us to remember him. It was the only way to say farewell.

It was decided we would travel south, back into the Desert. Out there, hidden in the dreary scrub, bleak dunes and rocky terraces dwelt the Wraeththu who could take me to Brynie. The desert people: Kakkahaar. I had been told of their cautious instincts, their preferred solitude. It would not be easy to find them, even less so to enlist their help.

Once again, Cal and I had to stock up on supplies and Seel advised us to purchase things that the Kakkahaar might find appealing. Runes, incense and colored scrying beads from a Wraeththu shop in Greenling center. We also bought weapons, long knives that were expensive but essential, from a surly, lank-haired man in a cluttered shop reeking of human sweat. Afterwards, we loitered round Feeny's till noon, drinking sour coffee at the bar and laughing at our occult purchases. But our humor was underscored by sorrow. That afternoon, we would make the final break with Saltrock and sanctuary. I think in our hearts, both Cal and I longed to say, "Damn it, Seel, we're coming back with you." But to do that would have been to go against destiny. There was no way back; for me especially, and Seel, beautiful Seel, who in times to come became a great leader, a tactful and trustworthy politician, his future too would have been spoiled had we returned to Saltrock. It is also true that someone else was marked for death that day.

When the bar began to fill with lunchtime patrons, both human and

Wraeththu, Cal and I prepared ourselves to leave. Outside, we blinked in the brilliant sunlight. Red and the other horse, Splice, were already loaded up and waiting, sleepily kicking the dust.

"Greenling might be the last peaceful place you'll visit," Seel said, musing aloud. Leather creaked in the hot sun and we gathered up our reins.

"Goodbye Seel." I reached for his hand. Splice's head went up, ears flattened, as Cal made him prance into life.

"Come on, Pell!" he said irritably, and his horse sprang forward, half-way up the road in seconds. I looked at Seel but he shook his head.

"It's alright. Go on."

And so we left him, Cal galloping Splice into a lather, an expression like fury on his face.

Two miles into the desert's perimeter, a jeep screamed out of a dust cloud and swung to a halt beside us. Red stood stock still, ears pricked, muscles tensed, while Splice made a scene, sidestepping, half-rearing. Someone jumped out of the driving seat, leaving the engine running. It was Kate.

"What the fuck do you think you're doing?!" Cal exploded at her, attempting not too successfully to get Splice under control. Kate came straight to me.

"Pell, I'm sorry, I meant to catch you earlier. I went to Feeny's but you were gone. I've got something for you."

She pointed to the jeep and I followed her over to it. "Here," she said. "Guns." She was smiling up at me with that deceptively innocent expression, holding out the weapons.

"Where did you get them?" I had never handled a gun before, but I knew weapons were probably the only thing that would ensure our survival, and bullets were more effective than blades.

"My father," she explained. "He deals with many things. He'll probably miss them, but what the hell. It'll be too late then."

Cal snatched the other gun from her hands, weighing it up, gazing over the barrel. Kate frowned at him, not really understanding his ignorance. She handed me a peeling box of ammunition.

"Don't mind him," I said, nodding at Cal. "Thanks anyway. How much do you want for them?"

She laughed. "What? Oh, nothing, nothing."

"We'll think of you, then, when we're fighting for our lives," I joked and she nodded.

"Till we meet again," she said, swinging back up into the jeep, "and I'm sure we will."

"I fucking hope not!" Cal replied, thankfully drowned out by the roaring engine.

As we rode away, he said to me, "Don't be like Seel. Don't bother with men and their bitches. Remember, they'd kill us all if they could."

"I'll remember that with the first bullet I fire," I answered. Cal gave me a sour look but said nothing.

It seemed we traveled in circles. The ground underfoot was too stony for us to go faster than a walk and the landscape so monotonous, it was difficult to tell which way we were going. I thought of Saltrock, where everyone would be sitting down to eat after a day's work. Cal and I did not feel hungry and certainly did not feel inclined to stop and make camp. We would have felt vulnerable and unsheltered trying to rest out in the open. The light had gone from the sky by the time we found a tall, stark rock poking without welcome from the dry stones. Grumbling and unhappy, we tried to make ourselves comfortable beneath it. I felt guilty. If I had not been so insistent about the Kakkahaar, we could have traveled east, where there were other Wraeththu settlements, though small and of low caste. I had discovered that the majority of Wraeththu rarely passed to a higher level than Acantha, which is the first of Ulani. I could not progress without the aid of adepts, the knowledge-seekers. In a fit of self-pity, I started apologizing to Cal. It was my fault. We could have stayed in Saltrock for longer. The desert might starve us to death. Something of the old Cal broke through his reserves of grief at leaving Seel and the miseries of our position. He held me to him.

"Oh, Pell. Don't ever think me selfish. Never. I knew the moment I saw you, you were special. Brynie you shall have to be, and more. Tomorrow we shall set out and find the Kakkahaar. Without fail!"

It took slightly longer than that, however. We wandered about aimlessly for three days, eyeing our dwindling water with concern. The only pool we had found had been in the process of dissolving the carcass of an unspecified animal. Large, scraggy birds trailed us hopefully; flies appeared from nowhere, clustering like grapes around the animals' eyes, leaving unbearably irritating bites on our faces, hands and ankles. We were so dejected, we did not even notice the Kakkahaar had been trailing us along with the birds for about forty-eight hours. They made their presence known in the late afternoon of the third day.

CHAPTER FIVE

The inverted pentagram

They rose up out of the sand, unfolding like dune snakes ready to strike. Faceless, hooded, motionless. Cal drew Splice up sharply, biting his lip. He had no experience of the Kakkahaar and was unsure what our reception would be like. I was feeling dizzy with heat-sickness and in no mood to put up with any ritual feinting. Something made me draw Orien's talisman out

of my shirt. I lifted its leather thong over my head and held it up for all to
see, urging Red forward at a walk at the same time. The nearest figure
strode toward me, his robe blowing all about him, the color of the desert.

"What is your business?" he asked in a low, rasping voice.

I could see little of his face; a moving mouth, a strong, well-shaped chin.
"We are from Saltrock," I began. "The shaman, Orien Farnell has bidden
me seek out the Kakkahaar."

"For what purpose? Why tempt danger in the desert?" He spoke as the
wind speaks, whistling over the shifting sands in the dead time before the
dawn. A dreadful cold that changes the desert to a different kind of wilderness.

"I am Neomalid," I answered. "I have to pass to Brynie. There are not
enough hara of Algoma level at Saltrock . . ."

Red was sniffing the stranger's robes, inquisitive. The whites of his eyes
were showing.

"Give me your hand." I leaned over and reached down. His fingers were
dry and hard, and from that position I could see his eyes sparking beneath
the folds of his hood.

"There is more." His voice was little more than a whisper now; his
followers still as sand-stone behind him.

"The one named Thiede incepted me." There was no choice. I had to tell
him, even though there was a risk that that information might go against
me. I had no way of knowing what the Kakkahaar thought of Thiede.

The stranger drew his breath in sharply and stared at me intently for a
moment. "We are a nomad people." He stepped back a pace or two and
with careful grace, lifted both hands to his head to throw back his hood.
"Our camp is not far from here. Welcome. I am Lianvis."

The Kakkahaar are steeped in mysticism; there are few amongst them
less than Ulani, although they keep a choice selection of Aralids as servants. I expected them to lead an austere life, but in fact found them to be
a luxury-loving tribe. They loved to be waited on, hungered for comfort
and trinkets; their Ara attendants were dressed in diaphanous silks and
heavily hung with gold adornments. I could tell Cal disapproved. He
thought the Kakkahaar treated their Aralids like women, and although I
could not disagree entirely, at no time did I meet anyone in the camp
dissatisfied with the arrangement.

Lianvis, asking us polite questions about ourselves, but not too prying,
led us to a tasselled pavilion; his home. Inside, it reminded me of Seel's
living-room, though Seel would have been sick with envy had he seen it.
The color scheme was dark bronze, dark gold and black. Tall, decorated
urns spouted fountains of peacock feathers, canopies hung down from a
central pole sparkling with sequins. The tent was so large it had several
different rooms. A near-naked har with hair to his thighs bound with black
pearls, rose from the couch. A book lay open there beside a half-eaten
apple. He bowed before Lianvis. "Ulaume, barley-tea for my guests. They
need refreshment." The Aralid looked at me from beneath long, thick

lashes. His dark eyes looked bruised, his lips full as if aruna was never far from his thoughts. Never had I seen such a breathtaking, sulky beauty. Lianvis caught me staring. "Magnificent, isn't it," and then ushered us to be seated, I would not help but remember, with amusement, Seel's introduction of Flick. Enormous cushions, slippery silk and satin, littered the floor. We sank down into them and Lianvis sat down in front of us.

"I know of your Orien," he said. "A well-respected har among Wraeththu-kind, though it is some time since we met. How are things at Saltrock?" All the Kakkahaar wear their hair incredibly long. Lianvis's pooled about him, the color of honey.

"It progresses in leaps and bounds," Cal told him. "The terrain is difficult, but at least they can grow things." Lianvis leaned back sighing.

"Ah yes. They work hard at Saltrock. Not the life for me, I fear. Not a day passes that I do not give thanks for how we earn our living."

"How's that?" I asked, hoping it would not sound impertinent. Lianvis smiled, tapping his head.

"This. We are seers by reputation and people pay highly for glimpses, hints of their future. Men and hara alike."

Cal shook his head. "You amaze me and I respect your genius."

"Oh no, not genius, my dear Cal, oh no. Shrewdness, sharpness, cunning and a good sense of the dramatic."

"You don't fool me," Cal said with a smile. "The Kakkahaar are full of genius. Cunning, maybe, but extremely clever cunning."

Lianvis was enjoying himself immensely, lapping up the compliments. Ulaume brought in the barley-tea and a silver plate of thin-cut aromatic bread spread neatly with butter. Cal and I were so famished we fell upon the food like wolves.

Lianvis was apologetic. "How foolish of me, you must be ravenous. Ulaume, something a little more substantial, if you please." Cal slid an embarrassed smirk at me but we made no comment. "The desert is an unpleasant road to suffer if you are improperly equipped. You have no pack-horse, I see?"

We both had our mouths full and there was a strained silence broken only by the sound of chewing. Cal wiped his hands on his knees.

"No. We wanted to travel swiftly," he said.

"Oh, but we have brought you something," I put in quickly.

"Cal, where are they, those things . . .?"

"Later, later, please," Lianvis urged, but looked interested.

Later, while he watched contentedly as we feasted ourselves on the meal Ulaume had prepared, I asked him how long it would take for me to be ready for the ascension to Brynie. He told me that they would assess me in the morning.

"Business tomorrow," he said. "You are tired and need to relax. Ulaume shall make ready a bath for you both." He immediately made us conscious of our travel-stained, unwashed appearance.

Ulaume led us to another room. Cal's trousers were ripped across the backside. I thought it looked very becoming, but Ulaume snatched them out of his hands with a quick murmur about laundering and sewing. We splashed into a huge, dark-wood tub together while Ulaume hovered around, eyeing the rest of our clothes with aversion.

"I'll find you something else to wear," he said finally, scooping them up distastefully and marching out, holding them at arms length. I laughed, hoping Ulaume would not hear. I did not want to be cruel.

"Pell, you're so beautiful," Cal chanted, feeling sensual in the scented water. There was hardly enough room and most of the water fell out onto the floor, soaking the scattered goat-skins. We were half-drowned, high on aruna, when I noticed Ulaume watching, half concealed by the door curtains. Inscrutable, he caught my eye, twitched his mouth and walked out. What the hell. The Kakkahaar thought we were barbarians. Now Ulaume would tell Lianvis we coupled like animals, when the mood took us. I spent several minutes mopping the rugs with the towels afterwards. It took some time for me to discover what true barbarism was.

We spent a couple of hours with Lianvis after our bath, conversing freely on a superficial level. Our host amused us with tales of people who had sought out his talents.

"Of course, all that men want from us is our secrets. They think we drink from the fountain of eternal life and that is what they crave more than anything. As their women are drying up, so too must the well-spring of their race; they know this . . ." Lianvis told us airily. On his fingers, rings set with huge tiger's eye gems shone dully in the lamplight. He asked me where I came from and I told him hurriedly; it was not a subject I cared to dwell upon.

He eyed me shrewdly. "Peasant stock, eh? Strange, Pellaz, I could have sworn you had an educated air."

"My father taught me some things . . . and he had the priest to teach us the rest. You know, reading, writing and of course, God's message. He had a lot of books . . ." I could not understand why he should think I was lying, and tried to make light of it. Cal was abnormally quiet beside me, never taking his eyes off Lianvis. He had a brooding, thoughtful look on his face.

"For a tribe that makes its living out of other people, you have an unusual reputation for solitude," Cal said after a while. Lianvis shifted his attention from me, smothering a sharp alertness that flashed across his features.

"It's all part of the allure," he said. "It makes our prophecies seem that much more real . . ." That made Cal laugh. It was not a pleasant sound and it embarrassed me. The tone was not lost on Lianvis.

Later, once we had retired to the chamber Lianvis had prepared for us, I tackled Cal about his behavior.

"I'm not stupid enough to trust anyone as soon as I meet them!" he snapped. "And our charming host is far from trustworthy. Can't you see that?! He lives on deceit."

I did not argue, but dismissed his suspicions in silence.

Some moments afterwards, the curtains twitched and Ulaume in-
sinuated himself into our presence, carrying two steaming tankards. "Lianvis sends you spiced wine," he murmured, holding them out to us and
glancing at me with those unnatural smoldering, smoky eyes.

"Put it on the table," Cal said. He was sitting on the low, furstrewn
couch and did not look round. Ulaume put one cup down, and with fluid
grace, held the other up to my lips. I sipped, spell-bound.

"I can stay," he said, his voice soft and husky. Oh, the promise! I half
reached for him.

"No," said Cal, "that won't be necessary." His smile, as he turned, had
the hard clarity of diamond. Ulaume slowly raised one dark, curving
eyebrow, still transfixing me with his eyes.

"Another time, perhaps," he said.

By the time I realized he had gone, I had finished my wine. Cal was
smirking at my awed stupefaction. "God help you, Pell," he chuckled, "you
are easy game—too easy!"

"But he's incredible," I protested.

"Perhaps, but he's a lamia all the same. Share breath with that and
you'll be so much dried gristle hanging from the nearest tree." He had
pulled off his Kakkahaar garments with some distaste.

"What do you mean?" I asked, still staring at the midnight blue curtains
where Ulaume had vanished.

"I mean Wraeththu have many interesting variations. I suspect Ulaume
is one of them. It's obvious. Aruna is only food and drink to him. He's
Lianvis's pet and should be kept chained up!"

But I was not convinced. "You're so suspicious," I grumbled, as he
pawed at the fur blankets, grimacing.

"That's why I'm still alive!" he retorted. "It's a bad old world out there.
God, these furs stink!" He reached for his wine, wrinkling his nose. "This
is foul as well."

Now I know better. Now I keep things such as Ulaume in pretty cages
to amuse my guests. Then I still saw good in everyone.

We slept late into the next day and then both woke with headaches. I
groaned and burrowed back into the blankets. Our journey must have
exhausted us more than we thought.

"Do you realize," Cal announced, "that we used to wake up from a bed
of stones with a bellyful of dehydration feeling better than this?" We
looked at each other, both thinking the same thing.

"Of course, how stupid!" I cried, sitting up in the bed and slapping my
head; it was too late to knock sense into it though. "The wine! It was the
wine, wasn't it? But why . . .?"

Cal curled his lip. "Perhaps Lianvis prefers to have any visitors dead to
the world at night. Knock them unconscious; keep them neatly in bed.
Other reasons, though?" He made a noise of disgust. "Watch me shudder!"

"If we get wine offered to us again tonight . . .?"

"Oh, it goes without saying, doesn't it. God, Pell, I know you need these snaky types for now, but tread carefully. Accuse me of paranoia, even hysteria, if you like, but there's more to this cozy little set-up than meets the eye."

I dropped back down onto the pillows, screwing up my eyes to ease the pain. "It would help, Cal, if I knew what ascension to Brynie involved. God, it could be so easy for them to . . . take control . . . let *something* in . . . you know."

"Mmmm, that's not impossible, of course. Look Pell, I've been through Brynie; I can tell you some things. That's highly irregular, but at least if there's any drastic deviation in the procedures, you'll know. Only ignorance makes you vulnerable."

All power lies within the mind. If it is said: "there is no magic," to a degree this is true. Magic is will. Will power. Ara and Neoma are concerned with the search for self-knowledge that is necessary before progression. (Try exercising your will without it! You can't.) I had learned how to discipline my mind, how to believe in myself. Brynie is the expression of this knowledge. Cal's memory of the actual rituals involved was sketchy but I gathered enough for what I hoped was safety. Perhaps we were being too cautious. I could not see what Lianvis would have to gain that was worth taking the risk of perverting my ascension.

Although I had been told my assessment would begin in the morning, it was not until the afternoon that Lianvis asked to speak to me. After lunch, Cal and I went to attend to our horses. They were looking tatty in comparison with the polished steeds of the Kakkahaar. At the back of Lianvis's tent was a cooking pit and a canvas-draped pit that served as a toilet. We tethered the horses there. I counted ten other large pavilions and several smaller, shoddier dwellings. From the outside, all were of a neutral-colored material that blended effectively with the surroundings. There was not much noise, not enough for a camp of that size. A sense of vague, unseen activity around us, but done silently. Sometimes, the warm breezes carried scents unidentifiable and unpleasant. Both Cal and I started to get paranoid, especially when Red or Splice threw their heads up in alarm and nothing was there.

I was squatting at Red's heels smoothing his legs, when something made my skin crawl. I glanced up quickly, and fell into the unwavering gaze of slumbering menace. Ulaume. He stood, half-wrapped in the door curtains at the rear of Lianvis's tent. All I could see of his face was his eyes and I did not like what I saw. It was a look to inspire fear and dread, even to one hardened by skepticism, and yet, there was an undeniable fascination. Ulaume wanted something of me, and because half of me wanted him back, I was powerless. "Lianvis has sent for you," he whispered and from ten feet away his voice was as clear as a bell. I stood up, dizzy in the hot light.

"Yes. I'm coming."

"Pell." Cal's voice reminded me of the warning. I raised my hand in a gesture of complicity and followed Ulaume into the tent. Inside, it was dark and hot, endless corridors of drapery. I could not see very well. The odor of heavy perfume masked other, earthier smells.

"Your friend does not like me," Ulaume murmured, somewhere ahead of me, his body luminous through a veil of hair.

"He thinks you are dangerous," I said, wishing I hadn't as soon as it came out.

Ulaume only laughed; a tinkling, restrained parody of amusement. "He is jealous."

"And what's that?" I sounded sharp. Jealousy, in that sense, was a word erased from the Wraeththu catalog of emotion. He must have realized his mistake. There was a slight rustle and then his warm, mobile arms were around my neck, his breath disguised with the perfume of mint, close to my face,

"I shouldn't have said that. He's right; I am dangerous. I can be. But you are safe; you know you are. I can smell the power in you. It smells like fire!"

"Ulaume . . ." I half-heartedly tried to break away, attempting to resist the onslaught of musky, sinuous allure. The heat and the gloom were claustrophobic; sweat began to creep from my skin.

"Are you really afraid to share breath with me?" His face was so close, we were nearly touching. I could see small, neat teeth shining like nacre between lips that were as well-shaped and smooth as swollen petals. A muscle twitched uncontrollably along his jaw. Part of me was still repulsed (the hint of the tomb . . . something), but I could not stop myself; the pull was too strong. He was a well and I was thirsty, it was as simple as that. His taste and his power poured into me. First the darker tones of earth, then hissing sand; sand harvested by the hot, desert winds; the metallic wings of the element of air prevailing. Ulaume: a dark vortex. But whilst I floundered on the edge of the maelstrom, afraid of slipping, of losing myself, exhilaration spumed through my blood. He tried to drag me down, take my soul, but I could match him. We embraced; we fought. He did not want to kill me, not that; it was a little violation he wanted. To rape my soul, perhaps; feel him there lapping at my strength. He had said he could smell my power but he was confident his own was greater. Now I could feel him scared, his heart pounding, his hands claws upon my chest. I could feel the weight of that waist-length hair shifting, lifting with a life of its own, lashing with reptile spite. There it was, tight as ropes around my wrists and whipping around my back. I tore myself away from his mouth, barely able to lift my head. Horror fizzed in my throat. Trapped, I was Ulaume's prey. We were so close; locked together in an embrace of tangles. There was only one way out for me. I looked once at his face; a pale and challenging oval suppressing its fear. One look, and then, with that supernatural strength I hardly knew, I directed one blasting surge of will at the strands around my left arm. Be free! Be free! With a screech and a smell of burning hair, Ulaume stumbled backwards. On my wrist, red weals began to rise where the hair had bitten into me. I could hear him swearing at me, low and guttural, but not quite a curse. He had that much sense, at least.

"Snake!" I cried, and hit him, hard, with the back of my hand across the face. He snarled, dropping to all-fours, bearing those immaculate, child's teeth, head thrown back; a neck of white cords. Then there was nothing. Then a shrinking howl; Ulaume vanished; upwards, sideways, backwards, in the smoke of his own hair.

For a moment or two I had to lean down; put my head between my knees. It was the first time I'd really tried to put into practice all that Orien had taught me. Supervised exercises, like moving a glass along a table-top are nothing in comparison. It was the difference between drawing a picture of killing someone and stabbing someone to death in cold blood. Although I had been trained to believe in my natural powers, some part of me was still surprised that it had worked. It felt like I'd been running. My chest ached, my heart raced and every breath was an effort. Blood had begun to bead on my wrist where Ulaume's hair had whipped around it. Lianvis, where are you? I wondered. Stumbling, absently licking away the blood, I went to seek him out.

Lianvis's pavilion was like a maze of shrouds. It seemed larger on the inside than it looked on the outside. Sometimes there were dark, deep-piled carpets underfoot, sometimes only sand. I felt disorientated with shock after my struggle with Ulaume. I was not used to dealing with such things, and knew I should have taken more notice of what Cal had said about him. At the same time, however, I was glad that I had found out for myself. It had also proved to me just what I was capable of. I had needed that moment of danger to channel my powers. It had been that or defeat.

Lianvis let me search for him for several minutes before he guided me to the inner chamber. It was draped in the darkest, non-reflecting black, and decorated with esoteric symbols. The curtains dropped behind me as I stepped into the room. I was still sucking my wrist which had begun to throb and prickle ominously.

"You did well with Ulaume." Lianvis's voice came out of the shadows. I could see him sitting on the floor on the far side of the chamber, cross-legged, robed in silvery gray, his hair pooled around him like molten metal, in the metallic glow thrown out by a single lamp that was on the floor somewhere behind him. Shadows arched and flickered among the curtains like mocking spirits. "Was that a test?" I asked.

Lianvis beckoned me to him. "Sit." I did so. "A test? Yes, of sorts, I suppose it was. I have been watching you Pellaz, while you slept, just now with my little pet, and I have reached a conclusion."

"Oh? You admit to drugging us then? Last night?"

Lianvis gave me a rueful smile. "Oh Pellaz, don't look so fierce. I only talked with you."

"I don't remember."

Lianvis shrugged. "Of course you don't. Now listen. My conclusion is this: it is not Brynie that you want or need."

"Why?" I could not hide my disappointment. I had been feeling good about myself, now this.

"Don't jump to conclusions. It is this. I shall raise you to Acantha, nothing less."

"But Acantha is Ulani!" I cried. "I'm not ready!"

Lianvis flapped a hand at me, leaning behind him and producing a long, carved wooden box. He opened it with leisure and drew out two long, slim black cigarettes, passing one to me.

"Your excitement is uncalled for," he remarked, lighting his cigarette from a smoking taper of incense. Heavy browny-gray smoke plumed from his nostrils. "I have examined you. I am of Algoma level. Therefore I know. We have heard of Thiede here. Few in the world of Wraeththu have not. He is a potent force, neither light nor dark, but something of both. Only a fool would not fear him. You say he incepted you, and from what I have observed I see that you are telling the truth. You have great power Pellaz, but you must learn to harness and use it correctly as of now. Brynie would be a waste of time for you. A redundant exercise. You already know that much. Few of Acantha level could have managed what you did with Ulaume. He possesses an untramelled elemental force."

"I could feel it," I said in wonder.

Lianvis nodded. "There is more. Sometimes even I am wary of aruna with him, Pellaz. He is what is called Colurastean. His tribe are the Colurastes; sometimes called the snake people, though that is a deceptive term. They have nothing to do with reptiles."

He remembered my unlit cigarette and leaned forward to light it for me. The smoke was acrid and burned the back of my throat although the aftertaste was pleasant.

"You do not trust me, do you," Lianvis remarked, without rancour.

"Not really," I admitted.

He smiled. "No. A little wisdom on your part perhaps, or your friend Cal's. Kakkahaar have somewhat different ideals from those of the Wraeththu of Saltrock. We travel different paths. But I shall help you if you wish it to be so."

"I have little choice. As you said, I can't waste any more time. The basic rituals must be the same . . ."

"Yes. That is only a formality. I shall instruct you as impartially as I can, but," here he leaned forward, just a little, "in my opinion, you would benefit from learning a little of the darker side of Wraeththu power. With abilities such as yours, any experience can only be advantageous."

I was not so sure about that. "Are you trying to glamorize me?" I asked him.

He feigned surprise. "Pellaz, please!" he exclaimed, throwing up his hands.

"Lianvis, I'm not a fool, not completely. Inexperienced, yes, but not stupid enough to stray off the path now. I know the dark exists, we all do, but you cannot convince me that looking into it will benefit me." I stood up. "I have to get this wrist seen to . . ." and made as if to leave.

"Pellaz, sit down!" His voice was an order, but I avoided his eyes and remained standing. He sighed. "Alright, alright, sit down. You'll have the straight ascension and nothing more. Now, show me that wrist." I sat down again and held it out to him. Three short strokes, an unutterable word. He wiped his hands. "There. Is that better?" I looked. There was no sign of injury.

"Fine," I said, gazing at it, flexing the fingers.

"You could have done that yourself," he told me. "Now, to work together, you'll have to trust me a little." I narrowed my eyes at him. "Look," he continued, "your friend is Pyralisit, is he not? He will watch out for you. He can attend your instruction if you wish . . ." I relaxed.

"Very well. I'll trust you a little." And I indicated how much with my finger and thumb.

"That much, eh?" Lianvis was amused. I raised my eyebrows at him and he said, "Ah, well, I suppose that is enough."

It did not take me long to realize that Lianvis had been astute in his judgment of me. He gave me instruction for two weeks, and during that time I was surprised at the ease with which I handled his complicated teachings. It seemed I only had to hear the words once or twice for them to lodge ineradicably in my memory. It was no problem for me to recite them at will, no difficulty for me to muster my strengths and utilize them. Once, back home, the old priest had told Mima and myself that one day we might find the knowledge we had acquired a burden, more than anything else. "Where will you use all this that's in your heads?" he had wondered. I feel sure he would have violently disapproved of the direction my search for knowledge had now taken and been horrified that the foundations he had laid within my head should support such timbers of information as Lianvis now imparted, but I, at least remembered the old man with thanks at that time. Without that first teaching, none of what followed would have been so easy, if at all possible.

Lianvis once told me I was "primal." He said this in a very grave and humorless tone, so that I was impelled to ask what he meant.

"Simply that," he answered, smiling. "Your aura is primal—back to the beginning . . . I get a feeling about you. Obviously, you'll have heard of the first Wraeththu; well, one of his names, used for invocation, is Aghama—that is an arcane word for "the first," literally, primary. His essence must be very strong because it is so pure. I sometimes get a whiff of that about you . . ."

"Is it possible to invoke the first Wraeththu then?" I butted in impatiently.

Lianvis sighed wistfully. "It is possible to try," he said.

Lianvis told me that two other Kakkahaar as well as himself would conduct my ascension ceremony. It would take place on the next night of the new moon, out in the desert, among the gray dunes. Only one thing bothered me. Cal would not be present. As he was of a lower level than the others, Lianvis pointed out, he had no place there.

Several days before the completion of my studies, a man came to the Kakkahaar camp. He was accompanied by a fair-sized entourage, all muscle-swamped, trained killers from the look of them, and they traveled in an impressive cavalcade of heavy duty vehicles. We had been sweating in Lianvis's inner sanctum when the approach had been noticed. One of the Kakkahaar Aralids had burst into the room (that alone was unheard of), and announced, "Tiahaar Lianvis, Mr. Shasco is here again!" An expression of unbridled avarice transformed Lianvis's face from adept to merchant in the space of a single second. He rose quickly in a flapping of garments and rushed outside. Cal and I raised eyebrows at each other. This was something we had to see.

Outside, the unrelenting sun flashed with the strength of white fire off the glittering chrome of Mr. Shasco's vehicles, that creaked as their engines tried to cool. Cal and I stood in the mouth of the tent, shading our eyes against the glare. A fleshy, red-faced man was descending from a hatchback, puffing with exertion and dressed in dripping khaki. He petulantly shrugged off assistance offered by his henchmen, and staggered forward; in appearance uncannily like an aggressive bulldog.

"I need your help again," he rasped at Lianvis, lurching past him into the tent, not even looking at Cal and myself.

Lianvis followed him, more slowly, grinning gleefully. When he saw us, his mouth pursed. "Pellaz, Cal, I'm afraid I have business to conduct now. You'll have to carry on without me today."

"But I can't!" I protested. "I've learnt the preliminary exercises, and the responses. I can't do any more without you."

Lianvis clenched his teeth. I knew I should have said something like, "Oh, it doesn't matter, we'll carry on tomorrow," but I could not resist being awkward. I disapproved of what he was doing anyway.

"Go back inside," he said impatiently. "I'll find you something to get on with." He tried to hurry us past Shasco who had sprawled uncomfortably into the floor cushions and was fanning himself with his hat.

"I'll be with you in a moment, Mr. Shasco," he said unctuously. "Ulaume! Refreshment, hurry up!"

I had never seen Lianvis so agitated. Money sat fanning itself in the main salon, of that I was sure.

Within the inner room was a black chest bound with iron. From this Lianvis produced a dense and ancient tome of thaumaturgical lore which he thrust into my hands. Decrepit leather flaked through my fingers. "The third chapter, read it and I will test you later!" he exclaimed with triumph.

"I will test you later," I mimicked, once he had gone, passing the book unceremoniously to Cal. Cal grinned with wolfish humor.

"Fuck this, my precious," he said. "I think now is the time to indulge in a little casual eavesdropping."

"He'll hear us!" I pointed out, none too keen. I was still sensibly wary of Lianvis, despite the amount of time Cal and I spent ridiculing him or lampooning his flamboyant mannerisms. I did not think he would take too kindly to us lurking in the draperies, listening to whatever transaction he was conducting with the corpulent Mr. Shasco. I felt sure he would catch us.

"He won't know," Cal argued. "Come on, where's your spirit? We might learn something useful."

"What, Mr. Shasco's fortune?" I asked scathingly, but followed him anyway. We crept stealthily back along the curtained corridors. I can recall, even to this day, the singular, pervading smell of Lianvis's tent. It was a burnt perfume smell, almost electric and hung like invisible curtains in the hot gloom of material curtains. Tendrils of less savory aromas mingled with it from the toilet facilities outside. In fact, we did not have to get too close to the main salon to be able to hear their voices. We could hear Shasco saying, ". . . superior quality. You can expect nothing less. The best; baptiscd, virgin . . ."

"And this *impediment* you mentioned. I trust you have brought some trifle, some personal trinket, with you." That was Lianvis talking. We could hear rustling.

"Yes," Shasco answered him. "I knew you'd need something of the kind. Here, will this do?" A moment's pause.

"Ah, yes. A ring. Yes, I can still get the feel of him."

"Lianvis, it is vital this matter is dealt with immediately. God knows what mischief has been afoot whilst I've been traveling here . . ." I could detect a note of panic in Shasco's voice, and could visualize Lianvis's expression of icy politeness.

"But of course, Mr. Shasco, of course. Don't worry, it is of minor concern. Rest assured your enemy will trouble you no more. Now, once again, as to the payment . . ."

"It is as I promised. When, where, shall I deliver it?" Shasco's voice was a disgusting wheeze, notes of lasciviousness vibrating within it.

"Tonight. By sundown I shall have concluded your business. After that. . . . There is a place half an hour's walk from the camp toward the west. There are stones above the sand, big stones. They are visible from some distance away. Deliver it there. Wait for me if you get there first; there are certain preparations . . ." Lianvis's voice was terse.

"And . . . you will let me stay?" An obscene plea. There was silence and I could sense Lianvis's disgust.

After a short while, I heard him sigh. "Very well. Yes," he said.

Cal put a hand on my shoulder and I jumped. The curtains trembled. "Come on Pell," he whispered. "I've heard all I want to."

Back in the inner room, we sat on the floor and looked at each other.

"God, I can't believe that!" Cal exclaimed, hitting the air with his fist.

"Is it . . . then?" I asked stupidly. Cal did not answer me.

"Lianvis is nothing more than a paid killer, and for *men* too! How could he?"

"Oh simple," I replied. "For money. Economies crumble like burnt wood all over the face of the globe, but there's no denying it can still buy a lot . . ."

"Oh grow up, Pell!" Cal sneered at me, making me feel ridiculous. "You can be really stupid sometimes! There's more to it than that. Didn't you listen?! Since when has money to be" (and here he struck a typical Lianvis pose) " 'delivered to the secret place when the moon is high'? Money? God! Pathetic!"

"What then?" I asked in a small voice but I thought I knew.

"Flesh," Cal muttered, with a grimace. "Of what kind, I'm not sure, but I'd swear to it. Flesh; Mr. Shasco pays in blood."

It was inevitable that Cal wanted to follow Shasco that night. I knew it would be an expedition fraught with the most horrible danger and told him so. "You were the one who warned me off Ulaume. You were the one that told me caution had kept you alive. Now this!"

"Now this!" Cal agreed, a fanatical light in his eyes. (A look I came to dread). "Remember, Pell, you'll be alone with these creeps and in a position of submission pretty soon. How long is it to your ascension ceremony? Two days? Three? Maybe after tonight, you'll decide to forego the honor. Maybe you'll learn something useful."

"Oh alright, alright," I said, giving in, starting to flick through Lianvis's book, seeing nothing.

"Look, Lianvis will be busy magicking Shasco's foes this evening. He'll have little time for us. Drugged wine again, perhaps? We'll take a romantic walk in the desert together, before the eminent Mr. Shasco trundles forth."

I could not really understand Cal's zeal for nosing into Lianvis's business. I felt it had nothing to do with us; the only interest I had was simple curiosity.

It was without surprise that we received the news that we would receive our evening meal in our own room that night. Ulaume had been efficient in his attempts of avoiding me since our skirmish, but it was he that brought our food to us. Cal was feeling bored, lying on the bed, and I could see a cruel mischievous light come into his eyes as Ulaume silently laid out our food. He watched the Colurastean for some minutes, various calculations slipping across his features, before uttering, "Come here, snake-beast," in a voice like ripping silk. Ulaume glanced up, his hands wavering above the plates. I still thought him beautiful and watched him carefully. He did not look at me. I could tell he was frightened of Cal. He started to back away, but with striking speed, Cal shot up and grabbed his wrist. Ulaume made a pitiful little sound, half whine, half cry.

"I said come here," Cal hissed through his gritted teeth. "Where's that offer now? You can stay can't you? Won't you share breath with me, Kakkahaar plaything."

"No," Ulaume gasped, trying to prize himself out of Cal's hold with his free hand.

"He's not Kakkahaar," I said, "Colurastes."

"He's Kakkahaar," Cal spat, shaking him. "You're Kakkahaar, aren't you, Ulaume. The Colurastes demand respect for their craft. What would your people say if they knew what you are now, Ulaume?" Cal shook him again.

"Cal, shut up!" I cried, afraid he would say too much. We could not risk alerting Lianvis to what we knew.

"It's alright, Pell," he answered, not looking at me, but the venom had left his voice.

I wished I had not told him about what had happened with Ulaume. Cal could be insensibly vindictive when the mood took him. He wound a handful of the threshing, tawny hair around his other hand.

"Come on viperling. Braid your hair. It gets in the way, doesn't it? It might creep around my neck. It might give my throat a little squeeze, accidently."

I was expecting Ulaume to muster his defenses at any moment, but of course he knew Cal was Ulani. When Cal let go of his arm, he did nothing but braid his hair. Cal smiled and lay back, arms behind his head. "Pellaz, commit to memory here another lesson. There is aruna, there is grissecon, and there is pelki . . ."

"Oh!" Ulaume's hands fell to his sides, clenching into fists.

"Oh. Yes. You think the hara of Saltrock are pious upstanding creatures, don't you Ulaume. But we're not from Saltrock, Ulaume. At least, I'm not. My tribe is Uigenna. Does that mean anything to you?" Cal, with the face of an angel and the sensual cruelty of a fiend.

Ulaume started to shake his head. "No, no, no, no, no," he wailed.

Something about this little scenario was beginning to sicken me. "Cal," I said, without emphasis. It is horrible when you realize that someone you think you know quite well could very possibly be a complete stranger.

Ulaume seemed to notice me for the first time. "Uigenna!" he said helplessly.

I could see him shaking. It meant nothing to me. I wanted to say, "Ulaume, I don't know, I don't know any of this," which I did not, but I stayed silent. Something inside me told me it was safer to remain uninvolved. Let Cal play this game himself. For a while there was a terrible, heavy silence. Cal stared without feeling at Ulaume, and Ulaume gazed beseechingly at me. I don't know why he expected my sympathy. I looked from one to the other wondering what the hell was going on. Suddenly Cal jumped up. Ulaume winced and covered his head with his arms.

"Oh, get out," Cal told him, smiling. "I don't have the time."

Ulaume fled without a further glance at either of us. I could not bear to look at Cal and started picking at the food.

"Don't eat that!" he said. "Remember the wine."

"Well, let's go then." I turned away from him, unsure of why I felt so angry, reaching for my goat-skin jacket; it would be cold later.

"Don't you want to know what Uigenna is?" Cal asked.

"No."

We went outside. In the distance we could see a smudge on the horizon. "That way, I think," Cal said. We trudged along without speaking. Eventually Cal broke the silence. "You're angry," he stated. I did not reply. "Oh, don't sulk Pell! I wouldn't have done anything."

My voice was harsh. "Wouldn't you?"

"No, of course not. I was just playing. Getting him back for what he did to you." He put an arm around my shoulder and kissed my cheek. "Forgive me?"

"Cal, he didn't *do* anything to me." It would not do for me to give in so easily.

"God, don't you ever bear a grudge? If you've forgiven the snake Ulaume, then forgive me." His face was the epitome of innocent charm and I could do nothing but relent.

"Very well, I'll believe what you say." After a while I said, "Cal, what is pelki?" I had my arm around his waist and felt him tense.

"You'll be angry again," he complained.

"I promise not to be." We both knew I might not stick to that.

"OK, you asked for it. I'll tell you this. I was incepted into the Uigenna. Their belligerence is famous. They are hostile to nearly everyone else on this planet except Uigenna. Pelki is a remnant of man's so-called civilization. It is something Wraeththu hate; it is anathema to them. Some will even deny it exists, but it does. It is rape." He stared into the distance, avoiding my eyes.

"And Uigenna and pelki are synonymous?" I enquired carefully. I was not as upset as Cal thought I would be.

He shrugged. "Not really, but it's where I learned the term. Mention Uigenna and most Hara with their heads screwed on start running, though. I was very young when I was incepted: thirteen. I suppose I had a hard time but it all had a kind of grim glamor. Two years later I defected to the Unneah. They are another northern city tribe, somewhat warlike, but honorable enough. I was really too young to be part of the violence of Uigenna, but I witnessed plenty of it."

"Cal, are you telling me the truth?" I asked him. He looked at me then.

"I've never lied to you, Pell. Never. OK, it might have been wrong of me to threaten even a reptile like Ulaume like that, but sometimes the beast just comes through in me, that's all. I didn't like what happened with you two, really I didn't."

"We cannot be selfish with each other," I quoted, reminding him.

"Oh, Pell," he said, rubbing my arm. "It's not like that, honestly it's not." I looked at him archly and he said, "Oh hell!," and leaned down to bury his face in my hair. I had been given a glimpse of the future, but I didn't know it.

CHAPTER SIX

Beneath the sand

The stony sand beneath our feet cooled for the night. Pebbles clicked in the shadows. Out there, in the desert, the cold and the dark creep up on you unawares. One moment it is balmy evening, the next it is a blue, gaunt, werewolf place.

Ahead of us, sand-sculpted ruins poked through choking, powdery folds, their carved summits eroded to formlessness. This must be the place Lianvis had spoken of. I could feel a hundred prickling emanations bouncing off my skin. It was a place that had felt Corruption's gingery touch.

"How old is this place?" Cal asked the darkness, his voice hushed with caution, echoing among the blind stones.

"God forbid it should answer you!" I replied in a quavery warble. "I think we should hide."

"We should fear least the creatures we *can* hide from around here," Cal told me cryptically.

I knew what he meant. Perhaps this jumble of disintegrating stone had once been a holy place. There was something of a feeling like that still lingering. Dark holes that were stone throats led down into the ground. Very little remained on the surface; most of the walls had toppled and the sand had swallowed nearly everything. I did not want to go underground. There were many places where we could crouch unseen (by hara and men at least) on the surface.

"Don't be ridiculous," Cal scoffed. "Nothing will happen out here!"

"We won't be able to see, if we go down there," I protested as reasonably as I could. It was true there were no lights, however dim, shining out from any of the tunnels.

"Well. Then we shall wait."

We leant against a half-wall, warmth oozing out from the heart of the cooling stone into our backs. We did not have to wait long. Soon a line of shambling figures folded out of the dusk, lit by the steady, orderly beams of flashlights. We crouched lower as they passed us; four or five individuals. Men or Wraeththu? It was impossible to tell from our position. One of them was obviously Shasco. We could recognize the stumbling step and labored breath.

"Now we wait again," Cal murmured, as their sounds disappeared into the earth.

Perhaps you have heard someone say: "My heart was beating so loud I was sure others could hear it!" and have thought it a colorful, exaggerated way of simply saying: "I was scared witless". You are wrong. It really does seem that way. Any moment I expected Cal to say, "For God's sake, stop making that noise!" There was no logical reason for us to be there. If Lianvis found us, we had no excuse. If I had argued more persuasively with Cal back at the camp, I might have been able to talk him out of this reckless folly. I cursed my weakness.

Out of the darkness came a muffled sound. Soft thuds, faint jangling. Horses.

"Two of them, I'd say," Cal whispered, lifting himself a little.

"Don't look!" I hissed, pulling him down. "It's Lianvis!"

He had to know we were there, had to! He was Algomalid. He must be able to sense my fear, at least. We heard them dismount, voices, the words indistinguishable. A horse snorted, hooves dancing on the cracked paving, its bridle jingling. We listened to the voices moving away. I had been holding my breath. Now I let it out, and my stomach ached.

"What now?" I asked.

"Oh, we'll give them a few minutes to get involved in whatever they're getting involved in." Cal stood up.

"Cal!" I squeaked, tugging his arm.

"It's alright," he said, "there's no-one here."

I stood beside him. Lianvis and his companion had hobbled their horses. They looked at us from lowered heads with troubled eyes and pointed ears, snuffling and backing away. Tassels on their bit rings brushed the ground.

"Which tunnel do you think they took?" Cal asked me, looking round.

"Who cares!" I replied.

"That is not the spirit, Pellaz," Cal chided me in a voice that betrayed not the slightest hint of fear. "You must learn to face danger with strength and courage. You won't last long if you don't."

I will last even longer if I avoid danger, I thought.

"That one looks vaguely lit up," I said, pointing.

Keeping to the shadows, we crept toward it. No sound issued from the uninviting gloom, but a faint, ruddy, flickering glow. I felt as if we were being watched from every other dark entrance. Cal stepped inside and I followed. Shallow, worn steps, dusted with sand, curled down before us. Many thousands of feet had trod here in forgotten times. It was possible that once this building had been well above ground, perhaps even a tower, before the desert had got to work with its enveloping tides.

We descended for some minutes, progressing slowly. At the bottom a corridor with a damp, sandy floor stretched forward. The ceiling had once been plastered. We could see, from the light of a single crackling torch hung on the wall, that most of it had fallen away. The stone beneath was pitted and cracked, but there was no rubble on the floor. It seemed to indicate that the place was used fairly regularly. Wall paintings, obscured by black mold, depicted orderly rows of figures marching toward the end of the corridor, their expressions frozen in haughty piety. I had expected to hear the sounds of chanting, the preliminaries of ritual, but the single sound that echoed toward us was worse than that, much worse. It was the last, desperate cry of the irretrievable soul, still recognizable as human, or har; just. I froze in horror, and found myself gripping Cal's arm. He touched my hand. "Let go. Come on."

The corridor was not really that long. At the end, the remains of huge, wooden doors sagged inwards. Beyond that, the light was stronger. The gap between the door lintel and the wood was so large, we could look through easily into the room beyond. It was a high-ceilinged chamber, columned, camerated; a temple.

Several figures stood around a central bowl of fire. Lianvis, clothed only in his hair and a black loin-cloth threw grains into the flames, which spurted up, amethyst, sapphire and ruby. His eyes shone like a wolf's in moonlight. Reflective, milky and opalescent. Ulaume, robed in diaphanous gray stood at his left side, holding a metal dish. His face was arrogant, yet disassociated, fronds of hair wafting about him as if in a breeze. There was only one man there and that was Shasco. He stood a little apart from the others. I counted six hara, including Lianvis and Ulaume. Candles, thick as my wrist, stood upright in thick pools of their own wax upon the floor, illuminating the circle and the signs that had been chalked there.

Lianvis spoke a word of power, and cold, luminous light filled the entire chamber. The candles guttered fitfully as if the luminence choked their flames. I could see then what had passed unnoticed before. Curled up on the ground at Lianvis's feet, moving feebly like a weak puppy kept from its mother too long, was a child, presumably human. Ulaume clicked his fingers and two of the Hara stepped forward to lift the boy; his feet trailed in the chalk as if the bones were broken. When the light touched his face . . . God knows I never wish to see such a thing again. He knew he was to die, wretched hopelessness was etched across his features, frozen in a rictus of a scream. It must have been his cry we had heard at the mouth of the corridor. I wondered what they had done to him for him to make such a sound. There was no mark upon his body. Lianvis stepped forward, his head thrown back; a wolf's head, his eyes beacons of destroying power. Ulaume bent to untie the cloth about his master's hips and I could see the corded muscles in his lean thighs straining and trembling with restrained energy. Realization made me utter a single, shocked "No!" and Cal elbowed me in the ribs to silence me. I did not want to see any more. Lianvis's face was changing into something demonic, the lips pulled back, long teeth shining in the sulphurous radiance, his neck twisting, twisting, his hair lashing like frenzied snakes. The boy began to howl, to struggle, his feet paddling helplessly in the dust, and I pressed my eyes against Cal's shoulder. There was nothing we could do; nothing. Whatever power we possessed was no match for Lianvis in that state. I clapped my hands over my ears, but it could not shut out the sound, the dreadful, dreadful cries and Lianvis's snuffling, guttural snarls.

Suddenly Cal pulled me upright. Whirling noises, shrieking out from the chamber broke up his words, but I made out, "Now . . . now . . . the power . . . him . . . the power . . . back! Back!" Reeling backwards, we started to run, the appalling, scraping screeching chasing us down the corridor; the smoke, the stench of burning flesh.

I shouted, "Does he know?! Does he know?!" as we ran. Cal did not answer.

Blue light flooded the tunnel as we reached the bottom of the steps. Slipping, grazing myself against the stone, I scrabbled up after Cal, his long limbs sure and swift above me. Outside, the stillness of the night was unnatural. Cold air hit our lungs with a breathtaking chill and I gasped, hardly able to breathe. Cal hauled me out of the tunnel, dragged me across the paving and threw me down behind the wall we had first hidden behind, covering me with his body. Arcane words ripped from his throat, his breath wheezing and shuddering. It was a simple protection. I was in no position to augment his strength with mine. I tried only to press myself into the stones, to become invisible. For a second or two there was only silence and then the night exploded with sound and blue luminence. Cal buried his face in my hair. I could feel his heart racing manically in his chest against mine. "Oh God, oh God, oh God," he kept repeating. I had never seen him afraid. We hugged each other, eyes shut tight. Something formless and huge spurted out of the ground, out of the tunnel. Its light burnt through our closed eyelids. Stricken with terror, I held my breath again, feeling the awesome, devilish fever pulsing round us. Lianvis transformed into elemental power. We were lucky that in that elevated, supernal state we were beneath his notice. With a dismal scream, he shot toward the stars, fizzing and hissing like a monstrous rocket, the air cracking around his phantom shape in shards of lightening. I opened my eyes, looked up over Cal's shoulder. It filled the sky. Lianvis, barely recognizable as he but for the suns that were his eyes. I felt he looked right into me, mocking. He could have reached down and plucked us off the earth. But the night just filled up with his demon laughter and the light that was his greedy soul reached up for the sparkling darkness. He blazed away from us like a comet. A word sprang uncontrollably to my mind. I still don't know why exactly, unless it was some kind of obscure presentiment concerning later events in my life. The word was this: Aghama.

Cal rolled off me and lay on his back, blinking at the sky.

"Your idea," I said, sitting up and brushing sand off my coat.

Cal closed his eyes and swallowed, clenching his jaw.

"We could steal the horses and leave," I added, tentatively.

"What horses?" Cal said in a flat voice. I peeped over the wall and could see them lying there; the black humps of their bellies.

"Dead," I murmured rhetorically.

Cal sighed. "There's no cover on the way back to the camp. We'll have to wait for the others to leave," he told me.

I said nothing, although I could see no way we could get back inside Lianvis's tent without being seen.

"Maybe we should just try to get back to our horses and get out of here," I suggested.

Cal rolled his eyes. "Are you joking? We have no supplies, no idea which way to go. Lianvis would know then that we'd seen something. He wouldn't let us get away. No, we wait, and then follow the others back. Once we're in the camp, we could bluff our way through if anyone sees us."

"Cal, he knew we were here, he must have!"

Cal stared at me and then shook his head. "No, I don't think so, no."

We lay in the dark, still breathing quickly. After a while I said, "Cal, what happened in there?"

"Murder," he replied. "Murder for power. Wraeththu essence is death to humankind, remember. But it is a sweet way to kill for those on the dark path, a sweet way to feed on souls . . ." He motioned me to silence then, for we could hear them coming up out of the ground. I heard Ulaume curse when he saw the dead horses, and that was all. There was no sound of conversation as they headed back into the desert.

I turned to Cal. I spoke to him. I said, "What are we, Cal? What are we part of?" He did not answer.

After maybe fifteen minutes, Cal stood up. He said he could see their flashlights in the distance and it was safe for us to follow. Luck was on our side. When we reached the camp, sounds of revelry reached us from around a leaping fire by Shasco's vehicles. His men were getting drunk and the witnesses of Lianvis's conjurations, doubtless desperate for a drink themselves, had joined them. As we slipped silently back into the tent, I saw Ulaume standing staring into the fire, a tin cup pressed to his chest. Even in the orange glow I could see his face looked gray.

I still feel that it was by some miracle that Lianvis did not become suspicious of my behavior from that time on. When, on the following day, Cal and I went to the inner room to spend more time with him on my studies, I could do little more than twitch and mumble at him. Terrible images of a gaping mouth uttering only a heart-rending mewl paraded indelibly across my inner eye. What made it worse was that Lianvis had conducted that ritual for no other reason than sheer, dissipated pleasure. I had thought at first that the whole exercise must have been for Lianvis to gain some kind of extra power, but Cal informed me otherwise.

"What we saw was sheer decadence," he said. "Nothing more. Lianvis took life as we take alcohol. The effect is similar, but as you saw," (and here he smiled) "so much stronger!"

Now, facing our charming host every day was a nightmare. Lianvis sat, composed and neat upon the cushions, but somewhere inside him the rushing wind spirit, star power, still glowed; a hidden, dense-white core. He had trained me well to focus my strengths; there was little time left to spend with the Kakkahaar and I wanted to make that time as short as possible. I visualized the shining symbols of protection against evil above my head and kept them there. If Lianvis guessed I knew something of his activities, he gave no sign, but knowing his level and his art, I think it virtually impossible that he did not know. It seemed he did begin to accelerate my studies toward their conclusion, but I may have imagined that. Of course, Cal and I had considered leaving the Kakkahaar before my ascension but we did not want to risk making Lianvis suspicious of us. We were afraid of him and it was fear that kept us there beside him.

Two days later he told me that my ascension to Acantha would take place that night. I asked him where and he replied it would be at the ruins some way west of the camp. He watched me sleepily as horror must have thrilled across my face. But that was all. He said, "It may be a good idea for you to ride out there this afternoon. Look at the place. Take Cal with you."

Of course, once we were there, in radiant daylight, there was no sign. The underground corridors smelled old and unused. Flaking cobwebs dangled from the crumbling plaster. Perhaps we took the wrong route down. The vast temple chamber was lit hazily by smoking bars of sun. There was no blood on the floor, no marks at all. Cal and I did not speak, but looked at each other in the gloom. Cal moved into the radiance and looked up through the cracked ceiling. It was a perfect picture. I poked among the rubble; not even a candle had been left behind. Nothing spoke to me there; it was thoroughly cleansed.

I had to fast that day. At sundown, Lianvis put me in a different room. He would come for me at midnight, he said. I lay down on the couch, uncomfortable in the hot, close atmosphere of the tent. My mind was in a daze; my ascension seemed something of an anti-climax now. The pleasure, the pride, the excitement had gone out of it. Kakkahaar's noble Hara were bloody with unhallowed crimes. I knew that what we had witnessed under the ruins was no isolated incident. The memory of it would not leave me and I knew it never would until the desert was behind us. One awful thought, that I could not banish, that made me feel sickened, saturated with sickness, was this: me going with trusting innocence with Cal into the desert. Me leaving my home with a stranger whom only Fate had decreed had not been a Kakkahaar, or something like them. Visions of me smoking, writhing, sizzling in the most unspeakable of agonies kept rising before me. Me, unconsciously flirting with Cal, tempting a possibility I could never have dreamed of.

So, here I lay, still in Lianvis's tent, awaiting the hour of my ascension ceremony. I vowed we would leave as soon as I was rested the next day. Perhaps then the bad thoughts would fade. I threw my arm across my eyes and pressed down hard, making the colors come. I knew that outside, in the real outside that is, far beyond the sand, the rocks, the scrub, the world of men still struggled to maintain their supremacy. I knew that the things that had frightened me so far were mere nothings in comparison with what might await us beyond the solitude of the sand.

Outside, muted voices called mournfully on the night air. The sun, a great, boiling, ruby globe, would be sinking in a haze of colors behind the ruins. Bars of light sneaking in through the cracked vaults of that unholy place would be crimson now, the chamber suffused with bloody light. And later I would go there, later bite my tongue whilst Lianvis stands in that same place; different, calmer forces bowing to his touch.

I turned on my side and curled my knees up to my chest. The room looked tawdry, the air stale beneath its veil of incense. I felt hot and dirty, hungry and anxious to be free to leave. The hours till midnight seemed interminable. I rolled around on the couch, trying to get comfortable and reciting rituals in my head until I hated them.

It was almost dark when I heard the curtains rustle behind me. Someone came in on silent feet, bringing with them a hint of the freshness of the air outside. I rolled over quickly. It could not be Lianvis; it was far too early. A dark figure, barely visible, stood at the side of the couch. All I could see was one pale hand holding the folds of its hooded robe together. I made no sound, but waited. The figure pulled itself up to its full height and gradually unfolded the draperies that swathed it, raising its arms above its head. Pellucid skin glowed like phosphorous in the shadows; yet I still could not make out the face. There was a cloud in my head forbidding recognition. I held out my arms and the strange, silent, pliable visitor curled into them. I found a mouth tumid with desire and I drank from it dark and secret things. All the colors around me were mazarine blue and richest purple; a taste of ink. A burst of starfire. I was ouana, violet and gold, tongued with flame, seeking ingress, conquering and revering. Streams of ice flowed from my heart, meeting fiery air, hissing, swirling, making steam. It may only have been an erotic dream; a temptation, an illusion, or it may have been a living, hungry thing.

I was sleeping when Lianvis came through the curtains. He shook me and smiled at my waking eyes. My mouth was dry, my body slippery with sweat. "Come now," was all he said. I looked. There was no-one on the couch beside me, though my arms felt cold as if only recently emptied. Lianvis watched me sit up, rub my face, reach for my clothes. His secret smile led me out to the desert.

Perhaps if I had known more of the way things really were in the world, I would not have been so desperately anxious to leave the camp of the Kakkahaar. All things in life are merely relative. The evils we had encountered in the desert were extremely bad compared with our time at Saltrock; later events would make our time with Lianvis seem like days of peace, a holiday. Never, there, had I been under direct threat. Things we had seen had been only an education, perhaps a warning. Then I was still afire with the ingenuous idealism that the haven of Saltrock had formed within me.

My ascension to Acantha had concluded when the first predawn gray had diluted the pristine darkness of the desert night. I did not feel as if my body was brimming with new-found power exactly, but what I did feel was an inner kernel of calm and confidence, something that could be called upon, should the need arise. I rode back to the camp with the echoes of ritual ringing in my head; exhausted, but still determined to leave the place that day. Lianvis insisted, I broke my fast with him. He told me he could not see why I was in such a hurry to leave.

"Whatever's waiting out there for you will still be there tomorrow," he said, flinging his arm to the east.

"I don't want to waste time," I told him, lying glibly.

"You *could* rise to Pyralis here," he pointed out, avoiding my eyes and picking at the food on his plate.

"No!" I cried, too quickly. "No, I mean, I mean we have to go on."

Lianvis shrugged. "Your choice, of course. Where do you plan to go?"

I looked beyond him, out through the door of the tent. Where? "Oh, Cal will know. Somewhere."

"You would be wise to return to Saltrock, you know," Lianvis said, wiping his hands, slowly. "We are fairly isolated from any trouble here in the desert; it's too far and too inhospitable for us to be a threat to anyone, and Saltrock too, but other places . . ." He drew his breath in sharply and shook his head. "Pellaz, some of the towns north of here are painted with Wraeththu blood. There is hell beyond the boundaries of the wild country."

I could have told him that even before I was har I had not seen the towns and cities of men. My experience did not extend further than pictures in books the priest had shown me. Now I wanted to see. But what I said was, "I do not want to hide forever. There is a world out there and a great war perhaps. Wraeththu will win that war because of the simple fact that they have Fate on their side. Cal and I are going to be part of it . . ."

"Why risk your life?!" Lianvis exclaimed. "It would be more sensible to wait a few years at Saltrock. Maybe, by then, things will be a little more . . . resolved."

I did not think he was right, which of course he was, and I was exaggerating slightly about our sense of heroism. Cal and I had no plans at all. He wanted Immanion and I wanted to live a little. We had not even discussed where we wanted to go next yet.

It was late afternoon by the time we were ready to leave. Lianvis equipped us richly with food and water. He had also donated a pack horse to carry it, ignoring our protests. There was a multitude of useful things: rope, salt, a knife sharpener, clothes and a tinder box. I thought Lianvis was just trying to get around us for some reason (and was probably right), but was grateful all the same. I had given him very little in return for the training he had given me, and now he showered us with gifts. A Kakkahaar guide would take us to the edge of the desert.

As we left, Lianvis came to bid us farewell. There was no sign of

Ulaume, which surprised me. Lianvis said, "You mustn't waste your talents, Pell; try to stay alive until you have matured enough to use them properly."

"I shall certainly try!" I replied. I gathered up Red's reins and he lifted his head, ready to leave. Cal was talking to the guide some feet away. "Oh, one thing, Lianvis," I said quietly, leaning down. "Last night; was it you who sent Ulaume to me?"

Lianvis laughed. "I did not send Ulaume to you," he answered, but his face looked sly. "You never saw Ulaume last night."

I was puzzled. "But his *hair* . . ." I said.

"No. It was not Ulaume. Farewell Pellaz." He turned quickly in the usual swirl of sandy cloth and strode back into his tent.

As soon as we rode away from the camp my spirits began to lift. The desert, past its cruellest mid-day heat, shone with barbaric splendor. Red and Splice, rested and well-fed, were anxious to please and light on their feet. Lianvis had given us a tent of sturdy black canvas. When we camped for the night, there were whole chickens to eat and pale, yellow wine to hasten our sleep. The Kakkahaar guide had told us that he would leave us at mid-day tomorrow. In less than a day the desert would be behind us, yet it would probably have taken us weeks if we had not had a guide.

As we lay in our tent that night, Cal quizzed me about the previous night's events. His voice sounded strained and he was lying on his back, not touching me.

"I'm sure all the ceremony bit is just decoration," I said. "It's the instruction that's important. That's what raises your level. Look at this!" I materialized a glowing crystal in the air before us. Cal slapped it with his hand and it vanished.

"What is important is common sense, that's all! You are Wraeththu. The power is there anyway. It is in man too, but they ignore it . . ."

"What's the matter with you?" I snapped, leaning over him. His eyes were cold, the darkest violet. He pulled his blanket tighter around his neck.

"Why won't you tell me?" he said. "I have never kept anything from you!"

"What do you mean?" I had an inkling however. He just looked at me and I dropped my eyes. "It is no secret," I said defensively, "I just forgot." His expression did not change. "I feel as if you expect me to apologize."

One side of his mouth twitched in a tentative grin. "Forgot? Oh Pell!"

"It's the truth! It all seemed like a dream anyway. I still don't know if it was real. How did you know?"

He raised one eyebrow. "I know; that is all. I can see it around you; something dark." The coldness had left his voice and I lay down, resting my head on his chest through the blanket.

"It was all so strange. I don't even know who it was. I did think it was Ulaume, but I asked Lianvis and he said it wasn't."

Cal said nothing for a while. His hand crept under my hair and stroked

the back of my neck. Outside, I heard the Kakkahaar cough in his sleep.
"I know who it was," Cal said. Something in his voice scared me.
"Don't tell me; don't," I murmured. "Just make me Light again."

CHAPTER SEVEN

They that have fallen . . .

To the east of the desert, a long, straight road winds straight across an
unrelenting plain. There are a few farms there; some dealing in livestock,
some in grain. We could see smoke rising thinly from their chimneys. The
Kakkahaar had said that we should begin to avoid the habitations of men.
There were only two of us and men might be tempted to shoot on sight. Cal
said we should forget the road and head north. Although that might mean
we would risk encountering danger, there would be more of our own kind
that way. We still had plenty of supplies and we could travel fairly fast
across the plains.

Now we changed direction again, abandoning our journey to the south
and heading north once more, away from the arid country toward greener
lands. For several days, we did not meet any hara or men. In the distance
we could see the land begin to rise. There, the blue of the sky started to mist.
Cal taught me how to use a gun. We did not want to waste what ammunition we had, but we shot at small animals, which supplemented our diet.
Sometimes I would dream of our being attacked by men, (shadowy creatures with pale, dead faces), and not being able to defend ourselves. I was
not a good shot. Our horses grew sleeker and fatter on the lush grass of the
plains. When the wind blew it billowed like a vast, green sea.

The first town we came to seemed inhabited only by ghosts. Only litter
moved on the empty streets; a makeshift garrison sagged unmanned. Cal
left me with the horses under cover and went to investigate. I fretted
impatiently while he was gone. Surely it should not take this long. I could
see him killed a hundred different ways, mostly shot and shot and shot. He
returned an hour later, sauntering back to me, biting an apple.

"It's safe," he said. "I think."

I could tell it had not been that long ago that this had been a thriving
town. Something had made the people leave. Just the fact that they appeared to have left their vehicles behind (we saw many parked along the
streets), made me uneasy. Cal said that wasn't too ominous a sign. Fuel was
becoming scarce, after all. I looked inside one of the cars and it appeared
long unused, but I was still unsure. Had this place been abandoned or
attacked? There were hardly any indications of destruction; what there was

could have been caused by neglect. The buildings were for the most part undamaged and we could see nothing of the more grisly remains of conflict; dead Hara or men. Cal showed me the fruit tree where he had picked the apple. It was in the garden of a large, white house. It reminded me of the Richards house back home. "Let's explore," Cal suggested, but I was not very keen. As a child I had often dreamed of big, empty houses, and the dreams had never been pleasant. I think that deserted houses have person-alities of their own, and once deserted, resent the intrusion of living things. Cal laughed when I told him about it, but he did not insist on going inside. We walked up the wide, main street, where once a community had bustled, ignorant of their fate. The horses hooves made an alarmingly loud clatter, which echoed all around us. I hoped frantically that the town was as empty as it appeared. If anyone did still lurk there, I felt sure it was unwise of us to advertise our presence. But no-one came. The town held its breath or slept or dreamed. The empty eyes of the shops, the cafes and houses watched us implacably until the hair stood up on the back of my neck. Once out of the center, we remounted our horses and cantered out through the suburbs.

On the very edge of the town, down a sleepy road of middle-sized, family houses, just as our fears were beginning to subside, a single, sharp, arresting sound shattered the air around us. Gunfire. Cal reacted immediately, swinging Splice sharply off the road and crashing into a nearby garden. I kept so close to him our knees were touching. Chewing up an unkempt lawn, we collided to a halt behind a shield of fir-trees. Cal hauled me to the ground. At first we could hear nothing.

"We should have the weapons ready all the time!" Cal hissed, speaking more to himself than to me.

"What now?" I asked, rubbing the rein-burns between my fingers.

"Men or hara?" Cal muttered to himself, ignoring my question.

"They must have been watching us. Damn! I should have known. It was too quiet. Pell, find out. Help me put out a call."

Now was the time for me to put Lianvis's tuition to the test. A call; to men it is a science fiction of telepathy. To Wraeththu it is just another way of communicating, conveniently without sound. If it was something other than hara out there, the chances were they would not pick up on it. We clasped each other's hands and focussed a channel of receptive thought out onto the street. I could feel Cal's nails digging into the backs of my hands; his arms began to shake with effort. We amplified the force, but nothing came back—at first. Then, I could hear it inside my head. Cautious, reti-cent.

"What tribe?"

Cal was controlling his thoughts with cool dexterity. He answered, "Saltrock," and did not waver. It is extremely difficult to lie, or even attempt half-truths, when communicating by thought, but Cal could do it easily. There was not even the faintest whiff of Uigenna or even Unneah. Thank God.

"We are Irraka," came the mind-voice once more, "You can come out now."

Cal smiled uneasily at me. "Let's go," he said. Our pack-horse, Tenka, had scrambled off up the garden. I could see him staring defiantly back at us with lowered head. Red and Splice, trusting creatures that they were, still stood behind us, breathing down our necks.

"I'll get him," I said, "You go and shake hands with the Irraka."

"Well, thank you Pellaz," Cal muttered scornfully. He led Red and Splice out onto the street. Tenka decided to be awkward and it was some minutes later that I emerged from the garden. Cal was talking to a tall figure clad in thick, black leather with cropped hair. He had a fierce, sharp face and unsettling gray eyes that were almost silver.

"I am Spinel," he announced, folding his arms so that the leather creaked.

"Pellaz," I said, resenting strongly the stripping directness of his gaze.

"I know. Your friend tells me you're heading north."

I looked at Cal whose face had assumed the blank look he reserves for strangers. "Yes." I confirmed. Spinel sniffed and shrugged.

"Brave Hara," he said with the faintest hint of a sneer. "Though you'd better learn to be more cautious. We could have finished you easily back there."

I almost said, "We thought the place was empty," but thankfully realized the folly of it before I opened my mouth.

Spinel spoke again, "You're from Saltrock, eh? Everyone's heard of Saltrock. Seems stupid to leave there . . ." He did not trust us, that was clear.

"Oh, we have business farther north," Cal told him. I was wondering what this stilted conversation was leading to. Was he going to offer us hospitality or order us on our way. I did not understand why he was cautious of us or that he had good reason to be. He obviously came to the conclusion, however, that as there were only two of us, we were not much of a threat. He raised a hand and snapped his fingers. Instantly, a dozen Hara materialized from concealment, all pointing weapons at us.

"There's no need for this," Cal's voice was beautifully clear and steady. "Let us pass. We mean you no harm."

It seemed ridiculous even saying it. Cal and I; two of us, and a dozen guns aimed at our heads. What did they expect us to do? Shape change into something large and numerous?

"We have to be careful," Spinel said smoothly. "As you see, the town is empty. Varrs were here. About a mile out of town, there's a place that's a heap of death. One whole heap of death. Men, women, children. We come from Phesbe; that's a town up there some way." He pointed. "We saw the smoke. Investigated. Varrs tried to burn the dead, but there were too many."

"Oh?" Cal said daintily. "And how long ago was this?" I caught on to what he was thinking; there was no smell. That much death and no smell?

"Very smart," Spinel sneered. "We dealt with it. You could smell it at Phesbe two days ago."

I could tell Cal was beginning to get annoyed with this pointless altercation. "We're not Varrs," he said.

"Varrs have whores," Spinel countered, aggressively.

Cal just laughed. "Do they? Saltrock whores even? Oh spare us the shit, Mister Irraka, and good-day to you. Come on, Pell." With remarkable sang-froid, he put his foot in Splice's stirrup and started to mount. I swung up onto Red's back hastily, hoping Cal knew what he was doing.

"Are you planning on passing through Phesbe?" Spinel asked him gruffly.

"I don't think so," Cal replied stonily, urging Splice into a trot. I followed.

"They'll shoot us!" I squeaked, catching up with him. Cal did not answer.

Some moments later, I heard hoofbeats behind us and looked round. Spinel and his troupe were galloping toward us on enormous black horses. Spinel caught up easily. His brute of a mount had a huge, curving head with red nostrils. Its mane was cropped, like its rider's.

"You'd be fools to carry on north just now," the Irrakan addressed Cal. "Chances are you'll meet the Varrs. We've decided you can come with us back to Phesbe. Wait a couple of days there."

Cal did not slow Splice's pace. "So kind of you," he said. "Well, what do you think, Pell?"

"It's up to you," I replied.

"OK, lead on," Cal smiled at Spinel.

The black horses poured past us, their hooves throwing up grit from the road. They were very impressive, like part of an army. Soon, all we could see of them was dust, but their trail was easy enough to follow.

"I wonder what they want," Cal mused.

"I won't say it!" I said.

"And what's that; 'Oh Cal, you're so suspicious'," he pantomimed, imitating me. "They probably want to steal all we have and ravish our silky bodies!"

"Why are we following them, then?" I demanded, in alarm.

"Because a thorough ravishing is good for you now and again!" he joked, or at least I hoped he did.

Just before we reached Phesbe I asked, "Cal, what are Varrs?"

"Oh, they eat Uigenna for breakfast, darling," he said.

"Be serious for once!" I snapped. He loved to irritate me.

"They're just another northern tribe," he explained. "Hideously arrogant and shockingly ferocious."

"Thank God it was only the Irraka we met then!" I exclaimed.

Cal pulled a face. "I should save thanking Him for a while yet if I were you," he said.

It seemed that with each Wraeththu tribe we came upon, we were slipping one note lower on the scale of civilization, comfort and morality. Phesbe was a stinking husk of what once might have been a decent, and fairly affluent, community. Now it was merely a rat-heap of broken concrete spiked with rust, rank, seeding weeds and ungodly stenches. Most of the buildings were crumbling into a rapid dissolution, gaping roofs were hastily patched with flapping canvas. All the streets, mostly insurpassable with rubbish, bore a sad wreath of mulching newsprint nurturing a surprising burst of late summer poppies. I saw two dead dogs and a dripping carcass of what might have been human hanging from a pole.

In the center of the town a rococco town hall stood bravely and still intact. Spinel had made this his palace. He was waiting for us at the foot of a sweeping flight of steps that led to the hall's porticoed facade. Bitter-looking hara with cruel faces lounged about him, all dressed in black leather uniform. Many were heavily tattooed, none wore their hair long, and I noticed quite a few had shaved their scalps completely and scored the white skin with black patterns. Their expressions ranged from outright hostility to mere boredom, and I could not suppress a shiver as we dismounted. Spinel snapped his fingers (all he ever had to do to summon his aides), and a skinny har with pale eyes shambled down the steps to lead Red and Splice away.

"Hold it!" Cal ordered, and removed as much of our luggage from Tenka as we could carry. Why tempt Fate, or indeed the fingers of the Irraka? We followed Spinel into the hall.

Inside, a sickly sweet odor of corruption mingled with a smell of wood smoke. Horses' hooves had cracked the marble floor and it was no longer the least bit white. Tatters of cloth hung without apparent purpose from carvings around the walls. Spinel studied our stunned appraisal of the surroundings.

"We are fighters, not thinkers," he said bluntly. "We have no time for Saltrock fancies here."

Cal raised his shoulders eloquently. "Quite," he said.

There was one large room where all of Spinel's immediate retinue appeared to sleep, eat and lounge around. Rags partitioned the room's perimeter into separate sleeping quarters, but there could be little privacy. In one of these makeshift holes I saw a pitiful creature, little other than a skin-covered skeleton, lying on a pallet. Spinel caught me staring.

"Leg broken" he explained. "The bone came through. Time says he might not heal."

I felt sick. The Irraka were without hope. They did not have any healers and, as there are few Wraeththu who cannot effect some measure of healing, this betokened more than anything, more than the filth and the squalor, that this tribe had fallen from the path. Wandered off it, more likely. I realize now that they must have been a splinter group of Aralids somehow separated from their main tribe. Without the strength of the higher castes behind them, the troubles they had suffered had dragged them down. They had no sense of productiveness; their fire and imagination had been doused by hardship. Most of them seemed healthy enough, however, in a lean, hard way, and their animals appeared well cared for. Two hounds had bounded over to Spinel and he absently touched their heads as they scrabbled to lick his hands. I dreaded that we might be offered something to eat. The smell alone was enough to turn the stomach. I remembered with regret Lianvis's heavy-perfumed chambers. The windows here were mostly broken and stuffed with cloth. Smoke had stained the ceiling and walls; there was little light.

Cal dropped his luggage onto the floor and uttered a long, low whistle. I knew we still carried bread and fruit and cheese from the Kakkahaar. It may have been foolish to waste it then, but I suggested Spinel should share it with us. Cal obviously shared my thoughts for he agreed immediately. I could only admire Spinel's restraint as we unwrapped the food. The dogs were more honest; they howled to get at the cheese, which was dry, fragrant and crumbling.

"How did you get this town?" Cal asked, tearing at a hunk of sweet bread. Spinel did not seem to hear him; he was chewing with utter concentration. Cal repeated the question.

"Eh? Oh, the Varrs had it first. Took what they wanted and left. We were traveling around. Moved in. The men who lived here had fled to Stoor, the town back there, you know . . ."

"What? And they leave you alone?" Cal sounded incredulous.

"Sure. We got nothing they need."

I could not resist asking, "Why did you go to Stoor when you saw the smoke? If you thought it might be Varrs, I mean? Would you have helped the men who lived there, if it had not been too late?"

Spinel's face creased with thought. He brooded over this question for a while. "Fight for men? Help them?" He laughed bleakly. "By Aghama, men are dead already, but the Varrs are a big badness. They make the sky go black. They should be made gone." He stood up and the dogs pressed around his legs. He still had pride, if little else, looking down through the remaining mired window-panes at the street.

"Why don't you all leave this place?" I asked him, rather appalled that he had used the name of the first Wraeththu in oath.

"For what?" He did not turn away from the window.

"Things are better elsewhere." It was so simple and so true I felt foolish saying it.

"Better!" Spinel scoffed. "Where? All the north is plagued by the Uigenna and Varrs have all the rest. No-one bothers us here. We have nothing. We have nothing for them to take." Muscles twisted in his face. He looked briefly at the figure I had seen lying on the pallet and then back to the window.

"It *is* safer down south," Cal put in, in a clear, even voice. He was sitting cross-legged on the bare boards of the floor, unhurriedly rolling himself a cigarette. Lianvis had donated tobacco too, apparently. He looked luminous, soaking up the only available light; almost unearthly; illustrating, by contrast, the dismal squalor of the room. Spinel stared at him stonily. He would never like Cal; Cal was everything he was not.

"There is a town called Greenling on the other side of the desert. If I were you . . ." Cal paused, licking the thin paper and pressing it down, "I'd take my people there. Have you got a light?" Spinel ignored his request. Cal shrugged, turning to search our bags, the cigarette dangling from his mouth.

"There are desert tribes. We could never get across." Spinel threw himself away from the window and squatted down beside us again.

"Ah, you mean the Kakkahaar," Cal said with a smile. I wished he would not make his contempt so obvious.

"Look Spinel, we've been that way," I told him. "The Kakkahaar are not as threatening as you imagine . . . well, nothing like Varrs anyway. There's a Kakkahaar Algomalid named Lianvis. We are known to him. If you mention our names he may well sell you the services of a guide. You could get across the desert that way . . ."

Spinel looked at me with suspicion. Though he did not know the Kakkahaar's name, he obviously knew of their reputation. Perhaps I had been too forward. The patronizing tone of our comments and the implied criticism of the Irraka and their hovel-town did not land lightly on Spinel's ears. He was obviously thinking; "Who the hell do they think they are." Cal was grinning happily to himself.

"Some time, perhaps," Spinel said at last. "Sometime, we may move on."

Sometime perhaps. The Irraka would linger in Phesbe until they were all dead.

As the sun sank behind the bones of the town, someone lit a fire in the enormous, soot-coated grate. It filled the room with leaping shadows and smoke, but hid most of the unpleasantness. Spinel left us alone. I guessed we discomforted him. I was annoyed by the waste and apathy we had seen. I could not understand why the Irraka wanted to stay here. They did not want enlightenment, that was clear. There was one thing I *could* do, however. Lianvis had given me instruction on the art of healing the body by force of will. So far, I hadn't had the opportunity to put this talent to the test properly, but if there was a case of having to try, this was it.

Close to, the Har with the broken leg looked even more pathetic. I knelt beside the pallet and drew back the revolting blanket that covered him. He started like an animal and snarled at me. Dirt was scored into the frown of pain on his caricature of a face. I attempted conversation by thought and projected a calming form. Some of the aggressive fear left his eyes. The leg was not merely broken, it was shattered. Shattered and putrifying. "Why have you no healers?" I asked him. It was all I could say, congested with anger. He stared defiantly at me, a look which told me he was only waiting to die. I put my hand above the wound and my arm went cold. Lianvis had taught me thoroughly the practice of healing. He had been surprised I had known so little. Most Kakkahaar could effect simple cures at Neoma level. I sensed Cal at my shoulder. He threw a shadow over the injured har.

"Why bother?" he asked, with cruel indifference. It did not deserve an answer. "I suppose you are going to invoke water elementals to get rid of the dirt?" he continued, with cheerful sarcasm.

I ignored him. First I had to draw out the badness. Cal was right; the wound did need to be cleaned.

"Have you water here?" I asked slowly.

"Don't waste your time playing with me!" the Har croaked at me with surprising venom.

"Find some water, Cal!" I ordered. He did not move. "Please." I heard him sigh.

"Alright, alright. If you must. Don't make a habit out of this kind of thing, will you!" He stomped away, still sighing.

"Do you have water in this building?" I asked once more. The har turned his face away.

"Yes. There is water . . ." He looked at me again. "I despise you! I hate you that you can help me!"

I did not argue. His hopelessness and bitter rage could not be fought. "Hate me all you want, little animal," I said.

Cal brought the water and Spinel sauntered over to see what I was doing. I expected him to complain, but he passed no comment, just watched as I cleaned the wound. This was the first time I had ever put these skills into practice and I was not very quick at it.

"The bone is shattered," I remarked, over my shoulder.

"Yes," Spinel confirmed.

"How did it happen?"

"In one of the old factories through town. He fell." Spinel stared into the Har's face without compassion.

"Why have you done nothing for him?!" I demanded angrily. I could not keep my feelings out of my voice.

"That's none of your business." Spinel did not sound offended. He meant simply that. "Anyway, you're helping him now." He went away.

I did what I could. Only time would tell if that was enough. I asked him his name and he replied, "Cobweb, Cobweb, Cobweb!" straining to lift himself up off the rags to shout in my face.

"You're mad to be in this place!" I hissed at him, casting a wary eye about the room for Spinel. "You hate us, you say; I know why! You could be out of this. You could be in a tribe, a real one. This is a shambles!"

Cobweb tried to push me away as I started wiping his face with the wet rag, but I was stronger. "I can't leave. I am Spinel's," he said.

"What?" I could not help laughing. "You are nobody's. You're just yours!"

"You don't understand. You're talking shit," he replied in a dull mumble. "The Varrs left me behind, 'cause I busted my leg. I guess I was still

pretty when the Irraka came, so Spinel didn't kill me. Now I have to die
to be free and, thank you, thank you, now it seems I'm not dying anymore!"

"I can tell you're not Irraka," I said. His eyes appraised me with weary
intelligence.

"Yeah." I offered him what was left of my food and he observed, "Well,
if I'm to live, I might as well eat."

"You could starve yourself to death," I pointed out, and he smiled
weakly, propping himself up on one elbow.

"Well, maybe life is worth living. Make me stronger and I'll feast on
Spinel's guts. He wanted me to host his progeny because my blood is better
than theirs, but he's so low-caste he can't, thank God! He wanted me lying
here like a crippled brood mare . . ."

I still did not know much about Wraeththu reproduction and was keen
to question him, even began to, but he would not listen. How long had he
been here, hostile, silent and suffering?

"You're from Saltrock," he gabbled. "I heard them talking. They're
fucking stupid, all of them. Stupid and ugly. They ought to be afraid of
you, oughtn't they? You fixed my leg, didn't you? Why don't you kill
them?"

I smiled and shook my head, looking at his leg. I had cleaned it, bom-
barded it with my strength and splinted it with wood, but I knew it was far
from healed. "Your leg has a better chance of healing now," I said, "but
it won't take your weight for a while."

"How long?" I did not know. "How long?" he repeated. "Look, I have
a chance now. I can get out of here and find my people." His feverish
excitement alarmed me.

"You must eat properly. And exercise the leg." Privately, I thought if
Spinel noticed Cobweb's condition was improving, there was no way he
could escape. "Why do you want to find your people again?" I asked.
"They did abandon you after all." His face curled into gaunt ugliness.

"What do *you* know?!" he spat at me. "Terzian did not see me fall. None
of them did. It was crazy out there; too much smoke. I heard him call me.
He didn't know I was there. He thought I'd got out. I heard him call me,
but I couldn't answer . . ."

"He never came back though."

"No, no; never." He lay back, grunting with pain as he moved his leg
for comfort. Orange, flickering light smoothed the sharpness of his features. It was easy to see beauty had been there once.

"Don't let Spinel know how much you did for my leg, OK?"

I nodded slowly. "OK." I stood up. "Good luck, Cobweb."

"Luck? Who needs it? I'll bust my way out of here!"

I went back to Cal feeling heavy with depression. Cal had been out to
see our horses. They were stabled in an old store next to the hall. He said
our possessions seemed to be intact so far and had brought two of our rugs
back up with him. We found a corner as far from the Irraka as possible and

tried to get comfortable for the night. The fire had died low; we could hear hara grunting like animals. One of the dogs gnawed on a bone too close for us not to hear the cracking. I thought of Cobweb's leg and pressed my face in Cal's fragrant hair to quell the nausea.

"We're leaving tomorrow," Cal decided. "I've had it with this rabble. The Varrs could not be worse. God, I'd sell my soul for a bath!"

We had not bathed properly since we had left the Kakkahaar, but I knew what he meant. Phesbe made cleanliness seem suddenly more important.

"Go on, argue with me!" he said, but for once I agreed with him completely. "Amazing!" he exclaimed. "What did the shriveled one say? It looked quite intense."

"His name's Cobweb. He's a Varr. Spinel's prisoner, or viciously reluctant concubine! He was planning on dying, only now he's decided on escaping." I laughed bitterly, dreading the guilt about him that I felt sure would haunt my path out of Phesbe.

"So. He's a Varr, is he?" Cal's voice sounded calculating.

"You don't know everything, Cal," I warned.

"There's nothing to know but the fact of his miserable existence and, perhaps, possible usefulness." He propped himself up on his elbow. Faint light from the window spun and glowed in his hair. "We'll have to take him with us," he said.

"What?! No!" I protestd. "No, no, no, no, no!"

"And if we don't? And if we meet the Varrs on the way north? Do you suppose they'll ask us in for dinner?"

"Only if they're cannibal," I remarked. "But it's useless. Spinel won't let Cobweb go. He plans to found a dynasty with him."

Cal laughed at me. "You're joking! There's no pearls in his loins and that's a fact." He lay down again, wrapping me in his arms. "Just leave it to me," he said. "Take your cue from me. Tomorrow."

In the grayness of an overcast morning, the room looked even more dreary than it had the day before. We started to gather up our belongings and before long, Spinel came over to see what we were doing. It was morning, yet there was no smell of cooking or even coffee. Nothing but the filthy stink.

"Leaving are you?" Spinel asked us.

"Well yes," Cal confirmed. "We'll take our chances with the Varrs. We can't afford to waste time." He was squatting on the floor, carefully folding the rugs.

"I see." Spinel sounded put out. I looked at him hard, pleased to note the trace of weakness in his chin, his small, silver eyes. He stared back at me. "Him with the leg. How did it go?"

Cal would not let me answer. "Oh, it's a shame about that. Too late to do much, or enough anyway. Sorry." Spinel grunted, looking even more displeased. I realized it was not beyond him to blame me if Cobweb died.

"He wants to go back to his tribe to die." Cal glanced quickly up at him. This was the test, the bait.

"They left him here." Spinel did not look exactly suspicious but I hoped Cal would not push it too far.

"I know. Pitiful, isn't it. Pell, pass me that bag there, will you. It would be best, Spinel, if you got that har out of here, you know. The poison's in his blood; he may even contaminate others."

Spinel's eyes opened a little wider. He knew nothing about medicine or poisoned blood and was in no position to argue.

"Even if he had lived, his essence would have been tainted," Cal continued smoothly, buckling up the bags. "Put him outside the town. Maybe the Varrs will find him. Maybe he'll poison them!" He laughed. Cal had lying down to a fine art. Even I was beginning to believe him.

"Hmmph!" Spinel grunted and went back to the fire.

"They're going to try and stop us," I sang.

Cal stood up and swung one of the bags over his shoulder. "Possibly, possibly. Get the rest of the stuff, Pell. Come on."

Our guns were still packed safely in the bottom of our luggage, but we had tucked our knives into our belts. All the Irraka carried guns, of course.

"Now may be the time, Pell, for you to exercise those talents Lianvis has been grooming for you. I won't be able to handle this alone."

"Oh no!" I spoke to his back. He was sauntering over to the group of Irraka huddled round the fire.

"Right. Thanks for the hospitality," he said to Spinel. "We're leaving now."

"You're mad!" was the reply. "You won't get very far." I sensed a growing alertness in the hunched shapes, but I would not look at them.

"Oh, it's not that much of a risk really. We can handle ourselves," Cal told them. "Like this!"

One arrow of thought reached me: there! Our strengths mingled. Together, we had no difficulty in bringing down a corner of the ceiling. The Irraka jumped like a pack of dogs. The dust settled; a few more pieces dropped from the ragged plaster.

"You see," Cal shrugged. "If the Varrs try anything, we'll turn a few of them inside out. It might dampen their ferocity." He adopted his most dazzling smile. "Think about what we said about Greenling, Spinel. Oh, if you like, we'll dump the crippled Varr outside the town for you."

Spinel only wanted to see us gone. He nodded nervously, his little eyes avoiding Cal's. I went over to where Cobweb lay, watching the show with relish.

"You said you didn't need luck, but you've got it," I said. "Come on, we're taking you out."

Cobweb hid his relief and his gratitude with abuse. "My leg, my fucking leg. I can't walk!"

"That doesn't matter."

He was so light, I could hoist him over my shoulder easily. Spinel's crew watched us leave with the expression and posture of beaten dogs.

CHAPTER EIGHT

>–◄►–◉–◄►–◄

. . . CHOSEN gods of carnage voice,
Dictate in etiquette tease . . .

North again. The land began to rise and was cut through by the wide, straight roads of men. We passed by several towns during the next few days; some were still smoking. Only one or two still showed signs of habitation. Cobweb, riding Tenka along with the baggage, was fractious with pain. For the first few days he hardly spoke at all; his face set in a sour expression of discomfort. Under the revealing light of the sun, we could see clearly the sad condition he was in. We had no opportunity to bathe and the filth of Phesbe, still saturating his clothes and body, could have done little to lift his spirits. I attended to his wounded leg each evening and morning, but I knew there was little more I could do. Even the most accomplished healer works better under sterilized conditions. At the very least I needed salt water to clean the wound and although we carried both salt and water, Cal would not let me use any of our drinking supply. Cobweb said we would eventually come to a river, and I hoped his condition would not worsen until we did.

There was no sign of the Varrs, other than the dead towns they had left behind them. Cal had told the Irraka we could deal with the Varrs, but that was just another of his convincing lies. The Irraka had seen us work magic, but the Varrs were a true Wraeththu race, and Cobweb told us they included many Ulani in their ranks. Parlor tricks would not deter them. Cobweb was our only protection. We did not really know if the Varrs were habitually hostile to hara of different tribes, but it was safer to expect the worse. I worried privately if Cobweb's patron would be pleased to see him again. The Varrs did not seem to be a tribe given to displays of compassion, and Cobweb's appearance was far from attractive. It might be that the mighty Terzian would be happier believing him dead.

The river, when we came to it, bore the signs of heavy conflict upon its banks. The dead were only men. If any Wraeththu had been killed, their tribe had either burned or buried the bodies. With typical inconvenience, dead men littered the stream. We would have to ride some way up the bank before the water would be clean. I was still a stranger to the reality of death, and the sight of the empty, staring bodies, sprawled in unnatural distortions disturbed me deeply. It was unbelievable that those clay-like puppets had ever thrilled with the spark of life; perhaps only the day before, thinking, talking, eating and sleeping. To see the dead like that can leave little doubt in even the most skeptical of minds as to the existence of the soul. Once the soul has gone, the flesh looks barely even human.

That night, Cal looked worried for the first time in ages. He watched me as I bathed Cobweb's leg with the long-awaited salt-water.

"Pell," he said. "This land is dying." The sound of his voice more than the words, sent a bitter chill through my stomach.

"What? Why?" I asked quickly. Cobweb had closed his eyes.

"A few years ago, we came this way. This was man's land; it was full of them. Now they are all gone," Cal replied.

"Then it is only the men that are dying, not the land," I argued, with relief. He had painted a terrible, dark picture for me with those words.

"It is closing up. The land is taking over. Once more, as it was a long, long time ago. Can't you feel it, Pell? Feel it! Mankind's funeral. You can feel them, can't you? All of them, somewhere around. Empty, but full of them."

"Shut up, Cal!" I shouted. Suddenly the dark was full of eyes. Unseen at that, which was worse.

"Spooking you, am I?" He picked up a stick and scratched in the dirt round our little fire. The only sound was the comforting crackle of flames and vague animal rustlings in the distance. "The sky's very high here, isn't it?" he remarked, looking up.

"Cal!"

"It's just changed so much, that's all. And in such a short time. Centuries of civilization wiped out in a couple of years. It's awesome!"

"We knew this is what it would come to!" I retorted, irritably.

"Are you feeling guilty, Cal? Are you thinking of all the pain and suffering and wretchedness of innocents just born in the wrong time and the wrong place?"

"And the wrong body," Cobweb added drily. I looked down at him. He seemed like an untidy bundle of rags thrown down in the grass. A sudden thought prompted me to speak.

"Maybe they have the choice . . . all of them. Perhaps every man on this earth could be incepted to Wraeththu—even the women! Does anyone really know? Has anyone ever tried to incept a full-grown man, or a woman?"

Cal looked at me with distaste. "You can be quite grotesque sometimes Pell," he decided.

To my surprise Cobweb agreed with me. "No, Cal," he said. "It is grotesque to think otherwise. That is man's smallmindedness; man's fear of questioning important issues. You know what I mean." Cal also looked surprised that Cobweb had spoken.

"Well, I suppose it has a certain grim fascination. Shall we try it on the next woman we find?" His voice was caustic with sarcasm. Female was just a symbol to him of something that made men hate us. Even if it were possible, I do not think he would want to share our Har-ness with women. Cobweb's comments had astounded me too though. The only way I can describe it, is that it had sounded very un-Varr.

"I thought your tribe had dedicated themselves to speeding up the extinction of Man," I said.

"They have," he answered simply. "But it is different for me. I am not a warrior. The Varrs all have very set roles. I am a progenitor. Killing does not always seem the best way."

"Yet you were there when your tribe sacked Phesbe," Cal commented sardonically.

"Yes, I was there," Cobweb agreed.

"Ah," Cal began, relishing the moment before the next thrust.

I did not want to give Cal the opportunity to exercise his love of quibbling and spoke quickly to dispel the tension. "Cobweb, you say you are a progenitor. Does that mean you have actually, er, you know . . . reproduced?"

He looked at me blankly for a moment. I could still feel irritation behind me in the silence.

"Yes," Cobweb said warily, after a while.

"You have Nahir-Nuri among you then?" Cal asked him suddenly, his curiosity overwhelming his desire to argue.

"No, that's not necessary. Given the right circumstances, we've found that Pyralisits or even Acanthalids can inseminate a host."

"God, that's amazing!" Cal exclaimed. "No, wait. That must be something fairly new. It must be. How long have the Varrs been practising it?"

Cobweb shrugged. "I don't know exactly. I came from the tribe of Sulh some eight months back. It was a common thing then."

"Events are moving even quicker than I imagined," Cal said softly, with a trace of bitterness. He looked at me. "God, Pell. One year in Saltrock. Time stood still for us, didn't it? But out here . . ." He shook his head. I had gathered that the knowledge Cal had of Wraeththu procreation was nearly as sketchy as mine. At the time when Cal had met me, it had been a shrouded subject, relevant only to the Nahir-Nuri. Yes, he was right. Everything was changing, speeding up. I had a feeling that the farther north we traveled, the more surprises would be revealed. At our backs, the trees. Beyond our fire, the river. All around us a haunted quiet, disturbed only by the water and the flames. Cal spread our rugs on the ground. He had lapsed into a contemplative silence and curled up with his back to me. I sat watching the fire and the darkness over the river. I thought Cobweb had fallen asleep, but I heard him say, "I have a son." The tone of his voice made me feel sad. I poked at the fire with a stick, sending sprays of sparks spiraling upwards. Cobweb was not looking at me. I think he should have been weeping, but all I could see was his thin, well-shaped lips twitching as he chewed the inside of his mouth.

"Terzian's?" I asked, and he nodded, once, just staring at the stars.

"I expect he's alright," I said, wishing I had never opened my mouth.

"Oh, I know that!"

I wanted to ask so many questions but at the same time, did not want to hear the answers.

"I know what you've been thinking," Cobweb continued.

"Oh?" I was not sure which of my thoughts he had in mind.

"I know what's happened to me. I know that. . . . In a way I don't want to go back, but I have to . . ."

"What have my thoughts got to do with it?"

"Oh, I can see you thinking," he said with a wistful smile. "When you do my leg. I can hear you say to yourself: there was beauty here once. We both know where that leads to don't we!" He did not want to say it, make it real with words.

"You're still the same person," I told him.

He grimaced. "Pellaz! If all the hara in the world were like you! They're not though, are they? I know it matters. It matters very much. Perhaps less so in a tribe where there is utter equality of status. The Varrs are not like that."

"You'll heal, get better." I did not like any of this. It made the peace of Saltrock seem like a crazed, idealistic dream. This was what was real. It mattered to be beautiful. Spinel had told us the Varrs had whores, and he was right. Where was the proof of the Utopian visions Orien had spoken of? We had seen only the ophidian cruelty of the Kakkahaar, then the sordid apathy of the Irraka, now this. What had really changed since the first Wraeththu had come into the world? One selfish, ignorant race had been exchanged for another, more powerful, selfish, ignorant race. Where was the great tribe of noble and elevated spirits to cleanse the world? Since Saltrock, all I had seen were magicians, villains and killers. Maybe Immanion too was just a hazy fantasy. If it existed at all, it was somewhere far, far away, where none of this sordid mess could touch it. I was overwhelmed by a swelling tide of emotion: anger, indignation and love. Perhaps it would be best to turn back and return to Saltrock. We could take Cobweb with us. Maybe, there, his body and his soul could be healed. The sanity and the care of kindred spirits would make him whole and proud again.

"No!" he said, and I lifted my face from my hands. "Do not think that, Pellaz." He was looking at me now, with a great weariness. "You look surprised. Am I reading your mind? It's there for all to see, isn't it?" I was dumbfounded. Cobweb sighed. "Oh Pell, it wasn't just for my pretty face you see. That's not just what Terzian wanted. I am Brynie and, they tell me, a gifted psychic. Not that it takes much of that kind of talent to work out what *you* are thinking! You must know you can't go back. You must. It's a wonderful idea, and I'm grateful that you're thinking it, but no. I'm strong enough to take any of the shit Terzian might throw at me, I really am!" He grinned. "You're tiring me out, do you know that? Tell me to shut up; I'm just moaning. Ignore it. I know I'll get better, and if Terzian tells me where to go, that's just too bad. I'll always have Swift; the son I still can't believe actually came out of me. You want to know about that too, don't you . . . I might scare him though, like this. How am I going to feel if he doesn't even recognize me? Why don't you tell me to shut up? Swift's not very old. Do you think he'll have forgotten me? I've not been gone that long, but, well children are strange, aren't they? *Their* children are strange, what are ours like? I don't know. He won't have to be incepted, will he? I'll have to tell him what men are. Won't it be crazy if he thinks that men and women are a kind of pervy idea? Only Aghama can help me now, if he's really out there; Aghama or God. Is there a difference?"

"Cobweb," I said, "shut up." He laughed, sort of crazily, and I leaned over him to wrap his blanket more firmly around his shoulders. "You shouldn't be in this . . ." I told him.

"Oh be quiet, Pell. I know what you think. Why don't you let me go to sleep."

I went back to watching the fire. My people. My race. I felt a hundred years old.

Two more days of traveling and then the spiky outline of a town appeared in the distance.

"This is where we'll find them," Cobweb said. He looked as if he was scraping the barrel of his strength.

Cal trotted Splice up alongside me. "Well," he said. "This is it. A meeting I would have preferred to avoid."

"Yes," I agreed miserably. We had started out from Phesbe regarding Cobweb as protection against a possibility. It had been clear for some days, however, that we had to actually seek out the Varrs. Cobweb was deteriorating. If we did not get him back to his people, the only alternative was to leave him to die. Cal often appeared hard-hearted, but I knew the limits of his coldness. It was a tough, thin shell around an extremely mushy center. Cobweb could no longer guide us; he lived in a solitary nightmare of delirium. So, without even discussing it, we had begun to look for signs that would lead us to the Varrs rather than away from them. After their ransacking expedition in Stoor, it appeared they had headed back to their home. It was not a difficult task to follow their trail of destruction.

About a mile from the town, a squad of mounted warriors cantered toward us. The horses were lean, breedy and polished; the riders fit, clean and lithe. Like the Irraka they wore mostly black leather, but it gleamed with the luster of matte silk. We halted our horses and waited for them. Their leader spoke to one of his troupe, who walked his magnificent, mincing mount to within a couple of feet of Red and Splice's straining, quivering noses.

"We would like to speak with the one called Terzian," Cal explained in his clear, careful voice.

"Why?" There was no hint of either hostility or cordiality.

"The one on the pack-horse back there," Cal indicated with his thumb, "he's one of yours. We got him out of a rather distressing situation and he's none too well. I understand Terzian would welcome news of his whereabouts."

The Varr warrior looked round us toward Tenka and the rigor dropped from his face. "Oh my God," he said, almost in a whisper. Cal and I exchanged a comforting glance. "Follow me!" The Varr trotted his horse back to the others and spoke urgently with the leader. They all looked at us with interest and suspicion. When we caught up with them the leader said, "We shall take you to Terzian. I am Ithiel." He held out his hand in a strange, old-fashioned gesture of welcome.

Cal took it and said, "Thanks," looking at Ithiel's hand with surprise.

"We had thought Cobweb was dead," the Varr remarked as we rode toward the town. "It is indeed fortunate that you . . . came across him." I had the feeling that he was finding all this very embarrassing. I did not know what Terzian was like, but I did not envy Ithiel the task of breaking this piece of news to him.

The town had been renamed Galhea, and was the largest I had ever seen. It was clean and boasted electric power. In fact, little appeared to have changed since Man had lived there. Shops were still trading, only the variety of their merchandise had changed. Music from inns and cafes gave the place an almost festive air. It was nothing like Cal and I had imagined. At home, the Varrs seemed relaxed and unexpectedly cheerful. Nowhere could we see the grim and deadly ranks of Wraeththu armies that we had anticipated. We rode through the town toward a residential area, bordered by tall, clipped trees and hedges of late-flowering orangeblossom. The perfumed air made me want to laugh with relief. It was a fragrance, a memory, of Saltrock.

Terzian's house was white and grand, approached by a winding uphill drive flanked by towering bushes of rhodedendron, rooted in turf as smooth as velvet. Order and cleanliness were everywhere. I did not catch sight of one stray leaf. We could see the house growing out of the top of the hill. It had once been a man's house, and he had evidently been rich. Slim, sparkling pillars framed the back of the building, leading to sloping, terraced lawns. The air held the faintest tang of autumn and the house stood out like a white tooth against the darker clouds of the sky. Inside, of course, it might have shared the same fate as Phesbe's civic hall, but I doubted it. Behind me, Cobweb began to cough. Only yesterday, the poison had reached his lungs. He said the Varrs had powerful healers and I prayed it was not too late.

Ithiel led us round the side of the house to an impressively neat stable-yard. As we dismounted, he said, "Your things will be safe here." Hara came to lead our horses away and we followed Ithiel and two of his troupe into the house. One of them carried Cobweb in his arms. He looked barely alive, the damaged leg dangling uselessly. I knew how little he weighed. Cobweb; his name was sadly apt.

Dark, wood-paneled corridors wound through the kitchens and domestic quarters. We could see many hara working there.

"It smells nice," Cal said.

"Better than Phesbe," I agreed and we laughed.

Ithiel turned at the sound. "Phesbe. Is that where you found Cobweb?"

Cal nodded cautiously. Neither one of us wanted to explain too fully about the Irraka yet. It was not inconceivable that the truth could cause a Varr-ish act of retaliation; depending on how Terzian felt about it. Terzian was an unknown quantity to us; we could not guess how he would react. The Irraka were pathetic and we held no sympathy for them, but we did not want to make more trouble for them. Time would see to their disappearance without any assistance from Varr revenge.

We were taken up huge, curving flights of stairs carpeted in dark red, to an enormous suite of rooms approached by white double doors.

"Terzian says for you to make yourselves at home here," Ithiel said, rather perfunctorily.

"Luxury we enjoy in the gilded chambers of the emperor!" Cal remarked sardonically, touching the heavy, floor-length, velvet curtains that bordered the windows. The predominant color was palest green; the carpet was like moss underfoot. Terzian, Ithiel informed us, would grant us an audience after we had rested and eaten. "Where's the bell for room service?" Cal asked him.

Ithiel sucked his breath in heavily, not smiling. "You will find everything you need in here. Food will be brought up to you presently."

"God, where have we found ourselves this time?!" I exclaimed once Ithiel had left the room.

"Nirvana?" Cal rejoined.

I looked out through the window. Below me, lawns and trees glowed emerald and viridian in the light of the dying sun. Rain-clouds of deep gray and purple massed on the western horizon. A great forest crept in toward the east.

"Things never turn out as you expect, do they Cal," I said.

He sighed and collapsed backwards onto the enormous, grass-colored bed. "No. The Varrs are very civilized killers," he replied. "Have I turned out as you expected?"

I looked away from the window, surprised, but he was not smiling. The pupils of his violet eyes were enormous. "Why?" I asked uneasily.

He shrugged. "I don't know . . . sometimes it seems . . ." He went silent, still fixing me with his lazy, cruel eyes.

I went over and sat on the bed beside him. "At first, I didn't know what to expect with you," I said. "Sometimes you frightened me, sometimes. Perhaps you still do. I get the feeling there are some things you will never tell me. But you are . . . Cal, what are you trying to make me say?"

He reached out with one hand and touched my back. "You're too good, Pell. I hope I don't see that pious, little angel knocked out of you."

"I'm glad it was you that found me," I told him, and he smiled.

That look, the fading light, the fragrant air of Galhea; they are with me for always. I took his perfect face in my hands. Our tired bodies, unwashed, underfed; hip bones sharp enough to bruise. We recaptured some of the magic of Saltrock then. Here we were; another oasis to shelter us in the savage waste of the world. It must have been on both of our minds: luck had been with us when Cobweb's had deserted him back in Phesbe.

As with the Kakkahaar, the Varrs brought us clothes of their own to wear. Black shirts of soft cloth and close-fitting black trousers. Boots of thin leather buckled to half-way up the leg. We were taken to Terzian well after the evening meal. Veiled lamps suffused the carpeted corridors with dim light. Downstairs, we were conducted to an enormous drawing room. Thick curtains shut out the dark. Terzian was alone. He was leaning against a huge, white fireplace, staring into the flames. It was all very self-conscious. He looked up when we were announced and said, "Please, sit down." It was clear he was a Har who was used to obedience and more. He was slim, tall, well-groomed and had the refined elegance of a torturer. It was hard to imagine him in the act of killing, but it was easy to imagine him ordering someone else to do it.

"I want to convey my gratitude for bringing Cobweb back to us," he said in a voice that betrayed no feeling. He asked us our names and where we had come from. Perhaps he had not visited Cobweb yet, or perhaps Cobweb could not talk to him, or he might have done both of these things, but just wanted to hear it from us. We told him anyway.

"Will Cobweb be alright?" I asked him.

"Oh yes. Our people know how to deal with the worst of wounds; they have plenty of practice of course. But for you, though, Cobweb might have died." He did not ask about the Irraka or even how we had found Cobweb. I do not think he cared. He offered us sheh, a spirit they distilled themselves. We accepted and found it pleasant enough.

"Where are you traveling to?" Terzian asked us.

"North," Cal replied. Terzian pulled a face.

"There is not much there," he said. "What there is, is horribly sordid. Tribes have broken up. Some of the splinter groups are like dogs. Men still have strong-holds in the cities. Time is spent there trying to stay alive by killing. But it's not organized enough. The cities should, in my opinion, be flushed out, evacuated by Wraeththu and destroyed. There is nothing there we really need."

What could we say to that?

"What of the Uigenna? I understand they had the balance of power in the north," Cal said.

"The Uigenna?" Terzian uttered a dismissive snort. "Where have you been? They had internal conflict, to say the least. Their leaders fell to

murdering each other; very artistically and no doubt spell-bindingly entertaining for the rest of them. Now, they spend their time bickering amongst
themselves, experimenting colorfully with new poisons and ways to torture
men and unpopular hara to death, and have little interest in maintaining
order."

"I didn't realize that they ever did. Chaos was more their style," Cal
remarked drily, sipping his drink. Terzian gave him a hard look.

"Although the Uigenna do have a reputation for a certain . . . reckless
nature, they at least once had some kind of organization. We never have
any trouble with them." I could imagine Cal saying: that does not say much
for Varrs, but thankfully he kept quiet, allowing himself only a private
smile.

"How about the Unneah?" he asked.

"I don't really know," Terzian answered him, moving away from the
fire. "They left the northeast cities. Can't say that I blame them. More
sheh?"

"Thanks," Cal held out his glass. Mine was still three-quarters full.

"You are lucky," Terzian remarked, looking at me directly for the first
time. "Cobweb gave you a ticket in here. We don't normally tolerate
strangers." All of this seemed very rehearsed to me. "However, the hara of
Saltrock do command a certain amount of respect. I have never been
there."

I hope you never will, I thought.

"Tell me about it," Terzian demanded. We painted a glossier picture
than reality, but Saltrock deserved it. Violence had no hold there. It was
not a place for Varrs and their like.

"They don't live in the real world," Terzian commented, after a while.

"Perhaps not," I said, thinking of all we had seen on our travels north,
"but their way of life is something all Wraeththu should want for the
future." Terzian flared his nostrils and looked away from me. I could tell
he thought that would be a boring prospect. I wondered what would have
happened to me if I had fallen into the clutches of the Varrs for inception.
It made me shudder. Varrs lived like men; their culture seemed just like
men's. They were living in stolen towns, acting out the lives that had left
them.

As we drank more sheh, conversation became easier. Terzian spoke
volubly of conditions in the north; the birth-place of Wraeththu. Men had
fallen because all the might of their weapons could not fight what was
meant to be. Tribes like the Uigenna were strong. Weapons could burn like
matchwood under the concentration of their force. They had the ability to
fill the minds of men with confusion and fear so that their leaders lost
control. Both the Varrs and the Uigenna had Nahir-Nuri in the north.
Dangerous, black creatures of heartless ambition. They had little time for
tribes of lesser strength, in fact, often regarded them as being as worthless
as men.

"We must cull the weak," Terzian declared. Like Cal, he was Pyralisit, unlike Cal, he had bred many sons. "This is not the time for braying and praying in the temples!" he told us vehemently. "We need new blood. Young, pure Wraeththu blood, growing up untainted by man." He stared at us hard. "You have lost some condition on your travels, it would appear."

Later, back in our room, Cal said to me, "Do you want to move on tomorrow?" We looked at each other, honest, and yet not entirely so. I shook my head.

"Not yet, not yet." I walked over to the window to look once more over the sweeping, lush countryside. "I think I like it here, don't you?"

"You just like the comforts!"

"Don't you though?"

Cal sat down on the bed, rubbing the back of his neck and looking at himself in the mirror opposite. "Their culture . . ." His hand touched his throat.

"There is much we could learn here. Maybe I do want the comforts; more than I want to winter in the north anyway."

Cal lay back on the pillows and closed his eyes. He sighed. "Something tells me: 'Move on!' but I don't want to. It's easy to see why Cobweb wanted to come back."

"There's nothing for us in the north, Cal," I said.

"Hold on a moment. This is all presupposing Terzian wants us to stay around. He's said his thank yous; that might be the extent of his gratitude." Cal sat up again.

"You don't really think that," I said, rather sharply. Cal did not ask me to explain what I meant. He knew.

I was not surprised when Terzian invited us to his table for breakfast the following morning. Again, he was alone. After we had sat down, I enquired after Cobweb.

"He'll live," Terzian muttered shortly and dismissed me from his attention.

His attendants brought us eggs, smoked fish and fruit juice served on thin white china. I asked Terzian if he lived alone. He did not answer me for a moment, dabbing his mouth with a starched napkin.

"No, not alone. I have hara that see to my needs." He tried to hide the fact that my question had irritated him. I wanted to ask where Cobweb was but feared his temper. After a while he said, "There is one other."

Cal and I exchanged a furtive glance across the table. The room was very light. Large windows led out to a terrace, closed against the chill, morning air. Black birds stalked across the tiles looking in at us angrily. Terzian lived like a lord; a warrior prince who had realized his fantasies. I could tell he was observing us, covertly, although he said little.

It was not a comfortable meal. I was trying to eat as quietly as possible when someone knocked on the door. Terzian bid them enter. The door opened a little way and a child ran into the room. It scrambled, chuckling, onto Terzian's lap, and I watched the brooding, sullen expression drop from his patrician face. I could understand, then, something of what Cobweb admired in him. "Quietly, little one!" he ordered gently. "We have guests."

The child turned to look at us with wide, intelligent eyes. He looked about two years old. "This is Cal, and Pell," Terzian told him, smoothing his fine, dark hair. "I'd like you to meet my son," he said to us. "His name is Swift." Not two years old, then; nowhere near that.

"That must be Cobweb's child," I said to Cal.

"My child," Terzian corrected mildly.

"How old is he?" Cal asked.

"Six months."

Cal and I both laughed. Terzian chose to ignore our indiscretion. "I'm sorry," Cal explained. "We don't have much experience of this kind of thing. Swift is the first Wraeththu child we've seen."

Terzian was not surprised. To him all tribes other than the Varrs were pitifully underdeveloped.

"He is perfect, isn't he," Terzian said to Cal. "This is our future; perfect and whole."

It was suggested that we spend the day sightseeing in Galhea. We were to be treated like tourists then.

"You'll find your baggage in the stable block," Terzian told us. "By all means, bring what you require into the house, but I would prefer it if you left soiled items outside. My staff will launder anything that needs it. You only have to ask." He stood up, lifting Swift in his arms. "Lunch is served at mid-day here. You are welcome to dine again with me, or in the town, as you prefer." He inclined his head. "Until later then." Swift smiled at us over his shoulder as he walked out.

"My God, what is this place?!" Cal exclaimed, pushing his plate roughly across the table. I stared at the wrinkles he had made in the white table-cloth.

"Two centuries in the past?" I suggested.

He grinned at me. "Two? Two! Three maybe, or three into the future, who knows!" He leaned back in his chair. "I wonder what they use for currency in this town?"

We had hardly touched Cal's stolen money, but both thought it unlikely we could use it here.

During our meal the previous evening, all our Kakkahaar clothes and any that were still wearable from before that, had been taken away by Terzian's staff. An abundance of Varrish garments had been left in their place. I had noticed that none of the Varrs wore jewelery; only those who we learned were the tactfully named progenitors wore their hair long.

"Male and female?" Cal queried with his usual acerbity, as we walked along the wide, manicured avenues of Galhea. It certainly seemed that way. "They are splitting off again," he continued. "Wraeththu combined the sexes, but they are splitting off."

"Is that so bad, so immoral?" I argued. "Wraeththu combined the sexes by favoring the male. There are too many issues unraised, too many uncomfortable questions unanswered . . ."

Cal glanced at me sideways. "You worry me sometimes," he said. "What's going on in that busy little brain of yours?"

"Some things worry *me*," I replied. "As time goes on, I get more questions in my head and no-one knows the answers. They don't want to. No-one knows the questions either, come to that. What are we? How? Why? To what end? It is more than just a fun time, running wild and screaming, 'Hey, let's get the bastards that fucked the world up!' It has to be. Perhaps the Varrs are on the right track about some things. Let the female side out . . . it is in us after all. Oh, I don't know!"

We came, at length, to an inn; old-world, gambrelled, and dark inside. Curious, we ventured through the door, and found ourselves in a large, low-ceilinged room which smelled of wine and food. The tables were highly polished and had lion's feet made of brass. Cal asked at the bar about currency. Could we use our money here? "You're staying at the Big House. Whatever you want is on Terzian," was the reply, given reluctantly, we sensed.

"Our fame precedes us!" Cal declared. We ordered food and drink at Terzian's expense. The menu was impressive. Long-haired, soft-footed hara, veiled and dressed like they should belong to an exotic harem, brought our meal to us. Slim, pale arms sliding from silk; their perfume eclipsing the aroma of herbs. They did not speak to us or even raise their eyes. Cal shook his head, his face grim.

"Cal, the Kakkahaar had Aralids as attendants," I pointed out, "and they were every bit as perfumed and delicate as they were." I indicated the swaying bead curtains that led to the kitchen with a wave of my hand.

"Not like that!"

I could not lessen his disgust. "What do you think about the child?" I asked, cutting into the fragrant, roasted fowl on my plate.

Cal raised his eyebrows and shrugged. "It's weird, I'll say that. Didn't Cobweb say he came here about eight months ago? That means it took him roughly two months . . . God! I wish I knew more about this. I didn't think it would be important until if and when I upgraded from Ulani. I suppose, deep down, I never really believed it was possible." He was showing no inclination to begin eating.

"Do you suppose," I began, trying to quell a rising discomfort, "that they bear their young . . . *live?*"

"What? As opposed to dead? Oh, I should think so!" Cal picked up his fork and started pushing food around his plate.

"Ha, ha! Come on, Cal, you know what I mean." I kept my voice low, paranoic about anyone overhearing our conversation, even though the place was nearly empty.

"Sorry." He reached over and touched my hand, lightly. "Don't look so scared, Pell. I know only this. It's something like an oyster and a grain of sand. You must have heard me mention pearls before."

I nodded. Cal twisted his mouth before speaking. "Well, it's like this. The har who is ouana, his seed is like the sand. The soft, passive, inhuman cavities of the soume; that is the oyster. Something happens that makes the pearl. It's not just ordinary aruna . . . something happens. That's all I know. The pearl becomes a Wraeththu child; how, I really don't know."

"Why have you never told me this before?" I demanded.

Cal gave another of his expressive shrugs. "The same reason you never asked me! Let's face it, Pell. We still think of ourselves as male, totally male; with a few pleasing adjustments, of course. We look male, don't we. We come through inception; wake up and it's just us. Don't you see? You never have to face yourself as some kind of monster. Your head's still the head you were born with; the same thoughts, the same memories. All this, it's a bit scary. It's having to face just how inhuman you are; what inception really did to you. All those female bits lurking inside you, where you can't see them, where you can forget them; but they're there!" Cal always had a way of putting things that opened doors onto a nasty, cold unknown.

"You were the one who was scorning the Varrs for, how did you put it, 'splitting off.' Are you now trying to tell me you've been actively suppressing half of your nature?" I tried to scoff, but my words sounded empty.

"And you haven't, I suppose?" He poured himself a glass of the pale, lemon wine. His fingers were wet, restlessly rubbing the glass. "OK, now's the time, Pell. Let's be painfully honest, shall we. When you first met me, your first Wraeththu chum, what did you think? Oh, here's a boy that's into boys, and as I'm an effeminate, spoiled little brat, living a boring life, I'll go along with that . . ." He made a hissing noise through his teeth. "Oh, don't look like that! Alright, that was a bit strong. I know it was more than that—for you. It was an adventure, the promise of life beyond the fields. But it was like that for me, can't you see? That's what I am. If I wasn't har, I'd be . . . you know what I'm saying don't you?" I nodded quickly, unnerved by his agitation. "But neither of us ever thought of this, Pell, did we? The responsibility of supplementing the race. Living things . . . oh God!" He put his face in his hands.

"Cal, Cal!" I said, reaching for his arm. "I didn't know it had . . . upset you . . . this much."

He did not look up. "Someone gave me a mirror and I saw the future," he said.

We wandered slowly back to Terzian's house. My head whirled with a multitude of questions and feelings. Cal was silent, looking at the ground, kicking up leaves. I looked around me. How come the Varrs had so much. Did they trade with other towns, other Wraeththu settlements? What did they trade? Perhaps it was all stolen; appropriated during Terzian's foraging tours around the country. As much as I tried to concentrate on how the Varrs obtained their wealth, the words, "you do not have to face yourself as some kind of monster" kept pounding between my ears. My body felt strange; even hostile. Cal did not touch me as we walked along. Above us, tumescent clouds boiled across a confused sky, echoing my mood.

That evening, after another fine meal at Terzian's table, he asked us how long we planned to stay in Galhea. There was a moment's embarrassed silence and then Cal said, "Well, that is really up to you, Terzian."

Our host smiled in a careful, controlled way. "I hardly think so," he said. "As far as I am concerned, you can stay as long as you wish. You can see my house is not exactly overcrowded."

"I must admit, we don't relish the thought of having to travel further north with winter approaching," I said, "And we haven't any plans to do anything else just yet . . ."

"Obviously we'll work for our keep," Cal put in. He was shredding a piece of bread onto his plate nervously.

Terzian laughed. "There's no need," he said pleasantly.

"We can't stay here for nothing," Cal insisted.

"I don't see why not! But if it will make you feel better, I'm sure one of my farms would welcome your help to gather the harvest. There is one just north of Galhea, not far." He stood up, neatly pushing his chair beneath the table. "Now, if you will excuse me . . ." Another gracious exit.

I told Cal that I did not trust Terzian. "He must have something to gain by having us here," I said.

"It was you that wanted to stay here," Cal pointed out, still fiddling with breadcrumbs.

"We must be vigilant."

"But I always am, my dear!" He reached forward to pat my cheek, making an effort to look unperturbed. I wish I had known then, that being vigilant is sometimes more than just having to look over your shoulder.

The following morning, we rode out to the nearest farm to offer our services. Terzian must have told them about us already. They treated us warily and with labored politeness. Most of the grain had been brought in, but there was still plenty of work to be done. All the Varrs are very hard workers, whatever else you might say about them. We were hard-pressed to keep up with them.

We did not see much of Terzian during the days that followed. Now that we ate most of our meals at the farm, there was very little opportunity to meet him. On our days off, and during the evenings, we kept to our room at first. Because we were unused to hard work, we were too tired to do anything else. But gradually, as we fell into a routine and began to befriend the cautious hara we worked with, we took to spending more time in the town at night. Several evenings a week, we would go out drinking with

Varrish companions, or visit them at their homes. Most of them were interested in our tales of Saltrock and the Kakkahaar; especially the Kakkahaar. My skin would prickle as Cal made Lianvis, in all his unholy glory, real again. When he finished speaking, we would all feel unseen eyes upon us and revel in the delicious fear.

We discovered that the Varrs had appropriated the remaining human population of the town as slaves. They were rarely seen; but we guessed the bleak nature of their existence; their hopelessness and utter despair was mirrored in the dull and wretched grayness of their appearance.

One evening, whilst we were sitting in a warm inn, quaffing large measures of ale, one of our companions brought our attention to a commotion that was going on outside. One har stood up to look out of the window. "They've caught something!" he cried. We all went outside to see. A group of Varrish warriors on horseback were herding a ragged group of individuals up the street. It looked like something from the Apocalypse. There were no electric lights in that area and the scene was lit by torches. Red sparks flashed off the horses' curbed bits and stirrup irons. Metal gleamed along their cheeks and their rolling eyes glowed red; their chewing mouths were laced with foam. The riders were like messengers of Death's angel; faceless and black. They ordered interested spectators to go back into the inns. We all shuffled back a few steps, but nobody went inside. At the end of the street was a small square, probably once used for open-air markets. We followed the procession and it stopped there. I saw Ithiel come riding across from the other side. His uniform was only half fastened, suggesting he had been summoned forth unexpectedly.

"What's going on?" I asked somebody standing near me.

"Intruders. Most likely caught thieving," he replied, craning his neck to see over the crowd.

"Are they men or hara?" I wanted to know, shaking his arm to make him listen to me.

"I can't tell from here," he said.

Cal had disappeared. I pushed through the crowd to get a better view. The prisoners were making pitiable noises; some on their knees. The great, black horses pranced about excitedly. I heard Ithiel say, "Let me see them." Horses blocked the spectacle, their hooves kicking sparks off the cobbles. I saw Ithiel frown and shake his head. "No good," he said, and turned his horse away. For a moment there was silence as the crowd held its breath. Then the horses back-stepped away and one of the Varr warriors raised his arm. I didn't realize what was going on until six evenly spaced gun-shots cracked the night air. Hara around me began to mumble, turning back to the inns, back to their half-finished drinks, and their half-finished conversations. Perhaps some of them looked over their shoulders at what lay in the square, but not many. I stood frozen by disbelief. Six twitching bodies were sprawled in an ungainly heap near the middle of the square; no, five. One had tried to run. He lay a short distance away. Blood pooled among the stones and the air smelled of sulfur. The warriors dismounted and began to talk amongst themselves. I saw the brief flame of a match. That, then, was the nature of Varrish justice. It was not messy, not zealous, nor even exultant in its savagery. It was merely brutal and to the point and without compassion.

Cal came and put his arm around my shoulder. "Not for them the fate worse than death," he said, with disgusting humor. I could not bring myself to speak.

Back in the inn, nobody seemed affected by what we had witnessed. One Har said to Cal, "This kind of thing often happens. Wraeththu stragglers or small groups of men stealing from the fields. Sometimes not even that. Sometimes they are merely passing through and run into Ithiel's watch-dogs. If they are har and presentable, or human, young and male and presentable, they are bestowed the privilege of slavery. Most of them end up as progenitors for Terzian's elite guard. If they are not presentable enough . . . well, as you just saw . . ." He drew his finger across his neck expressively.

"You can see how lucky you were!" another exclaimed with a laugh, fondling Cal's shoulder.

"Luck?! You think it's luck?" the one who had spoken first began to cackle. "Luck? Huh! Look at them!"

Because of Cobweb (just because of Cobweb?), we were Terzian's guests, and the respect that this situation afforded made life even easier. Both Cal and I enjoyed working on the farm and liked the hara we worked with. Of course, none of them were in the least bit politically minded and ac-cepted Terzian as their Autarch without question. He was admired, even deified by his followers. Terzian must know best, they thought. The average Varrish har was neither cruel nor ferocious; just stupid in that they never examined the way their leaders operated. But then, Terzian, to his people and his friends, was nothing other than sympathetic and just. Living inside all this, wallowing in the luxuries of Terzian's grand house, it was difficult to keep our situation in perspective. In a way, we had become Varrs and the Varrish way seemed right. We were protected from what Terzian's armies got up to outside of Galhea. Sometimes, Terzian's superiors would send representatives down from the north to keep an eye on what he was doing. When any of them were staying in the house, we were meticulously prevented from meeting them.

Sometimes, little Swift would escape from the vigilance of his attendants and creep into our room to chatter to us. He was a disarmingly attractive child and very precocious, but not annoyingly so. Cal studiously avoided contact with him, but I liked listening to his childish ramblings and would take him on my knee and tell him stories. It was almost disorientating to think that I held a creature who had not been born of woman or even heard of men. I had long since given up asking Terzian about Cobweb. He would never answer my questions and I did not like to try and ask Swift for fear of upsetting him. I often feared the worst. Perhaps Terzian was reluctant to admit that his celebrated physicians had failed in their ministrations for once.

One evening, after we had been at Galhea for about two months, Terzian sent word to us that he would like us to dine with him in the house. When we went downstairs, we were served the usual sumptuous fare, but there was no sign of Terzian.

"So what!" Cal declared. "Let's eat."

We thought he must have been called away to deal with some of his clandestine business. He was forever disappearing from the house for some reason or another; sometimes for days at a time. There was an unusual tension in the air that night, and I remember remarking upon it to Cal. He had rubbed his bare arms and shivered, although there was a huge fire burning in the grate. We had just finished eating when the door opened and Terzian came into the room. He stood there, one hand gripping the door frame, just staring. Cal and I both jumped with surprise. It was obvious Terzian had been drinking and the very fact of it was chilling. He was normally so contained; his every action controlled and precise. I could not think of anything to say and Cal looked cynical. He half twisted in his seat, leaning back, waiting for Terzian to speak. For one brief instant I was crazily frightened for him. Cal bloomed under the right conditions; at that time he was second to none. Terzian knew that, and in his intoxicated state could not hide that he knew. He stepped forward unsteadily and leaned on the back of a chair. I could see he was trembling; it was terrifying.

"Cal, I have to speak to you," he said. His voice was surprisingly steady. I noticed Cal's shoulders stiffen and I knew what went through his mind. His eyes kept flicking over to the door and back to Terzian. At any moment I expected him to make a run for it. Terzian guessed what he was thinking.

"Cal, please," he said, very quietly. "Why are you afraid?"

"Afraid?" Cal sounded dazed. I knew he feared Terzian, or more exactly, what Terzian might ask of him. I could not tell if that was a possibility or not. Terzian tore his gaze away from Cal to look at me.

"Pellaz?" he said, in the same quiet, deadly voice. I pushed my chair away from the table and stood up. There was still a chance he did only want to talk.

"It's OK," I said. "I'll leave you to your conversation. I was just going to go upstairs anyway." It sounded about as sincere as Lianvis at his worst. Cal glanced up at me quickly. I could not interpret his expression, but something said inside me, "He has been waiting for this." We both had.

I shut the door behind me and went quickly to our room. Everywhere seemed strangely empty. I kept repeating to myself, "We cannot be selfish with each other," but it was difficult for me. Cal and I were together nearly all the time. I remembered that night in the desert and a Kakkahaar incubus whose name I dared not guess. I remembered Cal's troubled eyes and the darkness he had sensed around me. It is not easy to be selfless in that way; it is almost unnatural, fighting against an inborn instinct.

I ran myself a hot bath (the water was always hot there), and miserably

misted myself up in it. We had heard that Terzian planned to make one
more destructive venture into the countryside before the cold season got its
claws into the land. I hoped he would leave soon. There was little left in this
area for him to deal with. Come the spring, the Varr armies would trek
north for some serious spring-cleaning amongst the colonies of humanity
that still stubbornly held on to their lands. We had overheard talk about
it. Cal and I had never seen the warrior quarters of the town but we had
heard about it. One of our friends at the farm had told us that Terzian's
fighters lived like kings; nothing was denied them. Sleek machines whose
only purpose was to kill and make Terzian more powerful. But, of course,
he had kept us away from all that. Whatever he thought of us, whatever
purpose he had in mind for us, it was clearly nothing to do with the
belligerent side of Varrish nature. He admired the way we looked and, I
think, liked to have us around the house for that reason. His house was full
of beautiful things. I had always known he liked Cal better than me; he
never looked me in the eye. Now he had obviously decided to take his
admiration for Cal one step further. There had been no hint of it before.

The water had begun to cool and I lifted myself out, reaching for the
thick, white towels, wandering back to the bedroom, drying my hair. I had
let it grow back again on the side of my head, but still tried to keep it short
there. I was still vain, but out of boredom more than vanity, I sat on a stool
in front of the mirror and messed up my hair with a comb. Unplaited, it
now reached my waist. For convenience, I had adopted the kakkahaar
fashion of braiding my hair; there had been little opportunity on our travels
of late for preening. Staring hard at myself at the mirror, I remembered
thinking: you can be taken for a boy no longer. What you are is Wraeththu;
male and female in one body. Then it was just an abstract, but now I know
we are made of the hardest part of woman and the softest part of man. Is
it any wonder then that we have to fight not to be cruel? Living in Galhea,
my eyes began to open, my thirst for knowledge increase. "What lies
outside, outside across the hills, the forests, the abandoned towns? Does
enlightenment lie that way? Does Wraeththu shine with a different kind of
light that way?" We are made in the image of the First, of the Aghama. If
he still watches us, have we lived up to his expectations? I doubted it. Weary
with a half recognized depression, I burrowed into my bed.

Sometime, in the darkest part of the night, when everything wears its
worst shadows, something woke me. I held my breath and hid under the
bedclothes, suddenly conscious of the size of that huge, slumbering house,
sentient in its hugeness. That someone, standing in my room unbidden,
spoke my name, and it was not Cal. I did not answer. Again, "Pellaz." Soft,
chiding; it was the voice of someone who saw me as a child, wrapped in the
heart-coccoon of blankets. I felt the weight of someone sitting on the bed,
and my skin prickled. (This house is so old, so many corridors . . .) I
thought of a vampire face and hollow eyes. Many faces look that way in
moonlight. "Pellaz, I know you're awake . . . look at me." The voice was

familiar and I threw back the covers. At first, I did not recognize him and he said, "Yes, it's me. You look like you were expecting a ghost."

"Looks like I've got one!" It was Cobweb. I could only just see him. The curtains were pulled tightly together at the window; very little of that pale light outside shone through. The room felt cold.

"Let me in . . . beside you . . ." Did he think I knew nothing, that I had not heard the stories of how the night creatures can only harm you if you invite them in? There was only werelight and cold; I was not sure about him.

"No."

He sighed and stood up, reaching to turn on the lamp by my bed.

"You look better," I said.

"Mmmm." I noticed he still limped as he came back to sit on the bed.

"Why are you here?"

He made a short, bitter sound. "I have not thanked you for saving my life."

His face was still too thin; the skin as white and flawless as ivory.

"Terzian sent you." It was not too brilliant a deduction.

"Well, yes."

"You don't look too happy about it." He shrugged and wrinkled his nose, running his fingers nervously through his dark hair, looking fragile enough to break. "It's taken a long time to heal, has it?"

He nodded. "Yes, a long time. I still get so fucking shaky, I hate it." He pulled at his hair again. "This house is so big, isn't it? I don't like it at night. Creeping along here, I felt like things were looking at me all the time. Lots of people must have lived here . . ." He shivered.

"You scared me."

"It's easy to get scared here at night. Anyway, part of you is still living in that old desert, isn't it. Peasants live on creepy stuff; it's in you."

"Oh, you've seen the sharp sticks under my pillow then?"

"And the silver crucifix!"

We were both silent for a while until I gave in and said, "OK, get in." He was wearing only a long, white shirt and felt as cold as death.

"I wondered what had happened to you," I told him. "Terzian wouldn't tell me."

He crept closer to my side and rested an icy cheek on my chest. "You're hot," he said.

"No, you're cold. Are you sure you're not a ghost?"

He laughed, "No, not sure. Stroke my back." I could feel every bone in his spine and was unsure whether it was attractive or repellant. He did look like a vampire. The ivory skin, the ebony, bruised-looking eyes; but he was not half as gaunt as the last time I had seen him. I put my hand to his face and tried to draw him toward me, but he pulled away.

"No. Not that. It scares me."

"Why? I don't breathe poison."

"Everyone breathes poison. Poison of themselves. It makes me feel like I'm getting lost, all mixed up in someone else; and their breath is always stronger. What if I can't come out again? What then?" I remembered Ulaume and knew something of what he meant. "Terzian is like that," he continued. "Like a big, black cloud filling the sky in the shape of a wolf."

I shuddered. "Cal . . ."

"I know." He sounded resigned, and not a little bitter.

Was it within me to warm away that kind of chill? Terzian had sent him to me and I wondered what had made him obey that order. In his position I wouldn't have done.

"I'm no substitute, am I, to either of you," he sighed.

I had forgotten he could eavesdrop on other people's thoughts. I held his face in my hands; his jaw trembled. "You are still beautiful," I told him, "and so is your son. I've seen him."

A faint cunning hardened his eyes. "Love me," he said.

"There is no love!" I replied.

"Oh, there is!" he said.

Masculinity in progenitors is considered unaesthetic and they try to hide that side of themselves. Aruna was a great skill to Cobweb; he teased me effortlessly. I could not understand why Terzian did not appreciate what he had; wit, sensuality and grace, if a little skinny.

"Why are you here?" I asked him. "With the Varrs, with Terzian. Why did you leave the Sulh?"

He smiled ruefully. "Ah, well, it is a simple story. Imagine this: Your tribe are a nomad people; fierce, strong, but not rich. You have traveled down from the north to trade with the Varrs. (Your leader carries a message from the Uigenna; that was our visa.) Conditions are bad in the north. It is all dried blood and the smell of burning and horrible black birds everywhere. Galhea looks like heaven and it's full of angels; black angels. One of them, a king of angels, looks at you and suddenly, before you can wake up, your tribe have left town and you're living with a Har who's like the beast in the middle of the maze. At first you don't mind because he's so wonderful, so tall, gold-haired and viciously handsome. He also has a metal heart. He doesn't say much but he knows the right way to touch you. All he wants is sons; he is ouana, never anything else. He takes beautiful hosts for his seed; but of course, you haven't realized that . . ." He sighed once more and I could feel his fingers flexing on my chest. "So there I am, Pellaz; innocent, wide-eyed, loving the warmth, the fine clothes, the rich food . . . and then one morning, I wake up retching my guts out, feeling like the sky's falling in. Terzian is actually pleased! He has his staff carry me off to the kitchen table and in a red, red, spiky haze, I know they tear something out of me. It shouldn't have been like that; not that exactly. Something went wrong. God, did I shout! I screamed and swore at Terzian and he told me not to swear. There was blood on the table and he put his finger in it, right as he told me not to swear. I can remember that so well. They carted me back to my bed and fussed around my fever and poulticed my torn parts, and so I got better again. Sometime, about a week later, I think, they came and put Swift in my arms. I didn't know he was mine at first. God, there he is; I can still see him. Perfect. He ate meat from the beginning, like some kind of reptile. A demon child. I wake up again and again and again; it's always real. Once I was human, a human boy with a mother that called me in for my dinner and mussed my hair and called me 'honey.' Now I'm something else. Maybe I don't even look the same. But you know something, it's a powerful feeling, very powerful. To make life out of nothing . . . Terzian. . . . if it wasn't for him, I could be happy, I guess."

"Why aren't you angry?" I asked him. "Why stay here? You're treated like a slave!"

He laughed at me again. "You're a real crusader, Pell. I'm lazy, really lazy. Don't feel sorry for me."

"You're lonely."

"Not really. Once I'm fit again, I'll start fighting. It takes time."

"Fighting! For what? For Terzian?"

"What else? He'll want other sons . . ."

I could not understand him. "Terzian left you for dead with the Irraka," I said, and he turned his face away.

"You don't know what's best for me, Pell. I am the only progenitor he keeps in the house. I am worth something to him."

In the morning, I could not face going to the farm and stayed in my room with Cobweb.

"We are on different paths," he said.

I braided his hair for him, fine as a child's. "You are a fool!" I told him. He only laughed. "Oh, go home, Pell. Sort the world out!"

He brought us food from the kitchens. It was like stealing. It was like hiding from stern and serious things not yet to be faced.

He said, "Cal will not be with you today," and I looked at him sharply, gut-cold. "Oh, you might see his body, later, but I know where his head will be. Far away. Somewhere deep in that wolfshaped black cloud I told you about. Up there." He pointed out of the window, where the sky was dark and heavy.

"Cal is not like you!" I answered hotly. "He can't be mesmerised by anyone. He won't be sleeping until it's too late to wake up!"

"You shouldn't have left him last night."

"Why tell me this now?"

"Because I'm a double agent." He put his hands on my face. "I may be wrong, of course, but I know Terzian. He ensnares people. Locks them away in that metal heart."

I was filled with a cold, condensed kind of anger.

"You can't kill him," Cobweb said. His cool, light hands slipped over my shoulders, down my back. "I am the chalice in the waters of forgetfulness."

"Perhaps you'd like to be!" I began to laugh. Cobweb had the power to make me forget. I couldn't see it. I should have searched the house, shouting, breaking the enchantment, but Cobweb made me forget. He was the web. He was the spider.

When evening came to draw its shades over the day, I wanted to go downstairs. Cobweb pushed me backwards, back onto the bed, laughing, smiling. His mouth was hot upon my skin and that room became the whole world again. I was hungry. We had eaten hardly anything since breakfast. He said he would go down later. There would be cold meat left from the evening meal. I wondered whether Cal and Terzian had sat, one on each side of the table, to eat that night. Did they talk together? "Don't think about them," Cobweb whispered. Cobweb. My head was full of cobwebs. I should have gone down, fought the lethargy, thrown off Cobweb's spidery, wispy magic. But I could not leave him. He could not (would not) satisfy me. I wanted more and more and more. In the dimness, he became more beautiful, more full and the sensations he aroused in me were unimaginable.

In the night, as Cobweb lay curled against my side, breathing evenly in contented sleep, the door opened. I was still awake, having slept for most of the day. I saw Cal walk into the room, without furtiveness, unenchanted, totally alert. He stood at the bottom of the bed, arms folded and slowly shook his head at me. He was smiling in his usual careless way; there was nothing different about him. After a stunned second or two, I hurled back the covers and threw myself at him.

"Cal, are you alright? Are you?"

He held my shoulders, laughing. "Alright? What do you mean? Of course I am." He looked beyond me to Cobweb, who had awoken and was crouching like a cat amongst the wrinkled sheets.

"Get back to your master," Cal chanted to him in a soft, chilling voice.

Cobweb's head went up. "You should not be here," he said.

"I am here though, now get out. You've done your part."

With dignity Cobweb hopped from the bed and went to the door. He had to get in one parting shot. "I don't know what you think you're doing Cal, but you won't get away that easily. And if you do, you'll be back some day."

Cal made a noise that was half growl, half laugh and raised his fist. Cobweb closed the door behind him.

Left alone, Cal and I embraced in silence. There were horrible words unspoken and I did not want to hear them. It was a crisis we had passed, that was all. There was no magic, no enchantments; just bodies and clever eyes, that was all. When I looked at Cal's face, his eyes were wet. Only two times, did I see that happen. This was the first.

"We cannot stay here," he said.

"No," I answered. My voice sounded as if it came from faraway; an insubstantial thread of sound. Cal let me go and sat down on the bed. He rested his elbows on his knees and put his face into his hands. His hair had grown longer since Saltrock; he had not bothered to cut it for a long time. Where it fell on either side of his bent head, I could see livid marks on his neck. My head went cold; loathsome, unwelcome pictures filled it. But I kneeled behind him and put my arms around his chest. I could feel him shaking. I did not know what to say. Outside, gray dawn started to creep up the sky.

After a while, Cal stood up. He took my hand. "I'm going to take a bath. A long, hot one."

"Shall I start getting the stuff ready?"

He paused at the doorway to the bathroom, rubbing his neck. "Yes, OK."

"Will we have any trouble?" I heard him turn on the taps.

"No."

I was anxious to know what had been going on, but also sensible enough to know I would have to wait. With some regret, I started hauling things out of the drawers and cupboards. Terzian had been generous. We would leave Galhea richer than we had found it. Curious. That statement works two ways. Maybe we should have left most of Terzian's gifts behind. Maybe not. We had a pack-horse now. Weight was no problem.

We walked through the great, silent house and met no-one on the stairs, in the corridors. Outside, in the courtyard grayed by mist, Cal turned and looked up. He pointed. "That's Terzian's room," he said. The curtains were closed. Red, Splice and Tenka had been shorn of their winter coats. It took some time to find traveling rugs to fit them. The remainder of our belongings we found amongst bags of oats in an unoccupied stable. Everything was floury.

We left Galhea and Terzian's big, white man-house. It was that easy. No-one came out of the house. No-one tried to stop us. The blank eyes of the building watched us impassively; Terzian's curtains did not twitch. All the time I was expecting somebody to appear; either to impede our leaving or just to watch us, make sure that we did leave. Would Cobweb show himself at an upstairs window to wave or smile or glower at us? No-one did. Something had happened and our presence was no longer important. Terzian, blind in grief, rage or humiliation had turned his back on us.

The horses had been shod with iron and the sound of their hooves echoed too loudly as we trotted out of the yard. Once round the front of the house, we turned them onto the wet lawns and urged them into a canter. Clods of turf flew everywhere, awkward carrion birds flapped up from the dew, complaining hoarsely. When we reached the gates of the driveway, Cal turned left rather than right, which would have taken us into the town.

"Where are we going?" I asked.

"South." Cal kept Splice at a trot. He could not leave Galhea fast enough.

"South? Again? But why?" Red was trying to go sideways, frisky, with a bellyful of oats.

"It's the way to go."

"The way to go for what?"

"Immanion, maybe? Who cares!" He looked so angry, I let it go at that. He would not talk, his head haloed by a nimbus of quick, shallow breaths.

CHAPTER NINE

>-!-+)-+-O-+-<>-!-<

Release, resist; you're on a leash

At least if we traveled south again, I thought, to comfort myself, and kept traveling for long enough, we would out-distance the winter. Although the climate was not too harsh in that part of the world, it was very wet, and a misery if you were stuck on a horse all day. At mid-day, the skies opened. Rain slashed down with merciless gusto. We had to dismount and unpack the enveloping cloaks Lianvis had given us. The material had been treated (by some secret Kakkahaar process) to guarantee comfort to the wearer, be the weather hot, cold or wet. We did not want to sleep out in the open and kept riding until we reached one of the dead towns. It was hardly pleasant to stay there. The houses were mostly ruined inside, but we managed to find shelter. There were animals outside, we could hear them; quite large too by the sound of them. Neither of us went to look. Cal built a fire and unpacked some of what little food we had taken from Galhea. I hated the wall of silence he had put between us; it could mean so many things. Eventually, I could contain myself no longer.

"Cal." I reached for his arm. "Tell me, tell me what happened."

He put his hand over mine, carefully. "It's not that much," he said, but he would not look at me.

"Is it bad?"

"No, not bad."

"Did he want to make you like Cobweb?" Cal looked up at me then. His face was strange and guarded in the meager light of the little fire.

"Like Cobweb?" he laughed cruelly. "Cobweb's just a plaything to him. No, not even that . . . he's looking for something else."

I could feel myself withdraw as if scalded or pressed with ice. "I see."

"Do you?" He stared at me stonily. His hair was wild and matted, his eyes wide; he looked like a lion. "You don't see Pell. You can't. What I've seen, what I've known . . . maybe I'm the only person alive who has and that's it! And I really don't want to talk about it anymore, just now."

I was horrified. It was like he was slipping away from me. "Cal," I said, questioning, sorrowful.

"Oh, it's alright, Pell. It's alright." He forced a smile and rubbed his face with his hands. "We'll keep on going. We've learnt a few things, maybe. We're wiser, maybe. There's no harm done."

For several days he said nothing more about it. We kept on going, as he said, killing small animals when we could for food. Luckily, because of the time of year, there was a lot of fruit around. Leftover cultivations in disappearing gardens raped by wilderness. Red ate too many green apples once, and I had to spend a whole night walking him round to ease his belly. The land around us was eerily deserted. We saw no-one. Nature crept back across the concrete at her own pace.

One day, the sun shone a little brighter and the sky was clearer. The air smelled wonderful, full of mist and ripeness. Cal sang to me as we rode along. I told him he had a good voice. Then he said, "Pell, do you think we are in love?"

I was so surprised by this that I felt color rise to my face.

"Orien said there is only one kind of love," I said quickly. "And that is the universal kind. We love our race. Anything else is just a state of agreeable friendship colored over too hard by lust."

Cal laughed, apparently oblivious of my discomfort. "Yes, that is Orien talking!"

"Why did you ask me?" I feared for his mind.

"Because . . . oh because . . . look, I know they teach you at your inception that you should never lay claim over another emotionally. We are encouraged to be independent in that way, aren't we? Wraeththu must be free. We have examples to warn us. The history of Mankind; what they did in the name of love. It can make you kill; because love's shadow is jealousy. Men could not have one without the other. Can we? We claim to be free of such things, but are we?"

Cal did not normally ask himself these kind of questions.

"Cobweb said love existed . . ." I said, not meaning to.

Cal reined Splice in to a halt. "You've said it, Pell, that's it. The Varrs, what are they? Selfish killers, pillagers? To us, they appear to have deviated from the pure beliefs. They do not want to progress spiritually, they are content the way they are, but they do not deny love."

"Don't you mean 'and they do not deny love'?" I added cynically.

"Love itself is not a terrible thing," he said.

"I know that. Orien knows that," I conceded, "but as you said, it has its shadows."

"We must bring it into the light then, where shadows cannot exist."

"This is all hypothetical," I pointed out.

Cal laughed, "Look at me and say that," he said. What I saw in his face almost frightened me; I could feel a frightening tide in my blood.

"I cannot say that, you are right," I answered.

"Then it must be true; we are in love."

"If a name has to be put to it, I suppose we are," I said.

"Yes, I thought so. Then I made the right decision."

I leapt off Red's back; he began to eat grass. "Cal, get down." He smiled at me. "I want to know what you're really talking about," I said.

He swung one leg over Splice's lowered neck and slid to the ground beside me. We had been riding over wide, sprawling fields; there was no cover. In the distance, trees crept forward from the horizon.

"We shall walk to the wood," Cal said, "and by the time we get there, you shall know everything."

We walked side by side, the horses trailing behind.

"You must have realized Terzian asked me to stay with him," Cal began.

"I think so," I answered (untruthfully).

"And you must have realized I was in two minds whether to leave or not . . ."

"No! Were you?"

His arm went around my shoulder. "Keep walking. Yes, I was. Terzian seduced me with the fire power of a volcano."

"Yes," I agreed, cynically. "Cobweb said he could mesmerize people!"

Cal gave me a dry look. "Oh, I expect he can, but it was nothing like that. Do you want to know?"

"If you like."

"Well, after you left us at the dinner table that night, he just came straight out with it. 'Cal,' he said, 'I want you to stay here.' 'But I am,' I replied. Then he told me. He had been watching me. He had seen no-one else like me. I was wary of the flattery, of course. It all seemed too glib. All his life, his Wraeththu life I might add, it appears Terzian has been waiting for someone like me. He said he wanted me to share his life, his powr and everything else; for ever. And he meant it, I have no doubt of that. It was all so serious; not just a seduction scene. I think it must have taken tremendous guts for him to say all that to me. He's proud, you know that, and rigidly contained. That kind of demonstration doesn't rest easily on him. We went to his room and for a whole day it was . . . just . . . it was just . . . well, you know." (The immediate thought, what, better than me? sprang to my mind, but I would not say it.) "Terzian said, 'Cal, we can be great,' and I believed him. He was as fine as a panther. I was waiting for him to say something about going that one bit further, further than ever before. That was what we were expecting, wasn't it? All those shrouded conversations. I was dreading it, feeling him there, knowing he had the power to open me up, to touch the place that would open me up and plant his seed there. But he didn't. He must have been sure I would stay, otherwise . . . when I think rationally about it, there was no reason on Earth why I should not have stayed with him; it is somebody's destiny after all. My dreams of Immanion are just that; dreams. What am I looking for? What was I looking for, way back, on the road, when Zack . . ." His face looked bleak; he turned to me. "I found something, didn't I, back then? The one thing that made me say no and turn my back on all that comfort, that easy way out of life. I would have missed it had I let it go, that something."

He waited for me to ask, "Which is?"

"You," he answered. "Simply you. That's what made me think."

I smiled at him, although strangely, it was hard. "You know I would have been lost without you, Cal," I said, which was true in the literal and emotional sense. "Most probably dead within a week."

"Most probably. Anyway, it's over now. How easy it is to say that. It was nothing, really; so quick. Now, I just feel one hell of a lot wiser. Some things I'm not ready for. Spawning brats is one of them; you know about that. But one day, when all this (and he flung his arm toward the sky), when all of this belongs to Wraeththu; Wraeththu building new cities here, *sane* people, not the crazy man-killers, there will come a time . . . God knows I want us still to be together then. If we are, we can begin new life with each other; I don't want to discover that without you."

"That's quite a speech, Cal," I said, embarrassed, but not for him. Seel had once said to me (and it seemed so long ago); "Cal's so emotional, I sometimes think he's still half-human," and he was right. What he had not thought of, however, was that we were all still half-human. Perhaps our sons would be for ever. Not all of mankind had been bad. I think humanity's main downfall had been that they had just over-civilized themselves, and as a result, surrendered themselves to isolation. Lonely, solitary creatures trapped in the darkness of their own frightened minds, and cruel because they feared the dark. They forgot how to trust, be trustworthy and how to see beyond the mundane. Because of that, as they slipped further and further away from the Truth, some great thing, the thing they had simplified to God, had made Wraeththu happen. Mankind, you had your chance with the world and you failed. Now it is our turn. And to succeed where Man did not meant there could be no Varrs, no Uigenna, no cruelty. Since Saltrock, the Wraeththu tribes we had encountered did not inspire hope, but this was a big country and we had seen so little of it. One country in a big world.

As we reached the shelter of the trees I asked, "Why are we going south again? Is there a reason?"

"Oh yes," Cal replied. "Terzian told me that beyond the desert, much farther south than we've been, there may be a way to Immanion."

"You still follow your dream then?" I pointed out, rather acidly.

He laughed. "We have to go somewhere."

"How can Terzian know of this?"

"How indeed! Who cares? It'll be a hell of a lot warmer down there."

I said, "You mentioned Zack back there. You never have done before."

"Before. . . . Don't try to draw me out on that subject, Pell. Let me forget that."

The forest was a big one. Matted, heavily scented with evergreen resins; dark and haunted. But we were not afraid. Light folded down into the Earth; the forest vibrated with the sibilances of night. Absorbed as we were in a new process of discovery within our hearts, the darkness, creeping and rustling, could hold no terrors for us. We found a clearing and lit a fire. When Cal reached for me, he drew me toward him in spirit and mind as well as body. We were truly one creature, and fierce and terrible in the strength of that knowledge. His mind was a shining city for me to explore; even the shuttered doors seemed to whisper to me, "one day, one day." A lonely voice called at the end of the darkest avenue. If only it did not have to end. If only. The end. Cal. I was soaring like a bird, my nerves bursting with a sizzling, gunpowder radiance. Totally unafraid, elemental, letting go; experiencing the unspoken word, loving him. There blinked the half-closed eye of God. Ouana pressing against the seal to another cosmos. I could have opened up to that strange, new universe, could have. But he ended it there. In a sigh, in the night-time, in the dark, glowing together, by the dying light of the fire.

I should have known. Perhaps I did. It was the last time.

BOOK TWO

CHAPTER ONE

➤—┤ ◆ ❯—⊖—❮ ├—◄

The thunderstruck tower

In the morning, we packed away our belongings, ready for the next day's ride in our journey south. A low breeze, tinged with the promise of ice, fretted the damp ashes of our fire. Daylight stripped the magic from the place where we had lain. The air was moist around us and we both felt sad. Cal held me in his arms beside the snorting horses. It was as if he knew our love was ephemeral. We had given it a name, a substance, and somehow, by doing that, we had condemned ourselves. We did not know the truth, not then, not for a long time, that we had never been alone. Forever at our heels, unseen eyes, all-seeing eyes. The gift of my inception. Cal had become too important to me. To the mind behind the eyes, I was no longer safe, no longer theirs alone.

By mid-afternoon, the trees began to thin around us. Where the horses had once pushed breast-deep in thick foliage, they now trod a sandy soil. Leaves above us tapped to the rhythm of a fine rain. Between the leaves, the swaying black branches, we could see it: a village.

Now is the difficult part. Now. I have thrown down my pen and picked it up again a hundred times. Even now it makes me feel sick and cold to think about it. I can remember the feelings, the smells, the sounds, everything. Just by closing my eyes I can bring it all back.

There were no people there. No hara. Everything was still, under the whispering mist of the rain. It was an enchanted place, asleep, dreaming, red brick and lush greenness. A place waiting to fulfill its destiny; its one true purpose. Something made me say, "Cal, let me go first." My voice sounded slow and deep.

He replied, sleepily, "There might be danger."

I looked straight at him. "Might be . . ."

Pain shadowed his eyes. It was impossible that we could not have known. We knew. Inevitability. It could not be fought. Our mood had become silent and somber as we had pushed through the trees, because we had felt it closing in around us. Fate. The great invisible hand. I made a clicking noise in my mouth and urged Red forward. My legs were frozen.

His neck was up, ears flat. I did not look back, but I could feel Cal's eyes burning into my back.

The woman was crouched in a doorway. I saw her first, but could not stop, my legs still frozen to Red's damp sides. I could not take cover. How her eyes hated me; black, almost blind with hate. She held the gun, really too large for her to use, against her belly, rag covered, twisted with poverty and tongueless rage. She saw me, wretched, weak as she was. Wraeththu, shining Wraeththu. Sleek with health, she saw the blood of her kind light my flesh from within. She struggled with the gun, raised it . . .

The shock came before the sound, the single, rolling, echoing sound. Something cracked against my head. At the front. At the back. There was no pain, no further sound. My body started to fall, but the essence of me still stared out between Red's ears in surprise. Vaguely, like a phantom, Cal flashed past me, red over white, like a scarf on the wind, and the woman died in silence. No resistance. Nothing. Just a weary confusion in her eyes as she looked at the knife. As it rose. As it fell. Slowly. I could see all around, colors bright enough to ache, the sky a white, white light. I saw Cal, his cheek cut by flying bone, stand over the shell that had been Pellaz. Red and white. He could not take it in. Then he kneeled. Warm lips against the cooling flesh. I could not feel it. In his confusion he could not feel me. I did not want to leave him; I could smell his tears. He gently pressed his fingers against the red star above and between my eyes. The ground, Cal's knees, were dark red. So much blood in one small body. One body containing all that red. The horses were shaking, foam along their sides. Cal threw back his head and screamed, howled; an animal cry. All feeling was leaving him; I could sense his numbness, his rage; all of this. For a while, I ignored the insistance, the calling. I wanted to watch Cal. I still needed him. We belonged to each other. If I left, I was afraid he might forget me. Already the scene had become unreal, like watching a moving picture, dusty with age.

The Call. Above the houses, the light had condensed into a star. Not really me, half me, I went up to meet it, I could not resist, and the eyes in the light were familiar, knowing. That was when I wanted to scream, but it was too late. I had no throat.

It was . . . rushing. Rushing past me, over me, through me. Moving black air, threads of light; spiraling curls of ether. I felt my murderer wailing at my heels. The soul, no longer she, a nebulous, tumbling light; afraid and screaming the voiceless fear of the newly dead. Our journey; a squealing, aching descent, ascent, through black gulfs and summitless cliffs. We were the only light between obsidian crags that were frozen forever beneath a black sky. No time; the limitless yawning of aeons. And then faster; something zooming in. Gold and shining. I wanted to throw up my arms before my face, but I had neither; nothing to shield me from the brightness. Reality shift. Upsidedown, inside-out. Impossible shapes scored my substance; sickening impossible, zigzag agonies. I was drawn, sucked, inside the golden columns. Inside a temple of light, its glory turned toward the starless dark of infinity. The soul, my companion, denied access, fled shrieking upwards and away. That was all. I can remember only that I remembered. It is no longer real. Like I only heard it somewhere, read it in a book. Do you understand? It was a split-second, a micro-unit, of time that my memory has retained. I can get it to replay, sometimes, on the blank screen between my eyes. I just have done. Do you understand?

It was sound that first came back to me; a voice. I could not understand the words, yet at the same time knew their meaning. It said, "He is perfect," and another voice answered, "Yes, he is." After sound, I became aware of solidity, my soul again encumbered by flesh. I accepted this without question. Then the flesh gave vent to its pain and poured its torment into my brain; stretching, searing, burning. Tears formed in my hot eyes, my hot, blind eyes. I could sense movement, life, around me, but could not see it. Everything was blank; not dark, just blank. Color was a concept I could no longer grasp. Voices came at me again, fluctuating in volume and pitch.

"Pellaz! Pellaz!"

No! I tried to move the awkward flesh.

"Pellaz, you are with me. Don't fight it!"

Drenched with recollection, I knew, I knew that voice. I wanted to scream and die.

"Open your eyes!"

I can't, can't.

"Open your eyes!"

No, no, no, no.

Something hard like glass was pushed between my teeth. Sour liquid scalded my sealed throat, but I had to swallow. Coughing, spluttering; liquid in my lungs. Rough, wet cloth scored across my closed eyelids, dabbing, then pulling.

"Open them, Pellaz; you can."

Fingers prised at my skin; it felt like tearing, the edges of my lids were sealed and gummy. Lashes tore loose and tears poured down my face. Light pushed into me like hot pokers and I cried out. I heard myself cry out. The agony was insufferable. A hot thread pricked the inside of my arm, followed by a cool wave creeping up toward my neck. When it reached my head, I stopped screaming.

"There. Pellaz?"

My mouth felt thick and numb. I could barely move my lips, and my voice, when it came, was like a breeze through tissue, but I said, "Thiede . . ." I could see him. Tall, shining, flames for hair; his eyes were black with curiosity. He wore a white robe that showed his chest hung with pentacled chains; behind him the room was white. I could see his hand, resting against his cheek, long pointed fingernails tapping thoughtfully.

"Thiede, why?" I croaked. He did not answer, but covered me with a fine sheet up to the neck. I could not feel it.

"Rest now," he said, smiling gently his dragon's smile. "You must rest."

"How can I?" I hurt so much; the deepest hurt in my heart. I knew nothing, was incapable of knowing anything; too tired to care, yet my mind churned backwards from a fear of sleep.

"Take this," he said and his hand arched over me, the nails glistening with the luster of pearl. "A temporary oblivion."

Dust was falling, falling, falling; the dust of centuries. I would fall back into a lighter slumber where dreams would walk once more. Up from the eternal pitch, the senseless peace. I slept.

For days, perhaps weeks, Thiede kept me in a semi-stupor, bringing me back to reality only at mealtimes. Even then, my limbs were too feeble to guide the food to my mouth; others fed me. Half-seen attendants saw to my bodily needs; cleaned me, turned me to prevent sores. My mind was switched off. I thought of nothing; watching only colors behind my closed eyes. My dreams were just of colors. Even so, I was fairly comfortable; just a little stiff. Hara came to massage my limbs three times a day. I could smell the light fragrance of the hot oil they kneaded into my skin. Sometimes, propped up on the pillows, I would stare at the room. It was sparsely furnished, but functional and tasteful. There were no mirrors and the windows were shrouded by gauze; I could not see what lay outside. Concealed lamps comforted me in the dark hours, so that I was never left alone in blackness. Sometimes, I thought I could hear music, wistful music or the tinkling of wind-chimes. It was so quiet there, no voices in the other rooms; the only sound, the only regular sound, was of footsteps outside my door, quick and light. The food they gave me was necessarily easily digested yet tinged with perfume I had never smelled before. Its fragrance would linger in my throat and nose long after the food had gone. After some time, I became alert enough to see properly the hara that fed me. Every evening, during my massage, a stern-faced, red-haired Har came to look at me. I guessed he was inspecting my progress. Thiede never came; not then. Reduced to the status of a child, I trusted completely my silent attendants. Not once, that I can remember, did I think of Cal.

One evening, the red-haired Har came alone to my room. He brought with him a tray of food, which I obediently began to eat. I was surprised when he spoke. "Pellaz, do you feel stronger now?" I must have looked startled, jolted out of my mindlessness. I had not thought about myself or my condition since waking up here. He did not press for an answer.

"I am Vaysh," he said.

"Vaysh," I repeated, stupidly.

I think it genuinely hurts him to smile, he so rarely does, but he did try for me that night.

"You must bathe," he told me. Silent-footed hara drifted into my sight and, at his signal, raised me from the bed. Dizziness blinded me again. All I could see was flashing light as they eased my arms into soft cloth. "Slowly!" Vaysh instructed. Slung between them, they carried me off.

When my vision cleared, they were lowering me into a bath set into the floor, steaming with greenish aromas. I know this ritual, I thought. It was all so familiar; only the room was different. Flickering recall of Mur and Garis . . . Saltrock . . . inception . . . Cal. . . . Then the knife twisted in my heart. The veil in my head turned to glass, thin as ice, and shattered. I made noises, horrible, unintelligible noises and all the time, the ghostly, silent hara just kept on smiling their soothing smiles, caressing my skin, their fingers lathering my hair. Weeping, in a hopeless, monotonous way, I lay in the bath, salt in my mouth, behind my eyes, saying his name endlessly in the tortured dark of my mind.

They put me back into the bed, oh so gently, their soft sighs filming my pain. So beautiful they were, so beautiful, but surreal and heartless. They laid me naked on the bed, on my back and drew back the light, gossamer linen. The room was warm and I did not shiver. Vaysh was standing at the foot of the bed, clothed in violet, holding a purple, glass vial. He gave it to one of my attendants. "Make it easier for him," he said and turned away. I could hear his footsteps, soft as a cat's, fading down the hallway outside my room. I was turned onto my stomach, arranged neatly, and salve from the vial was applied to my body. It felt cold as ice. I was rolled over and the procedure was repeated; I could hardly keep from laughing. Laughter through tears; I kept switching from grief to hysteria. "Who is it?" I asked, but they would only shake their silken heads, like slender flowers. With a glass rod, one of them filled me with unguent that spread sleepily its insentient cold through my loins. Perhaps they could not speak. Perhaps he had taken that from them. They straightened my legs and flicked invisible creases from the sheet. I was not afraid. Nervous of the waiting, yes, but not afraid. They stood, one each side of me, by my head, their faces turned to the door. I had expected them to leave.

Then there were footsteps outside, faraway, coming down the hall, brisk but unhurried. Nearer they came and it seemed to take forever. I knew. I knew and my heart was bursting. He was coming. Thiede was coming. Yet I was still surprised when it was him. He came into the room and stood there, where Vaysh had been before, arms folded and the disguised light of enthusiasm in his eyes. I spoke his name.

"Yes," he said. "Do you remember Saltrock, Pellaz?" I nodded at him. "I remember."

"Was it so long ago I wonder? Can you remember the things I told you?"

"No, not now."

"And the things I didn't tell you?"

"I remember all of them."

"Am I a god to you?"

"No, not that. I don't know what you are."

"Are you ready for me?"

"I can't ever be . . . can I?"

"You realize what must be?"

"I think so . . ."

He wanted to say more, he was enjoying it, but then thought better of it. I could see him, his shining robe shifting with subtle colors, his flame eyes. His lips parted to release a Sound. He began to . . . sing? No. A Sound; like a different language of gentle vibrations. His arms dropped to his sides, his head went up. I could see his eyes . . . shining. Reflecting light; they were white stars. All the light in the room went dim but for him. My heart! A pounding that sent the blood cataracting to my loins; my heart sucked dry. The Sound filled up the room, rising, becoming louder, more strident. I knew that sound. Knew it, knew it. His face; changing. His neck, cording, twisting, hair writhing, crawling, lifting.

"No!" I whispered, in disbelief, in denial, yet I still felt my body call to him. His teeth, his lambent eyes . . . taller. His hair was crackling with orange flames. It could have been Lianvis standing there; the elemental Lianvis of beneath the earth. He was naked, his body coursing with colors; colors I had never seen before, that hurt my eyes. He was above me, hovering, crouching. I tried to move, but his hara held me down. I could see their teeth; they smiled. I screamed in agony, but then in ecstasy; his smoldering, smoky breath bringing me to the lip of the abyss that was lit at its deepest point by a star of pulsing red. Movement there; bats, ravens, demons, all the creatures of the lake of fire rose up to claw my hair; their talons in my flesh that shuddered to a nameless delight. I wanted the pain, craved it; reduced to an animal fury. He filled me with the hot, smoking essence of his incomprehensible soul. It ripped me, scoured me, ate into me like acid. It was melting me apart, the sizzling rain of hell and I screamed, and I screamed again.

Is it a nightmare, is it? When I came back to my senses, I was alone, and at first I thought, "What have I been thinking?" But then I saw that the room was full of smoke, and the smoke was full of the smell of seared flesh. Then I began to moan. It was the right thing to do. I called upon God, "Help me! Help me . . ." I was sure I was dying again and it was a slow, lingering death. I did not want to die. Not again, I pleaded, please, not again. I could sense myself ruined. Sense myself used up, burnt out, finished. You have to die! You have to! Vaysh materialized beside me, out of the vapors. His hand hovered over my shoulder.

"Don't try to move," he said.

I could have laughed. Move? Could this charred remnant move? Vaysh was pushing tubes down my throat. "Open the window!" he called, over his shoulder. Cold air sucked the heat from the room and blew away the smoke. Vaysh was touching me with one hand, sitting on the bed. I tried to raise my head. One glimpse was enough. The bed, the pristine whiteness of my bed, was polluted with the dark stains of dried blood. It looked like dried blood. My body was purple and black and blistered.

"Don't move," Vaysh repeated. My eyes felt cracked and shriveled; it was a miracle I could still see. It hurt to close them, yet I longed to do so.

"I don't ever want to have to do this again," Vaysh said to someone I could not see. Disgust filled his voice. I began to slip and Vaysh said, "I'm losing him!" Another voice answered him, calm and confidant. "It proceeds as it should." As it should.

Thiede. I contemplated on his magnificence in the higher spheres. He had brought me back to him from death; this personality. Now he had mutilated me; he held me dangling on the end of a silver thread. Why? But I knew he would not let go.

For days I must have hovered on the threshhold of a second death. Vaysh was in constant attendance. He was there to heal me and he succeeded. Thiede knew that. Vaysh is one of his best. My mind was nearly broken and I retreated deep inside myself, seeking once again the comfortable idiocy of my first days in this place. Yet I could not shut out my senses completely. They drugged my body, but not my mind. Even though I feared insanity, I was aware of everything that happened around me, no matter how hard I tried to escape inside myself. My poor brain, exhausted, stunned, but still laboring on. I made an impossible vow never to speak again, and banished all memory of Cal from my thoughts. It was the only way I could cope. When they took away the tubes and tried to make me eat, I vomited with uncontrollable force. The tubes were put back.

One day, Vaysh put his hand on my paralyzed legs. "Tomorrow, we shall leave here," he said. I whimpered and wept, and he did not comfort me.

CHAPTER TWO

>-·+>-·O-·<+-·+-<

The symbolism of the thirteenth key

Winter; white, crackling, numbing. Vaysh rode a black horse, I was strapped onto a gray. Behind us, Thiede's marmoreal palace reared like a vast, sparkling bird of prey. Before us, dark canyons wreathed in drifts of snow. The sky above was pale. I had no idea where in the world I was. It was the first time I had ever seen snow, the first time I had ever been this cold. I was anaesthetized almost senseless, unaware of where we were heading and for what purpose. Wrapped in thick furs, strapped with leather, lolling with slack face upon the back of my silvery horse.

I had been given no explanation for anything that had happened to me or for what was to come. That Thiede had a definite plan was obvious, but I was only his pawn and as such, it was unimportant that I should know what was going on. I was changed for ever; into what I did not yet understand. There had been no mirrors, no words to tell me. Vaysh hardly looked at me. He had my horse on a leading rein. I could see his long, red hair, powdered with white, blowing back on either side of his fur hood, his straight back; a prince of Wraeththu. All sound was muffled in the pure and crystal landscape. No tracks other than our own marred its virgin shrouds. I sat and dreamed and sat and dreamed, as the sun arched from one horizon to the other. Once darkness fell (but it was never completely dark), we came to a wooden cabin under a sheltering overhang of rock. Icicles fringed its porch; drifts of white fingers reached toward the windows. Vaysh unstrapped me and hauled me to the ground. He had a key to the cabin and dragged me inside, leaving me alone as he went back into the snow to see to the horses. Some of the drugs were beginning to wear off and I began to whimper. I felt so *different;* distorted, heavy. Crippled and tied into the furs.

Vaysh methodically built a fire in the dusty grate and unpacked food to cook. He had paused only to feed me with milk from a beaker that was nearly frozen. Now I could smell rice simmering in a froth of garlic and my mouth filled with reluctant saliva. Once he was content the food was cooking slowly, Vaysh turned his attention back to me. I was lying on the hard, wooden floor, trussed like a chicken. Vaysh moved his mouth a little. It may have been a smile. "Let's unwrap you then," he said. It was the first time he had spoken to me that day. It took him some time to undo all the straps and pain was waking up in me with greater and greater strength. I was groaning and trying to twist around. When I was naked, I could see my body had become gray and misshapen like half-worked clay. The sight of it silenced my noises. There was a low, wooden bed, barely softened by a thin mattress. Vaysh lifted me as if I weighed nothing and laid me out on it. They had packed cloth around my loins and I had helplessly soiled it. Vaysh heated water on the fire and silently cleaned me. Incontinent cripple. His eyes held no expression other than concentration for his task. He did not have to offer me an explanation. I was reduced to the state of nothingness; something like before I was har. But he did speak. Vaysh the cold; Vaysh the silent. My loyal assistant, always; scarred frigid by distant pain. He lifted his head and looked at me with his hard, gray eyes. I saw him properly for the first time. His face almost makes you jump when you see it. A wistful, childlike beauty, until the flint in his eyes makes you look away. He looked so young, yet I had thought him older.

"It will not be long," he said. A boyish, soft voice, but so cold. "Three days? Maybe. Maybe four, it's different for everyone."

I was still adhering to my vow and swallowed the questions filling my mouth. Vaysh stood up and went back to the fire, staring into the pot of rice.

"You must eat some of this. Don't try to be sick, don't try to be awkward; I don't want any of that."

I moved my head as far as it would turn to look around me. The room was rustic and coarsely furnished, but a haven from the snow. Heavy dark curtains, grimed and colorless with age, hung against the windows and the back of the door. It was becoming quite warm.

Vaysh lifted my head and spooned small portions of rice into my mouth.

At first, I refused to chew, like an obstreperous child. Vaysh put his head on one side. "Damn!" he said, without rancor. "Come on, eat it. Hurry up; I have to eat as well." He prodded my lips with the spoon. "Come on!" Churlishly, I opened my mouth. It did not make me feel sick, but I could manage only half the bowl. Vaysh covered me with a hairy blanket and sat by the fire to eat his own portion. He consumed it as neatly as a cat only without the relish. After that, he spiked my neck and pumped a soporific into my veins through a tube, his face serious with concentration. As I drifted away, I wondered what he was thinking . . .

I do not really know how long we journeyed for, but from what Vaysh had said, I think it must have been for about four days. Thiede's horses were tireless; we rarely paused to rest them. At nearly the same time every day, sundown, a wooden lodge would appear through the dusk. Thiede's people must often take this path, I thought. I had hoped that my condition would improve, but each day I felt sicker and sicker. By the fourth day, I did not even have the strength to swallow and Vaysh gave up feeding me. He seemed strangely unconcerned. I kept mumbling inside myself: I am in hell, I am in hell . . . I suppose I should have been grateful he spared me any pain (Thiede had supplied him generously with drugs), but I was far from comfortable. Every few hours, Vaysh would dash our water leathers against a rock or a tree to smash the ice, and then dab at my congealing mouth with water and wipe my eyes.

On the fourth day, we rode through a forest of giant firs. In the silence I heard the muted thud of snow dropping off the highest branches. Everywhere seemed devoid of life; an enchanted waste. On this day, we came upon a great abyss cutting deep into the Earth. Black, jagged rocks reared aloft, the haunt of shrunken trees with twisted branches and huge, untidy looking birds with featherless necks, their eyes rimmed with yellow crust. One of them swooped right up to me and screamed in my face. Far below, the thunder and white spume of rushing water careered off the walls of the chasm; it sounded like vast, underground machinery. Rising up from the spray, mid-way across the gap, a single stone tower weathered the torrent. Spindly, wooden bridges swayed from it to either side of the canyon, creaking in a mournful voice. Here we would have to cross. Vaysh shook his head and made a noise of discontent. Icy wind rolled between the rocks, plucking at our hair and furs.

I do not think any horses other than Thiede's, half supernatural as they were, would have dared to set foot on the bridge. But with shaking muscles and tensed haunches, ears and eyes pivoting wildly, they cautiously edged their way forward. Below us, the water roared its anger, flinging up fingers of spray as if to pluck us from our fragile pathway. I cared nothing for our danger. It was all one to me: whether we made it across or plunged to our deaths, but I could see Vaysh's face looking back at me sometimes, his face bleached with fear. Once we had reached the far side, he dismounted and leaned against his horse's trembling flank. I was still slumped as before, strapped upright in my saddle. My horse began to sniff half-heartedly at the stringy plants along the side of the path. Vaysh looked at me for a moment without pleasure. I could see him thinking I was not worth all this trouble. Then, with a sigh, he swung back into his saddle, hastening the pace to a canter.

The road led once more into a forest, but this was a place of sweeping slopes and steep hills. The firs were dense, standing in neat rows and here, the snow underfoot was marked by the tracks of wheels and hooves.

At dusk, the forest fell away beneath us, thinning out to a valley floor, where a long, frozen lake glowed with the night-whiteness of thick ice. A small town curled around its edge. Directly beneath us, rising higher than the sentinel trees, a stone trident speared the heavy sky. "Phade's tower," Vaysh told me, pointing, looking round to see if I was interested. "Oh, what's the bloody point?!" he snapped, when he saw my face. I was looking beyond him, at the lake and the yellow lights of the town, reminded yet again of Saltrock. All memories seemed to lead back there. But here the warmth, the hell-soil of soda had been exchanged for the parchment purity of winter; endless white in a sleeping land. I was lulled by staring at the pale, pale fields and thought with longing of the powdery embrace of the deep drifts, and the sleep that has no end. My existence had become merely discomfort; no pleasure, nor even pain. I wanted only for it to finish, but was so weak, I could do nothing except what Vaysh ordained. He moved my limbs, he kept me alive and I did not question why. I had no interest in the answer.

Vaysh's horse skidded down the slope and mine followed dutifully. Phade's tower. I thought the windows looked like sunken eyes.

It seemed we were expected. Fur-wrapped hara bearing lights waited for us at the gate. They grabbed our horses' bridles and led us into a cobbled courtyard. Grim, high walls hid the sky all around. Windows in the wall appeared heavily shrouded with curtains. Very little light shone down into the yard, but I could see that large, silent snowflakes were beginning to fall. Hands unstrapped me and lifted me down. Voices to either side of me were cheery with welcome. I could hear Vaysh's surly replies. When the warmth hit me, they had stopped trying to talk to him. We must have been inside the tower, but my vision was beginning to blur and I was aware only of the change in temperature. Someone cleared their throat ahead of us and said, "Vaysh?" It sounded cultured, yet mocking; a voice of command.

"Phade," I heard Vaysh answer softly. He would have inclined his head, just enough for politeness.

"What's this you have here then?" Someone brushed back the furs from around my face. "Ye gods! A corpse, and, by the devil, it stinks!"

"Thank you, Phade, if we could be shown to our rooms?" Vaysh's voice; patient, soft, like the snow.

"What's going on here, Vaysh?"

Silence.

"Vaysh?!"

"Did Thiede tell you we were coming?"

"Yes; he didn't say why." (Sneering)

"That is Thiede."

"Yes, that is Thiede! Well?"

"You shall see when it is time."

I heard Phade laugh. "Oh no, not more of your mumbo-jumbo clap-trap!"

"The mumbo-jumbo clap-trap, as you so elegantly put it, that is responsible for your being here at all Phade, if you'll forgive my reminding you." Phade's laughter stopped.

"Oh, Vaysh, Vaysh! Still humorless, still the ice-maiden!"

"I'm not female, Phade." I could hear the rustling as he unclasped his fur cloak. "Our rooms, Phade?"

"This way, this way."

Phade wanted to stay while Vaysh undid my wrappings. He was full of morbid curiosity. "Why is he like this? What happened? Is he dead?"

"No, he's not dead." Vaysh's hand rested upon my swollen cheek for a moment. It may have been a gesture of reassurance or that he just wanted to note my temperature. I was heating up too quickly; my face burned and deep within the furs, my fingers began to tingle ominously. Vaysh stripped me down and rolled up his sleeves to perform all the distasteful duties of cleaning me. I could smell that the water he used was scented with pine.

"I don't like things like this going on here. Why did Thiede send you here?" Phade said.

"This town is on our way," Vaysh answered. They continued to argue mildly; Vaysh, I'm sure, deftly sidetracking Phade's questions, but I no longer listened to them. All my awareness centered on the heavenly softness beneath me. It felt as if I was slipping down, slowly, into a cloud of feathers. Comfort; I had forgotten it existed. Vaysh's voice came close to my ear. "Pellaz . . ." It was just a whisper. "You will sleep now; it is time. We got here in time . . ." Obediently, I let myself go into the feather darkness and there were no voices there.

CHAPTER THREE

>─┼─◆>─◆─O─◆─<◆┼─<

My truth, my destiny . . .

It was a noise that woke me. I do not know what. It had gone when my
eyes opened. I looked at the room for a moment. There were stone walls,
hung with tapestries, like a medieval castle from the picture books. A fire
spat and fizzled somewhere to my left; perhaps it was that which had woken
me. I became aware that my skin was itching and my hand shot to my
stomach to scratch. I could move! Startled, I sat up. Just like that. My head
swam for a moment, the room tilted, but then energy and strength surged,
with alarming confidence, right through me and my vision cleared. Something gray and papery littered the bed around me. It crumbled to dust when
I touched it. I felt marvelous; strange, but marvelous. Swinging my legs
over the side of the bed, it was no effort to stand. My toes buried themselves
in thick fur. Of course, I went straight for the shine, the glaze, of the mirror.
It hung on the wall beside the bed, framed in rather tasteless gilt gargoyles.
Golden light spun into my eyes and I raised my hand. My golden hand. I
could not look; it filled my chest to look. This . . . Thiede's essence. This
was what he had made me. The gold that was a reflection of the dancing
motes in his eyes. He had made me a god!

There was an adjoining room, which, although nothing as grand as a
bathroom, contained a pitcher of cooling water and a large porcelain bowl.
Clashing winds moaned outside and made the curtains shiver. It was colder
in here. I washed my face and relieved myself in the primitive toilet facilities
I found behind a curtain. Three candles peopled the room with eerie
shadows. I became aware of someone moving around in the other room,
and thought it might be Vaysh, but just peeped around the door in case it
wasn't. A har I did not know was inspecting the bed, picking at the gray
stuff and sniffing it. His nose wrinkled with aversion. He had thick, black
hair and was dressed in brown leather and fur. From the hooked, imperious
nose and hooded, sulky eyes, I presumed it to be Phade.

"Where is Vaysh?" I asked and he jumped, his hand flitting to the knife
at his hip. He narrowed his eyes. For modesty's sake, I had wrapped myself
in a towel I had found in the other room.

"What . . . ? Who . . . ?" Phade had drawn the knife. I walked a little way
into the room and his face lit up with gold flecks. He glanced nervously at
the bed and then back to me. He pointed at the bed, mutely, and I nodded.
"You've changed," he said, a little lamely. Straightening up from his position of defense, with some embarrassment, he tucked the knife back into
his belt. "What is going on?" he asked, in a voice that told me he expected
the most outlandish explanation.

"I don't know," I answered, and he shook his head in disbelief.

"If *you* don't know. . . !" he exclaimed and then muttered, "Thiede!" as if that explained everything. "Whenever life looks as if it might become *ordinary,* or even *safe,* up pops the omnipotent Thiede and everything gets weird again!" He threw up his arms and grimaced at the ceiling.

"Ah well, it is our luck, I expect, to be born out of weirdness!" Did I say that? It sounded like the Pellaz who was dead, and as I am very fond of him, I was glad to hear he was still around. I smiled, and then a dozen representatives were sent down from my brain, bearing angry questions. "I want to see Vaysh," I said, surprised that I was gritting my teeth.

Phade nodded; his face was also grim with displeasure. We were accomplices in our censure of Vaysh, that was clear. "Yes, so do I!" he said. He went to the door and bellowed an order. I heard footsteps scurrying away outside. Phade turned back to look at me. "He's worked a fine old magic on you, hasn't he!" he remarked. "His mightiness, the great Thiede. If you're one of his creations, he's more powerful than I gave him credit for." I only shrugged. All this seemed rhetorical. "Only a few hours ago you looked a week dead and now . . ." he shook his head, awed, and exaggerating this because he never liked to feel less than anyone, "you shine!"

"Something happened to me," was all I could say, facile as it sounded, coming from so resplendent a body. But it was all that I knew and I did not care to go into any detail.

Vaysh stalked in without knocking. He was dressed simply and elegantly in dark green. I could see now that his red hair was dyed. His expression did not change in the slightest when he saw me.

"Yes?" he inquired, looking at Phade. (He had, of course, been told that Phade had sent for him.)

Phade made an exasperated noise and slapped his thigh with one hand. "Vaysh, I hope we didn't disturb your rest . . ."

"No, I wasn't sleeping."

"Vaysh, will you just step out of your ice-castle for one second and look! Look! Your traveling companion has . . . hatched! We thought you should be told." Any sarcasm in Phade's voice glanced off Vaysh's composure.

"It was expected," he said. "It was time. An hour or two early, perhaps, but . . ."

"Vaysh, you have to talk to me," I butted in. His eyes slid over me like needles of ice.

"Ah Pellaz, you've found your voice." It is very difficult to hate anyone who is as beautiful as Vaysh, but his detached and disdainful manner made it easier. He turned once more to Phade. "Would you leave us please?"

Phade was not used to being addressed in that way. Clearly, no-one ever told him to leave anywhere. "No, I will not! I don't take orders from you, Vaysh! This is my home and you're in it at my pleasure and don't you forget that! I want to know what's going on!" I suppose it was reasonable enough. Vaysh swiveled his withering glance over our host.

"It is not necessary," he said politely. "I hate to be blunt, Phade, and

I am not totally ignorant of your position, but it really is none of your business."

"And I hate to be blunt, Vaysh, but what goes on in this place *is* my business! We all dance dutifully to our lord Thiede's tune, of course we do, but I want to know how all this affects me, and my people."

"It doesn't."

"Why here? Why? Thiede has his own strongholds." He wagged a finger under Vaysh's nose. "I am suspicious, oh freezing one, very suspicious. I do not trust Thiede, you or any of your magical charades!"

Vaysh sighed. "Phade, I know the hour is late, but I am sure you are a busy har. This is your little kingdom, I'm sure you have things to do." Vaysh picked up a crimson robe of heavy velvet from a chair and draped it around my shoulders.

Phade would not be put off. "You can't speak to me like that!" he objected, but he did not sound sure of that.

"You're only curious, Phade," Vaysh told him. It was impossible to anger him. "Suspicions! Worries!" He made a derisive noise. "Thiede helped you take this little town, and without him you would still be foraging around the country. Now tell me you don't trust him! When I tell you that what has happened here tonight is nothing to do with you, I speak with Thiede's tongue. Do you understand?"

For a moment or two Phade stood his ground. Then he hissed through his teeth and walked out, leaving the door open. Vaysh calmly shut it.

"Pellaz, you have been chosen," he said.

It was late. I had slept, but Vaysh had not, yet we talked till dawn. He told me everything, nearly everything, without emotion or opinion, just fact. Thiede had waited a long time for this, he told me; since my inception. He had decided then what to do with me. And what was that? I wanted to know.

"Do you know who Thiede is?" Vaysh asked.

"No, should I?"

"It doesn't matter."

Thiede had divined my possibilities, perhaps from the moment he had seen me laid out on the inception slab. He had seen within me an appealing unity of power, sanity and beauty. He had encouraged these qualities, in his own inimicable way, and made me what I am. Now it was intended that I should be put to work; I must fulfill my purpose as all things in Thiede's sphere of influence must fulfill their purposes. When he had taken aruna with me (if such a holocaust should be called that!), he had raised me to Nahir-Nuri, blistered away my lower caste.

"You are Efrata now," Vaysh said. "All thoughts in your head, you must voice to me alone. You need no-one else. You are apart from the others, all the others."

"What *is* the purpose of all this?" I asked him. He seemed almost reluctant to answer me.

"I shall take you to Immanion," he said. A single sliver of pain pierced my heart, and my head and my limbs went cold for a second. Vaysh looked at my face cold-bloodedly; it was likely he knew all about me, about Cal, everything. Those who walked in the white temple in the waste had seen it all: my tentative fumblings with the powers Thiede had transfused into me; my helpless idealism and finally, my discovery of love. To Vaysh, I was like an animal, whose habits have been observed until nothing is a mystery to the observer. It is an attitude that has never completely left him. Both Thiede and Vaysh know me better than I know myself. Vaysh said so easily, "I am here to serve you," and he knew that was his purpose in the scheme of things, but there is nothing remotely servile in him. Sometime, someone (Thiede?) had sterilized his soul. What is within Vaysh is truly a monster, clothed in flesh. Only his eyes betray him. He watched the memory of Cal haunt my eyes and said softly, "Yes, Immanion. Wraeththu are your people, Pellaz. Thiede has given them to you and you to them; you will become their king."

I must have stared at him like an imbecile for some time. All questions were frozen within me. "You are to become their king." It sounded final and beyond argument. For this purpose Thiede had groomed my flesh and tempered my spirit. Through suffering he had tried to raise me above the rest; he knew my mind, my feelings, my character and my weaknesses. I could hear myself asking, "Why?," but no sound came out. Perhaps Vaysh couldn't even answer that. Was it because Thiede had incepted me, or had that happened because in some mysterious way, Thiede had already decided what he wanted to do with me? Now I was refashioned, remoulded and improved. Physically, a perfect sovereign; I couldn't dispute that. But what was so terrifying was how much of this wonderful new me was Thiede's construction, Thiede's virtues, and how much my own emotions and opinions? I couldn't swear that I remembered perfectly how I was before. Too much had happened. That I still possessed sanity under the circumstances was remarkable. Something very cold and hard must live inside me. My flesh was numb, but I really couldn't tell if I was pleased or horrified by what Vaysh had said. All I could think was, "Well, so this is my fate." The words formed quite clearly in my head, several times. I had been awaiting its breath on the back of my neck for a long time. It should have been a relief to discover that it was not merely death.

Vaysh asked me, "Are you shocked? Are you surprised?" but there was no real interest in his voice, not even envy. Perhaps he had to report back to his master. (Yes, Thiede, he took it well.)

"Why?"

"Why not? It's what Thiede wants and that's the only reason I can give you."

"What if I don't want to . . ."

Vaysh laughed at this. One thing that could delight him. "By Aghama, you're pathetic! Yes, by Aghama." This obviously meant something to him for he positively bubbled with laughter.

"You have no choice, Pellaz. Can't you see that. This is your purpose, you have no control over it. I doubt he'd even kill you if you tried to refuse; he'd just alter your mind. You're helpless." Hadn't I always been?

"I shall see Immanion," I said, uselessly, suddenly, hopelessly missing Cal in a great wave of loneliness. Why do things have to fade? Why does reality only have to exist in the present second? We have no real proof that our memories are real. Once events occur and pass, they might well have never been.

Vaysh stood up and went to look at himself in the mirror, touching his hair. If he had lived before, in another time, he would have been a woman and a legend. It was not inconceivable that he should have been in my place, if he had possessed a conscience. I think I guessed then; this process had not always been successful, and I had not been the first.

"How shall we travel?" I enquired, and he tore his eyes away from his reflection.

"On horseback, as before. There is no fuel in this part of the world and anyway . . . things have changed, Pellaz. You must get to know yourself. The horses, Thiede's horses, are as different from man's horses as we are from men . . ."

"He *bred* them?!" I interrupted. Nothing seemed too bizarre for Thiede now.

"Not exactly. He brought them here from . . . they are . . . now you are ready, you shall see. The journey will not take long."

I watched his shrouded expressions, wondering. "What's your level, Vaysh?"

He smiled then; one of those rare frozen grimaces. "Oh, I don't know. I don't think I have one. More than Ulani . . . not quite Nahir-Nuri." He clasped his shoulders with his hands. "It's nearly dawn. I must rest. We shan't leave until tomorrow now."

"I'm not tired," I said.

"Oh, Phade's people will be around soon. Get them to see to the bed." We both looked at the drab, papery waste, some of which had blown onto the furred floor. Vaysh started to leave, but I called him back.

"What is it?" He was impatient to get out.

"Shall I glow forever?"

He looked at my luminous face. "On the outside? No, it is already fading."

Not long after Vaysh had gone, one of Phade's people knocked at my door. He did not raise his eyes as he entered. Phade must have told of what he had seen. "My lord Phade requests your presence at breakfast," he told me. As with all the other tribes I had visited, he had brought me clothes. It is something that is almost a fetish with Wraeththu. Wherever you go your clothes are replaced with the prevailing fashion. The Har waited in silence whilst I dressed myself. I was still numb, from moment to moment fluctuating in feeling from normality to stark terror. In a petty gesture of defiance against their customs, I braided my hair in the Kakkahaar fashion, even though it was doubtful that it would even be noticed. This was a different country. The land of my birth was far away. I did not exist there anymore.

I expected a vast hall furnished by an equally vast table, but found Phade awaiting his meal in a small, comfortable room on the ground floor, warming his toes by a fire. He smiled and stood up when he saw me in the doorway. "I am honored!" he said, sweeping a mocking bow.

I sighed. "It is your castle, Lord Phade, and as such, I suppose I should not be too surprised, or affronted, that you listen at your guests' doors."

"Not me!" he exclaimed, and I raised an eyebrow. "I have others for that duty."

"Hmmm."

"Please, sit down, make yourself at home. I'm no longer sure how to address you!"

I sat, resting my arms on the table. "Oh please! This is more of a shock to me than to anyone. I don't want deference. I would prefer it to be ignored, if possible."

"It's something you'll have to get used to, isn't it. King, well!" He laughed pleasantly. It sounded ridiculous, like some kind of child's game. Let's dress up and be kings and queens. I couldn't help wincing.

"What had Thiede done to you? You were in a terrible state when you got here," Phade ventured hopefully.

"Please don't try to interrogate me," I said. "I don't want to talk about it."

"God forbid!" he cried. I wondered how much Thiede trusted him. He remembered his manners and decided to steer the conversation onto safer territory. "We haven't been formally introduced yet, have we? As you know, I am Phade, but formally, you are the guest of the tribe of Olopade."

"Thiede brought you here?" I was beginning to feel hungry, and could hear my stomach complaining. I could not remember when I had last eaten.

"I suppose you could say that. The men that lived here were very wise. This town, Samway, it is a faraway place and its people were not like the men of the cities, the so-called advanced areas. They fought us in a strange, resigned way, and in the old way (he tapped his head), with the power of the mind. Olopade have been groomed by Thiede for this kind of skirmish. When we came here, the men fled to the forests. We have not seen them since. Thiede may have followed them, of course . . ."

At that moment, the meal arrived and seldom have I welcomed the sight of food more. Phade asked me what I thought of Thiede, and I answered with reserve, although without untruth. "I think he is probably the most powerful of Wraeththu and, although he is frightening, I do think we need him. We need order and Thiede knows that too. I don't think he is beyond cruelty, but he will eradicate it in Wraeththu as a whole if he can. He knows the truth."

Phade nodded. "Well answered!" he said.

"I hope Thiede thinks so," I replied drily.

Phade laughed. "You must learn to live with it; what kings really know freedom?" he pointed out and I shrugged.

"I may have been under an illusion before, about being free, but it was a comfortable illusion."

"Yes, ignorance is bliss as they say!" Phade sighed, attacking his helping of fragrant ham.

"You have met Vaysh before then?" I enquired, with my mouth full.

Phade poured me coffee into an enormous mug; he had no servants in the room. "Oh yes," he answered, in a somewhat confidential tone. "He's Thiede's right arm and sometimes comes here to cause discomfort in his master's name. He thinks I'm an inarticulate slob, I'm sure,"

"I doubt if you're alone in that category," I said. "My role seems to be defined as mere nuisance."

"What a challenge though, to break through all that ice!" Phade remarked enthusiastically. "Don't you think so? Is there a har of flesh and blood within perhaps?"

"There might not, of course, be anything left without the ice," I said.

Phade laughed. "Vaysh would consider my thoughts almost blasphemy!"

After the meal, neither of us made a move to leave the table, content to sit and finish the pitcher of coffee.

"This is sometimes a lonely place to live," Phade said.

"Too cold for me; I come from another land, it's warm there."

Hard sunlight was falling in through the leaded windows. Hara were clearing snow from the yard outside.

Phade said, in a different voice, "Do you know, last night it looked as if your skin was alight. Perhaps it was the dark . . ." He reached to touch my arm.

"No, it is fading."

"You are leaving tomorrow?"

"Yes, tomorrow."

He curled his fingers in the air, above my hand. "Pellaz." He said my name slowly, as if to pronounce it right, although it is not a difficult name. I looked up defensively. "It is difficult to speak with you . . . in a normal way," he said, and I sensed something of what was coming.

"You've had no difficulty so far," I answered tartly.

"About some things . . ." His fist clenched on the air. I could tell he did not want to miss this chance; not many hara like Vaysh and myself would visit him here. I did not blame him.

"Some things," I echoed. I looked at his face, his hair, his dark-colored arms. Some things. All people have a certain taste, a certain smell, an *ambiance*. Cal's presence was lodged within me in the ghost of his scent. Perhaps I feared the scent of someone else would exorcise it and then I would have nothing.

"Pellaz, I want . . ." Phade began, struggling.

"A night with the king of Wraeththu," I finished for him.
He smiled ruefully. "I can see your answer," he said.
"I hope so; there are reasons . . ."
"Are you another cold-store temptation like Vaysh?" I shuddered to
think that sometime he must have tried this with Vaysh. If he had, I could
only stand back in awe of his nerve.
"I don't think so," I replied, "but then, I don't know his reasons."
Phade leaned back in his chair; the coffee was finished. "What a pity;
you are a beauty." I did not resent the patronizing tone of that remark as
once I might. I knew Phade's position. He would remain here in a corner
of the world barely alight, whilst I would shine like a star. I could only pity
him. But if it had not been for Cal, well . . . maybe. Phade too, was a beauty.

I spent the rest of that day in Phade's library. They were not really his
collection of books, having been there long before Wraeththu had come to
the tower, but he was proud of them. He showed me the volumes that
interested him most; heavy, dusty tomes on magical lore, slim pamphlets on
herbalism and homeopathy, delicately illustrated with water-colors. There
were large picture-books of the world. I pored through them, searching for
the place from whence I'd come. Phade looked for me. "It was probably
here," he said, pointing. I stared at the photographs of yellow dunes, red
dirt and men smiling in the colorless fields. All the people I had known still
existed somewhere (why were their faces so shadowed in my memory?),
living, talking. Did someone else now walk the cable-fields each evening
with Mima? Would she say to them, "Here I remember most my brother
Pellaz; the Wraeththu took him . . ."? Had my father decreed, "He is no
longer my son"? Now they were a continent's, an ocean's width away.
When I'd woken up in Thiede's palace, I had left the country of my birth
behind. A great expanse of water was between us now, yet I had never seen
the sea! I turned the page. Here, a white house adorned the brow of a steep,
green hill. Pink flowers turned their petal faces and shiny, dark leaves
toward it. It seemed I was back there; yet the house was not really the same.
Did Cobweb still yearn for the attention of Terzian? Did Terzian yearn the
loss of . . .? Had the curtains ever opened again? I shut my eyes and quickly
turned the pages once more. He could have gone back there; easily. Bereft,
alone, seeking comfort. Or did he still seek Immanion? Would I find him
there again? Phade said, "Perhaps it is not a good idea, Pellaz, to look
back." Of course my distress must have been obvious. "I can force myself
to think of other things, but it is still there. The future is like tangled yarn,
but the past is woven thread." Phade put his hand on my shoulder, but I
could not be touched by sympathy. I made another vow, and this one I
would keep. There could be no other; I would find Cal again. I was sensible
enough to realize that time undoubtedly would lead me to the arms of
someone else; after all aruna is the lifeblood of Wraeththu-kind, but my
heart, for always, would be pledged to him.

*   *   *

Vaysh appeared at dinner, glacial and pale. "I hope the coffin we provided was comfortable enough to meet your requirements?" Phade joked and I began to laugh. Vaysh fixed him with a withering stare.

"It has become a custom of the Olopade, then, to bury their dead in four-poster beds?" he answered, but it was not meant to be funny.

Phade reached out and touched his white hand, which he snatched away instantly. "You really do ask for it, Vaysh," he said, "and what an effort it must be to keep this behavior up. Why not let your hair down for once? I promise not to tell Thiede."

I could tell Vaysh was confused, messing with his cutlery, eyes on the table.

"I don't know what you mean," he said stiffly.

Phade looked at me, and we both grinned. Because of the way he is, it is virtually impossible to resist the temptation to provoke Vaysh. You always long for a reaction. The chinks in his armor are well hidden, however. Only someone very clever or very familiar with him can find them. So Phade and I spent the evening meal slipping lines to each other and laughing at Vaysh's expense. I supposed he noticed it, but he did not care. Maddened by his aloofness, Phade's remarks became rather too brazen. I too began to speculate about what lay within the ice.

CHAPTER FOUR

>─┼─◇──O──◇─┼─<

On the nature of Vaysh and other journeys

Tomorrow we would depart Phade's tower. Traveling; it seemed I spent so much of my time wandering around. Perhaps I would feel uncomfortable settling down in one place. Once settled, it might be that the past would come back to haunt me with greater strength. I felt as if something hung there in the back of my mind, waiting to tarnish whatever happiness I might find. Is it safer to be unhappy? Nothing ever wants to take that away.

After dinner, I excused myself and went alone to my room. From my window I could see the virgin whiteness rolling out toward a shrouded forest. Mountain peaks rose above it. Would we go that way? I would not be sorry to leave this land. I have always hated being cold, and willingly dropped back the heavy curtains to turn once more to the fire. Phade's servants had prepared me a bath, but the ante-room had no fire and I was reluctant to undress in there. So I changed into a thick night-shirt and sat watching the fire. My hands rested on the padded arms of the chair and I disorientated myself by staring at them. These were not the hands that had worked in the cable fields nor taken up the reins of a horse for the first time. These were not the hands that had rested upon the warmth of another; he that was Cal. Those hands were moldering somewhere in another country. Beneath the ground? Had he burned my remains? He believed me dead and perhaps I was. I did not know how Thiede had brought me back to the world, nor could I tell if I still looked the same. I could not remember! It might be that if I ever met Cal again, he would look at me with the eyes of a stranger. But I was Pellaz inside wasn't I? Confusion; everything was misting up. (This is the boundary; what is behind it does not concern you now. You belong on this side Pellaz . . .) Even the memories of my former life were beginning to become indistinct, especially those of before I was Har. Faces were blurring; I could recall Mima only by her hair. I was suddenly terrified that even Cal would become erased from my thoughts. All the things I had learned, all the people I had met; so cherished. We need our memories; all of us. I dreaded that eventually Vaysh would become the only reality. Thiede's creature, my servitor and my guard. Oh, Orien had taught me well and I still remembered his words, those words that would never leave me: hide your tears, Pellaz. I have rarely gone against that advice, but that night I was alone, and the wind outside howled like a lost soul seeking warmth. No-one could hear me weep.

Vaysh woke me at dawn. He was already dressed to travel and carried a thick fur coat over his arm. I was glum and irritable as he supervised my dressing and made me eat an uninspiring breakfast of milk and oats. Perversely, at that moment I would not have cared if he had gone on without me. Let him take my place on the throne of Wraeththu. I would continue to molder away in Phade's tower, hating the cold in this frozen wilderness. (Was there ever a summer here?) More than this, I wanted to go back. I had dreamed of Saltrock the night before; a Saltrock of brighter colors, greater charm. In my dreams it had been Seel, not Cal, who had quickened with desire against me, but it had not spoiled the illusion.

"Hurry up, I want to get out of here!" said Vaysh.

I was pulling on my boots, sitting on the bed, hair in my eyes. I replied in the only fitting, possible way, "Oh, fuck off, Vaysh!" slowly and with venom. Vaysh blinked and flared his nostrils.

"We have work to do and quite some distance to cover," he said.

"I don't care!" I grumbled, pettishly.

"Are you always like this in the mornings, Pellaz?" A smile should have accompanied that remark, but when I looked up, Vaysh's face was expressionless, as usual. I wanted to make him angry.

"How much do you know about what . . . about what Thiede has done to me?" I asked. Vaysh turned away so that I could not see his face as he answered.

"How much? More than you . . . maybe. Is it important? It's happened, hasn't it? Would you prefer to be dead?"

A quick, cold anger flashed through me. I stood up and roughly grabbed Vaysh's shoulders. He tried to turn immediately; his hands came up and struck my wrists. I could almost feel his flesh crawling at my touch.

"Don't!" he shouted and I let go. His eyes were dark with the anger I had yearned for.

"My mind . . . I'm forgetting things," I told him. Emotions were pulsing in and out of his eyes as he struggled to control them.

"Forgetting things? What things?" he hissed and backed away about three steps, rubbing his shoulders. Even his own touch seemed repellent to him.

"Things that happened to me when I was alive!" I raved, and then, more soberly, "When I was alive before."

"Those things are not important," Vaysh said.

I could have struck him. "To you maybe not, but they are to me! I have to sleep, don't I? How can I sleep when my mind is draining away? Is it happening, is it really happening?!"

Vaysh stared at me impassively. "I don't have to tell you anything, Pellaz. I have only to deliver you to the right place in one piece. I don't give a damn what you think or what you feel . . . I don't give a damn about your precious, grovelling past. Don't you think that the only possible truth is that *he's* forgotten you already . . ."

He might have said more, but I could stem my rage no longer. In a second, Vaysh was looking up at me from the floor. He looked confused, perhaps wondering how he had got there, and touched his lip. My blow had split it.

"Now," I began patiently, "I can't make you concerned about me Vaysh; I don't want to, but I do want answers. Now, let's try again. Is my memory going?"

Vaysh stood up, the back of his hand to his mouth. He walked slowly to the fire and I gave him his dignity and remained quiet.

After a while he said, "I have something of yours," and left the room. Absurdly, I had begun to shake. It was rare that my temper erupted to violence and it always scared me a little when it did. Vaysh's teeth had marked my knuckles and if I was shaken, at least so was he.

When he returned, he held something out to me. "Take it," he said. It shone gold in the firelight, on a leather thong, worn with use. A sacred eye. I could not reach for it.

"How did you get that?" I asked in wonderment.

"It came with you . . ."

With me? I stared at the pendant turning slowly on its thong. "Orien . . . it was Orien's. He gave it to me." Whether Vaysh knew of whom I was speaking, it was impossible to tell. He would not meet my eyes, nursing his cut lip with his tongue. I took the eye from him and it felt warm in my hands. How? How had this talisman made that impossible journey with me?

Vaysh answered my question. "Someone made that trinket truly yours.

Thiede took it from around your throat. It made him uneasy; he did not want you to have it . . ."

"Why give it to you then?"

Vaysh shrugged and folded his arms. "Such a gift as that; even Thiede was wary of the charm. He gave it to me for safekeeping. I was told that if you ever asked for it, I was to give it back to you."

"But I didn't ask for it!" I protested.

"Didn't you?!"

I put the talisman around my neck where it rested with familiar comfort. "This is my past," I said, and it was almost a question.

Vaysh's voice was dull, "Your past? It is all in there, perhaps. Your body is new; nothing of your old life is relevant to it. Why should it adhere to events that no longer concern it? The talisman will give it back to you; that is its only purpose."

"How?"

Again, he shrugged. "Only your friend Orien knows that."

My skin prickled. "Does that mean . . . does that mean that Orien *knew?!*"

"Maybe," Vaysh replied with a sigh. "Thiede respects Orien. That should mean something."

"Vaysh, I want to know," I said. I went toward him and he backed away.

"Know? Know what?"

"Everything. How did Thiede do it? Where did this body come from? It looks like me doesn't it? It does look like me?"

"It looks like you," Vaysh answered, ignoring the first two questions. His voice sounded less harsh.

"You've seen me before?"

"Yes." He went over to the bed and started packing the clothes Phade had given me into bags.

"Where, Vaysh?" He looked over his shoulder at me.

"Where have you seen me before?"

He turned back to the packing. "Everywhere Pellaz, everywhere. I have seen through Thiede's eyes . . ."

All the chill came back to my flesh; my hand curled around Orien's talisman. Thiede's eyes; my life a spectacle. I was staring at a heavy pewter jug that stood on a table by my bed. I was thinking of the weight of it in my hands and the impact of it against the back of Vaysh's bent head. I was thinking of me, fleeing the tower and running just anywhere; all of this. Luckily, I was not thinking hard enough.

Vaysh stood up. "We must leave," he said. "Are you ready?"

We looked at each other without liking. He knew that I had the power, even the desire, to kill him, but he also knew just what had made Thiede choose me. I closed my eyes so that I did not have to look at him. "I am ready," I said.

Outside, the sun shone hard on the unbearable whiteness of the snow.

Only the center of the yard had been cleared. Phade, muffled in a wolf-skin coat, stood rubbing his hands by our horses. I was now in a condition to fully appreciate what magnificent creatures they were. Slim, long noses, intelligent eyes, dainty feet. They were draped with red traveling rugs, tassels dangled from their bridles. They did not appear to be laden with many supplies, however.

Phade came over to clasp our hands. "It was a pleasure to meet you," he said to me.

"We may meet again," I replied.

"What? When you are king and summon me to your court as an underling?" he laughed.

"Maybe."

Phade nodded good-humoredly and turned his attention to my companion. "Goodbye Vaysh, may your snow-lined knickers never melt!" He smacked Vaysh heartily on the backside as he was half over his horse. The animal jumped back with a start and Vaysh had to pull its mouth sharply just to stay aboard. He looked furious.

"See that, Pellaz?" Phade guffawed. "Emotion; pure and virgin loathing!" He laughed again and marched back to his tower, still waving at us.

We cantered out into the stinging, fresh air beyond the tower walls, heading toward the forest. I was wondering where we were going and how we were going to eat. We had brought nothing with us. Some three miles from the tower, beyond the lakeside town, Vaysh pulled his horse to a halt. We were on a snow-padded road, barely marked by tracks. Our voices seemed muted by the heavy clouds above.

"Why are we stopping?" I asked.

"I'm going to teach you how to ride that horse," Vaysh replied, deadpan as ever.

I laughed, "What?!"

"Just listen. You are riding a horse called Peridot. It is like no other horse you have ever ridden. Speak to it."

"Vaysh!"

"Just do it! Say Peridot and think the sound; like a calling."

"Peridot." I obediently sent out the name-shaped thought and felt it touch something disturbingly strange. The horse's head went up, its ears flicking back and forth. I had recoiled from the touch, but after the initial shock, tried again. My thoughts came to rest against an animal intelligence. It felt so different; frightening. The thought processes were so different. We made each other's acquaintance, Peridot and I. Animals do not look at the world like we do. It was a chastening experience to sense the way they do see things.

"We have to form a link," Vaysh continued. "I know the way we have to travel. We must communicate in the same manner for you to direct Peridot."

I did not welcome that. I expected Vaysh's mind to be a chilly, dark, inhospitable land.

"I like this as little as you do," he said frostily. "But you must trust me now. Take the information from me. Peridot is experienced in this method of travel; he will know what to do."

"Right," I muttered, cold inside my furs.

"Now . . ." Vaysh closed his eyes and for a moment, I just stared at him, before tentatively opening my mind to him. It was like an electric shock when we met and I pulled away. Vaysh waited with bitter patience. His thoughts were carefully protected; he exposed only the information we needed for the journey. I saw the place we would visit; I could almost feel the warmth, taste the air . . . "Link to Peridot!" Vaysh's voice whispered behind my eyes.

Beneath me, the horse's silver haunches began to quiver. He too could smell the salt-laced air of a warmer climate. I joined my mind with his, two completely different intelligences linking and mingling, until I was half-horse and he was half-har. I was blind, but I could feel Peridot begin to move; a great surging of white power. Contact with Vaysh became almost comforting. I was conscious of a gathering speed; the breathless impetus of flight. It was exhilarating. Air, vapors, formless, rushing, white noise poured through my skin. I could no longer feel the reins between my fingers. I had become inorganic movement; nothing else. I did not have to open my eyes that were no longer there to see. Two horses, two hara; one unit. Together, we sped through unimaginable space, stars hissing through our hair, laughter of alien forms at our backs; they could not catch us. Colors upon silken blackness undulated before me, through me, around me. There were worlds and worlds, hanging like glistening beads in an infinite darkness. I saw my father stride across a purple sky ahead of me, dragging a sheaf of cable plants that had comets for roots. The vision shimmered and became Seel painting his eyes with kohl before a mirror. In the mirror I could see Saltrock behind him. Then it was darkness again, and pulsing seeds of light, things like seaweed flickering at the edge of my vision. It seemed we traveled an eternity; perhaps it was only a minute. Suddenly Vaysh exhulted: through, down, out! In a burst of light, I followed his directions and the world shimmered around us, scattering sparks and laughter. We were galloping down a hard, brown road, red sunlight behind us, warm air melting a frost from our lips. The horses' coats crackled with ice that broke and faded onto the road. Vaysh was smiling. We looked at each other and I smiled too.

Ahead of us, a walled town massed gray against an encroaching dusk. It was like another planet; air powdered with fragrant dusts tickled the back of my throat.

"Is this Immanion?!" I called.

"No, no!" Vaysh shouted back, still beaming like someone who was used to smiling.

"Where then?"

"Ferelithia!"

Vaysh slowed his mount to a trot and Peridot nudged up against them, snorting through his nose, his head curved right over his neck. He could not speak to me exactly, but his kind, horsy wisdom congratulated me on my first out-of-world journey. I buried my fingers in his thick mane and scratched his neck appreciatively.

"We shall have to rest now," Vaysh told me. "It's not safe to travel that way for too long."

"Vaysh, that was incredible!" I exclaimed. Vaysh nodded.

"Pell, that is just the beginning. You have so much to discover. We have inherited a magical world."

It was the first time he had called me Pell.

We trotted toward the town and Vaysh explained a little about the place. I learned that our other-lane jump had carried us many hundreds of miles south, although we still traveled over the same land mass. "You will find Ferelithia different to most of the Wraeththu settlements you have visited before," he told me. "It is the home of the tribe of Ferelith. They're a showy and rather vain people, but much more advanced from Hara like, say, the Varrs . . ." A grimace crossed my face accompanied by a dozen uncomfortable recollections. "An unfortunate comparison, perhaps," Vaysh added, and I glanced at him sharply. His elation after our mad ride had begun to dissipate; he had started to solidfy again. "Personally, I find the Ferelith somewhat frivolous and thus rather irriating, but I expect *you* will like them." Accompanied by such a look of disdain as it was, this remark achieved everything it was intended to and offended me. But then, I looked at Vaysh's cut lip, which was still a little swollen, and began to feel better.

We must have looked ridiculous riding into the streets of that town, furred up to the eyes in thick coats. The air was so warm that both Peridot and I had started to sweat. Vaysh looked as cool as ever, but his horse shook moisture from his black neck. All the streets were lit with strings of multicolored lights, loud music, the like of which I'd never heard before, pounded from open doorways, along with the sounds of intoxicated merriment. Creeping plants, lush with heavy-perfumed blossoms, adorned many of the buildings, which were low and white and roofed with red tile. Vaysh struggled to undo the collar of his coat, looking down his imperious little nose at the hara who were strolling and shouting through the balmy evening. Through the scent of flowers, I could smell the sea.

We rode up and down for some time, looking for an inn. Several that looked suitable Vaysh shook his head at. I was not sure whether he had economy in mind or comfort. Eventually, he decided on a dimly-lit, small hostelry we discovered up a quiet backstreet.

"We need to sleep," he said, "and everywhere else is too noisy. Ferelithia never sleeps!"

I was tired too, the journey had sapped my strength, but thought with regret of the cheerful lights and thrilling music back in the town center. I did not know how long Vaysh planned for us to stay in Ferelithia, but I had seen enough of it to be eager to explore.

We tied the horses to a wooden bar outside the inn and went inside. A gleaming, red-tiled floor led to a low, stone-topped bar. Dim lighting revealed a group of hara sitting round a table near the window. They all looked up as we entered and one of them stood up.

"Are you the patron of this establishment?" Vaysh inquired haughtily. The har grinned and came toward us.

"I'm the landlord, if that's what you mean. A room is it?"

"Rooms," Vaysh confirmed.

The innkeeper looked with interest at our clothing. "Traveled far, have you?"

Vaysh glared at him rudely. "We may stay a couple of days," he said.

We ordered a meal and Vaysh told the innkeeper we would eat in our rooms. "We would be pestered downstairs," he said to me darkly, and then ordered the landlord to see to our horses. I was relieved to notice that Vaysh's high-handed manner provoked only amusement. Pausing at the door to my room, I asked him to eat with me. He thought about it for a moment and then said yes. God knows why I wanted his company; I was surprised when he agreed to sharing mine. We were served an attractive meal of smoked meat, rice and salad, accompanied by pale, yellow beer. There was a table in the room, but we sat on the bed to eat. Vaysh was silent and moody, consuming his food without pleasure.

"I'm sorry I hit you," I said, hoping to lighten the atmosphere.

He pulled a face. "I doubt it. I think you're still congratulating yourself for having done it!"

"You're weird," I observed, "and, I think, horrible." It cheered me up considerably to poke at his reserve. "What are you, Vaysh? Why are you like you are?"

He pushed his plate away, half finished. "We can stay here a few days," he said.

"What happened to you? Was it Thiede?"

He stood up. "The way we traveled; it makes us tire easily. I'm going to bed now."

"Oh Vaysh, sit down," I said, in a cajoling tone. "You haven't finished."

He hesitated a moment, clenching and unclenching his fists. Then he said, "Pellaz, I realize sometimes I treat you unfairly, even unfeelingly, but that's just the way I am. Also, I do not wish to talk about myself; ever!"

"OK," I agreed, placatingly. "I won't ask another question about your impenetrable self. Sit down, eat, tell me about me."

He sat down. "About you? What do you want to know?"

I laughed, "Oh God, Vaysh, everything!"

"I've told you all I can," he said. "There's nothing more. Some things only Thiede knows." He was staring at his food and then something made him grit his teeth and he threw down his fork. "Pellaz, I can see you are straining toward some kind of camaraderie between us, but that is impossible!" I suppressed an obvious wince as he fixed me with his heartless gaze. "You are very interested in what has happened to you; this is understandable. The future also fascinates you, but one thing you must realize, Pellaz, no matter how interesting it all is to you, it is only a bore to me!"

I suppose I should have let him stalk out after that, only more unpleasantness would follow if he remained, but it is difficult to act logically in the face of such excruciating indifference. I beat him to the door.

"You'll have to force your way out!" I cried, gleefully. Vaysh raised one hand to shoulder height. His fingers began to curl, his mouth to open.

"Just try it!" I snarled. Whatever words had been on his lips were never spoken. He could sense my counter-defense and thought better of attempting that kind of skirmish. His hand dropped to his side.

"I hope Pellaz, you are not going to make a habit out of tormenting me," he said. I watched him as he slumped miserably back down on the bed, one hand clawing his red hair. "Ask me questions, then, ask me!"

His defeat flummoxed me. "I can't think . . . well, OK, what happened to . . . what happened to my old body?"

Vaysh made a choking sound that might have been a scornful laugh. "Flirting with devils?" he asked, drily, leaning back on his elbows. Through that question, the balance of power had shifted.

"Just answer," I muttered, turning away; I did not want to see his face.

"It was burned."

I had started to shake. I knew what the real questions were, but could not voice them. I said, "Tell me what happened to it after . . . after I was gone."

I could hear him laughing. "Ah, I see, I am to be your crystal ball. Very well, I shall be generous. Are you ready? Turn around; I want to watch this."

I thought, "This is just another observation, this is unknown to him," but I turned around.

I wish you could see him as I saw him then. Dead loveliness that was inquisitive. A ghoul for the flesh of love.

"He wept for you, Pellaz. He soaked himself in your blood—for days. Sprawled in the rain and the mud until he was no longer rational; an unpleasant sight. Some time after, common sense got control of his hysteria and he burned what was left of you. Then, he went away . . ."

My jaw was frozen. I could not say: where? Vaysh knew the question. "We lost interest in him after that. He may have gone back north, or not, I don't know." He stood up. "I'm supposed to comfort you now, aren't I? Probably that is what Thiede expects of me, but . . ." I moved away from the door to let him pass. "Why be cruel to yourself?" he said. "Forget it, forget him; you might as well."

I know now that my pain pleased him, for reasons known only to himself. I let him leave to surrender myself to a nest of misery. In time it would not hurt so much, I was sure. Time fades everything to a degree; even the deepest wounds.

CHAPTER FIVE

> ﹥━┥◆﹥━◉━╉◆┝━┥﹤

New alliances and expectations; return of an old friend

The following morning, Vaysh being nowhere in sight, I breakfasted alone downstairs. The landlord waited for me to finish eating before sauntering over to my table. He offered me a cigarette. The smoke burned my lungs and I realized that this was the first time my new body had ever tasted it. I was subject to a subtle interrogation, which I equally subtly managed to side-step. The innkeeper laughed and called me a tease.

"Your companion has left money for you," he said, once resigned to the fact that he would get nowhere with me.

"Oh, has he gone?" I answered abruptly. (Surely I could not have been abandoned!)

"He said he would be back to eat at noon. Why don't you take a walk around the town? There is much to see . . . spend the money. I would be happy to show you around."

"No," I said, "Thanks, but I'll find my way about."

The landlord seemed rather put out that I had declined his offer and handed me the money somewhat churlishly.

Outside, the day was already hot. I stood for a moment in the doorway to the inn, soaking up the sun. Already I had forgotten what it felt like to be cold.

The typical Ferelithian is a sociable and contented creature. This does not come as a surprise after spending an hour or two exploring the city. The thriving markets and their bright merchandise betokened affluence and by the amount of ale-houses and live music venues (all bearing colorful, exotic names), I could see the Ferelith spent most of their time in recreation. Utter strangers stopped and spoke to me when they recognized me as a new face. Street-vendors entreated me to buy their wares; sparkling, cheap jewelery and colorful, gossamer scarves. By the time I reached the town center my mood was bordering on euphoric; friends could be made easily in Ferelithia and I could see no reason why I should have to spend another grim evening in Vaysh's company. I was intrigued by the amount of humans, most noticeably females, wandering around the streets of Ferelithia. Some even had stalls in the markets and were obviously enjoying a thriving trade alongside hara. Had the two races learned to live in harmony in this part of the world?

It was in the market-place that I saw her, recognizing her almost instantly. That a woman should have been there at all was remarkable, but that it was her was just too much of a coincidence. A fragment of my past here in Ferelithia. She was looking at some colored ribbons, a frown upon her face; the stallkeeper was bullying her to purchase. I hurried over, afraid that she would vanish, and tapped her on the shoulder. Her skin was dark brown and peeling. "Hello Kate," I said. She turned round with a smile on her face and I was surprised how much older she looked, but when she saw me her face dropped with bewilderment. She knew she had met me before but couldn't think where. "Don't you remember me?" I asked and she shook her head slowly, still thinking.

"I'm sorry . . ."

"Greenling. With Seel. You gave us guns . . ."

Realization dawned across her face. "Pellaz! Pellaz, isn't it? My God, you've changed! Sorry, I mean . . ."

"Oh, that's OK, I know. What are you doing here?"

"What, at the moment? Oh, visiting friends. I'm a bit stranded . . . waiting for a boat . . . waiting for work . . . you know . . . low on funds. How about you? God, I can't believe this! I never thought I'd meet you here!"

"I'm just passing through really. The power of coincidence . . . I don't even know how long I'm staying . . ." I said.

She laughed. "Long enough for a drink with an old friend, or shall I say acquaintance?"

"Long enough for that," I confirmed.

She took me to a quayside tavern where we could see the sleek Fereli-thian ships bobbing like impatient race-horses upon a dark blue sea. We sat outside at a canopied table, and Kate waved away my offer of Vaysh's money. "No, I'll pay. I'm not that broke." She was dressed like a man with her long hair clasped high on her head with gold circlets. But for her admittedly vestigal bosom, she could easily have passed for Har. She sat sideways in her chair, her nervous arms clanking with bangles. I could not remember her being that restless before, but of course it had been some time since I had last seen her. Now that we had said hello to each other, it was difficult to think of anything to say. I began with the obvious, "I'm surprised to find a woman here . . ."

"Why?!" she snapped. "I have no quarrel with Wraeththu, and neither have many other women . . ."

"You are tolerated here then?"

She rolled her eyes and rocked back in her chair. "God forbid! We're not back in the homeland now, Pell, thank heavens! There's quite a few women here. Ferelith like us, we amuse them, we have good friends. God knows womankind appreciates the vagaries of Man's nature just as much as Wraeththu. You've just got here I take it?"

"Mmm, yesterday."

She nodded, poking out her lower lip. "Have you any cigarettes?" she asked.

"For the first time in years, yes," I replied, thankful that I had actually bothered to buy some of my own at last.

"Where've you come from, Pell?" she asked. "You haven't stayed back home all this time have you?"

"No, not all the time . . ." Something about the tone of 'all this time' alerted me and I said, "How long has it been Kate?"

She smiled, flicking ask over the table, twirling the cigarette in her hand. "How long? God . . ." she screwed up her eyes. "Two years in Tahralan, some months in Lipforth . . . God, I don't know . . . what about five years?" She raised her eyebrows for confirmation.

"Five years?!" I slammed down my mug and ale slopped on the table.

Kate dabbed at her arm where I'd splashed it. "OK, OK, maybe not that long . . . four years something . . . What's the matter, Pell?"

I looked at her; I could not explain. "I didn't realize," I said. "Time goes so quickly doesn't it?"

"When you're having fun . . ."

"That's not always the case." Five years; I couldn't believe it. How much of that time had been spent in Thiede's care? I couldn't work it out.

"Where's your friend?" Kate asked and for a moment I thought she meant Vaysh. Then last night's wounds began to seep a little and the familiar cold numbed my head.

"Oh, you mean Cal . . ." Just saying his name brought me sorrow.

"We got split up," I explained and it came so easily after that. "That's when I came over here; I don't know where he is now . . ." (Now; five years later.)

"He really hated me, didn't he," she said, pulling her lip thoughtfully and staring into her beer.

"He hated all women. It was nothing personal . . . God, why do I talk about him as if he's dead?" Even in that hot, kind sunlight, I could not shake off the cold. I was shaking, my teeth were chattering. Kate was staring at my arms and must have seen the goosebumps.

"Do you miss him? Oh shit, yes, you miss him. Shut up, Kate." She took a mouthful of her drink. "He was gorgeous, can I say that?"

I laughed bitterly. "You just did. Hell, it doesn't matter. I'd like to tell you about it, but I can't. At least I think I shouldn't . . ."

"Where are you heading?" she asked, to change the subject.

I wondered whether I should tell her and then said; "Immanion."

She raised her eyebrows, swilling a mouthful of liquid thoughtfully. "Well, well, how privileged."

"Indeed. You must come visit me sometime," I returned sarcastically.

"Sorry, I'm only jealous," she said with a grin. "Look, I know it seems terribly ill-mannered, but I have to go soon, but I'll tell you what, meet me for a drink tonight; you can buy me one back. I might be in a sorry state if I don't get this job I'm after."

"I'd like that," I said. "I was hoping to find something to do tonight. I have a traveling companion who's about as lively as the grim reaper. Where shall I meet you?"

She quaffed the rest of her drink and wiped her mouth. "There's a leisure-warren not far from here . . ."

"A what?"

"A place to enjoy yourself, drink, dance, listen to music, whatever. It's called Temple Radiant . . . not far, OK?"

I watched her hurry back into the crowd, heading for the harbor. I had not even asked her how she had got here.

Vaysh was waiting for me in my room. "You've been gone a long time," he said, in his flat, disinterested way. I did not welcome the prospect of Vaysh destroying my mood.

"I met a woman in the market," I said. "From Greenling. You remember Greenling, Vaysh, surely!"

He ignored the implication. "What did you tell her?" he asked ominously.

"Nothing I shouldn't have!" I snapped. "I was surprised to see her though. Is it fate, Vaysh, or did Thiede organize it for me?"

"Shut up, you fool," Vaysh droned.

"Are all Wraeththu in this land kindly disposed toward women?" I asked, looking at myself in the mirror. I could see him behind me; his narrowed eyes.

"Some women are as pleased to see the decline of men as we are," he said. "It's a bleak prospect for them though and depressing for us. We have to watch them grow old alone. I had women friends once . . ."

"Vaysh, one more word and I'll consider you good-natured," I teased, making him pull one of his sour faces, of which he had an inexhaustive variety. I could still see him in the mirror. Sometimes, not often, Vaysh could be almost approachable and then he'd retreat behind a barrier of unpleasantness. He made disagreeable noises when I told him I was meeting Kate that night and then insisted on accompanying me.

"Ah, you just want to enjoy yourself," I said. "You're going to dance and get drunk aren't you?"

"I am not!" Vaysh snarled. "I just want to keep an eye on you."

We dined at the inn and Vaysh pointedly refused a glass of wine. He grumbled continuously whilst I tarted myself up to go out. The last time I'd had a social life was in Galhea; I was determined not to let Vaysh spoil our evening.

"Get changed, comb your hair," I told him.

"I don't have to," he replied haughtily, which was true. I had bought several brass bangles that afternoon and offered him one because I felt sorry for him. (Good humor often brings out a strange side to my nature.) Surprisingly, he took it. I had also spent a rather lavish amount of money on getting my ears pierced again, with half a dozen, heavy gold rings.

"The money's yours anyway," Vaysh said. "Waste it how you like."

We discovered that Temple Radiant was *the* place to be seen in Ferelithia. I was surprised how much it cost to get in. Inside, it was almost dark; what light there was glowed purple or dark green. The music was so loud and so *strange,* strident, pounding; I wasn't sure if I liked it.

"Stop gaping," Vaysh said.

"I've seen nothing like this," I murmured inadequately. Vaysh sniffed.

"I used to come here, before," he said.

Several rooms of varying murkiness led to the main auditorium. The furnishings were all of black velvet, leather and simulated animal skins. Black netting strung with painted bones hung down from the ceiling. Vaysh led the way into a room named Gehenna. I must admit I shrank at the door; its occupants, what I could see of them, seemed unpleasantly suitable for the name.

"Blend in, Pellaz; buy a drink," Vaysh advised, firing his basilisk stare at anyone who looked at us.

"Where's Kate?"

"Buy a drink first . . ." he said impatiently.

I didn't know what to order so Vaysh bought two glasses of something colored neon purple that tasted like acid perfume on first acquaintance and increasingly pleasant after the first swallow.

The Ferclith were undoubtedly the most exotic and colorful race I had yet seen. Their hair, their clothes, their careful mannerisms combined to form a breathtaking glamor. "*Do* stop gaping!" Vaysh said. I saw several women who looked just like hara; some of them may have been, it was impossible to tell. Vaysh pointed out Wreaththu of different tribes; most of them unfamiliar to me. Then someone touched my arm; a warm dry hand.

"Pell, you've come," Kate said, sounding surprised.

"I said I would."

"Yes I know, but . . . this way." She took my arm and hauled me into the darkness. I did not look to see if Vaysh was following. Kate and her friends had gathered round a table right next to the dance floor; the music was deafening there. Colored lights swept crazily through the smoke. I could see her mouth moving and presumed she was introducing us to the others. She couldn't stop looking at Vaysh. He was giving one of his virtuoso performances of astounding indifference, resting his elbows on the table, with his chin in his hands, looking bored. Kate was desperate to keep us entertained, although I would have been quite happy just watching the dancers. It was a strain to keep shouting over the noise. "I got the job!" she bellowed and insisted on buying us more drinks. Restless as ever, she kept leaving the table to dance. Her friends realized the futility of trying to get acquainted with us, so most of the time I was left with only Vaysh to mouth at. He looked sulky and lovely, and because of the drink, I remember trying to get him to talk to me. "You're drunk," he said.

Five empty glasses stood in sticky rings on the table in front of me when the music died down. My ears were ringing insanely; I felt pleasantly unsteady.

Kate leaned over. "Soon you'll hear the *real* music," she said, her face damp and flushed. "Are you enjoying yourself?"

I nodded and smiled and could feel Vaysh looking at both of us with scorn. Kate waved at someone. "Now be sociable, Pell, here's Rue. I want you to meet him," she said with a conspiratorial smirk. The one she called Rue sauntered over to our table; white light from the stage at the other end of the room shone through his hair. "Wait till you see this," Kate hissed to me through her teeth. "Hello Rue, mixing with the rabble are you? I'd like you to meet a friend of mine . . ."

That was where Kate faded out, more suddenly than she had intended, I'm sure. True magnetism is a hard thing to define, but Rue had it in abundance; shameless abundance. This was a classic example of what Thiede had once spoken to me about; instant gravitation. I suppose it was because he reminded me of Cal in a way; he had white-gold hair, but it was much longer. In looks, Vaysh could have outshone him easily (without the sulk), but what he lacked in symmetry of feature, Rue made up for generously with sheer sensuality and confidence. I could almost hear Vaysh thinking, "Ugh, how common!" and that in itself delighted me.

"Rue, sit down," Kate said, with the interested bustle of a voyeur, making room, patting the seat.

"I can't stay," he said, and looked at me. "Oh, hi," he added carelessly. I must have mumbled something inane. He smiled and walked away, leaping up onto the stage and through some curtains at the back.

"A singer," Kate explained and slid me a knowing glance. "Did you like him?"

"Mmm," I agreed, non-commitally.

Kate laughed, "You can't stay in mourning for ever," she pointed out incisively.

"Kate, shut up."

"You can't. I'm not psychic but . . ."

"Kate, shut up."

"Why are you grinning then?"

"Kate!"

"Pellaz, how much longer do you want to stay here?" Vaysh complained in his usual chilly voice beside me. He had barely touched his first drink. I had forgotten he was there.

"You can go back if you like," I said and we stared at each other for several excruciating seconds.

"Don't think about doing anything stupid," he said with a sneer.

"What's stupid?" I asked delicately and he would not reply. "Chaperone as well then," I said in a low voice. He still would not answer. Then all the lights dimmed out and I could feel heat rising in the darkness. Vaysh shifted awkwardly in his seat; his bangle knocked against the table. A sound, like a hissing heartbeat prickled my skin. It built up slowly, louder and louder, and the crowd cheered and whistled. The excitement was infectious; Kate climbed up onto her seat. For a moment, silence, and then with a flash of white light and plumes of steam, drums rolled like thunder and Rue was bathed in a cataract of spotlights upon the stage. I stood up. Primal and thrilling, the music roared through my head. Rue leapt around the other musicians; sparks of light lasered off the chrome of their instruments. His voice was a scream then a snarl; he crouched to tease the nearest of his audience, leaping up; his body supple as a snake. Kate leaned down and put her arms round my neck. "Dance with me," she said. The heat of other bodies pressed against us and for a moment I held her close. She laughed in my face, mocking, bitter, and pulled away. "Demon!" she said and then, in my ear, "but what a way to die!"

I had danced, as a child, in the sand. My mother had said, "What does he see that we can't? What does he dance to?" I had danced to the sky, reaching up for it, feeling a great and exciting void that had reached down for me. That had been so long ago but I could remember it vividly. I felt like that now. Before, the music had been only inside my head, now it filled my being and carried me. The sky had reached me.

At the end we cheered and shrieked and applauded; let it begin again. But the house lights came back on and Kate led us back to our seats. We were both drenched in sweat and exhausted to the point of collapse. I was surprised to see Vaysh still sitting there and steeled myself for the verbal assault. Unpredictable as ever he said, "You dance very well."

"Buy Kate a drink," I said. It scared me when he was nice to me. He gave me a sour smile and disappeared, sinuously, in the direction of the bar. Kate sat beside me, attempting to organize her wet hair.

"I really needed this," I told her and she looked at me quickly.

"I could see that," she said. "Your friend's a strange one isn't he?"

"He's not my friend!" I said, too harshly and she replied.

"Oh, really?"

Rue waited for quite a while before he came back to our table, as I had known he would. Outwardly tranquil, I was fighting the insufferable battle between guilt and desire. Could I forget so quickly? My feelings disgusted me, but I couldn't stop looking at Rue. He sat opposite me, the light behind him; his face was indistinct.

Vaysh leaned over and whispered in my ear, like a nagging conscience, "You'll regret it Pell, you will."

"Regret what? What are you talking about?"

"You know," he said.

"What do you care?" I retorted.

"Remember who you are," he said. "Anyway, it's too soon. If you weren't drunk, you'd see that. Remember last night . . ."

I turned on him savagely, "You love to make me miserable, don't you!"

He shook his head, "Not particularly." I sighed heavily. Rue was talking to Kate but he kept looking over at us.

"Look Pell," Vaysh hissed, conscious of Rue's vigilance, "we'll be here a few days. Just think about it."

I glanced back at Rue. He felt my stare and looked into my eyes. I was torn two ways; it was not easy.

"OK Vaysh, let's go." Vaysh was on his feet in an instant.

"Are you leaving? Kate asked, startled, seeing her plans disintegrate, whatever they might have been.

"Yes," I answered, and could not resist adding, "Where will you be tomorrow night?"

She seemed to relax then. "Oh, the bar on the quay, probably. The Red Cat; where we went today."

"Right, I'll see you there, then." The message was not just for her but I did not look at Rue. Vaysh and I walked back to the inn in frosty silence.

This was it then: the monumental choice. That night, I sat up alone in my room, chain-smoking, drinking cold coffee and trying to think rationally. All the windows were open; the night was very warm. I kept going to stare down at the gardens and heady perfume wafted up to me. My mind was in turmoil. Ferelithia was a night-time world of crazy fantasy. All of it was new, untasted and exciting. I had spent so little time quite simply enjoying myself. Life with Cal had often been hard; many nights spent in cold or discomfort. Now I had arrived in a land of plenty clothed in new flesh that was hungry for life; a body that was radiant with the finest of Wraeththu beauty. Most of the time I was unconscious of it, but tonight I had seen it work for me. Rue's eyes. . . . Something prim and small argued inside me against the glowing vivacity. Didn't I owe it to Cal to restrain myself? Had I forgotten my vow so quickly? Ah yes, my eagerness countered, but I had not vowed celibacy had I? I was too sensible for that. I had pledged my heart to Cal and yet, only that was sacred. Oh, come now! the primness insisted, you have seen an attractive har in a crowded, noisy place where everything was stimulating; music you'd never heard before, potent liquor, carefree Hara whose lives seemed enviably easy. It's not surprising you were tempted; it was just the atmosphere. I stood up and paced the floor. One thing I knew for sure, had known ever since my inception; Wraeththu-kind needed aruna. It was simply part of their existence and nothing to be ashamed about. Only love had made me feel shame. Perhaps this was the warning. Perhaps this was why Wraeththu scorned the relationships of men. Love means guilt means trouble. It was ridiculous; five years had passed. It was a concept that was almost too terrifying to think about and one, since Kate had made me realize it, which I had pushed to the back of my mind. Five years lost. Nobody knew; not those that had once cared for me. To them I was simply dead—mourned and forgotten. Just thinking of it chilled me. Mortal remains burned and rotted, skin, teeth, hair and bones. I looked down at my outspread hands. Had they heard of my death in Saltrock, in Galhea, at the Kakkahaar settlement in the desert? Did they ever speak of me? I summoned Rue's face to my mind's eye and sighed. He desired me. To him I was alive. It was inevitable that Cal had forgotten me, if indeed he still lived. I was just afraid; scared that in the arms of another, I would think only of him. "Pellaz, you are nearly a king!" I told myself. "Pellaz, you are har. What you feel is natural to you and you must obey

your instincts." But I could not climb out of the guilt. Then there was
Vaysh, his censure of my behavior. To him aruna would be viewed as
surrender at best and humiliation at worst, locked as he was in the ice-castle
of his pride. I could not rely on his advice. Tomorrow, I would see; what
will be will be. That was the only way out. Fate had me in her arms and
I would not fight her.

After breakfast, I decided to take Peridot out for some excercise. Vaysh
declined to join me; in his sullenness that day, he looked almost gray.

Peridot looked so pleased to see me I felt guilty I had not been to see him
the day before. Vaysh's horse watched us mournfully as we trotted out into
the sunlight. Now that I knew how to, I communicated with Peridot nearly
all the time, passing over my thoughts on Ferelithia. To him, it was just
bustle and color and pleasing smells. I could feel his mild impatience at the
chaos of my mind. I took him down to the beach and let him canter along
the damp sand, through the wavelets. Ferelithia had reached my heart; I
could have happily stayed there for ever.

Round lunchtime, hunger lured me back to the inn. I thought miserably
of the sour face that would probably be waiting for me and was therefore
gratefully surprised when I saw Kate lounging against the bar.

"How did you find me?" I asked and she tapped her nose and laughed.

"I wanted to see you. I feel a bit guilty about last night," she said.

"*You* do!" I snapped, not meaning to sound so angry.

"Oh, I'm sorry Pell. I was a bit drunk and," she shrugged expressively,
"well, you know. I shouldn't have said what I did about Rue or implied
what I did. It was awful of me; after what you said about Cal . . . and what
you didn't say! Is that why you left so early?"

"Oh Kate, you've done nothing wrong," I said to ease the worried look
from her face. "I didn't leave because of anything you did. I just had to
think."

She nodded abstractedly, "Yes, I understand. Anyway," brightening,
"what did you think of Temple Radiant?"

I threw up my arms and laughed.

"Yes," she said, "I felt like that at first. That's because there's a little bit
of peasant mentality lurking somewhere inside both of us, I suppose."

"Speak for yourself!" I chided. "It made me realize what I've been
missing. Everything's been so hellishly serious lately."

We ordered a light meal and went to sit at one of the low tables near the
empty hearth. I kept thinking of what Vaysh had said about the future of
women. Was Kate lonely? If I had known her better, I would have asked,
but instead inquired about how she had ended up in Ferelithia. She grinned
sheepishly and said she had run away from home. There had been no future
for her in Greenling, other than becoming some man's wife, and whatever
benefits that position had once offered seemed pointless now. "I want to
enjoy what's left of the world," she said, with a wide sweep of her arm.

"What's left of it for me, anyhow. It will soon all belong for Wraeththu and, although I can't be part of it, I can still enjoy some secondhand thrills."

"Have you ever thought, Kate, that it might be possible for women to share our future?" I asked.

"You obviously have," she answered evasively and I sensed her embarrassment. "You've touched a secret nerve there, Pell, you really have."

"It just doesn't make sense sometimes," I said.

"Oh, it does, there are reasons, Pell. Heavy, somewhat theosophical ones. Man before the Fall and all that. I'm just a spare rib and, I'm afraid, fearfully redundant. Woman is in you Pell; you know that."

"You seem to know more about it than I do," I observed.

"Well, that's obvious, isn't it. You don't really have to question things; you just *are*. I was full of frustrated anger at first. All of it seemed so unfair. Men, horrible things, seemed to have got away with lifetimes of mistreating women only to cheerfully phase us out with a timely mutation!"

"I must admit, that's how it seems to me," I agreed.

"Well, it's not like that," she said firmly. "It's purely biological, I think. Males are easier to mutate; but the female *is* there. You can't see it very easily, perhaps, but it is there."

"Why do we call each other "he" then?" I argued.

"Oh God, I don't know!" she laughed. "If it bothers you that much, think of something else. Think how easy it would be to get used to it!"

"Has anyone ever tried to incept a woman, do you think?" I asked.

She drew her breath in deeply and stared at the table. "Oh, yes," she said. Her voice was soft. I did not ask her to explain. "When I die, Pell," she continued, looking up with grave eyes, "that's when I get my chance. You should know that."

I shivered. Kate had accepted things so philosophically and worked out answers for herself. She had seen so plainly that which I had missed. We are all one. The bodies are different; but bodies are expendable. The soul goes on for ever.

Vaysh came to sit on my bed as I got ready to go out that evening. That he disapproved of my actions was obligatory; I only wished I could understand why. I was not so stupid as to think he was concerned for my welfare. He did not ask me any questions, just watched me steadily with blank eyes. Sometimes, I felt stronger than him; sometimes he reduced me to weakness. It was a constant struggle for supremacy between us; although for Vaysh it involved a deep fear of weakness. I just wanted to win for its own sake. I dressed myself in black leather and thin, white linen and was rather too lavish with the kohl. "You don't need that," Vaysh remarked coldly.

CHAPTER SIX

>─┤─◆〉─⊖─〈◆─┤─≺

The sacred pearl

The Red Cat was already busy when I arrived. The sun was setting in a blaze of color over the calm sea and some hara sat outside, laughing; the clink of glasses in the dusk. Not seeing anyone I recognized, I bought a mug of ale and sat down near the door. The room was much larger inside than I had anticipated and there was no sign of Kate. Absorbed in rehearsing a hundred different conversations, I did not notice Kate's friends sit down round a table nearby until they had been there for quite some time. Then one of them recognized me and called my name, beckoning me over. He had lilac hair plaited with feathers and earrings that brushed his shoulders. In fact, all of them were weighed down with gaudy jewelery. Two of them were musicians in Rue's band, which was named, somewhat esoterically, The Closets of Emily Child. They introduced themselves as Pharis and Amorel; the Har with the lilac hair was Karn. I had to fend off a rapid fire of quick-witted remarks and then a volley of salacious observations about Vaysh. Amorel asked, "Where is he?" and I replied, "It's still daylight isn't it?"

"Just . . ."

"Then he'll be in his coffin; ask later."

I did not see Rue until he walked up behind Amorel and put his hands round his neck. They all seemed pleased to see him and no wonder. The light here was much brighter than it had been in Temple Radiant and, if anything, flattered Rue more. His long, yellow hair was spiked up and crimped down his back and his face was unpainted, his skin tanned. A loose, white vest complimented his coloring and the customary black leather defined with pleasing candor, the slimness of his hips. I was virtually drooling into my ale. He must have sensed my scrutiny; one of the others looked at me and laughed. I wished Kate was there. They all knew what was going on. Rue was still draped around Amorel. He narrowed his eyes a little before he smiled at me. I found out later that his eyesight was not that good.

Pharis said, "Rue is short for Caeru, but we never call him that."

"He sings well," I said.

"He does!"

I guessed Rue was Ulani, but was unsure of his level; most probably Acantha. He did not look at me directly once after that first time.

Kate arrived about half an hour later. I had consumed several mugs of ale by that time and was feeling more relaxed. Pharis was discreetly trying to interrogate me and I was amusing myself by sidestepping his questions.

This, of course, only intrigued him more. I was talking to Pharis, flirting and teasing, but all of it was for Rue. We still had not spoken to each other and the glances we exchanged had been furtive. Kate raised her glass at me and smiled. When Pharis got up to go to the bar, Rue slid into his seat and my heart leapt into my throat.

"What did you think of the show last night?" he asked me.

I felt about fifteen again and prayed it did not show, mumbling my way through some embarrassing fatuousness, trying to remind myself, "You are not an idiot, you are a king, remember?"

Rue showed me a scar on his arm. "The spoils of inception," he said, "where's yours?" I rolled up my sleeve to show him, then remembered I no longer had a scar. If I did, it was in a place that could not be seen.

He looked at me suspiciously. "You don't have one."

I shook my head. "Not any more."

"Why?"

"It's a secret."

He rested his head on one hand. "You're different aren't you."

"Everybody's different."

"Not like you." He ran his fingers lightly over my arm. "You won't be here for long, will you?"

"No, not for long."

"Where are you going?"

"Immanion."

"I should have known." He took my hand and idly traced the lines on the palm. "Such destiny." He was only guessing.

Outside, the sky was pink and the air cooler. It was hot and noisy where we were sitting. The others had turned their backs on us.

"I'm going back to the inn now," I said. "Do you want to come?" My voice barely faltered. Rue just smiled and stood up.

We walked along the harbor and I could not think of anything to say. Rue threw stones into the sea; it was high tide. Ferelithia; the concubine of Wraeththu cities. Its ambience was that of lazy sensuality and its inhabitants were a reflection of that trait.

We came to a seat under a flowering orange tree. Rue sat down. I leaned on the sea wall and gazed at the horizon. For some reason, I felt nervous. Presently Rue joined me and our arms touched where they rested on the stone. "Kate told me some things about you," he said.

"Did she?" I must have sounded displeased.

"Yes. I lost somebody once, I know how it is. Don't feel obliged to do anything you don't want to . . ."

"Kate had no right to say anything!" I grumbled irritably.

Rue sighed and I looked at his profile staring at the sea.

"Rue, if I seem wary, it's not because of that, it's because . . . it's been a long time."

He tilted his head to look at me and I took him in my arms. His hair smelled of musk and smoke. It felt unbelievably good to hold him, something I'd forgotten. Warmth and friendship. I frantically implored heaven that Vaysh would not be still in my room when we got back. Hara walked past us; their voices muted. It was a place, a time, for closeness, and I did not want our simple embrace to end. But we started to get cold and Rue stepped back first. His eyes were saying, "I know you are different and I will give you my best. I want to keep part of you here in Ferelithia."

How thoroughly I took advantage of that.

Something about the atmosphere in my room, as if it held its breath, whispered, "What shall happen here will be almost holy." As before, the windows were held open to the night and heavy scents lingered in the air. We had taken a jug of hot coffee up with us from the bar. There was no sign of Vaysh; not even the faintest chill of his presence. We sat and smoked and drank the coffee. I ended up telling Rue all about Cal, right up until before, what I now termed, the "first death." Nothing more than that. In return, Rue told me something about himself. He had come down from the north about two years ago; Ferelithia seemed to be the goal of most Wraeththu in this country. More accessible than Immanion and very affluent. Its main trades, as in the Eastern cities of legend, were cloth-making and spice-growing. To the west of the city, a metal-work quarter was beginning to thrive. Work and money appeared to be in plentiful supply; there were no beggars on the streets of Ferelithia. In response to my query concerning the relationship between humans and hara in the town, Rue explained that it had mainly been women drawn to Ferelithia. The hedonistic easygoing Ferelith had no quarrel with anyone who was not openly hostile to them and their first reluctant tolerance of humans gradually softened to acceptance. Times had been hard in the surrounding country for women, where many human settlements, divided by civil strife and suddenly deprived of the over-civilization they were accustomed to, had regressed in temperament and life-style to something like out of the Dark Ages. What equality females had once enjoyed had been taken from them by brute force. I could sympathize deeply with those who resented the reversal of function to mere baby-machines and male pleasure-fodder. It was not surprising many had preferred to take their chances with the Wraeththu. Not that the women I'd seen in Ferelithia were soft or frightened creatures, far from it.

Rue confessed he did not like to work, not in the laboring sense, but as he was blessed with a good voice made an adequate living out of singing for the band. I asked about the name, where did it come from?

"It's an allegory," Rue explained mysteriously. "It means many things; choose your own meaning."

I like to think he guessed more about me than I told him. He knew I would go to Immanion as more than just a visitor. Half of me wanted to tell him everything, but I thought it would be unwise. Rue looked wistful when I skirted his questions. He wanted me to trust him, which I did, even on such short acquaintance, but trust was not enough.

The time came when our conversation came to an end. In the comfortable silence, Rue looked at me. We were sitting at the table.

"I was lucky to meet you," he said and stood up, lifting the white vest over his head.

I told him he was beautiful and he held out his arms for me. We were about the same height. Sharing breath had never been so easy on the neck. I think it frightened him, what he tasted within me, for he tried to pull away at first, but I would not let him. It was too pleasant for me, soaking in his warmth, his misty, sighing waves. He tasted lazy and I wanted us to meld; see him from the inside out. When he broke away from me, he kept saying my name, half in fear, half in desire. When we had scrambled out of our clothes, I said to him, "This body is virgin for you." He smiled, thinking I was a romantic fool, but it was the truth. He was soume for me; selfless compliance, and it was like coming to drink at a cool, dark pool after endless torment in a searing desert. I wanted to experience every second to the full; my body had truly come alive again. I thought, "After this, I will never be able to look at Vaysh seriously again." Perhaps he had known that; known that by experiencing something he never could, I would disregard the hold he had over me. His words could wound me no longer.

At some point, I realized my purpose, *the* purpose, for what had happened here in Ferelithia, and it did not matter that it was probably. Thiede's design. Rue tensed against me. He could tell something was happening but he didn't know what. "Pell!" he said, "Pell! What . . .?"

I put my hand on his face. "Hush," I said, "relax." I hope I did not cause him pain. Mostly, I think, he just found it strange, discovering parts of himself invaded that he did not know he had. I broke through the seal and his face flinched for a moment, but after that . . . Reality disappeared. With that unity we could have exploded the world. A microcosm flared in Rue's body, and I was the god that moved it.

CHAPTER SEVEN

>—⊱—⊙—⊰—⊰

Journey's end and the shining city

I often ask myself what made me, what exactly made me, run away so quickly. I like to think I had noble reasons, but if I had, I can't remember them. It was just an instinctive reaction. I did not want this complication; I shunned commitment of this nature. There were greater things waiting for me, after all. I said to myself, "It is Thiede's design that I should leave." I have no doubt that he deserved the blame for many things that happened to me, and would happen to me, but not everything. Thiede had become my personal (and often convenient) incarnation of Fate. All events were accountable to him. I could behave as I wished and declaim, "Oh, but it was not me; it was him!" and point the righteous, accusing finger. I can still do that now, if I wish. People will always believe me, liking as they do to believe the worst of Thiede. That is his fault. He has never exactly struggled to make himself either popular or trusted.

That morning, I woke to look at Rue's hair spread out over the white pillows; tangled and still damp at his neck, and knew instantly that I wanted to leave Ferelithia that morning; now, away from Rue. It was not, as Vaysh had predicted, because of regret; I regretted nothing. I just felt that I had fulfilled a particular path of my destiny and that was an end to it. Rue did not wake as I dressed, nor as I furtively emptied drawers of my belongings. We had had little sleep. Vaysh had left our bags under the bed. I hastily shoved all my things into them and pushed them back out of sight. I hardly dared look at Rue; I was afraid to wake him because I did not trust myself. I could not ignore the hundred screaming harpies in my head crying, "Flee!" but Rue had surrendered himself to me for that one night of bliss; he had made me happy. I don't think he knew what I had done to him. Afterwards, he had only laughed and praised my prowess, although his eyes had been shadowed with vague doubt. He would think more about that today. As I stood there, looking down on his wild beauty, I said to myself, "Rue, I will not forget you." That would be no compensation, I know, but it was the simple truth. I could so easily have reached for him again, but something stayed my hand. It was not meant to be. Perhaps he would come to hate me, or perhaps he would be glad and remember me with warmth. He did not know yet, but the fruits of our passion would linger here in Ferelithia long after I had gone. Rue had got what he wanted, but in a way he could not have imagined. He hosted the pearl that would become my son.

Vaysh was still asleep and took some time to respond to my knocking. He gave me a sleepy, contemptuous stare from around the half-open door.

"Get dressed, Vaysh, and get the horses ready to leave!" I ordered, and did not wait to watch his surprise.

Downstairs, the landlord was just preparing breakfast. None of the other guests had yet come down. I ordered coffee and bread rolls and asked for paper and a pen. Sitting by the window, looking out into the morning mist of a new day, I wrote:

Dear Kate,

I have no doubt that you will come here asking questions or looking for me. Do not be angry that I did not wait to say goodbye, or condemn me for running out on Rue. It may puzzle you that I have said that, but in time you'll understand what I mean. I know that you've probably got plans for the future which may involve leaving Ferelithia, but I would like, if you can, for you to stay here for a few months and keep an eye on Rue. I know

I've got a nerve asking you, but you remember once I said that you seemed to know more about Wraeththu than me? Well, this is something you won't have seen before and that's why I think you won't mind staying. Last night, Rue and I conceived new life. I'm afraid he doesn't know yet, and it's up to you when and if you want to tell him. I can't. I have to leave; I have no time. Finally, I want you to know that you'll always be welcome in my future home. Come to Immanion, Kate, and tell me how things went here after I'm gone. I shall leave money for you with the inn-keeper, whom I hope can be trusted. I know all this sounds very high-handed and mysterious, but when we meet again, I shall explain. I believe you shall be able to find me in Immanion quite easily.

Your friend Pellaz.

I wrote it out about three times before I was satisfied. Sentiment or something like it made me keep the other copies. One of them is reproduced above. Whatever else I wrote for her I've forgotten.

Vaysh and I rode along the coast road away from Ferelithia. Yellow beaches alive with shrieking sea-birds led down to the sea on our right. To the left, grassy dunes hid the fields that lay beyond them. Would Immanion be as beautiful or as welcoming as this place we were leaving? My heart was heavy but I had learned long before not to look back and did not turn in my saddle for one last look at the sleepy, white town whose mantle of flowers blew a haunting fragrance to us on the morning breeze. Immanion was three hundred miles or so south-east of Ferelithia; a shorter jaunt than the one we had undertaken from Samway. Vaysh was impatient to cross over to the other-lanes. He was eager to conclude our journey, but I still wanted time to mull over recent events and could only do that on solid ground. He reluctantly agreed to give me half an hour's respite and rode on ahead of me to sulk. I felt as if I was already out of this world; euphoric, yet at the same time a little sad. Soon my journey would end. On the other side of our next other-lane dash, Immanion lay waiting, waiting for me. So long ago, an ignorant peasant boy (who thought an awful lot of himself), had set out upon an adventure into an unknown world. So much had happened since then. That boy was dead. I thought of the time when I had lain beside my brother agonising over that first fateful move toward a beautiful stranger whom I had thought of as just a man caught up in a glamorous, perhaps impermanent, craze. What would I be doing now if I had not braved reaching out to him? My life would have been ordered for a time, I'm sure of that, but eventually Wraeththu would have had to touch it. Perhaps a different face of Wraeththu to the one I had been incepted to. I had been offered the best. Some suffering had come my way, but the good things outweighed it.

Riding along that road, with the tang of the sea in my nostrils and the claws of the wind in my hair, my heart rejoiced. I thanked God for everything; for Saltrock, for Cal, for Rue. I would not have lived my life any other way. Perhaps we were not as different from Mankind as we liked to think we were. Many Wraeththu would travel the same path of selfishness and greed. Within myself, I could recognize vestiges of those inherent traits. It will always be a struggle to combat these things, but it is enough just for some of us to recognize that battle. I had work to do, for my race and for the world, and I was now prepared to take on that responsibility. Ah, is that a cynical eyebrow I see raised? You must think that I had just run away from responsibility, but as an excuse, and excuse it is, I can only say that I had no time to linger. Rue had been the right person, only the place had been inopportune. I followed the current of my destiny. It would lead to a vast ocean of infinite possibilities.

Before we left Ferelithia, I had asked Vaysh to collect my luggage from my room. He had given me a knowing look but asked no questions. No doubt he thought I was wallowing in the corroding mire of regret that he'd warned me about. I did not enlighten him. He smugly disclosed that Rue had been awake when he went in. Neither of them had spoken. "He did not seem surprised to find you gone," Vaysh said demurely, obviously under the impression that Rue and I had spent a tedious night of uninspired and passionless gratification. I did not want him thinking that.

"You could learn a lot from Rue, Vaysh," I said. "He's sensual, warm, and *very* experienced."

"I don't need lessons like that!" Vaysh snapped, and I was satisfied to notice the self-congratulation drop from his face.

It was all so quick after that. A touch of minds, a shiver of power like white ice through the spine and we were up, up and slipping sideways into the otherworld night. Deadly chill smacked the breath from my lungs, a thousand screams echoing in a mind that clung to sanity only as a memory. In another world, so far from us, land shivered away from us in a shining, blurred ribbon, miles devoured, time become distance, become space. Sometimes, I felt the presence of others, whether fellow travelers or mere observers, I could not tell. I saw towers of light upon velvet blackness, pictures of the past frozen forever like photographs, but they were only memories. I could feel Peridot between my thighs, but I could not see him. He was sparkling dust. Vaysh was a curling spiral of steam, haloed by red hair. Once I think, he turned toward me for I saw twin stars that were the brightest jewels that were his eyes.

When we emerged once more, into the afternoon warmth of yet another land, we found ourselves careering down a gently-sloping, grassy hillside. Tall, white-barked trees with supple branches of pointed leaves that swayed like hair in the sussurating breeze, gathered together as if for company on the grass. Small, white flowers starred the sward. Where the ground evened out below us, a sun-speckled forest of widely-spaced trees was divided by a white-paved road. At intervals, statues stood like sentinels along its edge.

"Well," said Vaysh, good-humored again, at least for a while, until the madness of the other-lanes deserted him, "the road to Immanion, Pell."

The horses had slowed to a prancing walk and my heart began to pound. I did not know how I was to be received in the city. Did they know we were coming? Would the streets be thronged with cheering hara and the air flutter with petals? I hoped we could make a quiet entrance. I could not organize myself to prepare for a public spectacle.

Immanion was not as near as I imagined, however. Vaysh and I had been riding along the white road for an hour or more before the trees thinned out completely and the fields and farms of Immanion's lands appeared. A faint whiff of the sea blew toward us from the distance.

"You are nervous," Vaysh observed; a smile, straining to be expressed, hovered at the corners of his mouth.

"Yes," I sighed. "None of it seemed quite real until now."

"You were too preoccupied," Vaysh commented acidly. There was a familiar echo in his voice that made me look at him.

"Why does it bother you?" I asked. "I presume you're referring to Rue?"

Vaysh's fingers clawed his hair; it was always a gesture that signaled his discomfort. "To be honest with you, Pell," and here he paused, his face twitching with reluctance. I dreaded what he might be about to say. "I think it's because I nurtured you, made you live. You've always wanted to know this; here it is. Thiede materialized your flesh through the power of his will. Exact, precise and perfect. He remembered you well, didn't he? The only differences in you are that your slight imperfections have been smoothed away. Thiede said to me, the day he showed me what he'd created, 'Vaysh, this is your charge. This is Pellaz. He will be your king. He will be your life.' I was angry at first. For so long my home had been with Thiede. Now he was sending me away. I was not good enough for his purposes; now he had you. He was impatient with my bitterness. 'Pellaz must always have you,' he said. 'Your fidelity must be complete.' He did not mean, by that, that we should be close, the kind of close I can see you are thinking of; that was not my place. I was to attend your body like a servant, whilst you needed it, and after that, I was to be your confidante, your friend. After a while, it seemed as if it had been I that had made you. As if you had sprung from within me . . ."

I could not think of a single, suitable thing to say. That Vaysh had opened up to me like this was enough to stun me to silence, but I knew his revelations deserved a response.

"Vaysh, I. . . . Why did you not speak before? I would never have guessed from the way you've . . . behaved."

His eyes were dark as they stabbed me with reproach. "You know how I am; mostly dead inside. What feelings I have make me uncomfortable. Oh, it's something different with you; it has to be. Thiede's made you so much better than all the rest of us. You are his son—or as good as. Everyone wants you in some way, everyone! And you took that mouthy little roughy-toughie. . . !"

"Vaysh!" I could not stop myself laughing. His opinion of Rue, though cruel, was not altogether inaccurate.

He smiled back at me in a thin sort of way. "Yes, I amaze you don't I. Most of the time I'm jealous *of* you, with all your pompous warmth, goodness and beauty, which in itself is mind-numbingly sickening, but sometimes I'm jealous for you; all that you had with the incomparable Cal, and then with that . . . well, there are no words for that. What on earth possessed you?"

I felt it would not be a good time to disclose that Rue, for all his unplaned edges, now carried my son.

Vaysh mistook my silence for something else. "I see. Aren't you supposed to be elevated above all that now? I'd like to say, 'You could have had me,' but I can't. All that's gone now."

"Why is it, Vaysh?" I asked gently. "What has Thiede done to you?"

He gave me a sad smile. "Oh, Pellaz. You know. You've suspected haven't you? I'm burnt out. At best, barren and at worst gutted. No, you were not the first . . ."

My stomach shivered and writhed. There but for the grace of God, or Fortune . . . "I'm glad you told me this," I said. It was inadequate, but I could think of nothing else at the time.

"I'm sure you are," Vaysh replied bitterly.

I was beginning to understand the maelstrom of pain, frustration, panic and helplessness that was the essential Vaysh, but only a little. I was too privileged in my own circumstances to fully comprehend.

Then it was before us: white walls towering and crystalline, and the city itself; rearing like restless foam of sea-stallions into the cerulean blue of the sky. Towers, pillars and minarets convoluting, spearing, in a purity of grace. Immanion; first city of Wraeththu.

Vast gates in the walls were paneled with jet. They stood open. There was no guard. When I commented on this. Vaysh gave a dry laugh. Immanion did not need that kind of protection. No one would ever get this close who was not welcome. I wondered if Kate would ever be able to find her way here.

The streets were peopled by the most elegant and ethereal hara I had ever seen. If a man had ever chanced to find his way here, he would believe he had found the kingdom of heaven and was in the company of angels. A great atmosphere of tranquility calmed my thudding heart. It was hard to imagine the Wraeththu here cheering anyone. We rode into the city on our fine and magical horses, with their curving heads and proud steps, and the hara we met nobly inclined their heads to us as we passed. I'm sure that many of them (if they knew who we were), mistook Vaysh for their king and I for his companion. He looked impressively regal, riding just ahead of me. Immanion is a large city by any standards, but especially so to me as I was at that time. Riding through those evenly spaced wide avenues, I was

overawed by the grace and symmetry of the white buildings around me,
mystified by the utter calm and fragrance of the air. It seemed that Cal's
dream had been based on reality, for surely I now rode along the streets he
had once imaginatively described to me. Immanion felt as if it had stood
a thousand years, yet, of course, its age was only the minutest fraction of
that. How had Thiede done it?

Near the sea, in the heart of the city, a wooded hill afforded privacy to
the half-seen building that rested upon its crown.

Vaysh pointed, "Look Pellaz, forget the huts of Saltrock, the tents of the
Kakkahaar, even the human cast-offs of the Varrs; this is your new home."

It is not easy to describe. Not easy to do it justice. A list of words
presents itself: elegance, space, height, echoes, gold, black, white crystal,
silence, music. Terraces and rows of slim pillars. Patios of black and white
marble. The palace had a name, as all places of fable should: Phaonica. It
had a proud, female ambience. It was easy to turn to Vaysh though, and
communicate without even speaking; "I think I shall be very happy here."

We rode up the hill and through the fantastic hanging gardens, past the
cataracting fountains, the temples whose only function was ornament.
Hara tending the grounds, lowered their eyes as we rode by, and made, with
their hands, the genuflections of respect. I had come home.

My staff awaited us. Cordially, without fuss, our horses were led away
and Vaysh and I led into Phaonica. Up a snowy crest of steps, between
shadowed pillars, along lofty corridors, up more flights of steps. I could not
take it all in. It was a fairy-tale place; somber without brooding, shady
without darkness. Naturally, the first thing that our attendants wanted to
do for us, was to prepare the scented baths that would erase from our
bodies the memory of our journey. Vaysh had been allocated a suite of
rooms within my own apartments, which included his own bathroom presumably, for we were separated. My two servants were strange, elfin creatures with piebald skin, which may have been tattooed, and thick, black
hair. They introduced themselves as Cleis and Attica. I was still gawping
with wonder at my surroundings, but they passed no comment on my
stupor. My clothes were removed with downcast eyes; fragrant oils poured
into the bath-water. All the rooms were simple in design, high-ceilinged and
with painted walls. The prevailing colors were dark red, brown and gold.

"What have you been told about me?" I asked the har who lathered my
hair. He was clearly not sure how to answer.

"Our lord came to us and told us to make these rooms ready for
occupation. He has kept them empty since the palace was built. He said to
us, 'Your king is coming; I have chosen him.' That was all."

I did not have to ask who their lord was. "Is he here," I asked.

"We have not seen him," was the careful reply.

They dressed me in an elegant costume of black gauze. My hair was
crimped with hot irons, but when they asked what cosmetics I preferred, I
shook my head. "Nothing, thank you." And what food did I desire?
Anything, I wasn't bothered. Wine? Yes, anything. I kept getting faint

reminders of Mur and Garis. Did I detect just the faintest shade of mockery in their ministrations? None of this felt comfortable. Thiede had said to them, "Make sure you treat him well," and they were doing so, but it was Thiede who gave the orders, that was clear. I felt like a dressed-up doll to be exhibited in a position of prominence. "Ah yes," Thiede would say to his Nahir-Nuri peers, "and this is my latest creation." But I was Nahir-Nuri too, wasn't I? Although I felt no different. It was crucial for me to speak with Thiede as soon as possible, I decided. My role was vague. What must I do now?

I exercised my powers for the first time and asked Attica and Cleis to leave me alone. It was almost a surprise when they complied, backing, soft-footed from my presence. I spent some time investigating my rooms. There was nothing lacking. I found a bed-chamber which appeared to have been inspired from the pages of myth, two reception rooms, a library well-stocked with an eclectic array of titles (the literature of both Man and Wraeththu), and several other chambers whose function had not yet been ascribed. Glass doors in the outer wall of my bedroom led to a marble terrace which overlooked the sea. I went out there and leaned on the wall. To my left the terrace led to another door in the white walls. It was open. Inside, I could see Vaysh brushing his hair at a mirror. He must have been able to see me in it, but did not turn round as I approached.

"Do you think Thiede is here?" I asked him and threw myself down on his bed.

"Don't be inelegant, Pellaz. As for your question, I don't know. But if he isn't, he soon will be." Vaysh's steely defences were securely back in place.

"You look nice, Vaysh," I said.

He threw me a look of practiced disdain. "I always *look* nice," he said.

I was beginning to think more and more as Phade did; suffering an overwhelming desire to break through the ice. Vaysh was unconsciously seductive in his glacial loveliness, but he was also the only familiar face to me in Immanion. I was feeling insecure and needed warmth; Vaysh's manner was tiresome. I could not see why he should want to keep it up after our conversation on the road.

"I thought you were supposed to be my friend," I teased him. He shook his head, but covered his face with his hair so I could not see him smiling.

"Remember who you are," he said.

"And what's that, Vaysh?"

He looked up at me then and an unspoken thought passed between us. He shrugged. "It has to be faced Pell. This is Thiede's world now. We all just dance to his tune." (Phade had said that.)

"What if it's not our kind of music?" I asked.

Vaysh sat next to me. "Don't talk like that, there's no point."

He was dressed in green again. I put my hand tentatively on his back and the material was warm; which surprised me. He let me stroke him, like cats do when they're in the mood. It was possible to pretend, but I was sensible enough not to push it too far. I couldn't tell if he liked me touching him.

"What has Thiede got planned for me?" I asked.

"You will have to ask him."

"I intend to. Do you suppose he is watching us now?" Vaysh looked over his shoulder at me.

"It's best not to think about that, Pell."

"Make me think of something else then," I said. It slipped out before common-sense could block my throat. Vaysh kept on looking at me, straining his neck, but I still could not tell what he was thinking.

"I thought you were in mourning," he remarked. Perhaps he was trying to make me feel guilty, or perhaps he just wanted me to say that Cal was no longer important. Whatever the reason, it was pointless after what he knew about Rue.

"The truth is, Vaysh," I said, "that the time to mourn is sometime in the dead of night, alone, in bed. That's when I think, or get lonely. Nobody will ever take Cal's place, nobody. But don't think me shallow because I want company. I am Har; end of statement." I felt him sigh, through my hand.

"I can't help you," he said. "I'm not even sure if I want to. Oh Pellaz, I thought I'd got myself in order! What are you trying to do to me?"

"I don't think you're as cold or unfeeling as you like people to think," I suggested carefully. He did not comment. "Perhaps," I continued, "living with Thiede it was easy to imagine that you were . . ." He still did not move away. Every time I said something, I expected him to. I was desperate to bring out the real Vaysh; but my motives were not entirely unselfish. I could sense his confusion and only lay there, projecting all the sensuality Thiede had given me, tormenting him.

"I don't know," he murmured, his hands clawing each other in his lap. "I don't know . . ." I still did not appreciate how deeply he had been scarred. Wriggling around on the bed, I put my head in his lap (his hands flew up to his neck), and stared up through his hair.

"What color is it, naturally?" I asked, reaching up to put my fingers in it. Vaysh's face was so grave.

"Light colored," he said.

"The color of light . . ."

"No, just sort of yellowish, only darker . . ." Evening light shadowed his face. He stroked my face with his cool, white hands. "No more than this, Pell," he said, in his softest, gravest voice. I closed my eyes and smiled.

CHAPTER EIGHT

> ━ ⊹ ⟨⟩ ⊙ ⟨⟩ ⊹ ━

On the plans of the Hegemony and shattering ice

I could not remember where I was at first, waking up alone, opening my eyes to the swaying canopy above my bed. Then I smelled the air, purer than any other I had ever breathed. I had closed all the windows before retiring; someone had been in to open them. For a while I just lay there, staring at the fluttering folds of muslin over my head. My room did not catch the morning sun (an oversight?); outside the terrace was in shadow. I tried to imagine what it would have been like if Cal had been here with me; vividly picturing his cynical amusement. He would never have been comfortable here, not under these circumstances. I realized that when the time came for me to find him again, I would be ashamed to admit what Thiede had made of me. I feared his scorn.

Attica, or Cleis (I could not tell which, as they both looked the same to me), knocked on my door and entered the room without waiting for my answer. Breakfast awaited me. Would I dress first? I shook my head, reached for a robe to cover my nakedness and walked out ahead of him.

The table was decorated with flowers. Their incense perfume filled the room. Seating myself at the head of the table, I requested that Vaysh should join me. I was already eating by the time he sat down. As expected, the food was elegant and meticulously prepared, meticulously designed. Vaysh was robed in his favorite green and still sleepy. I had noticed it always took some time for him to wake up properly.

"Thiede will summon you today, I expect," he said, helping himself to minute portions of the food. I put my hand over his wrist and he looked at it with interest.

"You no longer stop me touching you, I see," I remarked.

He managed a bleak smile. "I trust you," he said. "I wonder what Thiede will say to you."

"I'm wondering what to say to him," I replied bitterly.

Cleis and Attica brought us coffee in a tall metal pot and cleared away the food before we could help ourselves to more.

"They appear to be hurrying," Vaysh observed. His meal had only been half-eaten.

Right on cue, the door swept open and my attendants all but threw themselves to the floor. Thiede, dressed in black and gray wolfskin, strode past them.

"Good morning Pellaz, Vaysh," he announced. "Ah coffee, good."

He sat at our table and snapped his fingers. My attendants moved in a blur to fill his outstretched hand with a brimming cup haloed by steam.

"Do you like your new home, Pellaz?" He looked around him. "I'm pleased with these apartments; they've turned out very well."

I was silent, remembering all too clearly the last time we had met. It was difficult to equate that kind of Thiede with the one who sat here now though. Less awesome, he appeared to have put aside the trappings of terrible power; no-one could exist comfortably like that all the time. Thiede is very hard to look at directly, because his beauty is so alien and stark. It is easier to look at his nose (aquiline, with delicately flared nostrils, of course), or his amber eyes or his cruel yet smiling mouth, but difficult to take in everything altogether. He is taller than most hara and his flaming red hair looks dyed, which it isn't. From the history books of Man, the nearest people I can compare him to are Salome and Alexander the Great combined in one body, with a dash of the witch Medea and the magician Merlin for good measure. He is deadly, but lovely, a little insane but clever. Shrewd Hara take great pains never to offend him although, mercifully, he rarely takes offense at anything.

Vaysh stood up and excused himself from our presence. Left alone with me, Thiede stared thoughtfully into my eyes for several harrowing minutes.

"I'm very pleased with you," he said.

"You compliment only yourself," I replied.

Thiede threw back his head to laugh. "Oh, you have such spirit, Pellaz. You are ninety percent yourself and ten percent me, if that much. I expect you feel obliged to be annoyed at how I've taken control of your fate . . ."

I did not answer. Thiede looked at me wryly. "I shall arrange a coronation for you. That will be an excuse for a celebration. I do so like celebrations, don't you? Your title will be Tigron; Tigron of Immanion and of Wraeththu." He folded his arms which had been gesticulating wildly.

"Forgive my ignorance, Thiede, but what exactly *is* my purpose? You are the true ruler of Wraeththu, that's obvious. Why do you need me?"

The smile never moved from his face. "I need you because you will rule *well*, Pellaz. I'm not interested enough to spend all my time attending to the affairs of the little hara. You must have seen; they are in such a mess. They need government, central government."

I put aside further objections to comment on what I thought was his simplistic view of things. "Thiede, I hate to sound pessimistic, but has it ever occured to you that the majority of the tribes of Wraeththu, who most need controlling, will fanatically resist anyone trying to wrest their autonomy away from them?"

He leaned forward and squeezed my arm. "Ah, Pellaz, this is what I was looking forward to! Your rational little mind wrestling with the problems of administration!"

"Thiede, there must be a hundred Gelaming capable, and more knowledgeable than I, of becoming Tigron. I don't understand; why me? All this fuss, what you put me through, what is it for?"

Thiede affected an expression of being downcast. "Pellaz, what must I do with all the power at my command? Call it a whim, if you like, but I had the desire to make you what you are. I wanted a new start, a new king, a stranger. Someone like you. You are still young, but I have always been able to see your potential."

I leaned back in my chair. "That is reasonable, I suppose. I hope you are right about me."

"I am. Now, as to the problems of establishing order that you mentioned. For the most part, of course, our authority must be implemented by force; distasteful though such measures are to the Gelaming. There are trouble spots, that must be cut out, and swiftly. You will have under your control an impressively adequate army; you shall meet your generals later. Obviously, major decisions of a strategic nature must be left to them. The majority of our tribes, however, will welcome my organization. Everyone shall benefit." He took a few mouthfuls of the coffee, staring out of the window. "I must begin to spend more time here in Immanion," he said. "It is the jewel of Wraeththu cities."

"Thiede," I began, having been thinking of it for some minutes, "how much of my life is an open book to you?"

He carefully replaced his coffee cup on the table. "You don't smoke much, do you." He removed a slim cigarette case from a top pocket. "This is one of the advantages of our hygiene-conscious bodies. They clean up after everything, even tar."

He offered me one and I accepted.

"These luxuries were not always available to me," I said, leaning forward to the flame he offered me. "Why won't you answer me?"

Thiede fidgetted in his seat. "Some sacrifices are necessary, for someone in your position, Pellaz."

"Privacy being the first of them, I suppose?"

"The very first." He inhaled deeply and blew perfect smoke rings at the ceiling. "I had to study you, to be sure."

"And since?"

He smiled and reached to pat my cheek. "Not always, my dear, not always. You handled Vaysh with princely sensitivity last night, though. You have a knack of getting your own way with people, haven't you; of making them love you. I'm very proud."

"Thiede, don't ever watch me with anyone," I insisted, "It can't be necessary now."

He raised an eyebrow at my audacity. "True, true; but I enjoy it. Vaysh is an interesting creature. Why didn't you reintroduce his miserable frigidity to the delights of aruna? He's not as disabled as he likes to make out."

I cannot understand why I was still shocked by anything Thiede could say. "I'm not going to discuss Vaysh with you," I said. "Whatever you did to him was despicable, merciless . . ."

"How do you know that?"

"He told me . . . some of it."

Thiede sighed. "Ah, well, what happened to Vaysh was an accident;

unfortunate, but still. . . . He's yours Pellaz. Do as you like with him. Be liberal with the famous healing touch and the ever attentive ears. . . . A pleasing challenge, I'm sure." He stood up. "Take time to relax, this morning. Have someone bring you to my apartments for lunch. Then I can introduce you to your staff."

"All of them at once?!" I cried.

"Oh, Pellaz, Pellaz; you are of my flesh, my blood, my essence. All these Hara are below you and you must believe that. They are naturally wary of you, but I have every confidence that you shall win them over." He squeezed my shoulder. "Until later then."

After he had left me, Vaysh came back into the room. "I listened at the door," he said.

"You and Thiede have a lot in common, it seems," I retorted, but I was not angry with him. Now I would not have to repeat everything, although some things I would have preferred Vaysh not to hear. "I am not what Thiede thinks I am," I complained.

"Think positively," Vaysh replied. "It is fairly safe to assume Thiede knows better than you."

My attendants reappeared and inquired whether I needed assistance to dress. Why not? I thought. I sneakily enjoyed being pampered.

"It's your birth-sign," Vaysh said scathingly.

I had found a box of jewelery in my bedroom and gave Attica and Cleis a different earring each. That way I could recognize them by looking at their ears. They thanked me effusively, the earrings must have been worth a fortune. I was no expert; cheap and expensive generally looked the same to me. Attica was the most talkative of the two. Because of the gift, he offered me some advice.

"It is not my place to say this, of course, but watch out for the one called Ashmael. He will try to trip you up."

"What, literally?" I had visions of flying, head first, into Thiede's apartments.

Attica did not laugh. "The word is, he disagrees with Thiede bringing you here. It is only rumor, of course, but many think he would have liked to see himself as Tigron of Immanion. No disrespect to you, my lord, but there are others who will say that he deserved the title; he is popular."

"Thank you, Attica," I said, awkwardly. Obviously, if spoiled, my two attendants were going to prove a fertile source of information. However, I was not blind to the fact that it could work two ways; I would have to watch my tongue. I asked them what their duties were and where they lived. It appeared that, since my arrival, their sole function was to attend to my needs. At present, they resided in a humbler region of the palace.

"It would be more convenient, I think, if you were to move into one of the empty rooms here," I said. They exchanged a glance of surprise.

"You have means of summoning us if necessary, my lord," Attica explained.

"All the same; I think it would be better," I said.

The rest of the morning was spent investigating my rooms. Vaysh assisted me, looking into every drawer and cupboard.

"It's amazing," he said. "You have everything; it's almost as if someone lived here before."

Thiede's apartments were similar to my own, except rather untidy. At lunchtime, I was conducted to his dining room, nervous and wary; I had no idea what to expect. Thiede obviously had his own reasons for not briefing me more thoroughly. Perhaps he believed in throwing people in at the deep end. Half a dozen Gelaming hara were already seated there and all went quiet when I entered the room. Thiede, at the head of the table, stood up, dressed simply, looking breathtaking, as usual. "Tiahaara," he announced grandly, "May I introduce Pellaz to you." This was met with stony silence. They all stared at me, but not one of them smiled. Thiede was not discouraged. "Pellaz, you must get to know these hara. They shall be working very closely with you." A prospect that was not greeted with pleasure on either side.

He introduced them as Cedony, Tharmifex, Dree, Eyra, Glave and Chrysm. No Ashmael. I sat down, braced for a trying meal. It was obviously not going to be an easy task winning acceptance from this lot, that was clear. More than likely, they were all supporters of the absent Ashmael.

"How much do you know of governmental procedures?" the one called Tharmifex asked me. He had long, pink and black hair which contrasted rather strongly with his taciturn expression.

"Nothing at all," I replied, thinking honesty was the best policy. Thiede was watching me through slitted eyes (what was he up to?), his head resting on his hand. Was he praying I would not let him down? This was a test of fire, which he could have made easier for me if he'd wanted to. Perhaps he realized his confidence in me was premature.

"Nothing at all, eh?" Dree remarked, throwing a weary glance at Thiede.

"He shall learn," Thiede drawled, not moving his position. "None of us came into this situation with vast knowledge, but we've coped. We need fresh minds, and this particular mind is of the finest quality."

"Being your own?" someone asked; I didn't notice who. Thiede laughed theatrically.

"It gives you such sport to inject my motives with cunning, doesn't it!"

"I shall try to fulfill my purpose," I said, realizing with shame how small and young my voice sounded.

"But do you know what it is?" This was Cedony, leaning forward over the table. I appealed to Thiede with my eyes, which he would not meet.

Tharmifex was seated next to me and turned in his seat to speak. Kind-hearted, he appreciated my difficulty. "We have no end of problems to solve," he said, taking the chance to assess me without appearing impolite.

"Thiede has told me a little about the outline of your plans," I said. "To unite Wraeththu into one nation. Is that possible?" Thiede's servant poured me wine, which was livid purple, and I sipped it nervously.

"The scale of this thing *is* vast," Tharmifex admitted. "But with co-operation from other tribes, not impossible. As a race, we desperately *need* organization. If something isn't done soon, it may be too late. We are a young race and for that reason, no-one has really become set in their ways. The way must be outlined as soon as possible."

"I have traveled around a little," I said. "So I can understand some of the problems you're likely to encounter. I should imagine some tribes won't be that enthusiastic about the idea."

"Mmm," Tharmifex murmured eloquently. "One thing I must stress though, we are not advocating mere oligarchy. The trouble with the world, or the civilized world as we know it, which at this time constitutes Almagabra and Megalithica, is that as throughout time, a few individuals of unscrupulous nature have seized power. They do not realize it, but they are a threat to Wraeththu existence. The Gelaming do not believe that we were put on this Earth to continue in the same way that mankind did."

"It is time wasted," Dree put in, "that spent on pursuing selfish ventures. This world has been neglected. It needs attention, not further abuse."

During these words, visions of the Varrs kept flashing before my eyes, but it was obviously not just of them that they spoke. "What we wish ultimately to initiate," Tharmifex told me, "is a world council of tribes, although that term is a little deceptive. Our own country and the continent west are what we mean by that. That is where the strongest Wraeththu tribes exist. At the moment, we can plan no further than that. It will require more than enough diplomacy and planning to achieve results in these two countries. But if we succeed, we will have something to build on."

The first course of the meal was brought in to us; savory soup made of shellfish, and fresh, warm bread.

"How do you anticipate beginning this campaign?" I asked Thiede.

"Well, that depends on how long it takes us to get properly organized. Naturally, I have other matters to attend to as well . . . Dree, where is Ashmael?" There was an uncomfortable silence. "Oh, I *see!*" Thiede said archly. "He is punishing me by his absence. If I was more suspicious, I would doubt his faith in my authority."

"Thiede," Dree cajoled. "You know Ashmael, always a law unto himself!"

"Yes," Thiede remarked drily, "his contrived waywardness has not escaped me." Thiede looked at me. "Unfortunately, the Ashmael we speak of is a brilliant strategist, a fearless warrior and a cunning diplomat. You will need his talents, Pellaz despite the fact (which I regret), that he may not be too willing to let you use them."

"I know about that; I've heard rumors," I said.

"Already?" Tharmifex grinned. "Something tells me it will be quite entertaining when you two come to cross swords."

"Metaphorically speaking, I trust," Thiede observed. "I will speak to him."

"Again?!" This was Chrysm speaking. Of all of them, I found out that he was the least sympathetic with Ashmael. "He is an infernal egotist! Because he had proved useful to you in the past, Thiede, he imagines you will condone all the absurdities of his behavior!" Chrysm was younger than the others. They looked at him with mild displeasure; his face was red.

Thiede stared at him for a moment and then smiled at me. "Ah, well, enough of that," he said to change the subject. "I've got some news for you, Pellaz; good news. An old friend of yours will be coming here to join your staff."

My stomach lurched, but I should have known better. "Who?"

"Seel, from Saltrock. I've always admired him. He has an enterprising spirit and these last few years have planed the edge off his temper."

I had never thought him bad-tempered, but I was surprised at Thiede's choice. "Seel? That's odd, I thought Orien, from Saltrock, would have been more suitable, if anyone."

Thiede took a deep breath and looked down at his plate. "Yes, you are right of course. Unfortunately . . . Orien is no longer with us; he is dead."

If you have ever received news like that, unexpectedly, you will appreciate how I felt; breathless and cold.

"How?" I demanded. "What happened?" Visions of a smoking Saltrock blackened my mind.

"Well, I . . . I'm not exactly sure," Thiede said, still not looking at me (that alone should have alerted me.) "Seel will be able to tell you."

What I thought he meant was, "I'm not exactly interested; Seel will be able to tell you."

"Why does Seel want to leave Saltrock?" I asked, my voice too urgent.

"He doesn't. I want him to. He's wasted there. We need hara of his caliber here in Immanion. Anyway, he won't be here for a while yet . . ."

"We have to improve communications," Tharmifex put in, impatient with what he thought were personal matters. Obviously, communication with Saltrock had proved a problem.

"Our technologists are working on it, Thar, as you know," Thiede drawled wearily, as if he had said that a hundred times.

Tharmifex flashed him an irritated glance. "I was about to explain things to your protégé actually, our proposed Tigron. I believe he will need to know about these things?"

Thiede inclined his head, smirking at the sarcasm. *"Please,* carry on." He leaned back in his seat and gazed out of the window. Tharmifex stared at him for a few moments before turning back to me.

"Clearly, in order to achieve any kind of union between the tribes of Wraeththu, we have to establish a reliable, far-reaching communication system," he began. "War, rioting, inexplicable dissolution; these factors have all contributed to virtually destroying those systems used by man, and as some areas no longer have access to the power supplies needed to run them, a completely new kind of communication network is called for. I'm sure I don't really need to tell you that we've not yet had the time to assess what may be salvaged of the world's technology and resources. It is a sad fact that many of the newly-incepted hara neglected their education; events conspired against them. Their belief was what use is knowledge of the old world when they are full of the fire of the new. It was an exciting and frightening time when Wraeththu first stepped out into the light, so to speak. Anyway, the situation now is that we believe all the finest, most capable minds Wraeththu have to offer are being summoned to Immanion. The Gelaming have been scouting around for some years . . ."

"Second to communication then, is education," Dree put in. "But that will have to come later, of course."

Tharmifex nodded. "Mmm. Fortunately, we think it will be possible to use our natural powers, those things that most Hara have been eager to explore and develop, to achieve things that Mankind had to carry out through science and machinery. Namely, our innate gifts for telepathy and telekinesis. Our technologists are working on an idea for communication involving the amplification of thought, the main problem being that over a long distance, this may not be effective for hara of lower caste. We shall arrange, as soon as possible, for you to speak with the technologists, so you may understand more fully."

"Representatives from Olopade, Unneah, Sulh, Colurastes and Smalt will be arriving here soon for talks," Thiede said to stem Tharmifex's enthusiasm. "Once we have outlined our plans and are confident of their co-operation, we can begin to devise a program for world domination!" He laughed. I suppose that was a joke.

"At no time, Pell," he continued, pointing a curved claw at me, "underestimate the scale of our proposal. It is vast, it will take time, and doubtlessly, lives as well. As Gelaming, we scorn the taking of life, but it would be naive to think we won't have to fight for our beliefs. Therefore, as with everything Gelaming put their minds to, our army is the best; the finest, fittest, fearless hara you could hope to gather under one banner."

Tharmifex laughed, unexpectedly. "If our Lord Thiede could remove his tongue from his cheek for long enough, I feel sure he could impress upon you that we will be well prepared for what faces us when the time comes. I wish we had more time to educate you, Pellaz; we need years really, and I fear we shall have only months . . ."

"Are you joking?!" Thiede exclaimed. "You'll have your years to indoctrinate him, Thar, you know that."

"I only know that we anticipate having years of preparation; we have no way of ensuring that the Varrs and their kind will allow that."

Thiede made a dismissive gesture. "Trust me, Thar, we'll hold them off for as long as it takes. Don't be frightened of Megalithica because of its size; it's a mess."

Tharmifex was clearly anxious not to continue this conversation in front of me. I had a feeling it was one that he and Thiede had had many times before.

"You must be able to talk to the other tribes' representatives as if you know what you're speaking about," Tharmifex said to me. "I'll give you a couple of days to settle in. After that, your education must begin in earnest."

As we ate the meal, I assessed what I had learned. Of the hegemony of Immanion, Tharmifex and Chrysm seemed the most inclined to assist me. The others barely spoke at all, but I was aware of their scrutiny. Chrysm reminded me of Seel; the same eyes, I think. Tharmifex probably disapproved of me in principle, but was prepared to wait for me to prove myself, one way or the other. I discovered later that he was Thiede's oldest friend and was, therefore, obliged to agree with him to a degree. The others were all staunch followers of Ashmael. The Gelaming had long since got their own country in order and Ashmael had been mainly responsible for that. It was not a large country, Almagabra (as I had learned it was named); bordered to the north, east and west by mountain ranges, the south open to the sea. Being an old race, and therefore sensitive to the true nature of Wraeththu, Almagabra's human population had not struggled too violently to maintain a hold on their lands, discouraged more by superstitious awe than anything else. Ashmael had organized the survivors (and there were many), giving them control of land to the north. They were councilled, naturally, by Wraeththu, but governed fairly and left, for the most part, to their own devices.

"Their women are barren, however," Tharmifex told me. "So we envisage a time when their aging population will become something of a burden."

"How come the women are barren?" I asked.

"Well," Tharmifex replied. "That is something that rests only in the hands of God."

I looked at Thiede, who glanced at the ceiling, whistling casually.

Gelaming technology is a strange marriage of the barbaric and splendid and advanced science, or para-science. Their architecture is classical, rhythmic and spacious, reminiscent of a much earlier time in the world's history and they have a fondness for labor-saving gadgets which sometimes sit uneasily in the lofty, camerated chambers of their homes. As with all civilized Wraeththu, the Gelaming have a love of beauty and harmony in their environment, and a great affinity for ceremony and ritual. Everybody seems to talk in long, carefully constructed sentences. Slang is rarely used. Cal would have considered them elitist and too concerned with appearances of all kinds.

I spent several hours in Thiede's dining room, watching and listening, and was in a thoughtful mood as I followed Thiede's servant back to my own apartments. There were so many people I had to meet and at the moment I was ill-equipped to discuss with them the things they felt so passionate about. Thus the thought would spring to their minds: where is Ashmael? Why is he not taking charge? It was easy for me to see why, even if the Gelaming couldn't. Thiede would have had a hard time controlling Ashmael as Tigron. Whatever meandering rubbish he fed me about my being "right" for the part, I knew the truth; he wanted only someone he could manipulate; someone whom he had formed, moulded, someone who was nearly himself.

I dismissed Thiede's servant at the doors to my rooms. They were huge, but opened silently. Beyond them, a skylit corridor led to the main salon, punctuated by doors to different chambers. The floor was pale, green marble. Large, dark, shiny ornamental vases filled with rushes and feathers stood in alcoves; statues posed unselfconsciously, half in shadow. I was anxious to discuss with Vaysh all that I had heard. His comments, though dry, were always sensible. I could feed all my confused thoughts into him and get them repeated back to me in some kind of order. I expected to find him in the main room. He had planned to spend the afternoon there, reading. I saw someone lounging on a low couch, idly leafing through one of Vaysh's books, but it was not Vaysh. He paused a moment (too long for politeness) before glancing up. I was presented with a face both elegant and bored, an expression laden with challenge.

"You must be Ashmael," I said, walking over to the couch so I could look down on him. "What are you doing here?" It was not the wittiest thing I could have said, under the circumstances.

"I'm here to see you, of course," he answered in a cultured voice, flavored by an accent I could not identify.

"You were expected at Thiede's for lunch, I believe," I said. "I've just come from there."

"I know," he drawled, sitting up, putting down the book, stretching. "There is a rumour going round, that Thiede actually *made* you. Is it true?" He did not concern himself with hiding his contempt.

"Believe as you like," I countered. "It is of no importance to me."

"You're pretty, yes; pretty. That's not enough, you know." He stood up and towered over me by some inches. "Don't think I'm unaware of why Thiede has brought you here. You won't be Tigron; Thiede will. He's too selfish or too greedy to surrender any of his power.

"You're just his puppet, you know. A glamorous sovereign for the people to fawn over so they won't get in Thiede's way. But it will be his words on your tongue all the time."

"Listen," I said in a low voice, but unconsciously moving away from his invasion of my space. "I'm not going to play any of your fucking games!"

His face hardened, almost imperceptibly. "Where do you come from? What antediluvian tribe spawned you?" His calm disdain was electric. His eyes steadily sought to hold my own; it was a simple technique, the most primitive of occult attacks.

I turned my back on him. "If you don't like the situation, I don't give a damn. Think what you like of me and enjoy it! Now get out!"

"I'll leave when I choose to," he said defensively. I mustered my strengths and turned back to face him.

"No, you won't. Attica!" I knew Ashmael would be loath to squabble with me in front of a servant and praised the moment when I had asked Attica and Cleis to move in with me. I could feel Attica hovering uncertainly behind me. "Escort Tiahaar Ashmael to the door," I said.

"You will regret this, I think," Ashmael said quietly.

"Save your complaints for Thiede, I feel sure he will be interested," I said with a smile. Ashmael uttered a furious snort and stalked out. Attica visibly flinched as he passed.

Perhaps my hostility had been too immediate. That, in itself, was a victory for Ashmael. Maybe I should have handled him differently; attempted to win him over. He was a forceful opponent and very strong. One show of weakness on my part and he would defeat me. I sat down on the couch, alarmed at how much I was shaking. I must learn to control myself, discipline my inner strengths. If I couldn't then I deserved to be beaten. This was no game of social etiquette; this concerned the future of our race. I needed the test to prove myself. To be Tigron, I had to be stronger than all the rest. Yet I was not too naive to recognize the seeds of truth in Ashmael's words. I was young and my position was uncertain; obviously not one from which to make a stand, because I knew so little. All I could do was be alert and absorb what I could.

Vaysh put his head around the door; his face was white. I imagined I understood why.

"He's gone," I said.

"Thank God!" Vaysh came into the room and sat down on the edge of a chair opposite me. "I must confess, Pell, I'm displeased, grieved, to find Ashmael here. I had hoped he might have moved on."

"Do you know him then?" It was disquieting to see Vaysh upset.

"Once, once I did." His hands were clawing his hair. "A long, long time ago and I was different then. It was . . . very awkward when he just walked in here."

I went to kneel by Vaysh's chair. "How intriguing, are you going to tell me more?" Vaysh sidled away from me.

"You sound like *them.*"

"Vaysh, this is not like you."

"No."

"Are you going to tell me?"

"No. . . . At least . . . not now." He clenched his jaw and swallowed. "How did your meeting go?"

"It's difficult to tell," I said, standing up because my knees had begun to ache. "How many of the Gelaming hierarchy do you know?"

Vaysh shrugged. "Not many. Tharmifex; he's OK. Cedony; he's a bit of a dreamer and worships Ashmael but apart from that, alright. The others I know by sight but that's all. I should imagine the ones to cultivate are those two and Dree; he has a big say in everything, but he's not that easy

to get on with. Oh . . . and Ashmael, of course. I'm sorry Pell, but I think
you will need him. If he's still here . . . well . . ."

"Hmm, you saw how we hit it off."

"I didn't but I wouldn't worry too much about that. He doesn't bear
grudges for long."

"It's more than that," I argued.

"Not really. He's bound to come around once he's seen more of you.
You're not what he thinks you are, whatever that may be."

"Even I'm not sure of that!" I said.

Vaysh scratched his brow. "He won't be like this for long; once he starts
fancying you, which is inevitable, I'm afraid . . ."

"I thought you disliked him!"

"I didn't say that, Pell. He's not the angel of Immanion for nothing.
He's probably hurt because Thiede doesn't think he's fit to be Tigron. It
might be hard going for a while, but he'll get fed up of being vile to you;
I know him."

"How well?"

"Well enough."

There was that strange echo again in Vaysh's voice. Maybe I was just
feeling very perceptive. "Is he your Cal, Vaysh?" His eyes flashed up to
meet mine, briefly, and then away. "Was it the same for you?"

He did not know whether to speak or not. I could understand. The act
of speaking your thoughts realizes them, somehow. Some thoughts are
often best left unvoiced. He stood up and paced the room, wringing his
hands, picking things up, looking at them, putting them down again,
opening his mouth to speak, and closing it again. I tried to imagine how I
would feel in his place, but the picture would not come. Vaysh's panic was
infectious. Then he stopped dead, in the middle of the room, fists clenched
by his sides.

"Pell . . . I don't have to tell you. You've guessed enough. Leave it at
that." He was the color of chalk; his hair livid about his face.

I feared for his sanity. "That's alright," I said in a gentle voice. "Don't
say anything." I sat down again on the couch. "But if ever you do feel you
have to . . . I'll always listen." I thought that would be an end to it for now,
but Vaysh sat down again, next to me. He looked ill and some small part
of me was selfish enough to consider getting up and walking out. I wasn't
sure I could handle him.

"Pell, I'm scared," he said. "I'm so scared."

Hating myself for wanting to leave, I put my arms around him. His rigid
body collapsed against me; he was cold and trembling. This was not the
Vaysh I knew.

"Scared, of what?"

"Breaking up . . . disintegrating." He made a sad little sound that was
half moan, half laugh.

"What do you mean?"

He raised his head and looked at me. "When I lived in the cold place,

I could be like that; cold. What had happened to me meant nothing to me. I made "myself strong. Now I've come back to the real world, having to face things again. Myself, for one. You're half to blame, Pell."

"Shit," I said and he almost laughed.

"I mean . . ."

"No, no, I know what you mean; and you're right. I wanted to crack the ice, Vaysh, I wanted to get in at you. But you heard what Thiede said this morning; ice preserves doesn't it?"

He lay with his head on my chest, chewing a lock of my hair, thinking about what I'd said.

"What did Ashmael say when he saw you?" I asked. Vaysh's glassy eyes did not flicker.

"Say? What do you think? A long time ago, I died in his arms."

CHAPTER NINE

This news may not be welcome . . .

Some days later, Tharmifex came to visit me in my rooms. I had seen nothing more of Ashmael and little of the other members of the hegemony. Vaysh had kept mainly to his room, listening to endless tapes of mournful music, but I had spent a lot of time with Thiede. He lavished attention on me, showing me the city ("Here we shall build the finest theater . . ."), dreaming aloud about how things would be when the Reign of Peace arrived.

"You have missed so much of it, Pell," he said, as we walked among the trees. "All the horror; the worst of it was over by the time . . . you were found. But *I* saw it; terror, panic, gluttony, fear and worse things besides. Boys dragged from the blackened ruins of their homes; firelight caught on steel and their screams as Wraeththu blood rained down upon them. That was often the way at first; that was why so many died. Inception, by its very nature, demands the discipline of ritual, of an educated mind; the other way was messy and for so long it was the favored way, because of our hate."

"I cannot imagine you young," I said.

"Perhaps I never was," he answered.

I loved to talk with Thiede and, although my opinions amused him, he always listened carefully to me. "Hara are not like that," he would say. "How you see them, Pell, perhaps that is how they should be; but they are not." We never spoke of my time in the other country. There was so much I wanted to ask him, but the subject seemed taboo. Perhaps when Seel came, it would be different.

Tharmifex brought me a gift; a spotted cat the size of a dog. He said he liked cats. "They never embarrass themselves," he said. Tharmifex, unlike Thiede, was not loath to talk about the tribes from across the sea. Gelaming call that country Megalithica; a somewhat tongue-in-cheek title, I suspect. Megalithica it still is. Tharmifex would frown a lot and say things like, "Time is running out. Once tribes like the Varrs have wiped mankind and all the weaker Hara off the surface of their lands, they will be at a loss for what to do. That's when some bright spark among them will suggest a coalition between them, and that's when they'll all turn their eyes toward the east and Almagabra and Immanion."

"Why are some Wraeththu like that?" I asked. "We happened; and our purpose was to change the world, yet so many Hara still follow the same path as Mankind."

"To understand that, Pellaz, you must understand something of the nature of humankind," Tharmifex explained. "Although there are two sexes, man has his female side and vice versa. In earlier times, the feminine principle was not denied and the world lived in a happier, peaceful age; a water age. All that changed and then, at the end, men came to uphold a rigid patriarchy; to be feminine was considered "unmanly"; all men were afraid of that. The age of Fire had come. So they buried the femininity in their souls, subjugated women, whom they feared, and took away their power. Women, too, were encouraged to think like men; motherhood was virtually scorned by all intelligent females, a kind of last resort when a woman was too stupid or uneducated to do anything else. Power, material power, was worshiped as a god; all other religions squeaked in comparison. Love between men was held in abhorrence; after all, feminine bits of the soul could then start leaking through and the warmakers feared that more than anything. Women, being discounted as worthless, were not as censured for seeking affection amongst their own kind (so long as its purpose was for the titillation of men!); they could do no damage to the myth, to the Fire God. Man could not grasp the truth; the power of sexuality and what it meant. A potent force was degraded to something animal, something steeped in guilt. Violence became the only true force.

"Warmaking is a strange disease, Pell, and goes hand-in-hand with greed. The majority of Wraeththu are those who have taken the Harhune; the changing. They are no longer men, physically, but the Harhune does not mutate the mind; that we have to learn. Until a new generation of Wraeththu children grows up, we shall always have this problem."

"But Thiede's power is great," I said. "Surely he will be able to quell the trouble?"

"Eventually, yes; but we are anxious to avoid as much conflict as possible."

My education continued along these lines. One day I asked, "And what of Man, is he no longer a threat to us?"

The world is large, Pell," Tharmifex replied, somewhat enigmatically and sighed. "Ah humanity! How convenient it would be to regard them

merely as ticks upon the back of Wraeththu!" Sometimes it seemed to me
as if the human race had ceased to exist; Thiede never mentioned them.

"In Megalithica," I said, "we traveled for miles and miles and miles and
there were no men there; only green stuff growing back over their towns.
What happened to them?"

"Death's angel assumes many guises," Tharmifex answered mysteriously.

"Were they all killed by Wraeththu, the *other* Wraeththu?"

Tharmifex shrugged. "It happened; they were decimated, but Wraeththu were not entirely responsible. Panic, disease, melancholy; all of these
things and many others too, claimed casualities," he said, "but you are
mistaken if you think men are beaten. To the east of Almagabra and in the
northernmost parts of Megalithica men still have control of their lands. At
present, they are still disorganized, demoralized, thoroughly shaken up and
afraid, but once they have finished licking their wounds (and they *are* a
remarkably resilient race), they will stand up again and think about re-
claiming their world. We must remember what happened when Wraeththu
was very young; men ignored us until it was too late and we were too
strong. Man's time is over, but I'm afraid he will be loath to agree with that.
Do not underestimate mankind, Pell; they are tough and tenacious. We
were lucky that they were in such a mess when we came into the world; that
gave us a start. Now we must discipline the rogue tribes of Wraeththu;
without unity men could inflict enormous damage on us when the time
comes."

Thiede had importuned most of Almagabra's population to assist in the
building of Immanion, although Tharmifex did say to me that buildings
had once had an unnerving habit of mysteriously appearing one morning
in places that had been but rock and rubble the night before.

"Immanion came into being surprisingly fast," he said. "We had a
brilliant architect working for us (not willingly, but his enthusiasm over-
came his reserve), a man; I can't remember his name. I recall him saying to
me once that the stone that some of the buildings were made of was like
nothing he'd ever seen before. He said it looked (quote) 'man-made,' glossy
and hard, but like nothing he'd ever worked with. At night it glows with
a soft and barely noticeable radiance . . . Thiede's magical city!"

We laughed, but there was more than a grain of truth in that.

Thiede, though rigorously tidy in his government of man, was not a
tyrant, and he paid his human labor fairly, if not extravagantly. By the time
I came to Immanion, the humans had been sent back to their own lands in
the north; Thiede did not want them lingering in the city once the bulk of
the construction work had been completed.

Almagabra was effectively shielded by mountains on all sides (apart
from the southern sea coast), which the Gelaming guarded zealously.
Beyond Almagabra, especially to the east, Tharmifex told me, unrest
seethed in an unknown and blasted territory. It was said that dark clouds
obscured the sun in those places and that men had become lunatic and

raving. What Wraeththu that lived there had submerged themselves in cultures of extreme eccentricity or, it was even suggested, had mutated further from the image of mankind than ever thought possible. Doubtless Thiede knew most of the answers, but as he wanted everyone's attention centerd on the west, he was not forthcoming, and evaded conversation on that topic. The Wraeththu of Megalithica, Varrs and Uigenna especially, posed a more immediate problem; the mysteries of the east would remain veiled for some time yet.

Representatives from the co-operative tribes would be arriving in Immanion in time for my coronation. "They shall see the new beginning," Tharmifex said. I wondered if Seel knew yet who was to be crowned Tigron, and if he didn't, the expression on his face when he saw it was me! He would ask me about Cal and I would ask about Orien. Our meeting was not destined to be a joyous occasion, I felt.

News kept filtering through to me about Ashmael's pronouncements concerning my competence. The meeting place for the hegemony was a grand building near Phaonica named the Hegalion. Attica told me that once Ashmael had stood up and publicly argued with Thiede, accusing him outright of having me crowned Tigron for his own selfish reasons. "You look down on us all," he had said. "None of us, in your opinion, are fit to lead Wraeththu but yourself!" Thiede, apparently, had taken this outburst with surprising calm. Until I was officially Tigron, I had no legal right to sit with the hegemony. Thiede explained to them, that when given the chance, I would be able to prove my worth easily. The hegemony was divided, but privately; publicly, they had sense enough to stand by Thiede.

I confided to him that I feared Ashmael's antagonism would cause too much damage to my reputation before I got the chance to speak up for myself, but he refused to take it seriously.

"Deep down, they all know I am right," he said. "Even Ashmael, though it would cause him a good deal of pain to admit it!"

I was not so optimistic.

"I have not heard bad of you from anyone but Ashmael," Attica said to me one evening. "It is Thiede that they think is wrong, not you. They do not blame you."

Only Tharmifex seemed to support me; Chrysm would commit himself to neither side.

I begged Thiede to let me be present at the next meeting in the Hegalion. "Let them speak with me; let them know me!" I insisted, but he would not agree.

"By taking our time, by not panicking, we expose their wheedlings for what they are," he said. "You must not present yourself at the Hegalion yet. Ashmael is attempting to force you to do just that, and at the moment, he will only make mincemeat out of you."

One morning, as I sat scanning the newsheet of the city, a har I did not know was conducted by Attica into my presence. He asked leave to speak with me and I agreed, requesting Attica to bring us refreshment. Orders were beginning to fall easily from my tongue. My visitor would not sit down, but told me his name was Phylax.

"Ashmael has sent me," he said.

"For what purpose?" I asked him.

He looked uncomfortable, standing there and I wondered if Ashmael had had to force him to come.

"Your presence is requested for dinner this evening," he replied.

Curiosity may have killed the cat, but it also opens many locked doors. After a suitable pause, I agreed to attend. When I told Vaysh about it later, he called me a fool.

"Ashmael means to humiliate you," he said. "It's too soon."

Thiede visited me in the afternoon, but I decided against letting him know about Ashmael's invitation. I felt sure he would forbid me to go.

I expected to walk in on a roomful of Ashmael's cronies, ready for sport at my expense, but there was only Ashmael. He lived in a residential area of the city, the home of many high-ranking hara of Immanion. The house was low and spacious, framed by spreading evergreens. Phylax and I had ridden there through the perfumed evening, along the moth-garlanded avenues. Phylax had hardly spoken; I was an unknown quantity to him. He had called for me at sundown to show me the way, but it was clear that I intimidated him.

Ashmael was like a combination of Terzian and Cal; Terzian's elegance and refinement and Cal's cynical good humor. It is almost too absurd to describe his appearance. He was, as you expect, one of Wraeththu's finest, and very comfortably knew it. He offered me a drink, politeness itself. Phylax sat down by the door.

"Tharmifex speaks well of you," Ashmael said to me.

"I can't see why that should sway your opinion," I answered, and he feigned surprise. "Ashmael, I'm perfectly aware of your feelings toward me and my position. If it's any comfort, I don't think they're entirely unjustified, but you must know yourself why Thiede has done this; you're not stupid."

He laughed, very quietly. "Well, Pellaz, you do believe in striking the first blow, don't you. But I didn't bring you here, sorry, *ask* you here, to squabble. Tharmifex has given me the sharp edge of his tongue over my behavior, so, I'm to make amends!"

That was too glib. I was still suspicious, but said nothing.

We dined on a terrace behind the house, talking mechanically at first, of inconsequential things. Then the wine began to flow more freely and I was given every chance to exercise the wit of my conversation. Phylax sat uneasily at the table, and his edginess, more than anything else warned me that Ashmael might not be as innocent of motives as he appeared.

"I look forward to working with you," he said and raised his glass.

I smiled. "Ashmael, perhaps I've spent too much of my life looking over my shoulder, but I can't get rid of this sneaky feeling that you're up to something."

He laughed, perhaps too loudly. "I've done my bit, being pleasant, haven't I?" I did not answer but looked enquiring.

"Alright, Pellaz, Tigron of Immanion and whatever else," he said, "I'll be straight with you. I don't know yet whether you're a pathetic and squeaking idiot, as I suspect, or an angel of salvation as Thiede would have everyone believe. I didn't like it when Thiede told us about you; petty, I know, but we can't all be perfect. I'm still not sure if I'm right to allow you even one chance to prove yourself, but only time and working with you will reveal your true nature . . ." He poured himself more wine.

"By that time, Ashmael, it may be too late to get rid of me, if your suspicions prove correct," I pointed out.

He shrugged and waved his arm at me. "Tharmifex is not a complete fool. If he's willing to give you a chance, so am I. I've had my say, to no avail. So, I'll give in gracefully for now. However, there *is* one thing I wish to discuss with you . . ." He looked at Phylax, who was virtually writhing on his chair, and turned on him savagely, "Oh, go inside! You know what has to be said, but you don't want to hear me say it, do you!" he raged.

"That was harsh," I said, once Phylax had gone. Ashmael leaned forward on the table. I could smell the wine on him and thought he had drunk too much.

"No, not harsh. He would just prefer some things, things that happened to me before, to remain buried."

"Oh, . . . I see." (Was this the reason then for the sudden change of heart?)

Ashmael looked up at me, resting his chin on his hands. "Yes, you do, don't you! Did he tell you?"

"Ashmael," I said, "have I got this right? Have you asked me here, your rival, your political opponent and a virtual stranger, to talk about Vaysh?"

"Well, it's given you something to think about, hasn't it?"

I dismissed this remark as rhetorical. "Surely you can ask Thiede about this . . . why me?"

Ashmael sprawled back in his chair and put one foot on the table. "Do you want to listen to this? I *am* rather drunk."

"I might as well."

"Well thank *you*, Pellaz! It comes as a relief to find that I can come to the Tigron with my problems! It was a shock when I went to your rooms and found Vaysh there. You must know why. Are you chesna with him?" he asked quickly. "Is this rather embarrassing to you?"

I shook my head. "No, to both questions," I said, and Ashmael shrugged.

"I had to ask. Anyway, I didn't say anything to him other than, 'Where's the master, then?' or something like that. It didn't sink in at first. I remember thinking, 'My God, he looks just like Vaysh!'; it's been some years, you see. Of course, he just shot out of the room as if I was the devil, and I sat down and waited for you . . . not long. Afterwards, I began to think about it and then I mentioned it to Tharmifex. I couldn't say any-

thing to Thiede. What if it hadn't been Vaysh? Thiede would have thought
I was cracking up; and it's not a very good time for him to be thinking that,
is it!"

"Tharmifex told you then?"

"Yes, all that he knew . . . sickening . . . terrible." Ashmael rubbed his
face with his hands, drank some more wine. "Whatever you think, whatever you thought, that wasn't the only reason for my asking you here. I
hadn't made up my mind whether to mention Vaysh or not until you
arrived."

"And the grape unleashed your tongue?" I suggested.

Ashmael snorted derisively. "That too, I suppose. Tharmifex has spoken forcefully for you; to me personally and to the hegemony. Thiede
would say nothing; that's his way. I suspect he knows the outcome of
everything in the world already . . ."

"Vaysh said you'd come around," I said, to bring him back to the
subject.

"Yes . . . about Vaysh," Ashmael's face twitched uncomfortably. "Does
he remember me? Is he the same? Should I speak to him?"

I paused eloquently before answering him. "He does remember
you . . ."

Ashmael looked at me stonily. "You have answered all my questions by
that," he said bitterly.

"You mind is as quick as they said it was," I said, smiling hopefully.

Ashmael did not smile. "Why shouldn't I speak to him? He was . . . and
here's a Wraeththu heresy . . . he was *mine.*"

"I wouldn't advise it; not yet," I said smoothly. "I don't think he could
cope with it yet." I realized afterwards that this was ultimately a lie; I don't
know why I said it. I should think the truth was, Vaysh really did want
Ashmael to speak to him, but I did not.

"Oh God, Thiede can be a monster, he really can," Ashmael murmured,
his eyes shining.

"It was an accident," I said.

This was like being an observer to a situation I could imagine happening
about me some day. Then too, people would doubtlessly try to keep Cal
away from me. I said, "Ashmael, you said it's been years since . . . how do
you feel about Vaysh now?"

He shrugged. "Feel? I can still smell his blood, even now. He was so
beautiful, so alive. Losing him was like losing life. Everyone worshiped
him . . ." I had gone cold, although the night was warm.

"But now, how do you feel now?" I insisted.

"Now?" Ashmael wrinkled his brow. "Now . . . something lives in a
body that looks like Vaysh, but is it him? I watched him die and spent a
year demented with grief. Now? What can I feel? Vaysh is dead."

Was this the way it would be then, when Cal found out that I still lived?
Would he be angry because all his grief and rage had been misdirected?

Would he feel cheated? That night, I tossed and turned in sheets that turned to wet rope against my body. I could not sleep for the thoughts that tormented me. Several times, I was on the point of going to Vaysh, but I did not want to answer the questions he might ask me about Ashmael. My thoughts turned to salt in my eyes. I could see Cal so clearly; time and absence had not blurred the memory of his face. I remembered the times we had sought each other's warmth in the dark, in the dangerous open country and by the stranger's hearth. The velvet texture of his skin, the flame of his violet eyes; all of this was lost to me. There could be no other to touch my soul as he had; no-one. Beauty could make me twitch (and laughter), but in my heart, in the deepest fibers, there was only him. Was I condemning myself foolishly to an eternity of loneliness? It was a possibility, but only if I stopped believing.

Seel arrived earlier than expected; Thiede brought him to my rooms. Vaysh and I were poring over some ornate and ancient maps in the library. They illustrated where dragons and trolls may be found and it was with amusement we discovered that one of the locations was right by Phade's tower. Gradually and carefully Vaysh and I had developed an easy friendship. Sometimes he was still staunchly unapproachable, but the cruel tormentor of our journey to Immanion had gone. His acid remarks were no longer tinged by hatred. We never spoke of how it had been before.

Seel had not aged in appearance, but as Wraeththu hardly do, this was not surprising. We began to greet each other as strangers, but then I threw my arms around him and the ice was broken. He still had about him a faint fragrance of soda.

He laughed and said, "Well, Pell, who could have guessed it would all have come to this?"

Later that day, over dinner in Thiede's apartments, I asked about Saltrock.

"Oh, it is bigger and better now," Seel replied in response to my questions. "I could have done more there, but not much. Thiede has impressed on me strongly how much work there is to be done elsewhere."

Thiede smiled gently at the cold edge to Seel's voice.

I waited until the last course was cleared away before asking about Orien. "He was murdered," was all Seel would say. I could tell he did not want to talk about it, but he had only made me more anxious to know what had happened. He asked me nothing about Cal, but that may have been because Thiede was there.

Time passed slowly in Immanion; every day was golden. I was invited to gatherings at Tharmifex's house and Dree's; in the latter case I sensed the invitation was wary. Delegates began to arrive from different tribes; they could easily be recognized by the expressions of bewilderment or wonder on their faces. To many hara, the splendor of Immanion seemed but a dream.

The time came when my coronation was but two days away. After that, talks would begin in earnest and there was a feeling in the air as of a holiday drawing to a close and the party that would mark the last night. Costumiers came to fit my regalia; an outstanding creation of black and azure feathers. My jewelery was made all of turquoise and silver. Seel wandered in to visit me, smoking a black cigarette and leaning against a table to watch the outfitters at work.

"You're still a wonder of the world Pell, and still to me that absurd little urchin who trailed after Cal into Saltrock burning with ignorance."

I could not move my head to look at him. "I had hoped you'd bring Flick with you," I said.

"Did you?" His voice was bitter and I jerked my head, to a chorus of complaints from pin-studded mouths.

I feared the worst. "Is he . . . alright?"

"I don't know!" Seel stubbed the cigarette out angrily in an empty wineglass.

"Don't know? What do you mean? Did you quarrel?"

Seel took a deep breath and something about his expression angered me deep inside. "Pell, there's something you should know, but I didn't want to tell you before the coronation . . ."

I was silent for a moment and then said, "Why?" Presentiment rattled my brains; I could feel the cold creeping in toward me. I knew already whom it would concern.

"Send these peacocks away, Pell," Seel requested, "It's now or never."

The outfitters looked at him with displeasure, but silently gathered up their things. I changed back into a loose robe and told them to come back later.

"Sit down," Seel said. He knew where I kept my liquor and went to the cabinet. "Drink this." It was a generous measure.

"Seel, what's all this about?" I asked, fighting my body's urge to start shaking. His face told me enough.

"God, where to begin?" He threw up his arms and walked to the window and back again. "Cal came back to Saltrock," he said. If I could have shrunk back into the chair, let the chair swallow me, I would. If I could have blocked my ears . . . and yet, of course, I wanted to know. "He would say nothing except that you were dead," Seel continued, still pacing. "We all tried to do what we could for him; he had lost far too much weight and spent most of his time out of his head; drink, drugs, whatever. I know grief has to work itself out. I was as supportive as possible. Flick took it very hard. He's very fond of you and it scared him to see Cal like that. One night, Orien was around, and to try and comfort Cal, he said that he thought you were involved in something none of us could understand. The fool! Cal's face went very strange. He just looked at Orien as if he'd said he'd killed you himself. He did not shout, his voice went very low. He said, 'What do *you* know about it, Orien?' By this time, Orien was regretting what he'd said; perhaps it hadn't sounded the way it was meant to. He shook his head and tried to mumble his way out of it. That was when Cal went wild. He grabbed hold of Orien and pushed him up against the wall. He was babbling that he'd had enough of witches and savagery. He blamed Orien for what had happened to you, in very graphic terms, and . . . Thiede. Well, he was right about that! Flick and I managed to pull Cal away, and then he appeared to calm down. When Orien had gone home, Cal apologized to me, but he said that he knew something had happened at your Harhune that had marked you somehow, and that Orien and Thiede were responsible. He asked me if I knew anything about it and I said no. Well, I didn't. We all had our suspicions at the time but. . . . Anyway, I think Cal believed me, although he did look at me hard for a few minutes. He looked at me and he told me that he loved you. Loved you . . . I felt terrible; his eyes were. . . . He was so, so *haunted*. I have never seen anything like that and I didn't know what to do, how to handle it. Cal said he wanted to be alone that night, so I was with Flick. We heard nothing. Next morning, we woke up and Cal was gone. Next morning he was gone and Orien was dead; hanging half-gutted from the roof of the Nayati . . ."

At some point I had buried my face in my hands. I cried, "It was *me* that did that!"

Seel squatted down beside me and pressed me to him. "No, it was not you. Some kind of craziness did that. The same kind of craziness that made men kill; obsession."

"Yet he called it love . . ."

"It was obsession; obsession and sickness. Perhaps he's never been truly well . . . since Zack . . ." I knew that was not true.

"Flick. . . ?" I said; dreading further revelations.

Seel sighed and stood up, rubbing his arms. "Flick . . . well, for a few days, he was just so quiet, listless, like there was nothing left inside him. I tried to make it better, say things . . . but there was so much to do. He left me a letter when he left Saltrock; it was a very nice letter, but he still went. I was left to clear up the mess. Everyone looked so wild and scared; things like that just don't happen at Saltrock. But then they started to forget, life goes on . . ."

I could feel the warmth of Orien's talisman against my skin. I should have known he was dead. I should have known it.

"Seel," I said, "I'm cold . . ."

We embraced and he said nice things to me to make me weep. It took some time. "I didn't want to tell you," Seel said, "and yet I did; *so much!*"

My tears were silent and I said, "You hate him . . ." Seel's arms tightened around me.

When Vaysh came in and found us like that, he thought it was something different at first. Then I stepped back and Seel turned away. Vaysh saw my face and I saw the fear come into his. I said, "Tell Vaysh, Seel, tell him for me," and went away to my bedroom. I could hear Seel's voice begin again, but not the words. My curtains shivered in a slight warm breeze, the day outside was golden. I lay back on the bed and put my arms behind my head. The aftermath of grief and weeping is almost sensual in its piquancy. Words composed themselves in my head. I could hear birds outside, singing on the terrace, see the pools of light beginning to edge toward my room. The day was black.

CHAPTER TEN

>─┤─◄►─●─◄►─┤─◄

He began it all . . .

Even when we think we are safest, we never are. Darknesses are everywhere. Both Vaysh and myself had become the victims of cruel shocks since reaching Immanion. We spent the following two days getting helplessly drunk together, licking each other's wounds by intoxicated ramblings. "You must put it behind you Pell," Vaysh advised, "there is nothing more you can do." Nothing more? Banish my fury, the fury I thought I felt, and the seething frustration? Some part of me kept saying, "This is not right; this is not Cal." It had crossed my mind that it might just be another of Thiede's games. What better way to drive all thoughts of Cal from my mind? But commonsense told me that no-one could have acted as well as the way Seel would have had to. Could he really have acted out so convincingly telling me that the har I loved had butchered the mentor and friend of my early Wraeththu days? Thiede was capable of such an obscenity, but I was sure Seel was not. The worst thing was, although I lamented and cursed the cruelties of Fate, scored by misery, some deep part of me was never touched. That part watched dispassionately, a core of cool rationality. It waited for the surface pain to pass; at night I could feel it lurking somewhere in my heart and it appalled me. On the morning of my coronation, I turned aside the measure of hot liquor that Vaysh offered me. Two days had purged me. My tolerance, my trust and my eternal hope had been battered numb, but some deep and healing well of strength overflowed within me and kept me sane, kept me safe.

They dressed me in the morning; the ceremony would begin at noon. Vaysh and I looked at each other and our eyes were full of granite exhilaration. We shared dark secrets but the terrible things we knew only fed our strength. There was a strained, tense atmosphere in the apartments that day, voices sounded muffled, as if on the eve of a great battle. Within us was the knowledge; we had both been singled out for greatness, Vaysh and I, and the harvest of the greatness had been emotional flaying. Yet neither of us blamed Thiede. He controlled us, bonded us to loyalty; now we had nothing, now we had everything; now we had nothing. It was endless.

We went out into the sunlight and for the briefest moment, the shade of

Saltrock blurred my eyes and the solemn, soaring temple up ahead became the wooden-roofed Nayati and the angels that lined Immanion's streets became the cheerful and scarred pioneers of another town. Vaysh sat by me in the splendid open carriage that was drawn by eight silver horses. He was the colors of alabaster, verdigris and rich henna, and among the feathers at my side, he held my hand.

Among the echoing columns, silvered by floating incense, I spoke before the hegemony of Immanion and the priests and the most exalted citizens, the sacred oaths that would bind me to them for evermore. Thiede's eyes, full of satisfaction and pride, watched me with ophidian constancy. He must have known what Seel had told me, yet there was no sign. He trusted me to be strong and indifferent. I was Tigron and I was changing. He would say to me, "You must listen to your wisdom now, Pellaz. See what the world really is and how we must cut out the dark and rotting places." He could never be termed benevolent, Thiede my holy father, but he knew what the Great Rightnesses were and no petty compassion would stand in his way of realizing them. From below, among the little Hara that toiled and scrabbled and tried to understand what they were, I had stepped up to stand beside him, to take my place upon the dais of knowledge and of Power. Wretchedness and fear were no longer equal to me. Tranquility smoothed my cares. I had lived and died and resurrected; resurrected to immeasurable power. I could no longer be patient with the twitterings of passion and pain.

When the last words had been spoken, the last thurible cast above my head, Thiede came toward me and took my face in his hands. I did not tremble when I felt his breath upon me; I was equal to it. "I have brought you through pain," his voice echoed in my mind. "Give me back some of the life I quickened."

It had not been planned, I was sure of that. Silence thickened among the congregation, yet I could feel their eyes upon me. I was heavy with silver and turquoise; feathers folded around us like wings.

The altar of inception, in that most sacrosanct of Wraeththu temples, is tasselled with gold. Power was red behind his eyes and his red, red hair fell into my mouth and eyes. "Pellaz, my jewel," he said, with a voice he had never used with me before. As with all Wraeththu temples, the place of inception could be veiled. Tumbling, black muslin shot with sparks, pooled to the floor, and it seemed we were alone. Tharmifex stood within the curtains. He looked at us once and we looked back with frightening unity. He twitched the curtains aside and stepped through. I climbed up onto the table and stripped the feathers from me. The Chosen One. He came to me and his heat was just har, nothing more. I cried out once, but not with pain. His eyes never left my own; he wanted to read everything there. When the moment came, it shocked me like electricity, switching on, opening up to a greater current. His flame hair crackled with static dust and I could see his face, so vulnerable in ecstasy. A god trapped in the anemone folds of aquatic soume. I could control him and make him writhe, and I did.

* * *

There was great feasting that day. The streets of Immanion were alive with celebration and so packed with hara; many had come from afar for the occasion. Thiede and I led the way back to Phaonica. Chrysm came up to me and embraced me.

"A coronation sanctified by aruna!" he exclaimed. "Will this become a custom?"

Now, it seemed, Immanion's reservations about me had been thoroughly quelled. I basked unashamedly in the admiration. This was my home, these were my people; for once everyone seemed happy.

Once evening had folded into dark, Thiede took me to his chamber of office. I was feeling dizzy with happiness and more than a little drunk.

"Pell," he began, "you might think it is too soon to discuss this matter, but it is important, especially as we may all be called away from Immanion in the near future to deal with potentially dangerous concerns."

I listened, still smiling. Thiede pushed me back into a chair and leaned on his desk in front of me. "Pell, you must know that as Tigron, we must be selective as to who shall host your heirs. Had you thought of that?"

I shrugged. "I can see that, even if I hadn't thought about it."

"You know, of course, that often hara are committed enough to each other to become chesna . . .?"

I could not keep the edge from my voice. "I think you could say I am aware of that."

Thiede nodded and tapped his lips with steepled fingers. "You need a partner, who is mostly soume, at least publicly, who shall host your seed. This har will also have to be trusted with domestic government in our absence, that is, government within our own lands."

I laughed. "What you are suggesting, Thiede, sounds almost like a marriage!"

Thiede did not laugh. "I suppose in a way, it could be seen as that. You need a consort, and you shall be united in blood at the temple to show our people that you are of one mind."

"Who?" I demanded.

"I haven't decided yet."

Anger shouldered aside the effects of alcohol. I could feel myself burning. It was not just that Thiede, as usual, was organizing my life for me; I was becoming used to that. It was that he expected me to commit myself in blood to another. I knew I could not do it; such a union would be a lie.

"Are we men then now?!" I stormed, "that we have to marry amongst ourselves?"

Thiede flapped his hands at me. "Pellaz, calm down, calm down. What I'm suggesting is not a stifling fidelity which might be alien to you. This is merely a political arrangement."

"But it's barbaric!" I cried. "I can't believe I'm hearing this!" I stood up. "And how many concubines will I be allowed? Is there a harem quarter in Phaonica?"

"Oh don't get emotional, Pellaz!" Thiede said impatiently. "Tomorrow, you will see the sense in what I say. There is no reason why you should not do this."

I read the challenge in his eyes immediately. Maybe I should have kept quiet. "Oh, I *see*. This is a test is it? Am I over Cal? Is that it?" Thiede said nothing. "It really bothers you, doesn't it," I said bitterly.

"Pellaz, he is not worthy of you. I should have stopped that relationship a long time ago, and would have done, if I'd guessed how deep your feelings ran. Don't you remember what I once said to you about how dangerous such feelings are? You must have seen within him all the time the possibility of. . . . He was Uigenna once; the fruits of that inception can never be truly eradicated."

"Why did you have to say this today?" I asked, but all I felt was anger, not pain. Thiede was not oblivious of that.

"I know, perhaps I should have waited, but I had hoped that this discussion would not become an argument about Cal."

"Thiede!" I cried. "That is bullshit!"

He twitched a corner of his mouth and walked to behind my chair. I sat down again.

"What if it was Vaysh?" he said slyly. "Would you be so angry then?"

"Thiede," I said in a patient voice. "We both know that it cannot be Vaysh."

"Yes, most unfortunate."

"But even if it could be, I would still say no. I can't. If you cannot understand that, I'm sorry. I will let you choose a consort for me to host my sons, and I will gladly hand over the reins of power to that har should I need to, but I will not, certainly and most definitely not, mix my blood with his in a vow of any kind involving spiritual communion. And that is my last word!"

He let me walk to the door. "Pellaz, all that I have given you; it could all be so easily taken away . . ."

I turned with my hand on the door handle. He had spoken so quietly I was not sure if I had heard it.

"Thiede," I said in a weary voice and shook my head, "are you incapable of compromise?"

He looked seriously at the ceiling in a comic display of deep thinking, then back to me. "Compromise? Are you joking?" He laughed. "Oh, Pell, get out of here. We've reached a stalement for now, that's clear. We'll talk again some other time. Tomorrow."

I went back to the party, but my heart was no longer in it. Cal's ghost had intruded once again. I could almost see him, standing in a corner of the room, among the tall ornamental plants, smiling, his hair matted with blood. But whose blood; mine or Orien's? I wanted him out of my head; that time was the closest I ever came to really hating him. He'd thought he'd had a murderer at his mercy. Did he feel elation as he tore Orien's life from him? (One for you, Pell.) Orien, no murderer, who had nurtured the seeds of my wisdom and kept my past in trust for me. My hand wandered unconsciously to the talisman. Cal, you fool! You blind, stupid fool! They thought he was mad, but I knew better. I had looked through the door with him, beneath the Kakkahaar sands, and seen Lianvis take life for power. We had seen that and we both knew, knew what lurked in the shadows of Wraeththu consciousness. Because of that, he would kill for me.

Back in my apartments, sounds of merriment still reached me through the open windows. I was feeling mellow and sad, but in a hazy, wistful sort of way. I was not unhappy. I went out onto the terrace to stretch against the cool, diamond-studded night. Tomorrow. . . . Something was over now, but I couldn't explain exactly what. The music sounded mournful below me. The gardens were in darkness, but thronged with rustlings and muted laughter. I looked along the terrace. Vaysh's window-door was open and a low light burned inside the room.

He was lying on the bed, half conscious. Two empty bottles stood upon the table where the light glowed. Nothing was knocked over. I went over and sat down beside him. "Vaysh." I shook him and he made a sound. "Vaysh." His eyes opened and I could see the redness.

"Pell, get out of here," he said.

"No, no." I took him in my arms and he wept anew. Vaysh was soume, more so than any other har I had ever met. The female was strong in him. He seemed made to be my consort, yet Thiede had scoured him barren; such justice.

"What is it?" I asked.

"His eyes," was all he said, but I knew. To someone, what lived in Vaysh's body was not Vaysh. "What am I, Pell? Why am I still alive?"

"Oh, Vaysh, Vaysh," I murmured and put my mouth upon his brow. His skin was hot and dry.

"I am a monster!" he said and tried to pull away from me. "You try to make me feel better, but I know, I know there is no hope for me. What hope is there for someone who can only repel, who makes Hara back away in revulsion?"

"That's not true," I told him lamely. I put my hand in his luxurious hair and touched his neck.

"Isn't it? Isn't it?"

For the second time that night I looked into eyes that offered me a challenge, but this was a hesitant, fluctuating challenge. At any moment, it might be withdrawn.

"You're beautiful, Vaysh," I said. "And because you're shamefully drunk, I intend to take advantage of you."

Outside the music had died away and the horizon was gray with the promise of dawn. Vaysh lay in my arms; we had pulled a sheet over our nakedness for the air was cool with dew. I thought he was asleep, but he put his hand upon my face.

"Pell," he said, "I'm going to tell you something that no-one else knows; or hardly anyone. It may mean nothing to you or it may explain everything. It's about Thiede."

I propped myself up on one elbow and leaned over him. "What?"

He smiled wistfully, seeming anxious about continuing, perhaps wishing he had not spoken. "We've had no time for gods really, have we?" It did not require an answer. Vaysh touched me quickly again and turned his head away. "Perhaps I should not speak," he said softly.

I took his hand. "It can't be that bad, Vaysh."

He shook his head. "No . . . not bad, but I may be betraying his trust. Then again, he may want me to tell you, I don't know. Do you remember me once asking you if you knew who Thiede was?"

I didn't, then. "Vaguely," I said.

"There is one Wraeththu har whom everybody knows . . ."

That disclosure implied nothing to me.

"Thiede is known to everybody?"

"Yes!"

"What do you mean? How is this important? He is notorious, I know. I've always known that."

Vaysh snatched his hand from my own. "It's more than that!" he hissed. "He is . . . he is the Aghama, Pell!"

"Aghama? What?!" I even began to laugh.

"Pell!" Vaysh's nails dug into my shoulders. "Don't laugh! Can't you see? He is the most powerful, the first, the last, the eternal. He began it all, Pell, everything. Wraeththu *is* Thiede! We are all his; like cells, like atoms of his own body! Aghama, Pell, think about it . . ."

I was silent for a while. I thought about it. Only the creaking of the palace walls and the call of early sea-birds broke the calm. I could not even hear Vaysh breathing, though I could see his chest rising and falling quite quickly. I did think about it. I thought of a wooden shack back in Saltrock that they call the Forale-house and sunlight coming in through a high window, falling onto Orien, where he sat cross-legged on the floor. Orien's hair shining around the edges, full of light, his mouth moving. I envisaged once again, after so long, a steaming, gray city, half rubble, dark and soulless and a mutant child-man scrabbling through the ruins, looking behind him, frightened and alone. Homeless, powerless; nothing. Thiede? Could the urbane, sophisticated, potent creature I knew ever have been so helpless? The first Wraeththu. On reflection, who else could he be? Through suffering we rise . . . I had been stupid not to guess. Had Orien known? In the beginning, once the Aghama had established his new, feral race, he had slipped into anonymity (changed his name? His appearance? Some people must know him, surely?). Perhaps he had been tired, needed time to recuperate, to plan. Perhaps he had simply become bored. Thiede divulges his inner feelings to no-one, except himself.

Wraeththu speak of the Aghama sometimes, not as often as they should, bearing in mind what he should mean to them, but when they do, it is in veiled terms of his still being involved in manipulating our race. A misty figure; part god, part monster. They are not wrong. The Aghama vanished from the chaos of Megalithica and built his stronghold here in Immanion. He had made the city the nerve-center of his operations, the heart of Wraeththu, and the communication lines he sought to install would become the veins and arteries, our thoughts the lifeblood. Had Thiede once needed peace? Was that why he had come here? Could he ever be allowed to experience it? He had never been human.

I lay back on the pillows and held Vaysh against me. Now I could hear him breathing; the sky beyond the window was faintest pink and gold.

Today, I would tell him; tell him that I knew. I could not anticipate his reaction, but I could imagine relief in his eyes. Together, we would walk outside and look toward the far horizon, where the sleek ships prance upon the skirling waves, and we would see the sky and we would see the future. It lay that way, didn't it? So much, so much; I wanted to know it all. I wanted to live the past through his eyes to understand what was to come. His blood, the primal blood, ran in my veins. His essence was my essence. He could see everything in the world and I would look through his eyes and see it too. I knew what to look for.

CHAPTER ELEVEN

>─┼─◆>─·O·─<◆─┼─<

Ending

It has taken me many months to complete this statement, and of course, other things have happened to me since the time where I wanted it to end. Parts of it I decided to rewrite; Vaysh pointed out to me the places where I'd been too vague or too hurried. Essentially, the writing of these pages has been an exorcism for me and surprisingly, a relaxation; one thing to look forward to every evening, even if I never actually get the time to write anything, which does happen. A year has passed since Vaysh told me the truth about Thiede, and already the Pellaz who lived then (and who began to write his story), seems such a callow, ingenuous person. I have been educated well. I am Tigron, and even if it suits some Hara to continue calling me Thiede's puppet, I have proved my worth, both in the Hegalion and among our people. I have pursued the desire to be thoroughly Gelaming with single-minded zeal. My ears are always alert; there are few things in Phaonica kept secret from me. Vaysh says I look taller, and it is true that I do *feel* taller. If the ghosts of my past have not yet laid to rest, at least I have learned how to silence them.

Thiede appears to have been right about the amount of time we shall have to prepare ourselves for the war against the Varrs (because no matter how euphemistically our invasion of Megalithica is referred to—that is what it boils down to), but we have learned that the self-styled supreme commander of the Varrs, known to us as Ponclast, has begun to turn back to the Path. The Varrs' weakness has always been their lack of self-development; now there are rumors that Ponclast seeks to rectify that. This news was not well received by the Hegemony. We shall have to move more carefully now. Ashmael has proposed that we should transport three divisions of the Gelaming forces to Megalithica and establish a garrison in the south. Around this base would be constructed a barrier that no enemy could penetrate; a shield of natural force. It is essential now that Gelaming personnel obtain a hold in Megalithica. We have supporters there who will need our help. I often hear Terzian's name mentioned nowadays; he is almost respected in Immanion. Every time I hear it, some part of me goes cold. It is because some instinct tells me, no matter how hard I try to ignore it, that Cal is in Galhea. He is with Terzian. I can sense it, and even now, if I dwell on it too deeply, I am filled with rage. Thiede knows for sure about this, of course, and in time will probably tell me. I suppose I am as close to Thiede as anyone can get, but he enjoys keeping secrets and I know he is still concerned about my feelings for Cal. I have hidden them very well. It angers me to say that I still love him, for I know it *is* a weakness and I can't afford that kind of weakness, but after all that you have read, surely you can understand. I feel that Cal and I will meet again, but I'm not sure about what will happen between us when that time comes. I've changed so much and I fear that living with the Varrs will have changed him greatly too. When Thiede reads this, as he will, he will be furious and we will probably argue. Occasionally, he makes some casual reference to finding me a consort, but because we are all so preoccupied with more important issues at the moment, I can generally avoid that one. Somehow I feel that the subject will be brought up again fairly soon.

Yesterday, Thiede and I traveled through the other-lanes to a small Wraeththu town, north of Immanion. I can't remember its name. Thiede thought we deserved a peaceful afternoon after a hectic morning of arguing with Ashmael in the Hegalion. (He thinks we are dragging our feet over when to move our people to Megalithica. He is too impatient.) I was in no mood to let Ashmael rant on and the debate got quite vigorous. Once I cracked a joke at his expense and everyone laughed. The atmosphere in the Hegalion had been sour when we left.

We found a quiet cafe and sat outside in the sunshine, drinking tart, sparkling wine. Thiede was amused by a fanciful statue that had been erected in the town square, supposedly in the image of the Aghama. It looked nothing like him. The har who served us our wine thought we were just high-ranking hara from the city. He spoke to us about the Tigron, whom he'd heard had more spirit than Thiede had bargained for and that they quarrelled incessantly. Thiede caught my eye and smiled. We confirmed or denied nothing. The Har went back inside the cafe.

"Well," I said, "Is that true?"

Thiede shrugged. "Sometimes you *do* say too much, but not enough that I regret my decision in bringing you here."

"Will we move to Megalithica soon?"

He looked away. "Not *you*, Pell."

"Why?"

"There's no need." Thiede has a knack of bringing down a cloud of silence that no-one dares break. He did it then. I watched him stare across the sleepy square, absently rubbing his glass with his fingers, frowning at the statue. Eventually, he said, "That isn't me, Pell," meaning so much.

"Yes it is," I replied, meaning even more.

He laughed, drank, laughed, drank some more. "I suppose you're going to put this in your book are you?" he said.

Everything of import, Thiede, everything.

Extract from "Immanion Enquirer," a weekly news journal, five weeks after the completion of Pellaz's manuscript

A press release from Phaonica today confirmed rumors that have been circulating within the city for over a week. It appears that yet another total stranger will ascend to the throne of Immanion, as Tigrina, consort to Tigron Pellaz. Without doubt, this is the decision of Lord Thiede, but it is stressed that the proposal has been given the full approval of the Hegemony.

It has been reported that a Ferelithian har, whose name has been given as Caeru Meveny, accompanied by a harling of indeterminate age and a human female, applied for an interview with the Tigron ten days ago, after traveling by sea from Ferelithia. Palace sources now reveal that the Ferelithian shall be crowned Tigrina in one month's time, and take the bond of blood with the Tigron. No comment has been forthcoming from either Pellaz or Thiede, but we are given to understand that up till now, the Tigron has refused to grant an audience with his proposed Tigrina or even acknowledge his presence through a third party. An employee at the palace has disclosed that the strangers have been allocated a suite within Phaonica itself and have described the child as having "weirding eyes." No confirmation has been forthcoming, but it is the widely held belief that the Tigron has been cited as the father of the child and that its hostling has come to Immanion in order to demand recognition and status for his son.

As the voice of the people of Immanion, this publication requests that the Tigron should make a public statement to clarify this matter as soon as possible.

THE BEWITCHMENTS OF
LOVE AND HATE

>━┼╉━○━╈┼━<

The Second Book of Wraeththu

*With very special thanks to
Valor of Christian Death for
creating the poems*

This book is dedicated to my long-suffering colleagues at the library, especially, Lynda, Claire, Karen, Michelle, Sheila and Gwyn. (See, you can get your name in print as well!)

With thanks to Jag for locking me in the workroom to get this finished, Sarah Wood at Macdonald for her insight, Rhoda King for believing in me, Nick Green for providing the hardware and software so promptly, to Sue Eley for her invaluable help and everyone else who has offered help and support and are too numerous to mention.

Energy is ectasy. When we drop the barriers and let power pour through, it floods the body, pulsing through every nerve, arousing every artery, coursing like a river that cleanses as it moves. In the eye of the storm, we rise on the winds that roar through mind and body, throbbing a liquid note as the voice pours out shimmering honey in waves of golden light, that as they pass, leave peace. No drug can take us so high; no thrill pierce us so deep because we have felt the essence of all delight, the heart of joy, the end of desire. Energy is love, and love is magic.

STARHAWK
The Spiral Dance, *Harper and Row, 1979*

BOOK ONE

CHAPTER ONE

>─┤─◀▶─●─◀▶─┤─◄

Made into Har

A lie from the lips of a hostling
Swimming in the irony
Gasping for breath of perfect wisdom
Whilst disgorging the relics.

Our house did not have a name until I was nearly five years old. Then, my hostling Cobweb (he that had brought me into the world), ordered that a board be nailed above the outer courtyard. It read, "We dwell in Forever."

Cobweb is afraid of dreams and sees omens everywhere. His life is governed by a chain of complex charms, cantrips and runic precautions, leading from one day to the next. Perhaps, he feared transience; to me the house became simply "Forever." Many things changed in my life at that time. I was now old enough to receive tuition, although Cobweb had been imparting his own particular brand of education for some time, so that now I habitually crossed my fingers and said a little rhyme whenever black birds flew from right to left across my path, and I never wished evil out loud upon anyone, in case the spirits heard and punished me.

"Each day has its own special character," Cobweb told me. "Today, for example, is a day of sharpness and crystal; you must learn to recognize the smell, the *ambience.*" It was true that the sky did look particularly brittle that day (could it really break?), and everything looked hard and shiny. On a metal day, my whole body would ache and the taste in my mouth would set my teeth on edge. By the time I was ready for schooling, other matters had taken precedence in my imagination, although I never confessed it to Cobweb, and the taste of the days would only come back to me on extremely summery days or extremely wintery ones.

Forever was enthroned upon a hill in the north of the town Galhea, my father's stronghold. We had farms to the west and in the valleys, hidden behind Forever's hill. In the summer, I could look from my bedroom window and see herds of cattle grazing the lush grass and the rippling seas of grain, green and silver, that were never still. In the autumn my father's house was filled with the smell of mown hay and wagons would come from the east, bearing produce from tribes who needed our grain and meat and leather. I once attended an autumn market in Galhea, shrinking against my hostling's legs, frightened by the noise and bustle. Cobweb gave me a newly minted coin that had come down from the north and I bought myself some sugar sweets with it that had come from a village on the other side of the great forest. Tribe leaders from miles around brought my father gifts, seeking favor in his eyes. It was usually in this way that our wine cellar became stocked for celebrations later in the season. Similarly, the larder shelves would become so full with preserves, delicacies, sweetmeats and cheeses, that jars would have to be stacked on the floor beneath. After the markets, it was customary for the people of Galhea to join together in the dusk to dance the harvest away from the town. It was a cheery lamplit procession of wagons and oxen and skipping feet. Blood-red flowers shed petals beneath the wheels and the air was full of music. Back in Galhea, the great doors to the grain stores would be closed, now half empty, but still holding more than enough for our needs.

Although my hostling could teach me to read and write (along with other more secret knowledge that Terzian would certainly not have approved of), it was not enough of an education for the son of a high-caste har. I was not allowed to attend the college in Galhea with other harlings my own age. Terzian, my father, preferred to find tutors whom he could trust, whose intelligence he respected, and who were happy to imbue my supposedly eager little mind with knowledge at home. I was not as intelligent as my father thought. It did not take my teachers long to realize this, but they were shrewd enough to continue entertaining my father's fancies by praising my progress. I suppose I was a late developer. Terzian lived by logic and strategy; I lived happily in a world of totally illogical imagination, inherited, no doubt, from Cobweb. I'm sure it always grieved my noble sire that Cobweb had ever had to have anything to do with my procreation and if he could have found a way to cope with reproduction all by himself, he most certainly would have done. He suspected every other har but himself of foolishness and fought constantly to discipline Cobweb's superstitious nature. Conversations at mealtimes were habitually punctuated by Terzian's impatient outbursts. "Clouds are clouds, Cobweb! That is not an avenging spirit, neither does it seek to recruit souls from my house! For God's sake!" and other such denials.

Forever is such a big house and so few of us lived there, yet I was never lonely. Cobweb once told me that he used to be afraid of it. "This house has been lived in for a long, long time," he said.

"Who lived here?" I asked.

"Oh, the *others,*" Cobweb answered darkly and would not explain what he meant. "You are young; it might spoil your innocence to know," he said. I was used to my hostling's somewhat gray remarks and had learned at an early age that some of my questions were not to be answered, at least not by him.

* * *

One day, I was playing at being a big, black animal in the green conservatory at the side of the house. Someone was paid to look after the plants there, but they did not seem to notice and continued to grow in unruly defiance all over the windows. The door to the garden could not be opened because vines had grown through the lock. It was one of my favorite haunts, a place where, when I was very little, Cobweb and I used to spend a lot of time together. The plants must have absorbed many secrets; Terzian hardly ever came there. But that day, he pushed open the window-door and stood in the darkness of the room behind.

"Swift," he said. "Come . . . Swift, what *are* you doing?"

Guiltily I told the truth because I was too surprised to think of a suitable lie. "I'm a big, black animal," I said nervously, and I could see my father gritting his teeth.

"Yes, well, the time for games is over!" he said with his intimidating air of authority. "Really, Swift, at your age, you must begin to put aside these infant habits."

I picked myself up off the floor, brushed down my clothes and went to stare up into his face. I have heard people call him wickedly handsome, but how can wickedness be seen in a face that is usually so cold? Although I was always conscious of displeasing him in many ways, I adored my father. Most of the time he paid me little attention, but when he did my whole world would light up with his special radiance. He was very different from me in ways I could not understand; there was something about him that made him seem very far away, but to me he was simply Magnificence Incarnate. I wanted him to like me. Most of the time, I was confident that he did. After all, Cobweb made a hundred mistakes every day that made Terzian angry and I had no doubt that my father was fond of him. I was canny enough to learn from Cobweb's errors. Terzian would never catch me making the secret signs, or talking to myself or watching the clouds; usually, I could sense his presence rooms away.

"Swift, I have chosen two hara to attend to your education," Terzian told me, drawing me into the dark room and closing the conservatory door. "The time has come for you to study properly, as befits a har of breeding."

"Yes, tiahaar," I said meekly. We rarely spoke to each other. Questions always died on my lips when he turned his eyes upon me.

He took me to another room, at the front of the house, where sunlight came in during the morning and the roofs of Galhea could be seen from the window. Two hara stood with their backs to the light, but I could still see their faces. One of them was smiling at me, one looked only at my father. The one who smiles will be the kindest, I thought, unconsciously shrinking back against my father's side, although I did not touch him.

"Moswell, Swithe, may I present my son Swift," Terzian announced grandly. I knew I was not at my cleanest and could feel my face uncontrollably twisting into an idiotic grin. I wanted Cobweb. Swithe looked at me for the first time; he still did not smile.

"Lessons begin tomorrow," my father said.

* * *

Afterwards, I ran straight to Cobweb. I found him upstairs, in his own room, where the light fell in so pleasingly, and everything was comfortable. He was sitting at a table by the window, painting strange faces on porous paper with black ink. I just ran to him and threw my arms round his neck. "Swift, be careful!" he said, but he turned to take my face in his hands with inky fingers. I was distraught, but I didn't know why. Dimly, I thought my father wanted to take something away from me, change my existence, yet I couldn't see how. Secrets can never be kept from Cobweb; he does not need words.

"He wants you to learn things," he said gently, "that's all."

"Will things be different?"

"Different?" He absorbed my fears and contemplated them. "Sometimes, Swift, it is better that Terzian does not know exactly the way we think and feel. He finds you teachers; listen to what they say. They are probably wise in their own way, but do not take their words as Truth, just because they are older and wiser than you. Just listen, that's all."

I crawled onto his lap, although I was nearly too big for that. "Things will change; I can *smell* it!" I said.

"Everything changes eventually," Cobweb said. "That's just the way of things. Not all changes are bad."

Not all, but more than half. Cobweb neglected to mention that.

"My father rules Galhea," I said to Moswell. It was the first day of my official education and I had been roused from my bed earlier than was usual. Moswell and Swithe had both eaten with Cobweb and myself in the dining room, though my father had not been there.

"Terzian is a great har," Moswell said stiffly. "And you are a privileged little harling to have him as your father."

Moswell was scared of Terzian. It was not until much later in my life that I learned of my father's reputation as an enthusiastic and callous warmonger. I knew that he was a warrior when he wasn't with us in the house, but I didn't really know what that meant. It didn't concern me, so I just never thought about it. Questions like "Whom does he fight with?" and "Does he really *kill* people?" never crossed my mind. Terzian would disappear from the house for months at a time, and the house would feel different then, more relaxed, and let itself get rather more untidy. Then he would be back; the big front doors would be opened and in he would come with the cold air and a dozen other hara, all dressed in black leather and talking in gruff, grown-up voices. Sometimes he would be scarred; once above the left eye, which made Cobweb moody and short with him. At these times, home from the fighting, he and Cobweb would be at their closest. I did not understand the needs of adults, but was intrigued by their brief caresses and the different tone in their voices, the exaggerated grace of their bodies. Cobweb was rarely to be found in his own rooms when Terzian came home.

* * *

Moswell's task was to instruct me in the history of Wraeththu. It was the first time that I heard of men.

"Before the rise of Wraeththu, another race ruled the Earth," he said. "Humanity. As Wraeththu are called hara, they were called men." I was instilled thoroughly with the knowledge of man's intrinsic badness; his pointless aggression (Wraeththu aggression, of course, was never pointless), his short-sighted pillage of the world and more than this (horror of horrors), his two separate *types*. Moswell struggled grimly with the necessary delicacy to impart this information; not an easy task as I was (naturally) ignorant of Wraeththu sexuality at that age. Humanity had male and female, their bodies were sort of *split*. This made me feel cold. How could humanity ever have felt whole? Half their natures simply did not exist. I was not sure whether I believed what Moswell was telling me. It was an inconceivable idea. The first lesson was merely a glamorous alleluia on how wonderful Wraeththu were and how vulgar and vile men had been. None of it seemed real, or even relevant, to me. I had been born in Galhea, sheltered in my father's house; the outside world was a mystery I had no inclination to penetrate. "You are just young," Moswell intoned, noting my impatience and wavering attention. "But your father would have you know these things, so, uninteresting as they appear, you must commit them to memory."

Moswell did smile a lot, but this was merely to cover up a numbing tedium of manner. What he told me should have been exciting. Wraeththu, after all, were a comparatively new race and their escalation had been thrilling, the foundation of legend.

After the first lesson, I looked for Cobweb; he was in the garden. It was the time of year when spring begins to get warm.

"What are men?" I asked him. He was dressed in palest green, some floating stuff, and his hair was braided to his waist. His skin looked very luminous that day.

"I was once a man," he said.

"You were once a man?" I repeated slowly, unsure that this was not one of my hostling's oblique jokes. He sighed and touched my shoulder.

"Ah, Swift, I would protect you from all this if I could. I cannot even see the purpose for you knowing it yet, but Terzian . . ."

An eloquent pause. He led me into the greenest part of the garden, where there are few flowers and the shadows seem alive. Sometimes there are lizards there. Paving stones beneath our feet were viridian with old moss.

"You mature so quickly," Cobweb said and we sat down on a wooden bench, which would undoubtedly leave licheny stains on our clothes afterwards. "When I was your age . . . well, I was just a baby."

I snuggled up close against him. That way most fears would disappear, but I could feel an unnameable sadness within him and our fears mingled. "I was human . . ." he said.

"When? When? Was I there?"

He laughed and squeezed my shoulder. "You? No, no. If I was human I couldn't have been your hostling, could I?"

"Why not?"

He took me on his lap and stroked the hair from my eyes. "Why not? Well, because, long ago, when I wasn't Wraeththu, when I wasn't har, I was the half of human that can't bear children, harlings . . . oh, do you know what I'm talking about?"

"No . . . I thought . . . what? What are you talking about?"

"It's so hard to explain." He sighed again and I pressed my head hard against his chest where I could sense his heart beating. "Swift," he said. "When Wraeththu began, we weren't born as hara like you. We came from human stock. We were mutated from human stock. I did not have a hostling like you. I had a mother; it's different. When I was sixteen years old, I became har. I was *made* har. That's when I stopped being a half and became a whole . . ."

"I don't believe you," I said. Time before my own simply did not exist for me and I could not imagine Cobweb as anything but my father's consort, gracing Forever with beauty and being there for me to run to for comfort.

"If I was human and you a human child," he said, "then I would be your mother and that's all. But as I am har, it would be quite possible for Terzian to be your hostling and me your father."

"But you're not!"

"No, but I could be. Oh God, now is not the time, Swift. One day you'll understand. Just see it like this . . . oh, like what?" He laughed. "Later perhaps."

"What's 'mutate'?" I asked.

"Change," he answered, and I became alarmed.

"Change? Does changing mean you become something else?"

"Sometimes, but don't worry, you won't ever change physically the way I did. That's in the past now." He sighed again. "I'm not very good at explaining things, am I?"

"Not really," I agreed.

"Look at the animals," he said, pointing vaguely at the unseen birds twittering above our heads. "Terzian's dogs, your puppy Limba . . ." He looked at me strangely. "Men are like that."

"Like animals?"

"In many ways!"

"Did they have whiskers, tails and fur?" My mental image of mankind was becoming a purring, cozy thing.

Cobweb laughed. "You are too young," he said mysteriously, but he did not answer my question. For several days after this, I became interested in the concept of male and female. Our cook Yarrow had a tabby cat named Mareta and apparently it was a female. Females are "shes," although we habitually called Mareta "he." I wandered around the kitchen driving the staff crazy, saying *"She* has she's kittens!" and considering myself worldly and clever. (Mareta watched me condescendingly from a cushion beside the stove.) One day Ithiel, my father's equerry, was at the kitchen window, taking a mug of ale, leaning on the sill, and he said, *"She* has *her* kittens, Swift, you little moonfly!"* and everyone laughed at me. I never said it again after that, but mulled over the concept of "her" for half an hour afterwards, in my private den among the shrubbery, beyond the gray garden wall. "Her" sounded suspiciously like "har" to me; was there a connection?

About this time (a natural progression from what I had learned), I began to wonder where harlings came from. Cobweb told me that Terzian and he had made me, which was an intriguing idea. Had I been formed from mud and sticks in the garden, perfected by one of Cobweb's secret charms? I preferred to think that Terzian had climbed the highest tree and found me inside an egg in a bird's nest. I fantasized them carrying the egg carefully back to the house (it would have been a moonless, windy night), and laying it gently on a fur rug before the great fire in the drawing room. Terzian, his chest swelling with the emotion of fatherly love, would have put his arm around Cobweb's shoulders and maybe even touched Cobweb's face with his mouth, which he did sometimes. Perhaps, creeping from the darkness outside, some little, furry men had pressed their whiskery noses up against the window to catch a glimpse of the infant as it hatched in the glow of the flames. They would have silently vowed me their king and would come back some day to take me to their secret land.

I told Cobweb all this one evening as we sat in his room, with the curtains drawn against the night.

"Terzian would never climb a tree!" he said, riffling through piles of different-colored paper. "Here is a picture of you when you were very young." He handed it to me, and I put my head on one side and squinted my eyes.

"I don't like it!" I said.

Cobweb shrugged, "You are vain, Swift,"

"What's that?"

"You!"

"Oh, Cobweb!" I ran to him and squeezed him hard, so full of love for him that I felt sad.

Moswell bored me to tears. He droned on and on every morning about Wraeththu this and Wraeththu that; I never really listened to him. It was far more interesting to watch the way the light changed color as it came in through the schoolroom window, dust motes dancing like insects upon the rays. My rangy hound Limba would lie against my legs and yawn, his yellow eyes appraising Moswell speculatively. Unfortunately, my father had trained him too well for his instincts to get the better of him. He would never bite Moswell, as I'm sure he longed to do. My tutor said that the world had once been full of people that had only wanted to take things away from each other. How could that be true?! Men were *so* bad, he said, and yet I secretly pitied them. I could vividly imagine shambling lines of pathetic, furry little creatures, leaving their homes with sorrowful backward glances, heading for the bleak north. That was when Moswell brought me books from my father's library and showed me the pictures of men. "Oh," I said, disappointed, "but they look just like us!"

"No," Moswell insisted patiently. "Men are crude, often ugly beings. The ones in the photographs are nothing to go by. Most of them are not half as attractive."

Physical ugliness was another new concept for me to ponder. Of course, I wanted to see it, but it was a few minutes' walk back to the library, and Moswell didn't want to go.

"Another time," he said.

"But what *is* ugly?" I wanted to know.

"Your questions are tiresome and mostly irrelevant!" Moswell said.

In the afternoons, Swithe took over as my mentor. He was a shy and introverted person, uneasy in my presence, but his head, like mine, was full of dreams. I could see that, no matter how hard he tried to conceal it. The first time we met he said, "What do you know, Swift?" with a shaky smile.

"Oh, lots of things," I answered airily. "I know the names of all the plants on the estate, the secret names that is, and I know where the spirit lives in the lake (it's near the drooping tree), and how to call him up to grant you wishes. I haven't tried it yet, but Cobweb told me how."

Swithe had difficulty maintaining a smile. He always looked as if someone was after him and I wondered if he had done something terrible somewhere else. Perhaps hara or even (with a shiver of delight) *men* would come looking for him some day. Perhaps he was a sorcerer. He had sorcerer's eyes. They changed color with the weather and Cobweb said that was always a way you could tell. I don't know what he was supposed to teach me, but mostly we spent our time together discussing the ponderous statements Moswell came out with in the morning. That was how I came to memorize what Moswell taught me. I needed to know just so that I could tell Swithe about it later. Swithe never actually criticized his colleague, but I could tell he did not like Moswell.

"You, and others your age, are the first pure Wraeththu," he told me, and I asked what he meant.

"Well, some time ago, but not that long, only men lived on the Earth. They had lived here for a long, long time and they changed gradually over the years. Not *all* of them were bad."

"I'm glad," I said. "Have they all gone?"

Swithe made a noise of amusement. "Well, hara like your father would like to think so, but no, they haven't."

"What happened to them?"

"To be honest with you, Swift, I don't know for sure. When it happened, and I became Wraeththu, I was too young and too interested in the newness of being har to take much notice of *exactly* what went on. It was important that I should have done; I can see that now. One moment, we were living in cities, hiding from men and killing them when we could and then suddenly . . . I realized. There were more hara than humans. The cities had died around us. It happened . . . silently."

"You were once a man then, like Cobweb?"

Swithe nodded. "Like everyone. Everyone but for our children."

As time went on, I began to learn more quickly, more from my interest in knowledge than any natural aptitude for study. Like all Varrish harlings, I had been taught to read and write at a very early age. It surprised me to learn that human children were not developed enough to understand these things until they were much, much older, nearly adult, I thought. Then came another surprise. Humans were not considered adult until they were about eighteen years old! How sluggish their brains must be. No wonder Wraeththu had taken their world away from them.

I had had little contact with harlings of my own age. Once, in a moment of outstanding bravado, I had mentioned it to my father and he had murmured obliquely that some day he hoped I would have brothers. He could not specify when. I wanted to go into the town because on those rare occasions Cobweb went there and took me with him, I had seen other harlings playing in the sun, laughing, running barefoot over grass. They had seemed so free and I could never join them.

"Swift," Terzian said to me, "the harlings in the town are . . . well, they do not have your *breeding*. You would gain nothing from mixing with them." Happiness, laughter; to my father these things were apparently nothing. "Anyway," he said with a smile, ruffling my hair, "you have Limba to play with."

This was true, of course. Limba was a good companion and fond of fun, but I couldn't talk to him, could I? If I did, he would just smile at me with his tongue hanging out of his mouth, but I don't believe he understood what I had said.

"All hara belong to different tribes," Moswell told me and then went on to explain what a tribe was. "Your tribe is the Varrs. You are a Varr, Swift."

Of course, I had heard this word before, but now it took on new meaning for me. I belonged to something, a great something. I was one of many. Swithe expanded on this for me later.

"All tribes live in different ways," he said. "They have different *cultures*. (Write that down, Swift.) Some of them live in deserts in the south and they do not look at things in the same way that we do. They are influenced by the desert. They are sort of *dry*, like snakes; deadly and quick. Some tribes care a great deal about magic (like Cobweb does). I'm afraid the Varrs are not one of them. Varrs have no religion, they shun the gifts that have bloomed within us, following man's path of fighting and greed." He remembered hastily where he was and whom he was speaking to and smothered the glaze of fervor in his eyes.

Swithe's often barbed remarks about my tribe and my father did not pass completely over my head. Terzian would of course have been furious if he had known. I said to Swithe, "You do not completely like the Varrs, do you?"

I could see from his face that he longed to tell me why, and I wanted him to tell me, but all he said was, "It is not my place to tell you about your father, Swift."

This did not frighten me as it should. It only added to Terzian's mystique. I never told Cobweb what Swithe said.

Naturally I was curious about Swithe's old home, where he and Moswell had come from. Swithe seemed reluctant to tell me, but I gathered they had sprung from a minor branch of the Unneah (who I later learned were allied to the Varrs only through prudence—or fear). Terzian had ears everywhere. He had heard of my tutors' reputation and had whisked them from under the nose of their tribe leader, whose sons would doubtless suffer from inferior education because of it.

All through the long, hazy summer, I stored knowledge from Moswell and then got Swithe to explain what it meant. Moswell neatened up my writing and polished up my ability to read. I could tell that he considered the tuition Cobweb had previously given me in these directions to be sloppy and undisciplined. Swithe said that my scrawly, illegible writing cheered Moswell up, because it gave him something to moan about. In the afternoons, we would sit in the garden and Swithe would tell me what to write in my notebook. Once, he recited a rhyme he had made up and I learned it by heart and then wrote it down.

> From ashes stumbled, whitened by the crumbled stone
> Of all Man's fears and exclamations
> Wraeththu rise and take the sword.
> Though we are red-pawed,
> Still panting from the kill,
> We say: "This is not ain but justice,
> This is neither shame nor pride."
>
> Where then the darkness
> Whose shadows we present as light?
> Must it not be buried with the debris,
> The earth stamped down in triumph.
>
> Ignored then, this black-hot cone,
> Suppressed beneath a grin of victory,
> But always pulsing, hidden:
> The lights within the tomb,
> Visible only to those who pass
> Its granite door, at dusk, alone.

Cobweb was not impressed by this. I chanted it to him in the evening and when I had finished, he threw down his book and turned on the light.

"God, Swift, that's horrible!" he said. "Don't ever say it to me again, especially after dark!" He was not very pleasant to Swithe the next morning at breakfast. I insisted that the poem had only sounded horrible because of the way I had said it. "It is vile and unfit for harlings to hear and that's that!" my hostling declared vehemently.

After this Cobweb often used to sit with us in the garden, a somewhat icy presence which was unusual for him. Swithe would stare at him and he would throw back his head, gaze at Swithe haughtily and then go back to his reading, never turning the page. Blind I was to the implication of this behavior. It was part of a ritual dance I was yet to discover in life.

Near the end of the summer, my father had to go away for some weeks and Forever breathed a sigh of relief and happily sagged in its foundations. Even Moswell became more likeable. The four of us, my tutors, Cobweb and myself, took to spending the evenings together downstairs in the house. We played games with cards and dice and talked. Moswell liked to steer the conversation in adult directions. Once he said, "No doubt Terzian has heard the whisper of Gelaming activity in the south." He wanted to appear clever and politically minded to Cobweb.

My hostling had been idly juggling a couple of dice in his hand. Now he threw them at the wall.

"In this house," he said darkly, "we shall have no talk of Gelaming!"

I could not understand why the atmosphere in the room became so cold after that. I knew that the Gelaming were another Wraeththu tribe for I had once heard Ithiel talking about them in the kitchen. Why the mere mention of them should anger Cobweb so, I could not guess. Moswell muttered an excuse to go to bed early and left the room. Cobweb sighed and rubbed his eyes. Swithe was hunched precariously on the edge of the sofa; Cobweb sat near his feet on the floor.

"I'm sorry," Cobweb said to the fireplace.

I had a feeling that one of those times was approaching when I would be reminded that it was time I went upstairs, so I tried to make myself invisible in a corner of the room. Swithe reached out gingerly and put his hand on Cobweb's shoulder, sensing what he thought was distress. Only I knew it was rage. Cobweb leaned his cheek upon Swithe's hand and said, "Terzian is my life."

"Terzian is not here," Swithe suggested and Cobweb smiled. That, of course, was when they noticed me.

"Go to bed now, Swift," Cobweb said.

When my father returned, when the leaves had begun to change their colors on the trees, Swithe's behavior became most eccentric. Several times I had to upbraid him, "Swithe, you are not listening to me!" and he would smile wistfully. I once went to his room and found it littered with scrunched-up pieces of paper, scrawled with verse which he would not let me read. I could not understand, for it was beyond me to work out the connection between my father's return and Swithe's behavior; beyond me to see the similarity between the discarded, savaged balls of poetry and Swithe himself. For Cobweb, the incident was over; his lord had come home.

Terzian had sustained a nasty wound in his thigh and had to rest. Cobweb never left his side, and Moswell and Swithe did not come to sit with us in the evening again for quite some time. One night, as I was lingering over my hot drink before bedtime, Terzian said, in a low faraway voice, "Cobweb, do you remember . . . ?" and Cobweb had interrupted him.

"Please . . . don't!"

My father sighed, touching his thigh. "It's just the leg . . . this wound, like yours . . ."

"I know." Cobweb went over to where Terzian lay on the couch and stroked his brow. "If it's any comfort, mine was a lot worse than that."

I was longing to scream, "What? What?!" sensing something agonizingly interesting.

"You've changed so much since then," Terzian said, taking a lock of my hostling's hair in his fingers.

"Perhaps we both have."

"Do you blame me for what happened?"

Cobweb shook his head. "You thought I was dead."

"Not just that . . . the other thing. It still makes you angry . . ."

"Not really. I think I was more angry for you than for myself." I recognized immediately an outright lie on my hostling's part.

There was a moment's silence, which gradually filled with tension.

"Cobweb, you know so many things. Do you know if . . . ?"

"It's unfair of you to ask!" Cobweb answered sharply and my father sighed and nodded.

The next day, I just had to question Cobweb about this conversation. He pulled a face and looked at me hard, deciding whether or not to answer me.

"You might not remember, you were so young," he said.

"Remember what?" I asked impatiently.

"When the Strangers came here; two of them. They stayed here in the house. Pellaz and . . . the *other one.*"

It was one of my earliest memories. People had been either hot or cold to me then, young as I was, and I vaguely remembered the dark-haired Pellaz and his golden warmth. I remembered also his companion, who had had yellow hair and the feeling of ice and who had not liked me.

"I remember them," I said and Cobweb nodded.

"In a way, we were talking of them last night," he said.

"I don't suppose you're going to explain it all," I said hopelessly, weary with the experience of someone who is always too young to be told things.

"The one with yellow hair (I cannot speak his name), he caused your father grief," Cobweb said, making the sign of the cross of power on his brow, his lips, his heart.

"He had the evil eye?" I enquired knowledgeably.

Cobweb wrinkled his nose. "Not *exactly*. He is just Trouble, standing up and walking about in a body!" We were in the drawing room. Cobweb walked over to the long windows and threw them open. Air rushed in smelling of smoke and ripeness, birds flapped noisily off the terrace in alarm. "Sometimes I am so afraid," Cobweb said, in a soft, sad voice.

"Of what?" I asked, running toward him. He bent down and put his hands on my shoulders.

"You're growing up," he said. "I suppose I still think of human children when I look at you. You are five years old, yet you look twice that age."

I sighed. "Afraid of *what*, Cobweb?"

"Let's sit down," he suggested and we curled up on the couch together.

"They brought me back home when I was hurt, those strangers," he began.

"How did you get hurt?" I demanded. "Where was Terzian?"

Cobweb pulled a face; his expression comprised bitterness, wry humor and disgust.

"Where indeed! Let's just say I was alone and they rescued me."

"Pellaz was nice. He talked to me," I said.

"I know he was . . . it was the other one." He began to scowl and his eyes shone with the kind of hatred that can quite easily destroy someone. I kept quiet, waiting for him to go on.

"I hate to say this, Swift, but I shall. Your father fell in love with him."

I did not think this was terrible, only understandable, because my simple grasp of "love" was then concerned wholly with what was pleasing to behold and what was not. The *feelings* were beyond my understanding. The yellow-haired har had been beautiful, in a cruel, lazy sort of way. This was clearly why my father had loved him.

"Was that bad?" I asked timidly.

"Bad?!" Cobweb screwed up his eyes and snarled. "It might have gone very badly for both of us if *he* had stayed here."

"Why?"

Cobweb looked down at me. "You love your father very much," he said, "as you should. But you are too young to understand him."

"It seems I am too young for anything at the moment!" I retorted hotly, mightily sick of hearing that particular phrase.

"Alright," Cobweb said, "Alright. If *he* had stayed here and given Terzian sons, there might have been no room in his life for us. He worshiped C—he worshiped *him!*"

"You're wrong!" I cried, pulling away, facing a Cobweb I felt I no longer knew. My hostling was too wise, too tranquil to come out with things like this.

"Oh, Swift, you know so little. One day, you'll understand." He stood up and walked back to the window. "Terzian needed me when they left here; his heart was broken. I suppose he's become fond of me over the years, but I am not deceived. That is why I am afraid."

"Why?" I pleaded, feeling tears building up inside me. Cobweb had never talked like this to me before; he had always protected me from things he feared might be upsetting.

"He . . . might . . . he might *come back!*" Cobweb pressed one slim, white hand against his eyebrows and leaned against the window. I could see his shoulders trembling, oh so slightly. I ran to him, sniveling and afraid, and we sat on the floor and hugged each other.

"Never speak his name, *never!*" Cobweb warned. "Never whistle in the dark for it summons evil and he will hear it. In the treetops, the feathered ones will know. Watch them, Swift, watch the birds!"

That night I had a terrible dream. In the dream, the yellow-haired har was standing in a wreath of shadowy flames and his beauty was ugliness. He saw me and snared me in horror. "Call me," he whispered and held out his hands, which were dripping red and shaking. I tried to turn away, run away, but I could not move. His eyes transfixed me. "Call me!" A terrible whine started in my throat, a sound I could not control. When I woke up I was shrieking, "Cal! Cal!" and lights were being turned on hurriedly in the hall outside my room; voices, and footsteps, running.

Next morning, I went alone to the long gallery on the second floor of the house, miserable and haunted. Cobweb had been very upset by what had happened in the night and Terzian very angry. They both blamed each other. I had heard my father shout when they had left me once more in darkness. The sound had come right through the walls. He had shouted, "What possessed you to tell him that? What possessed you?"

And my hostling's answering cry, "Are you ashamed that he should know?"

I could remember that things had changed when Pellaz and Cal had left Galhea. Of course, at the time I had not understood why. At first the house had held its breath, everyone speaking in hushed voices and looking over their shoulders. Ithiel had skulked about looking very embarrassed, but on hand in case my father needed him. He had wanted to go after them, I suppose. He had wanted blood; Cobweb too. He and Ithiel had had low, heated conversations together when they thought no-one was listening. My father had stayed alone in his room for three days, refusing food, accepting only wine and hot, potent sheh. After that, he had appeared once more downstairs, gray as with the aftermath of illness. That part I remember well. Cobweb and I had been eating breakfast together and my father had come into the room. He had stood in the doorway and no-one had spoken and then Cobweb had risen from his chair and Terzian had walked toward him; they had embraced.

Since that time, I had sensed them drawing closer to each other as the memory of the blighted Cal faded. We had built for ourselves an emotional haven within the walls of Forever; father, hostling, son. Now Terzian had come home from his fighting, sick and tired, and he had had too much time to think of the past, lying around the house all day. Now I had dreamed and called Cal's name. Now I feared I had opened the door to let him back into Forever. We had not thought of him for five years.

Swithe came to find me. "They guessed you'd be here," he said and squatted down beside me. I thought to myself, He is my only friend. I can tell him anything, and told him about the dream and then, after a split second's consideration, about the dreadful episode of Cal and how he had spurned my father. I suppose I should have been prepared for the warm light of respect that came into Swithe's eyes when I explained how Cal had refused to share Terzian's life, but I was still quietly outraged. "He would have made Cobweb and me leave the house!" I added venomously, forgetting that only yesterday I had denied that was possible.

"Come downstairs," Swithe said. "Moswell is fretting."

Later, I tried to apologize to my hostling for the dreadful thing that I had done, speaking the forbidden name, but he had only waved my apologies away with one quick movement. "I should never have spoken as I did," he said. "No wonder it gave you nightmares."

"But are we *safe?*" I begged.

"Yes, of course," Cobweb answered shortly.

CHAPTER TWO

>─┤─◆〉─◉─〈◆─├─◁

Coming of Age

Radiant angel; magnificent black hair
Prostration at his feet
Overwhelmed by the loveliest Har
Under the concave firmament.

Some weeks passed and then news arrived for my father from the north. There were cities there, Varr cities that had been seized from men. Varrs of high caste ruled in those places (of castes higher than my father's anyway), and sometimes their eyes wandered in the direction of Galhea and they would send emissaries down to see how things went with us. Terzian was never pleased about this.

One morning, three polished black horses trotted out of the mist, past the follies, the fountains of Forever's gardens, up the drive to the great, white steps where my father's dogs leaped up and howled and bounded round the horses' legs. They had been riding through the night. The riders' garments of thick black leather and metal were glistening with dew. Cobweb said that northern Varrs were hardy to the point of masochism. I was in the hall when Ithiel strode into the house, when he went straight into Terzian's study without knocking. They left the door open and I could hear my father's abrupt noise of irritation when Ithiel said, "There are three of them. Ponclast has sent them." Ponclast was Nahir-Nuri, the most elevated of hara. Normally, his name was heard only in oaths; my father resented Ponclast's interest in his affairs.

They were received in the red room that overlooked the lawns at the back of the house. It was the most uncomfortable room in Forever. I hung about by the door and one of them patted me on the head as he passed. Food was ordered, ale and sheh. I went into the kitchen where everyone was hurrying around looking harried. Limba was with me and he nearly made Yarrow trip over by getting under his feet. Yarrow boxed my ears and yelled at me to get the hell out of his kitchen. That was when Moswell put his nose around the door. I had hoped lessons would be forgotten for the day, but he dragged me off to the schoolroom and I did not see our visitors again until the end of the afternoon.

That evening, my father, looking much relieved and uncommonly cheerful because of it, made an announcement at dinner. We were eating off the best silver because the northerners were there. "Swift," my father said, and I turned red because I was uneasy with strangers then. "Swift," he said, "I know you'll be pleased; Tiahaar Ponclast's son Gahrazel is coming here to Galhea to stay in the house, to study with you." He addressed his guests. "My son has often wanted company of his own age." (I mentioned it once, I thought angrily, just once!) If the northerners hadn't been there I would have asked, "But why?" However, paralyzed by everyone's attention upon me, I was too shy to speak. It had nothing to do with manners.

Cobweb had a flinty look about him, caressing the smooth silver handle of his fork (maybe thinking it was a knife). He said in a clear, cool voice, "But why?"

One of them, who had sleek black hair and the face of a hawk (his name, I think, was Mawn), said, "Compared to how you live here, it is no place for harlings in the north. Ponclast feels the situation up there might adversely affect Gahrazel's development. He has always admired Forever, and is aware of Terzian's excellent choice of tutors." If Mawn was aware of the veiled hostility in Cobweb's manner, he forgave him. Cobweb, because of his charm and his beauty, could get away with murder. Mawn smiled toothily at him, helplessly enthralled.

"Swift's tutors are the best," my father said, rather unexpectedly. Cobweb looked at me and I could tell we were sharing the same thought. Ponclast's eyes in Galhea, in Forever, looking out from the face of his son. Cobweb smiled, partly because he saw in my recognition of that fact a developing maturity.

Later, I heard them talking, Cobweb and my father. I lay in my bed and their voices reached me through my open door. Since the nightmare, I was too afraid to sleep with it closed. Cobweb spoke with sarcasm. "You seemed almost *grateful* and so *pleasant!*"

My father answered irritably, "I have to be pleasant; we all have to be, damn them!"

"He's had trouble with this Gahrazel, I feel," Cobweb said.

"Who, Ponclast? Hmm, perhaps."

"Why else send him away from home? You don't believe that fawning rubbish about Forever being so *admirable,* do you?"

"He will be company for Swift. The child spends too much time alone."

I lay there, listening, in two minds about whether I was pleased or not. New people meant changes; I would have to talk to Cobweb about it.

The next day, all my hostling would say was, "It'll do you good, having someone else here your own age. Terzian is right, you live inside your own head too much!"

Feeling betrayed, I went to look for Swithe and he said, "Cobweb is right. Anyway, it'll make lessons more interesting, won't it?"

"Hrrmph," I consented glumly. "Anyway, what did they mean by it not being 'right' for harlings in the north?"

Swithe looked perplexed. I sensed him carefully preparing an answer for me. "This country . . . it is not . . . a *peaceful* place, Swift."

I must have looked completely blank. Galhea, after all, was very peaceful.

"There are two kinds of darkness," Swithe continued, still struggling. "Remember them now, even if you don't really understand what I'm saying. One darkness is the natural kind, like when the sun goes down, what you find inside a locked cupboard or the deepest glade of a forest. The other, well, it is a darkness *inside a person* and it can eat them whole! It can eat entire cities away, until only dust and shadows are left. It is what men called evil and the darkness in the north can be like that."

How could I understand his words? I couldn't; not then. But the feelings behind them struck deep. I never forgot them, nor how the room had seemed to chill as Swithe spoke, the sun beyond the windows to grow briefly shadowed.

Gahrazel was about a year and a half older than me, but he could not write as neatly and was always horribly restless. He was deposited one morning, without ceremony, at the gates of Forever, and Cobweb and I watched his hunched figure, carrying a single, bulging bag, trudge wearily up the wide, graveled road to the house. "It seems they are glad to be rid of him," Cobweb remarked drily. I thought so too. Gahrazel had seen fighting, real fighting. He had seen hara die and had actually touched the dead body of a man. "I cut some of his hair off," he said confidentially. I showed him all the secret places in the garden, including the corner of the lake where the spirit lived, which Gahrazel appeared eager to invoke.

"If I am to stay here, I suppose we must be friends," he said grudgingly, and went on to tell me how he would miss the hara he had known back home.

Lessons were over for the day and in the garden it was becoming quite dark. Nearly all the leaves were gone from the trees now and we had to wear coats when we went outside. "This *is* a beautiful place," Gahrazel said, "there is nowhere like this where I come from."

We had known each other only a week or so, yet already communicated in an unselfconscious manner. This was mainly because of the way Gahrazel was; spirited, confident and, to me, surprisingly mature. He had been sad to find himself in an unwelcome situation, but was prepared to make the best of it.

"Why did your father send you away?" I ventured carefully and he snorted angrily.

"Why?! You know what fathers are like," he answered scathingly.

I did not want to appear ignorant so I said, "I know what *mine* is like," and we laughed.

"I am near my time," Gahrazel told me. This was obviously something momentous.

"Oh?" I said.

"You know, Feybraiha, the coming of age."

"Oh, yes . . ."

"You *don't* know, do you!"

I shrugged helplessly.

"There was . . . someone, someone a lot older than me. That was why Ponclast decided to bury me in the country. He disapproved of my choice, and I knew I would disapprove of his! Our tastes have never coincided. There was an argument, so" (he threw up his hands) "here I am!"

Feybraiha: so, another new word for me to ponder. Was this another changing? If so, what? Pride prevented me from revealing my ignorance then, but something about it worried me deeply. A feeling of vibration; a sting. Presentiment perhaps?

For the first few days, Gahrazel was sullen and uncooperative. I tried to imagine how I would feel if Terzian ever sent me away to live with strangers. I strained to be tolerant. Gahrazel disliked his room (one of the best in the house), complained the food tasted strange and was sarcastic to Cobweb. It infuriated him that Cobweb didn't get annoyed. On the third day he joined me in my lessons, and to my delight, contradicted Moswell constantly. "This har knows nothing. He is a fool," Gahrazel whispered to me. From that day forward, the most crucial aspects of my education came from him.

Terzian gave Gahrazel a pony, solid and swift as my own, and we would often ride together, over the wide fields beyond the town and into the edges of the dark forests. My father did not approve of young harlings being out alone in the forest; stray men or hara of different, unfriendly tribes might lurk there, so either Moswell or Swithe would always accompany us. Gahrazel complained bitterly, once even to Terzian himself. "I go away for days by myself at home!" he said.

My father smiled. "It is not my wish, Gahrazel, to deliver you back to your father in pieces, however unlikely that might seem to you."

I had been brought up in Forever without ever feeling threatened by danger. I was not brave like Gahrazel, only ignorant. My father knew what lay beyond the fields of Galhea; I did not. Gahrazel knew too, to a degree, but it did not frighten him. In fact, he wasn't afraid of anything.

One night, Gahrazel came to my room when everyone was asleep, and we climbed out of my window, down the creepers. Outside, everything looked white and ghostly beneath the light of a round, white moon. I was terrified of the dark places, rustling with shadows that might not just be shadows, but it was an exquisite fear. Under the trees, we looked back at the house, standing huge, silent and gray; moonlight made the windows shine. Gahrazel said, "Do you know *all* of that house?"

I thought about it. "Well, no, I don't suppose I do," I replied, which seemed odd. It was my home after all.

Gahrazel put his arm around me. "Soon, we'll both know all of the house," he said.

And oh, how Gahrazel came to know the spirit of my father's house, what lurked in the shadows, much sooner than I did.

At mid-winter, there is a festival. Mostly it is to celebrate and welcome in the new year, but Gahrazel said that it was just another thing that Wraeththu had stolen from man. "It was once a religious holiday for them," he said. We were with Swithe in the schoolroom. Swithe always listened patiently to Gahrazel.

"In a way, I suppose it is for us too," he said. "A new year is a magic thing. We are still here and for the future, all things are possible. The rituals bring us together and it is good to have a time when hara can relax in each other's company and look forward to better things."

Gahrazel cast a cynical eye at our tutor. "I would say it is only an excuse for too much drinking and eating. In my father's house I would imagine that the future is seen only as a ringing head in the morning."

"You'll find it's different here," Swithe said gently and I noticed his pity of Gahrazel with amusement. Gahrazel turned his attention to me, his face brightening.

"Once, I heard some hara of the Uigenna tribe actually ate a roasted man at Festival," he said. The weather gradually became colder, the days shorter, and one morning, when I woke up, the ground outside was frosted with snow. Festival was but two weeks away, and the house was warm and vibrant with preparation. Exalted citizens from Galhea had been invited up to Forever to eat with us on Festival day, and the house would be decorated with branches from the evergreens in the garden. Cobweb supervised the stocking-up of the larder with a cool, efficient air. Moswell and Swithe took a holiday to go back to visit their own tribe farther south, accompanied by an escort of Varrish warriors, should hostile tribes or stray humans be abroad, braving the weather. Gahrazel and I now had time to explore the upper regions of Forever, where I had never been before. Gahrazel was puzzled by this, but I explained that I had always preferred to roam outside. Forever was the warm place to run back to when I was hungry or tired; at the top of the house it was neither warm nor welcoming. We found a way into the attics and it seemed we were in a different place; a house that shared the same space as Forever, while at the same time being in another dimension. It was forgotten, crumbling, resentful. One day we took food with us and ventured further into the cobwebbed rooms and corridors than we had ever been before. I took Limba with me because it made me feel safer. Gahrazel was never scared. "A madman must have built this place!" he said excitedly.

"Did men live here, do you think?" I asked in awe.

"Of course," Gahrazel said condescendingly. "This house is old; Wraeththu are not. Forever is just another thing hara have taken from men. Galhea too; it hasn't always been called that. It was a man's town once."

(I should have known that, I thought.)

"Imagine," Gahrazel whispered, "imagine if we found men still living up here, if they had been here for years, eating rats and waiting . . ."

I cried out and touched his arm. "They may want to kill us!"

"They may want to eat us!" Gahrazel added with relish.

We found no men, though. The attics were full of rubbish and treasures; a table whose legs were carved in the shape of hounds, a box of tarnished dress jewelery with half the paste stones missing, hampers of clothes that turned to dust when you touched them, bundles and bundles of papers and heavy, dark furniture with useless mirrors that I could not imagine ever having been downstairs, or even how anyone could have dragged it up there.

We came upon a grimed window that looked out over a flat roof and Gahrazel forced it open. Limba leading excitedly, we climbed out into the frosty air and, sitting with our backs to the sloping eaves, unwrapped our parcels of bread and cheese and apples, staring out above the chimneys.

"Swift, how old are you?" Gahrazel asked.

"Oh, nearly six years old," I answered importantly.

"Feybraiha is some way off for you then," he said. "Have they chosen for you yet?"

"Chosen? What do you mean?" I asked, no longer embarrassed when Gahrazel knew something I didn't.

"Someone for aruna. You know; the *first time.*"

"No, what's that?"

Gahrazel looked at me queerly, then laughed. "You are nearly six. In as little time as a year you may come of age, and you don't know what aruna is?"

"No," I admitted sheepishly. It seemed, in comparison to Gahrazel, I knew next to nothing.

"Then I'll tell you," he said gleefully.

I could not believe it; I had known nothing about sex. Suddenly, it became all too clear what had occurred between Terzian and Cobweb to occasion my appearance in the world. Gahrazel asked me if I ever touched myself and when I looked blank, went on to explain in what way. "No!" I exclaimed, horrified. Could our bodies have this strange life, this strange need, of their own; something we had no control over?

"All Wraeththu need aruna," Gahrazel said. "It is part of us; we are part of each other. I was told this long ago."

I hated the thought of it. I had spent so much time alone in my short life that I was perhaps too modest. But this concept of aruna seemed so sordid; something messy, without order. Two hara coming together, with utter lack of privacy, invading each other's bodies in their most secret places. It reminded me, strangely, of cutting. I kept seeing huge hunks of raw meat slapping down on the kitchen table and the great, sharp knife that the cook would plunge into it.

"It is supposed to be a wonderful thing," Gahrazel said earnestly, having grown up with the idea, but I was not convinced. I tried to imagine myself naked with Ithiel or Swithe and just the thought of it made me blush and I had to make a noise, like a growl in my throat, to make the thought go away.

"How do you know when you come of age?" I asked, and Gahrazel wrinkled his nose.

"I'm not exactly sure, but it's a kind of change, I think," he said.

"I might have known; a change!" I cried.

"Your father or your hostling will choose someone for you," Gahrazel said. "Someone has to teach you these things. It is usually one of their friends."

"Ithiel?" I squeaked, appalled. It would have to be him; there was no one closer to my father.

"Maybe. Would you mind? He's very slim, I like his arms, and he has hair the color of fur," Gahrazel said wistfully.

I shuddered, not sharing this sentiment. "I most certainly would mind!" I said.

We went back through the attics, Gahrazel happily oblivious of my confusion. I was anxious to return to my room, to curl up on my bed and think about what Gahrazel had told me. I would have to familiarize myself with this knowledge; maybe then its sting would lessen. When the time came, would Cobweb and Terzian really force such a thing on me?

We scrambled, sneezing, out of the attics into a disused room that had no carpet on the floor and no curtains at the window.

"We haven't been here before," Gahrazel said. He was nosing around the walls, looking as if he knew what he was doing.

"What are you looking for?" I asked irritably, hovering at the door, holding onto Limba's collar, looking out at the carpeted corridor.

"You never know," Gahrazel answered mysteriously. He squatted down on the floor. "Ah, your father's room is below here."

"I'm not allowed in there," I said, unnecessarily.

"Look at this!"

I joined him. Limba whined and put his wet nose between us. There was a small, splintery hole in the floorboards. Gahrazel bent lower, his fingers splayed out on the floor.

"Don't!" I cried and tried to pull him back.

"Why not?" he asked reasonably, and I could not think of a suitable answer. "You can see his things; there is his wolfskin coat with the tails on. You can see quite a lot; look." He tried to drag me forward.

"I don't want to!" I hissed, thinking, he will know! He will know! Gahrazel's eyes narrowed. He would think I was afraid of Terzian.

"One day," he said, "coming here, looking down here, you may learn quite a lot." And then he laughed and I smiled back nervously, thinking, Never!

Of course, I had bad dreams again that night, of imagined violations, my body breaking. I woke up sweating, tangled in the sheets, too hot and yet my breath misted on the cold air in my room. We had heating in the house, but it was never turned on at night. I needed to talk with Cobweb badly. I wanted to ask him why he had never told me about aruna. He had taught me so much, things I could never have learned anywhere else, and yet, this most private, crucial information he had kept to himself. Did he ever look at me and wonder? Had he and Terzian discussed whom they would choose for me when the time came? It is because he thinks I am too young to be told! I thought angrily, yet I was sure he would have a reasonable explanation when I confronted him. ("Oh, *that*, Swift! I didn't want to bother you with *that*" or something similar.)

I went to Cobweb's room, but it was cold and in darkness, the bed smooth, and the curtains had not been drawn. I stood there for a moment thinking and then crept stealthily back down the corridor and hovered outside my father's door. An impish voice in my head whispered, "Upstairs . . ." but I visualized a gigantic NO! and denied the forbidden thought before it could form properly. Pressing my face against the door, I could hear nothing; then it opened silently beneath the pressure of my hand flat against the wood and I jumped back in alarm.

The room was empty, silent and cold as Cobweb's had been. Where are they? I thought frantically, suddenly too aware of the dark, the cold. Running, I went to the stairs and leaned over the bannisters. The hall lights were off. The staircase looked wide and mountainous, the hall beneath massive and shadowed; above me, glass in the chandelier clinked eerily in a breeze I could not feel. I thought that my father must be in his study; he often stayed up late in there. A dim light glowed from the drawing room. No doubt Cobweb was in there, reading beside the fire, dogs and cats sprawled along his side. I wanted only to feel his strong, slim arms around me and hear his soft, low voice soothe away my night terrors. The marble floor of the hall was so cold beneath my feet, it hurt.

The door to the drawing room stood ajar. I had already decided to creep in quietly, tiptoe to Cobweb's side and curl up against him. I wouldn't have to say anything; he would *know*. He would sigh and say, "What, dreams again, my little pearl?" and stroke my hair. Then I could tell him. I put my head round the door, one foot over the threshold.

They were together beside the fire. My first thought was, No, not now! Why now, this precise, immediate now? and my second thought was, I'm still dreaming. I didn't want to look, but I had to, to be sure. I remember thinking, they are truly one creature; there is no division. It was slow, sinuous, like snakes sliding over each other in the summer, on the flat, gray rocks beside the lake. Cobweb's fingers lost in my father's hair. Terzian's lips upon my hostling's white neck. They did not see me. I don't know how long I stood there; a second, an hour, but they didn't see me. Perhaps it *was* a dream. When I woke up next morning, in my own bed, warm and rested, it certainly seemed that way, but on my way to breakfast, I saw Cobweb coming out of Terzian's room, putting his hands to the back of his head, lifting up his hair, and his neck was bruised. I can say nothing to Cobweb now, I thought. He is part of it.

Gahrazel was consoling and sympathetic when I told him about it, but eager for explicit details, which I was reluctant to give. "At first," I said, feeling important and grave, "I was disgusted, yes, disgusted! Now . . . well, I'm not so sure."

"Your hostling is perhaps the most lovely har I have ever seen," Gahrazel mused, having been pursuing thoughts of his own.

I nodded, still playing at being the somber keeper of knowledge. "Yes. Perhaps I have never seen him properly before, not all of him, not as a separate living thing. Now I know that people are still doing things when you're not there. Before it used to seem that they only existed when they were being watched. I thought I knew all of Cobweb, but I don't, obviously."

That morning, I felt as if a lot of questions I had not been aware of asking had been answered. It was a day of thin clouds, racing in wisps before the wind.

"How uncanny that you should have seen them like that," Gahrazel said, "after what we'd been talking about on the roof."

"No," I answered. "The truth is that it is not the slightest bit uncanny at all."

CHAPTER THREE

>━┥◀▸━◉━◂▸┥━≺

The Flesh

Coalesce the flesh; a splendor
Momentarily eclipsed by
The phenomena of the spirit.

On Festival eve, we heated wine with spices over the fire in the drawing room, Ithiel and some other of my father's officers came up to the house, stamping snow off their boots in the hall and grabbing hold of members of our household staff as they flitted past, for festive caresses.

Gahrazel drank two mugs of hot wine too quickly and sat, glazed, by the hearth staring dreamily at Ithiel, who did not notice. Cobweb, whose favorite colors were habitually pale, unexpectedly wore loose-fitting trousers and a shirt of deep crimson material, sashed with gold. Ithiel said to me, "Remember this time last year, Swift? You seemed such a baby then. Enjoy your childhood while it lasts; I feel it will be brief." It was the first time Ithiel had ever talked to me properly, yet I could not answer him intelligently. When I looked at him, I could only clench my fists behind my back and make the banishing growling noise. Ithiel laughed, surprisingly not surprised and brushed his hand against my face. I fled to Gahrazel's side by the fire, but of course he would not speak to me.

At midnight, my father called to Cobweb across the room. I heard him say, "Share breath with me," as they stood face to face with people all around them. Cobweb said, "This is an old custom, Terzian!" and their lips met. I had to look away. Was I to be faced with this kind of intimacy all the time now? Perhaps I just hadn't noticed it before.

Festival day means eating, and that is precisely what we spent our time doing. This year, hara from the town seemed to notice me for the first time and they were exceptionally polite to Gahrazel, who had gone to bed the night before sulking but was now back in a good humor. We ate our main meal seated around a gigantic polished table in the largest room in the house. It was only used for functions and was, therefore, only opened up a couple of times a year. Terzian rarely entertained on a grand scale. Seated next to Gahrazel, I asked him, "Do you miss your home?"

He shrugged. "I haven't been here that long; things *are* different here. It seems Forever is my home now."

After dinner in the evening, Terzian summoned Gahrazel to his study. Helpless with curiosity, I begged Gahrazel to come up to my room afterwards to tell me what it had been about. Had Gahrazel done something wrong? Was he to be sent home? I had got used to his company; we rarely argued and I did not want him to leave. I sat in my room, in darkness, on the window seat, staring out at the white garden. It is true that when a new year starts, everything does seem magical and sort of sad as well. It seems that everyone is given another chance, another year to get things right, the slate wiped clean. New beginnings. I sighed and misted up the windowpane. Already I could feel that unconscious childhood innocence slipping away from me. Outside the gray shadows were becoming just that. The spirits waved goodbye to a child who was solidifying, who would have to think about different things in future, until his casing cracked and a different being stepped out into the light. I had seen insect chrysalises hanging in secret places around the outbuildings in the garden. That was how I felt now. Insect! Insect! I thought angrily.

Gahrazel burst into my room about an hour later. He looked flushed, excited; I knew it could not have been bad news.

"Well?" I asked, and he threw himself down on the seat beside me, gripped my shoulders, shook his head, almost speechless. "Gahrazel, what?!" His excitement was infectious; I found myself smiling. He had become the light in the room; I could no longer see outside.

"Your father," he said.

"My father what?"

"We talked," Gahrazel said, settling down, letting go of me.

"Talked, yes . . . about what?"

"Well, he asked me how I was getting on, polite stuff, so awkward. As if he cared! He gave me a letter from Ponclast to read. It was quite boring, you know, 'Are you behaving yourself?' Things like that. He'd obviously got someone else to write it for him. But he must have sent a letter to Terzian as well, because after I'd finished reading, Terzian said, 'Well now, Gahrazel, your father feels the time has come for me to talk to you.' " (He mimicked Terzian so well.) "I knew straight away what it was, of course: Feybraiha. I tried so hard not to be embarrassed, but it was difficult."

I nodded vigorously in sympathy, only too aware of how he must have felt. I dreaded the day when my father would call me into his study to talk to me about such things.

"What did he say?" I asked.

"Well, after a few moments' temporizing, he told me that soon I would begin to notice changes about myself, physically and in mood. He said if anything worried me, I was to go to him, any time. As if I would! He asked me if I knew what Feybraiha actually was. Thank God I did. There's no way I could have sat there and let him tell me. I think I'd rather die! I explained I had been taught all that before and he said, 'Then you know I shall have to choose someone for you. Gahrazel, you have not been with us long, so I was concerned that there's no one you'd prefer it to be. I realize it will be hard for you, having to take your first aruna with someone who will be a virtual stranger to you, but I shall choose wisely, and naturally, once your coming of age becomes apparent, its syaptoms obvious, you will spend some time in his company, which may make it easier.' Oh, Swift, I couldn't help it. Maybe I shouldn't have asked, but I had to. I said, 'Who is it then? Do you know yet?' Your father raised his eyebrows and gave me what they call a scorching glance. He smiled, but not at me. He said, 'It is obviously important to you. Is there a reason?' I couldn't answer. He let me squirm for a few minutes, just looking at me. Then he said, 'Oh, I'm not blind, young har. Not much goes on around here I do not notice. Therefore, I feel sure it will meet with your approval that my equerry Ithiel is the har I consider most suitable for the responsibility.' I could have jumped up and hugged him!"

I winced. "I hope you didn't!"

"No . . . He said, 'Run along now. Go and tell Swift all about it!' and laughed."

"He knows I know then?" I asked quickly, breathless.

"What do you mean?"

"He knows that I know, about aruna, about . . . oh, he just knows, that's all!" Suddenly I felt irritable and exposed.

"Swift, it will be a long time before . . . well, before any of this happens to you. You'll be surprised how different you'll feel when the time comes," Gahrazel said, reaching to touch me. I shrugged him off and looked out again at the garden. We were silent for a while.

"It will snow again," I said. Gahrazel moved closer to me on the seat and put his arms around me. I did not draw away.

"You're a funny little thing!" he said. I looked at him, his open, rather cheeky face radiant with pleasure, his long, curling dark hair. Gahrazel was nearly adult. Just a few hours into the new year and I could feel him growing away from me.

"Don't forget me," I said, thinking aloud.

"Forget you? How serious you are!" Gahrazel put his warm, smiling mouth against my cheek.

"Why do things have to change?" I asked as Gahrazel and I scuffed through the snow. Festival had come and gone; now we were faced with the rest of bleak, sunless winter before the spring came.

"Swift, you've become melancholy recently," Gahrazel said.

"You seem to thrive on change," I remarked.

Gahrazel considered this. "I don't really notice it. I suppose it's because I get bored easily, so I must *like* changes. I think you've had an easy life so far, living here. Why should you want anything to change? It's so perfect for you, isn't it? Being Cobweb's baby, being spoiled, not having to make decisions . . ."

"Oh, Gahrazel!" I cried, but not too stubborn to recognize the truth.

We came to the tall trees where the crows lived. Cobweb had told me they were birds of ill omen and, when I was very tiny, their coarse, squabbling cries had always frightened me. Gahrazel looked up at the sky.

"Winter!" he exclaimed miserably. "Everything's so quiet, isn't it? Everything's sleeping."

"Or dead," I added. We stood among the gaunt, black trunks staring up at the untidy nests. Suddenly, the sky seemed to flash and I felt sick, so sick. "Gahrazel!" I screamed and sank to my knees in the snow.

"What is it? What is it?" he demanded in alarm. "Swift . . . ?"

"Look! Look!" I squawked, waving my arms.

"What? What?!"

"The *birds!*"

"What birds?"

"That's it!" I reached for him, half crazy. "There are no birds!"

"No birds?"

"Gahrazel, it's something I made happen! It's something I did! Oh God!"

I pressed my face against my hands. Suddenly the world seemed far too large. Gahrazel tried to make me stand up.

"Come back to the house," he said gently.

I told him everything. Perhaps I should have done so before. "The birds are gone," I moaned, "and now *he* will come back. Cobweb said so."

"Oh, come on, it may be just a coincidence," Gahrazel said reasonably. "There are a hundred reasons why the crows could have gone. Something may have killed them all, anything may have happened. Anyway, if they are birds of ill omen, it can hardly mean something bad if they decide to leave."

"You don't understand," I said grumpily. "They are trying to tell us something. *They know.* They are magical birds and the har with yellow hair is jinxed. That is why they left."

"Alright, alright, I *do* know about these things!"

"Do you think I should tell Cobweb?" I asked nervously.

Gahrazel shook his head. "No, it's obvious what we must do."

"It is?"

"Yes. We must protect the house." Here he smiled smugly. "I'm surprised you didn't suggest it yourself."

"But how?"

After lunch, Gahrazel went to the kitchen and asked the cook for a bag of salt. He must have made up some fantastic excuse for needing it, for Yarrow handed it over without question. For someone whose tribe supposedly shunned the use of magic, Gahrazel had a surprising grasp of occult lore. Perhaps he, too, had had a Cobweb figure in his formative years. In his room, we made protective talismans from herbs wound with horsehair and sanctified them with drops of our own blood. Then Gahrazel intoned a prayer over the salt and we were ready.

Outside, the afternoon air stung our faces with cold and the snow beneath our feet became really deep once we had left the neat garden behind. My trousers were soaked, my flesh smarting with chill. We trudged doggedly to the boundaries of Forever's lands, starting at the gate. Limba, who I insisted should accompany us, bounded ahead apparently unaffected by the cold. Gahrazel pinned one of the talismans to the gatepost, which was difficult as they were made of sandstone. "We must use only bent nails, made of iron," Gahrazel said. I was in awe of his knowledge. Then we made a trail of salt (very thin, to conserve the supply) from the gates along the edge of the high wall that hugged Forever's country. At intervals, we pinned up one of the talismans to the wall.

By the time we had got back to the gate again, it was really dark and well past dinnertime. We heard horse's hooves on the drive, and then Ithiel appeared out of the shadows of the overhanging yew trees, saying, "What on earth have you two been up to? Terzian's had people out looking for you!"

Naturally, Gahrazel and I were not exactly taken by surprise when we received a thorough scolding, first from Terzian, then further upbraiding from Cobweb. "Don't you realize how vulnerable you are?" Cobweb snapped.

No, I didn't! I couldn't see what harm could have befallen us within Forever's boundaries. It never crossed my mind that, because of the season, outsiders, enemies, might be drawn to the town, seeking food or shelter.

"Terzian is very protective toward you, Swift," Cobweb continued. "You are his only heir . . . at present. He is concerned for Gahrazel's safety as well. Can't you see that anybody could have come in off the fields? Anybody could have been hiding in the trees." He shuddered expressively.

Terzian decreed that, until lessons resumed in a few days' time, Gahrazel and I must be kept apart. This was humiliating, but inside myself I was once again contented. Nothing, nobody, that wished us ill could cross the magical threshold we had made. I longed to tell Cobweb about it, but knew instinctively that part of the magic was its secrecy.

More snow fell. Messengers came once again from the north. Now, my father considered me old enough to be included in the conversations at dinner. He said, "It seems the Uigenna have just disposed of yet another of their leaders. Sometimes, I wonder whether they are really quite sane."

"Are any of us?" Cobweb said drily. "Are we real, even? Do you think it at all unlikely that one day we might waken up in our beds to discover that all of Wraeththu was just a dream?"

"Well, I certainly do!" I answered hotly, and Terzian laughed, gesturing at me.

"There you are then," he said. "Did you dream up hosting the pearl that gave us Swift?"

Cobweb smiled. "No, at least I hope not. If I did, I expect I should wake up, not in my own bed, but in some kind of asylum!"

"They are all rather insane in the north," Gahrazel said then, in a thoughtful voice. He had been silent for most of the meal. "My father enjoys killing things. Do you know, it is a public spectacle when hostages are brought to the citadel. If they're human, some are incepted, made to be Wraeththu, some are just butchered. I saw it, many times. From my room in the tower, I heard it more times than I saw it."

My father looked at Gahrazel with embarrassment. "You must know that humanity has to be dealt with the most expedient way. Not all of them can be kept by Wraeththu."

"Oh yes, I am well aware of that. Another thing that I've heard many times. I also know that the humans would kill us all, if they could. Perhaps it is the only way, killing all of them. I can't answer that; I don't know. What I can't understand is why they have to suffer, why their screams are as music to my father's ear. They may be our enemy, but they're not animals."

Words cannot convey the stunned silence that followed that little speech. I was dumbfounded, not sure whether to believe what I'd heard. How lucky we were that Terzian would never allow such things to happen in Galhea.

After a while, Cobweb pushed his chair back and stood up. "Well!" he said brightly. "Swift, why don't you ask Swithe if we could all go riding together this afternoon? Look at the sun, the snow; we shouldn't miss it. Soon it will be raining and thawing and unpleasant."

"Alright," I said, still looking at Terzian, who was discretely observing Gahrazel with speculation.

Wrapped in furs, kicking up sprays of snow, we galloped our horses to the lake's edge. I looked at my hostling and thought, Gahrazel is right, he *is* the most beautiful har in the world.

Swithe pulled his horse to a halt and said, "Just look at this place! How hard it is to imagine we are struggling through a time of fighting, uncertainty."

"Oh, and are we?" Cobweb asked archly.

"Terzian keeps Galhea very . . . safe," Swithe replied in an unpleasant tone of voice.

Cobweb dismounted and walked toward the frozen edge of the water. Brittle, dead reeds rattled in the breeze like bones. I looked at the expression on Swithe's face and realized, Of course, they are . . .

A revelation that was cut, only half-formed in my head All that followed was simply a flowering of this realization. I had been within the flower; now I could see the sky.

"Swift, come here!" Gahrazel called and I jumped from my pony's back, running over to him, but reluctant to leave Swithe and Cobweb alone.

"What is it?"

"Look!" He poked something with a stick. Something dead. Its beak spread wide in a last obscene denial of death, a bedraggled black bird poked halfway out of the ice. I was chilled.

"Do you think he's noticed?" I asked numbly.

"Who? Noticed what?"

"Cobweb . . . about the crows . . ."

Gahrazel glanced over to where Cobweb stood staring into the ice, Swithe some distance away, arms folded. "Who knows . . ." he said.

Gahrazel and I walked back to the others. I felt on edge for some reason, nervous and twitchy. I could hear whistling in my head. Someone was watching me.

"Let's go back," I said and my voice sounded slow, echoing. Cobweb turned toward me slowly, his lovely, pale face smiling, a reflection of the wild, frozen landscape, his hair lifted by the breeze like wings. He began to speak, then a vague puzzlement came into his eyes; he winced.

"Cobweb?" I said, cautiously, and it echoed around us: "Cobweb! Cobweb!"

He shook his head once, as if something had got into his hair. "No . . . ?" he said.

"What is it?" Swithe asked harshly, still behaving in a way so that Cobweb would know that he'd been hurt.

"Nothing." Cobweb straightened up and began to walk back to the horses. I wanted to run to him, but my limbs were paralyzed. Above me, livid darkness was crawling across the sky from the south. Gahrazel was staring at me. Some feet away from us, Cobweb dropped to his knees in the snow. I could not move. He screamed. Swithe turned his head.

"No!" Cobweb slammed his fists into the snow, which flew up in glittering spurts. When Swithe went to him, Cobweb smashed his hands into Swithe's face.

We all called, "Cobweb!" me softly, Swithe indignantly, Gahrazel wonderingly. Cobweb sprang to his feet and ran to the jostling horses. Not bothering with stirrups, he threw himself over his animal's back and urged it furiously back toward the house. I still could not move. Gahrazel shaded his eyes with his hand and squinted at Forever. Swithe rubbed his chin thoughtfully, putting his foot in his stirrup, remounting his horse. "There's some kind of activity at the house," Gahrazel said.

I was first back at Forever after Cobweb. Leaving my pony loose in the yard, I ran, slipping, sliding into the house. I could sense the strangeness immediately. The house was outraged, holding its breath. I ran into the hall and I remember thinking, They have let the cold in; it is cold. Everywhere seemed empty, I could not hear anything. The drawing room, my father's study were deserted and the fires were low. I went to the kitchen. All the household staff were in there, talking in low voices. They went quiet when they saw me standing in the doorway. "What's going on?" I demanded. "What's happened?"

Yarrow spoke. "In your father's room," he said.

I ran out, up the stairs, stumbling. Of course, the door was closed. I could hear voices inside, speaking quickly. I could not go in.

Cobweb and I must have been guided by the same instinct. I found him in the conservatory. It was cold in there, colder than it should have been, and I was afraid that it might kill the plants. I put my hand on the radiator and it was hot. I rubbed my hands and shivered. Cobweb was slumped at one of the wrought-iron tables we had in there, elbows on the table, his head in his hands. I went to him, and put my arms around him, resting my chin on the back of his head.

"Don't kiss me," he said, "not from behind; it's unlucky."

"Cobweb . . ." I began.

"No," he said, quite emphatically. "No."

"Tell me, you must tell me!" My voice sounded alien to me, somehow stronger and older. Cobweb raised his head at the imperative tone.

"Can't you guess?"

I squatted down beside him and looked into his eyes. A single tear spilled and fell on my hands where they clasped his own in his lap. I knew; there was no way I couldn't have.

"Oh, Cobweb!" I said, and suddenly it didn't seem as bad as before, when it had been only a threat. This was real. This we could fight. "Tell me." My voice was calm.

"They *found* him, somewhere . . . I don't know. I don't know! He's here! Who the fuck cares how!" I had not heard my hostling swear in my life before.

"But he can't be," I insisted. "Gahrazel and I, we protected the house . . ."

"Swift, are you joking?" Cobweb spat sarcastically. He pushed me away and stood up. He laughed. "Destiny!" he said.

It was later, from Ithiel, that I heard how it happened. I cornered him in the kitchen, long after dinnertime (none of us had eaten), begging food and coffee off Yarrow. Limba was in there, crouched mournfully against the stove. Ithiel started guiltily when he saw me and said, "Oh, Swift." A brief wave of shame washed over me, for I was still troubled by my discovery of the existence of aruna, but I ignored it.

"Tell me what's happened," I said. It was one of those rare, magical times when I felt twice my age and others even treated me as if I was. Ithiel sat down again on the edge of the table, nursing a hot drink. I went over to the window and drew the blinds and turned on another lamp. Evidence of confusion was everywhere; unwashed pans in the sink, breadcrumbs on the table. Usually, this room was spotless. The cook was sitting by the stove, drinking a large measure of sheh and absently scratching Limba's back with his foot. "Yarrow?" Ithiel said and he replied, "This is my kitchen. If you want to talk in private, go somewhere else."

Ithiel inclined his head and ushered me out into the hall.

"My room," I suggested. "No-one will disturb us there."

It felt strange, preceding Ithiel up the stairs, feeling him tall behind me, passing hurriedly the closed door to my father's room. The first thing he said was, "Cobweb will need you now." He sat down on the bed and I on the window seat.

"Not just me," I pointed out and Ithiel looked at his hands and shook his head.

"No-one can predict what will happen now," he said.

"Who found him?"

"A patrol, three hara, south of Galhea. He was lying in the snow. They thought he was dead at first. God, maybe five, ten minutes later and he would have been!" Ithiel looked up at me. "They would have just left him, even finished him off, but one of them had to recognize him. That's when they sent for me."

"Ithiel," I said. "You needn't have brought him back here. No-one would have known."

He laughed. "You can't mean that! Three hara *did* know and is there any har in Galhea who doesn't know what that devil was, what he is? The patrol knew and I couldn't guarantee their silence. If Terzian had ever found out . . ." He shook his head and we both pondered the terrible consequences of that.

"What condition is he in?" I asked. "And why has he come back after all this time?"

"His condition is poor," Ithiel answered, with a bleak smile. "But I shouldn't raise your hopes too high. As you know, we're a resilient race and difficult to kill. As for why he's come back, well, your guess is as good as mine at the moment. I just think it means trouble, that's all. Terzian's always been obsessed with him and that worries me. It's unnatural." He stood up and looked at the door.

"How is my father?" I asked and Ithiel rubbed the back of his neck, flexing his spine.

"Oh, he behaves in his usual cool, contained way, but . . ."

"Perhaps we should kill him," I interrupted, "kill the devil that calls itself Cal!"

Ithiel grunted in derision. "A thought, I imagine, that will cross more than one person's mind. Anyway, I have to go. I have things to attend to. Our defenses must never slip, must they?"

He paused at the door, frowning and burrowing in a pocket of his jacket. "Oh, Swift, I meant to show you this," he said. "I found two of them on the gate this morning. Is someone casting spells on us, do you think? I thought I'd better take them down."

He threw them down on my bed. Two of them, bound in horsehair, blessed with blood. Our talismans.

After Ithiel had gone, I sat looking at my hands, afraid to look at the talismans. Eventually, I knocked them to the floor without turning my head. A sudden wave of anger made my eyes hot. I thought, I'm not going to skulk in a corner like everyone else! This Cal is just har. How dare he come back into our lives and destroy the harmony of this house? I stood up. Young though I might be, I was not going to let this upset me. I am Terzian's son, I thought, and I shall face this beast with his strength.

Hesitating at Terzian's door would have made it too difficult. I knocked once, loudly, and walked right in. My father was sitting at his desk, writing. Two hara stood by the bed, fussing over what lay in it. Terzian looked around as I walked in. It was the first time, that I could remember, that he seemed genuinely pleased to see me. Perhaps, because of that, I was more self-assertive than usual with him.

"Swift," he said. "I was beginning to think I was a pariah in my own house. Has Cobweb sent you?"

I shook my head.

"Come here," he said and I went to him. "You've grown up so much lately," he continued. "Perhaps we still treat you too much as a child."

Oh God, I was thinking, don't get emotional; I couldn't stand it! "What does this mean?" I asked clearly. "To Cobweb and me? What does it mean?"

My father bit his lip; not a gesture common to him. "Cobweb is naturally angry," he said.

"We want to know where we stand," I said stiffly.

Terzian laughed. "Oh, *I see!* Cobweb's told you that now Cal has come back, you and he will be cast aside, perhaps even thrown out of the house, hasn't he?"

I could not answer. Looking at my father's face, I realized that our eviction was probably the least likely thing in the entire world. Terzian touched my shoulder.

"You are my first-born," he said, and that was reassurance enough. "Swift, a long time ago, when Cal was here before . . . and afterwards, I explained to Cobweb how things were. Cobweb is your hostling and my consort and because of that, my people are fond of him. He belongs here, but if it hadn't been for Cal, well, maybe I would have had other hara in the house to give me sons as well. Cobweb's had it easy; I've spoiled him. There is no reason why his life should change now except that he shall have to learn to share his home."

"And you," I pointed out.

"Yes, that too," Terzian agreed.

I thought to myself, Father, you have no heart.

"Go and look at him, Swift." Terzian stood up and, clamping a firm hand on the back of my neck, half steered, half dragged me over to the bed. I thought, How lucky he has good bones. Starvation has barely marked him.

"Are you sure it's him?" I asked. "I remember him differently."

"It's him," my father said shortly.

Cal's eyes were closed, his head turned to the side. I could see so clearly the long line of his neck, the caress of hair against his cheek, his brow, the dark circles beneath his eyes. I could see his arms, outside the blankets, laid along his sides, smooth as sculpture, his long, sensitive hands. My first impression was unashamedly this: he is made to be touched. I hated him. I remembered a fairy tale that Swithe had once read to me from an old, old book, a man's book, about a magic mirror.

The beautiful witch queen had asked the mirror, "Who is the most beautiful in the land, magic glass?"

And the mirror had always replied, "It is you, Oh Queen." Until one day it had clouded and it had seen someone else, more beautiful still. When the witch had asked the mirror, "Who is the fairest in my husband's kingdom?" it had answered her differently and dark poison had flowered in her heart. Someone else, and here it lay, on my father's bed, and yes, more beautiful still. A Wraeththu child of snow and thorns whom we could not kill, because fairy stories just don't end that way.

The following morning, Cal was moved from my father's room, ironically, back to the very suite that he had occupied once before, with Pellaz. A circle in time; we begin again. Cobweb would not speak to Terzian, except with his eyes, which radiated contempt and fury disguised as pain, and all gatherings of the household became fraught affairs, where silence could be cut with a knife and knives glinted sharply.

Gahrazel and I philosophized endlessly about what all of this meant, the complexities of relationships, the capriciousness of feeling.

"Is Cal *really* evil?" Gahrazel asked me.

I had to admit, "I don't know. We all hate him because he broke my father's heart when he left and yet his staying here was the last thing in the world Cobweb wanted."

"Poor Cal," Gahrazel remarked cynically, "whichever way he turns the path is wrong!"

"We shall really have to wait," I said. "When he has regained his strength, then we may see him as he really is. Then he may try to bring about all the terrible things Cobweb is afraid of."

"But Swift," Gahrazel said, "Does anyone know for sure that Cal *was* trying to get back to Forever?"

I shrugged. "It does seem rather a coincidence . . . and the talismans, Ithiel *did* break the circle . . ."

That night, Gahrazel went to bed early with a violent headache and I was more or less compelled to spend the evening with Cobweb in the drawing room. By now, his martyred silence was beginning to get on my nerves. Had we been cast out into the wilderness? No. It seemed to me that my hostling was only driving Terzian farther away from him. His tactics were all wrong; it bored my father, which was perhaps the gravest error. Cobweb was displeased with me because Terzian talked to me at mealtimes, but that was only because he could not talk to Cobweb. Secretly, I thought that Terzian might need Cobweb more now than he had ever done.

On my way up the stairs that night, I heard Terzian and Ithiel talking in the study; low murmuring, the chink of glass. All the lights in the house appeared to have been left on; there were no shadows, anywhere. The corridors upstairs were tense and still, burning brightly. I could always sense the house holding its breath. Now I would go to the enchanted room; there are secrets there, an oracle. . . . Outside the door, I was alert for changes in atmosphere (would it be cold there? A spirit breath?). He lay as before, inert and splendid, carved from ice, asleep for a hundred years.

Now I was the prince of valour come to wake the sleeping beauty with a kiss. I found myself chanting, "Here is the room, the room of death!" At that time, I am quite sure, I was not wholly rational. I went to his side and said, "And what are you, white beast?"

His eyes opened, his hand shot to my wrist; not the grip of illness. Fathomless power, a sense of timelessness, burned right through me, but he could not have known it. His voice was husky, as if long unused. He said, "Pell, come closer, I have to . . . I have to tell you something . . ." and fell back on the pillows with a sigh, his eyes rolling upwards.

I ran back to my room, I sat down on the bed, I stood up again and walked to the window. "Must you always sit in darkness, Swift?" I said to myself, but I did not turn on the light. I flopped down, on my back, on the bed; strangely thrilled. In a month's time, it would be my birthday, I realized, wondering where the thought came from. I remembered Moswell telling me that at the growing stage, one of our years was equal to two of man's. I am a twelve-year-old human, I am a six-year-old har, I thought. When the time comes I shall be be fourteen, I shall be seven . . .

That week Gahrazel was confined to his room, afflicted by strange pains. I once heard him whimpering in the night; his room was not far from mine. Swithe told me that Gahrazel's coming of age was upon him, which sounded most unpleasant. "Men grow hair upon their faces, upon their bodies; we are not quite the same," he said. "Your flesh shall become furred with down as you mature," he went on, "beneath your arms, a thicker growth and between your legs, the silky mane that marks you as adult. Don't blush and writhe so, Swift! I am not your father after all."

I wondered what it was that caused Gahrazel pain. Swithe explained that certain internal organs (known as soume-lam) were coming alive, flexing, preparing themselves for the accommodation of aruna and pearl-hosting. "The phallus, the ouana-lim of Wraeththu, is a complex and wonderful thing, Swift," Swithe said, thankfully with his back to me. "Treat it with respect." (God forbid that I should do otherwise! I thought.) "Of course, some time from now you will be given thorough instruction concerning aruna and procreation," Swithe continued airily, "but if you are ever curious about anything, you can ask me. Of course, by that time, your friend Gahrazel will doubtless be answering all your questions!"

I went to visit Gahrazel in his room and his behavior was manic, more restless than ever. He said he itched unbearably all over and I charitably rubbed his back for him. The skin was taut and hot.

"How does it feel, this change?" I asked.

Gahrazel rubbed his arms, shivering, sweating. "Horrible!" he cried. "Horrible!"

He mentioned terrifying dreams that had been ruining his sleep, dreams about my father. At the time I thought nothing of it. We all have strange dreams occasionally; not all of them are prophetic.

Cobweb, nudged out of his self-indulgent moping, prepared steaming elixirs for Gahrazel to drink, which made him sleep. "I wonder how long this will last?" I wondered.

"Oh, not long," Cobweb answered vaguely, and by that, I guessed he had no idea.

Soon Gahrazel began to feel much better and told me that Terzian had been to see him to arrange for his coming-of-age celebration. "I suppose you're going to spoil my birthday," I complained. "Coming of age and having the lissome Ithiel to court you."

His face changed a little when I said that. I realized he was not quite as confident about his Feybraiha as he liked me to think.

"Will it be alright, do you suppose?" he asked. "I think about it often. It's an invasion and I'm afraid of conquest . . ."

"I hope it kills you!" I said and for a moment we stared at each other in silence.

"Is there a fate worse than death?" Gahrazel asked, and we both laughed.

All the snow had melted, the ground outside was dark and rich, green shoots sprouting beneath the trees. But no crows came back to their ragged nests in the high branches. Cal was brought downstairs in the afternoons to sit in the conservatory, which outraged Cobweb and put me off going in there. Terzian would spend an hour with him every day. Once, I crept to the door and eavesdropped on them. Cal said, "What am I doing here?" in a voice that was barely even a whisper, and my father answered, "Must you ask that every day?"

I peeked around the door, hidden in the curtains, and saw my father reach for Cal's hand, but it was snatched away instantly.

"Don't! Cal cried hoarsely. "Not ever!"

"It's alright," Terzian soothed. I was amazed by this reaction.

The idea of Cal fascinated me. He was a creature of mystery. We all presumed that only Terzian knew where Cal had been going, where he came from, when the Varrish patrol had found him. And what Terzian knew he told no-one. Not even Ithiel. Gahrazel was now allowed to spend some hours several times a week in Ithiel's company, under Moswell's watchful eye. I pressed him to drill Ithiel for information, which must have been difficult with Moswell there, but although Ithiel was not loath to divulge what he knew, it wasn't anything we weren't aware of already. One evening, afire with the spirit of rebellion, Gahrazel and I appropriated a decanter of sheh from the dining room and consumed it lustily in the privacy of Gahrazel's bedroom.

"I wish I knew what was going on!" I exclaimed. "He won't let Terzian touch him; I saw!"

Gahrazel was already rather drunk. "Why bother squeezing useless information out of everyone else?" he said. "Why not go straight to the source, the one person who will know. Ask Cal, ask him outright. It's your home too."

"Yes, you're right. Tomorrow then . . ."

"What?" Gahrazel snorted. "Tomorrow we have no sheh, tomorrow we are sensible and shy. Do it now!"

Spurred on by a tide of drunken bravery, I cried, "Alright, I will!" and rolled onto the floor.

Leaving Gahrazel giggling helplessly on the bed, I went to look for Cal. Of course, he was penned in his room. That was where they kept him at night. They had even locked him in. I turned the key and went right through the open doorway.

He was lying on the bed, dressed in a heavy, woollen robe. The curtains were drawn, the light dim. Books were scattered around him. We stared at each other for quite some time before I spoke. "What are you doing here?"

He smiled faintly; my voice was slurred. "And what are *you* doing here?" he replied

"It's my house," I said. "It's my father's house."

"Ah, you are Swift," he said. "I remember you." A dry remark which made me uneasy.

"You did not like me," I accused.

His smile is constant, words move around it. "I was afraid of you."

"Afraid!" I laughed and went to sit next to him. "What are you reading?"

"Tales of the night," he said.

"Why did you come back?"

"I didn't. They brought me back."

"I don't believe you," I said. Until I looked at his eyes, close up, I still felt strong. Now I was a child again. He smelled of smoke and flowers.

"Where's Pellaz?" I asked and he shrugged, bland as a cat.

"I don't remember."

"Where have you been? Why are you ill?"

"Who knows? Who cares? Give me the strongest light and I shall carve an axe for you."

"What?"

"It was in the book."

"Oh." One thing that is remarkable about Cal was that he was so easy to talk to. He appeared to have no side to him, communicating as easily as water running over stones. People did not perplex him and he cared about nothing then.

He said, "I have sobered you!" and laughed.

"My father's sheh," I explained. "My friend Gahrazel has come of age and we were celebrating together."

"I *see.*" He sat up and rubbed his face. "Be a friend to me, little monster, little reptile child, and bring me some of your stolen sheh."

"Alright," I said, and swung my legs over the edge of the bed.

"They lock me in," Cal said. "Lock the door behind you. The stairs are very steep and oblivion is heaven to me at the moment."

Strange he should say that when we both knew he would never kill himself. I smiled uncertainly, pausing at the door. "Cal," I said, and his name felt strange in my mouth. "Why were you afraid of me?"

"I told you," he answered. "You're a monster; you shouldn't exist. Men can't bear children, it's not possible."

"But we're not men!" I protested.

"Aren't we? Sometimes I wonder," Cal said.

I went to fetch the sheh and Gahrazel, reassured that Cal wasn't about to attack us, insisted on coming back with me. I was afraid Terzian would find out, convinced he would be angry. Gahrazel and I sat on Cal's bed and watched him gulp down the sheh, holding the glass with shaking hands.

"Aren't you bored?" Gahrazel asked.

Cal screwed up his face. "Bored? I can't feel anything. Only the evidence of my eyes persuades me that, in fact, I possess arms and legs." He held out his glass and I filled it dutifully. "This will make me sleep," he said. "The little death."

"Cal thinks we are monsters," I remarked to Gahrazel.

"My father thinks that too," he replied. "He often called me a little monster."

"Varrish brats," Cal said good-naturedly.

When Cal got sleepy, Gahrazel and I went back to Gahrazel's room. "He doesn't seem evil," my friend said thoughtfully. "Only rather pathetic, rather hopeless." I could say nothing. I was no longer sure of what I thought about Cal.

Gahrazel's coming of age was now just a week away, my birthday but two days. Terzian told Gahrazel to cut his hair, but Gahrazel told me he had no intention of doing any such thing. Among Varrs, only those hara whose life-work has been designated as hostlings wear their hair very long. Later, I learned that this was seen as a sign of femininity. Like men, Wraeththu want the bodies that carry their children to be lovely. What I did not know then was that among other tribes, all hara are considered equally masculine and feminine; anyone can host a pearl and it does not matter how you dress or how long your hair is or whether you're a soldier or a clothmaker. To a man, someone like Cobweb might appear superficially female, because that side of his nature has been unnaturally encouraged. Terzian was obviously worried that Ponclast's son might be too feminine. Ponclast wanted to breed warriors, not hostlings. Gahrazel and I discussed this and, of course, his disregard for authority meant that his hair stayed long.

Messengers came frequently from the north now and sometimes they would bring a letter for Gahrazel from his father. I began to sense something huge, an uprising, great activity, in the world beyond Galhea's fields. Terzian would sit at mealtimes with a frown on his face, ploughing his food with his fork. I think Cobweb was almost disappointed that the arrival of Cal had prompted no dramatic change in our lives. Now he had nothing to complain about. Naturally, I had told him what I had witnessed in the conservatory and this had made him smile.

One day, I said to my father, "What *is* happening in the world?" We were in the stables. One of Terzian's horses had gone lame and he was supervising the application of poultices.

"Rumors, rumors," Terzian replied vaguely and I knew he could not be bothered to tell me.

"What rumors?" I insisted.

"Rumors that Thiede is becoming active," he said.

"What's Thiede?"

"Not a what, a who," he said. "And a very dangerous who at that. Of another tribe; Gelaming."

"Oh, Gelaming," I said, remembering the incident with Moswell and Cobweb the year before. "Will they come to fight you?"

My father laughed. "It is suspected that they covet this land. There is a possibility we may have to fight to keep it."

"Oh," I said. I was used to my father disappearing and I had a vague idea what he got up to on those occasions, so I was not unduly alarmed. To me, he was omnipotent. I could not imagine him ever being beaten.

"I understand you've been to see Cal," Terzian said carelessly, but I could sense the slight tension in his voice.

"Sometimes," I admitted. "He's strange." Terzian did not comment on this.

"I think perhaps he is well enough to eat with the rest of us now," he said carefully. "Perhaps it would be better if you informed Cobweb of this."

As I grew older, I discovered I had a new role in life; that of intermediary between my parents. I realized that, although Terzian considered Cobweb to be alive solely for his personal use, he was also slightly afraid of him. Cobweb lived in a strange, magical world, but because he believed in it, the strangeness became power. When Cobweb became angry, he was a thing to be feared, because his power was invisible. I told him what Terzian had said and he smiled fiercely and said, "I see." That was all. I dared not tell him that I sometimes went to visit Cal in his room, but it was more than likely that Cobweb knew about that already. Because of his art, it was virtually impossible to keep secrets from him. I was torn two ways. Curiosity, and loyalty to Terzian pulled me one way, devotion to my hostling the other. Whomever I sided with, there would be unpleasantness. Cobweb and I had always been close, now he was reserved with me. I had a suspicion that the friendship with Swithe had been resumed as well, but I could not be sure.

Our first meal with Cal was a nightmare. If I thought the atmosphere had ever been bad before, I was now horribly enlightened. Cal, with a definite air of self-preservation, treated Cobweb's hostility with light amusement. I cringed when he had the nerve to say, "Well Cobweb, you've certainly changed since we last met. You're quite stunning now, aren't you! How lucky that injury to your leg didn't leave you with a limp. Did it scar? I seem to remember that the last words you said to me were something like, 'You'll be back some day.' I never thought you'd be right. Here's to your gift of intuition!" And he raised his glass, sipped daintily. If Cobweb had been a cat, he would have fluffed up his fur to twice his normal size, but he was har and therefore only simmered silently with rage. Gahrazel and I dared not look at each other, for fear of giggling. My father had a tight, uncomfortable expression on his face as he stared at his plate.

That was perhaps the only reference Cal had made to his past. I noticed that his hands still shook, although he tried to hide it, and his eyes were still shadowed, but he was no longer locked in his room at night. I wondered what had transpired between Cal and Terzian that my father should no longer worry about Cal trying to leave. It was hard to imagine them actually talking to each other.

I had got into the habit of seeking Cal's company virtually every day. He fascinated me so much, I couldn't keep away. I never got the impression that he didn't want me around, but at the same time he never said anything *important* to me. He asked me questions about myself and my family and his mordant sense of humor always made me laugh, but he never talked about himself. It wasn't that he was being secretive, it was more as if his life had only really begun once he had woken up in Forever. It didn't seem as if he was interested in what had happened to him before. He would never stare out of the window with a faraway look on his face, or stop talking as if a memory had walked across his eyes. His whole existence was simply "now." This irked me because my curiosity about his past was overwhelming. I wanted to know why he had left Terzian before, what had happened to Pellaz and, more than either of those things, why he had come back. He had evaded that question once, and I didn't believe the answer he had given me then. Was he evil? Sometimes I was troubled by my fascination for him. Alone, at night, I was often afraid of him, but I was always drawn back, for I had met no-one like him before. Each time we met it was as if I learned something new about the world that would never be put into words. It was as if I was learning his secrets, not through concrete ideas, but just from feelings that were nearly smells and sounds and tastes. On several occasions, after I had left him, fleeting pictures would flash across my inner eye, like memories, but they were of places and people I had never seen.

I once remarked upon Cobweb's hostility toward him and Cal laughed and said, "He is lovely now. Who would have thought it!"

"He will never like you," I said swiftly. Cal ignored this.

"I would like," he said wistfully, "to bind him naked with green, shining ropes of ivy and cover him with kisses."

I went cold, a strange, numb feeling. "More than you would like to touch my father's hand?" I snapped, a question which had come out before I could think better of it. Cal looked at me startled for a second, then he made a noise of amusement, as if at a private joke.

"In dreams, Terzian and I may be together. Is that what you wanted to know?"

Heat suffused my face; I could not look at him.

"If you want more of an explanation," he continued, "then let me say that reality may make me come alive, and I fear life. Can you understand that?"

It was the first time he had ever spoken to me like this, and I was unsure of his motive. "Do you mean that aruna may make you remember?" I asked cautiously, hating the feel of that word on my lips. Would he answer me? Cal wrinkled his brow and twisted his mouth to the side as he considered what I'd said. He did not appear embarrassed and chose not to show me he knew that I was.

"Aruna will open up all the blocked circuits in my head, I'm sure of it," he said. "It's an electric thing, after all."

"But can you live forever like this, now knowing?"

He shrugged. "I never think about it."

I wondered if that was true.

I was given gifts on my birthday, small things, and Cobweb and I had a small party with Swithe, Moswell and Gahrazel. My father was away for the day and Cal kept to his room. I knew he had started to write, but he kept the subject a secret. He spent most of his time writing now. Later, when it began to get dark, Ithiel joined us in the drawing room and Cobweb mixed us drinks of sheh and herbs and piquant essences. We all got happily drunk. Moswell, in a rare mood of abandonment, stood up and capered and sang. Everyone laughed till it hurt. I was sure that Cal would be able to hear us in his room. Did he throw down his pen in annoyance or think wistfully, If I was with them . . .

The day of Gahrazel's Feybraiha arrived; a sunlit morning, where yellow flowers glowed brighter than ever before under the trees and young leaves of an acid green color filtered all the light and made the garden secret and exciting. As Varrs don't hold much with religion and ceremony, Gahrazel had neither to fast nor pray. I understood from Swithe that in other tribes, Feybraiha was surrounded by ritual and meant a lot more than just losing your virginity. Cobweb plaited flowers into Gahrazel's hair and Terzian invited friends and officers of his guard to share our meal at lunchtime. The table was strewn with greenery; hara murmured in Ithiel's ear and laughed. Clear sunlight streamed in from the garden, making the curtains look transparent at the edges and spinning magic gold in Cal's glorious hair, where he sat with his back to the light. Cobweb forgot to be angry that Cal was there and I saw Terzian take Cobweb's hand and they looked into each other's eyes, smiling, half ashamed. I could not tell what Cal was thinking, watching them. He had a faint smile on his face and drank wine at a steady but consistent pace. Terzian made a speech and congratulated Gahrazel on reaching the lofty state of adult. "Today, you are no longer harling. Today you have a caste. I pronounce you of caste Kaimana. Your level is the first of that caste; it is Ara. You are Aralid, Gahrazel."

In the evening, much to everyone's surprise (and I'm sure, Gahrazel's horror), Ponclast arrived from the north. Terzian and he embraced and slapped each other's backs.

"My little Gahrazel is no more!" Ponclast boomed. He was a big har, though not fleshy, and had short, dense black hair, like fur. His nose was the fiercest I had ever seen and his eyes could have seen through steel. It was clear that, like my father, he made no concessions to the feminine side of his nature. "So *you* are the one!" he exclaimed to a white-faced Ithiel. "Take care of him!" When Terzian introduced him to me, he picked me up bodily and shook me as a dog would do with a rat. "Fair of face, as both his parents!" he shouted, close to my ear.

We had music and dancing in the big room. My father persuaded Cal to dance with him (which embarrassed me), and at the end they hugged each other. Cobweb hissed at my side.

Then the time came for Gahrazel and Ithiel to leave us and repair to the room that Cobweb and the house-hara had strewn with grasses and flowers. My heart was thudding so, it was almost as if it were me who would walk up those stairs with Ithiel, not Gahrazel. He came over to me and we pressed our faces together, cheek to cheek. I could smell sandalwood and fear.

"It's almost like goodbye," I said, surprised to find my voice was shaking. "You are leaving me behind."

"No," Gahrazel said. "No, Swift."

I could not imagine that one day, a celebration like this would be held in honor of my Feybraiha. On that day, my body would come alive. Another har would touch me and nothing about me would be private any more. I knew that aruna was more than just a communion of bodies; my mind as well as my flesh would have to be surrendered.

Must we do this? I thought. Can we never be alone?

After Gahrazel and Ithiel had gone upstairs, accompanied by ribald cheering and shouting (which disgusted me), everyone forgot about them and the music seemed to get louder, the lights brighter. Cal sauntered over to where Cobweb and I were sitting, looking this way and that like a cat. I wondered if he would sit down and begin washing himself without looking at us, but he said, "Cobweb, I would like to make you dance."

"Over my dead body!" was the predictable response.

Cal looked thoughtful. "To dance on your dead body, hmmm . . . An attractive prospect perhaps, but impractical; too lumpy. Maybe you are too drunk to stand?"

"I have changed since we last met," Cobweb hissed icily. "In those days, I would have told you to go fuck yourself; now I am contained and civilized and merely shake my head with a condescending smile. Now I visualize your extinction, now I dismiss you from my attention."

He rested his chin on his hand and gazed glassily at the dancers. Cal smiled as he always smiles, relishing any contact with my hostling. After he had gone I said, "Why do you hate him so, Cobweb?" and my hostling answered.

"Outside the trees are alive. I can see them moving, although the garden is dark. All trees have spirits . . ."
It is a wonder I was ever born sane.

CHAPTER FOUR

>━┼━<>━━○━━<>━┼━<

Enigma of the Beast
Incarnate war, captives clamoring,
Pangs of Trojan endurance.
Never suffering the distant humility
Of the human incarcarates.

Our house, throughout the ages, may always have been a place of secrets. Among the curtains, whispering, all the long corridors rustling with the confidences of unseen lips. We that lived there eventually got to hear everything. We were close-knit, and at that time, Forever was our only world.

Ponclast and my father spent several days after Gahrazel's Feybraiha locked in Terzian's study, deep in conversation. (Not just for his son's coming of age, then, had the mighty Ponclast left his northern realms.) I had often wondered what it was like in the north; what it would be like to have to live there. My imagination supplied dark visions of Hell; smoke, livid flame, shattered buildings, creeping forms, faraway howling. I could not imagine daylight in such a place. (Later, I learned that my visions were not that inaccurate.) Gahrazel had always been reluctant to describe in detail his old home, yet I could tell he had never been really unhappy there. I knew the names of his friends, that he had two rooms of his own in his father's palace, that his relationship with Ponclast was not as bad as he sometimes made out and that he did not know the har who had been his hostling. I knew all this, but very little else.

Through Ithiel, via the house staff and finally from Cobweb, I learned most of what my father and Ponclast had discussed. Because of my ignorance or because of the security I felt surrounded me, I was neither shocked nor worried by what I heard. It was unreal to me, only words, and the meaning of them could not touch us. I felt we were distanced from everything, that Galhea existed only in its own universe. To a degree, I suppose this proved uncannily true, for my home was never marked by true conflict, but I was wrong if I supposed what lay beyond our fields could not summon me out to meet it. Our country, which the Gelaming (and finally all Wraeththu) called Megalithica, was controlled for the most part by the Varrs and the Uigenna. In the south, other tribes held sway and northern Wraeththu had little congress with them for they were sorcerers and, while uninterested in accruing more lands, people to be wary of, for it was said that their currency was souls. Swithe said that the southerners did not seek conquests in this world and that even the Gelaming might avoid confrontation with them. I knew that Cobweb's tribe had traveled south all those years ago, when Cobweb had turned his back on them and remained in Galhea. I asked him if he knew about the currency of souls, but he only laughed and ruffled my hair. "And how many souls would it take to buy meat to fill the belly of my child?" he said, but I could tell that he knew. Cobweb knew many things and some of them he would never speak of. He said, "Swift, the rumors are true." He had known that for a long time.

For nearly a year, snippets of news had been filtering through to Galhea about the Gelaming. Terzian had no doubt that one day, they really would descend on Megalithica. "They are too powerful not to," he said. Now it was true; they were here, a long way to the south, just north of the desert, but too close for comfort. Some said that they had come across the sea in long, pointed ships that sailed against the wind, powered by silence, and others said that they had traveled through the air by means of magic.

Terzian scoffed at these ideas. "However they damn well got there, one thing is sure," he said, "they mean to take Megalithica away from Varr control. Mission of peace? Bah! That is rot, and the first to believe it will be the first to die. If they take control, the pestilence of their beliefs will infect us like a plague; masculinity repressed, all this talk of peace and harmony. . . . They will leave us half dead, like a race of women, twittering helplessly, seeking maleness, until the next tribe crosses the sea from the east and makes slaves of us! Can we allow that? It will happen if we don't fight and I shall fight until my last breath!"

It was in the town that he said that, and it is now quite a famous speech. All the people cheered him as he stood there so tall, so handsome, with the fires of courage and action burning in his eyes. Cobweb stood at his side like a queen, dressed in a robe of green. Afterwards, hara came to kneel before him and kiss the jewelled serpent's eye he wore set into a ring on his left hand. It was lucky. They gave him flowers. Cobweb the witch; they entreated him to pray for victory. Inside every Varr, it seemed, the seed of religion still waited to be nurtured. Terzian's sarcasm might turn them away from the light, but the light was patient. It could wait.

The Gelaming were giving no sign of what they intended to do next. They had installed themselves in the south and had so far, made no move toward the north or even tried to communicate with anyone. The Varr leaders refused to be discomforted by this, treating it as a rather obvious ploy to engender panic. I asked Cobweb why the Varrs and their allies didn't move first and drive the intruders back across the sea.

"Why?" he replied mysteriously. "Why indeed! It is because of Fear, little pearl, no other reason. Now Terzian and his friends may come to regret turning away from the path."

"The path?" I queried.

Cobweb smiled. He lifted one hand and twisted the fingers. Out of the air three colors merged and danced for a full half-minute before fading away.

"Imagine such a thing as that, Swift, but more powerful by a thousand times. Enough to take off your head! Now do you see why they are afraid?"

For a while, I too was scared by this, but then, as the days passed and nothing changed in the house, my apprehension faded. Terzian was all-powerful. The Varrs could repel any threat; we were safe.

Once Ponclast returned to the north, Forever closed its doors and again turned its back on events occurring beyond its walls. As before, we, its little occupants, became more interested in the convolutions of our daily lives. Terzian was absent much of the time, but I never thought to ask why. I was more interested in the blossoming of Gahrazel and asked him endless questions about the practices of aruna. He infuriated me by refusing to answer, saying, "To tell you would spoil it for you." He enjoyed annoying me, smug beast, and would only laugh when I lost my temper with him. Sometimes, Ithiel would stay with Gahrazel in his room and because I was excluded, I would get angry and bored. I bullied Swithe and Cobweb to take me into Galhea with them and occasionally they would relent and we would go into the town, perhaps to eat at the best inn, where they treated us like royalty, or to walk in the market where traders would respectfully entreat us to inspect their wares. I would see other harlings watching me curiously, whispering among themselves. I had learned to be haughty and kept my nose in the air.

Predictably, Swithe became friendly with Cal and they had long conversations about our race, most of it meaningless to me, all of it dull. Cal enjoyed arguing and I noticed that he often completely changed his opinions from day to day. This confused Swithe, who sometimes found himself defending a point that previously he had argued against fiercely. Cal would catch my eye and wink at me while Swithe spluttered for words. I was glad Cal had someone else to talk to, for it worried me that he spent so much time alone. He *seemed* to have recovered from his illness, but I could sense that not all was well with him and that he put a lot of energy into appearing healthy. The mask may have been convincing, but it was brittle. Once, it nearly broke completely. Once, we nearly saw him as he really was. I have found that in our house, a lot of important things were revealed during mealtimes. An idle remark, a seemingly innocent occurrence. This time was no exception.

Terzian had just come home and Ithiel had joined us for dinner. Outside it was dusk although the days were lengthening. Everyone was talking when suddenly Cobweb said, "Cal, you never told us, but what did happen to Pellaz? Did you fall out?"

Nobody else even stopped their conversations; it was perhaps only me that heard it. I looked at Cal. His fists were clenched on the table. He was staring at Cobweb, who stared back, a gentle smile misting the challenge. It happened so quickly. Cobweb said, "I see death in your eyes."

My father stopped talking to Ithiel, mid-sentence, and looked at them. Cal made a noise. Cobweb said, "Well?"

Cal cried, "Don't! You are . . . you are . . . !" He had lost the words; he couldn't speak. Terzian, reacting quickly, anticipating trouble, reached for Cal's taut hand. Cal barely winced; his face seemed to ripple, like wind over water. He picked up the nearest object, the nearest weapon, fumbling as if he was blind: a silver fork. His face was blank. Suddenly it was in his hand, my father was speaking his name, and suddenly Cal had plunged the pointed tines into Terzian's hand where it lay over his own on the white tablecloth. Ithiel stood up, pointing, making a sound. My hostling laughed and Cal ran from the room, knocking over his chair as we went. My father stared in amazement at the sharp fork still half-hanging from the back of his hand.

It was all so quick. Of course, Ithiel wanted to go after Cal. One does not attack the person of the ruler of Galhea and get away with it, but my father shook his head. "It is not as bad as it looks," he said and carefully removed the sharp points from his flesh. It did not bleed at first. Terzian looked sharply at Cobweb, who blithely offered his napkin, which Terzian wrapped around his hand.

None of us felt much like eating after that. At the end of the meal, my father said to Cobweb, "Don't ever say anything like that to Cal again. We can't guess what he's suffered to be the way he is!" But Cobweb only smiled. He was as aware as I was that Terzian had not gone after Cal to comfort his distress.

Naturally, I was the one that finally went to look for him. He had only gone to his room and was reading through some of his notes at the desk that my father had brought into the house for him. When I asked him if he was alright, he laughed and said, "Of course!"

It occurred to me that he might have forgotten the whole incident, but I said. "You stabbed my father's hand with a fork!"

"Yes," he agreed.

I was exasperated. It was like trying to communicate through a mist. "Why? Why?!" I shouted. "What was it that happened to you? Where *is* Pellaz?"

Cal turned his back on me, adjusted his lamp and went on reading.

"You *are* mad!" I cried.

"Very possibly," he said quietly. "Get out, Swift; I'm working."

But I had more to say. "Cobweb knows everything. He *knows*, Cal. He will have seen it in your mind and he will use it to destroy you. Can't you see that?" That thought must have been in the back of my mind for quite some time; now it seemed blindingly obvious.

"I don't want to talk about this," Cal replied. "Cobweb knows nothing about me."

I rushed forward, tried to take his shoulders in my hands, turn him toward me. His body felt rigid. His eyes were inches from my own and cold as death. I couldn't speak. He smiled.

"Do you see it too, Swift?" he said.

After this, I said to Gahrazel, "How does Cal sleep, do you think? Is he troubled by dreams?"

Gahrazel and I spent a lot of time discussing Cal. "I should imagine he sleeps very well," Gahrazel replied. "I don't think he remembers his dreams."

I watched Cobweb warily. His acceptance of Cal into our household had been too easy, too quick. What was he plotting? I had no doubt he knew a lot about what had happened to Cal and *would* use it, but carefully. It would have to be in a way that Terzian could not notice or even suspect.

One day in the late spring, one of the ever-vigilant patrols cornered a group of humans south of Galhea, some miles away from the town. No-one knew why they had been there, where they had been going, or why they had forsaken their cover. My father had been summoned to the town after Ithiel's troup had rounded them up. Inevitably, several humans had been killed. Now Terzian would decide the fate of the survivors and supervise their interrogation. Gahrazel and I were delighted. Men! At last, and in Galhea. Gahrazel had seen humans before, of course, but only as flitting shapes in the dark or dead bodies. We were both eager to see living humans. They were some kind of strange animal to us. I knew that, years ago, there had been human slaves in Galhea, but they were no longer around. I could only guess at what had happened to them.

Terzian was approached, first by me and then by Gahrazel, both of us requesting that we might see the captives, but he shook his head. He did not want to be bothered with harlings and our demands annoyed him. He would not give us a proper reason.

Gahrazel said that my father had looked almost guilty when he refused our request. He was so angry at having anyone saying no to him that he devised a plan. "We must sneak out of the house at night," he said, "and go to Galhea ourselves."

At first I protested violently. It would be too dangerous, my father would find out, we would be caught and punished. Gahrazel sneered at my objections and argued with me until I gave in. He was restless and craved adventure and I really wanted to see a human. I tried to imagine what it would be like speaking with one. Would it be astounded by my wisdom?

Gahrazel managed to find out that all the humans were kept penned in a fenced enclosure near the soldiers' quarters, where I had never been. This was not too far from Forever and we could walk there within fifteen minutes. Gahrazel planned our adventure down to the finest detail. He charmed, bribed or threatened the guards who would be on duty to let us approach the enclosure. We would be able to get really close.

When the night came, I could not sleep for excitement. Gahrazel waited until he was sure the whole house was asleep before he came to my room. We dressed in dark clothes and clambered down the ivy outside my bedroom window, as we had done many times before. This was the first time I was scared of being caught. I was unsure of my father's reaction. I could equally imagine him being furious or amused; it was impossible to guess his mood.

Running through the dark, I held Gahrazel's hand and the town below me glowed softly with the memory of light.

The guards did not know who we were. I waited while Gahrazel spoke to them. It was not a cold night, but I could see that the humans had built themselves a fire. They were sitting miserably around it, making very little sound, hunched shapes against the flames. The earth looked raw where the stakes of the fence had been punched into it. Behind the enclosure I could see the outlines of the soldiers' buildings against the sky, sounds of merriment and music reaching me from the open windows.

Gahrazel beckoned me over. He was speaking to two tall hara, resplendent in dull leather of deepest black. Gahrazel's voice was low and confident. "Can you get one of them to come over? I've never seen a human close to."

We approached the fence. If only I did not feel so small and nervous. A voice behind me, one of the guards. "Get one to the fence? Do you think they want you looking at them? How do you think we can make them do that?" He was laughing at us.

"Can't you offer them something?" Gahrazel asked indignantly. He hated to be laughed at.

"What, like throwing sugar to a horse?" the other guard joked. "Maybe they'd prefer a few handfuls of hay. Have we any hay?"

I could only think, "They do not know who we are. I must not be afraid." I could not turn round and look at them, but I could feel them behind me, slightly threatening, slightly wild. The one who had first spoken to us walked forward and put his hand in Gahrazel's hair. Gahrazel did not move; I jumped for him. "Share breath with me and I'll offer the rest of my sheh to them. It is said they crave alcohol."

I could tell he didn't think Gahrazel would say yes. But he did not know Gahrazel. My friend, whom I trusted to keep me safe, folded his arms, wrinkled his nose and then said, "Alright."

"Gahrazel!" I squeaked with horror.

He looked at me like a stranger. "Don't panic, Swift," he said and to the guard, "Afterwards, OK?"

I thought, Ah, this is a trick, and partially relaxed.

The guard cheerfully shouted a few insults at the humans by the fire and then made the offer of the sheh. One of them called back, "What is this?" I had expected human voices to sound completely different to ours, like animals perhaps, but they weren't. It could have been a har calling out.

"Whoever comes to the fence gets the sheh! Two of our citizens want to have a look at you!"

"We are not animals!" an angry voice shouted back, but two of them stood up and came toward the fence. I was almost too scared to look. I was afraid of their difference, but one of the guards laughed and said, "Kids!"

Their appearance was dreadful, but not alien. We could look like that, if we were half starved and filthy, dressed in rags with ragged spirit. I could smell them and it was the stink of stale bodies and wretchedness. They were young, but I could not guess what age or whether they were male or female. (Was the difference apparent on the surface?) Their arms were thin like flesh-covered sticks, hands like paws on the fence. Only their eyes showed any sign of brightness and there I saw the strength of humanity, the instinct to fight until weakness or death prevents it. One of them put its fingers through the slats and said, "Sheh!"

The guard looked at Gahrazel. "They are little more than children," he said, "but probably ten years older than you. This one's a female." He poked through the rails with the butt of his gun. The female did not move but reached toward us with her eyes. Perhaps sheh could ease her misery, perhaps she craved numbness more than anything. For that she would let us make fun of her; us, in our fine clothes, flaunting our clean, well-fed bodies before her poverty. For a moment she looked me in the eye and I was nearly physically sick. For the first time in my life, I felt truly ashamed. We should not be here. I could see myself tearing down the fence. I could see it so clearly, but all I did was lower my eyes.

"Where have you come from?" I heard Gahrazel ask.

"We are from nowhere," she answered in a clear, high voice. "We having nothing; you know this. We are nothing to Varrs!"

"The Gelaming!" the other human, a male, said suddenly and the female turned on him like lightning and pummeled him with her fists.

"Shut up!" she cried. The male backed away, panting.

"They're going to kill us," he said, pointing through the fence with a shaking hand.

"Will you?" the girl asked, pressing her face against the slats. "Are you going to do that?"

"We might!" The guards laughed.

"Oh, we are nothing!" she screeched, shaking the fence.

"The beast will come! The beast will come!" her companion raved madly.

"That's enough!" One of the guards slapped the fence with his gun. The humans hissed like animals and withdrew a few paces. A bottle of sheh landed in the dirt at their feet. I was surprised that the guard had kept his word. The female leaned down, picked up the bottle and wiped it, strangely fastidious, on her ragged clothes. I found myself against the fence with my mouth open. I said, "Female." She looked at me. "What is your name?" I asked.

She smiled, and nodded, almost imperceptibly. "Bryony." They both turned back to the fire.

"Wait!" I called. Their pale faces stared at me through the darkness, but they would not come back to the fence. I wanted to ask, How much do you hate us? How much? Something foolish. I wanted them to say something bad to me. I wanted to say, "I am different." They walked away. Gahrazel touched me on the shoulder.

"The guards are called Leef and Chelone," he said. "They have more sheh in their rooms, and the guard is changing now. They're going off duty. Come on."

"No, I think we should go back now," I said, uncertainly.

Gahrazel laughed. "Are you joking? Go back alone then! My adventure does not end here!"

He knew I would not go back alone.

Their rooms were in a house shared by several other hara. A splendid creature, dressed in blue and gold, opened the door to us. His face was heavily painted, jewelery hung heavily from his throat and ears. "Hostling stock," Gahrazel whispered to me confidentially. "Only the best for your father's warriors!"

We were offered sheh in crystal glasses. The painted har served the drinks and then left the room. It was a sumptuous salon, all comforts provided for. I was desperate to get home but too scared to do anything but stay by Gahrazel. Chelone unlaced his leathers and shook the creases from the linen shirt he wore beneath. "I am hot," he said. "Later, I must remove these as well." He stroked his black-clad thigh and Gahrazel laughed. Leef told me to sit down and I balanced myself on the edge of a chair. I felt my presence invaded the room; I was not supposed to be there and the room knew that but the guards did not. Leef asked me how old I was and I told him. He looked over his shoulder at Gahrazel sitting next to Chelone on the couch and back again. "Where do you live?"

"I . . . somewhere . . ." I shrugged helplessly. At the time I was more afraid of Terzian's wrath than what the soldiers could do to me. All I could imagine was these strangers telling Terzian what we had done. Shaking with a cold I could not feel, I drank some of the sheh. It was rougher than the drink I was used to. Leef took the cup off me when I winced.

"I think you're too young to be out taking sheh off strange hara," he said.

Why must they always laugh at us? I wondered angrily.

Leef leaned against the wall and stared at me. All my limbs felt enormous. I know the way back, I thought. There is no reason why I should stay here. I know the way back. I will leave Gahrazel. The door seemed a hundred miles away. When I stood up, Leef put his hand on my arm.

Apprehension turned to terror in my heart. I was so young, but would that be important to him? Meat cutting . . . I looked at Gahrazel, frantic, but he did not notice. He had his arms round Chelone's neck, his mouth on Chelone's mouth; I felt queasy watching them. Leef's hand slipped under my hair. I froze.

"You're afraid," he said. "Don't be." He tried to pull me against him. I could not resist; he was much stronger than me. With my head against his chest, my body shuddering as he stroked my back, I spoke the only words that could save me, "I am Swift. I am Terzian's son."

Leef hesitated for only a moment before he virtually threw me away from him. "Terzian's son!" His eyes rolled upwards. He laughed. "Do they know where you are?"

"No," I said miserably, close to tears. "No!" I wanted to make the growling noise and run, but snared by shame, I only backed slowly toward the door. Leef watched me speculatively. Then he shook his head and reached for the sheh bottle. My fingers touched the glossy wooden panels of the door and then I was in the hall, running toward the main entrance, and outside, gulping air, hurrying as if the devil's own hounds were on my heels. Someone shouted out as I ran past the humans' enclosure, perhaps one of the other guards stood up, but then there was only cruel laughter and the dark mouth of the avenue that led back to Forever. My mind kept repeating, "What if . . . what if . . ." and I growled and growled and growled.

Half a mile up the road, my chest aching, I slowed to a wobbly walk. Damn Gahrazel! I thought furiously. I shall never speak to him again! Never! Some moments later, I heard the pounding of hooves on the gravel behind me and slipped in among the trees at the side of the road. "No-one can see me, no-one," I chanted under my breath and leaned against one of the smooth trunks. Looking up, I stared through the waving branches at the stars and the dark, dark sky. Up there are eyes, I thought and felt the warmth of a tear escape my blinking eyes. Am I safe? Am I? How far is it back to Forever? Do I have to go past anyone? When the horse slowed down and snorted, I dropped to my knees and pressed my face against the tree. Will I die? I thought. Somebody touched my shoulder and I turned and snarled and lashed out with my hands.

"Hey!" the shape snapped and I knew it was Leef, that he had followed me, and though I was Terzian's son, I was in the dark, alone and helpless, and if I was dead I could say nothing.

"Don't touch me!" I screeched.

"Don't hit me!" Leef said, laughing. "Stop it! If you are who you say you are, you have nothing to fear, do you?" His voice was not threatening. I stopped striking out.

"That's better," he said. "Now, my lord Terzian will not thank me for letting his beloved son roam the streets of Galhea all alone, will he?" He took my hands in his own. "Come on, I'll escort you home."

"Don't tell him!" I cried, pulling away. "Please don't!"

He laughed again. "It might be dangerous for me not to," he said reasonably. "If this was ever found out . . . well!"

"It won't be!" I pleaded desperately. "Please, it won't be. Just let me go. Go away. Forget you saw me. Please!"

He thought about my fear. "Don't be foolish, get on the horse!" His voice was sharp. When I wouldn't move, he sighed. "Alright, alright, I won't say anything to anybody. Not a soul. Just come with me, *please.*"

He held me in front of him on the saddle and we cantered back along the avenue, all the trees rushing past us in a blur. At the gates of Forever he said, "What possessed you to do this?"

"I only wanted to see the humans," I said. "My father wouldn't let me."

His hand tightened on my waist a little. "Humans, was it! Your friend didn't seem very interested in them. He seemed more interested in Chelone."

"Yes," I agreed quietly.

"I wouldn't go wandering with him at night if I were you," he said. "At least, not for a while . . . God, Terzian! You must be brave!"

"No," I said. "Can I get down now?"

He hesitated a moment and then said, "What a pity. Alright, off you get!" When I stood on the ground, he added, "I'll watch you for a while, OK?"

I nodded, and because I was safe again, I remembered and asked, "The humans, will they be killed?"

"Killed? I doubt it, not yet. We need the labor."

"Labor?"

"A nice way of saying slavery," he said. "But never mind that! Start walking up that drive, now!"

I smiled at him shakily. "Thank you, Leef," I said and slipped between the gates of Forever. Soon the dark limbs of the trees hid him from me. I looked back twice. I could hear the horse snorting and stamping by the gates, but I could not see him.

Next morning, I went early to the kitchen. Yarrow was surprised to see me before breakfast. Our meal was already prepared, waiting to be taken to the dining room. Yarrow was now concentrating on lunch. "Yarrow," I said, walking around his huge, worn table. "How often I've heard you complain you do not have enough staff! Always you complain the house is not kept up as well as it might be." Yarrow looked at me suspiciously, still slicing vegetables at the speed of light.

"And what is this to you?" he asked.

I shrugged carelessly, watching him. "Oh, nothing really. I was just wondering; I might be concerned for you." I picked up a crisp finger of raw potato and chewed it thoughtfully. "Yarrow?"

"Now what?" He stopped slicing, pushing back his hair, which he always tried to tie back, always unsuccessfully.

"I need you to do something for me."

"Do something . . ." Yarrow repeated ominously.

"What do you think of humans?" It was one of our cook's privileges that he could virtually say what he liked to any member of the household, even Terzian himself to a certain degree. Cobweb said it was because Yarrow was an artist and the best cook we could ever possibly hope to get. He was young and he sometimes got too drunk, but even if our tempers often got sick of him, our stomachs were in love with him. Now he narrowed his green eyes at me and said, "Why?"

"If the opportunity presented itself, would you have them working for you?" I asked carefully.

Yarrow sighed and went back to his slicing. "Do I like the sound of this? I think not!"

"But *would* you?" I insisted.

"What, do you mean preparing food?" He wrinkled his nose. "No, I don't think so. Would you eat it? They are different from us. As for working about the house, I don't know. They're not supposed to be trustworthy and the fact that they loathe Wraeththu must be taken into account. Why, Swift, what is all this?"

Now I would have to trust him. First making him swear not to tell anyone, I told him about the humans in the town, that they might be killed, that I wanted him to get around my father and have two of them brought to the house. "There is only one person who can get his own way with Terzian over something like this, and that is you," I said.

Yarrow was flattered. "Mmm, maybe. Are you sure you wouldn't prefer another puppy instead? Mareta will be having kittens again soon. Won't a dog or a cat be less trouble than humans?"

"I don't want them as pets," I said. "I feel sorry for them."

"Really! This is worrying, Swift. How did you get to see them anyway? How do you know about them?" I smiled and shook my head.

"I just know, that's all. Will you do it?"

"They are children?"

"Yes . . . well, not that old." I walked around the table once more and put my arms around him. "Yarrow, if you do this, I will love you forever, I promise!"

"Ha! Love me, will you?" he said and laughed, and by that I knew that he'd agree.

"One of them is named Bryony," I told him. "One of the guards will know. His name is Leef."

"Leef!" Yarrow exploded, obviously knowing more about Leef's reputation than I did. "Swift, what have you been up to?"

"Hush!" I said. "Nothing. See my father after breakfast. I shall be especially well behaved to soften him up."

It was a tribute to Yarrow's powers of persuasion and my father's fear of upsetting Yarrow that within two days, Yarrow and two of his staff went into the town to choose human slaves to work at Forever. I was a little worried that Leef would not cooperate. After all, he would be afraid that my father might find out that he had spoken to me in the dark, and thought of me as older than I was and put his warm, forbidden hands on my waist when we were on the moving horse. He might say, "Terzian's son? What are you talking about?" and laugh. There was a very good chance he might do that and then Yarrow might bring the wrong humans back to the house. Not that it mattered, I suppose, a charitable act was a charitable act, whoever it was that benefited, but I was particularly interested in those two.

I had been ignoring Gahrazel very thoroughly for the past two days and Swithe and Moswell could not understand what was going on. Gahrazel had said the next morning, "Look, Swift, I'm sorry that—" But I had not let him finish and had walked away, head in air.

Cobweb said, "Have you and Gahrazel quarrelled, Swift?"

I just shrugged and said, "He's changed."

Cobweb smiled and touched my hair. "Poor little Swift," he said and went back to his painting.

One evening, I went to see Cal in his room and, even though he looked even more tired than usual, told him all about it. He laughed. "Oh, Swift, all that trouble, all that secrecy! If you wanted to see humans, I'd have taken you myself, in daylight even!" and I thought, Of course, why didn't I think of that?

"Cal, do you like my father?" I asked, knowing he would have taken me to Galhea because he cared so little what Terzian might think.

"Your father is a complicated har," Cal said obliquely.

"But do you like him?"

"Like him . . . like him . . . ?" Cal tapped his lips with a pencil, thinking, his eyes glowing like coals in dark, ravaged sockets. "I think perhaps I do. I don't dislike him, certainly. Pass me that green pen, Swift, will you?"

"Can I read what you're writing, Cal?"

"No," he said.

Yarrow spoke to me about the humans. "I told them if they tried to run away, or steal anything, or not work hard, I'd have Ithiel slit their throats," he said. "Their names are Bryony and Peter and they are brother and sister." He told me that the rest of the staff were rather pleased about the new arrivals because it meant that all the most shunned, arduous or unpleasant tasks could be allotted to them.

I wondered whether the humans were pleased that they had been saved from death or working for someone worse than Yarrow, who, although he exacted hard work from his staff, was never deliberately cruel. He might treat the humans differently, of course. When they had first arrived, Terzian had told everyone about it at dinnertime. "Yarrow is behaving strangely," he said. "He's asked for human slaves! Cobweb, do you think that latest batch of sheh was tainted or something?"

Gahrazel looked at me slyly while everyone laughed politely at Terzian's joke. Cal saw me going red and said, "Well, Terzian, this does dispel an illusion! There was I thinking that the only human you'd tolerate within a mile of your august presence was a dead one."

Terzian's responsive laugh was a little strained for some reason. Cobweb refused even to smile.

"Oh, you know how Yarrow is," Terzian said. "We suffer his whims. No doubt he'll get sick of trying to discipline them and get rid of them."

"We must examine carefully then all the meat we are served in future," Cobweb remarked drily and I saw Cal look at him. Did Cal ever tell the truth? I wondered.

A few days afterwards, my father was summoned north by Ponclast and we all looked forward to a relaxing few weeks while he was away. I thought the humans were quite attractive once they were cleaned up. Good food and comfort would restore their flesh. I was glad that they did not appear to recognize me. Yarrow suddenly found jobs for them to do that had been building up for ages. There was a cupboardful of linen to be repaired and all the silver and brassware needed a good polish. His racks of herbs needed labelling; the list was endless. Sometimes we could hear Bryony singing while she worked, that strange, high, female sound. Perhaps they were not too unhappy. Once, when I went into the kitchen, she was sitting by the hearth with Mareta on her lap, peeling vegetables (so Yarrow had relented about the food). She looked up and said, "You are one of the pure-born, I can tell." Then she said, "The Varrs live differently to how we imagined."

I was quite surprised that she dared to speak to me, and without any shyness, too. "And how did you imagine it?" I asked.

"Oh, we thought that with all the killing and because you have no craft, you'd live like pigs!"

"You're not afraid of us, are you?"

"No," she said. "I'm not afraid of anything any more. This house is like a palace and you're all like people from a story. Peter and I thought Cobweb was a woman at first. Will they incept my brother, do you think?" She gave me a dazzling smile.

"I don't know." I was not sure what she meant. "You don't seem to mind being here; do you?"

"No, I don't mind being here. Isn't it strange? Our tormentors are now our saviours. We were foolish to get caught, though. The winter made us foolish."

"Where were you going?"

She didn't answer for a moment. "Oh, south," she said finally.

"Are there humans in the south?"

"Not many." She had finished the vegetables and carried them over to the sink. It looked so natural, the sunlight coming in through the window onto her face, the brightness splashing from the taps over her hands, as if she had always lived here in this man's house that Wraeththu had taken for themselves. Her face was shiny and she pushed back her hair. "You don't seem much like your father," she said. (They must have been asking who I was, then.)

"They say I resemble my hostling more," I replied, missing her point.

"Hostling," she said and laughed. "I can't remember my mother. It must be really odd having two fathers!"

"I don't. I have a father and a hostling."

"Oh, I know. It's just that Wraeththu look more like males to us. Strange males, like angels and elves and demons all mixed up together. Some of them are angels, some of them are demons. In the north, there are more demons than angels, that's for sure!" She carried the cleaned vegetables back to the stove and began dropping them into a saucepan.

"This was once a man's house," I said.

"This was once a man's world," she replied. I could imagine Cobweb saying that.

"I don't think you're that different from us," I said.

"Perhaps not, but you're supposed to be. Our father (his name was Steven), he said that Wraeththu came into the world because men and women had forgotten how to open their eyes properly. I was younger when he said that and I didn't understand. He said it in church and everyone was angry with him and after that, the Wraeththu came, and they took away our homes. They only killed the ones that tried to fight them; they were not one of the very bad tribes. My father spoke to the Wraeththu, he wanted answers, and sometimes people would throw stones at us because of it. But it wasn't too bad until the Varrs came on their black horses and the Wraeththu began to fight. Things happened . . . we knew we had to leave."

"Wraeththu fighting *each other?*" I asked in a small voice.

She looked at me strangely. "Well, yes. Varrs kill nearly everything, don't they?"

"Not here."

"Well, you're all Varrs here, aren't you? And I suppose you're a sort of prince and you haven't killed anybody at all yet, have you?"

"Cobweb said . . ." I began and then couldn't continue. I had been about to say that Cobweb said that to kill was an extremely bad magic and one for which I would have to pay dearly if I ever did it. Just to wish someone dead was bad. But I couldn't say it because Bryony had seen Wraeththu kill Wraeththu and Wraeththu kill men and saying it was pointless. Bryony had seen all this, yet she could still sing and be happy. She had no proper home and had lost most of her family, yet still she smiled. I thought she must be very strong.

"Swift," she said. "Can we be friends?"

I looked up startled. "Don't you know your position?" I asked sharply, not really offended but just surprised.

She nodded. "Yes, I know my position, but I also know that I owe you my life. That's why I know I can suggest it."

"You *do* recognize me!"

She smiled. "How could I fail to do that? When I first saw you, I saw a girl and a boy superimposed over each other with the most wonderful eyes I had ever seen. I felt your shame. When you asked my name, I knew.

I only had to wait and then Yarrow came. I want to thank you. We never thought we'd find someone like you this far north."

I was too embarrassed to speak.

"Friends?" she said.

I nodded. "Bryony, what is the beast?"

Her face clouded. "What do you mean?"

"You know, your brother said it, when I first saw you. He said, 'The beast will come.' What did he mean?"

She looked at me hard and I could see she didn't want to answer. "It is just evil," she said.

But it was more than that and I didn't learn its form for a long time.

One day, hara came to the house with Ithiel and one of them was Leef. It was early summer and the weather was already very warm. I didn't know where they had been, or what they were doing at Forever, but they were very dusty. Leef had stripped to the waist and was washing himself at the pump in the stableyard. Gahrazel and I had just finished lessons; we were going into the house for tea with Swithe wandering behind. I stopped and looked at Leef, intrigued by his lean, tanned body. He sensed he was being watched and looked up. "Oh, it's you!" he said. "Been wandering among the common people again recently, have you?"

I looked around nervously but the others had gone inside and no-one was listening. I couldn't think of anything to say to him and yet I wanted to; it was very strange.

"Have you still got those humans here?" he asked, and I nodded.

"Yes, I can't understand it, they seem quite happy."

Leef laughed in a not altogether pleasant way. "Wait until you see the world outside, son of Terzian. Maybe then you'll understand only too well!"

I wished it was not always so obvious that I knew so little about the world. If I felt strong, it always happened that I was made to look foolish and it kept me in a childlike state. I wanted experience. I wanted to stand up and say to someone, "Oh, one day you will understand," complete and smug with my own special knowledge. I was the only person I knew that never did that. Leef put his shirt back on, but left it open. Now, most of Ithiel's guard affected the fashion of wearing their hair long at the back while still kept short over the crown. Leef tore the band from his hair with a grimace and scratched it loose. Was it a sign of growing up, I wondered, that he fascinated me? Yet if I dared to nurture any fantasies about him, I was too young to realize them, and by the time I was old enough, perhaps he wouldn't be around any more or would still see me as a spindly harling. Uncomfortable thoughts like that seemed to be springing into my head with uncontrollable regularity nowadays. Leef was no longer paying me any attention. I said, "One of the humans told me that up north Wraeththu are fighting Wraeththu. Is that true?"

"Why don't you ask your father?" he replied, and stung by a shame so deep I could not understand it, I turned away and ran back to the house.

That evening, Cal did not come to eat with us. After the meal, I went to his room and found him lying on the bed, staring up at the ceiling. "What's wrong?" I asked. "Don't you want anything to eat?" He turned his head in his lazy, Cal way and looked at me with his lazy, Cal eyes.

"Maybe I don't feel too well," he admitted. I sat next to him on the bed and put my hand on his face. He flinched so slightly, I barely noticed it.

"Do you hurt?"

"My head's black inside," he said.

"I could read to you," I offered cautiously.

He sighed. "No . . ."

I didn't want to leave him. To me he was like an injured wild animal that had been brought into the house. I couldn't understand him, it seemed unlikely we could heal him properly, he didn't really belong here, yet still I did not want to open the door and let him out. Half of me thought, Only what's outside can heal him. I was not exactly right about that.

Inspired by a memory of infant sickness, I said, "Turn over."

"Why?"

"You'll see. Something Cobweb used to do when I felt ill."

Sighing, reluctantly, he turned onto his stomach and I lifted his shirt and pushed it up above his shoulders. He laughed and said, "Swift?"

"Hush, now listen. I will draw you a story." His skin was hot beneath my fingers as I began a tale of creatures living in the dark and eating only sticks and mud.

"Do they hate the light?" Cal asked sleepily.

"But of course!" I answered. "Here is the big stone they use to block the entrance to their tunnel."

"It is my story you're telling then!"

"No, they are ugly creatures. They have little sense of humor and they don't know how to write."

"How do you judge ugliness?" Cal asked suddenly, half turning over and looking at me.

I shrugged. "I don't know. When you can't bear to look at something, I suppose, or worse . . ."

Cal shook his head. "No! You can't see true ugliness," he murmured and his eyes looked past me. "It is on the inside. It is always hidden . . ." Our eyes locked. "Always!"

"Cal . . ." I said softly and he replied, "No, no," just as softly. What was he denying? He looked dazed, almost delirious, turning his head this way and that on the pillow.

"What can I do?"

"I'm being attacked."

"But there's no-one here!"

"There's no-one here. Look! Look!"

It was on my mind to fetch Swithe or even Gahrazel. I was afraid.

"What is it, Cal? What is it?" I shook him, and his hand crept beneath his pillow.

"I'm being attacked," he said and pulled something out to show me. A card. On the card someone lies prone in the mud pierced by ten swords. A divining card and one of evil omen. Only one person would put that there. I took it from him and tore it to pieces. He watched impassively. We said nothing. His face twitched and he pressed himself into the pillows. His voice was muffled. "Draw me another story until I fall asleep," he said.

The next day, as it was the end of the week, we had no lessons, and Gahrazel and I went out into the garden to talk. I had eventually come to forgive him for the incident in Galhea although I still harbored a prudish disapproval of his behavior. We never talked about it. It was a strange day, hot and close. The kind of day that makes you nervous and I could taste it clearly. It tasted salty and sour. "There will be a storm later," I said. Gahrazel rolled onto his back on the grass, looking lovely and wild and secretive. Sometimes I could not control my jealousy of him, although our relationship did not appear to have changed that much since his Feybraiha.

"I want to stretch and stretch and stretch!" Gahrazel cried.

"You!" I snorted. "All the secrets of the world are yours!"

He laughed and sat up. "You are growing up to be another Cobweb," he said.

"What? Because I shall be a dark and wondrous beauty, or because I shall be slightly mad?"

"Oh, both, I think. Definitely!"

We saw Peter come into the garden and start digging around in the flowerbeds. Gahrazel called to him and demanded that he bring us refreshment because it was so hot. I knew Peter disliked talking to hara or even being near them. Gahrazel enjoyed making him uncomfortable.

"Peter could be har," Gahrazel said.

"Could he? How?" I hoped Gahrazel was not making fun of me.

"Like our fathers, like Cobweb, like everyone," Gahrazel replied, in a reasonable voice that was not the slightest bit mocking. "Do you think Wraeththu came from nowhere? Most of them were human once."

"Oh, I know that!" I said scornfully. "How, though? How do they do it?"

"It's our blood," Gahrazel explained, stroking the blue vein just visible on the inside of his arm. "It makes humans become like us. Male humans develop female parts as well. It can't work the other way. I saw it once at home."

"But how do they change? Is it really possible?"

Gahrazel laughed. "Give Peter a cup of your blood. Let's see!"

I shuddered. "Ugh, no. Gahrazel, you're disgusting!"

When Peter brought our drinks out, Gahrazel laughed because he would not look at us. I felt embarrassed. I did not want the humans to hate us.

"There may be thunder," I said, squinting at the deceptive sky.

"And great tearing gouts of lightning!" Gahrazel added enthusiastically. By lunchtime, the sky had become green and boiling.

Looking back, I can't decide whether it was the tension of the approaching storm or some kind of presentiment that made me so jumpy. I could barely eat my lunch. My head was full of strange, high-pitched sounds that I could not hear properly. Sometimes, ghostlike zigzags of light would flit across my vision. Cobweb ate daintily as usual, but I could feel the power in him and he scared me. I kept thinking of the Ten of Swords. A black sky, blood and despair. Gahrazel chatted with our tutors, sensing nothing.

After lunch, I went to my room and sat on the window seat. Vague growling echoed deeply in the sky from the east and the air was very still, as if holding its breath. The eerie green light outside made the garden darker, untamed and sentient. I pressed my face against the cool glass, feeling my heart flutter in my throat, the sound of blood in my ears and the dull pain that echoed it. Something is going to happen, I thought, and with that acknowledgment, another thing, shapeless and wild, released its terrifying grip on me. I opened up and let it flow into me; the power of the storm and something else, something more controlled and yet less understandable. My body shook, my throat was dry.

Outside, a white shape flickered through the gloom, passing beneath the mantle of the evergreens, into the darkness that lay beyond, toward the lake, toward the summerhouse, out in the living air. My skin prickled. Was it someone? Was it? While my mind still seemed to hover at the window, my body launched itself across the room, out of the door, down the corridor, dark and silent, down the stairs, toward the outside. Beyond the door, in the garden, the air was still hot, yet moist and scented. I ran into the trees, not looking back, sure-footed. I could see the white shape ahead of me. It was not running or even hurrying. By the time it reached the summerhouse, I had slowed to match its pace, and I could see that it was Cal.

A crooked finger of light snaked across the sky, flashing off panes of glass, off Cal's hair, off the water through the trees. The ground beneath my feet was moss. I crept toward the summerhouse and Cal opened the door. Was I so totally silent that he did not hear me? Inside, the summerhouse was strangely dark. There was a shallow stone basin in there, full of water, where orange fish lived among the lilies. It was in the center of the summerhouse. A stone animal curved uncomfortably out of the water. It was a fountain, but it was not turned on. Seated on the edge of the basin, holding something in his hands, on his lap, looking more lovely, more pale, more smoky, more deadly than I had ever seen him, was Cobweb.

I stood in the doorway and watched Cal walk toward him, his feet barely lifting, his head hanging. Cobweb looked only at him. If he knew I was there, I was of no importance and no hindrance. Cal stopped moving. Cobweb stood up. Cal looked around him, as if suddenly unsure of where he was or how he had got there. My sorcerer hostling smiled. "I am pleased you came," he said.

Cal looked confused; he said nothing.

"I knew you would come back one day," Cobweb continued in a conversational tone and he began to walk, around and around the basin pool. "I knew this, as I know many things. I know *you*, Cal, perhaps better than you know yourself. I have never liked what I have seen." He stopped and hugged closer to him the secret he held in his hands. "Sometimes when I look at you, Cal, when you sit at my table, drinking from my crystal goblets, using my silver knives and forks, with my Terzian's heart on your plate, I think to myself, 'There is blood on his hands,' and I can even see it. It is thick, dark blood. Blood from somewhere deep; lifeblood. And I can't help wondering how it came to be there. Can you tell me perhaps?"

I looked at Cal. His face was gray, his body strained and tense as wire, shaking as if it would break. Cobweb would wind him tighter and tighter, and then . . . a single touch would . . . I think Cal tried to speak. He made a noise. Cobweb laughed.

"It seems to me that you are no longer beautiful, Cal. Look into the water. See how I have brought all the foul ugliness that is within you to the surface. Look . . ." His slim, pale arm gestured toward the pool. His hair, unbound, was like creepers of ivy. I thought, I should stop this, shouldn't I? But how? I could no longer feel my hand where it gripped the doorpost.

Cobweb spoke again, so low, I could barely hear it. It was a lover's voice, caressing, reassuring. "I will make you remember, Cal," he said. "Will you thank me for it, I wonder?" He paused and tapped his lips thoughtfully. "The past, the webs, the fragments, all there. Like a locked chest full of treasures."

Cal tried to shake his head. "No," he croaked, but he could not move.

Cobweb revealed what he held to his breast. He held it up and in the green light I could see liquid in glass, moving slowly, like thick waves on a tiny sea. There was a mark on my hostling's arm, a thin smear of dried blood. Cobweb's eyes flashed. Lightning outside; lightning within. From his lips came words that hurt my ears, that I could hear and that were without sound. He raised his arm, higher. The mark on his skin cracked as if a great force from within had burst its seal. A single drop of red peered from the whiteness and began slowly to investigate the length of his arm. I tried to run forward, but it was too slow, as if all the world had become too slow. A hundred visions of my hostling's arm flickered down to the lip of the stone basin, a sound like a soul in torment, splintering, laughter; shards of light spinning outwards. My slow hand had closed on Cal's arm and it was cold and shuddering. Cobweb saw me and in an infinite space of time, recognition stripped the triumph from his face and made it anger. He screeched. He raised his arm. I tried to pull Cal away, but it was too late. Red lightning arced across the room, splashing down on Cal's face, his clothes, the floor behind him.

For a second, for an hour, there was only stillness and the phantom of a booming sound in the sky outside. Then the infant patter of raindrops. I think I said, "Cal . . ." or I thought it. Cobweb stared at him, his dark eyes immense, the whites of them showing all around.

Cal raised his hand. He looked at it almost inquisitively. He touched the redness on the front of his shirt, rubbed it between finger and thumb, sniffed it, tasted it. He looked at Cobweb, puzzled . . . for a moment. Then he looked at his hand again, it was wet and scarlet, and it started to shake. Cobweb and I were held in stasis while the terrible thing happened, while the thunder crashed in Cal's head and the lightning spurted out of his eyes. He threw back his head and the howling raised the hair on my head. His hands flew to his face. They *clawed.*

I was crying; I couldn't help it. I screamed, "Cobweb! Cobweb!" help-lessly, impotently.

My hostling did not even look at me. His voice was hoarse, his clothes, his hair seemed to billow around him. "Know yourself, Cal!" he snarled. "Know yourself! You are evil and death, the lord of lies!"

Cal twitched as if the lightning had coursed right into him. His face was the face of a demon, twisted, gaping. Through the glass above, the sky crawled with fingers of light.

"Go to the elements!" Cobweb screamed and Cal was blown past me, a scrap of flesh, light as air, into the rain, into the thunder, and my hostling laughed. "Not even all the hosts of Heaven can save him from himself!"

I heard it in my head as I ran out into the rain. Whether Cobweb had actually spoken it, I could not be sure.

Lightning had carved a great, seeping, pale gash in one of the gnarled yew trees by the lake. Perhaps at the same moment as the lightning struck, Cal's shuttered mind had opened up to him. I walked to the water and looked around me, still sobbing, tears and rain on my face. I was dazed, unsure of what had happened except that Cobweb's insane jealousy had been ap-peased. I called Cal's name, not really expecting an answer. Thunder was my only reply. I was soaked to the skin, my hair flat to my head. Cobweb would wait in the summerhouse until the rain stopped.

I kneeled in the soft, damp earth at the water's edge. Last year's dead reeds had not yet been cleared away. Among the stronger, greener shafts they juddered beneath the firing-squad bullets of the rain. I looked across the water, toward the half-tumbled temple folly that nestled into the trees on the other side. I could see a patch of white there. Before I realized what I was doing, I had started wading out into the water, mud and reeds swallowing my legs. Splashing, panicking, I turned round, waded back and scrambled round the sucking banks toward the stones.

He lay among the gray, licheny rocks as if he had been thrown there, his shirt torn off, his skin filthy with leaf mold and dirt, scratched and bleeding. I hurled myself toward him, wrenching my ankle, feeling the arrow of pain shoot up my leg. "Cal!" It was a scream.

He moved feebly. He curled away from me and put his arms around his head. I was so relieved to find him alive, I tried to pull his hands away, but he pushed me back and hit my face. "Fuck off, Varr brat!" he snarled, but I am sure he did not really know who I was.

I thought I would know madness when I saw it. The face that looked at me was not mad. There was anger, pain, despair, but also frightening sanity. "I'm sorry," I said feebly.

He sneered at my tears. "Get out of here!" He tried to lift himself and his face creased with pain. He punched the rock. "Get out of here!"

I put my arms around my knees and howled. Cal said nothing more. I didn't even know if he was watching me. After a while, I lifted my head and he was sitting with his knees up, his elbows on his knees, the heels of his hands pressed into his eyes. "Cal," I said again, hopelessly.

After a moment, his hands dropped and he looked at me. It seemed he was saying, "Go on, look at me. This is grief. I weep real tears and only I have the right to."

"You're all dirty," I said in a small, husky voice. Cal swallowed and blinked.

"Swift." It was just a whisper.

"Yes?" Only the leaves dripped around us. Long, pointed, shiny leaves. It was still dark, but the rain was stopping. Cal's face was a pale glow. He was filthy and haggard, attenuated, perhaps the ultimate evil, and yet. . . . Can this be? I wondered.

"Swift," he said again and again I answered, "Yes . . ."

"I never really forgot everything you know, at least . . . I don't think so." He held out one hand and looked at the water. "Little monster, little friend, come here, sit beside the lord of lies. I shall tell you such tales . . ." I did not move and he turned his face toward me and smiled. "Please don't be afraid of me; that's absurd!"

Scrambling, I tumbled over the stones down to him and came to rest against his cold side. He put his arm around me. "Cobweb—" I began, but he put his other hand over my face and I could smell the rich, dark earth smell.

"No," he said, "don't try to apologize for him. He was only doing something he thought was right, and he may *be* right . . ." Whatever result my hostling had hoped to achieve, I did not think it was this. Perhaps Cobweb thought that Cal was dead, destroyed by magic or by his own hand.

"Swift, you must understand, I don't think I am consciously wicked, but I have done wicked things. Some of them nobody knows about, but others, they have driven me across the land, this way and that, always wandering . . ." He sighed and closed his eyes. "What brought me back here? What?" His fingers squeezed my arm. "I must admit, my travels have brought me to good places sometimes, where good things can happen, things that can . . . touch me somehow. I'm here for a reason. What is it? Oh, Swift, you are the special one here, I think."

"Me?" I could not follow his ramblings. What did he mean?

"You remind me of someone I once knew," he said. "Not in looks, certainly, for there is too much of Cobweb in you, but that crazy, totally misguided, idealistic, childish view of things, *that* is very familiar to me. Very." He sighed and looked at me. Part of my soul seemed to melt right out of me into the ground. "This is the part of the picture story where I draw my confession on your skin, I suppose."

"You don't have to," I said quickly, for I was afraid of hearing it.

"But there *is* only you!" he said. "Who else could I tell? I have to tell someone, don't I? That's the way things happen, isn't it? Now I've regained the burden of my lost memory, I have to share it with someone."

"Terzian will be back soon," I said, glumly.

Cal laughed. "Oh, Terzian!" He leaned his head back against the rock and I stared at his throat because it looked so long. "Terzian," Cal continued, in a thoughtful tone. "My confession would bore him. He is not here to absolve me, no, not that. I've been out of my mind and out of my body, now I'm back again. If I returned to Galhea because of him . . ." He trailed off and smiled secretively.

"I'm cold," I grumbled. Cal snickered and I wondered, if like Cobweb, he could see into my mind. His free hand cupped my neck.

"Little Swift," he said.

"Let's go back to the house," I suggested, afraid that he was laughing at me.

"In a moment," Cal replied and before I could blink, he had me thoroughly in his arms and his mouth was on my own and my mind was full of red and black and rushing air. It was like dreams. I could see flames, only beyond the flames was a field of golden corn caressed by sunlight. I could smell it through the fire. I was not afraid. After a moment, it returned to merely flesh on flesh and the aftertaste of his tongue, which was like fresh apples. He put his lips against my closed eyes and held me to him.

"I once dreamed of you," I said. "In the dream you made me speak your name."

Cal rested his chin on the top of my head. "Did I?" he said.

We did not speak of what had happened in the summerhouse. I did not know how badly he had been hurt, but I had realized his strength was immeasurable, perhaps more so in spirit than in body. He was cut and bruised, but his injuries appeared to be only superficial; a scraped elbow, scratched shoulders. I wanted to lick his blood, I wanted to be like him. We walked back to the house.

I was afraid of meeting Cobweb, but Cal wasn't bothered about that at all. "So let him see me. What harm can he possibly do me now?" When he first stood up, Cal had complained of dizziness but by the time we walked in through the back door of Forever, he had completely recovered. The house was full of the smell of fruit cooking and I could hear Gahrazel's laughter coming from the drawing room. Sunlight filled the hall; the storm had passed us. I followed Cal into his room. "Just wait here while I take a bath," he said.

After a while, I plucked up the courage to go over to his desk and look at the papers lying on it. If I thought I'd find answers, I was wrong. I could understand nothing of what he'd written. It was complete gibberish, but dark in mood and disquieting. It was inevitable that he should come back into the room, a towel around his waist, rubbing his hair with another, and catch me red-handed, but he did not seem to mind.

"If you were older," he said, "we'd have taken that bath together."

I looked away. "But I'm not."

"No. I forget how old you are sometimes; you look much older. I'm sorry, it must have been confusing for you." He sat down on the bed.

"You mean what happened at the lake?" I asked, hesitantly.

"Yes, the legendary, essentially Wraeththu sharing of breath. Don't tell your father. It was very impulsive of me, and no doubt very corrupting."

(Don't tell your father, he said. Of course not. No. That part of Cal, the hands, the lips, the eyes, that was reserved for Terzian alone. I have not enough to offer; I am empty.) I tried to smile and watched him stand up and stretch. Magnificent, and forever beyond me. I turned to the window.

"I don't understand you, Cal. How come you always spring back like this? Nothing bad ever seems to affect you."

He shrugged. "Oh, I wouldn't say that. But I'm not self-indulgent, if that's what you mean. Anyway, as I said before, I don't think I'd really lost my memory. Cobweb just made me face things and it was for the best. I'm glad that he did now."

I had to smile at that. "Cobweb will be furious. None of that was supposed to help you, you know."

"But it did." He looked over his shoulder into the mirror and examined his back.

"You're incredible."

"Years of effort have gone into that effect," he said and winked at me.

He went back into the bathroom to dress and I sat at his desk. Soon I laughed out loud. Perhaps we were still at the lake; perhaps this was just an illusion and we were still melded mouth to mouth, living dreams. (If I think hard enough, can I make it true?) Cal walked up behind me, but he didn't touch me. I had the absurd feeling that he never would again, but at that moment, I felt too intoxicated to care.

"What are you laughing at?" he asked.

I shrugged helplessly; I couldn't explain.

"Pellaz is dead," he said.

I turned in the seat and looked at him. "Dead?" Cal saw what I was thinking and shook his head quickly, frowning.

"No, no, *I* didn't kill him. That's not the death the incomparable Cobweb saw around me. Let's sit down together, Swift. I want to talk to you.

"You are virgin in every conceivable way," he said. "Untouched, unmarked. Incredible really, when you think that you're a Varr and Terzian's son at that, but then, he's always looked after his own. Pell and I noticed that when we were here before. The Varrs are cattle and Terzian is the big, black bull!" Cal told me something of how he had met Pellaz, who had been unhar at the time, totally human. "He seemed about the same age as you then, but of course probably eight or nine years older." I learned about the Nahir-Nuri whose blood had made Pellaz har, whose name was Thiede. My skin prickled. I remembered my father speaking of him. Cal's eyes seemed to go black when he talked of Thiede. "It was he who murdered Pell!"

"You *saw?!*"

Cal shook his head. "You don't understand. I saw Pell die, and the person who did it, but it wasn't Thiede who fired the bullet. He's too clever for that, but I do *know.*"

"Why would he want to kill Pell?" I asked.

Cal laughed bitterly. "Why? Oh, who can understand Thiede's reasons for doing things? One day I shall know the reason. Unfortunately (and here it comes, Swift), I killed the one person who could have told me. That's the blood your charming hostling sees dripping from my hands all over the dinner table."

I looked at his hands, but I could not see death in them. They were the hands of love, if anything. "Beautiful, aren't they?" he said, lifting them up. I knew that; I had felt them upon me.

"Were you in love with Pell?" I asked. Perhaps that was impertinent, but I had to know. Cal did not hesitate.

"When someone says they are madly in love, there is no more fitting description for it. Madness, yes. It is worse than dying to lose it. It's like having your brains unraveled and squashed back into your head the wrong way. I loved him, I still do, very much." He thumped the bed with the flat of his hand and smiled and sighed. "Of course, out there, in the wonderful real world, love is an outlawed concept. Pell had a teacher once upon a time. His name was Orien, he was my friend; I killed him. It took me a long time to get Pell to unlearn all the pious things Orien taught him about love."

"I don't understand," I said.

"No, of course you don't. Let me illustrate it. Your hostling is in love with Terzian and then I come along and Cobweb is so scared of losing Terzian that he wants to kill me, or at least drive me insane. Now Wraeththu don't like that kind of thing; it's messy. The real Wraeththu that is. We're supposed to exist sublimely together, scorning the passions of jealousy, seeking aruna as a spiritual exercise and beaming with tranquility over everyone. It's a horrendous idea! So dull."

"Are all Wraeththu like that except for us?"

"Mostly, I suppose they're scared of becoming too much like men, yet you are pure-born and born with the ability to love. That proves they're wrong, doesn't it? OK, so my heart isn't exactly overflowing with positive feelings, but I *do* know what I'm talking about."

"I don't think I do," I confessed.

He laughed at me. "It *is* gibberish, isn't it? How can I illustrate it?" He twisted his mouth in thought. "Ah yes. You'll have to pretend. Imagine we are Gelaming and this is Immanion, not Gahlea. Immanion is the first city of Almagabra; the Gelaming capital, if you like. For a start, Cobweb would have welcomed me with open arms, delighted to have someone to smother with concern, and by now, he would be very worried that I'm not taking aruna with Terzian yet. He would want me to. In fact, I'd probably be sleeping with both of them by now. That's the difference."

"And that's bad?!"

"You don't understand," he said. "I'm not saying it is; I'm just explaining the difference. The thing I hate about the Gelaming and their kind is their hypocrisy. They can't be perfect; it's not possible. All that fawning niceness turns my stomach."

"Does that mean you prefer evil?" I asked in a small voice.

"What?! Oh!" He sighed and closed his eyes. "What the fuck am I talking about? It's so complicated. Today, I remembered. My beloved and one of my best friends are dead. One murder I had to watch helplessly, the other was by my own hand. Do you know what I did? We argued, I hit him, he went away. Does a sane har cool down after an argument and go after the other person and apologize, seeking comfort, take aruna with them and then murder them in cold blood? Does a sane person do that? God knows! I don't. They are good people, they are knowledge-seekers and I'm just a dangerous crazy!"

"What did you argue about?" I asked.

He was looking around the room. He was remembering.

"Cal?"

"I think," he said slowly, "I think that Orien watched Pell drift into some kind of trap because he thought that as Thiede was Nahir-Nuri, everything he did must be right. If Pell was to die, then that was right as well. I think Orien could have warned us, a long time before Pell was in danger."

For that, Cal had sentenced him to death.

It was starting to get dark. We stretched out on the bed and were silent for a while. There was one more question to be asked. I waited until the room was at peace.

"Tell me about my father, Cal."

He did not open his eyes. "I can't, Swift." The tone of his voice chilled me.

"Why not?"

He shook his head. "I just can't. Decisions have been made. My decision is to stay here . . ."

"A lot of hara hate him, don't they, even here, like Swithe." I hoped to prompt him, but he would not respond.

"The Varrs are hated everywhere. Let me tell you about Varrs."

"Is there a difference?"

"In this case, yes."

I already knew it was us versus them; the timeless formula. Cal told me that the Gelaming are the peacemakers, who want only to restore harmony to the world (did the world ever have it, I wonder), while my own tribe, the Varrs, just want to own it. Varrs kill everything, and what makes it worse is that they enjoy doing it. Apparently, it wouldn't be such a bad thing if they killed with distaste. Cal hadn't been there, but he'd heard that northernmost Megalithica (the stronghold of Ponclast) had been reduced to a scorched wasteland, punctuated only by ruined cities and stark fortresses. Obviously, the Gelaming were concerned that once the Varrs had exhausted Megalithica, they would turn their attention upon the east, the countries across the ocean, Almagabra in particular. More than assuaging the oppressed minorities of our country, I suspected that the Gelaming were, in fact, worried by eventual invasion of their own territories. It explained a lot.

Cal was scatching about my tutor. "Swithe is an intellectual. He takes your father's money while privately deploring his obsessions. I despise him."

"Yet you talk to him, often."

"Yes," he admitted, "but it doesn't stop me thinking he should leave here and go to the Gelaming. He's living a lie if he doesn't."

"What about you, Cal?" I asked. "What are your beliefs?"

"I don't care," he answered. "I just hope I'm with the winning side when it's all over!"

I lay down again on the bed, in the creeping twilight, and let the silence form around us and thought, Out there . . . ? No more than that. Why couldn't I understand? Why couldn't it become real in my mind? I had no fear, yet I knew that the Gelaming were here already, only to the south of us, and they had come to take our lands away from us. So near, and they had magic. . . . The name of peace. Would it be soon? No, I couldn't imagine it. Tomorrow would dawn fragrant with the smells of yesterday, until tomorrow becomes yesterday and so on. Nothing changes in Forever, nothing. Something had happened to me. It seemed that Cobweb's storm magic had opened up my mind as much as Cal's, but in a different way. I stared into the darkness, I felt powerful, my body brimmed with a nameless joy that was sharpened by sadness. That night I had the first dream.

Before dinner, I went to see Cobweb. I left Cal asleep on the bed and walked slowly to my hostling's room. My mind was still buzzing. It was as if I was afraid of something I'd forgotten about, that could come back to me at any moment. Cobweb opened the door to me; we looked at each other. He reached out and touched me lightly on the face, the arm, the chest. I knew what he was thinking.

"I thought I'd lost you," he said. I shook my head and went past him into the room. He observed me carefully, alert for changes.

"Swift, don't be taken in." So, he was prepared to be magnanimous, perhaps recriminations would come later.

"Then tell me the truth!"

"About what?"

"I don't know!" He watched me sit down miserably on the end of his bed. Did he know about my father, the secrets? He must do. What were they?

"You shouldn't have seen that this afternoon," he said, incapable of controlling the cold that crept into his voice.

"I had to."

"Cal is stronger than I thought," he conceded reluctantly.

"Perhaps he is just different to how you thought."

"I'm not beaten yet," my hostling said.

The first dream:

I am drowning. There is water in my mouth, but I am calm. There is no pain. Through the water, I can see something shining, far away. Two lights. That is all. I woke up laughing.

CHAPTER FIVE

> ━◆━━◆━

Shrinking out of touch

Belief in magic,
Of a power over zenith
Asphyxiation of the lesser legerdamain.

Two days later, Terzian returned from the north, with a face and a mood like thunder. His only welcome to me, as I lurked conspicuously in the hall, was a kind of surly growl. He stalked into the house, trailing bewildered hara in dusty uniforms, and bellowed for Cobweb, going directly to his room and slamming the door. Some moments after, my hostling ran through the hall and up the stairs, two at a time. We saw neither of them until the next morning.

It was from Ithiel that Gahrazel and I learned the reason for my father's ill humor. The talks with Ponclast had not gone well. Apparently, Ponclast had attacked the other Varrish leaders for their lack of foresight. He had ridiculed them for abandoning the powers inherent in our race. For some time, he had been grooming his own occult abilities and now was the time to fight fire with fire. The fire of the Gelaming was magic, the power of the mind, will pitted against will. Then he began to speak of a tribe that dwelled in the southern desert, the Kakkahaar. The tales of their art and cunning were widespread, and it was professed they had no love of Gelaming. Ponclast spoke carefully, each word chosen to instil fear into the hearts of his generals. As the Varrs stood now, the Gelaming would defeat them effortlessly, for the Varr's powers had been neglected, but with the Kakkahaar as Varrish allies, the invader would not find such an easy defeat. "I propose," Ponclast boomed, "that without delay, representatives are sent south to contact the Kakkahaar, with a view to combining our strength!" He delivered this final statement with gusto and sat down.

For some moments, the other Varrs had not moved to speak, only whispering among themselves. It had been Terzian who had eventually stood up and I could imagine vividly all eyes turning toward him. It was no secret how highly Ponclast valued Terzian and most hara would have expected Terzian's opinion to sway the vote. It must have been a hushed moment as he arranged his notes to speak. How would the Varrs' brightest star react to Ponclast's suggestion? From the moment he opened his mouth, Terzian lost no time in vehemently protesting against Ponclast's idea. Eloquent as ever, he said that he understood that different methods of warfare would have to be employed against the Gelaming, even to the extent of reassessing the worth of the effect of magic (the sarcasm would not have been missed there!), but he could only stress that in his opinion any alliance with such as the Kakkahaar would simply prove disastrous. The Kakkahaar had always been regarded with the highest suspicion by my father and his supporters. He reminded Ponclast that this was not the first time that an alliance with them had been suggested. As before, he could only urge that this proposition be abandoned. The Kakkahaar could not be trusted and it was not inconceivable that they might already have some arrangement with Thiede. "Both tribes are sorcerous," Terzian said. "How simple it would be for us to trust the Kakkahaar, have them privy to our plans, only to find ourselves in the midst of battle with our powers deserting us, with the Gelaming embracing the Kakkahaar triumphantly! I cannot support such a foolish intention!"

Ponclast must have been expecting Terzian's opposition. He had let the clamor die down before rising from his seat. My father had sat down again, staring at the table. Ponclast began by arguing reasonably that the Kakkahaar would never be allies of the Gelaming for the simple reason that Kakkahaar stood for everything that the Gelaming deplored. True, they were both masters of the occult, but their approach to it was entirely different. The Kakkahaar were not a large tribe. Ponclast thought that they would welcome an alliance with the Varrs. "Standing alone, both tribes are too weak to resist Thiede's advances, but together we can combine the physical might of the Varrs with the occult strength of the Kakkahaar. To an intelligent person it is obvious; this is our only chance!"

Ponclast had sat down again amid a burst of cheering. He had given the Varrs hope. Terzian could offer nothing better. No doubt my father's face had been black with fury. He would probably have stormed out of the hall. It was not often that his peers questioned his judgment. Ponclast had insulted his intelligence. Ponclast had won. Emissaries from the Varrs would ride south to contact the Kakkahaar. This in itself would be a hazardous venture. No-one was exactly sure how widespread the Gelaming were in the south. Many of the Varrish agents who had been sent to investigate had not yet returned. It was likely that the Gelaming had intercepted them.

Ithiel said that after the meeting, Ponclast had spent many hours arguing with Terzian alone. He must have been very persuasive. When the time came for my father to ride back to Galhea he had reluctantly conceded his support to Ponclast's action. Their farewells had been frosty, however.

"The Kakkahaar are dark creatures," Ithiel said ominously. "I, for one, would never trust them. They care for no-one's welfare but their own."

"A concept alien to the Varrs, no doubt," Gahrazel said acidly.

"For all we know, they might already be strong enough to protect themselves from attack," Ithiel continued, oblivious of Gahrazel's remark. "Why should they want to assist us?"

It was shortly after this that Terzian informed Gahrazel that the time had come for Gahrazel's instruction in caste progression. Perhaps this was another thing that he and Ponclast had discussed. Among other tribes, notably those farther south, this would involve rigorous and protracted spiritual training, but for a Varr it meant becoming acquainted with the regalia of warfare, the gun, the blade and the stomach required to perform the act of killing. I knew Gahrazel was far from happy about this and I sympathized deeply. To progress to the next level of his caste, he would not only have to learn how to fight, but how to survive in the wild, and, perhaps worst of all, how to endure pain. Further progressions would involve concentration of these activities and to reach a higher caste, that of Ulani, Gahrazel would have to kill. Now, for three days a week, Gahrazel was taken to the training yards of the warriors in Galhea and I continued my lessons alone. Swithe made one or two tight-lipped comments disparaging to the Varrs, while Moswell intoned that soon Gahrazel would be truly adult and that being able to take a turn at aruna was nothing to do with it.

Missing Gahrazel's company on those days when he was away, I took to spending more time with Bryony in the kitchen. I feared Terzian's disapproval of this, but he had much more pressing matters on his mind at that time. The humans had been warmly accepted by the other household staff, mainly, I suppose, because of their youth, together with the fact that they were willing workers. They were survivors, and somewhat manipulative in their charms, I think. It continually surprised me how alike our two races were (sometimes I forgot that Bryony wasn't har); our thought processes seemed entirely similar. Before, I had been taught to think very differently. As far as I could see, the main contrast between us was entirely biological, the division of male and female in the human. Bryony explained to me that it was more than that. "Wraeththu don't grow old like we do," she said and then explained it in more detail. I found this hard to believe. Looking at her tanned, healthy face, I found it impossible to imagine her shrivelling up until she died. "You are much stronger than we are," she said. "Not just physically, but in your resistance to disease and the control you have over your emotions. Less fear, more confidence. Mankind was always plagued by self-doubt."

Peter never joined in our conversations. He was a loner and shunned contact with everyone but Bryony. He was sixteen years old and feared that my father would force him to become har. I couldn't understand his terror, knowing as I did about the shrivelling-up process. "Once, every man who was unhar and under the age of eighteen was incepted by Wraeththu if he was caught," Bryony told me. "Now, they don't seem to bother about it as much. Since hara like you have been born, I suppose. They don't need to steal human children any more."

Her attitude puzzled me. Humans who became har were the fortunate ones, that was clear. Why should her brother be a slave when he could be made har, ageless and beautiful? Bryony could not answer me when I pointed this out. After a while she said, "I'm not saying I agree with Peter, but it's his life, isn't it? Perhaps it's fear of the unknown. . . . Our time is over, we know that. Wraeththu is the only future. If I had the choice, I know what I'd do, but of course, I don't."

One thing I learned from Bryony without her telling me, is that there are really three races upon the Earth, Wraeththu, Man and Woman. I think that out of the three, men are the odd ones out. Manliness is the side within ourselves that causes us most trouble. It is the fire principle, while feminity is the water principle. Water is magic, mystery and passivity. Fire is war, aggression and activity. Marriage of the two principles should produce a perfect, rational being: Wraeththu. Perfect theories are rarely perfect when put into practice, I thought cynically.

High summer unfolded around us. Terzian went away again to visit other Varr settlements in the east, and I arranged for Bryony to become friends with Cobweb, as I thought it would be good for both of them. My hostling had never harbored any particularly strong feeling against humans; he accepted all living creatures as individuals and I felt the girl was similar to him in many ways. He enjoyed sharing his wisdom with her, for she was eager to learn, and also found in her an ally in the house when everyone else had got fed up with being hostile to Cal. Bryony was frightened of Cal. Now, our soirées in the drawing room had expanded to include both of them, which created amusing atmospheres. Cobweb would pretend that Cal wasn't there, which was an art form in itself. Once I overheard Cal say to him, "I should thank you. You have made me well." Cobweb didn't even blink, only turning to speak to Moswell with a smile. Cal caught my eye and smiled ruefully. I disliked the way Cal looked at my hostling. I disliked even more the way Cal would not hate him, because I didn't understand it, and I thought I should have done.

One day, Gahrazel asked me to walk with him in the garden, something we had not done together for some time. He seemed preoccupied or troubled, but I was not as close to him as I had been so he could not speak as freely as once he might. "Peter is going to be incepted," he said. I looked at him aghast.

"What has changed his mind?" I asked. We were both aware of Peter's previous sentiments about becoming har.

"I have talked to him," Gahrazel replied rather frostily.

"I did not notice."

"You don't know everything about me, Swift!" he said.

After this, I tried to observe more carefully the transactions between my friend and Bryony's brother. Why hadn't I noticed before? Both of them nurtured very strong anti-Varr feelings, for different reasons, but it gave them a common ground. Gahrazel didn't care what happened to mankind; he cared only what happened to Gahrazel-kind. Peter was naturally bitter and restless, but since coming to Forever, perhaps he had come to understand more about what Wraeththu was. Perhaps he realized it was really absurd not to become har. However, I thought that Gahrazel's and Peter's encouragement of each other's hatreds was dangerous. They lived in Terzian's house, after all.

When I talked to Bryony about it, she told me that her brother had gradually withdrawn from her. "He is on fire and it is a strange fire that he cannot share with me," she said. "He is like the picture Cobweb showed me on one of his divining cards. Spears falling to earth and their descent is accelerating. He seeks a goal, but I fear for him."

"I didn't notice him becoming friendly with Gahrazel," I said.

"No," she agreed. "The secrecy of that is disquieting."

"You're worried about him," I said.

She smiled a small, sad smile. "As I said before, he has his own life to lead. He is flying away from me. I can do nothing."

So many of the inhabitants of Forever seemed disloyal to Terzian. There was Swithe with his wordy, arm-waving speeches, Gahrazel and Peter, hot in their fervor, and Cal, who didn't care about anything; we were not a large household either. One day, I felt sure, Terzian would stand still for long enough to notice, and then there'd be trouble.

When Terzian came home again, he consented without interest to Peter's inception. Swithe, who had taken charge of the proceedings, asked Cal to donate his blood. Cal laughed when he told me about it, but, I noticed wryly, he had still said yes. It was not the choice I would have made in Swithe's position. Cal was a wonder to me, but because so much of him was beneath the surface to be seen by no-one, I would have been very wary of putting his vital fluids into anyone. I am sure Peter had a worse time than was usual because of it. He fasted for a day before Swithe conducted the inception ceremony in the garden, beneath the canopy of the trees. I thought Cal looked like a white, shimmering spirit. His veins were blue and luminous, the life within them dark and poisonous. We could hear Peter's screams throughout the house for days afterwards.

It took a fortnight for him to recover fully, instead of the usual three days, but at the end of that time, his mutation was successful. Now he had a dash of Cal's weirdness to complement his revolutionary zeal. Gahrazel initiated him into the mysteries of aruna and the first time I saw them afterwards, Peter's eyes were full of prophecies that made me shiver. I saw Fate there, with a sharp knife held against the thread of life. Never again, that I know of, did Peter go to visit his sister in the kitchens.

At the end of the summer, we learned that the Kakkahaar, after some initial reticence, had agreed to combine their strength with the Varrs. High-ranking Kakkahaar would be traveling north for talks with Ponclast and his Nahir-Nuri. Because of its convenient position, Galhea had been chosen as the location for the meeting. Forever was an ideal conference center. Suddenly, the house was full of strange and important hara, and extra staff had to be engaged from Galhea to cope with it. Terzian surprised everybody by promoting Bryony to the position of housekeeper, which she said was to appease his guilt, while I thought it was more because Terzian realized the girl was capable of organizing the household to show him off in the best possible light. All the visitors thought it was a great novelty, as if we had a talking dog, walking on its hind legs, carrying the keys to the house and telling the staff what to do. I know that many of the northerners gave her tips in the form of money or trinkets, which was especially unusual, for the northerners had even less tolerance of humankind than most. Bryony affected an air of competent superiority, and what jealousy she might have aroused among the household staff was dealt with discreetly.

The Kakkahaar rode Arabian steeds. Cobweb and I watched their arrival from my bedroom window. I was intrigued by their strange, swirling clothes and their dark, interesting faces. "Their hair is so long!" Cobweb exclaimed, touching his own with a nervous hand.

Meals were always laid out in the main hall now, although Cobweb and I often ate in the kitchen with the staff. We did not like formality and were also wary of the Kakkahaar. I had been eager to meet them at first, but when their leader, Lianvis, turned his stone desert eyes upon me, I was chilled to the bone. I could see why Terzian was opposed to the alliance. I did not know the name for the darkness that came from their eyes, but I felt it touch me, and the touch was cold.

The Kakkahaar claimed to have had no contact with the Gelaming yet. They had monitored the invaders setting up their headquarters, but had made no overtures toward them, either conciliatory or hostile. No-one seemed quite sure what the Gelaming were actually doing, but their arrival had certainly caused a stir, and in more than one way. Reports were coming through that other, weaker tribes and even straggling bands of humans had been slowly, but consistently, making their way to the Gelaming base. Many people, human and hara alike, had very good reason to hate the Varrs in Megalithica, and it was only natural that they should seek the protection of the Gelaming. However, the Varr leaders were not oblivious to the fact that a lot of stragglers eventually become one large unit, all feeling righteous, and vengeful toward the Varrs. Security was increased across Varrish territories and anyone found making their way south was killed without question.

Bryony told me that her own people had been on their way to seek sanctuary with the Gelaming when Ithiel's patrol had intercepted them. Only a few months later and they would have been shot on sight.

Ithiel told me that he didn't think anything would happen until the new year. Preparing a campaign takes time. Our house was never free of strangers nowadays. Sometimes I would come across a strange har wandering round the corridors, lost. If it was a Kakkahaar, I would turn the other way and run.

I don't think anyone was too pleased to learn that we would have Kakkahaar with us for Festival. Most of them had returned south once the weather became colder (including their horrifying leader), but two of them had been elected to stay behind. I felt quite sorry for them because they found the cold so disagreeable, but I could never feel at ease with them. I always got the feeling they could eat you whole, if they had a mind to. Still, nothing could really dampen the mounting feeling of celebration. Snow fell and the garden was transformed into its winter fairyland of frozen marble. The house was fragrant with the smells of spice and cooking; the shelves in the larder were filled with Yarrow's creations.

One day, out of an upstairs window, I saw Leef in the stableyard, laughing with other hara, their breath like smoke on the air. I put on my coat and went down to speak with him. It pleased me that he did not recognize me at first. This meant I must have changed since we had last met. "You are taller," he said. I asked if he would have to go south in the spring and he replied, "I expect so. Nobody seems to know what exactly is going on at the moment."

"I hope you come back," I said, realizing immediately the tactless tone of this remark. Leef smiled, and I liked the way his face changed when he did so.

"I shall be here at the house at Festival," he said. "I've been promoted, so that means an automatic invitation to your father's celebrations."

"Congratulations," I said, "I shall look forward to seeing you."

Leef had a faintly puzzled, amused look in his eye.

"Me too," he said.

Events took a rather dramatic course before then, however. It was a week before Festival; each night the air was crisp with the anticipation of celebra-

tions to come, and all the curtains and corridors seemed alive with the
ghosts of songs brought back from other winters, other happiness. My
father had invited a few friends up to the house, a social evening, to sample
the festive sheh and for hara from the town to meet the Kakkahaar.
Everyone was in high spirits; noisy hara tramping through the front door,
trailing waiflike consorts, dressed in furs. Cobweb crimped my hair and
gave me new clothes to wear. "Quite the dashing young har!" he said and
stroked his throat with perfume. He seemed nervous that night, and his
smiles were forced.

Downstairs, among the lights and the perfumes, we were all intoxicated
by a wild kind of happiness, because deep inside we knew that everything
could change in our lives in the near future and our merriment was tinged
by a desperate flutter of hysteria. I had not expected Leef to be there, for
most of the guests were long-standing friends of Terzian's, but when I saw
him standing rather awkwardly in our grand drawing room, I knew that his
presence was right and sort of preordained, suiting my teetering euphoric
mood. I think I was trying to convince myself to be like Gahrazel was over
Ithiel and perhaps Leef guessed something of what was on my mind, but
he was not stupid enough to try and find out.

I asked him to come out with me into the hall to sit on the stairs, and
he looked quickly at my father before following me through the door. I
said, "He will not mind, you know."

"Who? What?" Leef asked and I replied, "Terzian; that you're with me.
Don't worry about it. He's not that fierce, or that bothered about what I
do for that matter."

"If you believe that, which I doubt, you are wrong," Leef remarked, but
he let himself relax a little.

We sat down on the stairs, but we were not alone. Hara seemed to be
everywhere that night. Leef said, "The atmosphere is strange. I don't feel
comfortable."

I thought about this. "Perhaps you are right. I've felt strange all day but
I thought it was just me."

We looked at each other and Leef said, "Well!"

I realized I must have changed quite a lot since the first time I had met
him. Now he seemed to be nervous with me. Most of his reserve, I felt,
could be blamed on who my father was.

"In the spring—" I began

"Yes, in the spring!" Leef interrupted, rather sharply. "Not one of us is
free from fear. Thiede has almost won before we even face the Gelaming.
He has been cultivating his reputation for years for just this moment."

"What, us two sitting here?"

Leef did not smile. "Everything," he replied. He looked at my hands
resting self-consciously on my knees for several minutes before he dared to
take one of them in his own. "Pampered hands," he said. "Aren't you
afraid that Thiede will come and make you work for a living?"

"No," I answered. "Does everyone think like you?"

Leef shook his head. "I don't know. I shouldn't be talking to you like this."

"Because of my father, I suppose! Do you really think I ever talk to him properly?"

"Don't you?"

"No, not about real things. We may discuss the condition of the meat at table, or the weather, or horses, but not much else. I think I am just a possession to him; like this house, like my hostling. Can houses or whores have opinions?"

"Swift!" Leef exclaimed, hurriedly scanning the hall to see if anyone had heard me.

"Can you deny that it is true?" I asked.

"Stop this conversation, stop it!" he said in a low but vehement voice. "We must be happy!"

"Alright," I agreed. It must be Cal infecting me, I thought. Perhaps I was becoming more like him, talking as he did. Was it me that had started this conversation? "I want to find out what my father thinks of you," I said and Leef looked at the floor and smiled. He knew what I meant by that.

Someone called my name and then Gahrazel was breathless on the stairs beside me. "Swift!" he said excitedly. "Come back into the drawing room. Now!"

"Why?"

"I think it will happen tonight," he answered mysteriously.

This was a kind of code between us. Ever since Cal's memory had been restored to him, both Gahrazel and I had been anticipating the day when Cal would give himself a shake and lower the defenses he had constructed against my father. It had always seemed inevitable. We could tell that Cal was naturally a sensual creature, and, although I thought that he had grand, if futile, designs on Cobweb, Cal would one day respond to my father's advances. I could not understand what was holding him back now. Terzian had never given up, and sometimes, his subtle, essentially Terzian method of wooing became rather too blatant; through sheer desperation, I think. Everyone knew, yet my father had not become angry. Another puzzle. Being made to look foolish was not a state that Terzian normally accepted gladly.

Leef followed me reluctantly back into the drawing room, with Gahrazel leading the way. I was suddenly angry at Gahrazel's eager curiosity, that all this was so entertaining to him. What was happening was a stately dance that had fallen into disorganization; it was not a joke.

My father was standing by the fire, leaning on the mantelpiece, caressing an empty glass, talking to the Kakkahaar. Cal was listening to Swithe on the other side of the room. Disappointed, I turned to Gahrazel. "I thought you said that—"

"Hush," Gahrazel interrupted, smiling, both hands on my arm. "Just watch them; absorb the atmosphere. You'll see." Still laughing, he sauntered away, no doubt to find a good viewpoint in the room.

"What are you up to?" Leef asked, once more nervously scanning faces.

"Oh, the Big Thing is about to happen," I explained. Leef shook his head.

"Is it? Will it hurt?"

"Who knows!"

I looked at my father. He is lithe, I thought, and tonight he looks so young. His heavy, golden hair was falling into his eyes. He raised his hand to push it back and glanced quickly across the room. I felt that look pass straight through my body like an arrow. I did not have to turn my eyes to Cal. I felt it. My father was like a stranger, no longer familiar to me. My head began to swim and I realized I'd knocked back two glasses of sheh without noticing. Is this what it's like? I wondered. This power, this hidden fire? Is it waiting for me some day? I looked slyly at Leef. Will it really be you . . . ?

"I've drunk too much," I said and Leef glanced at me sharply. He was so uncomfortable; I felt sorry for him.

"Swift . . ." he said and I could not see all of his face, only his mouth talking or his gray eyes, but not together.

"What?"

"I want to . . ." He put his fingers lightly on my mouth and shook his head. "Terzian's son!" he said and smiled.

Now it was me that felt uncomfortable. "I want to watch my father," I said. Leef followed me over to the sofa and we sat on the floor.

"Do you often watch your father?" he asked, wondering what kind of joke I was playing on him.

"Never!" I replied. "Leef, have you ever *wanted* Cobweb?"

"Stop it!" Leef hissed in a low voice.

"Another thing that is Terzian's. . . . He is smoke and ivy."

"And you are three-quarters sheh at the moment!"

"This is how we live; we are all quite mad. Don't be annoyed with me."

Leef shook his head and drew his mouth into a thin line.

I could see Cobweb talking to Ithiel, and his face was white and wild, his hair unbound, which always signified that he wanted to feel his own power around him. Ithiel looked as if he knew that he might have physically to restrain Cobweb before too long. Has anyone else noticed? I wondered. Desire in the air, so strong, it smelled like burning. I could feel it in my lungs, my head, behind my eyes. How can they stand it? I thought. Their need for each other is another being in the room, almost visible.

Eventually Terzian could stand it no longer. I saw him put the empty glass down slowly on the mantelpiece, rub his face, glance once more at Cal. He excused himself politely to the Kakkahaar, and began to make his way across the room, stopping to exchange brief conversation with other hara, smiling, gracious, signalling the staff to bring more drinks. As he passed me, he looked down and grinned and I grinned back; but we were strangers. I had no part in this event.

Cal was standing quite near to where Leef and I were sitting. I heard my father say to him, without deferment, "I have been waiting for you," and Cal's reply, "Yes, I know."

There was a pause, then Terzian said, "I know what happened while I was away."

"Of course you do, Terzian. You know everything," Cal replied, rather coldly. "What surprises me is that you haven't mentioned it before."

"Hmm."

They were so awkward with each other I began to think Gahrazel had been wrong. Leef said, "What's the matter?" but I waved him to silence. My father said, "You're still afraid, aren't you?"

I could imagine Cal shrugging but I dared not look around. "Afraid? Not exactly. Alarmed, perhaps. I expect your terms haven't changed."

"Terms?" Terzian's voice was raised, then he remembered he was in a room full of people, some of whom had turned their heads. "I am not so callous," he said quietly.

"You are! You know you are."

"*You* know how much I wanted you before. It wasn't just to sire harlings with you, perfect though they'd be . . ."

"But it's part of it, Terzian. Why can't you admit that?"

"Admit it?" My father's voice was almost sad. "You're a fine one to talk about admissions. Maybe you should admit to yourself that you're made to host sons, to sire them. You are Wraeththu. Admit that, Cal!"

Can no-one hear them? I wondered. Leef was staring at the carpet while my blood was in flames. Cobweb was a thin ghost, distant and in chains.

My father said, "I would never hurt you, Cal."

"I know that."

"It's in your blood; you need me. It's been too long."

"I know that. . . . There is one thing you must do." I heard the steel come into his voice, but I knew, if I looked, his face would be innocent.

Sensing triumph, my father said, "Yes, anything, anything."

There was a brief silence and I knew that Cal was looking around the room, making sure the right people were watching.

"If you want me, you must prove it. Nothing sordid. I think I deserve the status and demand recognition of my position."

"Cal, what are you talking about?"

"Don't laugh, Terzian. I know what your people think. Cobweb is like your queen. He's respected. I don't want anything less."

Perhaps it was only me that knew Cal cared nothing about things like that. This was just another move in the game and, of course, Terzian would fall for it, because it was the language he understood. Cal said, "Terzian, I want you to take me in your arms."

"Here?"

"Now! Share breath with me, here. Let them all see. I must be equal to Cobweb, nothing less."

"Is *that* all?"

All! I thought. Their embrace will take the form of a blade, more than one; ten. Who will lie face down on the bloody soil, pierced by swords, now? Terzian's consort, to be shamed before the elite of Galhea, that's who.

I sensed the silence fall around me and realized I had closed my eyes. I heard Leef mutter, "Good God, look at that!" His surprise was tempered by amusement.

The first thing I saw was Ithiel, trying to hold a feral Cobweb in his arms. Cobweb, with eyes like black saucers full of obsidian fire. He made no sound, struggling silently. I could not turn to look. I stood up, Leef tried to pull me back, he made some palliative sound, but I did not listen. I went straight to the door, across the carpet, past the faces who did not see me, a hundred miles away.

In my room, alone, sitting in darkness, I licked tears from my face, listening to the noises downstairs. There was still laughter, the buzz of voices, perhaps more so than before. The tension had disappeared. I voided my mind, letting it become a great and silent blackness, and into that emptiness I formed my hostling's name. Before too long, I heard the door open behind me and light from the corridor shone into the room.

"I had to walk past your father's door," Cobweb said.

"Already?" I asked and my hostling nodded silently. I must have been sitting alone for longer than I thought.

"You did this!" I pointed out cruelly.

Cobweb shut the door. He leaned upon the door and slid down it. I wanted to go to him, but I had no energy. I couldn't tell how I felt about anything any more. Cobweb was crouched against the wall, his hair touching the floor, beaten in so many ways.

"What is happening?" I asked the room.

"If it should happen tonight, then we shall feel it. We shall feel the soul when it comes . . ." Cobweb's voice was a whisper in my head.

I uncurled my feet from under me, touched the window with one hand. It was cold, much colder than the room.

Cobweb didn't resist when I went to help him up. He felt light, as if all his substance had drained away. I could smell moss in his hair. I led him over to my bed and he lay down on it. Standing there, I looked at the spidery, dark locks creeping over my pillows, his face that is a wood-creature's face, and I thought, So many times Terzian has stood as I am standing now and seen that lying there. Then I thought, My father is so greedy! and then, No, he is just very fortunate!

"Has the spring come already, Swift?" Cobweb asked. "Is it all over?"

"Not for you," I answered.

Cobweb laughed, an ugly, bitter sound. "It is the real magic that comes from within," he said. "We are all under its spell. It destroys us, yet we need it. . . . We should have destroyed it first. We are all tangled up, here in Galhea. We're not reaching out."

I understood some of what he was trying to say.

"It is said we are getting caught in the same traps that men once set for themselves," I said, and Cobweb sighed.

"We are all spiders; without the webs we cannot feed."

"You tried to kill him, didn't you?"

Cobweb turned his head slowly on the pillow, dark and lovely as a velvet poisonous flower. "I think my child attempts excuses for what has happened. Cal does not want Terzian. He seeks only to attack me. I need your support, Swift. Where is it?"

I fell to my knees beside the bed and took his long, cool hands in my own. "Cobweb, it is not a question of support! You tried to kill him! You're intelligent enough to realize that this is only the most predictable of reactions. You caused it yourself. You should have let well alone."

Cobweb threw his arms over his eyes. "I hate him! He makes me let darkness into my soul! I want him dead!" He sat up, wild-eyed, reaching with clawed hands for my shoulders. "Can't you see what he does to me? Worse than leaving me lonely, he extinguishes the light in me. It is a battle that sometimes I am too tired to fight and I let it come, and I let it take me over and then I hate him and wish him dead and find my hands around the things that could make him dead. He damns me!"

"No, it is you!" I cried. "You damn yourself! It is in your head!"

Cobweb pushed me away as if I repulsed him. "I'm going to Swithe," he said.

"No!" I would not let him stand. "Stay with me!"

"Why? Why should I? When I look at you, I see your father in your eyes; the same madness. You're as obsessed with that dark beast as your father is!"

I could say nothing. Immediately, "he is right" formed in my head. I lowered my eyes and a pane of ice was between us.

"I knew it!" Cobweb growled, very quietly.

And then emotion was bursting up, like a spire of blood, through my heart. I threw myself against him, curling my arms around him, very tight.

"I love you!" I cried. His body was cold and unyielding. "I do! I do! I swear it! I will never betray you!"

I felt his hands on my back, flexing from paws to hands to paws. I felt his leafy sigh through my hair.

"Mine," my hostling whispered. "Mine . . . Mine!"

Another dream:

A voice says to me, "It is nothing. Outside is the real Hell. This is nothing."

I must have been crying. My head is on my knees. When I look up, there are two eyes in front of me. I cannot see the face, I say, "Oh, I will never go outside!" and even in the dream, I know that this isn't true. I put up my hands. I shout, "I don't know you! I don't know you!" but I want to look into those eyes forever.

That is the way of dreams; they are never logical.

CHAPTER SIX

>—⁑⟩—○—⟨⁂—≺

Straw in the Wind

Straw in the wind
Blowing in my dreams.
A birth in the Spring
Sinking into pillows.

So for some of us, Festival was to be devoid of merriment that year. Admittedly, the house was full of hara blissfully ignorant of the dreadful stirrings in Forever's heart, and food and drink were in plentiful supply, everyone was smiling, but there was still Cobweb's gaunt and haunted silence to face every day. Terzian chose to ignore it. For various reasons, mostly, I like to think, because of loyalty to my hostling, I decided to stop speaking to Cal. Predictably, this only made him laugh. "Close ranks, Swift," he said. "The wicked seducer is loosed among you!" He knew, as we all did, that it had been Cobweb who had freed him from his fear of aruna.

At dinner, in the evening, I found that I was sitting next to Leef. He made several brave attempts at conversation and then commented drily on my sullen silence. I didn't want him to think I no longer liked him, but I was powerless to speak. I wanted to look at him helplessly, so that he might ask me what the matter was, but I could only stare at my plate. I couldn't understand myself, why I was locked in such a strange depression, and I wished desperately someone would notice it and say the right words that would release me, but Leef only sighed and turned to speak to someone sitting on his other side.

The new year had started with everyone in a sour temper, and that was a bad omen. The atmosphere did not improve when my father announced that he expected Gahrazel to accompany him to the south when the spring weather allowed it. I knew how Gahrazel felt about the approaching campaign. It wasn't that he was torn between loyalty to his tribe and loyalty to his beliefs; he just craved peace, an easy life, more than anything. He was angered by cruelty and killing appalled him. He knew Terzian was seeking to change all that about him. My father also sent Peter to work for Ithiel and we all knew that Ithiel and his staff would be remaining in Galhea when the Varrs set off to confront the Gelaming.

I had come to hate movement and rarely left the house. My sleep was often disturbed at that time by troubling dreams, whose main feature seemed to be the enigmatic eyes I had seen before. In a short time, I would celebrate my birthday. In a short time, I could expect to come of age. It was a prospect I anticipated with dread. Since Festival, I spent more and more time alone. My love was knowledge, not flesh. Swithe gave me books to read, and I virtually devoured their pages with my eyes, so eager was I to scour them for information, for answers. I learned a great deal about the world and about the past, but little about my own condition. Wraeththu had not been in existence long enough for anyone to have had the time to write serious books about our singular, wondrous estate. When I grew older, perhaps I could be one of the first to begin the analysis. That was when I started to keep notes, to write down my impressions of what was happening to us. The foundations of my life had become unsteady, the sacrosanct haven of my home soiled. Cobweb had become an icy and tragic figure, haunting the upper parts of the house or scrawling horrific, black pictures with splintered charcoal in his room. The faces he drew came into my dreams, the aftertaste of their anguish flavored my days. Even Gahrazel had become a bitter, fevered thing. The intrigues of Forever no longer seemed to interest him and he had learned how to kill. He gave Peter a Wraeththu name, Purah. They were together always, for their days together were numbered.

All I can say of Cal is that I could only look at him with painful anger. He would look back with smiling, knowing eyes. I heard him whistling in the corridor outside my room on those nights when he would go to my father. His presence burned me, and I tried to avoid him. It was clear he felt no remorse for the pain he had brought into the house, nor that he had lost me as a friend. I could not believe that he returned my father's feeling as strongly. It was all a game to him, to pass the time, to eliminate boredom. Time and again, I told myself to hate him.

As a fitting punishment for our ignorant behavior, Cobweb and I were the last to hear of the momentous news when it came. It happened only a few weeks after Festival and it was Bryony who told us. Cal was to host a son for Terzian; Phlaar had confirmed it. Just hearing about it made me see them together, in my father's bed, in that room. I was glad in a way, because I knew Cal would hate it. He was not made to be a hostling, no matter what my father thought.

Cobweb did not scream or rage as I expected. He took the news quite calmly, and I did not ask bewildered questions. We were quite, quite dignified, like something out of the history books. I remembered Cal once likening Cobweb to a queen and that was how I saw us now. The imprisoned queen and her son hearing news of the king's new wife; out of favor, out of mind. Cobweb and I drew closer together. I was wrapped in his ophidian hair, his inky eyes, and we caressed each other's black hearts with pungent fires and dark, whispered words. We nurtured our powers and found satisfaction in occult promises. "We too shall host a pearl," my hostling said, "the blackest pearl of regret!" It was a promise that was never realized.

* * *

When the first shoots found their way up into the light and the garden stirred and stretched into the spring, we watched them leave. Black, shining horses and the finest of Varrish hara. Terzian leaned down from his horse and embraced Cal for the last time, looking up to glance at Cobweb's expressionless face as he stood on the steps of Forever. My father called to me and offered his hand, which I took. "I shall bring you home a beautiful Gelaming slave," he said with a smile.

I grinned back weakly. "Good luck," I said.

Terzian raised his hand and they turned their horses toward the gate. Cal stood near to me but I did not look at him. Terzian turned in the saddle once and waved to us, before quickening the pace to a canter. It was an impressive sight. The main body of his army would be waiting for him in the town.

Afterwards, I paused on the steps of Forever and gazed up at its worn, white walls. It seems my story has ended already, I thought wistfully. All the happiness has gone from this house. Now it is forbidding and its secrets are cruel. Now, as long ago, a woman, a daughter of man, holds the keys to its rooms. Perhaps there was only Bryony left really to care about the place. To Cobweb, Forever had taken on the ghost semblance of a ruin of stark, poking rafters; a charred remnant of a home. His touch had palpably withdrawn from the rooms. Now he claimed only the darkest corners of the garden and his own suite on the second floor.

The previous evening, I had sat in Gahrazel's room and watched him pack away his belongings, as if he would never return to Forever. He is truly adult now, I thought. His enthusiasm is contained, his fire quenched. I watched him cut off his hair and burn it. There were few times we could reach each other now. After all, I was still just a child. Perhaps I bored this new, sophiscated Gahrazel. The Varrs, the state of being Varr, had come between us.

Not long after my father and his army had gone south, Cobweb and I celebrated my birthday together. Yarrow baked a big ginger cake, but no-one came to eat it with us. We sat in my room, drank sheh, and Cobweb cut my arm with a knife to take some of my blood. He made spells for my protection and put his hand on my face and said, "Some day soon, the animal sleeping inside you will wake up."

I remember I made an angry, bitter noise. "And what will happen then?" I demanded. "What will happen when my body takes over and there is no-one to take hold of it?"

Cobweb took me in his arms. "I would keep you as a child forever if I could," he said.

At night, lying awake, I would think of my father and of Gahrazel, wondering what they were doing and if they thought of home. Then I would drift off to sleep and the dream presence would visit me, the wondrous eyes, the hint of alien breath. In the morning I would wake afraid, but at night, in the dark, I felt comforted.

Sleeping late one morning, I was woken up by a female scream, coming from the Hall. Bryony's white face looked up at me when I leaned over the bannister, half dressed. "Swift, come quickly!" she cried.

Cal had collapsed, halfway through eating his breakfast. When I saw him, my heart missed a beat. Could he be dead? Could we be free once more? But he moved in our arms as we carried him up the stairs to his room. When we laid him on the bed, he moaned and threshed, curling and uncurling as if poisoned. Cobweb? I wondered. Someone had sent for Phlaar and I was left alone with Cal, while everyone raced around the house as if the end of the world had come. (Already he was Forever's heart.) He opened his eyes and saw me standing there. I stared back haughtily into his twisted face. We know each other now, I thought.

"Do you know what's happening to me?" he croaked.

"No," I answered, "but whatever it is you deserve it!" I was uncomfortable, thinking how not long ago, I would have been soothing him or stroking his face, craving his attention. It would have felt natural to go and do that now, but I controlled myself. "How things change," I remarked coolly, walking over to the window, so that he could not affect me. I could hear him groaning softly. When I could resist no longer and turned to look at him, he was clutching his stomach. His face was damp.

"Swift . . . don't hate me . . . please, not now." I began to speak, but he rolled around and shouted, "I need you! I need you! Swift!"

Even as I went to him, I was thinking, Surely you're strong enough to resist this?

His face was hot and wet between my hands; he was weeping. "You are witness to a miracle," he said, and laid his head in my lap. I put my hand on his arm where it lay across his stomach.

"What is it?" I asked.

"Life, I think," he said.

Cal was in torment for two days while his body sought to expel the pearl that would become Terzian's son. Phlaar did not seem unduly concerned about Cal's condition, and I shuddered to think that this agony was normal.

Only Cobweb had no interest in this momentous birth. Everyone else in the house was fascinated. Someone had to sit with Cal all the time as he struggled feverishly with his body. Phlaar would not risk leaving him alone, because sometimes he got violent and Phlaar was afraid he would try to damage himself. Bryony was particularly intrigued by Wraeththu birth, for the bearing of life had previously been a female prerogative to her. Near the time, when everyone was sitting up all night waiting for news, Bryony took me to the kitchens. We curled up in the darkness next to the stove, drinking strong, sweet coffee and talking of the mysteries of life. How intrigued she was (without actually saying so) about the secrets of Wraeththu physiology. I evaded her subtle questions for it was something I preferred not to think too deeply about. Not so Bryony. She explained with great candor a lot about woman kind and how their bodies worked. Then I learned about human procreation, so similar in some ways to our own, yet so different in others.

"The whole rotten business has been drastically improved in Wraeth-thu," she said. "I can see that, and it takes so little time. It's so unnoticeable. Women do not have it so easy. Oh no! We have to lumber around for months, growing and growing. It's something I've never cared for . . ."

Human reproduction did seem messy to me, and how inconvenient to have to look after such a helpless creature for so long. (No teeth, no hair!) Like little rats, I thought. I had seen Mareta's kittens take milk, but it seemed inconceivable that intelligent beings could be brought up the same way. What if they were separated from their mothers? How would they survive? Did many babies die?

During those strange gray hours before the dawn it was my turn to sit with Cal. "It will be soon," he said to himself and clenched his fists along his sides.

"Cobweb will hate me for this," I said, hoping to make him smile.

Cal barely recognized me and kept calling me Pell. "I've always lied to you!" he said. "You don't even know me, not really, but in spite of all that I've done . . . I do love you, Pell."

I sat beside him. He looked weak and helpless. His body was merciless; the personality was irrelevant at this time. His mind, set free, wandered at random. "Cal, you're a wicked, wicked person, but enchanting all the same!"

He did not hear me. "Pell, do you remember . . . that time . . . when was it? When I found you. Oh, there's something I've always longed to tell you . . . about the first lie, and it's so important . . . I must tell you!"

I put my hands on his face. "Hush, I'm not Pell. Be quiet." He tried to shake free of me.

"You must hear this, you must!" he whined pettishly. "It's important, because I mustn't lie to you any more. I want you to know everything . . . about Zack . . ."

"Zack? Who's Zack?"

"You know . . . have you forgotten? Years . . . years . . ." He lay back on the pillows, his eyes searching the ceiling frantically. "I told you he was dead, didn't I? I did say that, didn't I? Well, it's not exactly . . . true. I don't know. Not when I went back for him . . . he was alive then . . ."

"What are you talking about?" I asked to humor him. "Who's not dead? Pellaz?"

"*No!*" he said, as if angry with my stupidity. "*Zack,* before I met you. I ran away. I left him . . . I told you he was dead. It was a lie." He closed his eyes.

Thinking he'd be quiet for a while, I fetched a damp cloth and bathed his face. His eyes flickered, half open.

"There is no-one on this earth more lovely than you," he said, his hot hand seeking to curl itself around my wrist.

"Who, Pellaz . . . ?" I dabbed at his temples.

"No, no, Pell's dead. I mean you, now that he's gone . . . it's you, even though you hate me . . ." He sighed. His voice sank. "Unbind your hair, all over me. Fill me with your perfume, let me taste you . . ."

My hair grew only to my shoulders; I never braided it. Incensed, I threw the cloth back into the bowl of water and stood up, wrenching my wrist out of his hold.

"Why can't you see *me?*" I complained. "I'm Swift and I'm alive and I don't hate you, at least, not at the moment."

He looked confused. "Oh Swift," he said. "Yes . . . Swift. I was just thinking of a time, oh, it was a long while ago, before I met Pell. I was with someone else. We were in trouble and I left him for dead. I could have helped him, but then, maybe we both would have died. I had to save myself, don't you see? I told Pell I'd hurt my arm in a fall. Look . . ." He took my hand and ran my fingers over the long, white scar. "That was a lie as well. There was no fall, no. It was Zack's knife that did it. His curse and his knife thrown at me, while I saved my skin . . . ah well."

At dawn he was wholly lucid, the fever had gone, but his breath came quickly. "Fetch Phlaar!" he cried. "Quickly!" When I reached the door, I heard his voice behind me. "Don't come back in here, Swift."

They took the pearl from him and it was black and gleaming with the essence of his body. I saw them carry it down the hall like a holy relic. It was tested for life and washed. I wanted to look but they made it clear I was in the way, so I wandered back to Cal's bedroom to find him lying drained and relieved among the pillows.

"So, it's over," I said.

"Yes, it is." After a moment, he laughed quietly to himself.

I wanted to know how much it hurt him.

"Quite a lot, I suppose," he said, "But the memory of pain fades so quickly. It wasn't as bad as I thought . . ."

"You are pleased," I observed, conscious of a vague kind of prickly, edgy feeling within me.

"I'm pleased that it's over, certainly," he replied, but I knew it was more than that. His eyes were alight.

Not long afterwards, they brought the pearl back to him. It appeared to have nearly doubled in size already and its surface seemed to have toughened over. Now Cal would have to incubate it with the warmth of his body. He will hate this, I thought, he hates having to lie around. But he curled himself around it like a great, contented cat and closed his eyes. I once came from a *thing* like that, I thought. It was disorientating to think about it, so I chanted three words of terrible power to empty the mind and went down into the garden to think of other things.

We had had no news of my father. Rumors reached us, of course, but we guessed that most of them were untrue. From one source we heard that the Varrs had successfully exterminated the Gelaming with little effort, the

Kakkahaar allies wreaking havoc with their elemental force. From elsewhere, we heard that Terzian had been defeated and been taken prisoner, that Thiede now held him in Phaonica, subjecting him to torture, and that the Gelaming were marching on Galhea. It was said that they also possessed vehicles that ran without fuel and vomited demonic flames capable of incinerating whole cities. The Varrs had no fuel for vehicles. We knew that in the north, Ponclast had some kind of wide, black car that growled like a tiger, but his fuel conserves were precious and the car was only used on ceremonial occasions or to ferry Ponclast to executions of particular interest. Swithe told me that not all of the Earth's natural resources had been depleted, but that it would be a waste of time for us to try and go back to the old ways. "Now is the time for Wraeththu to seek a new way, a new source of power," he said excitedly. "Maybe the Gelaming have already found it. The less time spent fighting and squabbling over land, the more time we have for research, for rebuilding!"

I studied hard, using books from Terzian's library, marvelling at the sparkling metal cities that men had left behind them, touching the photographs. Had it all gone forever, this world of metal and glass? Gahrazel had once told me that the land was growing back over the cities of men, that vines had dragged down the buildings that once reached toward the sky. Often, he had said, only the creepers still stood, with stems as thick as oak trunks. Inside the cage of leaves, the buildings had crumbled away already.

"Things changed rapidly during the last forty or fifty years of man's rule," Moswell explained loftily. "Perhaps they advanced too quickly for their own good; their minds could not keep up with their technology. They lost control so that they craved extinction and sought depravity. In truth, men became demented by ennui, unnerved by so much leisure time, driven feral by lack of money. Their brains had been neglected for centuries, their spiritual lives were barren; they could no longer create through thought. Is it any wonder they turned on each other and their environment?"

I could not accept this explanation without question. It was too easy for Moswell to stand there and say all that, but I knew he had missed so much out. I wanted to know how Wraeththu had begun and what had made us happen. Was it a Grand Design or just a grand and cynical joke, or even merely an accident? Were we fooling ourselves that we were created to inherit the Earth?

Bryony was not so confused and she talked more sense than Moswell. As she was human herself, I valued her opinions and wanted to know how she felt about what had happened to her people. Had she looked for reasons? Her father, a devoutly religious man, had thought that most men were disgusting and selfish and godless, and that Wraeththu had been sent by God to punish them for their sins. Bryony said that she shared this belief to a degree, but she was not so sure about the wholly religious aspect. Perhaps humankind had just worn itself out. Her people had been seeking the Gelaming because everyone considered them to be the Great Saviors who had come to make everything better. Gelaming were thought of as the true Wraeththu, the pure strain. The Varrs and their like were considered deviants from this. Perhaps this was true. I lacked objectivity, I know, because I had never met any Gelaming, but one thing I was sure of: I felt very strongly about anyone coming to take our lands away from us, whatever their reasons.

"But it is not your land!" Bryony protested. "It belongs to everyone! Can't you see how wrong it is for your tribe to kill anyone they feel is weaker than themselves? They are in the position to be charitable, but no! They enjoy killing and making people suffer. They want slaves and sport . . . and worse!"

I couldn't be bothered to argue. I still thought the Gelaming were interfering and hypocritical.

"You wouldn't believe some of the things I've seen," Bryony said in a low, dark voice, "and yet now, I work for a leader of Varrs looking after his house, feeding his family. I should be ashamed of myself!"

"Run away then!" I snapped. "Go back to the wilderness. Take your chances there with a clear conscience!"

Bryony looked at me helplessly. "Don't think I haven't considered that," she said bitterly, "But the truth is, I like it here. I've found a home. I like you all. I'm treated well and I'm trusted with a position of responsibility. What's worse is that I've earned that trust. Me, a woman! Many would see me as a traitor to my race."

"You are like us then," I said, "Like Swithe, Like Gahrazel was before, like me, even. We philosophize about the state of the outside world and we argue and rant, but Forever is still our home and it keeps us safe. We don't want to go out there into the cold and *do* anything!"

"Forever is an enchanted place," Bryony observed wryly.

Just over a week after Cal had suffered delivery of the pearl, its shell became brittle, almost transparent, and a young, mewling har burst it asunder from within and crawled out into the world. So, Terzian had missed the hatching of his new son. He could have delayed riding south to be with Cal at this time, but to a Varr war always comes before life.

I had been out with Ithiel when the great event occurred. Ithiel always took me with him when he went about his duties, for he understood how I would have to learn about the administration of Galhea. We could talk together freely now and I came to realize why my father placed so much trust in him. Ithiel was thorough and economic and diplomatic in his dealings with other hara. He always introduced me as Tiahaar Swift, never Terzian's son. That day, when we got back to Forever, in the haze of a beautiful evening, everything stained red and gold, Bryony was waiting for us on the steps of the house, peering down the drive, still wearing the long apron she was rarely seen in outside the kitchen. She had matured recently, I thought.

"Where have you been?" she asked crossly. (We had paused in an inn on the way home for refreshment.) "You have a brother now, Swift."

A brother. I hadn't thought of it that way before.

Cal was in the drawing room waiting for me. He didn't have the harling with him. The room was cold: it did not seem the place I had grown up in.

"Ah, Swift," Cal said when he saw me.

"Congratulations!"

He smiled at my sarcasm. "Would you tell Cobweb that I'd like to speak to him?"

"Do you give the orders here now, then?"

"Would you *ask* him then?"

"You're wasting your time!"

"Maybe, maybe. Just ask him."

We looked at each other for a moment. Cal's face was inscrutable.

"Alright," I said. "But I'm warning you. Direct contact like this might provoke him into further unpleasantness."

"His unpleasantness is exhilarating!" Cal replied.

Cobweb was still punishing me in subtle ways for restoring my friendship with Cal. I was not sure how he would receive my news. On hearing Cal's request, he rose from his window seat and went to the mirror. "What for?" he asked, and it was impossible to tell whether anger or suspicion colored his voice.

I shrugged. "He didn't tell me, but I said it was a waste of time asking you anyway."

Cobweb slunk over to his table and aimlessly shuffled piles of paper in his hands. He was silent, but his silence lacked character.

"What shall I tell him?" I asked. "How shall I tell him to go to hell?"

"He asked for me?"

"Yes. I was surprised at his nerve. Obviously, you can't see him."

"Ah, Swift," my hostling chided gently. "Never presume to anticipate my actions."

He was out of the door before I realized. I called, "Cobweb, wait!" hearing his laughter ahead of me. He was already down the stairs by the time I looked over the bannister.

They had not really confronted each other since the incident in the summerhouse because there had always been other hara around. Now, they were nearly alone. I was unconvinced whether I was worthy of refereeing this encounter and wondered whether I had time to look for Ithiel, but I was scared to leave them. Cal was soaking up the sunset by the long windows; his hair looked red. I heard him say, "Cobweb," very softly.

I paused at the door. My hostling said nothing. He kept a distance between them and folded his arms, his eyes like flints.

"Thank you for coming."

Cobweb still said nothing but I could sense his excitement.

"I want you to do something for me," Cal said in a careful, reasonable voice.

Cobweb made a noise like an explosive snort. "So, the thief who stole my house requires something of me, does he!" he said, which was not quite the sort of thing I would have expected him to say. Cal turned away from him, as if he could not bear the sight of all that cold dislike.

"Yes, the thief who stole your house requires a favor," he said. There was a silence. I held my breath. Cal sat down on the edge of a chair. "Cobweb, I'm not a fit person to bring up a child, as I'm sure you'll agree . . ."

My hostling sighed through his nose. "Somebody thinks you're entirely fit, that's obvious!"

"Yes," Cal agreed bitterly. "Cobweb, I want someone to care for my son, someone who'll bring him up to think in the right way. I want it to be you."

Cobweb laughed, coldly. "Me?"

"You've done such a good job with Swift," Cal pointed out, somewhat ironically.

"You're mad! Can you really trust me with such a precious thing?"

"Yes," Cal replied simply. "There is no reason for you to hate the harling; he has never harmed you."

"But he's half yours!"

"Half Terzian's . . ."

"Half yours! I hate you!"

"I know, but I still want you to do this."

"You're the most impossible, insane thing I've ever met!" Cobweb raved, momentarily over the top in his indignation. "You want the child; you look after it! You took Terzian away from me to achieve it! I don't even want to see the creature! I can't believe your nerve!" He turned grandly, in a swirl of braids and ribbons, and stalked toward the door.

"Cobweb," Cal called softly. My hostling stopped. His head was up and I could see his fists clenched at his sides. "Why did you come?"

My hostling did not turn for a moment. "Curiosity," he said at last.

"You liar," Cal said, smiling, and my hostling's face twitched. He made a growling noise and stormed out, toward the stairs. "Don't you *know* everything, Cobweb?" Cal called after him.

This was the time I learned that it is possible to argue about one thing while really meaning something completely different. Words are flexible. Tone speaks more eloquently than words. Another move in the game.

I went to see the child and he was beautiful as expected. Cal took him in his arms, which I must admit looked unnatural. "Who could wish for better?" he asked, wondering.

"Yet you do not want to care for him," I remarked. Cal handed the harling to me, and he squirmed in my hold, sensing my nervousness. What disquieted me most was, despite his lovely face and small, perfect limbs, cherub-pale, his sentience was still only half formed, and his eyes were filled only by a kind of animal intelligence. "What shall you call him?" I asked.

"Perhaps I ought to wait for Terzian to come home before I decide."

We looked at each other, but neither of us could face saying the obvious.

Eventually, I thought of, "Oh, but that could be ages yet. What are you going to call him till then?"

"I haven't thought."

"Do you really want Cobweb to look after him?"

"I want my son to be like you," Cal said and touched my face.

The harling reached for his hand.

Before I went down to dinner that evening, a little later than usual, Cobweb came into my room. "Tell him yes," he said shortly. I had to turn away so that he could not see me smiling.

"You're an enigma," I said.

"I'm not sure if that's the word I'd use," Cobweb replied acidly. "I know you're laughing at me, son of my flesh, my faithful one."

"I'm sorry, it's just . . ."

"I always wanted another child," Cobweb said, uninterested in my remark, "but it was never . . . right, never possible. I agree with Cal in that I can't stand by and watch an innocent being indoctrinated by *his* sick-nesses and cruelties. The harling is your brother, part of this house, another Varrish heir. I know I'm capable of rising above personal feelings. I was trained once, not all of it has deserted me . . ." He turned his lambent eyes on me. There was more, both of us knew that, but it remained unspoken.

At dinner Cal said, "I'm sure Cobweb will feel happier now, and without guilt too. Quite an achievement on my part, I think."

I was appalled. "You're an absolute beast," I said.

"No, I'm not."

"You can't repair what you've done!"

"I don't want to. . . . More wine?"

"You knew Cobweb would accept, didn't you?"

"I wasn't sure, but I thought it was worth a try."

"I can see through you," I said uncertainly.

"Oh, can you? Do you understand my motives?"

"Implicitly!" I replied, but he didn't believe me.

Cobweb decided that the harling should be named Tyson, and baptized him into our tribe, although Swithe commented that this was a worthless practice. As soon as the child was delivered into Cobweb's care, Cal appeared to lose interest in him. Occasionally, pricked more by my reminders than conscience, he would come into the nursery that had seen generations of human children grow up and the first harish childhood, mine, and half-heartedly perform acts of what he supposed was affection. Tyson always looked wary and confused. In just a few weeks, he had learned to wobble around, careering off furniture, and say "Obbeb" and "Wift," which was how he addressed my hostling and myself. It was true that he helped to seal up the scars left in our household by recent traumas (even my nightmares began decreasing in frequency), for he possessed an inner glow of happiness that could not be affected by moods on either Cal's or Cobweb's part, but could only encourage to dispel them. I could see that Cobweb unashamedly adored him from the start, perhaps convincing himself that it was indeed his own child. In the afternoons, I would lift Ty out of his bed and wake him up and breathe in his wonderful, clean smell. Now his brown eyes were beginning to fill up with an eerie, knowing wisdom. I would hold him and hug him and he would nestle against me and whisper childish nonsense into my ear. It made me want to have sons of my own. Children are miracles, the living proof of the infinite. I had been told by Cobweb that only a special, vitally intense kind of aruna can bring about conception. "There has to be an utter mingling of souls for it to happen," he said, and then added drily, "Terzian has never found that easy."

One day, a messenger rode into Galhea and some hours later the news he bore reached us at the house. The Varrs were returning home. Cobweb went pale when Ithiel told us. I caught a glimpse of the visions of terrifying injuries and death that flickered across his mind's eye. But Ithiel could soothe his fears.

It would seem that the Gelaming were trickier than we thought. The Varrs could not even reach them. This demanded more explanation and Ithiel told us that there had been strange and potent spells cast upon the country. Places once recognizable had become territories of uncharted weirdness and the army had been traveling in circles. Their supplies and morale had dwindled. There had been one or two minor skirmishes with bands of marauding humans seeking to steal guns and food, and others with hara of hostile tribes, but these had just been irritations helping to cast a veil over the whereabouts of the enemy. Eventually, sensing the rising hysteria and depression among his hara, Terzian had ordered the retreat home. Ponclast would be summoned; there would have to be further debate. The Varrs had not been expecting this.

"The Gelaming do not want to fight," Bryony said. "It is because they know the Varrs would have no chance. Now, do you see, Swift?"

"We won't know what really went on until Terzian gets here," I said testily.

They returned in the mid-afternoon of a warm, glorious day. Terzian did not come up to the house for some time. I sat with Ty on the lawn and told him about his father. He would not listen, only chuckled and reached for my hair with handfuls of torn daises.

Everyone in Galhea was relieved that the army had returned alive, and there was great celebration that night. Terzian looked tired, but he managed to smile and take his new son in his arms. Tyson was frightened by all the noise and strange faces, and fretted until Cobweb came to take him away. Terzian looked after them speculatively. Leef came to find me and he looked thinner and exhausted. I suggested we go for a walk in the gardens. I was eager to question him, but waited for him to offer the information himself.

"I feel as if I've got someone to come back here to now," he said as we walked along.

"I did think about you sometimes," I said, which was not untrue, but there had been no sentiment involved.

"The whole thing, all that distance; it was a waste of time," he said bitterly.

"We heard something like that," I replied cautiously.

We had come to the lake. It looked eerie, with insects chirruping and the water shifting lazily in the darkness. I put my hand on Leef's arm, feeling his sadness.

"I really wanted to fight," he said. "I needed to. We all just wanted to *do* something. At night I could feel them watching us, but they never showed themselves. Terzian was furious."

"I can imagine," I said tartly.

"Everything got worse and worse. We crossed the great marsh Astigi but could get no further. Some of us became ill and there was the constant harassment of attacks by men and hara of small tribes. Things were always being stolen. It was so *strange*. Took a few days for us to realize what was happening. I began to recognize a tree we would pass every day, late in the afternoon. At first I thought I was mistaken, but no, we really were traveling in circles. The scouts' compass needles spun as if in a wind. Soon after that, Terzian gave the order to turn back. Every one of us was relieved . . ." He sighed and rubbed his hands through his hair, smiled weakly. "You've grown again, Swift."

I had been standing uncomfortably silent. Now I shrugged. "Well, I have no control over it."

"Out here, in this weird place, you look just like Cobweb." He laughed. "You see, I'm becoming used to magic!"

I wondered how long it would take him to get round to touching me. Leef was so hesitant, as if Terzian was always standing behind us, watching.

"I wasn't much fun at Festival, was I?" I joked.

"No, you weren't, but I know why now. It must have been very . . . stressful."

"Not compared with real things, what goes on out there." I waved my arm vaguely at the trees.

"Perhaps not, but troubles are always relative, aren't they?"

I sat down, on the spongy moss that is always a little damp. Leef hovered at my side. "Sit down," I ordered. "What's wrong with you?"

He sat. "You know, don't you? At this moment, I want to pour torrents of my breath into you, but I have to be careful."

"Not Terzian again!"

"It's easy for you to scoff; you don't know him in the same way that I do."

"You must have at least shared breath with a hundred hara. Am I so different?"

He sighed. "He may already have chosen for you."

I shuddered. That was quite, quite possible. Terzian would probably not think of consulting me. I stood up. "We'd better get back," I said.

I walked to my favorite yew tree. Once it had seemed such a long way to the nearest branch. Now I could reach it easily. Hanging upside down by my knees, I could see Leef smiling at me.

"Get down," he said.

"I feel like climbing to the top."

"Get down, now!"

He hauled me out of the branches and we ended up rolling in the springy, sharp leaves around the base of the tree. I wanted to taste him because it had only happened to me once before and that had been Cal. I needed to compare that time with someone else. Leef's breath was all dark, beating wings and feathery darkness. It reached right into me. I broke away and said, "Tell me how I taste."

"Of gold," he said huskily and sought my mouth once more, melding into me. My body felt strange. It almost hurt. It was the beginnings of desire and I was unfamiliar with it.

"You are near your time," Leef whispered, touching my face and neck all over with his lips.

"What will it be like?" I asked.

"Like heaven," he replied.

Terzian was worried and it was impossible not to be affected by it. Ponclast had been summoned and representatives from the Kakkahaar were expected any day. I kept trying to look at the situation objectively, to face the seriousness that might be hovering, waiting to surprise us with drastic change and discomfort at any time, but all that seemed real to me was a strange, half-waking, dreamy state where all that mattered was my own body, newly graceful, newly aware. My books were sadly neglected.

"Well, you've certainly changed your tune recently," Swithe observed caustically, but I could see that his eyes were smiling.

The Kakkahaar, whose names were Aihah and Shune, brought us gifts from the south. Exotic, spicy sweets, aromatic with honey and bitter, pungent nuts; glass beads that changed color in the light and dried herbs with arcane and special properties for Cobweb. I was intrigued by their strangeness, more aware of their presence than I had been before, when other Kakkahaar had visited us. They weaved and braided their thigh-length hair in convoluted styles and their eyelids were tattooed on the inside so that they never had to wear kohl. Of course, our lack of occult development must have been held in utter contempt by these adept practitioners of magic, but it was never shown. They were always gratingly polite. Aihah obliged me with special attention and from him I learned that they were still in communication with their tribe in the desert. I realized it must involve a similar practice to the one Cobweb and I used occasionally, when our minds could touch, but how much stronger the Kakkahaars' ability must be to be able to cover so many miles. Aihah corrected me about this. "Distance has nothing to do with it," he said. "We communicate *laterally*, not head on. Do you understand?"

"I'm not sure."

"It is something like visualization. A calling, and something more." He smiled at me. "One day, it might be possible for you to come south and learn with us. There is much we could teach you."

I had no doubt of that and thanked him warmly, but I couldn't imagine it ever happening.

CHAPTER SEVEN

>━┼━◆━┼━◆━━O━━◆━┼◆━┼━<

Seasonal Affliction

Tears of belated remorse
Swung from lashes
Worshiping manifestations within sexual glands,
To catapult assassins of beauty into erogenous zones.

I had always believed that the majority of harlings came of age in the spring, with the rising of the sap and the burst of new life. Perversely, I began to feel my Feybraiha approaching with the advent of the autumn. Since my father's return and my brief encounter with Leef in the garden, I had started to be aware of my body more than before, but that had been sort of exciting and secret, like hugging myself in private. Gradually, my advancing maturity began to get uncomfortable. Cobweb noticed it before anyone else; I had said nothing, half hoping it would all go away and I could resume my life peacefully. Blossoming sexuality raged within me like a fast-growing, strangling vine. I had no control over it. My moods swung like a great and sickening pendulum. One moment I was happy to the point of lunatic hysteria, the next plunged into a depression so black, only the thought of death could comfort me. As Swithe had once predicted, unexpected growths of hair seemed to burst from my skin overnight, beneath my arms, between my legs, and in those places the skin was hot and sore. I remembered what Gahrazel had gone through the year before and wondered whether I should talk to him about it, but ever since he had come back from the south, he had been like a stranger to me, no longer the elfin beauty with whom I had shared secrets and childish dreams, but a tall, tanned intruder that looked vaguely like a Gahrazel I had once known. He looked at me with different eyes now and appeared to shun coming into the house.

Cobweb made an ointment for my skin, using some of the herbs that the Kakkahaar had brought. Aihah expressed polite interest in my coming of age and taught me some relaxation exercises to try when I felt too manic. I think Cobweb would have liked the Kakkahaar to have given me some instruction concerning aruna and its practices, but my father was against it. I never knew for sure whether Cobweb had suggested it, but sensitive as I was at that time, I guessed some of what went on behind my back. As it was, Swithe and Moswell were entrusted with my education, as usual. Cobweb knew that the Kakkahaar could have taught me much more than either of my tutors could ever know.

Swithe was the most informative, which was not surprising as Moswell could never be termed a particularly sensual creature. "You must learn to understand your body in an adult way," Swithe told me. "It can no longer be simply a thing to giggle over in the dark. You must bring your sexuality to the forefront of your being and examine it carefully."

He told me that in humankind, where the sexes had been split into two different kinds, men and women were attracted to each other because of their opposite polarities, the positive aspect of male and the negative aspect of female. "They sought to make themselves whole through the act of copulation," Swithe explained. "We do not possess that confusing, desperate yearning; our desires are centered upon different aspects. As we contain both negative and positive elements within our own bodies, we can express through aruna a fusing of these elements to previously unattainable satisfaction. Men were unaware that through sex they could reach a higher form of consciousness. To us it is virtually commonplace. In the simple act of sharing breath, the minds of two hara can mingle and rise. During aruna, the manifestation of ecstasy can accomplish anything. It creates a living force that may be harnessed and used. If such an effect is desired, we call aruna Grissecon, which is aruna to perform magic. Varrs seldom practice it."

At night, I could rarely sleep. My skin burned, the moon called me with a soft, white voice and I sought the dew-soaked coolness of the shady trees outside. One morning, at breakfast, Cal said to me, "God, you look awful! What's the matter with you?"

Raging irritation made me run from the room, virtually in tears. Behind me, I heard Cal say sarcastically, "Oh dear."

Some time later, he came to my room. Swithe had obviously explained what was going on. His inquisitiveness was part ghoulishness, part concern. "Never was puberty so grim!" he said, pulling a face, which I guessed was supposed to make me laugh. "This must be one of the prices we pay for being so goddam perfect!"

"And what are the others?" I asked.

"One of them's learning, I suppose. A little of it is a dangerous thing, as they say. God, what a wreck you are!"

My face was red, the skin scaly, my eyes puffed and sore. It seemed to hurt me physically if anyone looked at me. Cal was interested in the concept of Feybraiha and what it entailed, but I shrank from explaining.

"So your honorable father selects some worthy har for the purpose of deflowering you," Cal enthused while I cringed with shame. "Who will it be, I wonder."

"Probably Leef," I said, surprised at a strange kind of anger that had crept into my voice. There was no way I could know whom my father would choose.

"And do you like him?"

"He's alright."

"Is that all?" Cal laughed. "How disappointing! I would have thought that for the first time you would have to be with someone who set your head on fire at least!"

"I've heard that soon just about anyone will be able to do that to me!" I said bitterly. I still spent a lot of time resenting the way my body was behaving, sailing happily on in the special life of its own that it was enjoying.

My little brother, Tyson, seemed more aware than most of what I was going through. He looked at me with strange, fearful eyes, bringing me presents in a pitiful, childish attempt to cheer me up. I now had two strips of rag, a pink stone and some of Cobweb's earrings (all mismatched) lined up on my windowsill. When Tyson thought I was particularly down-hearted, he would grab hold of my sleeve and drag me over to them, making me touch them. Perhaps Cobweb was indoctrinating him already.

One evening, the event that I had been dreading occurred. At dinner, my father said, "Later, Swift, I want you to come to my study." I went cold from head to toe, unable to eat my food for the hysterical beating of my heart.

He offered me a glass of sheh, diluted by cordial, leaning back against his desk, Master of Galhea, my father, lean, commanding and terrifying. I was insignificance itself, sitting there, looking up at him, glass clutched in my lap, waiting for the fateful pronouncement. Terzian seemed blissfully unaware of my discomfort. "As you know, Swift," he began, "for your Feybraiha, I have to choose someone I think right for the honor of . . ." (here he had the grace to falter) ". . . well, you've been told about it, haven't you?" He waited for me to nod. "Good, good. Well, I have talked about this with Cobweb and he agrees with my conclusion; it seems obvious to me that the warrior har Leef should be the one." My heart sank; I don't know why. I'd been expecting that hadn't I? Who else was there? My father looked at me strangely.

"That was why I had him promoted," he said. "I did hope you'd be pleased about this, Swift."

I shrugged helplessly. My father raised one eyebrow, stroking the edge of his desk with light fingers. "After I heard about your little escapade in Galhea with your young friend Gahrazel, I naturally assumed you had some interest in Leef . . ." My squirming was enhanced by savage blushing. "Nothing *ever* escapes my notice, Swift," my father chided gently.

I was choked by my own silence. Terzian carried on.

"I believe at Festival time and also in the garden some weeks ago, you indulged in some—er, petty frivolities with Leef. Is this so?" He was becoming impatient with my dumb stupidity. "Well?"

I nodded. Yes, it had been Leef. There was no-one else.

"Cobweb thinks you'll be ready in a week or two. Shall we say two weeks? I will arrange everything." And that was it.

Sensing my dismissal, I stood up. I wanted to say to him, "Can't you see that all this isn't just a case of 'being ready in a couple of weeks' for me, as if I was only being fitted for new shoes or something? It's my body! My life!" but he had already turned his back on me, sorting through papers on his desk, and anyway, I was too scared to speak.

"Oh, Swift, on your way out, could you find the Kakkahaar for me? Tell them where I am." He smiled wolfishly at me, but I could see he was already frowning by the time he looked back at the desk.

The weight of despair descended like a black cloud once I had closed the door behind me. Why hadn't I said anything? What could I have said? I knew Leef would be pleased and that annoyed me too. I did not dislike him, but I resented being handed over to him on a plate. It made me angry; I wanted something else, something more, but what?

When I delivered my father's message to the Kakkahaar, Aihah paused as he passed me and lifted my face with his hand. "I would like to speak with you later," he said.

"I'll wait for you here then," I answered.

Cobweb was sitting by the fire, on the floor. "It will do you good to listen to Aihah," he said, and by that I knew that they'd been talking about me.

"What is going to happen Cobweb?" I asked, curling into his arms. "It's all taking so long."

"What is? Your Feybraiha? Is your head hurting you again?" He pressed his palm against my cheek.

"No, not that! That's got nothing to do with me, has it! I mean about the Gelaming."

Cobweb sighed. "Oh, that! I don't know, I really don't. Perhaps they are playing with us. Perhaps they really are wary of the Kakkahaar. We can only wait."

"I wish it wasn't happening! What with that hanging over us and what my body's doing to me, sometimes I feel like . . . I don't know . . . like running or burying myself . . . Cobweb . . ." I clung to him. "If only we could go back!"

"If only!" he agreed.

By the time Aihah came back to us, my head was pounding with the inevitable nightly headache. Just when I felt so exhausted that sleep seem ineluctable, my body would wake up with a host of excruciating symptoms. I would ache and itch and boil inside. That night I wanted to cry and scratch myself raw. Aihah touched my brow. "Come to my room," he said and offered his hand. When I took hold of it, I felt a comforting coolness seep into my arm.

His room smelled alien, as if he had invaded it with his own scent and substance and made it Kakkahaar. I sat on the edge of the bed and he said, "I think you should weep. You want to. There is nothing to be gained by holding it back."

There was no way I could stop myself after that. He busied himself about the room while I lay on his bed and gave myself up to a maelstrom of howling. After a while he shook me gently. "Here, sit up, drink this."

"I feel wretched!" I said, sniffling into the glass.

"Of course you do," he said softly. "Back home we give that drink to our own harlings. It should make you feel a little better." I had never tasted anything so strange. Later, I learned it was a distillation of the putiri plant, whose effects played a rather dramatic part in my life in the future. Aihah was critical of the way I'd been treated. "Here in the north, hara appear to know (or care) so little about Feybraiha. I'm not surprised you're suffering. It is not something you should have to cope with alone. There's a host of things that could be done to ease your discomfort."

"I've forgotten what it's like not to be like this!" I said.

Aihah laughed softly. "You are so distressed," he said. "I don't like to see it. I don't like it at all."

"My father has chosen for me," I blurted, incapable of stemming the fresh tears building up inside my eyes.

"Not a welcome choice?" Aihah suggested.

I shook my head. "Not really. I can't tell. Once I thought . . ." I looked at him helplessly and he brushed my cheek with his thumb.

"Who is it now then?"

"There is no-one."

Aihah sat down beside me. "Now, you must never lie to yourself, Swift. That is perhaps the worst of Varr mistakes. Be truthful; who is it? Your body knows and it wants that one special flame that only one special person can give you. That is the way of Feybraiha. If not, well, just about anyone would do; like animals or (darkly) *men*. This will be your first time, Swift, and it is very important. It is something you will carry with you for the rest of your life and because of that, it must be perfect. Now, come on, don't let me sit here and lecture you" (he gave me a little shake) "search your soul and admit it."

"I can't!" I cried. "My head is too full. I can't see anyone. There is no-one!"

"You are afraid. Is your choice perhaps a controversial one?"

"There is no-one!" I was weeping again, my body heaving in great, agonizing spasms. I felt so much grief and I could think of nothing that would relieve it.

"Swift, look at me!" I thought I'd heard Aihah's voice but it had been only in my head. I looked at him. "Into my eyes . . . deep." He put his long-fingered hands upon my face, lightly rubbing the sore spots above my eyes. "Open up to me, Swift. Let your mind go blank . . ."

It was so easy to let go. I had been holding myself together by great effort, now I could relax and the Kakkahaar would be there to catch me if I fell. I acknowledged his unobtrusive presence in my mind. He calmed me and caressed my thoughts, and then, with gentle, painless thrusts, he began to search my feelings. Each soft probing brought a picture to my eyes and it was like dreaming. I could see Forever, huge and black and white like an old photograph. A younger me running through the snow. Gahrazel smiling. Talismans on a gate. Was that Ithiel there? I ran right past him. He looked away from me. Then I was mouth to mouth with Leef and we were great black birds, spiraling upwards and the trees were lifeless and the nests were empty. I twirled and spun, reaching up for the white, white sky. His face was there. He said, "You are the special one here, I think . . ." and then I had a glimpse, so quick, so brief, of a shining canopy lit by stars and the eyes of my dreams, my nightmares were there with hair all around them. But it was Cal who pulled me back.

I felt a real cry echo in the room around me and the force of Aihah's mind poured into me, compelling me to calm. "Face it!" he commanded and I sensed his awful, primal power held back. If he wished to he could have unleashed it within me, trusting as I was, joined to him by mind, unleashed it to swallow me whole, but he only ordered, "Face it!" and I did.

"It is impossible!" I cried. "My father would never allow it!"

Aihah sat demurely with his hands in his lap. "Terzian is Wraeththu. If he was doing his duty toward you correctly, he would have realized this for himself. It is not a question of what his feelings will allow. That is for humans, that indulgence! You must tell him, Swift."

"I can't!" Even though I was pacing around the room, wildly throwing my arms about, I knew that the grief had left me. I knew why. Once, beside the lake, I had let Cal into my head and his presence had lodged there. My body had fixed itself upon him. No other would do.

"Will you tell Terzian for me, Aihah?" I begged, but he shook his head.

"No, I won't. You must tell him yourself."

"But what if he says no?"

"He won't. He is Wraeththu. Although our differences from humanity seem little but an inconvenience to your father at times, he will understand this, Swift, I promise you that."

"Hmm. Maybe I'll ask him tomorrow."

The Kakkahaar laughed. "Why wait that long? Go and see him again now before he arranges anything. Tell him that you've talked to me . . ." (Ah yes, I thought. They know we are afraid of them.)

Just as I was steeling myself to go and face my father, a horrible thought came to me: Cobweb. I grabbed Aihah's arm. There was no need for words.

"Ah, your hostling," the Kakkahaar said. "I realize this might cause friction. I will speak to Cobweb for you; I can do that at least."

"Why do you want to help me?" I asked, wondering what he had to gain.

"Why? Well, that is simple. We don't know what will happen to us in the future, do we? If I am to die, then I hope someone will do the same for my own son. Every action has a reaction."

"I see."

"Not entirely. Your education has been sadly neglected. You are unusual for a Varr, Swift. You owe it to yourself to find that knowledge. Don't leave it too long. Now, go to your father."

Terzian was surprised to see me again, glancing impatiently at the clock on the wall when I walked in. He always worked very late, sitting alone, wrestling with his problems. The papers on his desk were covered in scratchy drawings, the odd word written thickly and underlined here and there. "What is it, Swift?" he asked coldly.

"It cannot be Leef," I said. It took a moment for what I said to sink in. He had probably already forgotten about our earlier conversation.

"What?"

I went closer to him. "I've been talking to Aihah."

Terzian rolled his eyes. "Go on."

"Well, it'll be my first time and I want, I need. . . . It has to be Cal, father." I hardly ever called him that. I hardly ever spoke to him directly. He stared at me thoughtfully and I like to think that then he saw me properly for the first time.

"You are so like your hostling," he said, lacing his fingers before him on the desk. "Perhaps I have never spent enough time with you, Swift. Sit down."

I had expected an outburst; now I had no idea what to say.

"How did you reach this conclusion?" he asked reasonably and I thought, My God, he is listening to me. He has actually heard what I said!

I related some of my conversation with the Kakkahaar and he pursed his lips.

"I had no idea you felt this way," he said at last.

"Aihah said you would understand," I murmured. Would that make him angry?

Terzian laughed. "Understand? I can't dispute that Swift! Cal does seem to have a traumatic effect upon everyone he meets."

"Are you cross with me?" I asked carefully.

Terzian leaned back in his chair. "Why should I be?"

"I don't know . . . I thought . . ."

He leaned toward me. "Perhaps I should have realized, but I've had a lot on my mind recently. Your choice is a good choice, Swift, but there is one thing. . . . Oh, hell, I don't know how to say this! Cal is a very strong person; his personality is strong. It may swamp you. I hope you can cope with it."

"I think I can," I replied.

Terzian smiled thoughtfully. "Hmm. It's as well you came to see me tonight. I was going to confirm the arrangements with Leef in the morning. He will be disappointed, Swift. I thought you liked him."

"I do," I said. "But, well, he was just not the one."

"I understand," Terzian replied. "You'll just have to make it up to him later."

We laughed together like adults.

Cobweb was waiting for me in my room. Aihah had lost no time in telling him about my decision. I was afraid he would strike me, but he contented himself with grinding his long talons into my arms as he shook me.

"Are you mad?!" he raged.

I tore myself away. "No!"

"He will poison you!"

"No!"

"What was it you said to me, Swift, that night so long ago? Wasn't it something like, 'I'll never betray you, Cobweb'?" He made an angry, sneering sound. "It didn't take you long to forget that, did it?"

"Alright!" I shouted. "You're right and I'm wrong. You're right to want me to surrender my body to the wrong person and I'm wrong to want to surrender it to the right person!"

Cobweb suppressed a smile. "He's really got to you, hasn't he? First Terzian, now you! Where will it end?"

"I wonder!" I rubbed my arms. My beloved hostling had drawn blood. Contrite, he drew me to him and kissed the claw marks.

"Hard to imagine you in Cal's arms," he said shakily.

"Thank you Cobweb."

His eyes were shadowed. He looked away.

I was so nervous of having to face Cal that I stayed in my room until the following evening. My head was aching and I could not eat. All I wanted to do was sleep, but because my skin was burning I could only toss and turn on the bed. At suppertime, there was a knock on my door and my heart seemed to jump into my mouth. "Come in!" I called, sweat breaking out all over my body, but it was only Swithe.

"How are you?" he asked. He had brought me some milk and a meat sandwich.

"I feel ill, of course!" I retorted irritably. "How are things downstairs?"

Swithe smiled. "Same as usual, I suppose. We haven't been invaded yet anyway! I heard that Ponclast is coming down next week. He'll probably still be here for your Feybraiha."

"Already the event is enriched beyond my dreams!" I groaned sarcasti-

cally. "Where's my father?" This was an oblique question, but its meaning
was not lost on Swithe.

"Oh, he's been talking to Cal in his study. They've been locked away
together for hours. Even had their meal in there."

"Oh God!" I pressed my arm across my eyes, every muscle in my body
flexing with self-conscious shame.

"Leef was here today," Swithe mentioned lightly. "Some say he left here
in a fearful temper."

Restless to the point of agony, I went down to the drawing room with
Swithe. Aihah and Shune and Cobweb were already there and they greeted
me as brightly as if I were a lunatic, to be humoured at all cost. I was bored
of constantly being asked how I was feeling. Cobweb offered me sheh and
rubbed the back of my neck. "It'll soon be over, Swift," he said softly.
Aihah smiled at me and his voice in my head said, "All is as it should be."
Feeling nostalgic, I wanted to see Gahrazel, but he never came to the house
nowadays, living with the soldiers in the town, being with Purah, no doubt.

When everyone was talking, Cobweb beckoned me to go and sit with
him again. I had been wandering restlessly around the room, going to the
window, looking for the moon with its vague face, its soothing radiance.

"Terzian is speaking to Cal," my hostling said.

"I know." We looked at each other and I was grateful that he did not
condemn me, as perhaps he should.

"You must know that from now on, you must not be alone with Cal,
don't you?"

I nodded. "Yes."

I put my arms around him, soft and hard, lean and full; my beloved
mother of mystery.

"You're shivering. You should go to bed," Cobweb said.

I had often wondered how, during aruna, it was decided which har should
be soume and which ouana, or if they could be both at the same time (an
intriguing thought. I tried to imagine the mechanics of it endlessly). Swithe
explained to me that the roles were interchangable and that, as far as he
knew, no-one had attempted to be both at the same time. We both laughed
at the thought of it. Apparently, the decision over who should take what
role varied from tribe and tribe. For some, it might involve occult ritual;
soume was the altar, ouana the blade of sacrifice, for others something that
was resolved naturally. Among our own people, I learned that many hara
(such as my father) had rejected the idea of submitting to soume and that
they always chose to take aruna with hara that were content to let them
take the dominant role. If this was not the case, foreplay to aruna often
involved a battle of strength over who would submit to whom. (Varrs are
never completely comfortable with the feminine side to their natures, hence
the need for those such as Cobweb.) As I was so inexperienced, it was taken
for granted that for my Feybraiha, I would be soume to start with. Swithe
told me not to be alarmed if certain parts of my body withdrew into the

safety of the pelvic cage while I was soume. "It is to prevent damage," he said. "Sometimes, aruna can be rather energetic and you know what parts of you are easily hurt."

"That will make me almost female," I said, uncertainly.

"Not entirely dissimilar, I suppose," Swithe agreed. "Although our sexual parts are much more complex than man's or woman's. Our ecstasy is so much more intense, because it can be used to obtain power. That is why our bodies are so refined in this respect." He smiled. "I can still remember when I was incepted and the har who came to me first."

"What was he like?" I asked. Swithe smothered the dreamy, faraway look in his eye, and I thought of Cobweb.

"It was a long time ago," he said.

Moswell, thankfully sparing me any graphic details (which were bad enough from Swithe) was concerned mostly with teaching me about etiquette. I learned that it would be proper to avert my eyes unless told otherwise and to do exactly as Cal wanted me to. By this time, I was wondering if I'd made the right decision, being familiar with Cal's instinct to make a caustic joke out of any trying situation. The chaperoned meetings I had to suffer with him were a nightmare. It was very difficult to talk under such constraint for we already knew each other quite well, so it seemed utterly ridiculous having Moswell sitting there, watching us like a hawk.

"This has come as a shock, Swift," Cal said and then laughed at my furious blush. "Not an unpleasant shock, of course. But what a responsibility!"

"It won't be your first time though, will it?" I reminded him, meaning Pellaz.

"No. I must have an extraordinary talent for educating virgins."

"Cal, shut up!"

"Well, I've had no complaint so far."

It was impossible to suppress his carefree attitude and he was determined not to instil the slightest note of gravity into the proceedings.

The day before my Feybraiha, Ponclast and my father received momentous news that sent a hush and then a babble right through the house. Through Shune and Aihah, the Kakkahaar had communicated that they had achieved massive breakthrough with the problem of the weird barriers the Gelaming had constructed about themselves. Soon, a passage would be completed through which the Varrs' armies could pass. The time had come. Restlessness spread through Galhea like a plague. Terzian would be leading his hara south within a week. This time, I felt I would be sorry to see him leave. He had been surprisingly understanding about Cal and also, this time, I was not so sure he would be back as quickly.

Terzian organized a great feast for my Feybraiha. It was to be the Varrs' leaving party just as much as my own coming of age. Yarrow roasted a whole ox in the yard and managed to procure sparkling Zheera, which is an extremely potent form of sheh and supposedly aphrodisiac, which made my father laugh when he heard about it. All the eminent citizens of Galhea were to be invited to the house and Ponclast gave me a gift to mark my coming of age, a jewelled, curved knife. It was very beautiful, but would undoubtedly snap like matchwood if used to defend myself. Gahrazel had turned out better than he had expected and he must have been feeling grateful to my father, whom he considered to be responsible.

On the morning of the great day, Bryony and Cobweb shared the task of choosing my clothes, brushing my hair and discreetly painting my face. "Not that you really need it," Cobweb remarked, "but it's nice to dress up for special occasions." The image that faced me in the mirror seemed like a stranger. Cobweb had made me trousers of pale, soft material in his favorite color, lightest green, almost white except in the folds. He weaved small, starry flowers into my hair and dabbed my skin with an expensive perfume which Terzian had once procured for him from some far place.

Bryony sighed at me and said, "You look so lovely, Swift, like a woman, like a beautiful boy. I don't know whether to fancy you or feel jealous of you. I wish I could hug you."

"But you can!" I said and opened my arms. She felt small and slim and helpless in my hold and when I kissed her lightly on the lips I could see tears in her eyes.

"You are so lucky," she said.

On our way downstairs, I turned to Cobweb. "We are all happy," I said. "For now, maybe," my hostling answered, "so we must enjoy it!"

All my father's friends were waiting for us in the Big Room. It was nearly midday and the sun was streaming in through the long windows in great gold bars. Everyone was dressed in finery, everyone was smiling. Red leaves blew along the terrace outside. "Swift, you are beautiful," Ponclast said, taking my hand and sweeping an exaggerated bow. I felt I could never tire of this attention. My childhood had been torn from me. Now I was adult and hara could flirt with me without reproach.

Custom dictated that Terzian perform some kind of ceremony in my honor, although, Varrs being what they are, there was nothing written down to give him any guidelines. I think he made the words up as he went along. I remember him touching my shoulder and saying, "This body blooms, this Wraeththu flower," and before all our guests he joined Cal's hand with mine and told him, "Bring this flower to fruit." Terzian is an accomplished speaker. Even Cal could not bring himself to smile as my father delivered solemn words about deflowering. I was relieved when it was over.

House-hara mingled among the guests dispensing sheh and wine, and many people came to speak with me. I can remember nothing of what was said. At some point I saw Leef standing with a group of friends near the windows. He saw me looking and we both froze and quickly turned away.

The whole day was one of happiness and feasting and dancing. I was floating on air the whole time. All my discomfort had gone. All that was left was a tingling in my skin that was a yearning for the dusk and the time that would follow it. When my father pronounced me Kaimana at lunch, Cal, seated next to me, took my hand and kissed my cheek. (Why was it Leef's eye I had to meet across the table?) My body surged with untapped power. I felt capable of anything.

Gahrazel came to speak to me in the afternoon. "It doesn't seem that long ago that it was my Feybraiha we were celebrating here," he said. "My God, Swift, you've changed since then!"

"It wasn't that long ago and you've changed more than I have," I replied. "When did we last see you? We used to be such friends."

"I know . . ." Gahrazel sighed heavily and looked at the floor. When he raised his eyes again, I felt he was trying to tell me something.

"Gahrazel?"

He shook his head and reached for my hand. "It's nothing. Look, I'll come and see you before we go south again, I promise."

"Forever used to be your home."

Gahrazel looked at the room around him, beyond the faces, at the walls. I saw him shiver.

"And how is Purah?" I enquired, but Gahrazel only smiled.

"I'll see you soon," he said. "And good luck for tonight!"

In the evening, after dinner, all the long windows in the Big Room were thrown open to an autumn evening still warm with the memory of summer. Hara wandered out there to dance in the moonlight and the smell of cooking meat drifted in from the remains of Yarrow's ox in the stableyard. I had had to speak with so many hara that day, I had hardly seen anything of Cal. Now, in the dusk, he came toward me and took me out on the terrace.

"Can you believe this, I feel nervous!" he confessed. "It's such a responsibility, what with all these hara here and everything. I hope Terzian doesn't ask you to write out a report for him tomorrow. What if I fall asleep?"

"I think I'm too drunk to be nervous," I replied. "Nothing seems real yet. I want to put my arms around you, but everyone's watching us."

"Feybraiha seems to be a spectator sport, I agree. I expect they'll all cheer if you do."

"I expect so too. Oh, what the hell!"

We embraced. They cheered.

At midnight, my father called us to the middle of the room and delivered another embarrassing speech, which everyone applauded with deafening enthusiasm. When he finished speaking and everyone was toasting my health and fortune, Cobweb came and touched my arm. "I think it's time, Swift," he said. "Come with me. It won't be so noticeable if you and Cal disappear separately."

I followed my hostling up the great, wide stairs to my room. Always, on those stairs, my mind is flooded with memories. That time was no exception. I felt that at the foot of the stairs was my past, a forlorn child looking up, while at the head, my future, as yet unknown, gaped before me.

My room had been strewn with ferns and smelled deep, dark and mysterious. "It's like a forest," I said.

Cobweb took me in his arms. "Dear, dear Swift," he said. "If he hurts you, I will kill him!"

"Will it hurt me then?" I asked, alarmed.

Cobweb shook his head quickly. "No, no. I shouldn't have said that. If it does, it will be a sweet, sweet pain, and short in duration."

He dressed me in white and took the flowers from my hair. I said, "My God, it's real, isn't it!"

Cobweb smiled. "As real as anything can be. Don't be afraid."

He folded back the sheets and I slid between them. The pillows were fragrant with perfume. Cobweb lit a dozen long, white candles and turned off the light. The room became an enchanted place. My heart beat fast and I was deep within the forest.

"It is like a dream," I said.

Cobweb was at the door. "Goodnight, little pearl," he said.

I lay there for what seemed hours, drunk on my own heady turmoil and the rich scent of the room. I tried to rehearse what I would say to Cal when he came in, but none of the conversations had any end that I could imagine. Now it was real; now. Before that moment I could not visualize reaching it, even during the day. I remembered once sitting on the roof with Gahrazel when he had told me about aruna and how I had felt about it then, thinking of Ithiel. Now I was afraid, now I craved its consummation.

Cal knocked on the door before he opened it, probably to give me time to compose myself. "Swift," he whispered. "Are you awake?"

I laughed nervously. "I feel ridiculous."

Cal crept stealthily across the room as if wary of others listening outside. "I know what you mean. It's a bit like Grissecon, having everyone there watching us. Hopefully, they're all too engrossed in drinking and dancing again by now."

"Grissecon. . . . Have you ever done that?"

He paused to examine himself in the mirror. "Yes. Once at Saltrock. That was where Pell and I stayed for a while."

"Why did you do it?"

"For magic, of course. There was a sort of plague, but it was man-made. Aruna is stronger than anything man can devise. We performed Grissecon to kill the plague."

"Who . . . you and Pell?"

"No . . . it was someone else." He smiled. "I don't want to talk about that now. You look lovely, Swift."

"Everyone keeps saying that today," I said. "But will they tomorrow? Is it just a temporary thing?"

Cal shook his head. "I could keep on extolling your virtues, but it might make you conceited. Shall we have a drink?

He poured us sheh and sat down beside me. We could hear the music from downstairs; the window was open.

"I wonder what will happen when Terzian goes south," I said.

"It's best not to think about that now. You might end up as Master of Galhea sooner than you think."

"God, Cal, that's awful. Don't say that!" I cried, appalled. I hated to think my father was vulnerable, but Cal was probably right.

"At least you'll be here if anything happens," I said.

"And what could I do?" he asked, laughing.

"Not *do* anything; just be here. I'd feel safer somehow."

He took the glass from my hand. It was empty. I tried to smile.

"Don't be afraid, Swift. Aruna is the most normal, commonplace, easily accomplished thing Wraeththu can do. We spend most of our lives being concerned with it."

He stood up and carelessly pulled off his shirt. His skin was dark, his hair almost white. I looked away and after a while he said, "Oh Swift, can't you bear to look at me?"

"Moswell said it would be indelicate to stare."

"Nonsense, it turns me on. I want you to admire me." I turned my head. His skin was tawny and soft with a sheen like fur. He turned round three times. "Front and back elevation," he said. "What do you think?"

"Wonderful . . . a bit frightening . . ."

"You think so? Come here." He held out his hand. I struggled from the bed in a knot of nightshirt. "I don't like that. Take it off," he said and I hesitantly pulled it over my head. "I can't imagine anyone finding a garment like that erotic, but still, concealment is enticing, I suppose." We went to the windowseat and looked out at the garden and it felt wild and magical to be naked. Anyone might have looked up and seen us. Cal put his arm around me, stroking my skin, staring out into the darkness. "The Gelaming might have a price on my head," he said.

"What, because of that Orien?" I asked.

"That Orien!" Cal mocked. "He was a respected shaman, Swift. I have a feeling that Seel . . . that Seel won't rest until I pay for what I've done."

"Who's Seel?" I felt I'd heard of him before.

"He founded Saltrock," Cal explained. "We were good friends once but I doubt if our friendship could weather my murder of Orien."

"You were sick, though, weren't you?"

"That is not an excuse, though I wish it was." He pulled me closer against him. "You feel so warm . . . I have a feeling, I don't know, I feel as if Seel is . . . is *coming closer* somehow. Sometimes it's as if he's here in this house. I've woken up and smelled him in the room, smelled his perfume, his body. I've seen his eyes. . . . Oh God, why am I going on like this! It's your Feybraiha."

"It doesn't matter. I like you telling me things, I want you to," I said and pressed my face against his chest. "I never dreamed this would be possible."

"I wish I could regret it properly, but I can't," Cal murmured.

"Perhaps it's because you're still angry," I suggested.

"Oh, I'll always be angry, but I know I shouldn't have done that, never, never . . . but in a way, I don't care that I did."

"Well, *I* don't care," I said.

"Swift . . ." His voice was a whisper and his breath called out to me. I could feel my heart; my eyes were hot. When his mouth touched mine, I could see his life, moving quickly, like a never-ending picture, unfolding before my eyes. He trusted me. There was nothing hidden. It was all there. I relived with him that first time with Pellaz; that was all he could think of. I wished I could have known Pell better, but I had been so young when they had been with us before.

"There will never be anyone like him," Cal said.

"Don't be sad."

"I'm not, really. Come on."

He led me back to the bed and we pulled the blankets over us.

"I never thought I'd come back here," he said.

"I'm glad that you did."

"Mmmm. Me too." He put his hand on my back. I could feel him trembling. "Are you still afraid, Swift?"

"I don't think so."

"Good." We shared breath again and then he broke away and said, "Come on, Swift, don't just lie there! It works both ways, you know. I'm yours to explore, feel free to do what you like."

"But I don't know what to do," I complained. "Show me."

He took my hands in his own, his eyes were laughing. "Touch me." He threw back the covers to let me see him and his ouana-lim had become a gold and jade sentinel, pulsing with moving colors. "Vibrant, isn't it?" he said.

"It is a sword. It will kill me!" I cried.

"No, it won't. Your body will be surprisingly accommodating. I've never taken aruna with a pure-born before. I wonder if it will be different."

I took his ouana-lim in my hands and its petals opened around my fingers. It was so beautiful, so mysterious, alive and radiant, a thing created for the sole purpose of pleasure. Shining trickles of luminous blue-green touched my skin. I had never seen anything like it.

"Look at yourself," he told me. My colors were bronze and metallic blue, with the faintest hints of blood red appearing and melting away. When he touched me, a sun seemed to blaze behind my eyes. I was lost then, in the intoxicating splendor that presaged our union. Sometimes, it was as if I was out of my body, looking down, sometimes I was inside Cal's head, looking at myself. Then the moment came when he pressed me back. "Say a prayer Swift," he said and seared right into me in one, long, tearing sliding movement. It did hurt, but I craved that pain, moving to meet it. I had visions before my eyes, oh, such wondrous visions. Other lands, alien and beautiful, strange people walking along azure dunes. Some time in that exotic landscape I felt a nerve awake within me, deep inside, where he could not reach, and it wanted so desperately to be touched. I called his name, feverish and despairing, and just when I thought the torment would go on forever, I felt a snakelike movement within me and something shot out and made contact with that vibrating nerve. I could hear a scream, it may have been in my head, but a universe imploded in my body, all my limbs shuddering and twisting to a nameless ecstasy. Hot, glimmering liquid spilled onto the sheets, aflame like opals. Light flared behind my eyes. I was released.

Afterwards, he wanted to talk to me again. It was all Orien, Saltrock and Pell. No matter how much he tried to hide it, he was obsessed with it all.

"It was not me," he said, "and yet it was. I can remember it all perfectly, yet it was another mind that moved those events, not mine."

I learned that Cal and the one he called Seel had known each other for a long time, their relationship went back to before either of them were har. "Saltrock is a special place. It's a Wraeththu sanctuary. Madness rarely touches it," Cal told me warmly. "One day you must go there. I think you will anyway, Swift. I can't see you living here forever, in Forever."

I laughed and put my arms around him. "Remember I'm a Varr," I said. "Do you think I'd be welcome there?"

"Of course, why not? Can you help who your parents are? Anyway Seel's people are unique. I think they'd surprise you."

"Ah, the Wraeththu who call themselves the knowledge-seekers," I said, not without sarcasm.

Cal sighed deeply. "Again I've betrayed them," he said obliquely.

"How did it happen?" I asked. "I mean Orien and all that. I want to know. I want to know everything."

"What, everything about me? How charming. Alright, if you really want to, although it may bore you."

"It won't. Say it all!"

"God, that would take forever!" He snuggled down against me and his voice was low. The candles were guttering away; soon we would see each other only by starlight.

"I found Pell in a wilderness; an unearthly child. He was so beautiful I could hardly believe it and wild like a scared, sleek animal. I would have kidnapped him to make him har if he hadn't wanted to go with me. I had to have him. It was almost sick! I took him to Saltrock and Seel had him incepted. That was just the beginning . . . I should have known that there was something . . . not right, even then. It was Thiede, you see. It was Thiede that incepted Pell, gave him his Wraeththu blood. You have to understand that Thiede is. . . . God, what is he? It's so hard to explain. He's powerful, frightening, awesome. Perhaps beyond good and evil. He wanted Pell for something (who didn't?) but Thiede's desires are obscure, incomprehensible. I still don't know the reason, but I'm sure Orien did.

Orien. . . . He was perhaps the kindest, wisest person I ever met. He was Saltrock's shaman, high priest, whatever . . ."

"If he was that wonderful," I butted in, "why did you kill him?"

"Why indeed!" Cal sighed and pressed his face into my neck. "Why . . . I'll have to go back, Swift, to when Pell and I were in Galhea before. It's not easy. When we left here, all those years ago, we were planning to travel back toward the south. I wanted to find a way to Immanion, the first city of the Gelaming. I knew that was where it was all really happening, where Wraeththu had organized themselves, found order. . . . It seemed the logical place to head for. I had no idea where it was. Now I know it's farther than I realized, across the sea, a long way away. Anyway, we had only traveled for a short time, a few weeks maybe, when . . ." For a moment he could not speak. His silence made my chest ache. After a while he swallowed. "I watched him die, Swift, all his life running out of him. I couldn't do anything, just watch. Afterwards, I must have wandered around half crazy. I can't remember. . . . Somewhere along the way I lost the horses. It was like, like, how can I explain? My body was moving, feeding itself, sleeping, looking after itself in a way, but I was buried deep inside my own head, unaware of what was going on around me. One day I woke up and I was back at Saltrock. I don't know how I got there. They didn't know how to cope with me. I was out of my head, and when I wasn't I wanted to be. Anything I could get my hands on to escape reality, I shovelled it into myself. Seel must have been at the end of his tether trying to sort me out. It was all because of Zack too, you see. I thought I was being punished for what happened to him. I thought that losing Pell was the divine retribution for my sins. I couldn't face myself. My life was a series of lies, conceit and pride. I was unfit to live, a blight on Wraeththukind. It seemed that everyone I got close to was destroyed in some way. The fruit of my self-hate was the murder of Orien. Perhaps it was the worst thing I could do, and to do it would prove to myself how utterly loathsome I was. I don't know. At the time, I blamed him for Pell's death. Now I can see that was . . . not stupid . . . just wrong."

"Oh, Cal," I said. He looked at my face and his fingers touched my cheek.

"Oh, don't weep for me, Swift," he said. "You see, the worst thing is, I haven't changed. I learned nothing from all that. I'm still selfish. My path is uphill. I don't struggle to climb it, I don't even slip back or seek the easy path. I just sit down where I am and think, 'Oh, to hell with it!' I'm too human; I shouldn't be har. Look at what I've done here. Don't think I'm not aware of it and don't think I don't enjoy it."

"But do you still hate yourself?" I asked.

"Inside myself . . . perhaps." He pulled away from me and lay on his back, with his arms behind his head. "Swift, I've never spoken to anyone like this, not even Pell. I don't think I ever will again . . ."

"Maybe you had to," I suggested.

"Maybe." He smiled. "This is depressing. Here I am again bringing up

reeking stomachfuls of confessions all over you! I *am* here for a purpose . . ."

He leaned over me and I closed my eyes. Already my body quickened
for the feel of him, desire of him.

"No," he said softly, and stroked my stomach with the gentlest possible
touch. He pulled me against him and lay back. I looked into his lazy, violet
eyes. This is too incredible, I thought. This is too much; it is a dream. So
close. His beauty almost withers me. Perhaps I shall be turned to
stone . . .

"Swift," he said, "I want you to—"

"Hush!" I answered. "I know."

It was frightening, like going into a dark place full of unknown things.
I could feel his strength, the great, beating pinions of his spirit. It was so
different. Before, when he took me, I had lived the ultimate of visions, now
I was part of his vision. He was an abyss and I was falling, a never-ending
fall. When I reached the end, I would fall again. His head was thrown back,
one arm pressed across his eyes. He murmured as if in pain, fretfully, then
his arm lashed back and hit the pillow. His eyes were blazing, I reared up
to escape them, but he caught hold of me, so strong, lifting himself. His
mouth found my neck; he wanted blood. I remembered for a fleeting
moment what my father had said: "He may swamp you." Of course,
Terzian was speaking of this, not Cal as ouana, but the devouring, lashing
female side of him, like a python, crushing me. For a moment, we were still,
staring at each other. Then it happened. That secret part of me snaked out
to ignite his pulsing nerve. He did not cry out, just hissed like a cat,
threshing around me. His hands, like claws, tore at my shoulders. He
lunged to bite me, snarling and crazed. Almost panicking, I hit his face and
he flopped back among the pillows. There was blood around his mouth.

"Cal?" I said, tentatively, feeling all my muscles shaking. I felt him laugh
around me; he opened his eyes.

"Pure-born, it *is* different!" he said.

In the morning I felt as if I'd been fighting for my life all night. My shoulders
had actually stuck to the sheet with blood. Cal fetched a cloth from my
bathroom and bathed my back. "Oh, hell, I'm sorry," he said. "I must have
got a bit carried away but it was pretty amazing, wasn't it? So much
stronger. God!" He laughed and stood up, throwing the cloth into the air.

"I've decided to become Varr hostling stock," I said. "If being ouana
means being torn to bits, I'll opt for submission any day."

"Oh, come on," Cal coaxed. "It's just me! You know how weird I am!
Terzian isn't exactly unscarred either."

"You enjoy being weird," I grumbled, wincing as I tried to get out of
bed.

"Yes, I have to agree with you there," he said cheerfully. "They'll have
finished breakfast, won't they? I'm starving!"

He was gorged on my vitality. I could hardly move.

* * *

I walked through the day in a daze. Everyone gave me very strange looks, except for my father, who probably understood. "Takes it out of you, doesn't it?" he said, and I felt he was glad to have someone he could say that to.

CHAPTER EIGHT

>─┤─◄>─◄O─◄>─┤─◄

A Deception

Swell upon sham
The autonomy of mosquito wings
Embarks on the spoor of a celestial bandit
Erudite killer, more stupid
Than peevish, human, monster freaks.

I had not really expected Gahrazel to come and see me before he left, and was therefore very surprised when he shook me awake the following morning. "I thought you were dead!" he said. "You used to be such a light sleeper."

I pushed my hair out of my eyes, still half asleep. "You're here early, Gahrazel."

He walked up and down at the end of my bed and the constant movement, made me feel sick. "Sit down, for God's sake!"

"It's not that early," he said. "Remember, I lead a soldier's life now. Gone is the luxury of lying in bed in the morning." His voice was bitter.

"Is everyone else up?"

"Yes . . . Swift?"

"What? Pass me my clothes, will you?"

He sifted through the pile on the floor and tossed bits of it over to me. "Swift, I've neglected our friendship," he said, not looking at me.

"What's happened to remind you of that?" I asked, pulling on my trousers.

"Oh, nothing . . . Good God, what's happened to your back?"

I wasn't sure whether to feel proud or ashamed. I said nothing.

"Oh, I *see*," continued Gahrazel, suddenly much more like the har I remembered. "If Ithiel had done that to me, I'd have blacked his eye."

"Oh, would you!" I retorted. "Just think about the fact that Ithiel didn't feel the need to illustrate his passion so emphatically."

"My little Swift!" he cried. "It seems you follow in your father's footsteps as a wielder of power."

"So it does," I agreed.

"I think I shall miss Swift the child," Gahrazel said wistfully.

"I get the feeling you're here for a reason," I said. "You're upset."

"No, no," Gahrazel denied quickly. "Not upset . . . perhaps I *am* here for a reason, though. I need to talk to you."

"After breakfast," I decided.

"If you like."

We went down the stairs together, laughing, joking, pushing each other around, as we had done so many times before.

"I've just realized how much I've missed you," I said.

"Blame Terzian," Gahrazel said caustically.

He was offered breakfast, but refused, just drinking coffee and messing nervously with the cutlery, always glancing at the door. Terzian had already left the table, and in a strange way I was relieved. There was only Swithe left in the room, pouring over a report my father had given him to read. I could see Terzian's mark of black humor in this, but Swithe just held the papers with distaste, totally ignorant of any intent.

"The Gelaming will annihilate them!" Swithe declared, throwing down the papers.

"That does seem likely," Gahrazel agreed. "But who can know for sure?"

"What do you think?" Swithe asked intently.

Gahrazel would not commit himself. He spread out his hands and shook his head. "I'm not paid to think, just to skin the hides off any Gelaming we might meet."

"You never used to keep your opinions to yourself," I said drily.

Gahrazel shrugged.

After breakfast, I took him up to the long gallery. I knew we would not be disturbed there.

Gahrazel took a slim packet out of a top pocket. "Cigarettes," he said. "Do you want one?"

"What are they?" I asked, eyeing with interest the slim, white stick he put between his lips.

"Smoke to combat nerves," he said, inhaling deeply.

"Oh, like hemp," I said knowledgeably. It was something I knew about, but I'd never tried it.

"Not really," Gahrazel said. "Do you want one or not?"

I shook my head. "No. You always know more than me, don't you, Gahrazel?" He made me feel young again, too young.

He pulled a face. "Do I? I don't mean to." He smiled at me, and it wasn't totally without condescension.

"Well then, Gahrazel, what's the matter?"

He sat on the floor, his back to the window, and once again inhaled deeply off his cigarette. "I trust you," he said, blowing smoke rings at the ceiling.

"Should you?"

"I think so." He looked at me intently. "Swift, I hate what your father's done to me."

"What's he done?"

Gahrazel stared at his hands. There was a moment's pause before he spoke. "What he's tried to do. Among other things, make me like him, like my own father. I'm not at all like them, you know." His eyes bored into me, full of words he could not speak.

"I've always known that," I said and squatted down beside him. "But I did think you'd adapted quite well. As we'd seen nothing of you . . ."

Gahrazel made an irritated sound. "Don't be stupid!"

"Don't speak to me like that!" I snapped, stung.

He sighed and rubbed his face with his hands. "Sorry Swift." His voice was mocking.

"What is it then?" I asked, standing up.

He looked up at me and squinted. "I can't stay here."

"I didn't think you would. You're going south again, aren't you?"

"I can't do that either."

"What do you mean?" I asked apprehensively. I suppose I knew already.

"If I tell you . . . you might have to lie to your father later."

I nodded. "Alright, alright, what is it, Gahrazel?"

He took a deep breath. "I'm not going south with Terzian again. I can't! There are so many reasons, Swift . . . I'm going to the Gelaming. I'm taking Purah with me."

I shut my eyes and turned away from him with a sigh. "God!"

"You'll wish I hadn't told you."

"Your father!"

"I know. I had to tell you, Swift."

"Why?" I demanded. "Why didn't you just go?"

"I think you know the answer. Someone had to know. The chances are . . . well, perhaps we'd better not dwell on the possible consequences. I had to tell you, Swift. There was no-one else I could trust."

"When?"

"Ah, well, that's something I think it's better you don't know about, don't you?"

"Yes, I suppose so," I agreed. "Gahrazel, do you know what this means . . . if you're caught?"

"Oh yes," he said softly. "More than anyone, I know *that.*"

I thought of Leef. Were there many of them, feeling as Gahrazel did now? True Wraeththu perhaps?

"Gahrazel," I said. "You're not alone, are you?"

He looked around quickly, furtively, as if suddenly chilled. "What do you mean?"

"That you're not alone. There are others, aren't there . . . others that perhaps lack the guts at present to . . ."

"If I succeed Swift, it may give others the courage to follow me, yes."

"Oh God!" I pressed my forehead against the long window. Surely my father couldn't be so ignorant of the dissension among his hara. Now I, Terzian's son, had been told. Terzian's son. Forever, my home. I looked down the long gallery, at its beloved, warm, worn, familiar length. "You shouldn't have told me," I said. "I wish you hadn't!"

"Swift!" Gahrazel stood up behind me and put his arms around me. "Remember, I once told you that we'd both know all of this house some day. Maybe I meant more than just the bricks and stone . . ."

"Let go of me," I said. He didn't for a moment, but I did not warm to him. He sighed and his arms dropped away from me. I felt cold.

"There's so much you don't know, Swift," he said.

"I don't want to know! Just go, Gahrazel!" I could not look at him.

"Not even 'goodbye,' Swift?"

"Goodbye, Gahrazel."

"Will you wish me luck?"

"I can't!"

I heard him sigh. "Farewell, my friend," he said.

I listened to him walking away from me, numb to my innermost heart. "Gahrazel," I whispered to the window, watching it mist. "Gahrazel."

It was a turning point in my life. I had to decide where my loyalties lay. If Gahrazel had told me everything, as he should have done, my decision might have been different, but, as he said, I knew so little. One thing I was sure of, if Ponclast's son successfully defected to the Gelaming, there would be many willing, if not eager, to follow him. At that time, I thought the reason was mainly fear of the Gelaming, rather than sympathy with Gelaming ideals. After Gahrazel had left me in the long gallery, I stood for a while thinking about what he had said. I wanted advice from someone I too could trust. I couldn't keep my mouth shut, could I?

I found Cal in the drawing room, lazing like a cat. He was idly tormenting Limba with a rolled-up piece of paper (Limba is trusting, but stupid). I imparted my news with a suitable note of dread in my voice. "Oh, Terzian will kill them," was all he'd say. I made an exasperated noise, annoyed that he was taking this revelation so lightly.

"And if he doesn't find out until it's too late?"

"Do you care?" Cal asked me in a tired voice.

"Care? Oh, of course I don't! Let all my father's hara desert him and run squeaking to the Gelaming! Let them destroy us all. Let them destroy this house!"

Cal smiled indulgently at my outburst. "Oh dear," he said, stretching. "And how many of Terzian's hara are you expecting to make a run for it?"

"Enough," I answered stiffly.

"If you *really* think it's such a threat, there is nothing to worry about," Cal continued, spreading his arms.

"What?"

"Terzian will kill Gahrazel before he gets away."

"Oh!" I shouted in exasperation, turning away from him. Cal came to stand behind me. He put his hands upon my shoulders.

"He will know," he said.

"How?" I demanded angrily.

"How? Well, that is obvious. You will tell him."

"Cal!" I cried, turning round, striking away his hands. He looked surprised for a moment. "How can I do that? I am not even convinced that what Gahrazel is doing is wrong!"

"Wrong for yourself, for us . . ."

"I can't!"

Cal threw back his head and laughed. "Ah, the gray specter of betrayal!" he mocked. I would not speak. "There is only one thing you should think of in a time like this," he continued blandly, "and that is yourself. In the end, there is only you; nothing else matters."

"Cal . . ."

"Master of Galhea one day, perhaps?" He took my face in his hands and I did not resist. I looked into his violet eyes and thought of all the things they must have seen. Was it caught within them forever somewhere? Could I see those things if I looked hard enough? "Learn well the lessons of self-preservation," he said. "Be subtle, my lovely. Be so subtle that you do not even realize yourself what you are doing. Gahrazel . . ." He sucked in his breath and shook his head.

"But it may be for nothing!" I protested. "I may only be delaying the inevitable!"

"Nothing is inevitable!" Cal replied, smiling gently. I could not be sure that we were not speaking about completely different things. "Your Kakkahaar friends should have told you that," he continued. "The path of our lives divides endlessly before us. We only have the power to choose which road to take, but even that road may be forked . . ." He led me out into the garden, through the long windows, to let me see it, to let me look back at the house. "This is where you belong," he said and blew a fleeting vision of his breath across my face.

"Gahrazel is a fool!" I said bitterly, still torn, gazing up at Forever's glistening face.

"He is more than a fool. . . . He should never have told you his secrets. So stupid! He is weak. I think his downfall can be blamed on that!"

"Are you saying that he deserves to die?" I asked chilled.

"We all deserve to die," he answered.

It is not enough! I thought. All morning I agonized over what to do, avoiding everyone, sitting among the trees, where it was cold and the sun could not reach. I had so little time. Gahrazel would not have told me if he wasn't planning to leave very soon.

My father was not present at lunch, and later I saw that his study was empty. In the peaceful, sunny afternoon, I went in there and sat down in his worn leather seat. Master of Galhea one day, perhaps? A consort of my own, all these halls mine? I closed my eyes, shook my head. Which is the right way? Would it be my father's blood in my mouth that would make me betray a friend? Subtlety, subtlety, that was the key. Cal knew all about that, and he knew all about betrayal. If the Gelaming should win . . . ? We dwell in Forever . . . I smiled. My father had been young once. Hard to imagine, but true. Had he ever doubted himself? "I do not want to lose you," I said aloud to the empty room.

It is a terrible thing to make your heart go cold; terrible because it is so easy. Every day, a couple of hours before the evening meal, a messenger comes up the house from Galhea, bringing papers and notes for my father that may have collected in his town office during the day. It is the messenger's custom to stop by the kitchen for half an hour or so for refreshment and to exchange idle gossip with the house-hara. During this time, he generally leaves his leather bag of papers on the table in the hall. Then either Terzian or Ithiel take the day's mail out and put back anything to be taken down to Galhea. A plan formed in my head.

In the privacy of my room, I wrote a note in block capitals using my left hand. It said, PONCLAST'S SON IS A TRAITOR. HE GOES TO THE GELAMING. THIS I OVERHEARD. My fingers were damp as I wrote it and it was with shaking hands that I stuffed it into an envelope. At any moment, as I stealthily scuttled across the hall, I expected the kitchen doors to swing open and someone to catch me fiddling with the messenger's bag, but luck was with me and I completed the task without detection. As I ran back to my room, I was thinking. Now I am truly a Varr. Now I have learned how to kill. It had not been an easy decision.

In the night, voices woke me from a nightmare of accusing eyes. Lights downstairs had thrown a spectral glow over the garden. Between my half-open curtains, I could see the waving shapes of the trees and hear the gusting lash of the wind. Someone ran up the corridor toward my room and threw open the door. A voice called my name and that voice was deeply troubled.

I shivered, still half asleep. "Ithiel, is that you?"

"Get dressed!" he snapped. "Quickly! Now! Come on! Terzian wants you!"

My blood seemed to cataract to my feet. Could he know I'd written that note? I didn't want him to know it was me. I didn't want anyone else to know that Gahrazel had spoken to me about his plans.

My father was in the hall, looking up, still wearing his wolfskin coat. His anger was contained, but I could sense it clearly. He said nothing, but pointed at the floor by his feet. I ran down the stairs, robe flapping, hardly daring to say, "What is it?" He blinked at my question, turning his back on me, beckoning me to follow him. In his study he shut the door firmly behind me. There were just the two of us.

"My son," he said softly. I was quaking, grinning fatuously, and went to sit down. "Stand up!" he bawled. I nearly shot back to the door.

"What's wrong?" I asked him, innocence itself. Now, I realized, it was vital for me to be innocent.

"Don't you know?" he sneered. I shook my head. He stared at me until I dropped my eyes. "Well then, Swift, I shall tell you." He paced around the room a few times. I could tell he was longing to go absolutely mad, but that was not his way. "I've just returned from Galhea," he said. "Tonight, I find our enemies are nearer to us than I thought. Much nearer. Not in the south, not even beyond the fields of Galhea. No, it is closer than that!" His fist slammed down on the desk top. "Here!" he cried. "In Galhea, perhaps even in my own house!" I thought, If he shouts any louder my eyes will roll out onto the floor.

"I don't understand," I said, striving to inject a certain amount of indignation into my voice.

"Don't you? Don't you!" my father raged, lunging toward me. I toppled backwards into the chair behind me. His face was inches from my own.

I thought, My God, he will kill me too! and at that moment I could have confessed that it had been me who'd sent the note, but all I did was splutter, "I don't know! I don't! Whatever it is . . ."

His hand gripped my throat. I tried to writhe, swallow. With a wordless exclamation, he let me go and went to sit in his usual seat, putting his feet up on the desk, tearing and scattering the papers that lay on it. He rubbed his eyes with one hand. I felt as if I was swallowing acid. "Gahrazel," he said, and that one word froze my flesh.

"What . . . ?" My voice was barely a squeak.

"Gahrazel," Terzian said again. His hands clasped on the desk. He looked at me, directly. "Surely you remember Gahrazel, Swift. Ponclast's son, in *my* care? Surely you know the one!"

I stared at my hands. "Yes," I said.

"Well, apparently, he wants to leave us," my father continued.

"Leave us?" I peeped. "I don't understand. . . . What do you mean?"

"What I said. Perhaps I should add that his intended destination after departing Galhea was the south and the Gelaming!" His use of the past tense did not escape me. I managed a pathetic laugh.

"Gahrazel? Never!"

My father looked at me with an expression that was nearly dislike. "Never, Swift?" My mind was racing. All I could think was, I shall have to be clever . . . Terzian sighed deeply. "Let's not waste time, Swift. I know you were Gahrazel's closest friend. He must have talked to you. I can only assume you knew something of what he was planning. Look, I hardly ever spoke to him and *I* could see how dangerous he was becoming, his strange fancies! Don't tell me you knew nothing! Are you such a fool?"

I lowered my eyes. "I . . ."

Terzian snorted angrily and stood up. Papers flew everywhere. One fell at my feet and I bent to pick it up. My vision was blurring; I stared at the paper blindly. Terzian snatched it from my hands and I almost cried out. Did he relish the terror in my eyes? "Swift, nothing that happens in this house escapes my notice; nothing! You can be sure of that! I know Forever inside out. I know its deepest secrets, but . . ." He squatted down before me and took my shoulders in his hands. I was shaking uncontrollably. His voice was quieter. "But . . . there are two things, Swift, two things that I shall never know, never understand, completely. And those two things are Cobweb and yourself. . . . You're closed doors, both of you. Too much Sulh blood in you, too much magic. I am . . . wary of that, my son, very wary. If either of you should ever want to betray me . . ."

"Terzian! No!" I cried and his name felt unfamiliar to me. "Never, I swear, never!"

It was the truth, in a way; I think it was the truth.

"Swift," he said and there was pain in his eyes. "I have seen Gahrazel. This afternoon someone, I don't know who yet, gave me a message that implied something of what Gahrazel was up to. When confronted, he tried to deny it at first, but then his quarters were searched and all the supplies he'd been hoarding were found. He was taken into custody and . . . after a while admitted the accusation was true. I asked him one thing only and that was 'Why?' All he did was laugh and the one thing he said to me was, 'Ask your son, Terzian!' "

I tried to look away, but his hand caught hold of my chin.

"What did he mean by that, Swift?"

"I . . . I don't know!" I stammered, squirming in his hold, feeling my face fold and twist. At that moment, I hated Gahrazel more than I would have believed possible.

"What do you know?!" Terzian demanded.

"Alright!" I said, still trying to free myself. "Let me go. Please!"

He stood up and leaned against the desk, arms folded.

"I've never wanted to know about what Gahrazel believes in, father," I babbled helplessly. "We've drifted apart. We're no longer close friends. I don't *know* him. Not any more. Not since Purah came. . . . Once, once he did try to tell me something, but I didn't want to know. I told him that. I wouldn't listen . . ."

"When?"

I shrugged, resisting the urge to wring my hands in my lap, but only just. "I . . . I can't remember exactly."

"Swithe tells me that Gahrazel was here at the house yesterday," my father prompted. I could feel a laugh, uncontrollable and stupid, building up inside me. Swithe! All his high and righteous beliefs. The only truth is his own hide, I thought.

"Yes," I said, biting the inside of my cheek until the laughter went away. "Gahrazel was here." I looked at my father with Cobweb's eyes, huge and shadowed, hoping to melt him. "He came to say goodbye to me. By that I assumed he meant because he was going to go south again, with you . . ."

My father sighed and looked up at the ceiling.

"And why did you take him to the long gallery?" Why? I started to panic. Did he know everything already? Was he only tormenting me to hear my confession? "You needed privacy, Swift, that's obvious. What did you talk about?"

"Nothing, nothing important!" I insisted. I was so scared, reality started to shift. There was a buzzing in my ears.

"Why there? Why?"

"Because . . ."

"Why? Because why, Swift?" The whole house must have been able to hear him. I could imagine Yarrow and Bryony quaking in the kitchen, all the pots rattling around them, but of course, they were curled up in their beds asleep.

"Because, because . . ." My mind suddenly cleared with inspiration. "Because we . . ." I lowered my eyes modestly and made my voice quiet. "He didn't want anyone to know . . ." I looked up again beseechingly.

"What?"

"That . . ." I touched my brow with one hand trembling. "He wanted to take aruna with me. He said I might never see him again . . . but he didn't want anyone to know. Because of Purah, because of Bryony . . . oh, I don't know!"

"Because of me . . ." Terzian whispered softly to himself.

"I just went along with it. It was like a game . . ." I sighed deeply. My father must have been holding his breath. Now he let it out in one long, shuddering gasp. He rubbed his face with his hands. "So Swift, Gahrazel really didn't tell you he was thinking of running away . . . or anything else? You knew nothing. Can you swear to this?" From his voice, I could tell how important it was to him. What was it he feared Gahrazel might have told me?

"I knew nothing," I said softly. "His mind was closed to me of all but memories of our friendship. Nothing else . . . at all."

Terzian went to the cabinet where he kept his liquor and poured us both a glass of sheh. His hands were still shaking slightly. So were mine.

"I'm sorry," he said, clearing his throat and handing me a glass. His fingers, where they touched me, were cold. "I had to ask you, Swift. I hope you understand."

"Of course," I replied. "I should have told you at once, but. . . . What will happen to him?"

Terzian sucked in his cheeks, staring at the floor. He sighed. "I'm afraid I can't say. I don't know. Ponclast went to a settlement farther north two days ago. He's not expected back until the end of the week. Of course, I've sent messengers. Obviously, I can't make any decisions about this. It's his problem, I would say, wouldn't you?" He refilled his glass.

"Who do you think sent you the message?" I asked.

He did not even glance at me. "I don't know. Someone who's well known to Gahrazel, I'd have thought. Someone loyal to his tribe, who would prefer to stay anonymous because he had to be disloyal to a friend. I think it's best to leave it at that, don't you?"

I nodded vigorously.

"Swift, there is one thing I'd like you to do for me. You're friendly with the girl, aren't you?"

"Who, Bryony?" (Bryony was always "the girl" to Terzian.)

"Yes. Well, I had to have Gahrazel's accomplice shot. I don't need Ponclast's permission for that. I believe he was related to the girl."

"Brother," I said.

"I thought so. She's a good worker, I've no complaint about her work. She's good for the house. Cobweb likes her."

"You want me to tell her Purah is dead?"

"Yes. It would be better coming from you."

I stood up and put down my empty glass. Terzian touched my arm. "Swift, come here."

I found myself in the totally unexpected embrace of my father's arms. "I'm very proud of you," he said and kissed my hair. "Don't ever—"

"Terzian!" I interrupted gently. Was there strength in me he did not have?

"You must . . . you must take care of your hostling and little Ty when I'm gone," he said, with difficulty.

"I will, but of course Cal will be here too." My father's arms tightened around me.

"Yes, I know, but . . . Cal is not of our blood, Swift. It's different for him. I leave Forever in your hands. Soon, in a few days . . . I shall be gone. You must progress, Swift. Ithiel will help you. He knows. Realize what is important. I have to trust you! You will have to be wise beyond your years."

I understood then just how afraid he was, that he doubted whether he would ever return to us, yet he had to go on. "I hate them!" I cried. "The Gelaming; I hate them!"

"Yes, yes," he murmured. "Hate them, Swift, hate them with all your strength. That is something they have no control over . . . perhaps the only thing."

That day I'd learned two important lessons. The first, as I said before, was how to kill. The second, perhaps even more insidious, was how to lie. It didn't matter to Gahrazel which way I chose to betray him, but it did to me. I had not told my father what he'd said, not in words. Gahrazel had been right. I did have to lie to my father, but not in the way he'd thought.

In the morning, Bryony came to the drawing room in response to my summons, smiling and carefree, chattering until I wanted to scream. Obviously, gossip concerning events of the previous day had not yet filtered through to the kitchens. I looked upon this as my first act of responsibility as Terzian's son. I leaned against the mantelpiece as my father would have done. I began to speak and watched her as all the color and gaiety gradually drained from her face and a look of bewildered anguish came to take its place.

"We can only assume that he knew what he was doing, Bryony," I said. "He must have known the risk . . ." She shook her head and would not speak. Her eyes were dry, but I could see the muscles moving in her jaw. "It was Gahrazel!" I exclaimed. "He did this! It was his idea!" There she sat, small and hunched on the edge of a chair, while I tried to convince her that a terrible act was not terrible. All I wanted to do was shift the blame in her eyes, absolve my people, heap Gahrazel with culpability because he would never be able to speak for himself.

"Is Gahrazel dead too?" she asked at last.

"No. . . . His fate has not been decided yet," I answered.

"No, of course not," she said bitterly.

Once again, Forever held its breath. Terzian carried on making preparations for the trek south, grimly waiting for Ponclast to return. I had word that Gahrazel had asked for me, but I turned my back on him. I felt he had tried to drag me down with him, and wondered if this was because he suspected it had been me who'd betrayed him. Nobody had a good word for him any more. Suddenly, everyone had been suspecting something like this happening for ages, even Swithe. Cal made a half-hearted attack on Swithe one evening over his rather abrupt change of heart, but was not interested enough to pursue it. I could see that Swithe had been thoroughly shaken up by what had happened. It was one thing to moan about Terzian behind his back, but it was something else entirely to stand up and be honest and face Terzian's wrath. Gahrazel was being held captive in Galhea. He never set foot in Forever again.

When Ponclast returned, an emergency meeting was held in the house. I saw Ponclast once in the hall. His face was gray; he looked right through me. I felt quite sorry for him. Obviously, both Terzian and Ponclast were aware of the detrimental effect it would have had on their warriors' morale if Gahrazel had got away with his defection. The whole affair was seen as high treason and the punishment would have to fit the crime. Terzian asked me if I would like to be present at the meeting. This was an honor, but I declined. Terzian did not press it. He was still under the impression that my last moments with Gahrazel had been spent aflame with the ecstasy of aruna. It is a sacred act, even to Varrs. "This must be hard for you," he said.

Ithiel had been sent some miles east on some errand or another. I heard my father say to him before he left, "Take the girl with you." I was surprised by this act of understanding. I knew that he looked upon humans with the same amount of respect as he looked upon dogs. I don't think Purah had ever ceased to be human in his eyes, but because Bryony was part of his staff and had proved her worth, she was less human than honorary har. Terzian always looked after the things he valued, or so I thought.

On the evening following the meeting, Leef came to the house to report to my father. Now he had been promoted again, to Ithiel's second in command, and was currently carrying out all Ithiel's duties while he was away. Perhaps his second promotion had been some kind of consolation because he had lost the honor of taking part in my Feybraiha. It seemed likely. We passed each other in the hall as he went to my father's study and he gave me a curt greeting. I suffered a pang of remorse, being only too aware of how once I had led him on to believe I desired him. Still jumpy because of Gahrazel, I decided I'd try to smooth things over between us. Secure in a new sense of power, I summoned one of the house-hara and told him to wait outside Terzian's study until Leef came out. "Take him to the red salon," I said. "And have someone build a fire in there."

It was a room we hardly ever used and all the furniture was uncomfortable in there. It was a room for formality, perhaps not the best that I could have chosen, but I knew there would be no privacy anywhere else and I shrank from asking Leef to go anywhere upstairs with me.

Fortifying myself with several glasses of wine in the kitchen, not even sure why I wanted to see him, I made Leef wait for ten minutes before I went in to him. "Oh, have I kept you waiting?" I asked, pausing at the door, with what I hoped looked like magnificence. Leef smiled uncertainly, standing in the middle of the room, awkward as ever. He never liked being in Forever. He never relaxed there. Now I too had seen a little of the Terzian he knew and feared, so I was more sympathetic.

After a few minutes' stilted conversation, I said, "So, now that you're Ithiel's second, you won't have to go south with my father again, will you?"

"No," he agreed warily. "It was rather a surprise. Unexpected. Ithiel never paid me much attention before." I could see him wondering what I wanted, what he was doing there.

"In a way, it was because of me that you were promoted," I said, hoping to make him think better of me.

"Was it?" he said, wondering whether he should thank me or not. His pride won; he didn't thank me. I offered him some wine, one of Yarrow's best, and he sat down hesitantly in a stiff chair, appraising the room, no doubt thinking how horrible and unfriendly it was. "Why did you want to see me?" he asked.

"I don't know," I admitted. "When we passed each other in the hall, I thought . . . You're cross with me, aren't you!"

"Cross with you? Why should I be?" he asked defensively.

"I'm not teasing you," I said.

"No?"

"No. My Feybraiha . . . it was something I had no control over," I said.

"Look!" Leef stood up hurriedly. "I don't want to discuss anything like this with you."

"Don't go! I just want to apologize . . ."

"Apologize?" For a moment he relaxed enough to be angry. "For what? Maybe I presumed too much. Hints dropped by you, then by Ithiel. Next, I'm told that circumstances have changed. I need no explanation other than that! Now, if you don't mind . . ." He put his glass down clumsily on a spindly-legged table that rocked dangerously.

"I didn't know they'd actually asked you!" I exclaimed helplessly.

"They didn't! I made a fool of myself, that's all!" I envisaged how he must have told all his friends. It must have been excruciating for him, even more so, having to be at the house attending the celebrations.

"I'm sorry," I said inadequately.

"Is there anything else?" he asked, with the coldest of eyes.

"No . . ."

"Then if you'll excuse me . . ."

He sidled past me as if I would strike out and bite him.

Later, my father summoned me to his study. I was still feeling distressed over the incident with Leef. Terzian looked very tired, his face white, his hair disheveled. It seemed to me that he was in no condition to begin traveling. From his appearance, it looked as if he hadn't slept for a week.

"It's over," he said, as soon as I'd shut the door behind me.

For a moment we just looked at each other. I thought he was upset because he'd been wondering about what it would have been like if it had been me and not Gahrazel. I reached to touch his hand.

"What happened?" I asked.

He closed his eyes and curled his fingers over my own. "Poison," he answered, as if he had a mouthful of it himself. "They . . . they made him drink poison."

"Were you there?"

He nodded. I had never seen him so distressed, but then Gahrazel's death could not have been a pleasant spectacle. Few substances are lethal to Wraeththu. Only the tribe of Uigenna have the art of it and what deadly elixirs they possess are death in its most agonizing, terrible form. Ponclast had obviously considered the bullet or the blade too quick a release for his traitor son.

I went to Cal with my grief. "This has been one of the worst days of my life," I told him.

"It is only the beginning," he replied mercilessly. "Just a foretaste of horrors to come. I know. Life just works that way."

CHAPTER NINE

>━┝━⟨╋⟩━✛━⟨╋⟩━┥━◄

Destiny

Callasity gaping through the gashes
At tender, childhood dreams,
Can no longer recognize the fruit
Disfigured on indignant vines.

I began my training in earnest. Once the Varr armies had headed south once more, amid pomp and sorrow, Ithiel started to teach me how to fight, how to defend myself, how to kill. I applied myself to my studies once more. Aihah, the Kakkahaar, had left me several books to look through; far from enough for me to gain any great benefit, but at least it gave me something to build on.

Sometimes, Cal would come to my room at night. Sometimes we would only sleep together, needing company, but other times, we would scream and struggle and tear at each other until the dawn. He was voracious and the merest touch of him kindled my responsive frenzy. I knew that it didn't have to be that way, but we needed that rage somehow. We had so much pent-up energy, there was no other way to release it yet. Once, while we were feeding upon each other like vampires, howling like animals, Tyson woke up in the next room and started to cry in terror. For a moment, we were still, staring wide-eyed at each other. Then we began to laugh. I seemed to have changed so much, the sensitivity of my childhood dulled, a new hardness flowering within me.

News rarely reached us from the south. The supernatural mist of the Gelaming seemed to have closed around the Varrs. They had found a way through, but nothing could follow them. Could anything come back out? Once, I tried to communicate with the Kakkahaar, but could not manage it. Either my art was too feeble or the Gelaming's power too strong. Most likely, it was a combination of both. With Cobweb's help, I could achieve the right state of mind, but where there should have been light was only a grey, impenetrable void, and I shrank from that.

Dreams of greater power began once more to prowl through my sleeping mind. Often, Cal would have to shake me awake, alarmed by my muffled cries. Now, I could rarely remember the events I dreamed, even though I longed to. I knew I dreamed of a face that both scared and thrilled me, but I could never recall its appearance on waking. Cal would pull me from sleep and cry, "What is it?" and all I could reply was, "Eyes! Eyes!" Such haunting. It filled me with grief.

* * *

At Festival, the household tried to carry on as usual. Cobweb invited Ithiel's hara up to the house and Yarrow began to prepare his customary, sumptuous fare. We got most of what we needed from Galhea, but the other things, more exotic foods and drink, which had once been obtained from farther afield, were no longer available to us. Two days before Festival night, we all gathered branches of evergreen from the gardens and decorated the house. That was when my father's presence was missed most. It was the first time since I had been born that he had not been home for Festival.

We had a small, miserable party in the drawing room, where everyone drank too much and didn't get happy. Leef was there, but he barely looked at me. Bryony sat by the fire and, after her third glass of sheh, began to weep silently. Cobweb went to comfort her and I saw Cal looking at him.

"Do you still think about the ivy?" I asked him.

"Most days," he admitted. I laughed and everyone looked at me.

When everyone had gone home or gone to bed, Cal and I lay beside the fire, sharing our cynicism. Some part of him was strangely distracted.

"He hasn't slept much recently, has he?" he said, unexpectedly. "Haven't you noticed?"

"My hostling, I presume," I answered acidly. "No, he looks tired. He misses Terzian, I suppose, in spite of everything."

"In spite of me, you mean."

"Yes, in spite of you."

"Do you think he knows something?"

"He tells me everything," I said. "What can he know that we don't?"

"You know him better than I do."

"Oh, I don't know. What with your constant and careful study of Cobweb . . ."

"Are you jealous?" he teased.

"No, of course not." I rolled onto my back.

"He must be lonely."

"Cobweb is always lonely!"

Cal stood up and looked at himself in the mirror above the mantelpiece.

"Swift . . ." he said.

I sat up. "I wouldn't advise it, Cal." I could see clearly what he was thinking.

"Now or never," he said, cheerily. He went to the door.

"Will I see you later?" I called.

"I hope not!" he replied.

For a while, I just sat staring at the shapes in the flames, shadows leaping beyond the hearth, thinking, what is happening to us? We are slipping, we are slipping. . . . Had Terzian ever said to Cal, "What is mine is yours"? Had he? Wood popped in the fire. I threw on another log. Behind me, stretching away, the house was silent. My ears strained to hear through that silence. There was nothing. I went out into the hall and stood looking up the dark stairs, one hand on the bannister, one foot on the bottom step.

Bryony came out of the passage that led to the kitchen. "Shall I turn off the lights down here?" she asked and I must have nodded. Her footsteps died away, into the house. The hall was full of the smell of greenery; ivy hanging down from the lights, softly moving with the chime of glass, torn ivy on the red stair carpet.

Cobweb's room was empty but his chair had been knocked over and there was a faint hint of outrage in the atmosphere. I ran up the corridor, up the few stairs that led to Cal's room, thinking that Cal had dragged or led Cobweb there, but the door was wide open and the room beyond in darkness. I was experiencing a strong sense of *déjà vu*. This had happened before. I looked in on Ty, but he was sleeping peacefully. All the doorways looked hostile and silent, sealed mouths. Behind any one. . . . A single, slight, echoing noise reached my ears. Prickles of cold broke out all over my skin. I prowled back down the haunted corridor and paused outside my father's door. Was anyone in there? I reached to knock, then hesitated. Perhaps Cobweb did know something. Were they in there? My father's room . . . Gahrazel's face was suddenly before my eyes, laughing. I could see him young again. Again, almost inaudible, a muffled sound reached me from within the room. It could have been anything; fear, anger, pain or submission. We shall know all of this house one day . . .

Before I realized what I was doing, I was pelting back along the corridor, toward the steep, forbidding stairs that led to the upper stories. Winter lived there, my breath was steam and the eerie, violated darkness was terrible. But instinct guided me and horror of the waiting dark could not touch me. I could almost hear the echo of our voices, Gahrazel's and mine, so long ago, a lifetime away, scampering through these forgotten halls. His voice was so real to me. "Do you know nothing, Swift?"

I found the room quite easily. Something flaked from the handle when I turned it. A supernatural rod of yellow light pointed upwards from the floor within. I went toward it and bent my face into its glow. Traveling down this ray of light, I saw below me, through a splintered hole that had waited here all this time for just this moment, my father's room. There were leaves everywhere as if the garden had bursting through the windows; a feeling of cold. I could sense the sparking presences of Cobweb and Cal, facing each other like unleashed elementals, but I could not see them. I heard Cal cry, "What will happen to us?!" and his voice lacked its usual confidence.

My hostling, when he answered, sounded chill and distant. "I have seen it . . ."

"Seen? Seen what?"

Cobweb's voice was merely a whisper. "I saw a great smoke. You went into it. Swift was with you . . ." There was a pause and then he spoke again, ragged with haste. "You must go that way. It is your destiny . . ."

Cal moved into my line of sight. He had hold of Cobweb by the wrist, which was bloodless, the hand curled into a dead claw. "Don't speak in riddles!" Cal cried impatiently.

"That's what I saw."

Cobweb's dead voice made me shiver. I steadied myself and bent lower to the floor.

"When?" Cal demanded. He did not get an answer. "Oh yes, of course! This is what you've been waiting for, isn't it? Have you made it happen? You will be glad to see me gone! Is this a lie?"

"No, I have not lied."

"But you hate me!"

"I speak the truth!" Cobweb wriggled away from Cal's grasp and put his taloned hands on Cal's shoulders as if to shake him. "Their Tigron is with them!" he cried, and his face was unbelievably white. The white of marble, of death. He crumpled into Cal's arms, so utterly without design, and it seemed Cal was nearly weeping.

"What do you mean? Tell me! Who are they?"

"Gelaming," my hostling rasped. "I have seen them . . . Not here . . . in the smoke, in the mist above the lake. You will go to them, both of you, through the forest of fear, into the mouth of your sin, where the beast speaks, where the beast walks and his blood is our blood. Oh! There is no escaping . . ."

I too wanted to scream, "What are you talking about?" but it was Cal's voice, not my own, ringing in my ears.

"Soon . . ." Cobweb straightened up and his hands fluttered to his face. "You want to bind me, but I am bound already," he said.

"Cobweb . . . ?"

My hostling backed away, very slowly. "You must take me; flesh to flesh, soul to soul. I have seen that too . . . many times."

"Is it something that you want?"

Cobweb frowned, shook his head. "It is just something I have dreamed of."

"Tell me about the dreams."

"Not yet. Oh . . ." Cobweb sat down on the edge of my father's bed. "I shall be left alone and there will be a time of glass, like shattering, like shards of light, and the past shall come back like a shimmering veil . . . I shall be left alone, but not for long . . . Cal?"

Cal did not even bother to conceal the fear in his face. Mostly I could see only the top of his head, but his body was held rigid as if ready to flee.

"I want you now," my hostling said, with bizarre sanity, and held out his arms. I denied the vision of sanity. He is mad, I thought, quite mad.

"I remember you, how you were before," Cal said to him.

Cobweb shrugged. "Faces from the past are always with us. They follow you too, Cal."

"Is it Seel?"

"You are obsessed with that. Too much is hidden from me; I cannot say."

Silence settled around them like dust. They were both staring at the floor deep in thought and then their heads rose like snakes, their eyes met.

"I don't like this room," Cal said, rubbing his arms. "It is cold."

Cobweb tried to stand and faltered, his body trembling, shivering, his breath misting. Cal lifted him up, trying to gather, control, the sprawling, shuddering limbs. Cobweb appeared to have sunk into a trance. His head lolled over Cal's arm; his eyes were open, but blank. Cal held him reverently, gazing with undisguised tenderness into his empty face. They did not know they were being watched.

I heard them leave the room. The light went out and I was left in darkness, conscious only of the wind-sounds beating at the house, windows rattling. Gahrazel was in this place, poisoned and bitter. I shuddered and ran quickly to the door.

I didn't think I'd be able to sleep. What were Cal and Cobweb doing? Did they share aruna or anger and bitter words? I surprised myself by waking up and realizing that half my thoughts had been dreams.

Cobweb came to my room soon after. I had never seen him so radiant, but it was under the surface. Superficially, he was nervous and harried. He didn't know how to tell me, yet he felt he had to. I made it easier for him.

"So, what happened with you and Cal then?"

Cobweb grimaced at me and then came to sit next to me on the bed, plucking restlessly at the covers. It was hard to believe that we were not the same age, harder still to believe that he was my hostling. He shook his head and said, "Oh, Swift!"

I touched his face. "Jealousy and desire are not the most comfortable of friends," I said.

Cobweb smiled ruefully. "It must always have been there, of course. Strange, I don't often deceive myself, only other people. Now I remember I am not only soume, but ouana too. Perhaps I have woken up, perhaps some part of me shall die."

"We've had enough talk of death!" I remarked sharply.

Cobweb stood up and shook out his hair. "Strange that someone else should find me real," he said.

Later, Cal told me about Cobweb's visions. I could see how much he thought of my hostling by the fact that he would not speak of anything else that had happened between them. "It seems that one day we'll be heading south together," he said, corroding a certain dreaminess with cheer. "I wonder when."

"We must enjoy this Festival," I said dubiously. "It may be our last."

Cal laughed when I said that. It was just the kind of thing he liked to hear.

* * *

It took some months for something to happen, however. Spring was approaching and our lives had lapsed into a regular, if tentative routine. I thought that my brother should begin his education far sooner than I had done and spoke to Moswell about it. Tyson might not be allowed a proper childhood. His would certainly be nothing like mine had been, whatever happened. I used to think that, but for the threat of the Gelaming, we could have been truly happy at that time. There seemed to be no hatred in the house any more. All the disruptive spirits had left it. But we all knew how temporary this contentment might be. My father had been gone for so long and we had had no word from him, not even rumor. It was as if the Varrs had simply vanished into the mist, as if they had never been.

It all crept up on us stealthily. I, and Ithiel too, had expected messengers, torn and wounded, galloping madly, riding north to bring us news. But it was nothing like that.

One evening, Ithiel came to me while I sat in my father's study. I liked to spend time in there, for it seemed to bring me closer to Terzian. Also, I found it interesting to read through his notes and books. I learned much about how he ran Galhea and how he had organized his war-torn people when they had first arrived there. Already the days were getting longer and the house was full of sunset, sleepy and relaxed. I was sipping coffee, feet up on the desk, gazing out at the garden. One thing that I had initiated since my father's departure was that intruders were not to be shot on sight as Terzian had once ordered. I gave the excuse that more could be learned by interrogating strangers than by butchering them, but the truth was that indiscriminate killing appalled me. Perhaps it was because I always imagined being in that situation myself. Anyway we had no other way of getting news.

It seemed I'd had to change so much and in a short space of time. Galhea needed my father; he was not there. I was all they could have, the only son. Daily, I would go to the administration office my father used in Galhea and listen to his people's problems. I was not a trader or a farmer and had complained to Ithiel that he was surely far better equipped to deal with the people's queries and settle their disputes than I. Ithiel only smiled and patted me on the shoulder. "Trader, farmer, you certainly aren't," he said. "But you are *fair*, Swift. That's what they need. You are Terzian's son and I shall help you as much as you want me to, but it must be your mouth they hear the words from, not mine." Help me he did. It was obvious why Terzian relied on him so much.

Now Ithiel came into the study and smiled, amused at my unselfconscious imitation of my father. "Intruders have been found in the forest," he said. "They were making for Galhea . . ."

"Human or hara?" I asked.

"Well, both actually," he replied. "A band of wanderers, like gypsies. They call themselves Zigane, which I understand means gypsy anyway. Tribeless people banded together. Their leader is a woman . . . she is what they call a pythoness, a sorceress and . . ." He looked uncomfortable. "Swift, she has asked to see you."

"By name?"

He nodded. "Her name is Tel-an-Kaa."

"How strange," I said, more to myself. "You had better find out what she wants of me, and who sent her!"

Tel-an-Kaa, the pythoness, would not speak to anyone but me. To Ithiel, she would only keep repeating that her message was for Terzian's son alone; when I sent Swithe to her, she would not even acknowledge his presence. Something about the Zigane commanded respect. They had hara among them; Ithiel's soldiers were loath to use aggression against them; it was a superstitious fear, more than anything. I held my ground for three days and at the end of that time, sent Ithiel to the pythoness with word that I would visit her at midday.

The Zigane were indeed gypsies, or at least had modeled themselves upon gypsy appearance. They had set up a camp in the middle of the town, already selling trinkets and cloth to the Varrs. They lived in gaudy, decorated caravans and affected a matching mode of attire. We were told they worshiped snakes and that the pythoness could scry in reptile tongue.

It was not easy to tell the humans and hara apart. Both races were lean, tanned and sinewy, their clothes entirely similar. Ithiel conducted me to Tel-an-Kaa's caravan. It looked no larger than the rest, although it was bigger on the inside than it appeared on the outside. I ducked into the perfumed gloom of the interior and had my first glimpse of her. She was sitting on the edge of a couch, like a girl, her velvet gown worn and shabby, long, pale hair falling over her shoulders like rags, yet I could tell in an instant that I was looking at a queen. Her small face was serenity and splendor, half smiling, full of secrets. It is in the blood, true royalty. Perhaps we recognized that feature in each other.

"Greetings, son of Terzian," she said and her voice was low and clear.

I motioned for Ithiel to leave us and he shut the door behind him. Now we were in another world, contained and silent. "What is it you wish to say to me?" I asked.

She grimaced. "Please, sit down. Would you like wine?"

I sat beside her and she handed me a long-stemmed glass.

"I was sent to find you," she said.

"By whom?"

She smiled, shaking her head. "We are not fond of this land, but we were persuaded by the fact that Terzian and his executioners would not be here . . ."

"Who sent you?"

"I regret I cannot answer you. I bring news."

"Of my father?" I asked quickly, noting my voice rise uncontrollably in timbre.

"It may not be welcome . . ."

"Not . . . is he . . . ?"

She shook her head before I could speak the word. "Not that. He went into the mist."

"I know that!" (Was that all she had to tell me?)

"Of course. They may have taken him, Swift. I don't know. It would be so easy for them, so exquisitely easy. He just went right to them, didn't he?"

"The Gelaming!"

She reached to touch my face with one small, white, childlike hand, and I thought, This must all be a dream. I shall wake up in a minute.

"You must not wait here for them, Swift," she said.

I looked into her eyes, which were hesitant and grave. She was old-young, as Wraeththu are old-young. She was tired and she was powerful.

"Tel-an-Kaa, you must come to my house," I said.

Tel-an-Kaa: a name of power, a sound of mystery. I never found out how old she was or her origins, or even how she had formed her band of wanderers. Perhaps it did not interest her to tell me, perhaps she only guarded the shroud of her enchantment. She was naturally wary of going with us alone to Forever, but adopted a pose of being too polite to suggest that any of her people should accompany us. Out of courtesy, I invited five of them to make up her party. "We rarely have guests now," I told her. "Our cook is one of the best in the country and he will be pleased to be able to show off his art again." Ithiel and I had arrived on horseback, and as it would have appeared improper for her to walk beside us (none of the Zigane horses were exactly what you'd call riding stock), Ithiel ordered some of his hara to bring a cart. Once more I reflected upon the indefinable quality of the pythoness that demanded respect. Even Ithiel felt it and he had never admitted to a great love of humankind.

On the way back to the house, I trotted my horse beside her. "Why is it that you have sought me out?" I asked.

She smiled her careful, cat's smile. "Oh, but I have already said, I had a message."

"Someone has paid you well then?" I suggested, but she would not answer. I caught Ithiel's eye and could see that he was sharing my suspicions. Varrs are the most feared of Wraeththu in Megalithica, yet this outlandish gypsy queen had wandered insouciantly into our lands, without precaution or defense. It was uncanny. Perhaps more uncanny was the way in which we treated her. Was it just my influence? Because of Bryony, women fascinated me for their mercurial minds and their unpredictable disposition, but I would never have imagined that I would come to treat a human with such deference.

Tel-an-Kaa appraised my home with a critical eye. She bowed before Cobweb and said, "Your name is known to us," which, as she had anticipated, pleased him greatly.

Yarrow prepared us a sumptuous lunch, which the Zigane consumed with undisguised enthusiasm. "It is some time since I have eaten as well," Tel-an-Kaa confided to Cobweb. She resisted all attempts by our household to draw her out about the message she carried for me, light-heartedly mocking all serious questions. Cal watched her steadily and I could tell that she was conscious of his dislike.

"You are lucky our noble lord is absent," he said to her. "Only Swift is against the slaughter of strangers. Perhaps you owe your life to him."

Only when Cal spoke to her did the Pythoness look uncomfortable. "We would not be here if Terzian had not been away," she said. "His leaving is the sole reason for us being here."

"Oh?" Cal said archly. "And perhaps you'd like to expand on that sole reason . . . ?"

"What I have to say is for Terzian's son alone," she replied, but she did not touch her food again after that.

After lunch, I took her to the conservatory, where it was warm and private. Bryony brought us wine and honey cakes. I could see that she was not impressed with Tel-an-Kaa either, but that was probably just Bryony being female and territorial.

"I am surprised to see a woman in this house," the Pythoness remarked. I decided not to answer her. Perhaps she was here to gather information about us. I resolved to reveal as little as possible.

"I think, perhaps, you had better tell me the real reason for your being here," I said. "You spoke obliquely of my father being taken by the Gelaming, but I doubt if you can produce proof of that. You spoke of messages, while telling me nothing. If you think I am unlike my father in some ways, you are right, but my patience is not limitless. If I decide you are a danger to us, I will not hesitate to order your extinction."

She inclined her head graciously. "But of course! I respect your position, Swift. In your shoes I would think likewise. I admit I have walked into your home with only a handful of vague hints and rather too much bravado, but I too have to be cautious. You are spoken well of and we expected to feel safe coming here, but I could not be entirely sure. You are Terzian's son after all and I am convinced his blood is thicker than most."

I smiled, relaxing enough to sit down.

"Well then, why *do* you want to see me?"

"Why?" Her eyes swerved away from mine with the grace of flight. "You will be annoyed when I say that some things I cannot tell you . . ."

She looked surprised at my laughter. "Oh, I have grown up with that sentence ringing through my head!" I explained. "Throughout my life I have had to put up with hidden things. That you should say it now seems only natural."

"It is true. I cannot tell you who sent me. My master would remain anonymous," she said. Her fingers idly traced patterns in the wrought-iron table at her side; the honey cakes were untouched. "In the south . . . there is a great strangeness in the south. Magic, conflicting magic has warped the land. Time and space have been injured. It is true that your father went straight to the Gelaming. Although the desert tribe, the Kakkahaar, breached the Gelaming's defenses, the Gelaming still had the power to choose where that breach should be. . . . Through my master, Swift, they have asked for you. They have no love of war, no desire for pain. Through you, pure-born as you are, they hope to unite the northern tribes—"

"Wait!" I interrupted quickly. "I can never speak for any people other than my own, here in Galhea. It is true that I too have no love of war, and I would like to see peace restored to our lands, but the hara further north have never seen me. They have probably never even heard of me. How can I speak for them? They are Varrs. In Galhea, our way of life has maybe made us soft, but I can assure you, that is not the case in Ponclast's domain. The har who can cold-bloodedly order the murder of his own son will not listen to me. I can do nothing!"

She nodded thoughtfully. "You are right. Perhaps that is not exactly what I meant . . ."

I stood up. "Have the Gelaming sent you, Pythoness?" I demanded. "Is this their way of defeating us? Are you here to worm your way into Galhea's heart and set poison there?"

"No," she replied, unruffled. "I told you; my master sent me. Let us say that, in this matter, he adheres to neither side. As for the Gelaming's motives, I am not qualified to say . . ."

"You must agree," I told her, "that this all seems highly suspicious. Only a fool would trust you. Only a fool would ride south into what is literally the unknown, because you suggest it."

She rubbed her forehead. "Yes, I suppose so . . . I realize I have to convince you. I would be held in contempt if I could not succeed."

"Convince me then."

She looked up at me wearily, leaning on her hand. "Convince you? How? All I have to say is that you must ride south and trust in Fate. Perhaps your father's life depends on it . . . perhaps. In your heart, you must know you are irresistibly drawn to what is waiting for you. Your dreams will have been forewarning you for quite some time, I think. Remember them now. Do you sense danger? You don't, do you! You think you ought to, but you can't. You are strong, Swift, strong and good. I can see that for myself. Galhea seems like yours now. It seems like a place untouched by the horror beyond its fields. I speak from experience. It would astound you."

"It seems you know me," I said, wondering.

"I feel I do," she replied. "Give me your hand."

Her female flesh felt no different from mine, yet we were worlds apart.

"See this," she said stroking my palm. "This is the line of destiny. It cuts deep; so straight, so true. Heart and head without blemish. The line of head is separate from the line of life; this symbolizes your intellect, your early development. You are passionate, but not governed by your passions. The only difficulty is . . . now."

"Now!" I exclaimed.

"An artistic hand," she said, thinking aloud.

"Is it really possible," I said softly, "what the Gelaming believe, human and hara sharing this world; the concept of harmony? Is it really possible?"

The Pythoness pulled a wry face. "They do not doubt it," she said, "but if it is possible, it will be sanctified by blood."

"Fighting is a dream to me," I said. "I have only heard of it. I have never seen death . . ."

"You will," she answered. "Long ago, I have heard, maybe in a saner, more aquatic age, when a temple was built, it demanded a life. Perhaps the temple that the Gelaming seek to build is so great, so beyond our grasp, only a thousand lives will make it live; I don't know. I'm only a poor girl after all."

We both laughed and I took her hand. "I do believe you," I said.

"Your instincts have not failed you," she replied.

So, my destiny would lead me at last to the south and the wild magic that lay there. In my heart, I was afraid that I could never be ready to face whatever might be waiting for me, yet I heeded the call, like my father had done before me, perhaps. Would I find him there? He had been gone for so long without us hearing news that it was as if he had already died. Perhaps he had. Would we have known? Could Cobweb's intuition penetrate the barrier that kept him from us?

After my talk with the Pythoness in the conservatory, my mind was already made up. Hadn't my hostling known this would happen? It was Fate, and there could be no other way. Even so, I was nervous of telling anyone. I anticipated their scorn, their amazement, their anger.

In the evening, we ate out on the lawns, the smoky aroma of cooking meat drifting around us, the light of torches eating at the sky. I could smell the vitality of spring in the air. It was a smell of something rushing in, a focusing, and great excitement. Something was waiting for me. Now I turned toward it and the pull was stronger. I wore a fur coat draped around my shoulders, but could not eat. Two of Tel-an-Kaa's troupe were musicians, and soon the darkness was alive with the fairy music of their strange echoing strings, the rhythmic mumble of a speaking drum. Shapes swayed in the leaping light of the torches, hissing fat spat down onto the glow beneath the meat and I could hear laughter. It was as if I was somewhere else, looking through a window at the lawns of Forever. Fighting disorientation, I walked toward the lake.

There is nowhere on this earth so eerie, so haunted or so beautiful as that spot in my father's garden. Moonlight touched the uneven surface of the lake, around me tall cypress trees nodded their lofty heads in a slight breeze and I could see the flicker of white that was the summerhouse between the branches. I had not been there since that time when Cal and Cobweb had been there. When I tried to open the door, it was stuck, but eventually, in a sigh of flaking paint, it gave in to my demands and squealed open. I sat down on the lip of the lily bowl. Pale light fell in through the glass across the tiled floor. My heart was heavy. I was grieved and exultant at the same time. (Is that possible?) No-one could tell me exactly what Fate had in store for me. Would I go to my death?

I reached down, under the rim of the stone bowl, searching for the tap that would turn on the fountain. I shivered as webs brushed my skin. Resisting, as the door had done, the fountain tap gradually turned and life spurted into the ancient mechanisms. With a shudder and a few abortive bursts, water finally shot upwards out of the stone animal's mouth, turning its scaly flanks dark with moisture. I watched it. Everything was black and white, or gray. I listened to the water sounds. I dipped my fingers in the pool.

When I heard the door to the summerhouse scrape open, I looked up, thinking it would be Cal, or Cobweb. Only they knew me well enough to know where to find me. Instinct guided the three of us in scented circles around each other. But it was neither of them. I saw Leef standing there and knew immediatly that this was just another intrinsic rightness of the whole situation. Leef and I had had our differences in the past, it is true, but circumstances, even roles, had changed in Galhea. Maintaining a worn-out atmosphere of resentment and bitterness was something none of us had time for any longer. I smiled and said, "Come in, come in."

"What are you doing here, all alone?" he asked. His voice was slightly slurred.

"Oh, just thinking," I replied. "Did you follow me?"

"Mmmm. To my cost, no doubt."

"Ah, there speaks a sore heart!" I said lightly.

Leef pulled a face and leaned against the doorframe. "There is no shame in wanting only the best, is there?"

I shook my head. "No, but I feel that what you say is only flattery."

"It's just my opinion, of course."

We both started to laugh, the fountain sounds seemed to fade right away, and he walked across the floor toward me.

"What's going on, Swift?"

"What do you mean? Is this why you followed me?" I asked, playing for time.

"One of the reasons . . . Zigane! A woman demanding to speak with you and then you allowing it, even inviting her and her ragged followers into your home. . . . What did she tell you, Swift?"

"A message, that's all. Come here. Sit by me."

I didn't tell him everything, of course, only what was necessary. He made a few indignant noises, but did not interrupt me. After I had finished speaking, he said, "And of course you've decided to ride south now." I ignored his dry tone.

"Yes. What else can I do? Wait here forever . . . or until it's too late? I'm not sure I have anything to lose. I'm not sure."

Leef shook his head at the floor. "Are you going alone?"

"I don't think so . . ."

"Swift, it will be dangerous!"

"Yes." I stood up, pulling the fur closer to my body. For a while we argued half-heartedly, he pointing out the dangers, me justifying the cause. I told him that Ithiel had taught me how to defend myself; I was not completely helpless. Leef pointed out that I would never know how to fight until I had had to put it into practice.

"Look, I'm going! There is nothing you can say to dissuade me!" I shouted.

"I don't want to dissuade you, but you have to be made aware of the pitfalls."

"Cal will be with me," I said airily, not yet sure if that was true.

"Just the two of you?"

"Yes, I suppose so."

"That settles it," he said.

"Settles what?"

"I shall have to ride with you."

"You!" I exploded. "You can't! You'll be needed here."

"Needed? Maybe. But it seems to me that the fate of Galhea is to travel south. I'm a fighter. I'm well trained, and I also know the way." He paused and smiled. I could see his teeth in the pale light. "Perhaps you are concerned I am not . . . har enough to travel with you and the celebrated Cal."

"I don't doubt your ability, Leef."

"Then trust my maturity too. You have nothing to worry about. What is done is done. The flower of Galhea rides south; he needs an escort. Much is at stake, Swift."

"Well, if you're sure . . . Thank you, Leef."

He stood up and came to stand behind me, circling me with his arms.

"You are braver now," I remarked.

"Terzian is not here, and you're no longer a child."

"But I'm the beast that rejected you. I may do so again. Are you so confident or is it just the enormous amount of liquor that you've consumed, whose odor is now overpowering me?"

I could feel his laughter. "Liquid courage," he said. "I want to take aruna with you. Shall we go back to Forever or shall we ride into town?"

"You are impertinent!" I snapped. "Town, I think."

Since his promotion, Leef had been given his own house and staff to care for his needs. It was not a large house, but comfortable and warm. We drank wine beside the fire downstairs, sitting on hairy deerskin rugs.

"This may sound a bit well-worn, but I have waited a long time for this," Leef told me with a grin.

"Your hair has grown," I said and reached to touch it. I could smell his desire, which is indescribable and different for everyone. He took my hands and kissed them. "You're always losing weight," I said. "You look even thinner."

He shook his head. "No . . . Swift, was it marvelous?" I thought he was still teasing, but when I looked at his eyes, they were serious.

"Yes, it was. I'm not going to say it should have been you, because it shouldn't . . . I want you now; is that enough?"

"Enough? Let me answer that properly. Come here!"

Aruna with Leef was nothing like the way it had been with Cal. He was gentle and lazy and loved to be fussed. When I stroked him, he could purr like a cat. For a while he was content to lie there and be pampered, but once I began to show signs of being more ouana than soume, he laughed and threw me onto my back, lying over me so I could not move. "Swift," he said, "let me at least pretend I am the first! Be scared and shy and compliant. Be water to quench my heavenly fire!"

His hand slid down my back, competent and caressing. I smiled in the firelight.

"Look at me; already I am yours."

Later, we went up to his bedroom and we sleepily began to make plans.

"Tomorrow I shall have to tell them," I said, glumly.

"I shall come with you." Leef decided. "It might make it easier."

"No, I shall have to tell Cobweb, at least, alone. I suppose he knows already, but . . . half of me still doesn't want to go but I can't waste my life here."

"Ah, all the action's in the south and you want to be part of it!"

"Yes, if you like. I'm curious as well. What are they like? I know their culture is different from ours. Bryony says that Varrs are more like men. Perhaps the Gelaming won't even look anything like us."

Leef took me in his arms, seeking my neck with his mouth. I could feel his tongue on my skin. "Are you scared?" he asked in a muffled voice.

I thought about this for a moment. "Scared . . . scared. . . . Not really, strangely enough. If the Gelaming have really asked for me . . ."

"If! Has it occurred to you that you may be a threat to them in some way? Perhaps it is a trap."

That thought had already occurred to me. "I shall soon find out," I said.

I went home early to find Cobweb and Cal conversing furtively in the drawing room. My absence had been noted and considered. Cobweb took in my rather bedraggled appearance with one chilling glance.

"Well, when are you leaving?" he demanded. I looked at Cal, who smiled and nodded.

"It's up to you," I said to him.

He shrugged. "As soon as possible, I suppose. We don't want to deprive the jaws of fate unnecessarily, now do we?"

"Leef is coming with us."

"How cozy."

There was a moment's silence. I wanted to run to both of them and hold them to me.

Cobweb leaned back in his chair. "I hope you're ready," he said ambiguously.

"It's more than dreams," I said, and when our eyes met, I could tell he knew what I meant.

BOOK TWO

CHAPTER ONE

>━┼━◀▶━◯━◀▶━┼━◁

Phantom Evil

Panopy, ardor, ritual, pain,
Death-stench, blood-stain,
War-magic, music-thrill,
Weary limbs, love and kill.

Our day of departure was warm and cloudless, acid green mantling the trees to herald our way. "Once more into the jaws of chance!" Cal exclaimed in a weary voice. It was a sentiment he was fond of, but I guessed he was not too sorry to leave. Our goodbyes on the previous evening had been emotional and wearing. Most of our household shared the suspicion that we would never return and probably cursed our folly.

I had asked Tel-an-Kaa to remain in Galhea for a while, thinking that Cobweb might find her presence a comfort. Some of the Zigane obviously welcomed a chance to rest, and I suspect that the Pythoness was one of them. As she had said, life beyond the fields of Galhea would astound me.

I had appropriated three of my father's best horses (his stables were always well stocked) and a packhorse from Ithiel. We were bristling with weapons and had a large tent so that our nights could be spent in comparative comfort. Cobweb loaded me with charms and packets of healing herbs. Tyson gave me a stick to ward off devils, casting mournful glances at Cal as we mounted our horses.

Leef said that we would have several weeks' traveling before we even began to approach where the Gelaming's defenses started. We set off at a brisk trot, westwards to avoid the forest, across the cropped fields. Herds of animals lumbered from our path, birds shrieked a warning of our intrusion. I could not accept that I was really leaving. It did not feel like it. Behind me, on their tree-mantled hills, the windows of Galhea sparkled in the rising sun. I could still make out Forever on the steepest slope, outlined against the sky. Bryony and Yarrow would be in the kitchens. Tyson would be waking up. Life would go on, as always.

Leef knew of several Wraeththu settlements to the south. We anticipated being able to restock our supplies there, all of us agreeing that to strangers we would no longer be Varrs, but just three travelers of no particular tribe, making for the Gelaming. We had tried to make our clothing as anonymous as possible, shrouding ourselves in gray, hooded cloaks, concealing our weapons.

For the first three days our traveling was uninterrupted save for sleeping. We were lucky that my father's horses had been kept in prime condition and that we could keep up a steady, consistent pace. The first night we had some trouble in erecting the tent. Leef found out that some vital part was missing and we had to improvise. We made ourselves a small fire and cooked some of the meat we had brought with us. I had been wondering about the nighttimes, that time for starlight and stirrings. Neither Cal nor Leef was a stranger to me physically. I wondered what would happen should either of them approach me. We had only the one tent after all. This, of course, was yet another aspect of my inexperience. For the first two nights, we curled up separately in our blankets, too tired to think of the solace or the fire of aruna, and I began to think that this was the way it was to be for the entire journey, a thought which I found strangely comforting for it avoided awkwardness.

On the third evening, we camped on the edge of a dense pine forest; rustlings behind us in the darkness. I kept having to look over my shoulder. Leef crept off into the trees in search of prey for our supper, while I untackled the horses and brushed the dust and dried sweat from their coats. Cal came over to watch me for a while. I knew he had something to say; I just brushed and waited. Eventually, he said, "Tonight."

"Tonight what?"

"Oh, just arrangements," he replied. "Up till now there has been slight reticence, mostly coming from you, I think. This is the world of adults, little Swift. This is the way we do things from now on. The lifeblood of Wraeththu, remember?"

"Oh," I said dubiously. I carried on brushing the horse vigorously. Cal reached out quickly and covered my hand with his own to stop me.

"You're not in Galhea now," he said. I tried to smile at him, but his eyes were too dark.

"You must do as you think is right," I said.

Leef brought a large rabbit back to the fire, which he skinned and gutted and spitted on a stick. Cal shared our bread and cheese from our supplies and we drank wine from a bottle. Yarrow had only given us half a dozen; we had no room to carry more.

After the meal, Cal stretched out on the springy turf and said, "Ah, Paradise! Imagine this is Eden and we still have all our ribs!"

Leef laughed. "Hail, Lucifer!" he said. "Fallen angel."

"Angels have wings," I said.

"Six!" Cal propped himself up on his elbows. "Mine must have been burned off in the fall to hell. Where are yours, Swift?"

"Oh, in my heart."

"And yours, Leef?"

"Hidden; as all Wraeththu organs of magic. If you have no wings, Cal, I could take you flying."

All of this conversation was conducted with much grinning and laughter, but there was no denying the undercurrent.

"We must all fly," Cal said coolly. "We must fly together." He stood up, in the purple gloom lit by firelight, and shrugged away his clothing as if it had no substance. He stretched toward the sky, throwing back his head, a slim, white flame in the dusk. Leef's eyes gleamed with hunger, but the feast was before him. Cal reached for the moon, swaying, humming beneath his breath, summoning forth his inner strength. "Moon of radiance," he whispered, his hands twisting like moths. "Pale swimmer of the skies, I entreat thee by the elements to sanctify our communion in thy name. Before thee, I sacrifice my fire. Before thee I am aquatic. Hail Ofaniel, angel of the moon! Shine upon us."

Only the sound of the crackling fire broke the velvet silence. The waning moon shone back impassively at Cal's prayer. He shivered. Leef leaned forward on the grass. There was only one mouthful of wine left in the bottle. He threw it into the fire and murmured, "Ofaniel."

I too leaned toward the flames. They fought with the wine that had sought to smother them. I blew softly and the red glowed brighter. "Ofaniel," I said.

Cal looked over his shoulder at us. "Beyond Galhea," he murmured, "we must abide by the rules. We are in another land. It is safer." He reached out his hands and we took them in our own. "Complete the circle," he said. "Feel the current. I am soume. You must be fire. I am the altar."

This was something I had never experienced. Aruna as it was meant to be; an act of magic. Leef and I shared breath above Cal's body and when Leef slid like a fish into the soume sea, I covered Cal's mouth with my own, filled with his sighs. Watching them, the fire of desire consumed me from within. I was almost delirious by the time Leef guided me gently into the moist folds, slippery with his seed. Cal's body shone beneath me and his hair was wet. This was true soume; he did not fight me. Afterwards, he collected our mingled essences in a cup and dug a hole in the earth with a stick.

"What are you doing?" I asked, too exhausted to move. I saw his eyes glow in the last of the firelight.

"We must bury our sacrifice," he said.

We had been traveling southwest. In the morning, Leef consulted his compass and we turned true south. Banks of thick cloud filled the sky before us, untended fields and defiant stands of trees undulated away from us to the left, while on our other side, the skirts of the great forest hugged the cracked surface of the road we followed. In places the surface had been burst asunder by the roots of trees; we passed bundles of rag that looked too hideous, too suggestive to investigate. Sometimes, we passed dead, burned out vehicles, sagging and rusting at the edge of the road, long abandoned. I wondered why they had been left there. Had men died in the rotted seats? Had the fuel just run out? I tried to open the door of one but was greeted by a puff of evil air, so did not look further.

I learned how quickly the earth takes back what humankind had taken from her. Buildings like empty skulls could be seen amid riotous growths of weeds and grass. A field of corn surged unchecked across the neglected yard of a farm. We passed a crossroads where something hung crucified, its legs hugged by clinging vines, white flowers blooming among the rags of its rotted belly. Cal was quite impressed by that sight. When the wind blew from the south, we could smell magic, the hairs on the backs of our necks would rise and we would be filled with dread and joy. Overall, the countryside seemed deserted.

One morning, as we packed up our belongings at the side of the road, half hidden by a scrubby copse, a galloping troupe of hara thundered past us on large, glossy horses. They wore long feathers in their hair, their faces were painted to look like demons; they paid us no attention. Cal looked at Leef and said, "Kheops?"

Leef nodded. "Probably."

They had no interest in us.

We came upon an inhabited town quite unexpectedly. Leef ordered us to halt. "We'd best go around. Into the trees," he said. Someone fired one or two warning shots over our heads, but no-one came after us. Whether humans or hara occupied the town was impossible to guess. Leef made us keep going for another two hours until he considered it safe enough to make camp for the night. I thought he was being too wary and mentioned it to Cal, who declined to comment.

We set up our tent among some thin, widely spaced trees. Noisy birds squabbled in the darkening foliage above us and feathers fell down into our fire. Leef organized us to keep watch for enemies throughout the night. When it was my turn (in that dreadful cold time before the dawn that is truly the dead of night), I wrapped myself in my blanket and sat hunched by the fire, occasionally feeding it with small sticks and leaves and watching the sparks spiral and burn. I could hear Cal's gentle snores behind me; now and again Leef would mutter something incoherent. He had wanted us to put the fire out for, he said, the light might attract unwanted guests, but I had argued that the night was too cold for that. We were miles from anywhere and we hadn't seen a living soul for two hours. Eventually, if only so he didn't have to listen to my moaning, Leef relented and the fire stayed lit. Resting my chin on my raised knees, nursing a long-barrelled gun between my legs, I smiled to myself as I thought back on our conversation.

I must have been dozing; there's a vague memory of a dream even now, for suddenly I found myself thrown backwards with sickening impact. My mind immediately tried to rationalize: What is this? Has a branch fallen? As quickly as I thought that, rough hands covered my mouth; I had no time to call out. A voice said "Freak!" quite sanely and something punched me between the legs. Sparks seem to shoot right out of me, pain contorted my spine and the reek of foul breath blew over me like the stench of death. They covered my head with the blanket; I tried to struggle, but whatever had hold of me was too strong. There was a taste of vomit in the back of my throat; they were still kicking at me. I was facing death. I was powerless. Then there was a shout behind me, a sound as low and clear as a bell, followed by musical laughter. Had these attackers thought I was alone? Gunfire rolled across the night air in an echoing peal; there was a sound like a sack falling to the ground, guttural curses. Suddenly, not so many hands seemed to be pinning me down. On my back I tried to wriggle away, fighting with the blanket that filled my eyes. Another lightning crack and something heavy fell across my legs. I cried out as my groin reminded me of the assault it had suffered. In an instant the air became full of the sound of bullets flying, ricocheting off trees; horses jostling and groaning in panic. I heard Cal swear and Leef shout, "To your right, Cal!" "Oh, the sweet wine of blood!" Cal exclaimed lightly. Another heavy thud. Then he was untangling me from the blanket and laughing in my face, his eyes shining like stars. "You OK, Swift?" he said.

There was little to see really. A vile creature, quite dead, lay by my feet, gaping at the stars. Two others were sprawled over the remains of our fire. Cal was leaning forward, his hands braced on his knees. "God, I'm out of condition!" He did not look it.

"One to you, two to me," Leef observed cheerfully, counting bodies.

"You fight like the devil," Cal remarked, bending to retrieve his knife from one of the corpses.

"I'm a Varr." Leef looked at me. "Swift, you were supposed to be on watch! Be more vigilant next time, will you? We were lucky; it could have so easily gone in their favor."

It had been men who'd attacked us. Now I had the chance to appreciate what Moswell had once told me about ugliness. The bodies were filthy. Inside their open mouths, I could see the blackened stumps of splintered teeth. The smell was abysmal. We dragged the corpses some yards away from our camp and covered them with branches and leaves. Leef decided we should leave the area straight away. It was possible that others might be near.

After that, we were much more careful, avoiding any signs of habitation, veering away from plumes of smoke above the trees.

"I think the settlement of the Amaha lies this way," Leef said, as our horses plodded along through a pelting rain.

"I hope so," Cal replied drily, "otherwise we starve."

We had used up the last of the food from Galhea two days before and had been living off the land as best we could. Because of the time of year, there wasn't any fruit around, but we raided a field of root vegetables (tough and stringy, but still nourishment), close to a town we passed, and loaded our packhorse with them. I congratulated myself on my first kill. It was only a small animal, but it gave us a meal.

The Amaha are only a small tribe, and while not warlike, vigorous in defense of their own property. They professed to have little time for the Gelaming, mainly because they were more interested in getting on with their own lives, tending their fields and caring for their animals. Their existence seemed simple, but I envied their contentment. The Varrs had traded with them for some years, as Amaharan cured meats and cheeses were regarded as a culinary delicacy in the north. The steady affluence such transactions had encouraged meant that the Amaha could decorate their most favored hara with gold and defend the walls of their town with weapons more effective than knives and spears. Not all the town of Ahmouth was supplied with electricity for they had only one generator, which, by the sound it gave off, seemed none too reliable. The buildings were single-story and sand-colored; many had thatched roofs and carved lintels. I was impressed by the neatness of the few short streets that composed the town.

Leef had been to Ahmouth a couple of times before and was familiar with Hiren, the Firekeeper, ruler of Ahmouth. Hiren was surprised to see Varrs abroad at this time, but did not ask too many questions. The Amaha had heard of Terzian's foray south but told us that, as travelers north had dwindled virtually to none, they had heard neither rumor nor truth about the Varrs' fate. They were not really concerned with the outcome but were interested in gossip. I heard Hiren muse aloud about whether the Gelaming would be interested in reopening trade with Ahmouth, should they take over Galhea. I think this, more than anything, made me realize that Varrs are not the center of the universe as I'd been brought up to think.

We were lucky that currency from Galhea could still buy us supplies. Hiren offered us the hospitality of his house and then proceeded to name prices for the things that we required. He and his consort were like identical twins; both tall, fair and slim. They had three harlings, the oldest of which was about two years younger than myself. His name was Throyne and he seemed very interested in the fact that I was Terzian's son. Sitting next to him at the evening meal that first night in Ahmouth, I answered his questions as best I could, though there was a lot about my own tribe I was ignorant of. Throyne asked me what my caste was and what level I was on. It wasn't a subject I thought about often, but I was rather ashamed to admit that I was only first level Kaimana. Throyne thought my training had been neglected because of the troubles with the Gelaming and expressed condescending sympathy. I remember smiling thinly. "My hostling has taught me many things," I said.

Later that night, because we were feeling comfortable and rested, Cal, Leef and I took aruna together, sharing our strength. I was soume and it was almost too intoxicating to describe what it was like to have both of them caressing me and penetrating me, filling me with the blue cloud of their spirits. Cal laughed and said, "Swift is insatiable!" and Leef had added humorously, "Swift is incomparable!" It was a happy time. Lying awake afterwards, while Leef and Cal greedily smoked cigarettes that

Hiren had sold them, I found myself wondering if, on the road south, my father had sought company to relieve his spiritual and physical needs. I wondered whether, as the Varrs had eaten their evening meals beside their camp fires, Terzian had chosen someone and beckoned; whether that someone had been pleased or annoyed and whether I knew him. I told Leef what I was thinking (he would obviously know, if anyone), and there had been a moment's uncomfortable silence. My heart quickened its pace a little. "Well," I said, "who was it? You'll have to tell me now."

Leef reached over Cal to stroke my arm. "I don't really know why I'm reluctant to tell you. How can it possibly hurt now?" (That meant it probably would.) "It was Gahrazel. On that first time south, it was always Gahrazel. Sometimes we heard him cry out. Once I saw Gahrazel come out of Terzian's tent in the morning and take a knife and cut his own flesh. He watched the blood fall. It explains nothing, yet it explains everything. I was not surprised at what happened to Gahrazel."

"Why didn't you tell me before?" I demanded. My flesh had gone cold.

"I didn't want to. Why should I? Gahrazel is dead now; another Varrish casualty. He was born in the wrong place, I suppose. He rarely spoke to me."

I remembered the long gallery in Forever, morning sunlight coming in over Gahrazel's shoulder where he sat on the floor. "I hate what your father's done to me, Swift . . ." I shivered. It was merely the tip of the iceberg.

We stayed in Ahmouth for two days and, I must admit, I was reluctant to leave. Our quest had become unreal. Away from Galhea I was no longer sure if the threat of the Gelaming still existed or if it ever had. I thought about going home. Dark clouds still hung in the southern sky. I did not want to go toward them. Leef did not ask me what I was thinking. He just said, "We must keep going, Swift; all of us." Cal had spent too much of our currency on tobacco. We squabbled amiably as the Amaha watched us ride away from their homes.

We headed back to the old highway and once the fresh, crisp air got into my lungs and the horses were trotting nimbly through dew-soaked grass, my spirits began to lift again. Cal started to sing and eventually Leef and I joined in. Near noon, the gray ribbon of the road could be seen snaking across the countryside ahead of us.

"Soon we shall reach the city," Cal said.

"What city?" I asked.

"A dead one." Leef's voice sounded bitter.

"An amazing sight," Cal remarked.

"Not the word I'd use," Leef said coldly.

The road became wider, its surface more broken. The abandoned vehicles we rode past were no longer intact but scattered like insect shells across the tarmac. Buildings became more frequent sights, but they were all horribly vandalized, as if torn apart by frenzied hands. Disturbingly, some of them gave off a feeling of still being lived in. We kept our guns in our hands and quickened the horses' pace, which was difficult, for there were so many obstacles to negotiate.

"Few ever come here by choice," Leef said. "The city is close. We shall pass around it."

"Is it safe?" I asked. "Is it deserted?"

"Yes," Leef answered shortly, but his eyes were never still.

"It was a man's city," Cal told me. "The reason it's now in such a sorry state can be put down to one cause; man himself. Unrest, poverty, bitterness. Bitterness that became anger and then hysteria. They tore it down themselves. Such a waste. Wraeththu consider it an unlucky place and sensibly shun it whenever possible. Some years ago, I passed this way and took a look around. I sort of liked it."

We breasted a steep hill, and the road fell away into a valley before us, the contents of which took my breath away. Once, towers of glass must have reared toward the sky; now they were broken off halfway up, fingers of steel poking through concrete, strangely sparkling, heavy vines creeping over them like a shroud. Listing telegraph poles leaned drunkenly away from us in disordered rows, streetlights stood intact, watching mournfully over flattened rubble. I could still feel the life that had once bustled here, just a vibration of the past, the thousands of lives that had once filled its buildings. It could have been only yesterday or a thousand years before. I stared entranced.

"Do men still live here?" My voice was an awed whisper.

"If they do, I don't want to find out," Leef replied.

"I never saw anyone when I was here before," Cal said.

It took us several hours to skirt the city. I had never imagined a town could be so huge. It was scary, but the kind of scary that makes you want to explore. Cal and Leef wouldn't hear of it, and I was secretly relieved, though I pretended bravery. "It's just wasting time," they said, "and it may be dangerous. It would be senseless to go in there."

Before then, I had not thought that men had had real technology. I had only seen photographs and it was like looking at something out of a story. In that gaunt, sprawling ruin, I could see the vestiges of past greatness. Now it was too far gone for Wraeththu to rescue it. Cal said that Wraeththu should concentrate more on building their own cities anyway. They had stolen enough from men. It was too easy to do that. Nothing new could be gained from it. He began to speak, then, of Immanion, the Gelaming's city, that Thiede had built. He said that it was a true Wraeththu city.

"Thiede must be very strong," I said.

"He is," Cal agreed, suppressing a shudder, but not before both Leef and myself noticed it. "He is strong, ruthless, clever . . ."

"What does he look like?" I asked, and Leef repeated my question. Cal had actually met Thiede; to Leef and myself he was just a terrifying name.

"He looks like God," Cal said grandly, but that wasn't enough. We pressed for more details. "Well, he's very tall," Cal continued, screwing up his eyes to remember, "and he has red hair which is very long and spiked up over his head like a halo of fire. Naturally, he possesses unnerving beauty, and his eyes sometimes look yellow. He looks like a child and he looks a thousand years old. His fingernails are varnished claws that could take your eye out. He talks like an actor and pretends weakness. I must admit he scares the shit out of me!"

For a while we were silent, all of us thinking of the omnipotent Thiede. I was terrified that it would be him waiting for me at my journey's end, waiting to throw me my father's head before he killed me too.

Being on horseback all day and sleeping rough at night had been a great shock to my system at first. I never thought I'd get used to it. On the day after we'd left Galhea, my thighs had been rubbed raw, and the skin between my fingers. My horse was a headstrong yellow mare called Tulga. It amused her to fight with me constantly, tugging the reins through my fingers, never keeping her head still, walking sideways when the mood took her, no matter what instructions I tried to give her. It also grieved me having to feel dirty all the time. I was used to creature comforts and now it seemed I had only the comfort of creatures! Both Cal and Leef were used to traveling. They soon fell into a routine; it neither inconvenienced them nor did they appear to dislike it. I had to get used to eating partially cooked food peppered with soot and grass and leaf bits. I had to get used to feeling tired all the time. After some weeks, the discomfort did seem to lose its sting; I became inured to it. As we traveled towards the south, the air gradually became warmer; nights became more bearable.

Sometimes we faced hostility; it was impossible to avoid everyone. Once I had to fight for my life. I killed a man. It was not a momentous event for me, not even sickening. It had been either me or him; that simple. Luck had been on my side. Warm blood had touched my skin and I didn't even bother to wipe it off properly. Round about that time, we lost the pack-horse. We never found out what happened to it, for it just disappeared silently one night. Someone may have stolen it, or its tether may have come undone and it wandered off. We never found out; but of course, a lot of our supplies disappeared with it. Leef was furious.

I began to dream of floating hair and beckoning eyes again. When I had those dreams I would always wake up craving aruna with a bitter taste in my mouth.

Cal and Leef did not pamper me. I learned how to survive and my conscious self forgot the Swift that had lived within the nurturing womb of Forever. I could feel myself maturing. I felt stronger and crueller. Traveling became my life until it seemed I had known no other. At first I had felt hungry all the time, but I became accustomed to that and started to smoke Cal's thin, acrid cigarettes. It helped me get over the hunger.

We stole, we fought off hostile strangers and we rode. Aruna was our only luxury. Through that we became close. Through that we became one unit, anticipating each other's thoughts, moving forward like a well-tended machine; it seemed nothing could touch us. We occasionally gleaned snippets of news about the Varrs, but never anything much. People had seen them pass. They had seen no-one return.

One day, Leef's horse broke its leg and we had to kill it. Impassively, we cut some of it up for meat and left the rest for the scavengers. Leef had to ride Tulga with me until we came across a small Wraeththu settlement where we could buy another horse. We had to pay much more for it than it was worth, for it was not nearly so fast or so fit as our Varrish mounts and it slowed us down. As we traveled, tension and strangeness reached out to us from the south. I could feel it most at night and we took more care with our rituals than before. Once, when we took aruna together, a spirit manifested itself in the air above us. Cal told us not to be alarmed even though it trailed us for about two days. Above the trees, the air seemed to shiver with electric currents; hair-raising noises, just audible, fingered the darkest corners of our souls. We could sense it. Unearthly power grew in strength around us, reached out tentatively to touch us. Plants along the way sprouted in giant abundance, dappled animals that we had never seen the like of before scuttled half seen through the foliage. If you gazed at the air in front of you for too long, faces would appear with gaping mouths and empty eyes. It was as if the land were cursed. Settlements of hara became less and less. What towns or villages we came across looked abandoned.

One night, as we made camp skittishly at the edge of a drooping forest, Leef said, "Tomorrow we reach the marshes."

"If they are still there," Cal added drily. He drank deeply from a water bottle, grimacing at the staleness. His horse kicked gnats from its belly in the dusk.

As we approached the Gelaming, I could feel Cal's apprehension building up. He had once said that the Gelaming might have a price on his head, supposing there was some connection between Thiede, Seel and Saltrock. The land was in turmoil, nobody really knew what was going on, everyone was concerned only with their own survival, which generally meant leaving the area altogether. Only misfits, loners and rogues appeared to remain. If any hara ever came to share our fire, we were always on edge, for we had seen too many crazy eyes, too many death carriers. As far as Cal's fears of meeting the Gelaming were concerned, after all I had seen, I felt that his murder of Orien was just one more forgettable atrocity in a wilderness of atrocities. I knew how afraid he was, yet he had still agreed to ride with me, without reservation or question. I knew my mission, or part of it. Cal also followed a quest, but he had no idea what it was.

That night, I hugged him to me, his head on my chest, and he spoke of Pell once more. After some time, he also began to speak of Seel, somewhat disjointedly and nervously, but I learned how deep their relationship had once been.

"Seel was a dear friend whom I once tried to love," he said with a sigh. "But Seel's ideals are beyond that. I watched him change until the child I had once known died forever. That spirit in the air we saw, floating above us, tasting aruna with us, that is like Seel. Available, physical, but just when you think your arms are full of him for good, there is only mist. He is a true adept and I fear him. I fear we will meet again."

In the morning, we woke up beneath a blanket of fog. The horses were jumpy and Leef spoke of heavy movement in the undergrowth around us, although we could see nothing. Since we had left Galhea, the three of us had got along together very well, but that day saw us arguing and snapping at each other; me bemoaning my discomfort, Leef getting annoyed at my moaning and Cal becoming fed up with the pair of us. "Let's get moving!" he said. "This place is dank; we should not have stayed here."

By midday, a pale sun was trying to burn through the mist. Ahead of us, huge, straggling tufts of waving reeds signaled the edge of the marsh.

"This is it," Leef told us, "Astigi, home of the Froia." The Froia were a tribe that Cal knew very little about, although Leef was vaguely familiar with them.

"Here be magic, Swift," he said, light-heartedly. "I hope they'll be friendly. Most tribes are edgy nowadays and fear to welcome strangers."

It was clear that we could no longer travel on horseback; most of the land was flooded and the roads were now dark waterways between banks of lofty reeds. Leef said that we would need a raft and that if we waited in the right place for long enough, hara of the Froia would come along. They habitually acted as guides through the marsh and accepted payment for providing transport. Leef only hoped they still provided the service.

The marsh was motionless and silent, but for the soft song of the frogs, unseen among the reed roots and the occasional rattle of a startled bird. We walked the horses for some miles along the edge of the waters, until we came to a rough jetty, poking precariously into the marsh. Here we would have to wait.

Cal was impatient; he could not keep still, insisting it was dangerous for us to sit out in the open. Leef calmly pointed out that we had no other choice. When he had last traveled south with my father, the Froia had still been hiring out their rafts. He did not *think* the situation would have changed, but . . . Cal snorted and threw stones into the water. Our horses jostled and groaned behind us. I sat with my chin on my knees and tried to think of home, but it was like a dream. I didn't think we knew where we were going, perhaps Tel-an-Kaa's message had been false; we could die here waiting for the Froia.

Leef came to sit beside me. "They will come, Swift, I can feel it. You will go into the marsh and out the other side. That Pythoness woman knew your destiny and I reluctantly agree with her."

I smiled weakly at him, thinking, Oh, we are vagabonds, we are filthy. No-one can mistake us for Varrs, at least! We had not taken aruna together for over two weeks. Our bodies were wretched, our spirits low.

Leef laughed, guessing my thoughts. "Yes, we are a sorry sight," he said. "I have only dragon's breath, but it's yours if you want it."

"My dragon is lonesome," I said and we embraced, clinging mouth to mouth, in an attempt to shut out reality. After some minutes, Cal kicked me on the leg.

"Break it up, we have company," he said.

Sliding over the misty water like a wraith, a large raft sliced through the reeds. Two tall figures, swathed in concealing robes, poled it toward us. Leef jumped up and signaled them. One of them raised a hand in response. Our supplies were low, we were exhausted and needed rest; Leef asked for us to be taken to the Froia settlement of Orense in the heart of the marsh. We goaded, shoved and shouted our reluctant horses on to the raft. Tulga seemed obsessed with throwing herself over the edge into the weed-choked depths; I was hard pressed to calm her.

We traveled for about an hour, through narrow waterways and avenues of tasselled reeds, through whirring, hanging balls of mosquitoes, into unexpected lagoons thronged with white birds. It was a place of pervading stenches, hidden dangers and eerie beauty. Eventually, we could see humped dwellings rising up above the reeds; the floating town of Orense.

At the prospect of comfort, food and drink, our good humor was restored almost immediately. We had reached a new level of existence, where pleasures were simpler and easily gratified. Barrel-vaulted buildings constructed entirely of reeds glowed pale beneath the watery sun. Only the electric shiver on the horizon reminded us of absurdity. Orense was placid, a pocket of tranquility within the boiling magic that existed beyond the marsh.

As was customary for visitors, we were conducted to the Braga, leader of the Froia. It was more than politeness or respect; they were naturally wary of strangers. His palace of reeds was roofed with mats of muted gold and pink, and carefully woven stalks formed a palisade at the front. All the time I was conscious of slight movement beneath my feet as the great platforms shifted upon the water below. We could smell pungent coffee. Voices called softly in the distance. Tulga stamped the ground behind me, nervous because she could not feel the earth. I was smiling with relief and Leef put his hand on my shoulder.

The Froia are extremely reticent about revealing their skin and affect clothing of the most concealing nature. Only their hands, feet and faces are habitually visible. At the door to the Braga's house, we had jasmin water poured on our wrists and an aynah bud tucked behind our ears. This was to banish any evil we might be carrying with us. Inside, the light was golden. Tiny shafts of sunlight penetrated holes in the woven roof. Froia in hooded robes regarded us implacably from around the walls. Veils of pale muslin drooped to the floor and in the center of the room was a wooden throne containing the august presence of the Braga. I was unsure what to do. Was some kind of obeisance required? Fortunately, Leef stepped forward, bowed gracefully and requested if he might be given leave to speak with the Braga. The Braga raised his hand carelessly: Leef may speak.

I looked at Cal and he smiled and shrugged. "I hope all this ceremonial crap doesn't go on for too long," he said. "I'm starving and I itch and I can think only of cool water and hot coffee."

"You have no respect for other people's cultures," I replied lightly.

"No," he agreed. "What is culture, after all? It's like incest or inbreeding; everything gets too involved, too tight, too crazy. It bores me, actually."

After only a few minutes, the Braga's attendants conducted us to a separate building, where we were supplied with warm (not hot) water for bathing and clean clothes and food. The Froia do not eat meat, except for fish on religious occasions. The brown goo we were offered for consumption looked disgusting, but its taste was savory and pleasant enough. After we had eaten, Cal fastidiously inspected the robes we had been given. "No chance of giving offense in this, is there!" he said.

Leef explained. "The clothes we are wearing at the moment are looked upon as erotic. Among the Froia, the body is revealed only for aruna. While we are here, we shall have to abide by their customs. Imagine that you are walking naked among strangers. Now, put that robe on!"

The Braga requested the pleasure of our company for the evening. We were now clean, fed and rested, but I thought this would hardly be apparent because of the enveloping robes we were wearing. The atmosphere in his reedy house was thick with the smoke of incense, curtains of smoke almost indistinguishable from the curtains of muslin. Young hara sat on the floor on cushions, playing music upon instruments of the strangest design. It sounded to me like the music of nature; the abrupt trill of a bird, the plash of raindrops or the echo of a storm that wakes you from sleep. Tame lizards stared out from the folds of the musicians' robes with eyes like jewels.

The Braga, seated on his cavern throne and surrounded by acolytes, beckoned us to his side with an imperious gesture. I could see that he had dark skin with very bright eyes and a mouth that was used to smiling. His forehead was tattoed with intricate black lines, thin gold chains fell from his headcloth around his face and the rings that reposed upon his outstretched hand were like a swarm of brightly colored insects. One of his teeth was gold.

"I understand that you are Varrs," he said, "and that one of you is the son of Terzian." He was waiting for me to introduce myself, not wishing to ask directly.

I stepped forward. "Terzian is my father."

"He passed this way . . . a character of strength and courage."

I accepted this as a compliment and inclined my head. The Braga did not try to interrogate us about where we were going or why. He was used to strangers passing through his domain, perhaps his people's livelihood depended on it. He was wary, but he knew when to be discreet.

We were offered a drink distilled from honey, whose effects shot without hesitation straight to the brain. Gradually, it seemed that the noise around me became louder, the music more strident, the air thicker. Cal and Leef began to share breath, inexplicably, for normally they did not initiate anything between each other without including me. I turned away from them, and the Braga put his jewelled hand upon my face. "Of royal blood," he said. I smiled uncertainly, wondering whether that was some kind of oblique proposal. "For your honor, there shall be dancing."

He clapped his hands once and the clamor around us ceased. Into the ensuing quiet, the Braga clicked his fingers once, and once again. Smoke rose lazily into the gently swaying gauze around us, sparkles like jewels or fireflies coruscating in the deepest shadows. One of the musicians stood up and walked to the middle of the floor. His instrument was curving, flutelike and made of wood. He raised it to his lips. Notes that rose from the dawn of the earth cut with purity through the curtains of smoke and incense. Every voice was hushed, while the young har swayed before us. His hood fell back. Beauty, I thought, and they keep this hidden! Beneath the haunting call of the flute a sibilant rattle rose and fell, rhythmic, beating, summoning. At first I did not see the figure emerging through the pall of smoke. Suddenly, it had solidified in front of me and the beating of drums vibrated the floor beneath us. Diaphanous veils concealed the body within them, but I could see a vague outline undulating and swaying below the folds. Even the face was hidden. Then two sinuous arms snaked out, glistening with heavy gold; bracelets and rings. When this happened, everyone in the room began to clap their hands softly in time with the music. The Braga leaned down and murmured in my ear. "Does this please you?" I nodded. Something was reaching out to me; unseen and insistent. It was the rhythm of the drums, the heat of the room, a swaying, inviting phantom. There was a flash and a sound like gunfire or sharp thunder and I saw the veils float up into the air as if sucked away by a powerful wind. For a moment, I looked only at that . . . spiraling, billowing, and then . . .

The Braga's hand gripped my shoulder. "For your blood, for your father, for what is to come; you shall be the first," he said and his voice was a gasp. I almost turned round to look at him, puzzled by his words, but the dancer was revealed. That describes it, but it was more than that. These people were used to concealment. To them it was something powerful and secret and forbidden to reveal themselves. There is a word for it: "veyeila," that is untranslatable to anyone who is not Froia. It means something like forbidden, taboo, desired, abandonment, frenzy; all these words and more. As I saw that har writhe barely clad upon the mats before me, I understood for just a while the eroticism they heightened within themselves by their austere code of dress. His skin was dark and oiled, his black hair curled to his shoulders, and he knew how to dance. All the invitation in the world reposed within his slender form. He danced before me, he smiled, his body gyrating inches from my face. His smell was amber and myrrh.

I heard the Braga's voice behind me. "Swift, son of Terzian, this har is soume. His water must quench your fire. It must be now!"

I started to laugh, to protest, "But I have no fire . . ." but even as I thought it a flame was lit inside me, spontaneous as lightning, igniting desire; I had no choice. It is magic! I thought, and then the dancer was in my lap, straddling me, arranging my robes with experienced hands.

It was all so quick. One moment, I had been half-drunkenly watching a desirable har dancing in front of me, the next my back was pressed painfully into the carving on the Braga's chair and my ouana-lim was buried to the hilt within the dancer's body. My modesty was not forsaken, the robes saw to that. For several stultifying seconds he moved upon me, clenching muscles within himself, expertly bringing me to a quick and paralyzing climax. Then he was gone, jumping up, flicking back the folds of my robe, dancing once more. For a moment, I could not move, but I could sense strongly the surprise in Cal and Leef as they stared at me. Had it really happened or had it been some bizarre hallucination, brought on by the strong liquor we had been drinking? Then I saw the dancer pick someone else from the crowd and I knew it was no dream. I felt the Braga's hand once more, squeezing my shoulder.

"He has brought you luck, son of Terzian. Good fortune will follow you out of Astigi. Speak to Nepopis later and he will tell you your destiny. You have my permission."

I suppose it was a kind of Grissecon. The dancer was blessed and to embrace him worked a charm of good fortune. I learned that strangers were not often witness to the experience, let alone participants. Nepopis the dancer was "theruna," a holy person, practiced in the art of sex magic and held in the highest esteem among his people. He lived in seclusion, on the edge of Orense, coming forth only for the dance, but if he had a whim to, he would allow visitors to enter his home and speak their destinies for them.

Cal and Leef amused themselves by trying to embarrass me. I realized the futility of trying to silence their remarks and turned my back on them. It was difficult not to get annoyed. At midnight, a Froia har came to take me to Nepopis, and I got up and walked out without a backward glance.

Nepopis lived in a single-roomed hut among a tall stand of reeds. It was surprisingly roomy inside. Now the dancer was thoroughly concealed by the customary robe, with only the hood thrown back. He bade me be seated and offered me coffee. It was as if the incident in the Braga's house had never happened. Nepopis was unselfconscious yet reserved. His smile was sincere, but guarded. As I drank, blinking into the steam, he stared at my face.

"You carry a burden," he said, and I shrugged, wondering how much he could tell me. "It is not yours to carry," he continued. "You would be advised to cast it aside. The past cannot be undone. Your father is beyond salvation—" I made a noise of exclamation but he raised his hand to silence me. "You must seek the path. You have neglected your training. Ah . . . !" He closed his eyes and rubbed them with one hand, throwing back his head, as if seeking a message only he could hear. "There is one . . . I see blood and it is old, it is dry and there is a fire that is not the fire of desire; it is something else. There is a cloud that is . . . that is . . . yes, it is emotion and it is seething. It will have to be . . . *unmisted.* Two of you follow a destiny that is cut so deep. The third . . . he is . . . he is a follower, he is your follower . . . he can be trusted. The time will come . . . beyond Astigi . . . first, beware the forest of illusion. The illusions are truth, but you will need strength to face them. You will understand the nature of the beast. He is still there . . . in the forest . . . echoes . . . of . . . no! In the future, you will see a face that you have known in dreams, and it will be burned upon you; you won't escape it; there will be no escape. You must follow your destiny, you must train because that is the only way. . . . His face. He has almond-shaped eyes and he is wise. He is held in high esteem. He bears the Tigron's mark . . ."

Nepopis sighed and bowed his head, silent for a moment before looking up at me. "I have held your seed within me," he said, "and I felt its destiny too. There will be a child of royal blood . . ." He shook his head. "It is all so unclear, usually I find it easier, but the aether is disturbed . . ."

"Can you give me a name?" I asked quickly, feeling the magic settling round me, back into the earth. Nepopis shook his head.

"I don't think so. It is guarded. I think they sense me."

"They? Is it the Gelaming? Will I meet this person among them?"

Nepopis raised his hands. "Enough. Enough. I've told you what I can." He smiled. "I'm sorry. I didn't mean to be sharp, but times have changed. What is going on out there affects my vision; it disturbs me, it leaves too much unseen." He stood up and went to look out of the doorway. "Swift, come here."

I could not remember having told him my name. At his side, I looked out at a pink and cobalt sky, misting into the fronds of the reedbeds. Dark, winged shapes wheeled on the cooling air.

Nepopis reached for my hand and squeezed it gently. "I have seen your home," he said. "I have seen your hostling and the long, dark gardens. All goes well with them. He is lonely for you, but . . ." He turned to face me with a smile. "I feel so many hara walk this earth bent double with the direst of destinies! It is a time for it; we live in a time of legends. Man had that time too, you know. I hope ours does not fade . . ."

"It won't," I said.

"You were born har."

"Yes. I thought that you too . . ."

He shook his head. "No . . . it was a long time ago that I was human, but I am not pure-born. It feels different with you, you feel so different; everything is stronger. It's like a weapon, that strength. Your seed is the color of dawn, did you know that?"

"Yes, I know that."

"It shines with force; I would like to keep some for the sake of its power. I will never use it against you."

If that was a question, my reply was to take him in my arms, bending to taste his liquid breath of dark lagoons and deep waters.

At dawn, Leef came to the door of Nepopis's hut and requested entrance. He said that he and Cal wanted to leave Orense midmorning. I'd only had about an hour's sleep and traveling was the last thing I felt like doing. After several minutes' argument, Leef bad-temperedly agreed that our journey could resume the following day. I didn't think that so short a delay could possibly have a dreadful effect on our progress, so I stayed with the dancer of dreams. Cal and Leef could do what they liked for the day; I wanted this time for I knew it would be the last chance I'd get for relaxation for a while.

"If only," Nepopis said, "if only this were another time and you did not have to leave. If only that mist wasn't waiting for you. The eyes in that mist have already claimed you as theirs, even though they have not yet seen you, even though they do not know . . ."

I told him he spoke like my hostling, in puzzles. "It is our way," he replied. "We must speak the way we think and we never think in straight lines." He held me in his arms, a dancing snake, supple and strong. "If you had not neglected your art, if you were Ulani as you should be, I would demand that you let me host your seed. But it is not to be. I know it would be pointless to ask you to return some day . . ."

"I may do . . . you never know."

Nepopis laughed and stroked my face. "Ah, but I do, Swift; I do!"

At dawn, the next day, we loaded our horses once more upon a raft and glided away from the floating pads of Orense. I looked back for as long as I could, until the reed buildings disappeared into a haze. Cal and Leef were surly with me. I think it was because for so long, it had just been us three together and they were a little put out that I had taken aruna with someone else. Probably, I would have felt the same way if it had been one of them that had been chosen. Not only had I neglected them for two whole nights, but I had held up our journey for an entire day! I apologized for this in a very scathing tone which brought a ghost of a smile to Cal's lips.

It took us two more days to cross the Astigi. Each evening we paused at one of the many floating villages where we were welcomed with food and drink, but no more exotic theruna. Occasionally, most often at dawn and dusk, something strange would cross our path and our Froia guides would elaborate signs of protection upon the air with rippling fingers. Once we nearly got caught in a loop of time, going round in circles that made our heads ache, but the Froia divined the weakest spot and we managed to break through into real time.

"What is most depressing," Cal observed, "is that all this messy, Gelaming hoodoo frolicking is going to get much worse beyond the marsh."

"When I last came here, we wouldn't get much further than Astigi," Leef told me. "We got caught in time weirdness. I only hope we can get through this time."

"Sadly, I think we can be assured of that!" Cal said bitterly.

The Froia helped us unload the horses at the brink of the marsh and Leef gave them as much currency as we had left. We felt that it would no longer be of use to us, so they might as well have it all. We rode away from the water into a liana-hung forest of dampness and haunting calls among the treetops.

"I wonder how long this place has been here?" Cal asked no-one in particular, and neither Leef nor I could think of a suitable answer. We followed the pull of the strangeness to its heart, and it let us pass.

CHAPTER TWO

>━┼━◆>━◯━<◆>━┼━≺

Mystical Convulsion, Tender Caress
Bony frame's loathsome degradation,
Eyes seek the mark of wounds.
Palpitating universe fallen unto me,
Membranous skin expands into wilted flowers.

It was like stepping into a dream. As that enchanted wilderness closed its green arms around us, reality faded and absurdity became the only truth. At first, we rode in silence, our horses pushing breast-deep through lush greenery. There was little sound and what sound there was existed high above us. I was lost in reverie, my skin becoming damp, brushed by a vague stream that rose from the soft ground. If I thought hard enough I could still feel Nepopis's slim, dark arms around me. Now that I had left him, his image began to crowd my head. I did not want to go back, but I wanted him here, now, before me on the saddle, pointing the way, unveiling his witchery of wisdom. Suddenly, I could feel flesh against me, fragrance all around me and Nepopis's low voice was in my ears. "The eyes; they are blind . . . as yet!"

I thought I was falling asleep and blinked and sound rushed in; squawking, clamoring cacophony, and there was no-one on the saddle before me.

"Swift, are you alright?" Cal's face swam pale, disembodied at the corner of my vision.

"Yes. Yes," I answered, still blinking, swallowing, gulping.

"Be strong, Swift." Leef's voice was low and cautious behind me. He, more than Cal or I, had an idea of what to expect from the forest.

"I shall be afraid to sleep," I said, with a shaky laugh.

"There will be no difference." Cal clicked his tongue and hastened our pace to a trot. The swifter, jolting motion cleared my head a little; the branches of wide-leaved shrubs hissed around us.

We had no way to measure time and time was stretched and condensed in that place. Was it possible that we were not moving forward at all? The air around us became hotter and more humid, strong aromas of dark earth and rotting vegetation filling our heads, clinging to our clothes and hair. It seemed that we had been riding for at least half a day without stopping; we were tired but too scared to rest. We feared that by resting we would enable the forest to claim us completely and we would wander crazed for the rest of our lives. It was an unspoken fear, but I have no doubt that it was shared by each of us.

Half-seen figures flickered on the edge of my vision, half-heard voices whispered urgently in my ear. Grasping at sanity, I remembered calling, "Cal!" and my voice was deep and slurred, slowed down. Cal was ahead of me (we were riding in single file), and he turned on his horse, raising one hand. He did not speak.

"Swift!"

My eyelids jerked open. Where am I? The forest was hidden by jets of green steam, spurting with a putrid stench from the rotted ground. I was on my knees. My knees and hands were wet. I was alone. I could not remember what names to call out. Who were they? Had I always traveled alone?"

"Swift!"

Louder this time, yet sibilant, like an echo. I tried to see into the viridian gloom, waving shapes that might only be leaves, shivering away into an impenetrable blackness.

"Swift!"

I saw him. He was holding broad leaves about him, half concealed. He did not want me to see him. Was he naked? Was that it? I tried to reach for him. Where am I? I tried to speak his name; then I remembered he was dead. He smiled, threw back his head and laughed. "Beloved friend! Do you remember our last meeting? Was I that good?"

"Gahrazel."

I lurched to my feet and he backed two paces into the trees.

"Back!" he hissed. "I don't want you near me!"

His hair was long and curling. He was eight years old. My father's training had not marked him.

"You betrayed me!" His voice was a thin scream, whose anguish and emptiness, both apparent, raised the hair on my head.

"No! I said nothing!"

"*He* told you to! Cal the devil, Cal the devil . . ." His voice, sing-song, trailed away to nothing. His jaw hung slack, his eyes were two black stones.

"I didn't say anything!" My voice too had become high, the screech of a black crow, most deceitful of birds.

"You spoke of something, though." Gahrazel's voice had become sly. "To your father. I know about that. I know what you said. *Every word.* Did you wish that it was true?"

"I wish you had been different. I could not help you."

"Not without endangering yourself perhaps . . ."

"I could not help you."

The Gahrazel that was not Gahrazel raised one pale hand to his face. He was weeping; his tears streamed like acid on flesh. "I died . . . they killed me."

"Gahrazel . . ." I reached toward him.

"No! No!" The foliage around him was shaking. He pointed at me with quivering fingers. "You! You must hear it!" His words came quickly, their speed increasing all the time. "Someone must hear it, that it died with me, dear God, that someone should know the truth. You! You! Terzian's brat, his blood, his seed, his damn eyes. His eyes! Steel they are, no laughter, no pity. When he killed me, when he killed me, my God, I saw his eyes, his eyes!" Gahrazel's sobs overtook his ability to speak. He pressed his trembling hands into his eyes.

"My father killed you?" Such a whisper, such a fateful phrase. Gahrazel stopped sniveling to look at me. His ghost tears were dry already.

"Yesssss!" Leaves scratching along the terrace in autumn; that was how he sounded. So dead. "Didn't you know that, Swift? Didn't he brag of that to you?" He laughed cruelly. "Ah, of course, you know nothing, do you? The babes of Forever, wrapped in all that glorious stone. Stolen stone!" He flapped his hands at me. "Now I'll tell you! Now I'll tell you! Your father, Terzian, he is the beast! He ate flesh, drank blood; mine! Ponclast poured the poison into an iron cup. It had to be iron; only iron can hold it. He handed it to Terzian and kissed him and told him to give me the cup. I took it. There was nothing I could do. Only pride left. They would not see me beg for life; I knew it was useless. So I drank it. In one draft. It tasted . . . peppery, but not too bad. Only when it hit my stomach, then, you see, it began to work and the moisture in my throat, that helped it too. A cupful of poison and it began to burn. Burn me from inside out. I fell to my knees. The floor was cold. We were way underneath the ground. I was not afraid of death, but I hoped it would be quick. So strange it was, knowing I was dying. So inevitable, there is no fear. I was kneeling there on the floor, waiting to die, not moving much, for the burning was not pain exactly, only I knew that it was killing me, numbness spreading all through me, when my father said, 'Now, Terzian.' Behind me, he clicked his fingers, and hands were upon me, pulling me back. I lay there, my legs melting, and your father, Swift, he took a knife and slit my clothing, pulled it away from me, not smiling, but grave, looking at my eyes. . . . All the excitement of the world was condensed in his body. He opened his trousers, just that, not even naked, and took my melting flesh; he was covered in unguent to protect himself. How lucky I could no longer feel it! Even as he shrieked in orgasm and put his hand through my rotting chest, even as he tore my purple, gasping heart from my chest, I could not feel it. Of course my mind had gone completely, you can understand that. As I died I watched your father eat half of my heart and hand my own father the other. When my spirit left that place, what was left of my body was unrecognizable . . ."

I was lying in the leaf-mold; I had vomited. My body was shaking. "Weep now, Swift," Gahrazel said.

He watched me weep. I thought, No, this cannot be true. This is illusion. This side of Terzian cannot exist. I would have known. Cobweb would have known. No! But even as I thought it, some deep, instinctive part of me knew it was senseless to doubt what I'd heard. Senseless.

After a while, I struggled to rise. Gahrazel was still a pale, insubstantial shape among the wide leaves. "I died . . . they killed me . . ."

"Gahrazel, can I come to you?"

"No!" He retreated further into the trees. I could barely see him; his face, a white oval, that was all. "You must not come to me," he said. "That must not be. Swift?"

"Yes . . . Gahrazel?" My eyes ached with searching for him, my chest, my throat, with grief.

"Did you love me?"

"Once . . . I think."

He sighed, a faint breeze that shivered the leaves. "You did not come. I asked for you, many times. I died alone . . . quite, quite alone." His voice was the sound of a bell, tolling over bare and shadowy hills, summoning nothing to a devotion that had lost its purpose.

"I'm sorry . . ." How could I have said that? It means nothing. I could imagine him smiling, sadly. "No-one is without sin," I said. "Not one of us. My sins are selfishness, fear and weakness. I was afraid, Gahrazel, not just of blame, but for my home, my people. Yes, I betrayed you; we both know that. I cannot apologize, because the consequences were so . . . so . . . beyond apology."

"I'll forgive you, forgive you, only say it, say it now, the one thing I can take with me. Forever. Do you know what to say?"

I knew what to say. I closed my eyes. I summoned it up within me, a maelstrom of feeling, and let it spill from my mouth. "I love you, Gahrazel."

"Do you forgive me?"

"For what?"

"Do you?"

"Yes, yes; I forgive you . . ."

All around me the greenness whispered and writhed. Darkness all around. I sank to my knees.

"Swift!" Hands upon my shoulders, shaking, shaking. I opened my eyes. Tulga beneath me, half-seen sky above. Cal's anxious face. I shook my head.

"It was nothing. I dreamed."

We came upon a clearing in the forest. Cal said, "I have been here before," and his voice was full of grief. All the ugly, dripping trees had become straight pines. Birds called. We found the damp remains of an old fire in the center of the clearing.

"We are safe here," Leef told us, but he did not sound sure. We dismounted and our horses began to crop the sward, unaffected by the atmosphere. Leef built a fire. I sat beside him, too shaken to move. Cal squatted some distance away from us, his face in his hands. Once timid flames began to leap from the damp tinder, we relaxed a little. The fire was comforting, normal. Leef unpacked food. "Look, we have wine!" he said and held out a green bottle.

Cal sat down next to me and I took him in my arms. He was weeping silently into my hair. My eyes were dry, but my chest felt as if it was stuffed with sawdust. After some time, Cal sniffed noisily and said, "What happened to you?"

I wiped his face with my hand, for a moment or two, unable to tell him. "I saw Gahrazel. I spoke to him."

"You too?"

"Gahrazel?"

"No . . . not him!"

I held him to me tightly, afraid to let go, afraid of the contact. I told him what I'd seen, what I'd heard. Cal said nothing. Perhaps he had known already, but I didn't want to find out. I had once asked questions about my father, now some of them had been answered. Of course it was something I had to know. I wish I didn't. "Gahrazel asked for me," I said, "and I turned my back on him. If I'd known what fate was awaiting him, would it have changed the way I felt? I hope so. Today, I said to him the things he should have heard before he died. His death was lonely, people there, I know, but it was true loneliness. Alone, unloved, unforgiven. Now I have said it. Was it real, Cal?"

"A spirit," he whispered, "or a conjuration of your own mind, or a conjuration of *theirs;* does it matter? If you have not appeased the shade of Gahrazel, you have appeased yourself."

"Was it just within me? Was it guilt?"

"Pray that it was not guilt!"

If it was, perhaps we were all doomed. I whispered Cal's name and held him and shared his fear. This place was not just a place of the dead, no, never that.

We ate the food that Leef gave us. Leef was a tower of strength; the forest seemed to have the least effect upon him. His mind was ordered; he denied what was not real. "There is no-one here," he said, when I told him about my experience, omitting the details about my father. I did not want to discuss that with Leef. "It was hallucination," he insisted, "that was all."

Cal said, "This place, this clearing . . . I recognize it. Pell and I were here once. It was the last time we were together."

"That's not possible," Leef replied emphatically.

"It's the same country!"

"No, your mind is playing tricks on you."

"That was our fire; it has always been here."

"No!" Leef stood up, running his hands through his hair. "Are you both cracking up on me?" he demanded. We stared at him silently. "Look, this is Gelaming work. You must regain control! They will break you!" He shook a warning finger at us.

"Every sickly bloom has his face, every whispering leaf speaks with his voice," Cal murmured. I reached for his hand. I understood.

"You will die here!" Leef exclaimed. "Pull yourselves together, for God's sake!"

"There is no God here," I said.

"Oh, there is," Cal answered. "He fights with the Gelaming. He's here, more than anything. They have his light, you see. They are his angels."

"Have some wine, Cal," Leef said drily, thrusting the bottle at him. Cal drank, deeply. "Was this from the Froia?"

"No," Leef answered. "I don't know where it came from."

Night and day had no proper sequence in that place. We took turns at sleeping and rested well enough; we could not remember our dreams.

Once we had slept, we began our journey again, leaving the clearing behind. Cooling sticks and ashes cracked bleakly in a curl of smoke as our farewell.

We rode into the forest, down a steep slope carpeted with fallen pine needles. It descended into an impenetrable gloom. Stark, black branches, fallen from the trees, littered the path, cracking abruptly as the horses stepped on them. It felt as if others had passed this way not long before us. I could sense life. After an hour, we came upon a ruined house, strangled and beautiful with flowering creepers. Its empty windows watched our approach. It was Forever. I made an exclamation, pointed.

Leef did not even turn his head. "Ride past!" he ordered.

I had to look. Was this Forever's future? Was it doomed to die? The roof was nearly gone. At an upper window, I caught a glimpse of something pale, flitting quickly from sight. Was it Cobweb I saw there, haunted and sad, clinging to a memory blighted by truth? There was only silence and I was afraid of sound. I was afraid I would hear voices and that they would be voices that I knew.

It felt like afternoon, golden sunlight through the leaves. Laughter in the distance. My father stepped out in front of us. "You are welcome, strangers," he said and his smile was a predator's smile and I knew he held a gun behind his back. I looked away. Through the trees, human children scampered and screamed in innocent delight, through the sunlight, until the light was gone and inky blackness smothered their cries to whimperings of terror. Now they ran with white faces and gaping mouths, silent in their horror, bearing scratched limbs and torn clothes. Behind them, with grave expression, my father rode a heavy, black horse. The children ran from him in fear. He and Ponclast suddenly blocked the road before us, dining on human flesh, holding goblets of blood in their bloody fingers, toasting life. They had the faces of wolves and their long muzzles were red. "The beast will come . . ." Wolves' heads. A horde of Varrs with wolves' heads. A screaming town, running with red, people running. Human, hara. The Varrs had torches, setting light to the buildings, the people. Wolves' heads, forever grinning. On a broad road, under the streetlights, my father dismounting from his black horse, lifting the wolf helmet from his shining hair, brushing it back, handing the helmet to a soldier at his side, smiling. Ponclast striding over, embracing Terzian. He says the words, "My star." They kiss. Ponclast hands him a human heart and, staring into Ponclast's eyes, Terzian bites . . .

I looked away. My throat burned; I retched.

Then a figure rushed out of the trees, light spiraling in, a euphony of birdcalls. It brought the afternoon back in. Someone grabbed Tulga's reins by the bit-ring. He looked up at me, smiling. "I knew you would come!" His beauty was like gold in my eyes. So beautiful, after what I had just seen, I wanted to weep. He wore a ring that was like a seal. His ears were pierced with gold, three times on each side. Hair that was a luxury of blackness, lifting like wings, braided with pearls. His smile touched my heart. I knew him. It was Pellaz.

"Are you afraid?" He laughed. Tulga sniffed at him and he cupped her velvet nose with his hands.

"No . . ."

He touched me, lightly, upon the leg and my flesh tingled beneath the cloth. "What your friend Leef said was true; it *is* only illusion," he said, "but illusion of the truth nonetheless. It will soon be over. Look after him."

"Who?" Of course I knew.

The vision shook its head, smiling sadly. "My love, my tormentor, my dearest memory, my Cal. Calanthe; slayer and beloved. It will be some time . . ."

"He has seen you."

"Not like this. Only you have truly seen me and it will not happen again. Be strong, Swift. I have faith in you and I will give you such jewels as you cannot imagine . . . when you find my people." He was fading.

I reached for him. "Pell, what is real?"

"You are. Remember that." He was gone.

Cal urged his horse to my side. "You spoke his name!" he cried, his eyes all wild as if I had spoken blasphemy.

"He was here," I said. "Cal, he was here. It was different. Cal, oh, Cal, I know it . . . he . . . Cal, Pellaz is not dead!"

Leef had to pull him off me. He was hysterical; he cut my lip. Tulga neighed in terror. "But it's true!" I wailed. Leef restrained a sobbing, broken Cal in his arms. How could he know what visions Cal had suffered in that place?

"Swift, for God's sake, shut up!" Leef cried angrily.

"What is real, Pell?"

"You; you are real."

A sandy trail the color of sandy hair, winding through a deciduous wood, whose trees are girded with moss. Green light everywhere. Fluting birdsong. "You are real. You are real. You are real." I am riding. Because Cal is in front of me, I realize quite quickly that this is his illusion, not mine.

I am here as a witness; that is all. I can hear water. Cal's horse snorts and shakes its head. I can see Cal's clothes are torn. He is wearing a white shirt and the rips across his back are fringed with red. It is claw marks, a whip's teeth, the last desperate scrabbling of someone dying. He turns to look at me and his face is greenish, perhaps it is because of the strange light; he smiles and his gums and teeth are red. "You are with me, Swift?" he says, and I nod my head.

"I am with you."

I will look after him, Pell; never fear.

Ahead of us a spreading oak grows in the middle of a glade. Sunlight reaches it, but there are no birds here. Leaning with its back to the tree, a figure stares up through the leaves. It is robed in white, long brown hair around its shoulders. I don't think it sees us. I think it can't sense us. Cal's horse stops in front of me and bends its neck to begin eating. Cal slips from its back to the ground, over the neck; it's quicker. Would he dismount any other way? Tulga wants to eat and I let her. I see Cal lifting his ragged, soiled shirt over his head and his back is livid with long, angry weals. He reaches round and tries to rub them, but he cannot reach. I want to go to him, but I can't. I am frozen. I am mute. Observer; nothing else. Cal is walking toward the tree and the figure looks at him. It smiles sadly. It shakes its head; lifts its hands as if to say, "Go back, go back." Cal keeps walking. The figure says, "You do not have to see this, Cal. You can turn around."

Cal says nothing.

The figure says, "Face the past."

"Have I ever faced any other way?" Cal asks. The figure smiles and opens its arms. "You seek absolution, Cal."

"Never that. I have always been aware of everything I've done."

"I know that. I had hoped . . ."

"You have no substance to hope!" Cal says bitterly. The figure is still smiling sadly. Its hands are upon the neck of its garment. Cal's fists are clenched at his sides. I cannot see, but I know that he is staring straight ahead. I hear material ripping; a lazy, elegant sound. I think, it is expensive cloth, even though I can see what lies beneath. It is no longer red, no longer shining; just ravagement. Cal and the figure are inches apart. Cal raises one hand.

"Touch me within; touch your sin, Cal."

It was once flesh, now it is nothing, a shell, nothing more. It is hard and dry. I can see the dull, brown bones of a shattered ribcage and I can see Cal's hand reach inside. Once he has touched, the spell will be broken; I know that. He reaches for the heart that no longer beats. He leans forward. The face; a dry mouth full of small, moving things that scurry upwards from the empty lungs. Their lips touch; one living, one who is beyond life. I see Cal wince; so slight a reaction. Corruption has him in its arms. It is pouring foulness into him. A head creaks back and there is no peal of godless laughter; just a thought. "It is done."

Like a fountain turned on, life comes back with a torrent of sound, wings in the treetops, whirring, whirring. Cal is alone and he is soaked in blood; blood in his mouth, his eyes, his hair. He shakes himself and red droplets fly through the air like bright, hard insects. He is sick with the taste of blood, but his eyes are dry, his back unbent. He comes back to me, fallen angel, evil incarnate, a spirit of love. He says one word as he remounts his horse. As he pulls up its head, one word. The word is this: "Orien."

In a viridian shift of time and space, we were riding through a forest of pines once more. Leef, leading, urged his horse into a canter. Ahead of us, bars of light were an avenue to the mouth of the trees. Beyond that, all I could see was hazy. Cal was behind me. I could feel him, but I dared not turn around. Faster. The horses galloped to the end of an enchantment. Colors flew past us, voices called, becoming fainter, birds spiraled upwards, their wings like metal. I wanted to cry, "I am free! We are free!" but I could only laugh. My skin still burned where a golden hand had touched it. I could see his face in the haze. "There is something waiting for you, Swift!" Like a bubble bursting upon the face of the earth, we exploded out of the forest, like bullets, like fear running. A sound of water, laughter, blazing light. Heat hit my skin. Perhaps I had been cold. My head swam. I had to believe it: I am real. The ground roared up toward me, like a green wave starred with white and amethyst. I melted into it, a green darkness; the peace of eternal green.

They let me sleep. When I awoke, it was night-time and Leef had built a small fire. The light was fading rapidly. I noticed at once that the air was clean, untainted. We had passed the barrier. Leef came to my side and offered me a drink of water. It was tepid, but I drained the cup. "Nervous wrecks, both of you!" he said. Leef had seen nothing in the forest.

There was a river nearby and Cal had gone down there to bathe. I found him thoughtfully rubbing his skin with a handful of leaves, naked at the water's edge. He turned round when he heard me approach. We smiled at each other.

"Was it true, Swift?"

"Which part?" I sat down beside him.

"About Pell. Nothing else matters."

"You are single-minded in your obsession."

He laughed and rubbed at his arms. "It was real blood, Swift. It's hard to get it off."

"Here, let me help." I ripped grass from the riverbank, moistened his shoulders with a handful of water and began to rub.

"I shall turn the river red."

"Then it will be someone else's curse. The river flows away from us," I said. His skin was cold.

"You have not answered me . . ."

"About Pell? How can I? It was just a feeling. Leef was right; I shouldn't have said anything."

"Could you be right, though?"

I shrugged. "Anything is possible. That is one thing I've learned!"

Cal took the matted sheaf of grass from my hands. I took him in my arms. Just us two; it had been so long.

We were naked in the water together, ribbons of red flowing away from us. Beneath the surface, it was brighter, tangles of waving weed and dark, darting shapes. I clasped him in my limbs like something drowning, or drowned, and pulled him into me. It was all silver bubbles, in our hair, on our skin, rising, rising. No prayer. Were there angels under the water? I opened my mouth, delirious, forgetting where we were, and he had to drag me to the surface before I filled up with water. As my being ignited in an ecstasy of steam, I saw flaming stars scream across the blackest of skies above us. His breath still tasted of blood, but it was behind him now. The Gelaming had taken their price, or so I thought.

"So, where do we go now?" I asked him as we strolled back to the fire. The dark evening was still faintly pinky-red around us, fringed with insects and wings. We walked among banks of waving pampas grass.

Cal put his arm around me. "Away from the forest—obviously! Straight on," he said.

"You don't really know, do you! You are afraid."

"They will come to us."

"Can you be so sure? Will it be that easy?"

His hand dropped away from me. He reached for his eyes. Only the stained dusk around us and a feeling of imminence, unfightable and shining with power. Suddenly, I felt very small. I could feel the immensity of the world around me, seen and unseen. I was shooting upwards into the sky and the body of Swift was becoming smaller and smaller, trees like pins, redness seeping into my soul. I had to shake myself to dispel the illusion. It was so close.

The glow of our fire was almost indistinguishable from the light of the sky above the forest behind it. But we could see it, as the tall grass parted before us. We could see it . . . and something more. There were voices, muted like echoes. Cal made a hissing sound and pulled me down into the undergrowth. We looked at each other. His breath was sobbing. I tried to struggle. I think I said, "Leef!" I was thinking of him.

Cal shook his head urgently. "No, Swift, no!" His voice was high with panic as I broke away from him. I ran toward the fire and I heard a horse neigh, through the night air, high and shrill. I could see Leef, two figures holding him down, although he thrashed and writhed to escape.

He cried my name when he saw me, his face stricken. "Swift, go back! Go back!" he screamed. Go back? I hesitated. Cal was behind me. I felt his hands land upon my shoulders and curl around them. I could hear his breath. It was as if we were frozen. We could not go back. Around our fire, maybe a dozen tall figures sifted through our belongings. Behind them, horses gleamed like marble and there was a smell, like jasmin, only stronger. One of them was kneeling by the fire, a hand stretched toward the flames, as if he had never seen fire before. He raised his head slowly and it seemed to take an eternity. I saw a curtain of tawny hair and a face that showed only curiosity. For a second, only curiosity, and then something like pain or fury made him turn away. He stood up and turned his back on us, shouting something incoherent to one of the others, who stepped forward. Cal's fingers spiked into my flesh like steel. I wanted to cry out or move, but I could do neither. The one who had stepped toward us spoke.

"Son of Terzian?" His accent was soft and fluid and he was very tall; his clothes were like nothing I'd ever seen before. I can only describe his dress as scanty but complicated. His neck was hung with chains and talismans and black beads, his ears with silver. His hair was also silver, and shaved away from the sides of his scalp, but long over his shoulders. He smiled. I must have nodded or spoken—or *twitched.* "I am Arahal," he said. "We are Gelaming."

So, they had found us. And so soon. They had been with us in the forest, they had watched us in the water, they had waited by our fire.

"You are wet," Arahal said with a laugh, flicking my hair. I could see his aura, all the colors of strength, yet they spoke like us, smiled like us. "Calanthe, you were expected," he said to Cal, with the slightest of coolness. Cal was still clutching my shoulders as if his life depended on it. I knew he had drawn blood.

"He is *different,"* he blurted. "He . . . his hair is different."

The Gelaming looked puzzled for a moment. I had no idea what Cal was talking about.

"Oh, you mean . . . I wouldn't know," Arahal said. He shook his head and then glanced quickly behind him. "It must have been some time ago, Calanthe."

"It was."

Cal withdrew his nails from my skin with a sigh. I wanted to crumple; I don't know how I managed not to. My fingers strayed to my shoulders, encountering moist warmth. It may have been sweat.

"Just wait here a moment, please," Arahal told us. "We would like you to accompany us back to our headquarters, where members of our Hegemony are anxious to meet you." He made it sound like a request, but it was clear we had little choice. I could see them packing up our belongings, stifling our fire. Leef still stood between two Gelaming, now staring at the ground. He no longer struggled.

"Who was it, Cal?" I asked, in a voice that seemed to come from some distance away. "The one by the fire. Who was it? Was it Pell?"

Cal laughed, but there was no humor in it. "Don't be stupid, Swift! Another ghost, that's all. One that has haunted me for some years, one that I have been waiting for . . ."

Something from the past then. I knelt on the grass, my hands on my shoulders, and I could feel it rushing in. The inescapable, the inevitable, a focus of time. It has always been here, I thought. Someone has always known this would happen, and yet I didn't know. How could I not have guessed, not imagined? Not enough magic within me, not enough hope . . .

I looked for him; Cal's ghost. It would have been easier if he'd had no substance. It is hard to look at him directly. I could see that he'd been tempered by fire, by all the elements until the blade of his spirit was made deadly. His hair was smoother than the others.' He was not so tall. He must have felt my scrutiny. I saw him pause, as if in irritation or regret, before he turned to look at me. He had almond-shaped eyes. I could not see the color; I never would. He was something of Cobweb, something of Cal, something, even, of Pellaz. I could tell he did not want to look at me; there was no smile, his brow was furrowed.

Cal's voice came to me with bitterness. "Just witchery, Swift, that's all. Don't let it get under your skin. He's so sincere, and his bland sincerity can dry the blood in your veins . . ."

"But who?" I asked, and my toes and fingers were numb.

He turned away from us and his hair swung like silk. It was more than beauty. It was waking up and realizing there are things in the world so far from us, yet we yearn for them so, even before we've seen them, and when, if we're lucky, we finally do see them, it is a torment, because they are like smoke or fantasy, it is pain; you resent that they exist, yet they are your life, so far . . .

Cal made a choking sound behind me. "Same old magic!"

"His name?"

"His name is Seel," he said.

The Gelaming had given their camp a name: Imbrilim. It was only an hour's ride from the forest. When we reached it, we found that it was more than just a camp, it was a city of canopies and gauze and soft lights. We heard distant, lilting music and the air was full of the scent of flowers. A fragment of Heaven, here on Earth.

On the way there, Arahal rode beside us, making desultory attempts at conversation, seeking to dispel any uneasiness, while knowing instinctively that he probably couldn't, as yet. However, out of the three of us, only Leef looked truly worried. These people were his enemies, more than they were Cal's or mine. He had sought them once before, with the Varrish army, his head full of anger and a thirst for blood. Now they had found him and he feared their justice. Cal kept a constant stare directed at the back of Seel's head, where he rode some way in front of us. "I want to get my hands on him!" he said out loud, and it was impossible to guess exactly what he meant by that. Seel must have heard him, but he did not look round or even move farther away from us.

"What do you want of me?" I asked Arahal, hoping to divert his somewhat affronted attention from Cal.

"You sound weary," he answered. "After the forest, you must rest. The real answers can wait. Time has little meaning here."

We rode through billowing avenues of silk, shadows gliding at the edge of our vision. I saw hara who looked like gods and there was primaeval light in their eyes. Encompassed by fragrance, I was happy. It felt like happiness, anyway. A kind of relief. I wanted to laugh or weep or shout. It did not matter that tiredness had crept over me so deeply that I was at the point of hysteria. I had found the Gelaming and I thought that they were all that I'd imagined them to be. Hail, Ofaniel, angel of the moon, here on earth, riding a pale horse just ahead of us.

Arahal touched my arm, his knee touched my own as he brought his horse up against mine. I looked at him and his face was indistinct, but I knew he was smiling.

"Not far," he said. "You are yet young . . ."

Gelaming always speak like that when they get the chance.

Imbrilim was usually noisy at night. The dark seems to bring the Gelaming to life. I had thought them to be an austere race of people, grave-faced and full of ponderous thoughts. Now all I could hear was music and laughter and hara calling to each other. I had never seen an army camp, but I would never have imagined one to be like this. Even Galhea was never like this. We came to a pavilion of pale, green muslin, a soft glow showing from within. Most of our escort rode on ahead, but about half a dozen hara remained with Arahal to help us from our horses and take away our luggage. As soon as my feet hit the ground, I began to feel faint. I think it was more the effects of the forest aggravating my exhaustion than shock at finding the Gelaming. Arahal murmured an order and two hara supported me as we passed under the muslin canopy into the pavilion. The room within was spacious and furnished graciously. We were led directly into the sleeping chamber beyond.

The next thing I remember was opening my eyes to find myself lying on a soft, low couch. Hands supported my head and offered me something warm to drink from a cup. It tasted of honeyed milk and alcohol. I don't know how long I'd been unconscious, but my clothes had been taken away and I was covered by a thin blanket that was surprisingly warm.

Arahal came and looked at me. "It is important that you rest now, Swift," he said. The effects of the drink I'd been given were gently making their way through my blood; I could barely keep my eyes open. Thiede's people. I thought that angels stroked my face. I could hear prayers whispered in a language I had never heard before, but that I could still understand. Drifting on the edge of sleep, I sensed several hara come in from outside, bringing night coolness with them. One of them said, "Is the Tigron coming here now?"

"I don't think so," another answered. "I've heard he will send the Tigrina."

"Ah, such a neat sidestep. Our Tigron delays the inevitable, I feel!" I recognized that voice. It had spoken to me always, in my dreams, in my soul.

"Perhaps, Seel, perhaps . . . though a more charitable mind than yours might think that the Tigron only wishes to consider other people's feelings. These hara have been through a lot. You are too harsh."

"Too harsh! I know him. I know Cal too. They are both too strong for that!"

"Be quiet, both of you!" another voice warned. "The pure-born is yet awake."

I could not open my eyes, I was drugged by fragrance, yet I felt him lean over me, almost feeling his hair brush my face. The angel with almond-shaped eyes, force beating out, that was stifled anger; stifled because he was a stranger to anger. He did not speak, I wished I was Cobweb, mystical, lovely and deadly; a creature to inspire, but I was just Swift, bedraggled, unkempt and unremarkable. When he stood up, it was like warmth and light moving away. A voice said, "You are prepared to fight, I can tell."

"Arahal, I was born fighting!"

I could hear them still talking as they left us. Someone extinguished a lamp and there was only darkness behind my eyes. I slept. When I woke, I would remember every word of that conversation, and remember it for the rest of my life.

CHAPTER THREE

Nor shall ye have faith . . .
Bewilderment envelope the observer,
The patriarch vanishes
Like fodder into aqueous entrails.

Is it mapped out for us from the start, our destiny? Does the supernatural agent who charts our life create us equal to our discoveries? Leef had once said to me that troubles were always relative. I had come to view inner strength in the same way. There is always something stronger than ourselves, no matter how brightly burns the flame of confidence and power. There is always something stronger, something waiting to damn us for our weakness. Around every corner of the forest another monster lurks in wait for us; sometimes we can laugh at its feebleness. It appears horrible, but its substance is tissue-thin. It can be torn. The worst monsters we encounter have the faces of angels and the grace of devils flirting among the cold flames of hell. They can destroy us, merely because they scorch our souls unintentionally. Face such a creature and reason trickles out like blood from a cut vein. Is it decided before we are born whom we must love?

* * *

Filtered light falling through the floating gauze woke me with the softest of caresses. Beyond a curtain, lifted by fragrant morning breeze, I could see Cal and Leef curled up together on a low couch, childlike in the temporary innocence of sleep. Clothes had been laid out for us, new ones, essentially Gelaming in design. There was scented water and a bowl for washing; a mirror condemned me with brutal honesty. I had known myself once. Now I seemed physically a stranger. My hair and my eyes lacked luster; my skin no longer seemed to fit me properly. Facing myself caused me pain. I threw a cloth over the mirror and walked out, through the gauze, under the canopy, into the light.

They had come as strangers, as invaders; strange to our land, unmistakably foreign in their height, their dignity, their dress and their supple grace. Gelaming: God's children.

To this end men had struggled in agony across the face of the earth for millennia, sterile millennia. This was the goal toward which all threads of survival had strained. No-one had known it. Those that had guessed were madmen; unheeded, derided. For that mistake, mankind had been swamped. To an outsider, such as myself during those first few days, Gelaming perfection seems almost an obscenity, something that cannot be, yet something that I felt the need to stare at until I was sure I could only go blind. To me, it seemed that all their blemishes of character and spirit had been polished away. I found myself wondering how they could possibly exist comfortably when they had nothing left to strive toward, no inner struggle, no contest. I should have looked deeper, but that did not come until later. As I walked among them that first day, I felt no fear, for the inspiration of terror holds no pleasure for Gelaming. It is merely another weapon, to be used only when the occasion truly merits it. They barely looked at me. To them, I was just another refugee, wandering wide-eyed among the angels.

Imbrilim was the size of a small town, and full of life. By day all the swaying canopies were held back and as I walked through the avenues of pavilions, I could see right into them. It was apparent that there were several places where all the inhabitants of Imbrilim went to eat. These seemed open for business all day, so it was rare that anyone took meals in their own pavilions. All this was paid for by the Hegemony of Immanion; the only things that hara had to pay for themselves were narcotics and alcohol. Tents for the consumption of beverages were set apart from those serving meals.

Everywhere, the flags and pennants of Immanion flapped lazily in the breeze. Their symbols were the double-headed axe, the scarab and two serpents entwined around a sword. All these signified the two-in-one; hermaphroditism. Above a huge pavilion of purple and gold (which I later learned belonged to the Hegemony) shivered the black and silver banner of the Tigron; a lion with a fish's tail shimmering against a dark ground. I lost myself entirely, but I couldn't stop walking.

Arahal sought me out. He found me eventually by the horses, corraled on the boundaries of Imbrilim. They were snowy creatures of myth, whose feet danced with the ache for wings. I reached toward them, my hand like ivory, and a dozen blue-black noses blew warmth upon my skin. They absorbed me and turned their heads to look at me properly. One tossed his snowy mane and threw up his head, nickering softly. That was Arahal coming; they knew him.

"I have never ceased to marvel at their magnificence," he said.

I was too intimidated to speak. I could only smile in a way I'd not smiled since I could still climb comfortably onto Cobweb's lap.

Arahal insisted on taking me on a tour of Imbrilim; we passed many things that I'd already seen, but he explained a lot to me about the way the Gelaming conducted their daily lives. He pointed out a magnificent construction of sparkling white muslin. "That is where we remember the Aghama," he said.

"Aghama?" I queried. It sounded like an event.

"The first Wraeththu," Arahal explained.

I had no idea what he meant. Yet another area of my education so sadly neglected. It was strange that I had never wondered about it, really. After all, Wraeththu must have come from somewhere. Now I learned the truth of our wondrous genesis. We had sprung from one mutant; born to a human female, a hermaphrodite child, whose special talents were seen by his parents as freakish abnormalities. Through his blood, he had created the new race; Wraeththu. To his people he had become the Aghama, revered almost as a god. I had known nothing of this, not even Cobweb had ever mentioned anything about this shadowy, part-mythological figure of the Aghama.

Arahal did not seem surprised. To him, Varrs were nothing but godless barbarians. He was prepared to educate me and took me inside the Fane of the Aghama. It was barely furnished; just a few polished benches before a table on which stood maybe a dozen slim, lit tapers. There was no representation of the first Wraeththu, either in paint or stone. "We come here to think, to remember," Arahal told me.

"Remember what?" I asked.

"Our beginning," he replied, and in such a somber tone, I shrank from further queries.

Out in the sunlight, I remember wondering aloud, "What am I doing here?" Arahal only smiled. I recalled Cal once asking that question of my father, and Terzian's reply, "Must you ask that every day?" I don't think Cal had ever truly known the answer; now I felt my own question was doomed to the same fate.

Arahal said, "Megalithica. . . . It is a grand name. The hara that shall come to rule here will be equal in stature and their sons will possess the wisdom of the generations."

What generations? As Arahal walked beside me, glowing with an inner light of pride, I thought about how the Gelaming had plucked their culture, even their cities, from the air and imbued it with a luster of centuries. It was a lie. Their culture was still damp from its birthing, yet they talked as if they had owned the earth a thousand years. It had taken men so long to step away from the creatures of the forest and the plain, up from the slime, the first discovery of fire and shelter. Perhaps they had stepped too far, too far to get back, and their isolation had shriveled them . . . perhaps. Wraeththu are animals; they are not men, they will not call themselves human. I could say to myself, "I am an animal," and see something shining in the dark, powerful, sleek and close to the earth. My eyes can light up and my teeth are sharp enough to kill, yet now, it seems, I must fold away my fangs and claws and learn to lie down with the lamb whose flesh is so tempting. Gelaming taught me: there is no murder, just negative impulses to scorch the soul and a temporary destruction of flesh. The soul will always return. Only the murderer ultimately suffers from the act of killing. I wondered why they wished to educate me, what use I was to serve them, but my questions were sidestepped. Arahal would say to me, "Do you not want to be full of feelings that are smooth and straight? Don't you want to be able to see around corners? We can help you to speak in colors, to see the pattern of sounds that are other hara's thoughts. This is the true mutation!"

Mutation: change. It seems my childhood fears would surface once again.

If they had come to Galhea, the Gelaming would never have killed us, or even sent us away from our homes, as we'd feared. We would just have been smothered quietly, our bewilderment soothed, the knives taken from our hands. Their conquering power was not violence, but no less effective because of it. We had been so wrong about them, and my father had ridden toward this without knowing. If he *was* with the Gelaming, I was sure he must be dead. If his body still lived, the Terzian I had known (and the one I had not) would be quenched from the fire in his eyes. Whatever I had learned about him, I had enough mercy within me to hope that he had *truly* died, and in the only way he'd have been proud of fighting.

Back to that first day, strolling in the sunlight with Arahal, his hand upon my shoulder. The air around us was full of insects with wide, gossamer wings. They got in our hair and sparked there like gems as they fluttered to death. I felt disorientated, unsure of whether I was dreaming. None of this seemed real.

Arahal smiled benevolently at me. "Ours is the only way, Swift, You will come to know us. You will see this for yourself."

"Why me?" I asked him. "What do you want of me? I'm not ready for it, whatever it is. My soul is too young. It does not crave this." I did not even understand myself what I was trying to convey.

Arahal laughed. "You are still in the forest, Swift. You must let go and come out of the trees." Gelaming seem to hate answering questions. It's not that they prefer secrecy, they just expect people to find out the answers for themselves.

"I want Cobweb," I said, helplessly. "I want my hostling."

"He is always with you."

"No, not here." I could barely remember Cobweb's face.

We passed a large pavilion, whose awnings were of palest pink and gold. Later, I found out it was a meeting place for those of high rank; the Hegemony and their closest staff. At its entrance, a group of hara stood in conversation, their hands gliding to complement their speech. Pain brought a bitter taste to my mouth. One of them was Seel.

Arahal called a greeting. Seel turned and looked and shook out his hair and smiled. I had not imagined him like this. Cal had described him differently to me. This was the har who had built a town from bare, corroded rock and blistered his hands tearing at the soda valleys in the south. Now he was just Gelaming, sanitized and unsoiled. He should have had snakes for hair. He did not look at me once.

I was not taken to the Hegemony for three days. During this time, Cal, Leef and I remained in our canopied home, emerging only to eat, when we would sit together in the quietest corner we could find in the nearest pavilion that served food. Once or twice, strangers came to talk with us, refugees from the north, as they supposed us to be. We were afraid of revealing too much about ourselves (all conversation seemed to turn to the Varrs and their atrocities), so shrank from responding to any friendly overtures. We amused ourselves by playing with the pack of cards Arahal had brought us and drinking vast amounts of wine.

Far from recovering from my weakness brought on by our journey through the forest, I seemed to be getting worse. It was an effort to do anything. I couldn't eat, but I was still the only one who ever went for a walk outside the pavilion. I liked the way nobody bothered me. I could wander half drunk for hours in total peace with people all around me. That was the best thing about Imbrilim, I think. Cal was on edge all the time, dreading further contact with Seel, while Leef was sullen and silent. It was a relief to get away from them occasionally.

"Why doesn't he come?!" Cal shouted out, unexpectedly, one evening.

"He will never come!" I answered, knowing that to be unbearably true.

Cal sat down on the floor. "He's changed," he murmured, to himself more than to Leef or me. "Once he would have come storming in here, yelling at me . . . now it's like, it's like he's been gelded or something."

"Different fire, different fire . . ." I rambled.

Cal put his head in his hands. "I *must* see him!" he insisted.

Seel never came.

In the evenings, I liked to stand at the entrance to our pavilion, taking in deep lungfuls of scented air that always smelled of nostalgia to me. Often, laughing groups of humans and hara would stroll past, lost in conversation, lost in friendship, perhaps on their way for an evening drink in one of the ale tents. Once Cal joined me. "It's disgusting! I hate them!" he said.

Sometimes I could bear it no longer and would have to go looking around Imbrilim, looking for *him*. I usually found him. I seemed to have an uncanny instinct for sniffing him out. The best time was when I found him alone, in a field, beyond the camp. I don't think he was dancing, just exercising his body, but it was incredible to watch. There was no music, but I could tell he was hearing it. He was so slim, it seemed impossible that he contained all the right bits inside him. The thought of it was inconceivable. Such a perfect being could not be blood and bile and gut. Inside, he would be made of glass or crystal or cloud. Maybe all three. I watched him entranced, full of pain. Once he looked right at me and seemed to stretch just that little bit further. I hated him knowing I was watching, but he did not seem to mind. He was used to an audience.

Afterwards, I told Cal about it. He did not laugh, as I had expected. "What is waiting for us?" he asked me. "I can feel something breathing down the back of my neck, just outside, just above us, perhaps. Why do they make us wait?"

Miserably, I took him in my arms and we sat on the floor, among the silken cushions, in silence, tasting each other's thoughts without the contact of lips or flesh. After a while, Cal said, "I get the feeling . . . I don't think I'll be around here for much longer."

I could not answer him, for I knew that it was true.

In the morning, Arahal came for me. The sunlight beyond the canopies was hard and glittering, like Arahal's silver hair. He was dressed in skin-tight black trousers, with a confection of straps and silver chains adorning his chest and back. There were black feathers woven into his hair. He looked magnificent, a prince of legend. I was feeling horribly light-headed because of the skimpy meals I'd had over the past few days, but Arahal did not seem to notice or concern himself with my condition. I was sure that if I fell, he would just sling me over his shoulder and carry on walking, chatting amiably about things I would never remember or even hear properly.

He took me directly to the purple and gold pavilion and told me cheerfully that I was to be given an audience by members of the Hegemony. I was miserably conscious of my bedraggled and feeble appearance and knew I was in no state to present myself well. "Does it have to be today?" I asked.

"I thought you wanted your questions answered," Arahal replied.

An intensely beautiful har, dressed in floating gray gauze, with thigh-length platinum-colored hair, conducted us into an antechamber. "I am Velaxis," he told me. I got the impression that was supposed to mean something. "If you would wait here a few moments, Tiahaara . . ." He swayed off into the curtains.

"Velaxis is a creature of renown," Arahal said drily.

"Is he one of the Hegemony?" I asked.

Arahal shook his head and smiled. "Oh no, but he is very close to them. Thiede gave him to them."

This struck me as absurd, if not a trifle hypocritical. For a race who professed to believe so passionately in freedom, how could they countenance something that had more than a whiff of slavery about it?

Arahal noticed my expression. "Velaxis is paid for his services," he said. I must have looked even more surprised. "He was once in Thiede's employ as a personal assistant," he continued. "No doubt Thiede realized the Hegemony would need efficient personnel here in Megalithica."

Velaxis conducted us into the main chamber of the pavilion. We hadn't waited long. Our presence was announced. I was nervous, expecting formality of the severest kind.

In the middle of the room was a large table. A tall, half-dressed har was sitting on it, peeling a piece of fruit with a knife, his boots were scuffed, and long, fair hair escaped from a black ribbon at the back of his neck. He had a face that was used to smiling and very white teeth. Another, standing next to him, sharing a joke (they were both laughing), was combing out his hair, which was wet.

"Ah, the rogue Arahal," said the one sitting on the table. That anyone should even think of Arahal being a rogue, let alone actually say it, was a revelation.

"Ashmael," Arahal responded, bowing sarcastically. The fair-haired har put his knife down carefully on the table. He looked directly at me and I had to lower my eyes. "And this must be the spawn of the mighty Terzian," he said.

They offered me wine, which went straight to my head, and we sat on warm, wooden chairs around the table.

"Arahal, what have you been doing to him?" Ashmael asked, lifting my chin in his hand. His fingers were sticky with fruit juice. Arahal did not answer.

"Are you struck dumb or something?" Ashmael asked me. "Can Varrs speak?"

"I am dying," I answered.

Ashmael looked at Arahal and they grinned at each other. "I think I should talk with him alone," Ashmael said.

"As you think best," Arahal answered and stood up. He and the other har (who had not yet spoken) went through the curtains to another part of the pavilion. From this, I gathered that Ashmael must be of higher rank than the others.

"Are you hungry?" he asked me. I shook my head, then nodded it, unsure, sick and starving. The Gelaming called for food and then sat on the table again, where he was obviously more comfortable. He looked at me in silence. His charisma was almost stifling. I could sense his power and his fame, yet he was effortlessly informal. I felt so small beside him, yet even in my helplessness, I wanted him to respect me a little.

"I want to know . . . ." I began, and then trailed off, confused as to what to ask.

"You want to know why you are here," Ashmael prompted helpfully, still staring right into me.

I nodded and my head swam. "I feel so weak," I said.

"Then you must eat!" He reached for my face again. "You're all bone!

If it helps, I will tell you that this is only the effect of the forest; our little Purgatory. Your psyche has been wounded. I fear you will have suffered terrible revelations. Perhaps we should not have let you stew for so long, but we wanted to let you rest for a few days before interviewing you. It must be intimidating . . ." He smiled and then made a noise of annoyance, standing up and striding to the entrance of the room. "Velaxis!" he called. "I believe I ordered food some time ago!" Even his sarcasm was charming.

"Are you their leader?" I asked, once he had sat down again. He laughed.

"No; their leader, as you call it, is a grand personage known as the Tigron. He is a phenomenon of phenomena . . . oh, but of course, you've already met him, haven't you!"

"Have I?" I asked, thinking of Seel.

"Yes. To most he is only known as the mighty Tigron, but to his friends and those fortunate enough to share his bed, he is merely Pellaz."

I should have known, I suppose, but even so, it took some moments for this fact to sink in.

"Pellaz! Then he *isn't* dead!"

Ashmael pulled a wry face and sighed. "Just the opposite, I would say. Searingly alive! Even if he is Thiede's . . ." He paused and shook his head. "No, I must not speak out of turn. Such things are not for your ears, son of Terzian!"

All I could think of was getting back to our pavilion and being able to tell Cal about this. I wanted to go now. Suddenly, my head had cleared and I no longer seemed to be among strangers.

I must have tried to stand. Ashmael carelessly pushed me back into my chair with his foot. "Where are you going? You haven't eaten yet and I haven't talked to you."

"I must . . . Cal . . ."

Again, Ashmael shook his head. "No, you mustn't. Cal has his own path to follow and I dare say it's a long one. There's no fiery reunion for him yet. Your paths must diverge for a while."

"You're going to try and change him, aren't you?" I couldn't help saying it, but Ashmael didn't seem offended.

"We don't want to change anyone . . . well, perhaps . . . not Cal, certainly. He is a pawn in a mighty battle that concerns neither of us. Put him out of your mind."

Velaxis brought in the food. There was cold, roasted chicken, a salad of crisp greens and nuts, and strong, aromatic cheese with blue veins. Once I could smell it, food was all I could think of. Ashmael ate off my plate, not really hungry, but too greedy to watch me eat it alone. He poured me more wine.

"Now then, the first thing we're going to do with you is begin your caste training, of which you've had none, I take it." I shook my head. He smiled. "After that, when you've settled down a little, perhaps the real purpose for your being here shall be revealed. For now, you'll just have to be content with learning how to be Gelaming."

"Why is it all so secret? Why am I important? Until recently, my only claim to importance was the fact that I was Terzian's son. Is that still the reason?"

Ashmael shrugged. "In a way. You must understand that the plans of the Gelaming are vast, and that you are only a small part of them, but an important one nonetheless. We all have our part to play. Soon, you shall understand yours."

"You're not like Arahal and the others," I said, suddenly. It was a thought spoken aloud.

"Not like them? What do you mean?"

"You're . . . I don't know . . . *real*. I can understand you."

"Oh, don't let them deceive you," he said, grinning. "That's just their way. You'll soon learn. Terrific posers, all of them. Just remember; they all have to shit, they all sweat, they're all flesh and blood and bone. The rest of it they learned from Thiede, who is the archetypal cool person."

"I think it's more than that," I said dubiously.

He shrugged. "Perhaps, but I helped shape Thiede's little kingdom for him and he values me, so I'm allowed to think as I like."

I laughed with him. Whatever he said, Ashmael was not like the others. He had no time for trivia and was impatient with formality, but he could be a bitter enemy if you upset him.

He told me about the Hegemony, that there were three of them here in Megalithica; Cedony, who was here before with the wet hair, Ashmael and another, whose name was Chrysm. He told me that Thiede had kept them inactive for quite some time. All they had done since reaching Megalithica was provide sanctuary for refugees from the north and "worry Terzian and Ponclast a little." That was when I asked about my father.

"Where are my people?"

Ashmael looked me straight in the eye. "I don't know," he said, spreading his hands, "truly I don't. I had nothing to do with that. It was a morsel that Thiede and Pell kept to themselves. We get so little news here. All we do is wait for orders that never seem to come. One day, we are told, 'Terzian's son is coming to you and he has to be trained.' It wasn't quite the earth-shattering event we'd been anticipating. I don't know why Thiede wanted you to come to us. It would have been much quicker for us to come to you at Galhea and bring you back, but that was the way he wanted it, so we couldn't argue. Thiede's fond of upgrading unsuspecting hara to greatness, as he did with Pellaz. I should imagine he has some grand scheme in mind for yourself. Better lie back and take it and make the most of it. There's little point in putting up a fight, believe me!"

"Perhaps my father is still in the forest," I said, not wanting to be sidetracked from my original question, although what Ashmael had told me prompted a hundred more.

"I doubt it," he replied. "As I told you, dealing with the Varrish army was something that Thiede and Pell handled alone. It would have been tied up long ago."

"Then where . . . ?"

"Leave it, Swift!" Ashmael warned and the tone of his voice silenced me utterly.

After a while, the other members of the Hegemony, whom I had not met, came to join us. At first, I thought it was Seel and my skin crawled. He had similar slanty, cat's eyes, but his hair was darker and he was taller.

"I can't stand it! The shower spits rust down my back and there's a dead bird in our water cistern!" he cried, raising his arms, rolling his eyes upwards. "Ah, Immanion, I grieve for you!"

"Chrysm, this is Swift," Ashmael announced.

Chrysm put his hands in his hair. "Ah, at last, the Varr! Can we go home now?" he asked.

From the way I was treated by the Hegemony, I could tell that my status must be close to that of Arahal's. They spoke to me in the way that people of high rank do to those whose position is beneath theirs, but higher than most; the way that tries to convey equality, while still making it apparent that they are making a conscious effort to do so. I had always imagined the Gelaming to lack humor, to be utterly serious all the time, but as in most of my preconceptions about them, I was proved wrong. Apart from their stunning appearance, they were nothing like the way I'd imagined. I found I was rather drunk and told Chrysm of my earlier opinions of his kind.

"It is a strain being perfect, I suppose," he said, grinning. "For myself, I am not above the occasional orgy of bitching, which no doubt offends my guardian spirit to the point of apoplexy, but still . . . talking of which, is this rumor of the Tigrina's impendence rooted in truth or supposition or what?"

Ashmael shrugged. "I don't know for sure. You know how these things get around. Pell won't come himself, I'm sure of that. Everyone's sure of that! Perhaps the Tigrina is bored, alone in his ivory tower in Phaonica. Pell might send him to us to keep him quiet."

"Or to gratify his curiosity over certain people," Chrysm remarked cynically.

"Mmm, that too, of course. However, I'm sure Thiede would have assured our gracious Tigrina that Cal is no threat to his position . . ." He noticed me trying to follow their conversation. "I'd better explain to you, Swift, who the Tigrina is. His name is Caeru and he is the Tigron's consort. You will no doubt hear rumors that their relationship is not all it might be. It was Thiede's idea, of course. Pell never lets slip anything about his feelings, but it's no secret in Immanion about his relationship with Cal. Neither is it a secret that Thiede would do anything to prevent them resuming it. I think it's sort of inevitable that Cal should come back into Pell's life. He could so easily have vanished forever. Just because he's here with us in Imbrilim must be bringing the Tigrina out in a cold sweat . . . Something's going on, but no-one knows what it is."

"Least of all Cal," I said. "He doesn't even know Pell is still alive."

"I pity him, in spite of his sins," Chrysm said, and for a while, we all fell silent.

Eventually, I had to ask some questions about Seel. I noticed my companions pause and grin at each other before Ashmael answered me.

"What about Seel? He's a born organizer, I suppose. He enjoys bringing order out of chaos. He's a close friend of the Tigron's and through that, the closest link to home. It is said they communicate frequently."

"He's beautiful," I blurted, inadequately.

"We are all beautiful," Chrysm laughed, throwing back his head and gazing haughtily down his nose in a typically Seelish manner.

"Of course Seel has inner light," Ashmael said caustically.

"Don't you like him?" I asked, appalled.

"Of course we do," Ashmael answered quickly, patting my head. "It's just that he's full of Pell's essence and finds it difficult to keep his feet on the ground nowadays. Few can aspire to embrace him. His nights are spent in solitary meditation, enjoying our Tigron's touch on the astral plane, no doubt."

"No doubt at all!" Chrysm agreed, raising his glass.

At dusk I wandered back to the pavilion that had become my home, thinking about the afternoon's events. The visit to the Hegemony had been purely social, I could see that. They had wanted to put me at my ease and had succeeded effortlessly. I was no longer so anxious about my purpose for being in Imbrilim, for the Hegemony seemed as vague about it as I was, and that was comforting in a strange sort of way. Some of the elated mood that had accompanied my arrival in Imbrilim had come back to me. I had walked away from my pavilion that morning, afraid of what to expect and of no worth. Now I walked back a friend of august persons who had a definite place in the scheme of things, even if no-one was sure of what it was. I was full of Gelaming wine and felt like dancing. For the first time in ages, I felt once more like a son of a Wraeththu tribe leader. My shoulders drooped no longer and the effect was magical. Hara bid me good evening and waved. A woman carrying a child in her arms stopped to speak and told me she was glad I was feeling better. "I am Shara," she said. "My people came down from the north some months ago, and after my father died, it fell to me to take charge of them. We were driven from our homes by the Varrs."

I must have gone white. Shara immediately reached for my arm, flustered by embarrassment. "I'm sorry. Please don't think I meant anything by that. We heard you were coming here. We know who you are. Did you suffer terribly at the hands of your father?"

How could I answer that? To say yes would be a lie and to say no might go against me. "Many have suffered at the hands of my father," I said and she nodded in sympathy.

"Our tents are in the eastern quarter of Imbrilim. My people are known as the Tyrells. Please come visit us sometime. You would be most welcome."

I thanked her and she walked away from me. So humans too were forming into tribes, it seemed. As the Hegemony had treated me like an equal, so too had the human woman. There were many things I'd have to get used to. I also realized that everyone in Imbrilim seemed to know everyone else's business. I'd never seen Shara before, yet she'd known who I was and that I'd been feeling unwell. Isolated in Forever, I'd never known that communities can seem surprisingly smaller than they really are and that gossip travels faster than fire.

Leef was waiting for me outside the pavilion, staring anxiously up the avenue. When I saw his face, which was wretched, I was angry, because I could feel my mellow good humor melting away. "Cal is gone," he said.

He did not know where, only that Arahal had come back to our pavilion some time in the afternoon and told Cal to gather up his belongings. He had not owned much. "Say goodbye to your friend," he had been told, and Leef had watched helplessly as Arahal led Cal away.

"He knew it would happen," Leef said, shaking his head. "What's going to happen to you and me? What do they want with us?"

I put my hand over his and said nothing.

They would not tell me where Cal had been taken, nor what fate awaited him. I had to ask, I had to stand up and demand answers; Leef expected it of me.

I sought Arahal; I found him sitting outside a pavilion with a group of friends, sipping green liquor, absorbing the evening air, laughing softly. Never had a scene looked more inviting. He listened politely to my outburst, nodding at the end of it. "You must not be concerned," he said and offered me a drink. "Please, sit down, Swift. Join us."

"I had thought his suffering had ended," I said, complying with his request and accepting the cool crystal goblet he placed into my hand.

"What makes you think Calanthe suffers?"

I turned away from him, angry at the evening for being so tranquil, annoyed at myself because I knew my anger was only superficial and that I only wanted to get this conversation out of the way so that I could enjoy myself and talk with Arahal about my conversation with Ashmael. It wasn't that I no longer cared about Cal's fate, just that I had accepted it. Before Arahal even told me, I knew that Cal's future, his path, was divergent from my own. If I sound cruel saying that, then it must be read as cruel, but it is how things were, nevertheless. When I turned round again, I realized Seel was sitting at Arahal's side. He was looking at the floor, one hand in his hair. As soon as he felt me looking at him, he stood up, excused himself to the others and walked away. Nobody commented on it.

"Where *is* Cal?" I asked Arahal.

He refilled my glass which I'd emptied too quickly. "This is awkward,

"Swift. I can't answer you and you must stop wondering. There is no sense in it. It is Thiede's will, or the Tigron's, so you can do nothing."

"Can you blame me for worrying?"

"Not at all!" He smiled and touched my face. "If you are worrying . . . They said you had a look of your hostling about you. They are right."

"They?"

He shrugged. "Rumors, of course. Yet you have Terzian's steel as well. Let us hope you have not inherited his mania."

I shivered at the possibilities in that concept. "He was always a good father to me," I said stiffly.

"And a considerate friend to Cobweb, no doubt."

I squirmed awkwardly. "Do you know so much about us?"

"Only what was necessary for us to know."

I looked away, up the avenues of swaying silk, in the direction Seel had taken. I wanted to ask about him, but I couldn't. "Is it true the Gelaming deny love?" I asked instead.

Arahal leaned back in his seat. "Ah, love; what is it? Can we ever know? It defies analysis, I'm sure!"

"You have not answered me."

"No. Perhaps I can't. The whole concept is a web of subtleties. Where is the dividing line between a close friend, who cares for your welfare, who shares the intimate pleasures of your bed, and a lover? Is there one?"

"Cal told me that the Gelaming scorn what they call 'the passions of mankind'."

Arahal sucked his upper lip thoughtfully. "Passion of any nature is to be scorned, of course," he answered obliquely.

"You are evading me," I said.

"Not really. I don't want to give you the wrong impression. Being Gelaming is a way of life, a state of mind; not just Gelaming either, but many other tribes. It is difficult to convey in words. If you had been trained, if you thought in the right way, then you would know and I would not have to explain."

"But what if I don't want to think that way?"

Arahal smiled. "Then you really are the son of Terzian, to the marrow of your bones, and we are wrong about you."

Arahal became my tutor. For the next few weeks I had to undertake the training that would raise my level. It had nothing to do with warfare as Varrish caste progression did, but was no less rigorous because of it. I suffered gruelling sessions of painful self-examination, when Arahal dispassionately sifted through my innermost feelings and beliefs. It was only through severe concentration that I managed to keep my thoughts about Seel to myself. I dreaded Arahal becoming aware of them. It was obvious that he knew I was keeping something back, but he also sensed the embarrassment surrounding those thoughts, so for the time being did not press me to reveal them. All he said was, "Guilt is a tool of destruction, Swift, remember that!" His voice full of dire warning. Some part of me really wanted to confess, but I feared Arahal's displeasure, more so because I thought he would not show it.

"Must you know everything about me?" I asked.

He smiled. "You are missing the point, Swift. *I* don't want to know everything about you, but I want you to."

In the evenings, I began to spend an hour in meditation. Everything seemed clearer then. I was pleasantly surprised how, when my mind was calm and ordered, it was so easy to summon up and control my innate powers. Now I could visualize with ease, which meant that I could now operate the special shields that the Gelaming used as a barrier at the entrance to their homes. I had only to visualize the force field to be there and no-one could pass through without my wanting them to.

After only a few days, Leef had moved out of our pavilion and gone to live with a group of hara he had made friends with, who, like ourselves and many other hara in Imbrilim, had come down from the north. I knew Leef was displeased that I had been absorbed into the elite of the Gelaming and he told me that he believed I had forgotten all about my old home and Terzian and Cal. He did not actually say it, but I'm sure he looked on me as some kind of traitor.

Perhaps I didn't think of my father and Cal as often as I should, but my mind was often full of Cobweb. I wanted to see him so much and he was so far away; our minds could not touch. We had always been near enough to each other for that, ever since I'd been born. Only now did I realize it and miss it. I used to wonder what he was doing and what Swithe and Moswell and Tyson were doing. Did Bryony ever think of me? Perhaps, in the garden, she could feel me near. At night, I liked to pretend I was back there, lying on the damp grass beside the lake; that place where things of importance had seemed to happen to me. Then I would feel like weeping, for I knew those times would never return. My innocence was lost to me and when I thought of that, I was swamped with loneliness, thinking, Nobody knows how to love me here.

A result or cause of these thoughts, of course, was Seel. Every day, my desire to see him became worse. I told myself I was obsessed and that obsession was dangerous and full of lies and that I must deny it. Then I would open my eyes and be full of tranquility and confidence, believing all my demons exorcised. Then I would see him again and a searing flame of longing would open up the wounds within me; I would want him again and more than that, want to tell him terrible things, terrible, wonderful things. I would imagine it again and again and again. The story would have one of two endings. The first ending was Seel smiling and saying, "This was meant to be" and the other was his face convulsed with revulsion, backing away from me in distaste. Of the two outcomes, the latter seemed more probable. I kept my fantasies to myself.

* * *

One day Arahal said to me, "Swift, it would be best if you did not take
aruna with your friend Leef from now on." I was so shockeed by this that
I did not think to mention that we had not been close for some time now.

"Is there any reason why?" I asked.

"Yes," Arahal replied, but that was all I could get out of him.

I found that I could have a glittering social life in Imbrilim if I wanted
to, for I was never short of invitations to other hara's pavilions. There were
always parties going on. I had visited Shara's people several times, and
although these occasions were never as sophisticated as those spent in
Gelaming company, I always enjoyed myself. Most nights, however, I was
simply too tired to go out and, once Arahal had called a halt to my
education for the day, fell into an exhausted sleep, often without eating or
even undressing. The intensive training was worth it, though, because after
only five weeks, my level was raised to Neoma.

Arahal was quick to squash all my thoughts of relaxation. "It is essential
that your caste should be Ulani, at last," he said. "Once you have achieved
it, then you can think about enjoying yourself more."

"Why Ulani?" I wanted to know.

"Because I say so," he answered.

I was curious about what the Gelaming planned to do with Megalithica
now they were here. Were they eventually going to ride north and deal with
Ponclast once and for all?

"Eventually," Arahal conceded, in response to my inquiry. "But not yet.
Ponclast has constructed shields about himself. We shall let him think they
are effective for a while."

"I thought the Gelaming had no cynicism in their souls!" I joked.

Arahal shrugged. "The time is not right; that's all. When we ride north,
Swift, you will be with us. When we seize the reins of Ponclast's power, it
will be to hand them over to you."

I laughed out loud.

Arahal smiled. "Ulani at least, you see . . ."

My purpose for being summoned to Imbrilim was revealed as casually
as that. Thiede had once groomed Pellaz to govern Wraeththu as their
Tigron, and now he was having me groomed to oversee one of Pellaz's
provinces. Swift the Varr, whom Varrs would find more acceptable than a
complete stranger. Terzian's son, sharing his blood while not sharing his
beliefs. Who else could have more chance of claiming Varrish loyalty
except Terzian himself? The Varr now occupied virtually all the north of
Megalithica and their influence spread even further than that. Even bearing
in mind that the average Varr was little different from the average Gelaming of low caste, it would not be easy to overthrow Ponclast's dominance,
for his people believed in his power, and their belief made his power real.
I found myself wondering if Thiede had ever considered trying to win
Terzian himself over, offering him sovereignty of the Varrs. Had that been
the original plan? Terzian was worshiped by every Varr. He was a warrior

prince, handsome, intelligent and fierce; a natural ruler. But the canker in his soul had run too deep and I knew he would never have succumbed to accepting Thiede as his lord; never. Whereas I was young and idealistic and half Cobweb's. The only conceivable substitute. I think the Gelaming's main problem with me was that I did not look more like Terzian.

"There may be violence," Arahal said.

"I should expect so," I agreed. "I know what Ponclast's capable of."

"We hope to avoid conflict as much as possible, but I'm sure you're familiar with the nature of your race. Distasteful!"

"Arahal, I'm lonely!"

"Swift, you must be patient."

Sometimes, Ashmael would send for me and I would sit in his pavilion and listen to him talking with Cedony and Chrysm or other members of his staff. It was the best way to learn. Often, he seemed to forget I was there, but now and again, he would send the others away and talk to me. Once he asked me to massage his shoulders, complaining they were stiff. Beneath my fingers, they felt as supple as a puma's. He sighed pleasurably and said, "What do you think of me, Swift? Do I please you?"

I was so surprised and embarrassed that I backed away from him. My answer was a shaky mumble. "You are Gelaming, Lord Ashmael; that should be response enough."

He laughed and shrugged, turning to look at me. "Swift, I have told you about this before. You mustn't spend so much time looking up to us as if we were gods or something. When I asked you that, you should have just said yes and then seduced me. I was looking forward to it."

After that, nothing happened between us. I think he must have been teasing me.

One evening, I was invited to a gathering at Cedony's pavilion. Arahal escorted me. It was quite an important occasion because everyone of note was there. I had seen little of Seel over the past few weeks and was surprised to see him there. I had thought he was away from Imbrilim for he sometimes went back to Immanion, although his journeys were amazingly swift; he was never away for long. I longed to touch him or even speak to him, but his unbearable loveliness was intimidating. He must have dozens of hara paying him compliments constantly. Whatever I could say to him would bore him. When he walked past us, he smiled and nodded at Arahal and then looked at me. I felt color rise to my face, but thankfully he had gone before he could see it. Arahal threw me a shrewd sidelong glance, but said nothing.

Chrysm came over and asked me how my training was coming along. Arahal answered for me and told him it was coming along just fine, thank you.

"Your looks are improving," Chrysm said to me, touching my arm, so that Arahal couldn't interrupt.

"No, my looks are returning," I replied, somewhat coldly. "It was the journey."

"You are angry," Chrysm said, smiling ruefully. "Perhaps that was rude of me."

"Not really."

"Come and talk to me. Is that allowed, Arahal?"

"You are a stupid beast, Chrysm," Arahal replied and walked away from us.

"Can he talk to you like that?" I asked, rather shocked.

"We know each other very, very well," he replied.

"Oh, I see."

"Mmm, I think you do, little Swift. I expect you hate being called that. You're not that little, are you? It's those enormous eyes. You always look so defensive, or defenseless; I'm not sure which."

We went outside and walked in the cool, fragrant air. Because of the dusk and his shining hair, I could imagine Chrysm was Seel quite easily, but tried not to. It seemed impure to, somehow.

"Why doesn't Cedony live in the Hegemony's pavilion?" I asked. "Doesn't he get on with the sumptuous Velaxis or something?"

Chrysm laughed. "No, it's not that! He likes his privacy, I suppose. I take it you are unimpressed with Velaxis."

"He looks down on me."

"No, he doesn't! You are soon to be a mighty ruler, like your father. Why should he look down on you?"

"Oh, please! I'm not so sure about the mighty part or even the ruler, for that matter. Ponclast might take the law into his own hands and kill me."

"Oh, come now, Thiede would never allow that! Anyway, stop being paranoid. In the words of mankind, Velaxis is merely a whore. If he really does try to look down on you, all you have to do is laugh at him. If you asked Ashmael for Velaxis's company for a night and Ashmael said yes, Velaxis would have to agree. Then let him try and look down on you!"

I laughed. "Yes, I know. Sorry. I know I'm being stupid."

"Oh, Swift." Chrysm patted my shoulder and I reached to squeeze his hand.

We leaned upon a fence and I realized I was looking at the field where I had seen Seel exercising that day, which seemed so long ago.

"I once saw Seel here," I said.

"You hardly ever mention him, yet why do I get the feeling he's always on your mind?"

"You are very perceptive, my lord Chrysm."

"Swift, please! This is a forlorn shamble of tents out in the middle of nowhere. What is rank in a place like this?"

"It is part of Heaven."

"Only one part is, I think."

"You look like him."

"I know. But I am not so self-centerd as to think I am as desirable as the real thing. Well, not in your case, certainly!"

"Please don't tell anyone," I said, turning to look at him.

"Why are you ashamed?"

"I'm not. It's just . . ." I waved my arms helplessly.

"No aspiration is too high."

"You know that isn't true!"

"Mmm. Maybe." He leaned with his back to the fence and spread his arms along it, his hair falling down toward the grass on the other side.

"How old are you?" I asked.

He raised his head. "I don't care. It doesn't matter any more."

"Don't you like having birthdays?"

He laughed. "Birthdays? What are you thinking about, Swift, that you ask these banal questions? Can you say what you are really thinking?"

"No."

He leaned over and took my hands away from my neck where I found I was clutching myself. He put my arms around him, his warm mouth touched my own and it was a taste of light and swords. I pressed myself against him, appreciating the contact. It had been so long since I had touched anyone like this.

"Say what you are really thinking," he said inside my head and I opened up my mind to him and let him see.

"You want me to be Seel," he said, but he wasn't angry, just mildly amused, and I put my hands in his hair and dreamed.

CHAPTER FOUR

> ⊱┥◆〉•⊙•〈◆┝┤⊰

Magic Lost

Tears of anger flooded through pores,
Vulgarity stumbled cruelly across the
Tongue of jealous love.

Beyond the boundaries of Imbrilim, cool woodland undulates away toward the north. What magic exists within that tangle of trees is only of the most natural, unobtrusive kind. In the morning I went to walk there, looking up through the gently swaying branches toward a placid sky.

I had woken that morning, plagued by a black depression and numbing confusion. Yesterday, I had been in a good mood, now I was the victim of my own emotions. As I walked, I spoke aloud to my father, imagining him there. Unexpectedly, he was most sympathetic and I could almost feel his hand upon my shoulder. "What do you expect of these people, Swift?" he said. "Do you really think you've been truly accepted by them? Are you of equal rank to them? I once warned you about the Gelaming. Have you forgotten everything I told you? To them, you are merely a Varr; at best a novelty to be used as a pawn, and at worst an object of derision. You should not be here, not really. Don't you know this in your heart of hearts? Even their whores look down on you!" I tried to silence him, to block the scraping words out of my mind, but they would not go away.

"Terzian?" I asked him. "Did you ever find an answer to your problems?" He never replied; it was something I could not even imagine.

I sighed and gazed up at the sky, visualizing freedom and flight, hoping to improve my mood. Now I was the beginning to understand my true nature, the possibilities within me, yet I was still plagued by doubts and teetering confidence. Arahal often upbraided me for this. "You must believe in yourself, Swift!" he would say, but it was difficult. I told myself it would be so much easier if I was still at home among friends. It was too much to cope with, having to come to terms with a new lifestyle, living among strangers, while trying to discipline myself to be calm and tranquil. I was under too much stress. What I felt about Seel only made it worse. Frequently, I wished Cal was still with me; I needed his clear sight to guide me and sometimes I longed to speak with Leef, but something held me back from seeking him out. I condemned myself to solitude.

When I returned to Imbrilim, I could tell immediately that something had happened. The air was full of activity and restrained excitement. I approached the first person I saw and asked them what was going on. The young har was only too eager to tell me. "The Tigrina is here," he said. A shiver of anticipation ran through me. Straight from Immanion, Pell's consort. Would I get to see him?

One project that I'd seen initiated since my arrival in Imbrilim was the beginning of construction for a permanent Gelaming town, some miles to the south of where we were camped. Ashmael said scathingly that the only reason Thiede had ordered it to be built was that he needed an excuse to keep Gelaming personnel in Megalithica and was becoming tired of their impatience over their inactivity. Chrysm argued sanely that a proper town would have to be built because of all the refugees seeking sanctuary in Imbrilim. There were now too many to be comfortably coped with and it was clear that these people needed to become self-sufficient. Everyone seemed enthusiastic about the plan and labor for the building was not in short supply. Ashmael had taken charge of the operation and sometimes I went over to the site to work with him. I found it all very interesting. I had always thought a town was constructed simply by building a lot of houses and shops in one place, but Ashmael taught me that the precise site was very important, because of drainage, water supply and the fertile land that was needed for cultivation. Architects had been brought over from Immanion. Already I could tell that the new town would be a place of grace and spacious symmetry.

That afternoon, I planned to ride Tulga over to the site so I could speak with Ashmael. Maybe he could dispel some of my doubts. He had a soothing knack of making me feel important. It was there that I received my invitation to the presence of the Tigrina. Moments after I had walked into the low, roomy hut that Ashmael used as an office, a strange har knocked at the open door. I had just said to Ashmael, "I've heard the Tigrina is here," when the stranger interrupted us. He handed Ashmael a white envelope.

"What is this?" Ashmael demanded.

"The Tigrina requests your presence at an informal gathering in the pavilion of the Hegemony this evening, Tiahaar."

"How charming. I live there. I do hope I can make it!"

The messenger inclined his head and turned to leave.

"No, wait!" Ashmael said. "Have you any more of these?"

"Most have already been delivered . . ." The messenger faltered, unsure of Ashmael's motive, no doubt familiar with his hectoring manner.

"Have you got one of these things for Swift the Varr?" Ashmael continued. I winced.

The messenger did not know who I was. He said, in a scathing tone, "Why yes, I believe I have! I believe I have one for your dog, Lord Ashmael, as well. Perhaps the two creatures are included in the same invitation, I'll just see . . ."

Ashmael snatched the bundle of envelopes the messenger had withdrawn from a shoulderbag. He leafed through them impatiently. "Ah yes, here it is. Take it, Swift, and be sure to tell the dog not to dress for dinner!"

I accepted it and bowed gracefully toward the messenger. "You must tell the Tigrina I accept with pleasure," I said, "but as yet I'm afraid I can't speak for the dog . . ."

Ashmael and I both laughed and the messenger hurried away abashed.

"I don't want to go to this," I said.

"Why on earth not? Such an opportunity to pose, my dear!" Ashmael countered. "You must learn to cultivate your vanity, Swift. That's what will make you most convincingly Gelaming!"

I sighed deeply. "I know what they think of me, Ashmael. I'm a Varr; less than a dog!"

Ashmael shrugged and then came to put his arms around me. It is a touch that never fails to electrify, however brief. "Then show them, Swift. Let them think what they like, but we know better, don't we, and whose table will you be sitting at?"

When I got back to my own pavilion late in the afternoon, I found that new clothes were waiting for me in a carefully wrapped parcel at the entrance. Later, Arahal sent hara to attend to my dressing. The results were most pleasing. The sophisticated and elegantly dressed har who faced me in the mirror was my inner self-image expressed in flesh. Once I had not thought that was possible. The clothes, the painted face, the elaborately styled hair; these were a mask behind which I could try to hide my self-consciousness. No-one would see my heart beating quickly.

At sundown, Arahal came to collect me. He too seemed pleased with my appearance. "I am honored to escort you, Tiahaar," he said, and courteously took my arm as we strolled into the evening.

"He has asked specifically to see you," Arahal told me.

"Who, the Tigrina?"

"Yes, I'm afraid so."

"But why?"

"As Tigrina, he does not have to give his reasons to me, a mere underling. Not that we can't guess at them, of course!" By this, I understood that the Tigrina was not wholly popular among the Gelaming.

The pavilion of the Hegemony was a blaze of colored lights; loud music reached our ears long before we reached it. It seemed packed to capacity with milling hara, all dressed in the most exotic costumes you could imagine. The air was narcotic with perfume. How Cobweb would have loved Terzian to have given parties like this! He would have been in his element, gliding through a throng of social luminaries, being known by all who were worth knowing and lapping up the compliments. Gatherings I had been present at back home now seemed dull by comparison.

I was very nervous about having to speak with the Tigrina, though I said nothing to Arahal, and took it as a bad omen that the first person I saw when we entered the pavilion was Seel. He came straight over to us and pulled a face at Arahal. I was surprised by his vivacity; perhaps he had been drinking. "Arahal, I have been regally stared at!" he said.

Arahal laughed. "Then I hope you're ashamed of yourself!"

"For what?"

"Ah, such innocence! You know damn well for what! Pell's consort, remember!" Seel smiled; such a secretive, sensual smile. I could have wept. Arahal put his hand upon my shoulder. "Seel, would you look after Swift for me for a moment? I shall go and ask his mightiness if he would speak with our Varrish protégé before or after the meal."

He walked away so quickly, Seel and I could only stare at each other in mutual dismay. I knew my reasons (which I feared were written all over my face), but I could not understand his. I did not really know why Seel always wanted to avoid me. That he considered me beneath him was obvious, but I suspected he did not like to admit that, even to himself. He made an effort to smile (such radiance!), and we both began to speak at once. I apologized.

"Well, what do you think of Imbrilim?" he asked perfunctorily and gazed over my shoulder, taking a graceful sip of his drink.

I wanted to touch him so much, I had to clench my fists at my sides. I wanted to say to him, "Imbrilim? It's very interesting, isn't it, but of course, I got used to this kind of life in Galhea. Ponclast's people were always

coming down from the north; our house was always full. Get me a drink
and I'll tell you more . . ." but all I came out with was, "Well, I . . . I think
it's . . . um . . . wonderful." He looked at me then and gave me a caustic
smile, leaving me cringing at my own banality. I wanted to look away, but
I couldn't; his eyes were hypnotic. Perhaps our eyes locked for just a shade
too long. All the time, I was bellowing inside myself for that fabled inner
strength, but it appeared to have shot into hiding. I could think of nothing
to say. The silence was unbearable and I wanted to sink into the floor. I
visualized the thought, One day, wondrous Seel, you shall see me as I really
am, and then you won't despise me! It was small compensation, but all that
I could cling to.

"Shall I fetch you a drink?" he asked, and I nodded my head, babbling,
"Yes. Please. Anything."

It was Chrysm who brought it back for me. "Seel said to give you this,"
he said with a knowing smile. I grimaced and drank, gratefully. "I enjoyed
our walk last evening," Chrysm continued.

"I'm sorry about that," I said.

"For what? You are too hard on yourself. You must learn to handle Seel
in the right way. He is only har, you know."

"Only!"

"He doesn't know what he's missing; that's all I've got to say about it.
I only wish you'd wanted me to be me and not him!"

"Chrysm, stop it!"

He laughed at my flushed embarrassment. "Well, Swift, have you seen
the legendary Tigrina yet?"

"No, not yet."

"You will have to prepare yourself for an interrogation, I fear."

"Interrogation? About what?"

Chrysm touched my arm lightly. "Don't look like that! Not that kind of
interrogation. It will be about Cal. Probably his name will not even be
mentioned once, but I swear you'll find yourself talking about him endlessly."

"I'm not sure I understand you," I said.

"When was the last time you took aruna with anyone?"

"Why? What has that got to do with it?"

"Nothing at all!"

"You are mocking me!" I thought about walking away from him, but
could see no-one else that I knew. My glass was empty.

"Arahal means to keep you chaste." Chrysm held a bottle made of
lilac-colored glass and was twisting it between his hands. "Your body is
sacred, Swift," he said.

"Yes, it is!" I answered coldly. If I asked him questions, he would tell
me the answers; he was trying to without the questions being asked, but at
that time, I didn't want to know. I was afraid to or I just didn't care; it was
hard to tell.

I was not given a seat on the top table as Ashmael had implied, but was placed next to Arahal on the next one down. The tables were laden with fragrant food, steam rising from roasted birds, their skins scarlet with spices, soaking in a marinade of tart berry juice. There were bowls and bowls of vegetables, aromatic with sprinkled herbs, and salad and baked fruit simmering in a salty sauce. The Gelaming are fond of food; their meals are always exquisite. It was difficult to keep my eyes off the splendid sight of the Tigrina, who sprawled elegantly in his chair like a god, bending his head to listen to what Ashmael, seated next to him, was saying. I had imagined the Tigrina to be dark like Pellaz, but his hair was the color of white gold and teased out around his head like an enormous mane, tumbling over his shoulders like molten waves. I thought he seemed strangely vulnerable in a female sort of way, but Arahal brushed away my observation. "There is steel beneath that velvet," he said. "There has to be!"

"Have I learned my lessons well, Arahal?" I asked. God knows what made me think of it then.

Arahal raised one eyebrow quizzically. "I haven't taught you all that much yet, but I'm pleased with your progress so far."

"Is there more than one purpose to my training?"

"What do you mean?"

I shrugged, but didn't continue. I could feel Arahal looking at me, wondering. I could feel the words trembling on the tip of his tongue. He curbed himself.

"There is more than one purpose," he said.

Some time after we had finished eating, when I had relaxed enough to forget why I was there, the Tigrina sent someone to bring me into his august presence. Luckily, I had drunk enough by then not to feel too intimidated. Ashmael winked at me as I sat down. Close to, the Tigrina was an electrifying sight, his strong perfume was overpowering. He was dressed all in clinging black, with black jewels at his throat and in his ears and hair. His fingernails were incredibly long, lacquered to a sheen of lustrous jet and set with diamonds. Never had I seen a throat so long and curving and slim, or shoulders of such sculpted, precise proportions. Caeru was a vision and he knew it.

As I had expected, he spoke in a cool, measured voice. "So, you are Terzian's son," he said. I smiled weakly. "You have traveled a long way to reach us."

"It seems that way," I said.

"The Tigron has spoken of you. I have heard about the time Pellaz spent in Galhea. Of course, you would have been just a baby then." There was no mistaking the hardness in his tone. He turned away from me. "Ashmael has been telling me of the plans they have for your future. . . . How privileged you are, Swift the Varr!"

Ashmael smiled fiercely at him. There was a moment's uncomfortable silence, during which the Tigrina sighed four times. I counted, unable to look away from him. I wondered what it would be like to be in his position;

so high. Everyone knew who he was; his clothes, his jewelery were the best. His smallest whim must be gratified. He looked at me with dark blue eyes. "Did you travel here alone?" he asked.

I shook my head. "No, there were three of us."

The Tigrina gazed over my shoulder at the crowd beyond us. "Oh, and where are your friends now? You must point them out to me. I find Varrs most fascinating."

I looked beseechingly at Ashmael, unsure of how to answer this request, but Ashmael would not help me, hiding his smile in a goblet of wine and scanning the room carelessly.

"There are only two of us left in Imbrilim, my lord," I said. "Leef and myself. The other has gone. I don't know where."

"I see." He snapped his fingers in the air, and Velaxis, who had been hovering behind Ashmael's chair, swooped to his side. "More wine!" the Tigrina ordered. "Be quick about it!" He turned his glacial attention once more upon me. "Now, tell me about your home," he said.

He listened to me for about twenty minutes. During that time, I consumed two goblets of wine. At the end of this time, Caeru raised his hand and silenced me in mid-sentence.

"That's enough," he said, and turned to Ashmael. "Have one of your people bring the Varr to my pavilion later." I sensed dismissal and stood up. The Tigrina smiled at me, but his eyes were still cold. He raised his glittering glass. "Until later, son of Terzian."

"Well?" Arahal demanded, when I was sitting next to him once more.

"The Tigrina wishes to speak with me later on," I said woefully.

Arahal made an irritated sound. "Oh no," he murmured.

I leaned over and drank from Arahal's goblet, which he fastidiously took from my hand. The linen tablecloth was strewn with crumbs and ringed with stains. "You are concerned for me," I said flatly.

Arahal smiled. "Yes . . . but I suppose you will have to gratify his curiosity. Do you understand why he wants to see you?"

"Because of Cal?"

"Not just that. Caeru knows why you are here and he will misbehave by trying to interfere with your progress. I don't suppose it will matter that much, though. Just don't give too much of yourself."

"I don't like that warning, Arahal!"

"My only fear is that you will forget it," he said, and toasted my health with a smile.

Way past midnight, when everyone was talking more loudly than ever and the musicians were playing with more abandon, I asked Arahal, "About the other purpose of my being here; what is it?"

He pulled a face. "Do you believe in destiny?"

"I'm not sure what I believe in any more."

"Hmm . . . well, it's something to do with that. The inevitable; what must be. Imagine a focus of two points in time; a focus of two lives at that point. Often, important things can be gained from such events."

"You never answer me properly, do you?" I complained.

"Well, you must realize that enlightenment for you might change things. We have to be cautious."

"Is something going to happen soon?"

"Something will happen tonight," he answered evasively.

The Tigrina retired fairly early by Gelaming standards. Half an hour or so after he had left the party, Velaxis slunk over to where I was sitting, announcing rather bitterly that he was to escort me to the Tigrina's pavilion. Neither of us spoke as we walked through the cool night air. Moths fluttered blindly. There was a damp smell of grass. Some of the other tents were still glowing with subdued light; soft laughter and voices; shadows against the cloth. I was not nervous; I had some idea of what was to come. Both Arahal and Chrysm had hinted at it.

It was only a minute or so's walk from the pavilion of the Hegemony to that of the Tigrina and for all that time I was thinking about Seel. Since that first embarrassing exchange, when Arahal had left us together, Seel had managed to avoid me entirely. Perhaps I was reading too much into his behavior, after all, there had been so many hara there, most of whom were probably known to him.

The Tigrina's pavilion was constructed of sparkling midnight-blue cloth and adorned with silver tassels that hung motionless in the still air. A single torch glowed blue-white at the entrance. Within, the only light came from a cluster of tall, black candles in silver clasps. Light reflected from spilled jewels, silken cloth and metal. The Tigrina was ready for us, carefully reposing upon a mass of dark, shiny pillows. He was alone, looking up when Velaxis and I eased through the door curtains and dismissing Velaxis with an imperious wave of his hand. Affronted, Velaxis swept out without speaking.

I wondered what had been going through this gilded creature's mind as he waited for me, what plans he had prepared. I could not tell whether it was through design or unease that he did not speak, but I watched entranced as Caeru slowly removed his heavy jewelery in silence. He laid the glistening stones down carefully upon a low table at his side, where they rattled into an untidy, treasure-chest heap. He stretched his neck and rubbed it languorously. I could see the scar of his inception on his arm. Arahal had told me the Tigrina bleached his skin with the juice of lemons. I could believe that; he was as white and luminous as pearl. I think he hoped I was afraid, but that was not the effect he was having on me. It was a kind of morbid fascination that kept me staring at him.

He offered me coffee, which I accepted, and poured me some himself from a tall, awkward pot, which had been steaming on the table. "I expect you're wondering why I've asked you here," he said, which I found to be a very predictable question. Perhaps this, more than anything, proclaimed that he was not truly Gelaming.

"I should imagine it's because you want to ask me about Cal," I said. The Tigrina smothered his surprise. What did he think I'd say? I found it annoying that he expected me to be so utterly in awe of him, because I knew that Ashmael and the others were not. Did he really think that they wouldn't have spoken to me about him, and that their opinions, no matter how surreptitiously implied, would not rub off on me? I was not overly fond of Velaxis, but I had not liked the Tigrina's insulting attitude toward him. Ashmael, whom I respected intensely, never treated anyone like that, no matter how much lower in rank they were than him.

"You are just repeating what you've been told, of course," Caeru said suddenly. I was alarmed, thinking he'd read my mind, but he was still talking about Cal.

"Isn't it true then?"

"Already, it seems, Ashmael has taught you how to be disrespectful," he said.

I wanted to reply, "Doesn't respect have to be earned?" but realized this would be going too far. No matter what the Gelaming might think of him, he was still the Tigrina, and commanded respect simply for that.

"I don't mean to sound disrespectful," I said.

He smiled and leaned back among the cushions. The shoulder of his garment dropped away slightly, revealing more of that skin which was so perfect and pale. "Can't you understand my fascination?" he asked. I smiled to myself, amused by the ambiguity of that remark, which I'm sure was unintentional.

"Yes. I understand."

"Good. . . . You look nervous, Swift the Varr, sitting hunched like that on the edge of your chair." (I wasn't.) "What have they told you about me?"

"Nothing."

"Nothing at all?" He forced a laugh, throwing back his head, exposing that throat which seemed to have 'bite me' written all over it.

"A little, then," I conceded. "But I would prefer you to tell me about yourself. If you fear you've been misrepresented . . . ?"

His mouth dropped open in amazement. "How bold you are! How very Varr! Do you really want to know?"

"Yes."

"How unusual! Very well, sit here beside me and I shall tell you."

I stood up and removed Arahal's brushed leather jacket that I'd slung about my shoulders as protection against the cool, dew-laden air outside. The Tigrina watched me with interest. How I've changed, I thought. What Caeru doesn't realize is that this person here with him is as much a stranger to me as to him. I sank down beside him and he leaned away from me a little, as if uncomfortable having anyone so close. He tried to appear brittle and aloof, but now I could see the saddened, bitter creature that he really was. His eyes could not hide it.

"What do you want to know?" he asked.

I honestly think he was regretting having asked me to join him. This interview was not progressing the way he'd planned, although it was fairly obvious that some kind of seduction had been intended. I'd learned how to decipher Arahal's riddles enough by now to have gathered that.

"Tell me where you live."

"In Immanion. Phaonica, the Tigron's palace. It is on a hill. It can be seen from any point in the city."

"Do you like it there?"

"It's very beautiful. It is always warm."

"How many servants do you have?"

"I don't know. A lot. I don't know them all."

"You don't know their names?"

"No. Should I?" He sounded defensive. I suppose he hated his servants. Perhaps they despised him.

"Describe your bedroom."

"It . . . it is large."

"Black and silver?"

He laughed nervously. "Yes. I like those colors. The moon and darkness."

I leaned toward him and he backed away an inch or two. "What do you see from your window, Tigrina?"

"The lights of the city and beyond them, the sea. It is always moving. I look at it at night."

"Is the sea black and silver?"

"Sometimes."

My lips touched his neck. He was so tense, he could barely keep from quivering, but he did not stop me.

"Do you sleep alone, Tigrina, in that big, black room?"

"What?"

"Do you sleep alone?" I raised my head. There was hardly any space between us. His eyes darted everywhere but into mine. "Do you?"

He closed his eyes, long lashes against his cheek. "That question was impertinent. Why did you ask it?" I could smell his surrender, a smell like cut grass. I had asked the question that perhaps he had always wanted someone to ask, because then he could answer.

"Alone, Tigrina? Are you . . . ?"

"Yes," he said. "Yes. Yes."

There was only the slightest of resistance as I pulled him against me. I brushed his lips with my own and he opened his mouth, straining toward me. I raised my head and smiled at him so gently. I took his chin in my hand and pushed it back. He curled his fingers round my wrist, apprehensive.

"Isn't this what you want?" I asked, and put my teeth against his white throat, and bit down, hard.

His body arched against me, but he made no sound. I did not draw blood, but there were marks in his flesh when I raised my head again. "Varrs do that kind of thing," I said. "You must have heard; we are barbarians." He laughed and I held him tight against me.

"I will ask now," he said. "I will ask about Cal . . ."

"He has gone and I don't know where," I replied. Caeru stiffened in my arms. He said nothing. "One thing I do know, that I am sure of, is that either the Tigron or Thiede is responsible for his disappearance."

"Are you fond of this Cal?"

I lifted his head. "It can't be helped. He just has that effect on people. He makes them love him."

"I know!"

"Such bitterness!"

"Such bitterness," he agreed wistfully. "I would like to meet him."

"Would you?"

"Yes. Really. He can't take anything from me. I am Tigrina; Thiede made me so. That can't be taken away, and I have nothing else." He did not sound self-pitying, only fatalistic. Cal would have found him irresistible.

He took my head in his hands and offered me his breath, which I drank from fiercely. He was panting as we parted. "We are similar," he said. "Pariahs in the Gelaming camp."

"Not I!" I exclaimed vehemently. "I will not let them think of me that way!"

Caeru smiled. "No . . . I can taste your father in you.

"I hope not!"

He frowned and shook his head. "By that, I don't mean . . . bad things, just strength and power. It is forming within you."

"More so during the last few minutes," I said lightly.

He smiled once more and put his fingers lightly on my chest. "Have you met Seel yet?"

The sound of that name went through me like a javelin. "Why?" I was too abrupt. Caeru nodded and smiled wryly to himself.

"Yes, I can tell you have. He is close to Pell."

"I know."

His hand slid under my shirt. "Do you think I've brought you here for just this purpose, to touch you?"

I shrugged, but said nothing.

"Well, if you do, you are right, but it is more than that. I'm offering you a kind of protection. They have kept other hara away from you, haven't they? Nothing is coincidental, nothing!" he cried. "You are in thrall, Swift, but you don't even realize it! I know these people. I know what their magic can do. You have a strong will and you shall be angry when you find out how they've manipulated you! Your innermost feelings are nothing to them!"

His fervor alarmed me and I put my hand over his mouth. "Hush!" I did not believe him at all. He made a muffled noise and tried to pull my hand away.

"I am not a fool," I said, releasing him.

"You are!" he insisted, but he knew I would not listen.

"No. Forget me; I want to talk about you. You are soume-har. I want to fill you."

"I am Tigrina. You are insolent!" (Some vestige of pride perhaps?)

"Then why are you smiling?"

He shook his head, sighed, and lay back. "Very well, Swift the Varr . . ."

"Is that an invitation?"

He laughed, for the first time honestly, without control. "Invitation? No, no; it is a command!"

For a second, some sober part of me was aghast. This being, this whole and shining being, was Pell's; he had done this once. The Tigron of Immanion had done this, held this in his arms, and I was just Swift, who until recently had entertained very few grand ideas. When had I changed? When? I remember thinking, Why couldn't it have been like this with Seel? What is it about him that weakens me so much? Tonight, with Caeru, I have said all the right things at the right time; I have been powerful. Is it just the wine that's made me so bold? Why, why, why, couldn't I have been like this with Seel?

As we writhed together, in a haze of sweat and tangled limbs, Caeru said, "You will need this knowledge." I did learn a lot from him. I learned how to prolong the pleasure until it becomes pleasure no longer and the final release is like dying and almost like pain. "One day you will think of me with gratitude," he said, and part of me could sense that time to come; formless and vague, a tantalizing presentiment.

Afterwards, I would not let him sleep. "Now is the time," I said.

"The time for what?" he asked drowsily.

"To tell me about yourself. I want to give you something in return. I want to give you my ears."

He smiled lazily. "You have given me enough . . ."

"No, Caeru. Tell me. Tell me how it happened, how you became Tigrina, why it happened and what went wrong."

He put his arms across his eyes. "Do not call me Caeru. That is what *they* call me. It is the name that I was born with, it is true, but my friends have always called me Rue." He sighed. "Rue for sadness, who barely exists any more. Rue was happy; Caeru is not. Caeru is a slave, because Rue made a grave mistake . . ."

"Go on."

He sighed again. "Very well. If you insist. Hold me, Swift." He curled against me and I listened to the tale, the other side of the story. He began:

"Once upon a time a har named Rue lived in a very nice place called Ferelithia. It was a happy, rich town where humans and hara lived together and it was always warm. Rue was contented there. He earned his living through his voice; he sang. He had a lot of friends and life was kind to him. Only, one day, he fell in love with a beautiful face and a beautiful body, both of which belonged to an incomparable, mysterious har called Pellaz. Pell was just passing through Ferelithia and his relationship with Rue was destined to be a brief one. It would have been too, if Rue had not been so stupid and so naive as to let Pellaz take aruna with him to its furthest possible point. There was a child, and by the time I realized, Pell had long gone. It was so ridiculous, because at first, I didn't even realize what was wrong with me. I'd get strange feelings in my stomach, odd little move- ments and pains. I thought I was getting sick and tried to ignore it. Kate knew what it was, but she didn't tell me. She didn't have the guts to! Kate, by the way, is my friend; a woman, and perhaps my only friend. Pell had told her what he'd done to me before he left. Can you believe that I didn't realize? It's incredible, isn't it? One day, I just collapsed in the street. I thought I was dying because the pain was so bad. That was when Kate finally confessed what she knew. We had a raging argument that lasted all the way through my delivery of the pearl. I suppose it was good for me because it took my mind off the pain. 'Oh, Rue, I wanted to tell you!' she said. As if that was any comfort!

"I couldn't understand why Pell had done it; made a child with me and then just vanished. What was the point? Our son was exquisite, beautiful and weirdly wise. I named him Wolf because it was a name of power and also how I thought of his father at that time. As he grew up, I began to see that . . . he was different. I knew inside myself that he belonged with his father, because Pell had been different in the same way. What could I offer him? I loved my life in Ferelithia, but it wouldn't be enough for Wolf; he deserved more. At that time, I didn't know Pell had become Tigron. Maybe I wouldn't have made that decision if I had known. Kate agreed with me that Wolf should be taken to Pell. She said that Pell had left money for her, so that one day she could use it to visit him in Immanion. We scraped together a little more and the three of us set off across the sea on a wonderful, romantic journey to find Wolf's father. I think it was the last time I was truly happy.

"Of course, when we reached Immanion and found out exactly what Pell had become, all the Gelaming thought I was a callous adventurer, who had simply come to cash in on Pell's fame and fortune. They still think that, some of them. But it was only for Wolf. *I* didn't want to stay there. Thiede realized straight away that Wolf is a special child. It was Thiede who dealt with everything. Pell wouldn't even see us. He thought I was hounding him too, you see. There is only room for one in Pell's heart and that space is reserved for Cal; it always will be. I knew that. I've always known that. I didn't want to stay there; it was embarrassing. Then . . . then Thiede suggested the worst thing of all. He came to me one evening, as I was trying to leave yet again. He made me sit down and he said to me, 'Caeru, you are a shrewd har, you have common sense and you are beautiful enough to please any Gelaming. I want Pell to take a consort, for the people expect it. I have searched for quite a time to find someone suitable, but now I feel that search is over. I want it to be you, Caeru. I want you to become Tigrina of Immanion.' He expected my refusal and listened to it patiently. Then he said, 'I hope you've said everything you want to say, Caeru, for I don't want to hear anything like that again. You know who I am, you know that I have made my wishes plain. Out of courtesy, I have listened to your objections, but now you will have to forget them. It's unfortunate that you'll have to lose the lifestyle you are fond of, but you are destined for greater things, I'm afraid. You will be Pell's consort and I shall conduct the ceremony of your bonding in blood to him.'

"It was obscene, wasn't it? The most sacred, intimate thing any two hara can experience; the sharing of blood. It is an unbreakable bond, and for me, because of that, a living hell. Of course, Pell went berserk when he found out about it. He came storming into the elegant suite of rooms that Thiede had put us in. It was the first time that I'd seen him since I'd been in Immanion. It made me weak; I couldn't help it. Some selfish part of me thought, I will do what Thiede wants because it will keep me close to Pell. I didn't want to lose him completely again. How stupid I was! Pell called me every foul name he could think of. How could I do this? he wanted to know. Hadn't he once confided in me how he felt about Cal? Was I mocking him now? He offered me vast amounts of money to leave, which I refused. I said that Thiede wouldn't let me leave. Pell called me a liar and accused me of plotting against him with Thiede. That was when Kate walked in and tried to intervene. She could see things were getting dangerously close to being out of hand. Pell roared at her. He called her an interfering human bitch and to keep out of it. Kate was horrified. She'd known Pell a long time. It's not like him to be like that, but he was furious. I'd never seen anyone so furious. It was like desperate panic. Eventually, during the shouting, he took a fruit knife off the table and cut his arm with it. He said to me, 'Here! Here's my blood. Take it! Drink it if you like! Let's get Thiede to bless the act!' He smeared blood on my face; it was terrible. It made me as angry as Pell was. I'd had enough. I said I would leave but begged him to accept Wolf as his son and let him remain in Phaonica. Pell said nothing. He was just looking at his arm as if he was thinking, Oh hell, what have I done? I *did* try to leave, I really did, but of course, Thiede was waiting for me. Thiede knows everything. He told me not to be stupid, that Pell would calm down and get used to the idea. 'You are going to be his Tigrina, Caeru, and that is an end to it. Go back to your room.' It was impossible to argue with him.

"Well, as you see, Pell did agree to it in the end, but there is no affection between us. We are bonded in blood to each other forever, an insoluble link, and both of us hate it. Some part of Pell still believes I only went to look for him because I'd heard he'd become Tigron. It isn't true. We'd had a good time together in Ferelithia, Pell and I. I was fond of him. I still am. Now, he is courteous to me. Most evenings, he will come to talk to me. He says he doesn't blame me for what happened. He says he knew it was Thiede. I tell him he's lying when he says that but he only smiles. Sometimes, he wants to take aruna with me. He admires me as he would admire a well-sculpted statue. That's what I am to him, fleshless, but I can't refuse him. It's sick, isn't it? I think he has become genuinely fond of Wolf. They've given him another name now, one fit for a prince, but he is still Wolf to me. At least that turned out alright. Ah well, I have riches beyond imagination, I live in a palace and don't have to lift a finger if I don't want to. He touches me sometimes . . . I should be happy, shouldn't I?"

So many people have said that Pellaz, Tigron of Immanion, is the kindest, most compassionate person they have ever met. He appears perfect. In a way, it is comforting to know that he is not. I listened to Rue's story in silence and I said nothing after he had finished it. Once I would have wept, as I had when I'd heard Cal's sad story, but now I expressed my emotions in a different way. I made love to him, sad Caeru; it was not aruna, but truly the warmth of love, because he needed it so badly, and I, soiled Varr of less than perfect character, knew how to give it.

At dawn, he bid me leave. We parted awkwardly; the magic of the previous evening had gone. Such things were meant to be brief. I wondered if Caeru, Tigrina of Immanion, had got what he'd come seeking for in Imbrilim. I would never know. By noon, his dark pavilion was empty.

CHAPTER FIVE

The Axiom

Sublimation through the spheres
Respect delivered by destiny.
Desire, desire with the beast of fire.

For some days afterwards, I could not keep the Tigrina from my thoughts. He had given me so much more than a mere night of pleasure; he had given me self-respect. Now I felt I could walk among Gelaming and feel equal to them; I felt taller, both spiritually and physically. Arahal noticed the change in me; I could tell by the way he looked at me, yet he chose to say nothing about it. My night with Caeru was never mentioned by anyone in Imbrilim, yet knowing as I did the way news flew around the camp, I was sure everyone must know about it.

During the next few weeks, I devoted myself to caste elevation, and found that in some ways, it was similar to learning to ride a horse. Once the simple techniques have been mastered, the more complicated and difficult parts seem to come naturally. Arahal praised my progress, admittedly with undisguised self-congratulation. "It was hard for those of us that were born human," he said, "for the powers were not natural to us. We had to learn so much. I have never educated a pure-born har before, but it is obviously easier for you just because you are pure-born."

"Well, Cobweb taught me things right from when I could first speak," I said, feeling it was wrong I should claim all the credit. "We could never speak of it openly, though, for Terzian would not have approved. He wanted his son to grow up to be a warrior like himself, not a secretive witch, which was how he thought of Cobweb. Anyway, he called it all mere superstition."

"A foolishness which I should imagine he is regretting now," Arahal laughed. His smile faded to a frown when he saw my face.

"Where is he?" I asked. There was a moment's pause, and then Arahal shook his head.

"I've already told you; I don't know, Swift. That has nothing to do with me."

I wanted to believe him, for I looked on Arahal as a friend nowadays, but I knew he was lying.

One day, I woke up and knew I was Ulani. It was an instinctive knowledge. The ceremony seemed merely perfunctory, for it was inside myself that my caste was raised and no words or rituals could reinforce it, but, because of the Gelaming's love of celebration, Ashmael organized a grand affair to mark my ascension. Because my attainment of Ulani meant that now the Gelaming could plan their attack on Ponclast in earnest, the occasion was treated as a great holiday by the whole of Imbrilim. The atmosphere was intoxicating. Although the actual ceremony itself was brief and held in private in the pavilion of the Hegemony, the rest of the day was devoted to feasting, drinking and dancing. Leef came to congratulate me in icy tones, which annoyed me so much, I was rather peremptory with him. This brought a grim smile to his face as if his worst thoughts about me had been justified. Seel did not appear all day.

In the evening, Arahal said to me, "Ashmael will speak with you tomorrow, Swift."

"He speaks to me often," I said lightly, feeling my heartbeat increase.

"He will *speak* with you, Swift."

"Is it . . . is it time to *know?*" I asked. "The other purpose for my being here. Is that it?" Some of my forgotten fears fluttered at the edge of my mind.

"It is time," Arahal confirmed grimly.

That night, I dreamed of the eyes for the first time in ages. I threw handfuls of dream mist at them, but they never blinked. In the morning, I woke exhausted.

"You are a prince, Swift," Ashmael said to me. I looked in his mirror and saw him standing behind me, taller, his hands upon my shoulders.

"I am Cobweb," I said and he smiled.

"No, not him; something else."

My skin will never tan, my eyes will always look shadowed; that is Cobweb's legacy, I know that. I shall never be very tall as my father is, and I shall never have his frightening eyes. I am Swift, through and through, nothing more. I am Swift, and I have learned to like myself.

"Megalithica is ripe for the harvest," Ashmael said, and I waited for him to continue. "We shall take our power with us," he said. "It will be contained in a crystal and it will glow a dark blue-green. It shall be your power."

"Where shall it come from?" I asked.

"Within you."

I turned away from the mirror and saw that Ashmael's eyes were shining with a strange and terrible light, for he knew the meaning behind his words.

"How shall you take Megalithica?" I demanded. "How shall you *really* take it?"

"What is least attainable is the most desirable," he answered. A typically Gelaming evasive answer; it meant nothing.

"I will never get used to this!" I said.

He followed me across the room of dappled folds and stood with me at the entrance to his pavilion. "It is the truth," he said.

"If it is, speak it plainly. I am Varr, not Gelaming. I don't understand. You play with words!"

"Grissecon," he said.

I turned and backed away swiftly. "Me?" (The other purpose; of course. No wonder they were wary of telling me.)

Ashmael nodded silently.

"No!" I cried, already feeling publicly naked.

"You are inhibited."

"Yes, I am. I've been told that before. I can't do this, Ashmael."

He sighed. "Oh dear! Must we have these problems? This Grissecon is essential. Only two people can do it to make it work and both of you are fighting tooth and nail to avoid it, one way or another. Both of you!" He threw up his hands.

Suddenly, I was cold and my arms were about myself and my flesh was chilled. Oh God, no, I said softly, weak with relief and sick with despair. In an instant so many things had become so clear.

Ashmael did not touch me. "You know who it is, don't you," he stated flatly.

I nodded, straightening up, though my arms wouldn't uncurl. "Yes."

"It is Thiede's will."

"What an excuse that phrase can be! Everything it seems is Thiede's will. *Why*, Ashmael? Why not anyone else? I've never performed a Grissecon before."

"It is a focus. Two essences that shall meet, and if Thiede has manipulated fate, it is inevitable; whatever happens."

"Nothing has been coincidental, has it?" I said, remembering something Caeru had said to me. He had known about this, of course. "It's all been planned, hasn't it? Everything!"

Ashmael had the grace to look offended. "Not everything, no."

Now I understood completely. Thiede had said, "This shall be," Pellaz had implemented it and there could be no argument. I was to be the one and I was everything to be deplored; Cal's friend, Terzian's son, a Varr. In other words, tainted. My father fed on human flesh and committed pelki against his own kind. His blood ran in my veins. No-one could be sure that such traits did not lie deep within me too. Except Thiede perhaps and Thiede always got his own way.

"When is this to happen?" I asked in a chilled voice that did not seem to belong to me. I was numb, totally without feeling at that moment.

"Oh shortly, shortly," Ashmael answered. "It shall be arranged and you will be informed as soon as we know the details. Swift, I can tell you're upset about this. I must say, you must not feel this way . . ."

"What you mean is, I should not feel at all," I added coldly.

"No, that is not what I mean. I can't understand your turmoil. The Grissecon will not be public; they have spared you that. Just look on it as aruna . . . but there is more, I'm afraid."

"More?" I asked in a dull voice. I could sense Ashmael squirming inside. This pleased me as I thought he could say nothing that could make things more unpleasant. I was wrong.

"Thiede wants a child to be made of this union," he said quickly. I must have made a noise, like a screech or something. Ashmael jumped and even started to laugh.

"Can a child come from hate?" I raged.

"No," he said. "Of course not. But what makes you think it's there?"

"If it's not hate, it's something worse; indifference."

"You are guessing."

"No, I'm not! I know!"

"You don't, though! You read too much into things. Chrysm said so."

What else had Chrysm told him? I could listen to this no longer. Without a word, I strode out of Ashmael's pavilion and walked back through the camp. It had started to rain; a fine mist. Ashmael did not call me back.

Arahal looked up, surprised, when I walked determinedly into his pavilion, unannounced. He noted my expression with apprehension. "Ashmael's told you then?" he said, standing up.

"Damn you, Arahal!" I said, pointing a shaking finger at him. "Damn you, all of you! You raise me only to humiliate me. This Grissecon, this person I must share bodies with, share seed with; it's Seel, isn't it?"

Sometime, someone had taken Seel aside and sat him down and told him. He had learned that Cal still lived and where he lived and how he lived, and then he had been told that Terzian's son was being summoned to Imbrilim and that Thiede had decided upon the vessels for the ultimate Grissecon; world power. The force within, blue-green, shining, barely controllable; sex as magic, to wield, to conquer. Seel and Swift, two small parts of a prodigious plan, our bodies connecting like live wires to allow the current to flow. I think he would have just shaken his head at first, in disbelief. He would have been smiling, that slight, wholly luminous smile. Maybe he said, "Terzian's son? A Varr? Are you serious?" And then he would have realized just how serious they were. Then he would have stood up and let the bitter words flow out of him; Terzian, Varrs, Cal; all that was wrong with the world, that was blighted in the world. He might have said, "Do you hold me in such contempt that my body should be used, possessed in this way?" Perhaps it had been Pellaz who had told him. I like to think that it was. His voice would have been soothing. Seel soothed to acceptance until the bitterness was deep inside him and he had nodded his head and agreed, "Alright, if it *must* be so." (Wouldn't that have struck a chord with Pellaz?) Seel would have thought to himself, I trusted you, Pell, and I could imagine his eyes looking at Pell's back, disillusioned and defeated. Then he must have thought to himself, as comfort, I will never speak to that creature; I will never like him. He is beneath me and it seems I must host his son, but I will never like him. No-one can make me do that!

One day I would have to touch him and his eyes would be veiled like cat's eyes and his head would be held to the side. I never had to be told all these things, no-one ever told me, but I knew them as surely as if Seel had told me himself.

Arahal stood up. He took my shoulders in his hands and shook me slightly. "Stop this; you are hysterical," he said blandly. Yet I made no noise. Perhaps my eyes were hysterical. How could I tell Arahal about my dreams that I'd had for years, the dreams that had been an intimation of the person to come? That person had been Seel; I knew that now. From the moment I first saw him, recognition had woken within me. Now, that one thing toward which I had been unconsciously striving all my life had become, indescribably, something terrible that I wanted to run from. What should have occurred naturally had become contrivance, Thiede's contrivance, and because he had accelerated everything all the harmony had been destroyed. I was numb. Maybe, if it hadn't been for this, Seel would have come to like me. I could have made him like me, but now he was angry and affronted.

Arahal's voice broke through my thoughts. "Swift, be objective, for God's sake!" I looked up quickly, feeling my glance strike his eyes like an arrow. He turned away and poured me wine into a long, thin glass that felt temptingly shatterable when he handed it to me. I drank from it and tasted sourness; Gelaming wine was rarely sour. "You are reacting irrationally," he continued smoothly. "You think you are obsessed with Seel, but that is only the effect of a powerful psychic attack. You were *made* to feel this way. Time was running out. Now you can stand back and view things calmly."

His words sluiced over me like a stream of melted ice. Made to feel this way? It was laughable. They didn't have to do that. I was obsessed with Seel a long time before the Gelaming had even dreamed of their plans.

"I am . . . confused," I said. I couldn't bring myself to tell him what I was thinking. His hand rested lightly, for a moment, on my shoulder.

"Obsession is desire," he said. "Desire is the seed of power. You must fashion your thoughts into a cool blade. Focus your energy, Swift."

"You speak of me and my behavior," I said, "but what of Seel's?"

"What of it?" Arahal asked. "Have you ever really spoken to him?"

"No," I answered irritably, "but I've sensed things. He doesn't like me."

Arahal made an impatient sound. "You must remember Seel is Gelaming," he said, not without sarcasm. "He is aware of his duty. His mind is trained to overcome personal preferences."

"That's sick! This Grissecon will be impossible, and if it is possible, horribly humiliating for both of us."

"Oh, Swift, calm down! There are ways of overcoming any difficulties that may arise."

I shrank from asking him what they were. I put my empty glass down on the table. In a dish lay a lock of hair, shining, curled like a sleeping cat. Arahal saw me looking at it.

"Go back to your pavilion," he said.

Sitting alone on my bed, I found my thoughts drifting toward my father and Cal. Both victims of the Gelaming, I decided uncharitably. Perhaps I feared I was being lost, misplaced, in a similar way. I tried to recall the way I had once felt about Cal, when my Feybraiha had come upon me. I tried to remember if I had felt like this, but the memory eluded me. I habitually banned all erotic thoughts of Seel from my mind, because I found them too painful to think about. Now I tried to imagine the feel of him, but all I could see were those unfathomable eyes, cold and distant. I imagined Grissecon and our bodies tangled together, his flesh hot beneath my mouth, damp with a mist of sweat; our craving, our energy. Then in my thoughts I took his face in my hand and turned it toward me. His eyes were dead, his mind untouched, even as his body moved around me. Could we make magic that way?

I lay back and put my hands behind my head, sinking into the soft cushions, going down and down. I was aware that I needed aruna, my body felt strange. I had rarely been denied it before, not when I needed it. I thought about Caeru; another of Thiede's puppets. I wondered if I would ever see him again. Did Pell know what had happened between us? I turned on my side and thought I would sleep. Then I was listening to the eerie chime that signaled someone was seeking ingress to my pavilion. I made the thought-forms that would open the portal and, after a moment, someone came to the inner chamber and lifted the curtains. I looked up, and saw him standing there. He said, "I think we have to talk."

"I think we do," I agreed, surprised to find that I was not nervous at all.

He sat down on the end of my bed and looked at his hands and I wanted to say, "Seel, you are the most beautiful thing I have ever seen," even if it wasn't true, but all I said was, "Well, what?"

"I think this will be difficult," he answered, and I was not sure whether he meant this conversation or what was to come.

"I was told today," I said. He did not turn round, just nodded. All that hair; it was unnatural. I wondered whether it had a life of its own and just lay there around his shoulders and down his back, for convenience. Perhaps it would stretch and crawl around if I touched it. He must have known my thoughts. Cal had once called him a true adept; thoughts might reach him like a scream.

"You must understand," he said, "that this . . . *state* is alien to me. I don't know what Thiede's done to me, I don't know . . . I do know I dislike it!"

I made an impulsive decision and spoke plainly. "You've known about this since I first came here, obviously. You've avoided me. I can imagine what you've been thinking." He was silent. "First, they must have told you about Cal." His shoulders stiffened and he raised his head, but still he did not look at me. "Don't think I'm not aware what I am to you. It's blighted Wraeththu, that simple. You don't want to soil yourself. Am I right?"

"Yes, you are," he replied, somewhat in surprise.

There were a few moments of awkward silence and then I said softly, "You should have come to see Cal while he was still here. You should have spoken to him."

Then he turned round quickly. "Killing to you of course is commonplace!" he said angrily. "I suppose I should expect that! When I look at you, all I can see is Orien and Orien's blood on the floor and his guts hanging out of him. That's what I see!" He stood up, his arms waving. "Oh, the Varrs! So sympathetic, weren't they! Who else could he have gone to, whining and beaten? Did you soothe him? Did you say, 'Oh, never mind, Cal, what is one more death? It is nothing'? Is that what you said, all of you? As Terzian the murderer, your dear father, fawned over that perfect, demon body, was it all, 'Oh, Cal, you are so good, so one of us'? Of course, there was you too, wasn't there! I expect with you Cal let the beast well out of the cave. Did he bite you? Did he tear at you? It's good, isn't it, that perversion? Some sick part of you actually enjoys it while it's happening; afterwards you feel disgusted. Only I don't expect you or your father, did!"

He glowered at me, color pulsing along his cheekbones. I propped myself up on my elbows and stared back at him. He had made me angry. I wouldn't have thought that was possible. "Sit down, Seel!" He didn't move. "Sit down. There are some things I want to tell you." He hesitated a moment, and then half fell back onto the bed. "My childhood in Galhea was not the way you think," I said. "I want to tell you about it."

I began with that time when my father had come home with the wound in his leg. I spoke with love, for my family and my people. I had to make him understand the way we had lived, that our lives had not been full of death and evil as he thought. I brought back the memory of Forever in the spring and the gaiety of Bryony's laughter about the house and the happy times we had had together, all of us. I went back to the beginning and told him about Festival and the snow on the ground. It was a story all about when the crows left the trees and two small harlings had trudged the boundary of Forever to keep the stranger out. Then I relived the pain of when Cal had first come to us, and made Seel live it with me, and all that followed, until I came to the part about my Feybraiha. Seel didn't want to hear it, but I told him. There were Cal and I, sitting naked on the window seat in my bedroom in Forever, looking out at the dark garden, he telling me things about Orien, Pell and Saltrock. Then I was talking about Cobweb and how Cal had released him from a prison he had made for himself. "Good is disguised as evil," I said, "because some evil things have to happen to make the good things come about. There is no escaping that. Our world can never be that perfect, for then it would be out of balance and just fade away. What happened to Orien was abhorrent, for he lost his life, but Cal has lost some of his as well. He was a tortured being; still is perhaps."

At the end of this Seel said, "Cal is lucky. He is lucky that you all cared about him so much."

"I thought our comfort was worthless."

Seel smiled and shook his head and all his hair fell across his face. I could not see him. "You are stormy creatures," he said. "You love and hate as men once did. I pity you."

I laughed. "Pity us? But why? Perhaps you should have come earlier, your people. You should have come north with your bloodless violence and taken all the weapons away. Why didn't you? You let death happen because you didn't come and stop it. I am pure-born and I have feelings and the only way the Gelaming will get rid of them is to beat them out of me. I am not ashamed of them. I am prepared to fight the bad within myself. It can be done without an emotional vacuum."

"It's not like that!" Seel stood up again. "The difference is subtle. We have love in our souls, but it is not selfish. That is the difference."

"You should see my people," I said.

"Oh, I shall!" he answered. "Hordes of them, with Ponclast at their head, all planning to slake their thirsts on Gelaming blood. They do that, don't they? Drink blood?"

I would not answer that. "Where is my father, Seel?"

The pause was barely discernible. "He's alive."

"Does Thiede have him?"

Seel put his hands in his hair. He shook his head and then said, "Yes. Yes, he does. Terzian is in Immanion."

I wanted him to tell me more, but he would only shake his head.

"I can't. That's all I know. I can't tell you more."

"I don't believe you."

"Why not? Why should I lie to you?"

"Because I'm a Varr and because you don't like me that much."

He shrugged. "Hmm, I suppose so. But it is the truth. You'll find out about Terzian sooner or later, but not from me."

He went to the door. He was going to leave and I wanted him to stay, even though I knew the strangling knots were only being wound tighter by his being here. He paused and looked back at me. "You were right about one thing, Swift the Varr," he said. "I should have come and talked to Cal. You were right about that. Now it's too late." He ducked through the curtains and was gone.

My heart began to pound. I relived the past hour a hundred times, seeking hopeful signs, but I was sure there were none. What had he come to say to me? All he had done was listen to me, really. I lay there on my bed, wistful and sad and exultant, and let a long, slow admission seep comfortably into my eyes, my brain, my heart. Admitting it was a relief, a burden lifted. It was as if I had shaken myself and a lifetime's mantle of dust had fallen away from me. I felt lighter and steeled to face the future. I was not ashamed. The admission was this: I love him.

The next evening, Chrysm came to visit me. "You've been hiding in here for a whole day," he said. "Have you eaten? I've brought some food for you."

I wasn't that hungry, but ate some of it anyway to keep him quiet. I had been quite happy in my solitude; I hadn't thought about food.

"What have you been doing here all alone?" he asked.

"Oh, nothing; just thinking."

He carefully dissected an orange and handed me half of it. "Ah, thinking! Ashmael tells me Grissecon will be performed on the first night of the next full moon. Only four days!" He shook his head. "Is that something to do with what you've been thinking about?"

"Oh no!" I lied and we both laughed. Arahal had been to see me first thing that morning to tell me this news. I had thought of nothing else all day.

"Isn't it what you've always wanted?" Chrysm asked.

"Partly. . . . Has Arahal sent you here, Chrysm?"

He shook his head. "No. They've finished with mauling your mind. I'm acting autonomously! Now, all you have to do is wait; wait and think. They want you to be alone. They want you to fast. They want you rabid with delirium, I suppose. More cheese?"

"Yes, please! Suddenly I am ravenously hungry!"

I told him about Seel's visit and he uttered an exasperated snort. "Seel! I hope you knock some of his glib piety out of him! Still, you seem to have handled yourself better than in the past. It must be driving him scatty wanting you so much!"

"Chrysm . . . ?"

"It must be like being tempted by the devil for him!"

"Don't say that?"

"Why not?"

"Because it isn't true! I can't joke about it."

Chrysm smiled secretively. "It is true," he said. "You'd better believe it, Swift, but don't think too highly of yourself because of it. Thiede's sledge-hammer mindgames have been thrown at Seel too, you know. Desire! Think of it! Thiede being thoroughly entertained watching you and Seel both squirming frantically, chasing your tails in a whirlpool of confusion. I could have told you that before."

I should have been angry, I suppose. Chrysm had listened to me ranting on about my unrequited desire for Seel and he had known all along that Seel was suffering similar lonely throcs of dark, unwanted passion.

"You should have said," I told him abruptly.

"I couldn't. It might have interfered with the process of . . . shall we say, enchantment?"

I ate in silence for a while, listening to the inner tumbling voice of my heart. I could feel Chrysm looking at me. "The force you two will produce may explode the world," he said hopefully. I smiled grimly. "I'm sorry, Swift."

"Don't be. Thank you for telling me. I'm not angry, just numb. I've felt like this before."

"Has it made things easier?"

"Hard to tell yet."

"You must treat him with compassion."

"While knocking his piety out of him?"

"He is distressed."

"Really?"

"Have you started to hate him?" Chrysm feared he was responsible. I put his mind at rest, only to worry him more.

"No. I've realized I am in love with Seel."

Chrysm recoiled, not sure whether to laugh or remonstrate. "Swift!" he cried and then softly, "You are a Varr." It was full of meaning.

"Yes," I replied, smiling sweetly, "It seems I am!"

The day came when the dawn was lemon and rose, the air sweeter than usual and the feeling of life stirring more noticeable. Before Imbrilim was truly awake, Arahal came to me, robed in purple and gold. He brought with him, on a silver plate, a lock of tawny hair surrounded by seven buds of the putiri plant. An attendant, veiled and silent, carried a flagon of water.

"It will be tonight," Arahal said, perfunctorily.

"Yes."

His eyes looked kinder than the last time we had spoken. "I can see you have prepared yourself," he said. I did not answer. He indicated the contents of the silver plate.

"These buds must be eaten at regular intervals during the day, Swift. Their taste is not the most pleasant, but we have brought you plenty of water to wash them down." He took one of the dull gray-green pellets between thumb and forefinger. "You may as well take this first one now."

"What will it do?"

"A slightly narcotic effect; a relaxant . . . it will help you." By his evasive glance, I gathered there was something more, which he would not tell me. I did not care. Obediently, I took the bud in my hand. "Chew it well, Swift."

The taste was bitter and rancid, reminiscent of a hundred foul things. Even severe chewing could not reduce the fibers to anything that was comfortable to swallow. Arahal offered me water. My eyes were running.

"Not too bad, was it?" he asked lightly.

I pulled a face of utter disgust. "Delightful," I said.

He smiled. "We shall come for you later. Spend this day in tranquility and purify your thoughts. Calm your body; be still."

It was a long, long time to sundown.

At midday I forced down another of the nauseating putiri buds, eyeing my diminishing water supply with misgiving. I had been instructed not to leave the pavilion and to spend my time in serene meditation. I did, for a while, but then got bored and started to read instead. My stomach screamed for food, but after the second bud, it did not hurt as much. I began to feel light-headed and could not focus on my book any more. I lay down on my bed, staring up at the swaying canopy, and delightful shivers ran across my flesh. I put my hand to my face and could feel the contact of each pore, each atom. I sighed and could see the vision of my own breath. Two hours later, I ate another bud.

In the late afternoon, as I lay in a contented stupor, I became distantly aware that someone was requesting ingress to my pavilion. I could barely summon the energy to form the thoughtforms to let them in. I was wondering if it might be Seel, but I did not recognize the tall har that came in through the curtains. I would certainly have known if I'd met him before because he was like something from a dream or a vision, or, it must be said, a nightmare. In my drugged state, I could hardly see him; he seemed insubstantial, flickering, shining. His head was wreathed in flame and then I realized it was just his hair, bright scarlet and vivid orange. I decided I was hallucinating and just stared, my mouth hanging open.

Then the vision spoke. "Well, aren't you going to welcome me, son of Terzian?" Such a sound can only be described as the voice of the world. The visitor must be real; perhaps another member of the Hegemony.

"Welcome, stranger!" I slurred and tried to raise my hand. The striking figure glided into the room. "I'm afraid I'm unprepared for callers," I continued in an unsteady voice. "I have nothing to offer you . . ."

"A seat will suffice."

"I'm sorry. Please, sit down."

He did so, crossing his legs, steepling his fingers.

"You must forgive me, no-one told me you would be coming, I don't know your name . . ."

The stranger smiled. A predatory, weirdly inviting smile that for a second brought Cal's face to my mind.

"I think you may have heard of me," he said. "My name is Thiede."

He waited a second or two to let the impact of this revelation sink in. He noted with satisfaction my gaping mouth and startled eyes. It is a reaction that will never cease to give him pleasure.

"I expect you are now wondering why I'm here," he said and it did not sound at all predictable as it had when Caeru had said something similar. "The reason is simple; I wish to talk to you. You don't have to say anything, Swift, for there is nothing you can say that I want to hear. I don't mean to sound harsh by that, but time is precious to me. Do you understand?" I nodded fiercely, aware that my stupor appeared to have fled. "Now then." He settled down and leaned back. "You know that I had you brought to Imbrilim to have you prepared for the role I wish you to take in Megalithica. You are young, Swift, but flexible. I admire your spirit and your good sense. But that is not what I wish to speak about; Ashmael can deal with all that when the time comes. I am concerned with more immediate ventures. This Grissecon you are to undertake is very important and you must give it your best. I realize it might be a waste of breath to say this, but try not to let your emotions take control of you. There are two extremely crucial reasons for the Grissecon. First, the power of the essence. Its strength will be increased by the intensity of your pleasure. Seel will take care of that. It is your task to please him! Think of that; it may sound obvious, but don't be tempted to let Seel take control. Overpower him, Swift, drown him in his own desire, let the spirit come alive . . ." He grinned at the effect these words were having on me. "No, you don't really need me to say it, do you. You *want* to give him your best; how well my plan has worked! Now listen. This part you must understand fully. When the time comes for you to plant your seed within him, you must leave this plane, travel to the upper spheres. It should be easy by that time. When you feel the pull, follow it. You and Seel as one individual. Once you have left this place, you may separate. You must seek the fields of lemon grass. On the horizon will be visible the golden pyramids of Shekh. You will know the place by them. Take aruna together in that higher place and call to the spirit of your son. It will hear you. It must be conceived there. Do you understand?"

I spoke at last. "I don't know . . . I will remember the words."

"Good. That will be enough." He stood up. "I shall leave you now.

There is nothing more to say at present, but I shall look forward to our next meeting. Goodbye, Swift."

Before I had finished my own farewell, the room was empty of his presence. One moment he was there, the next not, in the blink of an eye, so that I doubted whether I had ever really seen him. I could remember every word he had spoken exactly.

I ate another bud, thinking about what the mighty Thiede had said to me. My body was tingling. I felt so powerful, I laughed aloud. Thiede had spoken to me. My purpose, my importance filled the world. Outside, the sun dipped toward a crimson horizon and evening birds called above the canopies of Imbrilim. The air was full of imminence, tense as pulled threads, pulling me in. My future began here. This was the beginning. This was where it would all start.

Two hara came to bathe me and Arahal was with them, soft-voiced and somber. As they sluiced my skin with salt, scented water, Arahal mumbled incomprehensible prayers above me, scattering dust that looked like ash. I was dried and clothed in white linen, my hair pinned up in a loose coil, my hands rubbed with oil. Arahal said, "Take the lock of hair," pointing at the plate where only two putiri buds remained. I took it. "That is Seel's hair," he told me. "Absorb its vitality, tune in to his vibrations."

"Does he have some of mine?"

"Naturally."

"But how?"

"It was taken some days ago, when my attendant came to dress your hair."

"I did not notice."

"No." I closed my fingers around that small part of Seel and the smell of him seemed all about me like a tantalizing ghost. A smell of spice and clean skin.

"Will we be alone?" I asked.

"Most of the time. Of course, the essences must be collected immediately, but your privacy will be respected. The first time you must not go too far, for the presence of yaloe in the essence may destroy its effectiveness. You will be tempted to break through the seal, but you mustn't. That comes later and is not Grissecon. I hope you understand."

"Yes, Thiede told me," I said. Arahal did not comment. He did not intend to be impressed by that.

"Come," he said. "We must leave now. The moon has risen."

Outside, but for the light of the spectral moon, Imbrilim was in darkness. All the lights were doused, and everywhere was shrouded in eerie silence. "They pray for you," Arahal said. In the center of the camp, in a place that was normally an open space of grass, a pavilion of dove gray had been erected. Multiple folds moved listlessly in the slight breeze. "This is the place," Arahal said. "May the spirit of the Aghama be with you." He placed two fingers on my forehead. "Let this body be strength. Let this spirit be dominion."

I watched as he and his attendants began to retreat, not walking, but simply receding, shrinking in size. For a moment I was afraid, suddenly sober and shivering in the cool air. It seemed I had stepped from the world of reality into one completely unknown to me, somehow threatening. Within the pavilion a siren was waiting for me and I was unarmed, save for the weapons the Aghama had bequeathed me that were supposed to subdue the monster that was the wondrous Seel's desire. My body was all I had and that seemed too frail, too unpredictable to trust. I stared at the place where I must enter, at that place where the gossamer folds writhed and curled. Imbrilim held its breath, waiting. I walked forward.

Lifting aside the drapes, I passed through a narrow corridor of hanging cloth until another door curtain blocked my way. I had to force my hand to move them. My palms were damp, my heart beating painfully fast. The room beyond was filled with the soft yellow-green radiance of two lamps, standing on the floor which was strewn with white fur rugs. In the center of the room was a bed made of plump cushions, blanketed with furs. I walked straight toward it and looked down. He did not look at me; his eyes were closed, his hair spread out like floating seaweed all around him. He was covered by the blankets from the waist down, but by gazing at his chest, his shoulders and his arms, I could see he was as slim as I'd imagined him to be. Not skinny, but svelte with muscle while still softly curved, the hint of femininity. I thought, Oh God, I can't touch him; I can't! and then he opened his eyes and slowly turned his head toward me and I literally dropped to my knees beside him.

"So, we meet again, Swift the Varr," he said softly and I could see his eyes were partly glazed from the effect of putiri buds. Some of his hair had stuck to his mouth and I reached to pull it away. My fingers touched his lips and I felt a shudder shoot right up my arm. He caught my fingers in his own and kissed them. I spoke his name.

"You are full of mystery," he said.

"Mystery, is that it? I thought it was blight."

He frowned. "Don't say that. Not here. Not now."

I felt as if I had never spoken to him before, yet at the same time felt that I knew him intimately. It was so easy to reach out and stroke his face. He rubbed against me like an animal. I put my hands in his hair as I had longed to do so many times. (Is this real? Is it?) "I have never seen anything like you," I said.

"Then see it all," he answered and opened up the covering of furs as if it was his own skin. I stared, entranced. He seemed to glow. (I must be dreaming. I must be!)

"Do you hate me, Seel?"

"Do you have to ask that?"

"Yes."

He shook his head and his eyes were shining like distant stars. "No, I don't hate you." He reached for me, his face like the face of a person who has seen the lights of home shining out to him through a storm. "Have you waited a long time for this?" he asked.

"Yes, a long time."

"You have searched?"

"I didn't know I was searching."

He smiled. "You were, though, you were. And now you have found." He put his hand upon my face and brought my lips to his own. What I experienced within his breath is beyond words. It left me gasping, as if I'd been drowned, yet I wanted more. I wanted him so much, it was like pain. He laughed and sat up, pushing his hair over his shoulders, easing my arms from my robe.

"We are perfect, we are beautiful," he said and bent to touch my throat with his mouth. His hair fell into my face and I breathed deeply of its fragrance. The touch of his hands upon my shoulders was like being burned; it was hot and it crackled with sparks. Seel, splendor incarnate, covering my body with kisses, dragging his wondrous hair across my chest, my stomach, my loins. His tongue, like a sinuous, questing reptile, exploring every pore of my flesh. As I lay there, shuddering, he raised his head. "It must be the best," he said. I opened my eyes. He looked so serious, his hands behind his head, staring down at me.

"It will be," I answered. "How could it be otherwise? You are the best in the world for me."

I pulled him to me and pressed him back into the cushions. His face was all covered with hair and I tried to push it away. "Open your eyes, Seel. I want to see them."

"Why? Now?"

"This moment!"

I paused then, almost afraid of what I must do, still half convinced I was dreaming. Where would I wake up? Only slight pressure made him swallow me up; color burst all around me. In his eyes, the pupils widened, but his face was so still. Then he said, "God!" and laughed.

"Hush!" I told him. "This is momentous." And it was. It was comfortable, something simple, like slipping into a favorite chair and curling up there. We were perfectly matched, as Thiede had known we were, anticipating each other's thoughts and desires. Usually, during aruna, reality takes flight and it is all a world of dreams, but that time, I was wholly conscious the whole time of where I was, and the sensations were wholly physical. We never stopped looking at each other. I had never looked into another har's eyes at the moment of orgasm before; never. How I made him wait for that, using what Caeru had taught me. When the climax came, I saw colors pulsing inside his eyes, pulsing to the beat of his heart, and there were fires burning deep within. He whispered my name and we were quite still, in our heads, while all that wild sensation flooded our bodies.

We did not want to part, but as a hail of sparkling dust settled around us, on the bed, our skin, our hair, the curtains behind us lifted and Arahal padded into the room, accompanied by his attendants. I was so drained I could hardly move and it seemed it was coldly, without ceremony, that they lifted my damp body off Seel's and laid me aside. I had fulfilled my purpose in their eyes. Seel whimpered as Arahal milked our mingled essences from his body and I reached for his hand. His nails dug into my palm.

Arahal stood up and examined the glowing fluid he held in a glass bottle. "Well done!" he said, which seemed somehow irreverent under the circumstances. Seel and I were in no mood for conversation and were glad when Arahal woundedly recognized this and left us alone.

"He has made me bleed!" Seel complained.

"Does it hurt?" I asked him, knowing that there was more required of us that night. He shook his head.

"I don't think so. Arahal isn't used to doing that; he shouldn't be so rough."

I took him in my arms, longing to crush the life out of him. At times, his beauty sets my teeth on edge. He squirmed.

"I fought so hard," he said.

I released my grip a little. "Fought what?"

"Against you. One time, I nearly gave in. Do you remember?" I shook my head. Seel had never seemed the remotest bit interested in me before. "It was in the field beyond Imbrilim, when you were watching me. I could always feel you watching me. I knew you followed me around. That time, I was thinking, 'This is it. I shall go to him. In a little while, I shall go to him and we shall speak together.' But when I looked again, you were gone. You had looked like something made out of smoke, so pale, yet I could see your strength. That time, I could not think of Terzian, nor Cal, nor Varrs; only you."

"Strength was the furthest thing from my mind then," I said.

He smiled and put his head against my chest. "Oh Swift, I knew that as soon as we touched, there would be no going back. It is something I've feared for so long. If I ever tried to imagine the har who would do this to me, he never looked like you. More like Cal, I suppose . . ."

"Most people's dream," I added drily.

Arahal had left us a tray of food and drink. We pulled the bedcovers around us, for we were starting to get cold, and ate and drank. I was full of curiosity about Seel. There was so much I wanted to know about him, but I was unsure how much he would want to tell me. There was no way I wanted to risk offending him. Cautiously, I mentioned that I'd been told he was fairly close to the Tigron. He didn't appear reticent about it. "I've worked with Pell from the beginning, when he first went to Immanion," he said. "And of course, we had spent some time together in Saltrock . . ."

I wanted to avoid that issue. "Tell me about Immanion," I begged. "Tell me about Phaonica and the people there."

Seel laughed at my eagerness. "I'm sure you'll see it for yourself some day," he replied. "It *is* a wonderful place, as you'd expect. Phaonica is incredibly huge; all the hara possess unnatural radiance there. . . . Oh, Swift, I don't want to talk about that. I want to know about you. It fascinates me, how you lived before and the people you knew. Tell me about that."

"Now I know how you feel!" I said. "I don't want to talk about that either."

"We have an eternity to discuss such things. Another time."

As he said this, warmth and joy spread through me like a flame. I took him in my arms once more. He sighed against my chest and then said hesitantly, "I have never hosted a child before, Swift. When you told me about Cal and your father, I couldn't believe it! Cal, of all hara! Still, if he can go through with it, there's no reason why I can't. But you must understand, it's hard for those of us not pure-born to feel comfortable with the thought of bearing life. It's not a function I was born with!"

In the small hours of the morning, while Imbrilim slept and all the lamps were out, I took Seel in my arms and pierced him and carried him with me to the higher spheres. We were in a world of lemon-colored light and long fields of pale yellow grass stretched away from us on all sides. As Thiede had told me, on the horizon shimmered the vague shapes of spectral pyramids, which made our eyes ache to look upon. Seel and I sat down upon the sward, joined only by my hand in his hand. His skin was shining and his hair moved like feathers. He lay back and spread out his arms and I entered into him through the body and the mind and we called together to the spirit world, and presently a funnel of light appeared above us, rotating slowly. It drifted down to us and we were filled with the presence of our child to be. Within Seel's body, I nudged so softly the special seal that would open him up, and with utter compliance the muscles relaxed and I sought the star of his being, where life could begin. Nothing could part us now; nothing. We were joined inextricably, in convolutions of shining flesh; we were one. For a moment, we screamed together for the ecstasy was almost unbearable and light shimmered around us. Then I was lying across him in a room of silvery drapes that was filled with the pale glow that presages dawn, and our skins were cool and damp against each other. We both knew, in our hearts, that we were the makers of the true magic, that gift from the Creator, unparalleled, incomparable, the gift of life.

CHAPTER SIX

> ⤞⊶⊙⊷⤝

Destiny of the Pearl
Barbarism thrives; such habits
Are frozen in time.
Perversity swallows up the world,
Goodwill to the mirror of crime.

Seel and I spent two glorious days alone together and then, feeling thoroughly rested and exhausted at the same time, bid farewell to the small, gray pavilion where we had worked our magic. In response to an unspoken agreement, I moved that day into Seel's pavilion. From being utter strangers, we had become chesna, as close as Wraeththu can get, in the space of two days. It is something that has never changed, nor ever will.

As I was unpacking my rather small amount of belongings into a chest in Seel's bedroom, Arahal came to request my presence at the pavilion of the Hegemony. "You too, Seel," he said. "I hope you've made the most of your holiday, for it's over for all of us now."

All the high-ranking Gelaming were there, seated around the large table in the main chamber. Seel and I were the last to arrive. I was overpowered by uncontrollable pride as we took our places together near Ashmael at the head of the table. All of them knew that the splendid creature that is Seel was mine, and I his. Whatever Gelaming like to call it, I felt we were in love and knew that the radiance such feelings gave us were apparent to everyone.

Ashmael addressed me. "Well, Swift, it is nearly time to get things moving. The crystal has been constructed and you and Seel have made the power to fire it. Soon, we shall have to travel north and sort this godforsaken country out once and for all." He smiled around the table. "Now, for the benefit of those of you who haven't been present at all the meetings we've held on the subject, Cedony will bring you up to date on our position." He leaned back and gestured to Cedony, who was seated on his right side. Cedony stood up, trying to shuffle a rather unruly mound of notes into a single pile.

"Central and north Megalithica have been thoroughly surveyed, as I'm sure you all know," he began. "Our findings show that the majority of Wraeththu settlements have fallen under Varrish rule, or Varrish tyranny, which might be a more accurate way of putting it. Those who have maintained their independence are tribes who either have some kind of trading agreement with the Varrs, or those whom Ponclast views as irrelevant, whose property will not add to the Varrs' wealth and power. We have been rightly disturbed by the small amount of time it has taken Ponclast to establish his empire in Megalithica. It is known that he subjugates through fear, of course, and Varrish callous brutality is legendary, but it was always thought that the Varrs had turned away from the path, either black or white, and for the most part abandoned their natural abilities. Now, we understand that this is not entirely the case. While Ponclast has never encouraged development among his lower castes, he has certainly nurtured occult powers within himself and among his generals. He has created an elite company of dangerous, murderous maniacs, of whom Ponclast's ally, Terzian, is, of course, most notorious."

Beneath the table, Seel reached for my hand. Through mind touch I asked him, "Does it show then, my distress?"

"No," he answered soothingly. "Only to me."

As if aware of our conversation, Cedony turned to me. "We appreciate some of what must be said may cause you discomfort, Swift," he said. "Terzian is, of course, your father, but not all the company here have all the facts about him. We beg your forebearance over this matter."

I shook my head. "It's alright. Please continue."

Cedony put his papers down on the table. "In the extreme north lies Ponclast's citadel of Fulminir. It is a place feared and dreaded by both humans and hara in that part of the world. It was here that Ponclast and Terzian committed some of their worst atrocities. The Hegemony is aware that there are those among you who feel that the Gelaming should not seek dominion over the Varrs, that this is merely substituting one kind of tyranny for another. There are those of you who feel that some kind of arrangement suitable to both sides should be suggested to the Varrs, that whatever we feel about Varrish culture, to a certain extent we have no right to interfere. It is said that now the Varrs control most of Megalithica, the time for bloodshed and fighting is over and we should let the continent settle down on its own. What I am about to divulge may change your minds.

"The Varrs, or more accurately the Varrish government, will *never* lose their thirst for blood. We know this because we have learned that the Path they have chosen is involved with occult practices of the most black and evil type. From surviving victims, we have discovered that the Varrish elite feast upon the flesh of their own kind, the most prized vintages in their wine cellars being barrels of Wraeththu blood. They must have started these practices using human stock, I would imagine, but eventually discovered that much greater powers can be gained from consuming the flesh of hara. Another of their cheerful little pastimes is ritual pelki, usually simultaneously with the slow death through poison of the victim. What we are dealing with here, Tiahaara, is not Wraeththu of a more basic culture than our own, but demonic, heartless beasts who have tasted blood and will want more. Now is not the time for me to go into more detail about other crimes we know are regularly committed in Fulminir (there is a whole file on the evidence we have gathered), but I must urge you all not to vote against Thiede's design to thoroughly cleanse Megalithica of any trace of Ponclast and his acolytes. The name of the Varrs must be expunged from the memory of Wraeththu!"

Cedony sat down again heavily and for a moment or two there was silence in the room. I felt dizzy, as if Terzian himself had stood there and confessed his crimes. Then someone from the lower end of the table stood up.

"You have spoken well, Tiahaar Cedony. Later, I would like to examine the file you speak of, but for now, I'm sure I speak for all who you implied were prepared to argue against the Hegemony's plans, when I say that we defer our privilege to speak out. Please tell us Thiede's intentions . . ."

Cedony looked to Ashmael and Ashmael nodded.

"My turn to speak, I suppose," he said wryly, but did not stand up. "We propose that a force of five centuries be sent to Galhea, which was previously Terzian's base and now left for the most part undefended, and establish a Gelaming base there. From that point we can launch our assault on Fulminir. Once Ponclast is subdued, we should have little trouble with the rest of the Varrs; *he* is their driving force and our main problem."

"And what of Terzian?" someone asked, who was obviously unaware of developments in that area. "Does Thiede have him or not? Where does he fit into this plan?"

"Terzian is no longer part of Megalithica's future," Ashmael said coldly. He would not look at me. "Are there any more questions?"

"Yes," I said coolly.

Ashmael slid his glance over me warily. "Swift?"

"There is something that hasn't been mentioned yet. The Varrish allies, the Kakkahaar. What do you propose to do about them?"

Ashmael looked surprised, then horribly sympathetic. "The Kakkahaar have already been dealt with, Swift," he said.

I squirmed with embarrassment. "I see. I didn't know . . ."

Chrysm rescued me gallantly. "When we first set foot in Megalithica, Thiede requested a meeting with Kakkahaar representatives. He made a deal with them. It is well known that they too are interested in the darker side of the occult, and perhaps under normal circumstances the Gelaming would have been as anxious to disband their tribe as they are the Varrs, but Thiede decided that in return for certain favors, he would grant them autonomy and a seat on the Council of United Tribes in Immanion. He did stress that the taking of life was still an offense in the eyes of God and har, and that any Kakkahaar convicted of such a crime would still pay the penalty, but that if their leader Lianvis was prepared to try to curb the Kakkahaar's more *beastly* activities, he would overlook past crimes. Thiede and Lianvis have a certain respect for each other. We cannot allow the Kakkahaar's darker practices to continue without making even a perfunctory attempt to curtail them; we cannot, under any circumstances, be seen to *approve,* but of course we suspect that it is something we could never have complete control over. However, Lianvis is aware of Thiede's power and he won't want to put the future of his tribe in jeopardy—"

"And what were the 'certain favors' that Thiede requested from them?" I butted in, fiercely. I had no right to be angry now, of course; I had forsaken my tribe, but betrayal still cuts deep.

"To appear to form an alliance with the Varrs, of course," Ashmael put in smoothly. "How else do you think we got so much information?"

"So Terzian was right," I said softly.

There was a mumble of voices around the table and a small amount of shuffling. My anger discomforted them. Wasn't I supposed to be Gelaming now?

"I met some of the Kakkahaar," I said. "I did not like them. I was younger then; they frightened me."

"Not an unhealthy attitude for a sensible harling!" Ashmael said cheerfully. "Anyway, those of you whom we would like to travel north to Galhea will be informed over the next couple of days. You may warn your hara. It is safer to believe that Ponclast will know we are planning to make a move. Security must be increased around Imbrilim. Cedony, I believe that's your department; I shall leave the preparation to you. Now, I think this is a good time to pause and refresh ourselves, don't you? Velaxis! Wine and a sumptuous repast are in order, I believe."

As we ate, I said to Ashmael, "Are you afraid of Ponclast then?" He looked at me sideways.

"Don't underestimate him, Swift. He could damage us quite badly. That is why we needed the elixir that was produced during your Grissecon with Seel."

"Can I see the crystal?" I asked.

"Of course, but not yet," he answered.

Talks went on until well into the evening. It was mostly about small details for the journey north. Not much was said about what we'd do when we got there. I was in a daze. I remember saying to Seel, "My God. I'm going home. I've just realized; I'm going home! Will they have been told there?"

Seel shrugged. "You'd better ask Ashmael that. I would have thought so, though. It might cause problems having large numbers of Gelaming appearing from nowhere. When Ash spoke of Galhea being mostly undefended, I think he was probably exaggerating. What do you think?"

"He was. There are enough of the Varrish army still there to look after the place. I presume Ithiel is still in charge. If I were Ashmael, I would try to get in touch with him. He's quite rational!"

"Actually, Swift, we shall be leaving that up to you," Ashmael interjected, having been eavesdropping on our conversation. "But we shall leave that until we get there. You are our protection, my dear!"

We laughed together. A kind of excitement was building up.

"We shall probably keep quiet in Galhea for a couple of months," Ashmael continued. "Because, of course, Seel shall be with us and due to spawn at that time. An important event, as Thiede has impressed upon us."

"There speaks the smug face of someone who does not carry a pearl!" Seel said caustically. "Ashmael, sometimes you disgust me."

That night, lying awake in Seel's arms I pondered aloud on what it would be like to return to Forever.

"I am Gelaming now," I said. "How will Cobweb react?"

"I should think he will just be glad that you are alive," Seel replied.

"Oh, I don't know. To a Varr, being dead is better than being Gelaming."

"I'm looking forward to seeing Galhea, Swift. Don't let premature worrying ruin that feeling for you. I know how much you love Forever, and Cobweb and all the others. Just think about seeing them again after so long. I'm sure everything will be alright."

I was grateful for his optimism, but not convinced.

Cedony and Chrysm were going to remain in Imbrilim, but Arahal and Ashmael would travel north. As part of the preparation for the journey, Arahal taught me something about the nature of Gelaming horses. I had always thought them unearthly and had not been surprised when I learned that they had the ability to travel through time and space in a completely different way to any that I'd imagined. I had always been nervous of trying to ride one in that way myself, but now Arahal told me that I'd have to learn. It would be impossible for me to ride Tulga home and arrive months after everybody else. I knew that these fabulous beasts could take you out of the world we know somehow and take you flying through a mad helter-skelter of star-trails and aether. I knew that journeys of hundreds of miles could be accomplished in seconds that way. I knew that when you were brought back to solid ground again you were still drunk with the weirdness of it for hours afterwards. You can see why I was a little nervous.

The first time Arahal took me riding through the other-lanes and I found myself speaking mind to mind with a horse, it was as distant and as vivid as a dream, if you can understand what I mean by that, but disorientating because I couldn't wake up. It made my jaw ache. Arahal laughed at me. His hair still sparkled with static dust when we came back to earth again. I was sitting on a horse that was all white and glowing and prancing. Arahal said, "She is yours now, Swift." Her name is Afnina; I still have her. No har less than Ulani can travel in that way. It demands severe control of the mind to achieve it, and to lose that control in mid-flight would mean disaster. The horse could lose you in the vastness of infinity and it would be virtually impossible for anyone to find you again. Arahal didn't tell me this until after we'd reached solid ground. I was grateful for that.

Seel was worried about the journey, for he thought traveling in the other-lanes might damage the pearl within him. Ashmael said he thought Seel was being overcautious, but he communicated with Immanion to put our minds at rest.

"Why hasn't Pell ever come?" I asked, as we waited for an answer.

"Think you're that important, Swiftling?" Ashmael snapped, jovially.

"No, not me, but Cal was with me."

"He's not with you now, though!"

This was true, of course, but I still felt disappointed that Pellaz hadn't tried to contact me again. Even Seel hadn't seen him in any shape or form for some time. I wondered if this might have something to do with Cal, but shrank from discussing it with Seel. He was becoming edgy and restless and I knew that mention of Cal disturbed him. I would hold him in my arms at night, still incredulous that I could do that, and put my hand across his lean, hard belly. "No womanish swelling!" he would say uneasily and tried to hide his pain if I prodded him too sharply. "Where is it? What is it doing?" he once asked in a panicky sort of voice.

"Just growing," I replied.

"Is it really there?" Seel mused to himself, as if he hadn't heard me.

We received word from Immanion that it would be advisable for our journey to be undertaken as soon as possible, in view of Seel's condition. No-one was really sure what the other-lanes would do to unborn harlings, but Thiede had said it was safe in the early stages, and no-one cared to argue with him.

The night before we left, Seel said, "Home, Swift; this is it. I expect your family shall hate me."

"My family of two. How awesome!" I pointed out rather glumly.

"Nonsense, Swift. From what you've told me, your family in Forever is quite large. They may not be related by blood, but they are definitely family! I can't believe that I'm actually going to meet the prim and fussy Moswell, the dreamy, romantic Swithe and the melodramatic, mad beauty Cobweb."

"I believe you're mocking me, Seel!"

"No, I mean it. It will be like meeting characters out of a book, that I've read about. I can't wait!"

Seel had a feral gleam in his eye when he said that. Some mischievous part of him would welcome the havoc it would cause in my household when it was announced that a Gelaming hosted a pearl for me, especially when they saw him. I knew that Cobweb would probably loathe him from the start.

After the journey, swift as a dream, we burst onto the earth, in a spume of smoking manes and tails, onto the flower-starred fields beyond Galhea. The horses jostled against each other in excitement and I laughed at Afnina's elation. The air smelled damper here. Afnina pulled against my hands, rearing up on her hind legs so that her luxurious mane fell over my fingers.

It was another spring in the fields of Galhea. I did not really know how long I'd been gone. At least a year; at least. Cal, Leef and I might have traveled through the Forest for months, we had no way of telling. Leef was with me again now, although still rather curt and unfriendly. I knew he had been in two minds about whether to leave Imbrilim or not; there was not that much waiting for him back home, but I had personally requested him to accompany us. I knew it would look better if two of us came home. Leef made me wait for two days before he gave me his answer, which of course had been yes. I think he'd been surprised how easily he'd adapted to the way of life in Imbrilim. It had taken him a little longer than me but now I think he was as eager to forget he'd ever been a Varr as I was.

I could see the outline of Forever, high on its hill, all its windows catching the morning sun. Seel came up beside me. His face was pale. "So, this is your home," he said, with a brave attempt at a smile.

"You are tired." I leaned to touch his face. The journey had seemed to have taken only minutes, yet I felt as if I had been riding for days. Seel looked exhausted.

"I am tired," he said. "I must rest." He slid to the ground and leaned against his horse's flank. The animal turned its head and sniffed him curiously. I saw his hand reach to stroke its nose.

"Swift!" Ashmael skidded his horse to a halt at my side.

"Well, what do you want me to do?"

"Your hostling . . . contact him."

Now: I was home. Forever squatted like some vast, brooding beast on its hill, holding within its walls those people with whom I'd grown and lived and loved. I was afraid. I was afraid that by coming back I'd destroy the dream of my childhood, that Forever would seem different and my loved ones strangers.

I dismounted from my horse. Beside me, Seel could barely stand; his face looked pinched and he was cold to my touch. I put my fingers against his neck, just below the ear, and tried to transfer a little of my strength to him. I could feel the pull; he needed more than I could give. I looked back toward Galhea. Nobody said anything. They were just waiting. I closed my eyes and called him: "Cobweb . . ."

Once was enough. A blast, a surge of energy smacked into my brain, powerful as a hurricane and just as disordered. I could make no sense of it, but I knew it was him. Standing there, knee-deep in lush grass, I could even smell him. "Cobweb, I'm home." He withdrew a little, tentatively caressing my mind. He would be able to tell how different I was, what I'd become. I felt his puzzlement, vague at first. I formed the words, "You must send Ithiel . . ."

"You are not alone . . ."

"No."

"There are strangers with you, many strangers. Who are they?"

"Friends."

"Friends? So many friends?"

"They are Gelaming, Cobweb."

"You have brought them here. I thought you would." He felt weary and resigned; his anger would come later. He did not ask about Terzian or Cal. Before he withdrew completely, to find Ithiel and send him to bring us into

Galhea, he said one last thing. He said, "Thank you, Swift." It could have meant anything.

I was walking with Cobweb in the garden. We had been fed, we had rested, and now Ashmael was talking with Ithiel. Ithiel had looked older; it surprised me. I took my hostling to the summerhouse by the lake.

"Do you remember . . . ?" I began to ask, and then couldn't say it.

Cobweb smiled and looked away. "You have not lost your impertinence, I see!"

We walked in silence, evening all around us. Cobweb was so full of questions, he didn't know where to start and remained quiet. He reached for my hand.

"I'd forgotten how marvelous, how wickedly beautiful you were!" I said lightly.

He laughed. "Me? All that? I'm surprised you say that now. After being with the Gelaming who are like . . . like . . . well, something like I've always expected."

The door to the summerhouse was open, some of the panes were broken, others were greened by lichen. "There was a great storm," Cobweb said. "All the lights went off in the town, some people were killed. I listened to it all night, all that howling. It was like angry spirits. I heard a tree fall in the garden. How it groaned! It must have fallen right through the glass here, some of it." Stark, leafless branches littered the floor like black, broken bones.

"You should have repaired it," I said, lifting a couple of the branches and tossing them out of the door.

Cobweb shrugged. "Maybe, but I think I prefer it this way. It's symbolic."

"You come here often, don't you?"

He didn't answer me, but went to sit on the edge of the fountain basin. I had a brief, painful flashback to that time when I had seen him sitting there before and Cal had come in like a zombie from the garden. Only now, the water in the fountain basin was choked with leaves, the orange fish long dead through neglect. Cobweb hadn't changed; for him that time could have been yesterday.

"I lost both of them," he said to the floor and then looked straight at me. "Thank God you came back."

I went to him and put my head in his lap and he stroked my hair, but I could never be a child again. In a way, I hadn't come back either, not the Swift that Cobweb had known.

When we walked into Forever, through the great front doors, Cobweb had been waiting for us, standing on the stairs alone, a slim and tragic figure. His hair had grown; he seemed robed in hair. I had feared the house would look different, but it didn't. Perhaps a little smaller, but then I'd grown so much. Once I'd been a child in this place, in this hallway sat with Leef on the stairs at Festival, put that fateful note about Gahrazel into the messenger's bag, danced in the dust and the sunlight on my way to morning classes with Moswell. It all seemed so inconceivably long ago.

I felt huge and awkward standing there now, all in leather, weapons at my hip, my hair shaved at the sides like Gelaming hair, smoking a black cigarette because I was nervous. Cobweb had looked at me. He recognized me instantly even though I knew I'd changed almost beyond recognition. I saw the muscles along his jaw ripple. Perhaps he saw something of Terzian in me then. But, hiding whatever emotions must have shaken him, he fell into his role of perfect host immediately, prepared to save all the questions until later; this was the role Terzian had given him. I was Terzian's son and because of that, Cobweb would not question my judgment about whom I brought into the house. My father was not with us; Forever was mine now. Cobweb ordered refreshment and ushered us into the drawing room.

I had Seel, Ashmael, Arahal and about five others with me. Everyone else had been taken to Galhea by Ithiel, whom I'd instructed to find accommodation for them in the virtually empty army quarters. Like Cobweb, Ithiel did not question my orders, but his eyes were very cold. He did not approve of accommodating the Gelaming in Varrish barracks. I invited him to join us as soon as possible and he smiled grimly. I suppose it was absurd of me to invite him to the place he had probably been using as home for God knows how long.

Cobweb had embraced me briefly and scanned Seel with a chilling glance. Seel was hanging onto my arm, occasionally resting his head on my shoulder. I could feel him shaking. "I'm going to have to lie down," he said. "Otherwise I might embarrass you and fall down."

Cobweb sniffed and summoned one of the house-hara with a click of his fingers. "We shall find accommodation for your friend," he said. "Is he ill? Would you like me to send for Phlaar?"

"Yes, if you could," I said. "I should have introduced you two before. Cobweb, this is Seel. Get someone to show him to my room."

"Ty sleeps in there now," Cobweb replied coldly.

"My father's room then," I said irritably.

Cobweb raised his eyebrows and stared at me stonily. "It isn't aired. No-one's been in there for ages."

"That doesn't matter. Have someone light a fire in there."

"As you wish, Swift." He turned to the house-har. "My son will be staying in Terzian's room. Have it prepared and escort Tiahaar Seel to it." He made it sound as if we wouldn't be staying there long. I hadn't wanted it to be like that, but Cobweb just made it that way. Full of Varrish jealousy; another thing that now felt strange to me.

"You've changed," he said, once Seel had left us.

"Of course I have!"

"That har is carrying your pearl, isn't he?"

"Yes. Still impossible to hide things from you, isn't it?" I said with a hopeful smile. Cobweb did not return it.

"Where's your father, Swift?"

I looked away. "Not now, Cobweb. Please. Questions later."

He snorted angrily and swept away, grinning ferally at Arahal as he passed him. Arahal sauntered over to me, bemused. "An amazing creature!" he exclaimed. "The stuff of legend!"

"Amazing, yes. Creature, yes," I agreed. "Arahal, you will have to tell him about Terzian. If you won't tell me, then at least tell Cobweb. I'll get no peace otherwise."

Arahal looked uncomfortable. "All shall be revealed when the time is right," he said edgily.

I went to Seel in my father's room. It smelled a little musty in there, but there was a welcome fire in the grate, which had already taken any chill off the air. The canopied bed looked ancient and uncomfortable; I hoped it wasn't too damp. Phlaar was washing his hands at the sink, behind a screen.

"Seel, are you alright?" I asked. He was lying, half-clothed, on top of the bed. His face and hair looked damp. He smiled weakly.

"Apparently, my energy is drained," he said.

"Will he be alright?" I asked Phlaar, who was watching us carefully, drying his hands.

"The journey here has taken too much out of him," Phlaar answered. "The pearl drains his energy enough as it is. It was foolish of you to travel this far in this condition!" Seel turned his head away from Phlaar's reproach. "You need utter rest and quiet," Phlaar continued.

"Like hell!" Seel snapped. "I need an infusion of strength, that's all. Tell Ashmael, Swift; he can do it."

Phlaar cleared his throat. "Well, as you don't appear to be needing my services any longer . . ." He moved toward the door. I thanked him and he smiled thinly. Later, he would tell his friends about Gelaming conceit.

Seel made a derisive sound. "Varrs!" he said. "They know nothing!"

"And you, being Gelaming, know everything of course!" I could never be angry with him. He held out his hand and I took it in my own.

"I'm sorry, Swift. I don't seem to have any control over my mouth nowadays."

I sat on the bed and took him in my arms. "It doesn't matter." Seel laughed against my chest. My hands couldn't keep from straying over his skin; he was so touchable. "Did that monster downstairs really host you?" he asked.

Living among the Gelaming, I hadn't really noticed myself changing that much, but now I was home, every mirror seemed to scream my difference at me, and every eye I'd known had become a mirror. I don't think Tyson recognized me at all. The last time I had seen him he had been such a baby; now he was a willowy harling with Cal's haunted, bony face and a glistening mop of fair hair. I could see a hint of Terzian in his eyes for they could turn very hard on you, but his spirit seemed wholly Cal's, unearthly and wild. He greeted me with reservation; we did not embrace. All he said was, "You've been gone so long." Two springs had passed in Galhea since I had last been there.

After my walk in the garden with Cobweb that first evening, I went to my father's study. It looked uncomfortably tidy; Ithiel had been using it. On the desk I discovered balance sheets for crops and supplies, with heavy pencil marks scored across them in places. I sat down in my father's chair and leaned back, gazing out of the window. It felt as if I had never left Forever. It felt as if Cal was in the house and we were still waiting for news of my father. Perhaps tomorrow the Zigane would come . . . Cobweb had asked me about Terzian many times that day.

I found myself wondering how much my hostling actually knew about Terzian. I didn't think he was aware of exactly what had happened to Gahrazel, nor how close Terzian's relationship with Ponclast now seemed to be. How could I answer his questions without telling him what I knew? How could I stand there and say, 'That har you loved, would give your life for, is a monster'? And yet, surely Cobweb would have known those things. Didn't he know everything about those he loved? Weren't all our minds open books to him that he could learn from whenever he cared to look? I did not want to talk about Terzian because it caused me pain. It was something I wanted to forget. He would hate me if he knew, he would call me a traitor. Could he then stand by and countenance what happened to Gahrazel happening to me? I shuddered.

Outside, the evening was fading into a red and purple sky, bare trees stark against the color. Inside, warmth crept through the long corridors from well-tended fires, there was a sound of footsteps, the smell of cooking. I love this place. I was glad my father had gone from it.

I had learned from Cobweb that the Zigane had stayed in Galhea only until the autumn of that year. It was clear that Tel-an-Kaa had been a great comfort to Cobweb when Cal, Leef and I had first left Forever. Her optimism for my future, indeed for all our futures, had never been shaken. When Cobweb feared for my life, she would calmly argue against his fears. I knew that he was sorry when she left. She had given no reason for going. Perhaps her master summoned her, another errand waiting, another message to deliver.

"I think there must be a lot of female in me," Cobweb said to me, seriously. "For I could understand that woman. When she left, I was not surprised."

"There *is* a lot of female in you, Cobweb," I agreed, hiding my smile.

He shrugged. "My fault, I suppose; laziness. Are women indolent, do you think?"

"No. I think it is more lazy to be predominantly male, but that is only my opinion, of course."

Bryony was the only person in the house not too wary of me to come and throw her arms about me. "Welcome, Swift, welcome back," she said.

I had gone to the kitchens as soon as I was able, again trepidly and a little nervous of what I would find. It twisted my heart with nostalgia to see the place. The worn table, the shining expanse of sink, the archaic stove covered in huge cauldrons of bubbling, aromatic Yarrow creations. He was still the same, strings of hair everywhere. We all drank a bottle of sheh together and I talked, with drunken enthusiasm, about my adventures. Strangely, it no longer seemed real. I found I was reluctant to speak about Seel, but Bryony had already heard about him and was armed with questions. Rather than answer them, I promised to take her to meet him in the morning. Bryony, no longer a girl, but now a strong, lean woman. Out of all the people I had known before, she had changed the most. She was human, she was older.

I slept with Seel in my father's bed; the room was free of ghosts. Lying in the dark, I searched the ceiling, trying to locate that spot where someone crouching in the room above could see in. I suppressed a shiver, thinking of Gahrazel. Was he still up there? Seel stirred in his sleep. I wanted to talk to him. I put my mouth against his hair. He twitched his face and mumbled some nonsense. I stared into the shadows, listening for smothered breathing, anything. All I could hear was Seel. I did not wake him.

Apart from the natural destruction of the summerhouse, it seemed time had not touched Forever. Perhaps it was the name that protected it: We dwell in Forever; dissolution could not mark it. My father's presence, even my own, had not been missed by the house. Only when within its walls did hara exist for it. Outside was death; I had grown up with this notion. I was anxious to establish some kind of rapport with Tyson, but he appeared to have little interest in me. As a child, I too had been content to experience only my own little world and had resented anyone trying to enter it with me. My brother resembled me in many ways and he clearly looked upon Cobweb as his hostling. He never asked any questions about Cal. That was how we differed; I had always been full of questions. Seel remarked on the fact that Tyson reminded him of Cal. One day, my little brother would learn how to touch souls and break hearts. Already his eyes hinted at the knowledge of it.

The Varrs warily accepted the presence of Gelaming within their town. Over the months, they had isolated themselves from their brothers in the north, being concerned only with their own survival, bread upon their tables, and disregarding the concept of the War. Most of the soldiers had gone south with Terzian anyway. Now Ithiel found his time filled with the problems of administration, delivering justice upon petty squabbles and organizing the way our land was utilized. Strangers in our fields now meant extra mouths to feed that were not welcome, no longer a threat in quite the same way that they had been before. I was surprised that after the Zigane had left Galhea, other bands of humans had passed through. Some of them, bearing provisions, hardware or skills that were useful to the Varrs had been persuaded to remain in the town and had taken over empty houses in the southern quarter. The army had once lived there and it was now three-quarters empty. Human children and harlings played together in the gaunt buildings, where once a throng of polished horses had stamped restlessly, awaiting their masters' hands, awaiting a journey south. None of them had yet returned. It was accepted among the hara that they never might.

One afternoon, after we had been in Galhea for just over a week, I took Seel on a tour of the gardens. Life was stirring. Overnight, bare trees had become garlanded with a green mist of young leaves. I took him to the lake and he made me tell him again the story of Cal, Cobweb and the summerhouse. While I spoke, the summerhouse seemed to watch me mournfully from across the lake, perhaps remembering too.

Seel stared at the water thoughtfully. "Did that really happen here?" he said aloud.

I looked around me. "It is the setting, certainly . . . but it *does* feel different."

We went to investigate the fallen stones where I had found Cal. They were now nearly hidden beneath a growth of ivy (how relevant). I could remember the smells and the sounds and the feel of Cal's arm around me; that first magic taste of another har's breath. I looked at Seel putting his hand against the stone, touching the moss and the leaves, and I felt as if I'd somehow missed half my life, as if that day of the storm and Cobweb's rage had only been a short time ago, and suddenly I was here again, full-grown, with a har who was remarkable in every way and had never known me untouched and shivering. What had happened to me? I felt disorientated, removed from reality. I sat down. Seel came to my side, smiling, pushing back that wondrous hair.

"Ah, time," he said, sighing. "When tomorrow comes, it often feels like there's never been a yesterday."

I took his hand. He could always tell what I was thinking. "Once it's past us, it's just like a story," I said, "like something we've only observed, or heard secondhand. How can I explain it?"

He shook his head. "You don't have to. Remember here is a har who once found the dead body of a friend who had been murdered in cold blood. Did that really happen? Now I am here and it's another story, another person's life. I can't believe it happened to me. All those threads weaving in and out, bringing me here to you . . ."

"Seel," I said, "you have never told me . . . about Cal, about you and him. I want to know."

He had been squatting beside me, now he sat down and turned my face toward him.

"I can remember the first time I met him," he said. I didn't speak. Seel looked away from me, at the water. "We were only children then. He was always . . . *strange.* Popular, but the other kids were afraid of him. He fascinated me, he bewitched me. . . . We became har in our early teens, but had been lovers for some time before that. He went to the Uigenna, while

I was incepted into the Unneah. I thought I'd never see him again, but he didn't stay with the Uigenna for long. When he came to the Unneah, I foolishly thought he'd come because of me, but then he had Zack with him. 'You're too good, Seel,' he used to say to me, as if that was something despicable. Zack wasn't good. He was mad and bad and beautiful. After I left the north and went to start the Saltrock community, they'd come visit me sometimes. I once took aruna with them and it was terrifying. They loved to hurt each other. But they did *love,* I am sure of that." It surprised me to hear Seel say that, knowing how the Gelaming looked on such emotions. "I don't often think of those times now," he said and stood up, walking to the water's edge. "Things happen, Swift, times change. We are conceited enough to think we can understand the future, even see part of it, but . . ."

We looked at each other and an amazing flash of insight passed between us. Understanding of something infinite. Within seconds, it had passed. I held out my hand. Together, we walked back to the house.

We prepared for our final journey north. Arahal took me to his room and showed me the crystal, lying in a silk wrap of deepest indigo, pulsing with restless life, throbbing colors almost too painful to look at directly. "It worked well," Arahal said and smiled at me. "Such power!"

"I can assure you the product was merely incidental," I said.

Arahal laughed. "It worked better than Thiede could ever have imagined."

"I doubt that."

"And soon your child will come into the world."

"Yes." I decided to confess an anxiety that had been bothering me for some time. "Arahal, Thiede wanted us to make this child for a specific purpose. What is it? Will he want to take the child from us?"

Arahal clasped my shoulder. "Don't be ridiculous! He won't take the harling away from you."

"No, perhaps not the harling . . . but the har?"

Arahal shook his head. "A childhood; seven years. Later you must ask these questions again. I don't know the reason behind all this. That's Thiede's business. We have more immediate problems."

"I want Seel to stay here when we leave."

"Impossible; he will never agree."

"But the child!"

"It will survive whatever happens."

My hostling had already been approached about fostering the harling while Seel and I were away. It was a role he enjoyed, I suppose, and one to which he was entirely suited. I did not argue.

I could knead Seel's stomach and feel the hard growth that was the pearl within him. He complained of pain occasionally and was becoming more and more restless, but I could soothe him by stroking his back or combing out his hair. If he relaxed the pain usually went away.

Ashmael asked for the stableyard to be cleared and disinfected, the walls repainted. This was done without question. He had a pentacle painted upon the ground and wrote strange words all around it. Nightly, we gathered in that place and Ashmael, acting as shaman, began the preliminary entreaties toward the seventy amulet angels invoked at the time of childbirth. Cobweb would never join us, but I often saw him watching us from an upstairs window. Seel was anointed and blessed; he shone with a radiance that made me want to break the circle and take him in my arms. Later, alone with him in my father's bed, I would tell him he was perfect, again and again, until he'd tell me to shut up. "If I was perfect, I wouldn't feel the way I do," he said.

"How do you feel? How?" I asked urgently, pulling him against me, feeling his hard stomach hot against mine.

"That I want to be with you like this," he replied. "That I want you selfishly. I am worried my feelings will infect the pearl."

"But they must!" I told him.

"Thiede chose me for my level head, among other things, remember."

"Then it will be our son's secret defense against Thiede," I suggested triumphantly.

"That is not the idea," Seel replied with cynicism.

I am glad that it happened at night; daylight would have been too harsh. Ashmael wanted Seel to deliver the pearl in the yard, within the pentacle, but we both protested violently against that. "I am not an animal!" Seel exclaimed. "I will not give birth in a stableyard. I will not be watched scrabbling inelegantly around!"

"Since when have you developed such an exaggerated sense of vanity?" Ashmael snapped.

"Oh, and who is without vanity?" Seel argued relentlessly. "Coming from someone who is so well acquainted with his mirror, Ashmael, I'm surprised you have the nerve to say that."

"You were never this bothersome before, Seel."

"I was never in this outlandish state before!"

Ashmael gave in reluctantly, but insisted that my father's room be prepared properly. Half the furniture was removed. Cobweb was far from pleased and watched the undertaking with a disapproving, beady eye.

I had tried to spend some time with my hostling each day, but he was still reserved with me. I imagined that Cal had spoken to him about Seel when they had been together and Cobweb made a great display of his loyalty to Cal and my father. I was shown up as a merciless traitor to my tribe, but because Cobweb is not especially hard-hearted, he softened toward me eventually, especially when Seel argued with Ashmael over where to deliver the pearl.

"I cannot see how it will be beneficial for hostling or harling if Seel has to suffer being made a public spectacle," Cobweb said to Ashmael.

"Your opinion is respected, Tiahaar," Ashmael replied. "But I don't think you quite grasp the semantics."

"Perhaps not, but I grasp entirely the reality of what it would be like to deliver a pearl onto rough stone in front of a cluster of gawping idiots," Cobweb replied, smiling.

One evening, Seel left the dining room, halfway through the meal, without explanation. I followed him out, and found him half hanging over the bannisters, trying to get upstairs.

"Do you have to tell them?" he begged me.

I carried him to our room and laid him on the bed. He immediately curled up into a tight ball.

"I must bathe your face," I said.

"What the hell for?" He uncurled, stretched, yelped and curled up again.

"You're sweating."

"Never mind that! Tie my hair back." I couldn't find anything suitable to do it with.

"I must fetch someone!" I cried. "I don't know what to do! What if something goes wrong?"

"No!"

I remembered Cal once being in the same state and also that I had not been in the room when he had expelled the pearl. I hesitated for a moment longer, watching Seel moaning softly to himself, and then ran for the door. "Swift!" Seel called after me, but I didn't stop.

Ashmael took control. He strode into that room and ordered, "Seel, sit up!" Seel put his hands over his ears and Ashmael pointed at me. Cobweb was with me. Together, we lifted Seel up onto the pillows. By this time, Seel was almost delirious and did not object when we undressed him. Arahal paced restlessly at the end of the bed. Bryony brought us hot water and a cloth. I asked for a ribbon and tied up Seel's hair. He opened his eyes and looked at me.

"God, I don't like this. I don't like this!" he said. "Hold me, Swift. Please."

"Don't get in the way now, Swift," Ashmael said.

Outside a wind had come up, howling round the weathered walls of Forever with an eerie shrill sound. Seel ground his teeth and whimpered into my shoulder. Arahal had set up a tripod supporting a shallow metal dish. Into this Ashmael threw dark, pungent dust to which Arahal applied a flame. With a gusting glow, the powder began to exude silvery smoke, whose thick perfume was so strong, Bryony, standing nearest to it, began to cough.

Ashmael began the entreaties: "Yezriel, Azriel, Lahal . . ." Cobweb and I held onto Seel's arms, while his body writhed in discomfort. "Chaniel, Malchiel, Ygal . . ."

As if his body understood that this was primarily a female function, all the masculine parts of Seel's body tactfully withdrew, as during aruna when a har is soume. He bit my arm. "I am being destroyed from within," he said.

"You must visualize it through," Arahal instructed above Ashmael's invocation.

This is being conducted on two levels, I thought. On one level we have Ashmael and the Spirit, on the other we have the rest of us and the body.

"Tell Ashmael his voice hurts my ears," Seel said to me.

It did not take that long, maybe fifteen minutes, but it seemed like an eternity. The room was full of incense, all silvery smoke, and Cobweb lifted the pearl from the damp bed and held it up. Seel was a dead weight in my arms. I offered him a cup of water and he said, "One day, I'm going to make you go through this," and we both smiled for the wonderful fact that it was entirely possible.

Seven days later, the shell of the pearl cracked and our son was real and breathing, mewling angrily at the world. I was disappointed that I missed it; someone was sent to fetch me from Galhea. Soon we would be going north and there were still many preparations to be made.

I ran into the house and up the stairs. Bryony and Cobweb were sitting on the bed on either side of Seel, and Tyson was prowling around the room, trying not to look interested. Seel smiled when he saw me. "Look, Swift, look!" he exclaimed. Cobweb stood up to let me sit on the bed. I stared in joyous disbelief at what Seel held in his arms.

"Weird!" I said, which was all I could think of at the time.

The harling turned its head shakily at the sound of my voice. Its eyes were enormous; Cobweb eyes. Dark hair curled down its neck; its skin was flawless. Cobweb stooped and put his arm around my shoulder.

"You were once just like this," he said.

"Take him." Seel held the harling out to me. It was so warm. Its hands clawed the air and it whimpered once out of Seel's arms.

"He can't see that well yet," Cobweb said.

Bryony's eyes were full of tears; she always seemed to weep when she was happy. Seel noticed and held her hand. He understood she was thinking about whether she would ever have a child of her own. There were no men in her life; she never mixed with the humans in Galhea, and even if she had a mate, there was no certainty that she was fertile. Many women weren't. I put my son into her arms and he seemed more comfortable there.

"You grew up so quickly, Swift," she said.

"It didn't seem that way to me."

Tyson strolled over to us. "I remember when you were born and when you hatched," I said to him.

His grave little face did not flicker. "I remember *you,* Swift. I gave you ribbons and stones once." It was the first time he had made any reference to having known me before. I put my hand on his shoulder and he did not move away.

* * *

"I am glad that your son was born here at Forever," Cobweb said to me that evening. "I am glad you came home."

I decided not to tell him that it hadn't been my decision exactly. "Tell me what you think of Seel now," I said.

Cobweb lowered his eyes. "He is exactly how Cal described him to me. I know I can't blame him for what has happened . . ."

"Have you answered me?"

"I don't know. Have I?" he replied.

Some moments later, Arahal came into the room. "Ashmael and I would like to speak with you now," he said to Cobweb.

I knew immediately that it concerned my father. I stood up, deeply aware of an urge to flee.

"Sit down, Swift," Arahal said sternly. "We would like you to stay. We would like you to hear this."

The Varrs had ridden south, into the mist, beyond Astigi. They had ridden into the forest, separating, getting lost, their minds wandering, panicking and helpless. Their weapons rusted away in hours. Their horses fell beneath them, mouldering away to bones in seconds. The sounds of their anguished screams had echoed around the treetops like the harsh calls of carrion birds.

In the center of the forest, in a clearing, stands a lichened, white shrine dedicated to the Aghama. It is doubtful that anyone ever prays there, but it was in this place that Thiede and Pellaz waited for my father. It took him days to find them. I wondered what he had thought about, wandering into that sacred glade and seeing them sitting there. Did he have the taste of blood in his mouth. Had he remembered Gahrazel? Ashmael told me that Thiede and Pellaz had played dice to pass the time while they were waiting. Maybe they had diced for the souls of my people, like Death and Justice, looking up when Terzian staggered out of the trees, letting the dice fall one last time. Their ultimatum had been simple: change your ways, Terzian, confess your crimes, beg forgiveness, or go to your doom. His response had been inevitable: go to Hell! It was unfortunate for him that he did not understand what form his doom would take. Had he expected a sword thrust to the heart, a cup of Uigenna poison, a bullet to the brain? But it was not death; not that. Not any of those fitting punishments.

They had taken him to Immanion, capital of Almagabra, lush, green Gelaming country. In some place there, which Ashmael did not describe to us, the Gelaming stripped my father's soul and regressed him to the blackest, reddest times and made him face himself; his weaknesses, his faults, his sins. Oh, they'd known who would have been the best Varr to make Gelaming and turn against Ponclast. It had not been me. Not at first. It showed me that Terzian had not been beyond redemption; they wouldn't have bothered with him if he was. But he would not break, he would not turn around. Instead, he raved, he wept, he flailed his arms helplessly against the truth, but he would not recant. I had to sit in the calm, golden drawing room of my father's house while Ashmael told us that Terzian had eventually begged Thiede's people to kill him. It had come to that. He would never try to kill himself and they knew that. They would not end it for him.

"Seek forgiveness from the souls you have wronged!" they ordered, but he still refused. Then they spoke about Gahrazel. Insidious voices. "Didn't you once have fond feelings for Ponclast's son? Do you remember the first journey south that you made and what you said to him then? Didn't you promise him protection? You knew he was different, didn't you, Terzian? You knew he held, deep within him, the urge to run. You could have protected him, couldn't you? You had the chance. But instead you chose to enjoy his death. Did you enjoy it, Terzian?"

Terzian had shaken his head at them. "No. I did not kill him. It was Ponclast. Ponclast did it!"

"You deceive yourself!"

"I never lie!"

"You took part in his murder."

"I had to!" His cry had been despairing. He thought he would never speak these words, for it showed his weakness, and it was a weakness of the heart. "My son was implicated," he told them. "They were close friends. Ponclast believed that Swift was involved in Gahrazel's defection. The only way I could protect my son was to comply with Ponclast's wishes. I always had to comply with Ponclast's wishes. There was too much he could do to damage me. I love my family!"

Did it bring me relief to hear that? It was an excuse, wasn't it? An excuse for all that bloodshed and bestiality. He had done it for love; for me and Cobweb. It sickened me. If Terzian had really felt all that, why, in God's name, hadn't he turned on Ponclast when he got the chance? I couldn't understand it then and I never will. Ashmael continued with the story of my father's imprisonment and my hostling and I sat apart on the sofa, listening with frozen faces.

They told us that most of the time, Terzian refused to eat, and he could not sleep. He was wary of drinking the water they brought him, in case it was drugged. Pellaz had spoken to him alone. "For your son's sake, Terzian, let the evil go!" he had pleaded.

My father had simply replied, "I am not evil. I merely did what I had to do."

In the end, they realized that Terzian really would prefer to die than turn to the Gelaming. He did not want their absolution. They could not release him from whatever private hell he had put himself in. He wanted to die; nothing else. He could see no other future for himself. And so, they had taken him from the place where they had kept him for so long and put him into a suite of rooms in the palace Phaonica. They had given him attendants to see to his needs (to guard him) and eventually they had left him alone. It was then that Thiede had said, "Terzian is finished. It does not matter what he's doing to himself." And it didn't.

There was no moment of silence to let these words settle on the room. Cobweb had cried immediately Ashmael finished speaking, "And what now? What now, for God's sake?"

Ashmael raised his hands. "Be still, Tiahaar," he said. "Terzian will be brought back to you now."

"What will be brought back to us?" I asked sharply.

Ashmael glanced at me quickly and then at Cobweb. "Terzian. Your father."

"Terzian is finished. You said that. What will be brought back to us, Ashmael?"

The room was full of darkness. I felt cold. Nobody spoke. Ashmael lowered his eyes. Arahal had been staring at his hands for some minutes. "It is only right that your father should return to his family," he murmured, with difficulty. He braved looking me in the eye. "It is only right. He is dying, Swift."

They left us alone. I took Cobweb in my arms and we watched the last of the light fade from the sky outside. Neither of us wept. When it was nearly completely dark, Cobweb said, "I did not know about Gahrazel." His voice was clear, thoughtful.

"Leef told me," I replied huskily. I could not tell him about the forest. Perhaps one day, but not yet.

"It changes things, knowing that, doesn't it?"

(Knowing what, Cobweb? How much do you know?)

"It did for me when I found out," I said. "It did for a time . . ."

Cobweb stood up and walked to the window. "I'm not sure if I'll be able to cope with this, Swift. I'm not sure if I want to. In a way, I've got used to the idea of Terzian being gone. I think I want to remember him the way he was. I think I'm afraid of what they'll bring back to us."

"We'll be together. I'll help you."

"You're going north."

"Then I'll tell Ashmael not to do anything about this until I return."

"*If* you return." He clasped his arms and sighed. "You're telling me I should trust these people, Swift? You're telling me I have to let them live in my house after what they . . ." He could not finish.

"You heard what they were trying to do."

"Swift! That doesn't make it right . . . does it?"

"I don't know. I don't know what I think, except that there are some things about Terzian, Cobweb, that *you* don't know about."

He turned on me, snarling, "Don't you dare to think that! Don't ever think you know more than me! I know what you're implying, I know all about that! I will never speak of those things, Swift, but just because of that, don't think I don't know about them!"

"Yet you loved him!"

"You think that's incredible?"

"Yes. You knew what he was, yet you loved him." I shook my head in disbelief.

"You don't know what he was, Swift." He stared out into the evening and there was utter, calm silence for a moment. I still did not think Cobweb knew everything.

"I can't believe that Pellaz did that," he said, shaking his head. "I was wrong about so many things, wasn't I? Right from the beginning. Pell and Cal. The light and the dark. . . . Which is which? Aren't they both a little of each? The Gelaming have destroyed your father, Swift; think about that. Think hard. All that strength. . . . Now they will not let us keep even our memory of him intact. They will bring a shattered husk back to us that might not even look like Terzian anymore. Even at the end, they will not let him keep his dignity. They could end it for him! They could! So easily. Painlessly, kindly. But no! They have to . . . they have to . . ."

He put his arm against the window and leaned his forehead on it. I had never heard him weep like that, loud, animal sobbing. His whole body shook. He had never wept like that. I went to him. Now we were the same height. I held him and kissed him, but I could not weep with him.

"Gelaming do not like to kill," I said.

CHAPTER SEVEN

>-!-◄>-•-Ο-◄>-!-◄

The Fall

Deviation is the hidden dawn of daunt.
Phalanxes huddle in the kismet of deceit,
Profligate cortege of freedom
Mustered by the sanguinary evil.

The sky is darker in the north; leprous clouds boil across it. When rain falls there, it smells bad, or maybe it is the wet earth that is noxious. Nothing is ever quite as you imagine it. Usually it is either worse or better. Ponclast's domain *was* different to the mental picture I'd formed when listening to Gahrazel, but the horror, the darkness, the sheer barbarity were utterly as I'd visualized them.

We broke through from the other-lanes onto a scorched plain. Nothing grew there; its surface was pitted and gouged as if by a great battle. In the distance the great black walls of Ponclast's citadel reared toward a turbulent sky. Fulminir, a gaunt and skeletal shadow, whose poison seemed to spread outwards, tainting the land. Above us, the clouds growled and crackled with subdued lightning. Above Fulminir, the sky was dark red. We rode to within a mile of its walls and from there we could see the raw light of naked flame upon the battlements and dark shapes that might have been vigilant hara. Ashmael was leading us. He pulled his sparkling horse (so out of place in that land) to a halt and raised his hand. The only noise behind him was the jangle of bits against teeth and metal, the occasional snort. No-one in our company felt like speaking. We numbered maybe three hundred. Sighting Fulminir, many of us realized how few that was. Maybe thousands of fit, vengeful Varrs waited in the darkness and we still had no way of gauging Ponclast's strength. A biting wind plucked at our clothes, our hair, the horses' manes. Beside me, Seel sat tall in his saddle and stared bitterly before him. I wanted to touch him, but it would not have seemed right in that place.

"This is far enough," Ashmael called, and the wind carried his voice away from us.

Arahal, just in front of me, backed his horse until we were level. "We don't want to have to stay here longer than is absolutely necessary," he said.

"That goes without saying," I answered. "But how long do you think this will take? Will it be a case of unleashing the power of the crystal and being back in Galhea in time for dinner, or are we going to be here for days?"

Arahal shrugged and gave me a hard look. My sarcasm wasn't lost on him. "Ponclast must know we are here. He will have felt us approach. It is a good sign in itself that there was no welcoming committee. He's still not sure of us. We could have been finished off easily coming out of the other-lanes."

"We must prepare now!" Ashmael shouted. "We are losing time." He gave the order for certain members of the company to dismount. We needed protection; they were to cast a web of power around us, which would hopefully repel any form of minor assault launched from the citadel.

I heard Seel sigh. "Look, Swift, look around you," he said with sadness.

"Mmm, grim, isn't it?"

"This was once a great city. All this black, barren soil. I can remember great buildings being here and thousands of people, and cars and televisions and cinemas and bars and . . . oh, what's the point of even remembering. It might as well never have happened."

"Seel, how old are you?"

He laughed. "I was dreading when you were going to ask that! In old time, old enough to be your father, now—" he shrugged carelessly—"ageless enough to be your lover."

I raised one eyebrow, a trick inherited from my father. It is a gesture which can put a pleasing emphasis upon words. "Heresy!" I said.

"You have corrupted me, it seems."

"Do I ever seem too young to you, too childish?"

"God! What a place to have this conversation!"

"Do I, Seel?"

"Often!" He smiled and reached over to touch me. "Oh, it's not naivety;

just exuberance! I can be a sallow, bitter creature if I get too wrapped up in the past. I'm still eighteen, my hair's dyed red, I smoke too much . . ."

"You never smoke!"

"That's now. Where do you want me? Now or then?"

"Shut up; you're mad!"

"No, this is madness." He indicated the land around us with a sweep of his arm. Cities once. Now a crater of despair. Hell had been there.

I wondered whether Ponclast was standing on the walls of his citadel, laughing at us. Three hundred Gelaming. Was he just waiting to see what we'd do before he unleashed his hordes? Did he know about the crystal?

The air smelled cleaner once the shell of strength had been constructed around us. Hara began to construct a tall tripod of black, gleamless metal. At its summit was a shallow dish waiting to receive the crystal. I watched Arahal take the simple wooden box out of his jacket. It was lined with velvet. Inside it, reposing in dull, dark silk, lay our only hope. I could see it shining through the wrapping, emerald green, mazarine blue; holy fire. Thin vapors coiled out of it like ice in warm air. Arahal would not touch it with his bare hands. He had put on leather gloves.

We spoke the prayers, intoned the invocations for spirits of protection. The crystal was raised into place and all our faces shone in the glow of its clear, fluctuating light. Ashmael clasped two legs of the tripod in his hands and gazed upwards. His eyes flared green like an animal's eyes. He spoke to the crystal, softly, encouraging. Its flickers ceased for an instant; *it listened to him.* Ashmael's voice was crooning. He used few words, but his meaning was clear. Within the glowing points, an entity writhed, a living form of the essence of two bodies. Conceived in desire and focused by will.

"Turn your eyes to the walls, beloved. They are weak. They are weak but they obstruct you. What is within them shall burn you if you do not burn it first. It offends you and it hurts you. Reach out and remove it. Make it disappear. Breach the walls and fill the space within. Make them feel your power, beloved. Enter their minds and make them sleep. Take the fire from them and all will be quiet. The badness that hurts you will die away. But first, you must breach the walls . . ."

Slow, lazy beams the color of spring leaves and dawn skies rotated leisurely in the air above us. Powdery azure smoke fell to the ground. The crystal began to sing. At first, a careless, humming sound. The beams moved slightly faster, reaching further. We joined in its song and it seemed a thousand thousand voices rose in response. I shielded my eyes; the brightness was so intense.

"Go to the citadel!" Ashmael ordered. The power needed little encouragement now. It was acting independently of him, mindless, but eager to instil its song into any mind it encountered. We were immune. We knew the song already. For a moment, the light bunched and reared into a great, spinning column, black dust rising from the earth, forming streaks within it, and then, with a great, shattering howl, the power surged toward the citadel, rolling like waves, cataracting, bounding, half-seen creatures riding its crests. There were shapes like vast wings, long, lidless eyes and lithe, clawed fingers within it. A peal like laughter or water.

It hit the black stone with a sound like the earth splitting and a massive crack snaked sedately through the walls. I was expecting foul ichor, black blood, to come pouring out of the breach, but nothing like that happened. As the greeny-blue light of our power crawled over the walls of Fulminir, something rose up beyond it. Something sickly yellow, high into the sky. It leaned toward the light; a column of leprous, evil smoke. When it touched the spirit of the crystal, a terrible sound brought the taste of blood to our mouths.

Ashmael shouted something. His eyes were wild. Everyone was tense, staring upwards, toward Fulminir. Seel was at my side, quite calm. He said, "Ashmael will now panic." I could only stare at him in horror. In the sky above Fulminir, the light, the child of our crystal, and the oily, black smoke demon that was the child of Ponclast's sorcery were entwined in combat. Horrible, deafening scrapings and squealings ripped the air.

"It will beat us," I said. "It will beat us." I felt Seel's hand take my own. "Never. Come with me."

We stood beneath the tripod, looking up. The beam was weakening. We could see that. I was trembling. Seel put his hands on my arms and turned me to face him. His eyes were the eyes of a stranger. His hair was moving, as I had always expected it could, of its own volition.

"That is another of our children," he said, jerking his head upwards. "The child of Grissecon."

I was numb. "Don't say that . . . it is *hurting*. Oh, Seel, I can feel it!" I could. It was like being ripped apart. Seel made that happen. He made us be in tune with it. Hysteria raised my voice to a squeal. Seel shook me firmly.

"Shut up! Listen to me. We have the power; only us. Do as I say! Do you hear me?" He looked incredibly fierce; a Seel unknown to me. I nodded. "Then be naked, Swift."

"What?"

"Do it, Swift!" There was no way I could argue with him. He scared me. He was different. This was a Seel who could kill. Ashmael, wide-eyed, stared at us maniacally through the legs of the tripod. "Seel!" he shouted. "Seel! Seel!"

"It's alright." That was all he said, all he had to say. Ashmael dropped his head. My fingers fumbled with fastenings to my clothes. "Help him!" Seel ordered and hands were upon me, ripping, not bothering with fastenings. I had heard of pelki and I thought it must feel something like that. To lose control of your body. To have other people move it for you. I resisted the urge to struggle. Shivering, I was on my knees in the black earth, naked and defenseless, three hundred pairs of eyes upon me and God knows how many more beyond the walls.

Seel dragged me to him and we sat on the ground beside the tripod. His hair was across his face; I did not know him. "Trust me, Swift!" My leg was twisted beneath me. I could not move. Seel straightened it out.

"This is the most vital Grissecon either of us will ever have to perform," he said. "Do as I say. It will not be much. But concentrate!"

We sat facing each other. He arranged my limbs and pulled me onto his lap. I was not prepared; it hurt horribly. Flashes of red appeared in the light around us. Seel held me against him and I could feel his heart beating and buried my face in his hair so I could not see them watching us. But I could hear the crooning. Seel threw back his head and screamed out in a language unfamiliar to me. It was like gibberish, but I understood the meaning. He called to the crystal, ordered it to feed from us, let our strength combine with its own. Seel's fingers pressed the base of my spine and he moved within me, seeking the special places so that desire flamed inside me; I had no control over it. I was mindless, like the power, just body, just essence. The pain made it like perversion. I was making noises and when I heard them, it was as if they came from somewhere else. I opened my eyes and saw a dozen greenish fingers of light tentatively reaching down toward us from the crystal. Seel bit my ear and I winced.

"Concentrate! Power!" he cried. "Power! Power!"

I threw back my head, my eyes snapped open again and the radiance burned into me. I howled and felt the core of heat build up within me. I dragged it out of myself. I was rising. I was becoming stronger and stronger. Bigger; rising. We were so tall, we filled the sky. Like Gods, like angels; pure fire, nothing else.

The moment came.

Deep within me, the burning serpent bit the star and with a wordless scream, a great tide of energy burst out, like an exploding sun. Around us, the Gelaming fell to the ground, hiding their faces, curled up. I was ignited again (it so rarely happens twice like that), and in a glorious blaze of light, shaped like a towering figure with wings across its face, its feet, its back, so full of light, so ultimately wondrous, the child of our essence reached out one lazy arm and touched the walls of Fulminir. Ponclast's demon seemed piteously small beside it, quivering, shrinking. I was laughing out loud, crazily. Through tears of laughter, I watched as, like powdering rock destroyed by rain, the walls of Fulminir crumbled. Great chunks of stone rolled earthwards, revealing the dank innards of the citadel, spiked towers, curving walkways and squat, blackened buildings. The citadel was wrapped in the blue-green radiance of aruna power. Frothing, fizzing, the child of the crystal jetted up into the air and exploded in a million droplets of sparkling foam, drifting downwards like bubbles, descending like sleep on the streets of Fulminir.

Seel and I shivered together, spent on the ground. The light had left us. The bowl on the tripod was empty. Someone came over and wrapped us in cloaks or blankets; something. Rain began to fall and I looked up into it, blinking.

High above, through the blinding sheets of water, a crack had appeared in the cloud. Beyond it, the sky was blue.

I turn the pages of a storybook. It is old, its pages thumbed by many human children. I come to the part where the prince comes through a barrier of thorns and finds a sleeping palace. The thorns are everywhere. Perhaps it was difficult for him to see the people. They would have been dusty, almost insubstantial, frozen forever at that moment when the spell was cast. Birds hanging in the air; impossible. A bee poised motionless at the brink of a flower and all the bodies. . . . Are their faces alarmed? Are they looking skywards, feeling the awful power descending, one last moment of dread before their minds are numbed? The book does not tell about that.

In the story, a princess sleeps in the highest tower and only the kiss of the prince will awaken her. In this palace, the one before me, the one that brought back the memory of a childhood tale, the only possible princess, the king's only child, is long dead. Not a spindle-prick, not death through innocence, but a father's hand holding out the fatal cup.

There is a tower in Fulminir. It is tall and it is perpetually dark. No princess ever slept there, I'm sure, but I ordered it to be forever sealed and I had them plant briars at its foot, so that one day thorns and flowers will cover its walls. It is a tomb without a body. It is for Gahrazel and to show him that I did not forget.

When our horses picked their way carefully over the fallen stones of Fulminir's walls, I did not know what we would find within. Neither did I want to find out. I was dog-tired, my body ached and I was floating in a half-dream state that little could penetrate. I stared at the city around me and it was like walking through a painting. A child's painting of hell; red and black too stark, gaping faces. Eerily, the only sound was the hungry crackle of flames and the occasional thump of falling masonry. We rode by Varrish hara standing like imbeciles, utterly immobile, staring at the shattered walls. They did not see us. Like the people of the fairytale, their minds had frozen at the last instant before the spell was cast. Tendrils of blue-green light still investigated the dark, labyrinthine streets. Streets that were like tunnels, some of them disappearing into the ground like open sewers. Everything was damp and stilled.

Transfixed hara were caught in attitudes of bursting from open doorways, alarm forever painted across their panic-stricken faces, arms raised as if to ward off a blow. We passed a young har dressed in fine white silk, curled up in the gutter, gold at his ears and throat, his back branded and striped with weals. In a square, three rotting corpses hung from a scaffold, their blind, white, ruined eyes staring down implacably at the tumble of enchanted Varrs lying on the cobbles around them. In another place we found beautiful hara tied up with their own hair, their bodies naked and bruised. Varrish torturers stood grinning like stone around them. Others, who had perhaps only been passing by, had stopped to spectate. Their faces showed only mild interest.

Arahal pulled his horse to a halt; it skipped nervously sideways. He dismounted and stared up at the victims.

"Will they ever wake up?" I asked. My voice was blown away from me.

Arahal took a knife from his belt and sawed at the shining hair. He spoke three words and the wind sighed. Three bodies fell, slipped silently to the ground and twitched there feebly. Arahal rubbed his face, groaned, squatted and lifted the nearest har in his arms.

This was only the beginning. Fulminir had many other darker, fouler secrets to disclose.

Ashmael trotted his horse up beside me, an absurd blur of movement within the tomb. "Wake up, Swift," he said, with obscene cheerfulness. "This way. Follow me." He reached over and took hold of Afnina's rein by the bit-ring. I clung to the front of my saddle and we cantered through the ensorcelled streets of Fulminir.

Not even by those who have the most bizarre tastes in architecture could Fulminir be called a handsome city. But its sheer size and ugliness do inspire a certain kind of awe. The buildings are built very close together and the majority of them are tall; narrow but with many stories. Evidence of extreme poverty was everywhere; the further we progressed toward the city center the more harrowing became the scenes we encountered. If ever I had doubted that Varrs ate Wraeththu and human flesh, now I was given ample proof. We found a harling crouched in a blind alley, gnawing on a dismembered limb, his eyes frozen in a glassy expression of defense.

Ponclast's palace squatted like a scrawny bird of prey at Fulminir's heart. We rode right into it. More scenes of darkness, more tableaux of despair. I tried hard to imagine the lively Gahrazel growing up in such a place, but it was impossible. There was a throne room, vast, black and vaulted. Seel and some of the others were waiting for us there.

"Is there anywhere here we can get hot coffee?" Ashmael asked, with abysmal cheerfulness.

Seel grimaced. "Save thoughts of refreshment until we are safely back in Galhea," he said. "You must find Ponclast."

Ashmael nodded. "We will. Come along, Swift."

We urged our horses up wide, splintered stairs, shadowy banners motionless above our heads. When we could ride no more, we walked. Ashmael dragged me. I was dressed only in a woollen cloak; my feet were bare, my skin still wet. I remember saying, "Is this my kingdom then? Is this what Thiede's given me?"

"We must find Ponclast," Ashmael answered, repeating Seel's words, pulling me forward by my wrist. We hurried along endless black corridors, shuttered doors punctuating them at intervals, terrifying in their silence. No windows, no light. A young har swathed in diaphanous veils, forever lifted in a breeze we could not feel, pressed his back to the wall, looking backwards. We walked past. He could not see us. I don't know what he saw, but his face was frozen in terror.

At length, we came out upon the battlements. In the open air, beneath a boiling sky shot with clear blue, we found them, Ponclast and his staff. They were leaning on the stone, looking down into the city streets, perhaps beyond them to the walls. On the stone floor was chalked a rough pentacle; magical implements were strewn carelessly around. From this point had the oil-smoke demon arisen. There were smears like soot and black liquid along the walls of the palace. A vague charnel stench still hung around. Ponclast's wide black cloak was lifted up behind him like wings, petrified in that position. I recognized him immediately. The first thing I thought was, Gahrazel's murderer, and this was followed closely, as more uncomfortable thoughts began to crowd my head, by: my father's seducer.

Ashmael pulled me to face him. "You realize I have to release him from the stasis, Swift."

I nodded. "As you must."

He spoke three slow words that sounded and smelled like ashes and lime, and then suddenly Ponclast jerked upright. He was so surprised, he nearly fell forward over the battlements. He uttered an exclamation and turned. I was a stranger to him. He did not recognize me, but he knew immediately that we were Gelaming and that we had defeated him. In one swift, supple movement he reached for the gun at his hip, but Ashmael had anticipated that, raising his hand, calmly, languidly. It was enough. Now Ponclast's arms were frozen again, his legs paralyzed. His eyes were wild. Any chance he'd get he'd try to kill us, and then keep on killing. He enjoyed it. Neither was he afraid of death.

Anger spurted through me in a hot, quick wave. "What can you do with him?" I cried. "You can only kill him! It's the only way to stop him!"

Ponclast looked at me directly for the first time. He almost smiled.

"Yes, I am Swift," I said in a cold, low voice. "I am Terzian's son. I am with the Gelaming and now your kingdom is mine."

For a moment, Ponclast was expressionless. Then he laughed. It was the most mirthless sound I had ever heard. Had he laughed like that as his son writhed in the final agony of death? "Terzian's puppy!" he boomed, tears of laughter running down his sooty face. "I was right about you. Weakness on my part not to get rid of you when I had the chance. So now you dally with those who destroyed your father—"

"No," I interrupted. "You destroyed him! You!"

"You think so?" Ponclast drawled. "I gave him everything."

"Including evil."

"Including a thirst for evil. He loved power and he loved what we would do together. You never knew him, puppy; he was always mine."

I thought, I will silence you, pig! I could not bear the sound of his voice. Before Ashmael could stop me, I lunged forward, taking Ashmael's knife from his belt, swift, swiftly. I lunged forward and struck at that hateful smile and then there was another smile on Ponclast's face, this one gaping red and toothless. He looked surprised.

"Swift!" Ashmael pulled me back. "That is not the way! Stop!"

I struggled away from him and threw the knife at the floor. "There is no *way,"* I said bitterly. "No right or wrong; not here."

I turned away. I walked back into the palace. Ponclast shouted empty threats behind me. I did not look around.

It seemed I walked for hours, always downwards, seeking the throne room where I thought Seel might still be. I didn't know exactly what Thiede expected me to do with Fulminir, but at that moment I was planning a thousand ways of pulling it down, burning it and mutilating Ponclast's elite dogs. It seemed such an anticlimax to find Ponclast like that. We should have fought. I should have sent him plummeting over the battlements; sent him to a bloody, crushing death. Gelaming do not like to kill . . .

Eventually, I came out into a courtyard, down a narrow, snaking stairway. I looked around myself. I was lost. In the middle of the yard was a well. Sitting on the well's wall was a splendid figure. It was Thiede. In that place of utter darkness he shone like an angel. He was an angel. Uriel for vengeance, clad in silver steel and silk, his hair like a nimbus, his eyes deepest black. I could see his long feet in thin sandals, the toenails curved like claws and lacquered with the luster of pearl. If ever I had thought our race resembled humanity, looking at Thiede dispelled that illusion. He smiled at me. For a face so beautiful, his teeth are quite long.

"Once upon a time," he said. "I lived in a city like this. It may even have been this city. . . . Do you like stories, Swift?" I limped over to him. My feet were cut. Thiede leaned over and hauled up the bucket from the well. "Come to me," he said. I sat on the wall beside him and he tore a strip of silk from his sleeve and, with the water, bathed the blood and soot from my toes.

"All lives are stories," I said. "To somebody, they're stories."

He nodded thoughtfully. "Of course, this is true. I enjoy making up my own stories, though."

"As you made up mine?"

"Yes. I construct the plot, place the characters and then they tend to become headstrong and run away from me. I lose control over them. Usually, it is because of Love, a thing I once sought to eradicate in Wraeththu. Now I'm not so sure I can, or even if I want to."

"It surprises me you say this."

"It surprises me too, Swift the Varr."

I shivered. "After today, the name of Varrs should never be spoken again. The tribe should perish, the memory of it should die . . ."

"Is this your first decree?" He wiped his hands fastidiously.

"What are you going to do with the people of Fulminir?" I asked him. "And the city itself; what will you do with that?"

"Isn't that up to you now, Swift?"

"No, I don't think so."

Thiede looked beyond me at the dark mass of Ponclast's palace rising around us. We were still nowhere near the ground. The wind was chill.

"Do with them?" he mused. "Well, it is a problem. They are no use to us in this world, that's for sure, but neither would we be thanked for sending such black souls into the next! Come now, what do *you* suggest?"

"I suggest, Lord Thiede, that we make a deep hole in the Earth and freeze them all forever and throw them into it. Then we should close the pit. I would enjoy particularly stamping down the soil."

"But nothing would ever grow there."

"We could pave it with stone."

"Hmm . . . a possible solution, I suppose!" He smiled at me, which I returned. "There is one place you have not thought of, Swift." He stood up and began to walk across the yard, beckoning me to follow.

"Another place . . . ?"

"Yes." He put his arm around my shoulder. "Another place. My forest, the forest of best-forgotten mirrors."

"But would people be safe from them there?"

"You should know that they would. You've been there."

"Then it should be properly named."

"Of course. I have been pondering upon it, waiting for you here. What do you think of this: Gebaddon? A marriage of the realms of hell. Not this world, not the next, but somewhere in between where the only things they can damage are each other. Of course, there is the possibility, however slight, that they might discover enlightenment there."

"A possibility, I suppose," I agreed, "but it would be unsporting to deny it to them."

Thiede laughed and squeezed my shoulder. "I chose well when I chose you, my dear."

"Chose me for what exactly, my lord? I still don't understand quite what you require of me."

The darkness of the palace had swallowed us again. We walked along a narrow corridor where there were open doors to either side. I did not want to look into the rooms beyond. There was no sound.

"Your purpose, Swift, is to govern for Pellaz and myself in Megalithica. Of course, you will need a full-size staff which will come together in time, and also I suspect there will be quite a lot for you to learn. Seel will be a great help to you; he understands about these things."

"Will we have to live in Fulminir?" I asked, aghast. It was the Varrish capital of Megalithica, after all.

"No," Thiede reassured. "Galhea must be expanded. We envisage that it will become the major city of northern Megalithica. It is more central anyway. Fulminir is best forgotten. I think you will have to come to Immanion for a short while. You may talk with Pellaz there . . ."

"Thiede," I said. "Who are you?"

He stopped walking, surprised. He inclined his head enquiringly.

"What I mean is, Pell is supposed to be Tigron of Wraeththu. Where do you fit into things? He answers to you; that is obvious. What position is higher than the Tigron's?"

Thiede smiled. "Only one," he answered, and, putting his hand upon my back, propelled me forward once more.

"Few know my identity," he continued, after a while. "It is best that way."

"Greater than the Tigron?"

"Wraeththu is mine, *are* mine. I've been around a long time, Swift. Since the beginning."

"The *very* beginning?" I squeaked, enlightenment dawning slowly.

"But of course!" he answered.

"But—"

"No more!" he ordered. "In the presence of the Aghama, you must learn to hold your tongue." He smiled again. "Don't take me seriously, I didn't give myself that title. Now, I have good news for you. I have decided to give Seel to you. If you like, I will perform the blood-bonding ceremony myself."

"My Lord Thiede!" I exclaimed. "What will Seel think of this?"

Thiede gave my shoulder a little pat. "Don't be ridiculous, Swift! That is a mere trifle. I thought we understood each other."

We came out into the throne room, where the Gelaming waited. We were on a balcony high above their heads. Seel looked up when he felt my presence, and waved. Thiede raised his hand. It dispelled the shadows. Dust fell from the torn banners around us. The light was with us.

CHAPTER EIGHT

>·┤·◆>·•·O·•·<◆·├·<

Furnace of Hate

Pilgrim of love suffering repudiation
As though having conspired with the beast.
Maneuvers in the vestibule of the heart
Crumble to dust in the palm of airs.

The journey back to Galhea through the other-lanes was a nightmare; I wanted to sleep for a week and trying to keep up the concentration required was horrendous. Most of the Gelaming remained in Fulminir, allocated the none too pleasant task of cleaning up and sorting out. As well as the citadel, there were numerous pockets of Varrs dotted about the countryside in settlements and small towns. It was doubtful that they'd put up much resistance, but neither would they welcome the Gelaming with open arms. I questioned the wisdom of trying to conclude such an operation using only three hundred hara, but Thiede pointed out that to use more would make them seem like an army, which was an impression that the Gelaming wished to avoid. I was told that many more Gelaming personnel would soon be arriving from Immanion, but even then they would not travel around in large numbers.

"It is inevitable that some remnants of the Varrs will want to fight us," Ashmael said wearily. "There is also the problem of the Uigenna, who, we understand, have fled into the extreme north of the continent. It would be politic to weed them out now, while they are comparatively weak. News of Ponclast's defeat must have reached them by now."

Thiede wanted to come back to Galhea with us. When we entered the house through the great front doors, with all the house hara and Bryony waiting to greet us and cheer our success, Cobweb's acceleration down the stairs toward a welcoming embrace was stopped dead. It was a passable imitation of running smack into a wall. Thiede has that effect on people. He looks ten feet tall, while being nowhere near that height, and wears his awesome power like extra clothes.

I introduced him to Cobweb and he smiled graciously. Cobweb was speechless, watching this apparition wandering around the hall, picking up our ornaments, gazing up the great sweep of the dark, polished stairs. "You are back so quickly," my hostling said, "so much sooner than we imagined."

"Taking Fulminir was a mere itch on the Gelaming skin which your son obligingly scratched for us," Thiede announced.

Our bedraggled appearance must have informed Cobweb otherwise, but he made no comment.

Seel and I went directly to bed, without bathing, without eating, even without undressing properly. Before we slept, he insisted on apologizing to me. "I hurt you; I'm sorry."

"You never hurt me. I love you, Seel."

He thought about what I'd said and then smiled. I wanted to tell him about what Thiede had suggested, about the blood-bonding, but something held my tongue. It must have been my guardian angel. Seel stroked my face.

"When I look at you now," he said. "I see so many things. Not death, certainly, not bitterness or revenge or any of those bad things. When I look at you now, I experience a kind of pain, and I know it's happened before, but a long time ago . . ."

"Pain?" I said sadly. "I cause you pain?"

"Yes," he replied. "It is a kind of disease that, as far as I know, is curable only by another dose of the same thing. It is a plague that's scoured this small, helpless planet since life first crawled up out of the slime. A phenomenon that cannot be explained."

"What are you talking about?"

I knew what it was and knew also that he was struggling to say it. To a Gelaming, because of his training and his beliefs, it was difficult.

"You have infected me," he said.

I laughed and pushed him back and grabbed his wrists. "Say it, Seel! Say it, or I'll break your arms!"

He howled and struggled and laughed and said it. "Alright, alright, don't! I love you, Swift."

We slept well into the following day and it was the smell of food that woke me. I spent a few, treasured moments gazing at Seel, who was still fast asleep and would not wake for some time. His face was dirty, his hair tangled and his clothes wrapped around him in knots. He was beautiful, and I knew I would never tire of gazing; never. Each time I looked at him, it was as if it were for the first time. With soaring spirit and singing heart, I took a bath and then ran down the stairs to the source of the delicious smells. Lunch was just over. Thiede had by this time thoroughly acquainted himself with my home and I found him sitting with his feet on the dinner table, indulging in leisurely conversation with Arahal and Ashmael. Moswell and Swithe were sitting there with dopey, sycophantic expressions on their faces, lapping up the pearls of Thiede's wit.

Thiede smiled brightly when he saw me, exposing those gleaming feral teeth. "Recovered, Swift? I hope so. There's so much to be done. Unpleasantness to suffer, rapture to enjoy!"

I grimaced. "Is there any coffee?" I sifted through the remains of the meal on the sideboard.

"We thought tomorrow . . ." Ashmael began tentatively, raising his voice, leaning back in his chair to watch me.

I forked meat and cold vegetables onto a plate. They had not left me much to choose from. "You thought tomorrow what?" The coffee pot was still warm at least. I began to pour.

"Your father. He will be arriving here tomorrow morning."

I virtually dropped everything I was holding, lukewarm liquid splashed over my hands. I appealed to Thiede. "Is this really necessary?"

Thiede raised an elegant hand. "No, of course, it isn't, Swift. I can understand your feelings. If you would prefer it, I could arrange for your father to end his days in Phaonica, or even in Gebaddon with all his friends. It's all the same to me. Just give the word."

I turned irritably back to arranging my meal. "No . . . this is his home. The point has been made. Pity it had to turn out this way though, isn't it?"

Thiede smiled at me ruefully. "I hope you're not becoming hard, Swift."

"Hard? Is there any other possible way I can face what's left of my father?"

Even Thiede could not answer that.

Mid-morning the following day, the rafts came out of the mist. It was something I'd never seen before, straight from Almagabra, something I could never imagine. Powered by crystals, aruna-fired, they drifted, alien and graceful, over the lawns of Forever, casting great oblong shadows.

Hazy sunlight was beginning to burn through the moist air. Rain had fallen; soon the grass would begin to steam. From an upstairs window, we could see the huddled shapes of many hundreds of hara crowded on the rafts. They made no sound. This was what remained of the Varrish army, scooped up from Gebaddon. War veterans who had seen no fighting or whose battles had been wholly illusory among the dense foliage of the forest. Minds irreparably damaged, bodies wasted, they had the eyes of those who had looked into the abyss, the image of which was burned forever into their minds. If they were glad to be home, they did not show it. Perhaps they did not realize their ordeal was over.

Cobweb, Seel and I were in Cobweb's room. Tyson was playing on the floor, oblivious. We spoke in hushed voices. Cobweb called gently to Tyson. "Your father is here." The harling looked up briefly and flashed a Cal smile, presently absorbed once more in his game of make-believe. Cobweb had tied up his hair and dressed himself in dark, brushed doeskin. He was trying to make himself strong.

Bryony came into the room, holding my son in her arms. A worried frown creased her brows. She stood very close to Cobweb. None of us were happy that day, apart from Tyson, and he was half Cal's, so that wasn't really surprising.

I said, "Seel, he has to have a name."

Seel was in a world of his own, gazing out of the window. He looked blank. "What?"

"Our son," I said. "He has to have a name. Now. For my father."

Seel nodded slowly. "Yes. I have been thinking about it." He uncurled from his seat and stood up, taking the harling from Bryony's arms. "Do you know, of those names, all those wretched names that were buzzing through my head when I delivered the pearl, there was one I liked. When Ashmael said it . . . I think I knew then it had to be the one. It was Azriel."

"Azriel. . . . A Gelaming name?"

Seel shook his head. "Not really. It's very old . . ."

"Oh, I see; an angel," I said drily.

"Well, yes."

I looked at the harling happily pawing at Seel's face. So innocent. Perhaps he would need a strong name. I had no idea yet what his future would hold, but I suspected that he would have very little control over it.

"Yes, I like it too," I said. "Hello, Azriel."

The rafts settled on the lawns, their unearthly mechanisms sighing to silence. "I suppose we must go down," Cobweb said dismally. I reached for his hand and it was cold and clammy. Seel handed the harling back to Bryony and we walked down the stairs together. It seemed to take ages. Lingering behind the others, I looked back, thinking of the past. I was remembering running up those stairs to my father's room on the day they found Cal in the snow, and then it was the day of my Feybraiha, and I was coming down again with flowers in my hair and the smell of autumn all

around. I shook myself. Cobweb was waiting for me. "We are still together," he said.

"All those times, though!"

"Yes," he said with a sad smile. "All those times."

I wondered how the Gelaming had managed to round up all my father's
hara. Had they really been wandering around Gebaddon all this time? I
shuddered. The thing that struck me first was their utter silence. It was even
more profound once we were outside. Beaten creatures, packed together
like prisoners on those sleek, magical vehicles, shivering as if they were
cold. It was a hot day, close and humid.

Ashmael came straight over to us when he saw us standing on the steps
of Forever. He blinked at Cobweb. This was an unconscious appreciation
of his beauty, which was at its most wondrous that day. My hostling was
feeling tragic and it always gave him a special kind of bloom when he felt
that way.

"We shall bring him into the house," Ashmael said in a confidential
tone. Cobweb nodded shortly and went back inside. He would go directly
to the sitting room and put his back to the window and not come out again
until Terzian had been secreted away upstairs.

The Gelaming seemed edgy, which I took to be proof of their shame.
Who else had allowed these bewildered hara to wander forgotten in
Thiede's hell forest? It was hard to imagine the broken creatures on the
rafts ever having had a thirst for blood. They would never fight again. Hara
had come up from Galhea, seeking lost, loved ones. Everyone milled uncomfortably, looking over the rafts as if they were open graves.

"Come with me," Ashmael said. Seel put his arm around me and we
strolled toward the rafts. My heart was pounding and I found myself
chanting words of power that I had not used for years. I was conscious of
eyes upon me; conscious also of their weary hostility. Heads raised. I could
imagine the thoughts. "There goes the one who sold us out to the Gelaming. Terzian's son, the traitor." If I had been alone, they might even have
mustered the energy to spit at me. Hara from the town just stared at me
with unashamed curiosity. To them I was a celebrity and my part in what
was happening now was just that I had initiated the possibility of it occurring at all. The Varrs of Galhea are really quite sheeplike. They need to be
led and now they were happy to follow me. Wars cause discomfort, after
all. Wouldn't peace bring prosperity? It was also the first time that most of
them had caught a glimpse of Seel. If circumstances had been different, I
feel they would have cheered us.

Seel said, "Your warriors are home from the war that never happened.
This should have been a day of celebration, but it feels more like a funeral."

Terzian was on the smallest raft. Small, but provided with the greater
comforts. Few hara were with him. I thought to myself, In a few moments,
I am going to have to look at my father, and found myself quailing, so I
looked instead at the har who held Terzian in his arms. I saw straight black

hair and a white face; I did not recognize him. His clothes were torn and colorless, his shoulder scarred as if by claw marks. The expression on his face was something like that of someone who has reached the end of his tether, someone whose strength is gone and who faces horror, someone who will protect to his dying breath the thing he loves. He convulsively tried to shelter Terzian with his body as we approached. He could not have known who we were, only that we were Gelaming, the enemy.

I had dreaded my father being totally unrecognizable, aged and toothless perhaps, or slightly decayed in some way. The reality, while nothing like that really, was just as shocking. He was so thin, lying on the cushions, his head in the strange har's lap. His once thick hair was lank and lusterless, his face gray, all the skin stretched over the bones. But he was still Terzian. He still looked like the father I had known. That was perhaps the worst thing about it. I put my hands on the side of the raft and he stared past me. Seel was standing there. He looked at Seel. I said, "Terzian."

His gaze flicked over me, surprisingly quickly. He blinked.

"It is I . . . Swift," I said.

He tried to rise then, stretching out a hand whose veins bulged blue through the white skin. His companion snarled at me. Terzian spoke, a small sound. "My son. It is my son," he said. There was no inflection to his voice. He just looked at me. I could not tell what he was thinking. Did he remember, as I did, that time he had spoken to me in his study, so long ago? The night of Gahrazel's arrest; something I will never forget. I remembered Terzian making me promise to look after his family, our home, as if he feared he would never come back. Now I thought that his homecoming was not part of the future as it was meant to be, or that he had ever wanted.

Terzian painfully lay back among the cushions and closed his eyes. He shakily raised a hand to his face. There was silence; we all just looked at him. I could feel Seel's hand on the back of my neck. "Bring him into the house," Ashmael said.

I could not watch them do it. I could not watch them lift him, helpless, limbs sprawling, like an invalid. Terzian's companion was reluctant to leave him. I heard a scuffle. Without turning round, still walking back to Forever, I ordered that the har be taken to the kitchens and fed. I understood how he felt, that he had cared for Terzian for some time and wanted to stay with him now, but I could not risk offending Cobweb. They took him away, dragged him to the house, and I heard him cry, "Terzian! Terzian!" My spine crawled with pain. Hadn't these people gone through enough? It hurt me to separate my father from his companion, but I felt I had no choice.

Seel did not speak to me. There was little we could say to each other; it was all so ugly. In the hallway of Forever, he made me stop walking. I looked at him fiercely and he took me in his arms. I pressed myself against him, wanting his mouth, his breath and the sweet taste of life, so fragrant, to eradicate the stink of death in my throat. Neither of us uttered a word.

* * *

I had already arranged alternative accommodation for Seel and myself, so that Terzian could have his room back. We could have had Cal's old room, but I settled for a smaller suite because I was afraid of ghosts. Seel took me there and laid me on the bed. He gently took off my clothes and massaged my skin with oil. I felt over-sensitive, too ticklish, and all my muscles ached with tension. Seeing my father again had made me fear that I hadn't really grown up. Perhaps it was an illusion, this power that had been given me. Could I really give orders in this house now that Terzian was home again?

Seel could see me thinking deeply. He sensed my distress. "You will have to be strong," he said. We both knew that anyway, but it helps to hear someone else say it.

I waited until I was sure that the house-hara had settled Terzian into his room before I visited him. It was late afternoon and I was feeling sleepy and tranquil after a long session of Seel's exquisite attempts to ease my mood. Terzian lay in the bed, staring at the ceiling, bars of sunlight falling across his hands where they lay on the coverlet. It seemed I could see the life draining away from him even as I watched, but I had made my heart hard and walked toward the bed.

He looked at me. I was afraid his intelligence might have been affected, but his eyes were still alert. The room was dark and full of a thick perfume, which could not totally mask the faint miasma of sickness.

"Don't come in here," he said. His voice was reasonable and slow, almost emotionless.

I sat on the bed and said, "Father."

He turned his head away from me. "They told me of your betrayal. Get out! You are no longer my son. Get out!" He looked at me again and his eyes were full of contempt. I could not speak. "Seduced you, didn't they?" He nodded to himself, a peculiarly aged gesture. "Yes . . . mind you, the prize was worth it. I've seen him." He was referring to Seel. I tried to interrupt him, but he would not have it. "All my lands as well, eh? My house, my town, my people. Oh, you've a shrewd business head on that skinny body of yours, Swift!"

I pitied him so much I couldn't make myself angry, which was cruel because he wanted me to be. If I remained calm, he would think he didn't even have the strength left to unnerve me. I knew I must try to argue, but my head was empty.

"Where's . . . where's Cal?" he asked. I heard the despair in his voice, as if he knew the answer to that already, as if he knew that I didn't.

"Cal? Oh, I betrayed him as well, father. I took him straight to the Gelaming. They have him. Didn't they tell you that?"

Terzian tried to smile. The effect was ghastly. "My son, a true Varr. You know nothing about loyalty, do you, only self-preservation. I would have liked to see Ponclast's face when he saw who it was that had defeated him. You should have seen mine when I found out!"

Those words finally got to me. "Me, a true Varr!" I exclaimed indignantly. "Let me tell you, father, it was only recently that I realized fully what being a true Varr means. I've learned the truth about a lot of things, not least the Varrish concept of loyalty, and the details of certain executions. Gahrazel's, for example."

How it sickened me to see the furtive wariness creep into my father's eyes. He could not look at me.

"And who told you that? Gelaming story tellers, I suppose. What lies have they filled your head with?"

"No-one told me exactly," I replied. "It was in the forest."

He knew which forest; I didn't have to explain. He seemed to deflate before my eyes.

"I don't have to justify any of my actions to you, Swift," he said peevishly. "You don't know everything. You weren't there. You can't possibly understand."

"I don't want to. I don't want to have the kind of mind that could understand something like that."

"Is that why you betrayed me?" He sounded so pathetic, I had to grit my teeth.

"I never betrayed you, Terzian," I said. "You knew the risks yourself when you went south. I only did what you once asked me to do. Your family is safe and their future is safe. I did that. Forever still stands untouched and your blood will always flow in the veins of those that live here. By securing our position, I've immortalized you in a way. You don't deserve it."

"Oh, don't give me that! That's Cobweb talk!" he spat viciously. "The truth is, my son, that you have come out of this very well, while the demon Thiede has punctured my soul. My life is running out of the hole that he's made . . ."

"I know what they did to you. I know what they were trying to do."

"Do you? Do you really? I don't think so!" He closed his eyes and I thought how transparent he looked, how impermanent. Talking had enfeebled him more than he wanted to let me see.

"The past is done," I said. "Nothing can be changed now. What is important now is the future. You have a grandson." Terzian didn't move. "His name is Azriel," I continued doggedly. "Seel hosted him for me. My prize, remember?" There was still no response. I stood up. "I shall send Cobweb to you."

"No!" It was a weak exclamation. His eyes were still closed. "Not yet . . . Swift, come back later." It was a child's plea.

"Of course I will."

"Bring Cobweb with you then." He could not face seeing Cobweb alone.

Bryony was waiting for me on the stairs. She was agitated because my father's traveling companion had vociferously refused the comfort she had offered and was currently threatening to search the house for Terzian. "Cobweb must not see him!" she cried, sharing my concern for Cobweb's state of mind, which was as yet undetermined. Ashmael and Arahal were still outside, supervising the dispersal of the bewildered Varrs. Thiede would not want to be troubled with domestic incidents. I would have to deal with it myself, distasteful though it was to me. "His name is Mengk," Bryony told me, disgruntled. "Oh, Swift, he will not go! What if—"

"Alright, alright," I interjected, impatiently. "I'll see to it."

We found Mengk prowling around the hall. I walked up to him with what I hoped was an authoritative air.

"Terzian is comfortable," I said. "You must now go to Galhea."

He turned on me like a frenzied animal, uttering every curse he knew, flexing clawed fingers dangerously close to my face. He was not prepared to leave. With horror, I saw Cobweb come to the door of the drawing room. So did Bryony. She tried to push Mengk into the kitchen and he resisted fiercely.

"What's going on?" Cobweb demanded and came toward us, arms folded. We all froze guiltily. He addressed Mengk. "What is it you want exactly?"

Mengk was momentarily silenced, faced with the commanding vision of dark loveliness whom he knew to be Terzian's consort.

"Well?" Cobweb looked at me. I shrugged helplessly. Bryony had the courage to speak.

"This har traveled back to Galhea with Terzian," she said. "Now he is concerned for his master's welfare. Swift was trying to explain that Terzian is comfortable . . . and . . ."

Mengk straightened up and shook Bryony's hands off his arms. "I must see my lord," he said. "I have cared for him a long time. Only I know what he needs at this time." I was rather awed by his nerve.

Cobweb raised his eyebrows and I thought, as I had thought so often, how it is never possible to anticipate my hostling's reactions. "You are probably right," he said. "Swift, take this har to Terzian."

I started to protest, but could see from my hostling's face the futility of such an act. Sullenly, I showed Mengk where Terzian's door was and left him to it. I felt ridiculed because Cobweb had overridden my order. Downstairs, I found him solicitously examining Bryony's cheek, which was beginning to swell along the bone.

"She was struck!" he said, with some surprise.

"Why did you do that?" I asked him angrily. "Why didn't you have him thrown out? He insulted you!"

Cobweb didn't look at me. "I don't think so, Swift. I didn't hear any insults."

"Just by being here, he insulted you!" I insisted.

"Put yourself in his position, Swift, and then remember that all we can do for Terzian now is try to make him happy in small ways. That vicious little brute has been looking after him. Terzian is probably used to him. I won't say 'fond' because Terzian is hardly ever fond of anything. We must be patient during this time and learn to bite our tongues. We must smile at each other and not raise our voices and let Terzian think he is still master of this house. Now we shall go into the kitchen and make sure Yarrow has put out enough sheh for dinner. I think we should sample it now, in fact. Tonight, I shall dress in black and take pleasure in the Gelaming Ashmael's attempts to interest me. Come along!"

We followed him.

The meeting that eventually took place between Cobweb and Terzian is almost too painful for me to relate. It gave me a glimpse of the private side of my parents, that side that most children never see nor want to see if they are wise. I think the whole thing was made worse because it contrasted too strongly with the very convivial meal we all enjoyed that evening. Hara came up from Galhea, and Forever felt very much as it used to feel in the past when celebrations were in order; relaxed and comfortable.

Braced by alcohol, mellowed by good food and conversation, Leef and I had the long-deserved talk about our differences. Some things I realized he would never agree with me over (namely the issue of Cal and his fate), but once he had reassured himself that power had not gone to my head, our friendship was firmly reinstated. Now we could laugh at incidents in the past. I was so relaxed, I actually forgot about what lay in my father's bed upstairs. Then Cobweb caught my eye meaningfully and mouthed, "Now," and I felt a great deal of my euphoria disappear.

Mengk opened the door to us in response to Cobweb's peremptory knock, and we went into the room. "It is time you ate something," Cobweb told Mengk. "If you would like to go to the kitchen, you will find that our housekeeper has prepared a meal for you." Mengk nodded respectfully and left us.

Then I had to see my father's face as he watched the radiant creature of mystery that is my hostling glide toward him. He must have recalled immediately fragments of the past and the feel of Cobweb's cool skin and the caress of his cool eyes. Now they both knew that the room within their minds where the delight of their union had once thrived had been irretrievably shuttered and barred. Terzian the shadow looking at the light. Cobweb's face showed only a kind of pitying disbelief. I knew that he didn't really want to see this new, shriveled Terzian, let alone speak to him. He felt ashamed to be so vibrant. This was ridiculous, as Terzian had wronged him in so many ways in the past. Cobweb had always wanted to shower my father with love, while Terzian had perfected the art of shutting Cobweb out of his heart whenever he wanted to. Now the tables were turned. Now who was helpless? I could see that something definite had happened to the love that Cobweb had felt for Terzian. It was not quite the same, still fervent in a way, but no longer essential. I suspected Cal might have had something to do with that, but it may just have been that Cobweb had been alone for so long and had got used to the idea of life without my father.

"So, we have you back again," Cobweb said awkwardly.

Terzian's face was dark. It was in shadow, but then that room was always dark. "You never *had* me, Cobweb," he replied inscrutably, "never."

I felt that Terzian should have died right after saying that. They would have been very profound last words. More than that, he deserved to die for it, because he wanted to punish us for living, especially Cobweb, who was beautiful and whom he would have to leave behind. Terzian would still look on Cobweb as one of his possessions and would no doubt be gratified if my hostling offered to throw himself onto Terzian's funeral pyre. Terzian was affronted that Cobweb should have a life without him.

"Is there anything you want?" Cobweb asked stiffly, even though he must have known that Terzian's every need was being catered for. He showed that my father's words could not affect him; it was incredible.

"Want anything?" Terzian's eyes narrowed. The cue was irresistible. "In this life there has only been one thing that I have truly wanted . . ."

Cobweb and I looked at each other, both painfully aware of what he meant. If only Terzian could have known how the implication in his words, the sting he hoped would poison, could not touch us. Perhaps Cobweb would tell him. Perhaps he would say, "Oh, you are talking of Cal. Of course. The one who gave meaning to your life and who came to my bed after you left Galhea," but no, unpredictable as ever, my hostling kneeled at Terzian's side and took one of his hands in his own. (Surely my father must be able to see how Cobweb had changed. He was no longer the bound half-har whom Terzian had manifestly tried to keep utterly female. Surely he must see the difference?) My hostling smiled.

"Terzian, if I could do that one thing for you, I would," he said softly. "If I could bring Cal back, I would." He stroked my father's face. I could not bear it. My toes were curling in embarrassment. Tears began to run from my father's eyes, trailing unchecked over his gaunt cheeks. His body began to shake; he sobbed. Cobweb gathered him in his arms and kissed him.

"Cobweb, I . . . I never loved you . . ." Terzian said in a horrible, gulping, cracked voice. I wished it would end. I could not move, transfixed by a kind of fascinated horror. My father looked dead from the neck down. Could he even feel Cobweb's hands upon him?

"Hush," my hostling murmured. "You don't have to say these things. You don't have to. I will say them for you."

"No!" I cried. I don't know why.

Cobweb smiled crazily at me. "It's alright, Swift. He just wants to say that he gave me the best he could, that's all. I've always known that. Terzian lost his heart to Cal a long time before he met either of us. It was meant to be. Cal was just the one."

"Cal is just 'the one' to many people, it seems," I said scathingly. They ignored me.

"Cobweb . . ." Terzian's voice was almost nonexistent now. "I never thought this could happen to me. I'm dying, aren't I? I really am . . ." Bewilderment, weak frustration, envy of the living; what was really going through his head? Cunning, I thought, uncharitably. "I never thought I'd say it, never," he wheedled, flopping a helpless hand against the coverlet.

"We must all die eventually," Cobweb soothed. (Pathetic! Could such an inane observation possibly help him?)

"No, no, no," Terzian groaned. "Not that. I never thought I'd say 'I love you,' not to anyone. Now I say it to him all the time . . . only . . ." He reached up, gasping, mustering his failing strength, and caught hold of Cobweb's clothes by the neck. "In Immanion, it's all I thought about, what kept me going, just one more day, just one . . ." He trailed off, wilting visibly. "I cannot die without seeing him again, not knowing whether he's safe or not. I've kept myself alive for that, for the hope that he might be here when I came home . . ." He shot me a withering glance. I wanted to say, "Any more clichés, you two? Oh, come on, there must be more! Please, don't mind me, just carry on!" but I said nothing. Cobweb turned the sad, sick face back toward his own.

"Terzian . . ."

My father started to shake again, his eyes rolled maniacally. "Cobweb, Cobweb," he wailed. "Your magic . . . your magic . . . how I've scorned you . . . what I've seen! The Forest! The Forest! Oh, Cobweb!" To watch my father weep was an obscenity that nearly made me physically sick. It seemed the Gelaming (or his own guilt?) had destroyed everything within him but for his bitterness and his obsession for Cal. I wondered whether Pellaz had ever interrogated him about that.

Cobweb spoke my name. My father lolled in his arms, spent and shuddering. I said, "What?"

"You may leave us now," my hostling replied, and I saw his anger at the relief those words gave me.

Downstairs, I found Thiede in the drawing room with the others, opened bottles of sheh on the carpet, the room thick with cigarette smoke and laughter. I found it hateful, yet I wanted to be part of it. I sat down beside Thiede and he thoughtfully thrust a full glass into my hand.

"Harrowing?" he inquired lightly. He was smiling, but I knew he understood exactly how I felt.

"Yes. Harrowing."

"Behind you now, though."

"Yes, behind me." I sighed. "My father needs Cal, Thiede."

Thiede sighed as well, but theatrically and embroidered by waving arm gestures. "Oh God! Must my life continually be plagued by love-sick fools continually bleating that particular demand at me?" he said.

There is little more to say now. The time of upheaval was nearly over. I have to speak of the end of my father's life, for that will truly end the tale. With his ending, there began a kind of peace for me. I had played my greatest part on Thiede's stage. For a while, he would let me rest. Fulminir was deserted, peopled only by winds and dust, her victims succoured, her cruel inhabitants transferred to the shadowy, make-believe land of Gebaddon. For them, the play was over, at least in this world.

Taking Fulminir, of course, was not really the end. Megalithica is a vast country and the Varrs were widespread. Suddenly, what was left of my tribe found that those they had looked on as allies had turned against them, their slaves had the courage to rebel, their own loved ones, sickened by bloodshed and cruelty, broke free and ran to the Gelaming. Of course, many lives were lost. We could not avoid fighting, much as Thiede and his Hegemony hoped we could. Magic is sometimes not enough. Some minds are too far immersed in darkness to recognize light even when it is thrown in their eyes. There are probably a thousand thousand tales to be told of my country at that time; the heroes that rose up, the monsters that were discovered, the legends that were born. One day, I might go looking for those tales, for even as a child I had longed to write, and as I have said before, Wraeththu have not yet had much time for making books of their history.

Seel and I mingled our blood beneath the heavy, shady trees in the gardens of Forever. Thiede's ceremonial blade made the cuts, Thiede's own hand pressed bleeding skin to bleeding skin. He smiled his long-toothed smile and blessed us. Cobweb watched us with wistful eyes, thinking of what might have been. His gaze flicked once to Terzian's window; that was all. My father would not even countenance my blood-tie to Seel. I offered to help him to the chair by the window in his room but he declined with scorn.

Later, I couldn't resist going to see him, brandishing my blood-stained flesh. "Look, father, a different kind of inception!"

He winced away from me. "And we were once accused of emulating men!"

"I pity you. You cannot understand."

He smiled wryly to himself. "Oh, Swift, must I bicker my way to the grave?" His voice was introspective.

I watched him looking at what was left of his body, hidden beneath the bedclothes. Half of me wanted to gather him into my arms as Cobweb had done, half of me didn't care about him at all. There was a few moment's silence, then I said, "Why, Terzian?"

He sighed. "Why . . ." Looked up at me, his eyes young, sparkling with shadows of the past. "What particular 'why' do you mean? Is it why didn't I say what the Gelaming wanted to hear or why did I ride south in the first place, or why did I ever become Wraeththu to start with? Or is it the darker 'whys,' those best not spoken, eh?" He smiled and I thought his face was so much as I remembered it, and I recalled how it had sometimes frightened me and sometimes filled me with fire. Of course I have always adored him, always feared his displeasure, always craved his attention, yearned his respect. It was still the same har lying there, only the balance of power had changed.

I said, "No, none of those things. The 'why' I mean is, why are you killing yourself?"

I thought he would wince again, but he didn't. There was silence in the room, deep but not uncomfortable. My arm had begun to throb a little and I sat down on the bed and sucked at the flesh.

"Let me see that," Terzian said. His hands were hot and dry, papery dry. He traced the line of the cut with one finger. "By this mark, you have committed yourself to another har—for life. His welfare is your welfare. You are prepared to uphold each other, whatever happens. It is not a vow to be taken lightly."

"I know that."

"Of course you do, that's not what I'm trying to say. Some vows are made when you are very young, Swift, personal vows that might never be spoken. I cannot go back on promises that I've made to myself, whatever others might think of my beliefs."

"Is it that simple?"

He shook his head. "No . . . nothing can ever be that simple, can it? I worked hard for Galhea, Swift, worked hard to make it what it is. Perhaps, in caring so much, I've done things that I shouldn't have. Bad, evil, whatever you want to call it. It was because I've always cared about my people, this town was mine and I didn't want anything or anyone to take it away from me. I thought that whatever I did outside Galhea could never harm it. Maybe I was wrong. I can offer no excuses for my life, Swift, and I don't want forgiveness, but I want you to know that I *did* care, even if the popular view of me in this house is of a hard-hearted monster!"

I laughed nervously and he squeezed my arm. "I know you've always disapproved of the way I've treated Cobweb," he said. "Will it help you to understand if I tell you that I've always feared him and, because of that fear, envied him? Yes, I've envied him in other ways too. I know I tried to make him weak, but I could never do that for Cobweb's strength is pure, elemental. If I'd had a little more Cobweb in me, who knows, I might not be lying here now." He sighed and lay back, blinking at the ceiling. "Oh, Swift, I thought I was so strong! I saw defeat as going down in a blaze of glory with a curse on my lips, a curse and a smile. I knew we could never win, of course, that was obvious from the start, but I also knew I could never wait for the Gelaming to come here. Neither could I have done what you did, and joined them. Perhaps I'm not as sensible as you or too vain, I don't know. I travelled south seeking a noble death, I suppose, but what happened . . ." He shook his head upon the pillow, his face twisted with pain as he remembered, as he went back in time.

"No," I said. "Don't say any more! Don't think about it! Let it wait for another time!"

"No! There might not be another time!" he said desperately. "I have to talk to you, Swift! I have to tell someone! It's all inside me, boiling away, I've got to let it out! Does my distress upset you? Is that it?"

I felt I should apologize, but could only hang my head.

"They told you about what happened in the forest?" he asked.

"Yes. They were waiting for you, weren't they?"

"Years, Swift, years!" he said, his mind jumping backwards and forwards. "In that place of hell, and then in the towers of Immanion. They pulled me this way and that. All I could say was, 'Why am I so important to you? Just kill me!' but they wanted me with them! They wanted me to confess my sins and seek absolution. But why? What am I to them?"

"They wanted to save your soul," I answered.

Terzian laughed. "Oh, is that it? Is that why they brought my thoughts into form and made me face them? Is that why I watched a thousand deaths a day, and torture and blood and despair? To save my soul?" (But didn't you watch it for real once, father?) "Oh, Swift, let me tell you this. One day they starved me and gave me salt water to drink. They would not let me sleep. I was woken again and again and again. Then I was taken to Pellaz. He's so radiant now. They've made him a god. He had a pool for scrying, in a wonderful cool parlor with plants and birds all around, and lovely hara to bring him all the things he needs. He gave me a crystal flute of wine, ice-cold it was, and he smiled and touched my face. 'Terzian,' he said 'drink the wine. Drink, and look into the pool with me.' I drank. I looked. I saw a room. Forever. Two hara glowing with aruna fire. I had to look away. It was an invasion of something so private . . . even though . . . Pellaz the golden spoke. He said, 'You see, Terzian, already they have forgotten you.' Cobweb and Cal. Together. Of course, I realized it was only an illusion. I laughed at him. They could not break me that way."

I pulled my hand from his hold and stood up, afraid my eyes would give away the truth. That was no illusion, Terzian. "You are letting yourself die," I said. "You still haven't given me a reason!"

"Well then, do you want me to live, Swift?" he asked quietly. There was silence. A silence too long. "There's nothing left for me," he continued. "I have no place in this new world you're all building, no function—"

"That's not true!" I said harshly. "They wanted you, Terzian! It was you they wanted to run Megalithica for them, not me. I was second choice. You would have had Galhea for eternity then and you could have made it bigger and better; nothing would have been denied you. You are a fool! When you say you have no function, that's just a self-indulgent complaint. You were never one for self-pity before, Terzian!"

"Well, maybe I am now!" he answered with equal venom. "Anyway, do you think I wanted to be another kitten chasing bits of wool that Thiede would kindly dangle for me? No thank you. I am my own master—"

"Liar!" I cried. "What about Ponclast?"

"That was different."

"Rubbish!"

"Anyway, you talk as if I had a choice of living or dying. How can I? This is Thiede's doing. He took me apart, he sapped my will to live. Blame him! Your friend Thiede! Or doesn't that suit you?"

It was pointless arguing with him. Neither of us could reach the other over this. We had no common ground. Perhaps he thought that his death would be the final insult for our allying with the Gelaming. That was the truth of it. He was blaming us, me especially, for his death. If he forgave me, he lost his reason for dying.

"I can't let you do this," I said.

"What makes you think either of us has any control over it?" he responded.

"You, father, you make me think it!" I shouted. I walked out, slammed the door, and leaned upon it on the outside, shivering.

CHAPTER NINE

>—!—‹›—☉—‹›—!—‹

Elysian Song

The pillar was risen to infinity,
The pyre has cast his throne,
The gates of Heaven have sounded the bell . . .
Calling me back home.

Days passed. Sunlight on the fields, life stirring. People from afar. Nomad tribes were made welcome for the first time upon Galhea's lands. We sought to annihilate the memory of the Varrs and our tribe was given a new name; Parasiel. It is the name of an angel and he is the lord and master of treasures. We have found treasure within ourselves and this name seemed truly apt.

My father hung onto life, though daily he seemed to fade. I visited him every evening but it was hard to talk. Perhaps everything that could be said between us had already been said. It was as if he wanted to linger in this world for as long as possible, in a distressing state, in order to inflict as much pain as he could upon my hostling and myself. Day by day, he released a little more of his life force into infinity. Mengk was with him constantly; another devotee made to suffer. Cobweb behaved like a kind of tortured saint, full of self-recrimination, solicitous to Mengk, calm and understanding with Terzian, unshakable.

Thiede left Galhea to return to Immanion, promising me a summons to Phaonica in the near future as official representative of Parasiel for the forthcoming talks concerning Megalithica's future. Ashmael had returned with Thiede, and Arahal had gone east to take charge of the Gelaming personnel in that area. At the moment, only a handful of Gelaming remained in Galhea. Later, this would change, as their architects and builders and technicians came to get to work on the town, but for a while our lives were our own.

It was not spoken of, but it was clear that we in the house were all just waiting for Terzian to die. Perhaps it sounds harsh to say that, but for myself, I was mainly concerned for Tyson and Azriel, who could not but be affected by the heaviness in the atmosphere. All conversations seemed to be conducted in whispers; the harlings could not run or shout as harlings should. Outside Forever, my people seemed content to forget that they had ever been Varrs. Ithiel took his orders from me. I was Master of Galhea and Terzian still lived.

One night, a strong wind came up from the south, bringing heavy clouds with it that shook all the trees in the garden, and a faint, acrid smell of burning. Bryony ran around the house closing all the windows, for we expected rain. I had already organized a refurbishment of the upper stories of Forever, for I envisaged a day that the house would be used to its full capacity and too long had those haunted rooms stood untended. Bryony came to us in the sitting room, her face pale. "I don't like the third floor," she said, rubbing her arms. "Something seems to watch you there!" We laughed at her fears.

In the night, with wind lashing at the walls, speaking in a fierce, incomprehensible howl, I was woken up by a sound. A sound within the house, whose echoes had vanished by the time I was awake. Seel groaned when I shook him.

"What was that?" I whispered hoarsely.

"Nothing," he answered, and rolled over, pulling the blankets over his ears.

Nothing. For a while I lay awake in the dark with my arms behind my head, listening. Nothing. Perhaps I had been mistaken. Perhaps a dream . . . I began to drift back to sleep, but just as I was slipping under, it came again. Low, booming. I was not mistaken. I was fully awake this time. Not bothering to tell Seel, I scrabbled from the bed, pulling on a robe, and crept to the door.

Outside, the corridor was in darkness. I could hear the wind all around me. Feeling my way to the stairs, I reached to turn on the light. The sound came again; deafening. A great, hollow thundering. The door. Someone demands entrance. Who. . . ? Someone. Three times. I had heard it three times.

Flooded with light, the hall beneath me looked tense and stark, the great front doors dark and solid before me. Why had no-one else woken up? I hesitated only a moment. My hands were upon the doors, pulling them open. Wind rushed into the house like an angry spirit, bringing a train of whirling leaves. My hair was blown up behind me, my robe flapped with life. Breathless, I cautiously narrowed my eyes at the garden beyond. Nothing. There was no-one there. Only the wind howling.

With effort, I pushed the doors closed again and turned the great key in the lock. It should always be locked, I thought. Then the back of my neck began to prickle. My hair began to rise. The hall was too quiet. For a moment, I did not turn round. My heart slowed down to a comfortable pace, I rubbed the back of my neck.

"Swift." A single word. A single sound. A hundred memories flooding in; the past around me. I turned round. He was carrying a canvas bag which he dropped to the floor. He ran his fingers through his hair, which was longer than I remembered, and windswept. He looked very tired.

I said, "Cal," and found my back pressed against the door. There was no way out for me through them, though. "How. . . ? How did you get here?"

"You're afraid!"

"No." I made myself step toward him. He stepped back. "How did you get in here?" I repeated. "How. . . ?"

"No!" He would not let me continue. "I'm here. That's all. That's all you need to know. I've been given time. Not much, but enough for what I have to do." He looked stern, but he couldn't keep it up. His face softened. "Oh, Swift, how I've missed you all."

I found myself smiling. How could I help it? "You're not a ghost? You're sure you're not a ghost?"

He shook his head. "Oh no, no, I'm not. They'll never kill me, Swift. You know that. Now, will you take me to Terzian?"

"Can't we talk first? It's been so long. I want to know what happened to you."

"I'm sorry . . ." He shook his head again.

There was so much I wanted to say. I could only stare at him speechless. "Please, Swift. Now." He lifted his bag.

I led the way upstairs. "Do you get a feeling, walking up here? Does it make you remember?" I asked him.

"Yes," he said quietly.

Two steps from the top, I turned on him. "Oh, Cal, is it bad? Are you alright? Where did they take you? Did they hurt you? Are you safe?"

He almost fell backwards in surprise at my outburst. "Don't ask me questions, Swift, please. I cannot answer them."

"Then let me touch you."

"Alright. For a moment." He held out his arms and I stood on the step above him so that our height was level. He felt cold, but it was only the chill of being out in the wind. His violet gaze was steady. "Take this back to your lover," he said. "My taste." We shared breath, but I could taste only blackness, like a veil. He would show me nothing. "There's not much time," he said.

At the doorway to my father's room, he touched my face and said, "Don't come in with me, Swift."

"There's so much I want to say. Will we see you again?"

He smiled that lazy smile. "Oh, can I come back here? Will I be made welcome in Seel's house?"

I lowered my eyes. I had forgotten that.

Cal laughed softly. "Oh, Swift, don't be ashamed. You are happy and I'm happy for you. Your life will be perfect. You have everything."

"You must come back," I said. "What is done is done, but you are still part of us. Your son is here. For him, you must come back."

"If I can, maybe. Personally, I think Tyson would be better off not knowing about me."

I shook my head. "Never."

"I'll always think of you, Swift, you and your mad hostling. The changeling. I've thought of you all a lot recently."

"Where have you been?"

"Places, that's all. This sounds dramatic, but I'm being followed. A har on a black horse. How symbolic! My trials are not yet over, I'm afraid. There are still ghosts snapping at my heels. They battle for my soul, you know. Succoring Terzian on his deathbed is a karmic point to me, I think." He laughed again, his face lighting up as it always did. A summer smile.

"No-one will ever have your soul," I said. "Cal, about Pellaz. He *is* alive, you know."

There was a moment's silence. His face shivered briefly. "Yes," he said, "I know, Swift." He pulled a forlorn face and shrugged. He would say no more. "I'll have to say goodbye now, Swift."

"I can't just let you go like this. Stay a while, it can't hurt, there's so much—"

"No! You have to let me go. It's out of our hands. Goodbye."

He opened the door, walked inside, into the darkness, closed it. I stood there for a moment or two, wondering. All was silence. Outside, the wind had dropped.

In the morning, I learned that my father was dead. The house was full of peace. When I looked at the body, I could see tranquility in that lifeless face. A faint smile. My father's spirit was free now. He had another chance.

I took Cobweb and Seel to the long gallery and told them about a dream I'd had the night before about Cal coming back to Forever. I half suspected that Cobweb was responsible, for he was a master of visualization, but his surprise was genuine enough.

"A dream, Swift?" he said.

"It may have been," I answered.

We left it at that. Cobweb covered all the mirrors in the house and had someone stop the clocks. He was serene. We burned Terzian's body on a great pyre in the fields beyond Galhea and the ashes were scattered to the four winds. With their scattering, we all knew that the last of the Varrs had perished. The name was only a dark memory.

Most days, I like to walk in the garden. I can think there. In the evening, the summerhouse calls me and I go to it, although it is barely recognizable now. Ivy has covered it and the lily bowl is choked forever. It is there that I can talk to you best, Cal. For sometimes, I am sure that you are near. It is where I can tell you to come back to us, that hate is banished for good from our home and even you could not bring it back in.

In the autumn, Seel and I are going back to Immanion, but it won't be for long. We shall be coming back for Festival and Ashmael will be with us. Seel says it is because Cobweb has bewitched him and I'm sure you can understand that! It will be a good Festival, Cal. We will remember, but not with sadness. I want you to know that whatever evil you think is inside you (and I *do* know that you think that), it is only part of the essential harmony of the world; the world needs you. Without pain, there cannot be pleasure, without darkness, light cannot thrive. We need contrast, and the lone wolves who stalk the earth, like yourself, they bring perspective and objectivity into our lives. We need you, Cal, all of us. Angel or devil, you hold the balance. You begin the tales, we end them. It is time that you began your own. Every day, I look at Tyson and see your eyes. One day, he will ask me about you, for you are in his heart. The hostling who did not care. That is something you must attend to, for your son is innocent and your trials are not his.

I often wonder if you and Pell are together again, if you have met, even. Would that be the prize or the punishment? Perhaps, when I go to Immanion, I shall find out. When I get back. . . . Remember, Cal, Cobweb and the harlings will be almost alone in Forever while Seel and I are away. That is the time. I am counting on it. We shall come back through the snow and the yellow lights of Forever will be shining out to greet us. The doors will be flung wide open and the house inside will be alive with celebration. We shall walk into the hall and I shall see you there. I think you'll smile in that lopsided way you have and stand before me and say, "You see, I couldn't keep away. I've come home."

It isn't long, Cal. Listen to me. The bewitchments of love and hate are perhaps the strongest magics in the world. Magic called you to us in the beginning, I am sure of it. I called your name in a dream. Now I'm calling you again. Listen in the shadows; I'm whistling in the dark.

THE FULFILMENTS OF
FATE AND DESIRE

➤─⟨♦⟩─◉─⟨♦⟩─❮

The Third Book of Wraeththu

*This book is dedicated to Roy Wood who
"discovered" me in Andromeda
and to whom I am deeply grateful for his help, advice and
encouragement.*

*With thanks to Sue Eley for her swift correcting pen and critical eye,
and also for the map, glossary and character guide; Jeanne Wheeler,
Alison Perry, Steve Allman and Jag for contributory ideas;
Steve Waters for illumination about androgyny,
and the remaining Wraeththu-ites who were
brave enough to be filmed as such; Jayle Summers, Phillipa Cotterell,
Richard Clews, Sharon O'Hara and John Matley.*

PROLOGUE

>─┤◀╲─◇─╱▶┤─◄

One day, a time will come when all that we are pioneering, praying (preying?), cultivating, is history. The past. It shall be analyzed; a subject for earnest scholars to pore over and dissect. Trivial events, accidents, coincidences, shall be imbued with great meaning. I can already hear the voices raised, confident they know it all. Oh yes, I can see it now; our far descendants, all gathered together, clothed in their perfect flesh. One shall say; "The first Wraeththu, of course, were little other than barbarians, hectic in their search for truth and so far from it, eh? All they could grasp at was their sexuality. What a shock it must have been! They were human to start with, after all. What a shock to find they were half-female after centuries of despising that sex." Ha, ha, ha. They will all laugh together smugly. Then another bright spark, perhaps younger or more controversial in his views, might venture; "But surely the reason they couldn't see the truth was because they were so shrouded in self-deception. Knowledge was so close, and yet . . . they couldn't see it through the shroud. How sad." Here, I feel, one of the older hara, stern-faced, will deliver a subtle reprimand.

"The first Wraeththu were without *discipline,* too outspoken perhaps, before considering what, in fact, they were *really* saying." This will be said with relish and the younger har will feel humiliated. He may look down abashed, he may not. But whatever, those sentiments may well be right, and half of me is inclined to hope so. If those highly advanced hara never *do* come to exist, if our race remains static or even slips backwards to the ways of men, then the struggle really was all for nothing. A cosmic joke. The biggest case of self-delusion in the history of the planet—and there have been many, let's face it. We were just mutants, freaks; end of story. Not saviors, not ultra-men, not sons of angels or deities—just accidents. The gods weren't looking; it just happened. And yes I have to admit it, the other half of me is lying back, sipping good liquor, with its feet up, thinking; "Yeah, fuck the heavy stuff. Let it all be—just this!" I don't think this earth should ever countenance a future scorn for what we are—what *I* am—for, after all, our descendants can never be here, now. They will never know us as we are or why we do things. The bloody times, the horror, will just be history to them, words on a page, so how will they dare to judge? Very easily, I should imagine. Will it ever be said that, in spite of everything, we all lived to the best of our ability? If life is a battle, then my inner scars are medals for valor, for swiftness, for courage, for passion. Evil is the dark-haired brother of Good; they walk hand in hand—always. And by the way, whatever it sounds like, that is not an excuse . . .

CHAPTER ONE

>━┼━<┼>━•━☉━•━<┼>━┼━<

Fallsend: Its Mud Patch
"The burnt out end of smoky days . . ."
—*T. S. Eliot, Preludes*

The years were numbered ai-cara from the time when Pellaz came to power in Immanion. Sorry, that should of course read, Pellaz-Har-Aralis, as lesser beings must refer to him. I am a lesser being, best forgotten, best reviled. I have no part in the future of kings. I lost my sense of chivalry an age ago. Thank God! This is my story and perhaps it will be the truth, for I suspect that there will be an awful lot of untruth spoken about me. I realize it's unlikely anyone will ever read it; more likely that it will lie forever in some unhallowed spot, deep in the earth, clasped to my shriveled breast. Who knows? (Who cares?) Will someone bury me when I die? Are demons allowed that privilege? This began as a diary but lost its way. This began as a confession and developed a life of its own. This is me.

I shall start in the middle of the story. That is a bad place to start, and because of that, the best one for me. Here goes.

And it came to pass, gentle reader, that I found myself sliding down the black, mud channel they call a road, into Fallsend, a town of reputation but not repute, in the tail end of the year ai-cara 27. Time to rest. Time to reflect. Time to get rat-arsed drunk and stop dissecting the past in my head. Some hope. My first impression of Fallsend was simply to register it as a cold town in a cold country where it always seemed to be late autumn. Never winter. This more or less reflected my rather down-hearted mood at the time, and later had to be revised when it started snowing. Fallsend never looks pretty. It's built on the side of a hill and the floor of a valley the shape of a teacup. After being incarcerated here for a few weeks it begins to feel roughly the same size as well. The name that the country used to have around here has fallen into disuse. Everyone forgot it. Now, it's a northerly, ill-policed fragment of Almagabra known as Thaine. Nowadays, hara (nice ones) don't want to stay here long enough to think about where they are—if they have any sense. I've never had any sense. Presumably, that's why I'm here. That and the fact I wandered into the place without finery or finance and my horse was about to die on me, or more accurately, beneath me. OK, I'll look on the bright side. I'd managed at long last to shake off the shadow that had been following me to this godforsaken place, but that's about as bright as it's going to get for a while, my friend.

Fallsend is damp and made a little of stone, but mostly of wood, which rots at a merry pace. There are lots of steps, most of them likely to collapse beneath the feet of the unwarily drunken. Planks across the puddles which are collared with scum and the occasional dead creature. Little color. It's depressing. Just about every Wraeththu criminal, lunatic or honest-to-goodness misfit has passed through this little town, heading east to Jaddayoth. Today, from where I'm sitting, it looks like most of them stayed here. Uptown, they call it Glitter, it will convince nobody. Up here, those sweet souls who make this shit-hole pay have high, gothic houses and you can buy almost anything here. Drugs to make you sane. Drugs to make you insane. Waters of forgetfulness, powders of remembrance. They have white-skinned, moon-eyed harlings of the Colurastes tribe up here somewhere, bought and sold like meat, kept in the dark. Two spinners buys you one as a whore for a night in the shadows. I heard some of them have their tongues cut out so they'll never scream. We are the race of peaceful equality, remember.

Now for the social comment. I suppose it's necessary, though tiring when you've heard it and thought it a thousand times. Back west, children, the supremely superior tribe of Gelaming have scoured the home country of evil, or so I've heard. As a matter of fact, it was still pretty suspect when I was last there, but I admit that was some time ago. Things might have changed. Everything changes on the surface. (But does it change inside? Can it?) The Gelaming also control the south-western part of this continent as well, where it's sunny all the time, I suppose. I've worked out they swept all their rubbish east and it ended up here. Someone built a town on it. Fallsend. Not a place you'd want to die in.

I'd had to leave Morass, a settlement some ten miles west of Fallsend pretty quickly. Painful as it is to recall, I'd got involved in some sordid argument concerning someone's virgin son, which had all got unpleasantly out of hand. I shine at quick getaways, but as I was drunk, I don't remember too much about it. I lie a lot and sometimes get found out when I'm drunk. After forcing my ailing mount over several miles of boggy ground, I was actually relieved to catch sight of the glum pall of smoke that always hangs over Fallsend. Of course, I'd heard about the place. Every town I'd passed through was full of horror stories about it. What could happen to the unwary traveler there; rumors of abduction, slavery, murder—all anathema to upstanding, Wraeththu-kind. After some of the throw-back, puritan woodpiles I'd visited, it sounded like a welcome relief. "Well," I thought to myself, threatening the horse with death if it dared to stumble, "here it is; a town named for yourself. Have I stopped falling now? Is Fallsend rock bottom?"

After half an hour of wandering aimlessly about, taking in the sights, I took a room in a leaning, listing hostel in the south of the town. Its proprietor didn't work out that I couldn't pay him at first. I sold what was left of my horse to a har that didn't ask any questions, and to further my investigations of the place, went for a walk through the streets. Nobody looks at you in Fallsend. This is because you may well be a homicidal (or should that be haricidal?) maniac with a sensitive spot about prying eyes. Nobody wants to take that risk. I bought a bowl of nondescript gruel in a shady tavern—puddles on the floor, blotted by heaps of soggy sawdust, that sort of thing—and asked the regular patrons about where I could find work. At first, they were reluctant to answer me at all, but because I have a deceptively honest face, they eventually plucked up enough courage to laugh. Someone took pity on me. "What can you do?" I was asked.

"Ah well," I answered, "I'm pretty good at killing people, or just fucking up their lives if you can't afford that . . ."

This was not a remark to be met with humor, which was how I'd hoped it would be. They told me gravely that there was really quite a glut of killers in Fallsend and that there was too much traveling involved, even if you could get work of that kind. Nobody wants to pay traveling expenses to a murderer, it seems. I tried not to look downhearted. The way I was feeling at that time, I'd have welcomed the chance to throttle the life out of someone, even for free! More pity came my way. Someone said, "You're quite a looker. Skinny, but some people aren't fussy. If you're not fussy, you'll find work in Glitter . . ." I'm fussy. I half-starved for a week before I reviewed my morals.

Because this is the beginning of a book, I think it is a good time to talk about the concept of Wraeththu, if indeed there is one. I can't say it's something I think about often—how many of us in this confused world are allowed the luxury of time to think anyway—and I'm not sure if it is important or not, but for the sake of posterity, I'll say what I think. I am har, a member of the race that came after man. Came *from* man. We are the race that solved that niggling problem of sexual inequality, not to mention sexual orientation, by evolving into one sex; hara. I have a female temperament at times and masculine strength at times. Usually these things manifest themselves at the wrong time. Masculine temperament coupled with female strength are guaranteed to land you in hot water, so we all have our problems, no matter how complete and whole we smugly say we feel. Most hara will tell you that all Wraeththu are beautiful, but this is not entirely true—and how boring if it was! What is inside a person nearly always influences what is outside. The most beautiful hara are the truly evil, the most powerful and the most clever. Don't believe it if you are told all hara are good. I've never met a thoroughly good har and I don't want to. Not even the Gelaming are all good, although I'm sure they like to think so. They are certainly the most beautiful, so draw your own inferences.

Philosophers might tell you that Wraeththu are a race of sorcerors and mystics, supposedly created to rid the world of evil. Now we have a United Council of Tribes desperately trying to convince themselves that this aim has been achieved, but, like I said before, the rubbish was merely pushed east. Northeast, to be exact. In the west, we have the large countries of Almagabra, Erminia, Cordagne and Fereng. In the middle, Thaine, which is where I am now. East of that lies Jaddayoth, but when I first arrived in Thaine I knew very little about Jaddayoth. Let's imagine a line drawn down this continent from pole to pole. West of the line we find law and order, the ability to get the world on its feet again and tranquility. East of the line is a delightful trip back to the Middle Ages and chaos. South on both sides of the line, we have a huge, hot country we now call Olathe. Humans fucked it up very thoroughly by tossing nuclear weapons around, before Wraeththu spread east from another great continent, Megalithica. Well, that's the essential geography of my tale.

I came from Megalithica originally, and I've been dodging the apparitions of my conscience around Fereng and Thaine for what I think must be several years. It's all very alcohol-fogged, I'm afraid. I don't look any older and I know it's impossible for me to feel any older than I do now. All I want to do is keep running and lose myself in the chaos I know lies east. Sexual inequality may well be a thing of the past, but believe me, there were a host of other, equally irresistible inequalities that had just been busting a gut waiting to take its place. The strong enslave the weak. That about sums it up. Rewind history. Replay. *Ad infinitum.* Oh, I'm sure that there's a warm hearth yearning to give me comfort in Jaddayoth!

Anyway, as I was explaining before, I starved for quite a time after reaching Fallsend, and then the hostel-keeper began to get suspicious. Mainly, this was because I never ate in the (dare I call it this?) dining room with the other residents. It was a cash for meals arrangement in there you see, and as I quickly got through the money I'd made from selling my horse, the dining room was deprived of my enlightening presence. On the sixth day, just when I was convincing myself that I liked eating out of trash cans and had nearly finished my last bottle of liquor, money was demanded for my room. The hostel keeper and I argued in a civilized manner for about half an hour, until he lost patience and had me thrown out, keeping my meager bundle of luggage as security until I could pay him what I owed. It was all quite undignified. Sprawled in a black, stinking puddle, sniffed at by a stray, mangy hound, I shouted that I used to be the consort of a prince, which was rather an exaggeration on my part, but I had no fear of being found out in that place. It failed to impress my friend the hostel keeper, however. He told me to piss off back west and claim alimony if that was the case. I acknowledged defeat and abandoned the argument. Too many people had gathered to watch, and even numbed by alcohol I hate feeling embarassed.

Remembering the conversation I'd had about finding work some days before, I quickly examined my feelings on seeking employment in Glitter. Strangely, I found I had none whatsoever. Hunger and misery do odd things to your principles. Dusting myself off or sludging myself off which is more to the point, I walked up town and knocked on the prettiest door

I could find. It had a string of colored lights all around it. Tacky, I know, but I appreciated that the occupants were trying to make an effort at decoration in the face of such overwhelming squalor. I had no idea if I'd chosen the best house. A musenda was a musenda to me. Men once called such things whorehouses. After some minutes of repeated knocking on my part, the door was opened by a har who looked like something out of my past. That is to say he looked clean, attractive and wore jewelery and cosmetics. It had been so long since I'd seen anyone wearing either, that I spared a brief, wistful thought for the days when I'd been adorned with them myself. I said, "Someone in town sent me up here. They said there's work . . ."

"There are no spare places here in Piristil," the har said frostily, trying to close the door.

I pushed it open again. "Look, I know I'm a mess at the moment, but I've had a hard time recently. I've no money, no place to stay. If I don't get work, I'll die of cold, of hunger and the stink of the town. Could you live with that on your conscience?"

"Have you had experience in this line of work?" he snapped.

"No, I've never been a kanene, I've never even set foot in a musenda before, but I swear to you, if you let me stay, you won't regret it. It's a line of work I'm eminently suited to if you'll let me prove it."

The har looked at me with about the same amount of enthusiasm (and belief) as he'd look on a turd telling him it was a diamond. We suffered in silence for an eternity, staring at each other. I sensed a growing refusal. He said, "You're filthy," which I presumed meant my appearance.

I shrugged. "Yeah, I know, but I've told you, I've had a run of bad luck. Clean me up and the Aghama will have to shield the angels' eyes from my wondrous beauty."

He wasn't convinced, although he allowed the corner of his mouth to twitch a little. It was then that I realized I'd have to do that thing I'd just about forgotten how to. It had always worked like magic. I felt my face crack and, for a moment, I was scared it was my skin. But it wasn't. Just dirt. It was my last hope: I smiled. The har blinked at me, a little dazed. Poor creature, poor sucker. He opened the door wider. "You'd better come in," he said.

And that, my friends, is how Calanthe, lover of kings and princes, slayer of friends, charlatan of wit, beauty and refinement, a legend in his own time in fact, became a whore. How much lower could I fall?

CHAPTER TWO

>─┼─◆>─○─<◆─┼─◄

The house in Fallsend
". . . prowling hungry down the night lanes."
—Robert Graves, *A Jealous Man*

*I am living two lives. I am not mad. Perhaps that is my punishment. Yesterday
is two places, each memory convincing, each incident clear as ice-water. I am
fourteen years old. Seel is with me, younger, eager, dog-like in his trusting
simplicity. The air smells bad around here. It is a dead part of the city. They say
that the Wraeththu live here. We have come to see. Seel's trousers are ripped,
his knees grazed. He is nervous. I am merely numb. It is the only way for us.
The others, the world, our families, what is left of the establishment on this
wasteland earth are on to us. We are so young. We are afraid yet brave, our
courage is a kind of contaminated innocence; we are human and we are lovers.
In the wake of various hysterias, our love is outlawed. We risk death every day.
(The first thrown stone; others would follow.) No-one must know about us. It
is a danger even to look at one another, in case the warmth of our eyes betrays
us. So little warmth in this world; we must stand next to it when we can. Flesh
pressed too long to ice brings death; death of the soul. Many soulless people
walk this land. Every other house stands empty in our street now. Doors and
windows silent, sagging, vomiting desolation. Our trysting places. We first
made love amongst the rubble, the sound of wailing outside, far away, in the
sunlight. A sharp report of gunfire. Summertime. Dogs barking on the hot
asphalt but no children playing. Seel shuddered and closed his eyes. We both
knew. There is no place for us in the grave of Mankind. Always smoke on the
horizon and the stink of recent carnage. Frightened eyes, sealed mouths.
Mankind are a frightened people. Demons without, demons within. They can
see the door closing on them, shutting off the light forever. It is the end.*

*There is a hole in the ground. A house once stood here. This was the cellar.
Seel and I look at each other. We are so young; we know that. Our hearts ache
with nostalgia for other summertimes, simple pleasures, a mother's voice
calling from the shade. We look back at the city. I see us as children, happy
in that forgotten sunlight, and I know that Seel sees it too. He smiles and puts
his hand on my arm. We both look into the hole in the ground. There is a
musky smell as would issue from the lair of a beast. Wraeththu live beneath
the city. What are they? We have heard they can take our humanity away
from us. Take us in. It is our only hope. We can no longer live above the
ground. I take the first step and still look back. Seel is a silhouette against the
white, summer sky. He reaches for my hand. "We are together," he says and
his lovely eyes are full of fear.*

"Yes," I say, and he follows me . . .

* * *

The name of Piristil irresistably conjures to mind a fairy-tale palace, a haunt of witches and brooding, satanic lords, but despite its pathetic gaudiness, there was little glamor to be found within the house. I learned it was occupied by eight kanene, including Astarth who had let me in. There was also a staff of four, including a cook, a stablehand and the owner of the establishment, a thin, mean-looking har named Jafit. Astarth was the favorite of Jafit and virtually ran the place.

He shut the door behind me and I stood, drooping and dripping, in the hall looking around myself. There was a grand staircase leading to a gallery that ran round the three sides of Piristil opposite the door. The light was gloomy, trailing plants looped desperately over a table, somewhere a clock was ticking. I could have been back in Megalithica, a hundred years before.

"Well," my host began, "I am Astarth. I suppose I'd better get you cleaned up. Jafit can see you later. I hope you've told me the truth."

I didn't answer. He took me upstairs, and several inquisitive pairs of eyes peered round open doors.

"Charge him double, Astarth!" someone called cheerfully.

"Haven't you any belongings?" Astarth asked, above the laughter that accompanied that last remark.

I shook my head. "I prefer to travel light."

He shrugged. "OK, in here. This is my room. Don't dirty it."

I was gratefully surprised by the warmth. There was a huge fire burning in the grate across the room. I could smell soot. Another har was sitting on the floor by the fire painting his toenails.

"Ezhno, get out!" Astarth spat unpleasantly.

"No, my fire's gone out. The chimney's fucked. Get it fixed, Astarth. That's your job, isn't it?" Ezhno looked at me. "Hello filthy one," he said and resumed painting his nails. "Who's your friend, Astarth?"

"My name's Calanthe," I said lightly and walked over to the fire, holding out shaking, white and gray hands to the heat.

"Well, hello Calanthe, in that case," Ezhno said, shying fastidiously away from the filthy rags dangling from my outstretched arms. When I squatted down, I could smell his cleanliness; clean hair and tooth polish. He had narrow, crafty eyes, a startling blue.

"The bathroom's through here," Astarth said, and I realized that was an order.

The rooms in Piristil are comfortable, but worn. They look better in lamplight, but all have carpets on the floor. Unfortunately, all the water is heated by the fires and it appeared that everyone had just taken a bath that day.

"I hope you don't mind the water being cool," Astarth said, in a voice that showed he didn't care whether I did or not.

"No, I don't mind."

He watched me rip off my rags, standing with folded arms and expressionless face across the room. When I stood there, naked and shivering, he

said, "I think these old garments should be burnt, don't you?" I agreed.
After I had lowered myself gingerly into the tepid water, Astarth emptied
a bag of fragrant crystals over me and asked, "Well, who was it that told
you to come here then?"

"No-one really," I confessed. "The lights outside impressed me, that's
all."

Astarth smiled grimly and rolled up his sleeves. I was happy to let him
scrub at my hair.

"Don't let Jafit know you're inexperienced," he said.

I laughed. "There's no way I'd ever describe myself as that!" Astarth did
not share my amusement.

"Everyone thinks that before they're a kanene."

That sounded ominous. I studied him through a tangle of soapy hair.
Astarth has the face of an impudent female and the body of a young god.
Some angry part of him makes him hack his bright red hair off very short.
He affects a noncommittal attitude to everything, which I quickly realized
was a complete sham. Many things hurt him, but he'd never show it.
Because of his relatively elevated position in the house, the other kanene
make his life a misery at times. I hate to think what miserable set of
circumstances brought him to Piristil and kept him there. It's not something you can ask. Kanene don't talk about their history if they can help
it. No-one would be doing this if there was an alternative. Wraeththu
culture is nothing like Mankind's. Our attitude to sex is utterly different.
Obviously, it would have to be, but there should be no need for kanene in
a Wraeththu world. This may give some kind of intimation of the sort of
hara who do business in a musenda. If ordinary aruna is available to
everyone for free, what kind of har wants to pay for it? What does he expect
for his money? Sitting in that luke-warm bath, it was about the third thing
that came into my mind, after comforting ones of food and sleep.

Astarth shrugged off my question about it. "No-one gets hurt," he
answered enigmatically.

"Now why doesn't that comfort me?"

"You wanted the job," Astarth pointed out reasonably.

I'd become so paranoid over the last couple of years, that I was dreading
someone asking me questions about myself. It was a needless fear. Nobody
in Piristil asks personal questions—or answers them. I suppose everyone
had something to hide. Astarth brought me a plate of food from the kitchen
(cold potatoes and lumps of fatty meat), and he and Ezhno watched me eat
it. It tasted like nectar to my deprived tongue. There seemed little to say.
When you meet a person for the first time, it is customary to strike up
conversation by asking them about themselves. This could not occur on
either side in Piristil. Any questions about the house or the work were
answered by, "Jafit will tell you the rules."

"You eat like an animal," Ezhno said at last, as the sound of my frenzied
chewing echoed round the room.

"That's because I feel like an animal," I answered, with my mouth full.

Astarth sorted out some clothes for me from his own wardrobe. We were roughly the same size. Clean, fed and clothed, I was already much more optimistic about my future. Ezhno was eager to paint my face, enthusing over my cheekbones and eyelids. He combed out my hair, and it felt like I lost a good deal of it in the process, if the pain was anything to go by. I regarded his handiwork in Astarth's mirror.

"I look like a whore," I said.

"That's the idea," Astarth answered drily.

Jafit arrived home in the early evening. He had been drinking the afternoon away with friends down in Fallsend. Astarth wasted no time in taking me to see him, mainly because he said that Jafit would probably soon fall into a deep and unwakable sleep. Jafit's office is on the ground floor to the left of the front door. It is where he generally entertains his best (richest) clients before Astarth shows them upstairs. Astarth knocked on the door and opened it just as Jafit was saying, "Come!" I could tell by first glance that Jafit is not a har easily fooled. Astarth had given me some advice on how to bullshit my way through this interview, but one glance into those shrewd, yellow eyes had me doubting myself.

"So, you're looking for work," he said, after Astarth had explained how I'd arrived. I murmured some assent. "Thank you, Astarth," Jafit said meaningfully, and Astarth backed out, closing the door gently behind him. Jafit offered me a drink and I poured myself gracefully into a chair. I could see the spinner-light crashing round Jafit's eyes like a cash-till while he looked at me. He handed me a glass of tart wine.

"And where have you worked before then, er, Calanthe?"

"Oh, in Wesla, Persis . . . places like that."

"You are familiar then with the advanced practices of chaitra and pelcia?"

Astarth had told me to say yes when Jafit asked me that. "I've had no trouble before," I answered carefully.

"Forgive my asking, but how come you're so far east? I detect a trace of Megalithican in your accent. You don't look like a kanene. I get the feeling that you're the sort of person who doesn't need to be one, either!"

I shrugged, pulled a wry face. "You flatter me. I did come from Megalithica originally, yes. There are reasons why I'm doing this work, which I'd rather not go into. But they won't cause you any hassle, I can promise you that."

Jafit grinned. "They'd better not. I don't relish the thought of angry pursuers materializing on my doorstep. You'd better tell me now if you're in any kind of trouble. That doesn't mean I won't give you a place, so don't be frightened."

"I'm not in trouble," I said. "Nobody's after me."

"Good." Jafit slapped his legs and stood up. "OK Calanthe, I admit I like the look of you. I'll let Astarth take you over the rails for a week or two and then you can come to me. If you pass my test, and it's rigorous, I promise you, we'll set you to work. Payment is seven spinners a week, plus bed and board. You'll live here, of course. There won't be any need for you to do domestic duties, we have a staff for that, so you can sit and rub lemon juice into those torn hands of yours every night to get them soft again. One thing; don't abuse the staff! They have to work for a living too. Don't get cigarette burns in the furniture. Don't waste fuel or food and don't go poking around in any areas of the house that are off limits to you. Got that? Any other rules of the house, Astarth can tell you about. Learn as you go along; they're mostly a good bunch here. They'll help you. Any questions?"

I shook my head. "No, it all seems clear."

"Good. Now one thing, Calanthe, that I have to say to all newcomers and I only say it once, so remember it well. I look after my hara. I look after them very well. So you work well for me, do you hear? If anyone pulls a fast one on me, they're dead. No questions asked. Got it?" I nodded. Jafit reached forward and shook my hand. "I'm sure you do, Calanthe, I'm sure you do. Now, once a week, I like us all to have dinner together, so I'll see you again then. Listen to Astarth; he knows his job. You'll learn well and quickly from him. I make sure my kanene are the best around here." He waved a hand at me and I stood up. Jafit didn't speak again.

I went out, my mind reeling. What had I got myself into? Jafit's little empire. What, in the Aghama's name, were pelcia and chaitra?

Astarth was waiting for me in the hall. He asked no questions, but told me that I would have to wait a few days until I could have a room of my own. Apparently, all the spare rooms were in varying states of decay, so one would have to be redecorated and furnished for me. At my request, Astarth reluctantly took me on a tour of the house. It is much larger inside than it appears from the front, and rather haphazard in design. It is constructed in a rough square around a central courtyard. Three-storied on two sides, where the main rooms and living quarters of the kanene are to be found, and two-storied on the remaining sides, which comprise the kitchens, domestic quarters and the stables. I heard that it could all get very fragrant out in the courtyard come summer. Refuse collection is not one of Fallsend's strong points. What community council exists is more interested in feathering its own nest rather than the welfare of the people, or so Astarth told me. I can belive it. In fact, I was rather surprised that Fallsend had a community council at all, however corrupt.

A bitter wind worried round the courtyard as Astarth and myself, standing in a kitchen doorway, studied the rear vista of Piristil. Astarth wanted to make it brief. Shivering and exclaiming, he began to close the door. "Wait!" I said, staying his hand. I pointed out into the gloom, toward the right of the house. There, the top story's windows were shuttered, in a disturbingly permanent-looking manner. Several were reinforced with iron bars. Light was leaking around the shutters. "And what's kept up there?" I asked lightly. "A mad consort of Jafit perhaps? A deranged kanene?"

"What do you mean?" Astarth responded frostily.

"Well, you have to admit, it does rather look as if something's being . . . *kept in* up there, or hidden at least. Very gothic, Astarth, a nice touch."

My laughter did not amuse him however. His face had assumed a curiously blank expression.

"You must be tired, Calanthe. Sleep is what you need now, I think," he said, and the door was firmly closed.

That first night in Piristil, I succumbed to an exhausted slumber, stretched out on the floor in Astarth's room. In the morning, I awoke with my feet uncovered, freezing cold, my neck complaining fiercely because I'd rolled off the pallet in the night and slept on the hard floor. Across the room, I could see Astarth looking blissfully comfortable, up to the ears in thick quilts, his head buried in a mound of white pillows. As soon as I looked at him, he woke up. He has the instincts of a wild animal.

"Well, I'm glad you look different. You were telling the truth, it seems. You *are* beautiful," he said.

Normally, such words would be taken as a compliment, but Astarth delivered them without feeling. Nothing for me to work on there!

"You will never catch me lying," I said.

Astarth ignored this remark. "At least your training will be that much more pleasurable, well *bearable,* for me. As a rule, ugliness revolts me," he said profoundly. His conceit amused me. Piristil was certainly a little world of its own.

"Training," I said, without inflection, somewhat affronted, somewhat amused. I didn't know Astarth's age, but I estimated that he was anything between thirty and fifty years younger than me; a second generation Wraeththu har. "It will be interesting to see what you can teach me." The matter would clearly have to be dealt with on a scientific basis. Astarth didn't answer. Secure as a princeling of his own little kingdom, he sat up in the bed and lifted aside the curtains to glance out of the window. "Rain again," he said.

"Well, what a surprise!"

"I would like to live in a warmer country, but Jafit thinks I would find it uncomfortable," he continued vaguely. "Orpah will be bringing our breakfast in soon. You'd better dress. You don't want the servants seeing you in that state."

I groaned and lifted my cursing body off the floor. Astarth brushed me with a fleeting glance.

"Oh, scars," he said.

"A few. Will that increase or decrease my value?"

"Neither."

"I hope I'm not going to regret any of this," I said, in a cheerful tone, pulling a shirt over my head.

"Hmmm," Astarth said.

"Have you?" I asked. "Regrets I mean . . ."

Astarth stared at me. I had offended him, asked a question he did not want to answer. I put up my hands in a gesture of apology.

"I don't intend to stay in this place for long," I said. Astarth was silent. He rose from the bed, crossed to the mirror, touched his face, stretched.

"Jafit is impressed by you," he said.

I am Uigenna. This is the tribe that took us in. Uigenna. We had no way of knowing one tribe from another; we did not know they have different beliefs, different ways, different breath. Inception was ghastly. A fire-lit cellar, leaping flame shadows on the walls, a stink of filth. Inception room. Their hienama wore feathers and fur, stripes daubed across his face and chest. He took glass, a shard of glass in his hands. Someone held me down. I felt the painless, sickening kiss of sharpness against weak flesh. A transfusion of Wraeththu blood. We'd heard it was something like that. Hienama and me. His blood into my veins, humanity dripping out of me onto sand and sawdust, with a halo of whimpering. I heard Seel crying, far away, nearby, in my head. Yes, in my head. Seel would not accept inception to this tribe. I had already made up my mind. The past was powerless to persuade me otherwise, whether through love or hate. Even in my pain and fear, I did not regret. Not once. Not ever. For the next few days, whilst my body churned and changed, it was that one, fierce thought that kept me alive. It was what I wanted. I would face death to get it; and I did. And now is the time . . .

Now is the time for this virgin body to flower. I have arisen, shining, from althaia to a waiting hunger. The leader of this Uigenna tribe is known as Manticker the Seventy. This is because he once slew seventy armed human soldiers in one frenzied outburst. I can believe it. He is scarred and muscled, his femininity betrayed by his temper, his inner strength. I have only been here for a short while, yet already it is clear Manticker is being rivalled for control of the tribe. His contender is one Wraxilan, a great favorite of the warriors. He is rash and careless, but fearless and strong and quick. He carries few scars. His blond hair is shorn at the sides of his head, but as the rest of it is so thick, he still carries a splendid mane. He is also known as the Lion of Oomar, which is how our branch of the tribe is named. Wraxilan has the broad shoulders of a man, the slim hips of a dancer, the hands and neck of a graceful Amazon, the shapely legs of a whore. He laughs nearly all the time. Like all the others, I am passionately intrigued by him. Slightly afraid, yes, but that is a wise precaution. Now, I lie waiting in the straw, by the light of a single candle, in a dank cellar. I am waiting for the one who will come to me, awaken my new, female crevices, seal the pact that I have made with Wraeththu. As he comes toward me, it is his hair that I recognize first. "You," I say, and in my voice I hear the echoes of welcome and fear.

"You think I would let anyone else have you, Cal?" he answers, smiling. "You're the best we've had for a long time. Lie back. I will make this good for you."

The Lion of Oomar. He says, "I am your first. You must remember this." "No," I answer, "you are not the first. It was Seel."

He laughs and cups my chin with his hand, squeezes hard. I wince.
"No, my darling, that was before. *All that is gone, do you hear? I am your*
first. Me!" As he says that, he plunges into me. Ouana-lim, the phallus of
Wraeththu. Bone and petals, with the tongue of a snake. He enjoys my
weeping. He licks the tears from my face, and even in pain, I cannot resist the
rising delight of aruna. That is the way of it. Irresistible. At the end, he takes
my head in his hands once more.
"What am I?" he asks, and through a haze of tears, half-delirious, I say,
"You are the first. The first."
"And will you ever forget that?"
"Never. I swear it. Never."
He pushes me back into the straw. Stands up. Rearranges his clothes. As
I lie there with tears falling down my face into the straw, I can hear him
whistling as he strolls away from me.

Breakfast in Piristil is necessarily a light meal. This is because most kanene
rise late in the morning and the mid-day meal follows soon after. It is
customary for most of the kanene to meet at lunchtimes, in the dark and
elegant dining room on the ground floor. Astarth told me I could use his
cosmetics until I had some of my own.

"Is it really necessary at this time of day?" I asked.

"It is always necessary," Astarth replied in a stony voice. "You had
better get into the habit of it quickly."

He was strangely modest about displaying his body and even reprimanded me about my own carefree attitude toward nakedness. "Your
body is the tool of your trade," he said. "Get used to the idea that it is to
be flaunted only in the presence of paying clients. If you like, this is a
psychological exercise in maintaining a certain mystery about what we do."

I did not bother to argue. It was a minor point.

About an hour later, we heard the chime of a gong from downstairs.
"That is for lunch," Astarth said. "Come on. Hurry up." I was still fighting
with my hair in the mirror, not possessing Ezhno's quick knack of arranging it. I followed Astarth downstairs. It is quite amusing how the kanene
look upon themselves as creatures of quality. All day, they maintain this
genteel code of manners and behavior that would have been more at home
in an upper-class girls' boarding-school of perhaps a century before. They
are obviously not blind to their station in life, hence the need for a pretense
of class and etiquette. Downstairs, I was formally introduced to the other
kanene. Several of them were natives of the fabled land of Jaddayoth.
Salandril and Rihana, languid creatures, came from the cat-worshiping
tribe of Kalamah in eastern Jaddayoth; Yasmeen, Nahele and Ezhno from
the gregarious Hadassah; and a gaunt, forbidding-looking creature named
Flounah from the Maudrah.

After polite greetings, I took my place at the table, between a delightful
imp named Lolotea and Ezhno. Of course, as before, the usual ways of
starting a conversation were taboo, and it seemed my presence inhibited the

sharing of gossip, so I opted for a safe subject, and one in which I had a deep interest: Jaddayoth. Nobody was loath to talk about it. I learned that there are twelve tribes of Jaddayoth and, from what I could gather, they were all equally eccentric in one way or another. Most of them had formed from groups splitting off from the Gelaming, who wanted to develop their own brand of Gelaming philosophy and lifestyle, whilst others had grown from bands of refugees fleeing Megalithica at the time of the Varrish defeat. Of course, during that time, many hara were reluctant to live under Gelaming rule. This would, naturally, have meant their giving up such practices as murdering, looting, raping and conquering, and most of the hierarchy of the Varrs and their chief allies, the Uigenna, did not welcome the prospect of a world of peace and plenty. Their rituals were too steeped in the previously mentioned depravities for that. In Jaddayoth, such a vast and empty place, they had been able to hide and lick their wounds, eventually emerging as new tribes. The Gelaming, true to their all-powerful reputation, do keep a cursory eye on what goes on in Jaddayoth. Several of the tribes are, in fact, still closely allied to Almagabra, but on the whole, it is still an unsupervised country, where new societies can blossom unmolested. All natives of Jaddayoth are surprisingly patriotic about the place, even those who, for dark and untold reasons, have obviously had to leave it, such as the kanene. Obvious too was the fact that Jaddayoth is a rising star in terms of affluence and trade. In Piristil, we eat Gimrah meat and vegetables off Hadassah plates. Our perfumes and cosmetics come from Kalamah, our oil and carpets from Emunah, our wine from Natawni. It didn't take long for one clear and radiant idea to settle within me. Once I'd saved enough of my immoral earnings, Jaddayoth was the place I'd go. Privacy and freedom; what more could I want?

After lunch, Astarth excused us both from the company and took me upstairs again. "Take a bath," he said. "The water should be hot now."

"Again?" I protested. One bath a month had been luxury to me for the past couple of years.

"Yes, again," Astarth replied. "I want you thoroughly clean, if you don't mind."

I thought, "Ah, training," and complied without further argument.

Sitting in a deliciously warm bath, soaking in bubbles and steam, I found a package of cigarettes on a reachable table, plus a couple of yellowed but professionally-produced newspapers. I lit a cigarette and lay back to examine one of the papers. It had apparently come from Maudrah. This was obviously the top cockerel in the pecking order of Jaddayoth tribes. I read with interest. It was mostly propaganda stuff; how marvelous the government was, etc. About every five sentences the name of the Archon cropped up. Ariaric, Lord of Oomadrah, first city of Maudrah. If ever an election was held in heaven, this Ariaric would definitely be confident enough to run a campaign against God. From what I read, he certainly seemed powerful enough. There were a couple of muddy photographs, showing an individual whose face held the same expression and air of potential destruction as the blade of an axe. I smiled to myself. Whiffs of Terzian, I thought. Astarth came bustling in.

"What are you doing in here? We haven't got all day!"

"Who is this character?" I asked, dripping soapy water all over the paper.

Astarth took it from my hands and wiped it. "Ah, Ariaric," he said. "I've only been in Maudrah once. I've never actually seen him in the flesh."

"Now there's someone I would like to meet!" I declared with relish, putting my arms behind my head, blowing a series of smoke-rings at the ceiling. "He sounds just my type. Rich and powerful."

"And complete with royal consort," Astarth added sharply. "You certainly have a high opinion of yourself, Calanthe, I'll say that."

"Certainly not. I am perfectly at home in royal houses."

"Yes, well, you're not in a royal house now! You are a lowly kanene, that is all. It might interest you to know that Ariaric's consort Elisyin is a har of the Ferike tribe, whose wit, charm, intelligence and breeding transcends all others. You think you will ever get to Maudrah? Ha!" He laughed coldly. "You think you'll ever get near such hara as the royal family of Ariaric? You are mad, Calanthe. Chances are you'll never see the outside of Thaine!"

"OK, OK, don't distress yourself," I said, rising from the water. Astarth stonily handed me a towel. Obviously, I had hit a raw spot. It didn't take much to work out what that was. Bitterness. Astarth looked around the four walls of that bathroom as if they were a prison. Perhaps they were.

He stalked coldly back into the bedroom while I dried myself. "Ill-humor!" I thought and expected a cold reception when I rejoined him, some moments later. He was sitting on his bed, pensive in the gray afternoon light. A winsome sight. He looked up and saw me. "Come here," he said, and held out his hand. I took this as an apology for his sharp words. "Well, let's see what you can do, Calanthe." I sat down beside him and he put his arms around me, for a brief second favoring me with the pressure of his bright head upon my shoulder. It was short-lived. The flavor of that afternoon in Piristil shall stay with me forever, I think. The damp air, the sound of rain on the windows, the half-darkness of a gray, hopeless day. Little warmth reached us from the fire. I had never partaken in such a passionless, empty coupling. Aruna should never be like that. Astarth seemed dead to pleasure, his mind buried deep within his head. There was no touching of souls, no sensation of shared thoughts; nothing. Confused. I tried to change things, to bring us closer. It seemed so long since I had touched another har. I wanted it to be good. Astarth pulled my hair. "What are you doing?" he asked coldly. How those words, delivered so emotionlessly, stung is hard to convey. I had always come alive during aruna. Perhaps it is my outstanding ability. Perhaps that was why I thought I'd make a good kanene. I was wrong. Astarth and his kind are not proficient at aruna, no way. If sex is a machine, then kanene are good mechanics, but there is no way I will call what they do aruna again. It isn't. Now, I'm glad about that.

"It seems you have a lot to learn," Astarth told me resignedly.

"I'm not sure I want to," I replied. He smiled cynically.

"There are two types of pain. Pelcia and chaitra. Now I will teach them to you. Forget what you know. That is no use to you here. No use at all."

Pelcia is a corruption of the word pelki, which means violation. It involves learning how to put up a convincing resistance to the sex act. I must allow myself to be raped. Is that possible? Chaitra, simply, is the same service performed for a client. They want pain, whether delivered or received. That is what they pay for.

"Learn," Astarth said. "They don't know much. There are a hundred ways to deceive, a hundred short-cuts to the desired result. As long as they hear you squeal, they will be content."

I sat up in bed. I actually thought about leaving. Staring out of the window, I could see the depressing vista of Fallsend dropping away into a murky mist. Where could I go next? I had no money, no horse, not even any clothes of my own. It was the closest I had come to despair for a long time. Now, some of Astarth's bitterness when I'd been waffling on about going to Maudrah began to take on deeper meaning. I was trapped in a vicious circle. Unwelcome memories were coming dangerously close to the surface of my mind.

"Astarth, I have to think," I said. "All of this is going to take a little getting used to."

"Of course," he answered unctuously, as if we'd just been discussing a business venture of an entirely dissimilar kind. "Think all you want. I will see you later."

I wandered downstairs, looking for warmth, looking for company, and went into the sitting room that led off the dining room. Only one other person was in there, sitting close to the fire. Once I'd shut the door behind me, cheerfulness invaded the room. "Hi there, come in. Sit down." It was Lolotea. I smiled dimly and sat down in the window seat, my knees up, my chin on my knees, brooding sourly at the yard beyond.

"Hey," Lolotea said softly. He came and drew the curtains in front of my face. "Don't sit there. It's cold."

"Is it possible to be warm here?" I asked.

Lolotea didn't reply. He led me to the fireside and poured me a cup of coffee from a pot standing in the grate. He studied me for a moment. "In a week, you'll forget you ever felt like this."

"Like what?"

"Like the expression on your face. Don't worry. You'll get used to it. We all did."

"I can't think of anywhere else to go," I said bitterly, unwilling to accept those last words.

"There can't *be* anywhere, that's why. I'm sure you wouldn't be here if there was. None of us would."

"I think I've failed Astarth's test. Perhaps I'll be asked to leave anyway."

Lolotea shrugged. "Hmm, maybe. But if I were you, I'd sit down here for a while, warm up, smoke a few cigarettes, have a few more cups of coffee, then go upstairs and put that right. You're not stupid, are you? Just put it right."

We smiled at each other; conspirators.

"Advise me."

Lolotea smiled into his cup. "Astarth has a way of intimidating people. He looks down on everyone if they give him half a chance. This is the result of a rather large and heavy chip on his shoulder. Don't let him look down on you. Get in the first blow, so to speak. Surprise is the key to success."

"Hmm, already I feel I've learned more from you than Astarth could ever teach me," I said.

Lolotea gave another expressive shrug. "That is because I'm not trying to impose authority over you."

"Is that what Astarth's trying to do then? Just that?"

"I would think so. Astarth will be jealous of you. You spoke of plans to leave here, plans for the future. That would anger him. He resents ambition in others, mainly because he's too lazy or complacent to do anything himself. Dog in the manger syndrome. Don't you think so?"

"I can't say," I answered diplomatically, aware that any careless remarks might be repeated as gossip. "I haven't been here long enough to judge anybody's character."

Lolotea smiled politely. As he suggested, after a few more cups of coffee, I went back upstairs.

Astarth was tidying his room, something he seems to spend an awful lot of time doing, mainly moving things from one end of the room to the other. He looked up at me with annoyance. Perhaps I'd disturbed some precious, private revery. "Yes, what is it?" he snapped.

"I've been teaching myself," I answered. Luckily, I was angry. My whole, miserable set of circumstances was making me angry. Astarth's caustic, condescending tone was the final straw. I half threw him across the room. He landed with a clatter amongst some of his precious belongings. That, at least, wiped the hauteur from his face. I *do* know how to be wild. It is not something I'm proud of and I don't care to remember it most of the time, especially how and where I learnt it. When I'd finished with Astarth, he looked as if he'd just fought off the Hounds of Hell. He lay on the floor, staring up at me, dazed, and not a little frightened. I squatted down and put my face close to his. "Now remember this, my friend. It is something I want you to think about very deeply. One day, while you're still here, working on your back, I shall be back up there amongst the royal houses. Don't doubt it for a second, my darling. I don't know what keeps you here, and I don't want to, but believe me, I've lived in royal houses, I've been right up there among the angels, and I intend to get there again! Not you, your sarcasm, or your little world of sin is going to stop me. Is that clear? I'm not a whore, Astarth. I never will be. This is just a stepping stone. Got that?"

Astarth put up his hands. "OK," he said placatingly. It was the beginning of a certain mutual respect between us.

That evening, instead of staying in Piristil for the evening meal, Lolotea suggested that he and I should go down into Fallsend for a "bite to eat, a skinful of good liquor and a change of scenery." He guessed that my first day in the establishment had been a little harrowing.

"No work tonight then?" I enquired.

Lolotea pulled a face. "Well, just one, as it happens, but I managed to farm it off to Rihana. I thought you needed the company more."

We trudged down the muddy streets, past the gray and brown stalls selling gray and brown merchandise, to a tavern that Lolotea called "passable." If the food wasn't exactly haute cuisine, at least it felt warm and friendly inside and the ale was decent. Lolotea had kindly lent me the money that I owed the hostel-keeper who had kept my belongings. Knowing the labyrinthine streets of the town as well as he did, we had only had to take a short detour to call in there on the way to the tavern. After we'd finished eating and the pot-har had removed our plates, I emptied the contents of my bag onto the table, to examine what mementos I had left of my past.

Lolotea picked up a small, jewelled pin and inspected it with interest. "Hmm, this looks Varrish," he said, before he could stop himself.

"It is," I answered, taking it off him. Terzian had given it to me. Holding it, I could see once more the imposing outline of his house. Forever, feel the warmth of its hearths, smell the sandalwood perfume of its rooms. There was a moment's silence while I relived those memories, all the more painful because of the contrast between what I'd been then and what I'd become. My grief must have been unmistakable. In sympathy, Lolotea broke the first rule of Piristil.

"I came from Megalithica," he said at last.

"Me too," I replied in a thick voice, although I knew Lolotea had already guessed that.

"Look, don't answer this if you don't want to," he ventured, "but are you, were you, a *Varr?*" I looked up at him, unable to speak. He mistook my silence for something else. "I'm only asking, well, because . . . I was Varrish once."

I smiled. "Yes, I too was a Varr for a time. In Galhea."

Lolotea rolled his eyes. "Ah, *Galhea!* The nest of all intrigue! Terzian's stronghold was in Galhea, wasn't it?" This was a rhetorical question of course, but I still nodded.

"It was."

Lolotea laughed nervously. "Oh, it seems stupid, doesn't it. All this secrecy about ourselves!"

"Not if you happened to be a Varr in Megalithica around about the time I left there," I answered.

"Yes, but what does it matter now? It's over and done with, isn't it?"

"I suppose so," I agreed cautiously, "but you have to remember that the Varrs had a lot to answer for once. I expect that there are quite a few blood-debts left hanging around, even over here in Thaine. I don't think anyone will forget completely all that happened."

"Yeah, you're right, but I think most of them in Piristil have worse secrets to hide than they once used to be Varrs!" he said fiercely. "I must admit, I feel quite a sham keeping it quiet really. Look around you. The chances are nearly everyone in Fallsend had some connection with the Varrs at one time. I bet Astarth, for one, has several dark secrets lurking in his past!"

I agreed readily to that, mostly because I still hadn't forgiven Astarth for trying to humiliate me.

"I lived north of Galhea," Lolotea continued. "I once saw Terzian when he rode through on his way to Fulminir. What a hero! Everybody was virtually falling down and kissing the ground as he went by!" I laughed at this, visualizing it easily. "Did you ever see him, close to?" Lolotea queried, still tentative. "I mean, living in Galhea and all, I suppose you must have, but, well, we often used to wonder what he was really like . . ."

"I saw him," I said. I hadn't meant to put all that feeling into those words. It wasn't a deliberate clue so that I could show off to Lolotea. I just couldn't deny the feelings inside me.

"And what about Cobweb, the famous consort, or should I say the famous *first* consort? Did you ever get to see him too? Is he as beautiful as people say?"

I made an exclamation, remembering. "Oh yes! You could say that Cobweb and I actually got to cross swords a couple of times!"

"Really?" Lolotea was not sure whether to believe me or not.

"I suppose I'm saying too much," I said.

"No! Not at all. Please go on." He wasn't stupid.

"It may just be stories. How do you know I'm not making it up?"

"I'll take that risk. It's entertaining anyway, even if it is bullshit."

"What do you want to know?"

"Cal . . ."

"No, *Calanthe,*" I butted in.

"Calanthe," he said thoughtfully, staring at me very hard. I could see a certain dawning of realization creeping over his face, but it was too wonderful a coincidence for him to believe at first. He said casually, "Wasn't . . . wasn't Terzian's second consort, you know, the one that caused all the trouble in Forever, named Cal? He had yellow hair too, didn't he . . . like yours."

"He was called Cal, yes, among other things," I replied, filled with a weird kind of relief. I wanted him to know. I didn't know why. Lolotea raised his glass at me and smiled.

"It's not a common name," he said and drank thoughtfully. "Well, I'm not even going to attempt to work out why the consort of Terzian the Varr is working as a kanene in a dead-end pit like Fallsend . . . er, if he is doing so, of course! I thought that all of Terzian's family came under the protection of the Gelaming after Fulminir fell. Terzian's son went over to the Gelaming, didn't he? Swift, wasn't it? As I recall, he came out of it all very well! Some say *too* well."

"You don't know the circumstances," I said, defending Swift who certainly deserved it. "He acted in the only way possible. Galhea must be quite a mighty metropolis by this time, I would imagine."

"I don't know," Lolotea said. "I came over to Thaine before the Gelaming ever really got a hold on Megalithica. It seems we're both old crows together, doesn't it! Maybe one day, I'll tell you my story. If you tell me the rest of yours, of course!"

"That's a deal!" I said, having no intention of ever doing so. We clinked glasses, laughed, and drank. Now I had a friend. Perhaps things were not as bad as I'd thought.

CHAPTER THREE

>─┼─◆>─◦─<◆>─┼─<

Body for Sale

"I have been one acquainted with the night."
—Robert Frost, *Acquainted with the Night*

I am Uigenna. I am sixteen years old. The world has gone now, the world that I knew. My family is probably dead. I don't care. I really don't. I tell myself they never liked me. I still don't know if that is true. Seel went to the Unneah. That was because the Ugenna were too wild for him, too ferocious. We meet sometimes, on those crazy borderlands that exist in cities like this. It has changed so much in such a short space of time. I feel like I've lived for a hundred years. There is Wraeththu blood in my veins and I feel like God. Human life means nothing to me. They are so small. I hate them. I have to kill. Every time I kill, I see a mocking, threatening face. Such faces followed me in the past. Such faces drove me to what I have become. They shouted out to me, menacing, vulgar, ugly. But no more. They are dead and those that still live shall die. In the shadows of perpetual night, in the light of dancing flames, I meet a har named Zackala. We intrigue each other in an outlandish courtship. Our nuptial bed is a heap of debris, broken windowframes, wreckage of love. He bites me. We laugh. Pain makes me strong. I live in this place. It is always with me. At night, I do not dream. I just remember. There are no nightmares.

Lolotea and I returned to Piristil very late. There were several minutes of drunken giggling as we tried to sneak up the creaking stairs.

Lolotea paused by his door. "You'd better go to Astarth," he said.

I pulled a sorrowful face. "I suppose I'd better."

"Goodnight Calanthe." He closed the door on me. Astarth was asleep when I went in. I did not wake him. I curled myself in blankets on the floor and lay staring at the ceiling until I fell asleep.

The following day, Astarth informed me, with unmistakable relief, that he would be working until the evening. My training session would have to wait until then. At lunch, I took the opportunity to examine in more detail the other occupants of the house. I entertained myself conjecturing whether their eating habits gave any clues as to their personalities. Flounah glared at his food, eyeing it with suspicion and chewing distastefully. Ezhno read a book throughout the meal, shoveling forkfuls into his mouth abstractedly. Both Salandril and Rihana sorted out their food, before eating, into piles of what they liked and what they wouldn't touch. This, of course, was the only fitting behavior for hara whose tribe were reputed to be innately catlike. All of them were of averagely lovely Wraeththu appearance, which to me signified that they must all be villains of one color or another. Astarth sat at the head of the table, moodily ignoring his food and taking only wine. I had been surprised by the quality of the wine, which was excellent. Piristil was a place of contrasts.

There was a knock at the front door, which we all ignored. It came again. Sighing, Astarth fastidiously wiped his mouth with a napkin and graciously rose from the table. "Orpah!" he yelled unnecessarily as he left the room.

I had come to realize in a relatively short space of time that the staff of Piristil were inordinately apathetic about many of their duties, answering the door being one of them. Presumably, this was why Jafit had seen fit to caution me about my attitude toward them. Apart from Orpah, there were three others in the house; Wuwa, Tirigan and Jancis, who was the cook. All of them had that half-finished appearance of the unsuccessfully incepted. Relations between the staff and the kanene were not of the warmest kind.

"You have ruffled Astarth's feathers," Ezhno remarked to me as Orpah put his head around the door and said, "What?" We ignored him. I made no comment on Ezhno's observation. "Don't pull his hair too hard, that's all," he continued mildly. "Astarth is lord of the hearth in this place. He won't like it if you challenge his authority too much."

"I didn't realize I had," I said, wondering how much Lolotea had been blabbing to the others.

"Astarth perceives challenges to his authority in all kinds of innocent behavior," Flounah pointed out morbidly. Of them all, he was the most bewitching creature. Pale, attenuated, with smooth black hair like a sheet of silk. His slanted eyes must be the envy of the Kalamah. He is not to be trusted, however.

On my way upstairs that afternoon, I had my first glimpse of one of Piristil's customers. He was coming out of Jafit's office, accompanied by Jafit himself. I'm not sure what kind of monster I'd been expecting, but from what I could see, the Har looked merely ordinary. No manic eyes, no clawed hands anxious to do business with the flesh of a kanene. I had seen many such hara as warriors in my late consort's army. This har looked no different, dressed in black, scuffed leather, his hair tied behind his head, his eyes tired.

"Kruin, I'd like you to meet our latest arrival," Jafit said indulgently, as if bestowing a great honor. I bowed appropriately.

The har named Kruin inclined his head awkwardly and said, "Er . . . hello."

"Be so good as to summon Rihana," Jafit ordered, so I called "Rihana!" and went upstairs to find Lolotea.

He was in his room and invited me inside. "Comfortable!" I said.

"I try. Do you want to go into Fallsend again?"

I could tell from his voice that he hoped I didn't. "No, I don't think so. What do you usually do to keep entertained when you're not working?"

"Sleep!"

"That boring, huh?"

Lolotea lay down on his bed and stretched and groaned. "Not really. We could be artistic and paint pictures, we could tell each other stories or we could get very drunk."

"The last of those suggestions seems the most promising," I said.

"I agree. What do you want, wine or betica?"

"I've never drunk betica, so I'll have that."

"You sure?" Lolotea laughed, but sprang off his bed and poured us both a large drink. The liquor was yellow and its taste better left undescribed. However, after half a glass, the mouth is sufficiently numbed not to be alarmed by it. Lolotea flopped down on his bed again. "God, I'll be glad when you get paid, Calanthe! I don't suppose you've got any cigarettes, have you!"

"No, but you have." I helped myself.

Lolotea laughed but did not protest. "So, mysterious one, tell me about life in Galhea."

"Oh, it's not that interesting," I said. Everything that happened to me in Galhea was, naturally, intensely interesting, but I didn't like talking about it.

Lolotea thought for a moment, stroking the rim of his glass. He looked enchanting and mischievous. "Is Terzian really dead?" he asked, "or is that an indelicate question?"

He was pleased with himself for being shocking. Kindly, I tried to appear shocked. "Foully indelicate!" I answered. Lolotea raised his eyebrows. "Yes, he's dead . . ." I sat down on the bed beside him. "And no, I'm not grieving for him, before you ask. I must admit, I do sort of miss Galhea though. I had a good life there. Besides, I was rich in Galhea, I lived in a grand house; now look at me!"

"You look just fine to me, Calanthe," Lolotea remarked. I was not sure of his motive in that. He might possess a perspicacity I'd not given him credit for.

"I'm a survivor," I said.

"You will need to be here," he answered, although I didn't agree. Piristil, in its way, is just as womblike as Forever had been. No outside world. I would have liked to enlighten Lolotea about just what real survival entailed, but there was little point, and I didn't want to reveal that much about myself. Instead, because I like to turn and turn and trample in a new nest to make it comfortable, I said, "Lolotea, I would like to take aruna with you this afternoon."

Lolotea laughed and I'm quite sure that his first reaction was to ask, "why?," but it was not part of the image that he wanted me to have of him. "I hope you don't want to try out your newly acquired skills of pelcia and chaitra on me," he said with a smile.

"Is that an answer?"

"You didn't ask a question."

"OK, will you? I know it's probably not the sort of thing you do for relaxation around here, but the truth is, I'm desperate for a cuddle and need my faith restoring in physical contact."

Lolotea pulled a face. "Do you know, when I think about it, I haven't taken aruna for years, not *proper* aruna. I suppose we get kind of sexless, what with our work being what it is." He looked at me. "Maybe I need my faith restoring too. Faith! Ha!" He threw one hand over his face and laughed coldly. "What did all our dreams come to, Calanthe? Have we realized any of them? Look at us! My self-development went right out of the window as soon as my need to earn a crust for myself came in! Were we kidding ourselves that it was all going to be better? Are we really better than men?"

"Oh, give it a rest, Teah!" I said. "Leave the heavy bullshit for those who've got the time to worry about it. Right now, I want you. That's magic. No amount of failed dreams can take that away from us."

He sighed. "You're right. Undress me. And do it slowly. Let's make the best of it."

We did.

Maybe taking aruna with Lolotea woke up parts of me that had been sleeping (or catatonic), I don't know. But I remember how when I left his room that evening, the sun had struggled from its mantle of clouds; the hall and stairs of Piristil were bathed in a beautiful sunset glow. I could feel my senses, lifted with the kinder light, waking up, sniffing, looking around and thinking, "Ah yes, time for work to begin again." For too long I'd been aimlessly shuffling around the countryside, with no direction in mind, abandoning my skills, living like a scavenger. Look what it had brought me to! I might as well have been human. OK, I'd got a whole book of excuses for what might be termed my "breakdown," but the time of healing was over. No more excuses. From here, it's one way: up.

I went to Astarth. "Reporting for training," I said, with a smart and sassy salute.

Astarth shook his head and nearly smiled. "I can teach you nothing, Calanthe. From now until your room's ready, sleep with Lolotea. He can train you instead. I've asked Jafit, so it's alright. In a few days, I'll see what you've learned. OK?"

"Very OK," I said. And that was that.

We come to a place where humans still have control. It is not a large city, but from where we are stationed on the hill, it appears to cover the entire valley floor beneath us. Zack holds up his knife to the hazy sun. The clouds have not yet lifted. Pale ribbons lead into the town below us; empty roads. There is smoke rising and little sound. We begin to descend the hill. There are maybe just over a hundred of us, well-rested, well-fed. Now our leader is Wraxilan; Manticker the Seventy is no more. Wraxilan, Lion of Oomar rides a slim, brown horse that tosses its head impatiently as it picks its way down the narrow path. The Lion's hair flows yellow down his back, like girl's hair, beneath a metal helmet that covers nearly all of his head, giving him the face of some feral, gleaming animal. We trot like wolves and, before us, we can now see the barricades that have been built around the town. Feeble fortifications. Do they really think they can hold us back, stem the relentless waves of Wraeththu? We that beat patiently, like water, licking like flames, like fire. Unbeatable. Weak sunlight picks out the deadly nozzles poking through the makeshift wall before us. Tumbled automobiles, masonry and skeletal woodwork, all clothed by a rotting flesh of torn fabric. They have plundered the body of the town; she will not aid them. I allow myself to laugh. What we are doing is merely as tiresome as having to rub the sleep from our eyes in the morning, and perhaps not even as dangerous. We can smell their fear because they will have heard the tales. Just the presence of their meager defenses speaks of the fact that they have not entirely believed them. If they had, they would have run and run fast, north into the great forests where it is still possible to hide—for the time being. Instead, the fools have chosen to stay and defend their territory. Just ahead of me, the Lion of Oomar reins in his mincing horse and raises his hand. We halt. His generals confer. Half-naked, their skin shining like oiled leather, their hair arranged in savage crests, they are proud beings, the cream of Uigenna. Now the humans will be thinking, "Oh, they are so exposed, hardly shielded, unarmored," and their spirits, their paltry hopes will begin to rise. I can feel it rising, like a weak mist over the town, so soon to be burnt to extinction. The light is getting stronger now. An order is given. We pull ourselves up straight and, around me, I can see a hundred pairs of eyes light up. Nothing can quell the hysteria of potential conquest, not even when it is so easily achieved. We begin to move once more and now I can hear the voices coming from the town, half-heard-shouts, the clank of metal. They will wait until we are closer before they begin to fire. Now our shaman walks before the Lion's horse. He is robed in pale, floating stuff, his hair unbound, his arms raised. I can see, where his sleeves have fallen back, the sunlight glinting off the golden hairs on his arms. He is famed among Uigenna. His powerful voice is famous. We can hear him crooning. There is an order being given behind the barricade. "Fire!" There is a sound, it is true. It is the sound of the earth cracking, the earth stretching, the call of the fire serpents deep in their earthy lairs, but it is not the sound of gunfire. We need no further order. Wolves again, we bay and lope quickly toward the town. As I leap the barricade, I look quickly into a pair of wide and stricken eyes, looking up. My knife obliterates their expression and, for the first time that day, my skin is sprayed with blood. They cannot fight us for our shaman has poisoned them with fear. Like children, they whimper and cower. Like corn, we cut them down. There can be no pity.

The shambles of the town opens up before us. It is another vista of decay and putrefaction. There are lights that will no longer shine, shops with broken windows, whose wares have long since been looted or burned. Cars sag dismally along cracked streets, their insides gutted as if picked at by carrion-eaters, the lamps that were their eyes dimmed for eternity. Of course, humanity had turned upon their own a long time ago. We pass human corpses dangling from the lamp posts. We pass slogans of despair scrawled across walls. And still we run. "This town must be cleansed," our leader tells us and we know that. We know that so thoroughly, so lovingly. I howl and kill like the rest. Even as I plunge metal into flesh, I think, "A pity; there will be little food here." By evening, it is over. All the surviving young males have been rounded up and now stand shivering in pools of their own piss and vomit, next to the fire we have built. It is a good fire, large and potent. The magic still eats away at the hearts of the remaining man-children. They cannot lift a finger to help themselves, but even so, we look upon this as sport. Wraxilan has already chosen the best. The boy is dragged forward, weeping, kicking the dirt. I choke on despising, even though I know his mind is not his own. I never blink as his flesh is cut, nor wince as he screams, screaming still as our beloved leader's blood is instilled into the wound. A small libation, but enough. When the transformation is complete, the Lion shall take him, but not before. We are not barbarians. We know the rituals, respect the Changing. We shall tend the Incepted and help them in their passing from humanity. This town is depressing. I shall be glad to leave it. The Changing takes three days. Then the inception is fixed forever by the sanctity of aruna. The newly incepted will have haunted eyes for a while, but then they will Accept and the power shall course through their once feeble bodies. This the ways of things. This is what we have to do to the world; cleanse it. Change it. We are young, yes. Our cultures are young, yes. But the world is ready for us, you see. She wants us.

She has waited a long time for our coming. She hates humankind. They have raped her and beaten her nearly to death. We are her angels and we are the voice of vengeance. The lights go out forever all over this blighted country and the Earth shall claim back what is hers and we shall be given what is ours and the temples shall be sanctified with blood . . .

The next two weeks passed very quickly for me, while at the same time instilling within me the sense that I had been in Piristil for a long, long time. Its routines became my routines; it no longer smelled strange to me. At night I slept in Lolotea's bed (he was excused "night duty" for the time being with the clientele), and it was from him that I received my initiation into the rites of a kanene. Most of it was absurd. We did it, but then got drunk and laughed about it.

After a week, my room was ready for occupation. Orpah and Wuwa had been responsible for the decoration, so it was with no surprise that Lolotea and I found paint smears on the window and across several of the floor-boards around the edge of the room. My bed hid a bald patch in the carpet. On the day that I finally moved into that room, I stared at the bed for quite some time, trying to envisage what I must eventually do in it. I wished I had a different place to sleep in. I did not want my personal nest to be crowded by ghosts. I resolved to try and do most of my business on the carpet. I sat down on the bed and thought, "And how long is this to be my little world?" I couldn't help adding to it though, striving to make it some kind of home, however temporary. Out of my meager wages, I resolved to save at least half. Clothes, food, cosmetics, I would not have to worry about buying myself. Jafit footed the bill for those. Liquor was always available about the house. So all I would have to spend my money on was small comforts for myself. Fallsend has quite a good market, selling merchandise from Jad-dayoth and sometimes from Almagabra. I decided that as soon as I could afford it, I would buy some patterned rugs to hang on the walls and to disguise the tired appearance of the carpet. It might also help to keep the room warm. Occasionally, the open fire belched unwelcome clouds of thick smoke back out of the chimney. You see, I was thinking in terms of a certain permanency. Dangerous. I should have kept the discomfort and saved *all* my money. At first, the place smelled damp.

The Dire Time was drawing near. Sometimes, I would pass customers on the stairs, or come across them in the two sitting-rooms we had on the ground floor. I had quickly adapted to the Piristil tradition of deeply loathing those that came to buy, and was only frostily polite to anyone that spoke to me. Only in the bedroom, Lolotea told me, do we have to put on The Act. "They don't pay for us to like them, after all!"

Near the end of my first two weeks, Astarth summoned me to his room again. It was another dreary evening. Astarth looked miserable and un-comfortable. "Now, we shall have to see . . ." he muttered, convulsively wringing his hands. Maybe he was psyching himself up to find out what I'd learned. Guessing this, I infuriated him by talking about the weather, a subject which holds not the slightest fascination for either of us. "Calanthe, listen!" he cried at last. "You know why you're here. Let's get on with it, OK? I shall take the part of a client. I have to see how you will react."

In the light of the fire, stalking me, he looked feline and dangerous; his tension was power. "I can see the Wraeththu in you now," I said, and I could, for perhaps the first time. Astarth made a noise like the fire crackling. When he put his hand on my shoulder, I could feel thin, hard ropes of muscle trembling up his palm.

"Begin. Speak!" he said.

"Have you already paid for me?"

"Jafit takes the money before anyone comes upstairs."

"How much?"

"Not your concern. Never ask about money." He squatted down before me, where I sat on the carpet. "They will begin by saying something like; 'You don't want me here, do you?' How will you answer?"

I laughed. "Well, that's obvious. I shall say; 'Yes, that's true.' it won't be a lie, after all."

Astarth shook his head. "Somehow, I don't think you'll look frightened saying that, Calanthe."

"I don't think I can be frightened. Alright, I know the game. Don't look like that. I shall say, 'Please Tiahaar, don't hurt me.' Will that do?"

Astarth smiled grimly. "Simpering and lisping do not become you, but they pay for the sex, not a command performance." He put his other hand upon me. "Say it then."

I looked grave and said, "Astarth, I don't want you to hurt me." He looked strange and old in the firelight (had I been wrong about his age?), holding my eyes with a steady, flickerless gaze.

"I won't," he said, and dropped his eyes. He stood up, walked backwards two paces, turned his back, flinched and wheeled around. Before I knew what had hit me, I was half-way across the room, stars in front of my eyes. Astarth was only a stooped, carnivorous shadow against the window. I crouched into a position of defense, quite instinctively. I could see him moving. "My God, I think he means this," I thought. Had Astarth been waiting for the right moment to attack me ever since the aftermath of our first training session?

"Don't move!" he said. I didn't answer. He came at me quickly, like some monstrous spider, kicking out sideways so that my shoulder slammed against the wall. He'd been well-trained at some point, but it must have been a long time ago. Already I could see his weaknesses. I waited, then thought clearly, "Right! Now!" and retaliated. He was unguarded. Surely no client would leave his neck exposed like that? I don't know. We're not supposed to fight back in this role, are we? My fingers clamped around Astarth's windpipe, forcing his head back. He clawed at me, but sensibly gave that up when my other hand punched him in the stomach. Now we are both snarling, rolling like frenzied wildcats across the floor. It *was* exhilarating. Astarth gasped, "What in hell are you doing, Calanthe?" but in the dim light, I could see him grinning.

"It's no good," I said, pinning him carefully to the floor. "I just can't let anyone kick the shit out of me and not fight back. Perhaps, when I'm provoked, I can give pain, but I can't lie back happily and receive it."

"You're a fool!" he said. I could feel the bones grinding in his wrists.

"Enjoying it, aren't you!" I replied. That set him off snarling and spitting and twisting and flailing. I let go of his arms, let him rave for a while before slicing him under the ribs with the edge of my hand. That shut him up. I carried him to the bed and dropped him on it. He lay silent, breathing heavily, one hand across his stomach. His eyes were glass, staring out of the open curtains at a sky where there was no moon. I sat down on the edge of the bed to catch my breath. Clearly, I was far from fit myself.

"I don't think I'm going to be of any use here," I said.

"You must!" he answered vehemently and then coughed for quite some time.

I politely allowed him to finish before saying, "And what is it to you, Astarth?"

"Nothing. But Jafit will be displeased if you don't work out, that's all. He wants you here, Calanthe, not me."

"And yet it was you who was stupid enough to let me in."

He ignored that. "It's not that difficult to learn," he said. "We all had to. It doesn't come naturally, I know, but you *do* need the money."

"Yes." I sighed and rubbed at my face. "The problem is, I've always believed in aruna, Astarth. I know its magic. This pelcia and chaitra business is an obscenity. It turns my stomach."

"I know. Just don't look on it as aruna. There are other things we have to do with those parts of our bodies. Look on it as that."

"Succinctly put," I said, impressed. "And yet, I get the feeling, Astarth, that . . . how can I put this? It seems to me you perhaps don't feel the same about it as I do."

"You mean I enjoy it?" he asked in a clipped voice without any hint of shame. "Perhaps I do. It lets the anger out, doesn't it? Sometimes I feel like I want to be beaten to death. Sometimes I want to kill. You have your dreams to sustain you, don't you? I can't dream like that anymore." He turned his head away from me.

I put my hand on his shoulder and felt the flesh tense beneath it. "You want me to finish what I started?" I asked. There was a silence. "Come on!" I chided and poked him in the ribs. "Come on, Astarth!" I tickled him under the arms and he couldn't help laughing. Astarth likes it rough, it's true, but I look upon him as a kind of highly strung horse. Treat him the right way, gain his trust and you can mount him, no problem. Crude comparison, I know, but that's what living in a whorehouse does to people.

Later, we drank a bottle of wine and Astarth advised me how to behave with Jafit.

"Just get drunk," he said. "Rave like a banshee. Think female; it helps!"

"I'll try."

"Sure you will. You'll starve out there in the winter if you don't. Anyway, Jafit likes you. He won't kick you out."

I had been careful in my buttering up of the patron of this establishment. I had only met him properly twice since my first interview and that was when everyone else was there, when we all ate together. Not oblivious to the extent of my acting ability in respect of the boudoir, I realized it was important to seem indispensible to Jafit, if only for my looks. He always complimented me and I always sparkled with wit and charm in return; I squirm with shame to think about it. As Astarth and I sat by his fire, staring into the flames, sipping our drinks, Astarth said, "Don't forget the royal house of Maudrah now, will you!" I appreciated all that he meant by that.

"Thank you for your faith in me," I said. We drank to that.

The summons came next evening. Following Astarth's advice, I consumed an entire bottle of betica in the space of just over an hour. Rihana, Salandril and Lolotea watched me carefully as I did so. None of them felt capable of remarking on it. I was thinking about the few times I'd spoken with Jafit. Of course, I'd studied him keenly on all occasions, but I still couldn't work out what kind of reception I would get from him. He treated his kanene indulgently, like favored pets. He stroked their hair and pinched their limbs. They did not dislike him. I had learnt, though, that he could deal harshly with anyone who did not perform their duties properly. He always carefully examined any complaints received from the clients, although he didn't believe that the customer was always right. Lolotea said that Jafit could always tell when you were lying to him. Pickled in betica, but able to control movements and voice through years of experience of being in that state, I went to Jafit's office.

There, he offered me another drink and said, "If I appear to insult you, I don't want you to take it personally, but I suppose you know what to expect by now, don't you?"

I grinned at him helplessly.

"Take me upstairs," he said.

In my room, he sat down and looked at the table, where I saw a bottle of wine had been left opened next to two glasses. The cork lay beside the bottle. I offered him a drink, which he accepted. When I did not pour myself one, he said, "Please, join me, Calanthe," and I had to force down yet another measure of alcohol. I was dressed in a black lace robe that Lolotea had given me. It was virtually transparent. A wide, soft leather belt hung with net and chains swathed my hips. Jafit stared at me with approval. He asked me to undress, which I did.

"You have a warrior's body," he said.

"I've lived rough for a while," I admitted.

"I expect you want to be left alone now, huh?"

"What?" He didn't look at me. It was part of the performance.

"Yes," I said with convincing bitterness. "I want to be left alone."

"Why, is no-one good enough for you?" he asked and I looked at him sharply. His eyes warned me to silence before I spoke.

I smiled to myself, tapping the table with idle fingers. "No, as a matter of fact, they're not," I agreed.

Jafit nodded appreciatively and for a brief time, we smiled together. "You're just filth," he said.

"You think so?"

"I'm going to show you just how much I think so."

I decided to scream. Jafit nearly laughed. Then he lunged at me. He didn't really hurt me, just pushed me around a little. We ended up on the bed, me struggling, him trying not to laugh at my amateurish lamentations and then, half-way through, forgot what we were supposed to be doing and started enjoying ourselves. I remember saying, "Why Jafit, you're not so much of a rat as I thought!"

"We all just try to make a living Calanthe," he answered, "but you're no kanene, that's for sure. What the hell are you doing here?"

I shrugged. "Being employed by you, I hope."

He shook his head. "Alright. I'm not sure what I can do with you yet, but you're beautiful enough to be given a chance. Just don't fuck up, that's all! Piristil's clientele can be very pernickety."

"I'll try," I said, meaning it, surprisingly.

In the morning, Jafit stayed with me for breakfast. I still thought he looked mean. He is dark-skinned and wears his black hair short. I bet he too had rather a colorful history. He dipped hot, buttered muffins in his coffee, and said, "You're going to be bored a lot of the time, I think."

"Oh, I've decided to write my life story," I answered airily.

"Really! As your employer, I think I shall have to demand that you show me every thing you write."

"And what makes you think my life story is worth reading?"

"Last night," he answered. "Your veiled mind. I'm curious about what's going on in there."

"Mmm, well, talking of veils, Jafit, why are *you* here? Is it just that you've always wanted to be a pimp? Have your realized your life's ambition here in Piristil?"

He laughed good humoredly. "Why are any of us here? It's a bolt-hole isn't it? I hope you're not going to record any of this conversation for posterity."

"Not if you'd rather I didn't," I lied.

"The Gelaming want to ask me a few questions . . ." he said darkly, which was all he had to say.

I nodded to show my understanding. "Ah well, come to think of it, I suppose Fallsend is quite a charming place to retire in," I said.

It is late in the day when the summons comes. A young har stumbles in through the broken door, tripping over the rubble; bricks, cloth, bones. Zack and I are eating dogmeat that we have roasted in the fire. Our companions hurl gentle obscenities at the newcomer. His face reddens. He says, "The Lion sent me." That shuts us all up. We are all thinking, "Have I transgressed at all? Have I?" It is rare that Wraxilan bothers with any har save his own elite.

"Which of you is Cal?" asks the messenger in a brave voice. He is one of Wraxilan's body-servants. We both envy and despise him.

"What do you want with him?" I ask.

"A message . . ."

"I'll take it!" Zack springs up and snatches the rolled missive from the young har's hand. The messenger protests, but Zack just pushes him aside. He unrolls the note.

"But it is for the yellow-haired alone!" squeals the messenger.

"What does it say?" I ask, my body heavy with dread.

Zack makes a sneering, angry sound and throws the note to me.

"What does it say?" our companions ask, all leaning forward. I stand up.

"That easy, is it?" Zack asks coldly. "He calls, you go. That easy?"

I am silent. I have been summoned, that's all, but I am silent. I buckle on my belt, which carries my knives and darts. Zack picks up a bone from the floor. "See this?" He says. "Dog-meat! Ha!" he throws the bone into the fire, where it sizzles for a while. We stare at each other.

"See you later," I say, and walk away. There is no sound from those sprawled around the fire, but I am quite sure, once I am out of earshot, they will begin to talk.

The Lion of Oomar has made his headquarters inside an old supermarket. I have never thought it a good choice, but apparently the liquor shelves were well stocked when his company moved in. A warehouse and storerooms at the back are the private living quarters of the elite. I am shown within. The Lion is there with a bunch of sleek hara, all sitting round a fire. They are laughing together. Wraxilan does not look up when I approach, but he knows I'm there, alright. He says, "Take him to the inner room," and the har who is my guide, grabs hold of my arm and drags me off. It is most unnecessary. I am locked in an unlit cell. I sit down on the floor to wait. He is not that cruel. He comes very soon. He comes in alone and sits with his back against the wall opposite me.

"I am glad you came," he says, as if I'd had a choice. I say nothing. He is magnificent, in the way that all conquering heroes are magnificent; intimidating, confident, strong. "Give me your knife," he says and I comply. It is not my best blade, however. Wraxilan makes a small cut in his palm, holds out his hand to show me. "See this, Cal," he says. "This is yours."

"My blade? My wound?"

"No; your blood. Here, take it." Warily, I put my hand in his. He squeezes it. "Outside, the shamen are waiting. The ritual will not take long."

"Hey!" I pull my hand away, hug it to my chest. "What are you talking about? What ritual?"

"Don't be afraid, Cal. Don't you remember? I marked you a long, long time ago. The Nahir-Nuri of the north were here some days ago. They are

pleased with my progress. Soon, I shall have my caste level raised again. You know what that means? Soon, I may activate the real magic, the one we're not that sure about yet. Can we conceive new life within our own bodies? That will be the test, won't it! If we're wrong, then we might as well give up and leave what's left of the world to Mankind. It is the test, Cal. I need a vessel. The best. I need a consort. The best. I need you."

During this speech, I have backed right up against the wall, trying to push my body through solid concrete. I have never felt such fear. I know he means what he says. The Lion always means what he says. True magic. No-one has achieved it yet. If it is possible at all, it may kill me. We know so little. We have never been women. These things are mysteries to us. Trial and error. We may be wrong.

"Come on now," Wraxilan says in a reasonable voice. He stands up and wipes his hands on his chest. "Cal, come on!"

"No." It is such a small sound. I don't think Wraxilan believes he has heard it at first.

"What?!"

My voice becomes stronger. "I said no, Wraxilan." I too stand up.

"Do you know what you are saying? I am your leader, Cal. You can't just say no! I've decided your future."

"No, you haven't." I back toward the door, still nursing the hand that has touched his blood, as if it were me that had been cut.

"Don't you understand what I'm saying?"

"Yes. I understand."

"Then . . ."

"I don't want to do it."

"I could have you killed."

"I know." For some reason there are tears in my eyes. We fight like men, we weep like women. "I know."

I reach the door. There is a brief, electric silence. He can now give the order if he wants to. He can shout, "Kill him!" but he doesn't. He says, "If you will not agree to this, you know you must leave, don't you."

Banishment, in these times, is not as trivial as it sounds. It is important, very important, to have the protection of a strong tribe behind you. Life is a gamble, dangerous, deadly. I nod my head. I understand.

"It is your choice," he says in a soft, venomous voice. If he could have said different words, if he could have . . . but no. We are Wraeththu. All that lies dead in the world of men. I walk away. By the time I reach Zack and the others, I am weeping openly. I am afraid of the Outside. I tell Zack we have to leave. He says nothing, but gathers up our belongings. Within an hour, Wraxilan's guards have burst into the ruin that is our home.

"To the perimeter, you!" one of them snarls at me and swipes me across the shoulder with the barrel of his gun. Zack puts his arm around me. We walk away and the guards follow us to the edge of the safe zone. "No Uigenna will take you in," they say. "Get going! Now!" They fire at our feet. Humiliated, we have to trot away. No Uigenna. We are unthrist; tribeless. We go to Seel, *of course. The Unneah know more of the ways of peace than the Uigenna. It is not that bad. Sometimes at night, I think of the Lion. I see his face. One day, when I am older, I might recognize that expression as being the one of hurt, of rejection, but not for a long while yet. Throughout my life, this scenario shall be replayed several times. In Terzian I loved the Lion. An exorcism? Maybe, but it is not over yet . . .*

CHAPTER FOUR

Discovery of the Big Cat

"And in the idle darkness comes the bite
Of all the burning serpents of remorse;
Dreams seethe, and fretful infelicities
Are swarming in my overburdened soul."

—*Maurice Bearing (from the Russian of A. Pushkin) Remembrance*

I have been writing now for over a week. I find it cleansing, refreshing; it is good for me. Perhaps I have grown stronger because now I am facing the biggest, blackest door in my mind and am prepared to open it a little. I must continue to heal myself by facing the past. Lolotea thinks he has discovered my secret and that it is Galhea and all that happened there, but the truth is my real secrets come from a time way before I'd ever heard of Terzian. The biggest of them remains yet undiscovered, unspoken. Once, in Galhea, Cobweb, who is a true mystic, had a vision. He spoke these words; "I shall be left alone and there will be a time of glass, like shattering, like shards of light, and the past shall come back like a shimmering veil . . . I shall be left alone, but not for long . . ." At the time, I thought he uttered those words for himself, but now I know better. It was spoken for me.

Once Jafit knew about my desire to write in my spare time, he presented me with utensils for the task. The pen has my name on it; how sweet. I think he must have had a glowing report about me from my first customer. It was luck rather than effort. He was yet another refugee from Megalithica. He asked me to twist his neck. I barely paused before obliging. Jafit obviously considers it safer to use me for chaitra rather than pelcia. Perhaps he guesses my inability to accept pain gladly. Part of me dreads that I may come to actually like it, like Astarth. I didn't tell the har I'd once lived with Terzian, although his name was mentioned. Terzian's name is always mentioned when speaking of Megalithica, even after all this time. Terzian was good to me. I must take care not to abuse his memory.

Last night, I was woken up by a terrible noise in the house. By the time I'd sat up in bed, it had faded away. I was still and silent, straining to hear more, wondering if it had just been part of a dream. Lolotea's room is next to mine. I thought about banging on the wall. Had he heard it too? But perhaps it was just another of the kanene entertaining a client. Although Jafit prefers most of them to be kicked out before we go to sleep, special customers sometimes stay all night. I lay awake for a few minutes, listening. The sound did not come again. It had sounded like an animal in pain; hair-raising. One single, desperate wail, cut off. The darkness around me seemed very thick, almost breathing. Outside, it was no longer raining, but I could hear loud dripping sounds in the yard. Whatever water fell there must be black, or red.

It was colder the next day. Winter is approaching fast. Soon, I hope, the cheerless appearance of Fallsend shall be covered with a cosmetic blanket of snow and ice. It had taken me a week to get round to writing again; I'd been rather preoccupied.

When I first woke up, I'd forgotten about the eerie howl in the night. I took my breakfast into Lolotea's room and we started some idle conversation about going into the town later on.

"By Aghama, but it's cold!" Lolotea said. "It's enough to freeze the howl in a dog's throat!" That reminded me.

"That reminds me, Teah," I said. "Last night, I was woken up by the most godawful noise. Is the place haunted or something? Did you hear it?"

"What kind of noise?" he asked, somewhat too warily, I thought.

"Well, it was rather like the complaint you might make if you'd discovered someone had just cut your throat. You know, kind of spooky, and, well, *despairing.*"

Lolotea laughed. "How melodramatic! Can't say I heard it and no, the place isn't haunted. Must have been a dream."

"I'm sure it wasn't."

Lolotea shrugged. I felt he was hiding something.

Strangely enough, nobody else appeared to have heard it either.

"Probably just a cat in the yard." Ezhno said. "Why let it bother you?"

But, by this time, my senses were alerted and I wouldn't let it rest. I'd not lived this long in the wilds, in war-torn cities and wastelands not to recognize a harish scream when I heard one. I don't like to be in a situation where things are kept hidden from me. It's dangerous. Because of that, it was no coincidence that my feet led me in the direction of those shuttered rooms I'd seen above the kitchens. Piristil is a confusing place to explore. I kept finding myself in dead ends off corridors that led nowhere. Retracing my steps several times, I eventually emerged into a passage that had barred windows on the righthand side, looking out over the yard. This was more like it. Several of doors I tried were locked. I turned a corner to the left. Here, the passage was darker. I came across another door, almost by

accident, in the shadows. I reached for the handle, turned it. It was un-
locked. Just as I was about to push it open, a voice shouted, "Hey!" and
a heavy hand landed on my shoulder. Ducking, I pulled away. Behind me,
a tall and impressively muscled har seemed to fill the passageway.

"What are you doing here?" he demanded, in a manner that was unmistakably hostile.

"I live here," I said, suitably affronted.

"Not in this wing you don't. Now get out!"

"Why? What's going on in here?" I did not expect enlightenment and
was not disappointed.

The har waved an enormous fist in my face, quite menacingly. "Out!"
he growled.

I stood my ground for a moment, before walking back the way I'd come.
This branch of investigation was obviously proving fruitless.

I went looking for Astarth. He was in the kitchens, menu in hand,
supervising the dinner arrangements.

"I've just been accosted!" I said. He raised an eyebrow and politely
listened to my outraged explanation; I know how to act when I need to.

"I'm sorry that happened, Calanthe," he said, "but I should have
warned you. Don't wander about up there."

"Why not?"

"That's Jafit's business."

"Oh, a house secret!" I cried, as if delighted. "How marvelous!"

"Don't go meddling," Astarth said. "Jafit will not be pleased."

What was behind the locked doors? I did not sense danger, not exactly.
It was just another flavor of the house; Piristil of soot and perfume and
forlorn, leftover food. The corridors were cold here. Someone howling in
the night. A sound like an animal, becoming clearer in my mind all the time.
It was not despair; it was anger. I would find out why eventually.

Kruin was my second customer, and one destined to become a regular. The
first time he set foot in my room, I could tell that half of him hates coming
to this place. He was uneasy, giving off whiffs of profound guilt and
self-loathing. I wondered what he wanted of me. I think I warmed to him
because he looks Varrish; the same ropy, muscled look, tawny hair, restlessness. "I am Natawni," he told me. The name was familiar; a Jaddayoth
tribe.

"You'll wear a hole in my carpet," I said. He ceased striding up and
down.

"I have to explain before we . . . well, in my tribe, some aspects of aruna
are forbidden to us."

"The delights of pelcia and chaitra? Don't worry. They are forbidden to
just about every tribe."

He shook his head in irritation. "No."

"Then please explain."

"It is because of our god," he said hesitantly. "The Skylording. Like us, he is the two in one; bisexual. His priests, the Skyles speak with Him often and He has decreed that for the warriors of the tribe, there should be a special code. Our affinity with each principle, either male or female, must change with the seasons. Thus, in spring and summer, we are female, and on the cusp of the changing season, the procreation of harlings takes place as our sexuality shifts toward the male. For the autumn and winter, we are masculine. It is the curse of the warrior caste! We must not deviate from our decreed affinity lest we harm the blood of our children. The other hara of the tribe respect this code; they would never transgress it. Why should they? It is not their problem. It is early winter here. I am in the masculine phase. I desire warmth. I desire . . . submission . . ."

"You desire to be soume," I finished for him.

He smiled timidly. "Of course, you find nothing unusual in that. Don't mock me, Calanthe! The code of my tribe runs very deep within me. By this transgression, I taint my love of the Skylording. I risk the lives of future harlings."

I doubt it, I thought, but kept it quiet. "You must be very weakwilled, Kruin," I said. "I've seen you here often."

He bristled visibly. "I'm a long way from home. I have no friends in Fallsend. I do not have to justify myself to you!"

"No, of course not." I shoved a drink in his hand. "Here. How come you're in Fallsend anyway?" I sat him on my bed and began to unlace his jacket. The workmanship was exceedingly fine, the leather soft as living skin.

"Trade," he said. "I come from Orligia, a town in southern Natawni. Once a year, we bring leatherwork to the market in Fallsend. That way, we pick up trade that might otherwise be missed if we operated only in Jaddayoth. The Emunah export to Fallsend, but of course, we would lose a lot of profit using them as brokers."

"How many of you are there?"

"Four. The others don't know I come here. They think I visit a har in some corner of the town, but they don't suspect it might be a kanene. If they did, they'd draw their own conclusions, of course."

It was clear why Jafit had sent Kruin to me, for he wasn't seeking the ultimate in pain and repletion, but merely aruna in its simplest and most pleasing form. I took delight in his lean, hard body, which is how I prefer them. Lolotea and Astarth were sleek, it is true, but they had a certain *softness* about them, which came from their easy existence. Kruin had warm skin. His limbs were supple and our melding was harmonious. His tribe are also called the People of the Bones. He wore thorns of bone in his ears. I learned he was anxious to return home before the snows became too deep. "Jaddayoth can be a harsh place in winter," he said. Before he left me that night, he gave me one of his earrings, placing it in my ear himself. Half-way through the night, it woke me up because it had happily burrowed itself into the side of my neck. That was the first time blood stained my bedsheets; hopefully the last!

* * *

We leave debts in every town. We are notorious. Our lives have become a sort of daring, a desire to tempt Fate. Perhaps we feel immortal. The Unneah are far behind us now; we had little in common with them. Hara are looking for us, some to settle scores, some to ask for our services. We have a lot of money because of that. Zack grows more beautiful every day. He blooms like a strong, dark-petalled flower on a grave; what sustains him, sleekens him, is probably corrupt. I am half afraid of him. He is too wild, too reckless, too ephemeral. Flowers only bloom for a short time, don't they? It is night-time and this city is damp. Yellow lights flicker, but don't dispel the shadows. There are noises in every alley. We are armed with knives and guns; we are sleek. There is a red light above the door to a bar, lending an alien cast to those that stand beneath it. They part to let us pass within. The place is packed with Hara, the air dense with smoke. Much noise; music. Zack sits down at a table and begins to clean his nails with the point of a knife. I go to the bar. Someone speaks to me there. They tell me something important. I give Zack a beer and tell him we have enemies in this place. He shrugs and smiles. We drink. We talk of where we shall go next. Zack's teeth are very white and feral in the livid light. Someone comes to our table. Zack doesn't stop smiling, although we alert each other with our eyes. There is a conversation and, during this conversation, I pull out a gun. There is a shot, the ripping of flesh and bone, a red spray. Those seated behind us make noises of disgust and annoyance, as the body falls across their table; glasses, liquor flying all over the place. Everyone is looking at us, some smiling, some shocked and, inevitably, some angry. People have died before in this bar. What I've done is not that unusual but Zack still thinks we should leave. I agree. There are too many of the dead Har's friends here. We walk to the door and, once outside, begin to run. We run through the wet, dark streets. Zack is laughing out loud. We become aware of footsteps behind us, running, echoing. The city seems empty. A car prowls by emptily; black, silent and shining. We do not know this place, but we are not afraid. We run. And. . . . They corner us at the end of a dismal, filthy alley. There are trashcans, boxes everywhere; a dead dog with an open mouth. Zack turns panting. A distant light reflects off the blade of his raised knife. The wall before us is high, but it is our only way out. Zack puts the knife between his teeth. "On my shoulders!" he mumbles, past the blade. "Hurry!" I tuck my gun into my belt and scramble up his body. His muscles are trembling. "Hurry, for fuck's sake, Cal! They're nearly here!"

"OK!" My hands curl over the top of the wall. It is wet and slimy. I don't feel strong enough to pull myself up, as if all my strength is draining out of my feet. Should we stay and fight? We will die, almost certainly, but can we escape? Is there enough time, is there?

"Cal, for God's sake!" Zack is angry. He pushes me up and I lie on my belly on the wall. There is a clatter. My gun drops down on the other side.

"Oh, fuck it!"

"Cal!" Zack's voice is low. I look up the alley we have just come down. A gang of hara is approaching. They are now only feet away from us. They have

stopped running. Their breath is steaming. They are so silent. Then one of them begins to move.

Zack turns his face up to me. "Pull me up!" he says and reaches toward me. There is no time. I have no weapon. There is not enough time. "Cal!" One by one, behind him, the predators begin to move. Some of them are smiling. They look so furtive. "Pull me up! For fuck's sake, Cal, pull me up! What's wrong with you?!" There is disbelief in Zack's voice, a certain crack, a certain realization that I cannot, will not help him. "Cal!"

I stand on the wall. It is just seconds, but seconds that pass like hours. Everything is so slow. I am turning. Below me, on the other side of the wall, is safety and another alley. Just seconds. I am turning, so slowly, steam-light, neon, damp, viscous walls. A distant shout. I am turning. Noises below me are the howls of the pack.

"Cal!"

At last, desperation. He is afraid. I love you, Zack. I pull myself up, to jump.

"You fucking bastard! Cal!"

He can't believe I'm turning away. But then, he does believe. I feel something hit my arm. A brick. A dead dog. A curse. Who knows? I have heard many curses. I land on the other side of the wall, closing my ears to the sounds; the sickening, dull sounds of flesh under attack. I land on feet and hands and my arm buckles. I look. I am wet and warm. It is blood; Zack's knife in my arm, to the hilt. With a sad, desperate cry, I wrench it from the flesh. I can feel nothing. I stumble, I start to run. I keep on running.

We thought we were immortal. Now we are both dead . . .

Jafit sent for me the next day. "Kruin speaks well of you," he said, sitting behind his desk, looking authoritative.

"Perhaps I've found my vocation then."

Jafit smiled thinly. "Sit down, Calanthe," he said. I did so. He leaned forward over his desk. "Now, Astarth tells me you've been asking one or two awkward questions, nosing around in places where you shouldn't be."

"Well, I . . . er . . ." I raised my hands in vexation, pulled an apologetic face.

"Hmph. Quite the curious cat, aren't you!"

The fateful proverb paraded before my mind's eye. "Mysteries intrigue me, perhaps. But if you want to rap my knuckles, Jafit, please go ahead."

"Does that mean you won't try to find out what's up there now?"

"I didn't say that! What's the matter? Don't you trust me?"

He laughed. "Trust you? That's a good one! We're both hara of maturity, Calanthe. Is there a place for trust in this day and age?"

"If there is, it is certainly south of Thaine," I said.

"Quite so!" Jafit agreed. "No, I don't trust you, Calanthe, but I'll let you in on the secret. You've been here long enough. Anyway, it's not that terrible a thing."

"I'm all ears."

"Drink?"

"If you like."

He went to his cupboard. "There *is* a har up there, you're right," he said, filling two glasses with betica. "Want to know why I keep him locked up? OK here." I took the glass. "Three years ago, I traveled to Meris, a town in Emunah. It is not a journey I make often, but some merchandise is only available to us inside Jaddayoth. Astarth had given me a list this long," he made an appropriate gesture, "of things to buy. Now, as you know, slavery is outlawed everywhere that the Gelaming's claws can burrow into, but if there is going to be such a thing, Emunah is the place to find it. I got wind of a black market slave auction. My contact was going along and he asked me if I wanted to take a look. I was curious. I went with him. Now, normally, I'd never even consider accruing kanene in that way. Slaves are more trouble than they're worth. They rarely provide a good service, but . . ."

"Ah, something out of the ordinary?"

Jafit smiled and sat down again. "You could say that. This one particular Har . . . I'd never seen anything like him. Obvious that he had Kalamah blood, but there was something more. Beauty didn't come into it."

"How romantic!" I said. "Of course, you bought him."

Jafit nodded, smiling. "Cleaned me out, naturally! Astarth was most put out! I came back to Piristil with nothing but a slave."

"So what went wrong? Why the bars?"

"Hmm, well, it was a nightmare from the start! I wasn't surprised that he was uncooperative—that was only to be expected—but his ferocity and sheer madness, that was not something any of us were prepared for. The first client I sent him barely escaped with his life. He lost an eye!" Jafit shook his head miserably at the recollection. "Could have been nasty, more than that, money completely wasted. Then Astarth came up with an answer. We would use the slave's violent nature as an attraction. Some Hara pay me dearly for that kind of sport. And here was a kanene who did not have to act! His name is Panthera, by the way. I sell him for the fight."

"And he still has to be locked in?"

"God, I should say so! He escaped three times in the beginning. Three times I had to pay trackers to bring him back. In every instance, they barely succeeded. Panthera is half-Kalamah and half-Ferike. Because of that, he possesses brains, stealth and cunning to an exceptional degree. The har you discovered in the corridor up there is a Mojag. I have three of them on my payroll. Mojags are the most fearless, warlike tribe of Jaddayoth. Only they can keep Panthera in Piristil."

"So, an insane beauty kept in chains," I said. "It really *is* romantic."

"There is little romance about Panthera," Jafit replied drily. "He is sullen, uncommunicative and vicious . . . but lovely. Some hara pay me just for the privilege of looking at him."

"Well thanks for telling me, Jafit," I said "It was a great story."

"Don't thank me yet," he replied. "There was a reason. The staff won't go near Panthera. Astarth and the other kanene see to his needs. They don't like it but that's just tough. Consider yourself in, Calanthe. If any one can handle that wildcat, I think it's you."

"From whore to housemaiden in a single step! Is this a promotion?"

Jafit smiled without humor. "You'd better meet him," he said. "I'll take you now."

Nobody had ever created a pedestal for Panthera, but from the moment I first saw him, I created one there and then out of pure thought-form, and put him right on it. Wreaththu have spawned many legends. I remember the ones I've known; the Varrish Cobweb, the Kakkahaar viper Ulaume and, of course, Pellaz, Tigron of the Gelaming. Men had their goddesses, women named as the most beautiful and potent creatures that god could create. Wraeththu surpass all that. In them, beauty is complete because it is both male and female; the way it should be. Jafit knocked on Panthera's door and one of the Mojags opened it to us. I could see the other two sitting at a table engrossed in some kind of boardgame.

"Well, there you are," Jafit said. "Feast your eyes on that."

Panthera sat apart from the others, straight backed, on a stool, looking down into the yard through the bars of the window. The room was very light, tastefully decorated, pale hangings on the walls, soft, pale carpet underfoot. Panthera turned and examined us carefully for a moment, as a cat may examine a movement in the corner of a room. His green eyes were as cold as stone, his wild, thick hair tied up, his shoulders bare and bruised. I noted that his hands clutched each other in his lap. He was chained to the wall. He was, as had been implied, incredibly lovely.

"Well, there you have it," Jafit said, "A Wraeththu legend." Panthera turned away quickly. "How's he been today?" Jafit asked the Mojags, Huge things, they were, magnificent and deadly.

"Quiet, I'd say. Quiet," One of them said and the other two laughed.

"What's all that?" Jafit inquired, pointing to Panthera's bruised shoulders. The Mojags shrugged. They did not think it was any of their business. "Here, let me see that." Jafit went and put one tentative hand on Panthera's arm. Panthera did not resist. He ignored Jafit. Jafit pulled the material of Panthera's robe down to reveal his back. He made an angry noise. "Look at this!" he said. "This is too much! What do they think they pay me for?"

I sauntered forward to have a look. It seemed like Panthera had been mauled by a pack of wolves. Some days ago, too, by the look of the damage. The bruises were yellowing, the scratches dark and crusty.

"Well that's somebody who won't be coming here again!" Jafit decided.

"What do you expect us to do about it?" one of the Mojags asked gruffly, sensing criticism of their work. Jafit shook his head. He brushed the comment away with a brusque wave of his hand. Panthera looked as if he was on another planet for all the notice he took of what was going on.

"I'll let you rest for a while," Jafit told him. Panthera still did not respond. I looked on in amazement. "Panthera, this is Calanthe," Jafit said as if speaking to an imbecile. "He's going to help look after you." Panthera actually looked at me. His disdain was withering. He sighed through his nose and turned away again. "Come on, Calanthe," Jafit said. "You can start your duties in a day or two."

Outside the room, I said, "Jafit, that isn't slavery. That's a life sentence in hell."

"Oh come on, everywhere in the world is somebody's sentence, somebody's hell," Jafit replied equably. "Don't be squeamish Cal, it could be you sitting there. Count your blessings."

"Maybe" I said. "And the name's Calanthe, nothing else."

Jafit smiled. We walked away.

It could be me sitting there. . . . A sobering thought. I really should not care about anybody else but myself. Why put myself in danger? What would it be like to be chained to a wall? That night a har came to my room seeking chaitra. I gave it to him alright. His was the miserable face of someone given all the gifts of God, who was throwing them back without gratitude. His was the face of perfection turned to corruption. His was the face of Fallsend. I knew it couldn't be the har who'd rearranged the flesh of Panthera's back, but it helped to pretend it was. He left me a chastened creature. I lay on the bed and smiled. There were no gifts for me that night.

Red sand. Red pony. I ride away from those that succoured me. I am healed— in body. The desert has power; Mankind has barely touched it. It is soothing. After a few days, I ride into a one-horse peasant town. I have a feeling something will happen here. It does. I see him, framed in a doorway. Peasant boy, all hair and eyes, but such eyes! They know so little here. They do not know what I am. I watch him constantly. Here is beauty, I think. Yes, here it is. A healing loveliness, but human. "I am Pellaz," he tells me and he smiles; a nervous, bright smile of the uncorrupted. I am death, little child. I will lie to you. I cannot let you know me because I want you. I ride through the mist on a steamy afternoon, through red mud on a red pony, stolen money in my pocket, a stolen smile on my face. I ride toward him and he tells me his name. The first, fateful magic. Now I will have you, little one. It is so easy. I steal him away, like the money, like the pony, into the wilderness, that is not just a waste of stone and sand, but a wilderness of the spirit because he is leaving the world he knows. He looks back and I think, he will go back. He has realized, and he will go back. But he merely sighs and follows me. There is something powerful and untrained inside him. He must become har—and quickly. Seel has a stronghold in the desert mountains. I shall take him there. He shall be made Wraeththu. Then he will be mine. Healing balm, healing feelings; his innocence shall cleanse me and make me whole. I'll wake up and the world shall be new and my smile shall come from the inside, black memories forgotten. Please don't let him see me kill.

* * *

"Tell me about Jaddayoth," I said to Kruin.

He smiled. "It wouldn't mean anything to you."

"How do you know that?"

He shrugged. "You're a kanene. Part of the Wraeththu rubbish heap. There are no kanene in Jaddayoth. No Fallsend."

I was stung. "You know nothing about me!"

"Only what I need to know."

"Fuck you, Natawni. Fuck you!" He laughed and I stood up, pulled aside the curtain to my window. Across the yard, a yellow light burned in Panthera's window. "Look at that," I said. I felt Kruin's warmth before he touched me. He kissed my neck. "Look at that."

He looked. "What?"

"The light. Do you know what they keep in there?"

"Yes; doesn't everybody?"

"I'm not part of that."

"You don't have to be here."

"That's where you are wrong my friend, I do."

He sighed and went to lie down again on the bed, pouring himself a glass of wine. "I don't care, Calanthe. I don't want to know."

I threw some more logs on the fire. All the light in the room was orange-red. Kruin didn't want to know about me because he despised me. It was I that broke his tribal code; not him. The scapegoat. Rubbish. God, I shall not stay here long, I thought.

"Tell me about Maudrah?" I said.

"What about Maudrah?"

"Ariaric." I was thinking of Terzian again.

"You wouldn't like Maudrah," Kruin said. "It's a gaunt, severe place. It's people are gaunt and severe. They have no sense of humor."

"Then I will feel very at home there. I'm rapidly losing my sense of humor!"

"Stick to fantasizing about the big cats in this place, if I were you! Forget the Lion!"

"What do you mean?" (Why did I go cold?)

"Ariaric. Panthera; you know. Panthera's half-Kalamah; his name comes from panther. They call Ariaric the Lion . . ."

I did not hear what else he said. My mind was singing with white noise. When I came out of it, Kruin was saying, "Soon I shall be going home, thank God!"

It was a coincidence, surely . . . *surely.* I shivered.

"I wish you'd known me before, Kruin," I said.

Later, I woke up from a terrible dream. I was standing before a huge dam, which began to crack. I knew I was going to drown, but the dam was so huge and I was so small. There was nowhere I could run to. The flood-gates to the past have been opened. It has found me. I never thought I could think of Pell, but I have. I have written his name and our beginning. Something I have been afraid to admit, but now I will; they are watching me constantly. The Gelaming. In daytime, I rarely think that, but at night . . . I can almost *feel them.* I am not afraid of Pellaz, but I know I would run if he appeared before me. It was all so long ago. Now he is Tigron and I committed murder because I lost him. No-one here knows this. No-one ever shall. Perhaps it's all part of an absurd dream I once had. Pellaz; we knew each other once.

Morning. I awoke with a thick head and Astarth ripping aside my curtains to let a brutal light into the room. "Come on, get up!" he said. "What's this? Two empty betica bottles? You're disgusting, Calanthe! Come on; up! Get dressed! We have work to do!"

"What time is it?" I croaked, squinting at my clock. "Jesus! It's the middle of the fucking night, Astarth! What the hell are you doing here?"

"Language!" Astarth corrected mildly. "Zoo duty. Come on."

My turn to help wait on Panthera. It woke me up a little. Still putting on my clothes, I followed Astarth who was stalking down the corridor. He carried a tray of food. "The staff are afraid of Panthera," he told me, when I caught up with him.

"Why's that? Blacks their eyes does he?"

Astarth laughed. "No, worse than that. He spits out very convincing curses."

"And as we despicable kanene consider ourselves cursed already, his words cannot harm us, eh?"

"Something like that. Hardfaced creatures, aren't we."

"I feel honored!"

"Don't be. Panthera will hate you as he hates all of us."

We turned the corner into the long, shuttered corridor.

"What do you think of him, Astarth?" I asked.

Astarth raised a thoughtful eyebrow. "He's beautiful. What else can I say? If you look like that, being conceited, arrogant and insulting doesn't really matter, does it!"

No pity on Astarth's part, obviously.

The Mojags opened the door to us. Two of them were going off duty. "Don't envy you today," said the third. "We've not dared let him loose yet. He's got killing eyes today!"

"Oh, come now Outher," Astarth said lightly, "surely you're not afraid of our little pussy cat."

"See this?" Outher said to me, displaying a splendid scar on his neck. "It's not fear; it's respect." I smiled politely.

"OK, take a break, Outher," Astarth commanded. "Calanthe and I can handle it."

There were curtains around the bed, blowing softly in a cold, light breeze. One of the windows was open. The bars beyond it were glistening with ice. I could see my breath. The room was freezing. Astarth pulled the curtains apart. On the bed Panthera lay spreadeagled, tied by ankles and wrists to the bedposts. It was not the most elegant of positions. His skin was dead white.

"I thought Jafit said he was going to let Panthera rest for a while," I said.

"He has! Panthera has to earn his keep too, you know," Astarth replied, rubbing his hands. "I'll get a fire going. God! It's like hell in here. Shut the window, will you."

It was stuck fast with ice. It had been a while since I had used any of my special abilities. I thought "warm" and was just successful enough to shift it. Standing back, wiping my hands, I felt a soft, hesitant mind touch. "You've taken the cold away . . ." I looked sharply behind me. Outher had gone out. Astarth was busying himself at the grate. I looked at the bed, straight into the direct gaze of a pair of green eyes. "The others have forgotten how to do this. You're not one of them, are you?" I flicked a quick glance toward Astarth. It was obvious he had sensed nothing of this silent conversation. To me it was like having someone confirm that, yes, I was alive—at least not brain dead. I had thought my ability to communicate in this uniquely harish manner had rotted through disuse, but apparently not. It reinforced my views about the pedestal. Panthera, I could love you.

Astarth wandered back to the bed, brushing wood dust off his hands. "OK, big cat. I'm going to untie you now. Just don't try anything stupid."

Panthera didn't answer. He was still just staring at me. I went over and untied his wrists. The flesh was like corpse flesh; icy. Half his long fingernails were broken off, raggedly, viciously. Once free, he sat up and rubbed his wrists. I realized he must have been tied up like that all night, yet how detached from it he seemed. As if it was nothing. Astarth handed him a robe which he wrapped around himself. Without a word, he went into the bathroom and, presently, I heard water running.

"He'll have a bath now," Astarth said.

"Does he ever . . . speak?"

"Sometimes. He's so arrogant, so high and mighty. It's not our fault he's here, is it! Some of us tried to help him, you know, make friends at first, but he didn't want to know. He's happy to stay in his tower of ice."

"Perhaps he'd be insane if he wasn't." I looked toward the bathroom. "I think I'll try and talk to him."

Astarth laughed. "You're wasting your time," he said. "We've got to clean up in here. Don't be long."

Panthera lay back in his bath, facing the door. His eyes were closed. "They are not true Wraeththu here," he said at once, again through direct contact to the brain.

I sat down on the edge of the bed. "So how do you know I'm so different?" I asked aloud.

Panthera opened his eyes. "They do talk a lot you know. I know all about you. You've got them guessing. I know you want to leave here."

"Can't you speak aloud?"

"It is dangerous. You'll know why when you understand what I have to say. I knew you'd be sent in here eventually. I've been waiting. You shouldn't confide in Lolotea, Calanthe, you really shouldn't."

I didn't comment. There was nothing I'd told Lolotea that I didn't want anyone else to know.

"Get me out of here, Calanthe . . ." A silver arrow of thought.

"What? Are you mad?"

"Not at all. I've thought about it very carefully. I'm not going to die here. I've tried every other way of escaping. I need help from the outside now."

"You can get lost!" I said, standing up. He *was* mad.

"No," he said silently. "I can't. That's why I need help, you fool. You are leaving eventually anyway. You're a Varr, Calanthe. You can get me out." He closed his eyes once more. "Come back. Talk to me."

"You've forgotten how to talk, I think."

Panthera speaks mostly with his eyes. I knew I'd help him. He knew it too. It was something that had been subliminally decided from the moment I first saw him.

"One more thing," he said. "It will interest you to know; my family will pay highly for my safe return to them." He smiled. "Until we meet again, Calanthe." He slid under the water, all his hair floating around him like weed, his eyes open, staring up through the water.

I went through the door. "Goddam!" I said. "Goddam!"

"I didn't hear him answering you," Astarth said smugly.

"Oh, he whispered!"

Astarth laughed. "Oh dear! Got to you has it? We've all been through it, Calanthe. We've all wanted him. He has that power."

"And where are your powers Astarth?" I asked.

There was a silence. Astarth uncovered the tray of food. "There is a price to pay for everything," he said.

CHAPTER FIVE

> + <+> • O • <+> + <img<

The Beginning of Plans

"Tell me:
Which is the way I take;
Out of what door do I go,
Where and to whom?"

—*Theodore Roethke, The Flight*

I could have told Jafit, of course. I could have gone straight to his office and said, "Guess what, Panthera has asked me to help him escape!" and, no doubt, we'd have both laughed about it. There were two reasons why I didn't do that. The first was that I hated what I was having to do to earn money, and Panthera had mentioned a substantial reward. The second was that I thought it would help me considerably to be in the company of a native Jaddayothite when I first went there. The fact that Panthera was irresistably lovely had nothing at all to do with it. It would not be an easy thing to accomplish though. Panthera was guarded night and day. We'd need horses, money. . . . Someone outside Piristil. Now then, who did I know who was also a native of Jaddayoth, who had horses and money and who was planning to return home soon? Kruin. I'd have to start working on him, and fast.

That afternoon, I went into Fallsend with Lolotea and Flounah. My mind was buzzing with plans. Lolotea said I was preoccupied. "What's the matter?" he asked.

"I know," Founah said darkly. I looked at him quickly. He smiled. "It's Panthera, isn't it? It bothered me too at first. At least I live this life by choice!"

I smiled carefully. Flounah nodded to himself. He understood quite a lot. We took wine together in a small inn near the market. Lolotea went off to buy himself some Gimrah cheese. Flounah glared at the passersby through the window, taking small, bird-like sips of his wine.

"So, tell me," I said, "what's it like in Maudrah at this time of year?"

Flounah grimaced. "Cold. The weather is the one thing that Ariaric has no control over."

"Ah yes," I said casually, "Ariaric. He sounds a fascinating character. What is it they call him? The Lion . . . or something?"

"The Lion of Oomadrah, yes. He is thought of as a god . . . lucky for him . . ."

Suddenly, I didn't want to hear any more. It was too much of a coincidence, that was all. How many self-styled leaders of Wraeththu tribes might identify themselves with the king of the beasts? Many. I broke quickly into Flounah's conversation, not wanting to hear anything that might confirm or deny my suspicions. "Why can't you go back there?" This was, of course, breaking the Piristil tradition, but Flounah didn't appear to object.

"What makes you think I want to?" he said.

"Well, working in Piristil is hardly a worthy way to spend your life."

"No, of course it isn't! Let's just say I'm licking my wounds here. Maudrah is not for me. I wanted to get away more than had to. In the summer I intend to head west, maybe southwest to Almagabra. I need money." I could sympathize with that. "Hara like Lolotea and the others, they will be here forever," Flounah continued, without malice. "They lack spirit. You, on the other hand, would be wise to wait until the spring before you leave here."

"You think I'm planning on leaving then?"

He gave me a stripping glance. "Oh yes, I think you are. Don't be hasty." I wondered how much he knew, or had guessed. Perhaps not all of the kanene were as helpless as I'd thought.

I nearly said, "OK, but I haven't got that long," but managed to check myself in time. For all I knew, Flounah might have been instructed by Jafit to question me. "I'm not planning on going anywhere yet," I said. "I want to save at least fifty spinners. That's at least seven weeks, if I don't spend a single fillaret. You think I'd head off into the great unknown with no money and winter coming on? You think I'm that crazy?" I shook my head, smiling. "No, I'm not leaving." Flounah raised his brows, sipped thoughtfully. Thankfully, Lolotea chose that moment to return. He offered us some of his cheese. It was really quite exquisite.

"I want to buy some," I said.

"I thought you were saving every fillaret of your money," Flounah mentioned accusingly.

"Oh, buy some!" Lolotea said cheerfully. "Don't be such a misery, Flounah!"

Flounah will watch me now. I'm certain of it. He doesn't know me. None of them know me. Once, long ago, I'd learned how to escape. That time, I'd left a lover behind me to die. I still haven't paid that debt. Maybe now is the time. I raised my glass and stared Flounah in the eye.

"To my cheese," I said.

Kruin came to me again two nights later. I'd been waiting for him, panicking, thinking, "Oh God, I upset him. He'll never come back again!" But he did. He came in through the door and said.

"I've been thinking of you, Calanthe. I was hard on you last time. I'm sorry. Here." He gave me a necklace of polished stones.

"Don't be silly," I said, putting it around my neck. "Thank you, Kruin. I like it. You look nice today too."

"Oh, come on!" Kruin sat down on my bed and kicked off his boots. "This town is a hole. Neither of us should be here."

"No," I agreed. "Wine?"

"Mmmm." He looked thoughtful. "I enjoy being with you, you know. Don't think that I don't."

"I'm glad. Get your money's worth, Kruin. It's always better if you enjoy it."

"I don't know how you do it; you're always so cheerful."

"Of course. I'm here to please. Drink up!"

I really worked hard for my money that night. Every possible permutation of pleasure, however small, I lavished on Kruin with convincing sincerity.

"Stay with me tonight," I said.

"I can't. It's not allowed."

"They won't know. We'll be quiet. Stay. Please." It didn't take long to persuade him, but then, it was cold outside and a long way back to the inn where he was staying. We lay together, on my new rug by the fire. I smoothed his animal skin, murmuring endearments. He lapped it up. "Be ouana for me," I said, "I want to know you that way."

"It's not what I come here for," he answered, but I knew he was pleased. I sneaked him out in the early morning through the kitchens. We had hardly slept. Because I had the following evening free, I asked him to meet me in Fallsend. He hesitated and took my hand. "Where is this leading, Calanthe?" he asked, not totally stupid.

"I like you, Kruin."

"It's not just that, is it."

"Will you meet me?"

He rubbed his eyes with one hand, sighed. "Alright, but you must tell me what you're up to. I wasn't born blind, Calanthe."

I kissed him. "Trust me," I said.

He shook his head, smiling. "I hope I don't regret this," he said, and trudged away, pulling his collar higher up his neck against the cold air.

I learn from him constantly. His goodness rubs off on me like an ointment, into my skin. The blackness just sinks in deeper. Pell has Thiede's blood in his veins now. Thiede the mysterious; too powerful, too cunning. What interest does he have in Pell? I shouldn't have let it happen, but Seel thought I was being too paranoid. "Pell will be incepted by Thiede," he said to me and then couldn't understand my fears. "Won't this be an honor?" "No, a travesty!" a voice screams inside me, but only inside. Now my Pellaz is Wraeththu, but he is Thiede too and I am afraid for him. He possesses a taint of ancient wisdom, a taint of feyness. In the moonlight he appears transparent, touched by death. I am mirrored in his eyes; pure and clean. Oh Pell, we must be together always. Without you, I might go back. *No, no, not that, not the darkness, the time of blood. And now I mount the stairs in Seel's house, dressed in white. Dusk is past us; now is the night. I have bathed in milk and perfumed oil. I have been blessed, kissed with sacramental balm upon lips and breast and phallus. My part of the inception is nigh. Pellaz is waiting for me. I have sat for an hour with Seel on the window-sill at the back of the house. The air was warm there. Seel smoked a cigarette, which was torture for me because I could not. Until this is over no stimulant, of any kind, must pass my lips. Seel and I were once chesna; perhaps we were remembering those times, although we did not speak our thoughts aloud. But memory certainly prompted the remark, "He seems so small, Cal, so fragile. Be careful not to hurt him. This is not the City." I did not answer him. Seel is wrong. I am incapable of hurting Pellaz. Not in that way. Now the bare wood of the stairs is creaking beneath my feet and I enter his room, and shut the world away from us. In our universe Pellaz is a radiant star, luminous skin, lambent eyes, power that leaks from his pores. I have been yearning to touch him for so long, now the moment must be savored, prolonged before I do. His body surrenders for the first time, and I watch him discover the delights of his new being. He forgets he was once human, forgets he was once male. We take aruna and we are invading each other, cautiously and reverently. This is not the city. Zack is dead. My flesh twinges at the memory of the savage bite. I hear laughter, but it is far away. Now I will weep inside because of the simple, giving pleasure we enjoy. There is nothing beyond Saltrock. This is sanctuary. It is not safe to leave. I vow to keep us there.*

We will stay in Saltrock for just twenty-two months.

It was my turn to take "zoo duty" again that day. Lolotea was with me. This time, Panthera wasn't tied to the bed. He was still asleep, or pretending to be, flags of dark hair spread around him on the pillows. One Mojag was on guard duty; the other two slumbering peacefully in an adjoining room.

Lolotea gave Panthera a shake. "Wake up. We have to change the bed," he said, beginning to pull at the sheets.

Panthera stretched and looked at me. It was a glance that had my common sense struggling to keep my libido under control. Fluid as quicksilver, Panthera rose from the bed and stalked arrogantly to the window. He must spend an awful lot of time gazing out of that window. How many fruitless plans had been hatched there?

"I'll run your bath," I said.

Panthera did not look at me or say anything, although Lolotea glanced up sharply, shaking his head and smiling to himself. I went into the bathroom with its high, pale walls and started to run water into the pale, high bath. Panthera came in silently behind me.

"Well?" he asked at once, in a voiceless arrow to my brain. "Have you thought about what I said?" He'd obviously been thinking about it, perhaps worried that my answer would be "no."

"I've said nothing to Jafit, if that's what you mean," I answered.

Lolotea must not hear us. We conversed by mind-touch alone. I felt Panthera's uncontrollable relief pass through me like a breeze. He glided past me and let his robe fall to the floor. The threat of being struck by blindness could not have stopped me from looking at him; this he refused to acknowledge, although I could tell he derived a certain satisfaction from it. His body is like Seel's, almost too slim, but malleable. He lowered himself into the water and closed his eyes.

"You mustn't stay in here long," he said. "The fool out there might get suspicious. I have no contact with any of them if I can help it."

I sat down on the edge of the bath. "I have been thinking, Panthera," I said, "and, if I can, I will try to help you. But it won't be easy. Too much for me alone. I'm going to need help from outside Piristil."

Panthera's eyes snapped open. "Who?! Nobody can be trusted."

"You had to trust me."

He sighed. "Alright, but be careful."

"You know you don't have to worry about that. You wouldn't have approached me if you didn't."

"True. Now remember, if we succeed, you will be well paid."

"That is not the only item of concern."

"No, of course not. You want to get into Jaddayoth; preferably into a royal house. See how much I know about you? I have royal blood . . ."

"I don't doubt that for a moment, Panthera!"

He smiled. "You're a mercenary, aren't you. You can be bought. Have you made any plans yet?"

"A few sketches. I'm working on it."

Panthera leaned forward with vehemence. "Make it soon!" he said. "I've waited long enough."

I met Kruin in a small tavern near his lodgings. He was sitting at a table in a corner of the room with an ashtray full of cigarette ends on one side of him and three empty glasses on the other. As I sat down, he fumbled to light another cigarette and began to look mournfully at the bar.

"I'll get them," I said, to give him a few more moments to compose himself. I bought him a beer and one for myself. It was warm and rancid, and left an unwelcome deposit of slime in the back of the mouth. I asked Kruin why he was so nervous.

"I prefer you to be . . . *contained*," he answered furtively. "The part of my life you represent should remain locked in Piristil."

"Let's have less of the 'locked,' if you don't mind!"

Kruin smiled at the table, stubbed out his cigarette and lit another one. "Well, why do you want to see me?"

"Maybe I just like you."

"Maybe. Like I said, why do you want to see me?"

I leaned back in my seat; a perilous action, it wobbled dangerously. "Hmmm, now tell me; you are a warrior? Brave, courageous, fearless, all that?"

He laughed. "Calanthe, what is this?"

"Are you?"

"I've escorted three wittering merchants from Natawni, that's all. It's hardly the stuff of heroism. OK, back home, I've been involved in scuffles with the Maudrah, nothing serious. Why are you asking? Are you trying to hire me?" He laughed again, nervously, his eyes scanning the faces in the crowd behind us, in case his traveling companions should show up.

"In a way, yes. When you leave Fallsend, Kruin, I want to come with you."

"What?! No! A kanene? Do you realize . . ."

I broke into his furious splutterings. "Shut up! The minute I leave Piristil, I'm no longer a kanene. In fact, I'm not even one now! Do you understand?"

He looked into my eyes, silenced by the tone of my voice, sighed and shook his head. "You don't look like a whore, Calanthe," he said, at last.

"Good, then stop being so worried about being seen with me."

He pulled an apologetic face. "That obvious?"

"Rather, yes."

"I'm sorry. Let's start again, OK?"

I rejoiced in the moment when my friend Kruin stopped seeing me as meat and started seeing me as har.

"Now then," he said, "I get a feeling it may not be a good idea to get involved in whatever scheme you have in mind. There *is* some reason behind all this, isn't there?"

"Could be that I just want you to take me back to your tribe. Could be that I'd ask to become chesna-bond with you; you're quite a catch, Kruin."

"Yeah, and hard nuts like you don't have any finer feelings, Calanthe. Let's not play games. What is it you want?"

"You're suspicious aren't you!"

"Ever looked in the mirror, tiahaar?"

"At least a dozen times a day, sometimes more, depending on the weather."

"Ever noticed your eyes never smile? That's what tells me to be careful!"

"Survival's a caustic process," I agreed. If his observations were supposed to disquiet me, he was badly misguided. No-one knew more than me how thorough my defences were. "Back to what you were saying," I said. "You're probably right that it might be bad for you to get involved with me. Worse than that it may be terribly bad. You may never be able to set foot in Fallsend again . . . safely."

Kruin raised his hands. "Forget it!"

"Sssh, just listen. There's money to be made . . ."

"Oh?" He raised his brows, drank some beer, grimaced. "Go on."

"It concerns the har kept locked in Piristil, you know, Panthera."

"Mmmm." Deeper suspicions began to cloud his eyes. He drank again, lit another cigarette.

"I've been approached, Kruin. Panthera wants out. There's a substantial reward waiting for someone who can get him home."

Kruin did not over-react as I'd expected.

"Too risky, Calanthe. What is this? Social justice on your part? I doubt it! Must be one hell of a big reward!"

"You lack subtlety, Kruin."

"Yeah, maybe. But how the hell do you think we can blast our way through those Mojags? It'll need more than two of us!" He whistled through his teeth, shook his head. "No, Jafit's security is impeccable. It will take more than brute force."

"Well done, Kruin!" I said, somewhat sourly. "The power of seduction accomplishes far more than blazing guns."

"You've got a plan then? A watertight plan?"

"Are you in with me or not?"

He shrugged. "Tell me how you're going to do it first. I don't see how you'll get away with it."

"If I set my mind on something, I always get away with it!"

"Convince me then!"

"I'm still working on it. Come to Piristil tomorrow night."

"Again?! This is going to cost me a fortune!"

"But it will be worth it," I said, and leaned forward to pat his cheek.

CHAPTER SIX

>━!━<>━O━<>━!━<

The Beauty of Poison

"Sure to taste sweetly,—is that poison too!"

—Robert Browning, The Laboratory

Pell and I are in Galhea. Terzian is lord here and we are in his house. Flashbacks to another time. Terzian is a powerful har. He likes me. He says, "Don't you get sick of traveling around, Cal?" Of course I do, but how can I explain that we are running, just ahead of something and that something is huge and dangerous. We don't even know what it is. "It's because of Pell," I say, and that's all I can say. "We have to . . . keep going."

"We?" Terzian smiles. "you don't have to surely!" He wants me to stay with him. He wants me to have his sons. Such an offer. This is not a burnt-out wasteland; this is real living. Comfort, security, affluence. But then, there is Pell. And there are memories. It was not easy when Zack and I were kicked out of the Uigenna. I was younger then. We suffered for a while until we reached the sanctuary of the Unneah. Terzian cannot banish me. I don't belong here. He doesn't own me. This time, when I say no, it will be because I have the power; not him.

"Cal, don't leave me," he says. "Don't." When I am sure he loves me, I walk out of the door. It is not a happy triumph. Empty victory. Pell and I ride toward the south. The clouds are gathering.

I scuffed back to Piristil, through the bleak, moist cold; wrapping my woollen cloak more tightly around me, head down against the wind, sucking on a sour cigarette clasped between rigid fingers. I thought about Panthera. Occasionally honest with myself, I questioned my motives in wanting to help him get away. What he said was true, of course. I did want to leave Piristil, and I did want to get into Jaddayoth, but it is also true that I could probably have persuaded Kruin to take me back to Natawni with him, without the added hassle of liberating Panthera. I am not a person easily bewitched. Not now. I have learned to recognize the sweet, unsubtle pangs of desire when they assault me and never euphemize them with titles of love and longing. I also know that no beauty, however thrilling, is worth risking life and limb for. What the hell am I doing? Money, freedom, desire . . . I looked up the hill toward Glitter. Narrow buildings seemed to lean toward me, all crippled, all hopeless. A light shone down through the darkness, making the damp streets gleam. It was an arcanc, eerie and almost stimulating scene. The town was hushed. I stood for a moment in the empty, almost gully-like street and absorbed the ambience. Perhaps I was waiting for an omen. I looked up, pulling the gray wool closer to my neck. I felt as if I was clamped in the jaws of Fate. I was being manipulated, things were getting beyond my control. It is not a comforting feeling. Very well, if Fate was involved, I would just wait. If it was meant to be, coincidence would bring me a way to free Panthera. "Do your worst," I said aloud. From the darkness of the sky, a single, spiraling mote fell to earth, practically at my feet. I watched its descent, watched its rapid merging with the flesh and bones of Fallsend. "Soon," I thought, "everything will look different." I raised my head once more and the sky above me was creeping with movement. After a moment, I continued to climb the hill. Around me, snow fell silently.

My room was cold when I returned; the fire had died. Winter suffused the place. It was squatting there waiting for me and what chill I brought in with me merged with it eagerly. Before going to find Orpah or Wuwa to light the fire, I crossed the darkened room and glanced quickly through the window, seeking the light in Panthera's room. It glowed as usual, but there were no shadows crossing the bars. Everywhere seemed unusually hushed that evening. The house was too quiet, creaking as if it thought it was alone. I wandered along to the kitchens, thinking only about my fire. Jancis the cook stopped me at the threshhold. "You'd better get back upstairs," he said ominously, with expressionless face.

"Why?"

"There's been an incident. Jafit says everyone is to stay in their rooms for now."

I felt chilled. "Incident? What kind of incident? What's happened?"

Jancis began to close the door in my face. He smiled. "A death," he said. "A killing."

"What?! Jancis! Who? Jancis!" The kitchen door had slammed in my face. I heard him turn the key inside. I heard him chuckling.

Panicking, I bolted straight to Panthera's quarters. If anyone was going to get himself murdered around here, he was the most likely candidate. Outher was standing guard outside the door. I feared the worst. "What's happened?" I asked.

"Trouble!" he answered. "Comes with the job, I suppose."

"Panthera?" I cried, horrified. Outher shook his head.

"Oh, *he's* alright," he said. "God, as if anyone could get away with murdering him!"

"Can I go in?"

Outher thought about it for a moment. "I guess that'll be alright." He opened the door for me.

I put my hand on his arm. "Thanks, Outher. I appreciate it."

The Mojag actually flushed. "S'alright, Calanthe," he said. "You got a thing going with our pussy cat, have you?"

I laughed, but did not answer.

Panthera was surprised to see me and uncommonly natural because of it. It made me realize what a creature of artifice he can be at times. I asked him if he knew what was going on.

"No," he answered. "All I know is that all clients have been canceled for the night and that two of the Mojags have been summoned to Jafit's office."

"Damn!" I said, annoyed enough to hit the wall. "If only this could have happened later! It's almost too good an opportunity to miss. One Mojag and the house nearly empty! Damn!"

"You mean we could . . . *leave* now?" Panthera sounded uncertain.

"We could have, but unfortunately we're not prepared and neither is Kruin."

"Kruin. Who's Kruin?"

I explained. Panthera sat down on the bed. "I hope Ferike and Natawni are on friendly terms at the moment. Things might have changed since I left home."

"Relations that flimsy between the tribes then?"

"Can be. It's hard to say. It all depends on Maudrah really." He smiled beautifully at me. "Still, this Kruin doesn't seem to be worried. It will cause problems in another way though. The Natawni's route home can't possibly take him anywhere near Ferike. Surely, if he drags the merchants south with him, they're going to want to share the reward."

"God, Panthera, that's a minor point. Let's just get out of here intact before we start quibbling over details. That's Kruin's problem."

Panthera looked at me archly, but said nothing.

"I suppose I'd better go and find out what's going on," I said.

"Not yet," Panthera decided. "Stay. Have some coffee."

"Lonely for company are you?"

"No. I'm used to not having any; you know that. I was just thinking we have to talk about our plans and there won't be many opportunities like this one." He stalked over to the fire and picked up a coffee pot. Only then did I notice the long, silver chains.

"Are those uncomfortable?" I asked him, pointing.

"Not as much as they were, no," he answered.

I asked him about Ferike. "It is beautiful," he said. "There are woods everywhere, hills and mountains. All I live for is to see it again. All the noble families live in great, stone castles. Jael, my father's domain, is quite near the Clerewater and the shoreside town of Clereness. Look, I'll show you."

He preceded me over to a low table where sheets of paper and colored pens were laid out. I picked up a drawing; dark and disturbing scribbles of torture. "Yours?" Panthera snatched it from my hand.

"Yes. Look, I will draw you a plan of Jaddayoth." I watched his slim, hard arm skim quickly over the paper. "Here is Natawni in the north, you see? Both Hadassah and Gimrah separate it from Ferike. The quickest route to Natawni is north from Fallsend, out of Thaine, into Fereng and from there to Jaddayoth. That's probably the way your friend Kruin would go home. Now, Jafit will expect us to go south toward Elhmen, so I think we should go north."

"It will be a much longer journey," I said, studying the map.

"Yes, but safer."

"OK what ever you say." Without thinking, I put my hand on his shoulder. Ah, such warmth, such strength, such softness and hardness! These are the most succulent sweetmeats in the market of life and often the ones most dear. Panthera shrugged me off and gave me a hard glance. I was irresistibly reminded of Cobweb.

"You must not stay too long," Panthera said, and thus concluded our conversation.

Plans were beginning to formulate in my head. After I left Panthera, I paused to share a cigarette with the Mojag. He could offer me no information concerning the identity of the murder victim. If it wasn't Panthera, I decided I wasn't really bothered who it was. "Don't worry yourself with that," Outher said. "Stay here for a while. We could . . . talk."

"We could, but. . . . Do you get any time off from this job?"

"Tomorrow afternoon is free," he said, without a tremor.

"Fine. We'll talk tomorrow then." I had a feeling that friendship with Outher might prove useful.

I didn't know what action Jafit would take over the killing, but I was surprised when I found him still at home. I knocked on his office door and Astarth opened it to me (so it wasn't him lying dead somewhere). The room was full of smoke, opened bottles on the desk, Jafit sitting behind it with his feet up. He didn't look exactly grief-stricken, although Astarth was a little green about the gills. The Mojags were sitting awkwardly in small chairs, clutching glasses of betica in their large fists.

"What's happened?" I asked.

"Come in. Sit down, if you can find a seat," Jafit replied.

Astarth clutched my arm. "Lolotea is gone," he said.

"Lolotea?" I said softly. "No . . ." It stunned me. Of all the kanene Lolotea was the least deserving of such a sordid end. Over the years, I have become inured to the death of friends, but it still shocked me. Astarth sat me down. "How?" I asked "How, Jafit?" A full glass was pushed into my hand. Jafit was comfortably exhibiting unconcern. "Don't you care?" My voice was near to breaking.

"Of course I care," Jafit answered sharply. "It was a har named Arno Demell, from the town. Don't worry, it will be dealt with."

"Has this sort of thing happened before?" I asked. Jafit made a noncommittal gesture.

"Yes it has," Astarth told me bitterly. I was satisfied to note that he looked quite ill.

"There are risks in every walk of life," Jafit said. Astarth sneered at that and I don't blame him.

"What are you going to do?"

Jafit smiled at my question. "Do, Calanthe? Why we're going to kill the fucking bastard, aren't we my dears?" The Mojags grunted uncomfortably in assent.

A voice sounded in the room. It said. "No, Jafit, you don't have to. I will." I was surprised to find it was mine.

"You?" Astarth said. "Why?"

Why indeed? I wasn't sure myself, but the feeling was there, gut-strong. Jafit didn't give a damn really; I did. They wanted reasons, so I gave them. "He was my friend. I liked him a lot. Let me deal with it. Don't you think I'm capable?"

Jafit smiled and poured himself another drink. "Capable? Oh my dear, you are obviously eminently capable. But you don't know Fallsend, do you? Think you could find Demell?"

"No he couldn't," Astarth said, and I turned around to protest, but before I spoke, he continued. "But I could. Calanthe is right in this, Jafit. It is our blood debt. It could have been any one of us up there." He looked at me. "Get your coat, Calanthe. I'll meet you in the hall."

"Astarth, do you know what you are doing?" Jafit asked, highly amused.

"Yes, give me some money. Twenty spinners should do it."

"OK, but you realize it will be too late to get help from us if you fail. Demell will be in hiding, I should think."

"We'll find him, Jafit." Astarth took the money that Jafit had taken from the drawer. "Come on, Calanthe."

I went to fetch my coat, pausing in the corridor outside Lolotea's room.

If I'd been in there. . . . If I hadn't gone to see Kruin . . . I shook my head.
A life for a life for a life; never-ending. I opened the door and went inside.
It was not ghoulish curiosity or even because I wanted to fuel the fire of the
vengeance lust. I just went in. Someone had thrown a sheet over the body;
a pathetic huddle on the floor. The light was on, the fire roaring away
merrily in the grate. There was little sign of a struggle. I lifted the sheet.
Whoever had done this was not on a blood and guts kick. Lolotea's neck
was neatly broken with little other damage. He stared in surprise at the
ceiling, his hands above his head. I squatted down and closed his eyes.
Someone should have already done that. It was wrong that he should just
be left lying there. I lifted the body in my arms and laid it on the bed. It
was limp and cooling in my arms. The feeling of dead flesh is like no other;
it is disorientating. The body of Lolotea was as empty as the clothes
hanging in the cupboard. I opened the window, put a robe over the mirror
and murmured a few soothing prayers to help the spirit on its way, although strangely I could feel no inkling of its presence. Someone or something had come for it quickly. I shivered, suddenly cold with the sense of
being watched. Of course, I am always watched. Perhaps to Lolotea's
advantage in this case.

Astarth had scrubbed his face and dressed in dark, sober clothes. This
was not the hard-bitten tart I knew. He looked very different; determined,
competent. He paused, one hand on the door, looked at me hard. "Were
you trying to shame me?" he said. I shook my head. "You know I wouldn't
be doing this if it wasn't for what you said."

I shrugged. "Does it matter?"

"It should." He shook his head fiercely, swore under his breath, and
opened the door. We went outside into the muffled snow-darkness and
Astarth closed the door behind us, pulling on thick, woolen gloves in a
manner that implied he meant business. We trudged down the hill toward
the town. Tiahaar Arno Demell, I learned, was usually to be found draped
over the bar and the pot-hara in the Red Hog Inn. Astarth suggested we
go there first, although neither of us had much hope of finding Demell
there.

"Jafit doesn't seem that upset about this," I said.

"No he doesn't," Astarth agreed in an uncommunicative tone.

"Would he have done anything?" I persisted.

Astarth stopped trudging. He turned to face me. "Oh Demell would've
been banned from the establishment, but not much else, no. If Jafit persisted, he may have been able to get financial compensation from him.
That, by the way, was what he meant by 'killing the bastard.' A momentary
killing. Arno Demell is not a rich har. Don't you see, Calanthe, there is not
that much of a difference between pelcia and murder. Sometimes a client
will get carried away. Once they've paid their money to Jafit, he has little
control over what goes on in those rooms."

"Astarth, that's . . . that's . . ." I could not think of a strong enough
word.

"Yes, isn't it!" We carried on walking.

"Why are you doing this?" I asked. "Why are you here, Astarth? What kind of life is this?"

"Don't ask! Don't ask!" He started running through the quickly deepening snow. I followed him and we did not speak of it again. We didn't have to. After all, it's no kind of life, is it?

We searched and we searched. From inn to musenda to inn. Astarth asked questions, paid for information. Every lead we gained led to a dead end. I was beginning to give up. Demell could be miles from Fallsend by now. Astarth was more persistent. At another musenda, we spoke with a kanene who had a stitched wound all across his face and neck. Luck was looking us right in the eye; he knew where Demell was. Apparently, our prey had turned up there some while ago, being a close friend of the owner of the place.

"He was obviously in a bit of a state about something," our informant told us. "OK, we weren't supposed to know what was going on, but, let's just say we're more resourceful than our keeper gave us credit for." He smiled and the scar wriggled horribly on his cheek. "87 Canalside Row. Remember that. It's where you'll find him." He pressed the handle of a long, barbed knife into my hand. "Give Demell one for me," he said, running a finger down his scar. "Tiahaar Demell's a regular customer here; you see?" I tucked the knife into my belt. Yes, I could see.

Outside, I laughed and brandished the knife in a threatening manner. Astarth put his hand over my wrist and shook his head at me. "No," he said. "The punishment has to fit the crime. Come on." I followed him up another narrow streetlet that was slippery with snow. We went into a large and noisy inn named The Stone. Astarth said that many of the Jaddayoth traders frequented it; some even stayed there. The Stone did look more affluent than the majority of Fallsend establishments. I wouldn't have minded pausing for a mug of ale there myself. Astarth said we didn't have enough time. I watched him asking a few questions of people, wondering what he was up to. We knew where Demell was now. Someone directed him to a thin-faced har wearing dark, purple clothes. He was leaning on the bar, smoking a long-stemmed pipe, staring at the crowd as if deep in thought. He inclined his head toward Astarth semi-interestedly. A brief conversation took place, and then the pair of them went outside. Astarth motioned me to wait in the bar for him. Never a person to miss opportunities, I bought myself a drink and sat down. Astarth was only gone a few minutes. He rejoined me looking furtive and edgy, manifesting dire impatience as I finished my drink. Outside, the freezing cold was as welcome as a hangover and just as mind-numbing.

"Well Astarth," I said, "what shady business were you up to in there?"

"The har I talked to was the Garridan Liss-am-Caar," he replied with reverent tones of dread. "He sold me this." A twist of paper was held out for me to inspect. I had seen such things before and opened it cautiously, sniffed the contents. This was something the Uigenna had once been most famous for; poison. "The Garridan deal in toxins and venoms," Astarth explained, taking the twist of paper back. Shades of Uigenna, I thought. Yes, definitely. We hurried through the streets to the place where we'd been told Demell had secreted himself. It was an unimposing house, close to the canal that was one of the trade routes between Thaine and Jaddayoth.

"Well, what do we do now?" I asked Astarth who had appeared to have assumed command. "Go up and knock on the door?"

"We wait awhile." It was terribly cold and uncomfortable. I smoked four cigarettes and then the door to the house we were watching opened. A solitary figure stepped out into the street, glancing this way and that. I saw the flare of a match. "It's him," Astarth breathed.

Arno Demell walked toward the canal. He exhibited no signs of worry, or fear that he was being watched. An average kind of har, unremarkable in appearance. He stood at the water's edge and threw something into the shifting, oily blackness. I'll never know what. For a moment, he continued to stare into the water. Then we jumped him. It would have been easy just to have thrown him into the canal; the freezing cold would have finished him off pretty quickly, but Astarth wanted to shake that packet of crystals into the poor fool's mouth. It was his moment of glory and I wasn't going to deprive him of it. I don't know whether he was genuinely grieved by what had happened to Lolotea, it was difficult to tell, but he certainly enjoyed making Demell suffer for it. The victim didn't ask who we were; he knew. Of course, he may have seen our faces before in Piristil, but I saw that resigned acceptance of doom as he witnessed Astarth's bared teeth and patient execution of vengeance. Demell knew what he had done and now accepted he had to pay the forfeit; in this case, death. The law of the jungle, the law of the world. Few poisons can affect a harish frame. We are a resilient race. We left Demell gasping and writhing at the edge of the water. I expect he eventually did fall in, but we didn't stay to watch.

We walked back to Piristil in silence, both of us wrapped in our own thoughts. Perhaps Astarth was thinking that one death can't pay for years of degradation, I don't know, but I was thinking of the Garridan. It was possible that they were derived from Uigenna stock. Suddenly, my mind was alight with ideas. This was it. Panthera's liberation was suddenly so much nearer.

The following day, a predictable pall of gloom and despondency hung heavily in the air in Piristil. The air smelled greasy; the air was cold. The kanene passed each other on the stairs with barely a greeting. We dressed in black and bound up our hair. There is a hill about half a mile away from the house. It is reached by a steep, muddy path. That is where Lolotea lies buried. There are no hienama in the town of Fallsend, no priests. Jafit, who had made no mention of Arno Demell and his fate, spoke a few hackneyed words over the open grave as Orpah and Wuwa lowered the rough, un-adorned wooden box containing the remains of the murdered one into the ground. The rest of us stood around, numb from cold and, in some cases, shock. Some of them wept. Flounah veiled himself in gray and stood with his back to the grave. Ezhno held onto my arm, looking aggressive. There was no-one of Lolotea's blood to mourn him there. No-one would ever even know he was dead; a group of desperate whores the only thing he had close to a family. It was pathetic really, but me, I felt detached. I've experienced worse things.

After a dreary lunch, shared with Jafit and the others in Jafit's personal dining room, I went to find Outher. "I have to go into Fallsend," I said. "Want to come with me?" I think this rather disappointed him as he'd been planning to spend the afternoon with me in a more secluded place. "We can eat in my room tonight, if you like," I added. That convinced him.

As we walked down the hill into the town, snow seeping through my boots, I was deep in thought. My mind was racing, but I strove not to show it. I remember forcing some inane chatter onto Outher. He must have thought me as empty-headed as the rest. Once the streets leveled off, I mentioned that I would like to go for a drink in The Stone. "It seems it's the best this lousy town has to offer," I said, and Outher agreed.

He took my arm. "It will make me proud to walk in there with you," he said. How gallant.

Unlike the previous evening, The Stone was relatively quiet when we got there. A sumptuously painted har was draped over the bar waiting for custom. Outher offered to buy me a drink. I must not move too soon. I smiled and nodded and asked for a beer. As he strolled up to the bar, I reflected that it was almost a pity that I would have to leave Piristil this way. I'd made good friends whose company I would miss, not the least of which, Lolotea. That resolved me. The sooner I left the better. I scanned the room. Being large, it appeared emptier than it actually was. I could see no face that I recognized. Outher came over to the table I had chosen with the drinks. I smiled. He sat down.

"Panthera seems to have taken to you," he said. "I've never seen that before."

"Oh, I don't know about that," I said. "I just get on well with anybody."

"I don't think I've ever heard him speak to any of the others."

"Have you *heard* us speak then?"

"No, but . . ."

I inclined my head. "Well then!"

"You know what I mean, Calanthe," he laughed. "By Aghama, you're a cagey creature—just like Panthera."

"Cagey are the beasts kept in cages," I replied lightly, while surreptitiously glancing over Outher's shoulder. I drained my glass. "My round, I believe."

Outher looked at his half-full glass in surprise. "You are thirsty, Calanthe!"

"Yes, burying is thirsty work." Outher had the grace to look abashed. I said no more and went to the bar. The pot-har slouched over to me after leaving me waiting for maybe a minute. I watched him fulfill my order with the same amount of enthusiasm. Ale splashed over my hands as he handed me the glasses. "Tell me," I said, "is the Garridan Liss-am-Caar staying here?"

The pot-har gazed at me stupidly. I sighed and threw a spinner onto the bar where it rolled for a full insulting twelve seconds before lying still. The pot-har continued to stare.

"Well?" I enquired sweetly.

"Who wants to know?" he said at last.

"I do."

"And who are you?"

"A potential customer of his wares."

The pot-har continued to eye me with suspicion. "And what wares are those?" he asked, with undiminished surliness.

"Look." I said. "I haven't much time. Just tell him, will you! You don't have to be afraid. I'm not Gelaming. I'm a Varr. I just want to buy. No questions either side. Do you understand?" The pot-har stared me in the eye. I stared back.

"You want I should send him to your table?"

"No!" I hissed emphatically. "Have you a yard here?"

The pot-har pointed sullenly to a half concealed door to the right of the bar.

"Ten minutes," I said. The pot-har shrugged.

"If he's in. I'll have to try his room."

"Yes, you do that!"

I took the drinks back to the table. Outher asked what I'd been doing. I lied glibly about some flirtation with the pot-har. Outher grinned at me engagingly. Such a simple soul. I watched the clock above the bar. Nearly time. After nine minutes, Outher said, "Calanthe, you really are special."

"Yes, thank you," I said. "Look I just have to buy a couple of things. Hang on here for me, will you?"

"But I . . ." Obviously more profound sentiments were about to erupt.

"I won't be long."

"That's alright. I'll come with you. It's no bother."

"No! I mean, no, don't trouble yourself. Anyway, I want to buy something for us to eat tonight. It's going to be a surprise."

Outher smiled. He really is quite handsome. "OK, if you're sure."

I smiled and held up my hand. "Five minutes," I said.

I thought it safer to leave The Stone by the front door and hope that there was another way into the yard from out front. I had to be careful not to arouse any suspicions in Outher. Luckily, there were a couple of hara carrying barrels of ale through an open door in the wall. I followed them into the yard. It had been cleared of snow and strewn with ashes. I stood stamping and shivering for what seemed an eternity before a light touch on my shoulder made me spin round, half-afraid it would be Outher. It wasn't. In daylight, the lean face of the Garridan seemed even crueler, more snake-like, but seeringly attractive. I could see easily the mark of his Uigenna history in his eyes. Perhaps we had even met before. It was possible.

Inspired, I held out my hand and said, "In meetings hearts beat closer," which was an old, clichéd but authentically-Uigenna catch-phrase. Liss-am-Caar raised his brow fastidiously.

"In blood, brother," he responded. "You're a long way from home, friend."

"As are many," I replied. Now, I hoped he would not try to cheat me. He asked my business.

"Should you ask?" I replied.

He smiled thinly. "Only the result, my friend, only the result."

"Not death," I said.

Liss-am-Caar registered no expression. "Then I can only offer Blood-shade, Diamanda and Rauspic." Only two of those names were familiar to me, and I was also familiar with their side-effects. Death may even be preferable.

"I need sleepers not shriekers," I said mildly. "What is this Diamanda?"

"Perhaps what you require, although the sleep is deep. The dosage is crucial, for heavy-handedness whilst dosing could initiate a sleep deeper than might be required."

"That should suffice. How much?"

"That depends upon how much you want."

"Enough for ten, I think."

The Garridan did not flicker. "A hundred spinners then."

"What!"

He shrugged. "Sleepers are more expensive. I could sell you Acridil for a mere three spinners and you could administer maybe a hundred doses."

I reflected for a few moments. Should I? No. I remembered the shadow that had been on my tail through Thaine. Chances were, once out of Fallsend and in the open country, vigilance on the part of my pursuers would be stepped up. I could not risk causing another death. I'd already been through enough for the ones I'd initiated in the past. Arno Demell was more than enough for one town. "Diamanda for three, a light dose; how much?"

"A light dose? Should be thirty, but I'll give it to you for twenty-five."

Sighing, I handed over the better part of my savings. The Garridan counted it thoughtfully. He opened his bag and gave me three twists of paper. "This is a child's dose," he said, holding up one twist.

"And how will that affect a fully grown Mojag?" I asked.

The Garridan whistled through his teeth. "Ah, you're cutting close to the bone there! A light doze for half an hour, maybe."

I sighed again. It would just have to be enough.

"The advantage is, of course," the Garridan continued, "that should anyone wake up from a Diamanda sleep, they'll be groggy for ten minutes or so, no matter how light the dose."

"Thanks!" I said, glumly.

"Pleased to do business with you!" Liss-am-Caar touched his brow politely and turned away.

"Oh, one more thing, Tiahaar," I said. He turned.

"Yes."

"Who is the Lion of Oomadrah?" There was an electric silence. The Garridan's face was stony. He looked briefly around the yard.

"A changed person, my friend," he said. "In view of your history, you would do well to stay out of Maudrah. The Lion has sharpened his claws, but he never laughs nowadays. If you're looking for old friends, come to Garridan. Here, have my card."

I took it. "Thanks again," I said.

"Any time, my friend. Goodbye." He went back indoors.

I hurried back into the street and recklessly spent a further three spinners at the food stalls. Outher was looking very harried when I went back into The Stone, perhaps afraid I'd ditched him. "A long five minutes," he said.

"I'm sorry," I purred. "Listen, I have the whole day free. Do you want to go back to Piristil now?" That brought the smile back to his face; he didn't know I was thinking how much more preferable it would have been making that offer to the Garridan Liss-am-Caar.

We sat and talked beside my fire, mostly about what I was going to prepare for our meal; an engrossing topic, as you can imagine. I was still indulging in casual fantasies about the Garridan, even as I discussed with Outher the superiority of Fallsend chicken-meat to Fallsend pork. After what I considered to be a suitable time, I went to sit on Outher's lap to share breath with him. He cupped my face with his hand. "You're too good for this place," he said.

"Yes," I agreed and slipped my hand inside his leather shirt. "No, don't do that now," he said gently. "Calanthe, I have something to say to you. In the spring, I'm going back to Mojag. Someone else will take my place here. I'd like you to come home with me."

I laughed. "Outher, this session is for free, OK. You don't have to say things like that!"

He flushed angrily. "I'm not joking, Calanthe! I want you, but not just for a sordid night. I want you forever. It's terrible thinking of what you have to do here. Tell me now, will you or won't you? There won't be many chances for you like this here."

"Oh, I know that! But this is unexpected, Outher. So quick. Have I made such an impression upon you this afternoon?"

"You are laughing at me."

"Well, you must admit, it's hard to take your suggestion seriously. After all, we've only just met really."

He looked perplexed, wondering how to convince me. I resolved to let him suffer for a while. How could I be so lucky? I felt like leaping up and dancing round the room, but not for the reason Outher would want.

"It sounds so corny," he said, "but I wanted you from the moment I first saw you." He was right; it did sound corny.

I smiled. "Do you think I'll like life in Mojag?"

"Anything's better than this, surely!"

I lay back on the rug and stretched. I made him wait for as long as possible before saying, "Alright, if you're sure you mean it. This isn't going to be retracted after tonight, is it?"

Outher stood up. "Now you've said yes, there won't be a tonight," he said. "When we take aruna together, it will be when this place is far behind you!"

"Fine," I said, thinking, you get away from that door, idiot; you don't get away that easily. "Look, you don't have to go just because we're not going to leap in the bed or runkle the carpet! Let's get to know each other a little, shall we? Tell me about Mojag. Come on, sit down. I've got all this wretched food now and there's some wine chilling on the window-sill." I snuggled up against him again and let him bore me stiff rambling on about Mojag, a place that seemed tedious to the point of incredibility. I made a mental note never to go there. I've met many hara who are more masculine than they should be; sometimes they can carry it off pretty well. Mojags reminded me of the worst type of men who were probably (and thankfully) the first to be removed neatly from the face of the earth when Wraeththu rose up and splatted the humans. Mojags are a complete waste of harish time. Sorry Outher, you've been put together very nicely physically but your brain would be more at home floating, chopped up, in soup. After he'd exhausted himself talking, we sat quietly and watched the fire. He thought we were sharing a peaceful, silent moment together, but my mind was racing, planning, trying to take advantage of this incredibly fortuitous event. Outher was my key for Panthera's locked room. "What do you do in the evenings?" I asked.

"Drink mostly!" He laughed and I tittered impishly, flapping my eyelashes in what Kruin would have thought was a demented manner. "There's little entertainment to be found here," he continued woefully. "Most nights we have to listen to what goes on in Panthera's room. You have to get drunk to put up with that!"

"Ah, but you have me now," I said, nuzzling his face. His rapture at this behavior was laughable. Even an imbecile could see I was hamming it up so much you could virtually taste the salad too. "Do you have the same nights off as Panthera?"

He looked sour. "In a way. We take it in turns. Jafit won't ever let Panthera stay unguarded."

"How many nights off a week does Panthera get?"

"Only one, and he never knows which one that will be."

"Do you?"

"Yes, of course. We have to organize our duties around it."

"And when's the next one?"

"Four days' time. Why? What is it to you?" He didn't have an ounce of suspicion in him, however.

"I just want to know, because that night, I'll send you a present. I don't want you having to be all alert and on duty while you're enjoying it."

"You're lovely," he said tenderly.
"Deadly," I replied and he laughed.

So, tonight is the night. No more waiting. Goodbye vulgar clients, hello freedom. When I write again, it will be to state whether our plans were successful or not. If they're not, I may not be able to write again! A less than cheering thought. The Mojags are to be drugged with the Diamanda, which will be diluted in the large carafe of expensive wine that I'm sending to Outher for him to share with his companions. Once they're asleep, Kruin will scale the wall outside and try to remove the bars. He has obtained a corrodant which takes about fifteen minutes to work. Panthera and myself will leave Piristil through the window, into the yard, where Kruin will have the horses waiting, loaded with supplies. This venture has cost Kruin and myself nearly all the money we have. Kruin, to get rid of his duty toward the merchants, even had to hire another guide to get them safely back to Natawni. The planning is all finished; we'll just have to pray we're successful. It all hangs on Outher's trust in me and whether he's generous enough to share the wine as I'll suggest. I've had to endure four days of his dull wooing, made more vile by the fact that it required convincing responses. Imagine, we've even been discussing names for children! Every moment he has, he swears undying love to me; I have to take it all in without laughing. The fool's so easy to deceive it's embarrassing to take advantage of it. I could almost serve him a dose of Acridil for being such a stupid bore. People have died for less, as they say.

CHAPTER SEVEN

>─┼─◆)─◆─O─◆─(◆─┼─◄

Flight toward Hadassah
"Where but to think is to be full of sorrow
And leaden-eyed despair."
—*John Keats, Ode to a Nightingale*

*D*ampness, warmth, rising steam. The sound of moisture dripping from leaf to leaf. Birds are silenced; our horses pushing through greenery. Ahead of us the trees are thinning. Pell is in front of me. I am filled with feelings that I cannot describe. It is as if Fate himself is looming above the trees, filling the sky. At the time, I am not afraid nor even do I try to fight it. A town has appeared. It is quiet, no smoke rising, no movement; the trees have peeled back to reveal it. The town is red, the trees are green. We walk our horses *upon the road. "Pell," I say, "let me go first. It might be dangerous." Pell shakes his head. We are both powerless, but we know nothing, only that we love. We do not realize that all the time something has been following us, leading us, directing us. I should have known. God, I should have known. Love blinds me. Now the time for such teasing has come to an end. Pell can play at life no more and my time of sanity is over. Back to the time of blood. The end. We are not aware of what controls us because, for a time, we were innocent and incapable of thinking about, let alone comprehending, a thing so lunge, so terrifying, so corrupt. We can only see each other and that is enough.*

The bullet, when it comes, surprises me only by its sharp, exploding sound. Pell is killed instantly. I see him jerk, fall from the trembling horse. What's happened? It takes a moment to sink in. My face is stinging. Why? Has a sharp twig snapped up and scratched me? What is it? Pell, what's happened? He doesn't answer. He can't. Never again. Never. I watch my life explode in a spray of blood and a scream; a horse's scream. Then madness takes me and everything is cold, cold, cold. I look at him lying there, his fingers twitching. Screaming horses. Death. The smell of burning. There is light above the trees, taking him from me. A cold light. I am crying out because I'm sure it is the end.

If only it had been.

Jaddayoth is near. We are high up in the hills and the sharp, chill air is free of the stink of Fallsend, which is now far behind us. A fox with silver fur was watching me some moments ago as I wrote in the light of our campfire. His eyes were disks of gold. He watched me. Was he really a fox? Kruin and Panthera are asleep, rolled uncomfortably in blankets under the canopy of rock behind me. I have to take my gloves off to write and it is bitterly cold, but if I don't get it down on paper soon, I will begin to forget and the narrative will lose its edge. We have been traveling for a week, with, as yet, no sign of pursuit. I should have begun this before.

I'd been worried that some of the others in Piristil were suspicious of me, perhaps anticipating my plans—Flounah especially. For days I'd had to try and behave normally, not let anything slip, no matter how trivial, endure Outher's plodding and serious attempts at wooing me, prevent myself from packing away my belongings too soon. We weren't as prepared as I'd hoped we could be. There were too many areas in our plans where things could go drastically wrong, that we had no control over. I was concerned that we had so little Diamanda. It would be so much safer (and would improve our chances of success) if most of Piristil's occupants were slumbering peacefully as we made our getaway. On the actual night, obstacles arose like the fingers of a corpse who would not stay dead. It had taken careful machinations to nudge our time of escape onto a night when neither Panthera or I would be working. Suddenly, after dinner, Jafit told me he wanted me to see a client; a last minute arrangement. Flummoxed for a moment, I had to pretend to be ill, which also meant that Jafit relieved me of my duty of taking Panthera his dinner that night. Panicking furiously,

I imagined Panthera would think our plans had been discovered if anyone else took my place of attending him. He might even do something rash. I thought it would be too risky and too suspicious to try and get a message to him. I'd just have to trust his faith in me and try to sneak into his room later. The drugged wine had already been delivered to Outher and his friends with a suitably simpering note. Timing was crucial. After the wine knocked them out, we had about half an hour to get out. I knew that Outher and the other Mojags usually ate their dinner about nine o'clock on nights when Panthera wasn't working. They would drink the wine after that. That gave me about two hours to get in there. I shut myself in my room and paced it from end to end for half an hour. Then Flounah knocked on my door and asked if I was alright. He'd heard the floor creaking. Irritably, I answered that I'd just got a stomach-ache; I'd be alright soon. He asked if I needed anything and I tried to calm myself by answering slowly. No, I didn't need anything, thank you. I would go to bed very shortly. I could sense him waiting on the landing outside my door for several minutes before he padded off. Did he suspect anything? Then Jafit came up, knocked and demanded to be let in. Feverishly, I opened the door.

"You look ghastly," he said, touching my face. "You should be lying down. Should I fetch a physician? Would you like one of the others to sit with you?"

I shook my head. "No, I'll be fine, honestly. I get this complaint sometimes." Once, such things would have been utterly plausible. But that was when I'd been human. Physical illness is not as common in Hara. Perhaps I'd been foolish expecting that they'd leave me alone. Jafit continued to fuss and I could barely restrain my temper. The thought, "Look, will you just fuck off!" was dangerously close to becoming a spoken reality. Eventually, after I'd uttered more than enough reassurances that I would be fine in the morning, he left.

I locked the door again and sat down on the bed. I turned off the light and stood up again, crept to the window, gazed over at Panthera's dim lights. I tried to see if Kruin was lurking in the yard yet, but of course, it was too early for that. I fretted the time away, checking and rechecking the clock as its hands crawled lazily around the dial. I smoked seventeen cigarettes, but refrained from consuming either of the bottles of wine standing on the windowsill. I would be needing a clear head. My bags were packed and standing together on the carpet. I regretted having to leave the rugs behind.

Twenty minutes past nine o'clock, I put my ear to the door. All seemed silent outside. Working kanene would be busy in their rooms. Those who were off duty would either be in Fallsend or in one of the sitting rooms on the ground floor. Jafit, as far as I knew, was conveniently visiting a friend down town. I opened the door, looked out, and there was Flounah advancing down the corridor. *(Quickly, throw bags, coat behind me).*

"Oh, Calanthe," he said, "are you feeling better now?" I hoped the stricken feeling of horror inside me had not manifested on my face.

"A little," I said weakly. "I was just going to the bathroom."

"The bathroom's that way," Flounah said, pointing behind me.

"And to get a drink of milk from the kitchen," I added stonily. Flounah smiled and walked past me. Seething with annoyance, I had to walk past the corridor that led to Panthera's wing and go downstairs. Now I would have to go back to my room to pick up my luggage. Nuisance, nuisance; damn these stupid whores! Lurking in the shadows of the hall, waiting to see if Flounah should come back again, I was surprised by Ezhno.

"Calanthe, are you alright?" he asked, as I physically jumped about two feet. Perhaps he thought I was delirious, standing there in the dark, peering up the stairs.

"Oh fine!" I said, "Much better."

"What are you doing here? Why have you got your outdoor clothes on?"

"I was cold," I answered. "I just came down to get a drink of water."

"Why didn't you get one from the bathroom?" (Thank the Aghama my room didn't have its own water tap; what excuse could I have given then?)

"There was somebody in the bathroom!" I said, through gritted teeth. I longed to turn and smack him in the jaw, but knew he'd make too much noise.

"Why are you looking up the stairs?" He joined me, peering.

"That's none of your business, Ezhno!"

"What are you up to?"

I sighed, turned and looked at him for a few moments, sifting, discarding desires of murder. "Ezhno, come with me," "I'll tell you."

Putting my arm around his shoulders, I led him up the stairs. He said nothing as I went back to my room, hoisted my bag, grabbed my coat and silently closed the door. Said nothing, but stared at me all the time. I think he'd realized that I wasn't (nor had been) in the least bit ill, but had perhaps lost my sanity. Wise in the more cunning avenues of self-preservation, Ezhno, dumb little tart, kept his mouth shut. Luckily, there was no further sign of Flounah. Panthera's corridor was in darkness. There didn't appear to be a Mojag in sight, but the shadows seemed alive with potential adversaries. With panicking heart and a desperate urge to flee struggling inside me like a startled, cornered horse, I knocked on Panthera's door. Softly, briskly, Panthera called out, hissed out, "Who is it?"

"Cal," I answered, forgetting the new form of my name in my urgency. I think that was the moment when Calanthe disappeared into oblivion for ever. Some disguise. To the people I tried to hide from, names mean nothing. I heard a key turn in the lock and the door opened, spilling yellow light into the corridor. I dragged a protesting, wide-eyed Ezhno into the room with me quickly and Panthera closed the door behind us, turning the key in the lock. Panthera, thrumming with an energy that had bleached his face, turned his eyes to dark, animal disks, looked at Ezhno with distaste.

"What's this?" he asked me.

"What the hell is going on?" Ezhno squeaked, trying to struggle away from me. Worry had broken through his sensible silence. His eyes darted round the room, seeking bolt-holes.

I gripped his shoulder painfully. "Keep your mouth shut!" I advised, giving him a small, warning shake.

Ezhno glared at me, but complied. He wasn't stupid.

"Oh wonderful!" Panthera spat. "What do we do with this? And keep your voice down; you'll wake the Mojags."

Behind him, I could see Outher and his companions around the table, all unconscious. One had slipped to the floor, while Outher and the other slept with their heads cradled in their arms on the table. They had suspected nothing.

"What kept you?" Panthera hissed. "I nearly died when Astarth came in tonight. I thought we'd been found out and the Mojags had already started to drink the wine. I wondered whether your friend Kruin and I would have to leave Piristil without you."

"Leave Piristil!" Ezhno had found his voice again. I twisted his arm until he yelped.

"He needs silencing," Panthera observed. Ezhno made some further noise of disgruntlement so Panthera spun lightly around and kicked him in the side of the neck. Quite a feat. Ezhno was still pretty close to me. All I felt was the wind of Panthera's passing foot. Ezhno crumpled to the ground without a murmur. I had an idea that he might sleep a little longer than the Mojags. Panthera was dressed in black and still had the remains of the silver chains round his ankles. I could tell he felt completely confident about all this.

"Any sign of Kruin yet?" I asked and went to the window. With superb timing, Kruin's face popped up and we both jumped, Kruin nearly to his death in the yard below. He waved a fist at me.

"Hurry up!" I mouthed. Panthera was pulling on a pair of boots behind me, which I supposed he must have stolen from the Mojags. They did look a little loose on him, but it was too cold outside for sandals or soft slippers; he had no heavy shoes of his own.

"They keep moving," he said, cocking his head at the table.

"Hmm, I'm not surprised. It was a light dose. (*Too light? No, don't think that.*) God, I hope we have enough time. Come on, Kruin."

Kruin did not hear me. He was busily applying a smoking liquid to the bars of the window, a scarf tied over his face.

"Think we could take these three on?" Panthera inquired. I looked at him, then at the powerful, lightly slumbering forms of the Mojags. Sometimes, the willowy Panthera can look surprisingly menacing, a creature who could kill by stealth rather than strength.

"Not three, no," I said. "Not even with your high kicks!" I continued to gesture encouragement at Kruin. Panthera opened the window, the sash squealing dreadfully, and overpowering, foul fumes began to drift into the room. Kruin pulled a forlorn face over his scarf as both Panthera and I began to cough.

"Shut the window!" Kruin ordered. "If the smoke reaches the Mojags, they'll probably wake up."

The window was swiftly closed. We looked through it anxiously. Kruin kept trying to break the bars, but they appeared unmovable. Eventually, after what seemed at least an hour, one of them moved in his hand.

"Thank the Aghama!" Panthera murmured beside me. His fear, anxiety had released an enticing Panthera-type aroma from his pores; a delicious scent of cinnamon and smoke. Even under such conditions of stress I couldn't help noticing it, wanting to fill my lungs with it, wipe out the corrosion-stink. All hara have their own, bewitching perfume; passions of any kind can release it. Panthera became aware of my subliminal interest. He moved away from me and the moment was lost.

Just as Kruin was tugging and wrenching at the third bar, whose removal would give Panthera and myself enough room to squeeze through, there was a noise behind us. The door. I wheeled around and saw the key hanging from the lock, trembling, rattling. It fell, landing with a dull plop on the carpet. Whoever was on the other side of that door had the master key. Panthera and I exchanged an agonized glance. To both of us, a monster Jafit was waiting out there. Panthera swore and threw the window up on its sashes. More foul smoke billowed into the room. Behind us the door swung open. Not Jafit; Astarth. An Astarth with a key in his hand, looking right at me. His face was expressionless.

As air and fumes rushed into the room, Outher uttered a groan and began to lift his head, shake it, make further noises. "Come on!" Kruin urged, panicking. He disappeared, dropping to the courtyard below. Outher was lurching toward us, looking about twenty feet tall, one hand over his eyes, unsure of what was happening. Astarth was feeling his way carefully into the room, one hand over his mouth and nose. It was getting very murky; smoke everywhere. Another Mojag began to stir and rise, the third still lay unconscious on the floor.

"Get going, Cal!" Panthera said. He was grinning from ear to ear, positively vibrating with force.

Suddenly movement seemed to erupt around us. The second Mojag scuttled forward, growling. Outher shook his head clearer, saw us properly and roared. Astarth ran forward, a bottle held purposefully in his raised hand. Panthera tried to push me out of the window, throwing our baggage down before me. Just as I jumped, I saw Astarth smash the bottle down onto the second Mojag's head, then I landed with a sickening jolt in the yard. Looking up, I could see Panthera poised on the windowsill. Silhouetted behind him was the lumbering form of Outher. Kruin helped me up, looking anxiously at Panthera. It was bitterly cold out there, our hot, steaming breath almost clouding the scene on the window-ledge.

"Jump!" Kruin called, but not too loudly for fear of attracting further attention. Pushing off, with an exhuberant cry, Panthera effortlessly kicked

Outher in the throat, kicked him senseless back into the room, and soared backwards through the air, to land on all fours beside me. Astarth ran to the window, put his hands on the sill, leaned down. We stared at each other. I could not understand his motives. I could not speak.

"Get going," he said, "and good luck. Give my love to Jaddayoth."

"Astarth?"

"Go on, quickly!" He smiled. "Jafit will come after you, Calanthe. Don't let him beat you. Don't. Now go!"

"But Jafit will know what you did in there! He'll kill you!" An impulsive idea followed. "Come with us, Astarth. Jump!"

He was still smiling at me, shaking his head. "Would Jafit kill me for protecting his prize pussy cat? It looked like the Mojags were attacking him, didn't it? Difficult to tell with the room all full of smoke. No, I didn't know what was going on, Calanthe. Don't worry about me; I'm indispensible. Just get going will you! Now!"

Then light was spilling out into the yard as the kitchen door opened. I heard Jancis's voice cry out.

"What's going on?"

I grabbed Panthera's arm and we ran after Kruin, both of us laughing hysterically in our mad panic. Our bags bumped into our legs, the one containing my notebooks thumping painfully against my back.

"Come on!" Kruin shouted. He was in the gateway to the street, already on horseback. Two other horses were prancing in the snow beside him. I could see the rolling whites of their eyes. Panthera, unbelievably, jumped on the nearest horse by vaulting over the tail. I chose a more conventional method by using the stirrup, slinging my bags over the saddle. Behind us, activity in the yard became louder. We didn't look back. We shrieked and kicked the animals' flanks and skidded, slipped, half-galloped up the road, north out of Fallsend. Kruin had bought Gimrah horses and had to borrow money from the merchants for that purpose. Gimrah horses are fast, very fast. We were away before Jafit could follow us. Of course, we knew he would hire trackers to bring us back, or try to, as he had done when Panthera had escaped before, but we counted on him thinking we would opt for the quickest route, which was south. Obviously trained trackers wouldn't take long to realize that was the wrong way, but it could give us a little more time, a little more lead. Filled with the exhilaration of our success, I felt that what we had achieved that night was more of a memorial to Lolotea than what I'd accomplished with Astarth the previous week. We galloped madly past the forlorn, funeral hill. I waved into the snow-lit darkness. "We did it, Teah!" Panthera's laugh echoed my cry.

"May Jafit drown in his own blood!" he said, and we all whooped and cheered as it began to snow once more. If it snowed thickly and quickly enough, our trail would be covered. We estimated that it would take some time for Jafit to engage the trackers—if we were lucky, as much as a couple of hours. We headed toward the main road out of the town so that our trail would be more difficult to follow. Few hara were traveling at this hour, but the main road had been strewn with ashes all the same. What hara we passed looked at us curiously for we were still traveling fast. Although this did attract attention, we felt that speed was more advisable than caution in this case. We rode all night, punishing the horses. By dawn, we were well into the hills north of Fallsend. All towns that we passed were deserted and overgrown. Kruin was familiar with this territory. "We must keep north for a few more miles," he said, "and then head east toward Jaddayoth, following the River Scarm upstream. It should be more sheltered."

As morning began to seep a red mist over the land, the cold crept back into our bones. Camp-fires would not be enough to keep us warm. It was going to be a long, uncomfortable journey.

CHAPTER EIGHT

>-!-‹›-‹-Ο-‹›-!-≺

A Tale by the Fire
"Two roads diverged in a wood,
And I—
I took the one less traveled by"
—Robert Frost, The Road Not Taken

Fereng will soon be behind us. We have had to cut across its corner to reach Jaddayoth. Here, the air is dry and bitterly cold, making our lungs ache and our eyelashes and nostrils frost over. There is no sign of pursuit from Fallsend yet, but we are not so complacent as to think they're not behind us somewhere. Up here, in the spiky, clean air, it becomes impossible to remember the details of life in Piristil; such things should never be possible. But if I can forget it with ease, I do not think the same can be said for Panthera. After the first flush of excitement and triumph, he became very subdued. Initially, I thought the weather conditions were getting to him. Kruin complained aloud and dreamed of the warm hearths of Natawni. I could not envisage the future, and I am used to cold (cold of heart and cold of body). All I could think of was putting enough distance between ourselves and Jafit.

One night, Panthera and I sat huddled around a meager fire and he began to talk. Kruin was asleep behind us.

"I can't believe I'm free," Panthera said.

"We're not yet!" I told him. "We're only free when we reach Jael and the protection of your family."

"Ah yes, my family," Panthera said in a soft, cold voice, staring at the fire. "They must think I'm dead."

"What happened?" I asked. "How come you were up for sale in Emunah anyway? Do you want to talk about it?"

"I'm not that sensitive about it, if that's what you think!" he said. "If you really want to know; I'll tell you."

"The night is long," I replied, waving a hand toward the hard, starry sky. "We're cold, without the support of alcohol or good food. Tell me your story, my pantherine. It may help to pass the time."

Panthera shrugged. "You're a ham," he said, settling his chin comfortably on his knees. "OK, here goes. First the background stuff. I was born to the family Jael in the land of Jaddayoth, among the forest hills of Ferike. My sire is the Ferike Castlethane Ferminfex Jael and my hostling an imported Kalamah named Lahela." He smiled wistfully at the fire. "Talk about myself? Very soon; maybe. Now I'll speak of my family, which is a story in itself. People back home write poems about my parents' courtship; I can't remember them though. But I do remember my father telling me about it, how one day, he was invited to the Kalamah city of Zaltana, by the Fanchon, its lord, and there it all began . . ."

It was not just a sweet tale of romance as Panthera implied, but also a sneak preview of the Jaddayoth I intended to squeeze myself into; the world of the royal families. Around about the time Ferminfex received his missive from the Fanchon, Zaltana was nearing completion. Panthera said that the Kalamah work very slowly (lots of time for refreshments, etc.), but their architecture is splendid. Zaltana is a diamond of Wraeththu cities. The Fanchon wanted the history of its construction documented, his own accomplishments immortalized by written word—well-written word. The Ferike are the scholars and artists of Jaddayoth tribes. They are often called upon to undertake such work. Ferminfex set sail.

Zaltana is made of creamy, peachy marble and stands upon the coast. Ferminfex was immediately impressed by the wonderful, perfumed air of the place; hanging gardens of riotous, exotic blooms flavored and colored the city streets. He was in awe of the grand, lazy grace of the soaring buildings and the languid, feline beauty of its people. Day after day, Ferminfex would sit in the great library of the Fanchon's palace, working at his papers. He had been given a blond, pinewood desk still smelling of the forest, and as he sat there sunlight would fall on his hands through the open windows. Pausing from his work now and again to drink citrus cordial or smoke a musky, greenleaf cigarette, he would gaze out of the window at the langourous activities of the Kalamah.

In the late afternoons, before the early evening meal, the sons of the Fanchon would come to the tiled terrace beneath the library windows. They would sit on plump, tasseled cushions around their teacher who taught them to play strange, meowing music upon strangely clawed stringed instruments. Ferminfex would gaze down at them, as he took another drink, and be reminded of a pride of young lions from the land of

Olathe. They always had their cats with them, purring and chirruping in cat voices to their small, feline companions. Delightful, artless creatures they were, with tawny, streaky hair like manes, and slim, supple bodies. Lahela was the eldest of them, past Feybraiha but seemingly unattached, and of such loveliness that even the austere and normally unmovable Ferminfex could not help but fall desperately in love with him. Every day, while watching Lahela, he would put aside the dry, dusty business of praising the Fanchon's achievements, to write long, passion-laden poems instead; hymns to the Fanchon's eldest son. Occasionally, Lahela would glance up at the library window and smile at him. He was not a proud creature. Perhaps Ferminfex even let one or two of his desperate odes float down to the terrace below, who knows. Panthera didn't say. I like to think he did.

The time came when the Fanchon asked Ferminfex to name his payment for the work he had completed. Without hesitation, the Ferike requested that he be given Lahela as his consort and be allowed to return with him to Jael. For a Ferike, this was not an unusual request; theirs is a tribe that often sells children to others who might want to improve their bloodlines. But it was not the custom in Zaltana. For a while, the Fanchon was quite taken aback, even affronted, by what he thought was Ferminfex's audacity. Lahela himself solved the problem by telling his father he was wholly agreeable to the arrangement. They were bonded in blood without hardly ever having spoken a word to each other.

"Romantic, isn't it," Panthera said, at the end of his tale, "and quite removed from what happened to me! My parents adore each other! True, the Jaels were annoyed by Lahela's Kalamah ways when he first came to Ferike, but I suppose they've got used to it now."

"Your home is a happy one then?" I asked.

"Very." Panthera frowned. His violation and degradation might offend that happiness.

"So, you've spoken mainly of Jael," I said, too heartily, "what about how you came to be in Emunah? I presume your family didn't sell you to slavers."

Panthera laughed. "No, but they were selling me in a way. That's what made it happen."

"Oh?"

"Yes. I was approaching my Feybraiha, you see, and they were all concerned about who would be 'the one' for me then, and all mixed up with that was Lahela thinking I should spend some time in Kalamah, because I was half-Kalamah, after all, and being cooped up in Ferike was denying me half my heritage, if not half my family. They came up with a cosy arrangement between them. The Fanchon had a spare cousin of mine knocking about who was quite a lot older than me but in need of a suitable consort. He was due to take over some far-flung Kalamah settlement on the Emunah border. Guess who was picked for him." I pointed at him silently. Panthera nodded. "Correct. Never mind the fact that I loved Ferike and didn't want to leave; that was irrelevant. 'Panthera, you will be more at home in Kalamah,' Lahela kept telling me. I knew he was wrong. I'm not that much like him; much more Ferike. I want cold and dark and trees all around me. I tried to protest but it was useless. Ferminfex said that I'd be able to come home whenever I wanted to; a chesna-bond was not imprisonment. 'Aghama willing, you may like each other,' he said, but I didn't hold out much hope. Cousin Namir. How I hated the name! To me it sounded cunning and sneaky. The name of a thief!

"I can remember the day we set out from Jael so well. It was autumntide and very misty and dank, Ferike looking its best to see me off and make me feel worse. I was being accompanied by a guard of ten hara, all armed with Maudrah weapons, all capable of being competent and deadly, should the need arise. First we were going to Gimrah to pick up a present for the Fanchon, a group of racing-steeds. Then we'd take a ship from the coast of Gimrah, straight to Kalamah. The guards barely spoke to me. I was full of anger. Even more so when I discovered they weren't nearly so efficient as my parents had thought. Crossing the plains of Gimrah, we were overpowered by a large gang of Emunah slavers. It was over in a trice. Me and three others were carted off to Meris; the rest of my escort was dead. For weeks, I existed in a kind of stunned trance. Things like this just don't happen to sons of castlethanes, surely? But they do. No rescue. No respite. Dignity stripped away until all that's left is self-loathing. And there were no Feybraiha garlands for me either, oh no! By sheer luck, I think, I remained untouched until Jafit got me back to Thaine. Then I lost my virginity to a half-formed har who paid Jafit a lot of money for the privilege." He shook his head. "Vileness! Never again. Never. If my family searched for me, they found no clue to my whereabouts. No-one to tell them. No-one to care. The last three years have been more than hell for me, Cal. Much more. I'm not going back there. Ever. I'll die first. I mean that."

"It's OK," I soothed, reaching to touch his hand. He pulled away from me.

"No, it isn't OK!" he said angrily. "You know how aruna is so important for us! All that is just a dim, dark memory of a possibility for me. Anyway, you're so keen to interrogate me, what about yourself? What secrets are you hiding, Cal?"

I don't think he expected me to answer truthfully. I shrugged. "I may not be safe anymore. Not out in the open."

"Is that all you're going to say?"

"It's all I can say. I don't feel anything yet, but I'm sure it will come. Fallsend was just a refuge. I could hide there, but not forever. There's no way I can hide out here; too big, too wide."

Panthera looked puzzled by that answer. "Who's after you?" he asked.

"I'm not sure. It could be one of several people. It could be many. I don't know."

Panthera leaned toward me, searching my eyes, which he would find empty of clues. "What have you done, Cal? Why are you being followed?"

I smiled. "Now, now, my pantherine, don't pry," I said lightly. "Have you considered that it might be because, not of what I've done in the past, but what they'd have me do in the future?"

Panthera narrowed his eyes. "You speak in riddles. Why?"

"To protect you. I don't want to involve anyone else."

"That's an excuse!"

"No, it's not."

"You don't trust me. I told you everything."

"It's not a question of trust, Panthera. Really it isn't. I can't explain. Please leave it be."

He fell silent, moody because he had been denied something he wanted. We were sitting by an inadequate fire, both wary of pursuit. That night, we did not sleep.

CHAPTER NINE

>·!·<>·O·<>·!·<

In Hadassah

"Reprieve the doomed devil—
Has he not died enough?"

—Robert Graves, *A Jealous Man*

Of course, Seel is being very civilized about all this. There can't be many times he's had a houseguest go for the throat of his best friend, but Seel is, after all, a diplomat. Orien has gone home, nursing a bruised throat; Flick is hiding in the kitchens, very silently. "What do you know?" I say to Seel. Seel shrugs, lighting a cigarette. "Nothing, Cal, nothing. Have I ever lied to you?" He is testing our friendship. I would like to believe him. I would like to believe them all; they that claim to know nothing about Pell's death. Do they really think I've forgotten Thiede came to Saltrock for Pell's inception? How did Thiede know . . . unless he was told?

"You're not well, Cal," Seel says to me. "You haven't been well for a long time, have you?"

"Always so goddamn wise aren't you, Seel!"

He smiles; tolerant. "Who knows you better than I, Cal?"

Oh, he can look right through me to the black and rotten core, I'm sure. Now I will avoid his eyes.

"Bed!" I say, standing up. It is late. There are wine bottles on the floor; I knock one over. Seel stoops to put it on the table; as he stands he lays his hand on my arm. "Alone," I say.

"You sure?" I'm sure; there's no way I could sleep next to those eyes. He kisses me on the lips. "Sleep well, Cal."

Sleep? What's sleep? I grab two opened bottles of wine off the dresser on my way out of the room.

My room is in darkness and I don't want to change that. I sit on the bed, drinking wine from the bottle. What the hell am I doing here? Saltrock can never be home to me now; too many memories. I drink, fumbling for a cigarette in the dark. Matches spill over the floor, the bed. Damn! Damn, damn, damn. I'm on the floor, grovelling, snatching at nothing. Then I'm curled up weeping; no violence, no punching the ground; just weeping. When someone comes into the room, I am beyond objecting. It feels as if I have no bones as they lay me on the bed. God, how I hate to cry. It hurts, contorts, makes me so vulnerable. Someone says, "There was nothing I could say, Cal. Truly, there was nothing." It is Orien. He's come back. He's come back because he cares. I look up, uncurl, at the sound of his voice.

"God, how I want to believe you," I say. I am aware how I must look to him. Red eyes; childlike, helpless. He sits down on the bed, strokes my wet face.

"Then do believe it."

"Oh, you knew, Orien; I'm convinced you did. Why didn't you warn us?"

He never stops looking at me, yet there is no guilt, no furtiveness in his eyes. "There was no need," he says. "There was nothing I could tell Pell that he didn't know already."

"What do you mean?"

"Just what I said. If he said nothing to you, that's not my fault. Or Seel's or Flick's or anybody else's . . . is it now."

I want to say, don't you patronize me, but I just bury my face in the bedspread. Orien stands up to leave. I look up. He's standing there all lean and tawny and gentle; perfect Wraeththu. God, how I want to believe him; I can't stop thinking that. "Don't go," I say.

He hesitates, looks once at the door. It is a long moment. He smiles into my eyes and it's a slow, sad smile. He pushes his hair back from his face. "If you need me, I'll stay," he says.

"I need you." Come to me, Orien, come to me. Let me feel your warmth; penetrate my eternal cold. Please. Oh, I am so desperate; I want to melt. Is he surprised by my desire? Yes, he is. Maybe, he thinks it's irreverent because of my grief, but he complies all the same. Soothing, slow, languorous; that's Orien. A skilled lover. Afterwards, I sit up in bed to watch him fall asleep. One arm is thrown above his head; blankets thrown off to below his waist. He looks like the son of God. After a while I get out of bed and squat down in the corner of the room, still watching him. He barely moves; just the rise and fall of his chest. Moonlight is falling through the window to burn me, my knees hunched up nearly to my ears. I don't feel well. My insides are aching. The room is black and white; no color at all. How come I'm dressed like this, dressed to leave? I don't remember. How come my bag is packed and standing by the door? Have I been awake for a long time? Have I blacked out? How come there's a long-bladed knife in my hand? My hands are trembling; the sharpness catches the moonlight and shivers between my fingers. Slowly, I run the

back of my left hand over the blade. So sharp. Hand to mouth; blood upon my tongue. Salt. Salt. I am not afraid of death. Are you, Orien? Are you afraid of death? He looks perfect. I stand up; the room tumbles, bars of black and white across my face, my hands. Adepts fear nothing. If he wakes up he'll take the knife away from me, won't he? His eyes will command me. There's nothing to fear, but I must go on. I can't stop myself, you know, I really can't. It's the moonlight; must be. It's hypnotized me. All these black and white lines; they're driving right through me. Won't go away until I've made things balance. That moon out there, it looks like an eye. (Why did he have to come back? Why?) I'm thinking of eyes even as I stand over him with the knife raised, but it's straight for the belly that I strike.

Twisting, tearing; quick ruin. Up, beneath the ribs, through flesh and muscle, scraping bone. I feel it. I feel it. He gasps and his eyes flick open. He grabs my wrist; my hands are still around the knife-hilt protruding from his flesh, but his hold just slips away. I am already greasy with his blood. The blade has gone all the way in. I rip it out. He says nothing, just looks at me, his face bleached white, his hair, eyes and mouth deepest black. Maybe I should have obliterated his face; I couldn't. I just keep on stabbing, ripping into his belly until there is nothing left to stab. He never even tries to defend himself. Why? No, I don't care why. He could have warned us; he didn't. If we'd known, maybe Pell would be alive now. With me. A life for a life. That is the law. Nothing unfair about that, is there?

I am warm with his blood and drag him from the house. Take him home. The temple, the Nayati. A fine surprise for the next blind worshippers. I hang him from the rafters by his own guts. My mind is blank; no feeling. It doesn't hurt me to do this, doesn't sicken me; nothing. There is a red film of blood over his dead eyes; he will watch the moonlight through the long windows forever. Let him remember. Let him rue the day he kept silent.

That's it. Nothing else. I steal a horse and leave, galloping north. By daylight, the lunatic remembers nothing.

It is surprising how quickly you get to know people, traveling together on the road. I found Kruin mostly easygoing, although he does like to take control, which Panthera doesn't like at times. Panthera himself is an enigma to me. In Piristil, I'd categorized him to be someone very much like Cobweb; proud, vain and veering sharply toward the feminine. Out here in the wilds, he seems completely different; competent, sharp and helpful. He has also shown, in sometimes hair-raising circumstances, that he has no fear whatsoever. He is frightened of nothing. Sometimes, this kind of thing can prove to be a disadvantage, like not being able to feel pain. It's convenient most of the time, but just occasionally it is extremely useful to feel the burn as you walk across hot coals; it preserves the flesh and bone of the feet! Sometimes, it is best to feel afraid. I've never been ashamed to admit when I've been frightened gutless.

We often wonder whether Jafit has worked out which way we've come yet. None of us has dared to think he's given up the chase. It is deathly quiet in this landscape of snow; all the land is sleeping. We are following the river canyon east, climbing all the time. Our supplies are running low. Kruin urged the need for haste. We rest the horses as little as possible.

Yesterday, we passed a small, snow-covered shrine nestling in a shallow hole in the rock face. There was a spring there, a wide, stone bowl, but the water was frozen. Kruin and I broke the ice and melted some of it in a saucepan over the fire. Our horses nosed dispiritedly through the snow, looking for something to eat. We'd had to be mean with their rations for some days now. One of them chewed bark off a tree.

Panthera said, "Well, well, this is a shrine dedicated to the Aghama. I wonder what it's doing here, in the middle of nowhere?"

An icy shudder, that was not caused by the weather, passed right through me.

"Gelaming use this road sometimes," Kruin said. I couldn't help glancing nervously behind me, down river. Panthera must have noticed.

"I doubt if they pass this way in winter," he said. "I expect they'll all stay comfortably in the sublime land of Almagabra, and I don't blame them!"

"Not if someone is due for relief in one of the stations they occupy along the Natawni/Maudrah border," Kruin argued mildly.

"They don't travel overland very often," I said.

"This must be a stopping point then," Panthera decided, stroking the stone of the shrine.

I shuddered again, not being able to imagine anything worse than a troupe of Gelaming materializing out of thin air at any time. Even Jafit and a horde of Mojags would be preferable. I was anxious to move on. Kruin and Panthera wanted to camp there for the night, as it was so sheltered. The rock wall on this side of the river was quite high and overhung with trees. I tried to argue with them but could give no good reason for my aversion. The rock protected us from the wind and it was doubtful anyone could sneak up on us unseen. It was eerily silent in that place; the river was frozen, its life hidden deep beneath the ice. As darkness fell, I wrapped myself in a blanket and climbed up the rock to survey the countryside. It was difficult to see anything.

Presently, Panthera joined me. "You're afraid of the Gelaming, aren't you," he said.

"Hmm. To them I carry the mark of Cain," I answered.

"And what's that?"

"It's something that tells me to keep away from them at all cost, if I value my sanity and my freedom."

"Oh." He thought about this, not sure if he was supposed to have understood my answer. Panthera was much younger than I, of course. He was born of another world, born har.

"There are stories, other legends, from a long time ago," I said, but then could not continue. The tale was too bleak. Wind sliced my skin; cold to the heart.

"The past *is* interesting," Panthera agreed, knowing he'd get no more out of me. He clambered back down the rock, leaving me to stare out at the endless landscape of gray and white and snow-covered pines, poking rock.

Several mornings later, we passed through the gateway into Jaddayoth. Totems along the path proclaimed that this was Hadassah territory. Kruin told me that the Hadassah are perhaps the most gregarious tribe of Jaddayoth, and never discourage travelers. "Smell the air!" Panthera cried joyfully, filling his lungs with it. Only seconds before, we had been in Fereng. The air smelled no different to me. I must admit that having Jaddayoth soil beneath our feet did make us feel safer. Slightly. Would Jafit risk pursuing us this far? Was Panthera worth that much to him? How mad was Jafit, how deep his thirst for revenge?

"I think we should head south immediately," Kruin said. "We can pass through Gimrah. The land is flatter there and we'll be able to travel faster."

"Elhmen might be safer," Panthera said.

"Hmm, perhaps, but I still don't feel happy about the Fallsend trackers," Kruin confessed. "We got away too easily. Only reaching Jael by the quickest possible route will make me feel safe!"

We didn't argue with him.

"Strange, in a way, I hope they *do* find us," Panthera said, after a while. Neither Kruin nor myself deigned to comment. It was clear from Panthera's tone that he still thought Jafit had a debt to pay.

The following day, about mid-morning, we rode into a Hadassah town, Caraway. It was quite a busy place, though not large, and had been constructed recently (during the last twenty years or so). Many—too many—harish towns are those claimed from humans. There was something curiously fresh about this little place that was not. Hara looked at us with interest as we rode by, but no-one stopped us and asked our business. I commented on the number of inns. Kruin laughed and pointed out that he'd already told me the Hadassah welcome travelers. Because of our severe lack of funds, it was decided, rather glumly, that we couldn't really afford the luxury of a decent meal at an inn, which was a shame because we were all starving. Our meals along the road had necessarily to be frugal, but we did agree to partake in one small measure of ale each, which was cheap.

The inn we chose was warm and cozy inside and, because of the early hour, nearly empty. We stood around the roaring fire and put our drinks on the mantelpiece, holding our stiff, unmittened hands to the blaze.

"We're going to have to find more funds," Panthera said.

Kruin agreed with him without argument for once. "We might have to sell one of the horses," he said.

"Won't that slow us down too much?" I asked, still the nervous one.

"Not as much as slowly starving to death," Panthera said wearily. "Why the hell does it have to be winter!"

Presently, the pot-har came from behind the bar to talk with us. He was dressed in brightly colored clothes and wore heavy brass jewelry. He commiserated with us over the bitter cold and told us that he, personally, would hate to have to travel at this time of year. We agreed earnestly.

"Will you be ordering a meal?" he asked. "We serve lunches from mid-day, but I could get you something from the kitchen if you're hungry now."

"No, thank you," Kruin said politely. "I'm afraid we are traveling with light purses. One glass of ale each is as far as we can stretch, and a free warming in front of your splendid fire of course."

The Hadassah smiled, and gestured toward the highly polished tables beneath the back windows of the inn. "Please sit down," he said. I looked in puzzlement at Kruin, who ushered me to the nearest table. Panthera followed. We sat, and the Hadassah disappeared through the door behind the bar.

"Ah, Hadassah hospitality!" Kruin beamed. I asked him to explain. "We'll be given a free meal, that's all," Panthera said. "The Hadassah are famed for their generosity. The pot-har pities us."

"I get the feeling that you anticipated something like this when you mentioned we had no money," I said, wagging an uncontrollably contented finger at Kruin.

He smiled and made a non-commital gesture. "A small gamble," he said. "We had nothing to lose."

I was quite impressed.

Hadassah fare was offered to us in the form of thick, vegetable soup, hunks of warm bread and sour winter fruit, softened with sugar and cream. The pot-har watched us devour the food with satisfaction. He refilled our glasses and sat down with us. "You've come down from Fereng?" he asked, Kruin nodded, assuming leadership, as usual.

"Hmm. We hardly get any travelers from out of country passing through at this time of year," the pot-har said casually. "Strange we should entertain two parties within two days."

Panthera, Kruin and I swapped uneasy glances.

"Another party from Thaine?" I asked.

"Well, to be honest, they were a little uncommunicative, in fact, quite rude. Because of that, I took the liberty of charging them more than usual for their meals. They were asking if we'd seen any other strangers recently."

"Which road did they arrive on?" Kruin asked, with enviable calm.

"The south road, I believe. Don't envy whoever it is they're after; they had killer eyes."

"They intimated they were *after* someone then?" I enquired.

The Hadassah shrugged. "It was reasonable to assume so. Certain questions were asked. Had I seen any other outlanders recently? I hadn't. They seemed satisfied with my answers."

"And where are they now, this other party?" I asked, as carelessly as I could.

"I'm afraid I'm not sure. They weren't staying here. They may have left Caraway."

"Thank you," Kruin said, and the pot-har inclined his head and left us. We resumed our meal in silence.

"Jafit's trackers?" Panthera asked after a while. An obvious remark which we'd all been contemplating, I'm sure.

"Seems likely," I said, convinced of the fact. "But from the south? How could they have followed our trail?"

"Maybe they didn't!" Panthera said. "There are few clear roads into Jaddayoth at this time of year. It wouldn't take a genius to work out which way we'd have to come."

"They probably went south into Elhmen from Fallsend," Kruin continued, "and when they realized we hadn't gone that way, simply circled around, knowing full well they'd have a good chance of intercepting us once we turned south. That Jael is our destination is unfortunately obvious. As Panthera said, clear roads are few and far between."

"It was luck, just luck, on their side!" Panthera interrupted bitterly.

"Well, they don't know we're here yet, hopefully," I said. "Perhaps we'd better move on as soon as possible."

Outside the inn, the friendly town of Caraway suddenly seemed threatening and hostile. Perhaps there were unseen eyes watching us, spies reporting back, even a Sensitive poised somewhere with probing mind. We set off at a brisk pace and were cantering down the south road out of the town within minutes. Our silence was only breath steaming on the air, panting breath. We did not look back. It is an ill-omen to look back. At noon we entered a dense forest, veering off from the main road, where the snow was packed and hard, into a desolate place of wind-sculpted drifts and stark pines. Kruin was vaguely familiar with the path, but it was difficult to follow under these conditions.

"This track should come out of the forest near the town of Jasminia," he said, shaking his compass.

We slowed to a walk and the only sounds were the muffled tread of our horses' hooves in the snow and the occasional, startled rattle of a bird spiraling up through the trees. There was no outward sign of anyone following us, but we were all plagued by the horrible feeling of being observed. As the sun began to sink and the trees cast gloomy shadows over the snow, we were still deep in the forest. There were no clouds; it was bitterly cold. Kruin annoyed Panthera and myself by continually muttering, "We *should* be out of the trees, we *should* be." We weren't. A painfully definite fact that was not going to change in a short time. And we didn't need reminding of that. Panthera said that the way things were going, we would just have to try and find work in Jasminia—if we ever got there. "There's no way we'll reach Jael on the supplies we have, and the horses are beginning to lose condition."

"Want to risk hanging around then?" Kruin asked tetchily.

"We have no choice! Anyway, we have no proof that it was Jafit's people who were seen in Caraway."

"Don't be stupid!"

"I'm not. Why don't *you* stop being paranoid! We have to face this problem. There's no way it's going to just vanish. I haven't broken out of Piristil just to freeze to death in Hadassah!"

They continued to snipe at each other, but not with any great feeling. Their eyes and their minds were kept mainly on the gaps in the trees. I rode along behind in a kind of idiot daze. Perhaps it was just the cold, but I'd felt strange ever since leaving the road, picking up memories like bad visualizations. Pictures kept surfacing in my mind like murder victims in a mud patch. Unfortunate simile. Feelings, smells, tastes, a snatch of words. It all just drifted over me. I should have known it was a warning that power was near. Before Fallsend, I'd have put spur to flank and ridden the horse to death to escape that feeling.

At sundown, we crawled beneath a fallen pine and curled up together among the roots, in our blankets. We did not light a fire and I, for one, was thankful for the hot meal the Hadassah had given us that morning. I could not sleep, discomforted by Kruin's elbow in my chest, the sound of breathing all around me, that distanced any sounds beyond the branches. I stared up through the black, root fingers hanging over us, that were dripping with frozen soil. After several cheerless hours, I must have drifted off to sleep, only to awake soon after with an excruciating urge to urinate. I was reluctant to leave our bony nest of shared body warmth, but the need was too pressing to ignore. Fumbling through the branches, I stretched into the icy air.

All around me the forest lay white and black and silent, the snow sparkling in the light of a white, round moon that sailed above the treetops. My nerves were still raw and itching, but I roughly tried to suppress such sensations. "Paranoia, Cal!" I chastized myself, which was foolish. I deserved what happened. There I was, in mid-stream, for want of a better term, when someone said softly, "Calanthe." It was not the best time to be surprised by an unwelcome visitor. I looked, squinted, into the trees and a figure materialized out of the gloom. My first thought was "Gelaming!" and I froze, helpless in blind panic. If I'd realized who it really was I might have reacted differently. A knife blade kissed my throat with its sharpest point. I could not turn my head without risking injury, but I knew it was Jafit standing beside me. He grabbed my hair as I modestly rearranged my clothing, his thickly-gloved hand yanking my face close to his own. He shook his head as if in sadness. "I'm disappointed in you, my dear," he said.

"Then you were a fool to trust me," I replied, finding my voice. "Get your hands off me, Jafit. You have the position of advantage here, I think."

"Haven't I just!" he agreed affably. "Where's my Panthera?"

"Not *yours,* Jafit."

"Be quiet. You are surrounded. You have no chance. Just hand him over, Calanthe, and I might, just might, let you off with a thorough beating."

"What, and then let me go free?" I laughed in his face. "You can drop dead, pimp! Both Panthera and myself will die before you take him back to Piristil!"

"Oh, how touching," Jafit said, nastily.

I realized that, by this time, Panthera and Kruin must be awake, but were obviously lying low, waiting to see what would happen. I was not entirely sure how I felt about that. Support would have been most welcome at that point. Jafit, barely able to suppress his nauseating, triumphant leer, clicked his fingers and five hara emerged fully from the cover of the trees, to stand menacingly beside him and around me. Three of them were Mojags, one of these was Outher. Outher stared at me blankly, obviously still raw from my betrayal. I had hoped never to see him again, mainly because he was not a bad sort, and I knew I must have hurt him.

"Search the area!" Jafit ordered, with a tasty mouthful of satisfaction.

"That won't be necessary, Jafit." The voice was cool, and there was Panthera with his back to the fallen pine, looking as mean and deadly as a she-cat about to defend her young. He held a slim-barrelled gun in his hands, which was pointed directly at Jafit's head. Jafit looked thunderstruck with surprise. Was he really so stupid that he thought Panthera couldn't defend himself away from his chains? The Mojags scorned firearms, but the other two (who were deducably trackers) quivered to draw their own. "Tell them to be sensible," Panthera said, still clear, still calm. He must have felt wonderful in those moments. Jafit didn't respond, but the trackers lowered their hands anyway. "Kruin!" Panthera called. "Get the weapons." Like a shadow, forest-creature that he is, Kruin slipped past us. Jafit's hara made several disgruntled protests as he took their knives and guns. The Mojags also had axes and slim, whip-like swords, which must look rather incongruous in their large paws. Kruin looked up and smiled at me.

Too late, out of the corner of my eye, I saw the quick gesture that Jafit made, and that was when Outher, obeying some subtle command, decided to become a hero. With a roar, he jumped Kruin from behind, his large, lithe body covering several yards in one leap. Panthera should have shot him immediately. He didn't. I don't know why. He'd kept his head until that moment. Outher was much taller than Kruin; an easy target. Instead, incensed by whatever inner rages were motivating him, Panthera decided to empty the contents of the gun into Jafit's brain. Jafit fell to the ground, grunting in surprise. One shot would have been enough at that range.

"What the fuck are you doing?" I screamed. "Stop it! There are *five* of them!"

Panthera remained staring at the twitching body of Jafit. The gun smoked in the chill air. Behind us, Outher and Kruin grappled noisily, though Kruin's cries were from pain and frustration. Outher's from glee. The others were advancing warily, perhaps unsure whether Panthera, in his new role of mad, indiscriminate killer, had any more weapons on him.

"Panthera!" I cried again. He seemed to shake himself, wake up. "The others!" I said, gesturing wildly.

"Oh, the others," he said and raised the gun, but of course, the barrel was empty and all the spare ammunition was beneath the tree. Outher threw Kruin, coughing, to the ground, where he lay groaning, knees to stomach. Outher appeared to have assumed leadership of his fellows.

"Bring Calanthe to me," he said and stood back grimly, with folded arms, to let the others take us. We fought as best we could but, in our defense, I can only say that three super-fit hara of any tribe are no match for a single Mojag. They really are a mutated strain of the Wraeththu type. Panthera kicked up and out viciously, and was nearly always on target, but free from the influence of Diamanda, they could shrug off his assault as if it was merely the brush of an insect's wing. I can remember clearly a pretty array of stars exploding inside my head as a Mojag fist (it felt three feet wide) smacked me heartily in the face. After that, things get a bit muzzy for a while.

Jafit's party must have made camp farther away from the road. When I came to my senses again, I found myself lying in a heap on the floor of a large, leather tent. It was quite warm and pungent in there. For a moment or two, I couldn't remember what had happened to me, then I became aware of the lumbering presence of Outher as he squatted beside me. The light inside the tent was dim and brownish, but I knew it was him. He was indistinct, but there was no mistaking the hostility of his manner. I pulled my aching bones into a sitting position. "Any chance of a drink?" It was difficult to speak. My face felt several sizes too large for my head. Outher did not answer me. It was clear that, as far as he was concerned, I was merely a wayward whore who had stepped above his station, fit only for the dubious practices of pelcia and chaitra. I could see he was regretting ever having offered me a way out. He'd misjudged me and that had made him angry with himself and me. He'd treated me with honor, which had been wasted. I was only a thing to be used. Never speaking, he lunged toward me, throwing me backwards, ripping at my bruised body with steel, wounding paws. I struggled gamely, calling on every forgotten god I could think of and screaming out withering curses, but it was all to no avail. Tense against his brutality, I felt my flesh tear. I don't know whether he intended to kill me or not, but it was one of the vilest experiences I have ever lived through. In the back of my mind lurked the horrid, saintly thought that this was something I'd deserved for a long time. As a Uigenna warrior, I'd thought nothing of violating those weaker than myself. Self-loathing, pain, and fear of death do not make a palatable cocktail.

When Outher threw me away from him like a used rag, I was weeping uncontrollably, blood and snot and tears hanging from my face in strings. It was the absolute depths of the abyss. He threw a cupful of water over my head, which brought me to my senses a little. It was too painful to wipe my face. I sat up, knees to chest, dazed, yet aware that something terrible was over. Outher was fastidiously rearranging his clothing.

"Where are the uvvers?" I croaked. He did not answer. "Outher?"

He turned and looked at me, perhaps surprised to see that I was not as beautiful as he'd once thought. He had no words for me though.

"C'n you really blame me for what I did?" I said. "If you'd 'ad any sense you'd 've done the same thing, years ago. Panthera's fam'ly'll pay 'ighly for'is return."

Outher stared at me stonily. "Panthera will be returned to Piristil now," he said.

I made an exasperated noise, which had me wincing in agony. It was becoming more and more difficult to speak as my face swelled with every second. "What for?" I asked, in a muffled voice. " 'Afit 's dead. Surely, 'n mos' people's eyes Piristil 's no more."

"In most people's eyes, Piristil is now Astarth's," Outher said, "and I have no doubt that he will continue to pay my wages just as Jafit did. Panthera earns a damn sight more for Piristil than his family will ever pay for his return, I can assure you."

" 'Ot abow moral obligation?" I managed to gobble out. It was surprising Outher understood me, but he did.

"Oh, and what can you tell me about that, Calanthe?" he asked meaningfully. The silence was tense.

" 'Ot're goin'' t'do wi'' me?" I mumbled at last. " 'Ot abow Kruin?"

Outher finished lacing his shirt. He paused to consider before answering. "You will be bled to death. Both of you."

"What!" Despite the pain, I couldn't help bubbling out an uncontrollable laugh. "Bled t'death? You serious?" I couldn't believe it.

"You want reasons, Calanthe? Shall I jog your memory? First," he held up one finger, "you have abducted a slave. Two," another finger, "you have murdered your employer . . ."

"No, Thea 'id dat," I interrupted.

"Two, *conspired* to murder your employer."

"Bullshit Outher!" I exclaimed, with remarkable clarity, but still emitting a spray of red-mottled saliva. "You're goin' t'kill me 'n yer own c'lorful way 'cause I . . . I . . . you . . . *hurt!*" My garbled speech, (which was probably even less coherent than I have related) dissolved completely. Before I could utter further painful truths (in both senses), Outher knocked me backwards with his foot.

"Quiet, Calanthe. If you annoy me again, I'll just have you tied to a tree and leave you to starve to death, if the cold doesn't finish you off first, of course."

"Kruin . . ." I said. "Why? 'Ot's 'e . . .?"

"I just don't like him," Outher said, as if that was a grand and flamboyant thing to say. He put his booted foot on my chest.

"The Aghama has given you a fine body, Calanthe," he said. "It is almost a pity to take its life, but then it will serve as a splendid sacrifice!" He snarled and walked out of the tent.

I longed to throw some smart remark out behind him like, "You're lousy in bed, Outher!" but it was too much effort. I heard him laughing as he ducked beneath the door-flap. Obviously, his friends were waiting outside. I lay on the floor for a long time, until I started to feel really cold. All the adrenaline had gone. I tried to sit up and my head protested with a furious swipe of pain. Squinting, I looked for my clothes. They were nowhere to be seen. The tent was virtually empty. I wrapped myself in the rough blanket of Outher's bed and staggered, nearly bent double, to the door-flap. All I did was lift the leather curtain a little before some over-conscientious guard outside slammed a gun butt down on my wrist. Cursing unintelligibly, I retreated like a beaten animal to the bed and eased myself down. Where were the others? Had they suffered similar abuses to my own? I desperately needed a drink and there was no more water. Outher had made sure of that. I needed to rest but my mind was too hectic. When was our execution scheduled to take place? How much time had we got? What, in God's name, could I do about it?

I fretted alone for what seemed hours, but which was probably just minutes, before the door-flap was lifted again and Outher's statuesque frame was silhouetted against the light.

"Right you; outside!" he ordered.

"Don't you mean 'outside *please*'?" I managed to inquire with quite a steady voice, whilst lurching to a swaying stand. "Where are your manners, Outher?"

In reply, he grabbed hold of my arm and hauled me out of the tent behind him, blanket trailing. He took me a short way to a small clearing in the trees, where the snow beneath our feet was muddied. My legs could not work; I let him drag me. In the clearing, looking embarrassed, and blue with cold, a defiant Kruin stood naked facing the Mojags and the trackers. One of the Mojags was restraining a bound Panthera by holding onto his luxuriant hair. Outher threw me into the clearing and Kruin broke my fall, he bent to help me up. "My God, Cal, you're . . ." He waved a fist at Outher. "Bastard!" he screamed, following that with a colorful string of profanity. The Mojags laughed. Outher sauntered over to Panthera and grabbed his gagged chin in his huge hand.

"Now, little cat," he said, "we're going to have an entertainment. Hope you're not squeamish; it's especially for you. In your honor. Now make sure you watch it."

Panthera moaned and writhed, helpless. A tracker and a Mojag hauled Kruin and myself over to a large tree. Our hands were tied and the rope nailed to the trunk, so our arms were above our heads. As they secured the nails, Kruin said, "I've heard of this; it's a popular method of execution in Mojag."

"Does knowin' that help us?" I burbled weakly.

"No." Kruin's voice was tight. I think he was afraid, although, strange as it sounds, I was not. Perhaps I was numbed by pain and wanted only to be released from it, or perhaps it was because I have never been afraid of Death. There are far worse things in this world to fear. I was prepared for unpleasantness, the sensation of slipping away, even more pain, and wished we were being dispatched by a quicker method, but my mind was uncommonly calm. My life did not flash before my mind's eye, but I did think of Pell. I wondered if he was still watching me, whether he was writhing in anxiety because we were so far apart. Could he have done anything to help us? Perhaps these thoughts were what saved us; I don't know. A shining thought of Pell. But of course, I'd had intimations of Gelaming proximity in the forest the day before, which I'd ignored.

Outher came toward us, showing us the razor-sharp knife with which he hoped to take our lives. It was all very solemn. No more laughter. I could see Panthera, dimly, struggling against his bonds. From far away, I could hear his muffled cries.

"Well, here we go then," Kruin said in a shaking voice. "See you on the other side, Cal. Better luck next time."

"Not till I've haunted these fuckers to death," I murmured. The blade touched my throat, forcing my head up. I closed my eyes. "Now," I thought. "This is it. Now. Everything for nothing. I've been such a fool. . . . Oh God . . ."

But the incisive kiss never got deeper. It was as if everything around me seemed suddenly to stop; no, not suddenly, it was more like a winding down, a film slowing down. I couldn't open my eyes. I couldn't even breathe. I couldn't move anything, but it did not matter. There was no discomfort. It was not like being frozen, but like being utterly incorporeal and numb. My soul should be roaming free but it was trapped within my flesh. Astral traveling within my own body? An odd sensation. Is this death, I wondered. Was it that quick? And then I became aware of people around me; movement and voices. I became aware of the cold blade still pressed against my skin and then it was taken away. Breath shuddered painfully through my lungs, sucked in powerfully as if into a vacuum. A few seconds later and I could move again. I opened my eyes and then shut them again quickly. There was a raw shout that cried, *"No!"* Mine.

"Oh, yes," another voice answered softly. "We meet again, Calanthe. Please, look at me." It would have been petty and futile to resist, even ungrateful; I presumed I'd just been rescued. I opened my eyes and looked at him.

"In the nick o' time, Arahal," I mumbled. "S'pose I shou' thank . . ."

He inclined his head, an outlandish vision of silver and waving black feathers. Tall as a Mojag, twice as handsome, three times as intelligent. I knew him as the Gelaming Arahal, a commanding officer in one of Pell's armies, and one of the most highly respected members of Immanion society. Through fate or chance or purpose, he had materialized here, in order to save my miserable skin. Gelaming do that sort of thing. It is not unusual. It is the kind of display of power that appeals to their naturally—aggressively—peaceful natures. Had they been watching me again? How long? Arahal took a dainty, ornate knife from his belt and cut my bonds. I fell into his arms and he breathed healing, anesthetic Gelaming breath all over my face. I could not help but welcome it, no matter how much I wanted to deny it. Effortlessly, almost without thinking, he drew the pain from my body, and fed me with his limitless strength. "Made a mess of your face, haven't they," he said conversationally.

"Why are you here?" I asked. He sat me on the floor, with my back to the tree and continued to explore my injuries with the light from his slender fingers.

"Hmm? Oh, we had a message." He threw this remark out lightly, hardly concerned with what he was saying. "Cal, you'll have to rest."

"Watching me. . . ? Have you. . . ?"

He smiled and stroked my cheek. "Now then, don't worry yourself about such things." He wrapped me in the fallen blanket. "Now, I'd better see about sorting out your friends, hadn't I?" He stood up and gestured toward the edge of the clearing. About half a dozen Gelaming were shimmering there, all mounted on the fabulous, white horses of their tribe, that do not just gallop over land, but through space and time and dreams. At Arahal's beckoning, the Gelaming dismounted and spread out through the clearing. Arahal twisted his fingers high in the air, cried out, and there were the Mojags, who had been immobilized, lurching to life again, just as I had. I smiled inside at their bewilderment. They staggered a little. Then Outher saw Arahal and pulled himself up straight, clenching his fists at his sides. Gelaming are unmistakable. Anyone recognizes a Gelaming when they see one, even a Mojag.

"Before you say anything," Arahal said to him mildly, "I must point out that under the ruling of the Confederation of Tribes, the coldblooded taking of life is a gross offense."

Outher spluttered for a moment, before crying indignantly, *"They* are the murderers!" pointing a rigid finger at me. I could not turn my head to look at Kruin, but I could hear him gasping heavily, obviously still disorientated.

Arahal made an irritated gesture. "It is not for you to take justice into your own hands, tiahaar, no matter how aggrieved you might feel."

"But . . . I . . . we . . ." Outher was lost for words.

"Be quiet. Now, you have a fire; bring hot water. Learn humility. See to these hara's wounds." Arahal shivered. "By the Aghama, it's cold out here! Zaniel, free the other two."

Once unbound, Kruin huddled up against me. "What's happening?" he asked. "What's happening? God, I *ache!"*

I shook my head. Presently, Panthera joined us, bringing a blanket for Kruin. Neither of them seemed to have been knocked about too badly; I felt crippled.

"They're Gelaming, aren't they," Panthera said to me, staring curiously at my battered, multi-hued face. "Why did they come? How did they know? They *did* know, didn't they?"

"No questions," I said. "Not yet."

"I'm sorry," Panthera said, lightly touching my blanketed arm. "Here, I'll help you to one of the tents. Come on, lean on me." Clutching each other, Panthera, Kruin and I shuffled past the dumbfounded group of Fallsend trackers and Mojags. They eyed us stonily. I could hear Arahal lightly issuing orders.

Arahal let me sleep for nearly a day. Early the next morning, he came into our tent and politely asked Panthera and Kruin if he could speak with me alone. He had brought me some hot coffee liberally spiced with fragrant shrake, a Gelaming liqueur. Gelaming always carry such luxuries with them.

He watched me drink, shaking his head. "You are a puzzle to me, Cal," he said. "When are you going to learn?"

"Learn what?"

He stood up, sighed. "Do you really need me to tell you? Are your senses that dull? I remember that, at one time, Calanthe would have had no trouble outwitting Jafit and his kind."

"I've been through hell, Arahal," I said. "When you're living from day to day like a sewer rat, it's hard to remember you were anything but a low form of life."

"Rats have instincts, surely!"

I lay down and put my arms over my face. "I don't want to argue about this, Arahal. You know as well as I do that I can either live like this or as the Tigron's little pet. I can't say either of those choices are good ones, but what else can I do?"

"Are you going to keep on running forever then? Let me remind you, Cal, that no-one has estimated a harish life-span; you might be running for a lot longer than you'd like."

"Did *he* send you?" I asked bitterly. Arahal didn't answer. "How do you think I feel, knowing he watches me all the time?"

"You don't know that."

I laughed without mirth. "Don't I? How come you arrived so quickly then? Why wasn't I left to die? If Pell hasn't enough guts to face me, he should let me die! He won't come himself; he sends you! The Pell I loved is dead. Maybe I should be too!" I didn't mean that.

"Lord Tigron, to you," Arahal said, out of habit.

"When we thought we were about to die, Kruin said, 'Better luck next time.' He's right, Arahal. Maybe it would have been the best thing. This life of mine is a mess. I'm involved in things I don't want to be involved in. I have a conscience that watches me do the wrong things just so it can make my life a misery afterwards. Why are you smiling? I'm desperately unhappy!"

"I don't think so!" he said, offering me another measure of shrake from a silver bottle he untucked from his belt. "Enjoy Jaddayoth, Cal. It is a colorful country."

"You mean I'm free to go?"

"Of course! We are not jailers. I, as much as anyone in Immanion, want to see you well again."

Meaning what precisely? I wondered. "This is a blood sport. You'll hunt me again!"

"We've never hunted you. Don't be absurd!"

"After Megalithica . . ."

"After Megalithica what?" he snapped brusquely. "You were given a choice, Cal, but we bear no malice against your decision, just regret."

"You've always hunted me," I continued self-pityingly. "I've always been followed."

"You're deceiving yourself, Cal. We never have."

I turned my face away from him. I did not believe it. "You're lying."

Arahal sighed and rubbed his face. "There is a limit to what I can say to you."

"Oh, run out of the lines he fed you, have you?"

He smiled sadly. "I will not comment on that, because I can understand your pain. As soon as you're strong enough, we shall escort you and your companions to the next Hadassah town. The Mojags too. You can all take penance there for your crimes. You would do well to remember a certain unfortunate har who now lies poisoned in the mud of the Fallsend canal, I think."

I snorted. "Oh, you know me, Arahal. Life means nothing to me!"

"Certainly not your own, it seems!" He ducked out of the tent and left me alone with a sour taste in my mouth.

Kruin and Panthera respected my desire to remain silent over the subject of the Gelaming, although I know that they discussed it thoroughly together when they weren't with me. Perhaps they even asked the Gelaming questions, but I doubt that they were answered. Only a privileged few know of the peculiar set of circumstances that link me to the Tigron and Immanion, and it's not something that the Gelaming would want to make public. They buried Jafit in the forest and brought our horses back to us. In two days, I felt well enough to leave.

CHAPTER TEN

>–1–‹›–O–‹›–1–‹

The Huyana and the Vision
"My body was the house,
And everything he'd touched an exposed nerve"
—Stephen Spender, An Empty House

Jasminia is a much larger town than Caraway, and only a few miles away from where we were camped in the forest. So close to safety, yet so far! The Gelaming escorted us so that, as they tactfully put it, the Mojags would not be tempted to explore further transgressions along the way. It was evening by the time we rode through the carved, wooden gates of Jasminia, but the town appeared to be as busy and full of hara as it would have been at mid-day. Snow had been cleared from the narrow streets, crackling torches threw sulphurous light across the rooftops. Most of the buildings in Jasminia are single-storied, but sprawling.

Arahal had already mentioned that we would all have to pay a penance here and, along the road, Kruin had enlightened me as to what he meant. The Hadassah have a strict custom concerning the penalty for violence and murder. If anyone should commit either offense, it is required by law that he present himself at the nearest temple of the Aghama, to confess to the priests (or huyana as they are known in Hadassah), and be given absolution. The soul is cleansed of negative impulses by partaking in ritual aruna with the huyana. All Hadassah abhor the taking of life, but they are a boisterous tribe, fond of their alcohol and not unknown to be consumed by fits of temper when drunk. The huyana must always receive gifts for their services, whether money, food or other goods. A good impression of the nature of Hadassah may be gained by examining the fact that the temples (and their huyana) are incredibly rich. I thought that the temples must be rather like musendas, but whose kanene have divine administrative powers and higher status.

The temple of Jasminia was concealed behind a high, wooden fence in the middle of the town. Arahal handed me a fat purse of money. "Now, don't think about sloping off to the nearest inn until you come out of the temple," he said, with a grin. As if I would! The Mojags had been firmly instructed to return to Fallsend without us. Outher could do nothing but agree to this. He was sensibly wary of the Gelaming and had realized we fell under their protection. This did not stop him hating us though; we would all feel more comfortable once Outher and his party were far away from us.

"So, it's goodbye again is it?" I said.

Arahal would not be coming inside the temple with us. He smiled down at me from his horse. "For now, Calanthe, although I feel sure we shall meet again, don't you? Perhaps when you finally come to us in Immanion."

"You think I want a home there?"

Arahal shrugged. "Only you can answer that, of course. Do you ever tell yourself the truth, I wonder?"

"It's my life," I said. "Tell the Tigron that!"

"Any other message?" he inquired bleakly.

"No, no other message."

"Until next time then . . ."

"Sorry, but I don't want there to be a next time."

Arahal merely smiled. He raised his arm and the Gelaming trotted behind him, down the road away from us, increasing their speed as they went, until, in a blinding yet invisible flash, they were gone from this earth, and the road was empty. Everyone stared at the place where they had vanished. I pushed past them and knocked on the temple gate.

"Who seeks ingress?" The voice was polite and business-like, anonymous behind the thick, wooden panels of the door. I was tempted to answer, "Miserable sinners, of course. Open up!" but before I could speak, Kruin had shouldered up to me and said, "Travelers, tiahaar, seeking penance."

There was no further word from beyond the door, only the sound of wood sliding back as bars were removed. The door opened easily, without creaking, to reveal a veiled figure standing just inside. I was instantly reminded of the holy dancers of the Froia, the marsh people of Megalithica. The dancers (or theruna) always appear veiled, and they too are adept in the art of aruna magic. The Har before us wore a thick, fur cloak around his shoulders and the veil over his face was so diaphanous and sheer, we could see the kohl around his eyes. He bid us all enter and stood aside. Before us stretched a wide yard, snow-covered except for a pathway through the middle which had been swept clear to reveal colored tiles beneath. Two Hara muffled in woolen cloaks came to lead our horses away. Kruin made plaintive noises about the baggage to which the huyana raised his hand.

"No need to worry," he said. "Thievery is unknown within the temple walls. Come, I will escort you all to the fane."

I kept my bag of notes well tucked under my arm. I had come to hate being parted from them. The huyana glided ahead of us up the cleared path. In spite of what Arahal had impressed upon Outher, I was still not happy about being so close to the Mojags. They wanted our blood and here in Jasminia would only have to pay a further penance if they spilt it. Now that the Gelaming had left us, I had no doubt that Outher would soon forget his fear of their word. Moonlight cast long shadows across the yard. It was getting colder as the dusk became deeper; another cloudless night. Behind me, I could feel Outher's eyes boring into my back, causing the flesh between my shoulder-blades to itch. Two immense statues of stone guarded the door to the fane itself. One held out the silken cloth of forgiveness, the other a broken sword. I was not sure of the symbolism implied in that; it could be taken many ways. The emblems of the Aghama were scored into the door-lintel; the double-headed axe, the winged beetle, the prescient eye of our god. Beyond the doorway, all was in smoky darkness. None of us made a sound. Intoxicating perfumes—chypre, mimosa, green sandal-wood—floated and merged in the icy air; twisted gray fumes that writhed like spirits. After passing along a high-ceilinged, columned passage, we were shown into a small chamber, where several other hara were clustered around a cheerful fire, murmuring softly together.

"Please wait here," instructed our veiled guide. "The hour approaches, but you are free to refresh yourself before the time." He gestured toward flagons of wine standing on a broad shelf near the fire; already well explored by the other hara in the room, I suspected. Outher and his cronies went directly to help themselves and our guide left the room, closing the door behind him. Kruin, Panthera and myself sat down on a bench by the wall.

"Well Kruin, you're the expert on Hadassah customs; what's going to happen next?" I asked, hoping it was not going to be some dull, spiritual flaying. I'd had more than enough of that kind of thing.

Kruin smiled, showing nearly all his teeth. "Ah, you'll have to wait and see," he said smugly. "I won't spoil the surprise by telling you!" He slapped his thighs, smacked his lips together and went to fetch us some of the wine, which was red and tart, but warming. Panthera grimaced and put his cup down on the floor, where it remained untouched. Across the room, Outher kept on delivering hostile glances. It is not pleasant to look into the eyes of someone who wants to take your life. All your instincts cry, "Flee! For fuck's sake, flee!" I sat there uncomfortably and tried to ignore him.

In a short while, the chime of a bell echoed through the room. What light there was began to dim; unnerving because the lamps were powered by burning oil, not electricity. Everyone stopped whispering and stood up, put down their wine-cups, straightened their clothes and their spines. I could almost sense every har in that room holding his breath; the atmosphere was full of suspense. The bell sounded again and I turned toward the direction it came from. The wall on that side of the room was curtained from ceiling to floor, and now that curtain was wrinkling back and upwards, revealing another room beyond suffused by an orange glow. Veiled figures stood in the gloom. "What now?" I hissed at Kruin. He laughed softly, put a finger to his lips and pushed me forward. One by one, as if bewitched, the hara in our side of the room began to walk slowly forward, toward the vacillating forms of the huyana. Slim arms emerged from floating robes to draw them further into the chambers beyond. I couldn't remember moving, but suddenly I found myself across the room and face to face with a creature, whose face was unseen, but whose overpowering scent of wood-musk made me feel light-headed. He put his hand on my arm to draw me away. I glanced behind me, looking for Kruin and Panthera, but they had disappeared. I did not like the idea of us being split up.

"Have no fear," my chosen huyana murmured. "Within these walls, you are safe. You are all safe."

That sent a little shiver through my skin. The huyana seemed to speak with more than casual knowledge. I narrowed my eyes at him, but I could not see through the veil. I could not see whether he was smiling. We drifted away from the other hara and he took me into a simple chamber, deep in the heart of the temple. Glowing glass globes on the floor provided light. A large wall painting of the Aghama's axe symbol was the only decoration. There was no bed, but a number of animal skins were scattered around the floor, some stuffed to form cushions. Against the far wall was a low, wooden stool. The huyana sat me down on it and kneeled before me with lowered head. "I am Lucastril," he said.

Totally ignorant of what was required of me, I answered, "Hello Lucastril. I'm Calanthe."

"You are Cal," he said and put up his hands to remove his veil. I was half afraid there'd be a face I recognized beneath. His cheekbones and eyelids were painted with gold, the forehead tattooed, his hair drawn up into a coil. Only the strength of his throat and jaw betrayed his harness. It could have been a human female kneeling there. In some hara, the female is very strong. My heart was hammering in my chest. It wasn't fear exactly, just a kind of presentiment. I had an awful feeling that the reins of control had just been snatched from my hands again. It is the sort of feeling that makes you want to look up at the sky and shudder; deeply.

Lucastril took my hands in his own. "We had been told of your coming," he said earnestly, leaning forward.

I snatched my hands away, roughly. "Gelaming!" I hissed and it was in me to reach for his throat. I didn't. "You know nothing about me!" Both outbursts (as my inner desires, no doubt) were met with amused patience.

"It is beyond my powers to absolve you, Cal," Lucastril said, with some regret.

I stood up and went for the door. "It's my life!" I shouted. "Mine! You can all keep your meddling, psionic hands off me! Good-day to you, Lucastril!"

He stood up and pulled me back, with strength that shouldn't have surprised me at all, but which did. "Don't go," he said. "You are here for a purpose. This is just the beginning and, because of that, important. Important, do you hear?" This slim, little creature shook me by the shoulders.

"What do you mean?" I asked. He would not let go of me, perhaps afraid I'd make another run for it and succeed.

"Listen. Listen and learn. We've been told you record everything, all that happens to you. Learn from that."

Another icy shudder, suppressed. Who gave these hara their information? Arahal? The Tigron? "And what am I here to learn, Lucastril? Who told you I was coming? What do you know?"

He shut his eyes, lowered his head, shook it. "I can't tell you."

"Can't? Surely that should be 'won't,' tiahaar!"

He shook his head again. "No. Just let me do what I'm instructed to do. It is for your benefit."

"I doubt that." I let him take me to the cushions however. I let him push me down. "What am I to learn then?"

"The first thing," he said. "The first of many."

"Will it take long?"

"That is up to you."

"Well?"

"My art," he said. "Allow me to demonstrate." He stood away from me and sinuously cast off his robes. Then he kneeled at my feet and began to unlace my boots.

"One moment," I said and he looked up.

"You will not leave here until we have taken aruna together; that is the law."

I shrugged. "Very well. I don't know what results you're expecting though."

He smiled, kneeled against me and took my face in his hands. We shared breath until he broke away.

"You have taught yourself well how to guard your mind," he said.

"Even from interfering little mystics like yourself," I agreed.

"There is much darkness."

"Not really. I don't think so."

"You are lying or you are wrong; no matter. This is the first step on a great and golden staircase. Who knows what lies at the top? Let me lead you a little of the way up."

I thought that Lucastril's job was simply to needle my mind during the ecstasy of aruna; either to extract information or implant feelings there. Now I'm not so sure. I knew he was doing *something,* but I was helpless to resist, physically, thinking that knowledge was resistance enough. For a moment, I remembered Terzian, and what Gelaming mercy had done to him, how his body and mind had been shattered by the strength of their will alone. Was that to be my fate too if I did not comply with them? Terzian had resisted them with all his might, and he had died for it. Not a warrior's death, as he deserved, but a slow, lingering, quenching of the flame, terminal illness. I couldn't stand that. I'd rather die . . . or comply? So, I let Lucastril happily invade my mind under the cover of invading my body. I could feel a strange sensation of stretching, flickering currents scraping my spine. I'm convinced that Lucastril was the first link in a chain of events destined to change my life. I also believe he was truly unaware of what part his small service would perform in the whole. My mind was a rusty, neglected machine. It had to be cleaned and oiled. Soon it would be reachable in every way. There was only one possible end to all this preparation. Only one. My life is not my own. Am I strengthening *his* power by repeating that?

After our bodies had parted and Lucastril was curled up against my side, I lay awake in the darkness. There was a high-pitched whistle in my head. My whole being was thrumming; an instrument plucked by an invisible, yet potent, hand. I could trust no-one. How was I to know that Panthera, or even Kruin, was not part of some huge, elaborate Gelaming scheme? Lying there in the musky, hairy darkness, it seemed like the whole world was closing in on me. I was floundering in a shoreless sea, trying to find ground beneath my feet, searching the horizon for land, finding none. My friends could not help me; I was alone. Even if Panthera and Kruin were not part of some immense Gelaming scheme, I could not risk involving them. I did not want to involve them; I could not speak of my past to anyone. It hurt too much. It made me feel ashamed. Was I afraid, that if I opened up, my confessions would be met with revulsion? Then a hot, sour tide turned my uncomfortable shame to anger. Yes, I had done all those things, but hadn't it really been Pell's fault? It had! Surely, *he* had made me what I was now. You see, in the depths of my self-indulgent wallowing, I had managed conveniently to blot out the entire time I'd lived with the Uigenna. Why do I still love him? I thought. Why? There's nothing left to even *like* anymore. He is Thiede's lapdog; arrogant, egotistical, condescending. It was because of knowing Pell that I'd risen from being just an average kind of har to being a huge kind of scapegoat villain. Just from knowing him. It all seemed so long ago. I could see his face before me, as I'd first known him, laughing, shining with innocence, utterly enchanting. Not a king; just Pell. How I wished that he'd stayed dead to me. Why had I ever had to find out? Now there is a monster clothed in Pell's flesh that follows me like a curse. Does some remnant of the old Pell still exist, yearning for the past? Is that it? Pell has the vast power of the Gelaming empire behind him now. He can have anything he wants, yet he still cannot face me in the flesh. Perhaps, like me, he is afraid of being consumed. I feel that should I ever let the gates of Immanion close behind me, I will be as good as dead. Pellaz would wither me. He could not be the same, yet too similar not to affect me. We would be unable to speak. It would be hell. It is something that, deep inside, in spite of everything, I still want more than anything.

In the morning, Lucastril woke me up from a disturbing dream of caves and ghost-lights. He stroked my face as I twisted and whimpered like a child, half-asleep in his arms.

"The first message will come soon," he said. "I have cleared the way as best I can. Wait for it."

"I don't want to hear it," I said. "Can't you understand that? I'm a prisoner. The world is vast and I wander in it like a gypsy, yet I'm a prisoner. Of the past." Tears spilled from my eyes; I couldn't stop them. They were hot with anger, not sadness; the culmination of my confused agonizing in the night. Soon I must go out there again, scurry haphazardly around, go where they pushed me. Perhaps I would have been wiser to stay in Piristil. At least there I'd owned a spurious kind of safety. Lucastril helped me dress. I felt dizzy; weak yet, at the same time, full of untapped strength. My head was whirling.

"You may eat here with your friends before you leave," Lucastril said. I took some of the money Arahal had given me and threw it on the floor. Lucastril picked it up and handed it back to me. "There's no need for this," he said. "We have already been paid."

"Keep it!" I said that more savagely than was necessary.

Lucastril took the purse from my hand and put the money back inside. "Don't be stupid. You may need it."

I stuffed the purse into my trouser pocket and followed him to the dining-hall. Some of the previous night's sinners, cheerfully cleansed, were still there, eating and talking, but I was relieved to see that Outher's party appeared to have gone. Panthera and Kruin were sitting alone at a table in the corner. I stood in the doorway watching them, not quite sure if I wanted to go over. Perhaps I should just leave Jasminia on my own. After all, I was in Jaddayoth now. I had Arahal's money and could find work for myself in somewhere like Gimrah for a while. Perhaps I should just go where Fate led me. It looked to me as if Kruin and Panthera would not welcome my presence anyway. Their heads were close together; they were talking earnestly. I could guess the subject of their conversation. Hesitating, I was just about to turn and leave the place, when Panthera looked up and saw me. He smiled and waved and all my plans disappeared in a puff of weakness. I went over to them.

"Are you OK?" Panthera asked. "Your face is still a bit of a mess."

I sat down. "I'm fine, just fine!" There was a pot of coffee on the table, nearly empty. I took Kruin's drained cup and half-filled it. Kruin handed me a roll of bread and some cured meat, inspecting me silently.

"So, where to now then?" I asked. It hurt to eat, but my stomach was aching from hunger.

"You sure you're up to traveling?" Kruin inquired. "You look terrible. It should be safe now to stay here in Jasminia for a day or two if you like."

I looked quickly at Panthera who appeared to be carrying no external signs of our struggle with Mojags. "I told you, I'm fine! For God's sake, let's get moving. I'm sure Panthera is anxious to get home."

Panthera smiled wanly. "Anxious yes, but a couple of days won't make much difference. It'll only slow us down if you're not up to it."

"Oh, please! It's just a few bruises. It's nothing!"

Kruin shrugged. "Very well, if you're sure . . ." He brightened up, his responsibilities absolved. "Anyway, how did you two get on last night? Civilized method of punishment, isn't it? No wonder the Hadassah are so fond of fighting!"

Panthera's face had gone a deep crimson color. He fidgetted uncomfortably. "Personally, I prefer to answer to nobody for any crimes I might commit," he said.

"And I'm naturally suspicious of mystics," I said. Kruin rolled his eyes. "Oh, I see! Well, I enjoyed myself thoroughly!"

Panthera and I did not comment. I had no intention of revealing what was happening to me and Panthera obviously still harbored deep misgivings concerning aruna. We let Kruin ramble on, lewdly and happily. We let it wash over our heads. Panthera smiled at me.

"Let's get you home," I said.

CHAPTER ELEVEN

The Message

"What we call the beginning is often the end
And to make an end is to make a beginning.
The end is where we start from"

—*T. S. Eliot, Little Gidding*

We left Jasminia around mid-day, taking the south road into Gimrah. The sun was shining, making the snow on the ground and trees sparkle like crystal. There were quite a few other travelers on the road; mostly Hadassah. There was a great sense of camaraderie. We joined a group of a dozen or so Hara who were traveling to a town on the border. They shared their liquor and biscuits with us. We sang songs to pass the time. I can remember clearly that I was filled with happiness. On such a beautiful afternoon, it was impossible to believe that the world was anything but the way it seemed at that moment; untainted. I felt free. Surely my fears about Pell were just the product of a paranoic mind. That still didn't explain Arahal's timely appearance of course, or Lucastril's meaning-laden words, but that day I was desperate to convince myself I was leading a simple, ordinary life; no part of anything great. Panthera was a joy to watch. I found myself thinking that over the past couple of weeks, I really hadn't noticed him properly, or maybe it was just that the air of his home country made him bloom and had blown away the cobwebs of his confinement in Fallsend. If, I thought, just *if,* I could act utterly independently, I could think about wooing Panthera. Then we could live together forever in a high castle in Ferike. I would write stories to pass the time; he would paint exquisite masterpieces. We would exist together sublimely, riding nervous, pale horses through the mountain forests every morning. In the evenings, if we should want company, we could invite lofty hara of neighboring castles to dine with us, drink wine from long-stemmed glasses and converse intellectually about the outside world which we would never see. Ah, such would be a life! Who could yearn for more? I have traveled too long. Perhaps my ghosts have worn themselves out. Living with Panthera, perhaps my dreams could only be those of the sweetest kind.

"You look pensive, Cal," Panthera said, breaking my reverie.

"Mmm," I agreed. "I was just thinking about the sort of life I would like to have."

"Then live it!"

"Too many factors are beyond my control, I'm afraid."

"It is never impossible to take control of one's own life, I believe," he answered. "That's what my father says and he never speaks unless he's sure of the facts."

"I wish I could agree."

Panthera brought his horse more closely up against mine. I could see Kruin watching us, perhaps straining to hear what we were saying. "Is it . . . it is *power?*" Panthera asked tentatively.

I looked at him steadily. Could I? Could I? "Some hara are very powerful, yes," I replied carefully. "Some seek to control the lives of others."

"Cal, the Gelaming. . . . What is it you're mixed up in with them?"

This was the first question of the many that I'd been expecting from my companions. So far they'd had the discretion to remain silent, keeping their observations to themselves, between themselves. It must be driving Kruin mad, because he's naturally a gossip. "Don't probe too deeply," I said. "I'm not being close out of stubbornness, Panthera. It may be dangerous for you. If I tell you, I automatically involve you, and then whatever is out there may decide to organize your life for you as well. I don't want that on my conscience."

"Cal, I'm not afraid of that! If you tell us, or even just me, I can add my strength to yours. You'd have an ally. Surely that would make things easier."

"For me perhaps, but what about you? You have a life waiting for you, Thea. What about cousin Namir? I don't want you to ask me again. Is that clear?"

Panthera's eyes went cold. He does not like being spoken to sharply and is also convinced that his wishes should be granted at every turn. "I think you're being very foolish," he said stiffly. "And your excuses are pathetic. What I do with your life is my choice. I'm insulted that you won't accept my assistance! Anyway, cousin Namir has probably taken another consort by now. Can't you see, that life you talk about, the one that was waiting for me, has gone? It went the minute I set foot in Piristil. You're not the only one with problems, Cal."

"Maybe not, but I'm the only one with my problems!"

This argument could have continued in similar vein for some time, but at that point, Kruin's curiosity overwhelmed him and he trotted over to join us, only to encounter a tight-lipped silence. I had no doubt that later Panthera would tell him everything I'd said.

It would take us at least two days to reach Gimrah, and then a further couple of weeks to get to Ferike. Now that we had money, we would be able to stay in inns rather than camp out in the open, which was a definite improvement! Whenever he had the opportunity, Kruin kept on praising our good fortune over the incident with Arahal, in the hope that I'd say something enlightening about it, which I wouldn't.

"Gelaming have lots of money," I said. "This is nothing to them. Now, if they'd really wanted to be generous, they'd have given us three of their horses. We'd have reached Ferike in a matter of hours then."

"Is that Arahal a friend of yours?" Kruin asked bravely.

"No."

"Is . . ." Kruin began again, but Panthera interrupted him.

"Don't bother, Kruin. He won't tell you." They exchanged a meaningful glance, which meant they thought I was enjoying needling their curiosity.

That evening, we decided to spend the night in a roadside inn; all that was left of an old human town. We were all in dire need of a good night's sleep. Our Hadassah traveling companions were all set for a serious evening's drinking first and Kruin elected to join them. Panthera and I went up to separate rooms. I locked my door and went to bed with a bottle of betica, which was locally brewed and a much finer concoction than that experienced in Fallsend. I lay staring into the darkness of the room, trying to get so drunk my sleep would be free of dreams. I must have drifted off, for suddenly I was wide awake as if I'd been shaken. I was bitterly cold, lying face down, and my bed was unbelievably uncomfortable, as if strewn with broken glass. I opened my eyes and for a second thought, "Oh, I am dreaming," yet the sensations were incredibly real. I was lying face-down on the road outside the inn, half-clothed; an icy wind ripping at my exposed flesh with serrated fingers. I pulled myself up on my knees, looked around. To my right the inn was in darkness, the only light coming from the sky, where a round moon bobbed on breakers of cloud. To my left, a pine forest steadfastly worked its way across a landscape of concrete and fallen buildings. The waving shadows might conceal anything. Through the wind, I could hear an insistent sound; rhythmic, pounding, getting closer. "Why, it is horses' hooves," I thought sagely. "I'd better move off the road." Whoever was traveling at that late hour, was traveling very fast indeed. Sluggishly, numbed by cold, slow as the urgency of nightmare, I tried to stagger toward the inn, but my limbs refused to cooperate. Sleep-walking was not a thing I could remember having done before. I fell to my knees again with the image of the inn receding as if being drawn away. Perspective became acute. The moon cast stark shadows; everything looked two dimensional. I was aware of time passing and it was a speed I was unfamiliar with. Squinting, I tried to peer down the road, toward the south, where the sound of hooves seemed to be coming from. A vague blackness was moving there, rolling like a ball of smoke, but approaching at speed. I told myself, "This is not real . . . *surely,*" and out of the distance, between a tall, shadowy avenue of snow-stippled pines and humped rubble, a pair of horses pounded along the road, their powerful limbs surging with unnatural slowness, the ripple of muscle, the swing of silken hair, all slowed down, shards of ice flying with the grace of birds off the hard surface of the road. I did not move. I did not try to. Mesmerized, I could only watch. The riders of those horses were swathed in black, their faces covered. They sat straight, not bending with the animals' pace at all. From their shoulders black spikes rose up behind their heads. I could see shining black gems upon their gauntletted hands. Riding close together as they were, I did not notice their burden until they were really close. Whatever they carried was slung into a white sheet, lolling with horrible suggestiveness, between them. I knew they carried a harish body. It was as if I could *see* it. They came to a halt some feet away from me. I could still see nothing of their faces. The horses blew plumes of steam into the cold air, tossing their heads. Their bridles jangled, their feet stamped. I looked up and the riders hurled their burden down before me. It landed on the road with a dull thump and rolled slightly before lying still. The sheet had fallen partly away. I could see the face of what it had concealed; eyes staring wide, the flesh white as bone and bleached even further by the light of the moon. I realized with an odd, analytical calm, I was afraid, no, more than afraid—stricken with terror. The body lying at my feet, the face so familiar, of course I knew it. It was mine! Me lying there as dead and cold as the landscape. I looked up helplessly at the riders. They must be Gelaming; they could be no other. Covering their faces could not deceive me; no. Then, a movement from the road attracted my attention. I didn't want to look, but a sick fascination swiveled my eyes downwards. Even as I looked, the dead lips cracked and worked. (Oh God, it's trying to *speak!*) I must have made a noise of horror, must have. The eyes rolled. The thing that looked like me wriggled foully from its confinement of cloth. I could see the body was not marked by injury at all. It rolled onto its stomach and lifted the upper half of its body like a rearing snake, not using its arms for support. The face was inches from my own. I could smell nothing. It spoke; a ghastly, rasping sound. It said, "Beneath . . . beneath the mountains of Jaddayoth," followed by a gulping sigh. That was when I screamed. I can remember that sound shattering the stillness of the night air. The wind had dropped, completely. There was no answering movement from the inn, no lights switched on, no windows thrown wide. The thing that was myself lurched forward as if to touch me. I covered my face with my hands, powerless to move and fell . . .

When I opened my eyes, I was lying face down on my bed in the inn. Wholly awake, I threw myself over the edge and hurried to the window, throwing it wide, wide. I leaned out, feeling the ice press against my naked stomach. The road beneath was empty, the new snow unmarked, gentle flakes still falling. The road toward the south stretched unblemished as virgin skin. Stunned, I sank to the floor and leaned with my back against the wall, my head resting on the wet sill. My mind seemed empty. I looked at my bed, which was rumpled, disordered. I made a sound, small, not frightened, not amused, but something of both. My blankets, my pillow, the floor around the bed, were sprinkled with snow and it was melting fast.

I slept for the rest of the night on the floor, covering myself with a blanket. Beneath the mountains of Jaddayoth. . . . Had I dreamed it? Was that vision merely a sick manifestation spewed forth by my own sicker mind? But if it was true. . . . *What* beneath Jaddayoth? What? Was death waiting for me there, or merely submission? My room was cold. In the morning, Panthera came in and eyed my position with suspicion. Snow had blown in through the window and there was a thin covering of it on my blanket.

"Drunk again were you?" Panthera inquired with derision. He snorted when I didn't answer and went downstairs. My limbs were stiff. I dressed myself slowly. Clearly Panthera considered me a drunkard. I looked at myself in the mirror. It was a far from pleasant experience, for my face still bore the yellowing marks of Outher's attentions, accompanied by bleary, bloodshot eyes. I looked, in a word, terrible. For a moment, I leaned on stiff arms, my forehead against the glass. "Pellaz," I thought, and then aloud, "Pellaz."

His name is a curse, a prayer.

CHAPTER TWELVE

>⋅⟨⟩⋅⊙⋅⟨⟩⋅⟨

In Gimrah

"You dozed, and watched the night revealing
The thousand sordid images
Of which your soul was constituted"
—*T. S. Eliot, Preludes*

I did not mention my nightmare (experience?) to my companions, but the feeling of it lingered like a sour taste in my mouth. I had locked my door before going to bed yet Panthera had walked right in unhindered in the morning. It didn't bear thinking about. I could deceive myself no longer; whatever I thought I'd escaped in Fallsend had found me again, but even so, nothing like last night had ever happened to me before. Goodbye castle in Ferike. Goodbye pleasant dreams. I felt I had no future; only the past, which stretched behind me raw and bleeding for examination. That day I could barely speak. Kruin and Panthera thought I'd got a hangover; I got no pity from them.

The road became quieter. There were fewer travelers. Townships we passed were prevalently areas reclaimed from nature that man had abandoned to rot. As the silence of the White—as Hadassah call it—became more intense, Kruin told us we were now near the border. One gray, overcast afternoon, our horses waded thigh-deep through a drift of snow from which reared the black, horse-hair-fringed totem of the Gimrah. Two more steps and Hadassah was behind us. A valley swept down before us; a carpet of pristine white. Kruin was worried. He said that this could be treacherous. The snow had drifted; we had no idea how deep it was down there. A slight, cold wind worried the edge of our furs, our horses' manes, carrying small, dancing motes of snow. Night creeps up on you quickly in the winter glow. Slightly behind the others, I experienced a sudden, sharp, bitter-sweet pang of déjà vu. If I narrowed my eyes, could it not be Saltrock down there; not snow-plains but caustic shores of soda? Just a hint of its bitter scent. Now I am back there, riding in. Drunk and wretched. I am thinking: how can I tell them? What can I tell them? My water bottles are empty. My knees and arms are scabbed, my lips cracked by desert scour. I am alone. Alone. Alone. How much it echoed then. How much it echoes now through the overgrown cavities of my heart. I can remember being in love, remember happiness, but it was short-lived. (*A scream; a horse's scream.*) No! Kruin urged his horse down the slope. It skidded, bunching its hind-quarters, head up, ears back. He becomes a moving thought through the vacuosity of a dead mind. He turns round. "Come on!" he shouts and Panthera and myself follow him down.

The sky was black by the time we saw lights shining in the distance. Kruin said he'd known there was a settlement near here. Lemarath, it was called. All Gimrah settlements are a combination of large farm and small town, proudly independent of each other, savagely competitive concerning their live-stock. As we rode through the snow toward the light, to keep our minds off the numbing cold attacking all extremities, Kruin and Panthera told me about the Gimrah. Originally of Gelaming stock, they had split off from the main tribe to pursue their own breeding programs for their horses. The founding hara had all been employed in Gelaming livery establishments and had constructed for themselves a whole way of life about the animals they nurtured; a whole religion in fact. Almost unique amongst harish kind, who generally worship aspects of the Aghama under various guises and aliases, the Gimrah worship a goddess. This is unusual in that while rejecting all human trappings of sexual division most hara can only countenance revering a super-being of dual sexuality like themselves, or the life-force of the Earth itself, which is predominantly female, but mated to the male aspect of the sun. The Goddess of the Gimrah is naturally equine in form. In worship, all Gimrah hara subvert their masculinity. To the Goddess, they are soume; all procreation must take place by sunlight. On top of this rather eccentric custom, the Gimrah are the only tribe in Jaddayoth who share their territory, even their homes, with humans. When staking their claim on the land, they offered aid, employment and support against less tolerant hara, to the ailing human population. As conservationists, the Gimrah have decreed that all human males must conceive a child or two with females of their own kind at an early age, whereafter they are incepted to Wraeththu. A strangely civilized arrangement. All adult humans in Gimrah are female. The two races exist together in perfect harmony, with the humans content to let the superior race take the upper hand. To the women of Gimrah, hara are not hermaphroditic, but merely other women who have absorbed the male; thus negating the need for them. It was unsettling to live with at first. There are no walls around Gimrah estembles, as their farms are called.

Frozen nearly to death, we threw caution to the winds and knocked on the first door we could find in Lemarath. A medium-sized wooden and stone house that had several larger outbuildings at the back; a barn, stables possibly. A lantern swung, creaking in the wind over the door. All the windows were curtained tight, but we could see light beyond them. The door was opened to us by a human girl-child who had wrapped herself in a thick, woolen shawl. She squinted against the nipping snow-flakes. "Yes, what is it?" she asked, quite impertinently I thought. I was used to surviving humans being subservient. Warmth swirled out into the night from behind her, a tantalizing hint of the comfort to be found within.

"We are travelers from Hadassah," Kruin explained. "We need lodgings for the night. We were hoping you could suggest where we could find some."

The girl looked up the road behind us, wrinkled her nose, pulled her shawl closer around her body and stepped toward us. She extended a thin hand to the nearest horse. "Have you any money, tiahaara? It is a cold, fierce night is it not!"

"We have money," Kruin answered carefully.

"One moment then. You may be able to stay here; I'd better check." She went back into the house and shut the door in our faces. We all exchanged a glance of surprise but Kruin waved his hand briefly and shook his head.

"It is a strange land and we are strangers," he said. It was explanation enough. After only a few moments, the door opened once more.

The girl came out to us, taking all our horses' reins in one hand. "You can go in," she said. "I'll see to your animals. My mother charges three spinners for a night's lodging and a hot meal—each."

Kruin sucked air through his teeth. "Expensive for country fare, isn't it?"

The girl shrugged, leading our horses behind the house. "It is a hard season, tiahaar!"

We went inside the house and found ourselves in a spacious, low-ceilinged kitchen, typical of any well-to-do farmhouse. Kruin went straight over to the roaring fire. Several cats and dogs raised their heads from sleep to look at us suspiciously. Panthera, carrying most of our luggage, threw it onto the floor and slumped in a chair.

"God, this is so welcome!" he said, in a dazed, chilled-from-the-cold voice.

"No more welcome than your money'll be at this cruel time of year!" A woman had come into the room through a door at the farthest end of it. We all turned quickly. She was drying her hands on her apron; a tall, bony creature, with rather a sour face. She wore thick, woolen trousers and shirt, her hair concealed by a patterned scarf. She took off the apron and hung it over the back of a chair, stretching, rubbing her neck and grimacing. "Not the weather for traveling, tiahaara! Please, sit down. All of you." She gestured toward the table. "Excuse me—we had an emergency down the road. An untimely birth you might say! I'm just about done for, but I think Jasca should have got my meal ready. You're welcome to share it with me." She sauntered over to a huge cooking range and lifted lids off pots. Tempting smells wafted toward our straining noses. "Ah, beef stew is all it is! Travelers are few at this time of year, tiahaara. I've nothing fancier." She continued to chatter as she set plates and food down before us. "More snow they say, up at the House. More! We spent the last two days digging a road to the south pasture where my neighbor Lizzieman nearly lost her yearlings! Then Clariez has to drop a child on us! By the Goddess she'll give us no rest till spring, I'll wager! Still, new faces are welcome, tiahaara, most welcome."

We learned that, during the summer, the woman (whose name was Cora) earned a substantial part of her living providing lodgings for travelers. Many hara travel south from Hadassah and Natawni for the horse-fairs. The stew was excellent. Cora offered us wine, which she boasted that she had fermented herself from rose petals and tree-sap. It was sparkling and delightfully delicate; I found my eyelids drooping. Cora must have noticed. "How many rooms will you be wanting?" she asked, in a straight-forward manner. There was a moment's silence.

"Can we get back to you on that?" Kruin inquired smoothly.

Cora shrugged, finished her wine and stood up. "Of course. Shout if you need me; I won't be far," she answered and disappeared into another room, shutting the door behind her. A tactful, perceptive creature.

After she'd been gone a few moments, Kruin cleared his throat and said, "Are we all comfortable?" I shrugged and Panthera didn't answer. "I think," Kruin began again, hesitantly, "I think that tonight . . . we should be together."

"I think not!" Panthera protested with rather too much venom and volume.

Kruin winced. "Suit yourself," he said drily. "Two rooms then, Cal?"

I sighed. "If you like. I'm afraid of dreams when I sleep indoors anyway."

Kruin reached for my hand. "Since Fallsend, I have longed to suggest this many times," he said.

Panthera made a derisive sound and rolled his eyes. "Oh, *please!*" he cried sarcastically. He is a rigorously unromantic creature.

I must admit it was a pleasure, almost a relief, to experience once more the langourous delights of aruna. Kruin's body had always pleased me, even when he'd been paying Jafit through the nose for the privilege of enjoying mine. Recently my libido had become subdued, which was an alien condition for me. Unlike Kruin, thoughts of closeness had not really crossed my mind since leaving Fallsend; the cold hadn't helped much, of course. Though perhaps the disgusting, debasing humiliations I'd had to endure (and initiate) in Piristil were more to blame, coupled with the violation by Outher. Such things do not exactly quicken the sexual appetite. The time with Lucastril in Jasmina had not been exactly inspiring either. Maybe it also had something to do with the fact that I feared Pell was watching me all the time, but in Cora's house, I felt safe, and curled into Kruin's arms I felt even safer. Now that we were nearer his home country, Kruin was adamant about sticking to his tribal code, which suited me utterly because I was feeling too pathetic and drained to be ouana. Even though we were dog-tired and further exhausted by aruna, neither Kruin nor myself felt much like sleeping. We spent some time gossiping about Panthera, which I felt was a timely change from them talking about me. I was surprised to learn that Kruin was really quite offended that Panthera didn't want to be with us. Knowing Harish nature not to be as straightforward as it's believed to be, I hadn't been offended at all, even quite understanding. I tried to explain to Kruin that Panthera would have to put Piristil a long way behind him before he could think about forming relationships with other hara. Kruin, naturally, did not agree.

"Such wounds should be healed, and healed quickly," he said earnestly. "You know that any har's life is incomplete without aruna; it's our lifeblood."

"Not all the time, Kruin," I replied. "In a perfect world, maybe, but occasionally circumstances intrude upon the well-being of our juices, so to speak. Panthera's young. He only needs time. Once he gets home, I'm sure he'll be alright. Someone will fall in love with him and coax him out of his shell."

Kruin was in the mood for debate, but I was too tired to argue further. Tired of the subject probably. Kruin rabbited on happily about the necessity of aruna (warm to the subject because he'd just had a good time) and then realized I wasn't really listening. "Cal, what *is* wrong with you?" he asked, stroking my face in such a way that it was impossible for me to turn away. "I know you try to hide it, but there is something wrong isn't there. It's to do with the Gelaming, isn't it?"

"You're too inquisitive," I said lightly, closing my eyes.

"It's not just that! I'm concerned for you. You're difficult to like at times, Cal. I don't know why, but I do care, no matter how much you might, wish I didn't. Why don't you trust me?"

I looked at him. "It's not a question of that, Kruin. I think I'd trust you and Thea with my life now; we've helped each other. We're friends, aren't we? That's why I can't open up to either of you. You're my friends."

"Can't we help you then? Maybe you're wrong about whatever it is; maybe we can help you."

I didn't answer. I couldn't. He may well have been right. It was as if there was a valve on my throat that wouldn't let the words out. Kruin sighed. "Alright, alright, I'll be quiet. But please remember, it's not that I'm being nosy, OK? If you ever want to talk, well, you know . . ."

I smiled at him and touched his sharp, elegant jaw. "Yes, I know, Kruin. Thanks."

He took my hand and kissed it gently. A small gesture of affection that reached my heart. There was a lump in my throat. Kruin gathered me close and I held onto him tightly. "Oh Cal, Cal, don't be scared, don't be miserable," he said, helplessly, not knowing what I needed reassuring about. For a moment, I felt as if I could tell him everything, but the moment was brief. Kruin was not destined to be part of it.

I woke up lying in hay; crying out. Threshing, hysterical, for a second or two, I thought: this is a dream. I'm dreaming again. I was in a high barn and, this time, my movements were unrestricted. I clambered down from the loose bales beneath me, across the dusty hay-strewn floor, to the tall, slightly open door. A heavy wooden bar lay across the threshold. Outside, across a snow blanketed yard, I could see the back of Cora's house; to the left and right of me were shuttered sheds and loose-boxes. It didn't feel like a dream; not at all. I was freezing, my clothes unfastened as if donned quickly, my feet bare. No lights showed from the house. Glancing behind me into the darkness of the barn, which was bare of everything except shadows and hay, I eased through the door. I must be sleep walking, I decided; an uncomfortable thought, but not as distressing as another hallucination. Above me, the sky was brilliant with stars, the air crystal hard. Snow had drifted up against the back door of the house. It must have started falling again in the night, although the yard was thickly covered; too thickly. Surely Cora and her household must clear it every day? I began to run, but the house never came any closer. I felt sick. Panic spumed through me on a crest of nausea. I was straining against an invisible wall. Choking on dry breath, I fell onto hands and knees, shaking my head, willing myself to wake up, but it was real. "Cal!" My head jerked up. The silence was stunning. What had I heard? My name? Where had it come from? "No," I answered sensibly and then quietly pleading, "no, no, no." Only stillness all around. I curled my arms around my head, kneeling in the snow, waiting, waiting. A faint, icy breeze lifted my hair. The stillness was pressing in, full of energy. "Show yourself!" My cry was oddly muffled; no echo. Still nothing. I scrambled to my feet which were now burning with the cold. I must cope with this rationally. I must focus my will. I must walk toward the house. I took one step and then another and then a hand grabbed my hair from behind, a strong arm was around my neck, pulling me backwards. There was a body; a person clad in leather and musty fur. "Always useless in times of crisis, Cal, always!" This voice against my ear, which I recognized at once. I could feel his clouded breath, warm and damp upon my skin. This could not be a dream.

"No, you're not here," I said empathically. And then, to convince myself further, "You *can't* be!"

He laughed gently, politely. "Oh, forgive me, but I *am,* Cal. Aren't I always with you? I feel I should be, if only for the sake of memory."

He turned me around to face him. His head was covered by a thick, tasselled scarf, only the eyes showing. His eyes haven't changed, but I remember that once he never had a deep, white scar through the left brow, a permanent frown. He unwound the cloth from his face with one hand. "My faithful one," he said. "Aren't you going to greet me? It's been so long. In meetings hearts beat closer . . . don't they?" Of course, he looked older, leaner and his natural wildness was somehow *contained.*

I had once known him, intimately, as Zackala; now I had no idea what or who he was.

He examined my thoughts. "I am not an illusion," he said, "don't ever think that. You must not deceive yourself, not even in daylight, my Cal. Admire my restraint. I could have made myself known to you a long time ago."

He was the hound on my trail. I should have known this. Perhaps, deep inside, I had. Perhaps that was why I'd been nervous of leaving Piristil, coming out into the open. My finer senses have become as dulled as those whom I had mocked in the musenda. It was my own fault; Arahal had been right, but it was too late to do anything about it now.

"Pellaz brought you back, didn't he," I said.

Zack laughed in my face. "Brought me back? From where? For God's sake, Cal! Did you really think I was dead? Did you see me die? No, as I recall, you didn't hang around long enough to see what happened. No, my dear, Pellaz didn't bring me back; I found *him."* An expression convulsed his face, which I suppose was disgust. He pushed me away from him.

"What do you want with me?" I asked, still not convinced he was really there.

"Don't you know? Oh Cal!" He laughed and pulled the scarf away from his neck. "See my scars? Thankfully not fatal; but nearly, very nearly." He is naturally dark-skinned; the scars glowed very white. "Someone dumped me on a good healer. Lucky, eh? It took a long, long time to get well though. The world's changed, hasn't it."

"Are you with *them?"* I asked.

"I'm with you, Cal," he answered silkily. There was an eerie glitter in his eyes; red fire. He reached for me. I backed away. "Oh come on, my dear; share breath with me, if just for old times' sake. Come on, let's remember . . ."

I put my arms up in defense, but too late. His breath was a roar, his lips peeled back, pouring himself into my silently screaming mouth. There was an immediate darkness in my head, a pounding, the slice of a knife, a silver scream. I was lost, losing ground, in a hurricane of feeling; hatred, bitterness, frustration, pain. I could feel his hands on my back, claws scoring flesh, his teeth grinding against mine, but such physical things were not reality. What was real was the poison of betrayal, the yellow, sweet perfume of the guilty. We were clashing, not like swords, but like oily liquids; colors blending and repelling. I could feel myself sinking, too weak, vitality atrophied, strengths withered. He was ink in my soul; I was drowning in it. Slipping, sinking, I fell. . . . And awoke with a start next to Kruin, a cry in my mouth and a taste of sourness. Kruin was alert in an instant, frightened to wakefulness, leaning over me, pushing me back, saying in a scared, quick voice. "What, Cal, what?" I wanted to scream. I needed that release, but could make no sound. My body was cold.

We have been in Lemarath for over a week now, because the south road is blocked. Cora is confident that it will be cleared soon, but everyone is very busy at the moment coping with other emergencies caused by the weather. The amount of snow falling is frightening, too fast for it to be cleared away. I can feel myself slipping into a comfortable decline. Lethargy caused by the cold, I tell myself, but I have been writing almost non-stop for two days now. I'm alone quite a lot of the time. Kruin and Panthera are helping the Gimrah. The kitchen is very quiet. Because of the thickly clouded sky, it seems to be dusk all day. I quite like this place; the people are cheerful and strong. Cora shares her house with three others; her daughter, Jasca, her six-year-old son, Natty, and a young woman named Elveny. They all work together every day, shoulder to shoulder, shoveling snow, humping bales of straw and hay, mixing feeds; never a cross word between them.

Last night, after dinner, Elveny read my palm and told me seriously, that I must let the woman in me bleed.

"And just what do you mean by that?" I asked her sweetly.

She had dropped my hand and was gazing into my eyes. "Beauty alone is not enough," she said.

Perhaps she thought I understood her, which of course I did, but I pretended not to. I picked up a kitchen knife. "See this?" I said, waving it. "This is the moon." I cut my wrist (on the back naturally).

Elveny pulled a face. "Oh don't!" she said. I let the blood run down my arm, but the scratch congealed before it could drip on the table. There is probably a moral in that.

Jubilee Hafener was here yesterday. The Hafeners are the Gimrah family who own Lemarath, who run it and sustain it. Jubilee is the son of Gasteau and Lanareeve who rule the roost. Natty told me the Hafener's house is called Heartstone, but we can't see it from here because of the snow. I was sitting at the kitchen table as usual, paper and pens before me, wine to the left, scrounged cigarettes to the right, when I heard a commotion in the yard. I went to take a look. The Hafener rode a tall and stocky horse which was clothed in fleeces. He was accompanied by two armed women and a young har who appeared to me to be newly incepted. Cora came hurrying out of the barn, pulling the scarf off her hair, which is thick and attractively streaked with gray over the left ear. Jubilee Hafener wore a heavy coat; his straight black hair was plaited to his waist. His skin was very white. I took a good look and went back indoors. More snow talk. The Hafener's women and the young har came into the kitchen. I thought I'd better be polite and said hello. "How about a hot drink?" one of the females asked. She looked as if she could skin an adult lion with her teeth. Smiling, I went to the range and poured the coffee.

"Travelers, Cora says," the woman said.

I presumed she meant my companions and myself. "Yes," I answered. "Dreadful weather isn't it."

She sat down with a grunt, in my seat, and took one of my cigarettes, offering the packet to her companions. This is, of course, normal behavior in Gimrah where everyone shares everything. They have no petty rules of etiquette. I sat down with the others and we ended up talking about Fallsend. Ghoulish curiosity on their part, but they were neither censurious nor shocked. I like these people. After a while, Cora brought the Hafener in. I half expected his people to stand up, but they didn't. He's not tall, but appears to be; the mark of true nobility.

"Are you ill?" he asked me. "You're not working with the others."

Because of that, I found myself offering to help with the feeds that evening, but my heart wasn't in it. I'm working on half-power, half of my brain is trying to sleep because it's too afraid to be awake. On the morning after my dream about Zack (I won't admit it was anything but a dream), I looked out of the bedroom window and found the yard utterly cleared of snow. I was the first up too. Explain that. Kruin is worried about me, as if he's afraid I'll damage myself. Panthera is aloof. I think he's decided I must be some kind of criminal, and a drunken one at that. I know I do drink too much, but who cares! Anyway, I need it and I deserve it. Yes, I know I'm letting myself go. This is a defiance. Perhaps Pell will leave me alone if I'm no longer desirable. As Elveny said, beauty alone is not enough. If that's all I've got, let's see what happens without it. It's frightening that I'm thinking like this. I always used to be so strong, so impermeable. Have *they* done something to me? I can't help thinking of Terzian again. Am I suffering the same fate? Time for another drink. Cora has been feeding me all kinds of concoctions in a desperate attempt to improve my health. She thinks I picked up some kind of infection on the road. She has also started watering the wine, I notice. If I look out of the window now, I can see Panthera playing with Cora's children in the snow. He has been created to torment me, I'm sure. He is dressed in furs and his mane of dark hair is laced with snow. Now I am aching to hold him close, because he reminds me of Pell, the real Pell. When these thoughts come to me, I must write them down, because it is cleansing. Today 1 am confused. How much longer can I continue in this way? What is going to happen next? Oh dear, stop it, Cal, you're becoming a dreadful bore!

Out of curiosity, I think, the Hafeners invited us up to Heartstone. We all went, Cora's family as well. The women treated it like a real occasion, dressing up in long, soft woolen skirts and painting their faces. Panthera borrowed some of Elveny's clothes and brushed his hair for half an hour. I watched them get ready with cynicism for a while, until my vanity got the better of me and I joined in. I dressed in white, washed my hair and painted my lips bright red. "That bloody enough for you?" I asked Elveny, grimacing at her.

She smiled weakly. "Made to kiss, I think," she said. "There's little power in that."

"You're wrong," I answered. "Continents can rise and fall on the strength of a kiss."

"Kiss me then," she said. Elveny is truly lovely. I've never kissed a woman in my whole life, not even when I was human.

"Aren't I poisonous to you?" I asked.

"No, of course not. Your semen is deadly of course, but I'm only talking about a kiss."

We were not alone, but no-one else was listening. I took her in my arms and kissed her. Her female body was naturally softer than a har's. It was interesting. I've never felt like that about a woman before, but then, the women here are virtually har anyway. Inside, they are just as male as we should be. Male and female. Kissing Elveny made me think about what it used to be like being a half creature. As soon as I'd recovered from my inception I realized what a dull, unexplored existence it had been. Gimrah humans seem to have overcome that. "I've always hated women," I said to Elveny.

She smiled. "Of course. When you were male you used to love men, didn't you?"

That floored me. I'd got too used to Wraeththu superiority. "You've found the Way here, haven't you," I said.

"We surely have," she answered.

"I'm glad that men have gone."

"Me too." She poured us wine and we drank to it. I was in a comfortable daze by the time we got to Heartstone.

The house was not as big as I imagined. Two-storied, roofed with tile, its windows quite small because of the bad winters they have in Gimrah. Gasteau Hafener is Tirtha of Lemarath; a tribe leader. A servant met us at the door to Heartstone and took away our wet furs and boots. Soft felt slippers were provided for the comfort of the Tirtha's guests. The house was warm, the ceilings low and beamed. We were shown into a dark, fire-lit salon, where the Hafeners were gathered together, drinking mulled wine and conversing politely with their other guests. We were introduced. One of the Hara was a Natawni; he and Kruin began to gossip. I sat down with

Panthera and Elveny and glasses of warm liquor were thrust into our hands. Panthera had been eyeing me very suspiciously since he had seen me embracing the woman. That he thought me rather strange already was a foregone conclusion, but now I felt he considered my strangeness to be a sort of madness; best not to be discussed. I didn't really care. Whatever motives my companions might want to read into it, both Elveny and myself understood the reasons for our brief contact and were not deluding ourselves in any way. Panthera lacked confidence in my judgment. As I said; I did not care. I drank my wine and looked around.

"Oh look!" Elveny hissed. "Here is Jubilee."

I would have known without looking across the room; first because I became aware of being watched, and second because Cora, standing near to us suddenly straightened up and became alert, like a hound desperate to show us how capable, trustworthy and handsome it is. I glanced at Elveny, raised a brow.

"Mmm," she said meaningfully. "Jubilee Hafener is as yet unbonded to another. As far as I know Lanareeve has more or less promised Cora that Natty shall be taken as Jubilee's consort once he has been incepted."

"Is that politics or choice?"

Elveny pulled a wry face. "A little of both, I think. Cora is a pillar of the human community; her words carry great weight. She is also a good friend of Gasteau and Lanareeve and it is no secret that she is very fond of Jubilee."

"Ah, I see; she will live out her desires through her son."

"You are cruel, Cal," Elveny scolded, shaking her head, although her smile did not waver. "And too critical. In actual fact, she has known Jubilee since he was a harling; don't misinterpret her feelings."

I laughed, unconvinced.

We were shown into another room to dine. The Hafeners are a handsome family. Both Gasteau and Lanareeve are tall, both pale-skinned and dark-haired, a trait that has been passed onto their sons. As well as Jubilee, there was Danyelle, his consort Onaly Doontree and an older har, who though unrelated in blood, had taken the Hafener name; this was Wilder. As we sat down to eat, Jubilee Hafener asked if he could sit beside me. This was not unexpected. "How long are you staying in Lemarth?" he asked me.

"Oh, as soon as the south road's clear, we'll leave," I answered.

"Where are you heading?"

"Jael, in Ferike."

He smiled. "Well, I doubt if you'll be here much longer then. This snow fall will have stopped by the end of the week. The road can be cleared after then. What a shame. I had hoped to spend the rest of this bitter season wooing you into a wild affair."

"How direct of you!"

"Brief affairs are always the most poignant, don't you think?"

I shrugged. "If you say so. I've had more pressing matters on my mind recently."

"Are you chesna with the Natawni?"

"No. Don't flirt with me, Jubilee Hafener; you are distressing the mother of your future consort."

He ignored this. "You don't have to go back to Cora's house tonight."

"I don't have to do anything, do I!" I replied awkwardly. He left it at that. The meal was excellent, the company sparkling. Across the table, Panthera watched me blandly, constantly. The robe he wore left his shoulders bare, where he made the bones glide and slide beneath his pale skin. Sultry in the lamplight he was, lovely as a white lily wreathed in vines. The most beautiful thing in the room, and so unattainable. The Hafeners flattered him. Only Jubilee had the sense to realize his barriers were unassailable, which was presumably why he decided to have a go at me. Hara in these rural communities must get so bored being cut off nearly all winter. We left the house late, singing in the snow as we tramped back to Cora's. Panthera walked beside me.

"Well," he said, "now we have fine new horses to ride back to Jael on. What did you get?"

I was surprised. "Nothing," I said. "Who gave you the horses?"

"Gasteau," he replied with a charmingly wicked grin. "You think I'm such a prig, don't you. I think I should be insulted that you're shocked."

"I'm not shocked. What did you have to do to get them?"

"Don't be coarse, Calanthe! All I had to do was smile." He laughed. "You do things the wrong way, obviously."

"And left Jubilee Hafener's side empty-handed. Clearly you are right, my pantherine!"

On the last night in Lemarath, I stood in my bedroom window and stared into the snow, in the direction of Heartstone.

Kruin came into the room. He said, "Oh, for God's sake, why don't you go over, Cal? We're leaving tomorrow. More days of comfortless travel! Why don't you go?"

We had discussed the Hafener heir's interest in me. I had a bottle of strong wine on the table. That was enough. "What's the point, Kruin?" I asked. "Why settle for something less than I want?"

"I don't know what you mean," he said angrily.

He didn't. I couldn't really explain myself. I sat at the table and drank the wine. Tomorrow we leave. Another long, dull, painfully cold journey. Panthera came and put his head around my door.

"Can you possibly remain sober tonight?" he requested wearily. "We want to make an early start tomorrow."

"Panthera," I said, "don't judge me!"

He twisted his mouth a little and raised one eyebrow. "I don't judge you, Cal. How can I? I don't know anything about you. You wanted your privacy. Do you want me to beg for confidences?"

I could not answer. This conversation was not going in the direction I'd intended. "Wait until we get to Jael," Panthera said, in a softer tone.

I looked up at him then, unsure of what I wanted to see in his face. "Why?" I asked sharply.

He leaned against the door and folded his arms. He smiled, and the room lit up. "It is a safe place," he said. "You will be able to rest properly."

I laughed grimly and reached for the wine bottle.

"You've changed so much," Panthera observed pensively. "Do you have to do this to yourself, Cal? I get the feeling you're falling apart inside. Whatever's bothering you, don't let it beat you like this."

"You have such clear sight, my pantherine," I said.

He shook his head. "Alright, I know what you're thinking. I'm much younger than you; I know that, but I'm not completely ignorant. You are in trouble, obviously, and I can see that you are making things worse for yourself. Don't say anything, Cal; I know I'm right." He turned away, began to close the door behind him. "Please think about what I've said," he told me.

I stared at the door after he'd gone. Panthera can be such a pompous little beast at times.

CHAPTER THIRTEEN

>─┼─◀)──○──(▶─┼─◄

The House of Jael

". . . (the) richly glowing
Gold of frames and opulent wells of mingling
Dim colors gathered in darkened mirrors"
—*Martin Armstrong, In Lamplight*

We left Lemarath early in the morning, as Panthera had desired. We had three new horses from the Tirtha, plus a mule for carriage, which would speed things up a little. Cora and her family bid us farewell, exacting promises from us that one day, in the summer, we would return. I would really like to. My promise at least, was heartfelt. New furs, new supplies, new horses. We began at a fast pace, our animals clad in fleeces because the Gimrah keep their best stock shorn of winter coats. We traveled across the country much quicker than we'd expected. The roads were not as bad as we'd feared. Each settlement we visited was hospitable and friendly, but none as welcoming as Lemarath. Every estemble has a governing harish family, although several families may be under their control. Every estemble has a Tirtha, who in turn is just one delegate of the Gimrah council of estembles. This council meets six times a year to discuss the problems and policies of the tribe as a whole, and to show off their prize stock, of course. In fact, these meetings are generally nothing other than glorified horse-fairs.

Now we are in Ferike, although the country has been changing for quite some time; more hilly, more forests. I've not written anything down for a long time, mainly because I haven't felt the need to quite so much. My sleep has been mercifully free of dreams. Perhaps I am being allowed to "recover." Maybe *they* knew they were driving me too far. I do feel slightly better; less harried. Looking back over all that has happened recently, I find myself wondering if Zack is really still alive. Of course, I had once thought Pell was dead, and I'd seen him die with my own eyes, so anything in this world is possible. I should be prepared for anything.

At the moment, we are staying at an inn in the town of Clereness, which is about twenty miles north west of Jael. Tomorrow, there is no foreseeable reason why Panthera will not see his home once more. Kruin, in his head, has already started spending his reward money. His plans are becoming rather tiresome. Me, I have no idea what I'm going to do with the money. Perhaps I could return to Lemarath. Ah, thereby hangs the tail. I have asked myself a hundred times; why didn't I? It would not have been beyond me to wheedle myself into Jubilee Hafener's affections to the extent that he would have taken me as his consort. I'm an old hand at that sort of thing, as Terzian's family will be able to tell you. Why didn't I? It would have effectively ruined whatever plans the Gelaming have in mind, wouldn't it! I don't know what I want; I can't even think about it properly. Places to go, to run to, to hide in; just excuses really. If I don't go to Lemarath, I could go back to Megalithica perhaps. Forever's the nearest I've ever had to a home, after all. But then, Terzian's son is now the consort of Seel Griselming, and Seel, I know, would prefer never to set eyes on me again. He has seen me kill. This is sad, because Forever is very close to my heart.

Sitting here now, I am thinking, if it is winter in Galhea now all the long gardens of the house will be covered in snow, the lake frozen, the summer-house dark within because of snow on the windows. I can see Cobweb, walking through the white gardens, wearing a long, flowing coat, his hair loose around him like smoke. There will be dogs bounding in front of him, probably harlings behind . . . harlings. Yes. Have I forgotten that so completely? I feel uncomfortable thinking about it, because I know it is just another example of my skill at betrayal. Forever holds more than just the secrets of my past. It holds a secret that flowered within myself; not thought, but flesh. My son. Terzian's son. His name is Tyson, and he would have become an adult a long, long time ago. I did not abandon him because I did not care (which I still do when I remember to), but because of what I am. I do not want my badness to taint him more than is necessary. One day, perhaps. . . . Oh, useless sentiment, but I would like to go back there. If I thought that Seel could find it within his heart to forget all that has happened, I would go tomorrow. Terzian went back there too, at the end. Oh God, I must get off this downward, melancholy spiral! Panthera is right:

I must start fighting. If I concentrate hard enough, I can draw my scattered strength back into myself. The past is done. I spend too much time wallowing about in it. I have a future, even if it is destined only to be a short one. I must seek my destiny. What pompous crap! I sound like Pell. It seems more than likely I shall spend my reward money seeking the answer to those riddles that have been set me. Trying to see beneath the mountains of Jaddayoth.

Ferike is an exhausting place; so many steep hills. Your neck is forever craned backwards, trying to see over trees. There are long avenues of pines, where the roads are in darkness, for no sunlight could ever reach them. There are many tiny villages, many abandoned, larger towns, almost unrecognizable under their winter, white blankets. Wild dogs haunt the ruins of Mankind's dwellings, but they are cowardly and would never attack unless they came upon someone alone and unawares. Some of the villages are built deep into the rock face. Clereness itself stands on the edge of a vast, still lake. Across it, rising directly from the water, are gaunt, gray cliffs, which Panthera tells me are named Fortress Shield. Birds have built their nests there. In the morning, I can throw open the window and see them swooping down, to glide above the surface of the lake. I don't want to be unhappy here, for, even in the depth of the season, I can smell the promise of spring. The Ferike are a contained people, quite unlike the gregarious folk of Hadassah and Gimrah, but they are not uncivil. This is a land of peace and healing. There is quiet here. I am no longer afraid of visitations, hallucinations and nightmares. A respite; probably brief, but I must enjoy it while it lasts.

Last night, I sat in Panthera's room, here at the inn, and watched him comb out his hair. We were feeling tranquil and relaxed. Panthera laughed and said that Kruin's hair was still full of the moss and leaves of Natawni; he would never get a brush through it. "But then, I suppose you know that," he added in rather a sharp tone.

"Thea, you were not excluded at any time; you know that."

He put his comb down quickly on the table, staring at his hands. "Cal, do you really think I can bear to let anyone touch me now?" I gave a non-committal shrug. "In Jasminia, I paid the huyana to let me off the penance," he continued. His face was flushed. He was ashamed of admitting that, even to me, whom he looked upon as a friend.

"In time, you might come to feel . . . differently," I said, which I knew was not much help.

"No feybraiha garlands for me," Panthera said wistfully, looking at himself in the mirror, as if trying to see the virgin thing he had once been. "No, you are not the only one with problems, Cal."

I sat on his bed, knowing that once I would have tried desperately hard to seduce him; I would have relished this ideal opportunity. Perhaps he was hoping I would. But I could only watch him and remember that. Panthera gave himself a shake, sniffed, and picked up the brush once more, raking his hair vigorously. He looked at me in the mirror.

"You are tired, Cal," he said. "You are always tired. It shows. Once we get to Jael, you must rest properly. Stay with us until the spring."

I smiled at him, unwilling to commit myself. I didn't want to appear ungrateful, but I was nervous of the Jaels being unwittingly drawn into something they might not want. I was not so stupid as to believe it was all over; this was just a lull, a freeze, like the season. Come spring, I felt sure the whips would be out, attempting to drive me in the direction of Immanion once more.

As if reading my mind, Panthera said, "Are they watching you now?"

The evening light was red when we started upon the upward road that led to Jael; a road that hugs the side of a tree-covered hill. Jael is at the top. It is a beautiful place, and very old. Panthera started to get nervous as soon as we could see the turrets of the castle above the trees.

"Cal, shall I have to tell them everything?" he asked me, and his voice was very young. The child who had grown up here was not far away, I thought.

"What do you think their reaction will be?"

He shrugged. "I'm not . . . I'm not sure." He did not want to put his fears into words, those fears that this parents would be ashamed of him, angry, would wish him dead rather than an ex-kanene.

Kruin had to say his piece. "They will naturally be surprised and pleased to have you home again," he said. "I should save any explicit details until you are settled."

"I'm not sure I'll be able to hide it," Panthera said dismally. "I feel as if it's written all over me."

"It's not," I said.

The castle has a thick outer wall, with a drawbridge over a dry moat. Panthera said that the bridge is never raised. We rode over it and Panthera pulled the bell-chain attached to the huge, wooden gates. I could almost smell his fear. After only a moment, the gates were opened and a servant came out to ask our business.

"Tell the Castlethane that his son is here," Panthera said with a shade of the old, familiar arrogance.

The servant looked at us all suspiciously and then told us to wait. Panthera explained that this was a har he'd never seen before, obviously someone employed since his disappearance. "Time waits for no-one," he said. "I wonder how many other new faces there'll be inside?" His hands were shaking, his face white.

I reached out to touch his arm, but then we could hear a great commotion beyond the gates. Panthera's father had obviously lost no time in answering this summons. Dogs came barking under the stone arch and the gates were thrown wide. We all looked within, at the tall har striding toward us, several yards in front of those that followed him. We all looked into the face of a har who dared not believe that his wildest hope had become truth.

"Ferminfex; my father," Panthera told us weakly and dismounted from his horse.

Ferminfex, like many hara, was very tall. Looking at him, it was not difficult to see how Panthera had been born so lovely, I reached this opinion even before I'd met Lahela, who is something of a legend himself. Ferminfex came to a stop a few feet away from us. He said, "Panthera," and Panthera walked toward him. They embraced each other in silence and then Ferminfex led his son into the yard. Hara respectfully backed away from them, staring. Neither Kruin nor myself had been acknowledged and we shared bewildered glances, unsure of what to do. "Oh come on," I said, "we might as well follow." A stable-har had come and taken hold of Panthera's horse. Kruin and I handed him the reins to ours and went after Panthera into the main house.

We stood in the hall and gawped around us. The sight was most impressive; marble, tapestry, stone and dark, polished wood. It was also surprisingly warm. A servant came to intercept us as we made to investigate one of the passages that led into the heart of Jael. "The Castlethane would like you to refresh yourselves," he said politely. "Please come with me."

We followed him up a red-carpeted corridor and were shown into a parlor, quite a large room, though probably small by Jael standards. Long, pointed arch windows curtained with floor-length, heavy velvet, offered a view of the gardens. The servant, an imperious creature, told us to make ourselves at home, refreshment would be brought to us shortly. He backed softly from the room and closed the door. Kruin, as he always does, went straight for the fire.

"Wonder when we get to talk business," he said, in rather a mercenary manner.

"Just look at this place!" I exclaimed, throwing myself down in a plump, well-cushioned chair. "The Jaels are clearly more than just comfortably off, by anybody's standards!"

"If that's the case, then they'll probably skimp on the reward money. That's how most rich people become rich."

I thought Kruin was being a little too hard. The walls of that room were virtually covered with oil paintings of various size and style, although most of them were portraits. From all around us the sultry, yet austere, arrogance of the Jaels looked down straight and imperious painted noses into the room. I recognized one picture as being of Panthera as a harling. He hadn't changed all that much. In the picture, he was leaning against the knees of a seated har who could only be his hostling. They shared the same deep, green eyes and haughty beauty.

Kruin broke my reverie. "Do you think we'll be given rooms in the servants' quarters?" he said.

Presently, our refreshment was brought to us. It took two hara laden with trays to bring it in. My appetite hadn't been that good for a while now, so despite the tempting smells, I only took a bowl of soup and a tankard of ale. Kruin fell upon the meal with gusto. One of the hara told us that the Castlethane would be along to see us very shortly.

When Ferminfex came into that room, Kruin and I stood up immediately. It was done without thinking, although I must admit I felt rather foolish when I realized I'd done it. Ferminfex has a regal air that commands that sort of behavior. He waved us back into our seats. Many Wraeththu hara take to autocracy like a duck takes to water. I was reminded of Terzian yet again. Once, long ago, I'd been in a very similar situation to this in Galhea. It was not Terzian's son that Pell and I returned to him, but his very sick consort. Unlike Terzian, however Ferminfex is not a person to be feared. I could see that straightaway. With Terzian you could see the steel inside him that lifted him above (or below) morality; Ferminfex has a similar steel but its blade is tempered—there's no savagery in it. He thanked us warmly for helping Panthera to get home and then mentioned that, in the morning, his secretary would speak to us about our "expenses." It was all very civilized. The word "reward" was not mentioned once.

"You are welcome to stay here in Jael for as long as you wish," he said, and then to Kruin. "You are Natawni? In view of the season and the exceptionally heavy snowfall in the north, I think you'd be wise to remain here until the spring. I also think it would help Panthera considerably if you, his friends, stayed with him for a while. He'll need some time to readjust." He sighed and rubbed his hands together. "Now, you must be tired. I think we should all meet again at breakfast tomorrow and discuss your plans. I'll have someone show you to your rooms. Excuse me." He inclined his head and left us.

"Rooms!" Kruin exploded once the door had closed behind him. "The cheek of it! No question of us being together, was there!"

"Oh, stop being so pernickety!" I answered, irritated. "This isn't Cora's, Kruin. That was politeness, he was avoiding being indelicate."

"You love this sort of thing, don't you!" Kruin said accusingly.

I could only shrug. "Yes I do. It reminds me of home." It was the truth.

I would have welcomed the chance to be alone that night, but Kruin insisted on sharing my room with me, which he claimed was more comfortable than his anyway. My bones were aching; that was always a bad sign, but I hoped that it was simple exhaustion in this case and not a presentiment of something worse. Panthera came to see us before we went to sleep. He looked very different; clean and well-dressed, his hair pinned up. Obviously he'd just attended a family reunion. He looked tired.

"How's it going?" I asked him.

"Oh, OK." he answered wearily. "I think Ferminfex has decided that I've picked up some dreadful habits in the outside world. If only they knew!"

"What have you told them?" Kruin asked.

"I haven't lied," Panthera answered. "I told them nearly everything. I told them I was a slave, but not what kind. So far, I've been asked no awkward questions; but that'll just come later. Once they start thinking about how I came of age away from home. Lahela will start worrying about my sex education; that's when it'll all start getting unpleasant. I won't be able to lie about that. I know I won't." He looked so down-hearted.

"Perhaps you should tell them before then," I said. He looked at the floor and shook his head. Rather him than me.

In the morning, Kruin and I were woken up by a servant bringing us cups of hot, herbal tea. We were told, as the curtains were flung wide to let pale, winter sunlight into the room, that breakfast would be served in half an hour. An explanation was given on how to find the breakfast-room and would we care to have our bath run for us? We said we would.

Kruin, despite his reservations about the Jaels, was enjoying this immensely. "Some servants' quarters, eh?" I teased him. Our room was round, on the third floor of a turret. I went to open one of the arched windows, leaning out to gaze down the smooth, stone walls. Kruin complained of the cold. It was a lovely morning; crisp and hard and bright. There was a smell of cooking, sounds of activity in the yard below. I felt warm and secure. If I closed my eyes, it could be Forever around me. Panthera had sent us some clean clothes, plain and dark, in the Ferike style, but eminently flattering and stylish.

In spite of the directions we'd been given, it still took Kruin and myself several tries to find the breakfast room. By the time we found it, the rest of the family were already seated. There were over a dozen of them, and that wasn't counting the harlings. The room was airy and light, carpeted in a pale color with matching drapes. The table was of highly polished black wood with all the Jaels sitting around it, poised in the act of politely inviting us to join them. Spaces has been left on either side of Panthera. We sat down. Panthera forked slivers of ham onto my plate. He looked very serious, his hair still pinned up, revealing the longest neck I'd ever seen.

"You smell wonderful," I said.

He smiled without looking up. "It's only the food," he answered.

"No, it's not. Don't you think I'd recognized the perfume of your soul if I smelled it?" He looked at me then, right at me, light off the cutlery high-lighting his skin; his eyes were luminous. He was thinking, I felt the breath catch in my throat. I smiled and he smiled back at me. It was our first shared moment.

Lahela made a splendid entrance when we were all half-way through our meal. He was dressed only in a bathrobe, his hair knotted untidily on top of his head, though most of it was dangling down his back. The art of stylish scruffiness. He looked marvelous. Ferminfex lit up when Lahela walked in the room and I don't blame him. Lahela yawned and slumped down in a chair at the opposite end of the table to Ferminfex. A servant skidded to his side and offered to heap his plate with food. Lahela groaned. "Coffee please!" he said, "And a lightly grilled piece of toast." Like Ferminfex, he thanked us for bringing Panthera home, except his gratitude was delivered in a far warmer manner. He drank his coffee without using the delicate handle of his cup, and smoked three cigarettes. I could see the other Jeals exchanging long-suffering glances. Lahela seemed oblivious, but because of what Panthera had told me, I knew that this was a staged ritual of Jael irritation that Lahela must perform fairly regularly.

"Has 'Fex has his little talk with you yet?" Lahela asked me.

"No, he hasn't!" Ferminfex answered stonily before I could speak.

Lahela smiled. "Don't look like that, Cal. He won't bite you, will you my dear?"

Ferminfex rolled his eyes, shaking his head, smiling.

CHAPTER FOURTEEN

Reliving the Past

"Take this white robe. It is costly. See, my blood
has stained it but a little. I did wrong:
I know it, and repent me. If there come
a time when he grows cold—for all the race
of heros wander, nor can any love
fix theirs for long—
take it and wrap him in it,
and he shall love again"

—Louis Morris

After the meal, Ferminfex took me to his study. "I would have left this until later, but as Lahela mentioned it, I thought we might as well get it over with."

"That sounds ominous," I said lightly. He didn't answer that.

"Please, sit down," he said. It was a pleasant, dark and cozy room. A fire roared in the grate and there was a heady smell of pine. The desk was enormous. We faced each other across it.

"I want to come straight to the point," Ferminfex said, and then watched me carefully for a second or two. "We knew, were informed, of your coming here." He offered me a cigarette, which I took automatically.

My body had gone numb with the familiar cold. The room was closing in. I wanted to get out. I couldn't breathe. Panic. *They'd* been here before me then. Nowhere was safe. Everyone was in on it.

"Now listen, Cal. I can imagine what you're thinking. I was only concerned about Panthera; that he was still alive and coming back to us, but someone is concerned for you too, Cal . . ." *(Don't I know it!)*

"No," I said eventually. "No, look I'm sorry, Castlethane; I don't want to involve you or your family in . . . whatever. I'm sorry they've . . . contacted you. I . . ."

"Shut up," Ferminfex interrupted mildly. "There is nothing to apologize for. All that happened was that I was . . . requested . . . enjoined perhaps, to offer my assistance to you if I thought it was needed. I didn't have to tell you this, Cal. You do see that, don't you?"

I nodded, carefully.

He smiled. "Good. Now that's understood, perhaps we can go on. I am supposed to talk to you, impartially, but I don't like deception. I thought it only fair to tell you the score. If you don't want my help, then fine, we'll leave it at that. Panthera is concerned about you though. He spoke a little last night about what has happened."

"Did he!" (Fine to reveal my secrets then, if not his own).

"Yes, he did, and with the best possible motive, Cal. Now, I don't know what you're mixed up in with the Gleaming, and I don't particularly care; whatever it is can't offend me. We all owe you a lot, Cal. I want to help you. What do you say?"

"You've been honest with me?" I asked.

"I have. I cannot ask you to trust me, because I can see you don't trust people easily, but I'm sure you'd be able to tell if I was deceiving you."

"You flatter me," I said. "I'm not sure of my own senses anymore. Anyway, I really don't know how, or where, to begin."

Ferminfex nodded in understanding, chewing his cheek thoughtfully. He took a long draw off his cigarette and spoke through a plume of smoke. "You could try starting with why the Gelaming have such an interest in you."

"I could, yes. I'm not sure if I want to."

"Hmm, of course, it's not really my business, but I feel you gain nothing from bottling all this up. How can it possibly affect me, or even you, if you let it all out?"

"I don't know. I've always felt it should be something I keep to myself. If I tell you, you're implicated, Ferminfex. Remember, you don't know what it is yet."

"If you're afraid you may cause suffering by telling me, forget it. The Jaels have a very secure position; excellent positions in the esteem of both Almagabra and Maudrah. That is unassailable. Do you really think you'd have been allowed to come here if they didn't want me to know?"

"Your arguments seem sound," I said, still reluctant to speak.

"Well?"

"Well. It's not the Gelaming exactly that have the interest in me. It is their Tigron."

"Ah, Pellaz-har-Aralis," Ferminfex said softly, looking beyond me. It was strange to hear that name quoted with such respect.

"Yes," I agreed, "it is he." I wished I didn't have to go on. It was like ripping out my own heart, to put it on the desk before us, and watch it bleed. Why, after all this time? Why should it still hurt? Am I just crazy? Is that it? I'd always sort of *knowns* that one day I'd have to tell someone, but it was still hard.

"So," Ferminfex prompted, "and what interest does the Tigron have in you?"

"It's hard to explain."

"Is it? Then try." Ferminfex leaned forward on his desk, his chin resting on his clenched fists.

I took a deep breath. I closed my eyes. "A long time ago, long before Pellaz became Tigron, he and I traveled together. We were . . . close. Of course, it had been mapped out for him from the moment of his inception what he was to become, but we didn't know, you see. We were aware of the fact that Thiede had his eye on Pell, and for that reason, Pell tried to progress in caste as quickly as possible. Looking back, I can see we were so stupid—blind. To Thiede, I started off being an admirable bodyguard, someone who could teach Pell how to survive, but eventually, I became rather an inconvenience. There was no place for me in Pell's grand future, as far as Thiede was concerned. He hadn't counted on our feelings for each other. It was because of my heritage, you see, which, I'm afraid to admit, is Uigenna."

Ferminfex sucked in his breath at that. "Ah, I *do* see! Now there's something Phaonica would rather keep quiet, I'd bet! The Tigron was once chesna with a har of the Uigenna; hardly a savory background. How embarrassing!" He laughed out loud.

"I'm glad you understand," I said drily.

Ferminfex waved his hand at me. "Sorry, it's just that the Gelaming are such a pompous lot; so sanctimonious. I find your relationship with the Tigron is simply poetic justice, which they well deserve. The Gelaming would do well to remember their own origins at times!"

"I agree."

Looking back, it becomes obvious that Thiede had planned to get rid of me from the start. He bided his time and then . . . smack; it came. I couldn't look at Ferminfex's face as I told him about it. Oh no; I didn't want to watch any pain mirrored there. I looked out of the window, speaking to the sky. I still feel that Thiede's plans were far too ornate and fanciful. Why kill Pell at all? Was it just to fool me, having him murdered under my nose? Did Thiede think I'd just forget about him then? Probably. Uigenna are not famed for the depth of their passions. It was only later that Thiede understood the extent of my grief, the madness that it inflicted on me. I'm still not sure if I've recovered my sanity. For years I believed Pell to be dead. I'd burned his body myself. I knew I had to try and forget, but deep inside, something must have told me. I don't know. It was as if I *knew,* because whatever I did, whoever I was with, I couldn't stop thinking about that hare-brained, idiot, lovely child; my Pellaz. It was totally uncharacteristic of me, and still is. As far as Thiede was concerned, as soon as he'd grabbed Pell from my clutches, I was simply past history. But there was something he hadn't accounted for; Pell had a heart and a mind of his own. True, he was still Thiede's creature, through and through, but as long as I lived, Pell would look for me, and if I was dead, Thiede was afraid Pell might still look for me. Dangerous. An unhinged and bizarre state of mind. A messy wound that Thiede just could not suture. What a dilemma. Eventually, I meandered my way back to Galhea; not intentionally. Terzian's people took me in and when Terzian's son Swift went in search of the Gelaming looking for his father, I went with him. Oh, I was petrified of meeting them, sure enough, but at the same time. . . . An exciting, but terrifying, thrill. I wanted it. Why? When I reached them, I still knew nothing about what Pell had become; nothing. I went to them unarmed, in every sense. Perhaps that was a big mistake, perhaps it wasn't. It was certainly inevitable. Seel was there with them, utterly Gelaming by then. He ignored me.

I stopped speaking; clouds had covered the sun outside.

Ferminfex shifted in his seat, leaning forward. "Did they tell you then about the Tigron?" he asked.

This story was delighting him. I put my head in my hands, the taste of Imbrilim in my throat, the memory of so many faces filled with contempt. I had dredged these thoughts up from a deep, dark dungeon of my mind. Difficult. It had taken years to suppress them. Now I felt dazed, swamped, unsafe.

"Tell me? I don't. . . . It's . . ." The room was electric around me, Ferminfex's fire crackling, popping like a pyre. Outside, black birds were lamenting, voices echoing.

"Please try, Cal." Now my host was blatantly eager. It was foul. When I looked up from the darkness the day was bleached and stretched. "You must let it out, Cal. Relax. Come on, it can't hurt you now." *(It can! It can!)*

I gulped air through a throat that was squeezing itself shut. Ferminfex squatted beside me, I'd literally collapsed. I was on the floor. He put his hand on the back of my neck, hauled me into a sitting position, pushed my head between my knees. "Are you alright?" Now his eyes were filled with concerned not morbid hunger. Had they ever been otherwise? I don't remember. I nodded weakly at him. He stood up to fetch me a glass of wine, which I had to hold with both hands.

"I'm sorry," I said, clambering back onto the chair. "I don't know what happened to . . ." And then the glass fell from my fingers to shatter on the floor. My body arched, all the muscles flexed to agony. The sound of my mindless, almost divine, grief was the cry of a huge, tortured beast. The room was full of it, more noise than my frame would allow. Ferminfex was white, unsure of what to do. I hurt so much, every fiber of my being vibrating with a real yet imagined pain. After a while, like a spirit wind dying down, the feeling began to recede, back into me. I sobbed, sucking air into my lungs, wiping tears from my nose and finding that it was blood.

A subdued Ferminfex offered me a soft cloth to wipe my face. I don't think he knew what to say. We'd touched on something forbidden. We both knew that, without even mentioning it. But it had to be faced; that was another shared certainty. I felt raw, opened up, ready to be examined. That was an accurate analogy, but we'd have to work fast before the wounds healed.

"Can you continue now?" Ferminfex asked me.

"Yes," I said. "I want to."

"Can you remember everything?"

"Not yet; but I will. I have to begin."

"Then take your time." He gave me another glass and sat down.

I remembered that day in Imbrilim so clearly. Strange that before now I hadn't really been aware of forgetting it. Habit; must be. We'd just been waiting around, Swift and I, waiting for something to happen. Swift was quite ill with it all. Me, I felt as if there was one hell of a big stone hanging over my head by one fragile thread. It was vile. Why couldn't they just get on with whatever they wanted to do with us? One day, when Swift was out of the way, they sent a guard to take me to Arahal. One of Thiede's top dogs is Arahal. Then they made me wait in his pavilion; more agony. When he came in, he was very brusque with me. I remember saying, "OK, do your worst," having no idea just how bad that could be. He handed me a photograph. It was of a splendid har, obviously Gelaming, robed in feathers, crowned in feathers and silver filigree.

"Do you know this har?" Arahal asked. "Do you . . . *remember* him?"

I must have looked at him stupidly.

"Why?" I looked at the picture again.

"Just answer. Do you?" He took it off me, leaving my hand in the air, holding nothing.

"Well, it looks a bit like someone I knew once, yes, but he's dead now. It looks like someone called Pellaz."

"Yes, it is," Arahal said coldly. "I was afraid you'd say that." It was then that the cold dread started creeping in from the diaphanous walls of the pavilion, invading my flesh, penetrating deep. With it came a vivid recollection. A scream. A horse's scream. Flying blood and bone. The rain. Cold. Cold. Cold. I thought I'd learned to control it. My heart was going mad. Panic. It hadn't happened for a long time. With that memory came the feeling of death; my death. My brain exploding, my soul being sucked away. I was frozen; an imbecile. "Calanthe!" Arahal said. After a moment, I'd mustered enough self-control to look at him. He smiled then and the smile was almost gentle. "I'm afraid I'm going to have to ask you to go to Immanion," he said.

"Why?" A husky little question.

"Because Thiede is anxious to talk with you." He waved the photograph at me. "You've caused no end of trouble in Pell's name, haven't you. Cal, that's bad for us. Very bad. For the simple reason that the har you thought was dead lives on. He is Pellaz-har-Aralis, Tigron of Immanion."

It was a shock. It was a great shock. What more can I say?

Another slice of the past removed from my heart. There was silence in Ferminfex's room. He lit another cigarette. Outside, it had begun to rain; the day was dismal.

"There's more isn't there?" he asked.

"Oh yes, there's more. But I don't think I'm supposed to remember it. What's happened? How come I can speak of it now?"

Ferminfex shrugged. "I don't know. Have you really tried to tell someone before?"

"I think so. I can't remember. This is scary, isn't it?"

Ferminfex nodded. "I'm afraid I must agree with you."

"It's not just my sick mind is it?"

He smiled. "No, it's not just your sick mind. I'd like to flatter myself that I was the key needed to turn those locks in your head, but if I am then someone else is turning it, not me. Are you ready to go on?"

I shivered. "I'm afraid. I don't feel safe."

"We have all day, no need to rush. Come with me." He took my arm and helped me to rise. My legs were like jelly. Why did I feel like this? What happened had been years ago. I'm not a weak person. Memories, however harrowing, should not affect me like this. I thought I'd got over all that in Galhea.

There was a couch at the other end of the room, next to the fire. Ferminfex told me to lie down on it. He wrapped me in the woolen, fringed blanket draped over the cushions. My fingers were freezing. He took my hand. "Let's make this a little easier," he said. "Relax, Cal. Let me take you back."

Simple hypnosis. His voice washed over me and talked me back. It *was* easier that way. Living the past, I could not experience the pain of the present. I found myself sitting in a small room. I'd been there for some time. The building was the administration office in a town some miles north of Immanion. I hadn't slept for several nights. Neither had I eaten anything. They kept bringing me food which I wouldn't touch and talked in whispers behind my back. I was sitting on the edge of a narrow bed with my eyes closed, thinking of nothing. Then someone came and touched me on the shoulder. They said, "Calanthe, Lord Thiede wishes to see you now." They had to help me walk. My mind was a blank. If I tried to think at all, I was flooded with images of Pell's blood. I could feel the sting on my cheek where a shard of flying bone had cut me. I could smell the hot, sweet perfume of fresh blood, I could smell burning. They led me into another room. The rooms were all the same there. Tasteful, functional, soothing. Elegant plants and comfortable furniture. A har sat behind a desk, his feet crossed at the ankles on the glossy surface. A har with flaming red hair and an unmistakable aura of immense power; Thiede.

"Ah Cal," he said sociably. "Oh dear, you don't look at all well. Come on, come in, sit down. Here." He clicked his fingers and someone swooped in with the inevitable hot coffee. Thiede heaped sugar into my cup and pushed it into my hands. He shook his head. "My, what a state you're in!" He laughed. I couldn't speak. Leaning across the desk, he took my face in his hand. I spilled coffee over my lap. "Now, you're really going to have to pull yourself together, aren't you my dear. We've got to have a little chat and I can't speak to a gibbering idiot, can I now?" He put his fingers over my eyes and blasted me with white, searing strength that nearly knocked me backwards. When my vision had cleared, all feeling had come back to me. One of those feelings was rage. I remember swearing at him, which he listened to indulgently. When my invective had run out, he said, "Finished? Good. Now listen to me, Calanthe, you really are proving to be rather a thorn in my side."

"Good!" I said. "I hope the pain kills you."

He laughed. "Oh, no chance of that! Very sorry."

"Why did you do it?" I asked. "Why? Just tell me that."

"Do what?"

I shook my head, unable to speak it.

He sighed. "Oh Cal, it really is all a bit beyond you, I'm afraid. Just live out your little life and let hara like me deal with the important issues. Pell's like you, you know. He won't let go either."

"Of the past?" I had visions of Pell flinging himself around, reliving his own death every day.

Thiede shook his head. "Oh, no, not exactly. He is everything I'd hoped he'd be. He rules for me, Cal, and one day, his authority shall be over the entire world. He was a good choice. No, what he won't let go of is you. I'm afraid I'm finding it hard to see why, looking at you now, but I suppose you have been through a lot. Every creature in the world has an ideal partner, a soul mate. Only a few are lucky to find each other. You and Pellaz did, but then, that was unlucky because you had to be torn apart. It damaged you both more than I thought it would. You are nothing Cal, you don't matter, but Pell can't afford such scars."

"So, what are you going to do? Kill me?"

Thiede pulled a careful, disgusted face. "Oh, please! We are not barbarians. We are not Uigenna. No, there is a much more palatable solution. Of course, as you are now, you're wholly unsuitable for Pellaz to be associated with. It would cause a terrible scandal. He holds a position higher than any other har in Wraeththudom. But he's had to pay the price for that privilege. He's had to learn to live without privacy, to be as spotless a creature as he can. He's an example to our race, Cal. He has to be perfect. Do you understand this?"

Oh, I understood it all right. "So, what's your solution then?" I asked bitterly, still thinking of death or banishment.

"Well, in a perfect world, you would be taken to Immanion to undertake a course of ritual purification, so that, eventually, you would be fit to take your place at Pell's side, and could be brought forth for this end as yet another example to the people of how even the most base creature can aspire to perfection."

I made an explosive sound, which Thiede raised his hand to silence. "But," he continued, "this is not a perfect world—yet. Pellaz already has a consort, which I, admittedly, did rather bully him into taking. They are bonded in blood, which is insoluble. I'm afraid the liaison has not been a happy one, but there you are! Even I can make mistakes. So you see, whatever vows you and Pell made before cannot stand up against a blood-bonding. You cannot be his consort; there is no way around that, unless Caeru the Tigrina was to die. Unfortunately for you, he is young and healthy and, although not entirely popular with the Hegemony (which I regret is probably Pell's doing), he is well-loved by the people. Although his relationship with Pell may be barren, Caeru has carved a niche for himself in Wraeththu's heart. He does his job very well. No-one outside of Phaonica would ever know they are not perfectly matched."

I felt sick. "What are you trying to tell me?" I asked.

"Merely this. You must take the course of Cleansing. There is a position in Immanion for you, Cal, in the royal household. I know I could use your talents, and what you and Pell decide to do between yourselves, behind closed doors, is nobody else's business. Naturally, you'll both have to be very careful. Can't afford to let anyone know what's going on. I'm sure you understand that. It will help if I can find you a consort of your own. Arahal can employ you in his staff. You are untrained, so he won't be able to offer you much at first. You'll have to work your way up, but I'm sure you won't find that difficult. Now, what do you say?"

What I said was, "How dare you! You think I can be brought to heel, trained like a dog, to wag my tail and fawn at your Tigron's feet? You must be insane! You say that Pell still feels strongly about me? Well, let me tell you, Thiede, I may be the lowest of the low in your eyes, but there is no way, even now, that I'd ever be bonded in blood to anyone else but Pell. I respect what we had before, even if he doesn't. No, I'm not a toy, Thiede. Not like he is!" At that moment, perhaps for the first time, I hated Pell.

"Now just calm down!" Thiede said, still grinning. I wouldn't. My anger got hotter and hotter. In the end, he had me taken away and locked in my room. "Obviously, we shall have to talk later," he said, and there wasn't even a hint of irritation in his voice. It was almost as if he was pleased with my reaction. As if it was a *relief*. We did talk later. We talked many times. I was moved from place to place, probably (or so I thought) to prevent Pell finding out Thiede had me in confinement. Strange things happened to my sense of time. Sometimes I'd wake up from a winter night's sleep and find that it was high summer outside my window. I began to lose time. This always happened after one of my intimate chats with Thiede. I tried to rationalize, thinking of it as an hallucination. Thiede had created purposely to keep me disoriented. I was treated very well, given everything except my freedom. Gelaming are rarely physically cruel, of course. They have more subtle methods of torture. At the beginning, they even let me out to visit Terzian when he was dying. I was followed just to make sure I kept in line, but it was still a sweet touch. I suppose Thiede tried everything to get round me. I slept with a silver-haired har who never spoke, whose eyes were completely black, who loved me in a silent, distant way. I never even knew his name. Thiede would sometimes come to see me three times a week, and then I wouldn't hear from him for a couple of months. Every time we talked it got around to the same subject. My character was undesirable. I would have to change. I must publicly speak out against my own past and praise the way that Thiede had made me see the light. And no, there was no chance of my going free. I must recognize my duty to Wraeththu and to the Tigron in particular. Had I no sense of responsibility? In public, I would be allowed to be Pell's colleague, albeit a low-ranking one. I would have to bow to him and call him Lord. In private, well, how could there ever be such a thing. I wouldn't even let myself think about it. In case some small part of me said, Yes, yes, this is what I want! No, no, it was against my nature; impossible! Thiede enjoyed our wrangling; I know he did. Afterwards, my black-eyed companion would try to comfort me, ease the stress from the back of my neck. Maybe I did forget for a little while then. I could see no end to it. I'd wake up and it'd seem like years had passed.

Eventually, I came to be confined within a tower. I'd had enough. I didn't know how long I'd been locked up. One day, Thiede came to see me and he seemed different, just a little tense, watching me carefully. We drank iced wine on the high balcony and I said, "Just let me go, Thiede." I hadn't said that for quite some time, knowing how fruitless it was to bother. I'd made up my mind to throw myself from the tower if things didn't change soon. How long I'd have gone on promising myself that, I cannot guess. Thiede tapped his fingers against his lips, looking down into his wine.

"You really want to turn your back on Pell?" he asked casually.

Hope leapt in my chest like a crazy bird. "Look, if you let me go, I'll disappear, go away as far as you like," I babbled. "Tell Pell I'm dead; anything! I won't be an embarrassment to you, I promise! No-one will ever know about Pell and me, I swear it! I'll never breathe a word to anyone. You have my word. Take my life if I break it."

Thiede just threw up his hands. "Impossible, I'm afraid! Pell won't ever stop wanting you, looking for you. I have . . . er . . . *spoken* to him, Cal. He does know I'm in contact with you. Naturally, he is distressed by some of the things you've done. The incident in Saltrock springs to mind. But it is beyond me to dissuade him from caring about you. The problem is, I *do* understand it. Though he and Caeru may be bonded in blood, I am convinced that you and Pell are bonded in soul. I must stress that your only course of action is to do as I suggest; take the Cleansing. Come to Immanion."

"And be there for Pell to play with whenever he feels the need to?" I butted in angrily. "How many times do I have to tell you, Thiede? The answer is no. It will always be no. I couldn't live that life. I need my freedom. I need my self-respect. More than I need Pell. Anyway, I know we could never be happy living like that. It would be nothing like we had before. I'd hate it and so would he, I'm sure. It's better for us to suffer being apart than learning to loathe each other together. I'm right, Thiede, we've both changed. The Pell and Cal that loved each other are both dead. And even the memory of it must die. You can't argue with me; you know I'm right."

He was silent for a moment. "Hmm. Now listen, Cal, I don't think you've quite grasped the extent of Pell's power here," he said wearily. "His word is law. He is your Tigron too, Cal. If he wants you, then I'm afraid he's going to have you. It's against my wishes, I've done all I can to prevent it, but there's nothing I can do to change his mind. I've tried! All I can do now, is nudge events along in the most civilized manner."

"Thiede, it's disgusting and you know it!"

"Oh, I agree, entirely. But Pell has more important things to worry about than this. For God's sake, realize how small you are in comparison and make things easier by doing what I suggest."

"Sacrifice my life for the good of Wraeththu? Forget it! Let me go, Thiede!"

"You will merely delay the inevitable by that."

"I can go far away. I've told you!"

"Nowhere will be far enough."

"I'll hide!"

"You can try—certainly." He smiled at me. "You're a problem, Cal. A bull-headed wild child, if ever there was one. No wonder he loves you! Please think about what I've said though."

"Oh, I do. Every time you say it!"

"I admire you. I really do."

"Yet you want to change me."

He shook his head. "I can see your side too, you know. You have my sympathy."

"Oh, sure I do. Look what a help it's been!"

He shrugged, stood up. I remained seated, staring at my hands. Thiede took a deep breath, stared out over the countryside.

"You have a good view here, don't you." I didn't answer. I felt him staring at me. "It's your choice," he said, in a silky voice.

"I've had enough, Thiede."

"Yes. I know." And then he left me.

I sat there for a while, finished my drink and then went inside. Everywhere felt strange, deserted. I couldn't find my companion anywhere. I ran down the winding steps to the door that was always locked from outside. The hall looked different that day. No wonder. I'd always seen it in gloom, now it was full of sunlight. The great door was wide open. The tower was empty. Outside, a white horse lazily cropped grass, loaded with supplies. I sat down on the front step and stared at the outside world for several hours. I did a lot of thinking. Pell is my life, but I also knew that what I loved most about him was his innocence, his freedom, his simplicity. I couldn't believe that had survived along with his soul. It was impossible. He was Tigron. It took some time, and even some guts, but in the end I just walked out of that tower and never looked back. I mounted the horse that Thiede had left for me and galloped it toward the north. Funny how the people you most hate can surprise you with sensitive gestures occasionally. Oh, Thiede understood me, alright. I kept heading north. There was money in the saddlebags; plenty of it to start with. In a week, I was in Thaine, shying at shadows, numbing my sleep with alcohol. I'd been in confinement for many years. Now I was free. No-one had won. There was no victory.

That was when Ferminfex brought me back. I was shaking as if terribly cold, yet my skin was hot. I drank wine and took the cigarette he offered me. "What can I do?" I asked.

Ferminfex kneeled down beside me. "I want you to rest now," he said. "Panthera tells me you've been keeping a sort of diary of what's happened since Fallsend. I'd like to read it while you're resting. Tell me where it is."

I hesitated, but then, hadn't he witnessed my soul already? I told him where it was, and he left me alone, hurrying to fetch it. I lay there feeling like I'd come around after an incredibly serious operation, which could have killed me, but hadn't.

Pages turning. I lay on the couch, watching Ferminfex reading my notes. I could almost tell which parts he was reading by the exclamations he made. A guilty thought stole through me. All of Panthera's secrets were in there too. "Ferminfex," I said, worried, "about your son. He . . . well, I wouldn't like him to know I've showed you that."

"Don't think I haven't realized some of what Thea's been through, Cal," he replied. "I'm not stupid. This manuscript might be painful for both of us, but I do want to read it; as much to learn Panthera's troubles as help you."

"That's sneaky, Ferminfex!"

"Don't worry. Panthera will never know I've seen this, I promise you." He looked up. "I hope that one day he will want to tell me himself what happened. If he does, I'll tell him how I feel about it, that I'm just glad he got out of there alive. Nothing else matters. I don't think he realizes that."

"He's a proud creature," I said.

"Yes, that's Lahela's blood for you," Ferminfex commented bleakly, although I thought that Ferike austerity was more to blame than Kalamah vanity. No matter what Ferminfex said, I could tell that it still shocked him deeply to learn of his son's humiliations in Piristil. At one point, he looked up at me and said, "I know the taking of life is the worst of crimes, and I wish Panthera hadn't shot Jafit, but for simply one reason: I'd like to have done it myself!" He rubbed his eyes with his hands. "Lahela must never see this," he said. At the end of it, he put his head in his hands.

It was late afternoon. We sat together in silence, me on the sofa, he behind his desk. A knock came on the door. Lahela had sent one of the househara with a tray of food. I was hungry, and went to sit at the desk once more. Ferminfex stared at me for a moment and then tapped the sheaf of papers with his fingers, smiling wrily. "I must say your feelings for Panthera cause me some concern!"

I squirmed in mortification. "Oh, I wasn't myself when I wrote that," I replied lightly.

"Now don't take that the wrong way! I don't think your blood is tainted. Let's face it, any one of us who was incepted to Wraeththu rather than born to it has shady areas in our past histories. It was just the time for it. You don't strike me as evil, Cal, far from it. Tormented, maybe. What I should have said was, does Panthera return your feelings? I don't want him to be hurt more than he already has been."

"Oh no," I said. "Panthera has no idea I was lusting after him on the journey south. Anyway, I'm sure you'll agree, he's in no condition to return anyone's feelings at present."

"Yes, he needs time, that's true. But anyway, we're here to talk about your situation, not Thea's. Let's just analyze what we know. Since leaving Thiede's tower, you have been plagued by dreams which lately have culminated in two very frightening experiences. You have been aware of being followed, perhaps by this shadow figure from your past . . ."

"I don't understand where Zack fits into all this," I said.

"No, neither do I. Perhaps it is to make you all the more keen to recant your past, I don't know. I think the main question you've got to ask yourself is, who is behind all this? And what is its purpose?"

"Well, that's obvious, isn't it? Pell and Thiede. The purpose; to drag me to Immanion, make life unbearable for me anywhere else."

Ferminfex shook his head. "I wouldn't be too sure of that if I were you. There is something you aren't aware of yet. The message that came over our thought transference unit was very carefully guarded; no visuals whatsoever. But there was no mistaking the fact that whoever sent it wasn't Wraeththu."

"What do you mean?"

"Just this; it was female. Must have been human, of course, but a terribly advanced human."

"Then it's obvious!" I cried, leaning forward, eager to explain. "Maybe I'm not being paranoid about feeling everyone I meet is in on this. The woman must have been Cora. She was the link in the chain before you. I'm being manipulated, nudged in the direction of Immanion."

Ferminfex shook his head. "Oh think, Cal! It can't be Cora. From what you've told me, it's obvious she, or even the girl who lives with her, isn't that far advanced. I'm talking about an incredibly powerful human mind. No, you're wrong about the Gimrah. They have no part in this."

"Then who has?"

He shrugged helplessly. "I can't tell you that. What we've got to remember is that there are powers in this universe stronger than Wraeththu, stronger even than Thiede. Cal, there is more to this than meets the eye. You've got to learn the real reason why it's so important for you and Pell to be reunited. I don't think Thiede revealed more than he had to. I'm only acting on hunches, but . . ."

"If I don't black out and lose all this information again!"

"That won't happen."

"Don't be so sure. It's happened before, in Galhea. My mind blotted out crimes I'd committed, Pell's death, everything. It took a blast of power to clear the blocks. Seems I did the same over my imprisonment; I can't trust myself. My machinery is faulty, somewhere."

Ferminfex didn't agree. "Have you ever thought that is precisely what you're supposed to think. It's obvious why you couldn't tell people; you were prevented from doing so. Hypno-suggestion, mind coercion, any number of ways."

"Then why could I tell you?"

"If Thiede put the block on you, but somebody or something else is behind all this, nudging you to Jael, then maybe the time was right for . . . God, I don't know! It's beyond me!"

"What is all the secrecy for then? Why can't I be told? Surely it's just wasting time."

"Mmm." Ferminfex leaned back in his chair and screwed up his eyes in thought. "You're on a journey," he said. "Self discovery? Maybe. Or something more? I agree that you are being driven in certain directions . . ." He sat up. "The message you had, what was it again?"

"Beneath the mountains of Jaddayoth. Is that referring to caves or a grave do you think?"

"Neither. I believe it's referring to Eulalee, an underground kingdom, home of the tribe of Sahale. Clearly, you've got to go there."

"And if I don't?"

Ferminfex made an exasperated noise. "Look, how can you fight when you don't even know who the enemy is? Don't be ridiculous. Go along with this for a while with your ears and eyes open. The huyana in Jasminia spoke of preparing you for something. He spoke of messages. You've got to face it, don't you see? And look at things another way too. How about Pell? He must know that a relationship with you is impossible at the moment, except under the most excruciating terms. What Thiede says he's demanding is like the demands of a child, and Pellaz-har-Aralis is far from a child, I can tell you! Perhaps Pellaz is being manipulated too. Think about it."

I let myself slump over the table, sighing. "I don't want this. I don't want any of this!"

"Of course you don't," Ferminfex soothed. "You want to make a life in Ferike with my son, don't you? Shall I give my permission for that? Will you do it if I ask you to?" We stared at each other. I shook my head and smiled. "Wait until the spring," Ferminfex continued. "You have plenty of time. We'll talk about this again."

So, it was settled. Come the thaw I would ride into the Elhmen; the only known route to Eulalee. I didn't know what I would find there. Coming out of Ferminfex's study that day, I felt ravished, but renewed. The boil had been lanced at last. That night, I dreamed of Pell, but he was far away.

CHAPTER FIFTEEN

>─┼─◀▶─●─◀▶─┼─◀

What He Learned from the Water

"Though lovers be lost, love shall not"

—Dylan Thomas, And Death Shall Have No Dominion

Life in Jael is conducted at a leisurely, sedate pace. Every morning, the family gathers together for breakfast, and in the evening for dinner. There are two separate rooms for this. Panthera now has two brothers, one hosted by Lahela, one by Ferminfex. There are also uncles and cousins, and cousins' cousins. Everyone carries the refined, attenuated features of the family Jael. Only Panthera, his hostling and his brothers have more of a sensual, languid Kalamah caste to them. Lahela told me he suspects Panthera and I have some kind of *relationship* (Lahela's italics!). Tactfully put, I suppose. Lahela still knows nothing about what happened to his son in Piristil. Because of this, I don't let on either way if his suspicions are true or not. The sun always seems to shine in Ferike. Every morning, we wake to another frosting of snow upon the trees and in the yard, but all day the sun reflects with hard, crystal brilliance off the land.

One evening, hara from a neighbouring castle came to dine with the Jaels. It was an elegant affair. After the meal, we all sat and listened to some of Panthera's relatives play music in one of the large drawing-rooms. Hara conversed with me in hushed, intellectual tones. I heard one or two disparaging remarks about the Gelaming, which pleased me. Gelaming artists were accused of plagiarising Ferike works. Someone said to me, "The Gelaming strive for originality, wishing to shine at everything, and hoping, I would think, to attract the interest of the royal houses of Maudrah and Garridan, who will pay highly for works of art." The har sniffed eloquently.

I sensed an opportunity to pry. "Ah yes, the Maudrah! I have heard much about Ariaric, their archon."

"Hmm, a charismatic character."

"Was he born in Jaddayoth?"

The har smiled. "Born here? Do you know nothing? I doubt that any of the Maudrah were born here, and let me tell you, they aren't too keen to tell people just where they were born either!"

"Would the word Uigenna have anything to do with that?" I enquired delicately, but it is impossible to be delicate using that particular word. My companion winced, drew back, and I realized I'd blown it; no more information would be forthcoming.

And so the weeks passed. I drifted into a womblike contentment; everything outside of Jael had taken on a dreamlike, insubstantial quality. The Ferike spend their time perfecting their artistic talents; painting, literature, music. I used those weeks to rewrite my notes neatly, but Kruin rapidly became bored, being more a creature of action. He was chafing to return home to Natawni. Panthera had closeted himself away in his studio, intent on making up for lost time. I saw him only at meal-times, and often, not even then. One morning, when I awoke, the snow was sliding from the trees and the long icicles hanging from all the windows were dripping into the yard. At breakfast, Ferminfex commented that the thaw had begun. Lahela spoke spiritedly about venturing once more into Clereness and beyond, to restock supplies.

I learned that very soon, representatives from other tribes would begin arriving at Jael to purchase items from all that the family had produced through the long winter incarceration. When I'd first arrived in Jael, I'd often been woken up at night by what sounded like a rhythmic thumping coming from under the ground. I'd been told that this was the printing press in the cellars of the castle. What was conceived in the high, airy rooms above was committed to paper down in the cellars. Pictures were also framed there. It was the workplace of the screen-printers, the potters, the sculptors. It wasn't just the family who were craftsmen in Jael. Panthera had painted me a picture of a dark forest, which I'd hung on my bedroom wall. Before falling asleep, I liked to stare into its haunting depths where the suggestion of secret life seemed to rustle. I would have liked to give him something in return, but I have never been much of an artist.

The thaw continued. A clear stream ran down the road from the castle; the bare branches of the trees were sprouting sticky buds. One day, Panthera suggested that now all the snow had gone, we should take a walk into the woods together. Kruin was too busy packing his things to accompany us; he was leaving soon. Panthera said he'd teach me how to draw. I didn't like to tell him he'd be wasting his time. We set off early in the morning, on horseback, which was my idea. Spring seemed to be creeping quickly over the land. The ground was damp and lush with new grass. Small, spring flowers were blooming around the trees, and sunlight came down through the high branches as we rode away from Jael. After a mile or so, we veered off the road and cantered up a steep bank of bracken-strewn peat. The colors were marvelous; so vibrant, as if they could only have come from an artist's palette. Panthera led me deep into the trees; these woods were like a second home to him. We dismounted and led our horses through clustering trees that ached with the most acid of greens.

"Let's stop here," Panthera said.

We had come to a fast-running brook, that cut a deep, chuckling channel between banks of mossy sand-stone. Branches dipped longing fingers into the water and the grassy ground seemed wreathed in a faint mist as the sun gently dried it out. We sat upon the bank and our horses began to crop the grass, tearing mouthfuls out by the roots, so sweet it was, so eager their desire for its taste. Panthera gave me a sheet of paper to draw on, but I lacked inspiration.

"Do you think that Astarth really does run Piristil now?" he asked me. It was the first time he had spoken of Fallsend to me since reaching Jael.

"Who knows?" I answered, because I wasn't really bothered.

"Why did he let us get away like that?"

"I don't know. Why do you care, Thea? It's over. Forget it."

"It'll never be over for me."

"OK, I'm sorry. You want a theory? Astarth wanted us to get away, he wanted us to be followed by Jafit, he wanted us to kill Jafit."

"Of course! You must be right, how stupid of me. With Jafit out of the way, Astarth becomes house-owner not whore."

"Seems likely, doesn't it. Although, in Fallsend Astarth could easily have bumped Jafit off and nobody would have raised an eyebrow."

"Don't count on that," Panthera said. "The musenda owners are all pretty close. Honor amongst thieves and all that. I don't think Astarth could have got away with anything too blatant."

"Oh well, so what! I hope he's happier now."

"I wonder if the others are though?" Panthera was concentrating very hard on whatever it was he was drawing. I'd thrown my paper and pencil down onto the grass.

"Look," Panthera said and handed me his sketches. Of course, they were of me.

"Am I really that emaciated?" I asked, rather appalled.

"Not on the outside, no," he replied, taking them back again. He looked thoughtful, put down his pen, and lay back on the soft ground, staring up through the branches above. "Cal, I've decided to accompany you into Elhmen," he said.

At first I made no response, but his look of inquiry was difficult to ignore. "There's no need," I said at length. "I've traveled alone most of the time."

"You don't know the country around here though."

"True, but I can follow instructions. It may be dangerous, Thea; I don't know. I've no idea what's waiting for me there. And I'm sure Ferminfex will not thank me if I take you away from home again so soon. He's worried about you. I don't think he'd like you to get involved with me any further."

"You're wrong!" Panthera argued hotly. "My father would expect me to go with you. After what you did for me, it's the only honorable thing to do."

"Honor!" I laughed aloud. "That outmoded concept? Men used to die for honor, didn't they? We must live our own lives, Thea, make our own values. I don't want to endanger you."

"A more sensitive person than I might suspect you were insulting their courage, or indeed ability," Panthera said carefully. "Are you afraid I'll be a hindrance to you?"

"Don't be silly! You don't mean that! I just don't want to involve anyone else in . . . well, whatever."

"In what?"

I didn't answer. Panthera sighed and sat up, resting his chin on his knees. "Don't you think it's about time you told me? You've spoken to my father about it, I know." I looked at him for a long time; the light patterns rippling off his face and neck, reflections from the water, his shaded green eyes. Oh Panthera, what I would give to have met you years ago! "Well?" he said.

And I began. It didn't hurt any more. I could speak freely without fear. Of course, I didn't give him all the details, as I'd done with his father. The forest around us seemed utterly silent, the sunlight was very hot. I got a creepy feeling of being watched, but still I told him. When I finished speaking, he rested his chin on his knees once more and gazed at the water. There was a silence I could not break.

Eventually he said, "I didn't think it would be anything like that. I thought you'd committed some kind of crime. I . . ." He shook his head.

"I have committed crimes, Thea; that's part of the problem."

"No more than any Har in Jaddayoth, I should think."

"Yes, maybe so, but Immanion isn't in Jaddayoth is it? It's different in Almagabra; very civilized."

"That's not what it sounds like to me. Why can't the Tigron accept it's over? Any normal person would. He must be power mad!" Panthera's ferocity surprised me.

"Stop it!" I said. "You've no right to say that! You don't know anything!"

"It's not over for you either, is it? Look at you defending him. You're both stupid! Oh, what do I care anyway! It's your life!" he picked up his pen and drawing pad once more and scribbled furiously. I took several deep breaths. The silence was electric. I lay back again with my arms above my head and gazed with slitted eyes through the leaves. Trees clung precariously to the stream banks, leaning out over the water. Eventually they will have to fall in. I must have fallen asleep. When Panthera shook me awake, my head was throbbing because I'd been lying face up in the sun for too long. We'd brought food and wine with us, which Panthera was now unpacking from a saddle-bag.

"Are you hungry?" he asked stiffly.

"A bit."

He cleared his throat. "I want to apologize," he said. "No, don't say anything. I suppose you just told your story so well; I got too involved.

You're right; it's none of my business, but I still want to come to Elhmen with you. Can I?"

As if anyone could refuse those eyes! "OK."

He smiled. "Good. We'll start making preparations then."

We drank wine from the bottle. I reflected that I'd be happy remaining in any of the Jaddayoth countries I'd passed through. Ferike would be no exception. Panthera must have been wondering what I was thinking about.

"Look, there's a waterfall upstream," he said. "It's very beautiful. You must see it before we go back."

I stood up and peered through the tunnel of overhanging trees. "Alright; are you coming?"

"No, there are a few more sketches I want to make."

"Another forest painting?"

Panthera wrinkled his nose. "I hope so. I want to make this one really *live.*"

Laughing, I ducked between the low branches and began to walk upstream. At that moment, I could not remember a time during the last few years when I'd felt more contented. A shame I would have to leave. In Ferike, there were no pressures of any kind. Not even, if I thought about it, those delightful, most welcome pressures of desire. My mind was utterly at rest. Perhaps that's what brought it on; what happened next. After a while, I could hear the rushing sound that presaged the waterfall. I took off my boots and stepped down into the stream. It rushed around my legs; icy, breath-takingly cold. I stopped to take a drink, and it was like a light, heady wine in my mouth. As I stooped, a blinding light reflected off the water, like sunlight on glass. I looked up quickly.

Ahead of me, through a tunnel of overhanging greenery, shining steadily, a white, powerful radiance reflected off the water. I waded forward, against the strengthening flow. The branches parted before me and I stepped out into an arena of light. The waterfall cascaded into what seemed like a roofless cavern, spilling over a lichened lip of rock. Sunlight fell right into the bowl and the water of the pool bubbled like sparkling wine. I could see glittering droplets hanging in the air, bursting in the air, rainbows of light shimmering around me like insubstantial, ethereal beings. Riotous ferns sprouted from the green, rock walls. A cluster of brightly colored lizards were curled together on a flat stone, taking the sun. Dragonflies skimmed the surface of the water. I was awe-struck. Nothing is so stunning as natural, pure, untainted beauty—beauty such as Pell's once was. I knelt down in the spuming water and let the spray soak me thoroughly. My chest was heavy with an emotion I could put no name to. This place was sacred. It was the home of a god, but the god was not at home. Such moments bring enlightenment. For a brief flash of time, it is possible to understand everything in the world, and in the wake of that realization comes a swelling, bittersweet sadness, that is also the most poignant joy. In that moment, I knew that I could go forward without fear, and face whatever lay in store for me. I thought, "No-one else can direct my life. I am important, but only to myself and, for that reason, shall take control." It was strength, pure strength. If a time should come when I finally do have to face Pellaz-har-Aralis, Tigron of Immanion, then I will do so without tremor, with a clear mind. I'll tell him that, yes, we had once loved—the memory of it will last forever—but time goes on and life goes on; now I must live my own, which is different from his and always shall be. The scars must be covered with new flesh, comprised of sense and reason, and clear sight. I decided that my future lay in Jaddayoth; nowhere else. Pell will have to listen to me. If some vestige of his former self still remains, he will agree that I am right. I'd convinced myself Pell had become some grim, egocentric tyrant; power-hungry, grasping. Had it been Thiede who'd made that happen? Can't my own heart tell me the truth? Old wounds had to be cleaned before they could heal.

I stood up in the water, looked one last time at the shining cataract, and thought of returning, back the way I'd come, to Panthera, who was lovely and young, who needed healing as much as I did. I should have realized this before.

I turned to follow the flow of the water and fell. . . . On my knees with glistening spinnerets of light flashing in my face. The sound of the water had become a roar, the roar of battle, of crowds shouting. "Oh no," I thought; just that. My skin was prickling with the presence of power, my bones aching. The air smelled of ozone and the magical strength of the place was increased a hundred fold. Then I thought, "Remember; you are strong," and stood up again. There was no-one there, only the unearthly crescendo of light and sound. "What do you want?" I cried, without fear. If it was Zack, I could handle it. If it was Gelaming phantoms, I could handle it. Even if it was a vision of myself, dead and shrouded, I could handle it. It was none of those. I heard a sound, another sound, above the crash of the water. It was like a single note, a voiceless voice. It hurt my eyes, that sound. A glowing bubble of misty light detached itself from the waterfall. It drifted toward me, turning slowly, enveloping my head, my shoulders, my body. I couldn't breathe, but there was no discomfort. I was filled with gold, a golden feeling seeping through the pores of my flesh, my open mouth, my staring eyes. And oh, that feeling, it was the warmest thing on Earth. It was love itself, nurturing, selfless, supportive love. I smiled, held rigid in the arms of that bodiless emotion. There was a voice in my head. It said, "You are my soul"; softly, chiding. What it did not say was, "Would you forget me, deny me?" but I knew those words were there. I gasped. "I love you," and the light contracted about me, squeezing the breath from my lungs. I could smell him, taste him, all around me. A cold wind hit my skin. I opened my eyes and a pulsing ball of light was spinning away from me, up into the white sky. I called him, but it was too late. I could hear birds singing, the water chuckling; he was gone.

In a daze, I splashed back downstream. Panthera looked astounded when I emerged, soaked to the skin, bootless, crawling up over the bank to lie gasping at his feet.

"Cal?" he said.

"Thea, it was him," I gabbled. "Pell was there. He spoke to me. I *felt* him!"

Panthera gritted his teeth and dragged me further onto the grass. He gazed up the stream toward the hidden waterfall, hands on hip; an aggressive stance.

"He's no fool, is he," Panthera murmured softly. He squatted down beside me and pulled a twig from my wet hair. "He'll not let you go easily. Is it a fight he wants?"

I was still panting painfully. I could not speak, but whatever Panthera saw in my eyes turned his own to flint.

"A fight it is then!" he decided.

It was not until later that I realized what he meant.

CHAPTER SIXTEEN

>─┤◆>─◦─Ο─◦─<◆├─<

The Land of Elhmen

"Nothing of him that doth fade
But doth suffer a sea-change
Into something rich and strange."

—*William Shakespeare, Full fathom five (from The Tempest)*

Kruin left Jael just as the deep purple flowers were unfurling along the castle walls. Our farewell was unsentimental. He wished me well and told me not to forget to look him up if I ever found myself in Orligia. He left Jael a comparatively rich har. On top of the reward Ferminfex had given him, he also took several Ferike paintings home with him which were probably worth more than the money.

The night before Panthera and I planned to begin our journey, we had a small, private gathering with Lahela, Ferminfex and Panthera's brothers. Ferminfex wrote a letter of introduction that we could use throughout the journey. Obviously, this would only be effective with hara to whom the family Jael were known, but at least it was some protection.

"It should get you an audience with the Lyris, leader of the Sahale," Ferminfex said. "Although I have never met him personally, Jael has conducted some business with the royal house of Sahen."

"Straight to the top, eh!" I joked.

"Why bother with anything less?" Ferminfex shrugged. "The Lyris is Nahir-Nuri; he, if anybody, should be able to enlighten you."

After the meal, Panthera and his father spread sheets of paper over the table to draw maps and decide which would be the quickest route to Eulalee. Only one gateway was known to hara of other tribes; Kar Tatang, some miles north of the Elhmen capital of Shappa. Lahela watched them introspectively.

"I did try to dissuade Thea from coming with me," I said, in apology.

Lahela smiled at me. "He's doing what he thinks is right. Panthera is a tough little brute, he always has been, but please, don't hurt him, Cal."

"I have no intention . . ." I began, blustering.

Lahela raised his hand, shook his head. "I know. Just think; that's all I ask."

We traveled light. The weather was warmer, so there was no need to carry heavy furs. We had been traveling for over a week and now, ahead of us, the sheer mountains of Elhmen soared into a pale, blue sky, their summits mantled with late spring snow, girdled with cloud. Panthera rode ahead of me, his hair flying back, clad in black leather, patterns burnt into the hide. He rode with a grim kind of determination as if it was his destiny we were following, not mine. Perhaps it was. Looking back, I know that I was afraid, although at the time, I just thought it was excitement. I was filled with a sense of "approach," which increased as the mountains loomed nearer. My sleep had become fitful; I was so full of energy. I thought it was some kind of climax building up. Perhaps, on the other side of it, I could find some peace, and if that peace meant death itself, I was not afraid to meet and fight it. It is a strange thing, and perhaps common only to Wraeththu-kind, that we expect death whenever we are gripped by spasms of presentiment. From experience, I already knew that this was rarely the case (well, obviously so, otherwise I wouldn't be here to write this!), but it is still something we all seem to dread. I suppose it is some vestige of guilt, left over from the dark times of our arrival in the world. We fear the heavy tread of the dark giant because we have thrown stones at him from afar for so long. Perhaps too it is the curse of the near-immortals; can death be cheated so easily?

By mid-day, the gently swelling hills had sharpened to younger, spikier ridges and valleys. Water ran swiftly, coming down from the mountains, where the thaw was not yet complete. Rocks had enclosed us; the land of Ferike seemed far behind. We had dismounted, leading our horses to give them a break. Predatory birds whirled lazily on the air over our heads, screaming fiercely.

"Don't you feel it?" Panthera asked softly. He had stopped walking, tilting his head to the side as if listening.

"Feel what?" I doubted that we could feel quite the same things.

"Power," he answered.

I looked at his face, his clear, luminous skin, the dreamy yet concentrating expression in his eyes. "Yes," I said, "there is certainly power here."

Panthera glanced at me archly, alerted by my tone of voice and caught me staring at him. His neck bloomed with color. "I don't think you understand," he said drily. "Or you do and are merely being facetious, as usual!"

"Sorry. What kind of power?"

"Elhmen. They must be watching us now. I can sense it."

"Friends or foes?"

"It is never possible to tell with Elhmen!"

We carried on walking and came into a deep canyon. Moss grew like alien flowers from the stones above our heads.

"Where are the Elhmen hiding then?" I asked in a loud whisper. Panthera shot me another derisive glance.

"Elhmen do not always tolerate strangers," he said, "not even from as near to home as Ferike. We are not known to them; we shall need their consent to pass through to Eulalee. It is unfortunate we have to pass through these territories; once we reach the city of Shappa it should be easier. My father is known there."

"Panthera?"

"What?"

"Tell me what you think I'll find in Eulalee."

He shook his head. "No-one can tell you that. You'll speak to the Lyris, leader of the Sahale, as my father suggested, but after that, who knows? I'm not even going to try to guess."

"It would help if we knew, wouldn't it."

"Naturally, that's probably why we don't."

Naturally.

By late afternoon, we had come to be riding alongside a cataracting stream between high, rugged walls of rock that sprouted acid green clumps of grass and was stained with dark red and gold lichens. Panthera was still edgy, alert for signs of Elhmen proximity, although I could sense nothing. Because we were out in the open, I hadn't been feeling safe since we'd left Jael. We made camp as the sun went down, planning to set off once more at dawn, and hobbled the horses. I made a small fire and Panthera went to fill our metal cups from the clear, cold water. "This is like old times," he said.

"Very much," I replied and I was thinking back, way back. Panthera sensed this and I could almost feel his inner wince at what he thought was his tactless remark. He rarely spoke of Pell (neither did I), but I could always tell when he was thinking about him. I suppose the same was true in reverse. Perhaps that's why we never spoke about it. I had no doubt that, for my sake, Panthera hated Pell bitterly. I ought to have told him not to, but I remained silent. Perhaps I was afraid of what might come out of such a conversation.

Once we had wrapped ourselves up in separate blankets, I heard Panthera say, "Are you afraid of the dark, Cal?" I could not think of a witty reply. I shivered.

"Sometimes I'm afraid of everything," I said.

He reached for me in the darkness and squeezed my shoulder. I could feel his claws graze my skin. When I touched his hand, he withdrew it quickly, as if scalded.

In the dead of night, I woke up, opened my eyes. Silence. Too quiet. I raised my head, conscious of the humped form of the sleeping Panthera. Our horses stamped and snorted somewhere in the darkness behind us. And then there was a ghost before me. This ghost wore a shimmering veil made entirely from silver-white hair that covered its frail, luminous body. Its eyes were slanting, dark in the marmoreal pallor of its face. Its mouth was smiling. I tried to rise, spring up, reach for a weapon, but I could not move. I tried to call Panthera's name but could force no sound from my throat. The ghost raised its arms. "Travelers," it said and lowered its arms again, gracefully. My body shuddered, and then, with a jerk, lifted itself off the ground. The ghost drew me toward it with the power of its eyes, and such power! Nahir-Nuri, must be. . . ! I could not turn my head, but became aware of Panthera suspended beside me. We bumped together; logs on a stream. His flesh felt rigid. In front of us, the white figure turned and began to climb up the rock face on the other side of the stream. As if on invisible tethers, Panthera and I floated eerily behind him. In pleasanter circumstances, I expect it would have been a wonderful feeling, like flying. Then it was merely imprisonment; frightening. Gathering my senses, I put out a mental call to Panthera. At least my mind was unaffected by whatever occult paralysis gripped our bodies.

"What is this?" I asked, and Panther answered, "Elhmen."

"Does he mean to harm us?"

"Who can tell?"

Ahead of us, the enchanter did not even look back, although he had probably overheard our thoughts. He was confident enough in his magic to know we would follow him helplessly. We drifted through a tangled forest that sloped downwards into a pine-ringed glade. The Elhmen flickered through the trees, pausing only when we came to the mouth of a cave, set in a huge, mossy wall of sandstone. We followed him inside, down a winding, natural passage, lit by torches, and at length into a rosy-lit chamber, where we could see several other Elhmen seated on the floor around a strange fire that did not smoke and whose light was blue-white. With a shiver of the Elhmen's hand, our enchantment was broken, and Panthera and myself tumbled to the floor in an ungainly sprawl.

"These people *are* powerful," I said to Panthera, rubbing my bruised arms.

He ignored this rhetorical remark. Psychokinesis itself is only a low-caste talent, but it is most unusual to find any har with an ability to sustain it, especially so over living beings.

"All Elhmen are the same," Panthera said. Five heads turned to look at us, all smiling gently, probably at Panthera's remark.

"Not powerful, Ferike," the one who had found us said quietly, "but simply dedicated. Hara such as yourselves spend too much time examining the mundane. Here in Elhmen, we devote ourselves to cultivating our innate talents." His smile broadened. "We do not like to have our soil disturbed, our waters contaminated, by alien disruptive auras . . ."

"Such as our own, I suppose," I said.

The Elhmen spread his hands. "As you like," he said.

"We are traveling to Eulalee," Panthera said. "We have business there. We cannot help passing through your territory, but if you wish us to pay a toll, we shall do so gladly."

"A toll!" All the Elhmen laughed gleefully. "Money has little value in Elhmen. You'll find yourselves handicapped if you wish to *buy* your way into Eulalee."

I had the distinct impression that we were being played with. Our chances of getting into Eulalee at that point seemed depressingly slim.

"I am Arawn," our captor told us, "and these are my brothers. Enjoy, if you will, the hospitality of Elhmen!" They all laughed sweetly and in a flash, Panthera and I found ourselves smack against the carved, ragged ceiling of the chamber, along with rather gamey legs of meat and strings of vegetables.

"They have devoted themselves to their talents, yes," Panthera said, in a strangled voice beside me, struggling, "but it is rumored that some of them have strayed far from the Path. Some Elhmen, if the mood takes them, have been known to be cannibal."

"Why didn't you tell me!" I cried. "You are a fool, Thea! We should have made proper preparations for contacting them."

"Waste of time," Panthera replied. "There is no proper way to meet the Elhmen. This is probably the only way."

"Then how . . .?"

"Shut up," Panthera said mildly. "I know what I'm doing."

"Like mentioning money, I suppose."

Panthera gave me a hard look. "Sometimes they will take it. It all depends on their mood. Now, be quiet; I need to concentrate."

The Elhmen appeared to have forgotten about us. They were whispering to each other across the flameless fire. Like Arawn, they were all clothed only in their hair, which came to their ankles. Exquisite creatures, attenuated and elfin. Beside me, arms outstretched along the uneven roof, Panthera began to hum. His eyes were closed, his brow furrowed in concentration. At first, he hummed one long, monotonous note, which gradually began to rise and fall in pitch. Now the sound was steady, and quite powerful. I would have liked to have put my hands over my ears. Shortly, one of Arawn's brothers looked up at us, touching those on either side of him quickly, lightly, on the arm. They watched us as if listening deeply. Whatever Panthera was communicating to them, I could not penetrate. My senses were too rusty from lack of use, the thought too deep. But Panthera obviously implied the correct message, for in a second we were plummeting floorwards again, landing awkwardly, missing the fire by inches.

"So then," Arawn said cheerfully, "you are offering us something without the implication of insult?"

"You must forgive my earlier solecism," Panthera replied gravely. He delivered this obsequious remark with admirable dignity. "We need to get to Eulalee. We have to pass through your territories and, for this privilege, feel honor bound to offer something in return. I will present you with a tale. It is a story of magic, whose beginning was in the childhood of our race. This story has no end . . . as yet."

"Please, be seated," Arawn said generously, gesturing to a space by his side next to the fire. He raised his hand carelessly and a flagon of ale and two metal cups disappeared from a shelf in the corner of the room to materialize at our feet. We sat down and Panthera poured us each a cup of ale before settling to begin his tale. Different Wraeththu tribes never cease to amaze me. Imagine paying the Varrs, the Uigenna, or even the Gelaming for that matter, with nothing but a story.

Panthera cleared his throat and leaned forward. "Many years ago," he said in a hushed voice, "and far, far away from this land, in a place of darkness and savagery, a city of gray ruins and blood flames, there lived a tribe feared above all others. This story begins with them, and with a young har stepping onto the Path for the very first time. He was beautiful, his hair was yellow, but his heart was gray. His name?" Panthera looked at me and smiled. "Ah, that I cannot tell you, but his eyes were the color of a stormy sky and indeed could flash with lightning sometimes . . ." He paused, glanced once more at me, then closed his eyes to continue. "One day, I met this har upon the bank of a stream and he told me this . . ."

Heard from someone else's lips, I must admit that my history does sound rather unbelievable. In fact, it's surprising anyone ever does believe it! Perhaps that's one of the reasons why I rarely talk about it. Of course, in a story, all the exciting bits happen together, which is far removed from real life. For every escapade with Pell, there were weeks and weeks of tedious riding around, being uncomfortable and hungry. But Panthera had a way of telling it, that made even the most trivial events sound magical and startling. The Elhmen appeared entranced by it. I wonder if they guessed that, even though all the names were changed, the story was based on fact. By the time he'd finished telling it, Panthera's voice was hoarse and the flagon of ale at our feet was empty. My legs were numb. I shifted uneasily to another position.

"Well!" Arawn said, putting his hands upon his crossed knees. "The mouth of Eulalee, Kar Tatang, lies just beyond Shappa, a city northeast of here. It is only a few days' traveling, not far. But now, it is nearly dawn and you must rest. There is a pallet over there which I suggest you make use of."

I presumed we'd won our passage through his territory. The pallet was nearly invisible in the shadows beyond the fire. The white heat had dwindled to a sullen violet. All the Elhmen, except for Arawn and one other, stood up and filed from the room. Panthera and I exchanged an amused glance. The pallet was strewn with blankets of fur. We took off our boots and lay down, Panthera wrinkling his nose in distaste as he covered himself with a blanket. Personally, I found the heavy, musky smell quite comforting. With my back to Panthera, I lay there watching Arawn and his remaining brother. They had a certain, furtive air about them. For a moment, they both turned their heads toward me, staring, then away, faces close together; the echo of whispering. Arawn stood up. "Nanine . . ." he hissed softly.

"It is I," his brother answered, and fluidly fell back beside the fire.

It looked as if he lay upon a silk-tasselled rug; but this was his hair, transparent, catching the light of the fire, turning lilac. I could see the bones of his hips protruding sharply, the concave sweep of his belly, the down, curling mane of fur that grew up from his groin. Arawn sprinkled herbs on the prostrate body, kneeling beside it, staring up at the ceiling. He spoke several arcane words and I heard my name mentioned. Ah, I thought, probably some ritual to guarantee our protection. It wasn't that exactly, however. Arawn took up a curious knife, curved and barbed, which he drew lightly over his brother's chest. Beads of blood burst from the skin, gleaming like jewels, each one perfectly formed. Arawn drew his right forefinger along the line and the jewels became smeared liquid. He looked at me, and I shut my eyes guiltily. "Calanthe, approach the fire," he said. Up on my elbows, I glanced behind at Panthera. Whether that was for reassurance or advice, I can't be sure, but he was flat out anyway (so quickly?), snoring gently in an impenetrable sleep. "Come," Arawn encouraged quietly, one arm extended from the robe of his hair to beckon me. Curiosity alone had me slipping from under the furs and creeping across the floor. "Look," Arawn said softly, and I followed the line of his pointing finger. Nanine's head was turned to the side. I could see a single tear upon his exposed cheek. "In olden times," Arawn said, "It was almost a custom for heroes to be offered gifts from the gods. A sword, perhaps, or a shield, a magic helmet. The concept of the Quest is an old one indeed, Calanthe. True heroes have always been watched over by intelligences of higher form."

"And what has that to do with me?" I asked suspiciously, sure I would not like the answer.

Arawn smiled. "Oh, come now, you don't need me to tell you that you follow a quest of your own. In times to come, your adventures may well be related as the exploits of a harish paladin."

"I've never thought of myself as a hero," I said drily, feeling that Arawn had drastically misconstrued my purpose in life. It was quite embarrassing. "I don't believe there's any such thing, except in fairy-tales."

Arawn inclined his head slightly. "What is a word, a term? Nothing. It is the deeds behind the words that are important."

"If you say so." I was impatient with what I considered to be his esoteric twaddle. Leave that to the Gelaming and other similar creatures, whose hedonistic, leisurely lives gave them the time to waffle on in such ways, to believe in heroes. To ordinary hara, this was out of the question. I have always found it exasperating.

Arawn shook his head. "You are bitter," he said, "which is understandable, I suppose. Have you heard the legends concerning our tribe?"

I shook my head. "Not really. I'm only just beginning to learn about Jaddayoth."

Arawn nodded thoughtfully. "Well, some people say that to take aruna with an Elhmen will raise your caste automatically by one level . . ."

I rolled my eyes and laughed. "Really! That good is it?" In recent times, my caste, which was Pyralissit (second level Acantha), had ceased to have meaning for me, coupled with the fact that my abilities had atrophied somewhat through neglect. Arawn was not offended by my laughter.

"You are right to scoff," he said. "Such legends are a wild exaggeration of the actual truth. Only the har himself has the ability to raise his caste; no-one else can do it for him. I'm sure you're aware of this."

"Yes. So?"

In reply, Arawn once again gestured to the recumbent form of Nanine. "Drink," he said, and began to walk away.

"Wait!" I cried, but he did not pause. A door at the back of the room closed quietly behind him. Panthera was still fast asleep. "Wait," I said again, uselessly, slumping. Now what was I supposed to do? I thought that Nanine was unconscious, but now Arawn had gone, he turned his head and opened his eyes. The scratch down his chest had dried already to a crust.

"You must open this up again," he said, running his fingers lightly over the scar.

"What!" Visions of blood-drinking rose uncomfortably to mind.

"Are you afraid?" He reared up like a snake, took my hand and pulled me forward. "Don't be." He put the knife in my hand. "Quickly!" I could tell this was not a part of the ritual he enjoyed. What ritual?

I kneeled beside him. "Must I?" He did not answer. Sighing, I put the hooked end of the blade against the flesh, hardly aware of what I was doing. Experience had taught me that once adepts get it into their heads to assist you, it is always better to indulge their generosity and get on with it. I wasn't sure what the Elhmen thought they were doing for me, but it was less hassle to comply.

Nanine arched his body. "Not . . . so deep," he said.

"Sorry." Shortly, my irreverence would start to annoy him, but of course patience in another virtue that Hara of high caste always wave liked a goddamned flag. Blood began to flow.

Nanine put his hands in it. "Disrobe," he said, in a choked voice.

After a pause, I turned my back and self-consciously pulled off my clothes. I could hear Nanine breathing deeply, changing the atmosphere of the room, summoning power. "So, what is it I must do?" I asked. Must I kneel to drink? I turned around. Nanine had adopted a position of submission, his male organs drawn in.

"Drink," he said, and then I realized this was not a literal request. Soume is water; it had nothing to do with blood. As I've intimated before, my libido was not exactly a frisky young thing, galloping through fields of desire at the time. I felt exposed, pale and unhealthy—and not in the least bit ouana-active. Nanine called to me. He said, "My brother spoke of legends, and beauty such as yours is indeed legendary."

"Is that supposed to encourage me or what?" I asked and he shook his head.

"Not at all. Come." Still sighing heavily, I lay down beside him. His flesh was unexpectedly cool, but, as they say, the touch of Elhmen is always cold. I did not find it unpleasant. I bent my head to his own to share breath, thinking that this was as good a way as any to begin, but he put his fingers on my lips.

"No," he murmured softly, "not yet." His arms came around me, pulling me close until I could feel the dampness of his blood against my skin. Far from repelling me, I felt a strange and insidious stirring within me. Nanine pushed me onto my back, leaning over me, showering me with hair. He took my wary, but not totally complacent, ouana-lim in his bloody hands, painting it with his blood, blessing me in the name of fire. The beast flexed its muscles and flowered beautifully. So fire and water must meet; to what effect I was unaware as yet. Bodies always take over when they get the chance, shouldering the intellect roughly aside. Mine has never been an exception. Sluggish maybe, but Nanine's touch gave it a whack on the back of the neck which woke it up. Consumed by a strengthening fire, I pushed him back and he offered himself passively. Without hesitation, I plunged deeper into the pool of his body, his soul, and drank deeply. Primary urgency subsided to a gentler tide; time was unimportant. Nanine could control his internal muscles; they felt as dextrous as fingers, regulating effortlessly the heights and calms of our communion. If I'd thought to be a fire to make steam in his water, I was wrong. I was merely a small, plunging ship cleaving a great and powerful ocean. One storm too vigorous and I'd be lost forever. The climax of this elemental fight was a roaring crack like thunder-bolts and lashing streams of ice. Panting upon Nanine's heaving body, I could feel that my hair and flesh were wet, not with sweat, but as if I'd been out naked in a heavy shower. I was cold. Nanine pushed me closer to the fire. I was trembling in every part of my brain and body. He whispered softly into my ear, small comforts one would give to an animal and, as I shuddered there, he bent his head to my own. We shared breath for the first time, and the warmth came back into my skin. In his mind, I could see a shining path, upon which I must walk. Terrors to right and left, but the path was strong. I sighed lay back, and Nanine wrapped me in his hair.

"The legends are right," I said, "and Elhmen must have immeasurable power."

Nanine just smiled. "Look to your soul," he said, "then, only then, speak of my power."

I was far too tired to think about souls or power. I fell asleep.

Concurrent with such events, you might expect that I woke up on the pallet, next to Panthera, trying to remember a weird and realistic dream;

but no. It was Panthera who shook me awake, yes, but I was still curled up with Nanine next to the fire. Sunlight was falling in shafts from cracks in the cave's roof, illuminating all the darkest corners. Panthera curled his lip at me disdainfully and ordered me to get dressed.

"We must get moving," he said sharply. "I don't want to be away from Jael for longer than necessary. I have work to do."

"I didn't ask you to come!" I pointed out, just as sharply. I could see that it was in Panthera's mind to say, "That may be so, but you need me," but he was looking at the drowsy, sinuous form of Nanine and said nothing. I could hear him slamming around unnecessarily, pulling on his boots.

"Will our horses and provisions still be safe?" I asked, wriggling into my shirt.

"Of course, we are not thieves!" Nanine replied, but without rancor. "Now we must eat and refresh ourselves. Afterwards, I will take you to Shappa."

"You!" Panthera snarled. "That won't be necessary. We can find our own way."

Nanine shook his head. "Perhaps you can, but it will take you much longer. Control your hard feelings, son of Jael!" He smiled and Panthera colored vigorously. Nanine and I shared a conspiratorial glance. I thought it was Panthera's repugnance toward aruna that was causing the short temper.

Arawn and the others began to drift in, bearing plates of food, greeting us politely. Nanine dressed himself in a robe of white muslin and let me plait his hair for him. Bound, it felt like rope. "Once," I said, "I was traveling in the southern desert of Megalithica. In that place lives a tribe named the Kakkahaar. It was there that we met a young har of the Colurastes; a venomous witchling if ever there was one. He had hair like yours. Occasionally, he would use it to throttle people."

Nanine laughed. "You must be speaking of Ulaume, the consort of the Kakkahaar Lianvis."

"Oh, you've heard of them?" I asked, surprised.

"Well, of course; hasn't everybody? Lianvis attained quite a high position in the Council of Tribes in Immanion, once the Gelaming took control of Megalithica."

"You're joking!" I exclaimed. The Kakkahaar, as far as I knew, were devout followers of rather dubious, dark practices. I couldn't imagine the saintly Gelaming tolerating any of it.

"No, it's true," Nanine continued. "More than a few hara questioned the Gelaming's judgment, or motives, for it, but Thiede and the Tigron must know what they're doing, mustn't they?"

"So we all suppose," I said drily, "or are led to believe."

"Double standards!" Panthera snapped, throwing me a meaningful glance, which I wasn't sure how to interpret exactly. Naturally, all references to actual tribes and places had been disguised in Panthera's story the previous night. I wondered how much the Elhmen knew. Something, obviously, but what? Had they guessed Panthera's story was about me? As we walked to where our horses still stood, hobbled under the trees, I attempted to draw Nanine out on this. I could get nothing out of him. Was it possible that the Elhmen too had had some forewarning of our arrival?

The horses' harness was wet with dew, our bags lying untouched beside our blankets. Nanine did not intend to ride, which Panthera complained would slow us down.

"I know the quickest routes," Nanine said, "and most of the way, it will be impossible for you to ride anyway."

We set off once more, following the course of the stream, up into the mountains. Panthera maintained a profound and sullen silence, which I decided was best to ignore. Round about mid-day, we approached a huge, natural arch of rock. It was possible to pass right under it, into a stone-choked gully which sloped briskly downwards, but Nanine pointed out an opening in the rock which appeared to lead right down into the ground on the left side of the arch. It was nearly hidden by bushes and tall, dead grass. Being on horseback was now out of the question; we were going under-ground. Nanine carried a carved, wooden staff which I thought was to help him scramble through the rocks, but as we entered the stone passage, he held it aloft and its farthest end began to glow with a soft, but penetrating light. We could see for about six feet all around, which was very fortunate, for once the passage turned a corner we would have been plunged into absolute blackness. The ground underfoot was packed hard, as if traveled by many feet, but Nanine explained that the passage was rarely used during the winter. Come spring, Elhmen hara started wandering about a little more. By summer, he said, the entrance would be clearly visible, even to those not looking for it. Occasionally, sections of the wall would be smoothed off and carved with patterns that were rather runic in design. The horses were awkward and nervous at first; the darkness worried them, the feeling of pressure, but Nanine crooned softly beneath his breath and it seemed to comfort them.

"Is this part of Eulalee?" I asked.

Nanine, ahead of me, looked back. "No, it is merely a place where we can travel as the crow flies. Eulalee is deep, much deeper, beneath the mountains."

"How far does it extend? Just the width and breadth of Elhmen?"

"I can't tell you that," he answered. "Only the Sahale, the people of Eulalee know that. Elhmen only supervise the main thoroughfare, north of Shappa. Doubtless, there are countless entrances to Eulalee that no-one but the Sahale are aware of."

"I see. Are the Sahale as hospitable to strangers as the Elhmen?" I enquired rather drily.

"Oh, was our hospitality that lacking then?" Nanine replied with amusement.

"Well, without Panthera's tale, perhaps . . ." It seemed impolite to continue.

"You are wrong," Nanine replied. "Arawn was only playing with you. We knew who you were."

Rather belatedly, a dull, cold shock coursed through me. I stopped walking and Panthera cursed softly as he bumped into me. "What do you mean?" I demanded, and the echo of it sailed past us down the passage. Nanine turned around again. "Was it the Gelaming that told you? Was it?" Panthera was exuding a weird kind of satisfaction behind me; I could sense it clearly.

"Not the Gelaming," Nanine said.

"Then who?"

"I cannot answer that. I'm sorry." He turned his back on me and continued to walk along the passage. "I can't believe you're surprised by this after what occurred last night, but if you are, then all I can say is, you must accept and learn. It is the only way for you."

I made an exclamation of disgust.

Panthera put his hand on my shoulder. "Let's keep moving," he said.

We passed through vaulted caverns, natural cathedrals of rock, whose roofs were open to the sky. We passed underground lakes, complete with solitary, stone isles that rose like petrified monsters from the black water. We rested only when we were tired, for underground, there was no precise way of telling whether it was day or night outside, on the surface. Panthera and I would spread out our rugs in smooth, sandy hollows in the rock, whilst Nanine sat apart, cross-legged, meditating on the high, secret things that Elhmen ponder upon. The first time we rested, Panthera lay with his back to me, rigid and sulky. Was this unusual? No, not really, but I still said, "OK, spit it out; what have I done now?"

"Nothing." His answer was muffled, but sharp.

"That's funny. I thought you were angry because I took aruna with Nanine."

"Oh, shut up!" he said, out loud and with disdain. The sound echoed clearly. Below us, Nanine did not stir.

"OK," I said. "I won't say another word." Panthera did not answer. More to soothe him than anything else, I lifted the hair from his back and kissed his neck. He was still silent. I lay back and put my arms behind my head, staring up into the blackness above. "I don't need this," I thought. "Leave well alone."

I dreamed.

It is a hot, hot day. The sunlight is almost too bright to bear. I am standing alone at the edge of what seems to be a great battlefield; it is scattered with the debris of conflict. I can smell a hot, sweet yet sour aroma and the air is full of small, desperate sounds. Ragged birds investigate the flesh of the fallen. I cannot tell which tribes have been involved, or whether the fight has been between hara and humans instead. The Gelaming are in black leather and silver, their hair like haloes of steam, turning bodies, looking for survivors. I decide to follow them because I know they cannot see me. As I walk, the smell of carrion becomes stronger, a taste of sweet metal. A pavilion appears on the horizon and suddenly I am standing right in front of it. Two hara of obviously high rank are seated beneath a tasselled canopy, one on each side of a wooden table. Attendants stand silently behind them in the shadows of the tent. The seated hara are drinking sparkling wine from tall, stemmed glasses. The battlefield stretches all around them; a testament of carnage. I recognize one of them. The recognition comes slowly, but soon I am sure it is Zackala sitting there. The other has fair hair and the confident aura of someone who knows fame and power. He has a nasty wound above the left eye, blood in his hair, which is tied behind his head. There is another stitched wound on his shoulder. I can hear them talking, but not the words. Then, Zackala lifts his glass; sunlight makes it come alive with bubbling fire. He smiles. "To Cal," he says, "wherever you are . . ."

I awoke with a start, jerking back, and the darkness above me was spinning, writhing. There was an echo of a cry in my throat. Panthera leaned over me. "What is it?"

"A dream," I answered. "Gelaming." There was a foul taste in my mouth, stale and sour.

"Forget them!" Panthera hissed wildly. "Don't let them frighten you."

"I'm not afraid," I said, and I could feel Panthera's breath above me in the darkness, but it was not the time. "Thanks," I said.

"That's alright." He lay down again and I reached for his hand. Contact of fingers in the dark. He did not move away.

CHAPTER SEVENTEEN

Sahale

"For they are creatures of dark air,
Unsubstantial tossing forms . . .
In mid-whirl of mental storms."
—Robert Graves, *Mermaid, Dragon, Fiend*

From a distance, Shappa is virtually indistinguishable from the surrounding mountains. It is built entirely from gray stone; built into the rock itself, in fact. Nanine pointed out a curl of smoke rising above the city. That's how we knew where it lay. We came to a paved road, and here the Elhmen consented to ride doubled with me to save time. As we drew nearer to Shappa, other travelers joined us on the road, appearing from other tracks that converged onto the main route. Panthera and myself were regarded suspiciously but hara spoke to Nanine without reserve. The gates of Shappa loomed up before us, casting a long, black shadow on the road. There was a lot of activity, but the guards on the gate were still sharp-eyed enough to order Panthera and I to halt, so that they could examine our luggage. I can't imagine what they were looking for.

Eventually, their curiosity satisfied, we were waved on into the streets of the city. As Shappa is built into the side of a mountain, one would expect the streets to be rather steep, but some of them are virtually impassable. All the ground is cobbled; mainly so that hara can have footholds as they climb. It is a very clean city; the buildings high and narrow. Shop-fronts are unobtrusive and not many of the inns provide tables outside; presumably, so that their customers don't go sliding down to the city gates after a few drinks! A lot of the buildings go way back into the rock, so that Shappa is a great deal larger than it appears from outside. Elhmen hara in Shappa seemed more sophisticated than Nanine and his brothers; they were primly dressed in long robes, their long hair woven, bound and confined in a variety of styles.

"Well, first we find an inn," Nanine decided, "then try and hire you a decent guide to take you to Eulalee."

"What do we need a guide for?" Panthera asked in a voice that implied he thought Nanine was spending our money for us unnecessarily.

"Ask that again after you've been there," Nanine replied.

It was late afternoon. Nanine led us to a hostelry he knew to be comfortable and cheap, leaving us alone while we scoured the streets for a guide. Panthera and I decided to sample some of the local food in the inn's dining room. We sat near the back window, which overlooked a yard whose floor was unleveled rock. Bright flowers bloomed in cracks; a chained, black dog stared contemplatively into space, head on paws. I could not help feeling that Shappa had almost a holiday atmosphere about it, as if it catered mainly for tourists.

"It is the only stopping place before Kar Tatang," Panthera said. "And of course a lot of hara come here from other districts to take the air and mineral waters. There is a meditation center in Shappa, quite reknowned further east. Many rich hara send their sons here for caste education."

"You haven't been here before though."

Panthera shook his head. "No, although my father has, many times. The Jaels trade with Elhmen here; we have regular customers. One of my father's paintings hangs on the wall in the foyer of the Meditation Center. Elhmen might be careful about which strangers are wandering about the countryside, but once you are known to them, visits are encouraged. If they feel they'll gain something from your presence, of course! You must remember, they have little to trade but their knowledge."

About an hour later, Nanine turned up again with a young Elhmen har named Kachina, who was looking for work. He told us he'd already made fifteen trips to Sahen.

"None of my clients ever complained," he said, earnestly. "I get them to Sahen by the quickest possible route."

Nanine assured us that we would be in safe hands if we agreed to hire Kachina, and in pocket because his services were cheap. We saw no reason not to trust his judgment, even though Kachina did look rather young. We took our leave of the city early the next morning. Nanine embraced me and wished us luck. As in Gimrah, an invitation to return some day for a social visit was extended. Panthera waited grumpily. I had spent the night with Nanine in a separate room and Panthera's foul silence because of that was almost unbearable. We followed Kachina to the east gate of Shappa, where we took a northern path, cut through the rock. Kachina told us that, at Kar Tatang, the gate to Eulalee, we would be able to stable our horses at livery for a reasonable price.

"The keepers of the stables at least must be confident that travelers will re-emerge from Eulalee," I said.

Kar Tatang was merely an hour's ride from Shappa. The gate itself was an awesome sight; a gigantic, gaping face carved into the rock, whose heavy-lipped mouth formed the entrance to the land below. The blind, stone eyes were turned skywards, as if each mouthful of travelers was exceedingly difficult to swallow. The village of Kar Tatang itself, clustered around the chin of the gate, comprised inns and stables and very little else. I had imagined that the doorway to this eerie, underground kingdom would be silent and lonely, but was surprised to find it a bustling, crowded place. There was much to-ing and fro-ing; that was clear. We found lodgings for our horses and paused to take a meal in one of the inns before venturing through the gate. I was beginning to feel a little nervous; anything could be waiting for me down there, but I was comforted by the thought that many other travelers would be following the same route as ourselves.

Elhmen guards, hooded and dressed in black, questioned all travelers as they passed through the gate. We were asked our business, whereupon Panthera produced our letter of introduction from Ferminfex. It was studied with insulting thoroughness before one of the guards thrust it back growling "Pass!" and waving us through. Beyond the gate, we came upon a vast cave. Stalls selling provisions (and, oh dear, talismans of protection) were set up precariously on galleries around the walls.

"From now on, it's downwards all the way," Kachina said. At first, the road was wide and gently sloping. We had time to admire the surroundings, which were impressive to say the least. In some places water ran down the walls, into clear pools where travelers could pause and drink. Great, white, gnarled stalactites depended ponderously from the roof. After an hour or so, Kachina pointed to a dark opening to our left.

"This is a short cut," he said. "Not as comfortable as the main ways, but it will save a lot of time." He looked at us hopefully. Panthera shrugged.

"Lead on," I said. "Whatever's down there, I might as well get it over with as quickly as possible."

The new path was so steep in places that it made me dizzy, as if I could pitch forward at any moment and fall and fall. We walked sideways. Sometimes, the passage would level out, and the ceiling would be lower so that we couldn't stand upright. I wondered whether the main routes became half as treacherous as this one. Presumably not, for how could the Sahale transport goods below if they did? Kachina informed us that the journey would take about a day and a half. This was a blow to me, who had estimated a figure of several hours at the most. Oppressed by the heavy weight of the mountain above us, I was already twitchy with claustrophobia, something I'd not experienced before. The air was stale, smelling oily and sour. Dim illumination was provided by strangely glowing bulbs of orangey-red light. I could not work out how they were powered, but there didn't appear to be any wires. It couldn't have been electricity. Kachina led us onwards effortlessly, knowing instinctively which branch of the road to take when it forked. I was curious as to where the other passages led. Kachina told us about other Sahale settlements; temples and havens of retreat. There were no signs to mark the way.

Inconvenience struck. Half-way along a twisting, narrow passage, the lights went out. Kachina swore mildly.

"What now?" Panthera asked nervously. "Can we continue?" He had reached for me in the dark; now we clung to each other's arms. I'm quite sure that, if it hadn't been for Kachina's calm, we would have panicked like animals.

"Yes, we can continue," Kachina answered. "We won't be in utter darkness. I have this." It was a kind of emergency light-cell, similar in many respects to Nanine's glowing staff, powered by psychokinesis alone. It only gave off a dull glow, but this was enough to stave off hysteria.

When we were tired, we lay down in resting places cut into the rock. Our water tasted sour and neither Panthera or myself felt like eating anything. Panthera confided that he too did not enjoy being so far underground.

"I don't like feeling trapped," he said. "We'd be helpless if anything should attack us, or if the roof fell in. I hate not being able to get myself out. Let's face it, we'd wander about until we starved to death or went mad if we got lost down here. My sense of direction has gone completely."

So had mine. Even Kachina's spirits had dampened since the lights went out. As we lay in the darkness, resting our protesting muscles, I thought, "Why am I doing this? Someone is going to pay, I swear it!" Then I slept . . .

. . . *And dreamed. I am in Phaonica, the palace of the Tigron in Immanion. The rooms are all of dark, Etruscan colors; red and brown and gold. Bizarrely patterned curtains fold to the floor, pooling on the lustrous tiles. Amongst the drapes, I see the glint of metal, the luster of jet. The floor is black and red, black and red. I walk across it. Here is the doorway to the Tigron's bedchamber. It is empty and I pass right through, past the canopied bed, whose hangings are waving in a gentle breeze from the open window. The room is dark. Beyond this room, I can see light, hear the sound of water. I follow it. This is a white and green place. The bath is really a pool set into the floor, approached by marble steps, the water gently spuming. Lilies ride the wavelets, cut petals and scattered ferns. There is a sharp, herby scent in the air. Oh, there he is: Pellaz, rising from the water like a young god; a goddess. His body looks harder than I remember it, but of course, he is much older now and this is a different body. He has bound up his hair for the bath, and now he is pulling out the pins. Hair tumbles down to stick to his wet flesh. He shakes his head. He is still beautiful. He is still dreaming. There is a small, private smile on his face. He senses movement and calls to the other room, "Who's there?" Does he sense* me? *No.*

"Only I, your humble servant!" a voice replies, and then a tall, scruffy-looking har is leaning on the door-frame between the rooms. His hair is gray from road-dust. He has a dried wound above his left eye and his face is still stained by old blood. This is a warrior; I have encountered many of his kind. His clothes are gray. He looks weary. Pellaz calls him Ashmael and, of course, I have heard of him. Who hasn't? Another of Immanion's immortal stars. Pellaz has wrapped himself in a towel. These two are close friends, I can tell, but not that close.

"You look a little unkempt," Pellaz mocks him.

Ashmael shrugs. "I just got back."

"Ah, you've completed the task of single-handedly subduing Megalithica then, have you?"

Ashamel raises an eyebrow. He says nothing. Pellaz flicks a towel fringe over his shoulder, pulls his hair from under it. He gestures at the water. "Take a bath, Ash; be my guest." He begins to call for servants, but Ashmael takes the Tigron's wrist, shakes his head.

"No, just let me soak alone," he says, and Pellaz pulls away fastidiously, somewhat affronted. I watch him wander through to his bedroom, but I do not follow. Maybe I can't. I watch Ashmael pull off his clothes instead. There is a dark, sulky bruise all along one side of him. His shoulder has been stitched together. I sympathize with his deadened weariness. He stretches and winces, testing the water with a grimed, tentative toe. He shudders, glancing around him, as if sensing unseen eyes. Mine? I don't suppose he has ever been watched before. He is one of the privileged. It is he, and his kind, who usually do the watching, the spying. He eases himself carefully into the water, grimacing. Bubbles swirl around him. He sighs and smiles, leaning his head back, against the side of the bath. After a while, Pellaz comes back, carrying two goblets of wine. Ashmael is dozing, and the Tigron watches him for a moment. Then he kneels down on the marble tiles. He puts the cups down beside him and reaches to touch the stitched wound on Ashmael's shoulder. Ashmael yelps in surprise and sinks, floundering, beneath the water. Pellaz is laughing. "Jumpy!" he says.

"Well, I expect to be safe in these rooms," Ashmael replies, shaking his hair from his eyes. Of course, he is safe, and so at home there; I hate him. Pellaz offers him a goblet and they drink together.

"Only the best," Ashmael says.

"Naturally."

I get the impression they are mocking their positions. Pellaz takes up a slim decanter and pours fragrant, liquid soap onto Ashmael's head.

"You shouldn't do this," Ashmael says, enjoying it immensely. He lies back and revels in the attention. I am familiar with that touch. I can only envy him. That should be me there, surely. This is my dream. Pell rubs the grime, the blood, the weariness away. His touch is magic. I know that look upon his face; he is considering, thinking. Just a whim. Rinsing the soap from his hands, he stands up and throws off the towel. He dives into the water and, for a moment, the stunned expression on Ashmael's face is unmistakable.

"Pell?" he says.

"Here!" And Pellaz explodes from the water, rising up, shimmering jewels of water flying everywhere. Now they look at each other and I am trapped. This is where I should wake up. It is a dream, isn't it? Why can't I make it end? I am in the water, dizzy, and I can feel Ashmael's arms around me, his mouth on my mouth, his breath in my chest. I want to devour him. I have wanted to do this for a long time. Come with me. Follow me. I lead him from the water. Dripping, we go into the next room. I lock the door. There is no-one else there. I draw the drapes across the long, open windows that lead to the balcony beyond. The room is now in sun-stained, afternoon dimness. I have not submitted to soume for a long, long time. This is because of . . . someone, someone who seems so part of me, I can hardly . . . feel myself anymore. We dispense with preliminaries because we are both so hungry, Ashmael and I. He spears me swiftly, mercilessly, and I cry out in pain, shuddering beneath his strength, which I cannot throw off. There is no way I could get out of this now; no way. Who am I? The visions come and I am deep beneath the dark earth. Against my lips, the taste of Ashmael's wound. I pull one of the stitches with my teeth and he laughs fiercely. A bead of blood seeps into my mouth. Who am I? Is this some kind of betrayal? But against whom?

I woke up twitching and snarling. Panthera shook me to my senses. The dark body of the earth was pressing against us, bringing dreams. I forced my eyes hard into Panthera's shoulder and he held me tightly.

As soon as Kachina was awake, we continued downwards. Still no lights. How could it have happened?

"Oh, it does sometimes," Kachina said. "You see, the Sahale do not need the lights to know the way and very few travelers follow this route. It might be days before they're fixed."

"All the other hara at Kar Tatang," I said, "where were they going? To Sahen?"

"Some of them, but a lot more head east to Pir Lagadre. That's a temple settlement, not so far underground. It is where the Sahale conduct most of their trade with the outside world."

We continued to walk. This was a fairly level stretch and we could stand upright. Sometimes, though, I was convinced I could hear noises ahead of us, rather chilling ones at that. Scrabbling, muttering.

"Kachina, is this journey dangerous?" I asked: "By that, I don't mean because of the dark, but . . . other things?"

Our guide didn't answer for a moment. "I've made this trip fifteen times," he said at last. "I've never come across anything dangerous, but I have *sensed* it at times. I believe the lights act as a deterrent to anything unpleasant."

Perhaps it was the morbid humor of Fate that made me bring it up, but it seemed best not to continue that conversation. Maybe half an hour later, Kachina stiffened and hissed us to silence. We all stood still, tense and listening. I could hear nothing.

"Sense life," Kachina whispered, and that slight sound echoed around us. Nothing happened. "Keep moving," Kachina said, "it's not far now . . ."

And then his words were cut off as something *large* rumbled swiftly from a side passage just ahead of us. I was dimly aware of teeth, eyes and hair and a miasmal stench. Kachina, in the lead, cried out and raised his staff, but it was too late. Before he could throw whatever power he possessed at the attacking beast, it clipped him with some gigantic, furred appendage and the staff fell to the ground, followed quickly by a stunned Kachina. For a second, the beast, whatever it was—and surely not sprung from this earth—hung between spidery legs, staring malevolently yet without expression at Panthera and myself. I could hear a whistling sound that may have been its breath or its voice.

"What is it?" I squeaked.

Panthera did not care about such details. "Quick, Cal," he hissed, "combine force. Acantha level. We must. Pyro—killing strength!"

"What!" I had entertained no doubts that Panthera's occult training had been more refined than my own, but this was something completely out of my field. Pyrokinesis is the ability to make heat, intense heat, even fire, by the power of the mind alone. Panthera groped for my hand to strengthen the bond.

"Open up!" he ordered and I automatically slipped into mind touch.

"Panthera, I'm not really sure whether I . . ."

"Shut up! We have no time! Follow my signal!" It happened swiftly. A fireball was igniting, swelling, between us. I didn't have much to do with its construction other than lending Panthera my strength. It was he who pointed the commanding finger, he who released a bolt of white-hot radiance from his taut body. With a thin screech, the beast scuttled backwards, but not in time. Within seconds, it was ablaze, moaning and screaming terribly. Fortunately for us, it decided to back blindly into the tunnel from whence it had come, instead of charging forwards. We could hear it squealing and creaking until it died away into the distance. Panthera leaned forward, hands braced on knees. He wiped sweat from his face. He was

shaking and so was I. "Oh God; Kachina!" Panthera went to kneel beside
the motionless form. "Oh God," he repeated and his disgust and horror
could not be contained. Whether the beast had killed him or not, we shall
never know. Unfortunately, Kachina had been in the line of fire of our heat
blast. Very little remained that was recognizable as Elhmen. "Oh Cal!" In
the light of Kachina's rapidly dimming light-cell, I could see Panthera's
chalk-white face looking anxiously up at me. He wanted me to reassure him
that we had not just committed murder. I would not comment, but picked
up the light cell.

"Can you operate this?" I waved it under his nose.

Panthera took it and examined it carefully, too carefully. Clearly, his
mind was in a whirl. "Yes," he said at length. "Yes, I can." Sparing
Panthera any further unpleasantness, I dragged the body of Kachina into
the beast's tunnel, going back for the bits that dropped off as I dragged it.
Panthera and I then walked on into the darkness, grimly.

"You are more accomplished than I realized, Thea," I said. "How come
you didn't use these talents to break out of Piristil, or to confound Outher
and his cohorts? It would have saved us a lot of time and bother!"

"You don't understand," Panthera replied, in a bitter tone.

"Try me."

"Alright. It is something to do with aruna." He spoke as if his mouth
was full of something noxious. "When I was captured and taken to Fallsend, I was only third level Kaimana and incapable of mustering my
powers alone. As I aged, I did try to improve myself in secret, but as you
probably know, hara are such sexual creatures; we need aruna to progress.
All that happened to me only served to hold me back. My powers were
minimal and unreliable . . ."

"And what has happened since you returned to Jael then?" I asked
sharply. "I wasn't aware that the situation had changed!"

"It hasn't! Not exactly. I've been purified, of course. My father raised
my level to Acantha to purge the contamination of pelcia and chaitra
away . . ."

"That still doesn't explain how you managed it without aruna . . . or
didn't you?"

"No, I didn't. If you *must* know, I've been taught some exercise in
auto-eroticism. It's intended that such practices will rid me of my distaste
for physical contact. But now I've learned a way to get on without it, I don't
see why I should ever seek it, if you know what I mean. I don't want anyone
to touch me again. It revolts me."

"Thank you for being so frank," I said, rather taken aback.

"You're welcome." He sighed deeply. "Oh come on, Cal, you're my
friend. Let's get the hell out of here. One wrong turning and neither of us
will have the chance to worry about such things again anyway!"

We hoped the road would not branch again, but since our encounter
with the beast, Panthera felt that his powers were completely trustworthy.

"If necessary, I shall *smell* which is the right way to go," he said. "I'm not afraid."

"Are you ever?" I enquired drily.

"Not really, no."

We kept walking. Sometimes, we could hear strange groanings from tunnels, that led off the main passage, causing us to increase our pace, but nothing else actually attacked us. I'm not sure what kind of beings stalk the tunnels of Eulalee, whether they have always lurked there unseen or whether they are the children of powerful and malefic thoughtforms, but it appeared they had been discouraged from molesting us by the fate of their fellow.

"I wouldn't like to have to explain to the Elhmen what happened to Kachina," Panthera said, meaning he was having trouble explaining it to himself.

"He was killed by the beast," I replied. "Believe it, Thea! Don't think anything else; there's no point."

Eventually, a red haze became stronger in the passage before us, which was widening considerably. Statues of naked hara wreathed in flaming hair stood in alcoves along the way, where offerings of fruit and bread had been left at their feet. Ahead, we could see the glow of an intense radiance, and within minutes, reached the end of the path, emerging onto a lip of stone. Below us stretched a vast, underground valley, lit by a thousand, thousand points of fire. Gases and multicolored bursts of flame jetted from cavities in the rocks and valley floor. The air was richly perfumed; very sweet and smoky. Sahen; uncomfortably like a vision of hell

CHAPTER EIGHTEEN

>━┤◆≻━○━≺◆┤━≺

Encounter with the Lyris
"All shall be well . . .
When the tongues of flame are in-folded
Into the crowned knot of fire
And the fire and the rose are one."
—*T. S. Eliot, Four Quartets*

"So, how do we get down?" I asked, peering over the edge. There was no apparent way from where we were standing.

"Look above you," Panthera said smugly, pointing.

"What is it?"

"Cables. My father talked to me of this. It's a kind of public transport here in Sahen. We'll have to wait." He reached up and pulled a white flaglet out from the wall, which would be clearly visible below. Shortly, a cable-car shaped like a vast, wing-furled bird swept gracefully up to us, and paused at the brink of the ledge. "Passage to Sahen?" Panthera said politely and the pilot answered, "That'll be three fillarets."

We didn't have anything smaller than a spinner, so Panthera was magnaminous and told him to keep the change.

"And where is your intended destination, tiahaara?"

"The residence of the Lyris," I replied, grandly, and without a remark, the pilot released the brakes and we were sweeping, as if in flight, down to the city of Sahen. The buildings were incredible; a forest of stalagmites, precarious walkways linking the gnarled towers, spider strands of cable sweeping between them. All the Sahale have ferociously scarlet or crimson hair (variation in hue depending upon cast). As we swooped along, the pilot's hair (far from all-enveloping as an Elhmen's, but still impressive) billowed out behind him like flames. Panthera and I huddled together on the floor, both of us rather concerned about our safety, for the car rocked dangerously at times, and we were given terrifying visions of the city beneath us. Tall spires seemed to graze the car's wooden floor, often rising right above it, as it weaved and skimmed its way between them. It was a rollercoaster ride to end all rollercoaster rides. Panthera, of course, had never heard of such things, and looked at me blankly when I mentioned it.

The car glided to a halt upon a large plaza in the center of the city. In front of us rose a magnificent confection; the palace of the Lyris. It resembled a crown of stone, spiked and starred, bridges swaying from spire to spire, where small figures could be seen mincing along them. Our pilot lowered the side of the car and we stepped out, none too sure of our feet. "Over there," he said, unnecessarily, pointing. "Go to the outer gate. If the guards consider your business worthwhile, you may be granted entrance. If not, allow me the liberty of recommending the inn on Ash Row. It is owned by my uncle, true, but good and cheap fare are to be found within, nonetheless. Good-day to you, tiahaara."

Panthera and I glanced at each other quizzically and advanced toward the palace.

"A strangely hospitable and amenable race considering their habitat," I commented.

"Well, I doubt that they ever encounter *unwelcome* visitors," Panthera replied. "No-one who was unwelcome would ever get this close, I'm sure!"

Thinking back on the oppressive darkness, snaking tunnels and unspecified, mannerless monsters, I was inclined to agree.

The guardians of the Lyris rival the palace itself in magnificence. Two of them stood to attention at the outer gate, their spears crossed. Helmets of spectacular design adorned their heads. From beneath, braids of flaming hair fell to their waists. Their armor was moulded to their bodies as if sprayed there. Long skirts of pleated silk hung from waist to ankle. They gazed at us mildly as we stood before them, but did not smile. Panthera produced the letter of introduction from Ferminfex, which he offered for their scrutiny. One of them took it, alternately peering at the page and glancing at us. Panthera shifted the weight of his bag on his shoulder and sighed.

"You seek an audience with Lyris," the guard said smoothly. We nodded mutely, wary of saying the wrong thing. "Well," he continued, "I cannot guarantee you satisfaction, but you are welcome to wait in the Hall of Hearkening with all the others who desire the same. Here, you better take this with you." He returned the letter to Panthera.

We thanked him profusely and passed through the gate. Within, the palace was like a town within a town. We came out into a vast, tiled courtyard, plunged into a bustle of activity. Hara milled around noisily, shouting to each other, pausing to examine merchandise for sale on the gaily colored stalls set up around the edge of the square. Nobody spared us a glance as we wandered wide-eyed and rather aimlessly toward the other side. Eventually, I stopped a passing har and asked him the way to the Hall of Hearkening. He rolled his eyes. "Ah, simple! Through the Red Gate over there, down the left corridor, take the third right, across the Fountain Plaza, then second right. The Hall's down that passage; you can't miss it!" He smiled at us and passed on.

"Can't miss it," I said, bleakly. Panthera sighed and took my arm. We walked on.

After several abortive attempts and further questioning of passersby, we finally found ourselves at the grand, open doors of the Hall of Hearkening. A Registrar sat in a booth outside playing chess across the counter with a soldier. "What's your business?" he asked us in a bored voice, not looking up from the checkered board. We explained, Panthera waving the letter, which the Registrar did not bother to examine. He wrote our names disinterestedly in a ledger and gave us a numbered ticket. It was stamped with a date (presumably) which neither Panthera or myself understood: "23 Blue Foresummer—12:05". It was also numbered 217.

"Are these issued from nought daily?" I enquired. The Registrar looked at me properly for the first time; answering that question was obviously one of the few pleasures of the job.

"Yes, tiahaar. Don't look so glum. This is a fair society.Therefore anyone may speak to the Lyris. But, needless to say, all the fairness in the world won't make more hours in the day."

"Does the Lyris spend *all* his time speaking to his people?" Panthera asked coldly.

"No. Two hours in the morning, two early evenings. Some matters are cleared quickly or passed to his clerks. You may have a chance . . . sometime this week." He went back to his study of the chess board. I had noticed the soldier moving men furtively around whilst we'd been speaking.

"Come on, let's go in," I said.

"Seems a waste of time. Perhaps we should come back tomorrow," Panthera replied. The Hall beyond was packed full of hara, all talking loudly. Panthera groaned. "You see? We could be waiting here for days!" He dropped his bag grumpily onto the floor. I couldn't disagree. Several hara were sitting huddled in blankets around the edge of the room among rows of black pillars. I had the sick impression that they'd been there for several days themselves. I threw my bag down as well. Perhaps I'd been wrong to complain about the Gelaming (or whoever it was) announcing our arrival in the right ears before we got anywhere. We could certainly do with that kind of help in Sahen.

After a while, a har selling provisions came over and offered to show us his wares. I enquired about the queueing arrangements to see the Lyris. He answered the query easily. "Keep your ticket," he said. "Let me see it. Ah, 217. The Lyris has enough time to see maybe fifty hara a day, if their business is quick. Tomorrow you may move up the queue, cash in your ticket for another one. It's all done fairly, no-one can steal your place, but don't lose the ticket, otherwise you'll be at the back again."

"In my estimation, that means we'll be here at least four days," Panthera said, none too cheerfully.

The vendor shrugged. "My brother is a coffee-vendor," he said. "I could send him over if you like. You look as if you need refreshment." To get rid of him, we agreed to this.

"Family ties are important to the Sahale, it would seem," I said.

"Mmm," Panthera assented, still sour.

"Now, I wonder if a brother, cousin or uncle of the Lyris is selling anything around here—like a few minutes of the Lyris's time, for example?"

"Don't be stupid," my charming companion replied.

"Actually, I'm not. Neither am I joking. Think about it! How much money have we got left?"

Panthera moodily examined our joint purse. "Not that much really. Just fifty spinners. Is the Lyris's time that cheap, do you think?"

I let this sarcasm wash over me. "No, I expect his time is priceless or at least beyond our bargaining power, but perhaps someone who can help us could be bought for less."

"Fifty spinners won't buy much," Panthera argued. "A floor scrubber in the royal apartment, maybe . . ."

"I was thinking more along the lines of one of the more upwardly mobile household staff, if you don't mind! They could show the Lyris your father's letter."

Panthera considered this. "Hmm," he admitted grudgingly. "If the Lyris *has* been given advance warning of our arrival, it may work. If he's never heard of you, he may use the letter to light his next cigarette. But you never know."

"If the Lyris has never heard of me, then I suspect we've come to the wrong place anyway," I said. Panthera gave me a hard look. "That's not conceit talking," I continued, "just logic." He shrugged. We sat down against the wall, and presently, as had been promised, the coffee-vendor weaved his way through the crowd toward us. We bought two coffees and he gave us a handful of change. I put this back on his tray meaningfully.

"Could you point out to us a member of the Lyris's staff?" I asked. "Maybe someone fairly high up in the royal household?"

The coffee-vendor laughed. No doubt our plan was a common one, he'd heard many times before. "Nobody that high-ranking ever shows their face around here," he said, "this is the pleb's Hall, but I am acquainted with Zhatsin, who's an under-valet of the Lyris. For a price . . ." He smiled.

"Would two spinners induce you to bring him here?" I asked sweetly.

"As it happens, it would, tiahaara," the coffee-vendor replied, "but I feel honor-bound to point out to you that just about everyone who comes here tries to buy their way into the Lyris's presence. Quite often, it's suspected that those who are hired to facilitate this need simply throw away whatever notes or letters they've been given and pocket their money with a smile . . ."

"Thank you—we'll take that risk," I said.

"Very well. Wait here. I'll be back as soon as I can." He held out his hand hopefully.

"You'll be paid when you return," I said, and he shrugged, disappearing back into the crowd.

"That's the last we'll see of him!" Panthera complained. "I doubt he knows anyone in the Lyris's household."

Thankfully, Panthera was wrong. Presently, the coffee-vendor returned accompanied by a startling, blood-haired har who smelled strongly of patchouli and looked down an aristocratic nose at us. He would not speak to us directly at first. His friend, the coffee-vendor, told us that Zhatsin would be happy to accept thirty spinners to deliver our letter of introduction to the Lyris. Like the coffee-vendor, he silently held out his hand for the money. Panthera was going to hand it over straightaway (he had learned nothing), but I stopped him in time.

"No," I said, "you get the money when we get to see the Lyris."

The Sahale looked indignant. He spoke for the first time. "That seems a little unfair. My delivering this letter does not automatically guarantee that he will see you, does it! What if I complete my side of the bargain and he throws your letter away? How do I get my money then?"

"Let's just say that I'm confident the Lyris will not disregard the letter," I said. "How about if we up the price to thirty-five spinners?"

"Forty."

"Thirty-seven?"

"Tell them I'll do it," Zhatsin said to the coffee-vendor, who duly told us and took the letter from Panthera's outstretched hand. Zhatsin snatched it away and whisked off in a boiling cloud of crimson hair and muslin.

"Beautiful, but haughty," the coffee-vendor said, as if in apology.

"As is often the case," I said, smiling benignly at Panthera, who snorted angrily, folded his arms and stared into the crowd.

After about an hour, I noticed two splendid palace guards asking questions of the crowd. Eventually, they sauntered over to us. "You from Jael in Ferike?" one of them asked. His arms were sheathed in beaten silver to the elbow and a fern-like silver chain hung from his left ear to join a sparkling stud in his nose. We introduced ourselves. The guard nodded. "Come with us. The Lyris wishes to convey that he is impressed by your letter of introduction and will grant you a few minutes of his time, even though the evening Audience is some hours away yet."

Just a few minutes of his time? I knew better but I still said, "We are grateful" and ducked a slight bow, to show we understood this honor.

We were taken through a side-door of the Hall of Hearkening and through a number of low-lit corridors, where the air became smokier and more pungent. A double row of fat, polished pillars led to an enormous pair of doors framed by snarling dragons painted crimson and gold with black tongues and white tusks. Here, our hireling Zhatsin was waiting smugly with outstretched palm. The guards waited patiently as Panthera completed the rather sordid task of counting out the thirty-seven spinners. I thanked Zhatsin for his help and he smiled at me narrowly before stalking away from us, jangling his bounty in his hand.

"Are you ready?" one of the guards asked. Were we? I nodded, and he rapped upon the impressive doors three times. After a moment, both swung silently inward and we were ushered inside.

"Good God!" I exclaimed, under my breath.

"By the Aghama!" Panthera echoed, illustrating for a moment our difference in age. We were both surprised by the opulence. The room within seemed to be have been constructed entirely from gaudy, flashing gold, the brightness only softened by diaphanous curtains that swathed the walls and tented the ceiling. Censers swung on chains, exuding thick drifts of sweet smoke and globes of light hung in clusters shedding ruby, violet and lemon vapors. In the center of the room lay a wide, round hearth, where a smokeless fire bloomed with heatless light. Around this, an oiled and naked har danced to the racing pound of hand-drums, held by shaved and painted hara dangling from the roof in jeweled cages. At the end of the room, directly opposite where we stood gawping, the Lyris reclined in a magnificent throne on a raised dais, his favorites draped sinuously across the steps. He watched the dancer with unflinching concentration. His hair was many different shades of red and gold, his chest and feet bare, his body glistering with jewels and precious metals. But more than this, he had the aura of power that proclaimed him king; a radiance that jewels and finery had no part in. Panthera and I were obliged to wait until the dance had finished. Then one of the guards indicated that we must follow him across the room.

"This is how royal households are supposed to conduct themselves," I said to Panthera. "Remember this when we return to Jael."

Panthera smiled thinly. Every eye in that room was turned upon us; not a comfortable feeling. Neither was the curious silence. I'd expected the Sahale to be very similar in their habits to the Elhmen. Not so. The Lyris looked up at us lazily as we approached, waited until we were within ear shot, and raised his hand. The guard halted our progress by slamming the butt of his spear across our chests.

"Which of you is Calanthe?" This came from a pinched-faced har, robed in blue, standing next to the throne. I pushed aside the spear and took a step forward.

"I am." It seemed best to bow. The Lyris bent his head to speak to his aide, who then addressed me once more. He beckoned me closer until I stood with my toes nearly touching the bottom step of the dais. The Lyris's favorites fixed me with eyes that were not hostile, but not without contempt either. I could feel them taking in my appearance, my shabby clothes and unwashed hair, my lack of jewels and perfume. Perhaps they thought nothing of it, but I certainly felt horribly conscious of my appearance.

"You are quite famous, it would appear," the pinch-faced har remarked, to which it was impossible to reply. I shrugged. "We have had notice of your visit," he continued. (Surprise, surprise.) Thanks for the welcoming committee, people of Sahen. "If you would be so good as to come with me, the Lyris has asked me to inform you he will speak with you later." Ignoring whatever my reaction to this might be, he looked over my head at Panthera. "Take this son of Jael to one of our guest-suites, see to his comforts!" I could hear Panthera's vague protests as he was efficiently whisked away. Pinch-face flicked his hard eyes back to me. "Come," he said, extending a clawed hand. I looked at the face of the Lyris. He looked back, but did not smile or even register that he could see me at all. His aide descended the dais and took hold of my arm. "This way," he said, pulling me.

"My luggage . . ." I said, looking back.

". . . will be taken care of. Come along!"

He led me through a door behind the dais into more corridors of dim lit and smouldering opulence.

I shook my arm free of his hold. "Do you speak for the Lyris all the time?"

He looked puzzled. "No. Forgive me; I haven't introduced myself. I am Iygandil, First Shriever of the Lyris. His second pair of hands and eyes, his second voice, if you like."

"Hello, Iygandil, and will the Lyris speak with me himself, or have you been delegated that honor?" The First Shriever saw no slight in this. "The Lyris himself will speak with you. And remember, it is *you* who is honored!" He smiled, baring his teeth. "In here, if you will." Another clawed gesture.

The room beyond was nearly in darkness until Iygandil raised his hand and ruby light blossomed from the walls. A sultan's den, fit for a clutch of concubines, I thought.

"I wait here?" I asked, flopping down with passable elegance onto a plump cushion.

Iygandil shook his head, looking worried in case I'd soiled the satin beneath me. "Not yet." He clapped his hands and two hara came into the room, ducking beneath a fringed curtain. Iygandil turned to me. "Get up," he said, flapping an impatient hand. I did so. "This is Tatigha and Loolumada, attendants of the Lyris. If you would go with them, Calanthe . . ."

"What for?"

The First Shriever rolled his eyes. *"Please,"* he stressed. "Am I forced to broach such indelicate matters? Through there is the bathroom. Need I say more?"

"You mean I need a good wash, is that it?"

"Please cooperate. The Lyris will be here shortly."

Sighing, I followed the attendants from the room. Without speaking, they led me past an enormous green pool, which was gently steaming, a wooden tub of bubbling, scented water and ultimately into a white-tiled room with a slatted wooden floor and benches around its rim.

"What's this?" I asked, standing there, but my words were swept away from me. Standing back, to avoid being splashed, the one named Tatigha turned a handle in the wall and hot, spitting water gushed from a dozen concealed outlets, soaking me in seconds. I spluttered, arms cartwheeling and tried to get out. The Sahale were laughing.

"We'll give you ten minutes. You'll find soap in that green jug over there." No sensuous massaging then. I rubbed my face. Steam rolled around me. My clothes had gone gray, brownish streams were pooling around my feet. I hopped around, and pulled off my clothes. The water in Sahen is incredibly soft, which I realized only after I'd doused myself with the liquid soap. Cursing, I was still trying to rinse it off when Loolumada and Tatigha returned. One of them promptly turned the shower to icy cold, so I was obliged to emerge half-slippery. I stood there shivering as they towelled me down. After this, I was conducted to a hand-basin and presented with a tooth-brush and gritty paste, designed to remove mouth slime. Perfumed powder was provided to blot the last traces of dampness from my skin.

"Much better," Tatigha pronounced, forcing my arms into a long robe. "This way please." I was taken to a room of mirrors where they dried my hair and painted my eyes with black kohl. The image in the mirror reminded me painfully of the har who'd lived and worked in Piristil; I don't think I'll ever be that comfortable wearing cosmetics again. The sweet smell of the powders and colors will always bring a vision of that place back to me. Now I was fit for a king. Water: fire. It was not a difficult deduction. I had a disturbing vision of Iygandil standing there to whisper the sweet nothings into my ear as the body of his lord plunged into me. Was this what I should expect? The Sahale are a strange people.

The Lyris was already waiting for me when his attendants took me back to the luxurious salon. He was reclining on a pile of cushions, sipping from a crystal goblet and smiling at the wall.

Loolumada cleared his throat. "My lord, may I present Calanthe, from the house of Jael, in Ferike."

The Lyris looked at me. He actually spoke. "Thank you Looma, you may go." He looked much younger now than I'd thought him to be; olive-skinned too, which seemed odd for someone who lived underground.

"Won't you sit down?" he said. I perched on the edge of an ornamental chair. He appraised me. I appraised him. No way would I be the first to speak.

"Well," he said, turning away from me to pour himself more wine. "So you have been sent to me."

"Not exactly," I replied. "Let's just say that I had a message that told me "beneath the mountains of Jaddayoth." Ferminfex of Jael interpreted it as meaning I should come here to Eulalee. For what purpose . . . I really don't know . . . fully."

"How unfortunate for you."

"Do you know why?" The question was perhaps a little bold.

He shrugged theatrically. "Do I know why. . . . Only that I have to complete a process that was begun in Elhmen and thereafter that you should be allowed to descend to the deepest caverns, which are my personal domain and known in Sahen as Shere Zaghara. Does that mean anything to you?"

Being coy would waste time. "The first part, yes. I take it I'm supposed to take aruna with you. It happened that way in Elhmen. Yes, I'd worked that much out; why else would you want me so clean? Purged by water, seared by fire. Symbolic. Why? I want answers and if the only way of getting them is to play along with this charade for a while, I will."

The Lyris nodded thoughtfully, unabashed. "The purpose of ritualistic communion is to recondition wasted souls, minds, whatever term you want to use. Whatever abilities you possess have been neglected, we are informed, and useless for what you have to do."

"Which is?"

He sat up and rested his elbows on his knees, caressing the winecup. "We were told only what we needed to know. Elhmen and Sahale are often called upon for this procedure. Yours is far from an isolated case, believe me. Rich fathers from Maudrah, Garridan, even Hadassah, often send their sons here for this refining treatment. It's an education into what can be achieved through concentrating the force of aruna. But clearly, you are not here because your father sent you! Who did?"

"I don't know. Who told you about me?"

His eyes didn't waver from mine. A convincing actor or an honest Har. Did it really matter which? "I received word from Elhmen. Arawn communicated with me. He told me little but did seem to stress that the matter was important. Oh, forgive me! Most remiss of me; here, take a cup of wine."

I did so, although I found it a little too sweet for my taste. "Perhaps you'll find the answers you seek in Shere Zaghara," the Lyris continued.

"Maybe. It seems too easy."

"You'll find an oracle there. However, it won't speak to you until you're ready, until I've *made* you ready."

I pulled a face. "Fire," I said, mulling that over toward unpleasant inferences.

"Not trial by it, but refining." The Lyris raised his glass and smiled.

The answer. Was it this close? Was it here in Sahen that I'd learn how to escape the clutches of the Gelaming, their Tigron in particular? (Yes, seems too easy. Scary.) If I was honest, did I really want them, those elusive, provocative, teasing answers? I'd chased them across a continent, and I wasn't convinced I'd cornered them yet. Even if I had, it might be that I'd be happier not getting acquainted with them. It was Ferminfex's pet theory that there was much more to all this than we could guess, and it would take an utter half-wit not to be somewhat frightened of that. In grand schemes small people are often expendable; especially after they've trotted off dutifully and completed their allotted quests. After all, it was not inconceivable that the aruna bit with Nanine and the promise of it with the Lyris was, in actual fact, the Cleansing (fanfare, fanfare) that Thiede had tried to force on me. He'd asked me outright; I'd said no. Was I now being tricked into going through with it? I'd had my own thoughts on what Cleansing would be; nothing like this. Was that a mistake? How could I find out? Visions, messages, proddings and pullings, signs and omens; a clever, intricate game, and here was I, a pawn, puffed up with his own importance, scurrying hither and thither, in the name of seeking answers. How could I be sure there wasn't a cold-blooded intelligence behind all that had happened to me saying, "Yes, this is the moment, soon he'll be ready"? I couldn't. I had the cards in my hand, but I couldn't read them. Throw down the hand on a gamble and I might find myself whisked off to Immanion on a pink cloud, grinning like an idiot, brain dead, scoured, sculpted and garnished, to be served to the Tigron on a silver platter. Powerless. If I still possessed a mind, my power could never equal his. In Pell's presence, my blood would be turned to powder, my brain to stone. Dilemma. Should I stand up now and walk out of Sahen? Would that be foolishness or just a way to save myself? OK, more-superior-than-human brain, work that one out, and let me know the result pretty damn fast.

The Lyris stood up, sauntered to my side. He sighed, crouched down and took my shoulders in his hands. I flinched. I didn't want him that close until I was sure what I wanted to do. "Why are you afraid?" he said. "Are you worried I'll hurt you?"

That simple? No. If only. The har thinks I'm an imbecile. Join the world consciousness, Lyris! "Hurt me?" I laughed, trying to get his hands off me. "No. At least, not in the way you're thinking of."

He didn't stand up, squatting there with his hands resting on his knees. "I'm not sure I understand you, Calanthe."

"OK, I'll explain. Will you answer my questions truthfully?"

"If I can." He was wary though.

"Fine. What I want to know is this. If I go through the *process* you were talking about, could anyone take advantage of me because of it?"

"What do you mean?"

"It's a kind of Cleansing, isn't it?"

He shrugged, pulled a face, then nodded. "In a way, I suppose so."

"Ah. And if I were Cleansed, might it be possible for hara of great power to impose their will over me?"

"Is that what you're afraid of?" The Lyris stood up, his knees cracking as he did so. "I don't know your circumstances," he said.

"No, you don't, but that shouldn't prevent you answering the question, should it?"

"In my opinion, you should gain strength from the Rituals, not suffer weakness. It is not a process completed for 'power over,' but for 'power from within.' I must say, there's no way I'd be a part of this if I thought it was being used for the wrong reasons."

"I wasn't saying you would, but as you pointed out, you're only told what you need to know."

He nodded, "True, but remember, I know the result of this communion. I've seen it, many times. You haven't. Unfortunately, I have no way of convincing you its effects are entirely beneficial until it's done. A risk you'll have to take . . . or avoid. It's up to you."

I stared at him hard. He didn't look like a liar. I know I'm too suspicious but who can blame me? I smiled, drank some sweet wine. "Take me, I'm yours," I said. He smiled too and put down his wine-cup.

"I'm glad you trust me! Now, I have to go to the Hall of Hearkening for a couple of hours. Are you hungry? Wait for me here, I'll get someone to bring some food for you."

"Thanks. Can I see Panthera of Jael?"

"Not yet, no. He's been taken care of, and there's no sinister meaning behind that! Just relax. Completely. Understand?"

I nodded, happy to cause him no further nuisance. After he'd gone, I sat there and thought of Nanine. I'd treated his part in this with a kind of irreverence. I didn't feel like that now. An insidious sense of solemnity was creeping over me. I was looking forward to the next stage. Perhaps I was just feeling horny.

Tatigha and Loolumada brought me food, but I didn't really have much of an appetite. I just needed soothing. The Sahale were sensitive to that. Tatigha began to sing to me, unrecognizable words, the ruby light casting violet shadows in his coiled hair. Loolumada came to kneel behind me, humming the tune beneath his breath. He stroked my neck and shoulders with accomplished fingers. Wallowing in this pampering, I began to feel drowsy, so they led me from the cushions and laid me down upon the floor, still singing, sometimes chuckling, an eerie sound. The light seemed barely light at all, just a slight, steady glow where figures moved as black shadows. I thought I'd been drugged, even while I knew that thought to be false. My body flowed into the carpeted floor. Now I was naked although I couldn't remember being undressed. I was clean and vibrant; floating free, like lying on the deck of a ship sailing on a calm sea. Sun beating down. Hot wood, the creak of hot wood and the breeze is warm. My eyes were closed. A bitter perfume crept into my lungs so I looked about me, too comfortable to move, eyes sliding this way and that. There was Loolumada, holding a candle in a long, pewter stick. I could see his skin, his solemn face. He kneeled, putting the candlestick upon the floor, his spine casting shadows across the flesh of his back. Something was coming back to me; a memory. A feeling. Tatigha was at my shoulders, laying down the flame. I could hear him whispering beneath his breath and I thought clearly, "This is a caste elevation. Of course." A long time since I'd thought of such things. I'd been second level Pyralis ever since I'd left the Unneah, and had allowed my abilities to sink into decline. Most of what I'd learned then was half-forgotten now, mainly because I'd considered it irrelevant to my existence. The huyana Lucastril had started something in Hadassah. I had a feeling this was the end result.

I was still drifting in a stupor when the Lyris came toward me from the dark. He stood at my feet and, with that immense vocal power only Nahir-Nuri possess, by words alone made me female. My body could not disregard the potency of what he said. He did not have to touch me to do it. He said, to my female form, "We deceive ourselves in so many ways. We are not perfect, not new, nor absolved from the laws of this planet. What we are about to do is as old as civilization itself. Think of the past. Honor it, for we are closer to Mankind now than at any time since the Destruction, when we were born. Man burned himself out from within. He had no balance; without it he perished. We have our own balance; it is flexible. Calanthe, for this time you are woman, an incarnation of the Goddess and I am man, incarnation of the God. Our communion is sacred and must be honored in love." When he spoke again, it was to pray and I closed my eyes. He kneeled to kiss me and said, "There is a danger in the world. You must go to the source, the source!"

I tried to lift my head. "What? How? But . . ."

"But nothing! Have you learned only how to carry a burden of guilt?" He stood at my feet once more, his attendants on either side, looking up at him. "Submission shall be praised as welcome. As you trust me not to burn, so I trust you not to engulf. Maiden and boy, guardians of the threshhold; open the gates unto me."

And at these words, his attendents each took hold of one of my ankles. Lowering their gaze to the floor, they gently parted my legs; sea-gates. I felt completely submissive, yet with the strength of a lioness. The Lyris lay upon me and his attendants did not raise their eyes again. In Elhmen, the experience of water had been wild and untramelled, elemental female. Here in Sahen, the experience of fire was governed, controlled, the elemental male, the emperor. When the heat came, it burned me inside from what felt like stomach to throat, but it was not a terrible pain. I had an intimation of what we were really doing, and how aruna is probably wasted a million times a day by two million hara. Most of the time we cannot see. Sometimes we can; this was one of those moments.

CHAPTER NINETEEN

>⸺◆>⸺Ꙩ⸺<◆⸺◄

The Oracle of Shere Zaghara
"Though art slave to fate, chance,
Kings and desperate men."
—*John Donne, Death Be Not Proud*

Panthera was shown into the Lyris's apartments early the following morning. I suppose it's strange that, away from the light of the sun and the moon, the Sahale should regulate their days as normal, but they do. Panthera studied me carefully, aware of a certain change about me, but not quite sure what it was. I was dressed and ready to begin the next stage of our journey; not a long one, thankfully. The Lyris had gone some hours before. I had slept alone.

"And what happened last night?" Panthera asked me tentatively, as if speaking to an invalid sensitive about the accident that had maimed him. He felt obliged to say something.

"Thea; I am now Algomalid!" This seemed the safest answer.

His eyes widened, then narrowed. "You've had no training!" he accused.

"Haven't I?" For a moment, I felt bitter. "Oh, I've had my training, don't you worry. Years and years and years of it! A lesson learned; or dozens of them!"

"So, you know the *answer* then, do you?" Why that note of sadness?

"No, not yet," I answered defensively. "Not *the* answer."

He wanted me to say more. "How many are there then?"

"Who knows? I have to go to Shere Zaghara, deep carverns, north of Sahen. Of course, you don't *have* to come with me . . ."

Panthera stood up. "I never have," he said. "When do we leave?"

The Lyris had granted us passage through his private conduit to the deepest grottoes of Sahale. "It is not a difficult or treacherous route," he told me, "so you may go there alone, or just with your companion, as you prefer. Go to the burrow of the fire-saucer. It is the chamber of greatest light and unmistakable. Your answers may come to you there."

May. We went down through the palace and at first the stairs had plastered, painted walls on either side. Eventually this changed to gnarled rock. Feverish cavern-lights cast eerie shadows in corners and across our faces. At first we traveled downwards in silence. I was thinking deeply and eventually had to tell someone.

"Panthera."

"What?" He sounded disinterested, but I carried on.

"I can see the end now, I think."

"Of these steps?"

"No! Of everything. Of trouble. I can see it all through."

"Have you only just decided that?" he asked wearily, perhaps doubting my sincerity. I didn't blame him.

"Perhaps it's been decided for me, but I don't want to be wishy-washy about it any more. The best form of defense is attack."

"Or a mirror." That could have meant many things, some of them not quite flattering. "So you've admitted to taking up the quest then, have you?"

"I'm not as weak as you think."

He glanced at me quickly then and I could see that he thought I was deceiving myself, wondering how on earth I could be third level Acantha when I was such a fool.

"Listen, Thea, you didn't know me before Piristil, did you, when I was in Megalithica, before Pell . . ."

"And during, and after!" He did not hide the bitter sarcasm. "It's all him, isn't it? The God figure!"

I ignored this. "Let's just say that after Pell died, I let go of the reins, lost control. That has got to end."

"Oh? And how do you plan to regain control of reins that curb the bits of other people's horses?"

"They were my horses once."

"Who rides them now, though?"

"This conversation is getting out of hand!" I laughed.

Panthera wouldn't even smile. "Maybe. Perhaps everything is getting out of hand."

"What do you mean?"

He would not say.

The steps beneath our feet were becoming warmer, the rocks glassier and the air held a hint of sulfur. We could hear strange booming sounds coming from a long way below us. "Are we on our way to hell?" Panthera asked, too wistfully for it to be a joke. Now the passage was levelling out, widening and heightening. Landings swept away from us to either side, offering glimpses of swooping galleries and dark or flaming caverns. Ahead of us, a smooth sweep of glossy, black stone led to a narrow slit in the rock wall. From here a sliver of intense brightness shone like a ray of sunlight into the passage. It was stronger than sunlight. "This is it," I said. Bulbs of spectral, red light clung to the arching, throated walls like clusters of bubbles, but they were hardly needed. My heart had begun to pound about twenty steps up from here, half with fear, half with excitement. As we approached the entrance, I could see that the gap was just wide enough for me to squeeze through. We paused at the threshold. Panthera put his hand upon the wall, running his fingers over the undulating grooves.

"Should you go in there alone, Cal?" he asked. For a moment, I thought he was afraid. There was a fine lacing of sweat along his upper lip, but then I looked at his eyes; they were dark and tranquil.

"Perhaps I should."

"I'll wait for you here then." He turned away and then, impulsively, wheeled around to embrace me. "Take care."

"Don't worry."

"And don't change too much." He smiled and put his cheek, briefly, against mine.

As soon as I wriggled through the gap in the wall, it was as if a heavy, impenetrable curtain of time and distance had fallen between us. I was alone. Beyond me, I could see the glistering walls of a huge and camerated natural vault. There were veins of micra, taut tendons of mineral splatterings, and a thousand, thousand eyes of warm, living gems, glowing from the walls, sullen in the light of a slowly licking fire. The saucer itself was maybe only six feet across and of simple rough stone, broken in places as if it had lain there unseen for millenia. I could not decide whether the flames rose from a cavity in the saucer's center, coming up from the earth itself, or if it simply existed upon the stone; a fire without fuel. I approached the light. A pottery cup and a flagon of liquid sat in the sand, attached to the stone bowl by a thin, metal chain. I had been instructed by the Lyris to take up the flagon, pour some of the liquid into the cup and drink it. Sitting cross-legged on the floor, I did so. It tasted like stale, warm water; a strong, mineral flavor. For a moment, I calmed myself, controlling my breathing as I'd been taught so long ago. Then, making the genuflections of entreaty,

I addressed the genius loci of the cavern, and opened up my mind for the reception of thought. The entity that lived within the flame, as if used to such encounters with harish kind, introduced itself without preamble and asked my business. As instructed, I opened up the part of my mind that was like an illustrated book of my life. The entity read it slowly, thoroughly, and took pleasure in it. My small life, entertaining at the best of times, apparently captured its interest; it read with relish.

"You seek answers to questions you cannot form," it decided. "If you knew the questions you would know the answers."

"May I ask one of you?"

"You may."

"Why am I important?"

"You are important only as all natural things are important," it answered obliquely, and then added, "If time is a tapestry, then you are one thread, whose color improves the whole, and without which some threads may become unraveled or cease to have been at all."

"This much was known to me," I said. "You must agree that it is a circumstance that could be applied equally to every living being on this planet."

"Precisely."

"I'm not asking the right question am I?"

It did not answer this, but instead honored me with a physical manifestation of itself, which appeared as a slim, rangy hound with glowing eyes, whose fur was brindled and short, and who had a crest of copper-colored fronds growing from its neck. It lay down some feet in front of me and licked its paws fastidiously with a blue tongue. The fronds all pointed toward me like eye-stalks.

"Must I go to Immanion?"

"Yes. Is that an answer you did not already know?"

I rubbed my eyes. The words were bitter in my mouth, but I had to say it. "Is my destiny to be the Tigron's concubine?"

The hound looked up at that and pricked its ears at my indiscretion. "If that were the case," it said indignantly, "then you would not be here now asking questions of me! Don't waste my time!"

"Sorry. No insult meant by that. Tell me then, what must I know?"

"One thing. What you are. Another thing; what must be done. The tying of loose threads. Finish what has been started, and in the right way. Make it smoooth."

"I still don't understand."

"What is most important to you?"

I pretended to think. It took some time to force the words out. "Pellaz and myself. . . . Are we destined to be . . . together again?"

"You will meet in Immanion."

"As lovers?"

I could hear the flames cracking, spitting in the fire-saucer. The fire hound looked at the flames. "You cannot do this alone. Help is needed. Go to the Dream People and join with them in the saltation of vision. They are to be found in the east, and are known in this land as the Roselane. All nears completion. A great cycle draws to a close and heralds the morning of a new age. Among the Roselane, you shall see yourself, and the mirror shall be clear. That is all."

I could feel the creature drawing away from me.

"That is not all!" I cried desperately as its image wavered upon the sand. "You did not answer my question!"

"I have answered as I can, and as I must. Do not believe everything you are led to believe. That, too, is part of it."

"But the visions . . . what are they? Is it real? The dreams? Are they?"

"You do not need me to answer that!"

"And Zack, what has he to . . ."

"No!" I was interrupted firmly. "That is not part of what I have to tell you. I've delivered my part. Remember it well. That is all. Now, leave quietly!"

The flames in the saucer suddenly jetted skywards and then abated to a dull, crimson glow. The pottery cup fell over at my feet. I did not bother to right it again. I walked straight out.

Panthera was sitting where I'd left him, his back to the wall. When he saw me scrambling through the rock, he got to his feet. "Well?" he demanded, searching my eyes for the answers I'd not received.

"Riddles! Just riddles!" I snapped and strode right past him, heading blindly for the stairs.

Panthera hurried after me. "What do you mean?" He grabbed my arm.

"There are no answers!" I turned on him viciously. "Can't you understand? There are no answers. Just another place to go, another move in the game!"

"Didn't you expect that?"

I couldn't answer.

"What happened, Cal. What did it say?"

"You really want to know? OK, I'll tell you. I had a cozy little talk with a supernatural beast. What it told me was nonsense. I'm no wiser. Go to Roselane, it said. Can you believe it? We came all this way, Kachina was killed, for *that!* If it's somebody's idea of a joke, then I'm not playing anymore. It's ridiculous!" I started running, not bothered whether Panthera was following or not. Near the top of the stairs, my chest began to ache. I could not continue. I had to stop; leaning down, shoving my head between my knees, I gasped for breath.

Panthera watched me for a while before coming out with the inevitable, "Cal?" and touching me warily on the shoulder.

"Don't touch me!" I yelled, shrugging him off. Oh, that felt good! I struggled onwards, one hand on the wall, feeling like about the biggest martyr in the whole of history. Panthera did not speak again. He walked behind me.

We returned to the palace of the Lyris, to pick up our luggage and see about finding our way back to Elhmen. The Lyris had just finished his evening audience in the Hall of Hearkening. More time peculiarities courtesy of fire-saucer beast-hound. There was no way the trip could have lasted a whole day. He told Iygandil to bring us a meal. Panthera was now touchy about being in the Lyris's presence, probably because he suspected something of what had happened the previous night. We were both anxious to get on our way, I suppose. The Lyris had good news for us about that. It would not be necessary to struggle all the way back to Kar Tatang and from there to Ferike. As Nanine had intimated, there were hundreds of secret entrances to Eulalee. Conveniently, one of them was just a few miles from Clereness. It would be much quicker to travel underground, especially as we'd be going by boat. Eulalee has an extensive canal system. Panthera asked the Lyris if he could arrange for our horses stabled at Kar Tatang to be given to Kachina's family or closest friends. I knew it could not appease Panthera's guilt over the Kachina episode, but I think it at least made him feel a little better. There was a cold and unfriendly politeness between us all the way back to Jael.

CHAPTER TWENTY

Coming of Age

"We have given our hearts away; a sordid boon!"
—William Wordsworth, The World

We've been back in Jael a week now. Over the last couple of days, I've sat up here in my room and read and re-read everything I've written. Piristil is no longer real to me. A blessing, perhaps. Sometimes I'm scared that I'm getting dangerously close to being the sort of Cal that Thiede wanted to drag back to Immanion. (See, I'm still not sure about the Cleansing.) Occasionally, I allow myself the luxury of thinking about Pell and about the type of reunion I'd like us to have. The destruction of Almagabran society predominates in these fantasies and it would be me pulling the sole survivor from the wreckage; the Tigron. Then we could resume our wanderings together, ride off into a glorious sunset. I know it's impossible. The chances are, that once in Roselane, I shall merely be given yet another clue to the puzzle, shoved off into the unknown on another journey. Bearing in mind everything else, this seems distinctly plausible. How can I believe, sitting here, that my life has great purpose? I look at my hands; they are scratched from rock clambering, yellow around the first and second fingers on the left hand through chain-smoking. They are not the hands of a hero;

no. To be fair to myself, I have started working again; you know, the *real* work of Wraeththu, flexing the muscles of my strange abilities. Every evening, I've taken to sitting in meditation wih Ferminfex. The visualization's OK, but I can't say I've learned anything dramatic from this battered head of mine. Most of it's memory, but I know that has to be relived until the stings have worked themselves out before I can get on with the heavy stuff. Self-examination. I've never really liked it. Demons with my face. I don't want to be faced with the gravity of existence, because it forces me to become obsessed with the concept of time, aware of how much of it I've wasted. Each moment is terrifying in its brevity, never to be relived again, for better or worse. Perhaps I'll be two hundred years old by the time I see Pell again and we'll both last long enough to say hello before death steps in to say, "That's long enough, you two!" It wouldn't surprise me. Not at all.

The family Jael celebrated themselves silly when we returned. It was all supposed to be nice and friendly, but nothing could breach Panthera's ass-stupid silence, which even caused his doting parents to look askance at him. I've not been alone with him since Sahen. It would seem that our friendship, which was never very close at the best of times, is doomed to wither. For some reason (unspoken) he has decided to take offense at something I've done or said. All of Panthera's actions (and reactions) are premeditated; I've learned that much. He is doubtless furious that I haven't worked out what I've done wrong yet. Ferminfex wants me to stay here in Jael for a couple more weeks before I set off for Roselane. (You see, I *am* going there.) By then the weather should have warmed up a bit. I haven't yet worked out my route, but it seems fairly certain that either by coincidence or design, it'll pass close to Oomadrah. After all, didn't the fire-hound tell me to tie off all my loose ends? Well, if the Archon of Maudrah is who I think he is, that is definitely a loose end I want snipped off, if not tied. Perhaps it is all circumstantial, just coincidence. The law of averages dictates that Wraxilan should have been killed a hundred times over back in Megalithica; he certainly deserved it. Wraxilan. We all go back to the beginning sometimes, don't we. For Pell, it would be me, but for me it is always the Lion of Oomar. Like a glamorous, brutal father, he influenced my Wraeththu shaping, is perhaps responsible for what I am now. I feared him, I supplicated at his feet. OK, I was sixteen, for God's sake! That's forgivable, isn't it? I want to see him again so he'll know I made it alright (comparatively) without him. It might not be part of the plan—it might be the ultimate self-indulgence—but it's something I have to do. Anyway, it's not going to happen yet. I have Jael to enjoy for a while longer. Now it is evening, and Jael is a magical place of soft shadows and fading spring sunlight. I can smell the dinner cooking; venison in wine. Yes, I feel good at the moment; about myself, about everything. This is probably transitory, and because of that, dangerous, but who cares! Soon, I shall go downstairs. Another evening of routine comforts.

Panthera was late for dinner. Lahela had to send a servant to fetch him from his studio high up in the castle. He came in smeared with paint, indignant at having been disturbed.

"Immerse yourself in work if you want to," his hostling reprimanded him politely, "but one custom I wish to uphold in this house is that we eat together in the evenings. It would be pleasant if you could avoid looking on this as an inconvenience!"

Panthera mumbled an apology and helped himself to food; small portions. He was sitting next to me, but I might as well have been a stranger. I wondered whether he was angry with me or disappointed, or had just decided he did not particularly like me.

"Panthera," I said, "I would like to talk with you after dinner."

"I'm busy. Can't it wait?"

"No."

He looked up from his food with cold eyes. My first instinct was to wince away, but I managed to hold his gaze. He snorted and pushed food around his plate with his fork. "Very well then, but not for long!"

The evenings were still cool in the high towers of Jael. Fires were still lit in the deep grates. Panthera and I went to sit in a comfortable, private sitting room on the third floor. Panthera stalked restlessly around. He found a pack of cards and suggested we play some game or another. I'd had more than enough of games, of any kind.

"Are you joking?" I asked, with pretended horror. "Do you know what those cards are?"

Panthera riffled impatiently through the pack. "Of course. They are divining cards. Nobody has used them for ages. Shall we gamble?"

"You lack respect for the unseen, my pantherine," I said gravely, still joking.

Panthera threw down the cards angrily. "You've changed so much!" he accused me bitterly. "You never used to be such a prig! What's happened to you? I almost prefer the seedy drunkard of our journey from Thaine!"

"You will never be satisfied, obviously. Here is a lesson from life, little cat. You can never alter people's characters to suit yourself."

"Oh, shut up!" He sank moodily to the floor, his back against the sofa arm, staring sulkily into the fire. Spellbound by his loveliness, I experienced those familiar feelings of longing to touch his untidy, black hair, coax desire from his sensual yet passionless mouth, and ease the frown from his autocratic brow. I watched him. He knew it. I picked up the deck of cards and shuffled them. Laying them down on the floor, I cut the pack. "Oh look! How appropriate!"

Panthera could not resist a look, bristling visibly when he saw what lay there. "Ace of Cups, of course. This clearly indicates the next drinking binge you'll embark upon once your shallow mind becomes bored of hidden knowledge," he said, pleased with himself.

"Cut them," I suggested.

He shook his head. "No need. Obviously, I will draw a reversed king and possibly the Devil."

"Is that how you see yourself?"

Panthera raised a sardonic brow. He said nothing. I cut the cards again. "What a coincidence! Two of cups," I said.

"Very clever! The cards have not been used for years. Possibly, the last owner died and left a binding of untruth over the pack. What are you implying anyway?"

I shrugged. "Nothing. It was you that wanted to play a game."

"You're insufferable!" he cried angrily. "No wonder Thiede let you out of the tower! There was a moment's hideous, electric silence during which, I should imagine, Panthera dearly wished he'd kept his mouth shut. Then he felt he had to go on. "You look down on everybody, don't you!"

"Well, I am quite tall."

"Oh, you make me sick! You know what I mean."

"In that case, so do you. I'm surprised you're not cross-eyed!"

Panthera ignored that. "Everyone tries to make you seem so special, don't they! It must have gone to your head over the years. The truth is, you're a selfish and deceitful charlatan. I've always been able to see right through you."

"Oh, I'm flattered! Panthera has spoken and the words of the mighty ones are leveled to dust!"

"Mighty ones!" he spat. "And who do you mean by that? No, don't tell me, it's the Gelaming, isn't it! Those honorable, smarmy trendsetters of our wondrous, blossoming culture. Don't make me laugh!"

"Why ever not? That was the intention of my last few remarks, after all!" I smiled at him engagingly.

Panthera ruminated on this, unsure of whether to laugh with me or not. He was afraid of looking foolish. "I'm not wrong, Cal," he said.

"Why did you come to Sahen with me then?"

"I told you; honor."

"Ah, so at least I'm worthy of that then."

He sniffed and stared at the fire. "This is getting us nowhere, Cal. I have work to do. What was it you wanted to say to me?"

Not the best of cues, but clearly the only one I'd get that evening. "Just that I'm sorry we've grown so apart."

"Why? We've never been close."

"No, not really, but I don't want things to get any worse. At one time, I thought we got on quite well. Can't we go back to that? What have I done? Have I really changed that much?"

He turned and looked at me thoughtfully. "I wish I could tell you the truth," he said. "I thought you'd guess, but you haven't. Too wrapped up in your own affairs, I suppose. We're really not that much alike, are we?"

"No. I don't suppose we are," I agreed. "but I've learned not to avoid the truth, so tell me."

He bowed his head. "I can't. It's no use. You must go from here and complete whatever quest it is you've involved yourself in. I know where it'll end, we both do. I've accepted that . . ."

"Panthera . . ." It was obvious what he meant. How could I have been so stupid? But what could I have done about it anyway?

"No," he said. "Don't say anything. I've told you; you've got your reason. Don't say anythng; it's best that way. I'm sorry. If you hadn't asked, I'd never have told you." He scrambled up and struggled from the room. I didn't stop him. I was dazed. Panthera had frozen me out because, dare I say it, he *wanted* me?

After a while, I went along to my room and lay down fully clothed on the bed. All the curtains were open and I could see a pale, round moon beyond the windows. I was lying there thinking of bodies, all the ones I'd touched, some of them now faceless to me. I'd always relished challenges, the slow, sinuous winding toward seduction of the glacial, beautiful creature who denied me. And there'd been more than a few. With Panthera I had made the decision not to bother, primarily because I respected him. Other reasons would include my obsession with the Tigron and, let's be honest, myself, my apathy, the certainty that seduction of Panthera would inevitably harm him in some way. He was right, wise beyond his years, not to pursue it. Most young hara would have done. It's what they grow up with after all. But Panthera knew I would leave soon; it wasn't just aruna he wanted. I must leave him alone so he could forget me without pain. And yet, much as I tried to dismiss the thought, I wanted to be close to him because nobody ever had been, and he stirred my soul. Between us lurked the specter of Pellaz and, perhaps eventually, the reality. I tried to sleep, but my body ached. I wanted to give my pantherine some of what Nanine and the Lyris had given to me; magic. Real magic, the kind that when it's over you know the world is just the wonderful place your dreams were always telling you. All the shit doesn't matter because your head has just exploded into somebody else with a thousand stars, and they felt so good; like fur, like ice, like flames, like silk, like feathers and, by Aghama, you want to experience that again. That's magic. I couldn't stop thinking about it; so maudlin and most unlike me really. After about an hour of this useless longing, I threw off my clothes and lay in bed, smoking a cigarette. Perhaps I should leave here sooner than Ferminfex suggested. Stubbing out my cigarette in the saucer I'd used that morning, I pulled the covers over my head and furiously tried to get to sleep again.

And eventually I slept. I know this because, when I sensed somebody come into the room, I thought I was dreaming. Then I realized I wasn't and I was reaching for a knife or a gun beneath my pillow which could not possibly be there. I held my breath, waiting. Someone crept toward me, my back was turned to the door. In a moment, I would turn and have somebody's throat between my hands. But first I wait. Weight on my bed, the covers lifted. I almost laughed. This was not threatening, oh no. I let my saved breath out in one, long hiss. He slithered into my bed, cold and shivering. He curled his arms around me and pressed himself hesitantly against my back.

"Cal, Cal, don't be asleep. Talk to me."

I recognized his smell, his slenderness and took one of his hands in my own. He gripped it hard. We didn't say anything at all. For a while, we lay like that, and it wasn't calculated when I turned to face him. I just did it. In the moonlight, I could see he was weeping silently, his face all wet, like he didn't really want to be there, but couldn't help himself. I understood that. Our first kiss was fumbling, like children, breath visions fleeting and undecipherable. He had never been touched before except in violation. He had never given love. His skin, perfumed with the earth smell of cinnamon, was like cat-skin, furred yet smooth. I wanted to pounce, plunder that lithe pliancy; only some vestige of good sense held me back. I had to speak, because they were necessary words; even though he knew I was thinking them anyway.

"Thea, I understand what you're giving me. I really do. Don't get hurt because of this, will you. Promise me that, you won't get all churned-up and grieving. In the future . . ."

"Hush," he said. "I'm not a child. I know what I'm doing; all of it." Nearly all of it. He smiled. "I don't want you to show me anything. It must be done my way."

No, he was not a child, but he *was* afraid. I knew that because the caressing went on for far too long. I was starting to think he wouldn't dare and I'd have to indulge in my original desire of conquest. I held him close, burying my nose in his wonderful hair, trying so desperately to feel passive to him, not frightening, not engulfing, just receptive, yearning. He stroked my skin, fascinated by it, because it was not a skin covering cruel desires to break and tear.

"You are scarred," he said. "Your flesh is soft yet you are hard beneath, I know it, like iron under moss in the forest. I thought you used bleach on your hair because your eyes and brows are so dark. You have cynical eyebrows, Cal. They always look so disdainful; they know everything and they love it when all the other poor fools don't."

"Just my eyebrows, Thea?"

He laughed. "Started off that way. I got side-tracked into the rest of you. I've wanted to touch you for a long time, you know. And so many people were doing it, all so experienced. I couldn't get near you. So many people have touched you, haven't they."

"My body, yes, but not often my mind."

He nestled against me, his head on my chest. "If we could just hold each other forever, the bad things will go away," he said. "I think I must love you, Cal, even though it's senseless and sort of self-destructive too. You belong to *him,* you always will." He sighed.

"We don't know what's going to happen," I said, rather untruthfully.

"No, we don't." There was strength in those words.

We shared breath again; I let him move against me. Clearly, his responses weren't damaged at all. I wriggled us around until I was under him, wondering what else I could do to help without being obvious. There was no need. Suddenly, unexpectedly, he just found his way inside me and let nature do the rest. The time was right. Everything was fine. He was nothing like I'd anticipated, not timorous, but powerful, vigorous, dominant. I'd have to sort that out later. At the moment of orgasm, he screeched like a wild beast in pain right in my ear, drowning any responding cry I might have made myself. I thought he'd hurt himself, but he only laughed at my concern. Could I have met my match? Calanthe is renowned across Megalithica and beyond for his savage, skillful aruna. Usually, it was me doing the gouging and chewing. I was quite alarmed.

Panthera said to me "Cal, I want to see Roselane," and lying there in his arms, feeling battered but lazy, it seemed like the only course of action.

That night it was decided. We may have been wrong, but if we were, it was because our hearts were taking control of our minds. Panthera would accompany me to Roselane, and beyond. We would take responsibility for the consequences, whatever they were.

CHAPTER TWENTY-ONE

>-+-<+>-+-O-+-<+>-+-<

Morla

"If I think of a King at nightfall."
—T. S. Eliot, Little Gidding

In spring, the steppelands of Maudrah are a glistening, undulating ocean of waving, feathered grasses. This can even be seen from the sea, as a faint and distant glimmering, like sheets of silk hung across the horizon. We'd had to choose the quickest route to Roselane, which was over water from the Ferike port of Saphrax, east across the Sea of Shadows, grazing the southernmost tip of the Thwean region of Jaddayoth. From there it was north into the Sea of Arel, passing the summer ports of Gaspard and Oriole, to Chane. After that, the journey would be continued over land, through Garridan to Roselane. At no point would our travels take us even within spitting distance of Oomadrah. I could not bear to leave my notes behind me in Jael, perhaps because I feared I would never go back there. Many times, I've sat upon the deck of this Ferike vessel, with my back to the coast of Maudrah and read through them. So many pages, and yet so little said really. I have spoken of my first client in Piristil, but to read what I wrote of it does not convey the disgust I felt or—no matter how hard I fought it—the shame. Neither can Elhmen and Sahen live as brilliantly, as vibrantly on paper as I experienced them in reality, nor does the time I first held Panthera in my arms convey the actuality of that moment. I suppose it is impossible. It happened. I lived it. Here the grass is glowing with light across a shard of sparkling sea. Can you picture it? Panthera and I are not blind to the possible consequences of our relationship. It may be doomed to ephemerality; it may not. We have no way of knowing. Because he does not read this, I can say that I do not love him—not in the same way as I did (do?) Pell. It is different, but no less genuine a feeling because of that. What we have we shall enjoy.

Ferminfex has no contacts in the land of Roselane, but has given us another letter of introduction all the same. This ship is named the *Auric Wing,* a merchant vessel, heading for the Emunah ports now that the ice has melted. The sea of Arel is impassable in winter. Yesterday, we stopped at the Maudrah port of Pelagrie on the tip of Thwean and I had my first glimpse of Maudrah society. Glimpse it was as well. Our Captain, Asvak, advised us not to go ashore, although the other two passengers ignored this. We are not sure whether they are Maudrah themselves or not, as they are surly and don't seem willing to make conversation with us. Panthera and I take our meals with Asvak, while they dine in their cabin alone. We were carrying several paintings which were to be picked up by some Maudrah family in Pelagrie, so the pause in our journey was only short. Panthera and I stood leaning upon the rails of the ship, gazing at the town. On the docks, black-haired hara, stripped to the waist, were heaving barrels and crates on board other vessels, taciturn as our fellow passengers. Asvak came to join us, smoking a long, curiously curled pipe. He gestured at the Maudrah with it. "Happy souls, aren't they!"

I looked beyond the docks toward the gaunt, gray buildings of the town itself. "Is the paw of the Lion that heavy then?" I asked lightly.

Our Captain made a disparaging noise. "Not heavy, perhaps, but it has an eye on the end of each pad! See them?" He pointed toward a group of Hara dressed in black, watching the workers. They were standing back from the proceedings, but clearly had a supervisory role. "They are the Aditi," Asvak continued. "The eyes and hands of the Niz."

"Niz?" I queried. "is that *another* name for the Lion?"

Asvak laughed drily, taking another draw on his pipe. Panthera squinted in distaste through a cloud of acrid smoke.

"No, far from it, or perhaps . . . well, judge for yourself. The Niz are the priest figures in Maudrah and to be honest no-one can say whether Lord Ariaric controls them, or vice versa. If you take my advice, you'll take great pains to keep out of their way."

"We don't intend to spend much time in Maudrah," Panthera said, looking hard at me.

"Is Oomadrah far from here?" I asked casually.

Asvak narrowed his eyes so that he could think better. "Quite some way, although once we reach the Sea of Arel, we'll be closer."

"Have you ever been there?"

Here, Asvak pulled a forlorn face. "Yes. Can't say I enjoyed that visit too much either. Luckily, I was with a har of Maudrah origin who prevented me from making any *noticeable* mistakes."

"What do you mean, mistakes?"

Asvak laughed and patted me on the shoulder. "Don't ask! Believe me, even drawing breath in the wrong way is a mistake in Maudrah. Now, if you'll excuse me, tiahaara . . ."

Asvak's footsteps hadn't even died away before Panthera launched into the attack. "We can't go there, Cal!"

"Go where?" I asked lightly. Panthera is sometimes annoyingly perceptive. I'd told him about Wraxilan some time ago, and had wondered then whether I'd regret it later.

"To Oomadrah, of course! Do you think I'm stupid? I think *you* are! Not only is it dangerous, but a waste of time! Are you trying to delay reaching Roselane on purpose?" (That was snide.)

"Oh, be quiet!" I said impatiently. "I've got my own voice of conscience, thank you! Just remember, I was told in Sahen to tie up all loose ends."

"I can't see how Ariaric or Wraxilan or whatever he calls himself can be one of them, Cal," Panthera said with dogged determination. "It's just your curiosity. You should let well alone. Haven't you enough on your plate already?"

"Oh," I replied drily, ignoring most of what he'd said, "and don't I get a say in what I consider to be my own loose ends?" Panthera pulled an exasperated face. "Look Thea," I continued bravely, "Wraxilan was my beginning; he's never let me forget that." Have I ever let myself forget it? "Perhaps I want to see where his destiny led him. It may be that I can learn from it." (How I'd come to dread those times when Panthera looked at me as if I was stupid.)

"OK, let's just imagine we *do* go there," he said, as if seriously considering such a suggestion. "Would you care to explain to me how we'd get to actually see him. He is Archon, remember; not just anyone can walk in and demand an audience."

"Don't be silly, Thea! We carry a letter of introduction from your father headed 'To whom it may concern' . . ."

"You are foolish beyond words or indeed comprehension!" Panthera declared as if it was written in stone. "We wouldn't survive five minutes in Oomadrah. We don't know the customs, we don't know the law. This ship can take us straight to Chane. We could be in Roselane within two weeks. Why can't you chase phantoms in Oomadrah after that?"

I could not say that, after Roselane, there was always the possibility I'd no longer be able to take independent action. For if I did, Panthera would first accuse me of acute pessimism and then chew it over privately and worry. I opted for an easier way out. "Because I trust my instincts and my instincts want me to go there now, that's why. There must be hara who can be hired as guides, interpreters, whatever, to take us there. I'll ask Asvak about it."

Panthera nodded sourly. "Oh yes, and supposing we are successful in meeting the Lion. What are you going to say to him, Cal? Have you thought of that? Do you think he'll be pleased to see you? Will he even recognize you after all this time?"

"Oh, he'll recognize me, I have no doubts about that! As for the other questions, I really don't know, but I'll have worked something out by the time we get there."

"It's decided then, is it? We're going to Oomadrah?"

I reached to touch his face. "Panthera, I must be honest with you; I decided that quite some time ago. Of course, you don't *have* to come with me . . ."

My sultry Panthera smiled then, and the sourness dropped from his eyes in an instant. "Oh Cal, as you said, I'm just an extension of the voice of your conscience. You must be asked these things. I'm not afraid of Maudrah. As a matter of fact, though I was loath to admit it, there is a distant relative of mine there, on my hostling's side. I believe he is employed in the royal house itself. Even if he agrees to see us, we'll need our wits about us though, and an efficient guide."

This was more than I could have hoped for, but I wasn't going to let my feelings show. "Can Asvak drop us off somewhere convenient do you think?" I asked coolly.

"Well, we can ask him to take us to Morla, although this ship would probably have called there anyway. We'll need the luck of the Aghama on our side for that; let's hope he's listening."

"Quite," I said.

Late afternoon, as the tide was turning, we set sail once more. It was a glorious day and the ensuing sunset was breath-taking. Asvak had a couple of his crew members set out a table on deck for the evening meal and brought out a bottle of his finest wine. A gentle breeze carried a smell of grass from the distant shore, which complemented the exquisite aroma of spiced meat, if not Asvak's rather overpowering perfume. Half-way through the main course, I mentioned that Panthera and I had decided to go to Morla instead of Chane. This was met with silence. Asvak was obviously suspicious of our motives. It was not an unreasonable misgiving. After all, he had to trade in Maudrah and didn't want to risk incurring the displeasure of the Niz. It was not inconceivable that ferrying dissidents of any kind to Maudrah would be regarded unfavourably. Luckily, Panthera managed to persuade him otherwise (his charm, when he deigns to use it, is humbling, to say the least). He told Asvak about the relative in Oomadrah.

"Our original plan was to pay him a visit on our way back from Roselane," he said, "but we've changed our plans in that we now intend to carry on to Kalamah instead, so Maudrah must come first. Roselane will have to wait a little while."

"Very well," Asvak assented, after another of his grinding thinks, "but if you should run foul of the Niz, you did not reach Maudrah through me."

"Naturally," I said. "Can you recommend a guide to take us to Ooma-drah, and who might be able to keep us out of trouble?"

Asvak was still wary. "There are one or two in Morla," he said. "I may be able to affect an introduction for you. You realize I take a considerable risk in helping you."

"My purse realized that before I even thought of it," I said, and Asvak managed a weak smile.

Dawn was just breaking when the gaunt spires of Morla appeared against the sky to our left. It had taken us about three and a half days to reach it. Panthera and I were up on deck, bags packed and ready, to watch the approach. Behind us, Asvak's sailors called to each other eerily from the rigging. Wide-winged birds hung in the sky investigating our presence. In the town, a bell was tolling, and light flashed off the tallest spire, which was crowned with metal. Ahead of the *Auric Wing,* the sky was opalescent and hazy; all the sea was shining like oil.

Asvak offered to take us to a guide he was acquainted with, and who was best suited to hara unfamiliar with the country. "It would be best if you wore dark clothes, cloaks if you have them, to go ashore," he said.

The streets of Morla are narrow and murky. It was strange and disorientating to walk upon solid ground once more and disappointing that we could not go into the nearest inn for a meal and tankard of ale. It is not that there are no inns in Maudrah, but because of the rigors of the local customs, it is inadvisable for strangers to go into them. We soon gathered that the best mode of behavior was one of steady inconspicuousness, which was difficult, for a har can be recognized as alien even by his stance. "You may come to regret this," was all Asvak would say. We descended a narrow flight of steps, leading to a gloomy lane, overhung by cramped, leaning buildings. Here, Asvak pressed us back against the damp wall to allow a single file of chanting, dark-robed figures to pass.

"They are novitiate Niz, combing the streets with the hems of their robes," Asvak told us. "It is a ritual performed every morning, whatever the weather."

Half-way up the lane, he knocked softly upon a low, heavily-linteled door. A code. Three knocks, pause, one knock, pause, three again. After a while, a window was opened with difficulty on the upper floor and a pale face looked out. "Dawn blessings," Asvak said, touching his brow and his lips with two fingers. The window closed and presently we could hear a series of bolts and locks being drawn and turned behind the door. It was opened by a har with white face and hair, dressed in dark brown and gray.

"Dawn blessings, Asvak of the Ferike," he said. "You are welcome in peace over this threshold." Asvak kissed this har upon each cheek and led the way inside. The house was dark and smelled damp. Our host lit a lamp to reveal a wide, sparsely-furnished kitchen. "May I light the fire?" he asked Asvak.

"The hour is early," the Captain replied. "I will lend you my hands also."

Panthera and I were left standing there, exchanging confused glances, while they made the fire and lit it. A much longer process than the task merited, I felt. Once this was done, Asvak deigned to introduce us.

"Lourana, this is Calanthe and Panthera of the house of Jael in Ferike. They would honor you with a request."

"Which is?"

"A guide to Oomadrah," I said, "if you would help us . . ."

Here, Asvak screwed up his face in mortification. Lourana had assumed a stony expression and slid his eyes to Asvak. Offense had been given. I assumed.

"You must forgive them," Asvak said. "They have not set foot in Maudrah before."

Lourana gave us an icy smile. "It is plain to me. If I can lapse into the common tongue here, Asvak, and address your companions?"

Asvak waved an arm. "You may."

"Please, sit down." Lourana gestured toward the table, where wooden benches were set along either side. We did so, and he took his place at the head, folding his hands on the worn surface. We were appraised, very slowly, one after the other. Then Lourana spoke. "This is a danger-frought situation, if ever there was one! Friends of Asvak, I must tell you that for the transgression you just unwittingly committed by speaking out of turn, you could have been taken into custody by the Aditi and asked any number of awkward questions. You look confused. Well, remember this: as an outlander, you must never speak directly to a native of Maudrah unless they have spoken first. If you wish to attract somebody's attention, you must speak your request out loud, to the Aghama, so that he may speak for you." (I dared not look at Panthera. Lourana was serious.) "If you really are ignorant of all Maudrah customs, you must remain silent and stooped at all times when other hara are present. Leave all communication to me. Now you must offer me payment."

I looked at Asvak and he nodded discretely. "How much do you require?" I asked.

Lourana shook his head. "No, that is not the way." He sighed. "Make me an offer, an offer way too high. Then it is for me to suggest a fair figure."

"A hundred spinners?"

"Thirty will be plenty." The Maudrah were cheaper to hire than the Sahale then. I shudder to think, how much Zhatsin would have charged for taking us on such a journey.

"Would it be possible for me to pay you now, plus any extra for the purchase of horses and supplies?"

"Payment in advance will be welcome," Lourana answered, "but horses will not be necessary. I have a vehicle."

"A vehicle? What kind?" Panthera asked, clearly unconcerned with whether that was a permissible question. Lourana had the courtesy to ignore any transgression.

"A crystal-powered car, such as are used by the Garridan and the Gelaming, and, of course," he smiled slightly, "the Maudrah."

"The journey will be quite swift then," I said.

Lourana inclined his head. "Very swift. I've found that this is the safest way with strangers. There are too many hazards upon the roads, too many encounters I'd rather avoid. The sooner you leave Morla the better. Oomadrah is more tolerant of outlanders. This is a small town. Everybody knows each other here." A strangely ominous remark.

Asvak stood up, as if suddenly remembering where he was. "Yes, I'd better be back on the *Auric Wing* before too many people are abroad in the streets," he said and held out his hand to us. "Good luck to you, tiahaara, may you reach your destination in safety."

I put some coins into his hand, to which he made no comment. He was eager to be gone. I experienced my first pangs of misgiving. Once the *Auric Wing* had set sail we were stuck here.

"You must have good reason for visiting Oomadrah," Lourana said, prying.

I waited until Asvak had closed the door behind him before replying. "I do. I want to speak with Ariaric."

Lourana did not flinch. *"The* Ariaric?"

I nodded and Lourana stared at me very closely. He reminded me a great deal of Flounah (which was not very comforting) even though his hair was white where Flounah's was black. They shared the same ascetic appearance however, and the same piercing gray eyes.

"You are a brave har," he said evenly. "I am not here to question your requirements, merely to do the job I'm paid for. It may be that you wish to harm the person of the Archon, in which case, by assisting you, I run the risk of displeasing the Niz—never a wise course of action—but, as I have accepted this contract, I must abide by my decision."

"I can assure you," I said, "I'm not an assassin."

Lourana held up his hands and closed his eyes. "Please, no more," he said emphatically. "I do not want to know what you are or what your business is. It's safer that way."

It was decided that, as anonymity was such a vital factor, we would wait until dusk to leave Lourana's house. He lived alone, in the dark and the cold, like a wraith-light. In fact, Lourana was the only touch of brightness in the place. From outside, he must look like a lonely ghost flitting from window to window, wandering the rooms, looking for life. He drew the curtains (dingy things) across the kitchen window and gave us bread and meat to eat, accompanied by large mugs of bitter, lavishly sugared tea. Every time we heard footsteps pass the house, Lourana winced and glanced at the curtains. I could not help wondering why he stayed in Morla; he seemed far from content there. Perhaps it was for love, though somehow, that explanation didn't ring true. It was a dismal day we spent there,

Panthera restless and pacing, Lourana tense as wire, wide-eyed, and infecting both Panthera and myself with taut nerves. We spoke little, only learning that once in Oomadrah, we should submit our letter to the city's
administrators and hope for the best. Clearly, Lourana thought his responsibilities ended there. I could not resist enquiring; I asked. "Lourana, if a
native of Morla wanted you to take them in your crystal-powered car to
Oomadrah, how much would you get off them?"

"Three spinners, maybe," he answered. "Now do you see why I have to
risk taking strangers there?" Yes, very clearly.

As the light began to fade, Lourana set about gathering the things we
would need for the journey. I helped him carry bags and boxes out to a shed
at the back of the house. Here, the sleek gray car lay like a prize cat, waiting
to be aroused to purring life. I can't say I understand the way such vehicles
work but they run without wheels and are not hampered by weight. The
yard was greasy and black. Lourana opened the double doors to the shed
onto another high walled lane at the back of the house. There did not
appear to be any sign of life in the other dwellings in the row, but of course,
quiet behavior is standard in Maudrah, so this was not really surprising.

"Now, get in the back," Lourana instructed, lifting up the transparent
dome of the car. "Hurry up, get that luggage in. Noise will attract attention."

He jumped nimbly into the front and breathed upon an oily-looking
panel beneath the control sticks. With a yawning whine, the vehicle shivered, sighed and levitated gracefully three feet off the ground. Spots of light
bloomed around the controls, which Lourana touched lightly, in sequence,
with the tips of his fingers. The car edged warily forward into the lane,
slanting slightly as it turned. There was no-one around.

"Strap yourselves in," Lourana commanded, still fingering the light
panels. "Please make sure the canvas over the baggage is secure."

Once satisfied that passengers and luggage were in place, Lourana increased the speed to normal walking pace. We emerged from the dank,
dark lane into a wider thoroughfare, where other somberly clothed hara
could be seen shuffling, head-down, along the pavement. I heard a metallic
swish and looked up. Another car flashed overhead, leaving a luminous
trail behind it which quickly dispersed. Even though Morla was lit by street
lamps, the feeling of darkness was not alleviated. We passed inns, but no
sound of revelry, or even conversation, drifted outside. Sour-faced hara
clutched glasses of ale in the doorways, looking at the ground. Lourana
pulled the hood of his cloak over his glowing hair.

"Keep your eyes lowered," he murmured over his shoulder, "and your
hoods up."

I was beginning to feel apprehensive. The appalling, oppressive atmosphere of the town was getting to me. Danger seemed to lurk in every
shadow. We drifted onwards at the same sedate pace. Occasionally other
vehicles would pass us, causing us to shrink back in our seats. Our direction
was north. It took us a good half hour to reach the outskirts of the town,

and Morla is not a large place either. Now the streets were wider and the houses spaced more widely apart; clearly a residential area. Perhaps this was where the Niz lived. Lourana increased our speed a fraction and the buildings fell away to reveal the grassy plains of Hool Glasting stretching away before us into the night. Lourana stopped the car, letting it hover a few inches off the ground.

He slumped forward, emitting a long, shuddering sigh. "The Aditi are very vigilant in Morla," he said. "You don't know how lucky we are to have passed through without them stopping us to ask questions." He straightened up. "Are you ready, tiahaara of Jael? Now, we may really *travel.*"

We were ready. Lourana savored this moment. He lifted the car to a height of six feet or so, before quickly touching the light panel. I had once owned a horse, who, at a command, could jump straight into a gallop from a standstill. Lourana's car had a very similar response. It seemed to bunch itself up, take a step backwards and then shoot forwards at sickening speed. Panthera and I were pushed hard against our seats, the wind of our flight whipping our hoods back, lifting Lourana's hair like a white flag. He touched the light panel and the dome of the car slid silently over our heads, sealing us from the wind. We shot like a comet over the land. Looking back, I could see the ghostly shimmery trail of our passage, dissolving and floating to earth. The car rose in the air until the ground was some thirty feet below us. Lourana told us he was setting the course. Now he could sit back and relax. I asked him if we could smoke. He said yes, so I offered him one.

As he took it, he said, "This is sinful," and then laughed as I offered him a light. Now that we were out of Morla, our guide seemed much more inclined to talk. He told us that he liked being with outlanders, because then it didn't seem to matter what he said or did. "Sometimes, I must admit, the strictures of my life do sit rather heavily upon my shoulders," he said.

"Then why live it?" Panthera asked. "Couldn't you find work in Hadassah or Gimrah?"

Lourana shook his head. "You don't understand. The way we live is the right way. I am weak to yearn occasional respite from it, and shall no doubt have to pay for it some day. We cannot live like men; look what happened to them! We need order so that we may develop . . ."

"Oh come on!" I couldn't help interrupting. "No-one I saw in Morla could be described as a particularly enlightened soul!"

"The individual may only learn through suffering. We carry a great blood-debt on our hands . . ."

"You do?" I couldn't hide the cynicism; I didn't want to.

"But yes," Lourana insisted with furrowed brow. "From the old times, the Destruction, the Agony of Birth. Wraeththu squandered their abilities; now they are undeserved. It will take many generations to appease the guilt.

I can see the sense of it all, but sometimes it's hard to live. That's part of it, I suppose."

Doors were beginning to swing open in my head. If Wraxilan had fled east, banished from Megalithica because of his evil, it was not impossible that he'd suffered some kind of warped revelation. He may be assuaging his own guilt by passing it onto his people. Curious. I couldn't wait to see what had become of the Har I'd so admired and feared in the past. Ariaric seemed the exact opposite of everything Wraxilan had stood for; which was riotous excess in everything and having a bloody good time while doing it as well. Perhaps I'd been wrong. Perhaps Ariaric wasn't Wraxilan; then we'd be in trouble. But then, hadn't Liss-am-Caar known what I'd meant back in Fallsend? I'd have to be patient. Soon I would know for sure.

Our flight was swift; by late afternoon the next day, Lourana was circling his car high above the outskirts of Oomadrah herself. To the north was the pale track of the caravan route, that looped around the farthest end of the gunmetal lake Syker Sade with its fringe of har-height reeds, its screeching birds. From there, the trail stretched southwest to Strabaloth (the second largest Maudrah settlement) and the plains of Wrake Tamyd. The flat grasslands roll from east to west unremittingly, unbroken by tree or hill. Herds of Maudrah horses graze unmolested, rubbing shoulders with cattle and deer, and beyond them rise the sheer, black walls of Oomadrah herself; female if ever a city is. Her walls are polished obsidian, soaring so high as to cast a perpetual shadow over the edge of the city within. Such protectiveness. Only the Rique Spire of the Lion's palace Sykernesse rises above them. Many gates stud the walls, but even as I was worrying about how we'd get past the guards, Lourana had dipped the car over the south wall of the city, which spread out her secrets before us.

"How come they let you pass so easily?" Panthera asked suspiciously.

"Because my car is known to them," Lourana answered. "I make this journey several times a week; I have to. To live."

We drifted down toward the black and silver streets below. To see it is to believe it. The predominant colors in Maudrah's streets, are silver, black, gray or darkest violet. Sometimes, high-ranking citizens can be glimpsed wearing clothes the color of dried blood red, indigo or brown, but for the lesser hara it's always unremitting gray or black. Maudrah hara have hair of deepest black or silver white. They are generally a tribe of striking appearance and their austere mode of attire somehow complements this. Outlanders—there are quite a few, which surprised me—can usually be recognized by their hair. Most people from outside affect Maudrah style of dress pretty quickly, but is never possible to blend in completely. This is because, more than a difference in appearance, Maudrah really do have a serene kind of inner quiet, which marks them, and is inimitable. It is said that they can kill and maim without a tremor in the name of progression, without even glancing away. They can love you and destroy you in the same instant; that is the legacy of the Lion.

CHAPTER TWENTY-TWO

>─┤─◆>─•Ο─•<►─┤─◄

Oomadrah

"A bloody arrogant power
Rose out of the race
Uttering, mastering it."

—*W. B. Yeats, Blood and the Moon*

Lourana brought his car to a swooping halt upon a gray plaza. The stone beneath us was as polished as glass. Other cars were clustered there, beads of black and silver. Hara walking sedately among them; no-one hurries in Oomadrah. Although Panthera and myself had stayed awake for most of the night talking to Lourana, we'd managed to catch up on some sleep during the remainder of the journey in the morning. Now we had to suffer stiff limbs and a lurking sleepiness.

Lourana suggested that he took us to an inn that catered for outlanders. "They are more lenient there, but it would still be best if you kept your mouths shut. I'll be staying overnight; I haven't slept for two days."

We were more than happy to let him take control of us. Lourana left his vehicle unprotected because stealing is unknown in Maudrah. This is because the inhabitants nurse a healthy fear of the all-seeing Niz. Lourana told us to keep our heads lowered as we walked, but I couldn't resist the odd sly peep. What I saw amazed me. Nobody turned their backs on a har of higher rank than themselves; peers must also pass each other frontways. So, whatever strictures are placed upon merrymaking in that part of Jaddayoth, the people of Maudrah certainly dance. They whirl and bob and glide amongst each other like the cranes nesting on the grasslands beyond the city. Everywhere the swish of robes, the tap of feet as the correct steps are made. Lourana made genuflections to indicate that Panthera and I were foreigners and thus absolved, to a certain degree, from the rules of their society. As long as visitors are seen and not heard, all seems to be well, but we were aware of the steely eyes of the Aditi vigilant on every street corner, alert for serious transgressions. Lourana had warned us what forms these could take; a sneeze in the street, an unfortunate raising of eyes should a high-caste har be passing by, an increase in walking pace when it was not warranted. I wondered what would happen were someone clumsy enough to fall over in the street. A hundred conventions would be broken in one stroke; a cry, an incorrect wobble, a flailing of naked hands. And yet, it must be said, the Maudrah are actually comfortable within the cage of their laws; they thrive. A perfectly executed walk through town, observing every nuance of custom and tradition, can provide untold satisfaction. Whatever outlanders may think of Maudrah, it would appear that the natives themselves are far from discontent.

Lourana took us to what he considered a commercial inn named the Grain and Bowl—no brimming tankards in Oomadrah! It was a plain but reasonably comfortable establishment. He signed the register for us and then announced that we must present ourselves to the Office of the Niz right away. Panthera complained of hunger. I would have welcomed a chance to freshen up.

Lourana shook his head at our complaints. "No. Take your luggage to your rooms. Don't do anything else. If you fail to identify yourselves with the Niz, you may find your next meal less than welcome—your toes for example. There'll be plenty of time for eating and washing later on. You need a Pass to come and go in Oomadrah; your letter of introduction should provide you with one. You are lucky that the name of Jael is fairly well-known in the city. I've heard that the palace is full of Jael artifacts, so the Niz should be willing to let you remain here. It's more than I'm being paid for, but I'll show you the way, if you like."

Panthera took a couple of spinners from his pocket and put them in Lourana's hand, staring at him owlishly. Lourana sniffed, put the money in his purse and led the way outside.

As we walked along the clean streets of Oomadrah, Lourana advised us on how to behave in the office of the Niz. "You would be wise to tell them that Panthera's father wishes him to make a tour of all the major cities of Jaddayoth as part of his education; that will appeal to their sense of pride. Mention that you are seeking out remote branches of your family and would like to be presented to your distant cousin who can be found in Sykernesse." This caused a moment's confusion because Panthera realized he couldn't even remember the name of his relative in the Royal House. This would not look very convincing. Lourana was outraged, his pale face actually flushed pink and he would not take a step further. "Are you out of your mind?" he hissed. "If you wander into the Office so ill-prepared, so casually, the Niz will have you flayed, and me too very likely!"

"Don't upset yourself," Panthera replied airily. "There can't be that many Kalamah in Sykernesse. From what I recall, he is employed in the service of the Lion's consort Elisyin, quite high-ranking too."

Lourana looked annoyed, mainly because that meant he had to say, "Oh, in that case, you probably mean Lalasa."

"In that case I probably do," Panthera replied, "the name does ring a bell."

"Let's hope it's the right one otherwise the Niz may wring our necks," I said; a weak joke, but still enough to start Panthera laughing. Lourana hurried us along, looking in every direction at once in case someone heard us.

The Administration Office of the Niz was a grim, imposing building, set in a square of its own, unadorned save for the main entrance. Here, polished columns reared somberly to an arch where squealing birds squabbled among pendulous, tatty nests. The reception hall inside was enormous, the only sounds being those of brisk footsteps and hushed voices. The floor was so polished it was like looking into a black mirror. Lourana approached the low, unfussy desk to our left, which was staffed only by a single har. As we waited, black-robed hara drifted past us, heads bent together, never lifting their eyes.

"Panthera, this place is *spooky,*" I murmured. Panthera pulled a forlorn face of agreement. He didn't want to risk speaking out loud. After a moment, Lourana came back to us, ushering us further away from the desk.

"You are to be interviewed by the Niz's Prefect," he said confidentially. This did not sound like good news to me. "Have you got your letter with you?"

"Safe in my pocket," Panthera said. "I never go out without it."

Lourana did not smile. Presently we were approached by a young har dressed in tight-fitting gray, who requested us to follow him to the Prefect's office. His hands were gloved, his eyebrows plucked bare. Lourana insisted on accompanying us, although the Prefect's underling made it clear that he was far from happy about it. I presumed we were being honored in a way that Lourana was unworthy of sharing. I said, "This har is employed by us; he is our guide, our teacher in the lore of Maudrahness. His vocation was outlined personally by the Aghama, I believe."

The underling gave me a hard look, but nodded his head briefly at Lourana.

"Remember," Lourana said as we were taken away, "do not speak unless you are spoken to. Better still, do not speak at all. Let me do the talking."

The Prefect's office was on the third floor. We climbed a wide, shallow staircase carpeted in dark blue. The office itself was immense, ridiculously so. White, marble floor, ten foot drapes of dark purple velvet, windows all along one wall offering a view of the square and one large, gleaming desk. A gigantic portrait of a har I presumed to be Ariaric hung on the wall behind it, so stylised it was impossible to tell if he looked anything like Wraxilan. The Prefect stood up as we entered and dismissed his minion with an imperious wave of his hand. Aware that we were outlanders, he addressed himself directly to Lourana. This was a complicated procedure, involving a lot of words, but where very little was actually *said.* The Prefect seemed satisfied by it, however. He nodded and sat down, scanning the papers that Lourana had brought with him from the reception hall.

"Panthera Jael," the Prefect said. Lourana shot Panthera a quick glance, nodded. "That is I, tiahaar," Panthera replied in his best clear, regal voice.

"Your letter of introduction, if you would be so kind . . ." The Prefect held out his hand. To me, he was an unimpressive har, medium stature, unremarkable in feature or style; soft yet mean. Panthera stonily handed him the letter. The Prefect looked up, caught my eye, sniffed disdainfully, shook the letter and began to read. Gripped by a spasm of annoyance, I wanted to stare at this insignificant creature, perhaps wither him to dust. It shouldn't be difficult. He examined the letter for far too long; maybe he was a pathetically slow reader, but I took it as measured insult. Really, the letter was nothing to do with him at all. Such things were for the eyes of Sykernesse staff alone. Lacking in glory, the Prefect made the most of his brief moment of power over us.

"Lalasa, I understand, a courtier of the third tier and a valet of the Archon's consort . . ." We all made various noises of assent. "Hmm, well, your application will be passed on. Perhaps in a week or so . . ." Here the Prefect sniffed again in an insulting and derogatory manner. "You must appreciate we are plagued by outlanders' petitions constantly. Many claim to have relatives in the Royal House. You must wait your turn, I'm afraid."

That was when I decided I'd had enough. I've suffered most insults in my time, but never have I had it implied that I was a parasite. Fighting with a red mist before my eyes, I found I had the Prefect by his collar, and had half-dragged him over his desk. Clearly, he was unused to such behavior. His eyes were so round, I could see the whites all about them. "Excuse *me*, tiahaar," I said, "but I feel you have misconstrued the urgency of our request. We expect to be presented at the palace tomorrow at the latest, and would be grateful if you could see to it immediately. Not only is my companion a close relative of Lalasa, but I am an old friend of the Lion himself. I feel he might be upset if I am forced to wait . . ."

For a moment or two the Prefect actually considered whether I was telling the truth or not. He looked once at the door, but decided not to summon help. I was Algomalid; I doubt if the Prefect was even Acantha. His will was like butter. He extracted himself from my hold, took great care to avoid my eyes, and wriggled back into his seat. His neck was red. He coughed to hide his embarrassment.

"You must forgive me, tiahaara; an oversight. Return to this office first thing in the morning and I will arrange for you to be accompanied to Sykernesse." He handed me Ferminfex's letter. "Here, take good care of this; it is precious."

Lourana led the way stiffly from the room. Once outside in the corridor he allowed himself the luxury of one or two repressed outbursts.

"You are both insane!" he decided. "Tomorrow, the Niz will be waiting for you! You have blown your chances of entering Sykernesse. By Aghama, to assault the very person of the Prefect! I can't believe it!" He shook his head sadly.

"You worry unnecessarily," I said, thumping him on the back. "That wimp in there won't risk his neck. His mind is empty; no match for mine."

"You are confident," Lourana remarked drily.

I shrugged. "Tomorrow the Prefect will have taken us to Sykernesse.

The only disadvantage is that Ariaric may have been informed of my presence, thus ruining my surprise."

"Shock," Panthera corrected.

Lourana had us back there virtually at daybreak. Perhaps he had developed a fondness for us; we could not persuade him to accept any more money than he had originally asked for. "Not even a couple of spinners for your nerves?" I asked. We were early. The Prefect had not yet arrived at work. A bland receptionist told us he was due at eight o'clock and, lo and behold, just as the clock above the stairs shuddered to the hour, the Prefect came bustling in through the door. He came over to us as soon as he saw us, smiling unctuously. I presumed he had already been in touch with Sykernesse about us.

"I myself shall take you to the palace," he said, grinning horribly, "but not until ten. May I suggest we offer you a light refreshment until then?"

Two hours. I doubted whether any refreshment in Maudrah could be termed as light.

We were taken to a small reception room, tucked away in the back of the building. Lourana tagged along behind, now more curious than loyal, I was sure. The room was pleasant enough, if featureless. The only decoration was another stern portrait of Ariaric that stared beadily into the room. I went to look up at it.

"Ferike work," Panthera said, taking my arm. "This style is formal, but far superior to that we saw in the Prefect's office."

The face was nearly the same as I remembered it (which was a relief, because I'd still had doubts about the Archon's identity), but the mane of the Lion had been shorn. He wore a close-fitting hat which covered all of his hair, if indeed any remained.

"I hope you know what you're taking on," Panthera said, squinting at the portrait critically. "I'm afraid I'm finding it hard to place any resemblance between the har you described to me and the face I'm looking at now."

I didn't answer that, mainly because I agreed with him. Had I been wrong to come here? Would my caste elevation be enough for me to cope with what might follow? I was going to meet a stranger without arming myself with weapons or foreknowledge. Beside me, I could sense Panthera's echo of my mood; fear and resignation, plus a certain relief that he had a relative in Sykernesse.

After a brief, but uncomfortable wait, a servant knocked on the door, bringing us a tray of cinnamon-milk served in cups of white china and a plate of hard, sweet biscuits. The drink was too sweet, but its aftertaste was pleasant, a hint of earth and bitterness. Presently, another door opened behind us to admit a pair of scantily-adorned entertainers. They bowed to us silently and then proceeded to enact a rather lurid drama, which involved too much scourging and suffering to be classed as entertainment. Panthera and I exchanged quizzical glances. Was this normal practice in

Maudrah? It was certainly a place of weird contrasts. A reputation of brutality, yet a society that appeared pious and humble. A ballet of bureaucracy followed by a performance of bestiality. I asked Lourana to explain.

He looked surprised. "I can't understand why you ask this. Surely, one of the first things you learned after Inception was that without pain, pleasure cannot exist. Beauty is worthless without the contrast of ugliness. An honest society must learn to balance these things. Justice and outrage. Strength and meekness, aggression and humility . . ."

"In other words, a society of ridiculous extremes," I said, rather pompously. "On the journey here you spoke of blood debts, a need to make amends for the past and yet Maudrah is regarded as one of the most power-hungry, blood-thirsty tribes of Jaddayoth. You must admit, these two facets do not really make sense."

"A diamond is multifaceted, surely," Lourana answered, just as pompously, before popping a biscuit into his mouth, munching in relish, while staring with shining eyes at the performance.

I couldn't watch it. There were too many unpleasant reminders of Piristil within it. Panthera looked positively green. His sickly drink was untouched, developing a thick skin on its surface. Those two hours passed with agonizing slowness.

The Prefect returned at ten minutes to ten. By that time, the bizarre entertainers had gone. "It is my pleasure to escort you to the palace," he said, savoring the words. An honor for him as well then.

Sykernesse has three spires. One, it is said, to celebrate the birth of each of Ariaric's sons. The Prefect took us there by public conveyance, a car very similar to Lourana's. We'd left our guide behind us. There was no way the Prefect would let him follow us into the Palace. In a way, I was sorry to say goodbye to him. His knowledge of Maudrah had made us feel safe; now we felt alone. Sykernesse is surrounded by a high, impenetrable wall. Cages upon the wall contain the remains of condemned traitors, or perhaps hara who had accidentally fallen over in the street. I shuddered. What in Aghama's name was I doing here? Madness. We were the cause of some minor fuss at the Main Gate as we sought entrance. The Prefect argued unintelligibly with the guards. Administration assistants were summoned to indulge in more earnest discussion, scanning forms and lists carried on clipboards. Panthera and I took the liberty of reclining back in the car to smoke. We'd had two cigarettes each by the time the problems were smoothed out. Then the car lifted itself with a sigh and swept grandly inside the shadow of the gates. The Formal Entrance to Sykernesse revealed itself in morning splendor. Wide, white steps, rows of columns, carved doors, heavy banners lifting sluggishly in a faint breeze. Braceleted ravens stalked and flapped and grumbled along marble terraces and velvet lawns. A groom, leading two glossy, enormous horses, excused himself as he crossed our path. The Prefect directed the car's driver to veer toward a smaller side door. The grandness of the front entrance was intended for the Archon and visiting lords alone. The side entrance was still fairly impressive though. We were ushered into a wide, dark passage by a grave and gracious servant and conducted across a polished hall. The Prefect followed us into a formal salon, furnished in deep crimson. I was beginning to doubt whether we would ever get to see the Archon himself. It was doubtful whether Ariaric, or even his staff, ever ventured onto the ground floor other than to leave the palace. The Prefect asked us to sign a document. Rather carelessly, I just scrawled my name without reading it. Panthera spent some minutes trying to scan the text, but just signed it and tossed it back at the Prefect in disgust after being unable to decipher the official jargon.

"Just a formality," the Prefect insisted sweetly, folding it tidily into an oblong. "We like to keep a record of all foreign visitors to Oomadrah. Now, if you would care to take a seat, someone should be along shortly to see to you." He backed from the room, bowing and smiling.

Panthera made an eloquent sign at the door with his fingers; a rare gesture for him. "Now what?" he asked accusingly. "Cal, we could be well on our way to Roselane now."

"Don't remind me," I said.

"Ah, prepared to admit you made a mistake then?" He smiled smugly.

I shook my head. "No. Let's wait and see, shall we."

He laughed. "Yes, let's see. You know, I never thought Oomadrah would be like this, did you?"

"No. I didn't think *anywhere* would be like this nowadays."

"What do you mean?"

"Only that life before Wraeththu would have held little pleasure for you, my pantherine." He raised his brows, but we were interrupted. The door burst open and a tawny-haired har, dressed in white, virtually exploded into the room. He looked around quickly, raking a hand through his hair when he saw us sitting apprehensively on the nearest sofa. He smiled, rushed forward.

"Greetings cousin," he said. "Whichever one of you *is* my cousin."

"Lalasa?" Panthera inquired hopefully. He extended his hand which the har took in his own.

"Ah, Lahela's son; I should have known. Yes, I'm Lalasa. Now, what godforsaken reason brought you to this little nest of vipers?"

"Of course, the rigors of Maudrah society are somewhat relaxed in Sykernesse," Lalasa told us, as he poured us coffee. Servants hovered in the background, anxious to be at hand should he need them. I admired the way he was so convincingly oblivious of them. He was a typical Kalamah, I suppose. It was easy to see that he shared Lahela's blood. "We get quite a lot of outlanders here," he continued, "many visitors, many hara presented at court. Elisyin won't have Maudrah restrictions anywhere near his apartments. Even the Niz aren't welcome there, except for Wrark Fortuny, but he's a friend of Ariaric's, so that's different. How long are you planning on staying here? What the hell do you want? I can't believe you've just come to see me."

"Well, we haven't," I agreed bluntly. "I want to meet Ariaric."

Lalasa did not gasp, or even change his expression. "That figures," he said, rather enigmatically. "If you're from Megalithica, you can expect to be sent on to Garridan rather swiftly. Our beloved Archon does little to encourage faces from the past to remain here. I guess it embarrasses him or something . . . I doubt if he'll kick you out straight away though, and he'll certainly secure a good place for you in Garridan before he does . . ."

"I don't think you understand," I said. "I'm not looking for a permanent position."

"Aren't you? Forgive this indiscretion, you know, mentioning the terrible word, but a lot of Uigenna have headed this way, thinking that now Ariaric has his own little kingdom, they'll be able to sponge off his good fortune and hard work. We have to be careful."

"Ah, so it's no secret he was once with the Uigenna then?"

Lalasa pulled a face. "Oh, *please!* He never was! You'd best remember that, my friend. Ariaric only left Megalithica because things got a little out of hand over there. He didn't like it."

"That's the official version?"

"It is."

"Do any of the visitors from back home ever get to meet him in the flesh?"

"Are you kidding?" Lalasa pulled yet another expressive face.

"No, I'm serious."

"Well, what do you think? I'm with Elisyin. I get to hear things. No-one with Uigenna blood gets past the first floor, believe me. They might get sent on with a full purse, but he won't see them, not even for old time's sake. If you knew Ariaric before, best not mention it. Understand?"

"Yes. Unfortunately, I was rather indiscreet with the Prefect. I mentioned I was an old friend of the Lion."

Lalasa shrugged. "I wouldn't worry too much about that. The fool's an insect, a pen-pusher. He has no influence and no contacts of importance here."

"If I write a letter to the Archon, will you see that he gets it?"

"No, not on your life. Write to Elisyin. I'll probably be able to get you onto his floor. He likes having pretty hara about the place and you'll certainly suit requirements there. Just don't mention past alliances. Say Ferminfex sent you to tout for business amongst the idle rich or something. Panthera, can you paint portraits?"

"I can paint anything," he answered sourly.

"Good, that's the way in then. All of Elisyin's court are extraordinarily vain. Let's get cracking." He called for paper and a pen. Servants were driven into a panic of activity. Whatever I might have said about Kalamah indolence before, forget it. We were installed in a suite on the second floor within an hour.

The opulence was exquisitely understated. We had two rooms, plus a bathroom, which was modest by Sykernesse standards, but probably more than we deserved. After all, we were far from official envoys from Ferike. The apartment had an air of impermanence about it, as if all of its previous occupants had never stayed there very long. All the furnishings were terracotta red and brown and cream. Panthera examined an object hung on the wall.

"What's this?" he asked, pressing various buttons.

Lalasa snatched it from his hands. "A telephone," he said. "Be careful."

"A what?" Panthera was only used to thought-transference units; even I was slightly surprised.

"A primitive form of communication device once used by men," I explained to him. "Well, it looks as if we might be back in the twentieth century, doesn't it!"

"We're not that far out of it yet," Lalasa remarked. He told us that Elisyin would receive us later in the afternoon. I wasn't convinced that the Lion's consort had any interest in us at all really, but obviously Lalasa had no small degree of influence with him. No doubt he had dropped heavy hints about how grateful he'd be to have his relative from Jael received at court.

"I don't feel safe here," Panthera decided once Lalasa had left us alone. "It all seems so genteel on the surface, but I feel that it is just on the surface, don't you? I feel as if it would be very easy to, you know, fall out of favor."

"Ah Thea," I replied, pulling the rank of my experience on him, "when you've been in as many royal houses as I have, you'll realize they're all the same. Even Jael to a degree. A code of etiquette must be maintained, an elegance supposed to transcend the grubbings of humanity. As a race, you'll find that Wraeththu are suckers for pomp and circumstance; they love playing Olympians. You just have to know how to play the game to survive. It's not that difficult."

"Hmm, as I recall, when we first met, you were working as a kanene after having 'grubbed' around the country for some time. Did you forget the rules, Cal, or was it a voluntary choice to opt out?"

"I always underestimate you," I said.

"Perhaps you look on me as a child," he replied. "I've found that first generation hara always do have a slightly condescending attitude to those of us who are pure-born, as if we haven't 'lived.' That's not fair, is it? Can you really say I haven't experienced anything?"

"I wouldn't dream of it, my dear. All I'm saying is, I've lived with Varrs, I've lived with Gelaming—even if it was under restraint. I know this scenario. Take away the grand buildings, the luxuries, the clothes and you have the leader's clique of the Uigenna. It's not that different."

"I hope you're right."

"So do I."

CHAPTER TWENTY-THREE

>─┤─◆〉─○─〈◆─┤─◁

Sykernesse

"I must be satisfied with my heart . . ."

—*W. B. Yeats, The Circus Animals' Desertion*

I always expect the consorts of Wraeththu leaders to be effeminate, gentle creatures, whose sole purpose is usually for the generation of heirs. Elisyin was an exception to this rule. His hair was hacked short, consciously unkempt, his attitude restless and self-willed. From the moment I first set eyes on him, I could see why he wouldn't have anything to do with the petty restrictions of Maudrah society. First, it would bore him to distraction; second, it would get in the way of more important things. Elisyin liked to be direct. Form and ceremony held no interest, no comfort for him. Ariaric probably adored and slightly feared him. Terzian had once felt that way for Cobweb; perhaps I was being too subjective about Elisyin because of that. Elisyin was not tall, but as graceful and aesthetic as you'd expect from a well-bred Ferike. He did not wear cosmetics except for painting his finger-nails deepest indigo. His ears were pierced at least a dozen times by earrings of all shapes and sizes, but he wore no other jewelry. His suite of rooms was sumptuous, but untidy; it did not feel particularly royal.

Lalasa led us through a gossiping cluster of courtiers to the couch where Elisyin was presiding over a game of cards. Nobody seemed to be taking it very seriously. The consort of the Archon smiled politely at us when were introduced, but it was clear that he had little real interest. Many people, seeking positions in Sykernesse, must be presented to him in this way, so that two more new faces were just too unremarkable for words. Elisyin didn't ask us why we were there; he didn't care. I have to confess that it pricked my pride badly. I wanted to show him how different we were to the sycophants that surrounded him. It angered me that we should appear as such. It would have been madness to consider attempting mind-touch with this elevated Har, but consider it I did. Only the desire to remain "faceless" for a while prevented it. Vanity was still something I had to get under control. Lalasa went to great pains to impress on us how privileged we were, being introduced into such august company. He showed us off to a few of Elisyin's cronies, some of whom actually stirred themselves to take an interest in us. One or two hara mentioned they would like to have their portrait painted. Panthera gritted his teeth, smiled and talked about making preliminary sketches. He considered such things beneath his art, but hid it well. After an eternity of endless chit-chat he came and whispered in my ear; "Roselane!"

"Soon," I promised. It shut him up but we both knew that wasn't exactly truthful.

For three days we played the game. For three days, we rose late in the morning, dined like kings, went on tours of Oomadrah with Lalasa, said the right things to the right people. In the evenings, we visited the theater, the horse-races, the art galleries, all within Sykernesse itself. All so civilized.

Panthera was going crazy. "You're wasting time, Cal," he said. "What the hell are you doing here? This is madness. Have you forgotten Elhmen and Sahen so quickly?"

Oh, I knew he was right. Elhmen seemed a million miles away, Immanion but a dream. The way things were going, it seemed unlikely we would ever get to see Ariaric. Elisyin's people rarely interacted with those of the third floor. We didn't even know if the Archon was in residence or not. On the evening of the third day, I was prepared to admit I'd been wrong about diverting our journey. What had I been expecting? A fiery confrontation with the Lion to show him how much I'd achieved despite having been kicked out of the Uigenna? You see, I couldn't even be sure of my motives any more. Perhaps it was simply pride. I said to Panthera, "Tomorrow we leave," and he had the grace not to say anything. "I told you so" would have been just too obvious. We began to pack our bags and there was a knock at the door. Panthera looked up at me dismayed; presentiment. It was Lalasa. He didn't even notice we were packing.

"You've got an hour to get ready," he said. "Look your best. Ariaric has returned from the Natawni border and there's going to be a celebration in his honor. Elisyin asked if you'd like to come." (I bet!) "It may be the only chance you'll get, Cal. Make a move—now." He swept out before we could say anything.

Panthera did not look exactly elated. He stared at me meaningfully, no doubt wishing he'd bullied me into leaving the day before. "Be careful," he said.

The bulk of Sykerness is four-storied. The ground floor is the domain of the servants and staff, offices and reception rooms for visitors, kitchens and store-rooms. The first floor houses the offices of state, suites for visitors worth more than the ground floor but not high-ranking enough to qualify for a suite on the second or third, conference room, libraries and the living quarters of those hara who administrate that floor. The second floor, as I've already intimated, is the territory of Elisyin, his friends and staff. The third is Ariaric's and the province of the Niz. They alone have access to the towers and spires of Sykernesse, the observatories and private temples. Most of the court, including the Lion's family, reside on the second floor. And it was there that the celebration to welcome the Archon home was held.

Lalasa took charge of us, ushering us into the right corridors, "Stay by me," he said. "Whatever you do, Cal, don't attempt to speak with Ariaric. He may notice you. He may not. You are in the hands of Fate. Tomorrow you may be requested to continue your journey east at once. We shall have to see."

The gathering was surprisingly informal, held in a large, but low-ceilinged room, where the colors of palest dove gray and darkest indigo melded to a refined and tasteful effect and the lights were discrete, flattering hara who passed beneath them. Tables were set out at one end of the room, laden with food, but there were few seats. Servants glided silently among the guests, supplying glasses of dry, iced wine. hara mingled, conversing softly, but all eyes kept flicking to the doors. Panthera and I accepted a glass of wine each and then secreted ourselves in a corner to watch the proceedings. My heart was racing. Lalasa hovered close by, keeping an eye on us. Presently, Elisyin made a grand entrance, and we were witness to a mind-boggling display of sycophancy; the court virtually fell to their knees as he passed among them. Elisyin appeared not to notice this. He had an autocratic young Har on each arm, whom Lalasa told us were his sons. At his heels came a tall, robed figure, who kept his hands hidden in his sleeves. That, we were informed, was Wrark Fortuny, High Priest of the Niz. It was the first Niz we had seen since entering Sykernesse. Panthera and I quickly became bored by it all. We were too insignificant for anyone to come and speak to us and we couldn't help scorning everyone's fawning behavior towards Elisyin.

After half an hour or so, the elite of Ariaric's army made their entrance. More swooning and grovelling on behalf of the court. Panthera rolled his eyes at me. But the best was yet to come.

Presently, Wrark Fortuny took his place on a raised dais at the far end of the room. The music which had been playing so softly I'd barely noticed it ceased immediately, and there was an audible sibilance from the room, which quickly lapsed to silence. Fortuny raised his hands, his head, and closed his eyes. He took a deep, deep breath. Exhaled.

"As you are gathered here," he intoned in a ringing voice, "so shield your eyes from the Light as it falls upon you. Keen your welcome for the Son of Brightness, the Breather of Life, the Stern Deliverer of Justice, Semblence of the Aghama on this Blighted Earth; Ariaric, Archon of Oomadrah, known also as the Lion for the Intentness of His Gaze, the Soft Walker of the Deserts, whose Eyes are the Twin Lights of Destiny and have looked upon the Mysteries. As the Spirit of the Aghama resides in Him, so do we recognize the Goddua within the har, and avert our eyes until he gives us leave to see . . ."

Within the room, every chin sank toward every breast. Breath was held as a single breath. Panthera and I exchanged a nervous glance. "Avert your eyes!" Lalasa hissed at us desperately. For the time being, I looked at the floor. Out of the corner of my eye, I saw the wide doors onto the corridor outside thrown open. A clarion was sounded; five, sweet, clear notes. Fortuny spoke a blessing and Ariaric, accompanied by his closest friends, came into the room. I had to look up. Had to. It was a vital moment to me, a sweeping clean of the path of time so that two points could meet and blossom in understanding. I did not raise my head; I strained my eyes to see. I was the only one. Ariaric turned and smiled at his friends, who smiled back. He approached his consort Elisyin, whose head was bowed as everyone elses, and kissed him on the cheek. Elisyin raised his head, nodded. He was saying, "I am fine, beloved." I'd known that language myself once. Fortuny, inhaled deeply, as if he could smell their contact. He opened his eyes and Ariaric raised his hand. "Look now upon the Light!" Fortuny cried exhuberantly, and everyone sank as one to their knees. A few outlanders like Panthera and myself were standing rather self-consciously around the edge of the room. The Archon took a quick look at us. Perhaps he was always afraid of seeing old faces there. He looked me right in the eye, but gave no flicker of recognition. Even so, I knew he had recognized me. I felt his blood run momentarily cold, his heart miss a beat. For a second, we were both back there in the past, knees touching as we squatted in an old warehouse store-room, he with a cut palm, me with a crazy fear. He had been so strong then, but I'd faced my fear. I'd lived it through. I had a son now; somewhere. What of Ariaric? Had he grown too? I was Algomalid, but to his people, the Lion was a god. An incarnation of the Aghama. Impossible. But I could not dispute it . . . yet. I had been mistaken about his hair, he had not cut it off. Whatever austerities his new role demanded, he was too fond of his mane to lose it. It was braided tight against his head, down his back, showing off the bones of his face and neck, and darker in color than before. Obviously, he'd been working on his inner balance. The aggressive masculinity had been tempered by serenity and grace. I expected his voice would be softer. He said, "Rise, my people," and they did so. His voice *was* softer, but it carried far. I could feel his power, which may just have been confidence. As Lalasa had said, we would have to see. Every face in that room was shining with pleasure; how they loved him. I just watched. He kept looking at Elisyin and Elisyin would grimace back and I wondered about what jokes they made about these fawning hara when they were alone together. Perhaps they didn't joke at all. For a moment, I was intensely envious. The thought, "That could have been me" sprang instantly to mind, but it was not as potential consort to the Lion that I thought it. No. For perhaps the first time, I found myself thinking, "If I had accepted Thiede's offer, if I had gone with him to Immanion, would there have come a time when I would have met Pell's eyes across a room like this? Would we have smiled together, sharing our secret, savoring it?" It was a far more complicated feeling than that, but difficult to put into words. Panthera put his hand on my arm and brought me back. Perhaps he had guessed what I'd been thinking.

"Is he as you remember him?" he asked me.

I shook my head. "No. Greatly changed . . . maybe."

I knew he would speak to me soon.

The evening wore on, swirling around us. The music became louder, voices higher as more wine was consumed. I kept thinking about the difference between this and life in the city below, and commented upon it to Lalasa.

He smiled. "Not really double standards," he said. "In ancient times, men did not expect to live like gods, neither would they have dared to criticize the way in which their gods conducted themselves. Ariaric is Divinity in Maudrah; his behavior is beyond reproach, similarly the behavior of his court."

"And what exactly is Goddua?" Panthera asked.

"Simple," Lalasa answered. "It is the God and Goddess combined; as are all of us."

Panthera was ready to argue. "God and Goddess cannot be termed as 'he' surely," he said.

"You think it should be changed then?" Lalasa asked. "Should a new term be thought of that is as androgynous as we are?"

I sighed, and let my attention wander. It bored me too much to point out that theirs was a subject that had been argued dry about thirty years ago. Who cares whether we call ourselves he, she or it? Not me. I scanned the faces in the room, but could not see the Lion anywhere. Many hara had drifted outside, spreading themselves throughout Elisyin's apartments. I decided to leave Panthera to it and sidled away. I wanted to explore, and yes, I was looking for Ariaric. Who wouldn't have?

I wandered around the second floor, drink in hand, looking in every room I came across. Nobody spared me a second glance. I passed a mirror, looked into it and thought, "Yes, OK, that'll do." I was rehearsing what I would say to him when I found him. It was all very dramatic. Almost surreal, but absorbing. Eventually, I found myself in empty corridors, without even a servant around. Walking mechanically, I found myself at the foot of a great staircase, that disappeared into a velvet gloom. I walked right up it. Darkness fell about me like a veil and the sounds of merriment seemed very far away. Miles away. Before me, tall, gleaming pillars stood sentinel to a cathedral calm. The ceiling was lost in shadow high above me. This was Ariaric's floor. I shouldn't be here. Perhaps I shouldn't continue, but turn around and go back to Panthera. If I was found here, it could mean unpleasantness, but even as I thought this, I was walking, walking, and the staircase was soon far behind me. Was Phaonica like this, noble, grand and silent? I could sense melancholy, but probably only because I wanted to. Something was leading me, of that I was sure. I let it happen. How could I have known which turnings to take, which stairs to climb? How could I have found my way to the studded door that opened upon the base of a spire? Almost in a trance, I closed the door behind me and began to climb. Round and round and up and up. I could hear the wind whistling its single, mournful note and feel the air become colder. Up and up. Panthera was far, far away from me and I climbed a finger of stone, distanced from all that I knew.

At the top of the curling steps, I came out, breathless, into a room with a black and white tiled floor. Black pillars and curtains; the smell of incense. This was a temple. Before me, I could see an altar supporting only a white, tasselled cloth and a drawn sword. Beyond this, was a statue. Bland of face, one hand raised, the other palm upwards in its lap. The face was a face I knew, a face etched indelibly on my brain; Thiede's. Perfumed smoke blew across its features as it smiled at the room. And kneeling before this altar was a figure robed in crimson. Ariaric, Wraxilan, Lion of Oomar or Oomadrah, what did it matter? I had found him. That was all. He appeared to be deep in meditation, his hair unbound, but ropy with oil. I crept up behind him, cat-footed, unsure of what I would say or do. He raised his head, but did not turn around.

"I did not think you would come," he said. "I hoped you wouldn't."

So these were the first words. Disappointing? What had I expected? Surprise for one thing.

Ariaric sighed and got to his feet, his knees cracking. He faced me, rubbing his eyes. "Cold in the marshes," he said, smiling. "I've seen too many battles, I think. Perhaps I've outgrown them, or is that a euphemism for saying I fear I'm growing older?"

"No-one will know that until some poor har dies of old age," I answered. "All the hara I've know who have died have met, shall we say, untimely ends?" (Flying bone, blood, a scream, a horse's scream. No! I deny this image.)

The Lion of Oomadrah nodded and chuckled to himself. He did not hear my thoughts. "A point well taken, my friend." We looked at each other. He shook his head. "Ah, Cal, we cannot meet as strangers." He held out his arms to me and we embraced as brothers. I felt like weeping. This was not happening at all how I'd planned it. Ariaric grunted affectionately and then held me away from him. "In meetings hearts beat closer," he said.

"In blood," I responded.

"In blood," he added quietly. His hands dropped to his sides. Now he could think of nothing to say.

"Do I take it you were expecting me then?" I asked. Why on earth I hadn't anticipated that, I cannot understand.

"It was a . . . possibility," he said guardedly. "Look, we cannot speak here. We'll go somewhere more comfortable. Please." He indicated the door.

"One thing," I said, facing the altar once more. "Why is it that the Archon of Maudrah pays homage to the image of Thiede the Gelaming?"

Ariaric stared at me for a moment. "Ah, he didn't tell you *that* then!"

"Tell me what?"

"Cal, all hara worship the Aghama don't they? Thiede *is* the Aghama."

A long time ago, a mutant runaway came alive into the city . . . Thiede? Frightened, and dangerous in his fear . . . (Thiede?!) Wretched, helpless, abused mutant freak. Our progenitor. Thiede. Reviled as vermin, revered as a god, full of hate and bitterness at his condition; it had flowered into an insatiable appetite for power. And he had succeeded. He had taken it, bleeding, with his bare hands from the under-nourished, pigeon-chest of mankind. Thiede. Yes, it made sense. By any god that still lived, the megalomaniac that styled himself our deity earned my respect in those moments. Whatever his faults, he had fought against incredible odds and won. Now, presumably, he was laughing. I don't blame him. It's a good joke. I could feel things beginning to tilt into place a little when the Lion told me that. Looking back, I don't think I was altogether surprised. I should have realized Thiede's mystique went beyond mere charisma. Many hara have that. Thiede was the first. He made us happen: Aghama.

"High-ranking hara of most tribes are aware of this now," Ariaric said, looking at the statue.

"Obviously I'm not high-ranking enough," I said. Ariaric looked at me quizzically.

"I hope you don't mean that."

"Of course I don't mean that." I laughed, a forced, harsh sound. "I have no tribe," Ariaric winced.

"Downstairs, please," he said.

So, now it appears that Thiede is truly the guiding force of Wraeththu. A concept that poses more questions as fast as it answers others. How would it affect me? I'd have to think about it.

As we walked together along lofty, paneled corridors toward his suite, Ariaric became formal. He apologized eloquently for the dismissive way in which Panthera and myself had been treated by his staff. "I hope you weren't insulted," he said, "but unfortunately only Fortuny and myself were privy to the information about your journeys in Jaddayoth."

"You're wrong there," I butted in, "there's nothing secret about it. Just about everyone seems to know. They know more than I do, in fact."

The Lion ignored these remarks. "Elisyin did not know," he continued smoothly. "I had hoped to be back in Sykernesse long before you reached Maudrah, but things have dragged on a little in Natawni."

"Trying to make peace were you?"

He smiled benignly at my clumsy sarcasm. "Trying to secure the border actually. Natawni would have the world believe that Maudrah are their wicked persecutors. They prefer to keep quiet about the lightning raids they make upon Maudrah territory, the thieving from Maudrah settlements, the frightening of their inhabitants. Not all Maudrah Hara are warriors, you know. Most are herders, especially in the North." He sighed. "However, I hardly think the differences between Maudrah and Natawni can be solved overnight . . ."

"There will always be differences, surely, as long as you insist on trying to make all of Jaddayoth Maudrah," I said. "How can you blame anyone objecting to that? Although you and your court live like kings, it's rather a different story for the hara down in the street, isn't it. Do you know how they live? Have you ever seen? Or is that the province of the Niz and beyond your control?"

"Our people are not unhappy," he answered vaguely. "When the time is right, their society will blossom. Winter-time is necessary, a time of replenishing. I'm sure I don't need to tell you that most Maudrah came from Megalithica originally, and had to leave it pretty quickly."

"Who decides when it's spring-time then? The Niz?"

"Yes." Such a direct reply surprised me. "Here in Sykernesse, we are privileged; I know that. In Maudrah hara are expiating the sins of the past. You were there, Cal; you should understand. It's a novitiate state; they are learning."

"Your education was rather different, wasn't it?"

He smiled ruefully. "I cannot argue with you, Cal, but you shouldn't really pass opinions on what you don't fully understand, should you. This way . . ."

He assumed I knew a lot more than I did, especially about himself. I wondered if I could find out what he had heard about me without giving my ignorance away. The last time we had met, he'd had me cast out into the cold night of North Megalithican society—if such chaos could be termed as that. He had been a big fish in a small pond. Now, both pond and fish had grown somewhat. He directed me through an enormous, dark doorway and closed it behind us. As I took in the grand opulence of the room, I was still talking, saying things that perhaps should have been kept for later, but I couldn't wait. The main reason I was there was to say them, after all.

"You've apologized for your people treating us with disrespect," I said, "but don't you think that now is the time to apologize for what you did to me in the past? A second-class suite of rooms can't really compare with being ejected into a burnt-out wasteland teeming with blood-hungry psychos, can it!"

Ariaric winced once more. Gracefully. "You have a long memory Cal."

"I've lived with it."

"Have you come all this way just to rake over old coals? The fire has been long cold, surely."

"Maybe, but I suffered first-degree burns from it, so did Zack."

The Lion stared at me thoughtfully for a moment. I wish I hadn't spoken; it had sounded so peevish, even if correct. I went to sit on the floor in front of the fire to escape his eyes. The rooms of a king; it showed. "So here we are," I said, looking fixedly at a green and gold tapestry hanging above the fireplace. "It seems Wraxilan is no more. His slate has been wiped clean so that Ariaric the Lifebreather can take his place. Are they that different?"

Ariaric laughed good-humoredly behind me. I heard the clink of glass.

"By Aghama, I really got to you once, didn't I!"

"Dear me, and there I was thinking the feeling was mutual."

He handed me a crystal glass over my shoulder. I could not feel his warmth; I was too nervous. I drank; a fiery spirit tempered by a cordial of lemon and herbs.

"Cal, I had a lot to learn. I learned it. There is nothing more to it than that. You've come a long way too, haven't you?"

"Have I? I had hoped to surprise you." I was deviating from the subject but he went along with it.

"You did. Satisfied? Even though I'd had word you might show up here, the moment I saw you tonight filled me with . . . what? Terror, shock, awe? Maybe all three. It took me back." *I know it did.* "A long way back. I want you to know that the choice you made then was the right one."

"Oh? Why?" I turned to look at him then.

"Well, after you . . . left the Uigenna, I chose another to host my heirs. We didn't know enough. I wanted a son too quickly. The har died. I'm glad you refused me."

I nodded. "Yes," I said.

"Did you ever regret your decision?"

I suppose that was brave of him, or completely egotistical. I wavered. I could not lie. "Sometimes," I said.

That must have satisfied him. He smiled. "Well, it's over now isn't it; all of it. You want me to apologize for kicking you out of the Uigenna? Are you sure? I'd say it was probably a blessing."

I raised my glass. "Let's drink to that." We drank for a moment in silence, then I said, "Elisyin is a perfect consort for you." I don't know what made me say it; I prefer not to think.

"I know," Ariaric replied smoothly. "He's given me three sons. All thoroughbreds like himself."

"Three? Oh, as many as the fabled spires, of course! How come only two of them were there tonight? Is the third out accruing more land for his noble sire somewhere?"

"Hardly. He's dead." He smiled gently. "Don't look like that. The earth won't swallow you, however much you try. I'm not offended. How could you have known? We all have our tragedies to live with."

"Don't we just!"

We looked askance at each other, over the goblet tops, between shuttered lids. We were strangers who thought that we ought to feel like friends. I was still wondering whether Wraxilan had moulted away from the core of Ariaric or had merely been hidden deep inside. The Cal that he'd once known had shed a hundred skins. Could he see that? I said, "I thought I was fighting a battle, but I wasn't, was I. All along, I've been doing the right thing. I was trying so hard not to as well. How depressing."

Ariaric may not have had the faintest idea what I was talking about, but he was too proud to admit it. He smiled only with his mouth and said, "Learning?"

"Is that what they call it? I've certainly suffered; maybe I've learned. Remember the past and how they used to say that no-one should be dragged onto the Path against their will? I feel I've been tricked, not dragged, but the principle is the same."

"Oh, come on, don't think you ever fooled me with that superficial, devil-may-care, live for today kick!" Ariaric scoffed. It was so honest; he meant it. "You've always been there, Cal, if only on the scrubby bits along the side. And the Path is *hard.*"

"You don't have to tell me that. Don't insult me. I just didn't want it. I still don't, but I've had no choice."

"Bullshit!"

"It isn't!"

"It is. You could have run away any time, surely."

"They said I couldn't."

"They? Who are they?"

I narrowed my eyes. "How much do you know about me?"

"Not much, but you obviously think it's important, so tell me."

"You're a bitch, Wraxilan."

He raised his eyebrows. So I told him. I began by saying, "You're not the only Wraeththu herd leader who's wanted me firm against their sweaty little flank, you know." It was the best way to tell it. Now it seemed like only gossip, all those secret thoughts I'd carried around with me for so long. Until I reached Jaddayoth. Shining country; I love you. I must also point out that at no time had I ever envisaged telling any of it to the Archon of Oomadrah. Now the blocks have been removed from my mind, it seems I have to gabble it out at every opportunity.

When I'd told him just about everything, Ariaric said, "You've never really fought it have you! The Elhmen, the Sahale, the visions, the Jaels. You must have loved it. Every minute. You still do. Why kid yourself? Being the center of attention has always appealed to you." Knife straight to the heart, as always. He hadn't really changed.

"Are you saying I'm enjoying this?"

He raised his glass at me. "Know thyself magician," he said. "You haven't spent much time in meditation have you. Why?"

"I have! Every evening once I returned to Jael! You don't know that you're talking about!"

"Oh, I think I do, Cal. Mainly because you haven't seen the blindingly obvious truth. I think you've only been skimming the surface; you're afraid of what you'll see in that beautiful head of yours, that's why. Funny. I never thought self-delusion was one of your faults. Other people, yes, but not yourself."

I was speechless with anger. Such arrogance! Such conceit! How dare he! I'd poured out my heart to him and he treated it as a self-indulgent joke. What made it worse was the infuriating grin he had on his face.

"Use these rooms as your own for a while," he said. "Just sit and think about what I've said. Do more than think about it; face that truth. Recognize it. You might find it will help. I'll be back later."

Ah, so he was a coward too! Were his observations so flimsy he had to leave the room? Obviously, he was afraid I'd knock holes in them. I seethed with fury. He left me alone for half an hour. I could have gone back to the second floor. I could have left the room. I didn't. I was numb. For five minutes, I didn't think anything at all and then I breathed. Deeply. Rhythmically. Drawing energy from the earth, sending it through my body; traveling inwards. OK, show me the worst, soul of mine. It did. And it hurt. But one thing I learned, that I'd known all along really; the answers weren't outside. No-one else was going to give them to me. *I* knew. It was in me somewhere. And Ariaric was right. A bitter draft to swallow, but swallow it I did. When I opened my eyes, I thought, "Pell, I want you. I have always wanted you." Any denials, any fighting I'd thought about were a sham. The truth was, I'd always wanted to go to Immanion, even in Thiede's tower, even on my darkest days in Thaine, but it had to be on my terms. Pride won't let me settle for anything less. I couldn't be the Tigron's lapdog because I knew I was worthy of equality. Pride? Yes, OK. A fault, maybe, but one that I knew. When I'd learend that Pell stil lived, my first feeling, after the shock, had been joy. I'd wanted to see him, speak to him, but something had gone wrong, got in the way. What? Just pride? Or something more? Once I knew that I'd have the answer to everything.

Ariaric came in softly. I was still sitting, cross-legged in front of the fire. He put his hand on my shoulder and said, "You still angry?"

I rested my cheek against his hand and said, "No."

He squatted beside me; we embraced. I found myself doing something I vigorously loathe. I was weeping. I said, "Stop me doing this," and Ariaric replied, "No, it is part of you. Live it."

Live it. We talked and drank and talked about all that happened to us, what we wanted for the future. Ariaric's story was an epic in itself and would take too long to relate. He told me he'd met Pell in Immanion.

"What's he like?" I asked. Here was someone who could really tell me.

Ariaric stretched out on the floor, held his glass to his chest and closed his eyes. "Let me think," he said, "I want to get it right. He's got black hair."

"No! Really?"

"Indeed. I liked him, even though he was rather cross with me and called me a, what was it?, 'menace to all free-thinking hara.' He was right of course. I've learned since then. I was too full of revolutionary zeal and images of Uigenna atrocities. Progression was impossible when I was so full of self-loathing. Pell taught me that. He's frightening in a way because you can't see the steel inside him on the surface."

"Really? Strange, I would never have described Pellaz as being steely, ever!"

"You must remember many years have past since you last saw him, Cal. Perhaps you should prepare yourself for the fact that he might be a completely different person now."

"I have thought about that, obviously. I wish I knew more. Prepare me; tell me what you know."

Ariaric smiled, stroked my hair. "I don't envy you," he said.

"That bad is it?"

He shook his head. "Don't get me wrong. What I'm saying is I'm finding it very hard to equate the Pellaz you've told me about to the one I've met. They seem like entirely different people."

"You sound like Panthera. He said something similar to me about you."

Ariaric laughed. "And have I turned out to be a monster?"

"No, but you used to be. Is that how you'd describe Pell then, a monster?"

"Yes, I suppose I would, in a way. Oh, not because he's fearsome to look at or malign or tyrannical, but because he has such power. You can almost see it, simmering inside him. Of course, I didn't get much opportunity to speak with him alone, but on my last night in Immanion, I was invited to dine with him . . . and his consort. Pellaz spent most of the evening talking about Megalithica. Sorry, but your name wasn't mentioned once."

"The consort . . ." I began.

"You'll probably see," Ariaric said carefully. "The Tigrina is paying us a short visit very soon."

"How soon?"

"The day after tomorrow. Of course, you could leave before then if you prefer . . ."

"Are you serious?"

Ariaric shrugged. "You may not like what you see. But you're welcome to stay."

As if I could leave!

It was nearly dawn when I went back to the rooms I shared with Panthera. My companion was nowhere in sight but there was a note which read, "Cal, you're so predictable" left on the pillow. I was piqued; it was unjustified after all. Aruna-type thoughts hadn't even crossed my mind when I'd been with Ariaric. I tried to sleep, but my mind was in turmoil. Pell seemed nearer to me. I wanted to see him now, this instant. I wanted to go to Roselane tomorrow, Immanion tomorrow. I also wanted to stay in Oomadrah so that I could see the Tigrina. I wondered if he knew about me too. If he did, it would be a confrontation that I'd relish. My claws were out. What was happening?

CHAPTER TWENTY-FOUR

>—·<>—·O—·<>—·<

The Arrival of the Tigrina

"Then hate me when thou wilt; if ever, now;
Now, while the world is bent my deeds to cross,
Join with the spite of fortune, make me bow . . ."
—*William Shakespeare, Sonnet X*

Our bags remained packed. Panthera reappeared late the next morning;
I did not ask him where he'd been. The news that I wished to remain in
Sykernesse for a further couple of days did nothing to dispel the atmosphere of furious gloom that Panthera brought in with him. He did not ask
me why, obviously having drawn his own inferences, which were undoubtedly way off the truth. Admittedly giving in to him, I said. "Thea, the
Tigrina is arriving in Oomadrah tomorrow. I want to be here." He skew-
ered me with a withering, condemning stare. Silence. "You think I'm
wrong then?"

He shrugged. "Do what you like. I'm only along for the ride. As a
matter of fact, I don't mind staying on in Sykernesse myself for a while,
perhaps even after you leave for Roselane. If you ever do!"

I realized we were having an argument. "Thea, I did not take aruna with
Ariaric last night, if that's what's bothering you."

"Not at all," he replied smoothly. "I'm in no position to censure you."

I drew my own conclusions from that, even though they did seem rather
unlikely. I wondered who had been the privileged har to spend the previous
night in Panthera's arms. It was not a train of thought that particularly
thrilled me. Maybe I'd taken him for granted; my personal property because he was too scared or revolted to seek warmth from somebody new.
Ah well, it seemed I'd been wrong. It caused a weird kind of tearing feeling
inside me, as if the air was too big to fit into my lungs.

"I was telling the truth," I said. "I'm sorry I wandered off like that last
night. I had to talk to him. Can't you understand that?"

Panthera did not answer me. He took some clothes into the bathroom
to get changed, emerging some minutes later to announce, "I'm meeting
Lalasa now. See you later perhaps." Then he was gone, and the door didn't
even slam.

Ariaric sent for me around lunch-time. I'd spent the rest of the morning
mooching about, realizing I really didn't relish having to travel on to
Roselane alone. I'd got used to company. Lonely journeys reminded me
too much of how I'd been before Thaine, and then I'd been out of my skull

most of the time. I thought the hours were going to hang heavily over my head during miles and miles of sobriety. But how could I blame Panthera? Wasn't it entirely possible I'd discard him at a moment's notice should the outcome of all my traveling and soul-searching bode well for the alliance of Calanthe and the Tigron of Immanion? I can be despicable, yes, but not that despicable. Perhaps it would be best if Panthera and I did part company now. I dragged this mood along with me to the Lion's apartments, furiously wishing I hadn't when I saw who he'd got sitting around his dinner table with him. The gracious Elisyin, his two sons and Wrark Fortuny. Elevated company, in fact the best Sykernesse could provide.

"Is your friend not joining us?" Elisyin asked politely when I was shown into the room alone.

"No, I'm afraid he'd already made arrangements for the day when I received your invitation."

"What a shame."

"Yes, isn't it."

I took my allotted place and proceeded to grin and grimace my way through the meal. Ariaric passed me one or two shrewd glances, but made no comment. He probably thought I was worked up about the imminence of the Tigrina's visit. Elisyin went through the whole procedure of apologizing for his dismissive treatment of me.

"I had no idea you were a friend of Aric's," he said. "You should have mentioned it."

"I would have, but I'd been advized against it," I replied. "I thought all visitors of suspect origin were swiftly sent on their way."

"They usually are," Ariaric agreed. "Otherwise I'd be swamped with useless Uigenna rejects all hoping for a ride on my back. It's happened before and will no doubt happen again."

"Would you like to change your rooms?" Elisyin asked. "We have better suites available."

"No, it doesn't matter."

I waited until half-way through the meal until I asked the most important question. "Was it the Gelaming who told you I might come here?" There was a moment's silence, and then Fortuny cleared his throat. He had hardly spoken before.

"No, it was Tel-an-Kaa," he said.

I could tell he was waiting for a reaction. The name was familiar, but I could not place where I'd heard it before. "Tel-an-Kaa? Should I know him?"

"Not a 'him'," Fortuny corrected, "a 'her'."

"Of course!" I exclaimed. "The Zigane tribe of humans and hara! She was with them in Galhea, before Swift and I traveled south to the Gelaming. I can't see what she has to do with me though. What's the connection? I know she was some kind of messenger and presumed she worked for a high-ranking harish adept. She wouldn't let on."

"No, she probably wouldn't have then."

"She must be very old now, surely."

Fortuny shook his head and swilled his mouth with wine. "Not in the sense you mean," he said. "Tel-an-Kaa is a parage of the Kamagrian."

"A what?"

"The Kamagrian are an order of adepts, a parage of one of their number."

"An order of humans?" I couldn't help scoffing.

Fortuny never changed his expression. "Far from it."

"Then what? And what is their interest in me?"

"Your questions will all be answered in Roselane," Fortuny said mildly, raising his hands at my swift intake of breath. "Yes, I know. You must have been told that a hundred times, but it is true nonetheless. All we knew was that you were having some kind of . . . bother with Thiede and the Gelaming. We often have dealings with the Kamagrian, usually via Tel-an-Kaa. I think we were told about you so your journey wouldn't be inadvertently delayed by misunderstandings."

"What are the Kamagrian?" I asked again. The Niz and Ariaric exchanged an agonized glance.

"Maybe, after Roselane, you will be able to tell us," Fortuny said.

"Oh, another secretive lot are they! You know what I really object to?" I waved a fork across the table at him. "The fact that so many people seem to know much more about me that I do. Why should anyone tell you my business? It was only a spur of the moment decision that I came here at all! It seems like I'm being watched. Is that the case?"

Ariaric burst out laughing and everybody looked at him. "Was it really a spur of the moment decision, Cal? Was it really? Do you mean to say that someone who knew quite a lot about you couldn't have simply guessed you'd call in here on the way east?" His amusement made me uncomfortable, especially in front of Elisyin who had raised one eyebrow speculatively.

"Well, maybe not," I grumbled hotly. "but that doesn't alter the fact that my path through this country seems to have been completely predetermined as if I've had no choice in it at all. Why? It's been like a wild goose chase, a waste of time. Couldn't all my progression have been seen to in Roselane if it's so necessary? I've been played with, cat's-pawed around. Is it unreasonable that I object to it? Even if it has been intimated that it's all for 'my own good.' That's no comfort! You might think I've enjoyed it all Aric, but there have been moments of hell, sheer hell!" They let me rant on in this vein for several minutes until I exhausted my vocabulary of complaint. It didn't escape me that Ariaric must have spread my life story around his whole family either. Both of his sons were looking very embarrassed, but they knew what I was talking about alright.

"You feel you have to blame someone obviously," Fortuny said, to break a rather painful silence.

"You know, I actually envy you," Ariaric said, leaning back in his chair. "Look at me, trying to carve my name upon the stone of Wraeththu history, whilst yours is there already it seems. Burned upon it indelibly, and without you even trying!"

"And what does it say after my name do you think? Calanthe: was once a nuisance, but everybody got to hear about it?" They all laughed at that.

"Perhaps, but I think it will say, Calanthe: conscience of kings." Ariaric decided, pleased with himself.

"Oh, does that explain why I don't have a conscience myself then?"

"Haven't you?" Elisyin asked innocently. It didn't fool me.

"Let him answer that in a year's time," Ariaric replied for me. He raised his glass. "A toast: to Roselane," he said. "Our hearts will go with you, Cal. Whatever your destiny is, it concerns us all. Isn't that right, Fortuny?"

The Niz smiled slyly. "There is no doubt of that," he said. "No doubt at all."

All they'd heard were rumors; of that I was sure. Their knowledge was incomplete. I got the strange impression that all these tribe leaders who'd played their part were counting on me for something. What?

I only went back to my room to sleep, the whole day having been spent with Ariaric and Elisyin. I envied their closeness. Sometimes, I forgot entirely who Ariaric had been. It was good to see him again though, the only person, apart from Zack perhaps, with whom I could reminisce about the bad old times. We had been lucky to escape with our lives. Even luckier to escape with our sanity. We had both changed since the days of the Uigenna; perhaps that was why I could forget our last meeting. It wasn't ignored though. We could say, "Oh, we were children then!" and laugh. If I could have looked into the future back then and foreseen this meeting, I would never have believed it. Panthera didn't come back to our room again that night. He obviously hadn't been there all day either; the place felt deserted. I tried not to feel anxious about it, telling myself there was no point, it was best this way, etc., etc. I drifted into a sleep crowded by neurotic dreams, in which the lovely Panthera played a very strong role.

I got out of bed early and shot to Ariaric's apartments for breakfast. I wasn't sure what time the Tigrina was expected, but I was going to make damn sure I was by the Archon's side when he arrived. Wonderful lurid fantasies paraded through my mind. The Tigrina knowing who I was immediately. A fantastic argument ensuing with me emerging triumphant, a defeated Tigrina accepting my victory and fading away to some far land. Me killing the Tigrina by poison so no-one could suspect me; him dying horribly in front of the entire court of Sykernesse. Such were the gist of my dreams. Obviously, I have never properly grown up. Ariaric had Elisyin with him; they were breaking their fast in bed together. I waited impatiently, only picking at the food Ariaric's servants set before me. By ten o'clock, the Archon and his consort emerged from the bedroom. I'd been frantically waiting for nearly an hour.

"Don't appear so eager," Ariaric said to me. "Knowing your history, I'm not sure whether it's a good idea to let you loose on the illustrious Tigrina . . . I hope you won't betray my hospitality by misbehaving."

* * *

Caeru Meveny, consort to Pellaz-har-Aralis, Tigrina of Immanion arrived
in time for lunch. To give the people of Oomadrah a fine spectacle, Ariaric
had arranged for a lavish procession of horses, warriors and Niz to accompany this visiting dignitary from the south gate of the city to the palace.
Ariaric and his court would wait upon a balcony on the outer wall of
Sykernesse itself, too high up for the Tigrina to hear him say "hello," but
of ample height for Ariaric and Elisyin to be shown off to their people. It
would be good politics for the Tigrina to report the Maudrah's devotion to
their Archon back to Immanion. Ariaric would use every opportunity to
show how popular he was with them.

I couldn't see very much, having been hustled to the back of the balcony
by jostling courtiers. It didn't matter. I wanted my first view of Caeru to
be closer than this anyway. Hysterical cheering coming from the direction
of the south wall presaged the arrival of the Gelaming party. It came closer
and closer, an eery sound, almost like misery rather than joy. To me it
sounded like a vast and moaning animal approaching Sykernesse from the
south, getting louder and louder, until I had to fight an urge to run. Once
the Tigrina was beneath the balcony, the voice of the city had become
deafening. It was like a nightmare; all those repressed souls giving tongue,
going mad. They weren't allowed to do that very often.

I backed away and descended the dark, stone stairs to the courtyard
alone. It seemed deserted, with all noise coming from the city beyond. Only
a few whispering servants around. Everyone was on the battlements and
the balconies. I stood in the sunshine and watched as guards turned the
wheels that opened the vast, wooden gates to the palace. Creaking, turning.
They were rarely opened. Smaller doors within the gates themselves admitted daily traffic. First came the soldiers on horseback. The animals hadn't
moved faster than a trot, I'm sure, yet they were sweating and snorting as
if back from a gallop. This was backstage. Hara dismounting, laughing,
calling to each other, lighting cigarettes, away from the public eye. Then
came the Niz. They spoke together in low voices, drifting toward the main
entrance in clumps. Now the courtyard was beginning to fill up with hara
as the people of Syknernesse came down from the walls. I didn't want to
be too prominent. I hung back.

The first of the Gelaming came in through the gates. Huge, white horses,
not even faintly damp, gentle eyes sparkling with humor, manes as soft as
harish hair. The riders wore thick leather armor, like insect carapaces,
carrying their helmets on their saddles before them. These were hara chosen
for their yellow hair, which they wore loose over their shoulders; the
Tigrina's elite guard. All Arahal clones, I thought peevishly. Gelaming
always make me feel inadequate. They seem so *big*. Tall, confident, beautiful and brilliant. Still, they fascinate me too. Must be a perversion on my
part. The Tigrina came in surrounded by his aides. He looked so much
smaller than I'd expected. Perhaps his horse was just larger than the rest.
Apart from that, all that struck me was his incredible white-gold hair, a

huge mane that Ariaric would once have envied, as light and soft as feathers. I couldn't really see anything else. Ariaric and Elisyin descended from the balcony and the gates were closed upon the city. I watched as the Archon and his consort walked slowly up the wide steps to the palace with Caeru between them. They all looked as if they were very good friends. Caeru was skinny, I decided uncharitably. Small and skinny. I followed the party at a distance.

CHAPTER TWENTY-FIVE

➤━┼━◆➤━━◯━◄◆━┼━◄

Caeru

"He that can love unloved again,
Hath better store of love than brain."
—*Sir Robert Ayton, To an Inconstant One*

A banquet had been prepared in Caeru's honor on the second floor of Sykernesse. I had been lucky to secure a seat in the main hall because all the rooms were full to capacity. High-ranking hara from every Maudrah town appeared to have converged on Oomadrah for the day. I tried to see if Panthera was around but that was impossible. Sykernesse being so large, I could have walked round that crowd all day and not seen someone familiar. No-one could get near Ariaric or Elisyin, so that it was with relief that I spotted their youngest son Zobinek speaking to one of Elisyin's valets at the door to the main hall.

"Will I have difficulty getting in here?" I asked. "I believe your father did reserve me a seat."

"Not if you walk in with me," Zobinek replied cheerfully.

I felt it would give him considerable prestige in the eyes of his friends to walk into that room with someone like me on his arm. I'd done my best in the grooming department for most of the morning and the results were so stunning I barely recognized myself. (Would I have to preen myself like this every day if I lived in Almagabra?) Ariaric certainly had a sense of humor; he had me sitting right on the top table. I could have easily spat at the Tigrina and scored a direct hit. Zobinek sat beside me and pointed out the various personalities of interest.

"See him," he said, pointing discretely to a venomously glamorous Har further down the table. "That's Lissilma the Kalamah. He killed my brother Ostaroth."

"What! *And he dines on the high table in Sykernesse!*" I was amazed.

Zobinek nodded. "Yes. He was Ostaroth's consort. It's a long story, but my father didn't think Lissilma was much to blame."

"What does Elisyin think about it?"

Zobinek shrugged. "He can't dispute Ostaroth asked for it. He treated Lissilma abominably. Kalamah are like cats, you see. You can be tickling their stomachs one moment and it's all purrs, the next . . . psshht!" He clawed the air expressively. "It's best not to upset them."

All this was effectively taking my mind off the presence of Caeru, perhaps a deliberate ploy on Zobinek's part. He clearly fancied his chances with me. A well-worn circumstance. Give me a chimaera to pursue any day. Caeru appeared to be utterly at ease with the royal family of Maudrah. I could hear him laughing. We were served the first course; spiced shellfish. Zobinek stopped talking so he could eat. The thought of food in my mouth repulsed me. I was thinking, "That creature is Pell's. He took my place," but even as I thought it, it didn't seem real. I had been told about the state of their blood-bond; it was ridiculous to feel jealous, except perhaps because Caeru had all the prestige and status that went with being Tigrina. Thiede had said he was good at his job. Could I have carried it off so well? I admit to vanity. Maybe I'd have enjoyed being fussed round, having people think I was important. At least I was being honest with myself now. I know I was staring; I wanted him to look at me. It took me nearly all the meal to get him to do it. He resisted my will, or he ignored it, but eventually, as Ariaric leaned back to speak to one of the servants, Caeru scanned the table and caught my eye. I have hardly ever experienced such a feeling of triumph, even as I realized how grossly I was overreacting to the whole situation. He looked puzzled. Perhaps he thought he knew me from somewhere. A brief, uncertain smile wavered upon his lips. He had an innocent kind of face, high-cheek-boned pretty, but wistful. I wished he could have been razor sharp like Cobweb, suave like Elisyin or recklessly carefree like Lahela. Just not this; haunted. I looked away and realized Ariaric had been watching me for some moments. A wary expression. The Tigrina whispered in his ear. It *had* to be about me. Had to.

Later, Ariaric hosted a small (fifty hara) gathering in his personal suite on the third floor. Zobinek dragged me along, although I was no longer sure I wanted to go. I felt bruised. My journey must be resumed. I must forget this. For a moment, however brief, as I looked into his eyes, I had put myself in Caeru's place. I imagined the pain of fear, of loss. Such eyes as his expected it at any time. Yes, I actually felt guilty. Strange, isn't it. I told Zobinek that I had to find Panthera. "We are leaving soon," I said.

"Oh, not yet, surely!" Zobinek replied. "Anyway, Panthera may well be there. You never know. Come on; let's enjoy ourselves!"

Ariaric's suite was a riot of loud conversation, smoke and laughter. Zobinek forced a drink on me. He had drunk rather too much himself. I was grateful that, because of the crush, I couldn't see the Tigrina at all. With a bit of shuffling, I managed to squeeze Zobinek up against the door, thinking that was the safest place to stand. He obviously misconstrued my intentions, but being a sybaritic creature. I've never objected to having my backside stroked, so it didn't really matter.

"You are like him in several ways," Zobinek said, with half-controlled slurring.

"Like who?" I humoured sweetly.

"The Tigrina."

"Oh?" I tried not to sound cold. "In what way? I'm ten foot taller than him surely, and at least twice as lovely!"

Zobinek laughed. "You may be right. It's just a feeling, and the hair of course."

"Same color. That makes us blood brothers does it?"

Ariaric's son grinned mischievously. "You want to meet him?"

"No. Do you?"

"I will. Later. Why don't you want to meet him? Aren't you curious?"

"Zobinek, I'm curious about ghouls, cannibals and people who believe they are werewolves, but I can't say I'd want to meet one. Just leave it!"

"You do really though, don't you?"

"Is this irrepressible youthfulness or just crass stupidity?"

"Neither; clairvoyance."

I rolled my eyes. "Don't be loathsome, Zobinek. Just get me another drink will you." He left me standing on my own for some minutes and then pushed his way back through the crowd, beaming happily. As far as I could see, he was not bringing me a drink. I sighed as he grabbed my arm. "The wine, witless child! Have you forgotten?"

He ignored my remark. "Come on!" he said, dragging me behind him, me still clutching an empty glass.

"Come on where?" I stumbled, bumping into people as he hauled me along. A drink splashed over my leg; somebody glared at me. Zobinek was relentless. I could see Ariaric standing with a group of Niz behind a vast sofa of black and gold brocade. Sitting on one end of the sofa were Elisyin and Caeru, with a cluster of hara around them who were all grinning like imbeciles.

"Zobinek!" I hissed. "Let me go!"

"You wanted to meet him, didn't you?" Ariaric's idiot son said happily. "I'll introduce you."

"No!" I hissed again. "No, Zobinek!"

"Don't be silly! Where are your guts?"

Somewhere in the back of my throat by the feel of it. This was going to be disastrous. I tried to escape but it was too late. Here was I, the beast who had relished the public humiliation of a certain Cobweb years before, struggling like a harling to escape an embarrassment that was far less harrowing really. Hara slid aside as we drew near to the couch, recognizing the Archon's son. It seemed as if I stood in the center of an arena.

"My lord Tigrina," Zobinek began. Caeru turned his startling, blue eyes upon us, smiling mildly. "May I present a good friend of my father's to you. He's been waiting to meet you." (Cringe). "This is Calanthe, formerly of Megalithica, currently of Jael in Ferike, I believe."

Credit where credit's due; the smile never dropped from the Tigrina's mouth, but his eyes told me he knew exactly who I was. He must have heard my name a thousand times. This was worse than the sick surprise I'd hoped to spring on Ariaric. I should imagine I must be about the last person that Caeru would want to bump into at a party. Whoever else in Immanion knew my every move, Caeru was not one of them.

He said icily, "How nice." A flush was creeping up his neck; the atmosphere was electric. Elisyin was looking daggers at his son.

"It is a privilege to meet you," I said, bowing slightly.

"For me too," the Tigrina replied, frost still hanging off his words.

Elisyin decided enough was enough. "Cal's glass is empty Zobinek," he said, "Take him to get a refill."

Gratefully, I let an abashed Zobinek lead me away again. I drank two glasses of wine in quick succession before sneaking out of the room while Zobinek went to the toilet. My heart was pounding. I could have smoked a hundred cigarettes at once, but one would have to do. Shaking, I paused in the corridor to light up. I was shaking too much. Then a considerate hand offered me a flame, which I made use of before looking up. The fact that the flame was offered without the use of match or mechanical means of any kind should have warned me. It didn't. I was in too much of a state. A golden-haired har with silver eyes blew on his fingers and smiled.

"My lord requests you attend an audience with him," he said.

Caeru must have reacted the minute I turned my back on him. I shook my head. "No, I don't think so. Convey my apologies, but it would serve no purpose."

"My lord thinks otherwise," the Gelaming insisted. I avoided the penetrating gaze. "Now. If you would be so kind." He directed the way with his hand.

"I have no choice, do I?"

"No. Sorry, but I have my orders."

Caeru's suite was the most splendid Sykernesse had to offer. Gifts from the Maudrah hierarchy were heaped on every available surface. I was left in the reception room to take all this in, while my escort went to tell the Tigrina I was there. He kept me waiting. I probably would have done the same. When he walked in, I wondered whether I'd been mistaken about his innocence. This was no melancholy victim. This was a har of stature who was plainly angry. He stood some distance away from me, hands on hip and demanded. "Well, was this planned?"

"What do you mean?"

The Tigrina snorted and flung himself into a chair. "Sit down!" he ordered. "Omiel, leave us!" His aide left the room quickly. "What are you trying to do? You think it's clever, throwing yourself at me like that? You think the Archon's cronies haven't heard the rumors flying about this godforsaken country? I don't like being embarrassed . . ."

What rumors?

"It wasn't planned," I interrupted him. "Just coincidence. At least on my part and your part." The implications in that only fueled his anger. He looked ready to explode. "I'm on my way east. Oomadrah was just a pause in the journey. I had no idea you'd be coming."

"Of course you didn't! Ariaric has some explaining to do, I can tell you!"

I couldn't reply, sure that whatever I said would only make things worse. Such restraint was doomed to be short-lived, I'm afraid. Caeru saw to that with his next remark. "Don't think whatever plans you and Thiede have hatched together can ever be successful," he said.

"Excuse me! There aren't any!"

The Tigrina sneered. "Oh yes. I've heard all about your lies! I'm not stupid. Recently, yours is the name I'm constantly hearing on everybody's tongue just as I walk into any room. The name I hear before whoever's talking sees me and changes the subject, I might add."

"That's just as much a surprise to me as it is to you, I assure you."

"Is it? Well, as a matter of fact, it isn't a surprise to me. What is it you want? Wealth?"

I had to laugh at that. "That's the most pathetic thing anyone could ever say to me! Do I want wealth. Are you mad? I think we both know what I want." I regretted that even as I was half-way through saying it.

The Tigrina's face had bleached from red to white. "I could have you killed," he said.

I shook my head. "I doubt it."

He rubbed his eyes nervously with one hand. "Why?" he said, and the wistfulness was back. "Why, after all this time? Can't you let it be? I've always dreaded this moment; you coming back into his life."

"I'm not. I'm not in his life."

The Tigrina slammed his fist down on the chair-arm. "Shut up! You are! You know you are! You always have been! I just can't understand why it's happening now. It's been so long. Is it the position you want? Is that it?"

"Caeru, I have no choice, really I don't. Whoever's behind all this won't let it be, and I don't think it's Pell."

Caeru glanced up at me. He looked wretched. "Don't call me by my name," he said hoarsely. "That's one thing I can prevent. I am Tigrina to you, for as long as I can be."

"That's not. . . . Look, I'm not angling to take your place, if that's what you think. I'm probably as confused as you are. I don't know what's going to happen, or where I'll end up."

"You're all that he said you were," Caeru said, unexpectedly. "I had hoped time and longing had blown up your image out of all proportion. It hasn't. When I saw you at table earlier you intrigued me. I actually . . ." He pulled a disgusted face, shook his head. "I asked Ariaric who you were.

'Just an old friend,' he said. 'No-one important.' " He laughed bleakly at the crushing irony in that. "I can understand what . . . people . . . see in you now. I wish I didn't. The image Pell has of you lives. Does that satisfy you? It doesn't mean you've beaten me, far from it. My position in Immanion is unassailable."

"How about your position in Pell's affections?" I couldn't help saying that, because whatever the answer, he was still by Pell's side and I was still the lunatic who'd murdered Orien and had to be kept away. The words struck home. If he hadn't been the Tigrina and groomed for his role, I think Caeru would have physically gone for me then.

"Get out of my sight," he said, softly, looking at the floor.

"I'm leaving Sykernesse in the morning," I said. "You won't have to see me again."

"Won't I? I hope you die, I really do. Now get out."

A more depressing, pointless interview is difficult to imagine. I found my way, somehow, back to my own room, my head in a whirl. I felt sure Ariaric would be displeased—no, furious—at the embarrassment I'd caused him. His fears had been justified. Yet it was Zobinek's fault really. I don't think I would have made my identity known otherwise, no matter how graphic my fantasies had been. To throw salt on my tender wounds, I surprised Panthera in bed with Lalasa. It was too much to bear. I just threw myself facedown on the coverlet beside them and groaned, much to their displeasure, I'm sure.

"Fuck the world!" I cried, muffled. "Fuck it! Fuck it!"

"Shall I go?" Lalasa whispered.

"No, stay and witness my immortal shame!"

"Cal, you're drunk," Panthera decided wearily.

"I'm not! Just cursed! The Tigrina wishes me dead and I die obligingly!"

"I really think I ought to go," Lalasa said again.

Panthera sighed. "OK, I'm sorry about this."

There was silence for ten harrowing minutes after Lalasa had gone until Panthera said, "You ask for it, Cal, you really do."

"Yes, I know. I'm utterly foul. Vermin! Diseased! But I still didn't sleep with Ariaric, Thea, so I don't know why you're angry with me. Or is it just lust for your cousin?"

Panthera sighed heavily again. "I only have one neck, Cal, and I suspect you're going to stamp firmly across its wind-pipe one day. I must be deranged. You want to leave tomorrow?"

"Desperately. Are you still with me?"

He took my hand, squeezed it. "Surprisingly, yes," he said.

Like a coward, I was going to sneak off without saying anything to Ariaric. A note would do; I couldn't face him. But he must have anticipated that because he came to our room in person just after it got light outside. Panthera excused himself and remained locked in the bathroom until the Lion had gone. I tried to apologize, but he didn't want to hear it.

"My fault too," he said. "Wasn't it me that suggested you stay? I didn't think Pell would have told Caeru about you. Stupid, wasn't it. Somehow, nearly everyone seems to know about you now. It was playing with fire. I also intend to beat several pints of blood out of my gormless son."

"Don't be too hard on him; he didn't realize the gravity of the situation," I said. "I hope it won't affect your position in the eyes of the Gelaming though. I feel bad enough about it without that."

He shook his head. "I really don't know. I'll do my best to butter the Tigrina up, profess my ignorance. It may work."

"Anyway, it should help not having me around. We're leaving today."

Ariaric didn't press me to stay. "You're on a hard path at the moment, Cal," he said. "My heart will be with you. We'll all pray things turn out for the best."

"Thank you." I stood up and we embraced. It was hard to let go. "Our reunion started so well. I'm sorry."

He took my face in his hands. "Sssh. Don't say that. It's like I said, hard times. One day, all this'll be over and you'll come back here and we can do it properly. OK?"

I nodded. "You've turned out well, you really have. It gives me hope."

He laughed at that. "Cal, Cal, I worked hard, that's all. We were all kids in Megalithica. It's so long ago. Let it go now. It can't be changed. Just let it go."

"Can I really do that?" Even to me, my voice sounded wistful.

"You can. Don't hoard all that feeling. Release it into something constructive." He held up his hand. "See this," he said. "It's yours; take it." Even after all this time, the scar was still there. Overcome by emotion, I took it in my hands and kissed it and kissed it. "The blood is long-dried, Cal. You can't take it to Roselane with you. Have this instead." We'd never shared breath. I'd not been worthy of such a caress all those years ago. He gave me strength. I took it eagerly. A true friend is the Lion. He always shall be.

The farewells were nearly done, Sykernesse nearly in the past. But there was one last question. "Wraxilan, what was your part in this? You did have a part didn't you?"

He stood at the door, smiling. "Of course I did. What harm can it do to tell you. Tel-an-Kaa said to me, 'Tell him my name. Tell him about me, that I know him, but before that, make him see himself.' She told me how. I wasn't that clairvoyant."

"Are you beholden to these Kamagrian then that you obey their orders?"

"No. I did it because of the other thing she said, and that was that Wraeththu's future is in your hands, Cal. Simply that. We need you, and we need you desperately. Could I need another reason knowing that?"

CHAPTER TWENTY-SIX

>─┤─◆>─◆─○─◆─<◆─┤─◀

Journey to Roselane
"Whereat I woke—a twofold bliss:
Waking was one, but next there came
This other: Though I felt, for this,
My heart break, I loved on the same."
—Robert Browning, Bad Dreams I

From Oomadrah, Panthera and I would travel east to beyond Chane, through a tongue of Garridan territory to Roselane. Our destination was the mountain retreat of Shilalama, high above the world. To speed up our journey, Ariaric kindly offered us the use of one of his private cars, complete with pilot. I was in two minds about accepting this offer. It meant we could be in Roselane within days. Overland, it could take weeks, even months, and that would give me time to think. Eventually, I decided that in my circumstances, time to think would be a bad thing.

We left Sykernesse before most people were even out of bed. It was a misty, chilly morning. I sat moodily in the back of the car, until I could stand Panthera's astute appraisal no longer and curled up, pretending to be asleep. I concentrated on the sigh of the vehicle's mechanisms, the feeling of weightlessness as we drifted slowly over Oomadrah's walls into the true morning, toward the plains of Hool Glasting. A mild humming indicated that the pilot had activated the car's roof. Soon we were cut off from the fresh air and with a shudder the vehicle sprang to life and shot toward the east. This was a much more sophisticated craft than Lourana's. Its speed was determined but effortless. We planned to spend the night in the Garridan borough of Biting; by mid-day tomorrow, if all went smoothly, I would be in Roselane. It was like facing major surgery. I was apprehensive but could not imagine it was really happening. I was still not sure what to expect, but it seemed like a good idea to seek out the cloisters of the Kamagrian, whom Wrark Fortuny had told me had their headquarters in Shilalama. I felt sick about my encounter with the Tigrina. Bad enough to be considered a gold-digging trouble-maker without having twinges of pity for the owner of those opinions. Just where would the Tigrina stand after all this? How could I tell, when I didn't even know what would happen to me? I curled myself around these uncomfortable thoughts and investigated them thoroughly until our pilot brought his vehicle down to land on the plains below, so that we could eat in the open air and perform whatever duties of nature had become pressing. The day had warmed up; now clear sunlight, shining through small, white clouds, dappled the plains with light and dark. I told Panthera in more detail what had happened the previous night. It didn't seem to matter that the pilot was listening avidly whilst pretending not to. My secrets were no longer that. By whatever means, the news had seeped out in Jaddayoth and spread; my alliance with the Tigron was known and it was expected that upheaval would come of it.

It was dark by the time we reached Biting. Our pilot booked us into an inn whilst Panthera and I stretched our legs around the town. Most of the shops were still open. We laughed at the blatant displays of the toxicologists. An establishment named Foul and Fair exhibited its wares in a well-lit window. 'Ash-wilt for the successful withering of limbs!' one advertizement boldly claimed. Yes, we laughed, but our joy was false. The performance progressed toward its final act, when the players might say their farewells and go their separate ways, never to meet again. We returned to the inn and took jugs of ale to our room. Now was the time for remembering.

Panthera talked of Piristil. "I can remember the moment I first saw you," he said. "Even then you smelled of freedom, my freedom. Have I ever thanked you?" We undressed and lay on top of the bed. Voices below; other lives carrying on oblivious. Panthera closed the window so that we couldn't hear it. "We are near the end, aren't we?" he said.

I sighed heavily. "I suppose we should hope so. Maybe you ought to feel relieved. After this, you can return to Jael and take up your life. You have friends in Maudrah, Gimrah, Elhmen and Sahale now. At least you've gained something from knowing me."

"Will you ever go back do you think? To the Hafeners, Nanine, the Lyris, Sykernesse . . . to Jael?"

"I would like to. I hope I can."

Panthera threw himself across me then, squeezing the breath from my lungs. "Oh, Cal, Cal," he said bitterly. "I wanted to fight for you, fight the Gelaming, the Tigron, whoever was there in the shadows. Back in Jael, I thought I could. But it's all too . . . big. I have no chance. I cannot lose you because I never really had you. You've given me so much, but if I want to share it, it must be with someone else, not you. That's hard. It's cruel. Why must we suffer? If there's a great power behind all this, why did it let me love you?"

I could feel his tears falling through his hair onto my chest. Part of life is learning to lose, to let go; something I was still learning about myself. "We must accept it, Thea," I said. "Whatever we do comes back threefold, or so they say. For this pain there must be equal sweetness waiting in the future."

"Do you really believe that?"

"I don't know. It's the best I can offer."

He laughed weakly, raised his head. "We must not waste these last hours," he said.

"No, my pantherine, we must not." We shared breath to share our souls' grief and in the communion of our bodies beyond that was a vast sea that was time and the Earth, but that sea had a salty shore and it was the salt of tears.

In the morning, we found that we'd adopted a determined good-humor. It must have come to us in the night; a gift from the angels. The ache of tears had become pleasurable, subdued. Now we went to battle with renewed strength. We left Biting immediately after breakfast. The car whistled through mountain peaks of gray and green and white. Clouds were sometimes beneath us. After some hours, the pilot pointed through the window. "That is Shilalama," he said. "Can you see? In the distance." We peered at the strange, craggy rock towers, catching the light from the morning sun.

"Looks like fungus," Panthera said.

"How long will it take to get there?" I asked.

"Half-an-hour maybe, not long."

Half-an-hour. Panthera and I clasped hands like children. I had to say, "Thea, if you want to go back to Maudrah with the car, I'll understand. Maybe it would be best . . ."

"Shut up, Cal," he said. "Stop playing the martyr. You might need me here."

There was no easy place for the car to land in Shilalama. In some ways it strongly resembled Shappa with its vertical streets and tiny plazas. But where Shappa was gray and smooth, Shilalama was pink and russet and yellow, and rugged. We circled the town a couple of times, flying very low. Hara looked up and waved. Everyone was dressed in pale robes like priests. The pilot was concerned. "This car is too big to land here. I'll have to put you down beyond the walls. Do you want me to wait at all?"

"No. We don't know how long we'll have to stay here," I answered. We were dropped off on top of a cliff, where a brisk wind whipped away our words.

"Down there!" the pilot yelled. "There's a track to the town." We called back our thanks. "Good luck!" he mouthed and then the car was lifting, dipping, heading west, its transparent roof sliding forwards as it increased in speed. Panthera and I watched it until it had vanished in the distance. No going back now. We pushed our way through stiff knee-deep bushes and scrambled down the stony path, hampered with luggage.

The gates to Shilalama were open; no guards to question travelers or stop us entering. "Where do we go?" Panthera asked. It was impossible to tell whether the buildings were houses, inns, shops, temples, or just natural rock formations. Two Hara drifted past, heads lowered, hands in sleeves, humming to themselves. They ignored my inquiry about directions. "Let's just make toward the center," I said.

"What center?" Panthera asked, looking around. "It's such a jumble."

"Just keep walking."

There were few proper streets. Rock buildings seemed to have been hollowed out or thrown up at random. Any Roselane we came across seemed to be on another plane and unavailable for communication. Where were the waving hara we'd seen from the air? The wind was making such a racket, we couldn't listen out for sounds of activity, but eventually, after an age of aimless walking, we came to a small square where market stalls were set up, and hara of more alert mien were wandering among them. I went to the nearest stall and asked to be directed to the cloisters of the Kamagrian, though how we'd fare following directions in this place, I didn't know. "Just keep going," the stall-holder answered, pointing across the square. "All paths lead to Kalalim."

"Kalalim?"

"Your destination. Pause a while and refresh yourselves first. No charge." He offered us cups of steaming herb tea. Panthera set down his bags and rubbed his shoulders. Mine were numb. As we drank the tea, I tried to extract information about the Kamagrian.

"Is there any particular way we should behave? Any rituals to observe?"

"Just be your own true selves."

"I see. Do we have to be announced or can we walk right in?"

"There are no locked doors in Shilalama. Have you come far?"

"Very," I said, darkly.

The stall holder smiled. "You are tired travelers. The comfort you seek shall be found in Kalalim."

We thanked him and crossed the square.

Kalalim was unmistakable. The stones of its sheer walls were golden, its crazy towers higher than any other and twisted like cable. Warmth seemed to seep from the very stones, welcome from its open doors and pointed windows. Panthera and I didn't stop to take it in properly, but walked directly up the shallow flight of steps into the golden gloom beyond. A har dressed in pale lemon robes stood up when we came into the hallway and put down the book he'd been reading. "Can I be of service?" he inquired.

"I'm looking for a parage of the Kamagrian named Tel-an-Kaa," I answered. "I believe she may be expecting me."

"You have come to the right place." The Roselane went to a desk by the wall and picked up a heavy ledger. "May I have your names please?"

"Calanthe and Panthera of Jael."

The Roselane nodded. "Ah yes, you *are* expected." He entered our names on the top of a new page. "Well, I won't keep you waiting. Come with me please."

We followed him down a skylit passage that led to a garden sheltered from the wind. Hara were working among the flower beds. Every one of them looked up and wished us good-day. Rather different to Oomadrah beyond the walls of Sykernesse, I thought with amusement. The Roselane showed us into a pleasant, airy room that overlooked the garden. The only furnishings were cushions and rugs upon the floor, a couple of low tables and a book-case next to the window. A brass censer hung from the ceiling, exuding a strong, aromatic smoke.

"If you would like to relax, I will tell Tel-an-Kaa you have arrived."

Groaning, I eased my bags off my shoulders, slumping gratefully into the cushions.

Panthera went to look out of the window. "What's going on here?" he asked. "Why should a woman have such a high position in Roselane? Who are the Kamagrian?"

"We can only wait and find out," I answered. "It's probably just a gimmick. I can't see me finding the answers to my problems here somehow. Its unreal. The Roselane seem to have lost touch with the real world. They're incomplete. Perhaps even weak."

"You are quick to judge, Calanthe!" A warm, musical voice. I turned to look at the speaker, started to stand. "No, you can stay where you are. I am Tel-an-Kaa. Perhaps you don't remember me." She came into the light, a yellow-haired waif, very similar to how I remembered her—and that had been quite a long time ago. Either she, or her master, were indeed very adept. To halt the human aging process requires great power. "I trust your journey was comfortable," she said, as if this was some regular visit of no importance whatsoever.

"Very, thank you," I replied. "The Lion of Oomadrah provided us with transport . . ."

"Yes I know." Naturally.

Panthera was staring at her quite rudely; to him she was an anomaly.

"You got here quite quickly," she continued. "Shilalama can be difficult for strangers to negotiate. Ah, refreshment. Thank you." A har came into the room behind her and set a tray down on the nearest table. Wine and cakes. Tel-an-Kaa sat down opposite me and poured the wine. "Won't you join us Panthera? I won't bite!" Such authority in a human was a little disconcerting. Panthera sat down gingerly beside me. I didn't really feel up to drinking wine (my stomach had enough acid to cope with as it was), but was pleasantly surprised to find it mild-flavored, gently sweet. "I expect you've been wondering what this is all about," Tel-an-Kaa said with a smile.

"Now and again," I replied.

She laughed. "All the secrecy, the moving about, it must have been very irritating but necessary all the same. Perhaps you realize this too now."

"I'm not sure I do. I must confess I sometimes wonder whether you've been picking on the right har."

"Oh, we haven't been picking on you! I'm sorry it felt like that. You were in such a mess, Cal. So damaged, so wounded. The healing had to take its course."

"Well, I'm here now," I said. "So what happens next?"

"You must dream."

"Dream?"

"Yes. You seek answers, but they are within you. They always have been. If this process had begun right after you saw Pellaz being shot in

Megalithica, well . . . it would have been a lot easier for you. That's when it should have happened, a similar education to the one Pell had."

"But it didn't, did it! What happened after that seems to have run up a karmic debt that I'm incapable of paying off."

Tel-an-Kaa laughed. "Oh dear, always the pessimist!"

"And what are you?" I asked. "Do I get an explanation for that? Why are you involved in my future?"

"I am Kamagrian," she replied.

"Is that a tribe? Is it the same one you were with in Galhea, the humans and hara together?"

"The Zigane? No. Kamagrian is not a tribe. It is a sisterhood."

"Human!"

Here she paused, uncertain. "No."

"Then what? You can't be harish."

"Not in the same way that you are, no."

"What do you mean? Was a way found to incept females after all?" That was incredible; too incredible to be true. If it was true, then all my conceptions about my race were about to be knocked off center.

"We are not Wraeththu exactly, neither are we human," she said.

"You're not explaining."

"I'm trying to. Listen. Wraeththu are hermaphrodite, mutated from the human male body. I say body because, as you know, the soul is androgynous anyway. It was found impossible for human females to be mutated in the same way. No-one knew why. Was it biological? Spiritual? Why? The female has always been the driving force of the universe. The Goddess is life itself, love itself. And as she manifested her love for herself, the Goddess begat the God. He the mirror image of she; her complement. Her son is also her lover. Wraeththu philosophers, once the dust of their inception had settled, wrestled with this concept in respect of their own race. They knew the Earth was female in aspect to the Sun's fiery male. Animals are still divided into two sexes. Everything has its negative and positive polarity. How was this new race to cope with its physical form, to understand it? Thiede tried to outlaw love, but he was wrong and thankfully realized it. Love is the fuel of life, the gift of the Goddess to her beloved son, who sprang from her alone, without father. Wraeththu too are the sons of the Goddess; androgynous, but in the image of the God. Kamagrian are few and far between, but are also hermaphrodite. Made in the image of the Goddess, but as complete as she in light and dark."

"Can the Goddess reproduce without the God?" I asked, somewhat cynically.

Tel-an-Kaa smiled gently. "Kamagrian are not blessed with the gift of procreation as Wraeththu are," she said.

"Then how do you . . . happen, if that's not a crass question?"

"Not at all. One in perhaps every thousand Hara is born Kamagrian; a sport, a freak. However, the first was born to a human being, like Thiede was, and around about the same time as well. Her name is Opalexian. She lives here with us in Kalalim. She is our High Priestess."

"If these Kamagrian are so rare, how do you find them? Do you have to go out and look for them?"

She laughed aloud. "Oh no!" As we have sacrificed the gift of bearing life, we have been blessed in other respects. The psychic powers of the Kamagrian are far greater than those of Wraeththu. Our people find us. We have no need to search. We have also found that it is possible to mutate human females to be like ourselves, although the process is not always successful. However, a failed inception in Kamagrian terms (unlike Wraeththu) does not mean death or imbecility. It simply fails to 'take.' The woman is as she was before."

"An advantage, but our way meant we only got the best."

"And how do you judge what's best? Physical endurance? Isn't that rather masculine?"

"No. I think you'll find the emotional and mental disturbance triggered the deaths, rather than the physical change. Does that screw your pious little theories up? You were human yourself once, weren't you?"

"You thought that did you!" She laughed. "It was a good disguise, that's all. Kamagrian aren't as obviously inhuman as Wraeththu are. When you met me in Galhea, I was collecting refugees from Megalithica, under the guise of the Pythoness, as they called me. Opalexian has a hand in everything. She is not overt, as Thiede is, more uninvolved, discrete, careful. Wraeththu is Thiede's domain. She has never sought to be a great figure in this new world of ours, but neither is she blind. She saw Thiede making mistakes and, much as she didn't want to, had to intervene. Opalexian sees Kamagrian as here for those that need us, but we do not like to advertise our existence."

"The Roselane know though. Will you be able to keep it a secret after this?"

Tel-an-Kaa shrugged. "Who can say? The way the world is at the moment, some Wraeththu may not be too happy learning of our existence. Opalexian wanted them to come of age before we interacted. Thiede has forced this to be otherwise. Never mind. We're survivors. We have to be. The Roselane began from humans and discontented hara that I gathered together in Megalithica under the banner of the Zigane. We all learn together. Shilalama is a place of contentment. A pity that the outside world needs our attention."

All of Tel-an-Kaa's disclosures were mind-boggling, to say the least. Wraeththu did not know as much as they thought they did. They worshiped the Aghama as a god, but now we discover he is neither immortal nor infallible. What were the mistakes Thiede was making? What had I got to do with it?

Panthera and I were given a room on the second floor over-looking the garden. It was simple but comfortable, the bed but a striped mattress on the floor, strewn with colored rugs. Tel-an-Kaa pointed out the shower room to Panthera. "Someone will be up shortly to show you around," she said to him. "I'm afraid I'm going to have to take Cal away now." She turned to me. "Unless you want to freshen up first?"

I shook my head. "No, let's get this over with, whatever it is. I've waited long enough." Panthera and I embraced in silence. There was little we could say. If and when I ever saw him again, it would be after all this was over. As I let him go, he said, "I'll wait for you here, Cal."

"No, not if it seems I'll not be back. Understand?" He nodded, looking so young and beautiful and sad. How could I leave him? Not without touching him again. I held him close and whispered in his ear, "Whatever else I feel for whoever else, I love you, Panthera. In my own way. I'll not forget you."

I picked up my bag of notes and small momentoes and followed the slim figure of Tel-an-Kaa down the stairs, across the garden, into a passage that led deep into Kalalim where no light came from outside. If Panthera watched me leave, I'll never know. I couldn't bear to look back. We thought we'd said goodbye, but now I know that this must come later, and with greater poignancy.

CHAPTER TWENTY-SEVEN

>─┤─◀▶─┼─Ο─┤─▶▶─┤─◀

Dreaming the Answers

"Farewell, terrific shade! Though I go free
Still of the powers of darkness art though lord:
I watch the phantom sinking in the sea
Of all that I have hated or adored."

—Roy Campbell, *Rounding the Cape*

As we walked into the dimness, Tel-an-Kaa asked me if I knew anything about the Roselane. "They are known as the Dream People," she said.

"I've heard that. Are the dreams prophetic?"

She nodded. "They can be, but mostly they are inner visions. Like those of meditation, but the trance is much deeper. This is the state you must achieve, to go into yourself. Usually, it takes years of training; you don't have that much time. The experiences in Jaddayoth, the attaining of Algomalid will help, of course, but I will take you in myself."

"In?"

"Yes, just in. You'll see. It will be a new experience for you, and I'm not sure how much I'll be able to help you should you run into trouble. You'll just have to try and listen to what I say."

"Thanks for the comfort! Isn't this rather a long way around though? It seems to me that the Kamagrian must know all about what's going on anyway. Why not just tell me? Wouldn't that save even more time?"

"And how much would you learn from that? You have gained much knowledge during your travels in Jaddayoth, enough to sort this out for yourself with the right help. The visions of Dream show you what is in your mind, as any trained meditator can do, but they will also show you things that are not in your mind as well. Other people's minds. From this you will gain strength, greater understanding. You will need it to deal with Thiede."

"Deal with Thiede? What do you mean?"

"Veils," she said. Very illuminating.

She took me to a small room that had no windows. Cushions upon the floor, a single lamp. "Make yourself comfortable," she said. I sat down. "We'll go right in. Is that OK with you?"

"Fine. I'm not very relaxed though."

"Then we'll attend to it." She smiled. "Don't worry. I'll help you."

It was all happening so quickly. Only a couple of hours ago, I had been sitting next to Panthera in Ariaric's car, flying above the mountains. In any other place, I'd have been given at least a few more hours (if not days) to settle in first. Wraeththu, generally, do not rush things.

"Lie back," Tel-an-Kaa murmured. She lit a nugget of charcoal in a brass tray and sprinkled it with pungent incense. "Close your eyes. Get comfortable. OK?"

I could hear the rustle of her robes as she sat down. Her gentle, clear voice talked me through a basic relaxation exercise, disciplined my breathing, opened my mind.

"This is the first stage," she said. "Normally you would not need to go beyond it. Let go, I will lead you." All that caste progression and struggle had borne fruit. My mind slipped easily from reality, through the veil and she was waiting for me. "Ready?" A voice without a sound.

I am falling, plummeting, down and down, faster and faster, almost catching fire with the speed of my fall. "Pull up!" Tel-an-Kaa commands. "Take control. This is not a visualisation." I "will" stop, and stop I do. We are in blackness. I cannot see the Kamagrian but sense her presence. "Make your world," she says. "Let it come."

My world. There it is, spinning slowly, silver and green, spinning, spinning, until it is a shining bullet and there's a horse screaming, flying blood and bone; rain and blood; red and white. No! The image disintegrates in rags, circling around me, still mewing. "Will you ever face that?" Tel-an-Kaa asks. My core aches with cold.

"Pellaz."

I hold his head in my hands. On his brow a single star of blood that goes back and back. His eyes staring up at the rain. Rain in his eyes and he never blinks. It was the screaming I hated the most. Those animals. Just mindless screaming. I lay him down on the wet earth and he becomes part of it, absorbed by the life-force. I look up. There's a spinning globe, green and silver, me on a red pony riding through a desert. Pellaz in a door way . . .

We share breath and the link is forged. (I knew he was different, always knew it. Others did too.)

I am walking down a narrow throat of rock, very dark. Doesn't smell too good either. I meet a har walking the other way, carrying a torch. He is robed in green, red hair, very beautiful. As we pass each other, he puts his hand on my arm. "You were deceived you know," he says.

"By whom?" I ask.

"Do you want to know? Then follow me." I turn around and walk behind him. The light from the torch is like a capsule; beyond it is black space. We come out onto a balcony, high above a city, and the torch in the red-haired har's hand has become a jewelled sword. "Take it," he says. "This is Phaonica." (Am I really here? Am I?)

"Where is the Tigron?" I ask. "Take me to him."

"Follow me." We walk along an opal collonade. Hara pass us by, hurrying alone or walking slowly in pairs. "Thiede has him," the red-haired har tells me confidentially. "He has the part of him that is yours."

"Who are you?"

"I am Vaysh. The Tigron's aide."

"Vaysh as I see him or Vaysh as he is."

"Reality in one context only. There are many."

We come to a white hall with a statue of glass in its very center. Within the glass is a figure, bound in black rope. It's head is thrown back, the mouth open wide in an endless scream of impotence. It is Pellaz. Must I free him? How? Obvious really, the tool is in my hands. The torch, the sword. Light and Air. No, I'm afraid. I cannot lift my arm. Around me the room becomes dim, all the light condensing into the heart of the statue. Tel-an-Kaa is at my side, dressed in fish-scale armor. "You must hurry," she says. "Thiede will sense you. He will come. You're not ready for that."

"Must I break the glass?"

"Do as you feel."

The sword is heavy in my hands. It takes an eternity to lift it. Then the air is full of chiming, of flying shards of light, stars spinning outwards, my face cut by flying glass and the statue is shattered. I can't remember doing it. I look around for Vaysh and Tel-an-Kaa but I am alone. Alone with the sinuously tumbled form of my beloved lying amongst the glass, cruelly bound. I kneel at his side. His eyes are closed. Black lashes against perfect skin. So young yet so old. This is but a dream. My lips against his brow where there is no scar. I cut the ropes and lift him in my arms. His clothes are dark and dusty. He is heavy. Through a dark doorway and into a garden, but all I am holding in my arms is a web of silk. I look behind me. There is no doorway.

In the garden, beneath a shimmering tree sits a woman. Her appearance changes with every passing moment. "Thiede fooled you," she says.

"What do you mean?" I ask and go to sit at her feet.

"You think he didn't want you to leave the tower?"

"He wanted me to return to Immanion."

"If you believe that, you deserve to be fooled," she says.

"It's just what I know. He wanted me to join the court." A wind comes up, suddenly, viciously, and the woman has become a black hag laughing in my face.

"Know this!" she screams "Thiede has to keep you and his Tigron apart at any cost! You helped him! Fool!"

I put my hands across my face, a reflex action. When I lower them, both garden and woman have gone . . .

I am underground once more. I think about what I've heard. The earth groans above me, the cracking of primordial stone bones. Why should Thiede have to keep us apart? Why?

"Because you are part of the same thing," a voice says from nowhere. "Light and dark. Malleable and unmalleable. Which is which?"

"And if we are part of the same thing, if we were united, would not our power be greater than Thiede's himself?"

"There would be no place for the Aghama in this world . . . *would there.*" The last two words are sly. A covetous longing. Can I trust my own visions? Cal, known for his lies, could lie to himself.

Vaysh appears beside me again. "Why linger here? He has waited and waited for, oh, so long. He has waited for you."

"He could have come to me any time."

"No, it does not work that way."

Then how does it work? I must tear these curtains of obscurity. Around me, a haze of gray, floating veils. I can barely see Vaysh through them. Just his bright hair, a smudge of green below. Where are we going? Does Pell know what I'm doing? He's so powerful; he must do. In that case, so will Thiede. I grow cold. "Control your thoughts!" Tel-an-Kaa's voice. She must be near. Vaysh takes my hand and leads me into a temple of light. Tel-an-Kaa is with us, brandishing a drawn sword. Her eyes are wide. I realize that Thiede must have been closer than I thought. "Where are we?"

"Within you, Cal." I see a glowing figure robed in star-rays. It is me. But a me beyond all that is possible. This me opens its mouth. A sound peals out that is the music of the world, holding within it all that lives, all that *is.* It takes time and yet no time at all for me to peel the music to its white-hot core. I find inside a moving nest of embryonic thoughts and hold each one up to the light of my being. It is so obvious. I laugh aloud and then I'm weeping and the radiance is raining down like tears. There are no answers because there are no questions. Only what is unseen. And now I see it. Simple because the great purpose is moved by something so small and earth-bound. Greed and jealousy. Wrapped up in clothes of righteousness, but now I see them naked. It is Thiede who should be seeking answers not me. And I know them too. Tel-an-Kaa says, "It is time" and it is indeed. Beyond the purple, sunset sea and the red sails of an eyed vessel, Phaonica shines on the horizon. It too is waiting. I am ready to fly but the Kamagrian holds me back. "Not that way, Cal. Earthly matters must be dealt with on the Earth. Follow me back."

I opened my eyes to a darkened room filled with the smoke of incense. Tel-an-Kaa raised her head, inhaled deeply. "It is done," she said.

"Thank you." It was not enough, but all that I could think of.

She shook her head. "No need for words, Calanthe. We are all traveling and must offer help to those we meet upon the Path who may need it." She stood up, smoothed down her robe, brushed back her hair. "Opalexian wishes to meet you," she said. "Later, at dinner."

"You don't rush everything then!"

Tel-an-Kaa laughed. "Took your breath away did it? No, not everything. But what point was there in waiting to know the truth? Your companion will be relieved. I think he feared he'd never see you again."

"A fear I shared. How long have we . . . been away?"

"Your friend Panthera has probably not yet dried off from his shower. Come along, I'll take you back."

She left me outside the door to our room. For a moment or two I lingered outside, almost too scared to go in. It was embarrassing appearing again so quickly. I need not have worried. When I opened the door, Panthera launched himself off the bed where he'd been drying his hair, and hurled himself against me. His pure joy at seeing me was humbling. A Roselane who introduced himself as Exalan came to escort us to dinner. He explained that he was Opalexian's assistant. The spring evening had become quite chilly. I felt cold walking through the garden.

Like Thiede, Opalexian is very tall, but where his hair is brilliant scarlet, hers is rich chestnut. I suppose they are quite similar in appearance though, except Opalexian is not as intimidating. This is quite deliberate on her part, as is the opposite on Thiede's. Dinner was served on low tables; we sat on the floor to eat. Panthera was quiet, almost dazed. I'd told him nothing of what I'd learned. Opalexian's apartments were no grander than any other rooms we had seen so far. Tel-an-Kaa had been waiting for us in the hall. I was grateful that she was there. I was afraid of meeting Opalexian. I was afraid of what she'd look like, but the power I feared merely allowed her to put us at our ease without effort. She greeted us warmly and inquired after my comfort. "You must not be afraid to tell us if there is a reaction to your experience," she said.

"I'm sure there won't be," Tel-an-Kaa added quickly, worried by my expression of alarm.

"You must feel you know me pretty well," I said.

Opalexian shook her head. "Not really. I have no desire to be that invasive."

"Yet you have monitored my every move."

"You make it sound so dramatic. It wasn't really. Perhaps the most manipulative thing we ever did was to influence the visions of Cobweb the Varr so that his son Swift took you with him to Imbrilim."

"Is that so! Why did Tel-an-Kaa bother coming to Galhea then if you could influence events from afar?"

Opalexian smiled. "True, I suppose. But at that time, we could only reach Cobweb. Swift was still grossly uneducated in caste progression. Do you really think Cobweb's visions would have been heeded if he'd ordered the pair of you south? Do you really think Cobweb would even have revealed them if we'd sent them? After all, it was he who wanted to keep you both in Galhea. No, it was too risky."

"And perhaps too slow," Tel-an-Kaa added. "The chances are Swift would have headed south eventually anyway, but we took the decision to speed things up a little."

"This was mainly because I had misjudged Thiede entirely," Opalexian admitted. She took a handful of spiced nuts and chewed them thoughtfully. "Warning signals were coming in thick and fast, so we had to get you to Imbrilim. I believed that once you actually made contact with the Gelaming, Thiede would realize that he should let events take their natural course. He didn't, wouldn't. By then our hands were tied; Thiede had you inextricably in his clutches. I truly didn't foresee all those years of incarceration he put you through. It would have caused too much of an upheaval for Kamagrian to have intervened overtly at that point; counterproductive. For that, I apologize. Thiede's proficient at keeping people in limbo. Mind you, without that talent, it's doubtful whether Pellaz would be alive now."

"Without Thiede's talents, he would never have faced death in the first place," I said. "At least not in the way he did."

Opalexian smiled. "Oh never doubt that Pellaz was meant to be Tigron of his people or that the method of making him so was correct," she said. "Thiede was right there. It was just you he was wrong about, and for selfish reasons."

I felt weightless. Suddenly everything was beginning to slide into perspective; everything.

"I can understand a little how Thiede feels," Tel-an-Kaa said. She turned to me. "In Galhea, you made me feel very uncomfortable, Cal. I could sense your ungoverned chaos. It frightened me. I kept thinking, 'By the Light, I hope I never have to cross swords with him!' I thought you'd see through my disguise and know everything before it was time."

"No chance of that the way I was feeling during those years," I said. "Chaos was a good word to describe me; there was very little else."

Now the sting was being drawn from my flesh; slowly. It was incredible. I could ask, and Opalexian would tell me. No more mysteries. But where to start? Obvious really.

"One thing you must tell me," I said. "How much does Pell know of what I was shown today?"

Opalexian sighed. "You must understand that Pellaz trusts Thiede more than he should. Mind you, Thiede can be convincing, as I'm sure you'll agree. Pellaz will tell you himself what he believes and it will be up to you to convince him he might be wrong."

"Does Pell know of the Kamagrian? You seem to know a lot about him. Surely he'd be able to sense your existence."

Again Opalexian shook her head. "No, neither Thiede or the Tigron know we exist. Our abilities are greater than theirs. We can hide very well. Only certain high-ranking hara of the Maudrah know of us and even then, don't know *what* we are. I have eyes and ears in Phaonica though; that was pure chance. Pellaz has a friend, a human female named Kate. He's very fond of her and was concerned about her future. He sent her to a group of ascetics in Almagabra for occult training, hoping she would learn how to prolong the life of her body and mind. It was there that one of our number encountered her and subtly persuaded her to take inception to Kamagrian. It was too good an opportunity to miss. Nobody female was that close to Phaonica's heart. Kate is not a fool, although at first she was suspicious that we might have been working against Wraeththu. It took a while to convince her. Pellaz does not know what she is. He believes her to be an adeptly trained woman. Eventually, he would have doubted that, as she continued not to age, but it would appear that Kamagrian will soon be out in the open anyway, so that no longer matters. I'm glad. It would have hurt her to move from Immanion as would, of course, have been necessary."

"Have you been responsible for everything then, all that time I thought the Gelaming were following me?"

Opalexian sat up and poured me more wine. "There is a lot that has to be explained to you," she said. "I appreciate what an enormous relief this will be to you. As soon as we realized Thiede had brainwashed you and let you out of the tower, one of our Roselane initiates was sent to keep an eye on you. It was necessary to watch you for a while to assess damage, to let your troubled mind settle down a little. Strange as it sounds, Piristil was more than we could have hoped for. You began to relax, free from obvious supervision. You began to examine the past, even though Thiede wanted you to forget it entirely."

"Excuse me," Panthera butted in. "Am I to understand that *my* being there was previously organized as well?" He'd gone very pale. I almost dreaded the answer. Opalexian and Tel-an-Kaa both laughed out loud. "Oh my dear child!" the High Priestess said, "I can see why you'd think that, but no, it wasn't. Lucky for you that Cal came to the same house. Lucky for us too. We couldn't direct his feet, after all! We were wondering whether we'd have to let our Roselane make direct contact to push Cal into traveling to Jaddayoth. Thanks to you, that wasn't necessary. You saved us an awful lot of bother, Panthera. You took Cal to Hadassah (even provided him with a genuine reason to visit the huyana in Jasminia), you guided him to Elhmen and Sahale. In fact, you effectively did more than half of the Roselane's job for him. That disappointed him quite a lot. He had his own karmic debts to sort out; Cal was part of it."

"Zack?" I enquired.

She nodded. "Yes, Zackala is one of us. He joined Tel-an-Kaa in Megalithica, not long after she left Galhea. We considered him a prize when we learned of his connection with you. A bitter young har, but we managed to sort him out eventually."

"Is he here?" I asked squeamishly. Somehow I didn't relish another meeting with Zack. More cowardice to be faced, no doubt.

"Oh, he's around somewhere, although I do need him out and about in the world most of the time. There's little chance of you running into him here, if that's what you are worried about! He's one of our best; indispensible." She leaned back in the cushions, smiling. "Yes, all the visions you were blaming the Gelaming for came from here. I hope you learned from them as you should. It was a sticky moment when that Mojag oaf had the knife at your throat though. You have Kate to thank for sending Arahal to you. It was difficult for her. She'd been supervizing your movements for us from Immanion; they have sophisticated thought amplification equipment, that allows for a much clearer picture of what we wanted to see. Kate was convinced you were going in the right direction. It seemed unlikely you'd run into your pursuers. When you did, she told us she panicked! Zack was too far away to be of any help at that time. Only Gelaming had the ability to get there quickly; to send Kamagrian would have blown everything. We still needed to remain unknown. Kate felt that only Pell himself would send you assistance. There was the chance that if Thiede knew about the situation he would simply rub his hands in glee at such a fortuitous way to get rid of you without dirtying himself. So Kate had to intimate to Pell that you were in danger without giving away how she knew. There was no guarantee Pell would even do anything about it. A sticky moment. She had to act fast. The Gelaming were your only defense. Using the oldest trick in the book she told him she'd had a vivid dream about you and dragged him to the thought transference unit to check if the details were real. Of course they were! He wouldn't look himself, but was concerned enough to send Arahal out. That really put the wolf into the sheeppen! Arahal lost no time telling everyone you were around again once he got back to Immanion. Rumors were started, a dozen inferences reached. Thiede had wanted to keep your alliance with Pell a secret. Those who'd been in Imbrilim put a stop to that. Now, after everyone thought you must have died or sought a hermitic existence, you were abroad again, in Jaddayoth. Questions were asked. What had happened to you after Thiede had taken you into his custody? Why hadn't Thiede told anyone? Immanion became a hotbed of supposition; poor Caeru caught in the middle of it, no doubt. You have become something of a folk hero to Wraeththu, Cal. You can thank Swift and Cobweb for that. They love you passionately. Swift has never given up trying to find out what Thiede did with you. He is a respected har; people listened to him. And because of that, many hara were considering the possibility that you might be a convenient tool to use against Thiede's increasing autonomy with the Hegemony. They all knew Pell was incapable of acting independently. Oh, don't get me wrong; he wants to, but his power is no match for Thiede. He can't do it on his own."

We all digested these words in silence. I could feel Panthera's agony. Even the sound of Pell's name caused him pain. I found myself wishing he wasn't there, because there were things I had to know, had to talk about, that I knew would cause him further grief.

"There's one thing I must know," I said, and it was not easy for me to say it. "If you were responsible for the visions, the pushing around, does that mean Pell himself has had no real interest in me?"

Opalexian answered me briskly. "One thing you must understand, Cal. Pellaz was under the impression you would seek him out as soon as you made contact with his people in Imbrilim. You didn't. Up until then, Thiede had told him you needed 'purification'—whatever he meant by that. That was to keep Pell away from you; it had worked for years. Pell knew you'd suffered penance in the forest of Gebaddon on the journey south. He knew you'd talked with Thiede after that. There was no longer any reason why you could not come back to him. The blood-binding with Caeru was just another of Thiede's smokescreens. It had nothing to do with love. The Gelaming were interested in you, they wanted you with them; you knew nothing of this, but there was no question of you being some underling skulking in the shadows to be summoned to the Tigron's bed when he felt like it. So, after you didn't turn up, it was easy for Thiede to convince Pell you had no further interest in him. The incident of you leaving the tower was his evidence for this. Pell is too honorable. Assured you wanted to lead your life without him, he let it be. Can you see how Thiede's been manipulating both of you now?"

"I can see it," I said quietly. "What I can't understand is why Thiede didn't just kill me. There'd have been no problem then."

Opalexian laughed. "Don't think that harshly of him, Cal! He *is* Aghama, and has considerable good sense. He's not a Terzian or a Ponclast who can kill willy-nilly to get rid of nuisances. No, that's not the way Thiede operates. Superficially, it's all above board. He is under the impression that what he's done is right. He believes it is for Wraeththu's sake he's keeping you away from Immanion, not his own. He's blinded himself too much. That's his mistake. It is your task to make him see the light."

"Your faith in me is frightening!" I said. No way could I imagine being able to convince Thiede of anything he didn't want to believe in, whether it was good for him or not. "Was it you that came to me in the pool near Jael too?" That was one thing I didn't want to be true.

The High Priestess sighed. "It was Pell's feelings, certainly, but he wasn't aware of projecting them." A tactful answer.

Panthera stirred uncomfortably beside me. "And how did all the rumors that are supposed to be flying around Jaddayoth about Cal get out? Do you know?"

Opalexian shrugged. "How do any rumors start?! One would presume they originated in Immanion and spread east via traders and travelers. Remember what I said, unbeknown to Cal, he has achieved quite a reputation in the west. No-one can answer your question properly, Panthera. Perhaps if we look upon it as a necessary thing that was bound to happen, we are touching on the truth." I could sense Panthera thought such a reply was far too glib.

"And have these rumors reached the ears of the Tigron himself yet, by any chance?" he asked.

"If they haven't, they certainly will once Caeru gets home," she answered. "Surprise would have been better, Cal. The incident in Sykernesse was rather unfortunate in that respect." She smiled placatingly. "Ah, never mind, what will be will be. Rest here for a few days. Such a short delay can't hurt the outcome; it's been waiting for years!"

We talked a great deal more, but now it was all talk of Jaddayoth. What did I think of different tribes? Had I enjoyed Gimrah, Hadassah, Ferike? And what had I learned? Opalexian was not above making one or two salacious remarks concerning Nanine and the Lyris. "I must admit it was quite exciting to impart these mysterious messages all over the place!" she said. "We followed your travels with great interest."

"I'm glad it provided such pleasure," I said, drily.

"Pleasure for you too in parts, you must agree," Tel-an-Kaa remarked with a smile. "The worst bit for us was when I told Ariaric about you. His face went white! For some reason, he was under the blithe misapprehension we didn't know who he really was, or what he'd done in Megalithica. Even when I explained your arrival wasn't going to provoke some wildly embarrassing revelation to us, we still had to argue with him about seeing you."

"Yes, here's another boost for your ego," Opalexian added. "Even for the Lion your image had assumed some strangely avatistic form over the years. Maybe something he couldn't forget, or something he had intense inner fantasies about. He was afraid of facing you again, and I don't think it had anything to do with guilt either."

"You'll swell my head," I said.

"No, we won't. You know what you are now, Cal." I thought about it and realized, for the first time ever, I really did.

"You must remember," Opalexian said, and now her voice was grave. "It is wrong to interfere in other people's lives, to try and change their destinies, even if it seems you are acting for the best. What must be must be. Everyone has their own path to follow and, inevitably, the times will come when their way is at extreme variance to yours. Even if you think that someone is acting utterly wrongly, think very carefully before trying to influence that situation. That is their path; they must live it. People may only learn by their own mistakes; you cannot learn for them. For that reason it was very difficult for me deciding whether or not I should take a hand in what was going on out there. Only the fact that Thiede was being deliberately wayward, and that he had such power, persuaded me. Perhaps I was still wrong, even taking that into account. But it is something I am prepared to take responsibility for. The rest is up to you, Cal. Do what you think is right, but remember what I've told you."

Later, we began to make arrangements for my journey to Almagabra. Opalexian had Exalan bring out a map. Most of the journey would be by sea. Kamagrian had transport like the Maudrah, but the High Priestess was insistent that once I reached Emunah, a more conventional method of traveling should be pursued. I didn't ask why she should want that, but assumed it was something to do with arriving in Immanion at the right time. That suited me fine. There was no way I wanted to reach it any sooner. I needed time to prepare myself.

Panthera and I returned to our room very late. My companion was silent. As we lay together in the darkness he spoke the words I knew would come. He must have thought about it for ages to say it so quickly. "Cal, I want to come with you." I didn't answer at first, so he felt he had to expand. "Not for the reason you might think; it's not selfish. I just don't want you to be alone."

"Have you considered I might have to be?"

"For what you have to do, whatever that is, having me along can't make that much of a difference. I want to see you safe, that's all. I couldn't live, not knowing. As soon as all this is resolved, I'll go back to Jael. I promise."

"It's not like you to plead."

"It's not like you to act sensibly. I want to be there."

"Are you sure?"

"I wouldn't have asked if I wasn't."

There was further silence whilst I examined minutely the relief his suggestion had given me. It was a selfish relief, I know that. If Panthera returned home to Jael now, I could contact him immediately my future was resolved without putting him in danger or the position of suffering further pain. God knows, I should have ignored my feelings, put my foot down and told him to go home. Yet I didn't. I knew what was supposed to happen in Immanion. OK, even with Opalexian's help, there was no cut and dried guarantee that all would go to plan, but there was no way I should take Panthera along. Whatever happened, it was certain we could no longer look upon ourselves as a pair. Ariaric is right about me; I can't let go easily. My pious words to Panthera in Biting meant nothing.

"Count yourself in then, Thea," I said.

He laughed and curled his arms around me. "Good to see you still can't resist my charm," he said.

Even as I held him close, even as I wanted him by me, I feared he was going to regret this move.

CHAPTER TWENTY-EIGHT

>━┼━◆>━◇━<◆>━┼━<

Aboard the Fairminia
"The foamy-necked floater went like a bird
Over the wave-filled sea,
Sped by the wind."
—*Beowulf*

The Emunah port of Meris was a lively place, bustling with hara of many different tribes. It was here that Opalexian moored her personal vessel, a sleek, red-sailed ship with painted eyes upon her prow. It was the ship I'd seen in my Dream. The trip from Roselane had been swift, though dreary; rain, rain, rain. Not a good beginning to such a journey, I felt. By late afternoon, it was almost dark in Meris, rain lashing down on the cobbled streets, shops closing early, hara hurrying along, muffled in waterproof cloaks, faces down. Tel-an-Kaa had come along to see us off. "Sail tomorrow," she said. "The weather will be brighter then." We booked into a small, crowded inn up a curling back-street. Tel-an-Kaa was in disguise; she looked harish. One day, a ghoulish curiosity within me decided, I'd have to find out what the Kamagrian concealed beneath their clothing. Humans must have once felt the same way about us. We ate together in a small back-room in the inn. The Kamagrian kept looking at the door.

"Nervous?" I asked.

She shook her head. "No, I'm expecting somebody. Opalexian wants one of our people with you on this. Not me, unfortunately. He should be here soon."

"A har, then."

"Yes, one you know; Zackala."

I was not exactly overjoyed. "Thanks for telling me. Why?"

"Personal feelings mustn't get in the way of this, Cal. He may be of use to you. The image you had of him in Gimrah was somewhat distorted. Purposely. He bears you no grudge, so don't make things awkward."

Zack didn't turn up until the morning however. Tel-an-Kaa was beginning to fret. We strolled down to the harbor after breakfast, where the sea was calm beneath clear sunlight. The air smelled fresh and full of promise. The Kamagrian wasn't sure whether she should let Panthera and I continue our journey alone. Opalexian's orders had been that Zack should come with us, but there was no Zack.

"What should I do first when I get to Immanion?" I asked, to take her mind off the problem.

"What? Get to Thiede, I should think. It's your finale, Cal, you decide!"

"Should I go in furtively, or through the front door?"

"I'd go in as if it was perfectly normal. Go to Phaonica; ask to see Thiede."

"I'm sure his people will let me! He must be more unapproachable than Ariaric, surely, and it wasn't exactly simple getting to see him."

"Luck was with you in Maudrah, so it will undoubtedly be with you in Immanion as well. Do you think Thiede's going to let you wander about his golden city at will? Just keep your wits about you; he'll attempt to seduce your common sense, steer you away. Remember what you've learned."

Opalexian's ship, *Fairminia,* was anchored at the farthest end of the harbor. As we approached, we could see hara busy at work on her decks. One figure waved us a cocky salute. It had to be Zack. My heart sank. I'd hoped we'd miss him. Tel-an-Kaa brightened up considerably when she saw him. Panthera and I watched dubiously as she ran toward him, up the gangway. They embraced; he swinging her around playfully. Oh, it was the har I'd seen *(thought I'd seen?)* in Gimrah alright. He smiled his crooked, scarred smile at us.

"Good to see you again, Cal," he said. "You look well. Better than you did in Gimrah, anyhow!" He laughed. "Welcome aboard; come on. Our captain wants us to be on our way, and it's a long journey."

Yes. Just how long, I hadn't really anticipated until I realized I'd have to spend the entire time with Zack. A past thorn. It still made me uncomfortable to recall those days, whatever he felt about it.

And so we left Jaddayoth. Slewing around, the graceful might of *Fairminia* cleaved her way through the waves toward the west. From the west shore of the Sea of Arel, a sea canal divides the lands of Huldah and Florinada. This leads to the Axian Sea and the coast of Almagabra; the way we would travel. Tel-an-Kaa watched us leave. Before her figure was too small to make out, we saw her walk away, back toward the town. Panthera went to sort baggage out in our cabin, leaving me alone to stare at the receding shores of Jaddayoth. I'd enjoyed my time there, made new friends, learned one hell of a lot. I could no longer isolate myself. It was Jaddayoth that had made me realize life just wasn't going to let me do that. But perhaps the hardest lesson had been accepting I was part of something huge; no amount of hiding or running could change that. Now I must bend to obey its laws, however obscure or beyond my grasp they were. People like Opalexian and Thiede can understand them; people like me just have to accept them.

For most of the journey, I've been catching up on my writing, as you can see. It surprised me that I'd written nothing since Ferike. This journal has been my life-saver in the past; my priest, my confessor. Perhaps I no longer need it. The har who scribbled the first sentences had no idea what he'd do or become. Will the har who enscribes the final word in Immanion be as different again? Impossible to tell. But for that reason alone I'll keep writing. It's a record of my metamorphosis. Zack and I are maintaining a polite, if distant, friendship. I get the feeling he's laughing at me sometimes and I hate the way he makes me feel inept. Perhaps it's not deliberate, but personally, I don't think he's forgiven me as much as the Kamagrian think. I can't help wondering, "What does he think of me? Why does he never mention the past?" I can't believe it's forgotten, yet perhaps it's only me that insists upon raking up the ashes of old fires. Maybe it really is no longer a cause of concern to Zack. How can I tell? We hardly speak. He gets on well with Panthera though. They've spent nearly the entire journey playing chess.

Panthera and I avoid talking about the future. It's too vague, too vacillating to think about. He holds me tightly at night and once I awoke to find him weeping. Silently. I never let him know I saw that. Zack has strong contacts in Immanion. (The dream I'd had of him on the battlefield with Ashmael was uncannily correct, it seems). As well as Kate, Zack too has infiltrated the Gelaming for Opalexian. He's decided we should go directly to Ashmael's residence once we reach the city. I'm not sure if that's a good idea, but I'll have to trust him. He reckons that Ashmael should help me get into Phaonica. But surely, Ashmael's loyalty lies with Thiede and the Tigron? He'll have been fed the same information about me as Pell has. Zack says, "Don't worry. Don't make problems." I can only hope he's right.

Immanion is near. It is nearly dawn, and I've been awake all night. A few minutes ago I was standing on deck, staring at the horizon. Threads of light from the rising sun picked out stars on the spires of a distant city. The jewel of the Gelaming, the Place of Light. It can sense me coming, I know. It understands what I must do to it and I can feel it trembling; half-thrill, half-fear. It is strong; made of stone and hara's will and desires. Made of souls. But it feels me and its open, glowing streets ripple. Transience; made in a moment, destroyed in a moment. Is that what it fears? Pellaz must still be in bed, perhaps writhing in the grip of nightmare. Unspecified terror. I cannot feel him yet, but he is there, encased in glass. We will soon be there. And now, I crouch in my cabin, hugging my knees, listening to Panthera murmer in his sleep. My fingers are cold. I am afraid; trembling. Have I learned enough? I never wanted to come here, but here I am. I turned my back on the past and found that time is a circle; I'm back there. I think I'm praying, but can only pray to myself. The Goddess and the God are within all of us; that's what they told me in Roselane. A small part or a large part? By Aghama, I hope it's enough.

CHAPTER TWENTY-NINE

>━!━◆>━━O━━<◆━!━<

The Crown

*"I drink him, feel him burn the lungs inside me
With endless evil longings and despair."*

—Baudelaire, Destruction

Immanion shone far beyond my dreams. We docked in the morning, stepping onto a harbour of sparkling mica. It was so clean. Unbelievably, shockingly clean. The brightness made my eyes ache. *Fairminia* looked tawdry, bobbing alongside the tall, stately craft of the Gelaming, whose colors were white and gold, whose figureheads were of eagles, dragons, plunging horses. From the harbor, tier upon tier of glowing, white buildings reared toward the crown of the city. Here, the coruscating towers of Phaonica, the Tigron's palace, reflected the morning light, visible from any point in the city. Roads were wide, and lined with spreading trees. It was a busy place, but not hectic; alive, but not noisy. Hara moved gracefully; the pace of life was leisurely. Zack led us away from the harbor, heading toward the north of the city. We passed through an open-air market, where food-stuffs from all the Wraeththu countries were available in profusion. Farther on, we crossed an avenue where open-fronted shops displayed their wares upon the street. The effect was unobtrusive. Was this an art-display or a gift center? We saw many other outlanders as we walked northwards; traders, tourists and seafarers. There were also plenty of natives. I felt as if every tall, golden-haired Gelaming we passed could see right into my soul. This caused uncontrollable flinching on my part; probably nobody noticed me at all.

About a mile from the harbor, Zack hailed a swooping hire-car to take us to Thandrello, the borough where Ashmael lived. We skirted Phaonica, high up. I could see figures moving in her tiled courtyards, along her terraces and cloistered walkways. Nervousness made me fearful of looking too closely, but even quick glances assured me of one thing. There was no way the Pellaz I'd once known could ever be comfortable (even convincing) living in a place like that. Why did I still nurture this image of him as he was? Common-sense alone told me not to be so stupid, but I just couldn't visualise him any other way. It was all I knew, all that had kept my love for him alive. God, this situation was a sleeping monster to end all sleeping monsters. The face of the creature was covered; I'd have to wait until it woke up to see whether it was a face I liked. And here I was, having these reckless thoughts, even as I trespassed in *his* city. I'd been warned, told, about his power; surely he could sense me now, close as I was to him. I felt the burn of an unseen gaze at the back of my neck and acted self-consciously because of it. Did he watch me? Did he? Did he already know I was there?

We reached Thandrello in half-an-hour, but Ashmael was not at home. This precipitated an ungovernable sense of relief within me, even though I knew it was only delaying the inevitable. Ashmael's house was fairly modest by Immanion standards, but spacious and comfortable. One of his house-hara offered to contact him for us, conducting us to an airy lounge, nearly filled with plants, whose northern wall, overlooking the garden, was all of glass. The furniture was low and stylised; not really the sort of place I'd have expected Ashmael to live in. From what I'd seen of him (admittedly only in dreams) he appeared to be the sort of har who would only be at home in a stable, or under canvas, or in the back-room of an exceedingly seedy inn somewhere. Zack and Panthera sat down; I paced restlessly about the room.

"Calm down, Cal," Zack admonished mildly. "You'll be fit for nothing unless you do."

Easy for him to say. I couldn't remember ever having felt so nervy. I wanted to fight. I wanted to get on with my task. I resented waiting. Affecting a cruel indifference to my inner turmoil, Panthera studiously examined the pictures on the walls. Zack picked up a book to read. I was not feeling particularly warm toward either of them. After all, they had nothing to dread, nothing to accomplish. Their minds were calm enough to look at pictures or read; mine could barely work out which way was up.

We'd only been waiting half-an-hour or so when Ashmael arrived home. His staff must have contacted him straight away. When he walked into that room, I recognized him immediately, which felt odd because we'd never actually met before. He smiled at me and said hello—he hadn't a clue who I was—and seemed pleased to see Zack. They spent nearly an hour swapping pleasantries; Zack was clearly being very careful, gently nudging the conversation along to provide him with a cue. I'd always suspected he'd have made a good politician; very good at manipulating things is Zack. As for me, sitting with my back to the window away from the others, I found it hard to keep my eyes off the star among Gelaming that is Ashmael. In my head, I kept replaying the dream (vision?) I'd had of him with Pell. I wanted to see the scar on his shoulder. He barely looked at me. Was I really there? Everything to fear had come so close so quickly. Only moments ago I'd been in Ferike surely? My thoughts tumbled over each other so swiftly, I could barely keep track of them. Conversation in the room washed over my head; I can remember none of it.

Eventually, Zack mentioned that he'd come, as he tactfully put it, on business. "Oh? What kind of business?" Ashmael asked him lightly. He'd obviously guessed we weren't there on a purely social call.

"If you don't mind, I'd like to discuss it with you alone first," Zack replied, not looking at me.

Ashmael shrugged. "As you wish. I have an office in the next room. That private enough for you?"

Zack nodded, and, excusing themselves to Panthera and I, they left the room.

Silence moved in to take their place. I was still sitting by the window, my forehead upon the glass. I could sense Panthera fidgeting. I felt like saying, "You still sure you should have come here?" but it would have sounded sour. Panthera couldn't speak. Oh, I was happy to indulge in my own agony; nevertheless, I was not unaware that he was suffering too. After several minutes, he had the courage to say, "We should talk now, Cal. Who knows when we'll get the chance . . ."

"No," I interrupted. "There's nothing to say. I'm sorry, but there isn't."

"Are you going to throw your life away then?"

"Thea, be quiet. We can't argue about this. You asked to come here and I believed you when you gave your reason why."

"I love you."

"Thea, don't! You'll only make it worse, for both of us."

If we'd been in a familiar place, he'd have leapt up and stormed from the room. We weren't. He couldn't. So we both fought for breath in that room of thick, heavy air until Zack and Ashmael came back in. It must have been hours.

It was likely Zack'd had some trouble convincing Ashmael he should help me. I wondered how much he'd had to reveal. Quite a lot, I would have thought, at least as much as Zack knew himself. Ashmael was tricksy; you see that at a glance, but he was not stupid. However small the amount of information Zack had been given, I was sure it would be enough for any sane har to realize what had to be done. Was Ashmael sane? Loyalty does strange things to people. I suspected Opalexian had decided the fewer people who knew everything the better. I was alone in this. I'd got to accept that.

The conversation had clearly been heavy-going. Ashmael's face was inscrutably grim (the only possible way to describe it), while Zack looked worn out. Ashmael went directly to open a window because the room was full of cigarette smoke, and then came to stand before me.

"So, you're the famous Cal, are you?" He stared, shook his head, stared again. I stared back. I wanted to say, "Yes, I know the feel of you" and perhaps he saw some of that in my eyes. He looked away eventually. He had reached a decision. "I have just heard the most incredible things about you. Things that are hard to believe. If it's true, then it's my duty to help you. If it's lies then I'm damned forever if I do . . ." He picked absently at the leaves of a plant by the window. "Tomorrow, I'll take you to Phaonica," he said. "Thiede will be in his sanctum until nine. I will get you there for eight. By Aghama, I hope I'm making the right decision!" This last part was said fiercely. He looked at Zack.

"I've told you the truth," Zack said, simply, shrugging. "You must know in your heart what is right."

"I've worked for Thiede for many years," Ashmael answered. "This feels like betrayal. I have only your word that it isn't."

"You've worked for your race for many years," I said. "You won't be betraying them, I promise you."

He looked at me coldly. "Damn you for coming here," he said. "Damn you for existing."

"It's not me," I answered, "just the Law. There'd be somebody else if not me."

"Would there?" He shook his head once more. "I wish I could believe that."

I made them uncomfortable in that room. The atmosphere was not exactly congenial, not even when the inevitable refreshments arrived, so more out of consideration for others than a desire for personal well-being, I intimated that I wanted to be alone. Now they could talk about me with abandon. Ashmael had me shown to a bedroom overlooking the avenue at the front of the house. I sat on the floor under the window, and the muted sounds of the city reached me in whispers. I stared at the ceiling, but there were no answers there. I was alone, alone, alone. Never had I felt so conscious of it. Not in Megalithica, not in Thaine; nowhere. The world felt vast beyond me, vast and incomprehensible. I was such a small part. A single particle and yet, within me, the whole. I am looking up at the ceiling and there is a point that I must reach. The sun went down beyond the glass and no-one came to disturb me. I drank the water that Ashmael had provided in a glass flask. It tasted like nectar, soothing my throat and the heat inside my head. The bed looked inviting in the gloom, all honey pine and striped rugs, so I went to lie down on it. Now my capricious mind had decided to go completely blank. Could I go downstairs again? A drink of something a little stronger than water would have been welcome, but I resisted trying to satisfy that craving. The end was merely hours away. I must wait here, find strength; I would need it.

It must have been nearly midnight when Panthera knocked on the door. I suppose I'd been expecting something like that happening. He came right in and said, "I can't let you do this."

This was the last thing I felt capable of dealing with. "Panthera, if I'd known you were going to be this way, I'd have left you in Roselane. There's nothing I can do. For God's sake don't take it so personally!" I didn't want to sound so heartless, but it was the truth. Truth often hurts. Perhaps that's why I used to lie so often.

Panthera ignored what I said. "Cal, I've stuck by you through every-thing; doesn't that mean *anything* to you?"

"Of course it does, Thea. You know that! But I have to go through with this. There's no way out. I'm not rejecting you, just moving on. We both knew this would happen."

He seemed caged in a world of his own as, I suppose, I was in mine. I don't think any of my words reached him. "I know there's something you've got to do with Thiede," he said earnestly, "but, for your own good, can't you just walk away after that? Come back to Ferike. You can't live here, Cal. It's not you. It'll kill you!"

"Kill me!" I jumped off the bed and he backed away instinctively. "What the hell do you know about it? It's me that's the expert on killing, Thea; that's why I'm here."

"Yes." Panthera's voice was soft. I sensed an approaching cruelty and was not disappointed. "I know that. You've been obsessed with it; one killing in particular. He's dead, Cal. Why can't you accept it? The Pell you loved is dead. What lives up there in Phaonica is Tigron. It's power; nothing else. Don't you know that? Or have you just conveniently put off thinking about it?"

I couldn't even bear to be angry with him. I drank some of the water. He knocked the flask out of my hand and it shattered on the floor, water spreading in a dark stain like blood over the pale, wooden boards.

"Thea, you're hurting only yourself. You can't reach me. Not after Roselane. I *know* now. You can't reach me." The calmness of my voice did not sooth him.

"What do you know, Cal? Tell *me!* If I know too, maybe it'll help . . ."

"*No!* I can't Thea. I can't." He looked wild, but he was trembling. I wanted to hold him, tell him everything would be alright. I wanted to strike him senseless so he'd leave me alone. Tel-an-Kaa had told me to watch out for sneaky attacks by Thiede. Was this one of them? I couldn't be sure. "Panthera, please, you must go. I have to think. Tomorrow's a big day." I tried a tentative smile. For a moment, he stared at me, full of rage, then he walked to the door. As he turned the handle, it seemed as if someone came and stabbed him in the gut. He doubled up, slid down the door and crouched on the floor, leaning against the wall. I really thought he'd been attacked. Anything was possible here. "What is it, Thea? Where's it hurt?" I tried to pull him up.

"Here!" he shouted, uncurling. "Here!" And he was thumping his chest with one hand, right over the heart. His face was wet with tears. Internal agony then; it had been me who'd thrown the knife.

"Thea?"

"I don't know why I'm doing this to myself," he said. "I don't know."

"I'm sorry . . ." It was all I could say, all I could think of.

"Cal, don't leave me."

We looked at each other in the half-light. He was so beautiful; it seems almost lame to say it. Why? Why, why, why . . .

"Don't leave me . . . *please!*"

My chest ached. My arms ached to hold him, but tomorrow would always be there. I could make no promises.

A long time ago, I'd been chesna with a har named Zackala. That's very, very close by Wraeththu standards. Some might say an insoluble link that exists even after hearts and bodies have waved goodbye to each other. It was simple to reach out with my mind and call him. Easy to intimate everything, by projecting the very least. He came through my door within seconds. I looked up at him helplessly, crouched on the floor by Panthera, who seemed almost senseless with grief. Zack shook his head, but said nothing. Between us, we got Panthera on his feet. He made an enormous effort to appear normal, perhaps embarrassed that Zack was there. He did not guess I'd summoned help, perhaps thinking Zack had passed the door and heard something. Before he left he said, "Goodbye, Cal. I wish you luck." I pulled a wry face. "I mean it," he said.

"Come on, Thea," Zack said, in a horribly cheerful voice. "Help me make a hole in Ashmael's liquor store! Cal can't afford to have a good time tonight!" He put his arm around Panthera's shoulder and dragged him away. When I closed the door, that white, stricken face was still looking back at me.

Alone, I sat on the floor with my back to the door and stared at the dark place where the water had spilled. I'd have trusted Panthera with my life. He'd trusted me with his heart which had been frozen nearly to death in Piristil. Now, in pursuit of my crazy, half-realized dreams, I was casting him aside like a meatless chicken-bone. (And, oh yes, I'd enjoyed consuming the meat.) I even loved him; but not enough. There was still that bewitching phantom waiting for me, that stranger, that immortal memory. Oh God, am I doing the right thing? Am I? Phaonica. . . . Through the window, I could look out and see those glistering spires. Beautiful, but spiky cruel they are. I want to touch them. It's as simple as that. Beyond the glass, as the hours progressed toward that single point in time, the light gradually changed. I sat on the floor, staring, staring, oblivious of anything but the mystery of Phaonica, and remained like that till dawn.

CHAPTER THIRTY

⊱─┼─◀▸─◉─◂▸─┼─≺

Phaonica

*"The agony is past; behold
how shape and light are born again;
how emerald and starry gold
burn in the midnight; how the pain
of our incredible marriage-fold
and bed of birthless travail wane;
and how our molten limbs divide
and self and self again abide."*

—Aleister Crowley, Asmodel

Zack was up to see me off. There was no sign of Panthera. Was he making it easier for me or for himself? Ashmael made me eat something but the bread tasted like ashes. I was afraid. "Remember, we are with you," Zack said, and I thought of Opalexian. I thought, "No, I am alone," but appreciated his concern.

Ashmael and I went out into the brightness of a fair and dreaming morning, walking because we didn't have far to go. Tall trees with glossy, dark leaves hid the palace from general view at first. We passed beneath them and I looked up. Imagine then the tremendous bulk of that fair edifice Phaonica. Effulgence upon shine upon brilliant haze. Darkness without shadow; the crown. And me. Shambling behind Ashmael; a mote of dark within the sphere of light. Dread had made me feel black; from the core out. Oh, I had worked hard to pay for my sins, but that could not erase the fact they'd been committed. Had my shadows any place within this splendor? My heart was aching because it was beating so hard, so fast. I followed Ashmael through the quieter courtyards, where he knew it was unlikely anyone would be about. And then it was deep, deep into the heart of the palace of light; to the inner sanctum of the Aghama. We saw no-one. The spacious corridors meditated in silence, columns and spiraling stairs, galleries and vaulted halls. A place of hushed magnificence. The Tigron lived here. Who was he really? Could he sense my presence? The rooms felt bewitched, enchanted into sleep so I could pass through them unnoticed. I felt Phaonica sigh around me, but there was no sign of Pellaz. We went down a flight of white steps and the light became blue. Thiede's sanctum;

the temple in the heart of Phaonica. Ashmael left me at the gateway, and I stepped inside.

It was like being surrounded by floating veils; everything was indistinct. I could smell cinnamon, strong and earthy. Where did the light come from? How big was this place? A single room, a labyrinth? I was stopped, limping toward the center, shivering like a rat crossing an alley. In Phaonica, I could no longer be beautiful. Ahead of me, an eternity away, I could see a pulsing core of light, solid brightness at its center. Power radiated out toward me, a slumbering power. It was Thiede, wreathed in blue flame, suspended in the webs of his own thought, contemplating beyond this world. As I approached him (oh, so slowly) the brightness changed color. Threads of red light streaked its purity. Thiede could sense me. He felt me drawing nearer, a smoking, black-rot presence. At first there was only a dim outrage that something unclean had entered his sacred space, then I caught it; fear! One pure beam of naked fear. He knew. Then I was right up close to him and it was like looking through glass and his burning eyes were upon me, spitting flame. He could not believe it. How could such a worthless beast as I breach his privacy without detection? What power did that mean I owned, or was lent? His face contorted with revulsion. My clothes had become rags.

I stretched a shaking hand toward him and it was caked with grime, so thin, almost mummified. "I know," I said, and my voice was the voice of the last doomed prophet. "I have seen." He raised his hand to banish me but I spoke first. "Is the one who would be Aghama afraid to hear what this foul creature might say?" And now it was Opalexian's voice that I spoke with. "Didn't you always want me to come here, Thiede? Didn't you once ask me to?"

He considered for a moment before saying, "Speak then," and there was a certain curiosity in his tone. Thiede still thought he had the ability to get rid of me when he wished.

"It began with a bullet," I said, "when the soul of a single har rose high, transfixed by your radiance, but unable to reach it. Prevented from reaching it. That suited you didn't it? Even the Aghama can know fear. Pellaz could not reach you because he had no complement. Now I know you wanted it to stay that way; always! 'Come to Immanion, Cal,' you said. 'Be the Tigron's plaything.' Clever of you I suppose. You knew I'd say no to that. You only had to twist the truth a little to keep us apart. Pellaz and I are *Wraeththu*, Thiede. Fate brought us together, but a very calculating Fate. Pell is Light and I am Dark, but without each other we cannot understand the real Light. Together, we can combine and reach for it. We *become you*, Thiede. We become the ultimate. You knew that, didn't you? That is why it was so necessary to keep me away from here. Oh, I thought you were being so understanding, so reasonable about it all, didn't I? It was Pell who was the villain of the piece, the spoilt child who wanted something, and stamped and screamed until he got it. I know better now. Thiede, you are holding Wraeththu back, stunting their development. There had to be a Tigron, but it wasn't your idea. No, your part of it was to keep the Tigron to being just one person. That way you could keep all your power. Phaonica is but an illusion, Immanion built of dreams. Your dreams. It shines, it is safe, but it is unbalanced. Pellaz lives in glass; you have made him so pure. But there is still the sleeping seed within him that reaches toward me; the seed that shuts the Tigrina from his heart, that keeps his belief in Us strong. You can cage it, Thiede, but you cannot destroy it."

"No, but I can destroy you," Thiede answered, and he was calm and unsurprised. One day, all this would have had to come to light. Thiede was not that blind.

"Of course you can, and you must," I answered. His face flickered with brief, unspecified shadows.

"Have you come here then just to tell me what you know and let me dispose of you neatly?" He smiled. "I think not, Calanthe. You're a survivor. You won't give in that easily. Are you trying to fool me?"

"Perhaps I'm just playing with words. The Aghama can't kill, can he? If he could, he would have got rid of me years ago. No, in destroying me, you destroy yourself. Life is precious isn't it?"

"What do you want?" His patience was ebbing. He was in no mood for games, which showed he was worried.

"What do I want? Oh, that's easy. I want you to kill me, as you killed Pellaz. You're going to have to do it, Thiede. You must."

He smiled wanly. "And create something more powerful than this world has ever known? Destroy myself?"

"Only in death can you truly become Aghama, Thiede. Why are you afraid?"

"You do not know what I feel. It is not fear as you can grasp it. I have always understood that I am mortal, as we all are. Because of this my weakness is my love of flesh, my love of this world; its people, its earth, its feel. I know that is weakness, but it is also my strength because I can admit it. I also know that I have been fighting against the inevitable. I knew you'd show up here one day, to claim what you think is yours. I didn't believe, for a moment, that I'd managed to get rid of you forever. Don't, in your arrogance, think that I'm unaware of that. If I want to, I can know every thought in every Harish head. I began this race, Cal."

"Yes, you did, and you must let it go on, Thiede. Wraeththu must progress. The next stage must be initiated. Now."

"And if I don't? What then?"

"Then Opalexian will make you do it, I'm sure."

"Opalexian." The name obviously disturbed him. Perhaps he'd heard it in dreams, banished it from his visions.

"Kamagrian," I said.

"And what is that?"

I could not believe he did not already know. "I can show you. It is all inside me. All of it."

For a moment longer, in those final moments, he stared at me deeply. What did he see? A Uigenna wastrel? A used-up kanene? A murderer? Or did he see Opalexian's initiate? He was afraid.

"Show me then," he said, and I opened up my mind to let him look within me and learn what I knew. She that taught it lived there. If he'd been ignorant of her existence, as, at last, I felt he must, he did not let me see it. He extended his hand.

"Let me look at you again," he said, and drew me toward him. He smiled sadly. "One of my children. Every har is one of my children. Have I been a harsh father, a useless one?"

"Neither, but you have not been a mother either."

He shook his head. His last moments. He looked around the temple, loving it, smelling it, absorbing it, afraid he would lose it for eternity. Until the moment of extinction, there is no real proof for any of us that life extends beyond it. "Pell is waiting to love you," he said. "That, in itself, has been an act of worship for him. I envy you. I envy you everything."

"You shouldn't."

He smiled more widely, a sparkle coming into his eyes. "A last fling at carnality, my dear. That's all. I must go back to the beginning, look at it again. Then we will speak some more."

"In this place, we will speak many times."

"Conceive your sons here. Bring your love here . . ." He sighed and took both of my hands in his own. "I am not a wicked creature, Cal."

"I know that."

"Then let us do what must be done," he said. There was no way he could fight it, for the only way to fight it was to destroy me, which is what had to happen anyway.

As a column of shadow, I rose toward a vacillating brightness that in the moment of contact exploded into me as a countless number of sparks. At that moment, throughout the world, every Wraeththu har would shudder, raising his head to the sky, feeling fear, wonder, power. Those that slept would dream my dream, those that were awake would live it. Me, as a mote of the whole, in that instant *became* each of those individuals. And they felt me. And recognized me. But in Phaonica, the Cal that had been was consumed in the fire, spiraling helplessly, at one with the elemental force that held the world together. The walls of that temple trembled. I heard a piercing, agonised shriek that was Pellaz wrenched from the glass, pulled gasping through a crack of infinite sharpness, that cut and tore and ruined. I was high above the city and Immanion shuddered and groaned, black tongues licking its streets, sweeping oily smoke behind it. Buildings listed, fell, twisted, screamed. Hara came out of their homes, still pulling on clothes, dragging harlings behind them, staring up in horror at a sky that was red and black; a kingdom of flame. I could see all this as I burned and it lasted an eternity. And yet it was just a moment. When the peace came, I was lying on a cold floor in the middle of a vast chamber that was completely empty. For a while I just experienced *body*. I hadn't been sure

I'd still have one. Now it was just harish, panting and winded, with aching guts and scraped lungs, dazed as a small child kicked over by a heavy foot. High above me in the arches of the temple, I could see a spark of light. That was all. I could not reach for it alone.

Phaonica was in darkness, its corridors and halls empty. Everyone was in hiding. I stumbled along the terraces for hours, seeking, seeking. There was no-one to show me the way and I was too confused and drained to use my mind to find him. I came to be standing in a garden and it was evening. I was looking up at a balcony and the open windows beyond it. Here must I climb. Creepers on the walls shook and shed their leaves as I clambered upwards, tendrils losing their grasp on stone. I nearly fell a dozen times, scraping my knees, my knuckles. As I climbed I heard a whimpering that came from above. It was the whimpering of an abandoned child. I swung my legs over the balcony and tried to wipe the dust and twigs from my clothes. Impossible. Easier to tear the rags from my body, even if it was ravaged and unclean beneath. But the filth fell away with the rags and, free of them, I was pale and pure of skin. Reborn. Maybe. For a moment, I stood at the window doors to the room beyond and I was just Cal again. A Cal who had a heart beating fast, whose breath caught in his throat because he faced the thing he desired and feared the most. I walked inside. The canopy was torn from the bed (shredded) and cast about the room. Tall, decorated jars filled with peacock feathers and palms had been thrown at the walls and lay smashed upon the floor. I saw a huddled shape lying amongst all this wreckage and recognized it as Vaysh, the guide of my vision. There was blood upon his forehead, a frown upon his face. Eyes closed. But he was not dead. A single glance told me that. I could feel his life, see it within him. Now I must look at the bed and it took courage to do that. Courage because it was Pellaz lying there, his body scratched and torn and bloodied, tortured in its posture, arms across his face. He was half-conscious, now mumbling, now silent, lying in a tangle of torn sheets and splinters of glass from the long windows that had burst inwards upon him. For a moment longer, I stood and looked at him. Was he different? Older, yes. He was no longer scrawny but lithe. I leaned forwards and uncrossed his arms. This was the moment then, when I looked into the face of the monster. I sat down on the bed, touched his cheek, his eyelids, his lips. The face of the Tigron. Beautiful and, in it, the ghost of my Pellaz. I was afraid to wake him, but knew I must. Standing at the foot of the bed once more, I raised my arms, reaching for the Light. (Here, Thiede, here. We shall reach you.) The bed was strewn with glass. I grabbed hold of the fringed coverlet and pulled sharply. Pellaz rolled onto the clean sheet beneath and groaned. He didn't open his eyes but reached up to touch his face. It's been so long since I touched him. So long. This seems like blasphemy. I lay down beside him.

My body was warm, his was cold. I fed him with heat so that he had to open his eyes and see that I was there. Such bewilderment. From me to the room to me. Confusion to start with. "What? What . . .!" Then he saw

Vaysh lying on the wreckage-strewn floor and screamed, "No!" thinking of
Orien. He wanted to leap up, whether to escape or attack me, I couldn't be
sure. I had to hold him down. He struggled, tried to bite me, but his
struggles were weak because his powers had been disabled by Thiede's
passage from flesh.

"Would I be here if it was simply death I was carrying?" I asked and he
replied, "You have always carried destruction. It is you."

His nightmares, his dreams had been realized. How many times had he
yearned to open his eyes and find me there? Even though he had known
about Orien whom I murdered, and believed the tales that Thiede had told
him, he had still hoped. Now it was true. "What has happened?" he asked.
"What have you done?"

"Only what had to be done."

"Thiede has gone hasn't he," he said. "You have destroyed us all." He
shuddered in my arms, looking around the room, seeing violation, just
violation, too weak to protest any further.

I pulled him from the bed and dragged him over to the window, forced
him onto the balcony. "Look at your city, Pell," I said and he turned his
head away, eyes closed, wincing. "Look. Really look!" I forced his head
around and made him see. On the highest levels, the stone still shone, and
there were wide avenues where, in the morning, the light would dance. But
now, there were also places where the light would never reach, the dark
alleys, the subterranean canals and thoroughfares, where rats would creep
and moaning ghosts disturb travelers from the lighter places above. Now,
Immanion was whole, a place of softness and harshness, of thieves as well
as angels, as all these things should be. Destroyed to be rebuilt. Not
Thiede's city, but Wraeththu's. Not just Pell's, but mine too, as we were
each other's. I led him back inside. He was still saying, "What have you
done? What have you done?" and protested when I laid him on the bed.
"You are the Destroyer, I'll have no part of you. Where is Thiede?"

"We shall find him," I said, "but you must trust me."

"Trust you?" he asked bleakly. "As I trusted you to come to me once
Megalithica had fallen to our people? In the forest of Gebaddon you
encountered the past. I made you ready to come to me, but you never did.
Thiede never agreed with me about you, but he tried to help. Even then you
rejected me. I was just Pellaz who had died to you. A past occurrence, easily
forgotten. It was never like that for me. I never forgot! Now you have
returned, and it's like it always was; Cal and the sword of ruin. My city has
gone. So too whatever power I once had, I expect." He sighed. "Life
without you was never easy, but at least it was life. Now what have I got?"

"Everything," I answered. "More than you ever had before. Give me
your hand." He pulled a sad, wry face, but did so. I opened up and burned
him. He did not pull away.

"You are different." It was a wary decision. "How?"

"I must tell you everything," I said.

"Of course you must." He smiled. "So tell me."

I had rehearsed this scene in my head countless times, anticipating his reactions, his outbursts, his silences. Now he just listened, nodding now and then, his face expressionless; the face of a king. For some reason I didn't tell him about the Kamagrian, feeling that should come later. He had enough to swallow without that. When I finished speaking, he lay face-down on the bed, his chin on his fists, his feet upon the pillow. I watched him digest what I'd told him. I thought about how you did not interrupt the thoughts of the Tigron; you waited until he spoke. I examined the curve of his spine, his black hair, tangled, that covered even his thighs. I looked at his straight nose, his dark eyes; everything. I could never get enough of that. It was like being starved to the point of death and then being presented with a freshly roast lamb accompanied by every exotic vegetable you can think of. One does not interrupt the thoughts of the Tigron, unless one is Tigron too. "Well?" I said. I think I'd still been expecting him to leap on me with open arms.

He laughed. "This is crazy. My city explodes, Thiede evaporates and you burst in here naked telling me that now you're Tigron with me! Hell, I'm cut all over! Is this real? Am I going to wake up in a minute?"

"Maybe, but not in the way you think."

He narrowed his eyes at me. "Cal, it's been over thirty years! This is just . . . oh, I don't know." He shook his head, pressed his brow against his arms on the bed. "I'm not the same person, Cal. You do realize that, don't you?" There was a hint, just a hint, of a certain wistfulness I'd recognize after a hundred years, never mind thirty.

"Neither am I, Pell, but we're not strangers are we?"

He smiled. "No. It doesn't feel like that. I don't know how it feels. Maybe we should see. The truth is I've waited a long time for this. Dreams, hopes; oh, I've had plenty of those! Now they are gone. If it's ruins beyond this, then it's ruins! I'll think about it another time." He turned over. "Pick the glass from my skin first, Cal. I may be immortal, but not impervious to pain. Here I am; yours. I always have been. Want to come home now?"

There were no shooting stars, no huge explosions. We didn't even know if we were truly in love as we'd once thought; only time would tell us that. We met as hara and conjoined as hara, but there was a difference. In the midst of our communion, when we were truly one, we could reach for the ultimate and it was there for us to touch. It was the true godhead, and when we joined with it we became Three. Divine. It will always be there for us and together we can touch it whenever we want to. The Aghama, a god of all attributes, the sum of our positive and negative, force and meekness, flesh and spirit, love and hate. I am the stone, Pell is the silk and Thiede has become the binding force that makes us mesh. This is what happened in Immanion in the year ai-cara 29. It should have happened twenty-nine years before.

CHAPTER THIRTY-ONE

>—I—‹›—•O•—‹›—I—‹

Caeru, the Hegemony and Beyond

"If this be error and upon me proved,
I never writ, nor no man ever loved."
—*William Shakespeare, Sonnet XVIII*

When we woke the next morning, we knew that it was real because the floor of the chamber was strewn with broken crockery, torn drapes, wind-hurled leaves. We knew that it was real because the smell coming in through the shattered windows was of smoke and destruction. Somewhere a bell was tolling, without urgency, desolately. For a while, we just held onto each other in the fragmented blankets, and we could weep without fear of weakness. A natural reaction; the numbness, the feeling of surreality, had gone. Pellaz asked me, "What have we become?" and for that first day, it was a wistful, melancholy sentiment, because the easy ways of the past were over. The real work had yet to begin.

We would rebuild Immanion, clear the debris; it was not as bad as it looked. Dreams had been shattered yes, but what would be rebuilt would consist of more than dreams. In that brief, eternal moment when I had become one with the lifeforce of Wraeththu, the truth had been revealed to me. As Immanion had changed, so too had other places, touched by the fire of the Triad. Now there was a small, scruffy town in Thaine known as Fallsend, whose grubby streets would open out into wider avenues where hara could walk free. I wondered what would be the fate of Piristil and its kind. Would there be a place for them now? Was the force that strong? Somehow I doubted it. One thing I had learned was the utter need for light and dark, nothing can be *wholly* good, but if Piristil still thrived, then to complement it, there would be other houses; places of healing and learning. As Immanion could not be utterly Light, Fallsend could not be utterly Dark. From the mud would come roads, and other travelers would follow them, bringing the warmth of wholeness with them from the south and west. And what of Jaddayoth? I'd only experienced about half of it, but decided that most of the twelve tribes had, in their own way, already balanced their societies. Mainly they had just got on with the business of living. Gelaming, clearly, had just been trying too hard to live up to Wraeththu's potential, their beliefs had been too subjective.

Perhaps it was wrong *(selfish, weak?)* that I actually considered avoiding facing Panthera again, perhaps merely wise, but it was still late in the day when I forced myself to leave Pell's side to go and find him. We'd spent most of the morning trying to sort the Tigron's apartment out with Vaysh, who was nursing a colorful black eye. I had explained to Pell something about my companion from Jaddayoth. At first, he'd been rather unsympathetic with Panthera. "Why bother seeing him again? It's over, isn't it?"

"We parted messily. I don't like messes. Anyway, I owe him a lot. He deserves more than a kick out the door."

"Hardly that, Cal, but I suppose you're right. Don't be too long. There are things that need to be seen to."

It was not an easy mission. There was no guarantee that he'd still be at Ashmael's house although I was confident that he'd stick around to see how everything turned out. Most of Thandrello still stood intact, but a tree had crashed through a window of Ashmael's house, killing one of his staff. Ashmael and his people were in the grounds of the house clearing up, Ashmael stripped to the waist, hauling branches away from shattered glass. He was quite businesslike when he caught sight of me walking up the drive. He sauntered toward me, almost as if nothing had happened and casually asked after Pell. There was no mention of Thiede.

"I'll be up at Phaonica shortly," he said. "You and Pell must call an emergency meeting of the Hegemony; you do understand that, don't you?"

What with all the upheaval, I hadn't really thought about it. Pell certainly hadn't mentioned it, which was odd, because as Tigron, it should be the thing uppermost in his mind, whatever else was going on. "I suppose you're right," I answered.

Ashmael laughed grimly. "You're worried? Don't be! You're lucky in that the Hegemony will be in a bit of a flap; they won't give you their worst. After all, their godhead has . . ." He paused eloquently. "Pell will be able to tell you about how he fared at the Hegemony's hands when he first came here."

"Pell had Thiede to protect him as well." I shook my head. "Oh dear! Will they finish me off do you think?"

Ashmael was stony. "I doubt it. The very fact that Thiede is no longer . . . *appears* no longer to be around will act in your favor. They will look to Pell now for guidance; they will have to. They thought they were so democratic, but they're useless without Thiede's brains and commonsense."

"What makes you so sure they've lost those things?"

Ashmael raised his brows. "Suspicions, hunches, how the hell will I know until you decide to tell me? Am I supposed to ask? Have you killed him?"

"You've been listening to too many stories about me, tiahaar!"

"Perhaps. Can't help it. They've all been so scandalous. So?"

"So, aren't we rather making light of a very heavy subject?"

Ashmael shrugged. "I've never been one for those kind of theatricals. If Thiede is dead, let's just get on with what we've got to do."

"Two days ago you spoke of loyalty."

"That was a millenium ago! Posthumous loyalty is a matter to be considered seriously. Maybe I will change my affinities in the light of what you know. Come on, tell me."

I sighed. "Oh, it's quite simple really. Thiede has become the Aghama."

Ashmael regarded me quizzically after this statement. "*Become the Aghama,*" he repeated slowly. "Does that mean he's dead or not?"

"It means that Thiede is no longer a har entirely of flesh and blood. It means he has become the god he's always styled himself to be. Let us just say that through sacrificing the flesh he has managed to attain the position he has always craved."

Ashmael did not look convinced. "Such words slip uneasily from your tongue, Cal," he said.

"Not my usual style no," I agreed. "We will have to talk later. I'm sure many hara are as anxious to know as you are. Now, I've got business of another kind to attend to. Is Panthera still here?"

Ashmael nodded thoughtfully. "Around the back. Are you taking him back to Phaonica?"

"Nobody *takes* Panthera anywhere! I expect he'll return to Ferike soon."

"What a shame."

I smiled carefully and started to walk away.

"Just a moment!" Ashmael called me back. "I shall be going to Megalithica next month, to Galhea. You'll have to start getting used to being a celebrity and Megalithica is a good place to start. Perhaps you should come with me . . ."

"An inflammatory suggestion, tiahaar! Let me sort out my traumas in Immanion first please."

"Of course!" He smiled sweetly and ducked a bow. "Just a suggestion, that's all, but please think about it."

"I'll think about it certainly. Now, if you'll excuse me . . ."

He waved me away, still smiling. I was not blind. Ashmael had talked about Pell having had a rough ride when he first came to Immanion, and I could guess where most of the trouble had come from. I wondered how long Lord Ashmael would consider it necessary to test me.

I found Panthera and Zack together, pausing for a break from the cleaning up, sitting on the trunk of a fallen tree, sharing a bottle of wine and looking very cozy. I sensed a certain closing of ranks as they saw me approaching. A sudden flare of crazy hope kindled in Panthera's eyes, but only for a moment. I went right up to them and took the wine bottle from Panthera's hand, taking a careless swig in an effort to conceal the fact that this was not easy for me. Panthera could not bring himself to stand up and embrace me. It made me realize in an instant that I was now a stranger to him. He hadn't been part of what had happened in Phaonica the day before; all he had experienced was the result. We were both held in an embarrassing kind of silence which Zack had the presence of mind to excuse himself from. We both watched his retreating form in an agony of blank minds. Eventually I thought of, "Are you returning to Ferike now?"

Panthera didn't look at me. "I haven't really decided yet. Zackala is traveling to Oomadrah soon. I had thought of going back there with him first. Somehow I think the peace and quiet of Jael would get on my nerves at the moment."

"Ah, so the 'party party' of the Sykernesse court attracts you, does it?"

He looked me in the eye then. "It would be more healing for me than sitting brooding in Jael, yes."

I looked away, nervously kicked a fallen branch with my foot.

"You look well," Panthera said.

"Do you want to know what happened?"

"No, not really."

"Will you ever come back here?"

He sat there on a tortured, torn tree-trunk, knees apart, strong and young. He'd changed so much since Thaine. Grown, and in so many ways. I considered for a brief moment the ideas I'd once had of shutting myself away with him in Ferike. I still wasn't convinced it wouldn't have been the best thing for me to do. Now it was an impossibility and I had to watch this dear friend walk away from me into the world. He would meet so many new people and inevitably forget the intensity of his feelings for me. It was not conceit to think that. I could see it in his eyes, honest and unashamed.

"Come back here?" he said at last, taking a cigarette from a squashed packet, lighting it and savagely throwing the packet onto the ground.

"Are you serious?"

"Is our friendship over too then?"

"Don't play with me, Cal. Not now. OK, you want to hear it? Yes, I may come back here, but it won't be to see you. I don't mean to sound harsh, or petty or jealous, or whatever. It just *is*. Face it. You gave me up the minute you walked out of here yesterday. Maybe you still had the choice then, I don't know. I never will. Just let me get on with my life now."

"You're bitter."

"Am I?" He took angry, deep draws off the cigarette. "This is distressing me Cal, much as I hate to admit it. Would you just leave please?"

"OK, if that's what you want." I sighed and turned away. He didn't stop me.

Half-way down the drive, I said, "Dammit!" out loud and ran back to him. He looked up at me, hostile and uncertain, but I still dragged him up off the log and wrapped him in an embrace it would have been difficult to pull out of.

"I never said thank you, you arrogant little shit!" I said, which seemed easier than murmuring something maudlin. He wouldn't relax for a moment, arms stiff at his sides. "I'm grateful for everything," I said, "everything."

"Then thank me," he said, and smiled. "After all, you'll never have anyone as beautiful as me again. Gratitude is hardly enough!" He squeezed me hard.

"Still friends then?"

"I'll think about it. Probably in Oomadrah. Then I might come back and see if you mean it."

"Yes," I said. "Do that. Maybe I'll need a little of your abrasive company after all these high and mighty Gelaming."

"Just make sure you never truly become one of them." Wisdom there from my pantherine, which I must never forget. "Right up until last night I still wanted to fight for you," he said.

"What made you change your mind?"

He rolled his eyes mischeivously. "I don't think I'll tell you, or maybe I will. It was Zack."

"He's always had a way with words," I said bleakly, rather disappointed.

"Words had little to do with it," Panthera replied, a brave effort at masking his feelings, which didn't fool me for a moment. If something had changed Panthera's mind it had been nothing to do with mere physical acts (whatever they'd been), but the vast, unimaginable glory of the Aghama's transmutation. It must have touched everybody. Panthera and I shared breath for the last time and sounds around us, which had seemed to fade away, came back as if someone had lifted a veil. I saw Zack wandering over in our direction again and let Panthera go. This strand of the past was now truly over and its frayed ends had been sealed to the best of my ability.

"I'd better get back to Phaonica now," I said and this time I meant it. Panthera waved and turned back to his work. I did not look back at him, mainly because Zack decided to walk down the drive with me.

"Don't damage Panthera in *any* way," I said.

"And now you have the power to know if I do, eh?" He kicked a stone. "Don't worry about him. You're not the only one to change, Cal. Perhaps we should have spoken of the past together during the journey here on Opalexian's ship, but it hardly seemed worth it. That sordid history of ours was so worthless, after all. But perhaps we should mention it. Didn't we think we were so good then? Such a game."

"And you lost. We both did. At the time."

Zack shook his head. "I disagree. What we didn't realize was, that none of it really mattered. I hated you for ages, but then one day realized that I would probably have done the same as you if it had been me up there on the wall with my gun in the next alley. Who knows? We were both foul bastards who got what we deserved."

"So you don't think I was to blame then? That's great. I'd always been proud to take the responsibility for that as well!"

"Oh, come on, no-one was to blame. It was just the way we were living. Taking risks, scampering along the edge of the abyss with one eye closed. It's conceit to nurture that guilt for so long; it's unimportant. Sorry to ruin your self-indulgent shame, but it's true!"

"Perhaps I should be glad that you think that. I don't know. At the moment it all seems so dim; I can't really care about it."

Zack laughed. "No. Why should you? I wouldn't! Enjoy being Tigron, Cal. The title suits you."

He left me at the gate and I returned to Phaonica alone, scuffing through the streets, somehow tired, somehow sad, somehow relieved. No-one knew me in Immanion; yet. I saw Gelaming sweeping away the past, some with tired, grief-torn faces, some with a smile and determination. They'll learn.

And there was black-haired Pellaz waiting for me, as he had always waited for me and always would. To be able to walk into those luxurious (if currently war-torn) apartments and just take him in my arms as mine was a wonder I was sure I'd never take for granted. He was new to me, yet familiar. Like a shining phantom of the Pell I'd once known. A succubus/incubus, waiting in darkness. But this was daylight and he had a dripping sandwich of spiced ham and savage mustard in his hand, which he thoughtfully pushed into my mouth.

"There is a problem," he said, wiping mustard from his chin.

"A problem? Surely not!" I gasped, with watering eyes, gingerly putting the sandwich, half-chewed, on a plaster-strewn table. The only available chair was lumpy with clothes so I sat on the floor.

"You will have to deal with it."

"What is it? And why me?"

"The problem is my consort Caeru, and you will deal with it, because now you are my partner, my twin, and therefore I feel guiltless burdening you with it."

"Ah, yes. Caeru. We have met."

"Yes, I know. I heard all about it in extravagant detail. Several times."

"Did it worry you?"

"Of course. I had no idea what was going on. My Tigrina, being self-obsessed at the best of times, could only rant on about how you must be planning to come to Immanion to roust him from his throne. He had totally ignored the implications of what it could all mean to me, but that's Caeru! You will have to get used to it, I'm afraid."

"What do you mean?" I asked suspiciously. I had come to see quite quickly in my beloved, a certain deviousness that I'm sure hadn't been there before.

"Quite simply, Cal, I mean this: I am Tigron, Caeru is my consort. Now you are Tigron too, and he is yours."

"*He is mine!* Have you told him yet?" Horror didn't come into it. It had already been impressed upon me how popular the Tigrina was in Almagabra. As he had said, his position was unassailable. However, this was a circumstance that I was sure he hadn't thought of. Neither had I.

"No, of course I haven't told him! Sometimes we don't speak for weeks! I haven't seen him since the day he got back from Maudrah."

"That was ages ago."

"Caeru's moods can last longer than that."

"*Caeru's* moods?"

Pell sniffed impatiently. "Alright, *our* moods. You can tell him. I'm sure he'll be delighted. After all, he was under the impression that you'd arrive here with a gang of mercenaries and run him through with a sword. Run him through, by all means, but simply to show him his position."

"Pellaz, you can be foul."

"I thought I was supposed to be sometimes. You did that."

"I did not bond you in blood with Caeru, did I. That was your decision."

"You think so? I had little choice. One day I'll, *we'll* need heirs. Thiede chose Caeru for that function."

"How callous. Can't we make our own now?"

"Caeru is Tigrina, Cal. That's not something that can be taken back. Unless you really want to run him through with a sword. Think we'd get away with it?"

I sighed. "Where is he?"

Pellaz smiled triumphantly. "I'll have Vaysh take you to him. Vaysh!"

I must admit, I found it quite amusing how far Caeru's apartments were from Pell's. Clearly they didn't need the convenience of proximity. I was finding it quite difficult equating the Pell who could treat someone so dismissively with the compassionate young creature I had known in Megalithica. I told myself, "Of course he had to change. Nobody could be in his position and remain so ingenuous," but it still made me feel a little uneasy. Selfish of me really. Had I really expected the young Pellaz to have been preserved in entirety just so that I could happily relive fond moments of the past?

Gazing in wonder at the tarnished splendor of Phaonica, I followed Vaysh through halls and corridors, stepping over tumbled furniture and tapestries that had fallen from their hangings. Vaysh told me, "Caeru will be at his wits end. Probably demented." He smiled. "Maybe even dangerous. May I stay and watch this?"

"It is my opinion that you and Pell encourage each other in a rather harsh treatment of the Tigrina," I said, which was meant to sound serious, but came out rather mocking.

Vaysh shrugged. "You're probably right. But you haven't had to put up with him."

"Isn't it rather sad? I can't help feeling sorry for him."

"Oh, Cal, you disappoint me! Pell always admired your clever sarcasm. Don't feel sorry for Caeru, just let your talents rip!"

If Pell had learned to be hard, I at least had learned to be somewhat more understanding. "Tell him I've come for dinner," I said.

Vaysh grimaced, pushing aside an obscuring torn curtain, and knocked upon a high, studded door.

The nervous face of a servant appeared round the door. "Tell the Tigrina the Tigron is here to see him," Vaysh ordered imperiously. He looked at me and repeated with jarring sincerity, "Tell him the Tigron has come for dinner." We walked inside. The place was a mess, dark with an air of desperate desolation.

"Vaysh," I said. He raised an eyebrow in anticipation.

"OK, I know. I can go now. You don't have to say it, although I must point out that I don't often take orders from the Tigron."

"I didn't say a word."

He smiled. "No, you don't have to. Have fun."

I wandered alone further into the room, a small, once-elegant antechamber with many doors leading off. One was open and I could see a lean, black-haired har in the room beyond picking stuff up off the floor. His face seemed somehow familiar, so I went and stood in the doorway.

"Need any help?" He looked up at me. I was a stranger, but disaster brings people closer, so he said, "No, it's OK, I'll manage. I've been away. They called me back today. Is Thiede really dead? What's happened exactly?"

"A coming of age," I answered. "Destruction, rebirth, you know, that kind of thing." The har smiled, wiped his hands.

"You've lost me! I can't get any sense out of my hostling either. Did you want to see him?"

"That depends on who your hostling is!"

"Sorry." He held out his hand. "I'm Abrimel, the Tigron's son." I took the hand and clasped it warily. Stupid of me. I hadn't anticipated that Caeru may have already produced an heir, neither had Pell seen fit to mention it. Probably because, bearing in mind the Wraeththu life-span, by the time Pell was ready to hand over his throne, Abrimel would be too old to take it on. However, the young har's existence did bring home to me that once upon a time Caeru and Pell must have been locked together in something other than hostilities. I could see the resemblance to Pell in Abrimel's face; that was the familiarity I'd sensed.

"Caeru is your hostling then."

He nodded. "Yes. He's around somewhere. Sorry, I don't know you. Should I? Do you want me to fetch him?"

"No, I should already have been announced. My name is Cal. You may have heard of me." I decided it would be better not to mention my new title as yet.

Abrimel's face clouded instantly, though he was polite enough to try and conceal it. "You could say your name is familiar," he said. "Is my father alright?"

"Yes. Whatever you may have heard, don't judge me until you've spoken to him."

"My father won't speak of you to me."

"I think he will now."

Abrimel pursed his lips and threw down the bundle of clothes he'd been gathering up. Caeru's clothes; elegant and destroyed. "I hadn't planned to visit the Tigron until tomorrow," Abrimel said. "Caeru needs me more at the moment. As I said, I can't get any sense out of him. What do you want him for?"

"I think you should speak to Pellaz about it," I said, thinking this was something I was definitely not going to deal with myself. This was family business, and although I suppose I should look upon myself as a member of the family, I was just a new member, and therefore exempt from the bulk of internal quarrels. Abrimel was uncertain.

"I'm not going to harm Caeru in any way, I promise you. Please, go and speak with your father."

"Has he sent you here?"

"Yes."

"Right!" Abrimel stalked out, his face dark with a hundred bursting questions. I smiled to myself, bent down, picked up the fallen clothes and draped them over a chair. When I stood up, Caeru was standing in the doorway staring at me. From the look on his face, I wouldn't have been surprised if he'd produced an axe from behind his back and run screaming right at me. He didn't. He just said, "Get the hell out of here. Now!"

"You're not pleased to see me, are you," I said lightly. Imminent attack was still not unlikely. His fists were clenched by his sides, his hair in disarray, his clothes torn and dusty, his face scratched and marked with dry blood. He looked as if he hadn't slept or washed for several days, yet he was still undeniably lovely, possessing the sort of attractiveness that would let him look well-dressed in the proverbial sack.

"I know what's happened," he said, ignoring my remark. "You think I'm stupid, don't you. Both of you do."

"I'm here for dinner," I said. "Do let's try to be civilized."

"Civilized! You've wrecked my home!" he screeched, waving his arms at the torn room. I instinctively backed away as he advanced toward me, still shrieking his displeasure.

"Look!" I said, when he was just inches away and I was pressed against the wall. "Cut the crap, Caeru. I'm Tigron, Pell's Tigron, not you. We have to talk. No-one's telling you to pack your little spotted hanky and leave. So calm down, remember who you are and get your people to serve us dinner, OK?"

He snorted in a fit of repressed, seething rage. "It'll have to be on the terrace," he said in a strangled voice. "The rest of this place is just ruins."

"Oh, come on, it's not that bad. Just a little messed up."

"The terrace," he said. "Would you care to follow me?"

It was evening out there, warm and fragrant. All the tiles turquoise beneath my feet. From the balcony we could see the half-tumbled towers of Immanion stark against a blood-red, smoky sunset. The sea beyond them gleamed like polished metal. A wrought iron table had been set out hurriedly, draped with a fringed cloth. Huge, cushioned chairs from some forlorn salon inside had been arranged on either side and looked rather incongruous. One of the clawed, wooden feet was broken.

"You'd better learn to be friendly," I said.

"Is that blackmail or just a simple threat?" Caeru responded, sitting down gracefully.

"Neither. Get it into your head, Tigrina, if you are the Tigron's consort, in view of all that's happened, you are now also mine." I let this statement sink in before sitting down. Caeru remained silent, probably stunned. I admired the view, wafted a napkin over my knees. The servants brought us wine, offered a glass to Caeru to taste which he waved away. I took it. "Very good," I said. "Pour the Tigrina a large glass."

Caeru stared fixedly at the table, at his servant's shaking hand. Wine splashed onto the cloth. "This is a farce. I cannot eat," he said. "Did you mean what you said? It's too disgusting to contemplate."

"More disgusting than what you've been living before?" I enquired delicately.

Caeru put his head on one side and sighed. "OK, I'm tired, I'm exhausted; I cannot fight. If it's going to save time and agony, I give in. I give in! What is it you want me to do?"

"Nothing. Just drink your wine and eat. Ashmael wants to call an emergency meeting of the Hegemony. That'll be tomorrow now, I suppose, although it's leaving it rather late . . ."

"No, that'll be tonight," Caeru corrected, looking at me thoughtfully. "They don't waste time. I expect they'll send for you when they're ready."

"You mean after they've finished talking about me behind my back."
(Aha, a suspicion was forming; an unpleasant one.)

"Yes." *(That confirmed it.)*

"Do you attend such meetings?"

"If it concerns me, yes. If it doesn't, no. Same as everyone else. Tonight I will definitely be there."

And so would I! I'd had some vague ideas floating around in my head concerning the Tigrina ever since my confrontation with Thiede, albeit abstract ones. I gave in to a warm feeling of resentment that my beloved had shooed me off to deal with Caeru, thus getting me out of the way, so that he could call the meeting of the Hegemony and start it without even telling me. The old Pellaz would never have done that. OK, at times his naive honesty had grated on my nerves, but at least I'd always known what was going on in his head. Now, I was not so sure. Cue *déjà vu* concerning my observations about beautiful hara being clever, cunning or powerful. Pellaz was frighteningly beautiful and I was no longer sure I could strike any of the other qualities from his list of characteristics. Now, he must think me naive! If we were to exist together, as we must, emotions must be put aside. Clearly intense wiliness was called for. I still had the ace up my sleeve. No my darling; you will not push me around. Not completely.

The first course was served. Spiced fish in aromatic sauce with wafers of toast. Caeru sucked a slice of lemon, but wouldn't eat.

"Don't you trust me?" I asked. The food was very good.

"What a stupid remark!"

"Why? I can make life a lot better for you if I want to, and, of course, if you want me to." I'd already swiftly knocked back two glasses of the wine which was extremely potent.

"Oh, can you indeed! I'm very grateful!"

"Yes, you should be. If Pell is a beast to you, it's because he's been bitter and misled, that's all. There's no reason why things can't improve between you now. It can't always have been this bad, can it? Conception, for example, demands more than mere lust to achieve."

Caeru's lips had gone pale with rather more than just lemon-juice. "I expect the ability to shock people is one of your more outstanding talents, is it? Am I supposed to be impressed? What happened between the Tigron and I in the past is none of your business, and as for you being able to improve things between us, which in itself is a conceit beyond comprehension, haven't you forgotten just one thing? Doesn't he now have you here for him to love?" Caeru put up his hand and shook his head as soon as he'd finished speaking as if to negate that last remark.

"Ah, but as I said earlier, Pellaz and I should be looked upon as one entity now. Don't you think I have a say in our emotional life as well as our political one?"

Caeru shook his head again in confusion. "Cal, are you just stupidly romantic, or do you know something I don't?"

I smiled secretively. "Just eat," I said, "then go and have a wash and comb your hair. Come with me to the Hegalion. Let's surprise them."

The Hegalion stood unmarked, a vast, imposing building, about half a mile from Phaonica. As Caeru had intimated, the meeting of the Hegemony was well under way by the time we got there. Perhaps the place had been cleaned up before the meeting started; there was no sign of debris. Polished columns and dark, carpeted stairs lent an air of solemnity. As soon as we were noticed standing in the hall, an usher in black livery hurried noise-lessly forward, bowed to the Tigrina. He conducted us up a sweeping flight of stairs and through the main door of the grand chamber. I saw Pellaz sitting at the head of a long, low polished table, his chin resting on his fist. A number of hara were spaced out around the table listening to someone who was standing up to speak. Surprise, surprise. It was Ashmael. The public gallery was full to capacity, with fidgetting hara all dressed in what was left of their best clothes. Pell looked up and saw me, instantly alert, perhaps wondering how I'd got there. Then he glanced briefly at the Tigrina who was standing a little behind me and a barely perceptible sneer crossed his face. I could tell what he was thinking. He had decided that Caeru wanted to cause him discomfort by bringing me here. Let him think that for a while. It didn't matter. All went silent. Then someone offered to show me to a seat, and a ripple of whispered conversation traveled round the gallery.

"No," Pell ordered, as I went to sit down, "he sits here by me! Cal?"

Caeru was already seated, staring at his fingers on the table. I took his hand, hauled him from his seat and dragged him up the room with me. I think he was far too mortified to protest. Pell looked me in the eye, speculatively. He was trying to imply: "No, the Tigrina sits down there with the others," without actually saying it. He also knew I was going to ignore it. The sussuration of noise had ceased, and now a profound silence filled the hall of the Hegalion as everyone held their breath in anticipation. They were all watching me, all waiting, wondering what was going to happen next. Pell's chair was higher than the rest. Now he was watching me wearily, but there was a slight smile on his face. I could tell that in a way, he was proud of my independent action, but he would still try to fight me. I wouldn't let him. Pell had had his taste of power; he expected to be obeyed by all but Thiede.

I stood up on the dais, Caeru at my side. I turned my back on the Tigron and faced the Hegemony. Ashmael was smiling widely with sheer delight. I addressed them all. I said, "I am disappointed that you have all seen fit to begin this meeting without me. Especially after I have come such a long way to be here, and accomplished so much for our race in such a short time. For that, I am indebted to our sister race, the Kamagrian, especially their high priestess Opalexian, without whose help the progression of Wraeththu would not be possible." A fierce grumbling of surprise echoed round the chamber at those words. Someone, whom I did not know stood up, near the end of the table.

"Would you care to expand on that statement, tiahaar? Are you implying that unbeknown to anyone another race has been developing somewhere and would I be right in assuming these *Kamagrian* are female?"

"What have they to do with us?" someone else called out.

I could detect a tiny, niggling thread of panic in those questions. Let them wait for the explanation. I put up my hand to silence them and shook my head. Behind me I heard Pellaz exhale, slowly, deeply. A sharp dart of mind-touch reached me: "What the hell are you doing. Sit down and shut up before you embarrass yourself beyond redemption!"

I ignored it. "There will be plenty of time to explain fully about the Kamagrian, their relationship to Wraeththu, and their future relationship with Wraeththu. What matters most now is something entirely different, but it is still something that must be explained before all else. As you all doubtless know by now, the Aghama is no longer completely a creature of this Earth. But that does not mean that he has left us; far from it. Thiede is now *above* us; trine in power with Tigron Pellaz and myself. Perhaps it would be to insult your intelligence to point out that what is spiritual must also be reflected in the matter, so I do so, not to inform but merely to place what I have to say in context. Simply; as above, so below. Three in one. Whatever any of you thought about my coming here, I can assure you it was not to remove Caeru Meveny from office. He has his part to play, as do we all, and it is a vital part, as the mundane counterpoint of the Aghama. I just wanted to make that clear."

"To who?" Ashmael mouthed, for me alone.

"To me," Pell answered resignedly, under his breath, having known that Ashmael would say something like that.

I turned to Pellaz and reached for his hand. He pulled a face at me, but gave it willingly enough. Then I turned to Caeru. "Three in one?" I said, holding out my other hand. He took it as if he expected me to burn him; his flesh was icy. "Pellaz?" For a moment, I thought he would refuse. He smiled at me cynically. "It seems you insist," he said, knowing full well he had no choice. He took Caeru's free hand in his and closed the circle.

"Remember the past," I said. "The good bits."

"Whose past?" Pellaz asked, but he knew. We opened up to each other and the essence of Tigron/Tigrina whirled into a spectral cone of light above our heads. For Pell, it was so effortless, trained as he was by Thiede. There were still some things that Caeru and I would have to learn, but, one day, we would raise some fearsome power together alright. This was the earthly Triad. Not even Pell could dispute it. Above us Thiede, below us Caeru. Absolute necessity. From us would have to come the strong heirs to lead this confused and potentially great race into the future. We raised our hands to spin the light and Ashmael was the first to stand and applaud. Within seconds, everyone had joined him.

In comparison to that, the rest of the meeting just seemed like small-talk. Oh, there was much to speak about. Rebuilding, reality. What should be, what *was*. What had started as a tense and formal affair, became a relaxed discussion. The minute-keeper was hard-pressed to keep up. I created a storm when I stood up and suggested that the people of Immanion sitting in the gallery should be allowed to have their say. From being normally quite a reserved race, the Gelaming suddenly seemed eager to put their views forward, in some cases at the same time as several other hara. Caeru suggested that Abrimel was now responsible and old enough to be allowed to sit with the Hegemony. Permission for this was granted. It was also decided, at the instigation of one particular forceful voice from the gallery, that three members of the public should yearly be elected to take their place in the Hegalion. It was politely hinted that perhaps the current Hegemony was somewhat divorced from common life, and that such new members might give a wider perspective of things. The Council of Tribes would also have to be re-organized. It was agreed that the working future of Wraeth-thu certainly seemed to be taking root in Jaddayoth, and representatives of the twelve tribes should be invited to help in the reshaping of Megalithica, which was really too vast to be coped with solely by Galhea, even though it did have the backing of Immanion. I found that an excellent time to reintroduce the subject of the Kamagrian. Everyone seemed a little squeamish about it at first, which Pell deftly pointed out was a human fault and one which should be discarded.

"If it is so that we must share our world with a race of androgynes more feminine in aspect than ourselves, then we should rejoice," he said. "For a long time I tried to reconcile myself to the fact that Woman as a divine form must necessarily become extinct. Now I am glad that it is not so. Are we still so attached to human failings that we shun those that are different to ourselves? Haven't we learned the price Man had to pay for such foolishness? Surely as true Wraeththu we should embrace Kamagrian as the sisters they are and work together with them. As Cal pointed out, without their help we, Thiede included, would have been wandering up the wrong path for a long time. Perhaps forever, or until some other race came to take our place, as we took Mankind's. Think well on this, tiahaara. To be great, don't we also have to be humble? Serve as well as be served? If the power of the Kamagrian is greater than ours, then we should not resent it, but see it as it truly is. A great opportunity for learning."

Enterprise was another new facet of Pellaz I'd have to get used to. I didn't think it would be a good time to tell him that Kate, his good friend, was Kamagrian, nor that she had been Opalexian's eyes and ears in Immanion. Perhaps she would want to tell him herself. I still had not seen her. From what I could remember, the last time we'd met (a long, long time ago), I'd been a little bit rude to her. That was when I'd hated women because, deep inside, I'd envied them. Strange to think that I can admit that now. Perhaps it is because I have learned to be truly Wraeththu, to see myself as male and female, as I should, and not just a modified male. A lesson that had to be learned by many I think.

And now my story is just about up to date. It will all take a lot of getting used to. Sometimes, I am sure, Pell and I will hate each other's guts because we have both changed so much. This is necessary because we could not function as a pair if we'd remained the same, but it is still hard. Sometimes he is a stranger and I have to fight a certain fear of him. Sometimes I find myself going to Caeru to escape that fear, that power, but less and less as time goes on. We have learned how to love again. That makes up for all the bad times.

The other night, after a ritual in the temple, Pellaz, Caeru and I ate together on Caeru's terrace and the atmosphere was congenial between us. We were talking about Galhea. Swift, once he'd learned what had happened to me, had lost no time in contacting me. He suggested that we should meet in Immanion before I went back to Forever myself. (Still having trouble with Seel over me, I wonder?) He also said that he'd very much like to bring Tyson with him. It was a request more than a statement. I'd asked how Ty felt about it. My son was now about thirty years old; a disorientating thought. "He is like you," Swift had answered, which probably meant he and Cobweb were still trying to force Tyson to agree to it. I'd said OK, but a little reluctantly. Ty doubtlessly felt the same about it. I wanted to see him, but anticipated difficulties in communication at first. He might still hold a grudge against me because I'd left him in Galhea and never bothered to get in touch. I was telling Pell and Caeru all about Galhea, making them laugh with tales of Cobweb's often absurd behavior which I expect they thought I'd exaggerated. I hadn't. I told them, "Cobweb hated my guts for ages! Can't blame him, I suppose."

"Yet you ended up quite close," Caeru observed wistfully. A certain awkwardness materialized. Relations between Pell and the Tigrina were still cool more often than not.

Pell said, "Rue, do you want to know why I hated you?" and the air went cold.

Caeru rubbed his arms. "If you want to tell me," he said, meaning, 'no.'

"It was because I wanted you to be Cal, and you weren't. I felt you were taking his place, and if I let myself grow to love you, I would be reinforcing that belief, doing what Thiede wanted me to do. In a way, it was pure stubbornness on my part. It must have hurt you a lot. I won't apologize because it would sound pathetic after so much mental cruelty, so let's just open another bottle of wine and talk about something else shall we."

But it was said; that's all that matters. I caught Caeru's eye and winked. He smiled back. Sometimes it would be necessary for us to join forces against Pellaz and keep his ego under control. Not too often I hope.

Eventually, it got too cold to sit on the terrace. We stood up to go inside. One of Caeru's attendants was going round drawing the drapes, lighting the lamps that would show the rooms off to best effect.

"It's quite cozy here, isn't it," Pell remarked. I thought we'd be leaving but he threw himself down in a chair. "Have we exhausted your wine, Rue?"

"Er, no. I'll have someone bring us more." The Tigrina was as surprised as me. Usually Pell couldn't wait to get away from him.

Left alone with Pell for a few moments, I said, "What are you up to?"

"What do you think of Caeru?"

"Why?"

"Just answer."

"Why?"

Pellaz sighed. "OK, you think our communion should become more than spiritual?"

"I can't believe I'm hearing this!"

"Do you?"

I shrugged. Caeru came back in, trailing a servant carrying a tray of wine. Caeru was smiling; he was happy we were still there.

"Yes, I think it should," I said.

"What's going on?" Caeru asked.

Pellaz sat up in his chair, smiled wolfishly. "Rue, I want you to think back," he said. "I want you to remember Ferelithia. Remember a romantic young har and the time you spent with him. He's not that far away. Think you can manage that?"

Caeru has a good memory; it wasn't that difficult for him.

Someday soon, the stories of our lives, Pell's and mine, will snuggle together on the shelf beside our bed, and that will be an end to all the frantic soul-searching we went through writing them. We have the future now, no need to cling to the past. When we go to the temple to join with the Aghama, we can see it before us. Thiede will always be with us. Not just in memory, but in each harling that is born, every decision that is made, every worship we make to the power that is within us. We call that power God and Goddess. Once it lived in man, but men and women couldn't

774   STORM CONSTANTINE

experience the light and dark of their natures without fear. Perhaps Kama-grian and Wraeththu are the answer. We shall certainly try. Our races as we know ourselves are just the beginning; there is so much more to come, and if we are wise, we shall greet it gladly.

THE HISTORY OF THE TWELVE
TRIBES OF JADDAYOTH

>─┼─◄►──◖─◄►─┼─◄

The country that became Almagabra was initially colonized by the Gelaming who came over from Megalithica. They found human society in a state of collapse, mainly through the effects of strange, incurable diseases, inner conflict between peoples and a marked increase in the suicide rate via mental disturbance.

After settlement, various splinter groups split off from the main body of the Gelaming and traveled east. Although the Gelaming did not exactly sanction these moves, no overt action was taken to stop them. There are twelve acknowledged tribes of Jaddayoth, varying in size from the powerful **MAUDRAH** (MAW-druh), **HADASSAH** (HAD-uss-ar) and **NATAWNI** (Nat-AW-nee). To the smaller, but mystically influential tribes, such as **ROSELANE** (ROZ-uh-larn) and **FERIKE** (FER-i-kuh).

Hierarchies vary within the tribes, but most have governing families that have either seized power or been elected to govern by the rest of the tribe. Among the tribes, alliances may be formed by the mixing of blood through mating. Hara such as the Maudrah may want to improve their royal bloodlines by breeding with hara known for their intelligence, such as the Ferike. The sale of harlings between tribes is not uncommon.

Some tribes are city builders, often cannibalizing what mankind has left behind to construct their own towns, whilst others live in scattered, smaller communities. The main interaction between tribes is for trade. The Garridan deal in toxins and stimulants, the Emunah (besides being brokers for many other tribes) deal in perfumes, carpets, household commodities, the Gimrah deal in livestock.

Religion among the twelve tribes is as varied as their systems of government. The Maudrah's priesthood, the Niz, are basically political, although the Maudrah do have a king, the Archon Ariaric. However, it is suspected that the Niz put Ariaric on the throne themselves and that he is answerable to them. Before the Confederation of Tribes was initiated in ai-cara 14, skirmishes and raids between the tribes were common, especially along the boundaries of territories. In ai-cara 13, Ariaric of the Maudrah commenced hostilities with the Natawni over some trivial offense, and the

Natawni applied to the Gelaming for assistance. Once the Gelaming forces arrived from Almagabra, Ariaric claimed that Natawni warriors had been raiding Maudrah settlements along the border (which was still indistinct), stealing livestock and burning farms. The Gelaming proposed that proper boundaries be marked out, and suggested that a permanent peace-keeping force from Almagabra be stationed along this boundary. Thus, the Gelaming inveigled their way into Jaddayoth; a situation regarded with mixed feelings by all tribes. At this time, the Confederation of Tribes was also formed; an attempt to prevent further incidence of hostilities occurring. Another outcome of Gelaming intervention was that slavery was outlawed in Jaddayoth, whether of remaining humans or hara. Slavery has always been abhorrent to the Gelaming, and they stated that allowing such a practice to continue would be a step backwards for Wraeththukind. Healthy respect for the power of the Gelaming meant that this request was complied with, but the ensuing systems of bondharing are little other than slavery, and it is clear there is still a black market for slaves, if one knows where to look for it.

THE TWELVE TRIBES: A TRAVELER'S GUIDE

The Maudrah

The Maudrah are the largest tribe of Jaddayoth, many of whom are hara who fled Megalithica at the time of the Varrish defeat in that continent. Their society is governed by many strict codes, one of which is their religious cult connected with the Aghama, the first Wraeththu. To the Maudrah, the Aghama is a ruthless and vengeful entity, whom it is necessary to placate in numerous ways. The Aghama may be offended by deviations from custom, such as wearing the wrong mode of attire in any situation, or utilising incorrect modes of address to other hara. If any har should invoke the displeasure of the Aghama, he is obliged to make the correct penance. Mistakes made by strangers to the region are barely tolerated, but small allowances are made for visitors who may be unfamiliar with the Maudrah codes. Repeated aberrations do tend to inflame the tempers of the Niz, however, so it is inadvisable for hara unfamiliar with the region to spend too much time in Maudrah. The capital city of Oomadrah is probably the most lenient. An efficient police force, known as the Aditi, are employed by the Niz to supervise the streets of towns and cities. They may invite transgressors to "partake of the hospitality of the Niz." It is strongly urged that any traveler receiving such a suggestion resist it strongly. Fleeing abruptly from Maudrah territory is the recommended manner of replying to it.

The Maudrah attitude to aruna is one shrouded in mystery as few have ever spoken of it outside of the country. It is safe to conjecture, however, that it is bound by the same set of rigid rules as govern all aspects of Maudrah activity. Not recommended to be sampled.

Within the palace Sykernesse, seat of the Archon in Oomadrah, it is rumored that the restrictions adhered to by the Maudrah community at large do not apply. This may be because Ariaric's consort, Elisyin, is of Ferike origin and has considerable influence within Sykernesse itself. The court of Sykernesse is on very intimate terms with the court of Phaonica in Immanion. This too may be a reason why regulations are relaxed within the palace. Visitors from Almagabra are frequent, and would no doubt be offended if asked to behave in any manner other than that of a respected Gelaming. The only other reason why conditions in the palace are as they appear may be because Ariaric and Wrark Fortuny, High Priest of the Niz, are happy to dole out laws willy-nilly to their people but can't be bothered with such things themselves. Conjectures abound, but surely only the most cynical har would suggest the latter.

The Hadassah

The Hadassah are the second largest tribe of Jaddayoth. They are also the complete opposite of the Maudrah, possessing a far looser social structure. In fact, they have an almost morbid hatred for the Maudrah and utterly despise that tribe's traditions. The governor of the Hadassah is a har known as the Lexy, who resides in the capital town of Camphadal, close to the Natawni border. The Lexy is chosen every five years by means of a strenuous competition which comprises tests of strength, intelligence and magical prowess. The current Lexy has been in office for six years, having won the competition twice. He is highly regarded amongst his people. The Hadassah also worship the Aghama, but the idea rather than the har. They do not worship the image of Aghama, but believe that the Aghama's presence is inherent in every har and that to abuse yourself (or any other hara) is to abuse the Aghama. Thus, when having to engage in battle, for whatever reason, every Hadassah has to make amends to the Aghama. Conveniently, this is usually expressed through sanctified aruna with temple soumelam, known as Huyana, who must also be offered gifts in the form of food, money or clothing. As the Hadassah are a race fond of drinking, conquest and brawling, the Huyana make a comfortable living from this practice. The Hadassah welcome travelers as they are gregarious people and also because they seek to make profit from any visitors. As opposed to the Maudrah, who dress only in somber gray, black or brown (except for the Niz who wear robes of purple), the Hadassah affect clothing of the brightest colors. They are fond of adorning their costumes with scarves, jewelery and tassels. It is customary for most hara to accentuate their features with cosmetics and they import many exotic perfumes from Kalamah and Emunah. The Hadassah attitude to aruna is more or less the same as that of the Gelaming, in that they believe successful aruna is beneficial both spiritually and physically to whoever indulges in it.

Travelers may expect to receive excellent accommodation and service in any Hadassah town, especially so if they advertise the fact that money presents no problem.

The Natawni

The Natawni, found in the north of Jaddayoth, between Hadassah and Garridan, are also known as the People of Bones. This is because they use bones, the primal building block, for ornament, scrying, and even in the construction of their temples. Bones are built into the walls and foundations of dwellings and the Natawni have also developed a deadly weapon in the form of a bone needle steeped in poison purchased from the Garridan—the tiek. Notably fearless, and not unwarlike, the Natawni nevertheless possess one of the more democratic societies in Jaddayoth. Whilst having no tribe overlord, each community has its own leader, the Askelan, elected from a council of ten individuals, known as the Taima. Natawni has a good relationship with Immanion, but one of severe bad feeling with Maudrah, whom they despise. While they are wary (often bordering on hostile) to strangers in their lands, once satisfied that newcomers are not Maudrah spies or trouble-makers, the Natawni are happy to let them come and go as they please. All travelers wishing to explore Natawni territory are recommended to seek an audience with the nearest Askelan to obtain written authority. This is usually granted at a nominal cost of twenty spinners or thereabouts. More adventurous wanderers may wish to save their money and risk unpleasantness.

The Natawni do not worship the Aghama as a deity, but instead revere a god of their own invention—the Skylording. This deity is hermaphroditic, as themselves, but changes his affinity with the seasons. The warrior caste of the tribe are obliged to follow this custom, hence they may only be soume during spring and summer, ouana during the colder season. Breaking this code threatens to bring disaster to the tribe's fertility. Two religious festivals are celebrated each year. The spring rites are known as the Greening, when harlings are ritually conceived upon the warriors, Feybraihas celebrated and the land blessed for fertility. The Autumn Festival, the Musting, celebrates the Harvest, the birth of new harlings and caste ascensions for the warriors. (N.B. Conceiving children and caste ascensions may take place at any time of year for tribe members other than warriors.) The Skylording's priests are known as Skyles, hara chosen for their beauty and tranquility.

Natawni wear clothes of forest colors, dark brown, green, russet and gold. They plait their hair with moss and leaves and scent their skin with the essential oil of pine and cedar. Their magic is of the earth which they look upon as the feminine aspect of their god. To take aruna with a Natawni is to experience the forest as a living force, to breathe earth and become at one with it. Those towns to be found along the Hadassah border are most receptive to strangers.

The Garridan

Inhabiting the northeastern mountains of Jaddayoth, bound on three sides by Roselane, Maudrah and Natawni, stretching a toe of crags into Mojag, Garridan is perhaps the land most feared by strangers to the region. Incorporating many rogue hara of the Uigenna tribe who had to flee Megalithica during the time of conflict (and who were rejected by the Maudrah—a warning note), the Garridan are a tribe well versed in the esoteric lore of Wraeththu toxins. The Uigenna were a byword in Megalithica for heartless cruelty, and were famous for their ability to devise poisons fatal or painful to harishkind, whom most toxic elements cannot harm. It is rumored that the Garridan salvaged much of man's technology, which they now utilize in the manufacture of their venoms. Needless to say, poison is the main export of Garridan, finding its way west, through Jaddayoth, to Thaine, Erminia and beyond. A death through poisoning was reported in southern Megalithica two years ago. It was thought that all Uigenna hara had been expunged or driven from the land at the time, which brought about the conjecture that the toxin responsible may well have originated in Jaddayoth, Garridan in particular. Whether Garridan exports are this far-reaching has never been substantiated.

The Garridan are a notoriously handsome race, inclined to tallness, long-limbed and gray eyed. Their ruler is the Archon Hillelex, their capital city the mountain stronghold of Nightshade. Nearly all Garridan towns and cities are named for various poisons; they have a rather mordant sense of humor. More than most of the tribes of Jaddayoth who have deviated from the habits and customs of Megalithican Wraeththukind, the Garridan have stuck more keenly to their origins, still instituting the exact same caste structure as the homeland, naming their temples Nayatis, their priests Hienamas, their marriages and alliances chesnabond. Though they pay lip service to the Aghama as a deity, most Garridan have little time for religion. This is because the Uigenna were one of the first tribes of Wraeththu and have passed to their descendants a strong sense of what it was like clinging to the ruins of human civilization, regarded as a dangerous freak, having to fight just to live every day. Most tribes nowadays have a far more diluted bloodline from the original strain than the Garridan, owing to interbreeding between different districts and tribes. Hence, the racial memory is perhaps blunted or at least distant enough to ignore. The Garridan are a one-generation descent group away from the Uigenna. Some part of them still lives in the burning cities of fifty years ago. There were no gods then; Garridan see little need for them now.

The Garridan maintain a cursory alliance with Mojag and Maudrah. They are strongly opposed by the Natawni, who disagree with the majority of Garridan customs and creeds. Emunah, however, never fussy with whose money it takes, maintains a healthy trading arrangement with Garridan.

Visitors to the region are not discouraged or hassled in any way, yet there are surprisingly few that brave the journey. Visitors to Nightshade report that the Garridan are excellent hosts, Lord Hillelex especially, but it is advised to examine carefully any food that you are offered, unless you are sure your visit is welcome!

The Gimrah

Known among the tribes of Jaddayoth as the Horse People, the Gimrah (GIM-rar) occupy the vast southern plains to the west of Maudrah and a long stretch of the coast of the Sea of Shadows. Famous for the quality of their animals, many Gimrah can boast that their steeds can be found in the stables of all the noble houses of Jaddayoth. Four different types of horses are bred in this region. Firstly, the working beasts; heavy, muscled brutes, found on all the richer farms in the area. Secondly, riding animals, famed for their elegant appearance, reliability and zest. Thirdly, racehorses, exported to Almagabra, Thaine and as far as Megalithica, and finally, Faraldiennes. These animals are bred from two Gelaming horses presented to Gimrah by Immanion itself. Faraldiennes are far more than just animals, being able to travel through the otherlanes, out of this plane of existence, thus enabling an experienced handler to cross vast distances of land in a very short space of time. The Gimrah have several small herds of these animals, but their sale is controlled by the Hegemony in Immanion, to prevent them falling into the wrong hands. Obviously, there are many brave attempts by would-be thieves to steal from the herd, but the Gimrah guard them with outstanding zeal and happily kill anyone stupid enough to try. Any Faraldiennes sold to other tribes are geldings, preventing any illegal breeding of the strain.

The Gimrah are solely a farming community, and have no cities. Each farm is really a large village, presided over by a headhar known as the Tirtha. All Gimrah Tirtha meet six times a year to discuss tribal matters and to show off the best of their stock. The Tirtha acts as law enforcer within his own community, usually assisted by his family.

The Gimrah worship the Aghama in the form of a white horse who may sometimes take the form of a Wraeththu har. They believe that on the eve of the new year, the Aghama may be seen galloping over the fields beside the herds, ensuring their fertility for the coming spring.

Of all the tribes of Jaddayoth, only the Gimrah have any dealings with humans. Whereas Mojag, Garridan, Maudrah and Natawni successfully exterminated, or drove away, any lingering human communities, the Gimrah allowed men and women to remain on their lands, offering them employment and aid. This was sorely needed at the time of settlement as all humans were desperately clinging to the last threads of life at the time, never mind the territory. The Gimrah assisted by using their power of healing over the minds and bodies of the humans, managing to halt the deadly advance of mental illness, ravaging disease and sterility. Because of this, the relationship between humankind and hara in this district is uncommonly good. Many humans now live better lives than before the Wraeththu came. Naturally, this situation invites censure from the less tolerant tribes, but as the Gimrah have the sanction of the Gelaming, both human and har can live together without fear of reprisal. The only problem that arises from this circumstance is that all male children, upon reaching puberty, want to be incepted into Wraeththu. Obviously, if this was allowed to occur without supervision, the humans would inevitably become extinct. To preserve the race, the Gimrah have stipulated that no young man may take inception until he has successfully sired a male child. Therefore, humans tend to breed at a very young age and all of the adult community is female.

Visitors are always welcome in the estembles (as the farms are called) of Gimrah, although they may be expected to pay for their keep with labor as well as money. The best time to visit the region is during the summer months when there are many colorful horse fairs to look around.

The Ferike

Other tribes describe the Ferike as a race of scholars and artists, and it is true that they are a people that devote themselves to learning and creativity. The noble families live in high castles in the hilly, forested districts of Western Jaddayoth. The rest of the community live in small towns, generally along the shores of the many lakes found in Ferike.

Rich hara from other tribes often buy harlings off the Ferike to breed with their own sons, hoping, thereby, to increase the intelligence and artistic natures of their own families. Ferike hara are fey and pale with large eyes. Their pastimes include writing long, fabulous poetry and poignant, convoluted stories. Ferike books (always beautifully bound and illustrated) often appear in Emunah markets, but selling at massively inflated prices. It is said that Thiede of Immanion possesses an entire library of Ferike literature. The Ferike are also renowned for their brilliant artists and musicians, but it is a rich har's hobby to try and collect any of their works.

Time spent in a Ferike castle is supposed to be sublimely relaxing. The occupants are ethereally lovely, soft music enchants the ear, splendid paintings welcome the eye and the food Ferike cooks prepare is reputedly the best in the world for its subtlety of flavor. Surprisingly, not that much is known about Ferike social customs, for they are a private race, but there are many tales about the fabled Elisyin, a Ferike legend whom Ariaric of the Maudrah took as a consort. Between them, they produced three sons of biting, shrewd wit, all the more deadly because of their deceptively pretty appearance. Those wishing to learn more of this history should look for the Ferike book on the subject called "The blade, the reed and the shadow." Because of the difficulty in obtaining any Ferike works, serious students are advised to obtain permission from the Hegemony of Immanion to examine those volumes held by Phaonica's library. Although the Gelaming are sympathetic to researchers, and happily open their archives to anyone willing to pay for the privilege, it must be stated that the cost may turn out rather higher than expected. Accommodation does not come cheap in Immanion. Travel in Ferike, however, is not quite so expensive. It is recommended that any visitors to the region find a comfortable inn and pay one of the locals in ale to tell stories of Elisyin and his sons. This works out considerably cheaper than using the library in Immanion and is far more entertaining, even if the stories are rather less accurate.

The Elhmen

The Elhmen (ELL-mun) are a mountain race found northwest of Ferike. They prefer to keep themselves to themselves and can be most unpleasant to strangers if the mood takes them. Whilst hardy and fond of a colder climate, they are markedly more feminine in appearance than most Wraeththu. This is not through sublimation of the male principle, but because of their religion, which is a celebration of water magic. They harness the power of the mountain falls and their appearance is uncannily nymphlike. Elhmen are mischievous and fond of playing tricks upon unwary travelers. They do not often show themselves, but it is said that if a wanderer should catch hold of an Elhmen har, he can ask for a wish to be granted. This is more likely to be a romantic rather than realistic premise, and probably a tale started in Ferike!

Although the Elhmen are not warlike in nature, they are quick to defend themselves and their privacy. This is usually effected by sending any interloper into an enchanted sleep before moving them to the boundary of their territory. The Elhmen also guard the entrances to the underground kingdom of Eulalee, home of the tribe of Sahale. Sometimes the Sahale and Elhmen interact for religious or magical rites, for the Sahale are also known as the Fire People; thus the two tribes' magics are complementary.

The Elhmen live mainly in small communities scattered among the peaks, and have only one city—Shappa. This is built high in the mountains, a dazzling creation of stone towers and vertiginous streets. The Elhmen have no overall ruler. In fact, whoever does govern the Elhmen (*if* anyone does), does so in utter secrecy, for nothing is known about social administration within the tribe. Holy hara, who are definitely something more than mere priests, but no-one except the Elhmen know what, are called Esh. Travelers with money are generally welcome in Shappa, and it is worth the visit if one is prepared to put up with antisocial treatment on the journey to reach it.

All Elhmen grow their hair very long, are generally fair in coloring and have ice-blue or cloud-gray eyes. Their faces are ascetic, their expressions dreamy, hinting at a secret smile. It is said that their touch is always cold. Whilst they are totally unaffected by cold conditions, and often go naked, clothed only in their magnificent hair, the Elhmen usually prefer to appear before strangers clothed in flimsy, floating robes. Another legend about this tribe is that taking aruna with an Elhmen har automatically raises one's caste by one level. As with many such pretty stories, the facts remain unsubstantiated.

The Sahale

As has been mentioned in the previous entry, the Sahale (SARL) are known throughout Jaddayoth as the Fire People. They live underground, beneath the mountain ranges of Elhmen and beyond, emerging only rarely for religious ceremonies. As befits their chosen religion, hara of this tribe habitually dye their hair red, but of varying shades to signify their position within the tribe, and their caste. Young harlings, until feybraiha, have hair of a strawberry pink color which changes to vibrant scarlet once they have come of age. On reaching first level Ulani, the hair color becomes crimson, whilst hara of Nahir Nuri level have hair that is so deep a color it is almost purple. Subtle shades within these four groups denote abilities, social standing and intelligence.

The capital city of Eulalee is Sahen (SARN), situated next to a vast, underground lake, framed by breathtaking stalactites, stalagmites and curtains of gleaming, mineral deposits. Other settlements on the same level as Sahen include the religious retreat of Pir Lagadre, visited by pilgrims from as far away as Megalithica. Of the lower levels of Eulalee, little is known by outsiders. There are rumors of strange, supernatural creatures living in caverns of fire, and of ancient shrines where lost gods live on unaware of the changes wrought upon the surface of the earth. Again, stories. There are many stories to be heard in Jaddayoth. The fires of Sahale heat sacred springs, where bathing in the water is said to promote health and beauty. Anyone brave enough to bathe in the actual flames can try and prove the myths that doing so gives unparalleled wisdom, never mind unparalleled third degree burns.

The ruler, or Lyris, of the Sahale dwells in the city of Sahen, attended by priest figures known as Lithes. Although, as a complement to the Elhmen, it might be expected that the Sahale present a predominantly masculine mien, this is not the case. They are typically harish in every respect, their only peculiarity being that, in spite of living underground, they all have rather dark skins.

The Emunah

Although the Emunah (Em-OO-nah) are principally a nonproductive tribe, they act as very efficient brokers for the other Jaddayoth regions. Emunah hara are a mixed bag of many different tribes. They inhabit the eastern coast of Jaddayoth, where their river- and ocean-going vessels can have easy access to other areas of Jaddayoth, the northern coast of Huldah and the sea canal to Almagabra. Law in Emunah is half-heartedly presided over (i.e., it can be bought) by a group of elected hara known as the Nasnan. They are presided over by a grand judge entitled the Garondel. It would appear that the only way to break the law in Emunah is to steal from Emunah subjects or to attempt to defraud the Garondel's authorities, which are concerned with the administration of trade. Therefore, all travelers are advised to arm themselves well in Emunah towns. The advantages of visiting this region are that strangers are never questioned (or even noticed for that matter), and can come and go as they please. Visitors bearing produce to trade are welcomed with open arms and entitled to reduced rates at many Emunah inns. The principle towns are Oriole, Meris, Gaspard and Linnea. The Garondel and his committee reside in the capital town of Oriole.

In this region, little importance is attached to religion, although shrines may be found to many of the Aghama's different aspects deified in Jaddayoth. This is mainly for the benefit of travelers. Native hara use their innate talents for telepathy and illusion to secure prosperous deals for themselves and, unfortunately, to outwit unwary traders from abroad. Emunah are notoriously untrustworthy, but not cruel. If found out in their machinations, they will apologize with a smile, and perhaps offer to make amends by buying the offended party a meal (thus presenting themselves with the opportunity to get the unfortunate victim drunk and doublecross them again). However, once an Emunah har's respect has been earned (which is never easy for a stranger), they can reveal a deep and surprising loyalty. It is said that an Emunah friend, if indeed such a creature can exist, is a friend for life.

The Kalamah

Known among the tribes as the Cat People, the Kalamah (KAL-uh-mar) live in the east of the region in elegant cities of rose and cream stone. At present, most of these are still in the process of construction, for the Kalamah work slowly and precisely, stopping their labors often for refreshment, rest and appraisal of their craftsmanship. Even so, the architecture found in Kalamah is unbelievably lovely.

The Kalamah are a philosophical race and have made a thorough study of the feline mind, which they strive to emulate in numerous ways. They are fond of luxury and comfort, good food, excellent wine and soothing music. One of their main incomes is derived from the export of their wine, subsidized by the industries of carpet-making and perfumery.

Their religion, as most other tribes, is worship of the Aghama, but naturally mutated to fit in with their own particular beliefs. Here we have the lion-headed aspect of the god, upon whose statues is to be found the legend, "To be cunning without beauty and style is to light a fire next to an open door in winter." It has been said that all the most enchanting and destructive of human female souls have reincarnated in Kalamah. Perhaps that is a little too harsh; Kalamah never kill for sport, but have been known to make a hobby of breaking hearts. Whilst they are a race not easily provoked into a rage, it is strongly advised not to aggravate any Kalamah har to extremity, for once roused, they can continue an argument beyond any reasonable point, or avenge an offense with horrible suffering. As with the Ferike, harlings of this tribe are often sought after by the Maudrah and the Garridan (the only tribes who can cope with Kalamah temperament perhaps), so that harlings born of a union between the tribes may be blessed with the gifts of stealth, cunning and agility, as well as languid beauty. The fabled Ariaric of Maudrah, who is renowned for enriching his family's blood with the best stock, procured a Kalamah consort for his eldest son, Ostoroth. Unfortunately, this union was not destined to thrive. After being on the receiving end of some cruelty or another from his partner, the Kalamah Lissilma murdered Ostoroth in cold blood and, furthermore, effortlessly massacred a great number of the palace Aditi before he was overpowered. Ariaric was so impressed by this feat that he claimed Lissilma for his own son, professing that Ostoroth had embarrassed him dreadfully by allowing himself to be killed by a concubine. How Lissilma reacted to this remark is not recorded, but, being Kalamah, he probably settled comfortably into this new elevated position and overlooked the insult. Ostoroth was not fit to be remembered. His body was burned without ceremony, while Lissilma came to sit at the Archon's right hand, where he was professed to have caused much catastrophe among the other noble houses of Maudrah. A book, written by the Ferike on this subject and entitled, appropriately, "The claws of Lissilma," describes many of the intrigues initiated in the Kalamah's name.

Visitors to Kalamah are urged to end their journey in the city of Zaltana, where, it is said, if the claws of the Kalamah embed themselves in your skin, you will never want to leave. It is true, the place is breathtaking, and if one is strong-willed, not too dangerous.

The Mojag

The Mojag (MO-hag) are regarded as cultureless barbarians by most of the tribes of Jaddayoth, although it would be a fool who did not regard them with healthy respect. Occupying only one small village on their arrival in Jaddayoth, within only a year or so, they had soon secured for themselves a huge area of land among the eastern mountains of the country. Only the formation of the Confederation of Tribes halted their advance toward other territories. This no doubt caused the tribes of Kalamah, Emunah and Roselane to give a sigh of relief, and those of Garridan and Maudrah to slacken their defences along the borders with Mojag.

Being a tribe dedicated to conquest and troublemaking of all kinds, the warrior castes of Mojag are generally found among the armies of other countries as mercenaries. Even the Gelaming have a troupe of Mojags, which they use for restoring order in any troublesome areas, and also as escorts for Gelaming personnel venturing into countries farther east than

Jaddayoth, or south into Olathe. Mojags are totally fearless and seem to regard themselves as indestructible. Because of the strength of this belief, they usually are!

The Princelord of Mojag is a har known as the Wursm, who resides in the capital town of Shuppurak. It is said that he has killed a thousand living beings, both human and har. Because Mojag make little concession to their feminine sides, one wonders how they manage to reproduce successfully. There is no record of them taking hara from other tribes for this purpose, so the subject remains shrouded in mystery. Because of the belligerent nature of this tribe, few scholars have been able to make a study of them. Mojags cannot see the point of hospitality unless it is extended to a possible ally in combat. Not an area recommended for travel.

The Roselane

The Roselane are a tribe of mystics, whose aid may be enlisted by hara of other tribes seeking guidance in spiritual matters. Often called the Dream People by other tribes, the Roselane have control over dreams and visions of the future; solutions to waking-life problems may be interpreted from their dreams. Their religion is based upon the essential male/female polarity within themselves; they have no desire for external gods. Their most respected hara are the most influential dreamers; they are known as Frodinne. These hara have incredible control over their dreams and can even influence the future, in some cases, by dreaming it. Roselane harlings are taught at an early age how to confront enemies or objects of fear in their dreams and overcome them. On reaching feybraiha, all Roselane hara have learned this technique. If, at this stage, they appear to be unusually proficient at dream control, they may be trained further to join the ranks of the Frodinne. Otherwise, they will take up some other profession, using their dream powers only for personal benefit. It is said that the most powerful Frodinne spend most of their lives asleep, dreaming, although periodically they may take holidays from this function, when they are termed as being "on adinne." Some Frodinne have achieved remarkable fame in the country of Jaddayoth, and hara travel from afar to seek their advice. The most celebrated of these is Edolie the Ighted, who has dreamed for many of the royal houses of Jaddayoth. It is rumored that he may sleep for weeks at a time when working on a particularly sticky problem and that his appearance is "seraphic." As few hara outside of Roselane have ever seen Edolie the Ighted in the flesh, this cannot be verified.

The Roselane share their territory with another group, known as the Kamagrian. Little is known about these people, whether they are a separate tribe or an offshoot of the Roselane. The Kamagrian have their headquarters, a kind of temple-school, in Shilalama, the Roselane capital town. This temple is named Kalalim and it is said, in Shilalama, that all roads lead to it. Certainly the Roselane regard the Kamagrian with the highest respect. It has been reported that the Kamagrian have human females in their employ which has led to the assumption that they may, in fact, be some kind of disguised human remnant. This seems unlikely, unless the Roselane are shielding them in some way. Though privacy is a byword in Roselane, visitors are not discouraged. The journey to Shilalama is hazardous and uncomfortable, but the city itself is splendid, appearing almost as a natural rock formation eroded by winds. Other Roselane settlements may be less inclined to be interrupted by travelers, so it is advised to head for the capital.

A GUIDE TO THE COUNTRIES AND CHARACTERS

Calanthe (Cal-AN-thee) A traveler (was once a nuisance, but everybody got to hear about it)

THAINE

Fallsend

Jafit	Owner of the musenda "Piristil"
Astarth	
Ehzno (Ej-Noh)	
Salandril (Sal-AN-dril)	
Rihana (Ree-ARN-a)	kanene of Piristil
Yasmeen	
Nahele (Na-HEE-lee)	
Flounah	
Lolotea (Loll-uh-TEE-a)	
Orpah	
Wuwa (WOO-wa)	servants of Piristil
Jancis (JAN-kiss)	
Kruin (KROO-in)	a client, trader of the Natawni tribe
Panthera (Pan-THEER-a)	a slave, son of royal house of Jael in Ferike
Outher (OW-thuh)	guard of Panthera, of the Mojag tribe
Arno Demell	a client of Piristil
Liss-am-Caar	a dealer in toxins of the Garridan tribe

JADDAYOTH: LAND OF THE TWELVE TRIBES

In the land of the Hadassah

Jasminia
Lucastril (Loo-CASS-tril) a huyana of the Aghama's temple

In the land of the Gimrah

Lemarath

Cora	human female, farmer and lodging-house keeper
Jasca	her daughter
Natty	her son
Elveny	a young woman of Cora's household
Gasteau Hafener	Tirtha of Lemarath
Lanareeve Hafener	his consort
Jubilee Hafener	
Danyelle Hafener	their sons
Onaly Doontree (ONN-a-lee)	Danyelle's consort
Wilder Hafener	a relative

In the land of the Ferike

Jael

Ferminfex Jael (JAY-el)	Castlethane of Jael, father of Panthera
Lahela (La-HEE-la)	his consort, of the Kalamah tribe

In the land of the Elhmen

On the road to Kar Tatang, the gateway

Arawn	an enchanter
Nanine	his brother

Shappa

Kachina (Ka-CHEE-na)	a guide

In the land of the Sahale (Eulalee)

Sahen

The Lyris	ruler of the Sahale
Zhatsin	under-valet to the Lyris
Iygandil (Ee-GAN-dil)	First Shriever of the Lyris
Tatigha	
Loolumada (LOO-luh-MAR-duh)	attendants of the Lyris
The Fire Hound of Shere	
Zaghara	an oracle

In the land of the Maudrah

Morla

Asvak — Captain of the *"Auric Wing,"* of Ferike tribe

Lourana — Maudrah har, a guide

Oomadrah

Ariaric, Lion of Oomadrah — Archon of the Maudrah

Elisyin (ELIZ-ee-in) — his consort, a Ferike

Lalasa (La-LASS-a) — a Kalamah, valet to Elisyin cousin of Panthera

Wrark Fortuny — High Priest of the Niz

Zobinek (ZOB-in-ek) — son of Ariaric and Elisyin

In the land of the Roselane

Shilalama

Tel-an-Kaa — a parage of the Kamagrian

Opalexian — High Priestess of the Kamagrian

Zackala (ZAK-ARL-a) — one of Opalexian's aides, a Roselane

Exalan — one of Opalexian's aides, a Roselane

ALMAGABRA

In the land of the Gelaming

Immanion

Thiede (THEE-dee) — The Aghama

Pellaz-har-Aralis — Tigron of Immanion

Caeru Meveny (KY-roo MEV-EN-ee) — his consort, Tigrina of Immanion

Abrimel (AB-ree-mel) — son of the Tigron and Tigrina

Ashmael (ASH-may-el) — a Lord of the Gelaming

Arahal — commanding officer in the Tigron's army

Vaysh — a courtier

APPENDIX I

>━┼━❭━⊙━❬┼━≺

Wraeththu caste system

Wraeththu hara progress through a three-tier caste system; each tier consisting of three levels.

KAIMANA (Ki-ee-marna)
Level 1: Ara (altar)
    2: Neoma (new moon)
    3: Brynie (strong)

ULANI (Oo-lar-nee)
Level 1: Acantha (thorny)
    2: Pyralis (fire)
    3: Algoma (valley of flowers)

NAHIR-NURI (Na-heer Noo-ree)
Level 1: Efrata (distinguished)
    2: Aislinn (vision)
    3: Cleatha (glory)

Natural born hara have no caste until they reach sexual maturity, when they are initiated into Kaimana. The majority of them rarely progress further than Level 2 Ulani: Pyralis. Wraeththu of Kaimana and Ulani caste are always known by their level, i.e., someone of Acantha level would be known as Acanthalid, of Pyralis, Pyralisit. Once Nahir-Nuri has been achieved, however, the caste divisions (mostly incomprehensible to those of lower caste), are no longer used as a title of address. Wraeththu of that caste are simply called Nahir-Nuri.

CASTE PROGRESSION

Training in spiritual advancement must be undertaken to achieve a higher level. Occult rituals concentrate the mind and realize progression. Progression is attained by the discovery of self-knowledge and with that knowledge utilizing the inborn powers of Wraeththu.

APPENDIX II

>━┥◄►━❍━◄►┝━<

Wraeththu special abilities: a comparison to man

The differences between Wraeththu and humankind are not vast in number, and not even apparent (in most cases) to the naked eye. Biologically their functions are similar, although in the case of Wraeththu many basic design faults present in the old race have been removed.

A. DIGESTION

Wraeththu digestion is not wildly disparate from that of humankind, although it is unknown for hara to become overweight whatever amount of food is ingested. Their bodies are so well-regulated that excess of all kinds are merely eliminated as waste. Perfect bodyweight is never exceeded. This thorough system cleansing also extends to most intoxicants or stimulants. Narcotic effects can be experienced without side-effects. Because of this, few poisons are lethal to Wraeththu. It has been rumored that the Uigenna tribe of North Megalithica are fluent with the use of poisons effective against their own kind, but this has yet to be proved.

B. THE SENSES

Wraeththu senses of touch, sight, hearing, smell and taste are marginally more acute than those of mankind. But the sixth sense is far more well-developed. This may only be due to the fact that Wraeththu are brought up (or instructed after inception) with the knowledge to glean full use of their perception. This is a quality which has become dulled in man. Some hara can even catch glimpses of future events or atmospheres; either by tranquil contemplation or in dreams.

Again, it must be stressed that this ability is not a fundamental difference from humanity, as all humans possess within themselves the potential to develop their psychic capabilities. Most humans, however, are not aware of this.

C. OCCULT POWERS

This is merely an extension of becoming acquainted, through proper progression, with one's psychic senses.

Magic is will-power; will-power is magic. Self-knowledge is the key to the perfect control of will.

Obviously, this particular talent may be used either for the benefit or detriment of other beings. As all Wraeththu are firm believers in reincarnation and the progression of the soul, most are sensible enough to realize the dangers of taking "the left hand path." Others, however, still motivated by the greed and baser emotions of human ancestors, are prone to seek self-advancement through evil means.

D. LIFE-SPAN

In comparison, to mankind, Wraeththu appear ageless, but this is not strictly the case. Har bodies are not subject to cellular deterioration in the same way as human bodies, but on reaching the age of 150 years or thereabouts, they begin to "fade," vitality diminishes and the dignified end is welcomed as the release for the soul and the gateway to the next incarnation.

APPENDIX III

⊱─┤─❬❭─⊷─◉─⊶─❬❭─├─⊰

Wraeththu sexuality

A. REPRODUCTION

Wraeththu are hermaphrodite beings, any of whom have the capacity to reproduce on reaching the caste of Ulani. This is mainly because hara of lower caste have insufficient control of the mind, which is required to attain the elevated state of consciousness needed for conception. Experienced hara can guarantee conception whenever it is desired.

Conception can only occur during the act of aruna (Wraeththu intercourse); hara are unable to fertilize themselves. The inseminating har is known as ouana (ooow-ana), and the host for the seed, soume (soow-mee). This corresponds roughly to human male and female, although in Wraeththu the roles are interchangeable. When conditions are propitious (i.e., when desired state of consciousness is achieved through the ecstasy of aruna), ouana has the chance to "break through the seal," which is the act of coaxing the chamber of generation within the body of the soume to relax its banks of muscle that closes the entrance, and permit the inner tendril of the ouana phallus to intrude. This act must needs be undertaken with patience, because of the inner organ's somewhat capricious reluctance to be invaded by foreign bodies or substances. Aggression or haste on the side of ouana would cause pain and distress to soume (or possibly to both of them) caused by the inpenetrable tensing of soume muscles.

Once the seed (aren) has been successfully released, the chamber of generation reseals itself and emits a fertilizing secretion (yaloe) which forms a coating around the aren. Only the strongest can survive this process, weaker seed are literally burned up or else devoured by their fellows. During the next twelve hours or so, the aren fight for supremacy, until only one of them survives; this is then enveloped by the nourishing yaloe which begins to harden around the aren to form a kind of shell. By interaction of the positive aren elements and the negative yaloe elements, a Wraeththu fetus begins to develop within the shell.

At the end of two months, the shell is emitted from the body of its host, resembling a black, opalescent pearl some six inches in diameter. Incubation is then required, either by the host or any other har committed to spending the time. After "birth," the pearl begins to soften into an elastic, leathery coating about the developing harchild. Progress and growth are rapid; within a week, the pearl "hatches" and the young har enters the world.

Wraeththu children, on hatching, already possess some body hair and have moderately acute eyesight. Familiar hara can be recognized after only a few days. Though smaller in size, the harling at this time is comparable in intelligence and mobility to a human child that has just been weaned. Wraeththu children need no milk and can eat the same food as adults within a few hours of hatching. Development is astonishingly rapid within the first year of life. Harlings are able to crawl aroound immediately after hatching, and can walk upright within a few days. they learn to speak simple words after about four weeks, and before that, voice their demands by exercising their voices in a series of purrings and chatterings. Sexual maturity is reached between the ages of seven and ten years, when the harling is physically able to partake in aruna without ill effect. At this time, caste training is undertaken and the young har is also educated in the etiquette of aruna. Sexual maturity is recognized by a marked restlessness and erratic behavior, even a craving for moonlight. Aruna education is usually imparted by an older har chosen by the child's hostling or sire. This is to prevent any unpleasant experiences which the young har could suffer at the hands of someone who is not committed to its welfare.

(N.B. Those hara who are not natural born, but incepted, are instructed in aruna immediately after the effects of althaia (the changing) wears off. This is essential to "fix" the change within the new har.)

A physically mature har, when clothed, resembles closely a young, human male. Hara do not need breasts for the production of milk, nor wide pelvises to accomodate a growing child. They are, whilst obviously masculine, uncannily feminine at the same time; which is a circumstance difficult to describe without illustration.

B. ARUNA

The act of sexual intercourse between hara has two legitimate types. Aruna is indulged in either for pleasure; the intimate communication of minds and bodies that all hara need for spiritual contentment, or else for the express purpose of conceiving. Although it is a necessity for Wraeththu, the amount of physical communion preferred varies from har to har. Some may seek out a companion only once a year, others may yearn for aruna several times a week. It is not important whether a har enjoys most performing ouana or soume; again this varies among hara. Most swap and change their roles according to mood or circumstance.

The phallus of the har resembles a petaled rod, sometimes of deep and varied colors. It has an inner tendril which may only emerge once embraced by the body of the soume and prior to orgasm. The soume organs of generation, located in the lower region of the body in a position not dissimilar to that of a human female womb, is reached by a fleshy, convoluted passage found behind the masculine organs of generation. Self cleansing, it leads also to the lower intestine, where more banks of muscle form an effective seal.

C. GRISSECON

Grissecon is sexual communion for occult purposes; simply—sex magic. As enormous forces are aroused during aruna, these forces may be harnessed to act externally. Explanation other than this is prohibited by the Great Oath.

D. PELKI

There are only two legitimate modes of physical intercourse among Wraeththu. Pelki is for the most part denied to exist, although amongst brutalized tribes it undoubtedly does. It is the name for forced rape of either hara or humans. The latter is essentially murder, as humankind cannot tolerate the bodily secretions of Wraeththu, which act as a caustic poison; pelki to humans is always fatal. Because aruna is such a respected and important aspect of Wraeththu life, the concept of pelki is both abhorrent and appalling to the average har. Unfortunately, certain dark powers can be accrued by indulging in these practices and this only serves as a dreadful temptation to hara of evil or morally decadent inclinations.

GLOSSARY OF WRAETHTHU TERMS
AND MINOR CHARACTERS

>─┤─<>─•─○─•─<>─┤─<

ACANTHA	See appendix one
AGHAMA (AG-am-ar)	Title of the first Wraeththu, worshiped as a god
ADITI (A-DEE-tee)	Military arm of the Niz in Maudrah
AI-CARA	Wraeththu calendar; years since Pellaz-har-Aralis became Tigron
ALGOMALID	See appendix one
ALMAGABRA	Country of the Gelaming
ARCHON, THE	Title of the lord of the Maudrah
ARUNA (A-ROO-na)	Sexual communion between hara
AURIC WING	Merchant vessel out of Ferike, on which Cal traveled to Maudrah
AZRIEL	Son of Swift and Seel
BETICA	Cheap, strong liquor
CASTLETHANE	Lord of Jael
CHAITRA (CHAY-tra)	Simulated rape performed by kanene for client
CHESNA	A close relationship between hara
COBWEB	A Varr, consort of Terzian (q.v.), hostling of Swift; a mythic and legendary beauty
DIAMANDA	Soporific drug
ESTEMBLE	Gimrah stud farm
EULALEE (YEW-la-lee)	Subterranean land of the Sahale tribe
EXALAN	A Roselane, aide to Opalexian
FAIRMINIA	Opalexian's ship on which Cal traveled to Immanion
FALLSEND	A town in Thaine
FANCHON, THE	Lord of Zaltana, a city of the Kalamah
FEYBRAIHA	A harish coming of age, and its attendant celebration
FILLARET	A coin of the Thaine/Jaddayoth currency
FLICK	A bar from Saltrock, Megalithica

FOREVER	See We dwell in Forever
FULMINIR	Varr city in Megalithica, stronghold of Ponclast
GALHEA (Ga-LAY-uh)	Formerly a Varrish town governed by Terzian, now capital city of central Megalithica
GEBADDON	Forest of nightmares and consciences in Megalithica
GELAMING (JEL-a-ming)	Superior Wraeththu tribe, originating in Almagabra
GLITTER	An area of Fallsend, famous for its musendas
GRISSECON (GRIS-uh-con)	Sexual communion between hara to raise power; sex magic
HAR	Wraeththu individual (pl. hara)
HARLING	Young har until feybraiha
HEARTSTONE	House of the family Hafener, in Gimrah
HEGALION	Chambers of the Hegemony in Immanion
HEGEMONY	Ruling body of the Gelaming
HIENAMA (hy-en-AH-ma)	Wreaththu priest
HOSTLING	Bar who carries the pearl (Wraeththu fetus), who hosts the seed of another
HUYANA (HOO-ya-na)	Priests of the Hadassah tribe
IMBRILIM	Gelaming camp headquarters in Megalithica
IMMANION	Capital city of Almagabra
KAKKAHAAR	Desert tribe of Southern Megalithica
KALALIM	Palace of the Kamagrian in Shilalama
KAMAGRIAN (Ka-MAG-ree-an)	A sisterhood of adepts, female complement of Wraeththu
KANENE (Ka-NEE-nee)	A harish whore
LIANVIS	Leader of the Kakkahaar tribe
LION OF OOMAR	See Wraxilan
MANTICKER THE SEVENTY	Leader of the Uigenna tribe at time of Cal's inception
MEGALITHICA	Western continent taken from the Varrs by the Gelaming
MORASS	A settlement in Thaine
MUSENDA	A whorehouse
NAHIT-NURI	See appendix one
NAMIR	Cousin to Panthera, and his intended consort. A har of the Kalamah
NAYATI	The temple in Saltrock
NIZ	Priesthood of the Maudrah

ORIEN	A Saltrock shaman, murdered by Cal
OUANA (Oo-ARN-a)	Masculine principle of hara
OUANA-LIM	Masculine generative organ of hara
PARAGE (Pa-RARJ)	Any member of the Kamagrian, an adept
PARASIEL (Pa-RASS-i-el)	Ruling tribe of Megalithica, governed for the Gelaming by Swift. Once known as the Varrs
PEARL	Wraeththu embryo
PELCIA	Simulated resistance to rape, performed by kanene for client
PELKI	Rape
PHAONICA (Fay-ON-ick-a)	Tigron's palace in Immanion
PIRISTIL	A musenda in Fallsend
PONCLAST	Former leader of the Varrs
PYTHONESS	A title of Tel-an-Kaa
SALTROCK	Wraeththu settlement in Megalithica where Pell was incepted
SEEL GRISELMING	A contemporary, and early friend, of Cal's; now a Gelaming har, associated with the Hegemony and consort of Swift
SHARING OF BREATH	A kiss of mutual visualization
SKYLORDING	A god of the Natawni tribe
SKYLES	Priesthood of the Skylording
SOUME (SOO-me)	Feminine principle of hara
SOUME-LAM	Feminine generative organ of hara
SPINNER	A coin of Thaine/Jaddayoth currency
SWIFT	Leader of the Parasiel (once Varrs), son of Terzian and Cobweb
SYKERNESSE	Palace of the Archon in Oomadrah, Maudrah
TERZIAN	A Varr, autarch of Galhea, master of Forever, father of Swift (deceased)
THAINE	Northerly region of Almagabra
THANDRELLO	Borough of Immanion, home of Ashmael
TIAHAAR	Respectful form of address
TIGRINA (Tee-GREE-na)	Tigron's consort; Caeru Meveny
TIGRON (TEE-gron)	Lord of the Gelaming, Thiede's protégé, Pellaz-har-Aralis
TIRTHA	Estemble governor among the Gimrah
TYSON	Son of Cal and Terzian
UIGENNA (EW-i-GENN-a)	Tribe of Megalithica, into which Cal was incepted, warlike and famous for their poisons

ULANI	See appendix one
ULAUME	Consort of Lianvis, originally of the Colurastes tribe, renowned for his beauty
UNNEAH (Oo-NAY-uh)	Tribe of Megalithica
UNTHRIST	Outcast, tribeless
VARRS	Former ruling tribe of Megalithica, before Gelaming takeover. See also Parasiel
WE DWELL IN FOREVER	Terzian's house in Galhea
WRAETHTHU (RAY-thoo)	The race of hermaphrodites that evolved from mankind
WRAXILAN (RAX-i-lan)	The Lion of Oomar, warrior leader of the Uigenna after Manticker the Seventy
ZIGANE (Zig-ARN-ee)	Tribe of wandering humans and hara in Megalithica